Martina Cole was born in Avely in Essex and brought up as part of a large, close-knit family, living in and around Dagenham and Rainham for most of her life. She has been writing since childhood, and was encouraged by her English teacher to try to earn a living from it – advice she didn't take until she was twenty-five, though for years she wrote romantic fiction in exercise books for a friend.

Her previous novels, *Dangerous Lady* and *The Ladykiller*, available from Headline, were major bestsellers and both warmly praised:

'Move over Jackie (Collins)! *Daily Mirror*

'All the ingredients to be a huge hit' *Today*

'A major new talent ... a roaring success ... a powerful tale of gangland London' *Best*

'You won't be able to put this one down' *Company*

Goodnight Lady

Martina Cole

HEADLINE

First published in 1994
by HEADLINE BOOK PUBLISHING

10 9 8 7 6 5

ISBN 0 7472 4429 4

Typeset by Keyboard Services, Luton

Printed and bound in Great Britain by
Cox & Wyman Ltd, Reading, Berkshire

HEADLINE BOOK PUBLISHING
A division of Hodder Headline PLC
338 Euston Road
London NW1 3BH

For my sisters, Maura and Loretta. We've held each other's hands, wiped each other's tears, supported each other, laughed together even when our world had collapsed around us and enjoyed every second of it. We are grown women now, but still at heart, we're the Whiteside girls.

Remembering Jonathan Peake and Eric Lane, with love always.

Many thanks to Marlene Moore for all her help and information on Berwick Manor.

BOOK ONE

'When I was a child, I spake as a child,
I understood as a child,
I thought as a child'
– Corinthians

'The children of perdition are oft'times made instruments
even of the greatest work'
Ben Jonson, 1637–1673

'Who controls the past controls the future, who controls
the present controls the past'
George Orwell, 1903–1950

Prologue
1989

The woman in the bed was impossibly old. Her face, still showing subtle traces of a former beauty, was a mass of criss-cross lines. The thick powder she wore had cracked and flaked in the heat of the room. The red slash of her mouth was sunken and bent, emphasising her baggy jowls.

Two things were, however, very much alive: her eyes, still a startling green, despite the yellowing of her whites, and her hair. The thick redness seemed to crackle on the shrunken head, falling across bony shoulders in a shower of electric waves. It was this, and the eyes, which showed a casual observer that here lay a former beauty, a relic of another time, another era. A time when she was a show stopper, a woman of account. Now there was laughter in those eyes as she watched, beneath hooded lids, the two young nurses tidying her room.

She knew she was old and she accepted it. Death would just be another great adventure, she was sure of that. It was one of the prerogatives of great age that you made yourself ready to meet your maker. Well, she had a few things to say to him when the time came.

'She was lovely in her day wasn't she?' The blonde-haired nurse picked up a photograph in a heavy silver frame. It showed a beautiful, doe-eyed woman, wrapped in fox furs, wearing a cloche hat. Her heavily lipsticked mouth formed a perfect cupid's bow. She could have been a silent screen star.

'Yes, gorgeous. Look at all that hair coming out from underneath that hat.'

The mousey-haired girl sounded envious. What she wouldn't give for the old girl's hair, even as it was now, speckled with grey.

'Did you read about her? In the *News of the World* the other week? She had a life, she did. All those scandals in the 'sixties! Politicians and that, even Royalty!' The girl lowered her voice now, as if remembering the old lady was in the room.

'You don't have to whisper, dears, I'm not dead yet!'

Both nurses jumped at the sound of her voice, low pitched and surprisingly strong. She looked so tiny, so tiny and vulnerable, until she opened her mouth.

'I was seventeen when that photo was taken. I was a looker and all. Had all the men after me!'

One of the nurses sat down on the bed.

'Is it true what they said about you?'

The tiny frame shook with a deep husky laugh that turned into a hacking cough.

'Let's just say that there's an element of truth in there, shall we?'

The two nurses exchanged glances.

'Is it true that Jonathan La Billière started out in blue films?'

Briony sat up in bed and scowled. 'He's got a knighthood, you know, but he always had a soft spot for me, did Jonny. I knew many men, my loves, and I learnt one thing. Never open your mouth about anyone or anything, unless you stand to benefit by it. It's a rule I've lived by for nearly ninety years! There's things that will go to my grave with me, and there's people who think the sooner I go and take me knowledge with me, the better off everyone will be!'

She laughed again then, pulling herself up in the bed, she lit a cigarette, drawing the smoke down into the depths of her lungs.

'Well, Miss Briony, you certainly have led a chequered life!'

'How about a drop of the hard then, girls? There's a bottle of brandy over there in the dresser. I'll have a large one please.'

The blonde nurse went to the dresser and poured out the drink. The old woman sighed. This place was costing over a thousand pounds a week, though it was worth every penny. But a thousand pounds was still a lot of money, even for two of them! A thousand pounds to someone from her beginnings was a small fortune, but money was a necessity in life; without it, you were vulnerable. She sipped the fiery liquid and felt it burn the back of her throat.

'One of the perks of having money – you can happily drink yourself to death and no one gives a damn.'

The nurses smiled.

'They're making a film about me, you know? About me and my sisters. My sister Kerry was the singer. She was the youngest. Five of us, there were, but I'm the only one left. Kerry was the gifted one, and like many gifted people she used her talent to destroy herself.' Her eyes clouded over, as if she could see her sister once more in front of her.

'But they won't mention my poor Rosalee, I made sure of that, nor too much about my Eileen. I brought up Eileen's children, you know. Then there was my Bernadette. The sweetest child God ever put on this earth, unless you upset her that is! I'm the only one left out of the five of us, and I'm well on me way to the century!'

The face closed again and the old woman became lost in another world. A world that spanned many years and that seemed more real to her with every passing day.

Chapter One

Molly Cavanagh shivered underneath the sacking. It was so very cold. She could feel the earthy dampness beneath the mattress with every movement of her aching back. She shifted position slightly and looked at the children huddled around the dying fire. The eldest, Eileen, turned to face her mother and lifted her eyebrows questioningly. Molly shook her head; the child was a long way from coming. Time enough to get Mrs Briggs when it was well on.

'Can I get you a drink, Ma?'

Molly held out a dirty hand to Eileen and she came to her mother's side.

'Go down to Donnelly's and get some coal. There's a few pennies in me skirt pocket.'

The girl turned from her and Molly grabbed at her hand. 'And keep your eye on that Brendan Donnelly. Make sure he weighs it properly, last time it was all slack.'

As she spoke her breath gleamed like white mist in the dimness.

'I will, Ma.' Eileen picked up a shawl and, pocketing the pennies, she left the basement room. The four other little girls watched her go. Kerry, the youngest, got up from her place by the fender and slipped under the covers with her ma.

Molly closed her eyes. When that Paddy got in today she'd cut the legs from under him. It was always the same when he was working: full of good intentions until payday. 'We'll pay a bit off the back of the rent. We'll have a grand dinner of pie and peas and taties. We'll maybe even send the little ones to school.' Then when the first week's wages came it was straight down The Bull for a jar of Watney's, without a thought for her or his children.

Her mind was jolted back to the present by Briony, her second eldest daughter. Never a child to keep her temper long, the crack as she slapped her younger sister Bernadette across the legs broke the silence of the room.

'Ma! Ma! She gave me a dig! Did you see that, Ma? Did you see that?'

Kerry sat up in the bed with excitement. 'Will you be slapping the face off of Briony, Ma? I saw the crack she gave our Bernie . . .'

'Will you all be quiet! And Bernadette, stop that howling and jigging about before I give you *all* a crack.'

Something in their mother's voice communicated itself to the children who all became quiet at once.

After a few minutes Kerry started to sing softly to herself. Bernadette sat beside Rosalee; taking her hand, she smiled into the vacant eyes. Molly watched, and as she saw Rosalee smile back, felt a pain in her chest. Why the hell had God sent her Rosalee? Hadn't she enough on her plate as it was without an idiot? Then, seeing her chance, Bernadette leant over Rosalee and pinched Briony hard on the inside of her leg. She leapt up in the air. Pushing Rosalee out of the way, she grabbed at Bernadette's hair, dragging the now screaming child across the dirt floor, shaking her as Bernadette grabbed hopelessly at the fingers tugging her hair.

Kerry sat up again in the bed. 'That's it, our Briony. Scratch the skin from her hands . . . The dirty bitch!'

Molly dragged her cumbersome body up. With one deft movement she slapped Kerry's face. A howl went up. Then she dragged herself from the bed and set about Briony and Bernadette. Her work-worn hands found legs and arms and she slapped them hard. Rosalee watched it all in the dying firelight and her expression never changed. Three shrieking voices rang

8

in Molly's ears. She held on to the mantelpiece for support as a pain tore through her. Bent double, she gasped and tried to steady her breathing.

'I'm giving you all one last warning,' she told them, 'I mean it. One sound and you're all out in the backyard until the birth's over. If you don't think I'd send you out in the cold, then you just try me . . . You just bloody try me!'

She staggered back to her bed. Briony tried to help her, sorry now for all the trouble, and Molly slapped her hands away.

'You, Briony, should know better. You're eight years old. You should be helping me, child.'

She dropped her eyes and her thick red hair hung over her face like a tangled curtain.

'I'm sorry, Ma.'

Molly climbed into bed once more. The bugs in it ran amok, this way and that, trying to get into the torn mattress before they were squashed by the bulk above them.

'"I'm sorry, Ma". If I had a penny for every time I heard that, I'd be living the life of Riley! One more word out of any of you and I'll let your father find you work. I mean it.'

Briony was scared now. Her father would farm them out in the morning; it was only her mother who'd stopped him until now. She took Bernadette's hand and led her to the fireside. Rosalee smiled at them both and Briony hugged her close. Molly resumed her wait. Kerry crooned softly to herself again.

'Sing us a song, Kerry.' Briony's voice broke the gloom. 'Send our Rosalee off to sleep.'

Kerry lay beside her mother, her little face screwed up in consternation as she tried to think of an appropriate song.

Her haunting little voice came slowly at first but Molly relaxed against the dirty pillows and sighed. Kerry's voice was like a draught of fresh air.

> 'In Dublin's fair city,
> Where the girls are so pretty,
> I first set my eyes
> On sweet Molly Malone . . .'

9

The mood in the room was once more homely. Briony smiled at Bernadette over Rosalee's short cropped hair, their earlier fight forgotten. Molly watched her children and thanked God for the peace that had descended. It wouldn't last long, she was aware of that, but while it lasted she would enjoy it.

Eileen's bare feet were frozen. The cobbles had a thin sheet of ice on them and as she walked with the bucket of coal it banged against her shins, breaking the skin. She put the bucket down and rubbed them with one hand. She could hear the singing and almost feel the foetid warmth of The Bull as she stood outside. The street lamps had been lit and they cast a pink glow around her. She straightened and pushed her thick curly hair back off her face. As she bent down to pick up the bucket once more, a man stood in front of her. Eileen looked up into a large red face.

'What's your name, little girl?' Eileen knew from his voice that he was class.

'Eileen Cavanagh, sir.'

The man was looking her over from head to foot and she squirmed beneath his gaze. He pushed her hair back from her face, and studied her in the light of the street lamp.

'You're quite a pretty little thing, Eileen Cavanagh.'

She wasn't sure how to answer the man who seemed to be dressed all in black, from his highly polished boots to his heavy cape and big black hat. He was well armoured against the weather and she wondered if it had occurred to him that she was freezing.

'Thank you kindly, sir. I . . . I have to be getting along, me ma's waiting on the coal.'

The man put heavy gloved hands on her shoulders and kneaded them, as if seeing how much meat she had on her. Then the doors of The Bull opened and a man stumbled out into the street.

Eileen recognised her da at once and called to him. 'Da . . . Da! It's me, Eileen.'

Paddy Cavanagh was drunk. Very drunk. And to add to his

10

misery he had lost every penny of his wages on a bet. His fuddled brain tried to take in what was happening as he lumbered over to his daughter.

'Is that you, our Eileen?'

The big man smiled at her father and Eileen, for some reason she could not fathom, began to feel more frightened.

'You have a beautiful daughter, Mr Cavanagh. I believe you work for me, don't you?'

Paddy screwed up his eyes and recognised Mr Dumas, the owner of the blacking factory. Straightening up he tipped his cap to the man.

'How old is the girl?'

Paddy wasn't sure how old she was. That was women's knowledge. Women remembered everything and passed it on to other women. How the Mary Magdalene was he to know something like that?

'Tell the gentleman your age, Eileen.'

She bit her lip. Her large blue eyes were filling with unshed tears, and Mr Henry Dumas felt a stirring in him.

Patrick cuffed her ear. 'Answer the man, you eejit. You've a tongue in your head long enough to talk the legs off a donkey any other time.'

'I'm eleven, sir.'

'Old enough to be working, then. Where do you work, child?'

'She doesn't work, sir.' This was said bitterly. Paddy had wanted them all out working, but Molly had been adamant. Schooling for them all, even if it meant no food on the table.

'You don't go to work, a big strapping girl like you?'

Eileen looked down at the shiny ground, afraid to look into the big red face with the large moustaches.

'I need a strong girl myself, Cavanagh. A strong young girl. I'll pay you a pound a week for her.'

Patrick's jaw dropped in shock. 'A pound a week, sir? What for?'

He looked into Dumas' face and it was written there, in his eyes and on the fat moist lips, and for a few seconds Paddy felt the bile rise in him.

11

Seeing the look on Cavanagh's face, Dumas added: 'Two pounds a week then.'

Paddy shook his head, not in denial but in wonderment. He looked at Eileen: at her shoeless feet, blue with the cold, at her scrawny legs and lice-ridden hair and suddenly he felt an overpowering sense of futility. Two pounds a week was a lot of money and Mr Dumas was a very wealthy man. He could make sure that Paddy stayed employed, no matter what. As for Eileen, she would be broken soon enough, the boys around about would see to that, and then there would be more mouths to feed. Dumas was offering her warmth and comfort, and she could be the means of helping her family.

Dumas watched the man battling it out with himself. Then opening his leather purse, he took out two sovereigns and laid them in the palm of his hand. The streetlight played over them, the gold glittering in Paddy's eyes.

'I'll take her with me now then.'

'As you like, sir.'

'What about the coal, Da? I have to take the coal home to me ma. She's waiting on it, the baby's coming . . .'

'Now shut your mouth, our Eileen, and go with Mr Dumas. You're to do whatever he tells you, do you hear me? Anything he tells you at all.'

'Yes, Da.'

The big man took her hand and pulled her away from her father. Paddy watched her go, his heart wretched. He squeezed his hand over the two sovereigns and felt a tear force its way from his eye. He tried to justify his actions all the way home. But even drunk and befuddled, he couldn't quite convince himself.

Eileen sat in the cab and listened to the clip-clop of the horse's hooves as it trotted through a residential area. She gaped at the big town houses in wonderment, her fear of the man gone a little now since he had wrapped her in his cloak. It smelt lovely.

Dumas studied her profile as she watched the houses. She was going to be stunning in a few years, but until then he would have her. He liked them young, very young.

Five minutes later they stopped at a small detached house. Eileen noticed the garden especially. Even in the cold it smelt of lavender. Mr Dumas lifted her from the coach and carried her up the pathway. The door was opened by a girl in her late-teens who ushered them inside. Eileen was placed on the floor in the hallway. It had carpet and she dug her toes into the unfamiliar softness.

'Get Mrs Horlock, would you, Cissy?'

'Yes, sir.' She gave a little bob and walked through a green baize door to the side of her.

'You're going to have a nice hot bath soon. Then we can have something to eat.'

Eileen didn't answer. This man was talking to her as if they had been friends for years. There was something not right here. But the thought of food cheered her.

Then someone came bursting through the green baize door. Eileen jumped with shock. Rushing towards her was a small silver-haired woman. Her teeth had long gone and her mouth seemed to have caved in around the gums. Her face was a mass of wrinkles that all seemed to criss-cross one another. Thick white hair was scraped back off her face into a tight white cap. Bright hazel eyes surveyed Eileen from head to foot.

'Cissy, take the cloak and leave it in the outhouse until we can disinfect it, then come down to the scullery and help me scrub this one.' She jerked her head at Eileen as she spoke and then pulled the cloak from her. Cissy grabbed at it and disappeared once more through the door.

Mrs Horlock sucked her gums and then felt Eileen's limbs, finally grabbing at her tiny breasts.

'Sturdy, Mr Dumas, sir. Not a bad choice, if I might say so. Got good teeth. A few good meals and she'll put some flesh on her bones.'

'My sentiments entirely, Mrs Horlock. Now if you don't mind, I'll be in the morning room enjoying a brandy. Send Cissy along with her when she's ready.'

He smiled at Eileen as he spoke and she felt terror grip her heart.

13

Paddy Cavanagh stood in the centre of the foetid basement room and stared around him. Rosalee awakened and began to cry. Briony immediately began to rock her gently, soothing her back to sleep. Molly stared dull-eyed from the bed, Bernadette and Kerry dozing beside her.

'The child's well on then, Moll?'

She nodded, then frowned as she saw him making up the fire. 'Where's our Eileen, Pat? I sent her out to get the coal a couple of hours since.'

He stared into the fire. Briony's eyes seemed to be boring into his.

'I met her on me way home. I'd got her a job and she went there tonight.'

Molly sat up in the bed.

'You what?' Her voice was low.

Paddy turned to face his wife, working himself up into a temper.

'You heard me, woman! I got her a job. Jesus himself knows we need the bloody money! She'll be well looked after, she'll get decent clothes and food . . .'

'Where's this job, Pat? Come on, tell me, where is this job?'

He could hear the doubt in his wife's voice and felt a wave of anger. She did not trust him at all. Not with anything to do with the girls.

'It's working for Mr Dumas, the man who owns the blacking factory. She'll be working in the house, Moll.'

'Go and get her this minute, Paddy Cavanagh. I don't want her working sixteen hours a day, running round like a blue-arsed fly for a few pennies a week.'

Paddy stormed to the bed and slapped his wife across the face. 'I've said what she's going to do, and now it's done. I want to hear no more about it.'

Kerry and Bernadette both inhaled loudly at the slap their father gave to their mother. Kerry's mouth was open in a large 'O' and Paddy raised his hand to her before the shriek came out.

She snapped her mouth shut immediately.

'I'll scalp the bloody face of the first one to whinge in this house tonight. I mean it.'

As he turned to the fireplace, the two sovereigns slipped from his hand and landed with a gentle chink on the dirt floor.

Molly pulled herself up on the bed and stared at them in amazement. Then, as her eyes flew up to meet her husband's, realisation dawned.

'You filthy bastard, you sold her to him, didn't you? You sold my lovely Eileen to that man . . .' She put her hands to her head and began to cry, a low deep moaning that wrenched Paddy Cavanagh's heart from his body.

He tried to take her in his arms.

'Molly, Moll . . . Listen to me, she'll be living like a queen up there. Look, we'll get two pounds every week . . .'

Molly pushed him from her in disgust. 'So it's come to this? You'd pimp out your own child, you dirty blackguard!

'We had to eat, woman, can't you see that?'

'Why couldn't we eat with your wages then? Because they all went in The Bull, didn't they? Didn't they? By Christ, I hope the priest's waiting when you go to Confession. I hope he chokes the bloody life out of you. As soon as this child's born I'm going to get Eileen, and if she's busted, Paddy Cavanagh, I'll have the Salvation Army after you, I swear it. I'll scream what you've done from the bloody rooftops!'

Molly looked like a mad woman. Her hair was tangled and in disarray, her huge swollen breasts heaving with the effort of making herself heard. Suddenly she saw her life with stunning clarity. She saw the dirt floor, strewn with debris. Saw the only chair in the room with its broken back, the small amount of tea wrapped up carefully on the mantelpiece to keep the rats and roaches from it. The smell of the sewers was in her nose continually. They ran alongside the basement, and when it rained human excrement was forced through the iron grid in the wall. It was as if something burst inside her head.

'You brought me this low, Paddy Cavanagh, and I allowed it. I tried to stand by you, with your drinking and your whoring. Never a full meal for any of the children. But this last act has finished you with me. My lovely Eileen sold to an old man! You sicken me. Sicken me to my stomach.'

Paddy picked up one of the sovereigns and walked from the room. As he opened the door a gust of icy wind blew in.

Eileen was lying in a big copper bath and Mrs Horlock was combing the lice from her hair. The smell of paraffin, sickly sweet, hung over them.

'You've got lovely hair, child. Nice and thick. Once you get some meat inside you, it'll shine. Like a raven's wing, it is.'

She smiled a toothless smile and Eileen smiled tremulously back.

Mrs Horlock stood up. 'You lie there now and Cissy will bring you in some more water to rinse yourself off. The scum in the bath is as thick as me four fingers.'

She walked from the room and went to the kitchen where she prepared a meal for the girl. She shook her head. Poor little mite. Still, Mr Dumas was a rich man, and in fairness not really a nasty one. Providing the girl did as she was told, everything would be fine, and she didn't look like a fighter. Not like the last one. A red-headed bitch with a tongue that could cut glass, and a scream to match. It had taken a few good hidings from her father and a stern talking to from her mother to bring that one round, and by then Mr Dumas was fed up. The mother had finally taken her to Nellie Deakins and if she, Maria Horlock, knew anything about it, the little madam would soon wish she was back here. At least Mr Dumas would only bother her once a day. At Nellie Deakins' she was guaranteed six or seven fellows, and not all as clean and kind as Mr Dumas. Once Nellie had got the big money for the actual breaking in, the girl was worthless to her. Unless she was very young, when Nellie would use the piece of linen and the chicken blood trick a few times.

Mrs Horlock shook her head at the skulduggery of Nellie Deakins. Well, at least that little red-headed bitch would get her comeuppance there. This one though, this Eileen, seemed an amenable little thing. When she had scrubbed the child's body she had checked for tell-tale hairs around her privates but there was nothing, not even any raised follicles, so she wouldn't get anything in that department for a while yet. And a few leading questions had ascertained she hadn't started her periods just yet. Oh, Mr Dumas was going to get his money's worth with this one. The tiny budding breasts were like little plump cherries. Hard little nodules, just the way he liked them. She'd fill out though, this one, be all breasts and hips in a few years. But by that time she should have learnt enough to keep her in good stead for the rest of her life. Plus Mr Dumas always gave the girls a decent leaving present. One young lass had walked out of here with fifty pounds in her pocket!

Eileen allowed Cissy to pour the water over her body, ridding it of the residue from the bath water. Then Cissy wrapped her in a large white towel and dried off her hair. Pulling a comb through it gently, she began chattering to Eileen.

'Mr Dumas will insist you bathe every day. Me, I only have to once a week. You'll have the run of the house, but you can't go out without Mrs Horlock or one of the stable boys with you. That's not 'cos you're a prisoner or nothing, it's in case you get robbed of your togs.'

'What work will I be doing, Cissy?'

She bit her lip before answering. This one was greener than the grass in Barking Park.

'Don't you know, ducks?'

Eileen stared into the troubled brown eyes before her and opened her mouth to speak, but nothing came out.

'You're living here now, Miss Eileen, with Mr Dumas.'

Cissy threw in the 'Miss Eileen' bit because they usually liked that. It made them more amenable to their situation.

'You mean, I'm living with Mr Dumas. What as? A kind of daughter?' Eileen had heard of rich people buying children, but they were usually babies.

Cissy frowned. This one was definitely green. 'Look, supposing you was to get married, right?'

Eileen nodded, unsure where this conversation was taking her.

'Well, you'd have to sleep with your husband, wouldn't you?'

17

Eileen nodded again. This time a feeling of panic was welling up inside her ribcage.

'Well then, just pretend Mr Dumas is your husband, see. It's simple really, and you'll get used to it. They always do.'

Eileen began to shake her head.

'No . . . you're telling me lies. My father wouldn't do that to me.'

Cissy was losing patience now.

'Listen, miss, if Mrs Horlock gets wind of what I've told you she'll slap the pair of us from here to Timbuktu. Take my advice. Just keep your head down, open your legs and think of England. The last one we had who caused trouble was carted off to Nellie Deakins' brothel, and believe me, you don't want to end up there! The master's paid for you fair and square, your dad's already got the money and it'll come in regular every week. If you've any brothers and sisters, then they'll eat well. Look on it from that point of view and just remember what Cissy told you. Smile at the master and you'll have everything you want. Cause trouble and you'll regret it to the end of your days.'

Eileen allowed Cissy to dress her in a nightdress of white lawn and followed her meekly up the stairs and through the green baize door into the morning room. Mr Dumas stood up as she entered and smiled at her.

'Come over here to the fire, my dear. That will be all, Cissy. Tell Mrs Horlock to bring up the food.'

Cissy bobbed a curtsy and, winking at Eileen, left the room.

Mr Dumas took Eileen's hand and led her over to a large chair by the fire. She sat in it gingerly. The unaccustomed softness of the nightdress made her frightened in case she tore it. Mr Dumas took a small foot into his hand and knelt in front of her, kneading its coldness. Eileen watched him fearfully.

'Your poor little feet are frozen, my dear. First thing in the morning Mrs Horlock is going to rig you out from head to toe. You'd like that, wouldn't you?'

Eileen stared at the big man kneeling in front of her. His hands were now on her shins and she suppressed an urge to scream. Cissy's threats of Nellie Deakins had had their desired effect, though. Everyone knew about Nellie Deakins' house. Eileen wasn't sure until tonight what actually went on in there, but she knew that once girls passed through the doors they were never seen again.

The man's hands were now lifting up the nightdress and caressing her thighs. She had no drawers on and tried to squeeze her skinny legs together, but the man was parting them, gently but firmly, with his fingers. Eileen closed her eyes as his moustache began tickling her legs, its wetness roaming up her shins and along her thighs. He was lifting her off the chair now and on to the rug by the fire. She closed her eyes tightly as he began to undo the little bows on the front of the nightdress. As his cold hand enveloped one of her breasts she bit down on her lip, drawing blood.

Mrs Horlock walked into the room with a tray. Taking in the scene before her, she hastily left again, leaving the tray on the table in the hall. She smiled to herself. This one was more amenable than the last, praise God.

She was humming as she passed through the green baize door into the kitchen.

Eileen lay in a dream. Every bone in her body was aching, a fire raging between her legs. As the man pulled away from her she expelled her breath in a long sigh. She closed her eyes as he lay beside her and caressed her open body. She felt numbness invade her mind.

'There, there, my beauty, that wasn't so bad, was it? Now you're busted, it'll be easier for you in the future. I'm starving. Shall I get us something to eat?'

Eileen kept her eyes closed until he called in Mrs Horlock. The housekeeper said it had been a long day for the child and she needed her rest after all the excitement. Eileen walked from the room with the woman, feeling semen and blood running down her legs. She was tucked up into a nice soft bed, a compress of rags dipped in icewater between her legs.

Mrs Horlock spoke to her softly and kissed her sweating forehead.

19

Eileen didn't sleep for three days. She never said a whole sentence to anyone for six months.

Her reign with Mr Dumas lasted one year.

Chapter Two

'Briony!' Molly's voice was harsh.

Briony, who had been sitting on the steps outside the door rushed into the room.

'What's wrong, Ma?'

'Go and fetch the money from Mr Dumas.' This was said through clenched teeth. Briony nodded and pulled on her boots. Molly watched her as she rushed from the room, a coldness settling on her heart. She would have to watch Briony.

She put the kettle on for a cup of tea and sighed. It was a year since Eileen had gone and the room looked a different place altogether. It now had two proper beds, with good feather mattresses. Two brightly coloured mats on the floor, and a table and chairs somehow squeezed in. The fire was always alight, there was plenty of food in the house – and all of it stuck in Molly's throat like gall. She had saved enough to move them to a small house in Oxlow Lane, which would be a step up after this place, and still she wasn't happy about it.

It was the way they got the money that tormented her, night after night. Her baby boy had been stillborn and Eileen, her lovely Eileen, who had been so full of life, so vibrant, was now a shadow of her old self. Withdrawn and moody, she visited once a fortnight, bedecked in her finery, her lovely face white and drawn. It was written there for all to see what Mr Dumas did to her. Eileen had been there a year and every day it broke her more.

Briony walked through the streets towards Mr Dumas' house with a shiver of excitement. She loved going there. She loved the little garden, the lovely carpets and the sweet-smelling warmth. She made her way past The Bull in Dagenham and into Barking, hurrying. She normally stayed and had a bite with Eileen, and tonight she had a little plan. She smiled and waved at people as she went, a familiar figure in her large black boots, courtesy of Mr Dumas' two pounds a week, and her long brick red coat, courtesy of Eileen. Her red hair had as usual sprung out of the ribbon and curled around her face and shoulders.

At just gone ten years old she was a tiny little thing. Her face was open, with milk white skin covered in freckles and green eyes that took in everything around her.

She skipped up the street that housed Eileen, her eyes taking in the lace curtains at the respectable windows, and the scrubbed doorsteps. No smelly children playing five stones out on these streets, no drunken brawling men. This was a beautiful place as far as Briony was concerned. Near to Barking Park, it exuded respectability. Briony walked up the pathway and knocked at the big green front door.

Cissy answered and Briony walked into the hallway.

'Hiya, Cissy. How's me sister?' Briony slipped off her coat and gave it to the girl.

Cissy took the coat and laid it across her arm. 'Not too good, Briony. I think she's gonna get her monthly visitor soon.'

Briony frowned and nodded. As yet Eileen had not had her period, but it was due. Her breasts had grown and she had developed pubic hair. Mr Dumas was not bothering her much these days, and it pleased Eileen but bothered Briony. Because Briony knew, through the talkative Cissy, that once his girls reached adolescence Mr Dumas wanted shot, and then the two pounds a week would dry up. She bit her lip in consternation. If the money went, then so would the food, the new house in Oxlow Lane and the schooling.

She followed Cissy through to the morning room where

Eileen was sitting in front of the fire with a tray of tea and scones. Cissy gave Briony a large wink and she nodded slightly then threw herself across the room into Eileen's arms.

Her sister's long black hair was tied back off her face. She smiled at Briony tremulously.

'Sit yourself down and I'll pour you a cuppa. Help yourself to the scones.'

Briony picked up a scone and placed the whole thing into her mouth, cramming it full. She surveyed Eileen as she chewed. Her hands were shaking as she poured the tea, and Briony felt a moment's sorrow for her. She washed down the scone with a big sip of milk from the little jug and smiled at her sister.

'You all right, our Eileen?'

Eileen nodded. She handed Briony the tea and then stared into the fire.

'I'm not too bad. I keep getting a pain in me belly. I hope it's me monthlies, Briony, I really do.'

She gulped at her tea and swore under her breath. It was steaming hot.

Eileen stared at her.

'You shouldn't swear, Briony, it's not ladylike. Our mum would go mad if she heard you.'

Briony laughed. 'Well, she won't.'

Eileen laughed softly. She wished she was like her sister.

'How's Mr Dumas, Eileen?'

She sighed heavily, her hands fluttering nervously in her lap.

'Oh he's all right, I suppose.'

'How's the . . . you know . . . the other business going?'

'Oh, Briony, it's horrible. Honestly, how people can do that to one another . . . It's disgusting!'

Briony raised her eyes to the ceiling in exasperation.

'I don't mean what's it like! I mean, is he doing it to you very often?'

Eileen shook her head violently. 'No, thank God.'

Briony screwed up her eyes and looked at her sister. 'That's good then.'

23

But it wasn't good. It wasn't good at all.

She heard the front door open and relaxed. Mr Dumas was here. Eileen stiffened in her chair and Briony winked at her.

'Relax, our Eileen, worse things happen at sea!'

Eileen stared into the fire again and Briony had to stifle an urge to get out of her seat and shake her sister by the shoulders until her teeth rattled in her head. Eileen was helping all the family and shouldn't make such a song and dance about it. That was Briony's opinion. She could be doing a lot worse things for a lot worse money. She could be up in Aldgate, in Myrdle Street, working in a sweat shop fourteen hours a day. That would soon sort her out! Let her know what side her bread was buttered. Briony knew what she'd rather be doing.

Mr Dumas walked into the room. He smiled widely at the girls and, walking towards them, kissed them both on the hand. Briony sighed with contentment. As if she was a real lady, she thought. She looked at Mr Dumas' striped tailored trousers and his single-breasted morning-coat and thought he looked like the King. She gave him her brightest smile and he smiled back. Briony slipped to the floor and sat by her sister's chair. Mr Dumas sat in her empty seat and beamed at them.

'I've ordered more tea, girls, and some more cake.' He looked at Briony as he said this and she smiled at him. He always filled her up with cake. He knew she had a sweet tooth. Eileen looked at him and his face sobered. The child's miserable face was getting him down.

'Go and get my wallet for me, Eileen, there's a good girl. Briony will be wanting your wages.'

Eileen stood up as if she had been catapulted from the chair, glad to get out of his presence. As she bolted from the room his voice stayed with her. 'And while you're there, ask Mrs Horlock what's for dinner this evening.'

She nodded and went from the room, her head down. That should give him five minutes with the little red-headed minx. As the door shut Briony stood up and sat in her sister's seat. She grinned at the man opposite.

'I love coming here, Mr Dumas.' It was said with every ounce of guile she had in her, and this was not wasted on the man.

'Do you, Briony?'

'Oh, yes. I wish I lived here, but I expect I'm not big enough yet, am I? I'm only ten.'

She fingered a tendril of red hair as she said this and sucked it into her mouth. Unbeknown to her she could not have done anything more erotic as far as Henry Dumas was concerned.

'I'd do anything to live here. Anything at all.'

The man and the little girl looked full at one another then. An unspoken agreement passed between them and the man was surprised to find such knowingness in so young a child.

Paddy Cavanagh walked into the office with his cap in his hand. 'You wanted to see me, sir?'

Mr Dumas smiled at him, a man to man smile.

'It's about Eileen – I think it's about time she went back home.'

He watched with satisfaction as Paddy Cavanagh's face dropped.

'What . . . I mean . . . Well, what's wrong, sir?'

His mind was reeling. How the hell were they to manage without Eileen's money? Even Molly had had to put up with the situation. For all her high falutin talk, she wasn't backward at taking her cut from it every week.

'I feel a yen for something different, Paddy. You know how it is.'

He stayed silent. No, he did not know how it was, little bits of children had never interested him.

'Briony now, there's a beautiful child. She was at the house last night and she made it quite clear . . .' He raised a hand as if Paddy was going to stop him talking. 'She made it quite clear that she would not be averse to – how shall we say? – taking over where Eileen left off.'

Paddy licked his lips. Every instinct in his body was telling him to take back his fist and slam it into this man's face. Into his teeth. Into his very bones. But he knew he wouldn't even as he thought it. This man was gentry, whatever the hell that was. He

25

owned factories and part of the docks. He was looked up to, made substantial contributions to all sorts of charitable causes. His wife's father was a lord. Paddy knew he was trapped. He also knew that Mr Henry high and mighty Dumas was not getting his Briony for a paltry two pounds a week.

'I thought we could maybe settle for two pounds ten this time,' said Henry persuasively.

'Three pounds.' Paddy's voice was clipped, and surprised both himself and his listener with its forcefulness.

'Three pounds?'

'That's right, sir. My Briony is worth that.'

Dumas bit his top lip and screwed up his eyes.

'It would ease the pain of her mother, sir, because she'll have a fit this night when she knows what's going on. She was bad enough about Eileen, but Briony, her Briony, she'll be like a madwoman. She was all for going for Mrs Prosser Evans over Eileen.'

Paddy had the satisfaction of seeing Dumas pale at the words. Mrs Prosser Evans was a force to be reckoned with in Barking and Dagenham, fighting for justice for the lower classes with a vigour that surprised everyone who came in contact with the tiny woman.

Paddy watched the man battle it out with himself.

Mrs Prosser Evans and a scandal, or a little red-headed child just on ten for a paltry weekly sum. It was no contest.

'Three pounds a week it is then. Bring her round to me at six this evening and you can take the other . . .' He waved his hand as he tried to think of the child's name.

'Eileen, I can collect my Eileen.'

Without wasting any more words, Paddy put his hat on and left the office. He picked up his coat from his workbench and walked out of the factory and along towards The Bull. Inside he ordered himself a large whisky, which he downed in one gulp. Wiping his mouth with the back of his grimy hand he laid his head on the bar and groaned out loud against the fates.

It never occurred to him not to take Briony. Three pounds a week was three pounds a week.

* * *

Molly was dishing up the dinner when Paddy rolled in the door. 'What the hell are you doing home at this time?'

Paddy grabbed her around her waist, breathing his whisky breath all over her. She drew away from him in disgust.

'Get away out of that!'

Kerry giggled. Taking the hot wooden spoon from the large earthenware pot, Molly smacked her across the hands with it. Kerry licked off the juices from the rabbit stew.

Briony sat at the table expectantly, feeding Rosalee. She was the only one with the patience. You had to force the food inside her at times.

'Bri . . . Bri.' Rosalee was catching hold of Briony's hair and calling to her gently. She leant forward and kissed the big moon face. Rosalee started clapping her hands together in excitement.

Paddy watched them and felt a tug at his heart.

'Well? Answer me, what brings you home at this time?'

'Mr Dumas sent for me.' He sat on the broken chair as he spoke.

'What about? Is it Eileen? Is she sickening?'

'No, woman. Nothing like that. Bejasus, would you let a man talk without wittering into his conversation?'

'Well, what's wrong then?'

'He's had enough of her. I'm to go and fetch her tonight.'

Molly pushed back her hair and her face, red and shiny from the cooking, looked relieved.

'I'll be glad to have the child home safe.'

Paddy got out of the chair and swept his arm out in a gesture of disgust.

'Oh, she'll be safe all right, here, 'cos this is where we'll be staying now, isn't it? She'll be safe when the real winter comes, and the shite's bursting into the room, and the cold would cut the lugs from yer. Two pounds a bloody week we'll lose, two Christing pounds! She's up there, dressed up to the nines and eating her fecking head off as and when she fancies it. Well, she'll get a shock when she gets back here, madam. She'll have to go out to work, they all will, if we're to get the house in Oxlow

27

Lane. Even that fecking eejit.' He pointed to Rosalee.

Molly sat on the fender and tapped the wooden spoon against her hand.

'There's that to it, I suppose.' All her dreams were dissolving in front of her eyes, of a nice little house, two up, two down, with a bit of garden out the back, and no more living in basements without enough to eat. Instead it was no more boots for the girls or tea for herself, as and when she wanted it. Once going to Uncle every Tuesday with the blankets and sheets and anything else pawnable had been their way of life, until Paddy brought home some money. Now it would be again, it seemed.

'Well, woman, it's done now and I expect you've saved yourself a bit, to see us over until the spring?'

Molly didn't answer. As far as Paddy Cavanagh was concerned, the less he knew about her money situation the better.

'Yes, as large as life he says to me, "Paddy, I don't want the miserable-looking item any longer." The cheek of it!' He sneaked a glance at Molly as he enlarged on his story, building up to the point of it.

'And then, Moll ... I was all for bashin' him, you know, except I don't want to go along the line. Anyway, then he says to me, "I'd give two pound ten a week for your Briony!"'

Molly was up in a flash.

'He what?'

'"Two pounds ten?" says I.' Paddy poked himself in the chest as he spoke. '"Two pounds ten," I says. "Not fifty pounds a week will get you another of my girls!"'

Molly nodded her head, the wooden spoon like a truncheon in her clenched fist.

'"Three pounds then," he says to me. "Three pounds and we'll negotiate again in six months."'

Paddy, warming to his story, began to embroider it freely. '"Never," says I. "Not for all the gold in London town. Be off, you bugger," I said, Moll. "Get yourself away out of that," I said ...'

28

She nodded again. 'You did right, Paddy. You did right. When I think of what my Eileen's suffered this last year . . .' Her voice broke with shame and remorse.

Briony, watching the proceedings, felt her heart sink down to her boots. Trust her father to botch it up with a drink in him. He was actually believing what he was saying now. Briony was cute enough to know that her father would sell his grandmother if he thought he could get money for her. Getting up from the table, she went to her mother.

'I'll go to Mr Dumas, Ma. Think what you could do with three pounds a week. I wouldn't mind what I had to do. And . . . and our Eileen would be back home like.'

Molly put her hand on to Briony's head. 'This family has been shamed enough, child.'

Briony started gabbling: 'But, Mum, you don't understand. I don't mind going . . . Really I don't! I think I'd be good at it, what Mr Dumas wants like, and the girls can carry on at school, and you can get the drum in Oxlow Lane, and Mr Dumas said last night . . .'

Molly gripped Briony's ear hard and cracked the wooden spoon over her head.

'What did Mr Dumas say last night, child? Come on then, enlighten us.'

Briony was aware she had made a fatal error and looked at her father, her eyes beseeching him to help her.

Molly twisted her ear and Briony screamed out: 'He said that he liked me, Ma, that I could take over from Eileen because she hated it there. That I could earn more money because I was a bit more lively like.'

Molly threw her from her across the dirt floor. Briony lay still staring up at her mother. Whatever happened, she was going to Mr Dumas tonight.

'My God, you want to go, don't you? You actually *want* to go. You know exactly what you're letting yourself in for and you want to go.' Molly's voice was incredulous.

Briony stood up. Facing her mother full on, she shouted at her: 'Well, Eileen went and she didn't want to go but you still took the two quid every week! I *want* to go. I can't wait to go, and get nice clobber and decent food and sleep in a proper bedroom. I bleeding well happen to like Mr Dumas, and nothing he could do to me can be any worse than being cold and hungry and dirty and poor!'

The room was deathly silent and Briony was frightened by her own outburst, but her mother was not stopping her from going to that house tonight. She was determined. She wanted some of what Mr Dumas had on offer. She wanted regular food and warmth, and if that meant she had to touch Mr Dumas and he had to touch her, then that was fine as far as she was concerned.

'If the child wants to go, let her.'

'Oh, yes, that's about your mark, isn't it, Paddy? She's just on ten but always older than her years. A slut in the making we've got here! It'll be down to Nellie Deakins next with her, I suppose.'

'Why is it that Eileen who didn't want to go went, and me who wants to go, and for a pound a week more, can't? You tell me that, Mum?'

'You wouldn't understand, Briony, because you take after him, your father. You'd sell your soul for what you wanted. Well, you can go, girl, but I tell you now – I don't ever want you back under my roof!'

Briony looked at her mother long and hard, then at the silent girls sitting around the table.

'Well, that's a funny thing, you know, Mum, because I'll be paying for the roof I ain't allowed under. I bet you won't throw his three quid back in his face, will you?'

Kissing her sisters in turn, she put on the brick red coat that she loved, pulled on her boots and, motioning to her father, went outside and sat on the steps to wait for him. Inside her chest was a ball of misery. She'd only wanted to help, but it had been thrown back in her face. Well, the three quid would soon soften the blow so far as her mother was concerned. But all the same, it galled Briony and hurt her too. Why was what she was doing wrong? When Eileen did it, when she didn't even want to do it, it had been right. She swallowed back a sob.

Still, she'd had her way, and she brightened herself up now by thinking of the hot bath, the lice-free hair and nice soft nightie that was to come. She closed her mind to the other. As Mrs Prosser Evans always said at Sunday school: 'Sufficient to the time thereof.' She'd worry about that bit when she came to it.

Paddy stood in the hallway of the house in Ripple Road feeling depressed. The smell of cleanliness and the absolute quiet of the place gave him the heebie jeebies, as he expressed it. He always felt clumsy and dirty when he came to the house, and it shamed him. It shamed him that he had sold off his Eileen to Henry Dumas; it galled him now that his Briony, the only one of his daughters with a spark of real life, wanted to come here. Couldn't wait to get here. It was all she had talked about on the way. And yet, as much as he'd hated listening, deep inside himself he didn't blame the child. Not really.

Briony had always had a bit more going for her than the other girls. She was quick-witted and quick-tempered and always seemed to be a bit ahead of her years, even as a tiny child. He could understand to an extent the need in her to better her way of life. Could sympathise with her absolute single-mindedness in wanting to come to this house.

Molly had never had a lot of time for Briony, except as a helper with Rosalee. Only Briony could get her to go to bed, and stop the crying fits which at one time had been frequent. Molly was all for Eileen and Kerry – Kerry being her golden child, her gifted girl, her reason for wanting the house in Oxlow Lane. Kerry must have a good home to grow up in, never mind the rest of them. Bernadette was the odd one out of the five girls. Quiet, placid, but with a devil of a temper when roused, Bernie always looked as if she was sickening for something. As if she was just a guest who would soon leave the household. His own mother had said that the child would not make old bones, and even though she was not actually ill, there was an apathy about her that frightened Paddy at times.

He put his hands in his pockets and stared down at his old boots. This was taking the devil of a long time and he was parched. His throat was on fire with the want of a whisky. A few whiskies would be better.

He heard footsteps on the stairs and Briony rushed down to him, her face flushed and rosy.

'Oh, Dad, I'm to have Eileen's room! She's nearly packed. Mr Dumas said she can keep all the clothes and things, wasn't that nice of him?'

Paddy licked his lips. 'Aye, very kind. Tell our Eileen to hurry up, I haven't got all night.'

The morning-room door opened and Henry Dumas walked out to Paddy and gave him three pounds.

'Eileen shouldn't be long. Would you like a drink while you're waiting?'

Paddy brightened. 'Yes, thank you, sir.'

Dumas noted the civility in his voice and smiled to himself.

For the first time, Paddy went into the morning room, and was impressed way beyond his imagining. There was a good fire in the polished grate. The walls were papered in a dark blue flock, and tall green plants grew upright in painted bowls. A leather chesterfield and two winged armchairs gleamed in the firelight, and small tables held all sorts of knick-knacks and frippery, the like of which Paddy had never seen before. On the floor was a Belgian carpet that even in his hob-nailed boots felt like grass beneath his feet. He sat on the edge of one of the chairs and took the glass of whisky offered him.

No, he didn't blame his Briony at all. She had seen all this. She had been allowed a small peep into the world of the monied classes and she wanted to be a part of it. Who in their right mind could blame her? Certainly not him. Even at ten years old Briony knew what she wanted. As Paddy sipped his drink he had a glimpse of the future.

With the brains she had been given, Briony would use this place as a stepping stone. He had a feeling on him that once she tasted the delights of this house she would only want better, she would only want more, and he, Paddy Cavanagh, downed his drink in a large gulp and gave her a silent toast. May you get everything you want, my Briony, but never what you deserve.

32

'Oh, Eileen, fold the clothes up properly, they'll be like rags by the time you get them home!' Briony's voice was annoyed. Eileen, in her haste to get out of the house, was just throwing clothes into the leather trunk that Mr Dumas had kindly given her.

'Well, Briony, they'll be like rags soon anyway, so it doesn't really make any difference, does it? Now just help me pack and let me get out of here.'

Cissy shook her head as Briony opened her mouth to answer. 'Go down to the kitchen, Eileen. Mrs Horlock has something for you.'

Eileen flounced from the room.

'She bloody well annoys me, Cissy, ungrateful little bitch she is – all this lovely stuff!'

Cissy began packing the case properly and spoke to Briony in a low voice.

'Listen, Bri, don't be too hard on her. She hated it here. Some girls aren't made like us. We get the most out of whatever situation we're in, but other people are weak like. They don't have any bottle, see? Now help me pack and we'll get shot of her then we can get you bathed. Mrs Horlock has the water all ready.'

Briony kept her own counsel, but no matter what anyone said, she thought Eileen was a miserable wet patch. She looked around the bedroom with a feeling of glee inside her chest. It was lovely. The whole house was lovely. Soon she'd have a good scrub in the tin bath in the scullery and from tomorrow she would use the big bathroom on the landing. Oh, she thought she was going to faint with happiness. She stroked the richly embroidered bedspread gently and bit her lip. This was all hers, and unlike that scut of a sister, she was going to reign here for a long time.

No matter what she had to do.

'All done, child.'

Briony stood up in the water and held up her arms as Mrs

Horlock wrapped her in a towel. The little ribcage was visible through her blue-white skin and the tiny nipples, no bigger than farthings, were hard with the cold of the scullery. For the first time ever Mrs Horlock hugged a little child and, after wrapping her in the towel, put her on her lap and cuddled her close.

Briony automatically returned the hug and made herself a friend for life. The smallness of Briony, the very vulnerability that inflamed Henry Dumas, made Mrs Horlock, for the first time, aware of what the child was to do. Maybe it was her complete acceptance of the situation that upset her, she didn't know, all she knew was that Briony Cavanagh was the smallest child yet, and no matter how much she dressed it up, it began to bother her.

But she dressed her in a white nightie and took her up to the morning room and Henry Dumas.

Henry was astounded at the change in the child. As she sat chatting with him in front of the fire, her hair began to dry. First one tight spiral of red hair sprang up on top of her head, and then another. It amazed him, and he smiled to himself. She was exquisite. Her little feet were long and thin, and what shapely ankles . . .

Briony was shocked a bit at first when he dropped on to his knees and pushed up her nightdress. Now the time had come, it seemed her big talk and lioness courage were going to fail her. But they didn't. Instead, she forced herself to relax, because Cissy told her it hurt more if you tensed up. Looking down at Mr Dumas' head, she saw her nightie all scrunched up and cried out. Henry Dumas looked at her in concern. He hadn't even touched her yet!

Jumping from the chair, Briony took off the nightdress and, folding it carefully, placed it on the chairback. Then, naked, she went and sat on his knee, slipping her slender arms around his neck. Looking into his face she smiled tremulously.

'Am I doing right, Mr Dumas, sir?' The little eager voice made him want to tear into her there and then, but he stopped himself.

34

Instead he laid her on the carpet in front of the fire and traced every line of her body with the tips of his fingers.

'You're doing very well, Briony, very well indeed.'

When he began kissing her body, she studied the room around her, and shut her mind off from what was happening by thinking of all the things she was going to get the next day when she went shopping with Mrs Horlock. Everything from long pantaloons to a good velvet coat. As he entered her, she bit down on her lip and closed her eyes. A rogue tear made its way down her face and she licked its saltiness with her tongue. It hurt, Eileen was right, it hurt like mad.

She opened one eye and looked up at Henry Dumas. His face was shiny with sweat in the firelight, and his tongue was poking out of the corner of his mouth. He was completely taken over by her body, and she knew it. Instinctively, she knew it. It was the mystery of men and women, and inside Briony a little bell went off. To do this to her, men would give anything. It was a revelation. She felt better now, because she suddenly realised that there had been a subtle shifting of power here tonight.

She realised that Mr Dumas wanted her very much. He wanted to do this to her much more than she wanted the nice things he could give her.

Well then, so be it. But she would make sure she got her money's worth.

Chapter Three

Molly stopped for a few seconds and rubbed her hands together. The cold had crept into her bones and pushing the handcart had skinned her fingers. She took a deep breath and resumed her task. Eileen carried a large box, while Bernadette and Kerry carried a case between them. Rosalee sat on the handcart with her thumb stuck firmly in her mouth staring ahead of her over the tables and chairs and the other items of furniture stacked up around her. Bernadette lost her hold on the case and it swung sideways and hit Kerry's shins heavily. Dropping her side of the case, Kerry, in pain and temper, pulled Bernadette's hair with all her strength, and within seconds both girls were wailing. Settling the cart once more, Molly tried to quieten them. They had just rounded the corner to Oxlow Lane and she wanted desperately to make a good impression on her new neighbours.

'Come on now, girls. Whist now, be quiet.'

Bernadette sniffed loudly and then smacked Kerry across the face with the flat of her hand.

Eileen, putting down her box, separated the two girls who were kicking and screaming. She shook them until they quietened. Pushing her face close to theirs, she whispered, 'I'm warning the pair of you, Mum's on a short leash today and you're safe while outsiders can see you, but once in the new place she'll skin you alive if you annoy her.' She stared into one face and then the other. 'Do you two understand me?'

Both girls nodded, and picking up the case once more they trudged ahead of the handcart. Eileen picked up her box wearily and the handcart's squeaking wheel was the only sound as they walked to the cottage that was to be their new home.

Molly stood in front of the black front door and sighed in delight. They really were here, they really had this place. They finally had a proper home. Her eyes drank in the leaded light windows that only needed a good wash, the red-tiled roof and cream-painted walls. It was all her dreams come true.

The cottages had stood there since the sixteenth century and had once boasted thatched roofs and large gardens. They had been farm workers' cottages until the mid-1800s when they had been bought up and rented out to any Barking residents who could pay.

Oxlow Lane was still countrified, wide and sweeping and bordered by fields. Most of the people who could afford decent houses wanted to live near Stratford and Bow, if not in Barkingside, where the docks were. But Molly was astute enough to know that Oxlow Lane would be quiet for herself and the girls, while still close enough to East London which was only a couple of hours' walk. Rainham-on-Thames was only another hour's walk along the London Road and Molly was determined to take the girls there for the day in the summer. She had been there only once herself, when she had first married Paddy, and carried the memory with her in a kind of reverence. They'd sat on the sands as the Thames rolled by, watching the passenger ferries from Gravesend in Kent disgorge day trippers, dressed in their Sunday best. They had eaten whelks and cockles outside The Phoenix public house, and Paddy had kissed her on the beach to the scandalisation of some older women near them. Oh, she was taking the girls in the summer if it was the last thing she did!

She felt in her coat pocket for the large brass key and once more marvelled to herself. A key. For the first time they had a dwelling with a key. With a real front door. She took it out of her pocket and inserted it in the lock – then all hell broke loose. Rosalee, for some unexplained reason, decided to get herself down from the cart. She stood up amongst the furniture and somehow managed to upset the whole thing.

Eileen watched in dismay as the child was flung on to the

38

ground with a hard thud, closely followed by the table and chairs. The door of the adjoining cottage opened and a large man rushed out. Molly saw white-blond hair and huge musclebound arms pick up Rosalee and pass her to Eileen, then the table and chairs were also picked up and stacked neatly in what seemed seconds.

Rosalee, winded from the force of the fall, gasped for breath in Eileen's arms. But she wouldn't cry, Molly knew she wouldn't cry. The last time she'd cried was when Briony left her.

'Hello, Mrs. Me and me mum's been looking out for you like,' their neighbour told them.

A little woman of indeterminate age came through the door. 'I thought you could do with a cuppa, love. I've had the kettle on all morning, waiting for you.' She looked at the four girls. Molly noticed the frown as she glanced twice at Rosalee.

'These all yourn?'

Molly smiled. 'Yes, but they're good quiet girls.' She looked at Kerry and Bernadette who had the grace to drop their eyes to the ground. Molly so wanted to make a good impression.

The old woman opened a toothless mouth and screeched with laughter.

'I'll believe that when I hear it! I had six, four girls and two boys. He's the last one at home.' She indicated her large son with a nod of her head. 'And I'll tell you now, give me a houseful of boys any day to girlies. Fighting and arguing and moaning and crying and pinching . . . Oh, I could carry on all day. Be nice to have a bit of life up the lane again, though, not enough children here any more.'

Molly felt her heart lift.

'Now then, how about a cuppa, and what about some bread pudding for you girls, with a nice cup of weak tea, eh?'

She put out a hand, and to the astonishment of Molly, Rosalee wriggled from Eileen's arms and, taking the old woman's hand, she went into the cottage with her.

The man grinned.

'I'm Abel Jones and that's me mother. We all call her Mother

39

Jones, me and everyone else that knows her. Now get yourselves in out of the cold and I'll get the furniture in for you.'

Molly smiled at him and followed her eager daughters.

Abel looked at her as she went through the door and smiled to himself. Not a bad-looking piece that. He wondered if there was a husband in tow. Must be to afford the rent on the cottage, but you never knew, Abel told himself. She might be free for a bit of a laugh.

He picked up the heavy wood table as if it was made of paper and walked into the cottage with it.

Briony had been living her new life for three weeks and she loved it. Well, she liked most of it, she told herself. The things that she had to do for Mr Dumas got on her nerves a bit, but she was getting to like living at the house and that was all that really concerned her. She put on a brown dress with a tiny lace collar, her walking boots and her large brown cape. Lastly she put on a straw hat with dried flowers that was totally unsuited to the weather, but she was so enamoured of it she didn't care. She walked down the stairs and went through the green baize door to Mrs Horlock and Cissy.

'Get us a cab, Cis.' Briony's voice was clear and loud in the kitchen and Mrs Horlock smothered a smile. She was a case, was this one. Not five minutes in the house and already she acted like she was born to it. If she used the toilet once a day she used it fifty times, though the novelty of the bathroom was wearing off now and she was down to only two baths a day. But Mrs Horlock was clever enough to let the child have her head, let her get used to her surroundings. If she was happy, Mr Dumas was happy and at the end of the day, that was what counted.

'You're going to your mum's then, Miss?'

'Yes, Mrs Horlock, I am. Don't worry, I'll tell the cab to come back for me at five. I'll be home in plenty of time for Mr Dumas and me dinner.'

'Shall I go with her, Mrs Horlock?' Cissy's face was expressionless but the hope behind it was evident.

'No you won't, Cissy. All the work I've got here today! Now

40

go and get Miss Briony her cab. And hurry up!'

Cissy ran from the kitchen.

'I've made you up a hamper for your mum. She'll need it today.'

Briony grinned at the old woman. She looked stern at times, and she could be sharp, but underneath Briony liked her. She cuddled Briony sometimes of an evening when Mr Dumas went home to his real house. Briony would come out here, to the kitchen and Mrs Horlock would settle her on her lap, tell her stories and feed her hot milk and bread and butter while Cissy was ironing or baking. All under Mrs Horlock's astute gaze, of course. The kitchen fire would be roaring up the chimney and the smell of spices and baking was very welcoming to Briony. The warmth and the good smells made her feel secure.

Briony opened the lid of the hamper and saw two small malt loaves, that would be full of the raisins that Rosalee loved. A small ham and a large lump of cheese. There were also some home-made scones and a jar of strawberry jam.

'Thanks, Mrs Horlock, she'll be very grateful to you.'

The woman waved her hand at Briony. ''Tis nothing. There's a screw of tea on the table to go in and some sugar and butter.'

Briony put these in the hamper and then went to the housekeeper and hugged her, pushing her face, straw hat and all, into the floury-smelling apron. Mrs Horlock looked down on the flame-coloured hair that spiralled out under the hat and felt a rush of affection for the child. She hugged her back.

Mother Jones was ensconced by her fire with Rosalee on her lap. She stroked the downy hair and shook her head. This was a child meant for the angels if ever she saw one. Abel watched her and smiled.

'Poor little thing. Must be hard for that Molly like, Mum. Having one like her. She'll never be able to earn.'

Mother Jones sniffed. 'No, true, but she'll never leave home either, so she'll never be lonely if she loses her man.'

Abel nodded and looked towards the dividing wall. He had taken a fancy to Molly Cavanagh.

41

On the other side of the wall, she was busy scrubbing the floor and watching Bernadette and Kerry at their task of cleaning the windows. She had eaten two slices of bread pudding and drunk two cups of hot sweet black tea and it had fortified her for the job in hand. Mother Jones had sent Abel in to show her how to get the fire going in the range, and now she had steaming hot water as often as she wanted it. This thrilled her to bits, though coal was being burnt like nobody's business. Still, it was only for today.

'Mum, our Briony's arrived in a cab!'

Molly sighed and opened the front door. Briony got out of the cab and the driver took down a small hamper and placed it beside her on the dirt road. Molly watched her pay the man and gritted her teeth. As the horse set off, clip-clopping down the lane, Molly walked out of the cottage.

'Hello, Mum. Mrs Horlock sent you a hamper, to help you get settled like.'

Briony's voice was wary as she spoke and Molly felt a moment's sorrow for her coldness towards the child.

'Come away in, Briony, it's freezing out here.'

She smiled and followed her mother inside the cottage. Kerry and Bernadette crowded around her as she opened the hamper and showed them what was inside.

'Where's Rosalee then?'

'Oh, she's with the lady next-door. She's really nice and gave us bread pudding and a cup of char, and her house smells really funny and she ain't got no teeth . . .'

'Shut up now, Kerry.'

Briony laughed. Trust Kerry to go too far!

She took off her coat and hat, rolled up her sleeves and, taking the chamois leather from Kerry, set about the windows.

Molly watched her as she worked away, and closing her eyes she prayed to God to give her peace of mind where her Briony was concerned. They depended on her wages, far more than they ever had on Eileen's. It was Briony who was going to keep them in Oxlow Lane, and as Paddy had pointed out, Molly didn't want to kill the goose that was laying the golden eggs, did she? Forcing herself to move, she walked to Briony and embraced the girl. Briony cuddled her back, joyful that her mother wasn't cross with her any more. For her part, Molly closed her eyes and swallowed down the disgust that touching Briony always made her feel.

Letting her go, she resumed washing the floor of the cottage and Kerry and Bernadette sorted out the bedding and curtains into neat piles on the table.

'Give us a song, Kerry.'

'What do you want, a happy one or a crying one?'

'Whatever you like.'

Kerry stopped what she was doing and thought for a second, then she began to sing. It was Paddy's favourite and Briony smiled as she began. Kerry sang this song like an angel.

> 'Oh Danny boy, the pipes, the pipes are calling,
> From glen to glen, and down the mountainside . . .'

Next-door, Mother Jones and Abel heard the singing and both laughed as Rosalee started to clap her hands.

'They're a funny family, Mum. Another girl just arrived by cab, dressed up like a kipper. Only about ten and in a cab mind, not on foot. Where are they getting the money for cabs and the like?'

'How the bloody hell would I know! They seem nice enough, Abel Jones, so don't you go snooping round there and put them off us.'

'I'm only saying, Mum . . .'

'Yeah, well, just you say it to yourself then. It'll all come out in the wash anyway. People's business rarely stays between four walls. You'll find out soon enough, son, and when you do I hope it's what you want to hear!'

'Here's Dad and Eileen with the beds, Mum!' Kerry shrieked out the words at the top of her voice, making Molly, who was upstairs getting the bedroom floors swept, cringe. The child thought she was still in the basement where you had to shout to be heard above the din coming from the other families.

'Shall I let them in?'

Briony laughed out loud.

'No, Kerry, let's leave them out there 'til the morning. Of course you should let them in!'

Kerry opened the door grandly. She had been locking and unlocking it all afternoon, and the novelty of the key had yet to wear off.

Briony stamped down the stairs and, after kissing Eileen, began to help while they unloaded the beds and boxes.

Abel Jones watched the proceedings from his window, studying Paddy closely. Then a cab pulled up, and the little one with the red curly hair was kissing them all and getting inside.

He shook his head. There was something funny going on with that family, he'd lay money on it. There was only one place that child would be going in a cab and that was Nellie Deakins' house.

Rosalee sat at the table and drank her broth, Kerry and Bernadette were putting the finishing touches to their room, and Eileen was making up her parents' bed. Paddy looked at his wife in the glow of the kitchen fire and, sober for once, he felt a stirring in him. As she tended the fire he saw the roundness of her large breasts, caught a glimpse of creamy skin. She wasn't a bad looker wasn't Molly, for all the childbearing. He pulled her down on to his lap, and she laughed as the chair creaked under their weight.

'Isn't this a grand place, Moll?'

She smiled and nodded. It was her dream come true. The kitchen was also their living room, but Molly didn't mind. It meant only one fire. The table and chairs were scrubbed and clean, the mats were down, and the new chair was by the fender for when she wanted to sew or just sit and drink one of her never ending cups of tea. Briony said she was going to get Mrs Horlock to let her have some of the old curtains packed away at Mr Dumas'. She'd fit them to the windows and the place would be like a little palace. She frowned as she thought of Briony.

She allowed Paddy to nuzzle her neck. He pulled her face round and kissed her long and hard, forcing his tongue into her mouth, and Molly, for the first time in over a year, responded. In her happiness at being in the house, she wanted everything to go well.

'Oh, Mum!' Eileen, who had walked downstairs, saw them kissing and all the revulsion she felt was in her voice. Molly pulled away from Paddy just as Eileen got to the sink and threw up, retching and hawking with the illness that engulfed her at the disgusting sight.

'Eileen. Eileen, girl.' Molly put her arm around her shoulders gently, trying to pull her into her arms.

'Don't you touch me, Mum!' Eileen pointed a finger into her mother's face. 'Don't you ever touch me after you've touched him. Not after what he's done to me and Briony. And who'll be next, that's what I want to know? Bernie, Kerry, our Rosalee?'

Rosalee, hearing her name mentioned, clapped her hands together and upset the broth.

'Bri . . . Bri.'

Bernadette and Kerry, who had come down the stairs at the sound of Eileen's voice, stood like statues staring at their mother and father, fear in their faces as they realised that something bad was going to happen, and maybe even to one of them.

Molly looked from her daughter to her husband who was sitting in the chair, his head in his hands. Then Paddy got up, took his coat from the back of the door and tried to open the front door. He rattled it hard, trying to force it open, until Kerry ran to him and unlocked it with the key, all her excitement gone now as she watched her father leave the house.

Molly pulled Eileen towards her and cuddled her tightly.

'Oh Eileen, my baby, my lovely girl. What did he do to you?'

She didn't say we – what did we do to you? – because the knowledge that she had eventually condoned what her husband had done would not allow itself to surface. She held Eileen while she cried and Kerry cleaned up the mess made by Rosalee's broth.

45

Henry Dumas stroked Briony's hair. It was like stroking silky springs. Briony lay beside him and let him cuddle her. She liked this bit. After all the other business was out of the way, he cuddled her and whispered things to her. She didn't always understand what he was talking about, but the tone of his voice always sent her off to sleep. She watched drowsily as he got dressed, saw him push his fat little legs into his trousers, and smiled to herself. He always looked funny undressed. But when he was dressed he was like a different person. Briony respected him when he was dressed, and didn't answer him back or make as many jokes as she did the other times.

She'd turned on her side and closed her eyes to sleep when there was a loud banging on the front door. She sat bolt upright in the bed and stared at Mr Dumas. Then she heard her father's voice, loud in the hallway, and her heart sank. He was drunk, she could hear it in every word he said.

'Where's me girl? I want me girl this minute!'

Briony heard Cissy's and Mrs Horlock's voices trying to quieten him. As Henry Dumas walked towards the door, Briony was off the bed and in front of him.

'Stay up here. I'll see to me dad.' Instinctively she knew that as her father was, if he saw Henry Dumas, all hell would break loose.

Paddy looked up and saw her walking towards him. She looked beautiful. In the white lawn nightdress and with her spectacular hair unbound, she was like a vision. Through his drink-crazed mind he realised exactly what he had done to her and to Eileen, and it made him sick inside.

'I've come to take you home, Briony, my baby.' His voice was drenched with tears.

She flicked a glance at Mrs Horlock and then back at her father.

'Come into the warm, Dad, you're freezing.'

She opened the door to the morning room and he followed her inside. Mrs Horlock lit the gas lamps and Briony pushed the poker in the fire to get a blaze.

'What's all the noise about then, Dad?'

Paddy settled himself in a chair and stared at his daughter.

'I've come to take you home, lovie. This is all wrong. Eileen's been . . . she's accusing me something terrible . . . Your ma . . .'

He couldn't get the words out to explain himself, but Briony understood him well enough.

'But, Dad, I like it here. I don't want to go home.'

Paddy blinked his eyes as if to reassure himself he had heard right.

'It's lovely here, Dad. Mr Dumas is really nice to me and I've got Cissy and Mrs Horlock looking after me, and I go out to Barking Park every day . . .'

Her voice trailed off. Her mother must have caused all sorts of trouble for her dad to be here now. Even with a drink in him, he was aware of what the money meant each week. Now they'd all moved into the new house, how the hell did they think they'd pay the rent?

'Why don't you let Cissy get you a cab home, Dad? In the morning, when everything's all right with me mum, everything will be better.'

Paddy finally understood what Briony was saying. He hadn't left her here like Eileen to make the best of it. She actually *wanted* to be here, and the knowledge hurt him far more than anything else she could have said. Even losing the house wouldn't have hurt as much as what his daughter had just said. No wonder Molly was dead set against her. Here was a whore in the making all right.

'You're coming home with me now.' His voice was harsh, and he was surprised when Briony shook her head.

'I'll not leave this house, Dad, I'm staying here whether you like it or not. You couldn't wait for me to get here not three weeks since, and if you think that I'm going back to Oxlow Lane with you, you're wrong. Dead wrong. If you take me home, then I'll just keep coming back.'

She stared into his face earnestly. 'Can't you see, Dad? I love it here. I'm happy here. And best of all, everyone benefits by it. Especially me mum. She might want me home now, but she won't when we're back in the docks, will she?'

Paddy knew when he was defeated, but at least he could tell Molly and Eileen the truth now. That he'd come to get her and she'd refused. A little while later, as he made his way home in the cab paid for by Briony, he realised something. For all the trouble he was having with Eileen, he'd rather that than have her thinking like his Briony, and that was a turn up because Briony was their golden goose. Yet Eileen, it seemed to him, was more of a decent girl than ever, for all she'd been through with that scumbag. Whereas Briony, who'd taken to it like a duck to water, had broken his heart.

Chapter Four

It was thick snow and Briony had had to brave the freezing weather to get a cab. Even in her thick coat and dress, fur hat and muff, she was still frozen. Her face was stinging with the cold and as the horse moved slowly through the icy streets she waggled her toes in her boots to stop them from going numb. It was her second Christmas at Henry Dumas' house and she was a different girl altogether to the one who had arrived there fourteen months earlier. At eleven, she had grown. Her breasts were forming and the good food had put flesh on her bones. Her face had rounded, giving her a look of a young woman already. Her hair was still a fiery red, only now she wore it in a neat chignon pinned to her head with expert precision by Mrs Horlock.

Briony had also changed inside herself. She wasn't as happy-go-lucky as she had been, and she was sensing a change in Henry Dumas as her body developed. She bit on her lip and watched the traffic in the streets, mainly pedestrians, a few ragamuffins running around offering to hold horses' bridles or carry people's shopping for a halfpenny. The majority of the people wore sacking over their clothes to try and keep the snow from freezing their bodies entirely.

As they approached Barking Broadway, the horse's pace slowed even more. Briony pushed down the window of the cab and stared out. Then she saw him.

He was a tall boy of about thirteen, dressed in ragged trousers and jacket though his heavy boots were obviously new. Brand new, not second hand new. Briony was struck by his appearance because he had the thickest, blackest hair and eyebrows she had ever seen in her life. As she watched him from the cab she saw him stumble into a well-dressed man and apologise profusely before walking on. Briony smiled. He was dipping. She watched as another boy stepped by him and was given the wallet. It was all over in a split second and now the first boy ambled on again, safe in the knowledge that if he was stopped, he had no evidence on his person. Briony was fascinated by it all, and from her vantage point kept a close eye on him.

His next victim was to be a young docker, the worse for drink and also stumbling. She noticed the way that the pickpocket kept his cap pulled down low over his face; his clothes, well-pressed though old, were obviously new to him. He couldn't quite carry himself in them properly. More used to being ragged arsed. Briony watched the boy bump into the docker, and then it all went wrong. The young man grabbed the boy's hand like a vice. Briony saw them start struggling and banged on the wooden side of the cab for it to stop. Getting out, she ran over to where the two men were arguing, attracting the attention of more than a few people. She pushed her way through and, without giving it a second's thought, dragged the dark boy free.

All the people there took in her clothes and assumed she was from the upper classes. She looked it, from her well-shod feet to her fur hat and muff. She looked into the dark boy's face and in her best imitation of Henry Dumas' voice, asked: 'Have you picked up my purchases yet?'

The boy stared at her. She could see his brain seeking the appropriate answer. He was quick enough to know she was trying to help him. It was why she should that was the puzzle.

'Come on, boy, we'll go and pick them up now.' She grabbed the sleeve of his jacket and looked at the docker.

'You should not imbibe so much drink, young man, you obviously can't take it. Now get off home.'

She pulled the boy back to the cab and he helped her inside, lifting her arm and guiding her in as if he did it every day of his life. Once settled, they looked at one another.

'You didn't get to lift his wallet then?'

Briony's altered voice was such a shock the boy started to laugh.

She frowned at him. 'What you bleeding laughing at then? I just helped you out of a very tricky situation.'

The boy roared.

'It's your voice! Just now you sounded like the bloody Queen. Now you're speaking like any other street slut.'

Briony felt herself pale and this was not lost on the boy either.

'What did you just say?'

He hastened to make amends.

'I didn't mean that how it come out.'

She pushed her hands into her muff with such force she ripped the lining and the sound in the quiet of the cab was like a pistol going off.

The boy ran his hands through his hair. Realising his mistake, he tried to make it up to her.

'I'm Tom Lane, Tommy to me mates. Thanks for helping me out like. I 'ppreciate it.'

Briony looked at his handsome but dirty face, and thawed a bit.

'I'm Briony Cavanagh.'

He grinned then, showing big strong white teeth. He settled back in the cab and Briony found herself grinning too.

'Where do you live then?'

Briony swallowed deeply before answering. 'I live in Oxlow Lane, but I work in a big house, just round the corner from Barking Park.' There was no way she was giving him an address, he looked the type to turn up there. The thought thrilled and frightened her at the same time.

'Oxlow Lane, you say? That where you're going now?'

Briony nodded. 'I'm going to visit me family.'

Tom nodded and looked her over from head to toe. A nice-looking piece, he thought, but too well dressed for service. She was on the bash or his name wasn't Tom Lane. He had two sisters and a mother on the game and neither of them had hit the big money like this one. But he didn't tell her his thoughts. He liked her, he liked her a lot, especially for saving his neck.

'How old are you then?'

Briony tossed her head and looked out at the passing road. 'Old enough. You?'

Tommy grinned again. 'Older than that, girl.' He glanced outside and saw that they were at the Longbridge Road. 'You can let me down here.' He banged on the wooden side and the driver slowed the horse.

'Tara then, Briony Cavanagh.'

''Bye, Tommy Lane.'

He hopped from the cab, and before shutting the door he winked at her. Briony watched him cross the wide road and make his way inside The Royal Oak. She saw him disappear inside the doorway and felt a moment's sadness that he had gone. For some funny reason she liked him.

Tommy walked into the public house and ordered himself a pint of beer. His eyes travelled round the crowded bar looking for a face he knew. He saw a friend called Willy Cushing and walked over to him.

'Hello, Willy, you're looking well.' And indeed Willy was looking well. He was wearing a suit more fitted to a lawyer than a petty criminal.

'He looks like a pox doctor's clerk, if you ask me.'

Willy smiled good-naturedly at the little boy sitting on the seat beside his friend.

'Me bruvver James.'

Tommy nodded at the little boy.

'He's got some trap, ain't he, Willy?'

Willy, a small dumpy boy with sandy hair and non-existent eyebrows, nodded his head vigorously.

'More front than Southend, mate, and he's only seven. Sit down, Tommy, I ain't seen you for a while.'

He sat on the wooden bench beside his friend and admired him openly.

'You're looking really prosperous, Willy, what's the scam?'

Willy took a large drink of beer and smiled. 'I'm in with

Dobson's lot now. I tell you, Tommy, all the stories about him are true, but he's a good bloke if you don't cross him.'

Tommy nodded. Davie Dobson was the local hard man. He was good to people hereabouts in a lot of ways. It was known he would give money to women whose husbands had gone down before the beak, but he was also known to break a few bones when things weren't going his way. He ran most of the girls on the streets hereabouts, as far as Stratford and some up West.

'So what you doing for him then?'

'I sort out deals for him. Little deals that he ain't got the time or the inclination to bother with.'

What he actually meant was little girls. Willy procured them from the poorer families and then delivered them to Nellie Deakins' house and other establishments all over the smoke. Dobson, who was trying to make himself look respectable in certain circles, needed stooges like Willy who'd go down if they got caught and do their time without a whimper, coming home to a good few quid and a steady job. Willy was to progress soon to delivering girls to the homes of certain prominent people whom Davie Dobson would then blackmail. It was the most lucrative business, because once they paid, they paid forever.

'Could you get me in with him like, Willy? I could do with a regular job, and you don't look like you're starving from it.'

Willy swaggered in his seat.

'I'll have a word with him for you. Me and Dobson's like that.'

'You do that for me, Willy, and I'll owe you one. Now seeing as how you're in the dosh, you can get the next round in.'

Willy got up and went to the bar.

'What do you do, young man?' Tommy addressed James, who looked at him as if he was so much dirt.

'Mind your own business, you nosy bastard!'

Tommy laughed and James frowned at him. He was only three feet six inches tall and already he was a hard man. That's what life on the streets did for you.

Briony swept into the house in Oxlow Lane in a cloud of cold air and perfume. Molly went outside and picked up the hamper, dragging it through the door. Briony helped her get it on the table.

'Where's the girls?'

'All gone up the Lane for some last-minute shopping. Eileen's been promising them she'll take them all week. Rosalee's asleep upstairs.'

Briony removed her coat and hung it carefully on the nail behind the front door.

'How are you, Mum?'

She and Molly had had a truce for nearly a year now. It was a truce that suited them both. Molly needed Briony's wages, as they were called, and Briony had no intention of ever coming back to her mother's house. Molly had resigned herself to Briony's choice of career and now the two got on quite well.

'I wanted to talk to you, Mum, I'm glad we're alone.'

Briony put the kettle on the fire and started to make a fresh pot of tea while Molly unpacked the hamper.

'It's Henry – Mr Dumas. He's losing interest in me.'

Molly pushed back her faded blonde hair and stared across at her daughter's beautiful face. Every time she looked at Briony she marvelled where she could have come from. With that red hair and white skin, she was unlike any of the others. Unlike her parents or grandparents, though the Irish were often red-headed.

'What you going to do then?'

Briony sighed. 'I don't know, Mum, but if I get me marching orders, the wages go with me.'

Molly knew this already and it scared her.

'Have you got anything down below yet?'

'I did have, but Cissy plucked them out for me.' Briony bit on her bottom lip. 'He can't stand it, see, Mum. Once I start to develop properly, he won't want me any more. I had a show last week. The curse is on its way, I just know it.'

Molly nodded. Briony made the tea and took the steaming pot over to the table.

'What am I going to do?'

54

Molly sighed. 'I don't know, girl. We'll put our thinking caps on and maybe something will come up.'

Rosalee started to cry and Briony went up the stairs and brought her down to the kitchen. 'Bri . . . Bri . . .'

Briony hugged her close and kissed her. 'Yes, it's Bri Bri, and she's got a lovely present for you for Christmas.'

Molly watched the red head and the blonde together and felt a sadness in herself. Both were tainted but in different ways. Of the two she'd rather have Rosalee any day.

Paddy was drunk; not his usual boisterous drunk but a sullen, melancholic mood. He staggered out of The Bull at twenty past ten. He would have stayed longer except he'd run out of money and his friends, on whom he had spent over a pound, were now preparing to leave as well. Paddy stumbled home.

The long walk, instead of sobering him up, only made him more peevish with every freezing step he took. In his mind he conjured up all the wrongs done to him by his wife. First and foremost in his mind was the fact she'd have no sexual relations with him. He'd get the priest round to talk to her about that. Then there was the fact that she doled out the money to him. He knew she had a good wad stashed away and, on the rare occasions that he was alone in the house, had searched for it fruitlessly. Then there was her attitude with the girls. By Christ, they were grown up now, except for Rosalee who would never grow up.

He felt his eyes mist up at the thought of her. In his drunken mind, Rosalee was the fault of his wife as well. He knew she'd tried to get rid of her, he knew everything about the bitch he lived with. Then the naked white body of his infant son came into his thoughts. It was the night Eileen left to work for Mr Dumas, and somehow, in his drink-fuddled mind, he decided that Molly had got rid of his son as well. The thought induced a rage so violent he felt he could choke on it. A man was judged by his sons. Splitarses – as girls were referred to – were a slur on a man's manhood. They were no good for anything except the begetting of more sons.

As he passed by the empty streets he thought of all the

setbacks he'd experienced in his life: never enough money, never anywhere decent to live. And somehow, all the blame was laid at Molly's door.

She'd never worked like other women. She used to clean doorsteps when he met her, had specialised in that. She'd been a tweenie since seven and at fourteen had begun specialising in her damned doorsteps! For a split second he saw her as she had been when he met her. High-breasted and tall, she had looked a fit mate for the big handsome Irishman he'd been. But marriage and the bearing of children had changed all that. Her and her fancy ideas about the girls going to school. Not working, oh no. Or even doing a decent day's housework until they were twelve. He gnashed his teeth in temper. With the four girls working they could have lived the life of Riley, but oh no. Not good enough for Molly Cavanagh. Her children, her girl children, were too good to slave fourteen hours a day in a sweat shop to earn their brass.

As he neared home Paddy's rage was reaching astounding proportions. He even began to blame his wife for his own drinking and gambling. If she had treated him as a wife should, he wouldn't stay out like he did, he justified it to himself. He omitted the fact he had always led the life of a single man even when married.

He opened the front door. His face was blue with the cold, but one look at his eyes and the girls saw their father was in the mood for a fight. Dressed in their Sunday best, they waited patiently for their mother to braid their hair ready for Midnight Mass at St Vincent's where Kerry had been asked to sing a solo.

Molly was busy buttoning Rosalee's dress. Hearing her husband enter, she cried: 'Where the hell have you been? You know Kerry's singing at the Mass. You promised me you'd be home early.'

She looked up into his face and her heart froze in her chest. He was drunk, roaring drunk. He wouldn't miss Midnight Mass, though. He'd stumble up to Communion like he did every Sunday, oblivious to the staring faces around him. Most of the Irishmen left it to their wives to attend church for them. It was no sin for them to sit in the pub all day Sunday, but let an Irishman's wife miss Mass with the children and she would be ostracised by all and sundry. Not for the first time the divide between men and women irritated Molly Cavanagh. Maybe it was this that prompted her to fight with him instead of ushering the children from the house to Mother Jones next door and then letting Paddy do his worst 'til he fell asleep in front of the fire. She resigned herself to a black eye for Christmas and decided that this time she'd get it for a good reason.

'I'll not walk in the church with a drunk, Paddy. You can either go alone, or sleep the drink off and go in the morning.'

He pushed Kerry and Bernadette out of the way. 'What did you say to me, woman?'

Molly pulled Rosalee into her skirts and glared at her husband.

'You heard me!'

Paddy stared first at his wife then at each of the four girls in turn. Eileen gathered her three younger sisters together and, slipping past her father, took them to Mother Jones. Knocking gently on the window, she held the three white-faced girls to her. Mother Jones was in the process of tying a large bonnet of dark green taffeta on to her wiry grey hair. She opened the front door with a wide grin on her face, thinking they were all ready to go to Mass. One look at Eileen's face told her otherwise.

'It's me dad, he's drunk as a lord and about to go at me mum. Can I leave these three here?'

'Of course you can, lovie.' She pulled Eileen inside her door, closing it against the bitter wind. As they settled the children round the fire they heard Molly's scream, and a sound like splintering wood. Rosalee whimpered and the old woman pulled her on to her lap.

'There now, me pet. Everything's fine.'

Eileen stood up. 'I've got to go in there. He'll knock her from here to next week if someone doesn't stop him.'

'Stay here, child. Abel will be here soon with the cart to take us all to Mass. He'll go in.'

Eileen wiped her hand across her face.

'I've got to get their coats anyway. I'll go in.'

She left the cottage and went back inside her own home.

Molly was crying, harsh racking sobs. Eileen saw her mother's eye already swelling and the blood from a cut on her lip. Paddy had punched her to the ground and one of the wooden chairs was lying broken on the floor. It was what her father was doing now that made Eileen pick up the iron from the fire.

He was pulling up her mother's skirts and dragging at her underclothes. Eileen knew what he was going to do because it brought back painful memories of Mr Dumas. She knew how much it hurt, and how sick and ill it made you afterwards.

Molly was staring at her daughter, beseeching her with her eyes and crying over Paddy's shoulder softly.

'No, Paddy, not like this, man! Not like this!'

Bringing back her arm, Eileen swung the iron down on the side of her father's head with all her strength. The spray of blood that shot up into the air covered both mother and daughter. Paddy slumped down over his wife, his legs twitching for a few seconds before death took him completely.

Eileen put her hand over her mouth to stem the tide of vomit rushing up inside her. Molly, with a strength born of desperation, pushed the lifeless form from her. Dragging herself upright, she put her hand to her mouth in shock. The two stood there like statues until Abel, who had arrived with the cart, was sent in by his mother.

He took one look at Paddy lying spreadeagled on the floor, his head a mush of blood and brains, and swore under his breath.

'Jesus sodding Christ! What happened here?'

Eileen began to shake. It started in her hands and travelled through her cold body until even her teeth were chattering. Abel dragged Paddy over on to his back. The unbuttoned trousers told him the whole story.

'Was he at the girl? Was he at Eileen?'

He assumed that Molly had taken the iron to him. She shook her head, and as he heard Eileen moan, Abel saw the iron still in her hand.

'He was at you, Moll?'

She nodded. Her blonde hair was in disarray and her clothes were ripped. A strand of saliva was hanging from her top lip as she tried to speak.

Abel took the iron from Eileen and put it into the sink. Then he went outside to the pump and filled a bucket with icy water. He washed the iron clean of blood, talking over his shoulder as he did so.

'First I want you to get some sheets to wrap him in. Come on, you two!' His voice was urgent. 'We have to get rid of him, girls, or else one or the other of you will be before the beak in the morning.'

Molly felt his words penetrate her brain and forced herself into action. Going up the stairs, she pulled the sheets from her bed and brought them back down to the kitchen.

Abel had put Eileen in the easy chair and was pouring out a cup of hot sweet tea for her.

'We'll wrap him up tight and I'll dump him somewhere. We'll think of a story later, let's just get rid of the . . . of Paddy's . . . of his body.' There, it was said.

'Oh, Abel, what are we going to do?' Molly's voice had risen now as the shock wore off and he went to her and put his arms around her.

'Listen to me, Molly. We must get rid of him now, before anyone finds out what's happened. I'll take him down to the docks, dump him in the water. Plenty of people turn up there dead. You report him missing tomorrow and the police will assume he was set upon for his wages.'

The words were tumbling out of him. One thing was sure, he had to help Molly. Since she had moved in next-door he had grown to care for her deeply. Many was the night he'd heard Paddy going for her and had wanted to do exactly what the girl had just done. As far as he was concerned, his main priority now was to get rid of Paddy's body and keep the girls safe.

He began to wrap Paddy in the sheets, covering the broken head as best he could.

59

'What about Midnight Mass? Kerry's to sing there tonight!'

'The Mass has started, Moll. We'll say you was waiting for Paddy to come home. Yes, that's what we'll say. Now help me to wrap him tight, and then I'll put him on the cart and you and Eileen can get this floor scrubbed clean of blood. Come on now, Moll, or we'll all be done for.'

Eileen watched as Abel and her mother wrapped up her father's body. She felt nothing as she saw Abel put the blood-stained bundle over his shoulder and take him out to the cart.

Molly put the kettle on for more hot water and drank her tea standing up by the fire, waiting for the kettle to boil. She was suspended between two feelings. One of shock at what had happened, and the other a drive for self-preservation. The world now consisted of herself, Eileen and Abel Jones. Because Abel had involved himself for her, and she knew why. Though Paddy's passing was shocking, it was also a passport to a better life for her and this thought kept her going through the gruelling night ahead.

Abel went in to his mother before he took Paddy's body off in the cart. She had put the children to bed in her own room and he explained what had taken place to her in hushed tones. Being a sensible woman she didn't moan or wail, but nodded at her big handsome son and then began to talk.

'Take him to Dagenham Docks, son, but don't put him in the water wrapped in the sheets. Bring them back and I'll burn them. Empty his pockets. Street thieves take everything, even a good coat, remember that. If his boots are in good nick, take them off and we'll get rid of them too.' She racked her brains for what else she should tell him.

Abel kissed her on the forehead and tried to wink at her.

'You know you'll hang if this is found out?'

He nodded. 'I know that, Mum. But if you could see those two in there . . .' His voice trailed off.

'You're a good boy, Abel. Too good sometimes, I think.'

On this he left the kitchen and, taking the blanket off the horse, covered the body with it and clip-clopped down Oxlow Lane in a light flurry of snow.

Briony turned up at nine on Christmas morning, laden with food and presents. As soon as she walked into her mother's house she knew that something had happened. The three younger girls ran to her and she kissed them, pushing gaily wrapped presents into their hands. The smell of roasting duck was heavy on the air, but her mother's wan, swollen face and the absence of Eileen told her that something was afoot.

'Where's Eileen?'

'She's lying down, Briony. Come upstairs and see her.'

Briony followed her mother up to the bedroom without even removing her coat. Once inside the tiny room, she gasped. Eileen was lying in bed staring at the ceiling.

'What's wrong with her, Mum? And where's me dad?'

Molly bit on her swollen top lip.

'Eileen ... she hit him last night. He was drunk and trying to ... Eileen saw him and something snapped inside her, girl. She hit him with the flat iron.'

Briony stared into her mother's face.

'Where is he then? In the hospital?'

Molly shook her head.

'He was dead, Briony. Stone dead. And Abel ... Abel ...' She swallowed back tears. 'He dumped him in the Thames. In the docks. She'd have been taken away otherwise.'

Molly's voice was rising and Briony put her arms around her. 'All right, Mum. All right. You did the right thing. What's the next step?'

'I'm going to report him missing like, this afternoon. I'm going to pretend that he stayed out often all night and that if he's been picked up drunk then they can keep him. Abel ... well, Abel says that's the best way. More natural like.'

Briony nodded, seeing the sense of what was being said. The police in this area were used to women like her mother who brought up families on the money they could slip from a drunken husband's pockets. But if they came to Oxlow Lane then they'd wonder where the hell the money came from for the house. Briony felt no loss at the death of her father, he had been

61

like a thorn in all their sides. All she had ever known was either the back of his hand or his drunken caresses. She was more interested in looking after Eileen and her mother.

'If they question you about this place, then you tell them about me. I'll deal with them when and if I have to, all right?'

Molly nodded. Briony went over to the bed and stared down at her sister's face. It was white and pinched. Her eyes, normally so blue and clear, looked dull. Eileen stared back at Briony and her lips trembled.

Kerry and Bernadette burst into the room, both waving pairs of shiny new leather shoes.

'Oh, Bri, they're lovely, thanks, thanks!'

Briony turned and hugged them, while Molly hastily wiped her eyes.

'Keep your noise down now, Eileen's not feeling well.'

Kerry jerked her head towards Eileen and frowned. 'Will I sing you a nice song, our Eileen? To cheer you up.'

Eileen nodded weakly, trying to smile.

Kerry put her new shoes on the bottom of the bed and, pushing back her thick black hair, began to sing.

Chapter Five

Isabel Dumas watched her husband closely as he cosseted his niece. He had pulled the little girl on to his lap and was caressing her blonde hair as he whispered endearments to her. Isabel felt a sickness inside herself as she watched him. She glanced at her husband's sister and saw that she was smiling benignly at her brother and daughter. Isabel dragged her eyes from the scene and, excusing herself on the pretext of seeing how dinner was progressing, went up to her room.

Standing in their brand new bathroom, a marble and brass affair that she thought vulgar in the extreme, she splashed cold water on to her face and looked at herself in the mirror. She was twenty-five years old and had been married to Henry Dumas for seven years.

Her dark brown eyes took in the slight droop of her generous mouth and premature lines under her eyes from sleepless nights. Nights when she tossed and turned until she saw the daylight creep under her heavy bedroom curtains and intrude on her private world. She had long thick brown hair that had lost its gleam; her whole appearance was dull. It broke her heart every time she looked too closely at herself. She fancied sometimes that she was getting so sad and grey that eventually she would pass through the world completely unnoticed. Her mind went back to her husband caressing his five-year-old niece and she felt a wave of nausea engulf her.

It was true about Henry, she knew it. There was nothing for

her with him any more, she couldn't hide from that fact. Her
marriage was a lie, a blatant lie that she was beginning to regret
with all her heart. All the long, lonely nights!

After their marriage her fine new husband had taken her up to
bed and, after kissing her perfunctorily, had left her. She had
assumed he was being kind, thinking of her, of how it was all
new and the wedding had been tiring, and at first she had
actually felt a surge of happiness to have such a thoughtful
husband. But as the months passed it had become a nightly
ritual. Henry pecked her on the cheek and went straight to his
own room or left the house altogether. She had begun to think
that something was dreadfully wrong with her. How was she to
get a child if he never came near her? The worst of it all was that
it was not something she could discuss with anyone. Her mother
would have a fit of the vapours and be taken to bed for the day
with a liberal supply of brandy if Isabel so much as mentioned it
to her. So she had kept it to herself, and every month the strain
was telling on her more. As friends had babies and talked of
their husbands' indelicate appetites she felt like screaming,
because everyone assumed her childlessness was her own fault.

'Oh, Isabel must be barren.' She knew what was being said
after seven years of marriage, and the sympathy all went to
Henry. Poor Henry. To be saddled with a barren wife. She
gritted her teeth together and pressed her forehead on the cool
glass of the mirror.

After a year of marriage, one night she had brushed out her
long brown hair and, when she was sure the servants were all in
bed, crept surreptitiously to her husband's room wearing just
her chemise. She was a buxom girl with large firm breasts, and
had slipped into bed beside Henry, thinking that maybe he was
shyer than she was. She had put her arms around him and tried
to draw him to her. In his sleep he had put out his own arms and
then, opening his eyes, had recoiled from her.

She would never forget the look of horror and repulsion on his
face. He had stood by the bed and upbraided her soundly on the
wantonness she had displayed. He had reminded her that good
women from good families did not lower themselves to the same

level as harlots. Isabel had sat up in the bed white with shame and shock and listened to him. But after that night a hatred for him had begun to grow in her.

Isabel wanted a man, and she desperately wanted a child. The two went together. But as the years had gone on she had despaired of ever getting what she wanted. Her father would not hear of divorce, and so she was stuck. Sometimes she daydreamed that Henry got hit by one of the new motorcars and died, or that he fell under a train. She knew these thoughts were wicked but his dying was the only way she could escape from this life.

She closed her eyes to stop the tears from falling.

'Isabel! Are you staying in here all night? My sister has come all the way to visit us and bring the children and you're not even trying to be entertaining.'

She faced her husband.

'I see you're quite enamoured of your little niece, Henry. You take no notice of the boy.'

Husband and wife looked each other in the face and both felt the subtle threat. Henry had the grace to lower his eyes first.

'She's a very engaging child. Now come along, Isabel.'

She followed him out on to the landing and persisted with her conversation.

'And you like engaging little girls, don't you?'

Henry turned to her on the stairs and whispered under his breath: 'I've been a very good husband to you, Isabel, never raised my hand to you, but you're sorely near to that now. Now come along, and forget this nonsense.'

Isabel followed him down the stairs and was surprised to find she was smiling. She knew a lot about her Henry, but it could wait until after Christmas.

Molly stood in Barking police station with Briony. Her hands were trembling. A man with large handlebar moustaches who had told them he was Sergeant Harries was writing down the description of Patrick Cavanagh. Briony watched him closely for any tell-tale signs that he was suspicious, but his eyes lingered sympathetically on Molly's black eye and swollen lip. Sergeant Harries had always had a loathing for wife beaters, even though it was a pretty common occupation. His own mother, God rest her soul, had always told her son that women were like flowers, gentle and fragile, and that they needed careful tending. He smiled at Molly.

'Was it a bad fight, madam?'

Molly nodded.

'And had the gentleman been drinking?'

She nodded again, afraid to speak.

'I take it your husband's Irish?'

Molly nodded once more.

'Have you thought of getting the priest out to him? I know many women in your position who've got the priest out, and their husbands haven't raised their hands to them ever again.'

Molly looked at the man in front of her as if he had just arrived from another planet. It was on the tip of her tongue to shout: 'Are you sure?'

'I'll . . . I'll try that, officer, when he comes home.'

'Good, good. Now where does he normally go like?'

Briony answered for her mother, her voice low. 'My father will go anywhere there's a drink. He'd been drinking all day yesterday and came home like the devil was in him.'

She had guessed the policeman was Temperance and embroidered her story with that in mind.

'Without a drink he's the most mild-mannered man in the world, but with it . . .' She rolled her lovely green eyes. 'He's like a demon.'

The policeman nodded his head sagely.

'So he could be anywhere then?'

Molly and Briony nodded vigorously.

'Once he didn't come home for a week, and then he couldn't remember where he'd been!'

'That sounds a familiar story, ladies, if you don't mind me remarking. Well, we've got his description and if he turns up we'll let you know. How many children did you say you've got, Mrs Cavanagh?'

'Five, sir. Five girls.'

'Well, you get home to them, and if we hear anything, we'll be in touch.'

It was three days after Christmas that Briony went with her mother to identify her father. He had been found by a man walking the shoreline looking for driftwood. His boots were gone as was his jacket and Molly and Briony were told that he had probably been set upon by thugs and robbed. He was to be given a funeral courtesy of the parish and Briony and her mother hoped that that would be the last of that.

Molly hurried home to tell Abel the good news and Briony made her way back to Barking with a dragging feeling inside her. Since her show the month before she had been expecting a period, and when none had come she had felt euphoric, though her breasts were still sore and tender. On this particular day she was expecting Henry at five-thirty and as he had lately taken her straight upstairs she was not expecting a long evening.

She was to be proved wrong, however.

While Briony had been identifying her father, Henry Dumas had been dealing with a crisis of his own. After taking a light tea with his wife, he had got up as usual to get his hat and coat. He always made a point of being very civil and kind to his wife whom he saw as an ornament rather than anything else. Today however, as he had stood up to leave her as usual, Isabel put her hand on his arm.

'I don't want you to go tonight, Henry. I think we should talk.'

He had looked down at her and frowned. But he had resumed his seat, and that in itself gave Isabel courage.

'I know this is a delicate subject, Henry, and believe me when I say I don't like discussing it any more than you do, but I feel we must get this thing sorted out. I want a child, Henry, I want a child desperately.'

She saw the look on his face and felt a knot of anger begin to form inside her.

'As you know only too well, Henry, it takes two to make a

baby, and I think that you should give this some thought.'

Henry stood up, gave her a cold glance and left the room. A little later she heard the door slam as he left the house.

Isabel stared into the fire. She would endure Henry's attentions to get a child of her own. She was trapped in this marriage whether she liked it or not. She knew that a lot of women took lovers but those opportunities never presented themselves to her, and as she was still a virgin she had no idea of the wiles women used to inaugurate such affairs.

In order to forget his wife's unpleasant suggestion, Henry went straight to Briony. She was playing with her kitten in front of the fire in the morning room, her hair braided into two plaits. She was wearing a simple lemon-coloured dress with matching socks and hair ribbons. When he was due she made herself look as young as possible.

'Hello, Henry.' Her voice was high and girlish.

Henry smiled at her wanly. She really was a pretty little thing and her beaming face when she saw him always made him feel better. With this child he was in control, master of everything. He sat himself in a chair and patted his lap. Briony picked up the kitten and went to him. She slipped on to his knee and kissed him chastely on the cheek. She knew exactly how to act with him. He rubbed her thigh under the silky dress and felt the first stirrings inside him.

'How's my best girl been?'

Briony dropped the kitten gently on to the carpet and put her slender arms around his neck.

'I've been good. I've been a very, very good little girl. You can ask Mrs Horlock.'

Henry grinned and felt the tension seeping out of him. He rubbed at her little breasts with his large hand and Briony stared at an oil painting over his shoulder. It was of a ballerina and she loved the brightly painted scene. Henry nuzzled her neck.

'Shall we go upstairs and play some games?'

Briony rolled her eyes at the ceiling, then putting her face in front of his, smiled engagingly.

'That would be lovely.'

68

As she followed him up the stairs to her bedroom she saw her father's face as it had been that afternoon, and tried to blot it out.

Inside the bedroom a small fire blazed in the grate. Briony went through the usual routine of letting Henry undress her, then in nothing but her long socks she sat on the side of the bed while he undressed himself, carefully folding his clothes and putting them neatly on to a chair. Once he was naked he went to sit beside her on the bed. Taking her tiny hand, he placed it on his member and Briony gently massaged it the way she knew he liked her to. He closed his eyes and let out a heavy breath. She looked down at what she was doing and saw that her breasts were much more prominent than they had been. Then she sighed. Her body was letting her down.

As Henry pushed her backwards on to the bed, she played her own personal little game. In her mind she was grown-up and famous, with lovely clothes and a lovely house and lovely friends.

Henry Dumas, unaware of his charge's lack of enthusiasm, drove her hard that night before leaving. But although her body ached with his roughness, Briony's mind stayed crystal clear and untouched.

It was two-thirty in the morning when she felt the first pain. It shot through her like a red hot knife, waking her from her sleep. She pushed her knees up to her chest in an instinctive move to stop the pain. But it came again a little later. It was like a cramp inside her. Pulling herself from the bed, she made her way to Mrs Horlock's room. Shaking the old women roughly awake, Briony explained what was happening to her.

Mrs Horlock leapt from the bed in her haste, her old bones forgotten as she took the terrified child back to her own room. It must be her period coming. The old woman went down to the kitchen and made her a hot drink of milk with a touch of whisky in it.

'There, there now, me pet. You'll feel better soon.'

But when Briony vomited and the pains got worse, Mrs

Horlock woke Cissy and went for the doctor. Mrs Horlock was very worried. The child looked as if she was about to give birth! She held her hand until Dr Carlton arrived and then thankfully gave way to him.

Dr Carlton was in his fifties and, though he was a respectable practitioner in many respects, was also known for his attendance on people with money who could afford to pay for medical services with no questions asked. He helped gentlewomen who, for one reason or another, needed an abortion, usually because the child wasn't their husband's. He also helped men who had contracted certain diseases and were worried they had passed them on to their wives.

Dr Carlton examined Briony with practised hands and then, after giving her a draught to make her sleep, stepped outside to Mrs Horlock and Cissy.

'You called me just in time, madam, the girl was about to miscarry. I can't guarantee she won't lose the child, the next couple of days will be crucial, but if she keeps taking the draught I've prescribed and sleeps as much as possible, she may give it a chance of survival. She must not be distressed under any circumstances. At this stage it's crucial she rests in bed. I can't emphasise strongly enough, madam, the need for peace and quiet.'

He looked at the old woman as he gave his speech. Always a lover of drama, he injected it into his work as often as possible. He was nonplussed at the old woman's look of utter astonishment.

'How old is the girl, by the way?' he asked in a whisper. He could smell a rat before it was stinking, he prided himself on that. It hadn't occurred to him at first that the patient was a young girl, he didn't really take much notice of women as a rule, but something in the housekeeper's face alerted him.

'She's just twelve, sir. We thought it was her periods like.'

Twelve! He had put her at about fourteen or fifteen.

'Only twelve, you say? Where's her mother and father?'

Mrs Horlock bit her lip and thought for a second before she spoke.

'Cissy, go down and make up the fire in the morning room. Dr Carlton, can I get you a hot drink or a whisky?'

He sniffed loudly.

'A scotch would be agreeable, madam.'

'Then follow me, sir.' Cissy was already down the stairs and rekindling the fire with the poker when they came in.

'Make me a pot of tea, Cissy, and bring it through here. Please sit down, Doctor.'

Mrs Horlock poured him a large scotch. The redness of his nose and the broken veins on his cheeks told her he liked his whisky and when he swigged it back in one go she replenished his glass without a word.

'I look after the girl, sir, for my employer. She's a distant relative of his, you understand, and her mother was just a bit beyond the pale. From a very good family, mind, but she run away when young and the child was the result of an unhappy union.'

She once more refilled the doctor's glass. 'I don't know how this could have happened. As for Mr Dumas – well, he'll be broken-hearted.'

At the mention of Henry's name the doctor's eyebrows rose. So, he thought, the child was his. Henry Dumas was married to a peer's daughter and was respected in the local community, indeed in the whole of London. He was wealthy, from an impeccable family, and would be able to pay well. Extremely well.

'What a wicked, wanton child, madam! Like her mother, I'd say. I can well understand the need for secrecy. Such a scandal! Not a word of it will pass my lips, madam, I do assure you, and you can pass that on to Mr Dumas as well.' He tutted. 'Poor Mr Dumas, to have his kindness repaid like this.'

He shook his head for maximum effect. 'Well, I have done all I can. I'll return in the morning to see her once more. I'll say goodnight to you, madam.'

Mrs Horlock saw him to the door and then went back into the morning room where she helped herself to a large whisky. The child was pregnant. She had another drink to help her think.

71

Well, maybe she'd lose it tonight. Then they'd all be able to get back to normal.

'I'm what!' Briony's voice was incredulous.

She looked from one face to the other. Cissy's looked as shocked as her own, but Mrs Horlock's face was closed.

'I can't be, there must be some mistake.' Briony was close to tears and Mrs Horlock took her into her arms.

'There's no mistake, my love. You must have fell just as your body was coming to womanhood, I've heard of it before.'

She didn't say she'd experienced it before and had helped get rid of the offending child. She knew Briony's temperament too well to say anything like that.

'What am I gonna do?' It was a childish wail.

'Now don't you worry, my angel, I'll sort it all out for you.'

This was comforting to Briony and she settled back against the pillows plumped up around her and held tightly on to Cissy's hand. For the first time in her life she was frightened, really frightened.

They heard the front door shut and Mrs Horlock smiled at the two girls and left the room. The sooner Henry Dumas knew what was happening, the better. He looked up at the old woman as she descended the stairs.

'What's the to do, Horlock? Is the child ill?'

He'd been dragged from his place of work by a note twenty minutes earlier and now he was worried.

'In a manner of speaking, sir. Would you join me in the morning room? I took the liberty of getting a tea tray ready, I'll just get the hot water.'

Henry went into the drawing room where there was a trolley full of tea things, cakes and sandwiches. He picked up a paper-thin paste sandwich and popped it into his mouth, carefully avoiding his moustache. He wished the old girl would hurry up, he was due home for dinner. His wife's father was coming today and he wanted to be with Isabel when he arrived. She was acting very strangely lately, and he was concerned about what she might hint to her family. Luckily Lord Barkham was not a listener to women's gossip, having no time for his wife or indeed his daughter. Henry was pretty certain he would pooh-pooh anything she said. Nevertheless, he would like to be there during the visit.

Mrs Horlock came in with the freshly made tea and as she sat down Henry smiled at her faintly.

'Well, what's going on?'

'It seems Miss Briony is pregnant.'

'She's what!'

'She's pregnant, sir. I've had the doctor in and he's certain.'

'God's teeth, woman, how did that happen?'

Mrs Horlock suppressed a smile. If you don't know, she thought, I'm not about to enlighten you.

'It'll have to go, Mrs Horlock.'

'My sentiments entirely, sir.'

'And so will the blasted baby!'

Mrs Horlock looked hard at him and he felt a flush of shame.

'With all due respect, sir, it's not Briony's fault, now is it?'

Her own words shocked her. Never before had she reproached the man for anything. She had always been a willing accomplice to his schemes, but Briony Cavanagh had got under her skin and into her heart. Oh, Maria knew the child was a mercenary little bitch, but she did what she did more for her family than herself, and for her corrupter completely to disregard the child after all she done for him over the last sixteen months brought a feeling akin to anger. Briony was the child she had never had. The girl trusted her, and there had been more fun and laughter in her life in the last year or so than ever before.

'Really, Mrs Horlock, I think you're forgetting yourself. Something like this is not to be taken lightly.'

Mrs Horlock smiled grimly and interrupted him. 'I understand the situation, sir, better than you think. I will arrange with Dr Carlton for the removal of the . . . of the baby. I don't think Briony would want to have it at her age. Then we'll have to get our thinking caps on about the best thing to do once it's all over.'

Henry relaxed then, and sipped his tea.

73

'Of course, Mrs Horlock. I'll leave it all in your capable hands.'

She smiled at him. Thinking to herself all the while: Don't you always leave your dirty work to me?

Five minutes later Henry was on his way back to his house, his wife and her father. This couldn't have come at a worse time. Damn and blast the little guttersnipe to hell!

Isabel sat with her father and mother in the drawing room. Her father was telling one of the long-winded stories that required no answers, just an expression of rapt interest. Her father's stories always entailed a long boring account of how he had done someone down, as he put it. He had no time for the King, the army, suffragettes, or anything else that might be a topic of conversation in more moderate households. Any mention of suffragettes would indeed result in a long diatribe on the failings of womanhood in general going back to Eve, the mother of all sin. Isabel noticed that her own mother had dropped off to sleep in front of the fire.

She was almost pleased when Henry came into the room. He walked across to her with his usual beaming smile and kissed her on the cheek. Getting up stiffly, Isabel excused herself and went down to the kitchen to see how the food was progressing, feeling the tightening in her chest. It was a feeling of complete hopelessness.

How long must I endure this existence?

O Lord, how long?

Briony lay back against the pillows and waited for her mother to arrive. She had insisted to Mrs Horlock that her mother be sent for as soon as possible and eventually, after some cajoling and a few tears, Mrs Horlock had reluctantly sent Cissy to collect her in a cab. Briony looked around the little room with wide eyes. Her longing for this comfort had brought her to this. She was just twelve and now she was having a baby.

A tiny part of her was thrilled at the thought. Having lived around babies all her life they were not an unknown quantity.

But with all the upset over her father, and Eileen's involvement in it, she knew that this was not a time for anything like this to be happening. It would have been bad enough at any time, but now . . . She bit her lip.

She heard her mother arrive and watched the door with trepidation. Molly came into the room like a whirlwind.

'Are you all right, child?' Cissy's arrival had frightened her more than she liked to admit. Briony, who had been fine up until seeing her mother, promptly burst into tears.

'Oh Mam, Mam!'

It was what she had called her mother as a small child and Molly was reminded of the tiny red-headed baby she'd loved so well.

She pulled her child into her arms, the first time she had touched her without shrinking for over a year.

'There now, me pet, what's wrong? Have you a pain?' Cissy had told Molly nothing other than that Briony wasn't very well.

'Oh, Mam, I'm going to have a baby!'

Molly pushed her back against the pillows and stared into her face. 'You're what?'

Briony nodded, her little face streaming with tears.

'Dear God in heaven, save us!'

Briony threw herself into her mother's arms, a child once more despite the life inside her. Suddenly, faced with her mother, the enormity of what had happened over the last few days hit her.

'Me poor dad. Me poor dad. I want me dad.'

Molly held her close, fear replacing the anger and shock. All she needed now was Briony to blurt out the whole sorry business with Eileen and her da.

'Hush now, Briony. You're not ever to tell about that. Promise me?'

She looked into the fear-filled face. 'Promise me, Briony?'

'I promise, Mum. Oh, what am I gonna do?'

'We'll think of something, Briony, I promise you.'

As she spoke Mrs Horlock brought them all in tea and for the first time the two women came face to face.

'Mrs Cavanagh.'

Molly curled her lip in distaste at the older woman, who was to her mind no better than Nellie Deakins.

'Mrs Horlock.'

The old woman gave Briony her tea and, looking at Molly, said gently, 'I think me and you should have a talk.'

Molly nodded, running her tongue around her teeth. 'I think we better had. The sooner the better, to my mind.'

Both women having established exactly what they thought of the other through a few choice words, they retired from Briony's bedroom and went down to the kitchen for the first battle between them.

It was a battle neither could win without Briony's say so, but they enjoyed it nonetheless.

Chapter Six

Henry Dumas had been watching his wife carefully during the meal. As usual the table was impeccably laid. In fairness to her, he conceded, Isabel really was an exemplary wife in some respects. The crystal gleamed, the cutlery was of the very best, and the food was well above par. Once Isabel lost these notions she had begun to acquire, she would once more be his meek and obedient wife.

He had just taken a slice of apple pie when his wife spoke to her mother loudly.

'Mama, are you still working in the East End? I understand they have just opened another home for wayward girls there?'

She glanced at Henry as she spoke and then looked immediately back to her mother.

Venetia Barkham nodded.

'Yes, God knows they're more in need than ever. Some of the girls are only twelve or thirteen.' She lowered her voice as she leant across the table towards her daughter. 'It's a scandal, Isabel, what some men will do!'

Lord Barkham, who approved of his wife's charitable works because she mixed with the cream of the aristocracy, nodded sagely.

'My dears, you don't understand the lower classes like I do. Some of those girls could turn a veritable saint's head. They're evil, preying on men who are otherwise exemplary.'

Isabel looked at her father, avoiding Henry's warning glance.

'So, Papa, am I to understand that men cannot help these appetites? Even men of good birth?'

Lord Barkham began to choke on his apple pie.

'Don't be silly, Isabel. A doxy's a doxy, whatever her age. There's many a good man who's been taken in by a pretty face. These girls, some of them little more than children as your mother pointed out, are natural sluts. It's inbred in them. A woman of good birth never acts the strumpet. You wouldn't understand, Isabel. You see, my child, men must be iron-willed and have faith in God and their own constitution. Look at me.' He waved his arms expansively. 'I attend church regularly, and even in the thickest snow I never wear a heavy coat. It's in the constitution, you see? Sound in mind and body, I am, and always have been.

'The namby-pamby men who get involved with these chits are obviously mentally unstable. They have no place in civilised society. They can't resist temptation, just haven't the willpower of stronger, more intelligent men, and these chits know it.'

'Thank you, Papa, for explaining it so eloquently. I really do understand exactly what you mean. Don't you, Henry?'

Henry paled and cleared his throat before answering. 'I think it's hardly a suitable subject for discussion in front of ladies.'

Immediately he realised his mistake. He had just implicitly criticised Lord Barkham.

Barkham glared at his son-in-law, a milkwater sop if ever he'd encountered one!

'How are your own charitable works, my dear?' he asked Isabel.

She looked at him and smiled. This was going even better than she'd expected. She knew her father was only asking her the question to force the issue with Henry.

'I still work with Mrs Prosser Evans, of course, though I am thinking seriously of joining Mother's Little Band of Helpers. I feel that the child prost— I mean, the poor children, really need a guiding hand.'

* * *

78

Molly and Mrs Horlock had finally agreed and both women were relieved. After the initial bout, where each woman had carefully sized up the other, they had realised their common goal and were now co-conspirators.

Both had one end in mind: the removal of Briony's child. Molly pushed her hair back from her flushed face and drew her legs away from the kitchen fire so she could face the older woman head on.

'But isn't that dangerous? I mean, Briony wouldn't die or anything?'

Mrs Horlock shrugged her shoulders. 'There's always the possibility of death, Mrs Cavanagh. Even if she went through with the birth. But Dr Carlton has been used by the richest in London. We're not talking about a filthy back room and an ignorant old woman.'

Molly nodded. 'I suppose you're right, but it seems so brutal somehow. Briony's only a child herself.'

Mrs Horlock smiled slightly.

'And a very lovely child she is too. She's a credit to you, Mrs Cavanagh.'

Molly took this compliment with a nod of her head.

'It was her father who brought her here, you know. And my Eileen. I was against it from the start . . . When I think of my poor Eileen, how she's suffered . . .'

Mrs Horlock put a hand on her arm, and squeezed it gently. 'Would you like a drop of the hard? I keep some down here for emergencies.'

She got up and, taking a bottle of whisky from the pantry, made two strong hot toddies. Molly watched her spooning in sugar generously and decided she could like the older woman, given more time.

'So I'll talk to the master tonight then?' Mrs Horlock's voice broke into her thoughts.

Molly sipped her drink. 'Yes. Do you think I should take her home with me?'

Mrs Horlock shook her head.

'No. Definitely not. The master needs to be reminded of his

obligations, if you get my drift. I wouldn't advise taking the child from under his nose just yet.'

Molly and the older woman found once more they were in accord and, raising their glasses, pledged a silent toast.

Henry looked down at the child in the bed and felt a sickness in his stomach. Suddenly, her little elfin face had taken on harsh lines and her abundant red hair seemed vulgar in the extreme. His father-in-law was right in one thing he had said earlier: these children would turn the head of a saint. Now, with all the annoyance from Isabel too, he was faced with this. It took all his willpower not to raise his fist and strike the girl in the bed, venting his frustration on her for all his troubles, real and imagined. Instead he forced himself to take the tiny hand in his and smile at the child. He saw the swelling of her breasts and shuddered inwardly. In his eyes she was a woman now, and women had never been of interest to him.

'Dr Carlton is coming tomorrow to look at you, Briony, and then all your troubles will be over.'

She stared at him with a puzzled expression.

'What's gonna happen, Henry?'

He gritted his teeth at the use of his Christian name. Out of bed he was Mr Dumas. This really was a liberty! But he overlooked it this time, afraid of upsetting the apple cart.

'Oh, nothing for little girls to worry about. I'll be in to see you after he's been.'

Briony licked her lips and looked at the man beside her. Since the news of the baby, she had felt a change inside her. She knew what was happening to her, had seen births enough times, even helped her mother with a couple, including the birth of her dead brother. It was as if all this had turned her into an old woman. She no longer felt the childish exuberance that shielded her from the horror of nights spent with this man. Now every little thing they had ever done stood out in her mind with stark clarity. She felt his revulsion towards her, saw it in his eyes and felt it in his touch. She knew with an inner certainty that she was dead already as far as this man was concerned. That her child, the

80

little life he had sparked, was also dead. That he wouldn't rest until it had been dragged out of her. She also knew that she was not having any part of it.

'I want to see Eileen and me sisters, please. Could you arrange it?' Her voice was low but strong.

Henry cleared his throat and was about to protest when she spoke again.

'I couldn't understand what was wrong with our Eileen for a long time, but now I understand exactly, Henry. No amount of money is worth all this, is it?'

It was said so simply, so honestly, that he didn't have the guts to answer her. Instead he walked from the room.

Dr Carlton had imbibed a generous amount of whisky and was waiting now in the morning room for a light lunch to be served before the serious business began. The old woman, Mrs Horlock, was like a cat on hot coals. He sighed. It was never a nice business this, but needs must when the devil drives. The older woman should be hardened to it by now. He remembered her from years back when she'd worked for a much more illustrious client. She'd had no qualms about holding the chit down then, while he saw to the business in hand. Got softer as she got older probably. Well, she'd need her wits about her today. He'd have a quiet word with her before the off. The girl would be nervous enough without the old woman frightening the life out of her.

He hated these jobs, but twenty pounds was twenty pounds, and who was he to sneeze at it? He got out of his seat with difficulty and poured himself another whisky. Just to fortify him. His hands were shaking again this morning, and he wondered, as he did every morning, if he was coming down with a cold.

Cissy saw his bloated, red-veined face and breathed in the whisky fumes on serving his lunch, and went straight down the stairs to give the information to Mrs Horlock.

'He's drunker than a Saturday night sailor! Bleeding old git!'

Mrs Horlock sighed. 'Maybe the food'll soak it up a bit.' She

81

didn't hold out much hope. 'Mr Dumas will be here soon anyway.'

She wiped her hands on a clean cloth and looked at the clock. It was just twelve. He was due at one and she'd made up her mind. Hadn't she done enough to the Cavanagh family, what with Eileen and now Briony, without being part of murder as well? She was going to talk him out of the abortion.

Isabel, sitting outside her husband's house in Ripple Road in a hired cab, was also waiting for him to arrive. Her hands were trembling at the thought of what she was going to do, but she took deep breaths and channelled her mind on to the job in hand. She was going to wait all day if necessary and then surprise him with her presence. She had convinced herself that by doing this, she could achieve some kind of power over him. Force him to give her a child. She had considered going to her father with her information and demanding he do something about it, but she knew it would be futile. He would never countenance a scandal of any kind. And a divorce? She laughed ruefully to herself. It would be unthinkable. His own sister had been married to a brute who had attacked her on more than one occasion. Isabel could remember, as a child, a badly beaten woman arriving in a governess cart of all things at nine in the morning, her face a bloody pulp. Her father had ordered a doctor, then given her aunt a dressing down for being a slovenly wife who had obviously asked for her husband's hand and had got it.

No, she would have to deal with Henry himself, threaten him with her father. It was a threat that would frighten him out of his very wits. She knew her family's social status gave her a small hold over him, and it was a thrilling feeling. If only she could control her own fear! With Henry, it did not do to let him know you were afraid of him, or indeed of anything. He hoarded that type of information away like a squirrel, dragging it out of its hiding place when the time was ripe. Oh, she'd learnt a lot from Henry Dumas. An awful lot.

She saw his cab arrive and braced herself. She would give him fifteen minutes before she entered the house.

Henry looked at the doctor in dismay. The man was drunk!

'Shall we adjourn to the bedroom, Mr Dumas?' Carlton's voice was slurred.

Henry looked at the man quizzically. 'Why on earth should I go up there?'

Carlton waved a hand at him. 'Sorry, Dumas old chap, got meself a bit puddled there. Always the same with this kind of job. Nasty business.' He'd remembered at the last minute that Henry was only there to pay him. Imagine asking him if he wanted to be there! In his drunken state this struck him as hilarious and he laughed aloud.

A silent Henry watched the doctor walk from the room with exaggerated care. He poured himself a brandy and sat down to wait. Upstairs Briony, Mrs Horlock and her mother were arguing furiously.

'I'm not gonna let them do it, Mum. It's wicked!'

Briony's face was white. The strain was beginning to tell on her and Molly felt her heart go out to the child.

'Oh, Briony, you don't understand! What are we gonna do with another child in the house? Now your father's gone, and your wages too . . . we'll end up back in the dockside slums.'

'No, we won't. I'll think of something, Mum. Won't I, Mrs Horlock?'

Briony turned pleading eyes on her in the hope she'd come up with something. Briony was frightened of having the child, but she was more frightened of the alternative. After Carlton had saved her from a miscarriage, it seemed evil to take the child now, why couldn't her mother see that? And her a good Catholic as well. 'I mean it, Mum. I'll not let that doctor near me, I'll . . . I'll scream the bloody house down!'

As she spoke he lurched into the room with his big black bag and three pairs of eyes looked at him.

All three registered the fact that he was roaring drunk.

'Jesus in heaven, save us!' Instinctively Molly crossed herself.

'You're drunk, man!' Mrs Horlock reproached.

Carlton stood on his dignity. 'Madam, I am never drunk. I had a medicinal whisky for medicinal purposes. Now if you'd be so kind as to hold down the patient, I shall begin.'

He opened up his bag and began taking out his instruments. Briony's eyes widened to their utmost and she began to scream – high piercing screams that went through the doctor's skull like a drill.

Both Mrs Horlock and her mother put out their hands to try and calm her. Briony, thinking they were going to hold her down, kicked out and, leaping off the bed, ran across the room, Carlton grabbed her flying hair as she passed him, and she screamed again as she was yanked backwards.

'Let go of me, you old bastard! Let go of me, I say.'

Twisting around, she bit his arm. He let go, she opened the bedroom door and, running out, flew straight down the stairs and into the arms of a plump dark-haired lady who was standing in the hallway with Henry.

'Oh, please don't let them hurt me, missus! Please!'

She clung to the newcomer as her saviour. She looked kind, with those big brown eyes in a white face. Please God, Briony prayed, let her help me.

Isabel wrapped the child in gentle arms. Looking first at her husband, then at the two women and the obviously drunk man standing at the top of the stairs, she said, 'What on earth's going on here?'

Henry's shoulders slumped and Briony heard a terrible groan come from him. It was as if he had been punched in the stomach with an iron fist.

Briony was sitting on the nice lady's lap being petted, her mother and Mrs Horlock telling her everything she wanted to know. Henry was sitting by the window on a straight-backed chair, biting his knuckles.

Isabel listened to the two women with growing amazement, every so often looking down at the fiery head laid against her breast. She knew this child should repel her, but all she felt was motherly concern. That the girl had been coerced into her

84

situation, she had no doubt. This beautiful child with the porcelain white skin and the glass green eyes should be outside in the air playing games, not sitting in this overstuffed morning room waiting to find out if she was going to be allowed to give birth to a child she should not be carrying in the first place. Isabel looked at her husband and felt an urge to rise from her seat and fell him to the floor with one heavy blow.

What he had done here was disgusting and cruel. And all the more so because this child had been handed to him on a plate by a father who needed to feed the rest of his family. Henry played on people's poverty, the big Bible-thumping bully!

'What do you want, my dear?' She looked down at Briony's face, her voice gentle.

'I want to have the little baby, missus. I don't want that doctor near me.'

Isabel nodded. 'But who will look after the baby when it arrives?'

Briony sat up straight on her lap and grinned. 'Well, I suppose I will. I know a lot about babies, don't I, Mum?'

Molly nodded, defeated by all that had happened.

'That's settled then.' Isabel's voice was brisk. 'She'll stay here, of course, until the baby comes, and then we'll sort something out. Henry will pay the bills, don't worry about that. I'll see to it personally.' Her voice was getting stronger. 'I shall undertake to oversee everything myself. Mr Dumas will not be visiting here any more, so any belongings of his should be packed and ready for him to take with him as he leaves.'

Briony looked at her saviour's face and smiled shyly. God had answered her prayers in the shape of Mrs Henry Dumas. Mrs Prosser Evans had been right. God was good. God was very, very good.

Henry waited until he knew Isabel had retired for the night before going to see her. He had eaten dinner at his club, trying to decide how to face the situation in hand. A few large brandies had given him the courage he needed but it was already failing as he listened at his wife's door.

Isabel was humming. The annoyance he felt at the sound was so profound, it made his hands tremble and his heart beat a tattoo in his chest. She was laughing at him. In his own house, dammit!

Isabel, brushing her hair in front of her dressing-table mirror, turned in her seat to face him as he strode in without knocking. She was wearing one of the lacy chemises that had come with her trousseau. Her large breasts spilled out of the tiny garment, showing dark pink nipples. She smiled at her husband. She had been expecting him and had purposely waited up until he showed himself. She watched the flicker of disgust as he eyed her bosom, and her smile widened.

Raising one eyebrow, she spoke softly.

'Why, Henry, this is the last place I expected to see you.' The inference wasn't lost on him.

'I want to talk to you, Isabel, and this place is as good as any.'

She interrupted him easily.

'No, Henry, you'll hear me out. You picked this room because it's farthest from the servants' quarters, so what we have to say you do not want overheard. Well . . .' she spread her hands, 'what I have to say had best be stated in private anyway.

'From now on there will be some changes in our marriage. We will still function outwardly as man and wife, I expect your full support when socialising. In public we shall carry on as the devoted couple.' She allowed herself another smile at that. 'But inside this house I do not want to see you unless I absolutely have to. You disgust me, Henry. When I think of that child . . . the position she's in because of you. Well, I intend to look after the girl, and when the time comes I want the baby. I think the mother will be happy, and the child will have every advantage here with us. It's your child after all, Henry Dumas, and your child should be brought up in this house, as you were.'

Henry's face was white with shock and disbelief. He took a step towards her and she slipped from the chair and picked up a large cut-glass perfume bottle.

'If you make one move to stop me, I shall go straight to my father and Mrs Prosser Evans, I swear that to you. If you touch

86

one hair on my head, or indeed Briony's, I will bring such trouble to your door your life will never be the same. I want a child, Henry. I want a child so desperately I am willing to take on a street urchin's brat. So now you know what's going to happen.'

Henry watched his wife, breasts heaving as she spoke. The vehemence in her voice was more frightening than anything he had ever experienced. He realised belatedly that she had an iron will, stronger even than his own.

Briony was looking forward to seeing Mrs Dumas; she liked her. She liked the softness of her hands and the nice smell that enveloped her. At breakfast today Briony had eaten two boiled eggs, with thick bread and butter soldiers, and washed it all down with a whole pot of tea. She had woken from her sleep ravenous, content in her child's mind to let Mrs Dumas take over her life. Her belly was much better, and the reality of the child inside her had yet to hit home. Her mother was still to get her money, Henry was already a distant memory, and her sisters could all stay at Oxlow Lane. Her three main worries were over.

Mrs Dumas arrived promptly at ten-thirty. Briony stood up as Isabel entered the room, smiling widely.

Isabel looked into the deep green eyes and smiled back. The child was far too knowing already, but whose fault was that?

'Hello, Briony dear.'

Briony waited for her to seat herself before sitting down too. 'I've ordered some tea. I thought that today we could get to know one another better.'

Briony readily agreed. As Isabel listened to the child's chatter about her earlier life, about her ambitions and dreams and hopes, she felt herself relax. She would enjoy looking after the girl, seeing that she rested properly and ate well. Her health was to be watched with the utmost care.

Isabel passionately wanted this child's baby.

Chapter Seven

Briony was five months pregnant and she looked blooming. Her face and body had filled out becomingly and today she looked a picture of health and prosperity, her hair tied back into a neat chignon and her feet encased in kidskin boots with tiny pearl buttons. She wore a blue velvet dress with a lace cape around the shoulders.

She was sitting on a bench by the boating pool in Barking Park, lifting her face to the weak spring sun. She closed her eyes as her mind drifted off to another place. Mrs Dumas had generously allowed her this hour's freedom every day. A cab waited at the entrance of the park for her so she had no fears about walking home alone. Briony liked Mrs Dumas, or Isabel as she now called her, but this hour every day was Briony's favourite time. Oh, she loved living in the house with them all, she loved Mrs Horlock and Cissy, but she craved her own space more and more as the days passed. The child had become more real to her, and she guessed, rightly, that it was the reason behind Isabel's kindness to her. Because of the child she could have anything she wanted, and, being Briony, she used this to the full.

Hence the afternoons in the park without Mrs Horlock, Cissy, or that awful boy Mrs Dumas had employed to run messages. Briony shuddered as she thought of him, with his forever running nose and his big bulbous eyes. She had made Cissy get him a pair of boots because the sight of his callused feet sickened her. She knew she was being unfair to the boy. He was no more than eight, and his mother was probably glad of the few pennies he made a week, but Briony hated him. He was a reminder of where she came from, what she could be again, and he disturbed her for that reason.

She sat back on the bench and let her whole body relax. The child within her quickened and unconsciously she put her hands to her stomach. A tiny smile still playing around her mouth, she jolted upright as a familiar voice broke into her thoughts.

'Hello again. I thought it was you.'

Briony opened her eyes to see Tommy Lane. He grinned as he saw her obvious surprise at his changed appearance.

'Well, sod me! Ain't you going to talk to me?'

His voice was deeper than she remembered. He sat beside her and looked her over, his eyes staying just a second too long on her bulging stomach. He took out a small cheroot. Briony watched as he lit it. He certainly looked different. He was dressed in a checked suit and wore a rather natty bowler hat. He was clean, shiny clean, and his hair was cut close to the head, with just the right amount of hair tonic on it. She was impressed. He was a very handsome boy.

'Look, are you going to sit there gawping or are you going to talk to me?'

Briony grinned back at him.

'You gave me a shock, Tommy. Last time I saw you, you was trying to save your arse. Now you look like . . .'

He took a puff on his cheroot and then clamped it between his strong teeth.

'What do I look like, eh? A man of substance and fashion? At least, that's what these togs are supposed to make you look like. The geezer in the shop said so.'

Briony relaxed once more and laughed.

'Well, let's just say you look all right, shall we?'

Tommy surveyed her once more through a haze of cheap tobacco smoke.

'Looks like you got caught then?'

He motioned with his head towards her swelling waist and Briony put her hands to it.

'Yeah, that's about the strength of it. I'm going to be all right though, I'm being looked after by a nice lady who wants the baby when it comes.'

Tommy pricked up his ears.

'I hope you've made a good deal for yourself? Nippers is worth a fortune. Especially if the mother's a looker and ain't got the clap.'

Briony looked so shocked Tommy felt guilty and tried hastily to make amends.

'I didn't mean that how it came out. But you're obviously on the bash . . .'

Briony sat up straight. 'Listen here, Mr Tommy whatever your name is, don't you come and sit here and speak trouble into my face, I won't have it! My business is my business, and I think I've said a bit too much to you already. If I want your advice, I'll bleeding well ask you for it. Until then, either go away, or keep your trap shut!'

Tommy looked away. His face had reddened and he smoked his cheroot in silence. She was a funny little thing. He should clout her across the lug for talking to him like that, but for some strange reason he liked her. He had liked her since she had saved him from a nicking, and for that reason he would swallow her words.

'Who's the father then?'

Briony looked at him and sighed. He really was the nosiest person she had ever met.

'A man.'

Tommy threw away the cheroot and laughed.

'No! I'd never have guessed that! I mean, who is he?'

'Never you mind. What about yourself? You're looking prosperous, what work are you doing now?'

Tommy flicked an imaginary speck of dirt from his trousers and sat back in his seat.

'I'm working for Nellie Deakins now... I was working for some bloke – a right villain he was and all. But Nellie asked me to work for her exclusively, and so I do.'

Briony was intrigued. Nellie Deakins' brothel was something

she'd heard talked of since she could remember. It was a standard threat to most of the children roundabouts. 'You do that again and I'll cart you off to Nellie Deakins.' But she had never spoken to anyone who actually worked there.

'What's it like?'

Tommy grinned.

'It's not so bad really, Briony. She gets a raw deal, old Nellie. The girls are looked after, she gets a quack to them if they're feeling a bit rough. My job's delivering them around London to private parties and that. I only deal with the women though, not the little girls.'

His voice was thick as he said the last sentence and looked back across the park at the people strolling around the boating pool feeding the ducks. Tommy had hated the job he had first taken with Davie Dobson. It had sickened him to be expected to drag kids, some no more than six or seven, around London. Boys as wells as girls. Then taking the poor little blighters back again, their faces filled with fear and their sobs reproaching him. He'd kissed that job goodbye without a backward glance. He had gone to Nellie's on spec, and with one look at the big strapping lad, she had employed him there and then. He had given Dobson the bad news through his friend Willy and had not looked back since.

Briony bit her lower lip. She decided that although he got on her nerves, she liked Tommy.

'My dad took me to the house I live at now. Me sister went first and then me. I like it there, I've always liked it there.'

Tommy nodded as if he understood. And the funny thing was, he did. He understood only too well what an empty belly and a dead fire could cause. People sold their only assets, whether it was a woman going on the game or a man selling off a child. It was some people's only way out. It had been his mother's and his sisters'. He smiled at Briony and she smiled back. They were both aware of the other's way of life and it bonded them together. Standing up, Tommy held out his arm and Briony took it. Together they strolled around the park and chatted. More than one pair of eyes strayed to the well-dressed young couple. Briony, with her brazen hair tied back, looked older and more mature; Tommy, with his new clothes and confident gait, led her around with the pride of ownership.

He looked down on to the china white face and felt a lurch inside his chest. Her green eyes were so trusting as they looked into his, he felt a swelling of his heart.

He gleaned from her that she came to the park every day for an hour, and decided there and then that he'd make a point of being here when she arrived.

Isabel poured herself a cup of tea. She had arranged dinner with Mrs Horlock and had set Cissy the task of hemming the remainder of the baby garments that she herself had made. She sipped her tea delicately, breathing in the aroma. Briony joined her a few minutes later.

'I really feel well, Mrs Dumas.'

Isabel smiled. The child did look well. The walks in the park were obviously doing her the world of good. Her white face had taken on a rosy glow and her body, nicely rounded now, looked more supple somehow, more relaxed.

Briony took a noisy sip of tea and ate a sandwich. 'I'm hungry all the time lately.'

'It's the baby, Briony. You're eating for two.'

She nodded and ate another sandwich. She had been meeting Tommy every day for a month now, and had gleaned a mine of information from him. Although she was shrewd in her own way, Tommy had first-hand knowledge of the world and relayed this knowledge to Briony in plain and simple language. She took a deep breath and spoke to Isabel Dumas.

'You want this child, don't you, Isabel?'

The fact she had called her 'Isabel' spoke volumes. The older woman looked into Briony's face, searching for the reason for the question.

'I do.'

Briony smiled widely.

'You can have it. I can't look after it properly, me mum's got enough on her plate as it is, so I think the best thing for everyone would be for you to look after it.'

Isabel swallowed hard. This girl-woman sitting opposite had answered all her prayers and she felt an urge to kiss the white face and embrace Briony in her arms. Instead, she nodded.

'Thank you. I do want your baby, I want it very much.'

Briony, in her youth and her naivety, just smiled. 'That's that, then. If you have it, I can see it sometimes, can't I? Not every day like, but now and then?'

Isabel nodded again. 'Of course you can, and my husband and I will see to it that you benefit by giving us your baby.'

Briony patted her stomach and said, 'I wish I didn't have to leave here. I love this house, and Mrs Horlock and Cissy . . . And you.'

It was a simple statement of truth and Isabel took it as that, but still she said, 'I'll give you this house as a gift once you're delivered of your child. I'll also arrange a substantial sum of money for you to live on.'

Briony's face opened like a book.

'Really, you really mean that?'

Isabel smiled. 'Yes, I do. It's the very least we can do for you.'

Briony jumped from her seat and flung her arms around Isabel, hugging her tight. Isabel hugged her back, breathing in the smell of her, feeling a surge of love and sadness for the girl as she held her. Knowing that she was taking from her an integral part of her life.

Abel looked at Molly's frightened face and sighed.

'How long's she been gone this time?'

Molly bit her lip before answering him.

'Well, since this morning. Oh, Abel, she worries me!'

He pulled out a chair and sat Molly down, then, chucking a solemn-faced Rosalee under the chin, poured Molly a large mug of black tea.

'Well, don't worry, Moll. I'll get out the cart and go looking for her. She'll likely be up on Rainham Marshes again.'

Molly nodded, dull-eyed, as he walked from the cottage. Rosalee, sensing that something was wrong, pulled herself up from the cracket and went to her mother, pushing her bulky body between her legs. Instinctively, Molly pulled the child's head to her breasts and stroked the short-cropped hair.

'Oh, Rosalee, Rosalee. Where's your sister?'

She hugged her mother back and said, 'Bri Bri.'

Mother Jones bustled through the door then, all energy and common sense. Molly smiled weakly at her.

'Now stop your worrying, Molly. Abel's off looking for her and I'll sit with you 'til he comes back.'

She didn't say 'comes back with Eileen', because it was Mother Jones' opinion that the girl was a few farthings short of a penny, and that what she needed was to see a doctor. If Eileen was to jump in the cut, it wouldn't surprise her. That dirty blackguard of a father had seen to her ruin and now it was just a matter of time before she went completely off her head.

Eileen stood alone on Rainham Marshes. The sun was warm on her face, though the wind was cold. She took a deep breath and looked around her. She felt cleanliness envelop her when she was here. Here there was no one, no one and nothing. Just her, clean and pure. She loved it. She began to walk down towards the dirt track that would lead her through the marshes to the little hamlet of Rainham itself. Sometimes she ventured that far and sat by the big pond, watching the people come and go. People she didn't know and who didn't know her. The anonymity pleased her.

Every time she stood in her mother's kitchen, she saw once more the flat iron coming down on her father's head. She blinked back the picture in her mind and unconsciously walked faster, as if she could outwalk the picture, run away from it.

In the distance she saw a hare, leaping in the long grass. She walked towards it. In the sunlight its coat had a red tinge and she saw Briony then. Briony lying in the big bed with Henry Dumas; Briony with her tiny hands and feet and her head of red hair. Eileen felt the familiar heaving of her stomach and swallowed hard. She hadn't eaten again today. She never had an appetite, and the more her mother went on at her about eating, the less appetite she seemed to have. She had taken to forcing down an evening meal and then, when no one was looking, forcing it back up, up and out of her body. Enjoying the emptiness once more. Hating the feeling of being replete, of being filled with the food her sister's degradation bought. It was evil food, bought with evil money.

She was walking fast again and the hare, seeing her approach, skittered away with wide, frightened eyes. A man was walking nearby with his dog. He noticed the girl and nodded at her. He frowned as she turned abruptly away from him. His dog, a small black mongrel, ran to her, jumping up at her dress in excitement and muddying the ragged hem with dirty paws. The man walked towards her and, pulling the dog away from her with one hand, put out the other to steady her.

Eileen saw his hard work-worn hand on her flesh and looked fearfully into his face. Pushing his hand from her, she backed away from him, eyes wild.

The man stared at her, puzzled. Thinking that the dog had frightened her, he walked towards her to apologise, to make amends, when Eileen opened her mouth wide and began shouting. She was threatening him, mouthing obscenities the like of which he had never heard before from a woman, let alone a young girl. She stumbled away from him, her arms outstretched, her face screwed up with hatred.

It was then that Abel came upon her. He had witnessed the scene and as the man saw the huge musclebound individual put his arms around the shouting girl, he felt fear overwhelm him.

'I swear I never touched her, mister. I never touched her! The dog was jumping at her, that's all. She just went mad, stark staring mad . . .'

Abel held tightly on to Eileen. Strangely she never tried to fight him off but held on to him, sobbing into his barrel chest.

'He touched me, Abel, he was touching me.'

'I know, Eileen girl, I know. Calm down and I'll take you home to your mother.'

He motioned with his hand to the man to go away and leave them. He grabbed his dog by the scruff of its neck and almost ran in his haste to escape.

Slowly Abel led Eileen back to the road and his cart. He lifted her up tenderly and placed her on the seat, all the time talking to her softly, calming her down.

'He was touching me Abel, look at my arm. Look where he touched me, on my arm . . .'

Abel looked at the arm and nodded at her. She kept up a conversation with herself in low tones all the way home, rubbing furiously at the arm as if it was covered in filth.

It wasn't the first time she had wandered off and it was not to be the last.

Briony and Tommy sat on their usual bench. As the weather was warmer they had both begun to bring picnics with them. Today, Tommy had brought some tongue sandwiches and a small stone flask of lemonade. Eating the sandwiches, they put down crumbs of bread for the ducks, laughing at their antics as they fought over the tiny morsels.

'How are you feeling in yourself, Briony?'

She patted her stomach and smiled. 'Not too bad. I've only a few weeks to go now, and I can't wait until it's all over.'

'Has that woman, that Mrs Dumas, said any more about giving you the house?'

Briony nodded. 'Oh, yeah, she's like a nervous wreck waiting for this baby.'

Tommy nodded solemnly.

'Well, you just make sure you get it all in writing. You're thirteen now aren't you?'

'Yeah, I'm thirteen in a few months, why?'

'Well, you might have to get it put in trust for you or something. With your mum. Either way, make sure you take any papers they give you to a good brief. I know a bloke who's well up on all this kind of stuff, I'll arrange for you to see him.'

Briony screwed up her little face.

'Mrs Dumas wouldn't tuck me up. She's lovely.'

Tommy swallowed the last of his sandwich and threw the crust to the ducks.

''Course she's lovely, she wants your baby. Once it's born and she's got her hands on it, you might as well piss in the wind with all the legal jargon they'll baffle you with. You just listen to me, Briony, I've got contacts that could help you. You must look out for number one. If you don't, no one else will.'

Briony digested this bit of logic and shrugged. She trusted Isabel Dumas with her life, but she didn't trust Henry. Though he was never mentioned by Isabel, Briony sensed his baleful influence. What Tommy said made sense, and when the time came she would take his advice and see his lawyer friend.

'Thanks, Tommy, I'll keep that in mind. Now tell me some more stories about Nellie Deakins' place. They make me laugh.'

He poured her another glass of cool lemonade and handed it to her.

'First of all you tell me what's been happening with you. Have you seen the doctor this week?'

Briony sighed and began telling him everything he wanted to know. Tommy relaxed on the bench and watched her tiny rosebud mouth. He could listen to her and watch her all day. They chatted until her cab driver came for her and then, after promising to see him the following day, Briony went off. Tommy watched her go. As she reached the park exit she turned and waved and he waved back, feeling low now she had gone. They had met nearly every day for over three months. In that time he had felt a closeness spring between them that was not just friendship. He found himself thinking about her at odd times of the day and the evenings. He would not call what he felt for her love, because in his youth he wasn't sure what love was.

But whatever it was he felt for Briony, with her little button nose and that crackling red hair, he liked it.

He liked it, and he wanted to keep it.

Isabel was staying in her own home tonight. She made a point of staying two nights a week, eating dinner, seeing to her household bills, ordering the different cuts of meat and overseeing the general upkeep. The rest of the time she stayed with Briony.

As she sat in her room, she brushed out her long brown hair and was delighted to see the firelight pick out golden highlights. Her skin looked creamy in the triple mirrors on her dressing table and she smiled at herself. Since the night she had rescued Briony Cavanagh, her life had taken on a different slant. Her depression had lifted, and even the thought of being married to Henry didn't stop her from enjoying herself. Briony had given her a new zest for living, and now she was certain to get the child, she couldn't be happier.

She glanced at her heavy breasts in the mirror. Their rosy nipples peeping out from behind the thin lace brought a momentary return of her old longings. She quickly pushed these thoughts from her mind, concentrating once more on the coming child. She hoped it looked like its mother. That way she could guarantee it would be a beautiful child. If it looked like Henry and it was a girl child . . . She picked up her hand cream and began the laborious nightly ritual of softening her hands.

Henry walked in the room without knocking.

Isabel looked at his red face in the dressing-table mirror and saw at once he had been drinking.

'What can I do for you?'

He sat unsteadily on the edge of her bed and looked at his wife. In his drunken state, he noticed everything about her as if for the first time. Her high breasts and slim waist, the length of her legs, her well-turned ankles. The dark brown hair that tumbled across her shoulders and down her back. And suddenly, all his hatred of her dissolved. He saw her for what she was in other men's eyes. To any other man, she would be a desirable companion, a good wife. She was pleasing in face and figure, intelligent and well educated. She could talk on almost any subject and could also listen exceptionally well. He could almost pity her for being married to him.

'It's about the child, Isabel.'

He watched her smile as she turned to face him.

'What child? The one you got pregnant? Or the child of the

child?' Her tone was sarcastic and Henry closed his eyes.

'You're still intent on bringing it into this house then?'

'I am.'

He shook his head.

'What about the talk it'll cause?'

Isabel laughed now.

'There's always talk, Henry. I am seeing my father tomorrow and telling him I'm barren. We both know that's not true, don't we? I will tell him that you have a mistress, a respectable widow of the lower middle classes who has found herself in an embarrassing predicament. You wish to take the child and bring it up as your own and I have agreed to it. My father will set the rumour abroad and everyone will think you are a rake who has taken on an illegitimate child because your legal wife can't produce one. You'll come out of it as rather a colourful character, a man with many women. I'll come out of it as the poor barren wife taking another woman's leavings. So don't worry about the talk, Henry. It will all be grist to your mill really. Who would ever think that a rake like that really liked little girls?'

Henry sat still under the onslaught of his wife's tongue, and as they stared at one another felt an urge to confess his feelings to her. To tell her about the demon that drove him to little girls. But even as he thought it, he dismissed it. She wouldn't understand.

'What if your father refuses to allow you to take on the child?'

'Henry, I'm not going to ask his permission, I'm going to *tell* him. I don't care what he thinks. All he is to me is a means to an end. I'll talk him round, don't worry. Now if you don't mind, I want to get into bed.'

She was dismissing him and they both knew it.

'I am the man of this house, madam. It would behove you to remember that.'

Isabel stood up and her laughter caused her breasts to shudder.

'If you were the man of the house, Henry, indeed any kind of man, we would not be having this conversation!' With that, she

100

walked past him and opened the door wide.

'Goodnight, Henry. I'll keep you informed of what's happening.'

He walked from the room. As he sat on his own bed drinking a large brandy, it occurred to him that she had won again. She would bring the gutter brat's child into his home and he was powerless to stop her. Her strength of purpose was terrifying to him. Never had he felt so powerless, so utterly powerless.

He lay back and closed his eyes. Seeing Briony in his mind, he shuddered. He would not be in this predicament if it hadn't been for her. Well, he had a long memory and a lot of money. He would wait for his chance and get his own back on her eventually.

Happier now he had a fixed goal in mind, he waited for a drunken sleep to claim him. But the light was already sneaking in at the chinks of the curtains before it came.

Chapter Eight

Briony sat on the park bench waiting for Tommy. She shifted her position slightly as she had a dull ache in her back. The child had dropped inside her and her stomach felt as if it was lying on her knees. She was wearing a large silk cape to hide the enormous bulge that seemed to be quivering and turning constantly. She took a deep breath as she felt a stabbing pain go through her body. She closed her eyes until it passed. Isabel had been right, she should not have left the house today. But the thought of seeing Tommy had been too much of a draw for her and after nearly having an argument with the nervous woman she had finally got her own way. Now, though, she wished she had heeded the advice and stayed home. The last couple of days she had been possessed of a great energy, feeling as if she could climb a mountain if she wanted to. In the space of an hour that feeling had been replaced by one of a dull lethargy.

She felt Tommy sit beside her and opened her eyes.

'You look ill, girl. Are you all right?'

Briony stared into his face and shook her head. 'I think it's on its way.'

Tommy saw her eyes widen as she sat forward, clasping her stomach with both hands.

'Oh Tommy . . . Tommy . . . I've wet meself!'

The boy jumped from his seat in panic. 'Stay there and I'll get someone . . . I'll get the doctor!'

Briony laughed despite the pain. 'Just get me to the cab and back to the house, as quick as possible.'

Her voice had a strength in it that calmed the youth in front of her.

'Here, give me your arm and walk me to me cab.'

Tommy helped her up and they walked slowly towards the entrance of the park where her cab waited. In ten minutes they were outside her house. Tommy helped her down while the cabby knocked at the door. Pandemonium erupted.

Mrs Horlock and Cissy took Briony up the stairs while Mrs Dumas sent the cabby for the doctor. Tommy stood in the hallway watching in amazement. Isabel turned to him as she went to walk up the stairs and looked at him as if just seeing him for the first time. She unconsciously took in the neat suit and the well-cut hair. His penetrating blue eyes stayed her and she walked towards him.

'I'm so sorry, young man, thank you for bringing my charge home.'

Tommy looked at her, decided he liked the look of her and smiled.

'I'm a friend of Briony's actually.'

The woman stood stock still.

'Really? I can't say she's ever mentioned you before.'

'Well, she's mentioned you, Mrs Dumas. My name's Thomas, Thomas Lane.'

He held out his hand and Isabel took it before she had time to think.

'How do you do, Mr Lane?'

'If it's all right with you, I'd like to stay for a bit, see that she's all right like . . .'

Isabel was nonplussed for a second. She wasn't sure what to say to the boy. She was saved from answering by Cissy running down the stairs.

'She wants her mum, Mrs Dumas. She's insisting on having her mum here.'

Tommy stepped forward. 'Tell me where she lives and I'll go for her.'

Two minutes later he was rushing from the house and on his way to Molly's.

Briony felt as if her whole body was being rent in two.

'Oh, Mam, Mam . . . it's hurting me . . . it's hurting me!'

Her voice was high and filled with terror.

'Calm yourself, child. Would you calm yourself . . . It won't be long now.'

Molly looked at the doctor and he nodded at her, confirming her own opinion.

Briony twisted her head on the pillows. Her whole being was filled with pain. It seemed to her at that moment that even her teeth ached with it. Molly stared down at her child and felt such love come over her she would gladly have borne the pain for Briony at that moment. The doctor suddenly pushed past Molly.

'This is it, it's coming.'

Molly stood by, helpless, as the top of the child's head appeared. She watched the opening of her daughter's body stretch and the tiny head, that looked so small and vulnerable to her and felt so big and cumbersome to Briony, push its way out into the world. Then its shoulders appeared and it slipped from its mother and into the doctor's arms where the baby immediately began to cry, big, gasping, lusty cries that made Molly smile in delight. The child had a reddish tinge to its downy hair and its face, unlined and smooth, had a peach colour to it that denoted health and strength. Looking at it, she felt a stirring inside her. This was wholly Briony's child, that much was evident.

Briony lifted her head from the pillows and tried to glimpse the baby, but she could see nothing. Then the doctor put the child on her now blessedly flat stomach and she looked into the sea green eyes of her son. He looked at his mother and his crying ceased immediately. It was as if mother and child sized each other up for a few split seconds.

Molly saw Briony smile at him and felt a great sadness for her. It would be hard to give up a big beautiful child like this, but give it up she must. Instinctively she grasped her daughter's hand as the doctor finished cutting the cord and Mrs Horlock swaddled the child. She kissed Briony then, tenderly, in a way she had never kissed any of her children before. It was as if she and Briony had become sisters, sharing now a common bond: the pains of birth and of motherhood.

Isabel was sitting in the morning room with Tommy Lane. They had hardly spoken to one another. Both sat silent, straining their ears to hear what was happening upstairs.

Tommy noticed that the woman was wringing her hands together. He watched her ample bosom heave as she waited for the outcome of the birth. Then they heard the long low shriek and the sound of a child's crying.

Their eyes met and of one mind they stood up and went to the door. They met Molly on her way down the stairs.

'It's a boy child. A big, lusty boy child.'

Isabel lifted her skirts and ran up the stairs like a girl, her face glowing with happiness and expectation. She burst into the bedroom where Briony lay in the bed with her son in her arms.

Looking down into his face, Briony experienced a feeling like looking forward to ten whole Christmasses rolled together. Like the excitement caused by a very high place or the opening of a large present. She traced his every feature with her eyes, drinking in the smell of him, the size of him, the shape of his jaw.

She lifted her eyes to Isabel Dumas, and saw mirrored there the same expression as her own. But she also saw the raw longing, the gnawing want that would never be fully assuaged.

Holding out the child to her, Briony smiled widely. 'Look at him, Isabel, he's beautiful.'

She took the child and sat on the edge of the bed with him.

Mrs Horlock watched the exchange and felt a surge of relief go through her. She had convinced herself that Briony would not let the child go. She bustled from the room taking Cissy with her, on the pretext of making Briony a strong cup of tea. The doctor patted the mother's hand and walked from the room, ready to get his money and depart.

Alone together, Briony and Isabel looked at one another.

'He's beautiful, Briony.' Isabel's voice broke and Briony

106

placed her hand over Isabel's so both of them were holding the child. He stirred in Isabel's arms and settled himself more comfortably. Staring at the two faces above his. Trying to focus on one and then the other.

'You'll look after him, won't you?'

Isabel smiled and nodded her head vigorously. 'I'll look after him all my life, I promise you that. Thank you for giving him to me, Briony. Thank you.'

Satisfied, she lay back against the pillows, her face white and drawn. She felt so tired and so sore all she wanted to do was sleep.

Tommy waited until he was sure that Briony was safe and then left the house, telling Cissy he would be back the next evening.

Molly was the next to depart, then Mrs Horlock and Cissy both drank a large hot rum to celebrate the safe delivery.

Briony awoke at eleven in the evening, after sleeping for nearly two hours. Cissy was sitting by her bed and as soon as Briony was fully awake, went for Mrs Horlock.

The old woman brought Briony up a simple meal of coddled eggs and broth, knowing that hunger would have made itself felt by now. After a few sips of the broth, Briony looked at the wizened old face and smiled.

'I feel much better now. Where's the baby?'

Mrs Horlock put the bowl of broth on the bedside cabinet and sat beside Briony on the bed.

'He's gone to the mistress's house, Briony.'

She sat upright in the bed, her face a study in disbelief.

'What? Already? But I only saw him once. I want to see him again. Now!' Her voice had taken on a strident quality and Mrs Horlock pulled her into her arms.

'It's no good, Briony. If you see too much of him at first you won't be able to let go. I know, I've seen it happen before.'

Briony felt a hotness behind her eyes.

'But he's my baby, Mrs Horlock. I want to see him.'

She started to cry then, her little shoulders heaving inside the nice white lawn nightdress with the pink bows that she had been so delighted with, had loved to think she owned.

Mrs Horlock held her while she cried bitter tears. When she quietened, the old woman went from the room to make her a strong hot whisky with lots of sugar in. She would ensure the child slept. It was a great healer.

Alone in the room, Briony looked around her. At the brocade curtains and bedspread, the carpeted floor, and the pictures on the walls. Above the bed was a tapestry, worked by her own hands in the long afternoons of her pregnancy. It was a proverb from the Bible and read: 'For whom the Lord loveth, he correcteth.' It was one of Mrs Prosser Evans' sayings and Briony had always remembered it. Now, though, she knew exactly what it meant.

All that she now had – this house, the money that was being given to her, the fact that her mother and sisters would benefit from her giving away her little child – meant nothing. All the nice clothes and all the good food and all the warmth would never replace the feeling she had experienced when she had looked at her son.

Her son. He was her son, her son and Henry's.

But he would live with his father, a man who only wanted little children. A man who had taken Briony and abused her, tempted her with his promise of luxury and warmth and three pounds a week.

Now he had everything and she had nothing.

She had lain racked with pain, had pushed a life into the world, and at the end of it all she didn't even know what they were going to call her son.

She didn't even know his name.

Isabel looked down at the well-shaped head in the crib and sighed with contentment. The baby moved, snuggling into the warmth then, snuffling through his button nose, drifted back off to sleep again. Sally, his nurse, looked on and smiled to herself. Her own baby, born two months previously, had died after a week as if he just couldn't be bothered to breathe in the slum he'd been born to. She had made sure of keeping her milk by letting her sister's children suckle her, now she was ensconced in this lovely house, had been bathed and given two uniforms. She had her own room with three guaranteed meals a day, and milk and beer as and when she fancied it. Even if talk in the house was rife, if they did say that the child was the master's by a whore, what did she care? As long as she kept her position she would look after the child of the devil himself.

Isabel was beside herself with excitement. She had a child, a dear and blessed little child, and felt as if she had been touched by the good Lord himself. Unable to sleep with excitement, she watched the wet nurse feed him, watched his strong lips find the nipple and suck on it hungrily, and wished fervently that she could do that particular job herself. She was gratified that he looked like his mother, that he would be a handsome boy. He was big, so big. She had not been prepared for the sheer size of him. For the force of love the baby would awaken in her. Already Briony was all but forgotten.

Hardly able to contain herself, Isabel took the child from the wet nurse as soon as he was replete and, taking him back to her own room, sat in front of the fire and just looked at him.

She held him in her arms and drank in every part of him. He grasped her finger and she laughed out loud in the silent room. He was strong and he was hers.

Her son, Benedict Dumas. All the frustrated longing and the unrequited love she possessed would be channelled into this boy. He would be loved, cared for and educated. He would have everything that money and her influence could give him. He was, from that day on, her boy.

Her darling boy.

Henry walked into Isabel's room as she sat with the child. She heard the door open but was unable to take her eyes from the child long enough to see who it was.

Clearing his throat, he walked across the room and stood behind the chair, forcing himself to look. He was unprepared for the sheer beauty of the child in his wife's arms. He saw the strong hand holding on to his wife's fingers. Saw the perfectly shaped lips and the button nose that were wholly his mother's.

He saw the startling green eyes and caught his breath in his throat.

Looking down on to the wide awake infant he felt a revulsion inside him that was so acute he could almost taste it. It was as if every nightmare he had ever had was there, in that body on his wife's lap. It was his flesh and blood, he knew that, but he wanted no part of it. No part of it at all.

Molly arrived at nine the next morning and was closeted with Mrs Horlock for a good hour before she ventured up the stairs to her daughter's room. She looked around her as if seeing everything for the first time. It amazed her that her daughter of only thirteen owned this house. Owned everything in it. That her child was now a woman of property.

She walked into the bedroom and forced a smile on to her face. Briony lay in bed, pale and wan. Her usually animated face was drawn and dark circles were visible under her eyes. Molly could see the expert bindings around her breasts through her nightdress, and the sadness in her daughter's drawn face.

'Are you feeling all right, Briony?'

She looked at her mother and sighed.

'She took him, Mum. Isabel. She took him home with her.'

Molly sat on the edge of the bed and grasped Briony's hand. 'Of course she did, love. It would do you no good to see too much of him.'

Briony pulled her hand from her mother's and her face set in a pout. It made her look very young and very spoilt. Seeing the look, Molly herself sighed. Briony was the only one of her daughters who had never been biddable. She had always gone her own way. Even as a tiny child, when Molly had chastised her for something, Briony had taken the punishment and then gone and done exactly what she wanted to. It was this trait in her daughter's character that was evident now. Briony was quite capable of getting out of bed and going to Isabel Dumas' and taking the child. Molly tried a different tack.

'Look, Briony, Mrs Dumas can give the boy everything. He'll be educated, he'll be well looked after, with all sorts of people

110

seeing to his every whim. He'll grow up with all this—' she gestured around her '—as part and parcel of his everyday life. Would you honestly take that chance from him and bring him up in Oxlow Lane? Because if you take that child now, you can kiss goodbye to this place, and the three pounds a week, and everything else you ever wanted. If someone had come and asked me for any one of you, I'd have given you up, and gladly. This is like a gift from the gods, girl. Your boy's being offered the chance to be somebody. Don't ruin it for him.'

Briony let her mother's words sound inside her head. It saddened her that she was in such a position. It was as if the three pounds a week to keep her mother and sisters at Oxlow Lane was the most important thing in the world. And the worst part of all was, she knew it was important. It was Briony's sole responsibility to keep them where they were now accustomed to being. How could she take Eileen and Kerry and Bernie and Rosalee back to the dockside slums? Eileen would never be fit to work again so it would all fall on Briony's shoulders and her mother's while the two younger girls would be left to look after Eileen and Rosalee. Their lives would all become set into a pattern that they'd never be able to change.

'Shall I get you a nice cup of tea, love?'

Molly's voice broke into her thoughts and she nodded. Unknown to her, all her thoughts were plain to her mother. Molly had deliberately set the chain of thought in motion and now she wanted to leave Briony alone for long enough to think through the consequences of any foolish action. No rash decisions must be allowed to wreck an otherwise harmonious arrangement.

Briony didn't watch her mother leave the room, just waited with bated breath until she was alone once more. It was the first time Briony had felt the full force of the responsibility she had assumed. When it had all been a childish game, when she had dreamt of being a lady in the eyes of the world, looking after her family and taking over where her father had left off, it had all seemed glamorous somehow. Now, after the birth of the child, her child, who was even as she lay here being looked after and

111

fed by a stranger, the sheer enormity of her own actions bore down on her, leaving her feeling crushed and afraid. She could no more ask Isabel for her son than she could ask the good Lord himself to take her to tea at Claridges. It was out of her control now.

What was it Tommy had once told her? Possession was nine-tenths of the law? Well, the Dumases had the law on their side and she knew that if they chose to use it, she would have nothing at all. No child, no house and no money.

She saw her baby again in her mind's eye. His big long body, the red tinge to his downy hair, and knew he was still hers in so many ways.

Biting her lip, she made a pledge to herself. She could do nothing about her son now; she was too young, too vulnerable and far too poor. What she would do was to let herself heal physically and then work out a plan of action. If it rested with her she would never be vulnerable again, never be in a position to be overlooked by anybody, least of all Henry and Isabel Dumas who had both used her.

For different reasons maybe, but they had used her just the same.

Isabel had left the child sleeping and made her way up to Briony's bedroom with light feet. She had not felt happiness like this for years. The sheer act of looking at the child made her into a happy carefree woman. She bounded through the bedroom door with a large grin on her face.

'How are you feeling, Briony?'

The girl in the bed turned to face her and immediately Isabel's expression changed. Briony looked ill and drawn. Her eyes were dead and even that glorious hair, which usually crackled with a life of its own, looked dull and flat.

Isabel went to her and embraced her, all concern.

Being taken into the arms of the woman who now had her child made Briony's shoulders heave. Tears seemed to burst from her eyes. These hands, so soft and gentle, the hands that had held her and petted her throughout her pregnancy, were the

112

same hands that would caress and protect her son. Would hold him when he cried, would rub a sore knee better. The very touch of the woman whom Briony both loved and despised brought out the tears that needed to be shed.

Isabel held Briony tightly to her. She stroked the hair that her son had inherited, whispered endearments. She realised that in her own excitement, in her own longing for a child, she had forgotten the very person who had made all her dreams possible.

It would take all her tact and diplomacy now to right the enormous wrong she had done. But one thing was for sure: Briony Cavanagh would not get her child back. Isabel could no more part with him than she could cut out her own heart.

When the crying subsided, she kissed Briony's cheek and under pretext of plumping up her pillows, tried to be as normal as possible.

'Are you feeling better, dear?' Her voice was all kindness and sympathy.

Briony nodded.

'I have heard tell that many women get crying fits after a birth. It's natural.'

'How's the child?' Briony's voice seemed harder than Isabel remembered it.

'Oh, very well. A big healthy child. Briony, how can I ever thank you for what you've done for me? I look at him, and everything in my life has taken on a new meaning. I'll give that boy the earth if he wants it. I'll give him everything he wants and more. Much more.'

Briony nodded, gratified to hear that. She could hear the love and the want and indeed the need in the other woman's voice as she talked of the child, and already it seemed he was long gone from her.

'Is he a good baby?'

Isabel heard the little tremor in her voice and found it in her heart to pity this girl-woman in front of her.

'Oh, he's a perfect little boy. Sleeps on his tummy, as young as he is. Not a day old! He pushes his arms from the swaddling and turns himself on to his stomach. He's a baby who knows his

113

own mind already. Like his mother, I would say.'

Her voice was jocular, and it pleased Briony to hear that, as Isabel knew it would.

'And Henry, what does he think of the child?'

Isabel took a small breath.

'Henry wants what I want. His opinion is nothing in this.'

Briony nodded again. It was as it should be. If Isabel had said that Henry was pleased with the child it would have troubled her. If the child was to stay with the Dumases, as it was, she didn't want Henry Dumas to stake too large a claim. For the child's own safety.

Isabel swept the hair from Briony's forehead and smiled. 'I know it's hard to give him up, dear. If I had birthed him, it would break my heart to give him up. But it's all for the best. After all, what would you do with a child, no man and no money? What would your mother and sisters do?'

Even as she spoke the veiled threat, Isabel felt a disgust with herself that was forced down by her need to keep what she had taken. It would do no harm to remind Briony of the consequences of any rash actions.

'I have arranged for two thousand pounds to be made available to you. Once you're up and about I shall take you personally to see the banker and to find out how to write cheques. The house is going into your name as well. You'll be a woman of substance and wealth. The next child you have will be born to something better than you were. The world's out there waiting for you, Briony Cavanagh, and I have no doubt, no doubt at all that, you'll be someone in it!'

Briony didn't respond. She was more than aware of what all this talk was really about. It was about Isabel's having the child in exchange for giving Briony comfort and money. The two things that had brought her to this house would now be used to trap her.

'Thank you very much, but I just want to get back on my feet for now. I'll think about the future then.'

'As you wish. I've arranged all your menus for the next few days and I'll pop in again tomorrow to see you.'

114

Briony knew the woman wanted to get away from her. Knew that she wanted to be back in her own home with the child.

Isabel kissed Briony's cheek with hot feverish lips. Suddenly, she had to get out of here and away from this creature in the bed. Even as she thought it she knew she was being unfair. But like everything that is used for the wrong reasons, Briony was a source of annoyance. Isabel admitted to herself that a large part of her feelings was of guilt. As she walked to the door, Briony's voice stayed her.

'What did you call him, Isabel? What's his name?'

She turned once more and smiled gently. 'He's Benedict. Benedict Dumas.'

Briony nodded and looked out of the window where she could see the roofs of the houses opposite and an expanse of blue sky.

She heard the door shut behind Isabel and clenched her fists together on the counterpane.

Benedict. Benedict, my son.

My flesh and blood.

It was not a name she would have chosen herself. It was a name for a child of the Dumases. Somehow, even the name made the gulf between Briony and her child wider.

Tommy Lane had had a good day. He was happy as he made his way up the path to Briony's house. In his hand he carried a bunch of flowers. Red carnations, blood red. He knocked at the front door with a flourish. He was looking forward to seeing Briony. The door was opened by Cissy, and he took in the split second hesitation as she looked at him and deliberately walked back into the hall. He smiled at her.

'I've come to see Miss Briony Cavanagh.'

'Well, I didn't think you'd come to see me, lad.'

Her sharp cockney accent made Tommy smile.

'I'm not sure what Mrs Horlock's going to say about this, I'm sure.'

'I'm not too worried about Mrs Horlock, love. You go and tell Briony that Tommy Lane's here and wants to see her.'

Mrs Horlock appeared as if from nowhere.

'You're not seeing anyone, young man.'

Tommy sized the old woman up and decided she sounded more ferocious than she looked.

'As I was just remarking to this young lady, you go and tell Briony that Tommy Lane's here. I think she'll see me.' It was said with an air of confidence that made Mrs Horlock bristle.

'She's only just out of childbed. It ain't seemly!'

Tommy rolled his eyes and started walking up the stairs. Cissy watched Mrs Horlock dart up behind him and threw her apron over her head in shock, closing her eyes tightly.

The cheek of him!

Brushing Mrs Horlock off like a fly, he opened all the doors he came to until he found Briony. Holding out the flowers at arm's length, he walked over to her with Mrs Horlock soundly berating him as she chased in behind.

'It ain't right, Miss Briony! This lout here needs a clout round the earhole. Pushing his way in and upsetting the whole house. Suppose the mistress had been here? What would have happened then, I ask you?'

Briony took the carnations and held them under her nose. She breathed in the scent of them and smiled. Her first real smile. Pointing them at Mrs Horlock, she snapped: 'In case it's escaped your notice, to all intents and purposes *I'm* the mistress here now! So take these flowers and put them in water, and then bring us some tea.'

Tommy stifled a grin at the look of utter shock on the old woman's face. But she did as Briony asked her, taking the flowers with a snatch of the hand and a glare in his direction, before stamping from the room, slamming the heavy door behind her.

'You look ill, girl, and I'm not surprised with that nutty old cow looking after you!'

He went to the window and opened it wide. 'Get some air in here, for Christ's sake.'

Briony watched him and felt a stirring inside her. She had needed a pick-me-up and it had come in the shape of Tommy Lane.

'So how are you then?'

Briony smiled at him. 'Not too bad, Tommy.'

He sat on the end of the bed and grinned at her. He knew instinctively that the child wasn't in the house. There was no evidence of it anywhere. He took in the white face and the bound breasts and his heart went out to the girl in front of him. He immediately launched into a convoluted story that made Briony laugh despite herself and forget her own worries for a few moments. Mrs Horlock, bringing up the tea tray, heard the laughter coming down the stairs and decided that she would not press Briony about the boy. If he could cheer her up, he could move in for all she cared! She brought in the tray of tea, and a little while later a tray of sandwiches and cakes, without being asked. As Tommy ate another sandwich in one gobble, Briony grinned.

'That means she likes you really, you got her angel cake.'

Tommy laughed. 'I don't care whether she likes me or not. We're friends, ain't we? Why can't I visit a friend?'

He finished his sandwich and then asked Briony the question that had been in his mind since entering the house.

'Where's the baby?'

She sipped her tea delicately and the natural grace as she did this made Tommy want to grab her and hold her to him. To look after her.

'Isabel – Mrs Dumas – took him last night.'

Tommy nodded.

'Well, it's for the best, girl. You're only thirteen, you don't want a nipper hanging around your neck at your age. Not only that, they can give him much more'n you could even if you had a man. Get yourself better, get yourself up and around. Start over again.'

Briony nodded at him, her face sad.

'Come on, Bri, you don't want to go worrying about what's done. You just start worrying about what you're going to do next. Now then, has she signed the house over to you?'

'Oh, yes, and she's put two thousand pounds away for me.'

Tommy gave a low whistle. What he couldn't do with that!

117

He had the lowdown now on how to run a good 'house'. Once he had the capital, he would buy a place and run his own. He wouldn't stay the rest of his life at Nellie Deakins'. He looked at Briony and a glimmer of a plan formed in his mind.

'Would you care to invest five hundred in a little business venture with me, Bri?'

She was intrigued.

'What kind of business venture?'

Tommy took a deep breath and began to speak. And as Briony listened to him, to his plans, to his dreams, she felt a faint stirring in herself.

Chapter Nine

Briony looked around her and took in first the high ceilings, then the grey and gold flock on the walls, and lastly the rather garish chandeliers on the ceiling. She looked at Tommy who smiled at her. She nodded her head, smiling back.

The small stocky man with the handlebar moustaches, Mr Tillier the builder, grinned at them, showing pointed teeth.

'I knew you'd like it. I ain't overdone it, see? Now Nellie's place is nice, but it ain't got no class. All that red and burgundy, it looks what it is. This place, it's got a bit of class, and as you're having only a select clientele, well then, Bob's your uncle.'

He watched the young couple as they walked from room to room. The boy, or man as he tried to think of him, was cute. Cute as a nine-bob note, and as bent, but the girl – and she was a girl – was a completely different kettle of fish. He'd put her at no more than seventeen or eighteen, though he had heard through the grapevine that she was only coming up to her fourteenth birthday. Well, he mused, she must have pleased someone into giving her the money that she'd been spending like water. Her voice was nice, she spoke well, but it was forced. She still slipped in a 'bugger' or a 'bleeding' when she spoke to the young man.

He watched her climb the staircase. He was proud of the staircase. It curved round, and any of the ladies who walked down it would be shown to their best advantage. The chandeliers above it were of real crystal, their light giving off a bluish hue that made even the worst skin look good. As toms grew older it seemed the skin was the first thing to go with most of them, so good lighting was a priority for a class house.

He followed them up the stairs and into the first bedroom. This was done out in deep blue and peach, the bed a large fourposter with deep blue velvet drapes around it. Hanging up on the wardrobe door was a woman's wrapper of the same colour, as sheer as a spider's web. This would be called the Blue Room. Briony checked that everything was to her satisfaction and, seeing a pair of ornate cherubs over the fireplace, their features picked out in gold leaf, shook her head decisively.

'They'll have to go, Mr Tillier. I don't like them. A big mirror would be much more appropriate, I think.'

He nodded and wrote in his little notebook. She was cute all right. He'd thought they were a mistake himself. Although the walls to either side of the bed had large mirrors running the length of the panels, he thought that another mirror would not go amiss, especially when you thought of what the room was to be used for.

Both men followed Briony through the rest of the house. Each of them seemed to expect her to give the expert opinion and this she did, in a low voice that brooked no argument. There were now ten bedrooms of different sizes. The original six had been divided and rearranged and now there was plenty of room to accommodate ten men at a time. Briony walked down the stairs and through the hallway to the small offices set aside for herself and Tommy. Unlike the rest of the house these rooms were plain with good solid furniture. These were working rooms, and they looked it. Briony sat herself behind a mahogany desk and gently fingered the inkwells and the leather blotter in front of her. She was raring to go. In forty-eight hours she was opening the doors to the most select clientele she could gather. Thanks to Tommy's knowledge of Nellie Deakins' customers, they had arranged discreet invitations to the cream of London's society. Briony looked at her tiny fob watch and stood up.

'I have to go, Tommy, I'll leave the rest to you. I want the cherubs gone by this evening, Mr Tillier. I'll wish you both good day.'

She left them. Both men looked at one another and smiled.

'How about a glass of madeira, Mr Tillier?'

'That would be most excellent, Mr Lane.'

He took the proffered drink and was sorry the young lass had gone. She would have had the sense to offer him brandy.

Isabel sat in the park and chatted to Benedict in baby talk. She made a point of sitting away from the nannies and they allowed for this. Initially, they had praised the child and tried to strike up conversations, but once they found out who Isabel was, they respectfully kept their distance as they realised she did not want company. Then the chatter about Mrs Dumas had reached their ears, through a grapevine of scullery maids, tweenies, and finally cooks and butlers, until the knowledge that Henry Dumas had saddled his barren wife with the child of an unmarried woman, supposedly a widow of good standing, had resounded around London. Now they watched her carefully, seeing her obvious love for the child, and were frankly amazed by it.

Briony got out of her cab and told the cab driver to wait for her. She walked into Barking Park with a feeling of excitement at the prospect of seeing Benedict. She was dressed all in lilac, her hair pinned up in glorious tendrils under a matching hat. She walked with a dignity that was envied by most of the women who saw her, and her small-breasted figure looked just right for the fashions of the day.

Isabel saw her walking towards her and smiled widely. Benedict noticed her and started to clap chubby hands together, crowing with excitement. Briony sat down on the bench and looked into green eyes so like her own.

'How is he?'

'Thriving. Look at him. He doesn't stop eating and poor Sally is run off her feet looking after him. How are you?'

Briony peeled off her gloves and took her son's hands in her own.

'I'm OK. We open up soon, so I'm really busy.'

Isabel just nodded at this. The fact that Briony was to open a bordello shocked her more than she liked to admit.

'How's your mother?'

'Funny you should ask that, I'm going to see her today. Eileen's bad again. It's a shame because she started to get well for a while. Kerry and Bernie are fine as usual, and poor Rosalee ... well, Rosalee never changes except to get heavier.'

'Did your mother take Eileen to the doctor I told you about?'

'Oh, him, yes. He wanted her put away, but we'll never allow that. We'll look after her.'

The two women were quiet now, both admiring the child in the perambulator.

'His hair's getting darker.'

'Yes, but he's still got your red highlights. I think he'll probably be a dark brown, like me.'

Briony nodded. She'd noticed that Isabel often tried to point out likenesses to herself in the child and far from being irritated by it, felt sorry for her. If poor Isabel had had a normal man and her own children she would have been an exemplary mother, her treatment of Benedict proved that.

'I have something to tell you, Briony. I've been trying to find the words ...'

She was alarmed at Isabel's tone.

'What? Is – is Ben ...'

'Oh no, nothing to do with him. Well, not directly anyway. We're moving up to the West End. Henry's bought a house in Belgravia and we feel it's about time we moved away. This house is far too small really, and my father would see more of Benedict ...'

There, it was said. She didn't add that this monthly visit from Briony was worrying her. That she was frightened that now Benedict was getting older he might become too attached to the young redhead he saw in the park. That she was secretly jealous of the time he spent in his mother's company.

She could not look into Briony's eyes and see the hurt and confusion she knew she would find there. Instead she busied herself picking up the child and settling him on her lap. She kissed his downy head and hugged him to her. Briony watched as her son put his fingers up to Isabel's mouth and she kissed them, pretending to bite them gently and making the child laugh. Briony felt as if a stone had been placed inside her chest. A big solid weight that would eventually drag her down.

'I see.' But she didn't see. She didn't see at all. She was shrewd enough to guess what was really behind the action. She wondered who wanted the move most, Henry or Isabel.

'When will I see him then?'

'Oh, we'll sort that out in due course. I think it's best if the visits are cut down anyway. He's as bright as a button and might start saying your name, or when he's talking he might tell someone about you. That would not be good for any of us, let alone the child.'

Briony licked dry lips.

'But I must see him, Isabel. I have to see him sometimes.'

'And you shall see him, I promise. Only we have to be careful. If Henry knew he was seeing you now . . .'

She left the sentence unfinished.

Briony put her hand out to the child and he grasped her slim fingers, bringing them to his mouth to chew on them. Briony felt the tiny needle-sharp teeth as he gnawed and the familiar love for him overwhelmed her. If she was denied access to him she would die inside. Not an hour of the day went by but she thought of him. Everything else in her life was as nothing compared to this child.

'But I have to see him, Isabel.' Briony's voice was louder than she'd intended and Isabel put her hand on her arm.

'For goodness' sake, keep your voice down. Do you want all the nannies to know our business and take it back to their houses with them?'

Briony shook her head and Isabel settled the boy once more in his carriage and stood up.

'I really have to be going. I'll be in touch soon.'

Briony nodded weakly as she watched her son being pushed away from her. Her eyes blurred as tears stung them and she stared after Isabel and the child until they disappeared out of the park gates.

Molly was force-feeding Rosalee when Briony arrived. Rosalee was going through one of her not-eating phases. She swung between a state of constant hunger and one of not eating a scrap. Either way she still got heavier and heavier. Briony walked in the door and, kissing Rosalee's face, took the spoon from her mother and began to feed her sister. Molly watched as Rosalee ate every morsel Briony gave to her.

'You've certainly got a way with her, Bri. I wish to God I had it.'

Molly poured out two mugs of tea as Briony finished feeding Rosalee, then, taking off her hat, perched it on Rosalee's head and grinned at her.

Rosalee, looking ridiculous in the lilac confection, grinned back, saying her only words, 'Bri Bri' and clapping her hands together.

Molly tried to grab the hat off Rosalee's head but Briony stayed her hand.

'Oh, leave her alone, Mum, it's only a hat.'

'A hat that cost a small fortune.'

'So what? I don't mind, and it's my hat, so why should you care?'

Molly sipped her steaming tea and shook her head.

'I just saw Benedict. Isabel and Henry are moving up West with him. I think the days of letting me see him are numbered.'

Molly put a hand over her daughter's and said, 'Well, what did you expect, love? They won't want you around now, will they? And it's better for the boy.'

'But I'm his mother, Mum. Me, not her!'

'I know that. But, Briony love, he's better off where he is and you must accept that. He's their child now. Theirs. Not yours. You just try and remember that this way he will have everything he ever wants out of life.'

Briony nodded. She knew that what her mother said made sense, but when you loved someone as she loved Benedict, it didn't make any difference.

'That Kerry is getting to be a handful, Briony. She was caught singing in the pub again. I've scalped the arse off of her but it's no good.'

Kerry, now twelve, was uncontrollable. She would sing in a midden if someone would listen.

'Where is she now?'

'She's out with Bernie and Mother Jones. They're pea picking.'

Briony was glad of the change in the conversation. She knew that her mother was all for Benedict being with the Dumases and it would only cause more rows if they discussed it further.

'Pea picking? Well, she can sing to her heart's content there.'

'True, and she will, knowing her. When's the house opening?'

'In a couple of days. It's finished, the girls are all interviewed and ready to go, and Tommy is sorting out the last few details today. We'll need a few more strong men like Abel to keep a modicum of peace.'

Abel was now one of the men employed to dress in dinner suits and mingle with the guests. If there was any trouble they would deal with it as quickly and unobtrusively as possible.

Molly shook her head and smiled.

'Imagine you owning two houses, I can't believe it.'

Briony smiled despite herself. Her mother had changed her opinion on Nellie Deakins and the like when she had found out how much money was involved in the business. Also Abel, whom Briony knew to be her mother's beau, had been offered a job at twice his old money and that made Molly happier still.

Kerry and Bernie burst through the door, bringing the smell of the open fields with them.

'Hello, Briony!'

Both girls kissed her and then Rosalee was clapping her hands together to show her excitement. They both screamed with laughter as they saw the lilac hat perched on her short-cropped hair.

Molly busied herself making them some tea and a bite to eat. Kerry sat opposite Briony and grinned at her.

'This house you're opening up, will you have any entertainment there?'

125

Molly looked at Briony with raised eyebrows. 'There'll be plenty of entertainment there girl, don't you worry about that.'

Kerry sighed loudly. 'I don't mean *that* kind of entertainment. I mean, will you have a band there playing music or anything?'

Briony shook her head. 'No.'

'Then you should. It'll make it a bit different, wouldn't it? From what I've heard, the people what go there have a drink and a natter first. Well, why not give them a bit of entertainment like?'

'Such as, Kerry?'

She stood up and opened her arms wide.

'Like me, of course! I know all the popular songs and I'd only need a piano player like. I don't need no orchestra nor nothing. I can sing everything, you know that, Briony. It'd be good for you and good for me. I don't want to end up in Myrdle Street in some sweat shop, I want to be a singer.'

Briony laughed at her sister's outrageous suggestion. Kerry singing in a bordello? It was absurd.

'Oh, come on, Bri. You know I could do it. Just give me one try and if it don't work then that's that . . . Oh, Briony, answer me then!'

Kerry's voice was sharp now. She wanted this so badly she could practically taste it.

'Look, you're twelve years old . . .'

Kerry interrupted her.

'I want to sing, Mum, I don't want to work there as a doxie, do I? I will put on a nice dress and hat and just do a few lively numbers to get everyone in a good mood. That's all. Abel will be there to keep his eye on me, and Briony and Tommy. Where's the bleeding harm in that?'

Striking a pose that looked ridiculous in her pea-picking clothes, she began to strut up and down the kitchen, singing:

> 'Jeremiah Jones – a lady's man was he –
> Every pretty girl he liked to spoon.
> Till he found a wife, and down beside the sea,
> Went to Margate for the honeymoon.'

Briony and Molly creased up with laughter as Kerry began. Coming to the chorus, she swept out her arms and roared at the top of her voice:

> 'Hello, Hello, who's your ladyfriend?
> Who's the little girlie by your side . . .'

Molly wiped her eyes with the back of her hand. As much as she scolded Kerry, she had to admit that the girl was talented and could be hilarious when the fancy took her.

Kerry knelt down in front of Briony and implored with her eyes. 'Oh, come on, Bri. Give me a chance.'

Briony grinned. She had needed a bit of fun today and should have known it would come from Kerry.

'I'll talk to Tommy about it. But that's all I can do, so don't get your hopes up.'

Kerry cuddled her sister close and shrieked out loud in excitement.

'Oh, thanks, Bri. Thanks. You won't regret it.'

Briony looked at her mother. 'What about you, Mum? What do you think?'

'Abel will be there as she says, and you and Tommy. It can't do any harm.'

None of them had noticed a jealous Bernie slip from the room.

Eileen came down the stairs and smiled at everyone and Briony looked at the thin vague-faced girl who had once been her bright and chatty sister, and felt depression descend again.

Sometimes life stank. And the worst of it all was, hers had hardly even started.

She tried to make conversation with her sisters for the rest of her time there, but her mind was on Benedict once more.

Briony had taken Kerry out shopping and bought her a green, high-necked, natural-waisted dress. It suited her perfectly and was respectable enough to please not only Briony but her mother and Abel as well. It had long sleeves with hanging three-quarter flounces in black lace. She had her black hair piled high on her head, and wore a large-brimmed black and green silk hat over it. She also had a green silk parasol which finished the outfit, and black button boots.

Briony stared at her, amazed. Kerry looked much older than her years, being taller than Briony already. She had on a small amount of make-up provided by Lil, one of the 'girls', and waited eagerly for Tommy to announce her.

'Oh, Briony, I'm so nervous, I could get tom tick!'

Briony laughed. 'Just relax. You're the one who wanted this, remember. Now just stay here until you hear the piano start and then make your way out.'

She kissed her on the cheek and left her in the small ante-room behind the main lounge.

Briony herself, dressed all in lemon, looked a picture. She had deliberately worn a close-fitting dress that accentuated her slim frame while revealing nothing. That much would be left to the working girls, who were all dressed in little more than stays and wrappers. The air was thick with cigar smoke and as Briony looked around her she felt a thrill of anticipation. It was their first night and the place was packed out.

She knew that most of the gentlemen normally went to Nellie's or other such establishments and wanted them to have such a good time here that they would come back again and again. Once more she blessed Tommy for arranging such a guest list. There were no Two Bob Joes in here, only men of means with respectable reputations. She was sure that the offer of a bit of entertainment would go down well, as the men liked to get a bit drunk before they retired to the bedrooms upstairs.

She made her way through the crowded room to the double doors where Abel stood surveying the room with a serious expression. A good-looking man grabbed her arm and tried to pull her to him. Briony shrugged him off good-naturedly and he grinned at her. Tommy, seeing the exchange, came over and introduced Briony to the man as his future wife. The customer apologised profusely before being dragged off by Tilly Rowlings who rolled her eyes good-naturedly at Briony as she did so.

'I'll just introduce Kerry and then I'll be back, OK?'

Briony nodded at Tommy and smiled. She watched him stand on the tiny makeshift stage and call for quiet. Everyone looked at him expectantly and he cleared his throat and introduced the new singing sensation, Kerry Cavanagh.

Kerry came out on to the stage, her face white with worry but, hearing the clapping and cheering from the men, she seemed to take on a different persona. A saucy wink at her audience and putting all her weight on to the parasol, she stuck out her behind. After nodding at the pianist who started to play her first number, she wiggled her rump, much to the merriment of the audience, and began to sing:

'Oh, what are we gonna do with Uncle Arthur?
Uncle Arthur! The dirty old man!'

Briony was laughing with the rest when she turned her head and her heart froze inside her chest. Standing at the front of the little crowd was Henry Dumas. She could see him perfectly, and as she watched him looking at Kerry she felt the bile rise inside her. He would like Kerry, she was just his type. No more than a child.

Briony grabbed Tommy's arm and pulled him from the room and through the hallway to the offices. Closing the door with a quiet thud, she faced him.

'What's Henry Dumas doing here, Tommy?'

He saw the whiteness of her face and shook his head.

'I don't know, he must have come with one of the others. Look, Briony, I'll go out and keep me eye on him.'

'I want him out of here now, Tommy, I mean it.'

'You what? Our first night and you want me to sling someone out? Let me find out who he's with first.'

Briony could feel her hands shaking.

'You find out then, and after you find out, you give him the bad news. I don't want him in this house. Not now, not ever.'

Tommy walked over to her and grabbed her arms.

'Listen, Briony, you're only a girl for all your grown-up looks and ways. If any of them knew you owned the best part of this place, there'd be trouble. As it is now they think I've got a sleeping partner. I let the word go round that it's one of them, a rich bloke who's invested in me. If I go out there and rock the boat with Henry Dumas, he could fuck all of this up for us. Get it? Do you understand what I'm saying?'

Briony saw the earnest expression in his eyes and felt the futility of it all. What Tommy said made sense. If Henry decided to make trouble for her then he could ruin them, and she knew he was capable of it. She heard Tommy leave the room and sat in the chair, staring at the blotter in front of her without seeing it.

You had to be rich as Croesus before you didn't have to worry about anything. You had to be as rich as Solomon to know that you could do anything you wanted. Until then you had to keep your head down and kowtow to everyone and anyone. It was like gall to her, this knowledge. Henry Dumas had taken her childhood and her child. And still she had to pander to him. Indirectly, he still ruled her life.

Well, one day she would finish him. One day she would get even.

She would not venture out of the night. She did not know what she was capable of if she came face to face with him. On top of everything else they were taking her child to live far away from her. It was this, more than anything, that broke her heart.

Henry watched Kerry singing and was enthralled by her. He had had a lot to drink and now he felt a rosy glow enveloping him.

He walked unsteadily towards the stage and clasped his hands as the girl sang. She was singing a slow song now, and all the men and women around him were listening to the haunting voice, enjoying the sound and the timbre of it. Her little elfin face was captivating to him. He saw the jet black silky hair that framed it and felt a stabbing pain in his heart. She was exquisite.

As Kerry finished her last number, she bowed to the audience who clapped her whole-heartedly. She was as good as any of the singers at Drury Lane, or indeed at any music hall. And she was no more than a child. A large man in the front of the audience, loving the ballad she sang, took out his purse and threw a sovereign on to the small stage. The other men in the room, not wanting to be outdone, did the same and Kerry scrambled around the floor in all her finery, picking up the coins.

The pianist began to play a solo number and Kerry picked up her money as fast as she could, amazed at the reception she had received and the generosity shown her. As she picked up the last coin, a plump hand covered hers and she looked into the face of Henry Dumas.

'Hello, my dear. You really are a very good singer.' In his drink-fuddled brain he knew she reminded him of someone but he couldn't quite place who.

Kerry, though, knew him and, pulling her hand from under his, said: 'Hello, Mr Dumas.'

Standing up, she walked across the little stage and back into the ante-room. She placed all the coins on the small table by the door and, taking off her gloves, began to count them. Henry Dumas followed her a few seconds later. Opening the door, he popped his head around it playfully, moustaches quivering in anticipation.

Kerry backed away from him.

'How did you know my name, dear?'

Without thinking, she said: 'I'm Briony's sister.'

She watched him sober immediately as he registered exactly what she had said.

'You're Briony Cavanagh's sister?' His voice was full of surprise. As she opened her mouth to answer, he grabbed her arm in a vice-like grip.

'Where is she? Is she here? Answer me, girl, where is the bitch?'

Kerry pulled away from him, rubbing her arm.

'You touch me again, mister, and I'll scream the bleeding place down!'

As she spoke Tommy came into the room.

131

'I think you'd better leave the young lady alone, sir. Come along, I'm sure we can find you someone more suitable.'

He took Henry's arm firmly and led him from the room. Kerry watched them go and bit her lip. How did he get in here tonight? Surely Briony hadn't invited him?

She looked at the pile of coins but the excitement had gone from her now. She leant against the table and absentmindedly rubbed her arm where he had touched her.

Henry was so deep in drink he didn't care any more. He had arrived at the stage where a shock or a loud noise can cause one of two reactions, maudlin sadness or great rage. Unfortunately for him, he felt great rage. As he walked through the room he tried unsuccessfully to shrug off the iron grip of the young man escorting him. He saw his friend John Dennings embracing a young woman in a blue gauze wrapper, her huge breasts spilling out from white silk corsets. It made him feel sick.

All this flesh around him! He could smell cheap scent and fresh sweat. He could see garishly painted lips and eyes. He could feel the sexual charge of the men around him as they feasted their eyes on a bevy of young girls. But not young enough for him. They were women in his eyes, with breasts that jutted from their clothes in a disgusting fashion, hair between their muscular thighs and under their arms.

Tommy dragged him into the hallway, trying to prevent the trouble he knew was imminent. Without thinking, he pushed Henry into Briony's office and the two came face to face for the first time in eighteen months.

Briony stood up, shocked, and as they looked at one another, Henry seemed to grow before her eyes. He stood erect and stared into the sea green eyes that his son had inherited. He laughed, a deep bitter sound that cut into her.

'So, the slut is working, is she?'

Tommy watched the two warily. It was as if an electrical charge had been placed between them and he stared, fascinated as Briony stalked around the desk.

'If I'm a slut, Henry Dumas, what does that make you? I can't think why you're here tonight. After all, the men who come to houses like this function normally. I wonder what they would say if they knew you were fancying a little girl – the girl they all clapped and cheered, without a bad thought in their heads towards her? Eh? Well answer me, Henry. If I remember rightly, you used to have a lot to say, most of it filth!'

'I'll finish you, Briony Cavanagh.'

She laughed at him now, her fear of him suddenly gone as she saw him for the pathetic fool he really was.

Her laugh goaded him. She was the cause of all his trouble. The reason for his wife's mutiny; for his father-in-law's happiness, that must therefore be Henry's apparent happiness. Here was the mother of the child he hated and despised because he had fathered it, because it had sprung from his loins and been birthed by the slut standing before him, laughing. Laughing at him. Well, he'd soon put a stop to that. He swung back his arm to strike her and she picked up one of the heavy inkwells.

'I'll split your head open without a second's thought, Henry Dumas! You think long and hard before you ever threaten me because I don't frighten so easily these days.'

Tommy grabbed at Henry and put his arm up behind his back.

'Come on, you, out! I don't think we want your sort in here.'

As he was pulled to the door, Henry faced Briony once more.

'I'll finish you, Briony Cavanagh. You and that bastard you saddled me with!'

She laughed again, louder this time, and it was as if the sound sent him into a frenzy. He threw Tommy from him and made to run at Briony. She stepped sideways and he hit the corner of the desk with all his weight behind him, sending him to his knees.

Grabbing his hair, Briony looked down into his face. 'You get out of here, you hear me? You get out of here because you don't know what I'm capable of where you're concerned.'

She looked at Tommy and waved her hand at the man on his knees before her.

'Take him away.'

Tommy did as she bade him. Dumas was quiet now. Tommy walked him out of the house and put him in his cab.

133

'You're not welcome here, keep that in mind. If I ever hear that you've tried to cause any trouble for her, or anyone to do with her, I'll see you dead. As rich as you are, as influential as you are, don't ever make an enemy of me, mate. You'll regret it to your dying day.'

Later that night, Tommy tossed and turned in his lonely bed. He knew that Briony had needed to face Dumas, it was something that had to happen eventually, and now it was over and done with. The rest of the night had gone well; they had pulled in over two hundred pounds. He shook his head in the darkness as he thought about it. The place was a success. All they had to do now was save up enough money to open another.

Briony had a natural talent for figures which amazed him. She had taken over the ledgers and the financial side of the business. Kerry too had been offered a regular job, her innocent little act having gone down very well with the men.

He turned over in bed. By rights he should be out celebrating the success of his new venture, but he knew that the only person he wanted to celebrate with was Briony. He was nineteen years old, soon to be a man of real wealth and property. He had worked all his young life with these goals in mind and they had been put within his reach by a little girl called Briony Cavanagh. He knew now that he loved her, really loved her. He turned over in the bed again. The pillow felt as if it was stuffed with stones and he was too hot. As tired as he was, he couldn't find it in him to sleep.

He had moved into Briony's house a few months previously, because with all the preparations to be made, they could not be parted for any length of time. They had spent long evenings together discussing everything from the decor to the clientele. During this time he had consciously endeared himself to Mrs Horlock and Briony's mother Molly. Cissy, he was aware, was half in love with him so she liked him no matter what he did. It was Briony he wanted, though. Briony with her outrageous hair and her deep green eyes. He had fallen asleep many times in the last few months with the picture of her milky naked body lying

134

beside him, his large rough hands caressing the tiny breasts. He turned once more in the bed.

As he closed his eyes tightly and tried to sleep, he heard the creak of the door opening. He sat up in bed as Briony, in a white nightdress, her red hair unbound, crept into his room with a candle in her hand.

'Are you asleep, Tommy?'

He was too astounded for speech.

Briony walked towards him and placed the candle on the night table. In the flickering light she smiled at him. He watched with fascination as she took the hem of her nightdress in both hands and pulled the garment over her head, revealing her body slowly and tantalisingly to him. She dropped the garment on to the floor and he pulled back the covers of his bed so she could slip in beside him.

He made love to her gently and firmly, taking in every part of her body with his hands and his tongue. It was like a dream come true to him. She had walked out of his mind and into his bed.

Briony for her part enjoyed the petting and the feel of him near her. She had needed someone after the events of the evening. She had needed strong arms around her and had got them the only way she knew how.

Tommy was not to realise that the feeling of closeness was the only part of sex that Briony enjoyed. So carried away was he in his own excitement he did not notice her mechanical responses. But that night, it didn't matter anyway. It sealed their fates. The coupling of their bodies was just an extension of their partnership.

At least, that was how Briony saw it.

BOOK TWO
1925

'My sister and my sister's child,
Myself and children three'
  – William Cowper, 1731–1800

'Affection beaming in one eye,
Calculation shining out of the other'
 – *Martin Chuzzlewit*, Charles Dickens

Chapter Ten
1925

'Oh, for Christ's sake, Tommy, what the hell has got into you?' Briony's voice was hard and Tommy clenched his fists in an effort to keep his temper.

'I don't like it, Briony. For one thing it's expensive, for another you can't guarantee you'll make any money out of it.'

Briony laughed out loud.

'Oh, can't I? Listen here, Tommy Lane. On the continent these pictures are all the rage, mate. The French are shipping them over here like they're going out of fashion. Private viewings are bringing in a fucking fortune! I've more than looked into all this believe me. That "useless ponce", as you call Rupert in your more friendlier moments, is the goose that's going to lay us some golden eggs. Tomorrow I put up a quick grand, then we sit back and rake the money in. We can show the films in the houses, have our own private screenings. We can get in on the bottom of the market before it takes off. And quite frankly, Tommy, whether you come in with me or not, I'm having some of it. It's the thing for the future, it'll make us untold money, I guarantee that.'

Tommy looked at the girl opposite him. Her face was alight, as it always was when she was talking about money. In fairness to her, he knew she had really done the groundwork on the films, she was too astute not to, but the thought annoyed him. Inside himself, Tommy actually found the thought of filming couples having sexual relations distasteful. He voiced this.

139

'I think it's perverted.'

Briony really did laugh now. A contemptuous sound that grated on him.

'Oh, Tommy, you're priceless, do you know that? Of course it's perverted! That's what makes the films a guaranteed money-spinner! Think about it. There've always been dirty pictures, silly naughty postcards with half-dressed women, that sell for a small fortune. Our boys even took them off to war with them. Where's the harm? In our houses we have paintings everywhere of couples having it off, they're part and parcel of the fixtures and fittings, so it seems logical to me to take it one step further. Moving pictures are what people want. All it takes is some girl flashing her clout and some bloke enjoying himself, and we're made. It's no different to what we do already.'

Tommy could see the logic of her argument, he was honest enough to admit that. It was more the fact Rupert Charles had approached Briony direct, as opposed to himself, that was the bug bear. But whatever way he looked at it all, the pictures – well, they didn't seem right.

Briony watched him battling it out with himself and felt the familiar annoyance. Every time they ventured into a new area it was the same unless: Tommy thought of it first, then she was expected just to nod and go along with whatever he decided. When she thought of something it was days of discussing the pros and cons, Tommy humming and hahing, working out the costs, the overheads, the benefit it would be to the business. She knew that at times she made him feel inferior. She didn't mean to, but the fact would always remain that she was much quicker on the uptake than he. He would be the eternal heavy. She was the real brains behind them. Artfully, she tried a different tack.

'Listen to this, Tommy.' She picked up a newspaper beside her and began to read: '"Josephine Baker, the sensational nineteen-year-old dancer of *La Revue Nègre*, is the talk of Paris. Her Charleston, slapping her buttocks in time to 'Yes Sir, That's My Baby!', and her bare-breasted mating dance, wearing nothing but strategic circles of coloured feathers, arouses audiences to frenzy. Colette calls her 'a most beautiful panther',

Picasso calls her 'the Nefertiti of today', and Anita Loos speaks of her 'witty rear end'. Poiret and Schiaparelli are designing clothes for her, painters are begging her to sit for them and the Folies Bergères are wooing her to join the show . . .'''

Tommy interrupted her.

'What's she got to do with all this?'

'On the continent they're more relaxed about sex and anything to do with it. The sodding can-can was performed originally by women with no drawers on! This is 1925. People want more. They aren't as shocked as they once were. We have a whole band of punters out there with money to spend and not enough to spend it on. They can either go to Paris for a bit of a thrill, or we can provide it for them here. Once this filming is off the ground, I'm going to open more houses. Places where people, men and women, can get exactly what they want. Fuck Paris, mate, we'll have it all here in London! We've the contacts and the clientele. We can have private screenings of the films and then live entertainment. Live shows . . .'

'You're deadly serious.'

Briony grinned.

'Too right I am. Now, I'm doing this whether you come in or not. I mean it, Tommy. The filming first and the houses after. I want to own every decent house in London, and I will.' She stood up. 'I'll get us some more coffee.'

She left the room, giving him time to think.

Tommy watched her leave. She was, as always, beautifully dressed. At twenty-two she was glorious. Thank God she hadn't succumbed to the Eton crop which most women now sported. Her hair was still elaborately dressed with pins, but her clothes were up to the minute – up to the second, in fact. She wore the drop-waisted dresses with a jaunty air, showing wide expanses of milky white arms and legs. She plucked her eyebrows and drew them back on in wide, painted arches, and she wore deep red lipstick, painted on to her lips in a perfect Cupid's bow. She was the epitome of the new modern woman and sometimes, like now, it broke his heart.

She was right in all she said, he conceded that. She was always

141

right. Maybe that was why she annoyed him so much. Like the jazz club she had insisted on opening, this very night in fact. Now it was up and off the ground she wanted another project as quickly as possible. And the pictures and the new houses were to be those projects. Oh, he had no doubt she would make a success of them, she always did. But he wished sometimes they could lead a calmer, more normal life.

He smiled to himself at the thought. Nothing about Briony Cavanagh would ever be normal. She was a law unto herself, had been from a child and, if he knew her, would be 'til the day she died. In fact, at times she wore him out with her endless enthusiasm. It wasn't natural to be driven like she was.

She wouldn't marry him, she was adamant about that. He had stopped asking her. But she slept with him, she ate with him, she dressed with him. That was as far as it went. She wanted no more children, she had made that as plain as day. In fact, it was only her sporadic visits to see her son that revealed any kind of human warmth or feeling in her. Then he saw the girl he had known before, the child, the Briony with whom he had fallen hopelessly in love. Her son, her sisters and the girls who worked for them were her whole life now. She looked after them all like a mother hen.

He knew she loved him in her own way, cared about him deeply, but not in the same way he loved her. Even knowing this, he couldn't leave her. He knew he would take whatever she offered him and be grateful, because he couldn't live without her. Acknowledging this to himself, he knew his course was set.

Briony walked back into the room with the tray of coffee and smiled at him, her tiny hands holding the tray steady. Placing it on the desk between them, she picked up the coffee pot. 'Shall I be mother?'

'You can be mother. And yes, Bri, I'm in on the new deals.'

She slammed down the coffee pot and rushed around the desk to plonk herself none too gently in his lap.

She kissed him hard on his lips and laughed.

'You won't regret this, Tommy. We'll rake the money in!'

He smiled and kissed her back.

'I know we will, Bri. We always do.'

He held her to him, feeling the smallness of her, the tiny waist, the firm breasts that poked through the thin material of her dress, and breathed in the scent of her. If only once he could spark some life into her sexually, he would be a happy man. He wanted to throw her to the floor and make love to her there and then, to make love to her and have her respond, just once, with the same passion he felt for her.

It was her total passivity that ensnared him, he knew. If he pushed her to the floor now, she would allow him to undress her, caress her body and make love to her as hard or as gently as he felt he wanted to. Then, when he was spent, she would get up, dress herself and smile at him, as she always did. He would not have touched her mind.

Instead he kissed her and petted her, the way he knew she liked, and held himself in check.

If she would only respond to him in bed . . . but he knew she never would. Though every time he touched her, he lived in hope.

Briony walked into her club The Windjammer at two-thirty in the afternoon. She smiled at the people milling around, putting the finishing touches to the place. As she passed the hat check girl she was amazed to see her bob a small curtsy. It made Briony smile widely. She walked into the club itself and eyed the room, taking in everything from the fresh flowers to the newly laid carpets. Briony was pleased. In the dimness she saw Kerry and Bernie on the small stage, talking to the piano player and saxophonist. She saw the excitement on her sisters' faces as they turned at the sound of her clattering heels on the wooden dance floor.

'Hello, Bri. I'm just going over the final numbers one more time. Want to hear them?' Kerry called.

Briony nodded and took a seat at one of the tables at the edge of the dance floor. She glanced around her as Kerry sorted through her music and was once more assailed with a feeling of happiness. She was more than satisfied with the place. The decor was brilliant: the walls painted a very pale gold and adorned with photographs, head and shoulders shots of the most beautiful women of the day. The largest was of Anna Pavlova, her eyes staring out across the room. Briony had also had musical scores framed and hung on the walls. The tables all had white cloths of pristine Irish linen and the glasses that sparkled behind the long carved wood bar were all good quality crystal.

It had cost a small fortune, but one of Briony's main beliefs was that you got what you paid for. Well, this was a jazz club, one of the first in London, and she had planned it on a grand scale.

She had hired a quartet of black American musicians who were thrilled to work at the new club, and even more thrilled with their wages. She dragged her eyes back towards the stage as she saw Kerry walk forward. She noticed the eyes of the pianist, Evander Dorsey, watching her closely. Their whites seemed to glow with the look and she smiled to herself. If he liked Kerry he would play even better. Everything had its good side for Briony. The fact he was black and looking at her sister did not shock her as it would have done others. She took everyone at face value. Always had and always would.

Kerry cleared her throat, and as the first few bars of the music struck up, Bernie slid into a seat beside Briony.

She watched the instinctive swing of Kerry's body. Unlike herself, Kerry was buxom and small-waisted. Her breasts looked too big for the fragile ribcage. She was also tall; her height giving her the grace to carry off the figure God had given her. Her short black hair, freshly bobbed, framed her face to perfection. Briony looked at her younger sister with a mixture of admiration and pride. Pride because it was she, Briony, who had made her sister's career possible. And it was she, Briony, who had looked after Kerry until now when she was making a name for herself with this new music called jazz. Unlike the majority of white women singers, Kerry could sing the blues, and everyone who heard her was spellbound. Briony knew that she was going to be big, much bigger than anyone had thought possible, and the knowledge was like balm to Briony.

Kerry's voice when she began to sing was as clear and haunting as the words of the song she sang:

'I don't know why, but I'm feeling sad.
I long to try something, I never had
Never had no kisses, oh, what I've been missin'.
Lover man . . . Oh, where can you be?'

The deep soulfulness of the voice carried across the room. Briony watched as the pianist shook his head in wonderment and delight and knew then that tonight her sister's career would be made. Her success was assured, and along with it the success of the club. Kerry would be their draw.

Ginelle Carson walked as if she owned the world. In fact, she felt as if she owned a small part of it. Ginelle was now a main attraction at Briony's top house. She had appeared in a couple of Briony's films and now her notoriety added to her value as a good-time girl. She was dressed in a long brocade evening coat and silver high-heeled shoes. She pulled her shoulders back as she stepped off the kerb and tottered slightly. A large arm came out and steadied her. Ginelle turned to face the man and smiled at him professionally. Her lips were a deep orange crescent and her eyes heavily made up, her youth hidden beneath a veneer of sophistication. She automatically put a hand up to her short cropped hair and patted it unnecessarily back into place.

'Thank you.' Her voice still held its East End sharpness, but she was working on it. The man gave her a smile that quickly faded.

'We're going for a little walk, love.'

Ginelle stopped dead and looked at him closely. Something in his voice made her heart beat faster. She tried to pull her arm from his but it was held in a vice-like grip.

'Here, leave go! Give over!' Her voice was rising and there was no trace of her refined tones now.

The man frog-marched her across the busy road and towards a

145

waiting car. He bundled her inside without ceremony and the car pulled away from the kerb.

Ginelle had regained her composure by now.

'What the bleeding hell's going on here? Stop this car and let me out now!'

Her abductor turned to face her. Slapping her hard across the face, he said: 'Shut your trap before I punch your head in now instead of later.'

It was said in a low voice, completely devoid of emotion. Ginelle stared into the hard face and felt a sinking sensation somewhere in the region of her bowels.

But she shut up.

One thing in Ginelle's favour, she was clever enough to know when she was in trouble and knew instinctively that tonight she was in the worst trouble of her life.

The thing that puzzled her was, why? What on earth had she done? She racked her brain for the remainder of the journey, staring vacantly at the red neck of the large man in front driving the car.

Ginelle was dragged from the car on the quay of the East India Docks. She stood in her ridiculous heels as various foreign sailors walked past, all looking at her with admiration tinged with fear, because of the two large men beside her.

They walked her between them, towards a small cabin that smelt strongly of molasses. Tearing her arms away, Ginelle began to run, her shoes giving the two men an unfair advantage.

The bigger man laughed as he caught up with her. He dragged her roughly back towards the cabin. By now she was shouting and screaming. Something inside Ginelle told her that if she entered that cabin it would be the end of her, and with a strength born of desperation she fought the man, her crimson-tipped nails flying dangerously close to his face. Taking back a large hairy fist he dealt her a blow to the side of the head that left her sprawling on the floor in the dirt and the mud, her ears ringing.

Men were watching the proceedings with shining eyes. Her

146

dress had risen up in the tumble and her stocking tops were exposed; her silk drawers, freshly washed and pressed, smeared with dirt. Picking her up by her coat, the big man half dragged, half-pushed her towards the cabin.

Ginelle was looking around her at the sailors, beseeching them with her eyes. She realised in a daze that some of the men were London dockers, all watching her and not one doing anything about it. They thought she was a dockside harpy. They didn't realise she worked for one of the most exclusive houses in the smoke, Briony Cavanagh's Mayfair house. That Tommy Lane was her boss along with Big Briony, as she was known, even though she was so tiny. That she commanded a fortune from men because she was a star of certain films shown to a select clientele, men who paid money to see her, and afterwards to bed her. She was someone of account, she was not a sailors' darling, she was important, important enough to be on first name terms with her employers.

She opened her mouth to shriek these facts to the spectators, but a filthy hand closed over her mouth and she was dragged struggling inside the cabin. The men watching all went on their way, the pretty young girl gone from their minds already. A prostitute being beaten by her pimp was an everyday occurrence here, part and parcel of dockside life.

Inside the cabin it was dim. Ginelle registered first the smell, the deep scent of molasses, and underneath another of dankness and dirt, that brought back the filth and squalor she had been brought up in. It was a slum smell, a sweet, bitter, cloying smell that stuck to the clothes and never entirely left the nostrils.

Sitting behind a small wooden crate was a man whose face was lost in layers of fat. His eyes were like slits. Ginelle felt a final sinking of her heart as she realised who he was.

Willy Bolger was a pimp with a reputation for nastiness, violence and his perverted sense of humour. He was obese, his arms and legs looking too short and feeble to be any use, yet he was surprisingly fast with a knife. His teeth were pristine white, small and pointed as if he had chiselled them into shape. Now he smiled at Ginelle, who shuddered.

He shook his head slowly, languidly, as if he had known her for years, as if she was a recalcitrant child. The smile even displayed a sort of affection.

'Please, sit down.' He looked at the big man. 'Get the lady a chair!' The word 'lady' was said with exaggerated politeness. The big man dragged up a small three-legged stool and slammed Ginelle down on to it hard, jarring her already bruised spine.

'Forgive Seamus, he's no manners at all, my dear.'

Ginelle sat there, her hands icy cold, even in the foetid warmth of the cabin.

'What do you want with me?' Her voice was small. She sounded like the child she was for all her expensive clothes and make-up. Willy linked his fingers together on the crate in front of him and grinned again.

'I am going to hurt you, my dear. Nothing personal, believe me. But I want to get a little message over to a certain lady, and you, so to speak, are going to be my messenger. Hold her there, Seamus.'

He held Ginelle's shoulders in his vice-like grip, but there was no need. She had collapsed with fright, her body held up only by Seamus, because as Willy had spoken he had unlaced his fat fingers and picked up a large knife.

Willy walked towards her and tutted. He had hoped she would have stayed conscious long enough for him to hear her scream at least once. Sighing hard with disappointment, he picked up a wooden pail which was used by the night watchmen to relieve themselves and threw it into her face.

Ginelle spluttered to life, the urine stinging her eyes. Then, humming softly between his teeth, Willy started cutting, and was pleased to hear her scream, not once but many times as he removed first her nose, then her ears.

Seamus watched the proceedings with a bored air. His eldest daughter was getting married and he had to take her to see the priest later that day. Now he'd have to go home and change first. Blood was an absolute bastard to get out, and his wife would have his guts.

Ginelle slumped to the dirty floor, her clothes staining crimson, the brocade of her coat soaking it up like a sponge.

Tommy looked around the club and smiled. The Windjammer's first night was better even than they had hoped for. It was packed to the rafters with people, the atmosphere was electric and the cash was pouring in over the bars. Tommy lit himself one of the cheap cigars which he still had a penchant for, and smiled delightedly.

The whole place stank of money and he loved it. He nodded and waved to different people as he made his way through the tables. The resident band, which was to play between Kerry's sets, had struck up with the 'Black Bottom'. Girls – some debs and some shopgirls – leapt on to the wooden dance floor and began to jiggle around, their dresses shimmering in the lights. There were more than a few bright young things, hanging off the arms of young men who had been boys in the war and were now the new monied generation. If nothing else the war had taken down a few of the class barriers, but Tommy knew with his latent shrewdness that it was only a beginning.

He scanned the room again and saw Briony. She looked stunning in a gold sheath dress that emphasised her fashionably boyish figure and was the exact shade of the walls. The glorious hair, that he loved to caress in the darkness of the night, was piled on top her head. She looked beautiful to him. She would always be beautiful to him.

He frowned as he saw who she was sitting with. Jonathan la Billière was an actor, or so he said anyway. Tommy had never heard of him. He was one of Rupert's little band, which meant he must be as queer as a fish.

Rupert Charles was the typical bad boy, handsome and rich. His father had died in the war, leaving a fortune to Rupert's mother, a ridiculous woman much given to wearing clothes too young for her and with an appalling taste in men, and to Rupert, a rather spoiled young man who had never had anything to do with the actual making of money, only the spending of it. Now he financed movies as he liked to call them, and everyone

149

thought he was quite the thing, and fought to claim friendship with him. Rupert in turn loved the notoriety of Briony and fought to become a crony of hers. It made Tommy smile sometimes, the double standard, but not tonight, because Jonathan was watching Briony with an intent gaze. It seemed he wanted her. Perhaps he wasn't queer after all. Tommy could see the tell-tale expression. He knew it well. But Jonathan wouldn't have her. Even if she succumbed and slept with him, he wouldn't have her. Not in the way he wanted. Knowing this pleased Tommy.

He dragged his eyes from them and made his way back to the offices. He wasn't in the mood tonight for all that theatrical old fanny. He needed a couple of stiff drinks.

Being a Friday evening, the Mayfair house was packed. The girls working nights started at six-thirty at weekends. Many men arrived at six, retired to bed at six-thirty and arrived home to take out their wives around nine-thirty. So at seven-thirty the house was already buzzing. Winona, the head girl, was counting out money in her office when a repeated ringing on the bell brought her out personally to answer the front door. Heidi, the young girl paid for this job, was at that moment helping one of the 'young ladies' to brush out her hair. Winona opened the large front door wearing her plain black dress and professional smile. It died on her lips as she saw a crate left on the doorstep and no one in sight.

She walked out of the house and down the front steps, searching the street for a messenger or someone who could have left the heavy crate. The street was as usual quiet and empty, except for a few motorcars. Turning, she walked back up the steps and sighed loudly. She called down the back stairs for two of the men who worked there, and between them they hefted the crate through to the offices. Winona finished counting her money before she once more turned her attention to the crate. There was no address on it, no message, nothing. Briony had not mentioned any deliveries. She frowned in consternation. The new club was opening tonight so Briony wouldn't thank her for calling her away over a crate, but something wasn't right here.

Winona had a long nose – her mother had always said it was long enough to pick a winkle – well, that nose was quivering now, scenting trouble. She went to the crate and looked at it just as Heidi, the young maid, walked through the door.

'There's a Mr Blackley up top, wants to know where Ginelle is. Says he'd arranged to see her tonight.'

Winona turned, pulling herself up to her full height. 'How many bloody times do I have to tell you, girl, knock before you enter a room!'

Heidi blinked rapidly, a nervous habit that drove Winona to distraction. 'And for fuck's sake, stop blinking blinking!'

Heidi, all of eleven and looking nine, blinked even harder. 'Me mum says if you shout at me it won't get any better, it's me nerves like.'

Winona raised her eyes to the ceiling.

'Tell Mr Blackley that Ginelle will be along shortly, then nip round her mother's and see if she's there. Since she became Briony's blue-eyed girl, she's really started pushing her bleeding luck! Well you tell her that she can get her arse round here, she still works in this house as a whore no matter what else she might be involved in, and I run this place for Briony Cavanagh. I am the head girl, and I ain't putting up with tardiness!'

'With what?' Heidi's voice was incredulous.

'Just go and do what I say, will you!' Winona made a conscious effort to keep her voice down, but this child really was the limit.

After that, Winona was called on to sort out more than one petty drama, so she didn't open the crate until nine fifteen. It was an act she was to regret all her life.

Briony watched with shining eyes as Kerry came on stage. The lights were dimmed and Kerry looked much too pretty and much too young to be a real singer, but the audience were with her, Briony picked that much up from the atmosphere.

The first few bars were played by Evander Dorsey then Kerry began to sing:

'I don't know why, I'm feeling so sad.
I long to try something, I never had . . .'

As she began to sing the people who had still been chatting paused to look and listen properly. The whole club seemed to quieten and Kerry, feeling the reaction, put more and more emotion into the song.

As the last few bars were played, she was greeted with a standing ovation, drinks were raised and feet thumped on the wooden floors.

Briony laughed with delight. She had known this was going to happen, she had counted on it.

She was still clapping and smiling when Tommy came to the table and whispered in her ear.

Jonathan, clapping and smiling himself, was shocked to see Briony's face drain of all colour. She got up from the table, smiled half-heartedly, said her goodbyes then immediately left the club.

Jonathan la Billière watched her leave. There was trouble brewing there, he would lay money on it. Well, he was seeing her next morning, and he was looking forward to that. He was looking forward to it immensely.

He turned his face back to the stage where Kerry had just started singing a lively number. He enjoyed the rest of the set. But the memory of Briony's white face stayed with him.

Tommy and Briony arrived at the Mayfair house just after eleven. They walked into its pink warmth, slipping off their coats as they entered the front door. Heidi took the coats without a murmur, her eyes blinking in overtime now with the shock the house had had. Briony and Tommy went through to the office where Winona was sitting at her desk, her face grey, hands clutching a large glass of brandy.

'She's dead, Bri . . . But it's Ginelle, all right.'

Tommy lifted the lid of the crate and stared into it. Ginelle, minus nose, ears and breasts stared up at them. Her hands were fingerless, bloody stumps crossed over her body in some grotesque parody of the funeral rite.

Briony felt first the burn of bile as it welled up inside her throat, then she felt rage, a white rage that there was no reasoning against. Ginelle was just eighteen years old. She kept her mother and her younger sisters on what she earned. She was a nice girl, a kind girl. Whoever did this had better start saying their prayers, because she, Briony Cavanagh, was going to have their balls on a plate!

'Who knows, Winona? Who knows in the house?' Briony's voice was hard and brooked no nonsense.

'Heidi knows. She came in just as I opened the crate. Denice knows and Lily. They're keeping it quiet. I told them not to alert the rest of the girls.'

'Good . . . good. You did the right thing.'

Briony looked at Ginelle again and then at Tommy. Her voice was shocked and disbelieving as she spoke.

'Why would anyone do this, Tom? Why?'

It was the first time in years he had seen Briony shaken, and it saddened him.

'I don't know, Bri. But I have a feeling we'll find out soon enough, love. This is a message of some sort. What we have to do is find out who sent it.'

She nodded and stared at Ginelle's remains again, remembering the girl's laughter of the week before, remembering when she had come to her for a job in her ragged dress and her mother's shoes. Remembered her chatter, her unaffected pleasure in life, and felt rage once more for the destruction of a young life.

'Yeah, Tom, we'll find out who sent the message and then I'm gonna muller them. Me personally. No one, but no one, touches me or mine . . . So whoever sent this so-called message better start saying their prayers because, as Christ is my witness, they'll need all the fucking prayers they can get!'

153

Chapter Eleven

Molly was brushing out Rosalee's hair. Unlike years before, when it had been cropped to keep the lice at bay, Briony had insisted on having her sister's hair left to grow. Now Rosalee sported a mass of thick blonde curls.

'Would you keep still, Rosie darlin'!' Rosalee was fidgeting, moving her head from side to side and making low guttural noises which annoyed the life out of Molly.

Eileen walked into the kitchen and Molly smiled, a real smile that encompassed the girl from head to foot.

At twenty-eight Eileen was much better. Her nerves were still bad, but she had stopped her wandering and the nonsensical conversations were long gone. She even had a beau of sorts, a friend of Abel's who took her for long walks and listened avidly to all her chatter. He was a good deal older than Eileen, but Molly wasn't against that. Eileen needed a man who was settled. A man who would look after her.

'I've had a really good time, Mum. Joshua took me to Bow. We shopped in the little market and stopped for pie and mash. And I bought some material, I thought I might make meself a dress.'

Molly was amazed at those words. Although Eileen was clean, God knows she was forever washing, she still had that unkempt look about her. The shapeless garments she wore were such a part of her that the thought of her wearing anything even remotely nice was like music to her mother's ears.

'But Briony is always offering you money for clothes and you turn it down.'

Eileen faced her mother.

'I don't want anything from Briony thank you very much. I know she means well, but the thought of wearing anything bought with the money she makes . . .'

'Oh, all right, Eileen love, leave it, leave it. You make yourself something nice if that's what you want.'

Molly sighed heavily. It was still a sore point with Eileen about Briony, and Molly, who had once been her daughter's most ardent opponent, was now her most ardent supporter. The girl had taken the bit of money from the Dumases and turned it into a small fortune. Also, Molly could deny no longer her own involvement in both her daughters' downfall. Though the word 'downfall' was certainly not how she would describe Briony's life.

'Kerry's not been then?' Eileen tried to make amends.

'To be honest, I don't think she remembers where she lives!'

This was said with pride and without any malicious feeling against Eileen who didn't work, let alone keep herself. It was this fact that galled Molly most about her eldest daughter. She balked at accepting Briony's money but had no intention of going out and earning any for herself. Molly didn't say this though, because now Eileen was back on her feet she didn't want to rock the boat.

Bernadette came down the stairs and both women smiled at her. 'Did our Kerry come home, Bernie?'

'I ain't her keeper, Mum, only her dresser. She probably stayed overnight with someone.'

She poured herself some tea and smiled craftily to herself. She knew who Kerry had stayed with all right, but she'd keep the knowledge to herself a while longer.

'How did it go last night? Was it a success?'

'Oh, yeah. Kerry went down a storm. Everyone was raving about her. But it's funny, Mum, Briony was called away quick like. She looked rough I can tell you. I reckon there was hag at one of the houses.'

Molly put down the brush and went to the table to pick up her mug of tea. 'What do you mean, trouble?' Her face was clouded.

'What kind of trouble do you normally get in those places?'

Eileen's voice was low and Molly stopped herself from clouting her. Sometimes Eileen's holy Joeing, as she called it to herself, really got on her nerves.

Bernie laughed.

'Look, stop worrying, you know our Briony. If there's trouble it will be sorted by now. It was a shame really because she missed most of the opening. Oh, Mum, you should have seen some of the people there! Really rich like, their clothes . . . Even the air in there smelt nice, with all the perfumes and that.'

Molly nodded, pleased. This was more like it, this was what she wanted to hear. 'Were there any titles there?'

Bernie pushed her face close to her mother's and smiled. 'The place stunk of titles, Mum, it was really, really impressive. Our Briony is gonna make a bloody fortune.'

Molly sipped her tea and grinned.

That was more like it all right. She lived now in Briony's shadow, loving her notoriety, enjoying the stir her daughter created. People spoke about her in tones of awe. She was both loved and feared, and that, as far as Molly was concerned, was exactly how it should be.

Evander looked down at the girl asleep in his bed and felt his heart constrict. What the hell had he done? She was no more than a child really, for all her body and her incredible voice. She was a white woman. He had spent the night with a white woman.

Now hold on, a voice whispered at the back of his mind. You ain't in the States now.

But if certain people knew about them, it would be like the States all over again. There was something about a black man and a white woman that incensed people. Women as well as men. He had grown up under that cloud and had thought to die without ever knowing the pleasure of a clean white woman. Oh, he had slept with white women before, poor white trash who had gone to the bad and were thought diseased so sold their body only to the black boys.

157

All this talk about niggers over here ... about how niggers could dance, niggers had natural rhythm. They liked your music and your soulful songs, they liked to be seen with the black musicians, it made them look very hip, but if they thought you were sleeping with one of their women they'd turn like a pack of bloodhounds. What was it that Shakespeare guy had said? There's an old black ram, tupping your ewe? Well, that was exactly what Evander had done. And he had loved every second of it!

Kerry was worth anything they might throw at him, though. The smell of her, the feel of her silky black hair, was like nothing he had ever experienced before. And she had been a virgin, that was the most fantastic part! A virgin. In the darkness of the night before he had been too carried away with wanting her to think of the consequences. Now, as she lay asleep and the sun burned through the dirty windows, the thought made him feel physically faint though he was aroused again.

'Evander, my love. Come back to bed.'

He looked at her face and saw her staring at his enlarged member with the same fascination as he had stared at her. He watched as her long thin white fingers caressed him, running down the length of him and caressing his genitals, and groaned out loud. He knelt beside the bed and caressed her large white breasts with their pink nipples, and knew he was lost then. Any sensible thoughts were gone now, completely overshadowed by the milky white skin and the wet pinkness between her legs.

Briony and Tommy were sitting down to lunch but Briony just pushed her food desultorily around her plate.

'Last night was a resounding success anyway, Bri.'

She nodded.

'Good. Kerry went down well.'

'Look, Briony, worrying about it ain't gonna make it go away.'

She shook her head.

'I tell you, Tommy, every time I think about Ginelle, I feel a rage in me. I can't stand this hanging around, waiting for the next move. Suppose they touch one of the other girls?'

'We've got them all watched. Fuck me, Bri, even King Street Charlie couldn't get in one of the houses at the moment.'

'I think we should tell the girls. They have a right to know.'

Tommy pushed his plate away in temper.

'Oh, yeah? Start a general exodus, why don't you? The less the brasses know the better. They've got mouths like the parish ovens. It'd be all over the smoke by tonight. "Briony and Tommy have got trouble. Big trouble." Once word like that hits the pavements every little ponce with dreams of the big time will be out mob-handed. We've gotta play this one close to our chests, wait and see what develops. If it was a loony, say a bloke with a grudge, he wouldn't have had her delivered to the house, would he? That was personal.'

'Did it ever occur to you that it could be a customer? A bloke who's got a grudge all right. It's all right for you, ain't it? You ain't gotta go round and give Ginelle's mother the bad news, have you? You ain't gotta go round and tell her that her daughter's died. I've got to make up a story that she had an accident or something. How can I tell the woman that her daughter, her main bread winner, was cut up like a fucking piece of meat on a butcher's slab!'

Briony stared at Tommy hard then. Something in what she'd said had sparked off a train of thought. Now it had gone. Disappeared as quickly as it had come.

'What's the matter, Bri?'

'Just then something came to me mind, and went again.'

Tommy got up from his seat and walked around the table to her. Putting an arm around her, he pulled her to him.

'Look, love, just try and relax. As soon as we get word, whoever it was is history.'

Briony nodded sagely.

'Oh, they'll be that all right, Tommy. I'm gonna pay this one back myself. Personally.'

He held her close. Never had he seen her so intent on anything in her life. It was as if Ginelle's death was a personal affront. As if the girl was a daughter or a sister. Tommy would never realise the feelings Briony had for her girls. She loved them. Each and every one.

'It had to come now, didn't it, when we was branching out? I'm supposed to be seeing Nellie Deakins this afternoon. If word's got to her ear then I'll be a laughing stock.'

Tommy kissed her cheek, a wet smacking kiss.

'Nellie's an old has-been, Bri. Christ, I used to work for her meself when I was a boy. No one will hear anything about any of this, I guarantee that. We have to sit on it, just be patient. Then once we know what we're dealing with, everything will come right. OK?'

She nodded. But the thought of Ginelle wouldn't let her rest.

Mariah Jurgens was a big woman. Her grandfather, it was said, had been a large and troublesome Swedish sailor; her mother and grandmother were what was termed Bog Irish. Her father unknown. Mariah had the white-blonde colouring of her grandfather and the Irish temperament of the women in her family. Six feet tall in her stockinged feet, she had a body the like of which was rarely seen. Twenty years before she had been a highly sought-after courtesan. Her huge breasts and tiny waist, coupled with her sheer height and unusual colouring, had been prized by rich men. She had known her high price was for her sheer novelty value and had enhanced it with a pair of shoes especially made with high heels so that she looked even taller than she actually was. The fact that the majority of her clients were small men had made her laugh as she salted away the guineas; as she felt like laughing now, at the little man in front of her. She watched him take a pull on his cigar. It smelt expensive and was nearly as big as the little man himself.

'So, Mariah, what do you say?'

She spat into the fire and shrugged nonchalantly.

'Let me think it over, I'll get in touch with you tomorrow.'

She watched the man frown and felt the urge to laugh again. 'You do realise what I'm offering you?'

She nodded, serious once more. 'I do.'

'So what's to think about?'

'Mr Bolger, I always think over everything before I commit myself. It is, to my mind, the only way to do business.'

'As you wish, Mariah. I will expect your answer in the morning.'

He stood up to leave and she stood too. Towering over the man, she put out a large hand with fingernails painted bright red and grasped his tightly, emphasising the size and strength of her own. He left the room and Mariah rang her bell. It was answered by a young blonde, at whom Mariah smiled sweetly.

'Bring me some decent brandy and something to eat.'

'Yes, ma'am.' The girl was nervous. Mariah changed with the weather. From being a big cuddly woman she could turn into a demon from hell in an instant. Mariah was known as a woman who could 'turn on a coin', so unstable was her temper. It was something she nurtured in her madam's role, a trait that was mandatory in her profession.

She relaxed back in her seat, her mind racing. Bolger was as bent as a two-bob clock. So he was, in reality, offering her something he eventually wanted to take back from her. She had settled that in her mind immediately. He wanted something that Briony Cavanagh had, and that meant he was willing to take on Tommy Lane. That in turn told Mariah he had a lot more backing than usual.

Bolger was just a small-time pimp, really. He now had visions of hitting the big time, and this could only be brought about by an alliance with someone else. An original thought in Bolger's head would die a slow death from loneliness. No, there was a bigger fish involved in this, a much bigger fish, but who? The girl came back with the brandy and food. Thanking her, Mariah told her to send in Big John. While she waited for him she wrote a note to Briony Cavanagh, asking her to visit her establishment at seven that evening. Two bitches had always had more going for them than one dog, and she had heard through the grapevine that Briony Cavanagh was as sharp as a razor.

Sandy Livingston walked along the Caledonian Road with his

youngest son, Pete. The boy was so like his father it was startling to see them together. Pete was only fifteen, but already he was as tall as his father. Both men had watery blue eyes, ruddy complexions and the sandy hair and eyebrows that gave the older man his nickname. Pete loved his father. He knew he was notorious as a heavy, that he was paid huge sums to hurt people, and looked forward eagerly to the day he could join Sandy in the family business. His eldest brother Joseph was already making a name for himself, as were Martin and Eddie, his other two brothers. The Livingstons were a force to be reckoned with around Silvertown, or anywhere in the East End in fact.

Sandy saw the woman approach out of the corner of his eye. He automatically faced her and nodded in a friendly fashion.

'Hello, Miss Cavanagh.'

Briony smiled lazily.

'Hello there, Sandy. Come inside a moment, I want to see you.'

Sandy looked surprised at the request but followed Briony into the tiny terraced house without a thought. He knew Tommy and through him Briony Cavanagh. He respected her, a thing that was previously unheard of as Sandy Livingston had never respected another woman in his life, not even the wife who had borne his sons with the minimum of fuss and then looked forward to nothing but the back of his hand at least once a week.

Pete followed his father into the tiny house with exaggerated nonchalance, hands pushed into the pockets of his trousers in a parody of his father and brothers. Inside the house they were startled to see Tommy Lane and two big Arabs standing in the front room.

'Hello, Tommy. All right?'

Sandy looked around him, a trickle of fear running up the base of his spine.

Pete watched as the two large Arabs grabbed his father and pinned his arms to his sides.

'What's going on here? You leave my old man alone!'

Pete was frightened now. His big dad, whom he took such pleasure in bragging about, was scared – and this fact terrified the boy. Briony pushed him out of her way and dismissed him.

'Shut your trap and you'll be all right.' She looked at Sandy. 'He's like the spit out of your mouth, ain't he, Sandy boy?' Her voice was low now, even friendly.

Sandy licked his lips with a yellow-coated tongue.

'Look, Miss Cavanagh, I don't know what's going on here, but I swear, whatever I'm supposed to have done . . . well, I never done it!'

Briony and Tommy laughed. Briony slipped her hand into the waist of Sandy's trousers and took out the large boning knife he kept there. She took it out of its leather sheath and stared at it for a few seconds before placing the tip at Sandy's throat.

'You could do a lot a damage with this, Sandy, cut someone to pieces. But then, that's what you do best, ain't it? Cut people? For a sum of money?'

'I swear on my boy's life I ain't cut no one you wouldn't want cut . . .'

'Shut your mouth and listen! I'm gonna ask you something and if you lie to me you're dead, Sandy, dead as a doornail. I ain't joking.' Briony held a finger up to his face. 'Did you cut one of my girls, Sandy? The truth now, I want the truth. A little blonde bird called Ginelle. As God is my witness, you lie to me and I'll cut your fucking throat meself.'

Sandy looked down at the tiny woman in front of him. He met her hard green stare and swallowed deeply before he answered.

'No. I ain't cut no brasses. I swear to you I ain't cut no brasses! Not for yonks.'

Briony nodded slowly, watching his fear and sniffing it into herself, trying to assuage the rage inside her.

'Then who has, Sandy? All you cutters know one another, you all talk. Who is cutting up my girls? You give me the name and I'll see you all right, boy, but I must have a name.'

Pete watched his father battle it out with himself. He knew that grassing was the worst thing a cutter could do. Because cutters were the bad men, the really bad men, and they were the hardest. Hard men did their time, kept their heads down, and emerged from prison with their reputations intact, happy to

163

take on the mantle of hard men once more. He held his breath as he watched his father.

'I heard a whisper that Willy Bolger done a brass yesterday, down the docks. It was just a whisper, mind, from another cutter. I don't know the strength of it like . . .'

Briony sighed heavily.

'That's all I wanted to know.'

She nodded at the two Arabs and they let Sandy go. Briony handed his knife back to him and smiled.

'No hard feelings, Sandy, this was just business, boy.' She looked at Tommy. 'Give him a monkey, he's working for us now. Exclusively.' She faced Sandy and smiled. 'That OK with you?'

He nodded furiously. 'Yeah, I don't mind. I'm ready when you are, girl.'

'Then you can go.' As Pete and Sandy were leaving the room, Briony shouted after them.

'One last thing, Sandy. I don't want any mention of what took place in this room, from either of you. If it did I would be very annoyed, you see, and let's face it, Sandy, there's more than a few cutters around, aren't there?'

He nodded again, his face serious.

Outside on the pavement he walked along with his son, quiet and subdued. 'Little Pete', as his mother called him, searched his father's face and swallowed down his disappointment. His dad was a grass. The knowledge broke his heart.

Even worse, though, was the fact that his father was frightened of a tiny little lady with red hair and green eyes and the smallest feet he had ever seen. Even surrounded as she was with big men, little Pete had felt the fire from her, had felt the menace, and as upset as he was, felt a tremor of pity for whoever had angered her so much. If she could frighten his father, she could frighten old Nick himself.

'Well, you was right, Bri. But it wasn't Sandy. I heard a whisper a while back that Willy was branching out, but I didn't dream it was in our game. He's more a heavies' heavy, if you know what I

164

mean. He pimps, but not for our kind of girls. He's always dealt exclusively with the rough trade.'

Briony nodded, her face set in a frown that etched deep lines on her forehead.

'I have to scoot in a minute, I have to see Nellie Deakins and then Mariah Jurgens. I wonder what Jurgens could possibly want? I have a feeling in me boots she's involved in this somehow. It seems more than coincidence that she wants to see me after one of my girls gets topped.'

'There's no harm in Mariah, I knew her years back. She was always straight, Bri, always fair.'

Briony laughed bitterly.

'Tell that to Victoria Staines' mother. Her daughter still carries the scars of her run-in with Mariah to this day!'

Tommy sighed. 'You'd have done the same, Briony. If a girl is thieving you got to put the hard word on them, otherwise before you know it all the brasses are having a field day.'

'I can see you like her. Well, I promise to be very, very nice, unless she upsets me. I'll hear her out. But if she tries to cross me, I don't care how big she is, I'll wrap her from one end of London to the other! I ain't in the mood for fun and games at the moment.

'Now, you find all the cutters in town, and see if they're working for Bolger. I'm going to see him, but first I want to know exactly how much muscle he's got. He's more slippery than a greased eel, but he's made two bad mistakes. One, he touched something of mine, and two, the bastard has the audacity to think he can frighten me. Me, Briony Cavanagh! Well, he's got the shock of his fucking life coming to him. I'll pay him back tenfold for Ginelle, and for taking the piss.'

Tommy looked at her with awe and a tinge of respect. Never before had he seen her like this, and much as it troubled him, he was happy to know she would always look after herself and her own.

'*We'll* get him, Bri. We as in us.' His voice was low.

Briony went to him then and he pulled her into his arms. 'Yes, Tommy boy. We'll get him.' She looked up into his face and

165

tried to smile. 'But I'll cut the bastard, you owe me that. I'll be the one to cut him.'

Tommy nodded almost imperceptibly. It was what he had expected.

Nellie Deakins had grown big over the years. Now she was ponderously fat. Her neck, which had once been long and smooth, sported several chins. Her eyes were embedded in the fat of her face. She looked constantly as if she had just run a considerable distance, though she rarely left her chair. She puffed herself through each day, and even her girls had begun remarking on the unsavoury smell emanating from her.

Nellie had always ruled by fear; nowadays she relied heavily on her reputation from her younger days to keep order in her house. Nellie had once beaten a girl nearly to death, her crime to tip her hat at one of Nellie's boys. As Nellie had grown older she had taken an undue interest in young men. Big handsome young men whose only duty was to treat Nellie with a bit of respect, light the cigars which she smoked constantly and hold doors open for her. It was the illusion of youth and desirability that Nellie still fostered, even though the illusion was nowadays quite incongruous. Nellie wasn't really a jealous woman; she had beaten the whore for the simple reason that, if you let them get away with the little things, soon they'd try for bigger. Nellie had lived by that adage all her life. Until now, that is. Nellie was only sixty-two years old, not a great age for a madam. But she was so fat and lazy that the day to day running of her establishment had become something of a bind to her. She knew, deep down, that she had lost the urge to keep the place going, keep outwardly respectable and, worst of all for a madam, the urge to look out for her girls.

Now she had that young scut Briony Cavanagh coming to see her. Nellie pursed her lips to stop them twitching into a smile. She was a clever girl, that Cavanagh. Clever, good-looking and sensible. A lethal combination for a madam. Opened her first house with Tommy Lane when she was just a little girl, a greenie. Now the word on the street was that Briony was branching out into all sorts of skulduggery, legal as well as illegal.

Nellie sat back in her well-padded chair and absentmindedly unwrapped a sweet. Popping it into her mouth, she waited patiently for Briony Cavanagh to arrive and say what she had to say.

Briony walked into Nellie's house with barely concealed shock. The door had been opened by a girl of about nine who had sniffed loudly as Briony introduced herself and said at the top of her considerable little voice: 'You'd better come in.'

She had then been left in the hallway a good ten minutes before she realised the little minx had forgotten all about her. Briony was usually calm and fair in her dealings with children, but today she felt she had taken just about as much as she could stand.

She walked unannounced into the large main lounge and surveyed the room and the girls in it while she pulled off her gloves. The room had once been beautiful, if overdone. The crystal chandeliers were now hung with cobwebs, and the floor covering was bare in places. Around the room were girls and women, smoking and chatting. They glanced at her and resumed their talking. Briony breathed in the foetid stench of unwashed bodies and lavender water. Nellie's establishment had gone down even further than she had anticipated. The girls sprawled around this room would have been long gone from one of her own houses. She guessed they were lice-ridden and shuddered inwardly.

'Where can I find Nellie?' Her voice was loud and all the girls turned to face her with raised eyebrows.

'You a new girl?' This from a thin whore with non-existent breasts.

All the occupants of the room were taking in Briony's pale green dress and coat and costing it in their minds.

'What's your name, girl?' Briony's voice travelled across the room and hit the skinny one full on.

'You what?' The voice was belligerent now.

'I said, what's your name? Not too difficult a question, is it? I presume you know the answer.'

The others laughed and this put the girl in a terrible dilemma. She either fronted the red-headed cow in front of her, who though small looked like she could handle herself, or she answered the question and lost face in front of her friends.

'I'm Jinny Collins. And who are you?' It was said without any respect whatsoever and Jinny was pleased with herself. She had answered the question and asked one. To Jinny this showed considerable wit.

Briony let her eyes travel the length of the girl's body before she said: 'I am Briony Cavanagh, and you, Jinny Collins, had better start talking to me with a bit of respect!'

Briony nearly smiled at the different expressions on the girls' faces. They ranged from fear to a healthy curiosity which she noted with pleasure.

'I am here to see Nellie, and one thing I'll say to all you girls before one of you kindly shows me where she is, is this. You stink! All of you stink, and you're lousy. You're also ignorant. I could have been anyone coming in here, and you let me. If one of my girls did that, I'd scalp the bitch. My advice to you lot if you want to carry on working here is this: get washed and get your miserable little lives sorted.' She pointed to the skinny girl.

'You, Jinny, show me where I can find Nellie. Now!'

She practically jumped from her seat.

'Yes, miss.'

They all watched as Briony followed Jinny from the room. So that's Briony Cavanagh, each thought, and then cursed themselves. Briony Cavanagh was the person to work for and they all had inadvertently buggered it up for themselves. It was quiet after she had left them. But the room was filled to the rafters with regrets.

Jinny showed Briony into Nellie's office.

'It's Miss Cavanagh to see you, Nell.' Briony noted the use of the Christian name and sighed inwardly. This place was really run down.

Nellie watched Briony dust off her chair before sitting on it. She noted everything about her, from the perfectly arranged hair to the pale green suit that was plain and simple yet screamed of money. She decided she liked the look of the girl. The only thing that threw her was the fact that Briony Cavanagh, the big Briony Cavanagh, was small. 'Petite' the French would call her. Nellie decided she would rather describe her as scrawny.

'Now then, what can I do you for?' Nellie wheezed with laughter at her own joke.

'I think it's more a case of what I can do for you. I am looking for some more houses. I want established businesses, like your own.' She held up her hand as Nellie's mouth opened.

'Just hear me out, Nell, then answer me. I walked in here today to a bunch of filthy dirty brasses, the place is in tatters and looks unkempt – like its workforce. You are obviously losing heart in the place. I know that, in your day, you were one of the best madams this side of the water.'

She saw the woman respond to the compliment.

'Now what I want from you, Nell, is to buy this house outright, but I would still want you to run it. I will have a big say in what happens here, I admit, as will my associate, Tommy Lane. But you will be our mouthpiece, Nellie. I'll clear this place of crooks and vagabonds and wandering thieves. I think the house is in a prime location, it's big, and all it needs is a few quid poured into it to make it one of the best houses in the business once more. Now then, Nellie, what do you say?'

She looked at the girl, because Briony was only a girl for all her sophistication and expensive clothes, and felt a grudging respect and admiration for her. She had simply and firmly stated her case which Nellie was shrewd enough to know she would carry, with or without Nellie's co-operation. Briony Cavanagh struck her as that sort of person. What she offered was fair, and was also exactly what Nellie had dreamt of in her darker moments. She would have the status of head of the house without the real aggravation. It was a dream come true.

'I'll tell you what I think, little lady.'

Briony raised her eyebrows.

'I think you should go to the cupboard over there by the door and get out a bottle of my good brandy. Then we can toast our partnership.'

Briony grinned and did as she was told.

A little while later they were both pleasantly discussing the influential customers Nellie had had over the years, when Briony said: 'What about Willy Bolger, Nellie? You ever had any dealings with him?

Nellie waved her hand dismissively.

'He's a ponce of the worst order, Briony, but I know one thing about Willy that's always served me in good stead with him: he's a coward. He'd cut a brass or a bloke, but only mob-handed. Get Willy on his own and he shits bricks. He was in here not a week back telling me he wanted this, that and the other, but young Barry Black was in here. I've been hiding him up because the Old Bill's after him for that jewellery robbery over in Kent. He saw Willy off, no trouble. Willy reckons he's got a right royal backing now. I nearly laughed me head off! I mean, who in their right mind would back William Bolger? I remember him when he had no arse in his trousers and an empty stomach.'

Briony smiled and changed the conversation again, listening with half an ear to Nellie telling her about Lord this and Lord that who'd frequented her house over the years. But her mind was on Bolger, and on Mariah Jurgens who was next on her list of things to do.

It stood to reason Willy had backing, but from whom? That's what she had to find out.

170

Chapter Twelve

'You're what?' Molly looked at Eileen as if she had never before clapped eyes on her.

'I'm getting married, Mum. Joshua asked me today and I said yes.'

Molly grabbed her daughter in her arms and squeezed her tight. 'Jesus, Mary and jumping Joseph! This is the best news I've heard for many a long day, and aren't you the dark horse! I never guessed it was gone this far. All your gallivanting around and never a word! Oh, Eileen, I could shoot meself with happiness! You've made a good choice, child, a good choice!'

Molly's voice was loud enough to carry through the wall and beyond. Her pleasure was written all over her face. Rosalee picking up on this, grinned widely and clapped her hands together.

'Your sister's getting married, Rosie darlin', now isn't that something!'

Eileen smiled at her mother's obvious happiness.

'Wait until I tell the others!' Molly sat herself down by the fire and carried on making the tea. 'Now then, first things first. He's Catholic, thank God, so we'll have to see the priest and put the banns up. Our Briony will have to be told first, though.'

'What's Briony got to be told first?' Bernadette's voice wafted in at the front door as she pushed herself in laden down with packages. Eileen took them from her and, blushing furiously, said: 'I'm getting married, our Bernie, to Joshua.'

171

Bernadette screwed up her eyes in wonder and said loudly, 'You ain't? But he's an old man!'

Molly, seeing Eileen's face drop, gave Bernadette a stinging blow across the face and shrieked: 'Shut your mawing, you jealous bitch! Your turn'll come, if you can keep that galloping trap of yours shut for five minutes!

'Our Kerry will walk down the aisle fastern'n you because she only opens her mouth to a bit of singing.'

Molly's hard eyes stared into her daughter's with a warning and Bernie shook her head hard before saying, 'Our Kerry won't be walking down the aisle, as you put it. Our Kerry just might find herself getting a bit of a shock...'

She stopped herself from saying any more because of the look on Eileen's face. Even Rosalee seemed subdued now. Bernie realised that, as usual, she had walked into a merry situation and ruined it. It was a knack she had acquired as a child. Everyone was now angry or depressed on the day Eileen had announced she was getting married. For one of the few times in her life, Bernie felt ashamed. Poor Eileen had been so unhappy for so long, and now she was taking the shine off the news. She rubbed at the handprint that was glowing bright red on her cheek and grinned ruefully.

'I'm sorry, Eileen, it's great news. The best news ever!'

She kissed her sister on the cheek and in all the consequent excitement and chattering about the big day, Molly ignored the quip about Kerry, but it stayed in the back of her mind nevertheless.

Briony stood outside Mariah's house in Hyde Park and gave the large imposing building the once over. It really was a lovely old place. Painted white, the four-storey edifice blended in perfectly with its neighbours. It was class, and Briony felt a grudging respect for the woman who owned it.

She walked up the flight of scrubbed stone steps that led to the front door and rang the bell. The door was opened by a finely muscled young man in his early-twenties dressed in the scarlet

172

and silver livery that, Briony was to learn, was worn by all Mariah's staff.

He took her through a large entrance hall and into the office area of the house. He asked her politely to sit while he summoned his mistress. Briony was now impressed beyond her wildest imaginings. She might have been calling on Isabel Dumas. She sat herself in a leather winged chair and pulled off her gloves, her eyes greedily drinking in her surroundings.

Mariah was like her; where she worked was obviously important to her. Briony scanned the rows of bookshelves along the far wall and smiled to herself. Other than the copy of *Fanny Hill*, she guessed correctly that none of the books had ever been opened. Nevertheless they gave the room an air of respectability that Briony admired. She would angle for a look around the house if she could. It was always good to get a look at what the opposition was offering, and Mariah was her only serious opposition as far as the houses went, which was why she had never tried to take over any of her properties. There was room in London for both of them, providing Mariah didn't blot her copybook with Briony personally.

Her mouth settled into a grim line as she thought about this. She would make that point clear enough. Mariah might have requested the meeting, but Briony had only deigned to come because she had an ulterior motive. No, Miss Jurgens didn't scare her at all. Big as the bitch was, and as hard a reputation as she had, it would take more than a whore to frighten Briony Cavanagh.

She settled herself in the chair and resumed her neutral expression.

'Well, you're a runt and no mistaking!' Briony heard laughter in the big woman's voice and said, 'Yeah, and you're a big bastard. So that makes us quits.'

Briony's voice was hard, her face set. She stared up at the huge woman in front of her, her heart beating a tattoo in her chest. Briony consciously kept her eyes away from the massive clenched fists of her rival.

Mariah watched her and felt a flicker of respect. As small as she was, and God knows this girl was small, she wasn't afraid. In front of Mariah that took great courage. Men who were feared across the smoke were wary of her, she knew this and used it to her advantage. Yet this little thing was actually fronting her. She sat behind the desk with as much dignity as she could muster and said, 'Anyone else said that, I'd brain them, but I invited you here today for a good reason. Are you after my houses? I know you're after Deakins' place. Old Nellie is a bit long in the tooth these days for rowing, but I ain't. So I want a straight answer from you. Whether I brain you or not depends on what you say.'

Briony took a deep breath. The woman in front of her was renowned for her size, her strength and her temper. Well, Briony could match her in two of those attributes. But Mariah was also known to be fair. Briony decided to tell her the truth.

'It had crossed my mind, as you must have guessed. But no, I don't want to take over your houses. Unless you want to sell them, of course? Is that all you wanted me for?'

Mariah sat back in her chair and sucked on her teeth. Her white-blonde hair framed her face becomingly and for a second Briony got a glimpse of the woman she had once been, breathtakingly beautiful.

'I was sorry to hear about Ginelle, she was a good kid. Now then, before you leap out of your chair and start shouting your mouth off, hear me out. I know everything that goes on in this town, I make it my business to. I can find out anything about anyone. Now I had a visitor here, but I need to know a bit more about what's going on before I tell you who it was and what they wanted. I ain't known for sitting on any fences, unless it earns me money or peace, so let's cut the fucking crap and get our cards on the table. What exactly happened with Ginelle, and what threats have you had? Is this all about you taking over other houses or what?'

Briony was having difficulty controlling herself. She knew about Ginelle, this woman knew, and now she wanted to know the score! Briony knew she was trapped. She would have to come clean and hope for the best.

'How do you know about Ginelle, Mariah? I need to know.'

'Let's just say a little bird told me. It's enough that I know. Now tell me the honest truth and I'll come out into the open. I think that you and me could do each other a favour here. Let's see, shall we?'

'Nellie's house is in the bag. The death of Ginelle had nothing to do with that, as far as I know. She was delivered in a crate minus parts of her body. Bolger is behind it, but I need to know who's behind him before I can make a move. And I swear to you now, I take oath, that bastard is living on borrowed time! No one, but no one, touches my girls. Whoever is behind him had better start saying their prayers.'

Mariah smiled then. A real smile. She had heard what she wanted to hear. This little woman was a madam of the old sort. No milkwater sop who would run at the first sign of trouble. Mariah decided she could even get to like the skinny little bitch, given time. She stood up and, going to her drinks table, poured out two generous measures of brandy. Giving one to Briony, she resumed her seat and said: 'Bolger's been here, offering me the earth and other things besides. I don't like him but that's neither here nor there, I don't like a lot of people I do business with, but worst of all I don't trust him. He's a two-faced ponce, a violent two-faced ponce. He cut Ginelle up, and I won't forgive him that one. The girl was nothing to do with anything. Then he came here and offered me your houses. He wants me and my muscle on his side. Personally, I don't want to get involved, but I have to. Because otherwise eventually he'll want what's mine. I think I can find out who's backing him, then together we can wipe them out. Now, what do you have to say?'

Briony smiled at Mariah.

'I think, Mariah Jurgens, between us we could frighten the life out of the little shit!'

That was exactly what Mariah wanted to hear.

'I'm going to tell Bolger that I want to meet the man behind him, otherwise no deal. Bolger is a showman, a show off. He'll enjoy setting up the meet and letting me see how much he's come up in the world. I'll relay the information to you and Tommy. Then we decide what to do next. How's that?'

'That will suit me fine. Tommy is as anxious to sort this out as I am. We've got some pretty impressive muscle on our side.'

This was a threat to Mariah who took it how it was intended. But she didn't say anything. Briony was giving her fair warning, exactly what she would have done herself.

Raising her glass she said to Briony: 'I don't know, girl, what the fuck are we breeding these days? People like Bolger are getting thicker on the ground. Sometimes I hanker back to the good old days when you worked your girls, you took the money, and all the house owners met socially. There's a new breed out there now and we've got to stick together to fight the fuckers at their own game.'

Briony raised her own glass and said, 'My sentiments exactly.'

The two women sipped their brandy for a while, lost in their own thoughts. The groundwork was done. They had called a truce, felt each other out, and now they would work together to find a solution to all their problems.

Evander's friend and confidant Glennford Randall shook his head as he looked at his friend.

'I'm telling you, man, that girl spells trouble for you. No white meat ever tasted any different to black. You're gonna get hurt, I know it.'

Evander sighed heavily, his deep black skin shiny in the lights of the club.

'Kerry's different, man. She's real, something special.'

Glennford laughed. 'She's got a pair of tits and a splitarse, she ain't no different to any other woman in the world! She can get pregnant and, boy, if she does, you're a dead man.'

Evander watched his friend walk away, his long rangy body loping across the wooden stage. Kerry came out of her dressing room and smiled at him.

'Why so sad? What are you thinking about?'

Evander looked into her lovely face and felt the familiar tightening in his guts. She was exquisite, she was young, she was exciting, and she was milk white. It was a heady combination.

'I wasn't thinking about anything in particular, baby. Are we still on for tonight?'

'Yes, and I have a surprise for you. Bernie's staying at my mother's so we have the flat to ourselves. You can stay 'til the morning.'

Evander went to touch her arm when Tommy Lane came bowling up to them.

'All right, Evander? Listen, Briony's going to be a bit late tonight but she wants the sets a bit longer. Another couple of numbers in each one, could you manage that?'

Evander and Kerry nodded. Tommy was too caught up in his own affairs to notice the redness of Kerry's face and neck.

'The punters like a dance so we thought a few more lively numbers wouldn't go amiss. Now before I forget, there's a men's outfitters in Dean Street and the bloke's going to measure you boys up for some new stage clothes. At the moment you're all a bit bland, you know? We thought a nice deep green or a deep blue, whatever. You see the bloke and choose for yourselves. We'll be picking up the tab so don't go overboard!'

'Yes, sir, Mr Lane.' Evander's voice held the bland neutrality inherent to a black man and Tommy whacked him on the shoulder and said, 'For fuck's sakes, call me Tommy. All this Mr Lane and sir is going to me head!'

He ambled off to find a drink and Evander looked at Kerry. She saw the stark fear in his eyes and felt a lump form in her throat. He was scared of Tommy, was scared of all white men. They slapped you on the back one minute and put you in your place the next. She knew what he was thinking and felt a great sorrow for him.

'Tommy's all right, Evander. He means what he said.'

'I ain't never met a white man yet who means anything, Kerry. I call him Tommy boy tomorrow in front of his fancy friends and he'll try and break my head! Believe me, I know.'

'Not Tommy Lane, Evander, you're wrong.' Her voice was

soft and reproving and for a second he felt the terrific pull of her, and at the same time was reminded of just what trouble this relationship could bring him. Tommy Lane slapping you on the back and buying your clothes was one thing. Tommy Lane with the knowledge he was sleeping with Kerry would be a different matter entirely.

'I'll see you tonight, Evander, won't I?'

He looked into her little face, full of yearning, and he smiled.

''Course you will, sweetheart. Now let's get on stage before the crowd gets restless!'

Kerry put on her widest smile and walked on to the stage. Evander followed but his smile didn't quite reach his eyes.

Rupert Charles sat with Jonathan la Billière and a rather pale young man called Dorian. His face lit up at the sight of Briony walking towards his table.

'Briony darling! Where have you been? We've missed you, haven't we, boys?'

Jonathan stood up as Briony sat down and he winked at her.

'How did the filming go?' she asked them. 'I couldn't make it, I'm afraid, but I have a lot of faith in you, Rupert.'

She took out a cigarette and placed it in a long black holder. Dorian struck a match and lit it for her. She blew the smoke out into his face and smiled her thanks.

'Dorian darling, this is Briony Cavanagh. Briony, this is Dorian Carnarvon, the Duke of Tenby's only son. A darling boy with the most delightful grey eyes, don't you think?'

Briony smiled absently at the boy and concentrated on Jonathan, the male star of the film.

'So what's the score?'

Jonathan grinned and, losing his gentlemanly manner for a moment, said, 'The girl was young, plump, and knew all the right moves. There's a reel of film in your office waiting for you. Have a look and tell me what you think.'

'Is it as good as the other films? The truth now.'

'Honestly, yes! It's not bad. We know all the pitfalls now. You have a look and you'll be pleasantly surprised.'

178

Briony nodded, satisfied.

'What happened to you anyway, Briony? I was looking forward to seeing you. I was going to take you out after the shoot.'

Her eyes scanned the club around her as she answered. 'I had a bit of trouble, but it's sorted now. Do me a favour, set up another session and I'll put up the money. I want this pukkah, I want it right.'

He laughed.

'Do you only ever do business, Briony? Don't you ever relax?'

She looked into his face and he saw the fine lines around her eyes and mouth. It occurred to him then that this woman had a lot on her mind of which he knew nothing. For the first time she frightened him. Her reputation had preceded her, yet on his first meeting he had been pleasantly surprised. Looking at her now, he was convinced she was capable of anything.

Chapter Thirteen

Briony woke up to a terrific thumping on her bedroom door.

'What's going on!' Tommy opened his eyes and stared at her.

'It's your mother, Briony, she's downstairs with Rosalee.' Cissy's voice was loud and Briony screwed up her eyes and groaned.

'All right, tell her I'll be down in a minute.'

'Your mother's like a bleeding jinx, always around when no one wants her.'

Briony laughed gently.

'Tell me about it.' She pulled herself out of the bed and, going to her wardrobe, took out a wrap of heavily embroidered Chinese silk. Her long hair was hanging down her back in tangles and she began to brush it furiously to try and tame it.

Tommy got out of the bed and scratched his belly while he stretched. 'I feel knackered.'

'Stay in bed. I'll get Cissy to bring you up some tea.'

'Nah, I've got to see some people today.' He sat on the side of the bed and closed his eyes.

'Who have you got to see?'

'Oh, no one in particular, just a few mates. Tell Cissy I'll have that tea now, if you don't mind. And tell your mother not to get me up in future.'

Briony grinned.

'As if she'd take any notice!'

'What kind of time do you call this, still in bed at ten-thirty in the morning. My God, child, you must be raking it in.'

'And good morning to you and all, Mum.' She knelt down and kissed Rosalee's face. 'Hello, Rosie darling.'

Rosalee clapped her hands together and said: 'Bri, Bri.'

Molly tutted loudly and poured her out a cup of tea Cissy had brought them. 'I don't know, Briony, you're a lady of leisure, sitting in your dressing gown like Lady Astor, and the day nearly over.'

'Oh, Mum, put a sock in it, for Christ's sake! My clubs don't shut 'til three in the morning, then I have to do the takings among other things, so please give me five minutes' peace. Now what do you want and how much is it gonna rush me?'

Molly screwed up her eyes and gritted her teeth. 'What makes you think I'm after something?'

Briony did laugh then, a real laugh that burst out of her tiny frame and caused Rosie to laugh with her.

'If I see you and her before noon, then you're after a few quid. Tell me what you want and let's . . .' The sentence was lost in a long loud yawn.

'I came here this morning to tell you that Eileen's getting married.'

Molly had the grim satisfaction of seeing Briony's eyes widen. 'There, I thought that would put a stop to your gallop! Joshua's popped the question and she's said yes. I thought me and you could have a little chat about the do. That's all.'

'The do?' Briony's voice was puzzled.

'The reception! For the love of Mary, would you pay attention, girl! She's getting married and I want it to be the biggest thing this side of the water. I want her to go off in style. The way you lot are going, she'll be the only one of my daughters wedded and legal.' Her voice became wheedling. 'I want me eldest girl to have a good weddin', Bri. I want her to be set up like a queen.'

'Our Eileen getting married? Bloody hell! Who'd have thought it.'

Molly wiped Rosalie's face with a hankie and said, 'I'll never marry off this one, will I? And you living over the broom, and

182

our Bernie without a man in sight. As for Kerry, well, she would marry her voice if she could. I want our Eileen to have something special. After all that happened to her, and all her troubles . . .'

Briony put up her hand for silence.

'Look, Mum, she can have whatever you like, so drop the sales pitch. You book it and I'll pay for it. In fact, if you like we can have the reception here, I don't mind. My garden's huge, we could easily get fifty, sixty people here no trouble. Mrs H can do the food and Cissy can bring in a few girls to help serve. What do you think?'

Molly smiled smugly.

'You're a good girl, Briony, you're a kind and decent girl. Only a saint would look after her sisters like you do.'

Briony drank the rest of the tea and poured herself another cup before she said, 'Why do I get the feeling, Mother, that you've just mugged me off?'

Kerry was lying in bed with Evander, at the quiet stage after lovemaking. When the only thing needed, or indeed wanted, is to feel your lover's heart beating with your own. He stroked her belly with soft fingers and Kerry groaned. The bedclothes had fallen to the floor and the remains of a bottle of wine and a platter of bread and cheese stood on the night table. They had yet to sleep, and were both dozing when they heard the sound of a key in the front door.

Evander sat upright, and Kerry hastily jumped from the bed and pulled a sheet around her when they heard Bernie's voice.

'Hello, Kerry, it's me!'

Kerry and Evander looked at one another and Kerry, putting a finger to her lips, went to the door and slipped through it out into the hallway. Bernie was hanging up her coat. She smiled.

'Morning, Kerry.' She looked her sister up and down and raised one finely plucked black eyebrow.

'What has the wicked witch stumbled on here then? Could you have a man in there!'

Kerry licked her lips nervously.

183

'What you doing back here so early? I wasn't expecting you until this afternoon.'

'Our mother's took Rosie and gone on the ponce round Briony's about the wedding – Eileen's wedding actually. So I thought I may as well come back here and get started on your dresses for tonight.'

'Eileen's getting married?'

Bernie walked through to the kitchen and started to fill the kettle.

'How many cups of tea shall I make, two or three? Or would the chap in there prefer coffee?'

Evander's love of coffee was common knowledge around the club. He had tried tea and it had made him violently sick. Suddenly it was crystal clear to Kerry. Bernie knew everything and she was going to use it against her. That had been her way since childhood. She looked for a handle on people then used it for her own ends.

Kerry drew herself up to her full height and walked into the bedroom.

'Get up, get up now!' Evander looked at her in shock. She threw the sheet from her own body and pulled on a dressing gown. Then she stormed from the room.

Bernie was getting the cups out of the dresser when Kerry stamped back into the kitchen.

'You bitch! You nasty, vindictive cow! You know exactly who I'm sleeping with. Well, yes, you *can* make him a cup of coffee. You can also pack your bags and get the hell out of here and back to Mum's. I don't need you on my back, Bernie Cavanagh, I never did and I never will. Take yourself and your arseholing ways back home to Mum!'

Bernadette turned to face her sister and her mouth opened twice before she could form any words.

'What? What did you say?'

Kerry snorted through her nose.

'You heard. What? You deaf now as well as stupid? I said, you can get the hell out of here. I know your game, mate. Well, you tell who the fuck you like. It won't make no difference to me. I

184

ain't ashamed of anything where that man's concerned, I love the bones of him. So now you know.'

Bernie's mind was working overtime. If Kerry slung her out now she would be back home permanently; she would also be without a job. As Kerry's dresser she got a good wage and did nothing really to earn it except iron her dresses or alter them if necessary. She was well set up nowadays and it was all thanks to Kerry and Briony. She also knew that no matter what Briony's opinion of Evander Dorsey might be, she would not like the fact Bernie had tried to deck one over on Kerry. She wouldn't like that at all.

'I don't know what you mean, Kerry. I guessed ages ago about you and Evander, saw you looking at each other. I knew what the outcome was going to be. If I was going to say anything I would have said it by now. I'm pleased for you. I'm glad you've found someone!'

'Oh, pull the other one, it's got golden bells on! I know your game, Bernie, you've always been the same . . .'

Evander walked into the kitchen. He had pulled on his trousers and vest. Bernadette looked at his muscled torso and his handsome face and found it in her heart to see just what had attracted Kerry.

'Stop all this shouting, ladies. It's wrong for you two to fall out over me. Now let's have a cup of coffee and try and talk this out.'

Bernie saw that his eyes were wary and her heart lifted. He was scared of her, of what she could say, of who she could tell. Unlike Kerry, he was more than aware of what the outcome could be if she walked from this house. After all, no one would physically hurt Kerry but he would be lynched.

'She's a vicious cow, Evander, you don't know her.'

Bernie was shocked at the vehemence in her sister's voice.

'Oh, come on, Kerry, what have I done to deserve that? I wouldn't do anything to hurt you, I swear. I'll keep this as close a secret as you. After all, if it got out . . .'

She left the rest of the sentence in mid air and Evander bit his lip. The kettle boiled and Bernie busied herself making the drinks. Kerry stood with her back against the table and her arms tight across her chest. Unlike Evander she knew what Bernie was capable of, though unlike Evander she wasn't as aware of what would really happen should the affair become public.

Bernie gave everyone their drinks. Putting her arm on Kerry's, she said sweetly: 'I don't want to fall out over this, Kerry. You're my sister and I'll keep this a secret for as long as you want. I mean it. If you're happy then I'm happy. If you really want me to leave I will. I won't stay where I'm not wanted. But even if you ding me out, I won't say a dicky bird to anyone.'

Kerry looked into the face so like her own and felt the sting of tears in her eyes.

She knew that Bernie was staying whether she wanted it or not, Evander's reaction had seen to that. But it saddened her that she could never trust her sister, or indeed understand the hatred in her. It had always been the same. Since they were babies Bernie had always had a vicious streak where she was concerned. It was jealousy, and jealousy made people do evil things. For the first time Kerry was really frightened, not for herself but for Evander.

Molly was putting the finishing touches to the lunch she had prepared for Joshua O'Malley and his mother. She swept her eyes around her house to make sure everything was gleaming. Satisfied, she went to the fireplace and, taking up a large brick, banged it on the back of the grate three times. The banging was answered by two knocks from the other side of the wall and two minutes later Mother Jones came in at Molly's front door.

'Oh, Molly, it looks a picture. Beautiful. Even that old bitch won't be able to find fault.'

Molly smiled in satisfaction. Elizabeth O'Malley was the only fly in the ointment as far as Eileen's wedding was concerned. Hated by everyone in Dagenham and Barking for her vindictive tongue and her holy Joeing ways, she was now to become a member of the Cavanagh family, and as much as the thought distressed Molly she would take a lot to see her eldest daughter happily married, even take on Elizabeth O'Malley if necessary.

'The food smells beautiful, now stop your worrying. Did I tell you what I heard the other week?'

Molly busied herself tidying Rosalee's hair and said, 'No, what?'

'It seems Mrs O'Malley was cleaning out St Vincent's Presbytery when who should come in but Jean Barlow. The woman's got a tongue like an adder! Well, poor Father McNamara was nearly shitting himself at the two of them in the same place. I mean, their hatred of one another goes back years! Barlow was knocking off O'Malley's man just before he died. Well, this is the rub. Barlow asks the priest if he could set the banns up for her next weddin', looking at O'Malley all the time like, trying to annoy the life out of her. So O'Malley says all innocent like, "Aren't you a bit long in the tooth for getting married, Mrs Barlow?" And that mare turns on her and says: "There's no set age for getting married, or indeed falling in love. Why, Mr O'Malley could have told you that, dear."'

Molly gaped. 'She didn't mention O'Malley's man?'

Mother Jones roared with laughter.

'She did! Well, the priest, God love him and keep him, had to separate them. Mrs McAnulty his housekeeper threw a bucket of water over them in the end. Like alley cats, she said they were, and the language! The priest was red-faced for days after!'

'Well, good for Barlow, I say. It's about time someone gave that bitch one in the eye. No one split on her old man because they were glad to see someone getting one over on the old cow.'

As she said that Eileen walked through the front door with the woman in question and her son, and Molly, being Molly and a mother who wanted her girl wed, held out her arms and said: 'Come away inside, Mrs O'Malley. This is indeed a pleasure!'

Tommy Lane and his close friend and minder Jimmy Reynard walked into the lunch-time crush of The Two Puddings in Stratford. They pushed their way through to the bar and Tommy ordered two pints of best bitter. He noticed he was being observed by a huge bald-headed man called Boris Jackobitz. Tommy looked the man in the face and, raising his pint, motioned with his head to the back bar. Boris nodded almost imperceptibly and five minutes later slipped through the curtained doorway at the back of the pub. Tommy and Jimmy followed.

Their disappearance went unnoticed by the clientele who were waiting for the result of a horse race. This was the place for betting. It was crowded out day and night with punters. From well-to-do middle-class shopkeepers to run of the mill petty criminals and local hard men, all had one thing in common: a love of the horses. It was the main topic of conversation and the only interest of most of the clientele.

Boris employed runners from the age of seven to fifty, and was the foremost bookie in London. He chased his bets like the fillies chased the Cheltenham Gold Cup: conscientiously and without ever letting up. If you couldn't pay Boris it was time to leave the country.

He closed the heavy wooden door behind the thick curtain and motioned for Tommy to sit. He didn't extend this courtesy to Jimmy because a minder should always stand and remain alert. Jimmy leant against the wall and crossed his arms, watching Boris all the time.

'So what can I do for you, Tommy Lane? Long time no see.' Boris's deep and throaty voice was accompanied by a chuckle. Tommy smiled and crossed his legs. Pulling out one of his cheap cheroots, he lit it before saying: 'You're looking well, Boris me old mate. Prosperous and happy. That's what I like to see.'

Boris shrugged his shoulders and clenched his fists, emphasising his muscular torso.

'I have to keep well, Tommy, there's so many people wanting to come up in the world over my back. And yours, I don't doubt. I keep my place with fear and a little bit of respect. Now, we've had the polite chit-chat, what's the rub? I'm a busy man.'

'You know just about everything that's going on. People owe you money, and when they can't pay they trade information. What's been going on in the streets that would interest me particularly?'

Boris digested Tommy's words and, opening a drawer in the

table, took out a bottle of red-eye whisky. Pulling the cork out with his teeth, he took a long drink before offering it to Tommy. He took the bottle and swigged from it, wiping his hand across his mouth afterwards.

'Is what you have to tell me so bad I'll need a stiff drink first?'

His voice was jocular and Boris, noted for his dry sense of humour, laughed out loud.

'Maybe, Tommy Lane. Maybe. It's Bolger you're interested in, isn't it? Well, I heard a whisper – only a whisper, mind – that he has been seen with Isaac Dubronsky. He's well in with the Jews. Now they've always stuck to trading and loan sharking, but I understand Willy wants them to branch out into the cat business. Never had no time for whores myself, prefer my females to have four legs and a good pedigree. But it's funny, you know, Tommy, you coming here, because I was going to see that woman of yours, Briony. It seems she's the one he's gunning for. He's been asking all over town about her. It sounds more a vengeance thing to me. You know, I wondered if she'd had a word with him at sometime, a run-in like? Because he was asking about her in Stratford not a week since. And around Barking. About her family. You might not believe me but I was going to see the lady in question myself, especially after that young girl was cut.'

Tommy stared at Boris with awe. There was nothing that escaped his notice. He rarely used his information, it was more of a hobby to him.

'You know about Ginelle?'

Boris grinned. 'Listen, Tommy, I know everything about everyone, yourself included. But I don't use anything unless it benefits me. If you have a handle on someone it brings in unpaid debts a lot faster than a hiding. Also, if I hear of a robbery and one of the people involved owes me money, I can collect it quickly and cleanly. But this Bolger I don't like. He cut a friend of mine a few years back, a young tom who liked a bet. He cut her face. I went to see him myself. That's where Willy got the scar across his back. I done him with a razor and Willy, being Willy, let me. That was why I wanted to see young Briony. I like

189

her. I liked her when she was a child and her father used to send her with a bet. Tell her from me, whatever happens, I will be on her side.'

'Thanks, Boris, I appreciate that.'

He smiled, showing black teeth, and shook his head. 'I always was a gentleman. Whatever my reputation, I would never hurt a woman. Bolger has made a career of it. The sooner he's cleaned off the pavements, the better.'

Tommy stood up and held out his hand. Boris grasped it and squeezed it tightly.

'Go and see Dubronsky. If I know him he's in over his head. He's strictly small-time.'

'I will.' Turning back at the door, Tommy said, 'I'll tell Briony what you said, Boris. She'll really appreciate it.'

He grinned.

'She's a good businesswoman, clear-headed and sensible. Most women are when you get to know them properly. I think they could even run the country one day!'

Tommy laughed at the incongruity of the statement and left. He made his way with Jimmy to Petticoat Lane, stopping to pick up two hand guns on the way. When you visited the Jews on their own territory it was just as well to go there with a little bit of insurance.

Kerry sat on her bed staring at the pile of clothes on the floor, trying to summon up the energy to get herself dressed. Evander had left and she could hear Bernie humming to herself as she prepared some food. She gritted her teeth together, making a grinding noise. Why did she have to be plagued like this. She wanted Evander Dorsey so bad she could taste it.

It was all she thought about, all she wanted to think about. If he had been a big blond Swede, no one would have said a word. But he was black, and because of that fact, he and Kerry had to skulk around like criminals. Now Bernie knew about them and that was the beginning of the end. Instinctively Kerry knew this.

In France she could live openly with Evander. They were

artists, and as such would be forgiven much. Here, and in America, if she publicly proclaimed her feelings they would be ridiculed. Hated. It was so unfair. Her mother would go mad if she heard about Evander. You could be a twopenny whore and get more respect than a woman who went with a black man.

It was so unfair. So very, very unfair.

Bernie bustled into the room with a hot drink. She looked at Kerry and smiled sadly.

'Come on, Kel, get yourself sorted.' She began to pick up the clothes on the floor and Kerry leant forward and grabbed her wrist. Bernie looked up into her face, stunned.

'If you try and bugger this up for me, Bernie, I'll kill you! Do you understand me? I'll kill you with my bare hands.'

Bernie nodded, her eyes filling with tears. What really hurt her was the fact that Kerry knew her so well, knew exactly what she was capable of. She could see through her like a pane of glass.

'I won't, Kerry. I promise.'

Kerry pushed the offending arm away from her and said, 'Too right you won't, because I won't let you!'

The two sisters stared into each other's eyes, and it was Bernadette who looked away first.

Chapter Fourteen

Brick Lane market was packed. The stall holders were shouting out their wares in loud voices. Children ran among the stalls, looking for a chance to swipe the nearest thing to hand. Old women and young mothers stopped for a gossip or to scour the second-hand clothes stalls, of which there were plenty. Barrow boys stood by with apples and oranges piled high, their dirty hands grasping money and weighing up their produce quickly and efficiently, always underweighing when possible and keeping up a stream of talk as they did so, chatting up customers, young and old.

The shops were open. Gold was displayed behind metal grilles, diamonds sparkled, and furniture was displayed outside on the pavements. It was the era of the never-never and the Jews cashed in on this. They had always been the Uncles, the moneylenders, they were established and commanded respect because of this. They were rich, owning property in Brick Lane and roundabouts, but lived in Golders Green, respectable lives, with respectable families. Many of the men started out making a small fortune from the cobbles, a term for boxing without gloves. They fought all comers at Victoria Park and when they had a stake eventually made their way into the garment or gold industry, always lending money as a sideline. The easy atmosphere belied the real dealings that went on here. The lane was open till late at night. The smell of gefilte fish and blintzes vied for a place among the smells of rotten vegetables and the ever present smell of steam from the hoffman pressers. Tommy walked along with Jimmy until he came to Dubronsky's small pop shop. 'Pop' was the term for pawn. It was not unusual for a woman to take her husband's good suit in on a Monday and get it back out Saturday, ready to be worn on Sunday. Pawning was a way of life for most people. It was the only way to stretch meagre pennies, and to keep children's bellies full. Inside the shop, Tommy closed the door and put up the 'Closed' sign.

The small Jewish man behind the counter smiled at him.

'Tommy, my boy. What brings you here?'

Dubronsky's exterior did not kid Tommy one iota. He knew the little man could blow his head off at a whim; his meek and engaging exterior covered a calculating brain and a violent streak. Until now, Tommy had always got on very well with him. He used this fact as he ambled over to the counter.

'I hear you've been making friends with the pimps? Is this true?'

Dubronsky shrugged.

'Since when have I had to ask you who I can be friends with? What are you, Tommy Lane, an Irish rabbi, that you come here on to my premises and question me about my likes and dislikes?'

Tommy grinned then.

'Jimmy, have a look out the back, would you?'

He walked through, slamming up the flap of the wooden counter noisily and walking through to the back of the shop. He emerged with a girl of about eighteen. She had thick black hair and a large nose. Dubronsky's daughter Ruth, the likeness was unmistakable.

'Leave my daughter be, Tommy, she's only a child helping her father.' Tommy detected the worry in his voice. Jimmy was well known for his vicious ways and his non-existent brain. Dubronsky knew that if Tommy nodded, Jimmy would just batter the girl without a second's thought. But Tommy was piqued that the man thought so little of him.

'I wouldn't hurt your daughter, you should know that. I

194

want to hurt Willy Bolger. I don't want to fall out with you or anyone else for that matter, but I will if needs be. Bolger has upset me, and now he has to pay the price. If you protect him, I'll raze this fucking place to the ground! I mean it. So you give him a little message from me. Tell him I'm looking for him, and I'll find him eventually. So he can make it a lot easier on himself if he makes a point of coming to see me. If I have to look for him, it will be worse on him and any of his so-called friends. Do you understand me?'

'Perfectly. Now if you don't mind, I have work to do.'

Tommy stared at the man for a few seconds, battling the urge to attack him. It seemed that whoever was behind Bolger was a bigger fish than he'd first thought, otherwise why would Dubronsky be so cavalier? Walking around the counter, Tommy grabbed the little man by the scruff of his neck and frog-marched him out to the back of the shop. Kicking open the toilet in the yard, he pushed the man's head down the pan, using all his considerable strength. The toilet, though well used, had not seen soap for many years. The smell of dank urine and mould hung in the air. Someone had used it a while before and the urine was deep orange, an oily film floating on it. He held Dubronsky's head under until the man's body began to sag, then he dragged his head up and threw him on to the ground outside the toilet door. He proceeded to kick him ferociously, concentrating on the chest and back.

Dubronsky lay on the ground heaving. Eventually he turned on his side and a trickle of blood-stained mucus came from his mouth. Tommy knelt beside him and grabbed his face, squeezing it.

'Don't you ever mug me off again, you ponce! Not ever! Now, you're going to tell me who's backing Bolger or I'll drown you in your own piss. Believe me when I say you've pushed me too fucking far. Out with it. I want a name and I want it now!'

The man looked up with fear in his eyes. In all his years of knowing Tommy, he had never seen him like this. It began to dawn on him that he had written Tommy Lane off too soon.

195

The boy, and he was still a boy for all his grown-up looks, was a person he should not have underestimated. Like the Cavanagh girl, he was part of the new breed, and the prospect of what they could be capable of was frightening. All Bolger's big talk was suddenly forgotten in the face of this boy's wrath.

'Tommy, leave go of me! Let's talk.'

He laughed low.

'I've had it with talking, you short-arsed runt! Now tell me who Bolger's new friends are, and me and you will get on a lot better.'

'I don't know, I swear. All I know is that Bolger came to me and a few others with a proposition. He has a lot of money at his disposal, and a lot of manpower has been bought and paid for. Believe me, Tommy, it was nothing personal, just business. But I swear to you I don't know who's behind him. He said once it was a businessman, a big businessman. That's all. He won't let on who it is to anyone.'

'You expect me to believe that and all, don't you?'

Tommy's voice held an incredulity that was forced. Dubronsky would save his daughter's arse if not his own. But he had to be sure the man didn't know.

'Tommy, listen to me, I don't know. Before God, I swear to you I have no idea . . .'

He let go of the man's face. Livid white fingermarks were indented upon it. Tommy wiped his wet hand on the man's shirt.

'Where will I find him? He ain't been seen in his drum for a while so where's he hiding out?'

The little man squinted. Without his glasses he was nearly blind.

'He's staying with the Olds brothers down by Upton Park. But I warn you, Tommy, he's well protected.'

'How much muscle has he bought? Who are they?'

Dubronsky coughed and spat the mucus out on to the ground before answering.

'The Olds, the Campbells, the Dennings. Not to mention a lot of the Jewish muscle as well as Maltese. The Marianos are considering his offer and I tell you now, he's spending money like water.'

Tommy ground his teeth together. Poking his head at the man before him, he said: 'I don't care if he's bought the whole of the smoke. He's a fucking dead man. And if he's dead he can't pay anyone anything, can he. I'll piss all over his fireworks, you see if I don't.'

Standing, Tommy walked through the back of the shop to where Jimmy was standing with Ruth. The girl's sallow complexion was now white. Nodding to her, Tommy walked through the shop and out of the door with Jimmy. Outside he took a deep breath. Picking up a metal dustbin from the gutter, he threw it with all his strength through the shop window. People watched the spectacle with bright eyes. Dubronsky was not well liked, the Uncles never were really.

Jimmy smiled as they walked towards their car. Sometimes he wondered why the hell Tommy wanted him along. He was quite capable of taking on anyone by himself.

In the car Tommy said, 'Home. Me and you are going to see the Olds tonight. There's a bundle tonight at Victoria Park, and if I know Ronnie Olds, he'll be there.'

Willy Bolger nodded at the man sitting behind him in the car. His face was set in a neutral expression and he coughed gently before he spoke.

'Look, trust me. I'm not afraid of Briony Cavanagh or Tommy Lane. They're history. Soon they'll be out of the picture for good. Between us we'll run their businesses. In six months' time they'll be folklore.'

The man in the back of the car whispered: 'They'd better be. I'm paying you a lot of money to get this off the ground. I want Briony Cavanagh wiped off the face of the earth. I want everything she owns, and I want her out of the way once and for all.'

Willy grinned, showing his tiny pointed teeth. 'It's as good as done.'

The man slipped out of the car and walked along the

Bayswater Road where he hailed a cab. Willy watched him go with contempt. What a fool. He'd handed over large sums of money and Willy had taken it without a second thought. If the man had had any sense he would just have had them taken out. It would have been cheaper. But for some reason best known to himself he wanted Briony Cavanagh stripped of everything she had first. Willy pocketed the wad of money the man had passed to him at the start of their meeting and smiled again. Who gave a fuck? he thought. So long as the money kept coming he could do what he liked. As he drove towards Hoxton he daydreamed of being the Baron of the East End. The first Baron who was also a pimp. He would be in control of just about all the women who worked the streets. The prospect pleased him. It was his dream come true. Plus he would enjoy taking out Miss Cavanagh, the feisty bitch! She needed knocking down a peg and he was just the man to do it.

He had heard the whispers that Lane was looking for him. Well, let the fucker look. There was no harm in that. But he wouldn't find him. Tommy would see him when the time was right, and then he would be the last person Tommy Lane saw in his life.

Briony had just finished drying herself when Tommy came in the bedroom. She stood naked, her tight belly emphasising her small breasts, and Tommy dived across the room and grabbed her. His hands were freezing and Briony screamed. He picked her up and carried her to the bed. Laying her down gently he kissed her mouth tenderly.

'You still look like a kid, especially with that mad hair all over the place.'

'Well, I don't feel like one. Let me up.'

Tommy leant on her with all his weight, pinning her to the bed.

'No. Why should I?'

Briony laughed. 'Because I'm bleeding well freezing that's why! Cissy never even bothered putting a fire up here today.'

'I'll warm you up, girl.' He felt Briony consciously relax and stifled a sigh. It was always the same. She would allow him inside her, that was all. He felt an urge to bite her, make her feel something if only pain. As if she read his thoughts, she whispered to him. 'I'm sorry, Tommy.'

The tiny voice was desolate and he pulled her to him, breathing in the mingled scents of soap and perfume.

Pulling himself back, he looked into her face. The deep green eyes had golden flecks that made them luminous. They were framed by deep, long black lashes, that were a startling contrast to her hair. As she was now, scrubbed free from cosmetics, with her hair tumbling around her, she looked good enough to eat. She looked like the girl he had fallen for. Only a few lines around her eyes betrayed her troubles and her age.

His eyes roamed over her body to the fine white lines just inside the pubic hair, the only evidence of womanhood she displayed. Her small breasts were unmarked, as were her thighs, but a few rogue stretchmarks glistened on her stomach and Tommy loved her more for them. Because they reminded him, as they did her, of what she had given up. Had had taken from her.

Briony ran her slim fingers over them tenderly.

'Sally's coming on Saturday, I'm going to arrange to see Ben if I can.'

Tommy nodded solemnly. Sally was Benedict's nurse. After Isabel Dumas had stopped Briony seeing the boy, she had cultivated his nurse. Briony now saw him only from a distance but it helped to soothe the ache inside her.

Lowering his head he kissed her belly tenderly.

'I love you, Bri.' His voice was husky with pent-up emotion and Briony pulled him on top of her and kissed him, her fingers expertly unbuttoning his trousers. As she caressed him he became hard. He pulled off his trousers and lay beside her, kissing her breasts and neck, murmuring his love for her. Briony slowly unbuttoned his shirt, running her nails gently across his back, feeling the goose bumps appearing on his skin. As he entered her, he groaned. She gripped him with her vaginal muscles, pulling him into her expertly, cold-bloodedly, like one of the girls who worked for her. He felt the familiar feeling of sadness envelop him. He rode her hard, thrusting himself inside her until he was spent. Then he collapsed on top of her, and she loved him then. Kissing him gently, whispering endearments. Enjoying his nearness. And as always he forgave her for his hurt. The feeling he was using her and being used in return. Because he knew that Briony was incapable of the feelings she generated in him, and the saddest part for him was what she was missing. But he petted her as he knew she liked, and kissed her.

They lay together for nearly an hour, both lost in their own thoughts. Both wanting to speak of their real feelings and both lost for words.

Finally, Briony stirred. Slipping from under him, she put on a silk wrapper and built up the fire. It was early evening and the sun was slowly disappearing. She put on the bedside lamps and smiled down at Tommy.

'What have you been doing today?'

He stared up at her and smiled.

'To be honest, Briony, I've been chasing up Bolger.'

'What's the rub? Have you found out who this mysterious backer is?'

Tommy shook his head. 'Nah. It seems our Willy is staying round with the Oldses. Ronnie Olds hates him, I know that for a fact. He's always hated ponces. Ronnie's strictly robbing and villainy. But here's a lot of dosh being spent, and I'll be honest, Bri, it's beginning to worry me. Someone wants us out of the picture for good. We're not talking healthy competition here, my love, we're talking death and destruction. Namely, mine and yours.'

She sat on the bed and put her hand over Tommy's. 'You're really worried, aren't you?' Her voice was shocked.

Tommy bit his lip and nodded.

'To be honest, girl, I am. There's something going down here and I can't get to the fucking bottom of it. I've been tramping the pavements like a madman and I can't get nothing from no one.

'Whoever's backing Willy is very shrewd, and I think we already know that, and he's arsehole fucking lucky. Because Willy ain't mentioned him to anyone. Also, whoever it is ain't a villain, because Willy's buying up anyone who's anyone.'

He sighed and wiped his hand over his face. His thick hair was tousled. Looking at him in the firelight, his face drawn, a feeling of fear stole over her. If Tommy Lane was scared then there was definitely something to be nervous about.

'So what's to do? Do we sit here and shit ourselves or do we go out and find the fucker? You tell me.'

Her tone was aggressive as she wanted it to be. She was frightened now herself, really frightened, and she didn't like it. She didn't like it at all.

Despite himself, Tommy laughed. Only his Briony would be prepared to go out looking for someone who could be the death of them. She'd pick up a chair and fight anyone!

'Tonight there's a fight over at Victoria Park. Olds will be there, maybe even Willy. I don't think we can wait for Mariah to have her meet. I think we need the element of surprise, don't you?'

Briony nodded and grinned.

Tommy leapt from the bed and lit one of his cheap cheroots. 'Ring for a bit of scran. Bacon and eggs will do, anything. I'm starving. Then I'll round up all the boys and tool them up. We'll go there tonight and give them a run for their fucking money. If I'm going down, I intend to take a good few with me.'

Briony rang the bell.

'I'll get myself washed and dressed. I think we should get there as the first fight comes on. That way we'll slip in easier.'

Tommy looked at her and shook his head.

'Oh, no! You're not going. That ain't no place for you, or any woman come to that. You're staying here. Sort out the clubs, the houses, anything. But you ain't going near the places tonight!'

Briony faced him. Putting her hands on her hips, she said: 'And who's gonna stop me?'

Tommy walked to her and pushed his face close to hers. 'I ain't never raised a hand to you, Briony, nor to any woman, but I'll give you the leathering of your life if you set one dainty foot near that place tonight!'

Tommy rounded up twenty of his best men, including Abel Jones and Jimmy Reynard. In the basement of a slum in Wapping, Tommy displayed his arsenal and the men each picked out a weapon and secreted it on their person. Knives, guns and coshes were the order of the day, and as they all left to go to the fight there was a general air of excitement. Most of the men had grudges against the Oldses and the Campbells, so were looking forward to the fight. Tommy smoked cheroots one after the other as the cavalcade made their way to Hackney. They arrived just after nine.

The first fight was already taking place and the park was literally packed out. Tommy and his men pushed their way through the crowds, looking for Ronnie Olds. He would be made to tell them where Bolger was hiding out, even if it meant losing his testicles during the conversation. Tommy was now acting on pure adrenaline. His heightened awareness made him more aggressive than ever and he pushed through the crowds with a grim look on his face. He wanted this sorted once and for all. The chance was he would end his life here tonight but it was a chance he was prepared to take. Tommy noticed Jimmy and another man buying themselves roast chicken from a vendor. Walking over to them, he grabbed Jimmy by the throat.

'What's this then, Jimmy, a fucking night out or what?'

Jimmy put the piece of greasy chicken back on the barrow and followed Tommy sheepishly. He was starving. Unlike Tommy he hadn't eaten since the morning and his stomach was gurgling now, with only a few pints of Watney's inside it.

Tommy walked along, keeping up a stream of abuse.

'I don't fucking believe you, Jimmy! What next? Shall we have a break and watch the poxy find-the-lady bloke? Or, I know, how about we go and have our fucking fortunes told?'

They were approaching the area where the fighters were; a ring had been roped off and the money men were milling around. Tommy spotted Ronnie Olds by a small marquee. He signalled to his men and they all surged forward together. Ronnie was busy taking bets and didn't see Tommy 'til it was too late. Tommy was beside him with a false smile on his face and a dangerous grip on Ronnie's arm. Looking at the old woman who was trying to place a bet, he said, 'Sorry, love, this bookie just closed. You'll have to go somewhere else.'

The woman, a known penny lender, looked at Tommy in temper and said: 'Balls! I wanna place a bet. I've been queueing for half an hour!'

Tommy looked down at her and said between gritted teeth: 'Fuck off, Grandma, or I'll shove your money right up your arse!'

People began to move away then, guessing there was trouble afoot. It was Ronnie Olds' trouble and not theirs. The old woman contemptuously spat at Tommy's feet and went along to the next bookie, complaining loudly.

Tommy pushed Ronnie into his marquee and the two men faced one another.

'You're out of order, Lane. You've no business coming here and pushing me around.'

'Bollocks, Ronnie. All I hear lately is you and the Campbells and that slag Bolger. Well, tonight's the night I pay my fucking debts, and I'm starting with you, matey.'

Ronnie Olds was a big man, big and cumbersome. Tommy knew this and had planned accordingly. Pulling a boning knife from his waistband, he slashed it across Ronnie's beer belly. The blade went in about an inch. Ronnie watched in dismay as blood began to seep out. The boning knife was so sharp he hadn't even felt any discomfort. But he was cute enough to know the pain would come. He held his stomach with both hands, unsure whether the knife had cut deep enough to spill out his guts. Once they left the body you were dead. White-faced, he staggered back, his heart beating too fast, sweat appearing on his forehead.

Tommy slashed him again, lengthwise this time. Making a red cross on his stomach.

'You fucking ponce! You thought you could fuck me up, didn't you? You thought that Bolger was the dog's bollocks. Well, he ain't, mate. He ain't, but I am. You want violence, I'll give it to you. I'm gonna take out every one of you, even your fucking drunken old man. You want fear, well, I'll make sure you get more than you ever dreamt of in your poxy little life!'

He took the knife and wiped it across Ronnie's face. Slicing through the skin until the cheek flapped down exposing the bone.

Both men stared at Briony as she walked into the tent with Mariah Jurgens.

'Hurts, don't it, Ronnie? Stings I should imagine. Well, thanks to you one of my girls was tortured like that by your mate Willy Bolger. Now, where is he? Tommy's mob-handed and so are we. Me and Mariah just picked up every piece of shite in the Arab quarter of the docks. So you'd better start talking or we'll just round up your brothers and cut them 'til they tell us what we want to know. Won't we, Tommy?'

He stared in amazement at Briony and Mariah. They stood there, dressed up to the nines without a flicker of fear on their faces. Mariah grinned maliciously.

'By the way, Ronnie, we've rounded up Micky Campbell too. He's outside in my car now with Marcenello, the Maltese hero. An Arab friend of mine is watching them for me. You know big Kousan, don't you, Ronnie? He's the one who chased you off his manor with a meat cleaver not six months ago when you was trying to get into the dock industry. Well, he don't like you and I think we can safely say, you don't like him. So tell us where Bolger is.'

Ronnie looked at the three people in the room. He was gradually feeling a faintness stealing over him. Not just from the loss of blood but at the realisation that here were three people who could not let him live after this night's work. It was all Bolger's doing, with his packed wallet and his smarmy tongue. He was as good as dead, and he knew it. Being a nasty man, if he was going he wanted to take as many with him as possible.

'He's round Valence Road. Bethnal Green. He's staying with a girl of his, Gilda the Pole. You'll find him there. But he's well protected. The Jews are seeing to that.'

Outside the fight was in full swing and the crowd screamed for blood. That meant an opponent was down. Briony, Mariah and Tommy left the tent without a second look at Ronnie who was still trying to hold his guts inside the large gaping hole across his belly. Ronnie Olds had lived by fear all his life. He was a known villain who dealt out death like other people dealt out cards. Now he was coming to the end of his life, inside a marquee in Victoria Park, a pile of money in his wallet and a bottle of whisky in his pocket. He slumped to the floor and, pulling out the whisky bottle, drank from it eagerly.

He died as he had lived, violently, and there was no one to mourn his passing.

Pushing through the crowds who were eagerly shouting encouragement to the two fighters on the stage, Briony fought down the urge to vomit. As bad as Ronnie Olds was, the sight of him bleeding like that made her ill.

She breathed in the stench of the unwashed bodies around her, the old sweat mingling with the new, the heavy aroma of food cooking on braziers, and the sweet smell of candyfloss and rock, and she emptied her stomach just as she approached her car. As she heaved, Mariah rubbed her back gently.

'Listen, Briony, if he had his way, he'd have stood and watched you die in agony. I know Ronnie from the old days. Put it out of your mind. He deserved it. And if Tommy hadn't done it, someone else would have.'

Briony slipped into her car, aware that Tommy had not spoken a word to her which was a sign of his anger. Closing her eyes she sat back in the car as they all made their way to Valence Road. Ginelle's face danced in front of her eyes, in her ridiculous cloche hat and her silk flapper dresses. And that imitation posh accent she had tried so hard to acquire.

By the time she reached her destination she felt infinitely

better, her resolve strong in her once more. She had to frighten people enough so that nothing like this ever happened again. She lived in a violent world where the law of the street was the only law you could live by and survive. Well, she'd made up her mind that was exactly how she would live from now on. She would rule through fear. No one would ever touch her or anyone to do with her again.

At the entrance to Valence Road Briony, Tommy and Mariah directed their respective men. Jimmy Reynard and two others, Abel and Kevin Rafferty, were to watch the back entrance to Gilda's house. The men rushed off to take up their positions. Micky Campbell and Marcenello sat terror-stricken in Mariah's car. Kousan, the undisputed leader of the Arabs, sat smiling at them, his huge head seemingly split by a wide grin. His men had stayed at Victoria Park and were rounding up the men belonging to Olds, Campbell and Marcenello. It was a well-planned and well-executed operation.

Mariah and Kousan were old friends and old adversaries. But he had listened to Mariah and Briony and had been persuaded into taking part in this war because he trusted them. It benefited him to have a good relationship with whoever run the East End. No one, but no one, got near the docks unless he allowed it. Anything that went missing off the ships went to him; he had no interest in prostitution whatsoever although a few of the dock dollies were under his protection. That was because they were with Arab men, or had given birth to Arab children at some point. He would enjoy having a good relationship with this Tommy Lane and Briony. It could only benefit them all.

An added bonus was that he could pay back a few debts of his own tonight, starting with Micky Campbell. He hated the Campbells and they hated him.

At this moment Micky was terrified because for the first time ever he was on his own, without a weapon, his brothers or his formidable mother, who was the real brains behind the Campbell businesses.

He and Marcenello watched as Briony, Tommy and Mariah

walked down to Gilda's little terraced house. Gilda the Pole was a woman of uncertain age with a pronounced limp who catered to the lower echelons of the docks, the African sailors and the Chinese. She was a small woman with a beautiful peach skin, and the worst temper this side of the water.

She was called 'the Pole' because she'd had polio which had left the limp, and had no other known last name.

The women's heels tapped on the pavement and Tommy heard the sound with his temper bubbling up inside him. When he got Briony home he was going to slap her face for her, hard. When she had walked into that marquee he had felt such a fool. So annoyed he could easily have throttled her.

This was men's work, they were dealing with the lowest of the low, and as much as he respected her cunning and her bravery, he couldn't forgive her for turning up there with those Arabs and that bleeding lanky bitch Jurgens! It made him look soft. As if he held on to her apron strings. His temper was so hot he nearly knocked Gilda's neat green front door into the hallway when he hammered on it.

Willy had seen their approach through the small front room window, and taking a gun he ran out to the kitchen, telling Gilda to open the door and try and stall them.

As she opened the front door, she flicked her head and said: 'He's trying to do a poodle out the back door. He's got a gun, and the hump. What more can I say?'

Outside in the yard Willy looked at the three men waiting for him and, hearing Gilda's opening words at the door, knew he was finished. He was supposed to have an armed guard here and there was no one but Lane's men. He looked around in the hope a couple of his minders would appear from the woodwork, but he knew instinctively that they were long gone. He didn't hold out any hope that any were sitting outside or watching from the road. The Jews had abandoned him. They obviously knew something he didn't. He could try and shoot his way out but he would be dead in seconds. It was the end of the line and he knew it.

He had been so close to achieving his aims! So very close.

Now it was all falling down around his ears. The thought amused him even in his terrified state and he began to laugh. As Tommy appeared at the back door, he grinned at him.

'Hello, Tommy boy. I hear you've been looking for me?'

Then, as Tommy watched, he put the barrel of the gun in his mouth, curling his tongue around the metal and still laughing as he pulled the trigger.

He had cheated them of his death and they were still none the wiser as to who had been backing him.

Going to the lifeless form, Tommy began to kick it in his rage. Briony and Mariah walked out with Gilda. Turning to Briony, Tommy bellowed: 'You lot had to stick your beaks in, didn't you? Well, he's brown fucking bread now, so that's an end to it. If you don't mind I'll sort out Campbell and the others. Or do you want me to put me hand up and ask permission first?'

With that he pushed through them and went out through the house. Jimmy and Abel looked at one another, eyebrows raised, before they left.

Mariah put her hand on Briony's arm.

'He's upset.'

Before Briony could answer, Gilda shouted: 'So what? I'm upset! That fat bastard was paying me a small fortune for staying here. Now I've got to get the Old Bill and report a fucking suicide!'

Looking at the little woman in front of her, standing awkwardly with all her weight on her good leg, Briony started to laugh. A laugh that rapidly turned to tears. Taking her by the arm, Mariah walked her back to her car.

Pulling away from Mariah, Briony went to Tommy and said in a low voice: 'All right, big shot, so you're annoyed, but think on this. Where the fuck are the Jews? They were supposed to be protecting him, remember? Someone got here first, mate. Bolger thought he was running out to help and security. There wasn't a soul there but us. Think about it. Come on, Mariah, we'll leave the big boys to their little games.'

When the women left, Tommy got into Mariah's car. It was

208

being driven by her minder, Big John. Nodding at Kousan, Tommy said to the men: 'As you can probably see, I'm fucking fuming so don't bugger me about because I ain't in the mood. I've got two dead men and no explanations. So have a good think before you open your traps!'

Campbell and Marcenello had no intention of aggravating Tommy Lane any more than was necessary.

They both began to talk at once.

Chapter Fifteen

Ma Campbell was sixty-eight, with a face like a walnut, and black hair liberally sprinkled with grey worn piled up on her head in a neat French pleat. As always she was in a shapeless grey dress, covered over by a large apron which crossed over her pendulous breasts and was tied in a neat bow around her waist. Her feet were swollen, and bulged out of carpet slippers cut at the side to allow her bunions free rein. She had just made her husband and herself a ham sandwich, and was settling by her kitchen fire waiting for her boys to come home and tell her the evening's doings.

As the door knocker was slammed against the wood she heaved herself out of her chair. Walking along her hallway, she bellowed: 'All right, all right, for fuck's sake! I ain't deaf!'

Pulling open her front door she closed her gaping mouth as she saw Mariah Jurgens and Briony Cavanagh standing there. She drew herself up to her full height and stood aggressively before them.

'Well, well, well, if it ain't the bleeding Tarts' Society on me step!'

Briony and Mariah pushed her into her hallway in a flurry of bad language and shoves.

'Who you bleeding pushing, you pair of whores? My boys won't take no sodding nonsense, mate. They'll cut your tits off if you touch me.'

Briony grabbed the woman by her immaculate French pleat

211

and practically ran her into her kitchen.

'Shut up, Ma, before I lose me rag. Your Micky is at this moment in a car with Kousan the Arab and Tommy Lane, and I don't hold out much hope of him coming home.'

Da Campbell, as he was known, carried on eating his sandwich without glancing at them.

'Everyone knows you're the brains, Ma, so why don't you just calm down and tell us what we want to know? Believe me when I say we've had enough for one night and we're rapidly losing our patience.'

Ma Campbell was so incensed her face was a bright red and her hands were visibly shaking.

'I don't know fuck all! Now get yourselves and your cheap perfume out of my clean kitchen.'

Mariah slapped her across the face, hard, making her head roll back on to her shoulders.

'You bitch! Raise your hand to me, would you?'

As Ma made to grab at Mariah, Briony took hold of her arm and twisted it up her back.

'Shut up, Nancy!' Da Campbell's voice was loud in the room and the three women stared at him.

'You bastard! You'd do a deal over your boy's life, wouldn't you? Wouldn't you?' The last two words ended on a scream.

Taking another bite of his sandwich, Da wiped his hands over his mouth and said through the food: 'If Kousan's got Micky, he's a dead man. I told him to steer clear of the screaming Ab Dads but he wouldn't listen. It's the other four boys I'm worried about now. What's gone on tonight?'

Briony pushed the old woman from her and shoved her into a chair. The tiny kitchen was silent as she began to talk.

'Ronnie Olds is dead. So is Willy Bolger. Me and Tommy come out in the open tonight, and believe me when I say we ain't having any more nonsense. This is our manor from tonight. There's no room any more for wasters or ponces. Anyone wants to work the East End, they've got to come to us. One of my girls was cut up and I ain't taking that lying down. No one touches me or mine and that goes for your precious fucking sons. It's all

212

over, finished with, but I have to know who the big man was, who Bolger was cultivating, because I won't rest easy until I've cut the bastard. You understand me? I want him, and I'll trade the rest of your boys for him.'

Da Campbell nodded, it was what he'd expected. Unlike his wife he had no personal feelings about anything. His boys were an extension of him and his own quest for survival; he was quite happy to sacrifice Micky for the good of the rest. Kousan had been one of his son's biggest mistakes and without doubt his biggest enemy. He had a grudging respect for these two women because to get the Arabs working side by side with you was an achievement.

Da Campbell swallowed the last of his food. Standing up he went to the fireplace. He picked up his pipe and tapped it against the bricks.

'I saw Bolger about a week since. He was with a gentleman, and I mean gentleman. I worked for him once – around the same time as your old man Briony, actually. Do you know, I remember you when you had the shit still running down your legs! Always had that flaming red hair though, even as a baby. Who'd have thought you'd have turned out like you did?'

Briony wasn't listening now. She knew who he was talking about but until she heard him voice the name she wouldn't rest.

'Who was the man? Tell me his name.'

'It was Henry Dumas. I was going down the Old Kent Road, up by The Apples and Pears. You can put on a good bet in there without the hag of getting paid out with an hammer. I saw them together. Now what would them two want with one another? I thought. But I knew straight off. My Micky was a prat. He should have taken Bolger's money and wasted the little shit. Never liked ponces, never. Dirty two-faced bastards, the majority. Whoring's a woman's game, the money's too easy. Bad as my boys are, they don't live off no tarts. You ladies know the game better than any man, I'll bet. And you've got the muscle behind you.'

Ma Campbell listened to her husband and then turned on him viciously.

'Hark at him! The bleeding oracle. By Christ, Da, you've sunk low before but, dear God, tonight you've sunk to the depths. Your son is sitting somewhere with that Arab bastard and you're telling this pair of whores what they wanna know!' Her voice was drenched with tears. Micky was her first-born, her baby. She knew he would never walk in her house again, never be there when she woke up, never speak to her again, and it broke her heart. Mariah patted her shoulder gently.

'Don't you touch me! I'll never forgive you for the news you brought here tonight. My boy's dead. My beautiful boy . . .'

Briony stared at the woman before her, at the tears bubbling out from underneath her closed lids, and felt a stirring of pity inside her. If her son was to die, was to die in fear and terror, without her near to try and help, to try and protect him, she would feel the same as this old woman before her. As bad as Ma Campbell was, and God himself knew she was a vicious woman, she loved her children. She had robbed, schemed and threatened to give her boys what she considered a good life. That meant plenty to eat, good clean clothes on their backs, and shoes or boots on their feet. Unless you were born as low as them, you couldn't understand in a million years what an achievement that was.

'You'll see me other boys come home, won't you now?'

Briony nodded at the man, who bit his lip and half smiled. 'Then there's nothing to do now but wait for the body to turn up.'

Mariah touched Briony's arm and silently the two women left the house, the only sound the heart-wrenching sobbing of Ma Campbell, which followed them out into the night.

Briony sat in her bedroom with a large glass of brandy in her hand and a cigarette dangling from her lips. She looked ugly and full of hate. Since finding out about Henry Dumas, she had felt a canker growing inside her. With every second the clock ticked, the feeling grew. She was now full of it, it consumed her until she was ready to burst. Everything she had ever suffered at his hands was there in front of her eyes in crystal clear detail. His flabby body, his roughness as he took her, the putrid stench of his breath on her face.

She'd been a child, and she had thought as a child. She had thought to save herself and her family from poverty by letting him have her. But he should have known how wrong he was, her father should have known! How could she have realised what she was doing? All she had wanted was the warmth of the house, the good food, the cleanliness. She had wanted it for herself and her sisters, and Dumas had made use of that. But what a price she had paid, still paid.

He had taken her child, and before that he had taken her very heart. Had helped strangle every natural instinct she possessed. Until now she was empty.

But she would pay him back. Dear God, she would pay him back tenfold, a hundredfold for what he had done to her. What he had tried to do to her.

She heard Tommy enter the house and held her breath. The front door was banged hard; she could even hear him throw his coat across the banisters, the buttons making a snapping sound as they hit the wooden balustrade. She heard him stamping up the stairs, heard Mrs Horlock's light tread on the landing and her voice as she spoke to him.

'What's all the noise? What's going on? Briony's not fit for man or beast, like a madwoman . . .'

'GO TO BLEEDING BED!' Tommy's voice echoed around the hallway, sending the old woman scurrying away.

Briony tensed in her chair, waiting for the onslaught that was to come. Tommy opened the bedroom door and it banged against the dado rail with a sickening thump.

She watched him as he walked into the room, his face set, his hair standing on end as if he had received a massive shock.

'You mare! You showed me up tonight, Briony. Never have I felt so embarrassed, so small. You charged in there like I didn't mean anything, I was nothing! I don't work for you, madam, let's get that straight. We're a partnership! A partnership. I ain't your fucking lackey, I ain't no one's lackey.'

He pushed his face close to hers. She could see the tiny veins

215

in his eyes and almost taste his breath as he bellowed. 'You ever do that to me again, put yourself in the frame like that, and I'll give you the biggest slap you've ever had in your life. Do you hear me?'

Briony took a long drag on her cigarette and blew the smoke into his face.

'Yes, Tommy. I can hear you, mate. The whole of Barking can hear you.' She pushed him from her with a strength that surprised him. Standing, she pointed at him with the cigarette.

'All I ever hear is *you*. You, me, I – sodding Tommy Lane! Well, for once I ain't interested. I've got a bit more on my mind than your stupid fucking worries about saving face. As you just said we're supposed to be a partnership so that gives me the right to do what I want, go where I want, and have a say in what I want too! *That's* a partnership, boy. Not sitting home like a fucking wife while you run around being the hero!

'And while you was ducking and diving tonight, running round like a blue-arsed fly, I went round and saw Ma and Da Campbell. It's Dumas we want Tommy. Henry Dumas. Da Campbell saw him and Bolger having a meet and put two and two together. So why don't you calm yourself down and use your head instead of your arse for once? Only I would be interested to know what the other half of this so-called partnership has to say about that?'

Even in her grief she was secretly pleased to see Tommy deflated by her words.

He was shaken and disturbed.

'Dumas?' His voice was low, incredulous.

'The very one.' She stubbed out her cigarette and immediately lit another, pulling the smoke into her lungs with a ferocity that stunned him. 'I want him. I want that bastard once and for all. I don't care if he has got a father-in-law who's a fucking lord, I couldn't care less if he is the Prime Minister or fucking King Street Charlie, I want that bastard cut!'

'Oh, Briony, come here, love . . .'

She screwed up her eyes and clenched her fists, her whole body tense.

'Don't try and make it right with me, Tommy, please. I don't want a cuddle or kind words, they don't mean nothing. I want that bastard prostrate in front of me. I want to pay him back for me, for my emptiness, for Ginelle, and most of all for daring to try and tuck me up.'

She looked at him and he couldn't meet her eyes. Couldn't acknowledge what he saw there: the pain and unhappiness. And the lust for revenge. She wanted revenge and he knew she would get it, with or without him. All the anger seemed to seep from his powerful frame in seconds. Compared to what she had suffered at that man's hands, his own feelings were as nothing.

'We'll get him, girl. Between us we'll get him, I promise you that.'

It was what she wanted to hear. The burden of her thoughts was lifted, shared now and taken on by Tommy. Walking to him, she let herself be pulled into his embrace. Over his shoulder she watched the cigarette smoke curling up in tendrils in the empty air and saw the faces of Ronnie Olds and Willy Bolger. Tomorrow Tommy and she would be the undisputed King and Queen of the East End, and the knowledge made her feel sad and bitter. It was a title she had never craved, wanting respectability through her clubs and money-making schemes. Now she would have to keep the title and fight for it, otherwise Dumas and people like him could get to her once more. Could try and force her back to the gutter she had crawled out of. Sometimes things were forced on you, and you had to bear the consequences. It was the story of her life.

Finally, after what seemed an age, she cried.

Benedict Dumas watched his father's moustaches quivering as he sat in his chair reading his daily paper. He pushed his own food around his plate, unable to stomach the kidney and scrambled eggs. He liked a boiled egg and bread and butter, his father knew this, but forced the kidneys on him every morning and waited until he ate them.

'What are you staring at, boy? Eat your food.'

'Yes, Papa.'

Henry clenched his teeth in anger. Every time the boy called him 'Papa' he fought the urge to beat him. He had to acknowledge the child. His father-in-law doted on him, his wife adored him, even the blasted servants pandered to him. Henry hated the sight of him. Hated what he represented.

Banging his fist down on the table he shouted: 'Eat your breakfast, boy!'

Isabel walked into the room with the mail and the atmosphere immediately lightened. Benedict smiled at his mama, and she kissed him on his cheek lightly.

'Your grandpapa is coming today to take you to see the trains at Paddington. Then, I believe, he is taking you to the zoological gardens!'

'Oh, Mama, how splendid! I'd better not eat too much breakfast as he always buys me an enormous lunch.'

Henry gritted his teeth and carried on with his pretence at reading the paper.

'No, darling. Leave that now and run up to your room and get your lessons prepared for Mr Bartlet. He has kindly allowed you to miss French today, but you must make up for it tomorrow.'

'I will, Mama.'

Isabel's eyes twinkled as the boy looked at her with the special conspiratorial look reserved for when Henry was near them. Already Benedict knew the set-up in the house. His father was a terror to the face, and a joke behind his back.

Isabel watched her husband as he tucked into his bacon, eggs and sausages. She had aged a great deal since the arrival of Benedict in her household. At first Isabel had been shunned by her so-called friends and contemporaries. But as her father had become besotted with the child and rumours had begun circulating that the child was actually his and not Dumas', people had begun to call again and life had resumed its normal pattern. Isabel adored the boy; she saw him as the only thing in her life she actually possessed wholly. He was also a stick to beat Henry with and she took delight in this, surprising herself with the keenness with which she pitted her wits against her husband.

218

Now the child was ten, he ate with them, as a boy was expected to at a certain age, was allowed to greet company, and was being trained in the niceties of being a young man of wealth and good family. The latter made her smile in her darker moments, knowing his stock so well: a father who was enamoured of little girls and a mother who was a whore of the first water. She shunned Briony now, hated thinking about the girl who had borne him. He was her son, wholly her son.

Henry's fork crashing on to his plate distracted her from her reverie and she looked at him, the animosity between them tangible in the confines of the room.

Folding up his paper, he stood and left the room without a word or a backward glance. Pouring herself more coffee, Isabel smiled and mentally chalked up another victory to herself.

Joshua was eating his lunch at The Chequers Inn. As always he had a pint of brown ale, and pie, peas and mash. He was swallowing down the last of his peas when his friend Billy Buggins started chattering about events of the previous night.

'Anyway, seems that Tommy Lane went to Victoria Park and caused all sorts! I heard this morning that Ronnie Olds is dead, Micky Campbell, Marcenello and Willy Bolger! Though no one's gonna miss him! Cut Ronnie Olds up right under his brothers' noses they did. The Old Bill has been crawling around like maggots on a bit of rancid bacon. Well, they ain't gonna find out nothing, are they? No one's gonna put their face in the frame for the likes of them, I ask you. That Briony Cavanagh was there by all accounts, with the big Swede Jurgens. Now there's two women I wouldn't fancy . . .'

His voice trailed off and Joshua wiped his tongue around his teeth before saying: 'Go on, Billy. Finish what you was going to say.'

Billy was terrified – not of Joshua, he had known Joshua for years. He was terrified of the fact Joshua was soon to be a part of that set-up too. He was marrying Briony's sister.

'Say what you was going to say, Billy, I ain't going to have a go nor nothing. I want to know what you was going to say.'

Billy was as red as a beetroot, even his neck was flushed. 'I never meant nothing by it, Joshua, everyone knows Eileen's a good kid. I mean, she can't help her stock, can she? Can any of us?'

This was a veiled reference to Joshua's father and he digested the words before he said: 'In future, Billy, think before you open your mouth. I'm a peaceable man but my wife's family is soon to be my family and I can't listen to anyone bad-mouthing them, can I?'

Billy shook his great head furiously. 'No, Josh . . . You're right, I was out of order.'

Joshua smiled and carried on eating his food.

But he was worried. Eileen's sisters had not really played a part in his life, not yet anyway. But all he had heard this morning was how Briony and Tommy Lane had taken on the hard men and won. It was just occurring to him that his sweet-faced Eileen, with her angelic face and compliant nature, might be more trouble than she was worth.

Bernadette and Kerry were sorting through a pile of clothes together. They'd had a truce since Kerry had made it plain she would brook no trouble. Bernie for her part was frightened of her sister now. Besides being her employer, she was Bernie's ticket out of the East End. Evander was not discussed by mutual consent and they played a game that everything was as it had been, though both knew that to regain their old easy footing would be impossible now. They walked around each other carefully, weighing up their words and phrases. It was exhausting for them both.

Now, though, they had a subject they could discuss freely: the events of the night before in Victoria Park.

'Our Briony's got it all now, Kerry. She's number one, the business as they say.'

Kerry nodded. 'Yes, our Briony is up there with the hard men. Jesus wept, I never thought she'd stoop to murder! I thought she was strictly a good-time girl, a madam. Oh, Bernie, what on earth will all this come to?'

She shook her head.

'Our Briony was always a law unto herself, you know that. It's why she got as far as she did and took us with her. We'll just have to hope she can take on contenders for her crown, because there'll be plenty of them, once the novelty wears off. She'll spend her whole life looking over her shoulder now.'

Kerry looked down at the dress she was holding and bit her lip. If Briony looked over her shoulder and saw Evander, what would happen then?

Chapter Sixteen

St Martin's Church was full. Ginelle's coffin was closed, the lid
screwed tightly down. Briony stood at the front of the church
with Tommy, Ginelle's mother and her elder children taking the
second pew. Briony's eyes strayed constantly to the coffin,
knowing exactly what was inside it. She heard the muffled sobs
of her girls, and the vicar's droning voice.

Unlike a Catholic Mass, with its pomp and ceremony, the
Church of England service seemed very shallow and unfeeling to
Briony. The vicar, a dour man in his sixties, kept referring to
Ginelle as 'the young lady', as if frightened to admit any kind of
association with her. There were no hymns, no real prayers, and
as far as Briony was concerned, no emotion. She grasped
Tommy's hand for warmth. He squeezed it tightly, as if
knowing the battle raging inside her, the guilt she felt. Ginelle's
death was her fault. Ginelle had become a valuable asset,
appearing in the films with Jonathan la Billière. She had been
the girl of everyone's dreams. Bolger had killed her because she
was worth money to Briony, a lot of money. If Briony hadn't
decided to branch out into the films, Ginelle would have still
been just a Tom. Would still be walking around with her phony
accent and her outlandish clothes.

Recognition of this caused her a great deal of concern.
Though Briony had fought for Ginelle, and now guaranteed her
girls a much safer life, she still couldn't rest easy in her bed. Not
even with the reassuring presence of Tommy beside her.
Because in her mind's eye, in the dark, she once more saw

Ginelle in the crate. Smelt the sticky blood. Saw the terrified face on the dead girl. Now there were other faces too. Bolger's, Marcenello's, Campbell's and Ronnie Olds'. Ronnie holding his guts inside the gaping hole of his belly. As soon as this service was over, and Ginelle had been laid to rest, she was going to go round and see the bastard who was behind all the carnage, and the death. She forced herself to concentrate and began praying.

Tommy watched as her lips moved in silent prayer, not at all sure what exactly he was doing in this church, burying a working girl. He sighed heavily. Briony gave him a quick look out of the corner of her eye and, feeling ashamed, he tried valiantly to remember a prayer from his childhood. As he began his 'Our Father' he smiled to himself. Only Briony could get the new governor of the East End to a whore's burial. But that's what he had always loved about her: her dogged determination to do what she considered right and just.

He finished his prayer and hastily blessed himself, feeling a glow of righteousness go through him. Then, bored once more, he concentrated his thoughts on Henry Dumas, and contemplated the vicar who was saying nothing and taking far too bloody long about it.

Henry sat in his office and looked over a pile of papers. His secretary, Miss Barnes, a recent acquisition, stood nervously by waiting for his approval. Henry took his time, enjoying her discomfiture. He had no real need of a woman in his workplace, but it was now the done thing. She stood there in front of him in her long grey skirt, high button boots and a sensible white blouse, her brown hair tied at the back with a black velvet ribbon, her hands clasped demurely together. At least she didn't smoke. He couldn't abide seeing women smoke.

'They'll do, Miss Barnes.' He held the papers out for her without looking up and the girl hastily took them and departed. Henry rested his elbows on his desk and glanced at the heavy mahogany clock on the wall. It was a quarter to five. He grinned to himself, contemplating the little girl waiting for him at a small house in Upney Lane. He decided to leave early and walk to his destination. It was only fifteen minutes from the dock offices. Nodding at Miss Barnes, he left the building.

Briony and Tommy watched him leave, buttoning his coat. They watched him walk down to the corner of the street and walk into a small shop. He came out five minutes later with a brightly coloured box of sweets. Briony felt her heart stop dead in her chest.

It was as if she was a child again and Henry was coming to visit her, with his little treats and presents. She gripped Tommy's hand on the steering wheel and whispered: 'Follow him, let's see where he's going.'

He shrugged and started up the car, the urgency in her voice communicating itself to him.

'He's got a girl, Tommy. The bastard bought sweets, and from what Sally's said they're not for Benedict. He can't stand the sight of the child. He used to bring me bits and pieces. The bastard, the dirty bastard!'

They followed him, matching his brisk pace. As he turned into Upney Lane, Briony held her breath inside her chest until it hurt. Henry's pace quickened and when he opened a small wooden gate and practically danced up the path, she felt the rage build inside her. The front door was opened by a young woman. Briony squinted. She looked familiar. The woman greeted Dumas effusively, and when the door shut behind them, Briony and Tommy emerged from their car on to the dirt road.

'I'll kill him , Tommy. I swear to you, I'll kill him!'

'Calm down. We'll go in and find out the score. There'll be no killing here today. If we top him it'll cause us too much trouble. It's a warning we're here to deliver, right?'

Briony stared into his face and the misery she displayed made Tommy want to wring Henry Dumas' neck.

'I hate him! I hate him from the very bones, do you know that? Even Olds, as bad as he was, deserved to live over that bastard. Had more right to life.'

Pulling away from Tommy, she walked over to the house purposefully, banging open the little wooden gate and tramping up the neat path as quick as her legs would carry her. Tommy followed her, a feeling of foreboding inside him.

This was more than a revenge. Briony was facing her own personal demons today, he understood that, and as the front door opened, he put his hand inside his coat and caressed the policeman's truncheon he had placed there earlier. He had a good few scores to settle this day himself.

Christine Howell opened the door smiling, her big moon face split in a grin that rapidly disappeared as she saw the two people standing before her.

'Where is he?' Briony's voice was tight.

'Who?' Christine's voice was high. Fright mingled with confusion making her panic.

'Who? Who do you fucking think! That nonsense who just walked in here!'

Pushing past the terrified girl, she opened the first door she came to. Bursting into the room, she stopped dead. Sitting by a blazing fire, his face drained of colour, was Henry Dumas, on his lap a little dark-haired girl of nine. Her hands were still clutching the box of sweets, her face a mask of dismay.

As if just realising the child was there, Dumas pushed her from him as if she was red hot, emptying her from his lap on to the carpet with a thump.

'What are you doing here?' His voice was high and incredulous. His mouth moved again, but this time no sound emerged. Henry Dumas was literally lost for words. As his eyes burned into Briony's he became aware of Tommy Lane picking the little girl up and leading her from the room. Heaving himself from the chair, he stood up, shoulders back, and in his most commanding voice, shouted: 'Leave that child alone! Now take yourself and this . . . this . . . slut back where you came from!'

His voice and demeanour triggered a reaction from Briony. He dared to shout at them? He dared to stand there in this house and order them out?

She flew at him, hair and nails flying. Instinctively she went for his face, dragging her nails through the soft plump skin of his cheeks, feeling it tear, a superhuman strength flowing through her body. As small as she was, she forced him to the floor. His

226

utter shock at being attacked gave Briony the edge over him. As Henry hit the carpet, his hands trying desperately to hold her clawing fingers away from him, Briony kicked him in the stomach.

He let go of her to hold himself and she picked up the poker from the embers of the fire and brought it crashing down on to his head, the smell of his singeing hair permeating the room. Raising the poker up over her head again she brought it down on to his shoulders and back, again and again, every blow easing the pain inside her until, spent, she looked down on to his bloody face and dropped the poker with a dull thud. She closed her eyes tightly, savouring the moment.

In the recesses of her mind she heard him groan and was aware he was still alive. Her breath was coming in deep gulps, a hoarse whisper escaping from her lips with each gasping breath. Her chest hurt, her arms ached, but she felt a sort of peace descend on her body as she stared at the man before her.

'You'll never do to anyone what you did to me, are you listening?' Her voice was low in the room. The three people at the door watched her in the firelight with a strange fascination. 'You tried to ruin me, Henry, and you failed, you'll always fail, because as God is my witness, the next time I have any dealings with you, you'll die. Ronnie Olds is dead, so's Bolger. You've no one and nothing on your side now. All you have left is me, and I'm gonna watch you from now on, mate. If you so much as shit I'll know what colour it is. That will be my revenge on you, boy. I'll see you never play your little games again.'

Henry looked up at her, and even through his pain he realised that in trying to destroy her, he had inadvertently destroyed himself.

'You so much as breathe at Benedict and I'll hear about it. I've eyes in your house and in your workplace. My boy is all I have in the world, and thanks to you and Isabel I have to look after him from afar. Well, you'll toe the line after tonight, Henry big man Dumas. You'll be a proper father to him. If you so much as look at him out of place, I'll ring your fucking neck. Do you understand me?'

227

He looked up at her, his face and mouth bleeding profusely.

'DO YOU UNDERSTAND ME?'

Her voice echoed around the room and Henry nodded, the action making him wince.

'You sicken me. You make me hate like I've never hated before. You made me what I am today, and I'll never forgive you for it.'

She turned from him and walked to the door. Looking into Christine Howell's face, she sneered, 'I know you.' She looked at Tommy who was still watching her with awe. 'We went to school together, we was in the same class.' Then, taking back her arm, she slapped the woman a heavy blow to the side of her face.

'You dirty bitch, you'd give your little child to him? Your own flesh and blood!' The little girl, her face pressed into Tommy's thigh, began to whimper. Briony shook her head in wonder.

'She's a beautiful child, and you'd let him touch her! You'd deliver her to him on a plate. Well, your game's over now. You and that child are leaving this drum tonight. I don't care where you go or what you do, Christine, but I'll keep my eye on this little girl. I'll make sure you look out for her or you'll answer to me. By Christ, you'll answer to me!'

Kerry watched Evander talking to Glennford. She smiled over at them and waved. They waved back and grinned at her, but Glennford's grin was forced.

'I'm telling you, Evander, you're in over your head, boy. From what I have been told, her dear sister, our employer, is now some kind of gang boss here. Her and that Tommy wasted four men the other night! They're bad people to mess with, and you're sleeping with her kid sister.'

Glennford's face was covered with a thin sheen of sweat. Since hearing the talk about Briony and Tommy he had become very worried for his friend, and not a little concerned for himself and the other members of his band. Mud tended to stick in his experience, and the mud would be flying in all directions if

Evander's association with Kerry Cavanagh came to light.

'I'll sort it out, don't worry.' Evander's voice was low. His athletic body moved away with speed and easy grace. Glennford stared after him, a feeling of foreboding inside him.

Evander walked to Kerry and smiled at her.

'You look beautiful.'

Kerry smiled up into his eyes and gave a low throaty chuckle.

'So do you.' Without thinking what she was doing, Kerry put up her fingers and touched his face gently.

Glennford watched the exchange and felt the feeling of foreboding once more.

'You look as white as a ghost, Briony. Are you drinking enough milk?'

Molly's voice was beginning to annoy Briony. Taking a deep breath, she said: 'Give it a rest, Mum. It's been a hectic few days.'

Molly wiped Rosalee's face with a handkerchief and grinned. 'It has that, child. Oh, you should have seen the way I was treated down the Lane. Like visiting royalty. "Yes, Mrs Cavanagh. No, Mrs Cavanagh. And how's the girls, Mrs Cavanagh? Give Briony my regards, Mrs Cavanagh." Huh! The two-faced bastards. I can remember when I couldn't get a fecking smile outa them. When I had a shilling on a piece of string to see me through the week. Collecting the rotten veg from the gutters as they packed up for the day to keep you lot fed. While that drunken sod of a father pissed away the money in The Chequers . . .'

Briony put her hand up to her head and groaned.

'Oh, Mum, we're not going through all that again, are we? You're all right now, aren't you? You've got plenty of money now. Don't I see you all right?'

Molly looked at her daughter with concern.

'Jesus and Mary, you're a daughter any woman would be proud of. Look at the way you handle your businesses. But sometimes, when I remember how it was, how it could have been, I feel the old sadness creep over me. It's hard to see your babies hungry, you know. To hear them cry themselves to sleep. It's a sound that never leaves you. You hear it sometimes on the wind when it's whistling around your house. It still taps on the windows, taunting you in the cold weather.'

Briony smiled a smile she didn't think she had in her.

'Well, stop remembering! The old man's dead, and we're all alive and kicking. We've plenty. Even if I never made another penny we'd have enough to keep us all for the rest of our days. So stop worrying. Now, what's happening about Eileen?'

'Well, we thought we'd have the wedding in six weeks' time. I've booked the church, and she's waiting 'til you've a minute to yourself to help her pick the dress. You, Kerry and Bernie and Eileen can all go out together one day. What do you think?'

'That would be lovely. I know a dressmaker in Bond Street who'll knock her up a stunner. Real silk and all. She makes my clothes.'

Molly felt as if her heart would burst. Wait till she bragged about this to everyone! A real seamstress making Eileen's dress. She'd knock their eyes for them.

'I don't think it'll be long before our Kerry's giving us a bit of news. She's got a man or I'm Anne Boleyn. Do you know who he is, like?'

Briony shook her head.

'It's news to me. I've never seen her with a bloke. No one in particular anyway. There's a young fellow at the club . . . he's an Earl's son. A second son mind, so he won't get the title, but he's besotted with her. Moons over her all the time. But so far as I know he ain't got anywhere. She's a dark horse, old Kerry. She'll do her own choosing, her, and once she chooses, that'll be it.'

Molly smiled and nodded.

'An Earl's son. Oh, that would be nice, that would.'

'Anyone you think is gentry, as you put it, would do for you, wouldn't it? Even if he had a hump on his back and a club foot! Mum, believe me, they're no different from us. They eat, sleep and shit, same as we do. They just do it in nicer surroundings!'

Molly flapped her hand at her daughter and laughed out loud.

'I'd rather my girls did it in nicer surroundings as well. When I think of what we came from and where we are now. Well, I tell you, girl, it does me heart good. Even my Rosie looks a different girl.'

Rosalee, hearing her name, grinned and clapped her hands together.

'Bri, Bri.'

'She loves the bones of you, Briony. You've done so well, child. I couldn't have been happier at the way you've turned out. You lot could have been living in the basements now with four or five children hanging round your necks and the back of some bastard's hand round your lug on a Friday. But not my girls! I can look people in the face now and say: "Not my girls." My girls are women to be envious of, and believe me, people are envious of you. That Nellie Flanagan – well, it's like a poker up her arse to think of you lot and what you've become!'

Briony laughed despite herself.

'I hope you won't use expressions like that if Kerry does bring home an Earl's son!'

Molly grinned back and said in her best imitation of a posh voice: 'I'd say poker up her behind if I was in good company!'

They laughed together loudly, Briony's laugh bordering on the hysterical.

Molly wiped her eyes with the back of her hand and said seriously to her daughter, 'You're all right, Bri, aren't you? I mean, now you're like you are. It's what you wanted, isn't it?'

Briony felt an urge to tell her mother everything in her heart, but she knew Molly wouldn't want to hear it. So instead she lit herself a cigarette and said brightly, 'Of course I am! You're looking at the first female Baron of this town, and I intend to keep me title, Mother, no matter what. Me and Tommy have this place sewn up.'

Molly laughed in delight. That was exactly what she wanted to hear. After experiencing life with an influential daughter, a really influential daughter, she couldn't bear the thought of having her new position taken from her.

To Briony, this knowledge was just another cross to bear.

231

Briony walked into the warmth of The Windjammer and listened to the sounds of conversation and glasses rattling. Giving her coat to Donna, the hat check girl, she smiled at her briefly before entering the club itself.

It was full. People who couldn't find seats were standing around in small groups, breathing in cigarette smoke and perfume. She pushed through the throng, greeting people as she went. Not stopping to chat, she made her way to the small dance area, scanned the tables, and was surprised to see Tommy sitting with Rupert and Jonathan. She saw his flushed face and guessed he had been drinking. Jonathan noticed her and waved her over. His face was flushed and sweating too. Briony walked across the small dance floor and deliberately ignored the people watching her. She felt as if she was in a glass bubble, on show to the world. She sat beside Tommy and he kissed her on the lips.

She had dressed in a deep crimson dress which accentuated her white skin and green eyes. She looked startling, almost too bright. The colour gave her a brittle quality, her rouge a deep stain on her cheekbones, her lips a deep crimson to match her dress. Tommy eyed her for a few seconds before kissing her again, this time on her cheek.

'Hello, darlin'. Have a glass of champagne.'

She took the fluted glass from him and sipped the cold liquid. Then, tilting her head back, she drank it down, holding the glass out again for another drink.

Five glasses later she was having a friendly argument with Jonathan about the films they were going to make. He wanted art, she decided to be contrary and insist on porn. Tommy sat back and listened to them with a smile on his face.

She was holding up. He had counted on that. While she was sorting out her mind, coming to terms with herself and her actions, he had been organising their protection and their new workforce. Tommy had no qualms about what he had done. It was over with, finished, done. Briony was a different kettle of fish; she needed to adjust to her new status. But he knew that once she did, the two of them would be a dynamite team, and nothing and no one could ever stop them.

People dropped by their table to pay their respects. Men who would not normally have been seen dead in their club had made a pilgrimage to the West End to offer their support and friendship, and Briony gave them just the right amount of her time and her interest.

Tommy sat back and relaxed. She was holding up all right, as he had known she would. By the time Kerry had finished her second set, Briony looked positively relaxed.

Chapter Seventeen

Briony lay in the bed alone, her head thumping. She closed her eyes tightly to stem the pain. She could hear the sounds of the household coming from below, the heavy tread of Mrs Horlock on the stairs, and the rattling of crockery. Her bedroom door was pushed open and the tray of tea was placed on her night table. Without a word the older woman went to the heavy curtains and opened them, letting in the weak sunshine.

'What do you think you're doing?' Briony's voice was low and angry.

'What's it look like? You deaf now as well as stupid?'

Mrs Horlock bustled to the bed and began pouring out the strong tea. Kitchen tea, thick and black, which she knew Briony loved.

She squinted up at the woman and said: 'What did you just say?'

Mrs Horlock laughed loud. 'So, the dead arose and appeared to many! My God, you look terrible. Worse than a Saturday night whore on Monday morning. How long are you going to keep this up?'

Briony was blinking her eyes rapidly and straining to keep her temper.

'Keep what up?'

'Drink your tea.' She thrust out the white china mug, spilling a few drops on the bedspread.

Briony sat up in bed and, taking the mug, slammed it down on to the bedside table.

235

'Keep what up, I said? Answer me, woman!' Raising her voice made her wince and she held on to her head gently. 'Oh, piss off, I ain't in the mood.'

'Look at you, Briony. You look a disgrace. You've bags under your eyes big enough for me to get me weekly shopping in. Your skin's in a terrible state, no doubt due to your drinking like a fish and eating like a bird. You was thin before, fashionably thin, now you're like a scrawny cat! Even your hair's in rat's tails. And don't think you can talk to me any way you like because you can't. I've put up with your bad mouthing for the last month, and all I can say is, grow up!'

Briony sat up in the bed, stunned.

'How dare you . . .'

'I dare, young lady! I dare. Because you might be Miss Big out there, but to me you'll always be a child. You've drunk yourself stupid now for over a month. Out 'til all hours, coming in roaring drunk and upsetting the whole house. Arguing with Tommy like a demented woman.'

'This is my house . . .'

Mrs Horlock stuck her face close to Briony's and cut off her tirade.

'Well, you might just find yourself all on your own in it if you're not careful. Because you pull another stunt like you did last night and we'll *all* bugger off!'

Briony racked her brains to remember the night before. 'What happened last night?' Her voice was low now, bewildered.

'Huh! Last night you picked a fight with your new minders, Jimmy and David Harles. You woke up first the whole street, then the whole household, and you told Cissy to fuck off out of it at three o'clock this morning. You took a swing at Tommy, which is why he's not in bed beside you. I don't know where he went, but if it was to another woman, who could blame him.'

Briony groaned, it was all coming back to her slowly, in crystal clear pictures.

'My God.'

'Well, I'm glad you think of him as yours because I've a

236

feeling on me you just might need him. What's wrong with you, girl? You've been like a bear with a sore arse for weeks.'

Briony shook her head and said sadly, 'I really don't know. I feel like I'm going to explode or something. Since we had all the carry on with Olds, we've had people constantly sitting outside the house. I can't shit but I have to have a minder with me! I feel as if my whole life's in everyone else's hands but me own. Even the clubs had to tighten security, the houses have more locks on them than Fort Knox! The girls treat me differently. It's "Miss Cavanagh" this and "Miss Cavanagh" that. I feel like a freak.'

'Oh, my heart's bleeding for you. Don't give me all that old fanny, Briony. You made your bed, as the saying goes. And there's another saying might interest you: Don't play with the big boys unless you know the rules to their games.'

'Oh sod off!'

'Drink your tea and get washed, you smell like a drayman's cart! Then get yourself out of that bed and come and eat something. Your mother will be here soon, about the wedding. Not that you've shown much interest in that either this last few weeks!'

The old woman took the mug of tea and thrust it into her hands.

'Get that down your neck and I'll run you a bath, then you can apologise to Cissy and the minders as well. No one, no matter who they are, is above common courtesy. Remember that, young lady.'

She flounced from the room and Briony closed her eyes and sighed. The truth hurt, but sometimes it was a welcome pain. She drank her tea.

Molly sat with Eileen and Rosalee, her face dark. Briony walked into the room and smiled widely, ignoring the pain thumping in her head.

'Hello, Mum, Eileen.' Kneeling down she kissed Rosalee's face. 'Hello, Rosie.' Rosalee hugged Briony to her.

'This is a fine time to crawl out of bed, I must say, and your sister getting married.'

237

Briony laughed.

'What? You getting married today then, Ei? Have I missed the service?'

Eileen burst into tears and Briony realised something had gone drastically wrong.

'Sorry, Ei, I was only joking.' She put her arm around her sister's shoulders.

'It's that eejit Joshua. He wants to postpone the wedding now. It's that scut of a mother behind it, I swear. He turned up last night all sweetness and light, saying they should wait, it was all a bit quick, and he thought they should have a bit longer together courting. The bastard of hell! And there's me, making them tea and leaving them together while I went in to old Mother Jones'. When I came home I found this one crying and your man nowhere to be seen. I'd have scalped the face of him if I'd have seen him.'

Briony knelt before Eileen and said: 'Has he mentioned anything before now? Anything that would make you think he'd changed his mind?'

Eileen shook her head. 'He hasn't said a word, but he's been funny for weeks now. For the last month. It's as if I got the plague overnight or something. And his mother, she cut me dead the other day at Mass . . . She doesn't like me, Bri. I don't know why.' She dissolved into tears again.

Briony's face took on a hardness noticed by Molly. Both women were thinking the same thing. Joshua and his mother didn't want to be related to her, Briony, in her new role. It was bad enough when she owned the houses, though her offer of help in buying Joshua his own home had been gratefully accepted. But now they were actually frightened of becoming involved with the Cavanaghs whose name was synonymous with violence. Well, Joshua O'Malley would find out what violence meant before he was much older! Briony determined she would see to that personally.

Elizabeth O'Malley shook her head at her son. 'Sure, you're better off home with me. That Eileen was a pasty-faced bitch if ever I saw one. Not a spark of life in her at all. Jasus, she'd breed you mewling brats.'

Joshua stared into the fire. It was Eileen's passiveness that had attracted him, but his mother was right on one thing. The Cavanaghs were not a family to get tied to. Not now anyway.

'That Briony . . . a murdering hoor if ever one was born! Your father must be turning in his grave. All those girls with skirts up their nostrils and legs bare to the world!' His mother blessed herself fervently.

According to her, Joshua thought, his father must be like the Spinning Jenny in that grave of his. Yet he himself had been a rake who had been finally driven from the house by the harridan standing before Joshua now. His mother's first sight of Kerry and Bernadette with their lipstick and bare-legged mode of dressing had incensed her, especially the short Eton crop worn by Bernie.

'To think you would have been a part of them! You're well out of it, son. You're a young man with your whole life in front of you. There's plenty of girls who'd be grateful to you for taking them on.'

'Mother, I'm thirty-eight years old. Hardly a boy. And in case it's escaped your notice there hasn't exactly been a stream of women beating a path to my door.'

'Men are fools! They shouldn't marry 'til they're in their forties. Even then they have to be careful. A pretty face can hide a multitude of sins, you know. You have to look at the stock they come from. If that Briony Cavanagh comes around here shouting her mouth off, I'll fill it for her meself. I'm not scared of her, or any of them for that matter. Let them come and see what I'm capable of! My son will marry who he bloody well wants and it won't be a Cavanagh. Over my dead body! You hear me, over my dead body!'

Elizabeth O'Malley was in full swing when Briony walked in at the back door of the tiny terraced house in Longbridge Road. She stood in the scullery for a few seconds before she made herself known. As she stepped into the kitchen Elizabeth O'Malley nearly jumped from her skin in fright. Holding her

239

hand over her mouth, she whispered: 'Jesus cross of Christ!'

Briony smiled widely.

'I take it you wasn't expecting me then? Well, you should have been. You should have been sitting here with locked doors pretending you was out like I was the tally man coming for me money. Only unlike the tally man, the chances are if I don't hear what I want to hear, I'll break your fucking necks! Starting with you first, Mrs O'Malley.'

Joshua stared at the little woman in awe.

'Shut your mouth, Joshua. You look like you should be on a slab at Billingsgate market. What's this I hear about you dumping me sister after promising to marry her?'

Joshua just stared at the apparition in front of him.

'What my sister sees in you I don't even pretend to know, Joshua. But she wants you so she's going to have you, see. Because you strung her along, you asked her to marry you, and now I'll see to it personally that you do. You are going to get washed and spruced up, you're going round my mother's at seven-thirty tonight, and you're going to tell Eileen all that old fanny you gave her was just wedding nerves. Do you understand what I'm telling you?'

Joshua nodded.

'And you're going to do what I say?'

He nodded again.

'Good boy. Now another thing while we're on the subject. I don't want you, Mrs O'Malley, within a ten-mile radius of my sister. If I find out you've even touched her without Eileen's express permission, I'll rip your ugly head off your shoulders and give it to me henchmen to play footie with.' She smiled at them. 'Well, I'm glad we had this little chat. It's good for families to talk and get things sorted, don't you think? Now if you'll excuse me, I am a very busy lady and you've caused me enough trouble for one day.'

Tommy sat in the Dickens Club in Soho nursing a large scotch. He had earlier met a man called Siddy Trundley, a small Jew who took the bets for the traders in Soho Market and aroundabouts. He was hoping Tommy would come into his business with him so he could have the protection of Tommy's men and also some extra capital. Tommy had been agreeable, seeing the chance to expand the business and double the turnover. He would give one of his more intelligent minders the job of managing it for him. That way everyone was happy. Now he sat thinking about Briony and the night before. She had gone off with Jonathan and Rupert again and got roaring drunk, coming home in the small hours causing havoc. It was becoming a regular occurrence. He was wondering whether to chance giving her a right hander, as he put it to himself, when her voice startled him out of his reverie.

'You gonna drink that drink, Tommy, or get engaged to it?' She sat beside him, smelling of musk and orange flower water. 'I've been looking for you.'

'Really, Briony, what for? To call me a prickless wonder again? Or to try and scratch me eyes out? Only your histrionics are beginning to get on my tits, know what I mean?'

Briony licked her lips and opened her eyes wide. 'I'm sorry. Honestly, Tom, I'm deeply ashamed of what I did last night.'

He looked into her innocent face and barely controlled his desire to slap her.

'You're mugging me off, Bri, and I won't have it. It's not funny. Sitting there all wide-eyed and trying to make me laugh won't work this time. You have been pratting about for a month. You ain't done a full day's collar in the houses or the clubs since we took out Olds. Either you sort yourself out or me and you are finished, over with. I mean that.'

Briony sat up straighter in her chair.

'You're right. I have been pratting about but it's over with now. I took a while to adjust to our new position but I think I've sorted meself out now. Come to terms with it like. I don't want you to leave me, I don't want to break up the partnership. I love you, Tommy, more than you will ever believe.'

For Briony to say she loved him in broad daylight in a crowded place spoke volumes to Tommy. Kissing her hand softly, he smiled at her.

'What's really wrong, Bri?'

'I don't know, Tommy. I found it all a bit scary, I think. Taking out Olds and Bolger, all that with Dumas. Everything just got on top of me and I couldn't cope with it.'

'And you can cope with it now?'

She smiled brightly. 'Yes, I think I can. I've come to terms with meself, with what we did.'

Tommy squeezed the tiny hand in his and smiled gently. 'I'll look after you, darling, you should know that.'

She smiled and nodded. Tommy knew that Briony wasn't as hard and calculating as she liked to make out. That she was just a young woman, for all her talk and her business acumen. She had taken the death of Ginelle hard, and the consequent deaths of Olds and Bolger and the others had given her many a sleepless night. He would stick by her, support her, and take the pressure off her for a while. She was his woman, his love, and whatever the right and wrongs of their life, he loved her desperately.

Briony pulled her hand from his. 'Have a guess what I just done?'

'What?'

She told him of her visit to Joshua and his mother, making it sound amusing, playing on the comic aspect instead of the real, frightening part of it. As they laughed together Tommy was aware that Briony's laughter was a bit too high, her gaiety too brittle to be true. He would keep his eye on her. In fact, he'd watch her like a hawk.

Chapter Eighteen

Henry Dumas sat up in the bed and made a pretence of reading the paper. Isabel watched him as she fussed around the room. His whole countenance was different, even his mouth had lost its arrogant sneer.

'Anything interesting in the paper, Henry?'

He shook his head. 'Not really.'

Isabel tidied the counterpane. 'What about this new thing, sending people to Australia? I think it's a wonderful idea.'

'If it gets rid of the working class, then it can only be good.'

Isabel sighed. A livid scar travelled up from the top of Henry's cheekbone and disappeared into his hairline. It was a startling white and when he was angry, as he was now, it seemed to raise itself from the skin around it. He also had scars on his shoulders and back. Whoever had attacked him had really meant to do him harm. She'd wondered at first why his attackers had not taken his wallet and watch. But the police said that maybe the men had been disturbed, it often happened in daylight robberies. Now her sympathy, and she had been surprised to feel any at all, was slowly disappearing. As he was getting better, he was getting back to his old self. Never an appealing prospect at the best of times.

'You're a very difficult man, you know. Since you were attacked you've changed. You haven't left this bed. God knows, you were bad enough before but now you're impossible. Even the doctor is getting worried. Your wounds are healed, you're fit and well enough to get up. So why don't you come down today, have your meal in the library? The garden looks lovely.'

'Isabel, do me a favour and leave me alone. I still feel unwell and if I choose to stay in bed that is my prerogative. I do not want to sit in the library or look out on the garden. I have no interest in the doings of little people who want to go to that Godawful continent Australia. I don't care what we're having for dinner or lunch. I don't care what you're doing or what your blasted father's doing. In short, you bore me. Please go away and leave me alone.'

Isabel pursed her lips and stood up. As she walked from the room, Henry called her back.

'And keep that child and his confounded dog away from me!'

As she opened the door, Nipper, a large German Shepherd, leapt into the room, closely followed by Benedict. Nipper bounded on to the bed and began a ferocious licking of Henry's face and balding head. Muddy paws ripped into his copy of *The Times*. He pushed the animal away with all his strength, knocking it on to the floor.

Nipper was an amiable animal. He was still young, and even though Henry Dumas had never given the dog a kind word the animal lived in hope. Jumping on to the bed once more, he resumed his frantic ministrations.

Benedict stood at the door, his face alive with fun, and called the animal loudly.

'Nipper, Nipper! Come here now. Leave Papa alone. He's not well!'

Isabel bit back a laugh as Henry's face appeared above the mass of fur and said through clenched teeth: 'Get this dog off me!'

Benedict pulled the dog from the bed bodily, heaving him on to the floor where Nipper sat with his huge tongue hanging out of the side of his mouth, panting from exertion.

'I'm sorry, Papa, but he likes you. I try and keep him out of your way . . .' His voice trailed off and Benedict hunched his shoulders in exasperation.

Henry looked at the boy closely. Other than those startling

244

green Cavanagh eyes, it could have been his own mother standing there. Benedict had unconsciously used a movement of his mother's. She would tilt her head to the side and smile at him, hunching her shoulders, exactly as Benedict had, when she couldn't answer his constant questions. For the first time ever, he felt a flicker of interest in the boy.

'Do that again, boy.'

Benedict shrugged.

'Do what, Papa?'

Henry parodied his action and Benedict laughed. He held out his hands, hunched up his shoulders and did as his father asked him. For the first time ever, Henry smiled at the boy, a genuine smile.

'Isabel, get my albums from the bottom drawer in my dressing room.'

Amazed, she did as she was told. Benedict stood by the bed and stroked Nipper's ears absently as he waited for his father to speak again. He was unsure what he should do. His father actually having a conversation with him was so rare. It normally only came about when his school work was not up to par. Then he was upbraided soundly.

Henry laughed again, a wide open laugh that showed his teeth. 'Here it is, look! Look at that, boy.'

Benedict took the photograph from his father's hand and looked down at a woman dressed in black bombazine. She had white hair and a sad smile on her face.

'That's my mother, your grandmother.'

Benedict looked into his father's face and said: 'She's very pretty.'

Henry nodded sagely. 'She was very pretty. Too pretty, some thought. But I always loved her dearly, she was a good woman.'

Isabel stood in absolute shock and amazement as father and son chatted for the first time ever.

'What happened to her, Papa?'

'Oh, she died when I was a lad. Not that much older than you. She had many children but they all died. My mother died because of that. Because she was too gentle, too fine-boned to

245

have children. She was like a child herself. Her laughter was so beautiful ... she was a generous woman, and doted on me of course. We would play hide and go seek and blind man's buff with my old nurse Hattie.'

He stared into the distance as if seeing them all again. Benedict looked at the old sepia photograph with interest. 'Have you any more photographs, Papa? I'd love to hear about my grandmother. I've seen the painting of her in the drawing room so many times and I've often wondered about her.'

Henry looked at him again, a piercing look. It was natural the boy would want to know of his background. He smiled then, a cruel smile. His mother would be a revelation to him if he knew.

'Come and sit on the bed with me and I'll show you all the photos I have. I've only one of my father, but his portrait is up in the attics. He was painted in his full dress uniform. He was a lancer.'

'Did you like him, Papa?'

Henry laughed at the childish enquiry and shook his head. 'No, I didn't, actually. He was a nasty-tempered man.'

Benedict bit his lips and stared trustingly into his father's face. The sentence hung on the air.

'You're thinking I take after him, aren't you?'

Benedict shook his head furiously, unwilling to break the friendliness of the moment; it was so rare to speak to his father like this he couldn't bear for it to end.

Henry sighed heavily. 'Maybe I do, boy. You inherit things from your parents, you know. I inherited my father's bad humour. I wonder what you'll inherit from me and your mother?'

As he spoke he looked at Isabel and she felt herself sinking inside at the expression on his face.

Briony awoke the morning before Eileen's wedding in high good humour. In the weeks since her showdown with Tommy and Mrs Horlock, she had gradually become more like her old self. Only now she had a touch of hardness to her that was not apparent before.

She opened the bedroom curtains herself and frowned slightly at the two men lounging against their Cowley motor car, smoking and chatting. She still hated to be watched like this. To have minders everywhere. They never did a real day's work and they ate their heads off. Tommy laughed at her complaints, telling her that if they ever had any serious trouble, the men would more than earn their dinners. But it galled her just the same to have those two standing around constantly, have them follow her everywhere she went, and even vet visitors to her home. It was necessary, but that didn't mean she had to like it.

'Come back to bed, Bri, it's too early to get up.'

Briony smiled. 'Listen, Tommy, I have a full day ahead of me. The final preparations for Eileen's wedding, plus a meeting with Mariah, and on top of all that I have a special date this morning.'

He pulled back the covers and Briony saw he was aroused. 'You can have a special date now if you like!'

'Oh, Tommy, you're terrible! I have to get bathed and dressed and off to Regents Park for ten-thirty.'

Tommy pulled the covers back over himself and said, 'Do you want me to come with you?'

Briony was nonplussed for a moment. 'Would you like to? Only you haven't really seen him, have you? He's beautiful, Tommy . . .'

'I know that, Bri, you tell me often enough.'

'Sally's taking him to the park, and while he runs his dog we chat. If Isabel knew there'd would be murders, but what she don't know can't hurt her. Sometimes I feel like just taking him, you know? He's ten now, he's growing up, and he doesn't even know I exist. It hurts, Tommy.'

He took her small hand in his and kissed it.

'We go through this every time. He don't know you, Bri, he's happy with them. Well, with Isabel anyway. He'll have everything we never had, he'll have the right friends, go to the right schools. Fuck me, Bri, he's got it made! I wish my old mum had given me to someone like that.'

'But I could give him all that now.'

Her voice was small, distressed.

'Oh, Bri, don't go queer on me again. You can offer him money, but you'll always be Briony Cavanagh. You're not even married. He'd just be an illegitimate kid. This way he's someone, someone important. He'll go to one of them university places, then he'll inherit all that old goat's money. Don't balls it up for him, Bri, because he won't thank you for it. Watch him from a distance, watch over him like that. When he's a man, then tell him the truth. Who knows? Maybe he'll find out himself. But for now, don't rock his boat, love, you don't know what the upshot might be.'

Briony's radiant face had paled. 'Tommy Lane, the voice of reason.' The words were bitter.

'Yeah, well. I'm only trying to do what's best for that boy. Think with your head, Bri, not your heart. Now then, let's get ourselves suited and booted and off out! I'll treat you to a nice Jewish breakfast in Brick Lane before we go to Regents Park, how's that? I ain't had no lox or bagels for ages. What do you say?'

'Who you got to see at Brick Lane?'

Tommy laughed.

'You always outthink me, don't you? I have to see Solly Goldstern. He owes me a whacking great sum of money and today I collect.'

'All right then, Tommy. I'll get Cissy to run the bath.'

As she busied herself getting ready, she daydreamed of having her son back home with her. Of her dressed in her best walking him to school. Dreams were free, and no one could stop you having them.

That was why, for Briony, they always had the edge over real life.

Solly Goldstern was thin to the point of emaciation. He was sixty-seven years old and was a gold merchant. A gold merchant in the East End bought for peanuts from the Jewish immigrants who were trying to get a start and a new life, and sold for a small

248

fortune to the wealthier jewellers in Hatton Garden and roundabouts.

Solly had borrowed a large amount of money off Tommy to buy a ruby tiara from an old Russian woman. She was shrewd, knew her tiara's worth and stuck out for fifty per cent of its real value. Solly had borrowed the money from Tommy, made the purchase and then sold it on for a huge profit. All was good, until his daughter's husband, Isaac, had taken the money, left his forty-year-old wife and five children, and run off with a little cockney girl called Daisy. The funny thing was, Solly was more annoyed about Daisy than anything. Isaac had run off with a *goy*, an English girl. His daughter's shame was worse because of this fact.

He had tried to locate the errant husband without any success whatsoever, and now Tommy Lane was coming for his money and soon it would be common knowledge. His daughter and grandchildren would be shamed, he would lose the respect of his usual clientele. People would think he was old, foolish, that if his son-in-law could rob him, he was easy prey. He knew exactly the East End mentality. It was what had shaped him from his first arrival in this country, when he still spoke Yiddish and had only his quick brain and business acumen to help him along.

He felt the sting of tears in his watery blue eyes and hastily blinked them away. He caressed the handle of the gun before him and bit his lip 'til it bled, licking at the salty droplets of blood. He tasted his own misfortune and felt the urge to cry again.

He had borrowed a lot of money for that tiara, and now he was expected to pay it back. He had nowhere near the amount Tommy would want. With the ten per cent interest and the five per cent handling charge Tommy had insisted on, Solly was just about broke already. Like a cornered rat, he was thinking in terms of death.

Vita, his daughter, came into the room with a glass of tea, her harassed face more deeply lined than usual. She had wanted Isaac desperately as a young girl. She had got him, thanks to her

249

father and a good sum of money, had borne his children and loved him. Now he had betrayed her, and not only her but his children and her father. She felt responsible for her husband's actions and as she looked at her father's grave countenance her heart constricted. She had brought him this low. Had been the instrument of his downfall. He owed money everywhere now, and it galled him. Soon the talk would start, and in the Jewish community that was fatal. If you had no money, you had no power.

'Drink your tea, Father. Tommy Lane will be here soon. He's a reasonable man, a decent man. He'll understand.'

'So, my daughter, you want me to beg to a street urchin, is that it? Me, the chief gold merchant in the East End, whose credit was always the best?'

'If he was good enough for you to borrow his money, the least you can do is give him the benefit of your honesty, Father. Who knows? Maybe he'll take an offer of so much a week until you're better fixed.'

Solly laughed nastily.

'Tommy Lane isn't a tally man. He won't want his five thousand pounds back at a rate of fifty pounds a week, for God knows how long! He'll want the lump sum, plus the ten per cent interest and the five per cent handling charge! Now leave me alone, for the love of God. Take your wittering somewhere else.'

Vita stared stonily at the gun in front of her father. He was still touching it and she shook her head.

'As if we haven't enough troubles, you want to give us more! Isaac has gone, your money's gone. We have to try and sort this thing out.'

'If he was here now I'd shoot him like a dog.'

She snarled through clenched teeth: 'If he was here now, I'd shoot him myself!'

The shop bell rang and Tommy's deep booming voice followed it into the back room.

'Hello, Solly me old mate!' As he walked into the room with Briony behind him he stopped dead. 'What's going on here then?'

Briony's eyes opened wide at the sight of Solly Goldstern waving an antiquated gun in front of him.

'Have you gone mad, Solly?' Tommy's voice was low now. He put his hand behind him and pushed Briony gently away. She stood in the tiny shop front, her hand to her mouth. She heard Tommy's voice as he tried to reason with the old man.

'Give me the gun, Solly.'

Solly's hand was shaking and Vita walked over to him and took the gun gently from his fingers.

Tommy said dryly, 'I take it you ain't got me money then? Or do you always try and top people as they come in here?'

Vita gave Tommy the gun. 'He's out of his mind with worry. We've had a lot of trouble . . .'

'Don't tell them anything, Vita! Let Tommy do his worst. You can't get blood out of a stone.'

The old man's voice, full of dignity, made Briony intervene. 'Look, Mr Goldstern, you remember me, don't you?'

His face softened. 'Of course I do. Every Monday regular you brought in your mother's wedding ring to pop. I gave you seven shillings and you brought back nine shillings on the Saturday. Briony Cavanagh . . . my wife Etta thought you were the most beautiful child she had ever seen.'

Briony sat beside the old man. Smiling at him she said to Vita, 'Make a cuppa, girl, we'll all have a little chat.'

Vita went to make the tea and Tommy pulled out a chair and straddled it, the old silver-handled gun still in his hand.

'By rights, Solly, I should knock you from here to Kingdom come for the stunt you pulled on me.'

Solly's face was grey. His skin seemed to become baggier by the second. Briony had thought of him as an old man all her life, it was the way when you knew people from children, but he seemed to be ageing in front of her eyes.

'Shut up, Tommy, let him talk.'

Solly shrugged his shoulders and held out his hands helplessly.

'Vita's husband Isaac, he worked for me. I borrowed the five grand off you, Tommy, to buy a particularly nice tiara from an

251

old lady. Beautiful workmanship, white and yellow gold, with diamonds and rubies. It was one of the finest pieces I've ever seen.'

'All right, Solly, we get the picture. What happened?'

'Well, Isaac, he has five children by my daughter Vita. I had him work for me because he couldn't keep a job down. Here I could watch him. Make sure the children were fed. You know the score.'

Briony and Tommy nodded.

'He waited 'til I resold the tiara to a jeweller up West who had a buyer for it. Then in the night he came and took the money, also every bit of the cash I'd saved over the years, and – even Vita doesn't know this – all my Etta's jewels. They were to be hers one day, Vita's. He had taken up with a young girl, a slut of the first water, a *goy*! We haven't seen him since.'

Briony laid her hand gently on the old man's arm, her heart going out to him.

Tommy on the other hand said waspishly: 'You was gonna top me over that ponce Isaac!'

Briony shook her head at him. 'Look, Mr Goldstern, listen to me. We'll sort something out, all right?'

'Huh! What, my little love? I am finished. I can't even scrape up enough to start my business again. I'm at rock bottom. I have Vita and her children to look after. Her eldest son is fifteen now. I have so much responsibility and I haven't the capital. I'm even behind on the rent for this place!'

Vita walked into the room with the tea as her father broke down crying. Placing the tray on his desk, she went to him, taking him into her arms.

'It's pointless beating him. He can't pull your money out of thin air. It's been preying on his mind for days.'

Briony began to pour out the tea. Giving everyone a cup, she smiled at Vita. 'Sit down and let's try and make some sense out of this. We'll look for Isaac, see if we can recoup any of your money, right? He's the main holder of the debt now so if he's still in the smoke, he's as good as crippled. I'll arrange for three hundred quid to be delivered here first thing in the morning.

252

You owe me then, Mr Goldstern, not Tommy. You pay me back at a pony a week, restart your business from scratch. I'll want a twenty per cent return on me dosh. What about that?'

Solly looked at the girl in front of him and had a sudden vivid memory of her father. Paddy Cavanagh had even brought in his children's boots to pawn for a drink. He was a waster, a schmuck, yet he had bred this beautiful girl with a kind heart. She had known only poverty and hardship. His own daughter, who had had everything a girl could want, had taken up with Isaac. Solly had bought and paid for him so she would once more have everything she wanted. It was a strange world when the girl with the least became more of a woman than the girl with everything.

His eyes were wet again. Unable to talk, he grabbed her small hand in his and kissed it.

Vita sipped her tea, her eyes watching the changing expressions on Tommy Lane's face. She guessed, shrewdly, that Tommy wasn't at all pleased at having his five grand scrubbed in such a cavalier fashion by Briony Cavanagh. But she also guessed that Briony generally got what she wanted, regardless of who she upset in the process.

Twenty minutes later, in Tommy's car on their way to Regents Park, Briony took the brunt of his tongue.

'I don't fucking believe you! Why didn't you offer to put him in your Christmas club? Five poxy grand down the crapper, and the old bastard had a gun! You've no right to countermand me like that, Briony, you was out of order.'

She smiled to herself. 'Shall I tell you something, Tommy Lane. When I was a kid I hated having to pawn me mother's wedding ring. I hated it. That "old bastard", as you call him, never once made me feel like the dirt I was. He always called me Miss Cavanagh, as young as I was, and he always gave me a sweet.'

Tommy stopped at a junction and shouted to a barrow boy: 'Oi, got any hearts and flowers on there?'

With a laugh, the boy watched him turn the corner.

'Very funny, Tommy. Why don't you do a turn at the club?

253

I'll tell you something now, for nothing. It hurt me seeing him brought so low. Even when he was on top – and he was, Tommy, he was the business as far as fucking gold was concerned – he still had the decency to treat me with a bit of respect. I owe him for that. After years of being treated like Irish shite, it was a welcome change!'

Tommy shook his head, and Briony watched him battle it out with himself. She knew exactly how he was feeling. She knew him better than she knew herself. Every mood swing, every nuance of his personality. He was fighting within himself now, because one half of him wanted to muller her where she sat, and the other half of him understood what she was saying, because being treated with respect was what they'd both fought so hard for. If you had money you automatically had that respect, even if only for the fact you were well heeled. To be treated with respect when you were no one, with nothing and no visible means of ever getting anything, counted for a lot.

'So old Goldstern gave you a sweet, and because of that you let him get away with pulling a gun on me? It's nice to know you care so much!'

'Oh, balls! That gun was so old it was positively ancient, it would have backfired and killed him, not you!'

'Oh, so now you're a firearms expert as well?'

Briony started to laugh then, a rollicking boisterous sound. 'Give it a rest, Tommy, you would have done the same.'

'Yeah, maybe. But I didn't get the chance, did I?' This was said seriously and Briony kept her peace. He was five grand down, and she knew when she had pushed her luck to its extreme.

Sally sat in Regents Park watching Benedict as he played with Nipper, rolling around the grass in his good trousers and shrieking with suppressed energy. She would spend the best part of the evening sponging his clothes down so all the tell-tale evidence of his supposedly sedate walk would be cleaned away. She didn't care, she loved him. Only with her could he be a boy, a real little boy who jumped and played. Even Isabel, who loved

254

him dearly, Sally conceded that, tried to make him into a little gentleman. Well, in Sally's opinion, there was plenty of time for that.

She saw Briony walking towards her with Tommy Lane and signalled with her head towards Benedict.

Briony and Tommy settled themselves on the wrought-iron bench beside Sally and started chatting. To passersby it looked innocent enough, their subject matter would be unheard and their interest in the little boy was cleverly disguised.

'Hello, Sal. You know Tommy, of course?'

She nodded.

'How's me boy?'

'You can see for yourself, Miss Cavanagh. Healthy as hell, eating like a horse, and more energy than a lightning bolt!'

Briony laughed. This was what she wanted to hear. 'How's things at the house?'

Sally looked her straight in the eye. 'Well, that's a funny thing, Miss Cavanagh. It's been strange since the master was attacked.'

Tommy pushed his face towards Sally and said, 'What do you mean?'

Sally shrugged.

'Well, lately he's took to playing with the boy like. Taking him out and that. The master wouldn't leave the house for weeks, then all of a sudden it's "let me take you here, let me take you there".'

'And how's the boy responding to it all?'

'Well, Mr Lane, he loves it. They play chess together, and you want to hear them laughing! It's like someone's switched masters in the night like. One day he was a miserable old fucker, the next all sweetness and light. It was strange, I can tell you, and the mistress ain't happy with the change. She don't like it one bit!'

Briony nodded, thinking. 'Well, she wouldn't, would she?' She wasn't sure she liked it herself. But hadn't she told him to be nice to the boy? Was this his way of doing what she'd said? 'Benedict's happy enough, though?'

'Oh, bugger me, yes! Never seen him so happy. He's been a little darling. Not that he was ever any trouble before, mind, but now he's got his old man behind him, it's put the icing on his cake if you see what I mean.'

Benedict ran and Nipper jumped up, sending him sprawling on to the grass. Briony nearly got out of her seat, thinking he was hurt, when high-pitched laughter floated over to them.

Sally grinned. 'He's a hard little sod, Miss Cavanagh, take more'n a tumble to set his waterworks off!'

Benedict ran over to Sally, holding out his sleeve. 'Oh Sal, Sally! Look what I've done to my jacket!'

'Come here, let me look.'

Briony felt the tightening in her chest as he approached. He smiled at her and Tommy before he held out the offending arm to Sally.

'Mama's going to trounce me, Sally.'

Briony and Tommy's eyes both opened wide at the expression.

'Now, young man, don't you be using those words in front of your parents! Your mother would have my guts for garters if she thought I was teaching you words like that!'

Benedict smiled craftily. 'As if I would, Sal! But look at it, it's covered in mud.'

'It'll clean, lad. You go and play with your dog.'

Nipper, deciding he liked the look of Briony, jumped up at her, putting his muddy paws on her coat.

'Nipper! Get down! I'm sorry about that . . .'

As Benedict looked into the lady's face his words dried in his throat. It was like looking in a mirror.

'Hello, Benedict. Your nanny was just telling me all about you. What a wonderful dog.' Briony's voice was quavering with emotion. It took every ounce of her willpower not to grab hold of him and crush him to her chest.

Benedict stared into the green eyes so like his own and said, 'Yes, he is a wonderful dog. Excuse me, but do I know you?'

Briony shook her head and answered, 'No, you don't know me.'

'How strange. I feel as if I know you from somewhere.'

Briony and Benedict locked eyes. Tommy watched them as they sized each other up. Benedict was so like her it was uncanny. The same heart-shaped face, the same high cheekbones, and the same green eyes. Benedict was like the spit out of her mouth, as his mother would have said. He was going to be handsome, and if he had his mother's nature as well as her looks he would be one hell of a man. Looking at Briony and Benedict together, he felt the pull that Briony must experience and understood then exactly what kept her going in life. She looked after everyone, even old Solly Goldstern, but the one person she really wanted to take care of was out of her jurisdiction. She couldn't put him to bed, wipe away his tears, or hold him in her arms. No wonder she had gone for Dumas as she had. At the end of the day, he had got everything and she had got nothing.

'Would you like an ice cream, son?' Tommy's voice broke the momentary closeness.

'Oh, yes please.' Benedict's eyes were bright.

'You take him, Bri, I'll chat to Sally for a while.'

Briony stood up and walked with Benedict to get the ice cream. He held on to her arm and they chatted together. Sally watched them go with fear in her heart.

'It's not a good idea, Mr Lane. He's at an age when he'll talk about things, in company like.'

Tommy lit himself a cheroot and shook his head in dismissal. 'Who gives a fuck. Certainly not me, love. She's every right to see him if she wants.'

Sally kept quiet but the thought scared her.

Briony and Benedict chatted together and enjoyed themselves. Briony listened to all his boyish talk and drank it inside herself. Benedict, guessing he had a sympathetic ear, poured out all his doings, good and bad, with a fervour.

When he was walking home with Sally later in the day he said, 'I don't think I'll mention the nice lady to Mama, she'd think she was a bit common. But I liked her, didn't you, Sal?'

Sally smiled in relief.

'I think you're right there, young Master Ben. Your ma or

your pa wouldn't like her one bit. But we can keep her friendship our secret can't we?'

'Do you think we'll ever see her again, Sal?' He stroked the dog's coat as it walked beside him.

'Oh, yes, young Benedict, I have a feeling we'll see her again. In fact, I can guarantee it.'

Chapter Nineteen

Briony liked Mariah and liked the way she ran her houses. Both women were fighters and survivors which gave them a bond, something neither had expected. But now they owned just about every house in London between them, they were also adversaries. Although both worked their respective patches it was only natural that they would at certain times poach one another's girls or customers. It was an unwritten rule of business.

Mariah wanted to cement their newfound friendship with something tangible. Not just because she liked Briony, though she liked her a lot, but because Briony's newfound status with Tommy Lane also made her a threat in certain ways. If push ever came to shove, Briony could take what was Mariah's at the drop of a hat. She was certain that Briony was too straight and fair for such skulduggery, but there was nothing in Mariah's book like an insurance policy. A guarantee. Which was the reason Briony was sitting in her house now, with a cup of tea and a slice of Battenberg.

Briony wiped her sticky fingers on a napkin and grinned at Mariah amiably. Her afternoon with Benedict had made her happy with the whole world.

'Now then, we've had the tea and cake, you've offered me a stiff drink, which I declined, and we've run out of chit-chat. So come on then, girl, spit it out, what's the rub?'

Mariah laughed with her.

'I have a proposition to put to you, Briony, which, if you agree, will really bring us in money.'

Briony lit a cigarette. Blowing out the smoke in a large billowing cloud, she said, 'Go on.'

Mariah sat back in her chair, her large breasts heaving under the strain of her tight bodice. Briony wondered briefly if they would escape their confines and burst out into the warmth of the room.

'There's a house up for sale, Berwick Manor. It was used through the war as a hospital. The place is in a right mess. It's going for a song, and I mean a song. The thing is, between us we could restore it. It's perfect for what we'd want. It stands in its own land, it's big, it's got plenty of rooms. We could really make it pay.'

Briony nodded.

Mariah took a deep breath. Briony was not making this easy for her.

'If we both invested equal amounts of capital in it, we could make it a showplace. Private functions, our best girls working there, catering for the elite. I know you have a few faces. Well, so do I. We could double up our clients *and* our takings. It's a good investment.'

Briony smiled slowly.

'I know the old manor. Who don't? We walked past it often enough when we was kids pea picking. Kerry used to say, "I wish I lived there!" It's a nice property, you're right. It's in a good location, too. We could cater to the London mob without them having to go too far. We could have weekend parties like, theme parties. Ancient Greece, French nights!'

Briony's enthusiasm pleased Mariah who knew now that the idea was sold. All she had to do was collect the collateral.

'Yeah, we could start them Friday and they could go on 'til the Sunday night. There's a banqueting hall there where the punters could eat, plus plenty of outhouses for livestock and that. It could pretty much be self-contained. The grounds are enormous, acres of fields, even the old Berwick pond, ducks and all! It's very picturesque, perfect for the monied man. Near to

London and discreet. Just the place for a weekend in the country.'

'How much is this going to rush me then? Only if it's going for a song, it must need a lot of work on it.'

'Oh, it does, Bri. I'm not gonna try and spin you about that, girl. It needs a major redec for a start, from carpets to curtains. It ain't been touched since 1919, then it was boarded up and put on the market. In the last six or seven years it ain't even seen a broom. But think of how it could be!'

Briony grinned. 'I am. I know just the girls to work it, too. Young, pretty, wanting to make a quick few grand to set up on their own. It would be so easy. So how much money are you looking at?'

'Off hand, Bri, I'd say about ten thousand each. To get it off to a good start. By my figures we'd recoup that within the first three months of opening.'

She passed over a book where she had broken down the costs. Briony scanned the pages for ten minutes while Mariah smoked a cigarette.

Briony was impressed. Mariah had even allowed for an odd job man. It was well thought out, and it was viable. Two things Briony found hard to resist.

'Shall I tell you something, Mariah?'

She smiled. 'What?'

'I'm in. I'm in up to me bleeding neck! This is going to be a real money spinner. It's class, Mariah, real class.' She shook her head in wonderment.

Mariah clapped her hands together in excitement.

'I'm glad, Bri. I think me and you could make a good team.'

'Plus, together as working partners, we can't tread on each other's toes, can we?'

Mariah saw the crafty look on Briony's face and knew she had been rumbled. Sobering now, she said, 'Well, Briony, there's that to it as well, I suppose.'

'Oh, don't take on, Mariah. I admire your foresight. I'd have thought of something like this in your position. But I can tell you now, I wouldn't turn on the hand that fed me. When we had all that business with Henry and his mob you was a good mate. I'd never forget that. Friends abound in our position, but good mates are few and far between.'

Mariah's face softened and Briony saw a glimmer of the girl she had once been. Big, beautiful and innately nice. Mariah was a nice person, except it seemed too small an epithet for her huge frame.

Rupert and Jonathan were roaring drunk and the noise was beginning to disturb the other customers. Tommy watched them without intervening. He thought they were ponces, though he had given up arguing the fact with Briony. He watched her, dressed in a cream sheath dress, walk over to their table and cajole them into quieting down. He shook his head and walked behind the bar to pour himself a decent scotch. When the punters first arrived, they were given real drinks. When they were drunk, they were served from the 'cottage' bottles, the watered-down versions. They paid top price and Tommy's excuse was, he was doing them a favour.

As Briony walked towards him he motioned with his head for her to the offices. Briony followed him, stopping at tables to chat for a few seconds and waving at other customers. In the office the thumping beat of the Charleston reverberated through the walls.

'How'd it go round your mother's?'

'It's like a mad house, but Eileen's all right. She seems happy enough. Tomorrow it will all be over!'

'You look really lovely tonight, Bri. Really beautiful.'

She kissed him. 'You don't look too bad yourself.'

He poured her a drink and she sipped it gratefully.

'That Ben . . . he's like you, Bri. I don't just mean in looks but personality. You had the same naivety when I first met you.'

'When I saved your arse, you mean?'

Tommy laughed, remembering.

'He is a lovely boy though, Bri.'

She pushed her hair into place with one hand and nodded. 'I know. It takes a lot for me to leave him. I feel like picking him up and taking him away. But even as I am now, with all my connections, my so-called friends, I know I couldn't do it. If push came to shove the courts would take that bastard's side.'

Tommy pulled her into his arms.

'You'll survive, Bri. That's your greatest talent. You see him, you watch him from a distance. He'll be all right.'

Briony looked up into his face and he saw the hurt she felt.

'Sometimes, in the night, I see him. I wonder if he's ill or feeling frightened, you know? And I'm not there to comfort him. To see he's all right . . .'

'Look, whatever you think of Isabel Dumas, she loves the boy. She loves him with all her heart.'

'But she's not his mother, is she? His real mother. I am.'

'And you're a good mother, in your own way.'

Briony pulled away from him and laughed scornfully. 'Oh, yeah, I was a great mother me. I let them walk off with him. Take him from me and bring him up, a pervert and a frustrated spinster! Because that's all she is, she's only married in name, no other way. He couldn't get it up with a woman, she told me that herself. I must have been stark staring mad!'

'Not mad, Bri, young. Young and foolish. But think about it. Without him, you have all this.' He swept his arms out to encompass the whole room.

Briony nodded slowly.

'Yeah, I have everything and nothing. Because without my boy, this is sweet fuck all.'

Tommy shoved her hard in the chest, sending her drink flying everywhere.

'Oh, save me the self-pity, for Gawd's sake, Bri. You can't have him and that's that! You have a lot more than anyone of our station could even dream of. You could have more children, but you won't. Don't you think I might want a baby, a child of me own? No, of course not. You only think of yourself. Sometimes, Bri, you really wind me up, do you know that? I sometimes dream at nights of a son or a daughter, our child. OURS, not fucking Dumas'. Mine and yours! A red-headed little girl I could take out, could love, or a boy with your eyes and my hair, a

263

boy we could bring up together, could give everything to. So don't try and put your silly poxy self-pity on to me all the time. I'm sorry, right, heart sorry. But don't you ever put down my achievements like that again. We worked hard to get where we are and if you would rather give it up for that boy, you're a fool. Because with him, you'd have been scratching in the dirt, his arse would be hanging out of his trousers, your sisters would be in sweat shops working for a living and the bleeding wedding wouldn't be taking place tomorrow, because you couldn't buy your sister a bridegroom!'

Briony stood stock still. Tommy had never spoken like this to her before. It was a shock and a revelation. Suddenly she saw the real loneliness in his face. The sadness in his eyes. He was right, of course, in everything he said. But being right didn't mean she had to stand there and take it. He had embarrassed her with what he said, stung her to the quick, humiliated her. She felt her face burning and before she could think the words tumbled out of her mouth.

'I'll never give you a child, Tommy Lane, you or anyone else. So think on that! You crawl all over me, night after night, and I hate it. I hate everything about it. I allow you to use my body, that's all. I feel nothing for you physically, and you know it. You've always known it. But still you want it, still you're there, night after night, with your stupid pawing and your wet lips. You sicken me! You're no better than Dumas, no better than the men who come to our houses. Your prick rules your head.

'But, not me, mate, not me! I have a child, and if I can't have him, I don't want any! Not by you or anyone else.'

As soon as the last words were out of her mouth she wanted to retract them. Wanted to tell him that it was sheer temper talking, that she was upset. Instead she stood silently as he recovered from the blow he had received.

'You bitch, you fucking bitch of hell.'

Taking back his arm he slapped her across the face, sending her flying across the office on to the desk. The inkwell crashed to the floor. In the silence, Briony pulled herself to her feet.

'I've tried, Briony, to be a good man to you. I've put up with

264

things off you another man would have scalped your arse for, and this is how you repay me, is it? Well, we're finished, girl, after tonight. I know exactly where I stand now, don't I? We'll sort out the pennies and halfpennies another day. For now, I have to get as far away from you as possible.'

Briony went to him, her eyes beseeching.

'Tommy, Tommy, listen to me . . . I didn't mean it.'

He held up his hands.

'Don't touch me, Bri. Not now, not ever again. You've finished anything we ever had between us. You always had the gift of the gab, didn't you? Talked us in and out of every situation. Well, you talked yourself out of me! I sat back today while you talked me out of five grand, lady. I've always listened to you, let you have your head, and all the time you had no more feeling for me than a mad dog. Talk about a fucking eye opener, eh! Get out of me way.'

Briony held on to him, grabbing the sleeve of his jacket.

'Let go of me, Bri, or I'll knock you out, I mean it.'

She held on harder, beginning to cry now.

'Please, Tommy! I never meant it, any of it, I was hurt!'

Putting the flat of his hands on her chest, he pushed her with all his considerable strength. She flew backwards against the wall, the force knocking the breath from her body. She crumpled down on to the floor, her back aching with the blow.

'Good night, love. See you around.'

She was crying hard now.

'Tommy, I'm begging you . . .'

He looked down at her and laughed.

'I've got to hand it to you, Bri, you never did know when to give up, did you? Your big trap will still be moving when they put you in the ground.'

He walked from the office and Briony sat on the floor and cried bitter lonely tears.

Tommy walked from the club and out into the evening air. He pushed his hands down into his pockets and walked quickly towards the East End, his motor car left behind.

He felt the sting of tears and blinked them back. All around him London was quieting for the night, the streets empty and void of life. He had loved her so much, so very very much. She had been like a beacon to him, calling him home to her. She was his other half, his second skin. In her, he'd had a deep abiding friendship and a love he thought could rival any in the world. He had been such a fool, a stubborn fool, not to see what was under his nose all the time! Well, they were finished, finally and irrevocably. He couldn't think what the upshot was going to be now. He still loved her dearly, despite what had happened this night. All he knew was that this was the end of the road for them. The final parting. He never wanted to look at her lovely face again.

In his mind's eye he saw her as she had been all those years ago, with her belly high in pregnancy, her blue velvet suit, her stunning hair. Even then, she had had something special about her. He saw her when they opened their first house, her face serious and exquisite. What was it that made one person more to you than another? What was the magic chemistry that made only one person your life, your love? Why was he plagued by her day and night, year after year, when there were women aplenty in the world? Other women as beautiful, with better bodies and sweeter natures. Why was he cursed with wanting her? Because he still wanted her, even now. After all that had happened, he still wanted her.

It was this that hurt him more than anything. Where Briony was concerned, he had no pride.

Well, he decided, he would find the pride. Nothing would induce him to have her back after this night's work. Not even her tears. From tonight, Briony Cavanagh was on her own.

And a little voice at the back of his mind said: So are you, Tommy Lane, and you'll be the lonelier in the end.

He stood on London Bridge later that night, and watched the traffic on the water, the boats' hooters sounding ghostly in the light of the dawn.

It was then, cold and tired, that Tommy decided just what he had to do.

* * *

Briony could hear the preparations for the wedding from her bedroom. She was sorry now she had decided to have the reception at her house. It meant she had to be nice to everyone, talk and chat and be the good hostess, when all she wanted to do was tell them all to bugger off out of it. Go away and come back another day.

It was overcast, and Briony hoped the heavens opened so the reception would be cut short. She looked in the mirror and groaned. Her eyes were swollen and red. Her face grey-tinged.

She knew that she had blown it with Tommy, that what she had said would always be between them. It was her wicked vicious tongue that had taken her over. It was not even the truth. Just words spoken in temper, a temper brought on by hearing the truth. She felt the useless tears again and swallowed them down. She had no time for tears now. But, oh, she was hurting inside, she was in an agony of pain.

The door was opened and Mrs Horlock bustled into the room. Briony looked at her with new eyes, saw the aged look of her face, the way the skin had sagged, the heavy jowls and ruddy complexion, and suddenly it occurred to her that years were passing with a sameness that was startling.

'Come on, girl, get yourself up and eat this toast! I'll cook you a proper breakfast later when the main work's done. The bloody help is no good at all, a couple of nervous children! By Christ, you get what you pay for these days all right. Still, they'll have to do and they're showing willing so I mustn't be too hard on them.'

She dumped the tray of tea and toast on a small table beside Briony's bed.

'Your mother's arrived, by the way, sticking her great galloping oar in where it ain't wanted!'

Briony ignored the tirade and sighed gently.

'Look, lass, I don't know what happened with you and your man, but he's sent a message for his bags to be ready to be picked up first thing tomorrow morning. Now I know you've had a fight, but this is your sister's wedding day and you've got to show willing. You and him have always fought like cat and dog. But he'll be around with his tail between his legs as usual, and everything will be all right.'

Briony shook her head. 'No, he won't, Mrs H. This is the finish.'

'Oh, Briony girl. Listen to me. Whatever has happened with you and your man, it'll all be resolved before you know it . . .'

'No, that's just it, Mrs H. Things were said last night that can never be retracted. Can never be forgotten. I blew it with Tommy. I pushed him too far this time.'

Briony started talking again, babbling, her words running into one another as she tried to make sense of them herself. 'It was seeing my boy, it was seeing him. Being near him. I couldn't get the thought from my head that if things had been different we would have been together. I could have looked at him every day. I hate the thought of him with them. It grieves me, it kills me. It should be me, not her. Then Tommy said we could have children and I said . . . I said no. Never. And I meant it. I realise now I really meant it because I only want my boy! Benedict. My son. Any other child would be like second best, you know?

'Tommy deserves better than that. And knowing all that, I still want him. I would have fifty children if it kept Tommy here, but now it's all too late. Too fucking late to try and make any sense of it all.'

'Then don't. Don't try and make sense of it. Try and pull yourself together, child, for God's sake. There's a whole army arriving here in a few hours and you've got to greet them with your sister. It's her day, not yours. It's Eileen's day. And let's face it, Briony, she deserves some happiness, doesn't she? Think of Eileen and your sisters and your mother. Everyone will be expecting you to be the life and soul of this gathering.'

Briony looked into the lined face and before her and sighed heavily.

'That's been the trouble, hasn't it? It's all always been for everyone else. Never for me. For me mum, me family. I even frightened Joshua into marrying Eileen. What about me? What about what *I* want?'

268

As she walked down the stairs forty-five minutes later, she was a semblance of her old self, a veneer of the old Briony that pleased everyone. They all looked at her and she could read in their eyes the same thought.

Briony was here, she would take over, and everything would be fine.

Only she knew that nothing would ever be the same again.

But Briony, being Briony, played the game she had started so long ago, the game where she set the rules and never told anyone else what they were. Least of all Tommy Lane.

Chapter Twenty

Briony stood in Saint Vincent's church with her mother and sisters, waiting for Eileen to walk down the aisle. She knelt down and made the sign of the cross, giving an offering prayer of two Hail Marys and an Our Father. As she kissed the cross of Christ on her rosary beads she noticed Kerry staring at her and dropped her eyes. Only Kerry had noticed something wrong with her, only Kerry had realised she wasn't her usual self. Kerry was to sing today, at her sister's wedding. It was a family day all right, and even though Joshua was giving Eileen his name, O'Malley, it was still a Cavanagh day.

Rosalee, dressed in a silver-grey dress and coat, looked at her and clapped her hands together. Briony smiled at her. Rosie was enormous now. Her flat face, so adorable to Briony, still made people stare at her. She trotted alongside her mother wherever she went, and was well known to all the shopkeepers. Her vocabulary was still limited to 'Bri, Bri'. It was the only word she had ever spoken, though Briony guessed she would talk more if she really wanted to. Briony straightened up the black silk headscarf Rosalee wore and gave her a little kiss. Bernie was tapping her foot against the wooden floor. She looked agitated and Briony didn't bother acknowledging her. She couldn't bring herself to have a whispered conversation, just wanted to take Rosalee and walk from the church, from all this pretence, but knew she couldn't. Instead she smiled wanly at her mother.

No one as yet had asked after Tommy, Briony's demeanour

had made sure of that. The fact he had ordered his clothes to be packed was common knowledge, though, thanks to Cissy. Dressed in an outrageous red silk suit, she was already crying before Eileen even walked down the aisle.

Kerry slipped from her pew and walked up to the altar. She knelt and blessed herself before taking up position at the side, ready to sing. Eileen had let her choose the hymns herself.

Joshua waited patiently for his bride. His new suit looked and felt incongruous. He had never owned anything so fine in all his life. He was frightened of all this sitting down because he didn't want to crease it. It had been provided by Briony, which he hated, but he consoled himself with the thought it would last him the next thirty years if he watched his weight. It was of good material and fully lined, a fact that had him swinging between pride and a kind of shocked wonderment. It was a suit you could take to Uncle's and get a good price for, and as it was no shame to pawn things, he was actually looking forward to doing so. It would only get damp or smoke-damaged hanging up in the house, depending on what time of year it was, and where the hell would he wear it, except maybe to weddings and funerals.

He bit his thumbnail, and quickly chastised himself. No biting nails in church, no crossing of legs or arms in church, and never, ever was one to think a bad word or thought in church. He concentrated on the pink roses on the altar. The church looked lovely. His mother and Eileen had dressed it early that morning. It looked a picture.

He smiled nervously at his friend Harry Higgins, and Harry patted his pocket to let him know he had the ring safe. The news Joshua was marrying Eileen, one of the Cavanaghs, had spread through the East End like wild fire. For the first time in his life he was treated with the utmost respect. Yet he wasn't sure he even wanted to be here. At first Briony getting the better of his mother had pleased him. He had been forced into this marriage, and being a weak man, there was a kind of pleasure in that fact. Always living by his mother's lights, he had exchanged that for living by Briony Cavanagh's. But Eileen now, she was a different kettle of fish. With Eileen he would rule the roost and she would let him. That fact pleased him enormously. He had a fleeting vision of her naked before him and squeezed his eyes closed. After this day, he could take her any time he wanted to. He would be master in his own house, and master of her.

Everyone looked towards the back of the church when Eileen began the walk down the aisle on Abel's arm. Kerry began to sing, low at first, her voice rising as she picked up the organist's tempo:

'Amazing grace, how sweet the sound.
To save a wretch like me.'

People sighed with contentment as she sang. Eileen looked at Joshua, and even the stern old priest, Father MacNama, smiled, shaking his head in wonder at the sound of her voice. As he thought to himself, the way some of the eejits in his parish murdered the good God's hymns, it was a breath of fresh air to hear that one sing them.

He opened his bible and blessed it. He was ready to begin.

An hour later Joshua kissed his bride and they went through to sign the register, everyone following, happy now the deed was done and all that was left was the merry making.

The sun had come out, and Briony was pleased. She was sorry for her churlish thoughts of the early morning. The heavens had not opened and the garden was jam packed with people.

As Joshua stood with a jar of ale in his hand he was more than pleased with the reception. There was a large four-tier wedding cake, and food the like of which he had only dreamed of. A large ham, turkey, chicken, beef. There were all sorts of salads and cold vegetables. He had even eaten curry for the first time, amazed at the skill of Briony's cook, Mrs Horlock.

He watched as his friends relaxed in the grand surroundings and sampled the fine foods and the plentiful drink. All the children had little cakes thrust into their hands and one of the men had made a swing on a large tree at the end of the garden. He looked over to where his wife was talking to her sisters and suddenly felt an enormous burst of pride. She was actually his, now, his wife. She looked beautiful and he knew this was being remarked on.

A normal East End Irish wedding reception consisted of some currant cake and a barrel of holy water. This was home-made scotch, or poteen as they called it. Then the next day there would either be a big joke, such as, 'Someone forgot to book the fight!' Or the talk would be of an actual fight that had ensued at some point in the drunken proceedings. Not on his wedding day, though. People were enjoying tasting a bit of the high life, as they would put it to themselves. They'd talk for years about this day, the only chance many would ever get to stand in a garden like this, with drinks and food, and not be either working there or watching from a vantage point. Joshua knew that the general consensus was he had done well for himself, and basked in his newfound status.

Eileen smiled at him tremulously, and he smiled back. Her tiny waist was emphasised by her ivory satin wedding gown, and he told himself that soon she'd be sporting a belly full of arms and legs. He couldn't wait to start the ball rolling. Tonight couldn't come quick enough for him. He'd drive her hard, by Christ, because after all, she was his wife, wasn't she? And a man was allowed to be a man in his own home, surely?

Eileen and Joshua were in their small terraced house in Bow. It had been presented to them a week earlier by Briony and now Eileen stared around her in wonder. It was hers entirely. In her name, in fact. She didn't even have to pay rent.

She had been all for refusing the place, her horror of how Briony accumulated her money still fresh. But Joshua had said it would be churlish to refuse such a magnificent gift, so she had acquiesced. Now she stood in the kitchen, with the freshly leaded range and the smell of lavender polish and coal, and gazed about her in wonder. It was fully equipped, she didn't even have to supply a tablecloth or a tea towel. Everything was already there.

Joshua put his arm around her waist and she pulled away from him as if she'd been burnt.

'Shall I make a cup of tea?'

Joshua smiled. 'It's not tea I want, Eileen love. You just get yourself upstairs and get into bed. I'll sit here for a while and have a smoke. I'll be up soon.'

The words were heavy with emphasis and innuendo and Eileen licked dry lips and nodded.

Upstairs she stared around her at the bedroom. The bed looked very big all of a sudden, and the lights from outside seemed to give the room shadows and dark corners previously unnoticed. She didn't want to turn on the light though, the thought of Joshua seeing her in the light frightened her. She sat on the bed and bit her lip. Unsure now why she had been so keen to get married. She liked the thought of having her own home, and cooking meals and looking after children, but that was all daytime stuff. She had not allowed herself to think of the nights. They were like her times with Henry Dumas, to be pushed into the furthest recesses of her mind. Only now, here she was married, and the night was here, black and ominous and threatening to go on forever.

She started to unhook her dress, unable to reach the tiny pearl buttons with her trembling fingers. She covered her face with her hands, seeing another bedroom, warm and pretty, and herself lying in bed terrified in case Henry came in and woke her. It was the fear of the unknown that frightened her so. Would Joshua want what he'd wanted? Would he want her to put her hands and lips in secret places that made her feel faint just thinking about them? Would he want her naked and open, kneeling on the bed, her tears seeming to spur him on. Was that what the priest meant when he said children were born through pain? The pain of rough hands and humiliation and fear?

She searched the room with wild eyes, as if expecting a doorway to appear so she could run through it and escape. She closed her eyes tightly and tried to stem the burning tears that were filling up her eyes. Tried to stop the erratic beating of her heart. She could smell her own fear and it spurred her terror on to new heights.

She heard him tapping out his pipe in the fireplace, the rat-tat-tat like an explosion in the silence. She held her breath, ears straining to pick up the sounds as he shut the kitchen door and made his way up the stairs. His tread was heavy, new shoes creaking with each movement of his feet. The breath was hurting her chest and she let it out noisily. A fine layer of sweat was covering her body. The armpits of the dress were wet now. As the bedroom door swung open she groaned in fright. Her whole body seemed to be stiff and unyielding, her legs rooted to the floor.

'Come on, Ei, aren't you undressed yet?' The words were low, spoken in a cajoling whisper.

Her face, strained and white, devoid of colour, stared at him in dumb terror. He unbuckled his trousers, a loud belch escaping from his lips. The trousers dropped to the floor and he stepped from them.

'Let's get some light in here.'

As he turned to put the light on she croaked out through stiff lips: 'No . . . No, please, Joshua. I'm frightened.'

He turned to her, a smile on his lips.

'I'm sorry, Ei, I'm forgetting it's your first time.' He sat beside her on the bed, taking hold of her hand. 'Stop your shivering, girl, we'll soon warm each other up.'

Eileen saw his face in the dimness. He had drunk too much and his face was ruddy. His thick lips gleamed and his eyes looked empty. Like vacant sockets. She pulled her hand from his and stood up.

'I can't, Joshua, I can't . . .'

He pulled her down on to the bed. Lying on top of her, he began pulling up her wedding dress. Feeling for her underclothes, he kissed her – wet, tobacco-tainted kisses that made her whole body shrink. She pushed his chest, feeling the roughness of his shirt on her palms. He laughed. Hitching himself up, he pulled off her drawers, tearing them with the force he used. Dragging them down her legs while his mouth sought her again. She tried to put her head on to her shoulder, the panic welling up inside her. Wanting to be anywhere but in

276

this room. She saw her father trying to take her mother, Henry taking first herself and then Briony. All the pictures ran through her mind and merged, until all she could see was Henry, her father and Joshua, all naked, all trying to pull at her, touch her. With one almighty push, she forced him from her.

She heard his muffled curse as he landed on the floor. Before she could pull herself from the bed, he was up, dragging at her dress. She could hear the material tearing, the pearl buttons coming apart with ease. She hooked her hands and tried to tear at his face, arms flailing in the darkness. He grabbed her wrists and a searing pain shot through her arms. Then he slapped her hard, across the face, knocking her head sideways with the blow. She lay then, stock still, looking at the man who loomed over her.

He pulled her clothes from her then in silence, meeting no resistance, his hands rough, his mouth spewing out reprimands and curses. He looked down on her nakedness, her heavy breasts and tiny waist, and felt the full force of his want. Kicking her legs open with his knees, he held on to her waist and roughly entered her, jabbing himself into her, careless now of her pain, of her fear. Enjoying the sensation of being the master of the situation. As he entered her he suddenly stayed still. Buried inside her, he looked down at her in confusion. There had been no resistance in her at all. He had slipped inside her, even as she was, dry and terrified, and had met nothing. He took her hair in his great fist, pulling it hard.

'You've been busted.' The words came out low and deep.

Eileen stared up at him, her mouth moving in prayer. She wasn't aware that he had spoken. She lay there staring up at him in terror, her mind blank except for the prayers that were crowding into her mind.

Joshua began to lose his erection, all desire for his virgin wife leaving him. In his drink-clouded brain he saw her as she had been when he met her. Never a real kiss, never a touch, nothing. And all the time she was busted, had been used. No wonder that sister of hers had been so quick to marry her off. Had threatened him. Some other man had known her, had touched her. They must all be laughing up their sleeves at him, like it was one big joke.

Eileen, realising that he had stopped, assuming it was all over, tried to rise. It was as if this action, the way she tried to get up, get away from him, finally finished him. Shoving her down by her shoulders he pinned her to the bed and began to ride her hard, thrusting himself inside her with every ounce of energy and strength he possessed.

He wanted to kill her, wanted to slip his hands around that slim white throat and squeeze the breath from her body. But he couldn't. Even in his rage he remembered she was the sister of Briony Cavanagh. Well, he decided, there were other ways to skin a cat, and by Christ he'd use everyone of them. Eileen O'Malley, as she now was, would never know another day's peace.

Chapter Twenty-one

Mariah looked at Tommy with shock tinged with well-concealed annoyance. She put her hands together and tapped her two forefingers against her lips. 'And what has Briony to say about this?'

Tommy shrugged nonchalantly.

'They're my halves of the businesses, I can dispose of them where I want.'

Mariah shook her platinum blonde head, a smile playing on her lips as she answered him.

'I don't see it that way, Tommy, and I have a feeling on me that Briony won't see it like that either. Now then, I don't know what has brought all this on, what's transpired between you, but I know this much. You're not using me to get a sly dig in. Me and Briony get along very well, we're going into business together on a house actually, and I have no interest in making an enemy of her. Not now, not ever.'

Tommy was surprised to hear about their business deal and looked at his hands, clasped together in his lap, while he digested the news. Briony had said nothing about it to him. Nothing.

'I see.'

Mariah grinned. 'No, you don't, Tommy Lane, and I think you should be ashamed of yourself. You walk in here, like the big "I am", offering me your half of Briony's businesses when they're hers really. Briony's the one who built up the houses while you concentrated on chancier deals. I know about your bookies, I know everything about everyone. I've made a career out of it. If you want shot, as you so eloquently put it, of any connection with her, my advice is to let her buy you out.'

Her voice softened and she leant towards him. 'Listen, Tommy mate, I don't know what's happened between you, but this ain't like you. Trying to tuck her up! Whatever she's done to you, remember the past. Remember when it was good and then decide on big things like the partnership. You might be having a nasty half hour today, but think, will you still feel like it a month from now, or a year?'

'To tell you the truth, Mariah, I can't face her. This ain't nastiness. I thought you'd be the best bet for a partner. You're alike, so bloody alike! But I can't face her meself. I'm sorry, I don't want to clap eyes on her now or ever. I don't really want to do her down, I swear that. But I have to sever the ties.'

'Do you need the money?'

Tommy shook his head.

'No. I don't need the money.'

'Then write to her, tell her from now on you're a sleeping partner. To bank your half of the profits. That way, you don't cut all your ties – you might be sorry you did one day – and also you don't have to see her until you feel you can handle it. And I'll give you some more free advice. Don't try and sell your half to anyone without consulting her first. That's taking the piss and you know it. If she done it to you, there'd be murder done. Try and keep an element of friendship there, Tommy. Give her first offer, then if she refuses, be a sleeping partner. But don't make things worse than they are. Trouble comes without you going out looking for it.'

Molly was shocked at the sight of Eileen. She had left the newlyweds for a week, restraining herself from going to the house, telling herself they would want a bit of time on their own. Finally, she had made the long awaited trip and now she sat in the little kitchen with Rosalee chewing on a slice of bread and wasn't sure what the hell she had stumbled into.

Eileen was as quiet as a church mouse, her face pinched and drawn. She was preparing her dinner, and such was her lassitude, even peeling the carrots was a long-drawn-out operation. She had made a pot of tea and had not opened her mouth since. Molly had talked about all her own doings, until now there was an absolute quiet that hung in the air like a silent cloud.

'Is everything all right, Eileen? You don't look yourself, girl.'

Eileen looked at her, her face strained. Molly felt a sinking feeling at the sight. Please don't let Eileen's nerves get the better of her now, not when she'd been better for so long. Holy Mary, don't let her be going off her head again, please.

'I said, are you feeling all right, Eileen child?'

She nodded.

Molly sighed loudly, wondering what to say.

'Is everything all right with you and Joshua?'

Eileen cut the carrots up, the scrape of the knife against the wooden chopping board the only sound in room.

'For the love of Christ, Eileen, will you bloody well answer me?'

Molly's loud voice made Eileen and Rosalee jump.

Eileen stared at her mother from fearful eyes. Molly noticed that in the week since the wedding her shoulders had acquired the old drooping look of before. Her face seemed to be on her collarbones instead of her neck.

'What do you want me to say?'

Molly closed her eyes. At least she'd answered, she wasn't entirely gone.

'Tell me what's wrong with you, girl? I'm worried about you. For a woman who's been married a week, you look suspiciously like one who's been married forty years, when the novelty's well and truly worn off! Is it Joshua? Is Joshua not nice like . . . You know. Is he doing something to upset you?'

Eileen shook her head, terrified, thinking of the taunts he constantly gave her, the way he asked her to tell him in detail what her seducer did to her, as if this spurred his own sexual appetite on. Telling her he would tell the world about her killing

281

her father, and about Henry Dumas. How the police would dig
her father up, and how she'd have to go to court . . .

'Is it that fucker of a mother of his then? Has she been at you?
Because if she has, you tell me and I'll wipe the floor with her!'

Eileen shook her head.

Molly gritted her teeth. She'd get to the bottom of this if she
had to throttle Eileen with her bare hands.

'Is it the bed like, the nights, love? Is that it?'

Eileen put her hand to her mouth and nodded furiously and
Molly sighed with relief.

'Listen, Eileen, I remember me own mother telling me on me
wedding day: "There's some that like it and there's some that
don't." I was an in-between meself. I liked it at first but once you
lot arrived, I soon went off it.'

Eileen didn't answer and Molly spoke again, her voice gentle.
'Look, Eileen, it's a part of marriage we all have to put up with.
It's the only way you'll get babies, and believe me, when you
have a little one on your breast, you'll see it was worth it. Do you
understand me?'

Eileen looked away and nodded.

Molly watched her as she made the dinner, and crossed
herself. She wouldn't like the bed part, that stood to reason,
she'd bad memories of it. But if she could get a child, then that
would straighten her out. Once you had a few babies, you didn't
have time for worrying about your troubles, and Eileen had had
far too long to dwell on hers. Joshua was a good man, he'd see
her all right. Molly consoled herself with that thought.

It had been over a week, and still Briony hadn't heard from
Tommy. She had sent three messages, and he hadn't answered
one. He had not tried to get in touch about any of the businesses,
or about their new ventures in the East End. It was as if he had
never existed. A young fellow had picked up his clothes from the
house and had refused down and out to tell Briony where he was
taking them. That had hurt desperately. Now she was to go and
look at Berwick Manor with Mariah, and pretend everything
was still tickety boo.

She felt the sting of tears. Well, he had to get in touch soon, even if it was just for the businesses, if she could speak to him once, she'd be all right. She'd convince him of how sorry she was, how much she missed him, loved him . . .

The door of her office swung open and Briony groaned as Bernie breezed into the office.

'What do you want?'

Bernie laughed. 'Oh, you're pleased to see me then!'

Briony half smiled. 'Sorry, that came out a bit vicious, didn't it? I'll start again. What can I do for you, Bernadette?'

'Nothing really, I just thought I'd pop in and see you, that's all. I've hardly seen you at the club and I thought, I know, I'll go and see her. See how she is like.'

Briony was inordinately pleased that Bernie, selfish, sharp-tongued Bernie, who could start a fight with her own fingernails, should be thinking about her.

'I'm all right, Bernie.'

'No word from Tommy then?'

'Nothing, not a whisper.'

'He'll be back.' Bernie's voice was strong.

Briony laughed. 'I hope so, Bern, but I have a feeling that this time he won't be coming back. Not now, not ever.'

'Balls to him if he don't, Bri, it's his loss not yours. Sod him, that's what I say. He was at the Ninety-Eight Club last night, Fenella told me. You know Fenella, the big girl with the huge buzumbas!' Bernie held her hands out from her chest to emphasise what she said and Briony laughed.

'Was he on his own?'

'What do you think? 'Course he was. Pissed out of his head and all, according to her.'

'No Kerry today?' Briony wanted to change the subject. Tommy going to the Ninety-Eight Club had upset her. He was going out then, even if he was getting drunk. She had waited in last night, as she had every night, for him to come round.

Bernie shook her head.

'Our Kerry is sleeping, she had a heavy night last night.' Her voice was heavy with sarcasm.

283

'What's that supposed to mean? She got a bloke then? It's true, is it? Me and Mother wondered. Who is it?'

Bernie smiled craftily.

'I've been sworn to secrecy about him, Bri, I can't even tell you. I'll give you a hint though. It's the last person in the world you'd expect.'

Briony picked up an air of malice in Bernie's voice and it troubled her.

'Is he married, is that it?' She was all concern.

Bernie shook her head. 'I don't know, do I?'

Briony stared at her for a long moment before she said, 'What's going on here, Bernie? You ain't come here to be Miss Nice Sister, you've come here to cause a bit of hag. Now if you've got something to say, spit it out, or else shut up.'

Bernie sat down and grinned. 'I ain't saying nothing, Briony. If you think there's something funny with our Kerry, you ask her yourself. You'll find her at home in bed about now. She don't get up 'til five these days. Like living with Dracula it is. Up all night and asleep all day. Even the cleaning woman asked if there was a coffin in her bedroom!'

Briony laughed and shook her head.

'You're a bleeding wind up, Bernie, do you know that?'

Bernadette smiled.

'Now, how are you really, Briony? We've all been worried about you.'

Her voice was so sincere, Briony left the subject of Kerry and started to reassure her sister that she was fine, knowing it would all go back to her mother. But what had been said about Kerry stuck in the back of her mind.

Kerry was not lying in bed, she was sitting in her small kitchen with Evander eating toast and drinking strong black tea, full of sugar. Evander was wearing just his trousers and shirt, Kerry was in a silk dressing gown.

'Tell me about Alabama, Evander, please? You never really tell me anything about America.'

284

Evander chewed on his toast slowly, deliberately annoying her. He knew that Kerry was impatient. Pulling his arms open, she sat on his lap.

'Come on, Evander, don't annoy me.'

He kissed her on the lips.

'There's nothing to tell, Kerry, really. Nothing that would interest you anyway.'

She took a bite of his toast. Licking the butter from her lips, she said: 'I'm serious, I want to know about your life there.'

Her voice had lost its jocularity now and Evander hugged her to him.

'Look, Kerry, let's just say it's very different from England.'

Kerry pulled herself up and looked at him sternly. 'For crying out loud, I'm not a kid, Evander! Stop treating me like one. If I ever go there, I want to know what to expect.'

He placed the remains of the toast on his plate and carefully wiped his hands on a napkin. This was becoming a regular occurrence. Kerry had a mad idea that they could go to Paris and live there, eventually going to America. No matter how hard he tried to dampen her enthusiasm, she would brook no argument on the subject. Looking at her now, standing with her hands on her hips, he knew the time had come for the real truth. He had to tell her everything. And somehow he had to explain to her exactly why they could never really be together. Not as man and wife.

'Sit down, Kerry. Sit down and keep your peace, woman. I'll tell you what you want to know.' His voice was low. Sitting herself in a chair opposite him, Kerry picked up her tea and waited, her face bright, as if lit from inside.

'Go on then.'

Evander wiped his mouth with his napkin and began to talk in a low sing-song voice.

'I was born in 1896 in a small place just outside Birmingham.'

'We've got a Birmingham here!'

Evander nodded and held his hand up for quiet. Now he had decided to tell her his story, he wanted her to hear it all.

'My father was a drifter, he was half-white. My mother, Liselle, lived on a small farm with her father. My three elder brothers were her father's children.'

Kerry screwed up her eyes at this and Evander could practically hear her mind clicking as she worked out the relationships.

'In Alabama, the blacks were treated worse than the animals. If a black man worked on a farm, then the horses and livestock would get priority over him for food, warmth and shelter. Most niggers slept in an outhouse. Some brought up whole families scratching in the dirt, working on a small place for food and maybe a few clothes. Children there worked from the time they could walk and feed the poultry. It's hot in the summer and cold in the winter. But it's hotter'n hell for a nigger come summertime and colder than an icebox for a nigger come fall.

'So, my mother picked up with a half-chat called Rusty Dorsey, a big, smooth-talking man. I can't remember him too well, but I can remember his voice. Like brown molasses, sweet and thick and syrupy. My mother bred four children in three years to him. I was the first. My sisters came after. He worked around, had a trade kind of, good with wood. My mammy always said that he could make a piece of tree bend itself whichever which way he wanted it to. Well, he left. We woke up one mornin' and he was long gone. Liselle, my mammy, broke her heart, and lived in hope of his coming back. Never did, of course, 'cept he'd turn up when he was rock bottom and then drif' off again after a while.

'My granddaddy liked him. They were both hard-talking, hard-drinking men, 'cept my granddaddy had the religion as well. We all lived in one small shanty, but it was ours. There weren't no bedrooms or toilets or nothing like that. You saw and heard everything about everyone. No privacy at all, but then children don't need none.'

Kerry nodded then, remembering the basements. The squalor, the tightly packed bodies in the beds.

'When I was five, I went to work with my mother at a white lady's house. She had a man servant called Tobias, a big nigger.

286

More a field hand really, than a lady's servant, but the woman, Miss Gloria Day . . . she was older than him, she was really old, you know. But she weren't ready to lie down, at least not in the ground anyways. Land's sakes, I watched her a watchin' him with that look!'

He laughed and Kerry smiled to hear him. Her eyes were boring into his face.

'Yes, sir! She liked black meat did Gloria Day! And Tobias, well, he was good to her. Anyway, Tobias took a liking to me. He knew I loved to hear the piano. Miss Day would play and I'd listen, getting a whipping for not sweeping the porch or cleaning the floor, whatever I was supposed to be doing. Well, Miss Day called me in and said to me – she had a high voice, kind of sweet but bitter, you know? – she says, "Evander, you like my piana playing, boy?" And I says real cute, "Yes, mam."

'So she shows me the scales. Anyway, for some reason she decided to teach me to play. I'd spend hours with her, listening to her. I could listen to her all night and day. She was an interesting person, you see. My mammy said, "Evander, she gonna get fed up soon so don't you be breaking your heart over it if she does."

'But God was good, and she began to teach me Chopin. Well, I picked it up real quick, and it pleased her. When I'd play, she'd laugh her head off. That went on for five years. The best five years of my life. By the time I was ten, I could play any damned thing she asked. Somehow, I think now, looking back, I was like the child she never had. She even tried to get me into a school, but the authorities wouldn't even listen. But I'd already accepted that so when she told me, I wasn't too disappointed.'

'It sounds wonderful. You had a great childhood . . .'

Evander laughed out loud.

'No, Kerry. That part of it was good, sure, but I was a nigger, and niggers don't have no childhood! You're a man from the first time you hold you own pecker and pee! Anyway, one morning we goes there and Miss Day is sitting on her porch, looking real bad. Her face was whiter than I ever seen it, and she was white you know. White skin, white hair, white clothes . . .'

He swallowed hard and took a sip of his cold coffee.

'"Look round the back, Lissy," she tells my mammy. "Look what they done."'

He looked down at the table for a few seconds.

'Who are "they", and what had they done?' Kerry's voice was serious now. She was frightened of what he was going to say, but had to know.

'"They" were the white men. They'd come late at night. Around the back of her property was an orchard. I'd spent many hours picking the fruit in the summer. There was a large oak tree. It had stood ever since I could remember. I'd climbed it so many times, chasing the coons. Well, hanging by his feet on the oak tree was Tobias. Only I didn't realise it was him at first. They'd burned him, burned him alive, but first they'd beaten him with sticks, kicked him with their boots. His face would have been unrecognisable anyways. They'd castrated him at some point, and pushed his pecker in between his teeth. That was the weird part, you see, because he was charred all over, his clothes were gone, everything, but that was still recognisable. You could see it hanging down.'

'Dear God, I feel sick . . . Really sick!'

Evander smiled.

'I got sick. I looked at that body and I brought up my grits like a hand was pushing up inside my stomach and forcing the food from me. My mammy was crying, she was crying hard, snot hanging from her nose and spittle hanging from her mouth. I ran back to my granddaddy and finally he came with Tobias's father and they cut him down.'

'What about the law, the police?'

'Honey, that *was* the law. It's still the law even now, all these years later. The law says a black man can't look at a white woman. If a white woman thinks a nigger is looking at her in lust, then he can be hanged. Someone at sometime had guessed about him and Miss Day. They didn't care that she wanted it, that she liked it, that she paid him! They wouldn't touch her, her family had been there for years. She had the security of money. So they touched the next best thing – Tobias. Black and

288

white don't really mix, girl, and it ain't no different in France. It's no different anywhere. You've got to understand that sometime.'

Kerry stared across the table at him. She saw his hair like coiled watch springs, his chocolate-coloured complexion. She wanted him so badly she could almost taste it.

'What are you trying to do? Why are you telling me this? You think I don't know about poverty, is that it? Believe me, Evander, I grew up in a slum, the worst kind of slum. We're Irish trash, we're paddys, even though me and my sisters were born here. Why are you trying to scare me, make me listen to such stories? If you don't want me, Evander, just come out and say it, because if you're waiting for me to finish with you, don't hold your bleeding breath, mate.'

Her voice was high, scared. The depth of feeling for him in it made him want to cry out at the injustice of it all. He went to her and knelt before her. Framing her face in his big hands, he tried to reason with her.

'I love you, girl. God help me, I worship you. But you don't understand what I'm trying to say! If anyone ever found out about us, you can't even begin to guess what trouble it would cause. I'm scared. Not for me, for you! You!'

Kerry tried to pull her face from his hands and he held her hard, digging his fingers into the white flesh.

'Listen to me. You think that love conquers all. Well, it don't. When me and you were living hand to mouth, you'd hate me, and if we had children, eventually you'd hate them too. We can't ever believe, either of us, that this is forever, because it's not, it can't be.'

Kerry began to cry then, her eyes filling with tears, blurring his face as she stared at him. Her whole body ached with the want of him, and the harshness of what had happened to them. He held her close, smelling her perfume, her hair. The gentleness of his touch was her undoing, and she cried bitter tears. Hard sobs that made her shudder, and soaked his shirt

'I should never have let it go so far, girl. I was wrong. But believe me when I say I love you, all of you, and I'd do anything

289

at all so we could be together always. But, Kerry, there's just no way. I've lain awake night after night, trying to think of a solution to our problems, and there ain't one.

'I'm going back to the States. I know a guy who can give me a job, I'll go and you'll forget all about me.'

'No . . . I won't, I'll never forget you. I'll follow you . . .'

Her voice was thick with tears. She knew she was babbling and couldn't stop herself.

'We'll find a way, I know we will.'

He held her away from him and looked into her face. Shaking his head, he said: 'I'm gonna leave you, baby, but I'm leaving my heart right here. You gotta accept that, Kerry. This ain't about what we want, it's about what we can and can't have, and we can't have our love. Not now, not ever. Maybe one day, who knows? Maybe one day it'll be different. But not in our lifetime, you can be sure about that.'

'But I love you so much, so much!'

He smiled, grateful for her undying love, even though he knew he should never have sought it.

'I love you too, baby, more than you'd ever dream. I want you so much. I've never had anyone like you before and I never will again. But let's be strong now. It's time for us to grow up and be big people. Big enough to finish what should never have been started and can only end in heartbreak. I'm going, girl, I'm finishing out my contract and then I'm off.'

'So all we have left is a month right? Just four weeks?'

He nodded, sorry to the heart for the sadness in her face, her voice, her whole being, but at the same time he was proud to know that she did love him, really love him. It was like a soothing balm to his wounds. It was sweet to know that he was the one finishing it with her, and he could finish with her for all the right reasons and come out of it with his dignity and his pride intact. He was, for the first time in his life, in charge of a white person's destiny. He was telling this lovely white girl enough was enough. It was a heady feeling.

Kerry sniffed loudly, her face still streaming with tears. 'Then we'd better make these four weeks the best of our lives.'

Evander kissed her then, pulling her face down softly on to his lips.

'We will, baby. Now that, I *can* promise you.'

Chapter Twenty-two

Briony watched the flickering screen with interest. Despite herself she was impressed with the way Rupert had made use of the girl and the camera angles. Jonathan's face was always obscured in some way, which was good, because the men who watched these films would want a faceless man. It stood to reason.

The girl was typical, which disappointed Briony. She had platinum hair, huge breasts, and a tiny waist. Briony detected an air of boredom emanating from her, but she knew that only she would notice that, and maybe the girls who worked for her. The men couldn't see it in the flesh and blood girls they bought and paid for, so a screen beauty would be no different.

The sex on the screen was hot and heavy, the girl's face expressing faked wonderment and lust. At one point she looked at the upright phallus in front of her and, staring directly into the camera, put a well-manicured hand over her mouth and opened her eyes to their utmost. It was what the punters would want, and exactly what Briony had invested in. As the girl turned over on to her stomach and stuck a perfectly rounded bottom into the air, Briony actually laughed out loud. Jonathan, naked except for a cape, entered her roughly, holding on to her hips. Tommy would hate it . . .

The thought brought Briony back to earth and her face clouded over. Tommy wouldn't even see it. It was ten days now since he had left and she had heard nothing, nothing at all. Oh, she knew he'd been out and about, she had heard that much, but he had not even had the decency to get in touch. Well, she wasn't going to get in touch with him again. He had ignored all her letters and messages, the ball was in his court now! Rage was getting the better of misery and she was glad. She preferred to be cross with him, it made his absence more tolerable. But she was getting worried. If they were still partners that meant she was still half-owner of the East End and she was acting accordingly. If Tommy didn't come back soon, then the rift would be open, really open, and that left her dangerously exposed. At the moment she was still protected, but if he left her high and dry, she would have to fight to regain credibility, and fight she would. No one, but no one, was going to pull her down or take what was hers. Not even Tommy Lane.

The two people on the screen began to flicker and dissolve. The film was coming to its conclusion and she forced her mind back on to the subject matter. She had to OK it with Rupert and Jonathan. She watched it end and then put the light back on.

It was good enough for what they wanted, it would do. She stared around the room for a moment, taking in the furnishings which she hadn't really looked at for a long time. A picture of Benedict stood in a silver frame on the mantelpiece. This was her private room. Only people who were specially invited ever came in here. It was her own private domain. Even her mother wasn't allowed inside. It was where she did her thinking, where she and Tommy had once planned and schemed. That seemed so long ago now. It was as if he had always been gone.

There was a photograph of her and Tommy too. It had been taken the day they had gone to see Charlie Chaplin in *The Kid*. They had loved little Jackie Coogan, loved the film. Both were smiling widely, her face partly obscured by a large hat. Briony picked up the photograph and stared at it, trying to remember everything about that day, every nuance, every moment. If only she had realised sooner how much they had meant to one another.

But that was the trouble, she never did think. Tommy had been there for a long time, she had thought he always would be. She had not realised you had to keep people. She collected people like others collected luggage, and kept them with the minimum of trouble. Her family, for example. But Tommy had needed more and she had been too wrapped up in herself to notice that. She sighed heavily. If Tommy truly abandoned her now, she was back where she started: a madam, a club owner, nothing more and nothing less. If Tommy wasn't there she would look after herself.

She placed the photograph back on the mantle, picking up the one of Benedict. He was grinning. Dressed in a dark suit, he leant against a pillar. It was a good photo, had caught his laughter. Sally had taken him to have it done, telling him it was for herself. He thought Sally looked at it in her room, never contemplating the fact it could be for someone else.

Her face broke into a small smile. Ben looked like her. Even in the sepia-coloured photo where you couldn't see the green of his eyes or the red tinge to his hair, he was wholly her child.

She felt the familiar tug of him, the need of him, inside herself. Replacing the photograph carefully, she walked from the room. She had to go to her mother's today. Another crisis in the family was beckoning. Sometimes she wished they'd all disappear down a big hole and leave her alone. She wasn't in the mood for trouble, she had enough of her own. But no one was to know that, of course. Briony had to be strong, morning, noon and night. It was the law of the Cavanaghs, and she wished with all her heart she hadn't been the instigator of that law.

Molly waited in Eileen's kitchen for Briony. She had left word for her to go straight there, threatening Mother Jones with death, pain, torture and destruction if she made her a cup of tea and delayed her. Elizabeth O'Malley sat wide-eyed, staring into the fire, her face swelling where Eileen had smacked her in the eye.

'Briony was coming to see me today anyway, I was going to tell her that Eileen wasn't right. I blame you and that son of yours, you bitch of hell! Torturing the poor girl out of her mind!'

Elizabeth O'Malley shook her head slowly.

295

'That girl is as mad as a March hare, you know that in your heart. You were here, you saw what happened. She attacked me for no reason at all. I only came to see how she was.'

Molly made a grunting noise of disbelief.

'That's what you say! You come here day after day. Oh, don't think I don't know. Driving my girl to fecking distraction with your mawing and your jawing! You think you had a smack off our Eileen? Wait 'til my Briony gets here, she'll wipe the fecking floor with you! And as for that great galloping eejit of a son of yours, my Eileen's never known a minute's peace since she walked down that aisle with him. Not two weeks wed and she's like a poor distracted maniac. He's like your husband, madam, one of them sex fiends! Everyone knew about O'Malley. By Christ, as long as it was breathing, he'd bed it!'

Elizabeth O'Malley's mouth stretched to its fullest. 'YOU BITCH!'

'Yeah, I'm a bitch, but you're a vixen of the first order and my Briony will take the jump from your gallop, by Christ she will. She'll maul the face off you!'

Briony walked in at the back door just as they started fighting properly. Separating the two women, she looked at them both in disbelief and said: 'What the hell is going on here?'

Molly pushed her rival in the chest, sending her careering across the kitchen and into the dresser, the plates and mugs dropping to the floor with a resounding crash.

'That whore of hell there, Bri, *her*, she's the blame. Her and that boy of hers. Call himself a man! Huh! I've seen better men laid out in coffins!'

'Where's Eileen?'

'She's upstairs, and if you ask me she needs to see a doctor. She's out of her mind and my boy ain't responsible for a madwoman, no way. She's your bad blood, not ours. Yours!'

Briony looked into Elizabeth O'Malley's face and said low, 'If I was you, old lady, I'd keep my trap shut. Only I ain't in the mood for hag, and I'm that far from losing me temper.'

She held out a finger and thumb to emphasise her point.

'That's it, Bri, rip the cheeks from her . . .'

'MUM! Will you give it a rest and let me see Eileen? You two can fight and argue the day away, but for fuck's sake take it out into the street. This is neither the time nor the place.'

Both women shut up then, though both would fight 'til the cows came home left to themselves.

'That's better. Now make a cup of tea, I'm gasping, and keep it down. I'll go on up and see what I can do.'

She made her way up the stairs with a heavy tread. The two older women were still arguing, but softly now, in vicious whispers. Rolling her eyes at the ceiling, she went into Eileen's room. What she found there shocked her to the core. Her sister was curled up on the floor, the quilt from the bed over her, a corner in her mouth pushed in as if to stop a scream from escaping.

'Eileen, Eileen! Are you all right, love?'

Briony knelt down beside her, her face and voice concerned. Eileen stared from pale blue eyes, as if unsure of who she was.

'It's me, love, Briony. Are you all right, what happened? Tell me what happened?'

Eileen's nose was running, and taking a hankie from her coat pocket, Briony wiped it gently. Then she pulled the quilt from Eileen's mouth, wiping the spittle away.

'I can't take any more, Bri. They fight all the time, the two of them. Shouting at me and at each other. Joshua won't leave me alone, see. He won't ever leave me alone. Night after night. I don't like it, Bri, I don't like him. He's nasty to me he is, makes me tell him things, and I can't stand it.'

Briony looked down at her sister, her elder sister, and shook her head, trying to comprehend what was going on.

'What do you mean, tell him things? What things?'

Eileen swallowed hard.

'You won't let on I told you? You mustn't let him know I said anything, see. Because he said if I told anyone, he'd kill me.'

Briony screwed her eyes up and said, 'Oh, he did, did he? Well, I won't let on, darling. You tell me and I'll see what I can do. How's that?'

Eileen grabbed Briony's hands in hers, relief flooding her

297

face. Briony saw the fear there, and the worry. She felt an urge to take Joshua and throttle him with her bare hands for putting that terror there in the first place.

'Come on, Eileen, you tell Briony. I'll look after you.'

'He made me tell him about us, Bri. About me dad, and Henry Dumas ... He knows everything. About the boy, about me dad, what I did to me dad. He says he's going to tell the police. And he makes me do things to him. Awful things. I don't know why he's doing it. He was nice to me, Briony, always nice. He never hurt me before ...'

She started to cry harder. Briony stroked the fine dark hair gently.

'Come on, up you get, I'll help you undress and put you to bed, then we'll sort all this out once and for all.'

Eileen sniffed loudly and allowed Briony to help her up. As she slipped her dress off, Briony saw the bruises and scratches on her body and clenched her teeth. She made the bed and helped Eileen into it, smoothing the covers over her with kind hands. Eileen's face, so white, so pinched, broke her heart. Briony felt responsible for all that had happened. Kissing her sister on the forehead, she left the room.

In the kitchen Molly and Elizabeth O'Malley were sitting at the scrubbed table, tea cups in hand, mouths clamped shut. Briony walked in and shut the kitchen door behind her.

'What's been happening here?'

Elizabeth O'Malley shook her head. 'I don't know. I came today to see her like and then your ma arrived. We had a row and Eileen just went mad. Attacked me. And her language!'

'She must have learnt that off your son, our Eileen never said a bad word to my knowledge all her life.'

'My Joshua is a decent man, I'll have you know ...' Pride in her son overrode any fear of Briony Cavanagh.

Briony poked her face into the older woman's.

'Your son is an animal, and that's what's turned our Eileen's head. Now get up off your fat arse and go and get the doctor. Then go home, go anywhere, but get as far away from me as possible. Oh, and another thing. Your son won't be living here

298

after today, so expect him home at some point.'

Molly grinned in anticipation of all that was to happen in the next few hours. Her Briony would sort it all out, she knew that without a doubt. When Elizabeth O'Malley had left, she smirked and said:

'That told her. If you'd have heard the carry on here today!'

'Shut up, Mum! You're as bloody bad, coming round here tormenting the life out of her. Eileen's ill. She's ill in the mind, Mum, and if you hadn't got me round that ponce's house to marry her, none of this would have happened. She should never have married anyone, not after what happened to her. Dad taking her to Dumas broke her; the day the old man died finished her. Remember when she used to wander off? How she couldn't cope with anything? Well, I think now she's gone over the edge and you can thank yourself for that, not the O'Malleys, mother or son. Yourself.

'Now listen to me and listen good. In future you leave everything be, and keep that big galloping trap and hooked nose out of other people's business, right? Because I blame you for all this today. You and myself. I should never have listened to you.'

Molly's mouth dropped open. That Briony could talk to her like this spoke volumes. Molly felt the first twinge of shame envelop her.

'I'll tell you something else, Mother, he knows all our business. About the old man, Dumas, my boy, everything. He made her tell him, been torturing the life out of her with it. How's that for the icing on the fucking cake!'

'NO! She told him? Dear God in heaven, the stupid, stupid girl.'

'Not stupid. Frightened, terrified, mentally ill, lots of things, Mum, but not stupid. We were the stupid ones to countenance the marriage in the first place. I'll see Joshua O'Malley meself, and shut his trap up once and for all if he ain't careful. He needs knocking down a peg and I'll see to it myself!'

Kevin Carter, Briony's driver, was surprised by the look on her face when she emerged from her sister's house. Her usual good

299

nature seemed to have deserted her and her face was a mask of anger. She got into the back of the car.

'Elizabeth O'Malley's, pronto.'

Without further ado, he drove. Briony sat in the back. Wrapped in her coat, she stared out of the window at the passing streets. Children played on the pavements, men lounged against the lampposts. It was like going back in time. The streets were no different from how they had been when she was a child. Since the war times had changed. Only the people in these streets had been passed by. They still lived in the same back to backs, soot-blackened and small. They still kept a few chickens if they could afford it, or a rabbit or two in a hutch knocked up out of a jerry crate. They still lived hand to mouth, still had that look of hopelessness about them.

The car pulled up outside Elizabeth O'Malley's and Briony got out slowly. It was seven-thirty, still light enough to see everything that was going on around her. A group of ragged children hunched around a doorway, their game of five jacks forgotten as they gazed at the lady in the deep green coat who owned a car. One little girl scratched at a festering flea bite on her ankle and broke the skin. She dabbed at the blood with dirty fingers.

Briony saw curtains twitching, and a mother with a young child on her arm stopped where she was and stared at her. Briony recognised her: Lily Bains, a girl she had gone to school with. She smiled and nodded and banged on Elizabeth O'Malley's front door. The knock resounded through the house and instinctively Briony knew no one was there.

'Lily, do you know where she is?'

Lily stepped back a pace, unsure whether to talk to Briony, a woman who was spoken of in hushed whispers these days; the girl with whom she had once played Tin Pan Alley and shared some childish dreams.

Briony walked towards her. 'Come on, Lily, cat got your tongue? Where's the old bitch O'Malley? Have you seen her son?'

Lily heard the gentle tone and shook her head. 'They went

out about an hour ago. I think Mother O'Malley was moving because they had some bags. I hope she was, I can't stand the old cow.'

Briony forced a smile.

'Any idea where she could be moving to? Has she anyone who'd put her up like?'

Lily shook her head again and the child smiled. Briony saw the caries in the child's teeth already; he was no more than a year old.

'The only place she's welcome is the church, and I don't think she's really welcome there. How are you, Briony? You look really well. Really smart.' The last was said with admiration.

'You look well and all, Lily. This your boy?' She stroked the child's face with soft hands. He chuckled. Lily puffed out her cheeks, aware that they were being observed. Now Briony had singled her out for attention, she could brag about how she had grown up with her and people would be impressed.

'I've got four, this is me youngest. I married Danny Little, remember him?'

'I remember him, he used to show us his birds' eggs.'

Briony knew the O'Malleys were long gone, and somehow she was reluctant to leave Lily, a reminder of times past. Of her real youth.

'He still collects them, Briony. Knows all about birds does Danny boy.' Lily's voice dropped. 'I heard you're doing well. I'm glad, Briony. I'm glad you got away from here. You was always a clever girl, always had your eye to the main chance, you did!'

Briony smiled. 'That was me, all right, Lil. It was lovely seeing you. You must know where I live. Come round one day and we'll have a cuppa, talk about the old days.'

'Maybe I will and all.' Both knew that she wouldn't, that her children were infested with lice and she wouldn't have the guts to take them to Briony's house, but it was nice to be offered and she respected Briony for that. Opening her bag, Briony took out all the money she had in it, about eight pounds, and pushed it into Lily's hand.

'No! No, Briony, I can't take that! No, it was lovely to see you, and talk to you. I don't want your money.'

Briony laughed then.

'Well, you're the only one who don't! But you're the only person I really want to have it. Take it, there's plenty more where that came from!'

Lily looked at the money in wonder.

'I won't say it won't come in handy, girl!'

'Listen, Lily, if ever you need anything, you come to me, right?'

She nodded, tears in her eyes.

'Thanks, Bri. It's funny but we was at rock bottom today. Danny got laid off at the docks. This'll keep us going for a good while.'

Briony and Lily embraced, the child between them crushed by their bodies. He shouted to remind them he was there.

'Tell Danny to go and see Bobbie Phillips tomorrow at the Royal Albert. He'll have a job, I'll see to that.'

Lily nodded, her throat constricted.

'Tara, mate, see you round.'

'Tara, Bri, and thanks again.'

Inside the car Briony was aware of Kevin Carter looking at her as if she'd gone mad.

'Saint Vincent's church, Kevin.'

Her face looked more relaxed than it had earlier and she waved at her friend until they turned the corner of the street.

Father McNamara was not surprised to see Briony Cavanagh in his hallway. He smiled at her and showed her into his library.

'Now then, Briony, what can I do for you?'

'I'm looking for Elizabeth O'Malley and her son, Joshua.'

The priest nodded. 'I see, and why would you be looking for them. You're related now, aren't you? Didn't I see him married to your sister not two weeks since?'

Briony smiled.

'You did, and now he's left her. I want to have a little talk to him. Only I can't find him, or his mother.'

302

The priest lit himself a cigar and puffed on it for a moment to get it fully alight.

'That woman is like one of the deadly plagues, a mouth on her like nobody's business. Has she put you out like?'

'You could say that, Father. Now have you seen them?'

'No, I haven't seen them.'

Briony stood up.

'Thanks anyway. I'll just keep looking. Do you know if they have any relatives at all? Someone they could go to?'

The priest looked at the girl before him, weighing up in his mind whether to speak out or not.

'Sit back down and tell me what's happened. Then I'll answer your question.'

Briony sat back down and told the priest about Eileen, a carefully edited version, leaving out the juicier bits.

'So Eileen's in a terrible state and he's to blame. I want to see him and set the record straight once and for all. I think I owe him that much.'

'Poor Eileen. She was never right, that one, I saw the change in her myself, God love her and keep her. Didn't she used to work for that feller with the moustaches who owned the blacking factory and half the dock properties?'

Briony screwed up her eyes to slits and nodded. 'As I did, Father. I worked for him as well.'

'Ah, that's right indeed.'

Briony and the priest looked at one another in unspoken communication.

'She wasn't right, poor girl. Maybe the work was too hard for her? I remember your father taking Communion afterwards every week, regular as clockwork.'

Briony didn't say a word. If you took Communion, you had to have your Confession heard. She knew the priest was telling her he knew exactly what was wrong with Eileen and still she didn't speak.

The priest sighed. He had hoped to trade information. This girl and her family intrigued him.

'Well now, if I remember rightly, Elizabeth O'Malley has a

303

brother in Islington. He's a bit of a demon by all accounts, another one with religious mania. I don't think they really get on, but that's not surprising, is it? You ask around Islington and I'm sure you'll find him.'

Briony nodded and stood up.

'Thanks, Father.'

'Would you like me to go and see poor Eileen?'

'My mother would like that, Father. There's just one thing, before I forget.'

'What's that, my child?' The priest looked up at her with his hands clasped together on his lap, cigar clamped firmly between his teeth.

'Don't ever try and find out my business or my family's again. What you guess and what you know is up to you. But in future remember where the money comes from for your expensive cigars and whisky, because there's plenty of other churches who'd welcome me with open arms. No questions asked.'

She left the room, leaving a stony-faced Father McNamara whose Havana cigar had suddenly lost its expensive taste.

Chapter Twenty-three

Eileen was tucked up in bed in the house where all her troubles had started. Cissy and Mrs Horlock fussed over her, Molly stared at her in bewilderment, and Briony soothed her. But inside her head nothing was right. Her thoughts seemed to run off on tangents; she wasn't sure what was fact and what was fiction. She stared vacantly around her, smiling at times but always quiet. Too quiet.

Briony left her in Mrs Horlock's capable hands and she and Molly retired downstairs to the library to talk.

'You're good to have her here, Briony.'

Molly's voice was stiff. She was still upset about what Briony had said to her, and wasn't sure how to approach her daughter now. Briony turning on her had shocked her more than she cared to admit. Molly liked to think that everything was fine, that the horrors her daughters had experienced were now relegated to the back of their mind, as they were to hers, but Briony had brought them all back. She had reminded Molly that in her own way she had played an integral part in their unhappiness, that in effect she had condoned what her husband had set out to do. Molly lost no sleep any more over Paddy's demise. In fact, since then she had experienced a measure of freedom which would have been unheard of had he still been alive. Now she had to try and ingratiate herself once more with this powerful daughter.

'I think I'll get another quack in to our Eileen in the morning, Mum. There's a bloke from up West, Scottish name, treats

Lord Palmer's son for shell shock. He's the best in his field for mental illness.'

Molly nodded but kept her peace. Only rich people could afford nerves and mental illness. She believed still that the devil made work for idle hands. In Molly's eyes a good day's work looking after a few kids and a husband and house was more than sufficient to keep a woman from thinking. Thinking was a bad thing. Too much time for thought and you started sickening.

'I've asked around and about. It seems Joshua has an uncle in Islington, I'm going there later. Kevin Carter's out now with a couple of others tracking him down. If he's there we'll find him. I've got to shut his trap up in some way. But the main thing at the moment is our Eileen. Getting her better if we can. Though I think, eventually, she'll have to go away.'

Molly nodded again.

'Oh, for fuck's sake, Mum, have a go at me, fight me, but don't keep being so bloody passive, it don't suit you. If you've anything to say, any thoughts on all this, say them! I can't stand you quiet, it's unnatural!'

Molly opened her eyes wide and nodded once more, infuriating Briony even further.

'God give me strength!'

'Oh, he's given you that, Bri. He's given you enough already for ten men.'

Briony laughed gently.

'Oh, it can speak then?'

'I can. It's whether or not you're interested in what I have to say?' There was a semblance of Molly's old spirit as she spoke and Briony was pleased.

'Mum, think about this. When did any of us ever listen to you anyway? That never shut you up before, did it?'

Molly grinned then. Briony was joking, she was over the worst, the sun was out and everything was going to be all right. Briony would look after them all. The weight was lifted from Molly's shoulders and she could relax again.

Kevin stood uncertainly in front of Tommy Lane.

'If she knew I knew where you were, Tommy, there'd be murders.'

'I know that, Kev, and I appreciate you telling me everything. Is Briony all right like, in herself?'

'Oh, yeah. Well, I mean, she seems all right. But I think all this with her sister has shocked her more than she'd ever admit. You know Briony, she's more close-mouthed than the government.'

Tommy smiled in spite of himself.

'True. So Joshua has something over her, has he? Well, ain't he the brave bastard! Milk and water, I booked him. Wouldn't say boo to a mouse on a mortuary slab. Well, we live and fucking learn, don't we? Still, don't worry, Kev, I'll find the ponce and sort him out. In fact, me and you can go and see this bible basher now. Maybe I'll get a bit more out of him than you did.'

'Suits me, Tommy. I just want to give Briony a break. Her sister's bad, I saw her meself. She's ill, mate. That bloke's worked her over and all, black and blue her arms were. But he never touched her boat race. Well, he wouldn't, would he? What a turn up, eh?' He shook his head in silent disgust.

'Sit down and I'll get changed. Help yourself to a drink.'

Tommy left the room and walked up the stairs of his new house in Stratford. As he entered the bedroom a female voice said, 'Are you coming back to bed, Tommy?'

Shirley Darling, as she was called, held out one long slim arm towards him. He smiled.

'Sorry, Shirl, but business beckons. Get yourself dressed and trundle off now. There's a good girl.'

Shirley sat up in bed, the sheet dropping away to reveal enormous breasts. 'Oh, Tommy! Can't I wait for you to come home later?'

'Nope! Dressed and home for you, young lady. I'm busy.' He pulled on his clothes with a nonchalant air.

'You're a wanker, Tommy Lane!'

He laughed out loud. 'Very ladylike, I must say.'

Shirley, who really liked Tommy, had always liked him and had been over the moon to climb into his bed, was upset that he was dismissing her like a two-bob tart. Her eyes screwed up and she said, 'You *are* a wanker. As for me being ladylike, I'm no more ladylike than Big Briony, as they call her. They also call her the Poison Dwarf, did you know that? What's the matter, Tommy? Frightened she'll find out I've been here and little Tommy Lane's been a naughty boy? Scared of her, are you?'

She froze as he yanked her from the bed by her arm. He ran her across the room and into the dressing room where her clothes were neatly folded on a chair.

'Get dressed and fuck off. As for Briony, you ain't even fit to walk on the same bit of pavement as her. Now take your stuff, take your big fucking trap, and piss off!'

Shirley sat on a chair naked, and rubbed at her arm. 'You hurt me!'

Tommy made a tragic face. 'NO! I never, did I? If you're not careful I might just tell Briony what I've been doing all afternoon. Now if she frightens me, what must that thought do to you, eh?'

He left the room but as he walked down the stairs felt a wave of temper wash over him. So people thought he was scared of Briony, did they? Then he smiled. The Poison Dwarf! Briony would laugh if she heard that one. Collecting Kevin, he left the house, Shirley never once entering his thoughts. Unlike Briony, she was over and done with.

Padraig O'Connor was a thin wiry Irishman with burnished red hair, a red bushy beard, and large rough hands. Not a tall man, only five foot four, he gave the impression of great strength in his compact, tightly muscled body. His deep-set blue eyes had the glint of a man on the verge of religious mania.

Padraig went into the lowest of pubs and drinking establishments, giving out the word of the Lord. He knew his bible backwards and forwards, believing in the pure and simple sanctity of living your life by the word of God, the ten commandments and *Leviticus*. He drank only water, Adam's Ale, and ate simple foods. He also worked hard as a coal man, delivering the sacks everywhere, his hands and back ingrained with coal dust, a sign to the world that he toiled hard at good honest work. Drunks, women of the night and local priests ducked into corners and under hedges when they saw him coming. As Father Kennedy had once remarked, the man could make a top of the morning sound like a declaration of war.

Padraig was in The Green Man, his bible open at *Leviticus*, regaling the rather drunken customers with the Lord's words on bestiality.

'"Thou shalt not lie down with the beasts of the field."'

A big burly docker shouted out, 'I'll agree with you there, mate, but what if your old woman looks like the fucking back end of a bullock? What then, eh?'

Everyone laughed. A tiny man with horn-rimmed glasses, carried away with drink and camaraderie, shouted out: 'Your old woman *sounds* like the back end of a bullock! She's got more mouth than a cow's got . . .'

The docker stopped laughing immediately and, turning to the man who'd insulted his wife, said: 'Do you want a bunch of fives or what?'

The little man's head disappeared into his glass of ale and the docker looked around him for anyone who fancied having another go about his wife.

Padraig O'Connor carried on regardless, his words delivered in a loud voice, his whole demeanour taut and intense. He believed every word he said and couldn't for the life of him understand how no one else could gain the enjoyment from the bible that he did.

The smoky atmosphere was burning his eyes and throat. He coughed loudly and the barman pushed a pint of beer on to the counter.

'Go on, man, drink that. It'll cool you down.'

Padraig shook his head.

'A glass of water will be sufficient, thank you.'

The barman got him his water, and handing it to him, said, 'Drink that and go. They're laughing at you, can't you see that?'

Tommy Lane and Kevin Carter walked into The Green Man. One look at the man at the bar drinking down a glass of water and they knew they'd struck gold. They stood watching as he started his preaching once more.

'"Thou shalt not lie with mankind as with womankind, it is abomination!" I see this all the time. Round the docks, men dressed as women, men looking for other men, like painted harlots!'

Tommy looked at Kevin and made a face. 'Fuck me, he's as mad as a hatter!'

Kevin laughed.

'Shall I get him outside so you can talk?'

'Yeah, I think this lot will probably be grateful to see the back of him.'

Kevin walked over to Padraig. Whispering in his ear, he half dragged and half cajoled the man from the public house. To the amusement of everyone there, the docker shouted: 'Oh, leaving so soon? And we hadn't got to the bit about whoredoms yet! Well, don't hurry back, mate.'

Outside Tommy looked at the man before him with sorrow. In his own way Padraig was a good man, only like most people who were too good, he got on the nerves of lesser mortals like Tommy himself.

'Hello, Mr O'Connor. I'm Thomas Lane, and I'm looking for your nephew Joshua.'

Padraig stared at Tommy intently, his hard blue eyes seeming to bore into his face.

'My nephew is no concern of mine, or yours come to that.'

Tommy smiled widely then, opening his coat, waited until O'Connor was watching this action before punching him with all his might in the solar plexus, driving the man on to his knees. Dragging him up by his shirt, he looked once more into his face and said: 'If you know where your nephew is, you'd better fucking tell me because the wrath of God is nothing compared to mine.'

Padraig weighed up his chances. His bible was lying in a small puddle, the pages open and getting soaked with dirty water.

'I've nothing to say to you.' Tommy began working him over then. Kevin held Padraig's arms behind his back and Tommy pummelled him in the stomach and head. Five minutes later, his face was bloody, his eye swollen.

Tommy looked at the man's destroyed face and said, 'I can keep this up all night if needs be. It's no skin off my nose. Now then, where's your nephew? He's hurt a woman I care about deeply. Sent her off her head, in fact, beaten her up and broken her heart. You're not telling me you'll hide someone like that?'

Padraig was shocked at the charges against his nephew. He had never cared for his sister much. They had tried to outdo one another on the religious front since childhood, but her husband had been a fornicator and a drunkard. Now it seemed the son was the same.

'Hurt the woman you say? Beat her?'

'Black and bleeding blue. I'll take you to her, if you like?'

'No . . . no. Joshua is at my coal yard in Shepherds Bush. At the corner of Scrubbs Lane. They're both in the shed at the back.'

Tommy smiled then, sorry for what he'd had to do.

'Thanks, mate. You can get on with your holy work now. We won't keep you a moment longer.'

Padraig wiped a hand across his mouth. 'The Lord is slow but he's sure, young man. "What ye sow shall ye reap."'

'God also has another little saying. It's: "An eye for a fucking eye." Well, tonight your nephew's going to find out exactly what that means.'

With that Tommy left the man and climbed into his car. He saw Padraig pick up his bible and wipe the pages lovingly before walking back into the foetid warmth of The Green Man, and in a funny way Tommy couldn't help but admire him and his principles.

'Come on, Kevin, let's get moving. All this do-gooding is making me feel ill!'

Joshua was chewing his thumbnail, a habit that had always annoyed the life out of his mother.

'I blame you for all this. I've had to leave me home, everything, because you brought the Cavanaghs into our house.

311

Two weeks you've been married, two weeks! And now we're hiding out in my brother's bloody coal yard! Me, a respectable widow, reduced to this!' She felt a terrific urge to brain her son where he sat. 'Will you stop chewing your fingers to pieces!'

'Listen, Mother, I can sort all this out. I have something Briony Cavanagh wants, in a manner of speaking. I'll get us the money to start up again somewhere else. Now, for goodness' sakes, give it a bloody rest!'

Elizabeth looked at her son, a weak man like his father. A weak and cowardly individual who had been both the pride and bane of her life.

'What have you got exactly that's so important?'

Joshua shook his head, annoying her once more. 'Nothing for you to worry about. Let's just say I have certain information that could help us, both physically and financially.'

As what he said sank in, Elizabeth O'Malley felt her legs begin to give way. She sat down abruptly on an old chair, glad of its support. Her voice low now, she said: 'You fool of hell! You stupid foolish boy. You're not seriously contemplating black-mailing the woman, are you? Jesus wept! She'll take you by your balls and hang you from the highest lamppost she can find, and she'll do it in public and all, because there's none will ever split on her. That's what this is all about, isn't it? You've found out something. This isn't over Eileen really. Tell me what you know now, before they find us.'

Joshua licked dry lips and swallowed hard. He was in over his head and he knew it. Now, worst of all, his mother knew it too.

'It's Eileen and Briony . . . they were both whores of Henry Dumas as children. Their father took them as little girls. Eileen attacked her father with the flat iron, and killed him stone dead . . .'

'Jesus fecking cross of Christ! And you thought you could use that to get us out of this trouble? You're even more stupid than I gave you credit for.' Joshua saw the fear on his mother's face and felt the heat of terror enveloping him, making him sweat.

'Briony Cavanagh kept that a close secret, boy, so do you think she'll ever rest easy again, knowing we have her marked down? Do you really think that? Could you be so bloody stupid! That Eileen, as mad as she is, was at least a decent wife in that she was quiet. Amenable and easily handled. You could have kept us both up there, living the life of Riley, but you had to push the girl. I can see now you pushed her over the edge. You've signed your own death warrant. Briony and that Tommy Lane rule the roost and, let's face it, there's more than a few people who'd like to see us out of the way. They'll have all the help they need to find us.'

Joshua jumped from his seat.

'Will you shut up! For once in your life, shut that great big gob of yours! If it hadn't have been for you, I'd have married Eileen fair and square. But no, you didn't want me married, not to her or anyone. Well, she was a slut like her bloody sister. Can't you see, I can get us enough money with this knowledge to set us up anywhere we want to go?'

For the first time ever Elizabeth O'Malley was lost for words. This great big son of hers really thought he could get away with threatening Briony Cavanagh.

'You're mad, son, stark staring mad if you honestly believe that. Briony Cavanagh will tear London apart looking for us. You have nothing on her, nothing at all. Because she'll see you don't live long enough even to breathe a word of what you know.'

Tommy Lane walked into the tiny cabin then and said: 'I couldn't agree with you more, love.'

Joshua felt a sinking sensation in his bowels as he looked at Tommy Lane's smiling face.

Elizabeth O'Malley took her son's arm, pulling him to try and get him to move.

'Come on, Joshua. At least walk out of here under your own steam.'

He allowed himself to be led from the cabin. Tommy walked beside them, his hand on Elizabeth's arm. The vicious-tongued old woman beside him looked very small all of a sudden, and very vulnerable.

Gritting his teeth, he helped her into his car. This one was for

Briony. He owed her this much at least.

'Who's at the door?'

Cissy marched across the hallway in her dressing gown. 'How the bleeding hell do I know? See through solid wood, can I?' She opened the door wide and gasped.

'Hello, Tommy . . . Briony's in bed.'

Mrs Horlock smiled as he walked into the entrance hall. 'I'll go up to her then.'

As he disappeared up the stairs, Cissy and Mrs Horlock clasped one another in glee.

'He's back then, I knew he would be!'

The two women smiled conspiratorially.

'Briony will be sleeping in, I'll bet!'

Cissy pushed Mrs Horlock in the shoulder gently. 'Oh, you're terrible you are!'

Tommy walked into Briony's bedroom, shutting the door gently behind him. Briony lay asleep, her hair around her head like a deep red halo. She had on a small night light which flickered as the door opened and closed, giving her milky skin a luminous glow. She turned on to her side, giving him a tantalising glimpse of breast, then as she began to burrow under the covers, she froze. Opening her eyes in alarm, she realised someone was there.

'All right, Bri, calm down, it's only me.'

She lay on her back once more, staring up at him in wonderment.

'Tommy?' She blinked her eyes a couple of times as if unsure what she was seeing was real.

Sitting up in the bed, her face glowing, she hugged her knees through the blankets.

'You came back? Oh, Tommy, it's good to see you.'

She flung her arms around his neck, pushing her body against his and feeling the comforting warmth as he hugged her back.

Tommy remembered the love he had had for her, felt the pull of her. He disengaged himself from her arms with difficulty.

'I'm not back for good, Bri, let's get that straight now.'

Her face darkened. 'What do you mean?' He could hear the confusion in her voice.

'What I say, Bri. We're old news, love. I came to tell you something important, something that has to be said face to face. Joshua and his mother are gone. They won't be back again. What he knew about you and Eileen is as safe as houses.'

'How did you know . . . How did you know he'd found out? No one knew, no one except me and me mum and our Eileen . . .' She was stammering.

'I found them tonight, and heard everything they said. At least his mother had the sense to know he'd gone too far. Well, I've shut the pair of them up, permanently.'

Briony's face dropped. Her whole countenance seemed to crumple before his eyes.

'You don't mean . . .'

He nodded.

'You didn't have to do that! I could have shut them up. Fear would have shut them up, Tommy, plain and simple fear. I wanted to kill them myself, but I know I never would have. It was just temper. I could have shut them up by myself!' She pushed him away from her then. Getting out of the bed, she pulled on a wrapper and began pacing the bedroom floor as she tried to comprehend what Tommy had done.

'My God, Tommy, you'd kill anyone, wouldn't you? Without another thought? I admit I could have wrung his bloody neck, and a good hiding would have been compulsory, but I'd never have topped them. They weren't worth topping. They were nothings, no ones. Shit on my fucking shoes! How dare you do that without telling me? How dare you take something like that on yourself and expect me to be grateful!'

'Well, that's rich, Briony, I must say. Here's me trying to help . . .'

'Don't give me that old bollocks, Lane. You wanted an out. Well, you've achieved what you set out to do, you've got your out, and your big fucking finale into the bargain. Only don't expect me to drop to me knees with thankfulness. It ain't gonna happen.'

315

Tommy stood up.

'Before I go – about the businesses. I'm staying as a sleeping partner. I'll send you details of where to bank me money.'

Briony cut him off. 'Sleeping partner? More like a fucking coma victim! You never ran the houses or the clubs – *I* did. And I didn't feel the urge to kill all and sundry while I did it. You know something, Tommy Lane? One day you'll go too far. You always did before. It was me who was the sensible one, the voice of reason. Remember that next time you feel the urge to batter someone's brains out.'

'Well, then. We know where we stand, don't we? I'm off.'

Tommy walked to the bedroom door.

'Goodbye, Briony.'

She watched him leave the room, then sat on the edge of the bed, her face buried in her hands, tears forcing their way through her fingers.

Tommy was gone, she was really alone. Empty at last of any real feeling, she dried her eyes. She herself was the only person she could ever rely on from this day forward. It was Briony Cavanagh against the world, and this Briony was a harder, sleeker version than the previous one. Because she had no one at all now except herself.

Tommy drove himself home, his heart light inside his chest. He had achieved what he had set out to do. Briony would be fuming with him for what she thought he'd done. But her mind would be at rest with the thought that her secrets were safe. She had broken with him, and so he would try and make a life of sorts without her. His need for her was as strong as ever, but he had to try and live without her.

As he parked outside his house he glanced at his watch. At this moment Kevin Carter was driving Elizabeth O'Malley and her son to Liverpool. They were frightened out of their wits, and both knew better than ever to open their mouths about Briony.

Tommy opened his front door, frowning. It annoyed him that

316

she thought him capable of killing an old woman, even if the old woman was Elizabeth O'Malley!

As he climbed his staircase though, he felt a sort of lightness come over him. He was young, he was unattached, and he was a man of substance.

He had severed his ties with Briony, even though they were still partners. He would still look out for her, no one would hurt her while he breathed, but now he'd look out for her from afar. Her status in the East End wouldn't change. Briony would still be the force she had always been, only now she would be on her own.

Chapter Twenty-four

Delilah Glasworthy was fifty-five years old and looked good on it. Her hair was still thick and dark, with only a sprinkling of grey, her eyebrows lustrous and finely shaped and her deep-set brown eyes were humorous. She was tall and slim with long shapely legs which she did not try to hide. A widow for over twenty years, she owned a house in Stepney, in East Street, and let it out to boarders – gentlemen of good standing, civil servants, engineers, and others of that ilk.

She looked down her nose at the people around her, watched young mothers giving their windowsills what she called a 'cat's lick', tutted over children with dirty knees and snotty noses. But in general she kept herself to herself. Today, though, she was sitting in Molly Cavanagh's kitchen drinking a cup of tea and trying her hardest to pluck up courage to talk frankly to the woman in front of her.

'You look great, Delilah, your hair is beautiful still. You always had the hair, even as a child.'

Delilah smiled tremulously. She had known Molly Cavanagh from childhood. Their mothers had known each other in Cork; their fathers had both been seamen, then dockers. Of an age, the two women found it easy to pick up exactly where they left off, even though they might not see one another from one year to the next.

'I still board, Molly. I have some lovely gentlemen at present. Refined types, you know.'

Molly stifled a grin. Refined my arse! she thought, but she nodded pleasantly anyway.

'But East Street! Molly, it's gone downhill, I tell you. We have some horrible characters there now. The young women of today. Make-up in the middle of the afternoon! Tally men banging their doors down at all hours, men coming home to ructions and fighting. It's a disgrace, I tell you. And over the road to me, well, they take blacks now. Nanny Carpenter lets to blacks!'

Molly looked suitably scandalised.

'Nanny Carpenter! Why she was always the one for respectability!'

Delilah raised her plucked eyebrows and said: 'You can charge them double, see? It's a terrible thing really because the poor people have no choice, do they? It's robbery. And the men seem quite refined and well dressed. In fact, I heard they work in your Briony's club. Must be her band, eh?'

She gave a tinkling little laugh that she thought sounded very ladylike, and which she practised when she was alone.

Molly's face dropped now. If they worked for her daughter they were her property, so to speak. Briony was responsible for them. Her eyes narrowed and she said, 'Charging the poor buggers double, is she? Why, them boys of Briony's are cleaner than most whites, my Kerry told me that herself! Works with them, doesn't she? She should know, it stands to reason. Can't stomach the buggers meself.'

'I've seen Kerry there, actually, Moll. A few times, in fact. That's what brought me here today. I don't want to gossip or cause any trouble, you know, but a girl's reputation is her greatest asset . . .' She foundered under Molly's direct gaze.

'Go on then, Delilah, spit it out.'

'Well, people have noticed. Look, Molly, I'm here as a friend so will you stop staring at me like that? You're making me nervous!'

'Are you saying what I think you're saying? That my Kerry's black man's meat. Is that what you dolled yourself up for today, to come and bring lies and filth into my home?'

Delilah stood up abruptly.

'I'm sorry, Molly, I thought you'd want to know. If it was my daughter . . . I mean, I'm not saying that anything's going on, but she picks him up from there in a car, they chat and talk like . . . well, like people who are more than friends. I'm telling you before anyone else does.'

Molly chewed on her bottom lip, her face a mask of dismay.

'I'll see myself out, Moll. 'Bye, Rosalee love.'

She kissed Rosalee and left hurriedly, rushing up the lane as fast as she could. Sorry now for interfering.

'They chat and talk like people who are more than friends . . .'

Kerry had no place being friends with blackies, that was what was bothering Molly. True, she was a singer, a bit bohemian, but that was Kerry. But Molly uneasily remembered her sitting in this kitchen one day and arguing the toss about black people when her mother had made some disparaging comments. She'd been defending her man, the big mysterious man they'd all assumed was married or, as Molly had thought, a man of substance, gentry, a lord. When all the time he was a black man, a dirty stinking black man!

Her disgust knew no bounds. That Kerry, her talented, beautiful Kerry, could sink to that level, broke her heart. Jumping from her seat, she pushed and pulled poor Rosalee roughly as she got her coat on her, dragging the protesting girl from the house on their way to Briony's.

She would know what to do.

Andrew McLawson held Eileen's hand. He had taken her pulse, checked her over physically, and now he sat looking at her, puzzled.

'Are you going to talk to me, Eileen?'

She opened her eyes and smiled tremulously.

'Come on, tell me about yourself.'

He watched the changing expressions on her face and sighed. He had seen people like her before though not many times, he admitted. But he had seen the same haunted look, the same fathomless eyes, the same symptoms. Yet this wasn't a family

321

who would terrorise a child, or at least they didn't give that impression. He had a girl at his nursing home, Sea View, who was the product of a very Victorian father and a weak-kneed mother. The girl had had all the life drained from her. The lust for life, the wanting of it, had been gradually beaten from her. Oh, not with fists, though this girl was still carrying the remainder of bruising on her arms and back, but with words and harsh behaviour. She'd been told she was worthless, and now she believed it. Quiet as a church mouse, she sat out her days, looking at the sea and drinking tea, constantly drinking tea, her hands clumsy and shaking. McLawson would lay money that the father had sexually abused the girl, he knew she wasn't a virgin. But the father was a man of wealth and position, and the doctor was employed to hide people's mistakes. 'Bad nerves' had become a catchall phrase for all the illness of the mind. At Sea View he had men, young virile men, who were still shell shocked from the war. He also cared for old spinster aunts or eccentrics without the private means to keep themselves who were shunted into homes like his by their uncaring relatives. Now he was to have this girl. The Cavanaghs were working-class, the voices betrayed that. But Briony Cavanagh seemed to have an inexhaustible supply of money, judging from this house. He shrugged. How she'd come about it was her business, but her concern for her sister was genuine enough. It was that concern which had prompted him to leave Sea View and travel up to this house to see Eileen O'Malley. Now he knew he would take her. She was like a poor broken bird. He'd take her to the home and try to look after her, but there was something her sister should know first.

Briony walked into the room. 'Everything all right, Doctor?'

He smiled. His dark eyes were sad and his thick dark unruly hair stood up as if he'd been out in a gale, though this was the result of his constantly running his hands through it.

'Sit down so we can talk.'

Briony sat beside the bed in a large leather chair. Andrew McLawson was surprised to see how tiny she was. Her feet were so small in her little white shoes they looked like a child's. And all

322

that hair, that beautiful red hair, with those startling green eyes. She was a lovely girl all right.

'As you know, your sister's not well.' He looked at Eileen as he said this and smiled. 'I think we could accommodate her at Sea View, but I really have to know all the details of your sister's illness first. Everything. If I'm to help her at all.'

He noted the whitening of Briony's face and looked at Eileen pointedly. He smiled at her gently. Briony was surprised to see Eileen smile back. She liked him.

'If you would like to follow me down to the drawing room, I'll tell you what I think you need to know.' Her voice was hard and for a fleeting second the man felt that this little woman could be dangerous. The feeling passed as quickly as it had come and he stood up to follow her.

'Anything you tell me will be in the strictest confidence, Miss Cavanagh.'

She looked into his face and said, 'The name's Briony, and some of the things I do aren't strictly legal. In fact, they're highly illegal. What do you say to that?

Andrew McLawson picked up his bag.

'I am in the business of keeping secrets, Miss Cavanagh. Many of my patients are from the cream of this country's aristocracy. I want to help people, not hinder them.'

'Then you sound like just the man for me.'

The fact that he had first called her 'Miss Cavanagh' pleased her, and he wanted to keep everything businesslike, which could only augur for the good.

'That is a very tragic story you told me there, Briony. I think your sister has had a very very sad life.'

She nodded. 'My father brought her here to this house. He brought me a year later. Only I was stronger, I survived it all. I'm now a very influential woman in my own right, Dr McLawson, and what I want, I generally get. If something upsets me, I leave no stone unturned to sort out the problem.'

The doctor laughed out loud.

'You're threatening me!'

Briony smiled now, but it didn't reach her eyes.

'Not threatening, Dr McLawson, making you a promise. I have been very candid here today. The knowledge you now possess is because I want what's best for my sister, but it has never been discussed with outsiders before. I want to make sure it stays that way.'

'It will. Your father was a very wicked and evil man . . .'

Briony cut him off.

'My father was a very poor man, a totally uneducated man, a man at the end of his tether, in fact. Born into the same circumstances, who knows what you would sell to keep your head above water?'

'I wouldn't sell my children.'

Briony smiled again. 'You don't know what you'd sell, young man, in the same position. You'd be surprised what I could get for you round the slums for five shillings. Every sexual act under the sun. It's some people's only saleable commodity. So don't be too harsh on them. If I can find it in my heart to forgive my father, I'm sure you can.'

Andrew McLawson bowed then to a will much stronger than his own. This was a strange household, with strange secrets. He was beginning to be sorry he had ever entered it.

'I'll bring my sister tomorrow and stay 'til she's settled in.'

'As you like. I really must go now, to meet my train in time.'

'My driver will take you to the station.'

'Thank you, that's very kind.'

He shook the tiny hand that fairly glittered with jewels. This was a strange household indeed. Thank goodness he'd left by the time Molly arrived, breathing fire and fury.

'Mum! Will you calm down?'

'Calm down, she says! Calm down when that black-headed whore has been running round with a black man!

Briony stared at her mother in wonderment. 'What! What did you say?'

'That Kerry, she's been running round with a mystery man all right. A fucking big darkie from her band! Oh, the shame of

324

it! How will I ever hold me head up if this gets out?'

Briony managed to laugh.

'You'll manage somehow, Mother. If you could live down me and Eileen and the old man, you'll live down Kerry. Now how do you know this is true?'

'Because Delilah told me. She has a boarding house in Stepney. Well, your woman has been seen there, picking him up and dropping him off, as brazen as you like!'

'She might just have been giving him a lift. You've no proof that anything's going on. Bloody hell, Mum, you know what people are like. They're still reeling from the disappearance of O'Malley and his mother. Don't tell me they've time to talk about Kerry and all!'

'Listen to me, Briony, I've had a feeling on me for a long time there was something not right with Kerry. Then the other week, I said something about blacks and she went mad. I should have guessed then. If she was here now I'd rip her sodding head off her shoulders, I would that! The thought of her and him . . . him touching her with his black hands.'

Briony saw the disgust on her mother's face. Going to her, she sat her on a chair.

'Calm down, for crying out loud.'

'You've got to do something, Briony. Smash him up! Smash his bloody face in! Teach him a lesson he won't forget! You have to put a stop to it – now.'

'Hello, Bernadette. Sit yourself down.'

Bernie sat opposite Briony in her office. The door was closed but they could hear Kerry's voice as she sang.

'Sounds well, don't she, Bri?'

'She does that. In fact, she sounds just like a girl who's getting a regular portion off a big black man. Am I right? Is Kerry having a fling with someone in the band? Because they ain't likely to be getting engaged, are they?'

Bernadette's face was a bleached white.

'Who told you?'

'Never mind who told me, it's enough I know. You were

obviously in on the big secret. You even tried to hint to me about it, didn't you? Is it that Evander then, the one she's so sure is talented and clever? Is it? Well, answer me then, you two-faced cow!'

'I ain't two-faced! I never said a word to anyone.'

'That's just the point, ain't it? Normally you've a mouth big enough to get your foot in it, both your feet, in fact. Why keep quiet about something like this, eh? Is it because you thought that once the shit hit the fan Kerry would be finished, is that it? You sat and watched your sister bugger up her life and didn't even try and do anything about it? You should have come to me, told me as soon as you knew or even guessed. Now I've got the job of getting rid of the ponce ain't I?'

'He's going back to the States anyway at the end of the month.'

'Oh no he ain't, love, he's going tonight. And he's going with a flea up his arse. Rupert Charles knows a bloke who wants to record our Kerry. He thinks she's going to be big, very big, and so do I. Unlike you, Bernie, our Kerry has a brilliant future ahead of her – and a black piano player ain't in the picture anywhere! Tonight, after work, you keep her in the club. Evander and his merry little band are going to leave tonight, leave this place permanently, back to the good old US of A.'

'But, Briony, they're going at the end of the month anyway. What difference does a few weeks make?' Bernie was amazed at her own argument for Kerry and Evander, but now the cat was out of the bag she genuinely felt sorry for them.

Briony shook her head in amazement.

'Can't you see? She's been tumbled. Someone came and saw the old woman. It's common knowledge, Bernie. We have to get shot now, as soon as we can. He has to leave with the knowledge that, if he ever comes back looking for her, there'll be big trouble.'

Bernie looked at her hands clasped in her lap. 'This will break her heart, Bri, she's mad about him. Honest, she really loves him.'

As sorry for her sister as Briony felt, she had to be hard, and when she answered Bernadette, she meant every word she said. 'Then that's more fool her, ain't it? But one day she'll thank me for this. One day she'll see the folly of what she's been doing. Can you imagine what the upshot would be? Can you? If this was public knowledge Kerry would be an outcast. No. Her voice is the biggest thing she's ever likely to have, and if it rests with me, she'll use it to its fullest potential. I'll see she don't fuck up. I'll see to that much personally.'

Bernadette stared at her sister for a long while before she said: 'Do you know something, Briony? It must be great being you. You just barrel through life organising everything and everyone. You play God, and we all play your disciples. Well this last lot stinks. I admit, I wanted to see Kerry get her comeuppance. Talented, marvellous Kerry, the girl with the golden voice. But now I'm not so sure. Because I'll tell you something for nothing – she loves the bones of that man, and you can send him off on his bike, do what you like, but you can't change people's feelings. I'd have thought you'd have appreciated that fact better than anyone? Look at how you feel about Benedict, and look who fathered him. You can't help where your feelings lie, Bri. Not you, not me, not Kerry. Not even poor old Eileen.'

Briony leant across the desk, knocking her glass of whisky flying.

'You've got a big mouth, Bernie, it's always been your downfall. From a kid that trap of yours has always got you into bother. Well, let me tell you something, girl. I ain't in the mood for you tonight. I don't want to hurt Kerry in the least, I want what's best for her. You're the one who wanted her to be hurt. Whatever you say now, the fact you kept that big mouth of yours buttoned speaks volumes to me. So you'll do what I tell you. You'll keep her back tonight, and if you let on about any of it, I'll wring your neck. Tonight this lot is finished and Evander Dorsey is history.

'Now piss off out of my sight, Bernie, before I forget you're my sister.'

Chapter Twenty-five

Kerry had promised Bernadette that she would have a quick drink with her at the bar to hear all the latest news on Eileen. The night had been a big success, the last of the stragglers were leaving and Kerry stood with a glass of champagne. She sipped it, and catching sight of herself in a mirror, automatically straightened up. Julian the bar manager watched her and smiled sadly. Kerry liked him, he was usually fun.

'What's the matter, Ju, you look miserable?'

'Well, to be honest, dear, your sister isn't exactly the happiest soul in purgatory tonight, know what I mean?'

Kerry laughed.

'She has a lot on her plate now, what with Tommy taking on more outside business...' Her voice trailed off. It must be common knowledge about Tommy and Briony, but it wasn't going to come from her. She knew that the word was Tommy was expanding, which was the reason he wasn't at the club any more. But people weren't stupid. She had heard herself he was chasing every bit of skirt that passed his way. You couldn't say that to Briony, though. Kerry was sorry for her sister, what with all that trouble with Eileen and Joshua, and now the split from Tommy. Their relationship had been so well established, it must be hard to live something like that down.

Evander walked past her and shouted, 'Goodnight, Miss Cavanagh.'

She smiled and said goodnight to him, keeping up the big

pretence even though she was aware that Julian had guessed months before about them.

'Goodnight, Evander dear, see you tomorrow!' Julian's voice was high and Evander smiled as he left the building.

'Very nice chap that. I like him a lot.'

Kerry smiled and sipped her champagne. Where the hell was Bernadette? Evander would have to wait for her on the corner now until she could pick him up in her car.

She swallowed down the champagne.

'Another?'

Kerry nodded, and studied herself in the mirror once more. She was looking forward to seeing Evander tonight, she had some news for him. A club owner from France had heard about her singing and had offered her a spot with her band in his club, the *Joie de Vivre*. She had told her agent she was very interested. It was the break she had been praying for. She had convinced herself that France was the place where she and Evander could be together. The French were much more open-minded. Somehow they would be all right there, if only they could get away from London. She felt a small shiver of excitement in her breast. Her main aim in life was to stop him going back to the States. Stop him from leaving her. And now she had the handle she needed. She was surprised to find her champagne glass was once more empty and, turning to Julian, said: 'Do you know where Bernadette is?'

He smiled and said, 'She left about an hour ago.'

Kerry frowned.

'Are you sure? Only we were supposed to be having a drink before we went home.'

Julian shrugged.

'Perhaps she forgot.'

Kerry smiled, but she was puzzled. Bernadette had been very insistent.

'Maybe. Goodnight, Julian.'

'Goodnight, Miss. You sang like a little bird tonight. It was a pleasure to listen to you.

'Thanks. See you tomorrow.'

Kerry left the club. Five minutes later she was on the corner of the street where she normally picked up Evander. He was nowhere to be seen.

She waited ten minutes and then drove herself home.

Evander was sitting in the back of a large car between two men he had never seen before. Kevin Carter, Briony's driver, was in the front. No one had said a word since they'd bundled him inside. He could feel the sweat rolling down his forehead and into his eyes. Evander was a big man, and strong, but there was no way he could hope to fight his way out of this situation. Knowing this, he became calm inside. He knew what they were going to do to him, he knew they were aware of his relationship with Kerry Cavanagh. He knew the time had come to pay the piper.

'Can I smoke?' His voice, he was glad to hear, came out strong, without a trace of terror.

'Only if I set fire to you.' Kevin Carter's voice was hard, but the other two men laughed as if it was a big joke.

'That's what happens to blokes like you in the States, ain't it? You get burnt alive on crosses. I read about it in the paper. The Ku Klux Klan, they're called, ain't they?'

Evander felt a return of the terror he had so valiantly suppressed. These men were no different from their American counterparts. No different from the people who rode up in the night and burnt out black shanties. Their sort was the same the world over. Red necks with cockney accents. He smiled in the darkness, watching the streets pass by, trying to figure out where he was.

'I wonder what that means?' Archie Tubby's voice was genuinely interested.

'What? Ku Klux Klan?'

'Yeah, funny name, ain't it?'

'It's Greek. It comes from the Greek, Kukos, meaning circle. Klan is from the Scottish clan. The first four Klansmen were confederate soldiers, descendants of the Scottish settlers.'

331

'How do you know that?' Tubby's voice was nasty now. He couldn't write his own name. A black man being educated was alien to him.

'A white lady told me, a long time ago when I was a child. I just never forgot it.'

Kevin Carter laughed.

'You won't forget tonight, either, you black ponce. What the fuck did you think you was playing at, dipping your wick with a white girl? You're scum, you're shit beneath my shoes, you're nothing. And you thought you could take a decent white girl and soil her? Well, you're going to learn a big lesson tonight, mate.'

The mood in the car was ugly, the atmosphere heavy with malice. Kevin Carter stopped the car in the East India Docks. They walked a now terrified Evander into a small warehouse. Kevin Carter picked up a large pickaxe handle, and when the two Tubby brothers had forced him to the ground, proceeded to beat Evander mercilessly across the back of the legs. Finally, when he was unconscious, they broke every one of his fingers. An hour later, they were banging on Glennford's door. When it was opened they threw Evander's bloodied and bleeding form on to the bare floor.

'Here's your tickets, you lot fuck off tonight! You're to be gone by the morning or there'll be more trouble.'

Glennford nodded, wanting to fight but knowing since his years of childhood and manhood it was a fight he could never win. Instead, he did as he was bidden.

They were all gone by first light.

Briony was impressed by Sea View. It was a large rambling Victorian house on the seafront at Southend. It had two large turrets either side of the roof, which provided bedrooms with windows that looked over the Thames estuary towards Kent. The round bedroom to the right of the building was to be Eileen's.

As Briony unpacked her sister's things, she noticed that Eileen was sitting on a window seat gazing out to sea.

'It's beautiful here, isn't it, Eileen?'

She nodded, her feet tucked underneath her. She looked like a child again.

'I like it here, Briony, it smells nice.'

'That's the salt, Eileen. Remember when Mum took us to Rainham on Sea when we was kids? And we sat on the beach and paddled in the water?'

Eileen nodded, smiling at the memory.

'We had jellied eels and whelks for supper and Kerry got sick everywhere on the way home.'

'That's right, Eileen.' Briony was pleased she was talking, pleased she seemed to like this place peopled with nuns and patients who seemed to move about as silently as the nuns. It was peaceful, though, with only the sound of the tide coming in. Briony sat on the seat beside Eileen. A few lone fishermen sat on the small quayside. It was overcast and they wore their oilskins and wellingtons with a jaunty air. This part of the coast was called Thorpe Bay. All along this road were large houses, imposing residences owned by people with money and position. She gazed out over the estuary, seeing the silent movement of the ships as they passed one another. It was a calm and beautiful place. It would do Eileen good. Make her happier.

A ship's hooter blasted and Eileen jumped. Briony laughed and put her arm around her shoulders, pulling her sister's head next to hers.

'Everything will be all right, Eileen, I promise you.'

'What's happened to Joshua, Bri? Where is he?'

Briony took a deep breath. 'He's gone away, love. He can't hurt you any more.

'Will he come back, do you think?' Her voice was low.

'No, he can't come back, darlin'. Not where he's gone.'

Eileen relaxed against her.

'Good, I'm glad. I can't face him any more, Bri, any of them. Keep Mum away from me for a while, will you?'

Briony started. 'Mum? Why don't you want to see Mum?' This request shocked her.

'I can't face anyone but you, not for a while. She bosses me about, you know that. Tells me to pull meself together. I wish to

Christ I could, Briony. But I have those feelings again, like I had before, remember? Sometimes I don't know for sure who I am or what I'm doing. I hear things, Bri . . . People keep talking to me, all the time. I know there's no one there really, but I have to listen to them. If I don't, then I feel like something bad will happen.'

Briony hugged her close. Her voice was thick with tears as she said: 'Nothing bad is ever going to happen to us again, not me or you or the others. I promise you that.'

'I really like it here, Briony, I feel safe.'

'You are safe, Eileen, as safe as houses.'

'And you'll keep Mum away, just for a little while, until I get settled?'

'Of course I will. Anything you want you can have.'

She looked at Eileen, but she was gone again, to wherever it was her mind drifted to. She pulled herself from Briony's arms and looked out at the seascape before her.

She didn't say another word the whole time Briony was there.

Kerry woke up alone. She stretched in the bed and put out her arm to a cold empty space. Opening her eyes, she remembered that Evander had not been there when she had got home the night before. She turned over on to her back and sighed. She had got used to having him beside her, having him there when she opened her eyes. Her neighbours were faceless people who kept office hours so she rarely saw them, and the fact that she was a singer, one who was becoming well known, gave her the perfect excuse to have a black musician with her. Now she wanted that black musician and he wasn't here.

She looked at the clock by her bedside. It was nearly ten-thirty. She sat bolt upright in bed. She had slept later than she had for a long time. As she pulled a dressing gown around herself, she heard Bernie's key in the door.

'Hello, Bernie, where've you been all night.' Kerry walked out into the hallway as she spoke, tying the sash of the dressing gown. The sight of Bernadette's face made her stop in mid-sentence.

'What's wrong? Is it Eileen?'

Bernadette shrugged off her coat and dropped it unceremoniously on the floor of the hallway. Then, yanking off her cloche hat, she dropped that on to the untidy pile as well.

'Come through to the kitchen, Kerry. Nothing's wrong with Eileen but there's something I have to tell you.'

'What? What's wrong, Bernie?'

Bernadette picked up the kettle and banged it down on the hob. She lit the gas then, satisfied it was fully alight, looked into her sister's face and said: 'He's gone.'

Kerry screwed up her eyes in disbelief. 'Who? Who's gone?'

'Evander. The whole band, in fact. Mother tumbled you, Kerry, she was told about you and him. Briony had him driven out last night.'

Kerry put a slim hand to her throat. Holding on to the table with the other hand, she whispered: 'He ain't dead?'

Bernadette, after a sleepless night with her mother who'd been cursing her errant daughter up hill and down dale, finally snapped.

'Oh, don't be so bloody dramatic! They got shot of him, that's all.'

Kerry sat on a wooden kitchen chair, her face grey now. 'Don't be dramatic, you say! She made short bloody work of Ronnie Olds, to name one of many! Dear God, my poor Evander. They must have taken him last night. I waited for him, but he didn't come.' She jumped from the seat and ran through to the bedroom.

Bernadette made the tea. She was bringing in a cup when Kerry emerged from the bedroom, dressed.

'Where you going?'

Kerry looked at her in amazement. 'Where the hell do you think? Stepney.'

Bernie put the cup of steaming tea on the small hall table. 'He won't be there.'

'How do you know? He might not have gone yet, she might have just told him he had to go, maybe he'll still be there, he

335

might have left a message for me.' Kerry knew she was babbling.

'Calm down, will you? You'll have the whole place on the knocker in a minute.'

Pushing Bernadette out of the way, she grabbed her bag and keys and left the flat. Bernadette followed her out on to the stairwell.

'For Christ's sake, Kerry, it's pointless going there, can't you see that? Please come back inside. We'll talk about it, try and sort something out!'

Kerry laughed nastily. 'You and me, talk? You must be joking! Who told on us, eh? I bet it was you. You vindictive cow! I bet you loved every second of it. I wouldn't put nothing past you. Nothing!'

Outside on the street she tried to unlock her car. Her hands were trembling so much she dropped the keys. Kicking them across the road in a temper, she flagged down a passing cab. 'Stepney, East Street. Quick as you can.'

The cabbie laughed.

'What's the matter, darling? Your old man doing a moonlight flit?'

'Just drive the sodding cab, mate, and shut your mouth up! If I wanted a fucking comedian I'd have arranged to have Stan Laurel drive me!'

The cab driver shut up. Dressed like a lady and with the mouth of a dockside harpy. Now he was sure he'd seen everything. She jumped from the cab at the top of East Street, throwing the man ten shillings as his fare. He took the money and saluted her like a general before driving off.

Kerry walked down East Street. She was dressed in a deep red brocade evening coat, with fur collar and cuffs. The coat swung as she walked, displaying a suit of pale pink wool that hugged her ample figure. She wasn't wearing a hat but her hair was fresh-looking, swinging healthily with each step she took.

East Street had once been a nice area. It had large imposing four-storey houses, with steps leading up to the front door. Years before these steps had been scrubbed every day; now the majority were filthy and chipped. Rubbish was strewn in the road – vegetable peelings, soiled rags and human waste where the children dropped their pants and defecated where they played. It smelt like the basements, only every now and then a billow of fresh air whipped through, giving the residents a welcome change. The breeze smelt of coal from the factories around and about. The houses were covered in soot. At eleven-fifteen in the morning the tally men were on the knockers, the children were out in force, and women were gossiping among themselves. Or rather the women who weren't trying to avoid a tally man, or the rent collector.

Kerry was aware of hostile eyes watching her as she approached the house where Evander and his band had lodged. Outside number two was a young boy of about sixteen. He looked her up and down with a surly leer as she stopped beside him.

'Would you like to earn a shilling?'

'Doing what?' His voice had a thick twang, affected and very unpleasant.

'I want a message taken to a Mr Dorsey in there.' She jerked her head towards the front door of the house.

'Cost you a bit more than that, darling. Messages for blackies is double.'

Kerry swallowed down the retort that came to her lips and nodded.

'All right then. Two bob. I want you to knock at his room and tell him that Miss Cavanagh is outside and wishes to speak with him.'

'Gis the money then.' He held out a dirty hand. Opening her bag, she took out a half crown.

'That's all I've got, I haven't anything smaller.'

'Well, I ain't got any change, girl, so it looks like the price just went up again, don't it?'

With that he disappeared up the step and into the house. Kerry stood uncertainly outside, wishing she had not worn such a striking coat. Wishing Evander would come out so they could get away from this place. Hoping against hope that he would tell her everything was all right and it was just another of Bernie's nasty jokes.

A figure appeared at the top of the steps and Kerry's heart sank.

'You've got a bloody nerve, I must say, you trollop! Coming here for your bleeding black fancy man!'

All the residents in the street looked in the direction of the loud strident voice. Kerry felt her heart sinking. The woman was old, her huge pendulous breasts hanging down to her waist beneath an old wrapover apron. On her feet were an old pair of men's issue army boots, minus the laces, and her stockings hung around the tops in wrinkles. Arms like meat cleavers were crossed before her and her face was screwed up in disgust.

'He left here in the night, love, they all did, owing me a bleeding week's rent! Someone must have tumbled your game, darling, because he was dripping blood. All down the stairs it was this morning! Up me bleeding walls, everywhere! My God, you've got a Christing nerve coming here to a respectable woman and looking for your darkie! Your black man!'

A few men emerged from doorways in their vests, obviously just woken by the harridan's voice and coming out to see the uppity bitch in the red coat get her comeuppance.

Kerry turned away and started to walk down the street, her heels clattering on the pavements, her head hanging down on to her chest.

'Gerroutofit, you whore of hell! Before I stick me boot up your arse! Black man's darling, are you? Go on, piss off!' The man disappeared into his doorway after shouting at her and Kerry began to walk faster.

A woman with a young child on her arm walked across the road. Hawking deep in the back of her throat, she spat in Kerry's face, the spittle running down her cheek and on to her fur collar.

'You filthy bitch, coming here for your darkie! Don't think we never saw you.'

Kerry was waiting for the woman to move when the man who had shouted at her came out of his house carrying a chamber pot. He threw the contents towards Kerry. A small amount hit the bottom of her coat and her shoes. Looking into the man's face, seeing the hatred there and all around her, she began to run, dropping her bag on to the pavement as she went. Never before had she felt such malevolence. Never before had she experienced anything so utterly shaming and humiliating. She ran until she was in the High Street, staring around her like an animal being chased by a pack of hounds, her eyes wild. She carried on running until she came to Victoria Park.

Sitting on a bench, she cried, bitter tears that seemed to wrench her whole frame in two. Wrapping her arms around herself, she caressed her belly underneath her ruined coat.

She had had such good news for him, such a secret. Now she could tell him nothing because he was gone.

Bleeding and beaten he had left, but if he was bleeding he was still alive. This thought, amongst so many other bad ones, comforted her.

If he could bleed, he was still alive.

At that moment in time, she hated Briony more than she had ever hated anyone or anything in her life.

It was late and the journey home from Southend-on-Sea had tired Briony out. Sitting alone in her small sitting room, she sipped a steaming cup of tea. She was supposed to go to the club tonight, she was supposed to go to the houses, and she was supposed to be seeing a man called Joey Vickers about some very cheap liquor. Eileen's blank face was haunting her. She looked at the photograph of Benedict. Bernadette had been right in a lot of respects. You didn't know where your heart was going to lie. The fact that his father was Henry Dumas, a skunk, a piece of filth in Briony's opinion, didn't stop the feelings she had for the son she'd borne him.

How many times had she heard people say, 'If I could have my time again, I'd do it all differently'? Well, she wouldn't really, because as bad as it all seemed now, it had been the means of her son coming into the world. Of Benedict's very existence. Although he was away from her, was in a different house, living a life she could only glimpse through Sally, he was still her boy. One day he would know that, when the time was right.

She drank her tea and poured herself another cup. The room was quiet, the house too. She was enjoying the peace when Cissy tiptoed into the room.

'Can I get you a bite?'

'No, thanks all the same. Sit down a second, Cissy. Take the weight off your feet.'

Cissy sat beside the fire and glanced ruefully at her swollen legs. 'Look at them, like legs of pork!'

'If they're bad, you should take the doctor's advice and keep off them now and then. There's plenty of help coming in now. You don't have to take the brunt of the work any more.'

Cissy blew out her red mottled cheeks, making a rude noise. 'What's that silly old bugger know, eh? I can't sit around all day, I'd go off me head . . .' She bit her lip. 'I'm sorry, Bri, that just came out.'

Briony laughed. 'You don't have to watch what you say to me, Cis, I was just thinking about her meself.'

'How was she? All right?'

Briony nodded. 'Yeah, she seemed to like it there. It's really lovely, Cis, the view from the place is gorgeous. I've never really seen so much water before. I know we used to swim in the cut when we was kids, but this was different. Clean-looking and deep green. It was lovely. And the smell! I tell you now, I felt like staying there meself. Getting away from it all. Never coming back here.'

Cissy made a loud noise.

'I can just see you now, in an early dotage, sitting on the prom in a bleeding bathchair. Listen here, Briony, you've got a lot of bother at the moment, I know that. You ain't been yourself since all that with Ginelle. That threw you. I watched you change. But even if you did leave this place, left London even, you'd soon be back. You're a woman who needs aggravation, you bloody well thrive on it. Otherwise, why the hell would you have opened up your houses? Look at this week. You've had no Tommy to back you up yet you've sorted out Eileen, in between running your clubs and your houses, of course.'

Cissy's voice was full of admiration. 'Me, I couldn't organise the proverbial piss up. Don't sell yourself short, and don't get maudlin. Get drunk if you want, let off a bit of steam, but don't let it all get you down now. I don't like seeing you depressed. Somehow, if you're not right, then the world around you don't seem right.'

Briony looked into the face of her old friend. Cissy was only a few years older than she, yet she looked ancient. She was a workhouse child, had known nothing but hard work all her life. Without it she was like a fish out of water. That's why she couldn't bear to let a younger girl take on any of her work. She had to be needed, to earn her keep. It was something that had been drummed into her at a very early age.

'I'm all right, Cissy, but I have a lot to think about these days. There's been trouble with Kerry. I don't think she's exactly going to love me for a while. I had to do something that won't make me the most popular sister in the smoke.'

'What happened then?'

Briony shook her head. 'I can't say, Cissy love. I think that's something best left between me and Kerry.' And me mother, she thought, because Molly was adamant that Kerry was never to darken her doors again.

Chapter Twenty-six

Briony had dressed carefully for her meeting with Mariah, the two women were going to look at Berwick Manor and decide if it was a viable business. Briony already knew the answer would be yes, because Mariah was shrewd. All they would do today was put Briony's stamp of approval on it and make an offer.

She put on a deep cerise suit, the skirt full, the waistband tight. As she walked it clung to her silk stockings. The jacket was long and shapeless, cut with a square neck, and she pinned a lizard-shaped diamond and ruby brooch on to the shoulder, giving the whole outfit a touch of class. She pulled her erratic hair up into a tight chignon, pinning it carefully, though tendrils of hair escaped, framing her face with their curls. Sighing, she gave up hope of getting it smooth and put on her make-up. Finally she buttoned up her shoes and looked at herself in the full-length mirror by her dressing table. She would have to do.

It was as she was sorting through her large black handbag that she heard the commotion in her hallway. Kerry's voice, loud and strident, and Bernadette's more modulated tones. With a grim face she left her bedroom and walked to the top of the staircase.

'So you're here then? I was expecting you sooner.'

Kerry stared malevolently up at her sister.

'You bitch! You bloody cow! You think you're so clever, don't you?'

Briony walked down the stairs. Cissy and Mrs Horlock watched with interest, Bernadette with fear.

343

'I tried to stop her coming here, Bri, she's out of her mind. Don't take any notice of her . . .'

Kerry looked dreadful. Her clothes were mud-stained, the hem of her brocade coat looked as if it had been dragged through the dirt. Her legs were filthy, her white stockings black and laddered, her hair uncombed and tangled. She turned wild eyes on Bernie and shouted: 'Oh, don't try and smooth this over. This can't be forgotten, swept under the carpet like the old man's death! This is my business, mine! So why don't you piss off out of it? Keep your nose out where it ain't wanted!'

Briony walked down the stairs. She looked at Cissy and Mrs Horlock and said calmly, 'Make some tea.'

The two women left the hallway through the green baize door, but Briony knew they would stand behind it listening. There was no way they would want to miss all this. Kerry tensed as Briony walked over to her, but Briony passed by and opened the door to the lounge.

'Come in here and do your talking. And I mean talking, not shouting. I've got a headache actually, and your voice is going right through my head.'

Kerry stood uncertainly. She had expected a lot, but not this. The calmness of Briony threw her, as Briony had known it would. Kerry watched Briony disappear and had no option but to follow, with Bernadette hot on her heels.

Briony was standing by the fireplace, her immaculate clothes and hair making Kerry more annoyed with each passing second.

'Look at you! I suppose you've got a red hat and all? What's the saying, Bri? Red hat, no drawers? That certainly sounds like you, don't it?

'Tell me, who beat up Evander? You? I wouldn't put it past you. You're like a man, do you know that? You think like a man, you act like a man, no wonder Tommy Lane dumped you. It must have been like living with a queer. Two men together, only one wore a dress.'

The barb about Tommy struck home as Kerry knew it would. As she'd wanted it to. She wanted Briony to hurt, as she was hurting.

'You're quiet all of a sudden, normally your mouth's going like the clappers. What's the matter? Truth hurts, does it?'

Bernadette tried to take Kerry's arm but she shrugged her off.

'Leave me alone, you!'

'Sit down, Kerry. Sit down, for Christ's sake.'

Briony's voice, so calm, so clear, jolted something in Kerry's mind.

'Don't you tell me what to do, you vicious bitch! You've ruined my life. Me and Evander was going away. I had a job lined up in Paris, I was going to tell you to stick your club right up your arse. We would have been all right there, me and him. But no, you had to have him removed, taken away, like so much rubbish. Well, let me tell you something else, Briony Cavanagh, I'm pregnant!' She laughed at the look of shock on her sisters' faces.

'Yes, thought that might give you a start. I'm in the club, up the duff, by a blackie. And shall I tell you something? I'm proud of it. I hope it's as black as night! I hope it's so black it shines! So what are you going to do about that, Bri, eh? How are you going to sort this out? You know, all your threats and all your money and all your trapping can do nothing at all because I want it. I really, really want it. Especially now you've driven my Evander away. It's all I'll have left of him, ain't it? All that remains.'

Briony heard a loud sighing noise, and it was a few seconds before she realised it was coming from herself. It was as if Kerry had stuck a pin in her chest and she was deflating slowly.

Kerry laughed at her sister's reaction.

'That's pissed all over your fireworks, hasn't it?' She rubbed her belly gently. 'Never banked on that one, did you?'

Briony pulled herself up to her full height and, walking across the room, slapped Kerry hard across the face. Then she grabbed her arm roughly and shouted: 'You stupid little bitch! You stupid little cow! You think this is funny, clever, do you? You think you've got one over on us? What are you, on a death wish or what?'

She threw her on to the chair by the fire, then leaning over her, screamed, 'You've ruined your life, you silly mare, if you could only see it! Pregnant? I could cheerfully throttle you!'

She began to slap Kerry around the head and shoulders, holding back the urge to punch her, rip at her hair, tear her skin with her nails.

'My God, girl, you've really done it this time. You're right, I can't help you. No one can help you now. You wonder why I stick my nose in your business? I'll tell you why. Because if it was left to you lot, you'd fucking crumble. You're all as thick as shit! You especially. You've got a talent, a voice, you had something going for you, and now that's nothing, that's all finished, because the day you give birth, you're a second-class citizen.

'I liked Evander, believe it or not, I liked him a lot. But liking him ain't enough. With him you would have been ostracised, shut out, people would have looked at you like you was dirt! Now you've got all that coming anyway, and for the rest of your life. And you have the cheek to come here and tell *me* what *I've* done wrong. It was a pity you didn't think of that when you was counting the cracks on the ceiling, on your back for Evander bloody Dorsey!'

Kerry looked fearfully into Briony's face. All the dark thoughts that plagued her in the night were being spoken out loud. The truth, as she had pointed out only minutes before, did hurt. It hurt a lot.

Briony paced the room, her hands shaking in temper. Bernadette lit her a cigarette and passed it to her.

Briony pulled hard on the cigarette. By now Kerry's white face and dishevelled appearance were making her feel sorry for her sister, despite herself. She wanted to take her in her arms and tell her everything was going to be all right. But how could she? Nothing was ever going to be all right for Kerry Cavanagh again.

'Are you sure you're pregnant? I mean, are you really certain?'

Kerry sat hunched in the chair. She looked very small and

forlorn, her face stained with tears and dirt. She nodded her head.

'How long gone are you? I mean, is there still time to do something about it?'

'I don't know, I'm over three months.'

Briony closed her eyes and stubbed out the cigarette, immediately lighting up another.

Sitting down on the chesterfield, she looked at her sister, now bowed down not just with the pain of losing the man she loved, but with the knowledge she also carried his child. A child that would be spurned because of its colour. In her heart of hearts, Briony felt a glimmer of compassion for the poor unborn child, nestled so cosily in its mother's womb. But she had to try to save the situation.

'I'll arrange for you to see Denice O'Toole, all my girls use her. She's clean and she knows what she's doing.'

Kerry looked up at her sister. Her face crumpled then, tears gushing from her eyes, a terrible low keening sound issuing from her open mouth. Briony went to her and pulled her into her arms, hugging her close, stroking the dark head, and murmuring words of endearment.

Later on that afternoon, when Briony had left Kerry in Mrs Horlock's capable hands, she and Mariah walked round Berwick Manor with Mr Jackson, the solicitor instructed to sell the property. He was a tall thin man with iron grey hair and a small moustache, perfectly waxed. He blew his nose often, to the amusement of Mariah who rolled her eyes at Briony, making her smile.

They toured through the rooms, taking in their size, the high ceilings and old fireplaces. There were four large reception rooms with huge windows which looked over the Essex countryside. There were two large kitchens, with pantries and what would once have been the butler's and the cook's sitting rooms. There was a huge cold store, with marble slabs to keep butter and milk cool in the summertime.

A large sweeping staircase led up to a galleried landing. Off

347

this were eight bedrooms, and above these a rabbit warren of servants' rooms. More stairs, steeper and narrower now, led up to the attics.

Briony saw the dilapidated state of the property, but she could also see its potential. From the upstairs bedrooms the whole of Essex seemed to have been laid out before them. The Berwick Pond Road was quiet, unsurfaced, and would ensure they kept their privacy. The outbuildings were still in a decent state. Even the stables were still usable. It was only the inside that had been allowed to deteriorate. The soldiers who had convalesced there after the war had used and abused the rooms terribly. Wood panelling was wrenched off the wall, the carpets were worn, and the curtains, once beautiful Austrian silk, were in tatters. Mr Jackson, to give him his due, pointed out the finer points as best he could. But even his powers of persuasion flagged as he surveyed the interior.

'Of course, ladies, the outside is still very much as it was before the war. A very picturesque property, don't you agree?'

Briony walked over to the inglenook fireplace and stared at the remains of a fire. It seemed the paintings and the furniture had eventually ended up as kindling.

'It needs a lot of work to bring it back up to scratch, Mr Jackson. It's Tudor, isn't it? Do the cottages at the beginning of the lane form part of the property, and if so are they occupied?'

Mr Jackson was in a terrible quandary. The big blonde woman was intimidating enough, but this little redhead was worse. He wasn't sure which question to answer first when Briony began talking again.

'Also, the stables will have to be turned into garages. Neither myself nor my colleague ride. So that will be an added expense if we do decide to purchase. Also the kitchens need refitting and I notice that electricity hasn't been installed. Another expense. How long has the house been up for sale? Since 1919? So it's been empty for six, nearly seven, years. I should imagine the damp's got in by now.'

Mr Jackson leapt to the house's defence. 'The roof is in perfect condition, madam, I can assure you of that.'

Briony wiped her fingers daintily on her handkerchief and said sweetly, 'I'm glad to hear something is.'

Mariah grinned.

'If you would be so kind as to leave my friend and myself alone for a few minutes, Mr Jackson . . .' With a last trumpeting blow of his nose, he left the room.

'I shall wait outside by my vehicle until such time as you have concluded your business.'

When he had gone, Mariah said, 'Well, conclude, Briony, conclude!'

'Is he all the ticket, Mariah?'

'I don't know about that, Bri, but if he blows his nose once more I'll scream!'

Briony grinned. 'It is a bit disgusting.'

Mariah looked around the large drawing room and said, 'So? What do you think?'

Briony looked at her friend and smiled.

'I think it's perfect. We can do a lot with it. I thought upstairs we could really go to town, you know? There's so much scope for the bedrooms, and even the servants' rooms could be made up to accommodate customers. It's exactly what we want.'

Mariah relaxed. 'I knew you'd like it. It's like a shithouse at the moment, I know, but that's to our benefit. It'll get the price right down, but think how it could look, eh?'

'I think I'd like this room in dove grey and deep burgundy, it would look stunning. We'd easily accommodate thirty or forty men here at any given time. If the cottages aren't part and parcel of the deal, we'll buy them somehow. They're too close for comfort. The people who come here want guaranteed privacy and we'll make sure they get it.'

Mariah laughed in delight.

'So shall we put in the offer today or let Mr Jackson and his client sweat it out?'

Briony shrugged.

'We'll put in an offer. Now let's get going, I'm dying for a cup of tea.'

They left the house, happy now they were both in accord. Mr

349

Jackson watched them emerge and sighed. They were not ladies, not by any standards. What was the world coming to?

Kevin Carter was at home having his dinner. He had three young daughters, all with dark hair and brown eyes. His wife Annie was a small girl with black hair and a small, pretty face. She opened the door to Briony and smiled widely.

'Hello, Miss Cavanagh. Kevin's just having his dinner. Come through, I was making a cup of tea anyway.'

Briony walked into the house and down the tiny hallway into the dining room. Kevin saw who the visitor was and stood up. 'Sit yourself down and finish your meal, I'm ready for a cup of tea anyway.'

She sat on a large overstuffed chair by the doorway. Three identical little faces looked up at her hopefully. Carmel, the eldest, said shyly: 'Have you got something nice for me?'

Briony laughed, and opening her bag took out three mint creams in bright green paper.

'You shouldn't ask, Carmel!' Kevin's voice was loud.

Briony flapped a hand at him and said airily, 'Leave her be, Kevin. If you don't ask, you don't get!'

Ten minutes later she sat in her car, with Kevin driving her to the house in Barking.

'By the way, Kevin, I want you to go and pick up a bloke for me today. Marcus Dowling. He's interested in becoming one of the team.'

Kevin whistled softly.

'He's getting a name for himself, is Marcus.'

Briony cut him off. 'When I want your opinion, I'll ask for it.' Her voice dripped ice and a shocked Kevin turned slightly to look over his shoulder.

'Drive the car, Kevin, that's what you're paid for. And one last thing. If I tell you to frighten someone, that's what you do, get it? If I want him cut, I'll tell you. Evander Dorsey was bleeding. I never asked you to do anything but scare him. You ever take something like that on yourself again, and you'll feel the full force of my anger. Do I make myself clear?'

Kevin nodded almost imperceptibly.

'Yes, Miss Cavanagh.'

'Good, now we know exactly where we stand, don't we?'

Kevin didn't answer, but Briony had not expected him to.

Briony could hear the new band through the walls of her office. The Velvetones were good, but they weren't Kerry. Bessie Knight, the singer, had a good voice, but it was Kerry people came to see. She sipped at a glass of brandy and lit herself a cigarette, dispensing with the holder while she was alone. She heard a small tap on her office door and bellowed: 'Come in.'

Jonathan la Billière walked into the office with a wide beaming smile on his face.

'Someone upset you, Briony?' His thick eyebrows rose quizzically and she smiled.

'I'm feeling a bit fragile to say the least.'

Jonathan sat on a chair and, crossing his legs, said jocularly, 'Drinking alone? Shouting? All the symptoms of an old maid, my dear. Be careful, you have been warned!'

Briony laughed gently.

'What can I do for you?'

'I want to ask a favour actually. We're filming again in two weeks. Now I have a little girl in mind to star with me, but Rupert's not too happy about her. He has another one lined up and quite frankly, Briony, I couldn't fancy her baked, fried or boiled! In fact, I want to concentrate more on a real acting career, you know. I've been asking around and I think I may be in line for a part. But it's Rupert . . .'

His voice trailed off and Briony nodded at him, and smiled.

'He's mad about you, Jonathan, you knew that at the start. What you're saying is, now you have someone else who can help you, you want me to give Rupert the bad news. Am I right?'

He had the grace to look a little ashamed.

'Well, I wouldn't put it quite like that . . .'

'Of course you wouldn't. But I would, because I always say what I mean.'

Jonathan squirmed in his chair.

'Look, Briony, the deal was a couple of art pictures then he'd consider me for something serious. And that isn't happening. Now you hold all the cards in your hand, he'll listen to you. In fact, you're the only person he *will* listen to, period. I deserve a break . . . just one break. I can act, I'm good. And I look good on film. I don't want to spend my life at Rupert's beck and call.'

Briony stubbed out her cigarette.

'Can I ask you something?'

Jonathan spread his arms.

'Of course, anything you like.'

Briony took a deep breath. 'Are you really the son of an impoverished vicar? Only, now and again you sound very South London to me.'

Jonathan looked at her for a second, his piercing blue eyes boring into her deep green ones, then he laughed.

'How long ago did you suss me out?' He'd dropped the affected accent slightly and Briony warmed to him then.

'From about five minutes of meeting you, actually. Look, Rupert will keep his side of the bargain, I know he will. You have to learn how to handle him is all. Drop a word here and there about your other offer. Don't tell him anything concrete, just hint. He is serious about going into the legitimate film business. As silly as he acts at times, he's shrewd. It's only with the young boys he loses his head. But I expect you've noticed that yourself?'

Jonathan rolled his eyes.

'You're telling me! Honestly, Briony, how he hasn't been locked up, I don't know. He sails really close to the wind at times. Now he's gone on Lord Hockley's boy, and I mean this kid wears full make-up! I've told Rupert to be careful, the boy's father's up in arms about it, but they're seen together everywhere. That's what bothers me, I don't want to be tarred with the same brush. In fact, Briony, he's never been near me. I wouldn't want that. I am mercenary, I admit, I want to get on, but not that way. So far I've kept him at arm's length, and young Peter Hockley's keeping him occupied. But now I want out.'

'I'll see what I can do. But keep your eye on him and the boy

in the meantime. That kind of thing could bring us all down.
Lord Hockley's got a lot of sway in this town. He's rich and
influential. If he decides to do something about his son, it could
affect us all. Me as well as you. Does the boy know much about
our business dealings?'

Jonathan nodded vigorously.

'He knows it all, Briony. I warned Rupert to keep quiet but
you know him after a drink, and the cocaine doesn't help. The
other morning I found them both lying on the floor naked with a
couple of Arab boys. It made me realise just how low Rupert was
sinking. I mean, he's not even trying to hide his preferences
these days. It's as if he wants everyone to know. When it was just
him, it was all right, but now that young Peter's involved, it
could all end in tears. The boy's only nineteen. I don't think
he even shaves. But he's hardly as sweet and innocent as he
makes out. It's him who arranges their little diversions.
Frankly, Briony, it's like a three ring circus in that house some
nights. Even you would be shocked at the goings on.'

She frowned.

'It's really worrying you, isn't it?'

'It should be worrying you, too, because he knows enough
about you and me and Tommy to get us all up before the beak.
Hockley threatened Rupert only a week ago because of Peter.
He's not a man to cross, Briony, yet Rupert refuses even to
countenance not seeing the boy. Peter seems to find it all
exciting. I think he's enjoying the stir he's creating.'

'I'll keep an eye out, all right? But if I was you I'd take up that
other offer, Jonathan. The way things are going, you might be
glad you did.'

After he had left she pondered the situation. If Lord Hockley
caused a ruckus then it would be a big one. He was a leading
industrialist, owned a newspaper, was a member of parliament.
All in all, a man to fear. If only Rupert could see that. Hockley's
son's sexual preferences would be hidden, no matter what it
cost. Hockley had the money and the influence to ensure that.

Chapter Twenty-seven

As Denice O'Toole opened the front door of her semi-detached house in East Ham to Briony and Kerry, her face was beaming smiles. 'Come in, my dears, I've just made a pot of tea.'

Briony and a white-faced Kerry were ushered through to a small overstuffed parlour that was far too warm and far too full of knick-knacks.

Kerry sat down on the edge of a chair, and Briony settled herself at a small table.

Denice bustled about pouring the tea, pouring milk and enquiring who took sugar and who didn't. Kerry felt as if she was stuck in some kind of bad dream. This was the last thing she'd had expected. In her mind's eye she had pictured a dim dirty room, with an old wizened hag holding a crocheting hook. Somehow that picture seemed more fitting for what she knew was going to happen.

Denice smiled at her in a friendly fashion.

'Don't you worry, my dear, everything will be all right, I promise you.'

Briony sipped her tea. The atmosphere in the room was one of gentle conviviality. Her girls had never seemed to mind coming here. Briony always asked them if they would like to keep their child, and was always amazed at the number who said no. A clear and categoric no. For them the child inside them was just a nuisance, a problem to be solved by Denice and her ministrations. It was their body and their life. Now she sat here with her sister who did not class her pregnancy as an occupational hazard, something to be sorted out like the laundry or a little domestic problem.

Denice stood up. Her attempts at conversation were falling on deaf ears.

'If you would care to follow me, we'll get down to business.'

Kerry looked at Briony wild-eyed. Taking her sister's hand, she pulled her gently from the chair.

'Come on, Kerry love. Soonest done, soonest mended.'

It was a saying from their childhood. Kerry stood up uncertainly, her hands icy cold. She felt sick with apprehension.

They walked slowly from the room, through the narrow hallway and up the stairs to the back bedroom.

Kerry hesitated at the doorway. The white room looked forbidding in the bright light. Briony pushed her gently through the door. Inside there was a large table, covered in newspaper, and a chest of drawers with all sorts of instruments and padding set out neatly along the top.

'Hop on the table, my love, and let me have a quick feel.'

Briony helped Kerry off with her coat, and in a dream she pulled herself on to the table top, her legs feeling like jelly, her hands trembling so she found it difficult to use them. She lay back slowly, her head touching a soft pillow.

'Relax yourself, dear, so I can have a good mooch around!'

Denice's voice was loud. It echoed in the hollow confines of the room. Unlike the rest of the house, this room was bare. No knick-knacks of any description, it was like a doctor's surgery. Even the blinds on the one window were plain black. They were pulled down and the artificial light cast shadows on the white walls. Kerry closed her eyes.

Denice pulled up her dress and began to feel around her stomach, digging her fingers into the softness of her belly.

'She's well on, Briony, over three months. It'll be the hook, I'm afraid.'

Briony licked dry lips. Kerry's face was as white as the walls around her. Her eyes strayed to the implements on top of the

356

dresser, and one large imposing piece of metal with a hoop on the end made her feel faint.

'Kerry . . . Kerry love, are you all right?'

Kerry opened her eyes and shook her head. Then, sitting bolt upright, she was sick. Briony stood by shocked as Kerry threw up, over and over again.

Briony went to her sister. 'All right, all right, Kerry. Relax, love, take deep breaths.'

Kerry looked at the instruments again and once more started heaving.

'Get . . . Get me out of here, please, Bri . . . I can't breathe, I can't breathe!'

Denice ran through to her newly installed bathroom and began to fill the bath, shouting, 'Bring her through, Briony, she's in shock I think.'

All the time she was praying that Kerry Cavanagh would not be sick again on her new lino or all over her new bathroom suite.

Briony put Kerry's arm over her shoulder and helped her to the bathroom. There she sank down on to her knees, her whole body shaking with fear.

Between them Briony and Denice stripped her of her clothes and placed her in the hot tub. She lay back in the hot water, breathing deeply, her breasts heaving with every breath she took.

'Feeling better, Kel?'

She opened her eyes slowly. 'I'm sorry, Bri, but I can't go through with it. I can't.'

Briony smiled half-heartedly. '*You* can't! *I* can't go through with it and it's not happening to me! You just relax. We'll get you home soon and then we'll talk. We'll think of something, love, I promise.'

Kerry grasped her sister's hand, all animosity forgotten in the closeness of that moment. Kerry and Briony had accepted the child. Between them it would be all right, no matter what else happened.

'What about me mum? She'll go mad,' Kerry whispered after a minute.

Briony sighed heavily.

'You leave her to me. Now come on, sort yourself out. This place is giving me the heebie jeebies!'

Kerry laughed, a choking, throaty sound that was heavily tinged with relief.

As she dried her sister's milky body, Briony felt as if someone had stepped on her grave. She fancied they were being watched by the ghosts of hundreds who had never had a chance of life. Denice O'Toole's calm and collected manner now seemed chilling. Briony was amazed by the way she'd never really thought like this until it directly affected her or her family.

Kerry's baby was going to cause trouble, she accepted that, but anything, no matter how bad, had to be better than the alternative offered by Denice O'Toole.

Molly's eyes were bulging out of her head in temper.

'You what? You're telling me you brought her back home here with the child? Are you stark staring mad?'

Molly started to pace the room in a blinding rage, her heavy body tense and erect.

'Sit down, Mum, and for once in your life think of someone else.'

Molly marched towards Briony and bellowed in her face: 'All I can think of is that my daughter is going to give birth to a blackie! Jesus suffering Christ! I could brain the bitch, I could. I could rip the hair from her bastard head. How will I hold me own head up once this gets out?'

Briony pushed her mother none too gently in the chest, sending her flying back across the room.

'All I ever hear in this family is me, me, me. How are *you* going to hold your head up? The same way you did when me dad died, and the same way you did when me and Eileen were whoring for you, and the same way you are now, with our Eileen in a nut house! Jesus Christ, this baby will be a godsend in some ways, give them something else to talk about at last.'

Molly's face was twisted with temper.

'Every time I think of her . . . with a black man . . . it makes me stomach turn. The whore! She's nothing but a dirty stinking whore!'

Briony's face went a dull white.

'Then she's in good company, isn't she? Because, quite frankly, give me a good whore any day of the week to a hypocritical old woman who jumps into bed with the man next-door. He won't even marry you, Abel. And why should he, eh? Talk about having your cake and eating it! He's got his mother running round like a blue-arsed fly after him in one house and you on your fucking back in the other! I don't think you've got much room to talk. You was at it with him before the old man was cold!'

Molly laughed nastily.

'At least he's white. I didn't drop me drawers for the first eejity blackie I laid me eyes on.'

'You know I have to laugh at you at times, Mother. As Irish Catholics we're the lowest of the low round here, always have been. Old shawlies shouting in the street – your own mother was one. Men who drink hard and work as and when it suits them. Evander Dorsey was a talented man, an intelligent man. Kerry's only mistake was falling for someone like herself, a kindred spirit. I can see that, so why can't you? I got rid of him before I knew what the full score was. I knew she was going to come a cropper, Mum. I knew that because there are far too many small-minded people like you around. Christ, you make me laugh. You was up in arms last year because Jenny O'Leary was marrying a Protestant, a ranter. You hated *him* and he had blond hair and blue eyes! Your prejudice knows no bounds, woman. That little child is the innocent party in all this. It's your grandchild!'

Molly grabbed at her daughter's hair, tearing at it as she pulled her across the room, her great bulk giving her added strength. Briony elbowed her mother hard in the stomach, making her double over in pain as she gasped for breath.

'You . . . you bitch! That child is nothing to me! Do you hear me? Nothing. It should be dead, I hope it's born dead. I hope she loses it now, while there's still time. I never want to clap eyes on it! If that whore has it, me and her are finished for good. And I mean that. She'll not drag this family's name through the dirt. No way. I'll disown the bastard first.'

Briony started laughing, a high vicious sound.

'Drag this family's name through the dirt! Well, that's not hard, is it? We're only accepted because I keep this family's name spoken with respect. Through fear, Mother, plain and simple fear. People are scared of me, Briony Cavanagh. They tolerate you because I do. If you disown our Kerry, then I will disown you and I mean that, Mother. Let Abel poxy Jones keep you in the manner you've become accustomed to. Let him pay your bills and put the food on your table. We don't need you, woman, we never did. You needed us more. You couldn't keep a sheep in wool and you know it! You've never got up off your arse and done a real day's work in your life! You swan around Brick Lane market like the fucking Queen of Sheba. Well, in future you'll swan around on Abel's money. Disown us, go on, disown the lot of us. See how far it gets you. You'll need us before we'll ever need you, I can guarantee you that.'

Molly stood and stared at Briony, the daughter she had found it increasingly difficult to like as a child yet the one who had grown into a woman of substance, a woman of renown. All Briony had said was true. Molly was respected only because of this daughter. Because she was a force to be reckoned with, a woman no one in their right mind would cross. Except, of course, her mother. Now Molly had crossed her, and had had her answer. Well, she had a trump card still and she played it.

'Take your money, see if I care. Me and Rosalee don't need it, we can get along by ourselves.'

She looked at Briony shrewdly, sure that she would not want to think of Rosie going without. But Briony had outthought her and answered equally craftily.

'That's all right then. You and Rosie fend for yourselves. You do what you have to. But that little child is here whether you like it or not. So if you disown us, do it now because I have a lot to do today.'

Walking past her mother she left the room. Upstairs Kerry

was lying on the bed, the screaming and swearing from below barely reaching her. Bernadette sat beside her holding her hand. Briony breezed into the room and said, 'How are you feeling in yourself?'

Kerry shrugged. 'All right, Bri, I suppose.'

'I'm very pleased to hear that, love, because you're going back to work tonight. You're not ill, you're pregnant, and we're all going to brazen this out. So get rested and bathed, and later on dress yourself up to the nines. My club is waiting for you, love!'

Bernadette laughed with glee. This was more like it, this was Briony at her best.

Waltzing from the room, she said nonchalantly over her shoulder, 'Oh, by the way, I've some news for you. Mother has seen fit to disown us. Personally, I couldn't give a toss!'

Bernadette was once more Kerry's dresser. In the few weeks since the run-in with their mother, everything had calmed down. Molly had kept a very low profile, and Briony had made a point of sending a cab to the house to pick Rosalee up for her visits to her sisters. Molly had been all for stopping her going, but had thought better of it. Rosalee came back flushed, excited, and full to the brim with dainties. Eileen could only be visited by mutual consent. If Briony was going, Molly kept away and vice versa. Bernadette had not been near or by her door which galled her, as it seemed three of her daughters had now formed some kind of unholy alliance, Briony and Bernadette both protecting Kerry.

In fact, it seemed to Bernadette that the three of them were getting on better than ever before. Briony was even talking about having Eileen home for a visit. Kerry didn't look pregnant to outsiders, so the secret was still closed. It would come out eventually, but they had an unspoken agreement that until it did, they would put it out of their minds. Kerry had a glow to her skin that gave her looks an added lustre. In fact, she had never been healthier, had never enjoyed her singing so much. She lost herself in the words of the songs, and gave them an added meaning.

361

Pieter Delarge, a small dark-headed man with a beaked nose, had been in the club frequently of late, and now, on a cold October evening, he sat opposite Briony in her office, drinking coffee laced with vodka and chattering amicably.

'Come on, Pieter, what are you really here for? I know it's not to talk about the weather or your health.'

Briony smiled to take the edge off her words.

Pieter shrugged expansively.

'I've come to ask you about your sister Kerry. I know through the grapevine that she's had an offer from Templar Records.'

He blew out his lips dismissively as he said it. 'I'm here because I can make you a better offer. A much better offer.'

'And what might that be?'

'I want to sign her for Campion Records. They're new, but they're going to be big. We want her to do four recordings over the next three months. We shall promote her well, her name will be everywhere. Even the music sheets would carry a picture of her, as well as her name in large letters. We want our own Billie, our own Ella. In short, we want a white singer for this new music. We want her to be the first big performer of this new age. We also want to pay her a great deal of money.'

Briony looked at the little man with shrewd eyes. 'A percentage of the royalties as well? That's what Templar have offered.'

'Then of course that would be fine by us. The girl has something about her ... youth, talent. My God, such talent! She also has a presence lacking in so many artists today. I have watched her, seen how she plays to her audience. The girl's a natural.'

Briony nodded in agreement. Her eyes were burning with ambition for her sister, with the knowledge that this little man with the bad breath and cocky manner could make Kerry into a star.

'Tell your lawyers to contact mine with the contracts. We'll talk again next week. How's that?'

Pieter smiled.

362

'That suits me down to the ground, my dear.' He stood up. 'I will leave you now. Thank you for the coffee, and I look forward to seeing you one week from today.' Clicking his heels together, he left the room.

Briony relaxed into her chair. She would get Kerry signed, sealed and delivered then they would drop the bombshell about little junior. If she went into recording, they could keep her from the public gaze for a few months, once the pregnancy became noticeable. Then, once the child arrived, they could get someone to mind it. It was the only solution. She knew through Jonathan that a lot of the stars in movies these days were hiding a multitude of sins. He was one of the few outsiders to be told about Kerry's child, and had been very supportive, telling Briony that he would do anything he could to help.

It seemed that his first legitimate acting part had made him overnight. He photographed well and looked the part of the movie star, even though he was far from being one yet. She would do the same thing with Kerry. Let her sign the contracts, get a few records under her belt. Become a known name and face. Then once the child was born, they would go on from there.

She had promised Jonathan that once Berwick Manor was underway, she would allow him to hold a big party there, a great big madhouse party, with her girls and his friends. Female as well as male. It would be a wonderful advertisement. The rich and famous gravitated towards one another.

Marcus Dowling, now her number two, walked into the office and Briony jumped. She'd been so deep in thought she hadn't heard him knock.

'Marcus! You made me jump!'

He smiled. He was big, blond and devastatingly handsome. He sat down opposite her and grinned, showing perfect white teeth.

'I'm sorry to barge in like this, Miss Cavanagh, but I needed to talk to you.'

Briony poured them both a drink.

'Go on.'

'Well, it's about the men you intend to employ at the Berwick.'

'What about them? I picked them all myself.'

Marcus smiled.

'Well, going over the lists, I found some of them were well-known nancies.'

Briony giggled. This man was so finicky it made her want to roar with laughter.

'Listen, Marcus, those men are part of my staff, not yours, love. They'll be working there just like the girls. You just worry about the heavies. Anyone else is my business, OK?'

Marcus relaxed visibly.

'Thank Gawd for that! I didn't really fancy keeping *them* in order. Give me a big burly docker any day of the week. Every place I've worked with them, they're murder.'

'Not all of them, love. Most are no different to me and you. They just have a different outlook on life, that's all.'

Marcus raised his eyebrows saucily and said, 'Well, I agree with you there anyway. Everything's running smoothly, I saw Mariah earlier, the work is nearly done. Another week or two at the most. The plasterers are finished. Soon it'll be ready for the redecoration.'

Briony nodded.

'Me and Mariah have that all in hand. By the way, I wanted to ask you something personal.'

Marcus scowled.

'What's that, Miss Cavanagh?'

'Next time you give my sister Bernadette a lift home, turn your engine off, would you? Only you kept half the bleeding street awake last night, and the night before.'

Marcus reddened and Briony laughed gently.

'Surely you didn't think you could keep that a secret, did you? Everyone knows. I was told about you and her within minutes of you being seen together. I look out for my sisters, you see, I take a deep interest in what they're doing.'

It was a veiled threat and he knew it.

'I happen to have a very high regard for Bernadette, but we've

364

only been seeing each other a week. So it's early days yet. We're friends, that's all.'

Briony nodded.

'Well, she's a big girl now. How's the recruiting going for the bar staff at the Manor?'

Marcus relaxed, back on his own territory once more.

'I've decided on the men. I thought the heavies could be incorporated better as barmen, etcetera. Then, they'll be there all the time, should any trouble arise. I'll suit and boot them up, give them a good talking to beforehand, and hopefully they'll blend in with the wallpaper.'

Briony grinned.

'I can't see Big Denny Callaghan blending in with pale grey walls somehow, can you?'

Marcus also laughed.

'Big Denny is on the door, Briony. It's the only place for him!'

'Good. Well, you seem to have everything in hand. I want you to take over a lot from me, Marcus, as you know. I want you to run the Manor, do all the heavying so to speak. But any major decisions will be mine.'

Marcus Dowling smiled.

'Of course.'

'And Mariah's. Who could forget Mariah!'

Marcus relaxed in his chair, crossing his legs.

'But, one day, I take over everything properly?'

Briony took a pull on her cigarette before she answered.

'Providing me and you don't have any major falling outs, that's about the strength of it, yes.'

'I'll go a good job, Briony. In fact, I'll work like a nigger for you!'

The smile faded from his handsome face at the look Briony gave him.

Chapter Twenty-eight

Tommy Lane was tired out. His face was aching with the cold and his hands were frozen. He turned to face the wind, his eyes immediately stinging with tears. He sank his hands deep into the pockets of his coat, wishing now he had put on his gloves. He saw a car coming towards him, its headlights bright in the darkness. He could see his own breath as he exhaled in relief. The car slowed and he walked to the passenger side and slipped inside.

'You're late.'

Marcus Dowling looked at him, a cigarette dangling from his bottom lip.

'Sorry, Tommy mate, but Briony kept me late then I had to take Bernadette home.'

Tommy nodded in the dimness of the car. He lit himself a cigarette and said seriously, 'I've had word that there's trouble brewing for Briony with the Ricardos, the Maltese ponces.'

Marcus scowled, his usually open face troubled.

'They've been in The Windjammer a few times, haven't said a word to anyone that I know of.'

'They think that now me and Briony are history, they can have a crack at her. Well, me and you are going to pop round and visit the old man, let him see a show of solidarity. He should be at his gambling rooms in Soho about now. So let's get going, me balls are nearly frozen solid.'

Marcus drove towards the West End. He was quiet for a

while. Then: 'They've got a fucking nerve 'ain't they?' He spoke incredulously. 'I mean, Tommy, even if you're off the scene as far as they know, Briony's no pushover and she's got me as her number two now. Her workforce are hardly bumboys, are they?'

Tommy laughed gently. His taut face relaxed. 'Listen, Marcus me old mate, I never met a Maltese yet who had an ounce of brain in their thick skull. She's a bint, so she's a prime target. As far as they're concerned she's got above herself, see. And if they think so, everyone else will, so tonight me and you put them all out of the ball game. I've got a shooter in me coat. You came tooled up, I take it?'

Marcus nodded. 'Of course.'

'Good. How is Briony?'

Marcus shrugged lightly.

'All right. Eileen's still bad, they've got to go and see her tomorrow. Kerry's getting heavier, but she don't look pregnant. Briony still ain't having none of it with her old woman, and Rosalee . . . well, Rosie's Rosie, if you know what I mean.'

'And how's Bernadette?' Tommy's voice was full to the brim with innuendo.

'Bernie's doing all right, thank you very much.'

Tommy laughed heartily.

'Touchy, ain't we?'

Marcus swerved round a corner fast, and Tommy held on to the dashboard to keep himself upright.

'All right, Marcus, I can take the hint.'

Marcus slowed down, his face grim now in the dimness.

'I don't know why you don't just keep in touch with Briony. I mean, you've me and Kevin Carter watching out for her, and reporting back to you. Wouldn't it be easier if you just kept up a full-time partnership?'

Tommy shook his head.

'No. It wouldn't.'

Marcus heard the hard edge to Tommy's voice and dropped the subject.

Tommy stared out of the window in silence, thinking of

Briony. He had had to leave her, to save himself. Briony was just too much, she had too many complications in her life. But that alone would not have been enough for him to have left her. He had left because, much as he loved her – and he did love her, deeply – she could never give him more than she had already.

But that didn't mean he couldn't look out for her, and he always would. No matter who he married, or who was the mother of his children, Briony would always occupy a big place in his affections. Without her, he would have had a much harder road. He owed her, and Tommy Lane always paid his debts.

Although he wouldn't admit it to a soul, he missed her at times so much it was a physical pain. If only they could be friends. But their relationship was such that that would be impossible. He either had her, one hundred per cent, or he had nothing of her.

At this moment in time, nothing seemed the better choice.

Victor Ricardo was a Maltese immigrant. Born in Buggiba, a small fishing village, he had come to England in the late 1800s bringing his fifteen-year-old wife, Maria. He had settled in Stratford where his wife had given birth to six sons in quick succession – all big-nosed, with deep-set dark eyes and thick unruly black hair. He loved to look at them, they were like his doubles. His only daughter, Immaculata, was tiny, pretty, and had the same modest demeanour as his highly religious wife.

Immaculata went to Mass, she cooked, she kept her lovely hair covered, and never spoke unless spoken to. She would not marry until her brothers had left home, as she was a great help to her mother with all the cooking and cleaning for the seven men of the household. Victor already had his eye on a husband for her, a Maltese baker who ran a bookie's on the side and had buried his wife a year before. He was older than Immaculata, but that was good. A man should be older than his wife. Women needed to be looked after. They had no right to opinions other than their husband's, and needed a man to guide them and their children. He himself was twenty years older than his wife and it had been a satisfactory arrangement.

He watched his eldest son Mario eject a troublesome man from the club, and smiled to himself. Mario was a good boy. Big and strong, he was not the most intelligent of Victor's sons, but his physical prowess was legendary around the East End.

Victor's little Soho club was in Greek Street. It was a basement really, but he had made it into a gambling house ten years before. He also allowed certain girls to work his place for a small percentage of their earnings. He treated the toms with contempt, not being a great lover of the female sex.

Tonight his eyes scanned the basement room with interest. The smoky atmosphere and constant buzz of conversation gave him a thrill every night of his life.

Victor poured himself a small medicinal brandy, staring at his bulbous hands which were becoming stiff with arthritis. Sighing, he went to his office and sat behind his desk. In front of him were the ledgers, telling him who owed what, and how long the debt had been outstanding. He would go through them tonight, then in the morning one or another of his sons would chase up the late payers. It was a good arrangement. He was toying with the idea of starting a protection racket in the West End. Now Tommy Lane was seriously East End, and his relationship with Briony Cavanagh was over with, Victor felt the time was right to make his own mark. He already collected from Maltese and Italian businesses in Soho. Now he felt he could extend his operation to the clubs. If he could get a madam like Briony Cavanagh to pay up, the others would rapidly follow. She was a woman without the guidance of a man, and no matter what anyone said about her, she was only a woman. He would prove that she was not indestructible, he and his sons would be the men to make her pay what she should have been paying for years – protection money.

Victor smiled to himself as he thought about it. The Irish were scared of her, the Jews were scared of her, even the German and Russian immigrants were scared of her. The Italians paid whoever asked them, so it was down to the Maltese or the Arabs to take advantage of this situation. It seemed the Arabs weren't going to, so that left the door open for him.

370

Victor sipped his brandy slowly, savouring the taste as it slipped down his throat and warmed his belly. He looked up as the door of his office opened, and swallowed heavily as he saw who was standing there with his son Mario. A very subdued Mario.

'Hello, Victor, how are you?' Tommy's voice was friendly and calm. 'Do you know Marcus Dowling at all?'

Victor stood up slowly and nodded at Mario who shut the door and stood in front of it, trying to look menacing. Tommy turned and faced him, saying loudly, 'Fucking hell, you two are so ugly you even look alike! Sit down, Mario, before I box you down. I ain't in the mood tonight for anyone trying to annoy me.'

Mario stayed put and Tommy shook his head at Marcus. At the signal, he pulled a gun from under his coat.

'Sit, Mario, or I'll blow your legs from under you.'

A white-faced Victor rushed around the desk.

'Mario, for God's sake, sit down!'

Tommy pushed Victor back towards his seat and, looking at the two men, said loudly, 'Did I ever tell you that I had a run-in years ago with Maltese Jack? Do you remember Maltese Jack, Victor? A big ugly bastard, a bit like you actually. He had a big hooter and all. Well, he tried to tuck me up so I shot him. No kidding, I shot him in both his feet. Now in the East End, if you shoot someone in the plates, it means they've tried to run you out of your business. Trod on their toes, like. Do you get my point? So in a minute, I'm gonna shoot you both in the feet, then everyone will know you tried to take what was rightfully mine.'

Victor shook his head.

'I swear, Tommy, I have tried to take nothing of yours . . .'

Tommy laughed gently.

'But you have. Because me and Briony Cavanagh are partners still. I've left the running of the businesses to her because I have other fish to fry. So if you go to her for protection money, indirectly you're stepping on my patch. Now my Briony would have sorted you, because she isn't as easygoing as I am. She would have got this young man here to blow up your club, or

371

maybe even your house. Because she hasn't got the patience I have. She's much more quick to anger than I am. Which is why I trust her to run my places. But me and Marcus here, we thought to ourselves, we'd better go and see Victor before Briony does, because me and you have known each other a long time, haven't we?'

Victor nodded slowly, his dreams and his hopes fading before his eyes.

'So when we shoot you in your feet, you'd better thank us, because we saved your lives.'

Mario looked at his father in shock. He tried to raise himself from his chair and Tommy shot him at close range in his right foot, shattering the ankle bone and the shin.

Mario dropped back in his chair, his devastated foot hanging loosely on to the floor.

All were aware that the hubbub in the club outside had dwindled into silence.

Tommy poked his finger in Mario's face.

'So, what do you say?'

Mario groaned with pain, and Tommy screamed at the top of his voice: 'What's that? I can't hear you, Mario. Did you say, "Thank you, Mr Lane"?'

Victor saw his son's face, the sweat standing out on his brow, the trickle of mucus running from his nose.

'Thank him, Mario. For God's sake, thank the man and get this over with!'

'Th ... Thank you.' Mario's voice came out stronger than he'd expected.

'Thank you, Mr Lane.' Marcus's voice was high-pitched, as if talking to a child.

'Thank you, Mr Lane.' Mario's voice had tears in it now.

Tommy grinned. Then, shooting Mario in his other foot, he said, 'You're welcome, my old son. More than welcome in fact.'

Victor looked at his child, his first-born son, and a seething hatred for Tommy Lane swept over him. He swiftly opened his desk drawer. Marcus aimed his gun at the older man and shot him full in the chest.

Victor slumped over the desk, his body twitching uncontrollably in the throes of death.

Tommy tutted loudly. Walking to the man, he turned him over. In the desk was a small revolver. Tommy took it and slipped it into the pocket of his coat. Then Marcus and he walked slowly from the office, and through the hushed crowd outside in the club itself.

As they drove the few streets to The Windjammer, Tommy was humming to himself. Marcus, on the other hand, had not reached the point where the use of a gun didn't bother him at all. But he was determined he would get there, in the end.

'You really expect me to believe that?' Briony stubbed her cigarette out with such force she pushed the ashtray across her desk. Only the quick action of the girl before her prevented it from crashing to the floor.

'Honestly, Miss Cavanagh, it's the truth.'

Briony walked around the desk and held up a finger. Pointing it into the girl's face, she said slowly, 'You ever try and muscle in on another girl's customer in my club again, I'll have your guts. Do you hear me?'

The young girl opened her eyes wide in alarm and once more tried to deny everything.

'But I never . . .'

Briony stared into her face, her green eyes glittering with malevolence.

'Are you calling me a liar? Because I was watching you, love. You waited for the girl to get up and go to the powder room. Then you sauntered over there like butter wouldn't melt and tried to muscle in. I saw you! Now I couldn't give a toss, but Betty wasn't having any of it. You two were fighting in my club.' She poked herself hard in the chest. 'My club! You hear what I'm telling you, girl? You don't fucking cause hag in my place. Now get your bag, and get your arse out of here. If I ever see you or your lousy mate on my premises, I'll see you never work the smoke again. Do I make myself clear?'

The girl nodded, her face frozen with fear at the change in Briony Cavanagh. Only a week before Briony had stopped by her table and said a friendly hello. It was silly to underestimate her, it was foolhardy. Now she well and truly had her card marked, and all over a punter who was only good for a fiver, top whack. She could cheerfully kick herself.

Picking up her bag, she left the room. Her face was drawn and her shoulders drooped.

Briony watched her leave and sighed heavily.

Brasses weren't worth the hag half the time. She was happy for the girl discreetly to ply her trade. It didn't bother her in the least. She was clean, well dressed, and blended in with the clientele. But two of them arguing the toss over a man was a different ball game. It lowered the tone of the club, and that was the last thing Briony wanted.

The door opened once more and she turned away in a temper. 'I don't want to see or hear any more about it, Julian!'

Tommy's voice was soft as he said, 'Hello, Bri. All right?'

Turning back, her jaw dropped with the shock.

'Tommy? Oh, Tommy.' Her voice was thick with pleasure.

'Can I sit down then, or is everyone getting a bollocking tonight?'

Briony laughed at his jocular tone.

'Oh, Tommy, you're the last person I expected. Sit. Sit down and let me get you a drink.'

She poured him a large scotch, her brain whirling with the implications of having Tommy Lane in the club, in her office, chatting to her as if nothing had happened.

He pulled off his heavy coat and slung it casually on to the floor. Then he sat down and opened the cigarette box on her desk. He blew out the smoke heavily, a large grey cloud forming around his head.

'Jesus, Briony, what's in these fags? Camel shit?'

She placed his drink in front of him.

'Could be, they're Turkish!'

'You're supposed to give this kind of crap to the punters and smoke the usual Gold Flake yourself! Now then, how are you?'

Briony sat down opposite him; and gazed into his eyes. 'All the better for seeing you, Tommy.' Her voice was soft, gentle.

Tommy looked at her for a long moment. Smiling, he said, 'How's the family?'

As she spoke of her sisters and her mother, he felt the familiar pull of her. But he also reprimanded himself for being weak enough to come and see her. She was like a dainty piece of Dresden china: her milky-white skin so flawless, her deep red hair emphasising the green glint of her eyes. Her mouth looked too good to be on a mortal woman. He could hear the deep longing in her voice, see it in the depths of her eyes, and just for a second he wondered if he had come here deliberately. To show her he could walk away from her again, maybe even to show himself.

'So Eileen's getting better? I'm pleased to hear that, Bri. Really. She had a rough deal, did old Eileen. I'm glad I got rid of the pair of ponces.'

Briony smiled. 'So am I.'

Tommy sipped his scotch.

'Actually, Bri, I helped us both out tonight. That's why I'm here. Maltese Victor was all for blowing this place up! Can you credit that? He wanted protection. Anyway, I heard a whisper so I got your new bloke, Marcus, and me and him went round to see the old bastard and gave him and his son the bad news.'

Briony's eyes had widened to their utmost.

'He was going to do what?'

'Give this place a quick singeing. Cheeky bugger! Anyway, everything's sorted now. That's why I came round.' He looked at his watch ostentatiously. 'I have to run in a minute. I have to see a man about a dog.'

Briony sat back in her chair heavily.

'I beg your pardon?' Her voice sounded small and hurt. Tommy found he couldn't look at her. 'You mean, you've come here to let me know you've slapped Vic the Maltese, and that's all?'

'I did a bit more than slap him, love. I shot Mario the wonderboy in his feet and Marcus shot the old man through the heart. I expect the Old Bill is having a field day about now. It's only round Greek Street, ain't it?'

Briony nodded, her mouth twisted in a grim line.

'Oh, I get it now. You had to show a front. You still own part of the clubs so you wanted to protect your investment. I'm sorry, Tommy. I thought maybe the years we spent together might have brought you back round here, but I was wrong. I won't make that mistake again in a hurry.'

Standing up she snatched his glass from him and slammed it down on the desk. 'Well, you've told me your bit of news. Exciting as it is, I think I have the details now. So why don't you piss off to wherever it is you're going? Or more precisely, whoever.'

Tommy stared at his empty hand, then picking up the glass he drained his drink in one gulp. Standing, he picked up his coat from the floor and walked towards the door.

'You dirty bastard, Tommy! You came here to see how the land lay with me. You're laughing at me, aren't you?'

He faced her then.

'No, actually, I'm not. You're still a big part of me, Briony. But I'll tell you something for nothing, love, something I've told you many times before – your big mouth and your attitude will always be your downfall. You couldn't swallow could you? Just for a few minutes. I always had to do what *you* wanted. Well, if you want me back, I'm sorry. Because at this moment I wouldn't have you gift wrapped.'

'You're too demanding, Bri. You have to take the lead. You have to be in charge. Well, you don't pay my wages, love, and you never have. I do what I want, when I want, and that includes visiting you or any other woman in the smoke as and when it suits me.'

He poked himself hard in the chest as he said the last word and Briony fought back tears of frustration and rage.

'Well, you don't visit no other woman while you're with me, I won't stand for it!'

Tommy laughed then. 'But we've already established I ain't with you, am I? We're partners, Briony.'

'Yeah, silent partners, and that suits me right down to the

376

ground. In future *I'll* sort out Vic the Maltese or anyone else who wants to muscle in, all right? You sort yourself out. I still own the lion's share of this place, mate.'

Tommy smiled sarcastically.

'Of course you do. You always owned the lion's share of everything didn't you? Well, now I've been put well and truly in my place, I'll fuck off.'

As he walked out of the door Briony threw her own glass of scotch at the door. It smashed into thousands of tiny pieces. Tommy shut the door quietly behind him without looking back. Briony sat down at her desk, the tears running down her face. How could he have done this to her? How could he have walked in here, all sweetness and light, and then dumped her back down on the ground so wickedly? She had felt so euphoric at seeing him, telling herself he could not live without her the same way she couldn't live without him, and all the time it was just business. Plain, simple business.

Stalking across the room, she opened the door. Spotting Julian, she bellowed, 'Get Marcus Dowling, now!'

Julian winced visibly as the door was slammed. Walking through to the club itself, he spied Marcus at the bar with Bernadette.

'Briony wants you, now. And I do mean now. She's rather upset.'

Briony was standing by her desk when Marcus walked into the office. 'Oh, so you've come then? I understand you did a bit of business with Tommy late tonight. A bit of business you should have consulted me about?'

Marcus licked his lips. 'That's correct. I did a bit of business. But I didn't see fit to bother you with it, Miss Cavanagh. After all, I am your number two. It's what I'm paid for. I deal with things as and when they come up.'

'Did Tommy Lane approach you?'

'Yes...'

Briony cut him off.

'You've been reporting to him, haven't you? Now don't lie to me, Marcus.'

He sighed. 'I have never lied to you, Miss Cavanagh.'

'No, you ain't lied, you just ain't said nothing. Well, I'm telling you now, as the person who pays your wages, you owe *me*, not Tommy Lane, your loyalty. He's a sleeping partner. I am the main owner of this place. I don't employ dogs and then bark myself. Do you get my drift?'

Marcus nodded. 'Yes, I understand. But we was trying to protect you . . . We was just . . .'

Briony flew across the room and grabbed his shirtfront. Shaking him hard, her tiny body possessed of the strength of great anger, she screamed: 'I don't need anyone to protect me, especially not a slag like Tommy Lane! Me and you could have sorted that out. Me and you! That's why you're my number two. How's it going to look now, eh? Tommy Lane still fighting my battles. Well, I can fight me own battles, and if you still want to work for me, you'd better get that into your thick head!'

Marcus grabbed her wrists and pulled her hands from his clothes.

'I'd thank you never to drag at me like that again. I know you pay my wages but I was doing my job. Believe me when I say tonight was well thought out and well planned, Miss Cavanagh. I am known to be your number two, and me and Tommy showing up like that only made you look stronger. More in control. Now calm yourself down. You're not acting rationally. I've never seen you like this before.'

His deep gentle voice was her undoing. Leaning against him, she began to cry, a high sobbing that wrenched at his heart. Putting his arms around her, he held her close, letting her cry herself out. He could feel her body shuddering with each breath she took, and for the first time ever he felt a twinge of sympathy for her. She seemed more human now than at any time before. Gone was the work machine. The hard-nosed businesswoman. In her place was a Briony Cavanagh who could be hurt, who was human and cried because she was hurting inside. All that he saw was pain, and an intense loneliness that made him ashamed of all his previous feelings about this little woman.

In the space of five minutes, he knew her better than he would ever have believed possible.

He held her until she had cried herself out. Then he lit her a cigarette and poured her a drink. Leaving her sitting at her desk, he went back to Bernadette, knowing in his heart of hearts that neither he nor Briony would ever mention this night again but that it would always be there between them. It would anchor him to her. Because it was proof that Briony Cavanagh could feel. Something he would have found very hard to believe had he not seen it with his own eyes.

Chapter Twenty-nine

Kerry sat beside Eileen, her hands resting on her belly. Her pregnancy was not yet evident to outsiders but her spreading waistline was now obvious to friends and associates. Kerry poured out the weak tea and, mustering up her best voice, said gaily: 'How do you fancy a nice cup of tea, Ei?'

Eileen smiled dreamily. Her deep blue eyes drooped as if she had just woken from a long sleep.

'A cup of tea would be lovely, thanks.'

Kerry gave her a cup, stirring it solicitously.

'You're putting on a bit of weight, Eileen. You look much better for it.'

Eileen nodded. She was staring out of the window at the sea.

'I like the ships, Kel. I like to watch them. They blow their hooters so loud. Sometimes I can almost feel the spray of the salt water on my skin. I wish I could be on a boat. I watch the sailors pulling up the rigging, or getting the little fishing boats off the sand. It fascinates me how you can live on the sea, be a part of it, and yet only a few miles away we had no real inkling of it. I wish I'd been born here. Born on the sea. It's clean here. Even the sailors' breath on cold mornings looks clean. Sister Mary Magdalene says you have to respect the sea because it's a stronger force. It can be calm and friendly one moment and like a raging tyrant the next. Her dad died on a ship, he was a merchant seaman.'

Kerry sat amazed at Eileen's monologue. Personally she couldn't give a tinker's cuss about the sea, but obviously Eileen had taken a fancy to it and that was good.

'It is very pretty here. That view. I suppose that's what it's named after. I expect you watch the boats all the time?'

Eileen nodded and resumed her contemplation. Kerry smoked her cigarette. She wished Briony and Bernie would hurry back from seeing the doctor. Eileen gave her the heebie jeebies these days.

Briony and Bernadette were sitting in Andrew McLawson's office, looking stunned.

'Are you sure?' Briony's voice was incredulous.

The doctor nodded seriously. 'I'm sure. Your sister knew, in fact. She's four months gone.'

'Bloody hell!' Bernie shook her head in shock. 'Does my mother know? Has she been told?'

'She was informed three days ago. She was very pleased, in fact. Over the moon. I was quite surprised, considering her daughter's illness. Personally, I'm not sure it's a good thing.'

'Do you think Eileen will be able to cope with this pregnancy?' Briony sounded agitated.

McLawson shrugged.

'I really can't say. Your mother thinks it will be the making of her, but in truth I'm not so sure. Your sister is physically very weak, has to be forced to eat. We have a nun here, Sister Mary Magdalene, who seems to be the only person your sister will do anything for. They have a very close friendship. Sister Mary is a very kind girl, only twenty, with a very deep vocation. She loves Eileen dearly. I think maybe she could see her through this pregnancy, but we have no facilities here for children. I'm afraid you'll have to make alternative arrangements. We'll keep her here until she's ready to give birth, then she'll have to leave. Once she's delivered of the child, if you can get someone to care for it, Eileen can come back. We all feel she's doing very well.'

Briony sighed. 'But not well enough to look after her own child?'

'Good God, no! I would be very surprised if Eileen ever went back into the real world. I think your mother will probably take on the child. At least that's the impression I got anyway . . .'

Briony interrupted him.

'Over my dead body! She ain't getting her hands on it, or my Eileen. She'll drive the girl stark staring mad, as if she ain't doolally enough as it is! I wish you hadn't told her, Dr McLawson, she is a very determined woman.'

Andrew McLawson smiled once more.

'I think it runs in your family, Miss Cavanagh.'

Molly was making a large loaf. Her huge arms were stretching and pulling the dough into shape, kneading it to give it a nice crisp lightness as it cooked. Her front door opening was nothing to her, she didn't even bother to look round.

'Come away in, woman, and make yourself a cup of tea.'

She expected to hear Mother Jones' voice. Instead she was surprised to hear Bernadette's.

'Hello, Mum.'

Molly swung around to face her. 'Well, if it's not one of me daughters. What do you want?' Her floury hands on her ample hips, she looked formidable. Bernadette swallowed hard.

'I've come for Rosalee.' She smiled at her sister as she spoke.

'Oh, you have, have you? Well, maybe I might not let her go today. It's very cold out.'

Bernadette raised her eyes to the ceiling. 'Don't start, Mum. Our Briony's expecting her, and you'd better not cause any hag. Marcus is keeping the engine running, so I've got to go.'

'How is Marcus? When am I going to meet him properly?' All her animosity was forgotten at the thought of Bernadette's beau. She was ecstatic at the thought of one of her daughters having a man, a decent man.

'He's fine, Mum, now can I please take Rosalee?'

Bernadette was already putting Rosalee's coat on. Molly watched her without speaking.

'Kerry's fine, Mum, if you're interested.'

Molly went back to her task of making bread, not even acknowledging her daughter's words.

Bernadette swallowed down an angry remark and instead

383

said, 'I'll bring Rosalee back tomorrow afternoon, OK?'

'If you like. And tell that Briony she's not to stuff her on cakes and sweets, she's a big enough lump as it is.'

'Okey doke. Come on, Rosie darling, we're going in the car.'

Rosalee grinned and said, 'Bri, Bri.'

Bernadette kissed her face and said, 'That's right, Rosie, we're going to see Briony.'

Molly wiped her hands on her apron and kissed her daughters on their cheeks.

'Watch her now, she's got a cold coming on.'

'See you tomorrow, Mum.'

Molly walked out to the car with them. Smiling widely, she waved at Marcus Dowling. She approved of this big man with his blond good looks.

Marcus waved back. Once Rosalee was settled in the back of the car with Bernadette beside her, holding her hand, he drove away. Molly waved until they were out of sight, then Mother Jones came out of her front door.

'He's a fine-looking specimen and no mistaking.'

Molly nodded in agreement, then in a jocular voice said, 'I wouldn't mind his boots under my table meself!'

Mother Jones cackled in agreement.

Rosalee and Briony were sitting on the hearth rug before a roaring fire. Briony was shelling monkey nuts and Rosalee was opening her mouth at regular intervals to eat them. Kerry sat on the settee, her knees drawn up under her, and Bernadette sat on a chair by the fire, her feet resting on the polished brass trim of the hearth.

'She eats so much, Briony, we should cut her down. Mum said she was getting too heavy for her to lift.'

Briony laughed. 'Mother always says that, then she feeds her a great slice of apple pie.'

Kerry was at the sleeping stage of pregnancy. At five and a half months, all she wanted to do when she relaxed was have a quick nap. She yawned widely, making a throaty noise. Briony laughed.

'Keeping you up, are we, Kel?'

'Oh, Briony, I feel so tired. I'll have to have an early night tonight.'

Briony was immediately concerned. 'Look, I think you should cut the club now until after the birth. Concentrate on your recording. I reckon that's where you'll be best off. The contract's signed and they can't do nothing. You just get that out of the way. Bessie Knight can do two spots at the club, she'll be glad of the dosh anyway.'

Kerry nodded lazily. 'I like Bessie, I like all the Velvetones. She goes down well and all, don't she? With the punters. Very good-looking woman.'

Bernadette said, without thinking, 'Marcus said she ain't bad looking for a . . .' She stopped speaking and the room went very quiet. 'Oh, Kerry, I'm sorry.'

Kerry pulled herself upright, awake now.

'For a what, Bernie? A blackie? A soot? What did the marvellous Marcus Dowling say then?'

Briony knelt up and put her hand on Kerry's leg.

'Come on, Kel, she never meant nothing by it. Let's not let this ruin a nice evening. It's bad enough we ain't got our Eileen here. Let's not have any rows. Not tonight anyway.'

Kerry made a moue. 'Well!' Then, her voice lowering, she said: 'I'm shitting myself about having this baby, Bri, I don't know if I'm strong enough to face what it's going to bring.'

Bernadette leant forward in her chair and said firmly, 'Don't you worry, Kel, we'll weather anything. That baby is going to be the best looked after kid this side of the water.'

Kerry smiled.

'I wonder what I'll have. And what Eileen will have. Mother's over the moon about Eileen's baby at least.'

Briony blew out her lips in a very unladylike way.

'It's your baby she should be pleased about, if anyone's. Eileen won't be able to cope.'

'Mum wants it, don't she?'

Briony laughed. 'Well, Mum ain't getting it! Eileen's coming here. Once she's delivered safely, we'll see how the land lies. If she still ain't all the ticket, she can go back to Sea View. I'll have the child.'

Bernie and Kerry both heard the deep aching longing in her voice and exchanged glances.

'You!'

Kerry's voice was loud and Briony looked her full in the face. In the firelight Briony's hair looked redder than ever, her eyes for once a glittering black.

'And why not? I'll get a wet nurse in to do the business with the feeding, and I'll oversee its upbringing. What's so bloody strange about that?'

Kerry shrugged. 'Well, ain't you got enough on your plate? In a way I think Mum would be the best bet. Let's face it, she's sod all else to do all day.'

'She's also got Rosalee and her life with Abel, such as it is. She's too old for a baby in the house. Not only that, I can give it more, give it a better start in life.'

Kerry sat back on the settee. 'I suppose so. Bri?'

'What?'

'Can I ask you something, without you getting all aereated?'

Briony grinned. 'Of course.'

'You really miss Benedict, don't you?'

Briony's face dropped. She bit her lip before answering.

'Shall I tell you something? I miss that boy with a vengeance. I'll be walking down the road, happy as a sandboy, and then I'll see his little face. Wonder what he's doing, who he's talking to. Whether or not he's happy.' She stared into the fire then, watching the flickering of the flames.

'In the dead of the night, I daydream. I imagine how it could be, you know. I imagine me and him living here, Tommy and me married and looking after him. Tommy taking him out to play in the garden, a swing for him, a rabbit. You know, things children like. I see him asleep in bed, and me kissing him goodnight, ironing his little clothes meself, ready for the next day. I see me combing his hair, smoothing it over his forehead. I miss him all right, Kerry. I miss him so much it's like a physical pain. Especially on his birthday or Christmas, because I can't ever really touch him, or smell him, or talk to him. He's my child and I have no contact with him at all.'

Her voice trailed away and Bernadette patted her shoulder. Rosalee leant towards her and kissed her, a whacking wet kiss that sounded loud in the quietness of the room. Briony hugged her sister close, smothering her with the little dry kisses she knew Rosalie loved.

'I think you're right, Bri. I think Eileen and her baby will be better off here. At least you'll really love it.'

Briony looked at Kerry and said: 'And I need a baby to love, don't I?' Her eyes were full of tears.

'You can have my baby and all if you want.'

Briony coughed to give herself time to recover.

'I'll love your baby, Kerry, I'll love it and care for it. I swear that to you.'

Kerry smiled. 'I feel just like you do, about Evander. I think of him in the night. It's as if the darkness makes you think more somehow. I imagine me and him married, and everyone pleased for us . . .'

Briony nodded. 'I know. I'm sorry I chased him away, Kerry. Honestly. If I could put the clock back, I would.'

Kerry answered her bitterly, 'But I don't want him back, that's the funny thing. Because it's only now, with this baby, that I realise I was chasing a big dream. A pretend life. Because I'm not strong enough to live a life with him. I know that now. This baby has taught me that much.'

Bernadette said softly, 'Are you going to keep the baby after you have it, Kerry? Have you decided yet?'

She shook her head vigorously.

'Ask me again after the birth. One minute I want it, I love it to death. The next the thought of its colour and the effect it's going to have makes me feel faint. I can't answer you, Bern, 'cos I don't know the answer meself.'

'Well, whatever you decide, I'll stand by you. And so will you, Bernie, won't you?'

Bernadette nodded her head. 'Of course. There's a girl at the club, her baby's with a woman in Devon. She travels down

387

every couple of months to see her. The baby's father is a married man, and she can't hack the thought of people knowing she has an illegitimate child. She says the arrangement works well, 'cos the father coughs up the money like.'

Kerry sighed. 'I don't know if I could have the baby too far away. Oh, to be honest I don't know what the fuck I want. I don't know whether I want a shit, a shave or a shampoo, as the old man used to say.'

They all laughed then, the atmosphere lightening. Rosalee pulled on Briony's sleeve and she said to her, 'What, darling, what do you want?'

Pointing to the nuts, she opened her mouth, opening it as wide as it would go.

Bernadette and Kerry both started screeching with laughter, Kerry's with a tinge of hysteria to it.

Briony picked up the bowl of nuts and said seriously, 'Of course, madam. If madam wants the nuts, madam must have them, tout suite!'

Rosalee closed her mouth and Kerry shook her head slowly. 'At least she knows what she wants, Bri, which is more than I do. Ain't that right, Rosie darlin'?'

Rosalee clapped her hands together and made the deep-throated gurgle that meant she was happy.

Chapter Thirty

Briony ran through her front door like a lunatic. Pulling off her coat, she raced up the stairwell, shouting to Cissy over her shoulder.

'Tea, hot and steaming. I'm freezing.'

Cissy picked up the full length silver fox coat and tutted to herself as she went through to the kitchen.

Briony went into Kerry's bedroom where the midwife was making Kerry comfortable.

'How are you, Kel, all right? I came immediately.'

Kerry lay against the pillows, her face shining with sweat. 'I'm all right, Bri.'

The midwife wiped her face with a damp cloth. 'This is a quick birth, I've seen the type before. One lady I had was up and over it all in less than three hours! She won't go long. The doctor's seen her and he's coming back later, he's got two emergencies. Christmas is always the same.'

Briony smiled at her. 'Go down and get yourself a cuppa, I'll stay with her.'

The woman left the room gratefully. Briony Cavanagh was paying her a lot of money to deliver this child and keep it quiet. She had no intention of blotting her copybook, not where Briony Cavanagh was concerned.

Kerry moaned as another pain shot through her. 'Imagine, a Christmas baby, Bri. In another half an hour it's Christmas Day!'

'And what a present, eh? A baby.'

'Now I know how poor old Mary felt!'

Briony laughed, pleased at how well Kerry was coping.

'At least she had a husband, Bri, that's one thing in her favour.'

Briony sat on the bed and said, 'Yeah, but he wasn't the father of the child, was he? Poor old Joseph got all the hag and none of the pleasure!'

Kerry grinned, scandalised. 'If Mum was here, she'd flatten you for that remark.'

'Yeah, well, she ain't, is she? And it's only the truth anyway. How are the pains?'

'Let's just say they're there, shall we? Give me a drink of water, Bri, I'm parched.'

She doubled up as another pain shot through her. The sweat was standing out on her brow and Briony picked up the cloth and wiped her sister's face gently.

'Oh, that's lovely, Bri.'

'Here you are, have a drink of water.' She held the heavy crystal glass to her sister's lips.

Kerry gulped at the water, the coolness easing the burning of her throat.

'Have a guess what I heard today, when I was shopping.'

'What, a bit of scandal?'

Briony grinned. 'No, nothing like that. I heard your record being played in all the music shops. It's selling wonderfully.'

'Oh, good.' Kerry had a lot more on her mind at the moment and sighed.

'I wish this bloody baby would hurry up and come, I'm starving.'

Briony laughed.

'Bri, would you do me a favour?'

'Of course, anything.'

'Get me Mum, would you? I want me mum.'

Briony heard the hurt in her sister's voice and said calmly, 'Of course I will, love.'

Standing up she walked to the door, saying over her shoulder,

'I'll send the midwife back up and go and get the old woman meself. Be back soon, all right?'

Kerry nodded, panting in the aftermath of a pain.

Briony ran down the stairs and through to the kitchen. 'Can you go back up, I have to go out.'

'I've just made your tea!'

'Then drink it yourself, Cissy. Mrs H, make Kerry something light – she's starving. Coddled eggs will do. Where's me coat?'

Cissy went to the scullery where the coat was hanging up, dripping water from the snow. Shaking it, she took it out to Briony.

Dragging it on her slim frame, she smiled at everyone. 'Be back in two ticks. I'm going to get me mother. Keep your eye on Kel for me, all right. And if Bernie rings, tell her to get herself home, though with a bit of luck Kevin Carter will have tracked her and Marcus down.'

'All right, Bri. Get yourself off. And drive carefully, the weather's atrocious.' Mrs Horlock's voice was concerned.

Briony felt a glow come over her. Kissing the old woman's wrinkled cheek, she said, 'Look after Kerry, won't you?'

Mrs Horlock smiled. 'Of course I will. Now you get going before this snow gets worse.'

After Briony left the kitchen, the midwife said: 'She's a lot nicer than you'd think, isn't she?'

Cissy nodded. 'Yes. But if anything happens to Kerry, you'll see a different side to her, so get yourself back up the stairs.'

The woman didn't need to be told twice. She left the kitchen in double quick time.

'If Molly comes, I'll be very surprised.'

Mrs Horlock shook her head sagely.

'If Briony wants her here for Kerry, then she'll come. Briony will see to that.'

Cissy poured herself a cup of tea and in her mind admitted to the truth of that statement.

If Briony wanted her, she'd get her.

Molly was trimming the small tree with Rosalee passing her the ornaments as she always did. Marcus and Bernadette had brought round presents for them both, and Molly looked at the gaily wrapped parcels with sweet anticipation. Briony's presents to Rosalee were with them; Rosalee's was a new coat of deep red wool that would keep her as warm as toast. Bernadette had told her that earlier. Briony had also bought Rosalee a collection of hand-made animals that she could put on to her dressing table. They were carved from hard wood and Rosalee would be unable to break them.

'This cake is lovely, Mrs Cavanagh, did you make it yourself?' He knew Molly had, but he also knew she liked to boast about the fact.

'I did, it's me own recipe. Boiled fruit cake it is. Quick and tasty, with just enough cinnamon to give it a kick.'

'And a drop of brandy as well, Mum, if I know you.'

Molly laughed.

'Of course. A drop of the hard doesn't go amiss with dried fruit. They complement each other.'

The feeling in the house was festive and cheery. It was into this happy warmth that Briony came, bursting through the doorway in a flurry of snow.

'Briony!' Bernie's voice was high with shock.

'Hello, Bernie, I've been trying to locate you all afternoon. Kerry's in labour.'

Rosalee had set up a screeching from excitement, her huge cumbersome body rocking itself in her chair by the fire.

'Hello, Rosie darlin'.' Briony kissed her sister who pulled her into a hard embrace.

Molly watched with contempt. So that whore's time was on, was it? Well she hoped she had a dead child. That would make Molly's Christmas.

Briony extricated herself from Rosalee's arms and said, 'She wants you, Mum.'

Molly carried on fiddling with the tree.

'Oh, she does, does she? Well, she'll have to know what it's like to want then, won't she?'

Briony stood up, staring at her mother with eyes narrowed

dangerously. Bernadette closed her eyes. Marcus, on the other hand, watched in fascination as Briony went to her mother and said: 'I don't think you realise, Mum, but you haven't got any say in it. You're coming if I have to drag you there myself.'

Molly looked down at her tiny daughter and smiled grimly. 'I'd like to see you try, madam.'

Briony lifted her arm and Bernadette jumped from her seat. Pulling Briony away, she said, 'Come on, Mum. How long can you keep all this up? It's Christmas. Poor Kerry's got enough on her plate as it is. Try and have a bit of Christian spirit, you're always going on about it.'

Molly sneered at her daughters.

'That bitch of hell can go and die for all I care, that child is a stain on the earth. It's . . . it's an abomination! She wants me – me! – to go to her in her labour. Well, she can want all she likes, the whore. I couldn't care if Christ himself or the angel Gabriel appeared in me kitchen this second, I still wouldn't go.'

'You're a vicious old cow, Mother. Come on, Bernie, help me get Rosalee's coat on.'

Molly stood in front of Rosalee and shouted, 'She goes nowhere.'

Briony laughed. 'Oh yes she does, because this house is still in my name. I put you down as the lodger, Mother. I handed it to you only as a lodger. You won't own it unless I die before you. It was my way of keeping Abel's hands off it. So if I'm going to put you out – which I fully intend to, legally mind – then Rosalee is homeless, isn't she? I don't suppose they'd welcome her and all next-door. Also, the allowance stops so you'll have to live off Abel who gets a good wedge from me, by the way, for doing fuck all! Or you'll have to get yourself a job.'

Molly's face paled.

'You wouldn't do that to me? You wouldn't use your money to force my hand, surely?'

Briony smiled nastily. 'Wouldn't I? You don't know me very well, Mother. In fact, you don't really know me at all. You get your coat on, or me and you are really finished, Mum, I mean it. Not another penny do you get. I'll make it my business to let everyone know me and you are old news. That anyone giving you a kind word will answer to me.'

Picking up her mother's coat from the peg behind the door, Briony threw it across the kitchen at her. Molly instinctively caught it.

'Come on, Kerry is well on her time and you must be there to greet your grandchild.'

Rosalee stood by the door, her huge bulk blocking it. She smiled at everyone with her wide grin and Marcus smiled back at her. He liked Rosie, which endeared him to Bernie and her sisters. It was not a fake liking. He genuinely accepted her.

'Come on, Rosie, you come with me and your mum in my car. Bernadette, you go with Briony.'

She could have kissed him. He was trying to defuse the situation.

Walking out of the door, he took Bernadette and Rosalee with him. Briony and Molly stared into each other's face. Molly was amazed at how beautiful this child of hers was. The white skin, standing out in contrast to her hair, and those deep green eyes really made for a beautiful woman. Yet at this moment she felt nothing for her except contempt. A deep-rooted contempt, because she was owned by this girl, owned by her own flesh and blood. Now she had to go to her whore of a daughter, the one daughter she had truly loved and who now disgusted her, or else give up her easy way of life.

Molly was an intrinsically selfish woman, and the decision once made was easy to accept.

She followed Briony from the house and out to her car.

Kerry was in pain, a deep racking pain that surprised her with its ferocity. Nothing had prepared her for the sheer agony, the feeling of having her body split into two.

'Oh, it hurts, Bri. It's a fucking nightmare!'

Briony smiled. 'I know. I remember me own labour. Not the pain, you forget the pain. But the memory of being a part of something bigger than you doesn't ever fade.'

'Never again, I'll never do this again.'

394

The midwife laughed now. 'If I had a penny, love, for every time someone said that to me, I'd be a millionaire!'

Kerry grimaced as she was once more torn in two. 'I want to bear down. It's coming. I can feel it.'

Molly sat in a chair by the window looking out at the snow which was now a blizzard. A thick whiteness covered the roofs of the houses and all the gardens looked beautiful. She heard the grunting of her daughter as she pushed and bit on her lip.

'Please, dear Mary at the throne of Christ, don't let this child breathe. Let it be born dead.'

The prayer came from her mouth in a whisper. She heard her daughter grunting again, remembered her own births, particularly the dead boy. She wished now he had lived. He would have been coming up to manhood. A big strong son, with her blonde good looks and his father's strength.

Kerry's breathing changed and the midwife pushed everyone away. Pulling back the covers, she exposed Kerry's bottom half. Her legs wide open on the bed, she lay back against the pillows and began to push.

Briony stared fascinated as a darkness appeared between Kerry's thighs. A deep blackness. Briony shrieked with delight.

'Its head's here, I can see its head!' She laughed out loud in excitement.

At the window, Molly closed her eyes, her prayers intensifying.

'Dear God, in all your wisdom, take the child from her. Don't let it ruin the rest of her life. Make it go away. Take its breath as it comes into the world.'

Kerry had her sweating face on her chest, a deep animal-sounding moan escaping her lips as she gave another great push.

Her whole body screamed out with the pain inside her. In her mind she begged God to take the child from between her legs before she fainted away with the pain!

Briony and Bernadette both clapped their hands in excitement as the baby pushed its head out from inside its mother.

The midwife looked at its face and stood stock still. It was so dark. Its skin was dark. Then, her natural instincts taking over,

395

she said, 'It's got the cord caught. The cord's around its neck.'

Hooking her little finger underneath the cord, she pulled it over the child's head.

'Now come on, Kerry, give one more push. It's nearly over, love, nearly over . . . Come on, push.'

Kerry answered crossly, 'I am pushing for fuck's sake.'

Then, after one more almighty push, she felt a queer sensation come over her body. The child slipped easily from her and she felt a great peace. Relaxing back on to the pillows, she let out a deep-throated, heavy sigh.

Briony looked at the child on the newspapers underneath Kerry's buttocks. It was covered in blood and vernix. It was not very dark! It was the cord around its neck that had made it look so black. It was nearly white. Foreign-looking, but not black.

'Oh, Kerry, she's beautiful. Gorgeous!'

Kerry pulled her head and shoulders off the bed and laughed delightedly.

'Is it a girl? Let me have a look then!'

The midwife cut the cord and the baby gave a lusty cry. Over at the window, Molly felt the sting of tears. It was alive then, this baby. It lived.

Briony picked up the precious bundle and gave it to Kerry, Bernadette was crying softly, and Briony, Kerry and Bernie all bent over the tiny scrap of humanity and admired it.

Kerry's voice was incredulous. 'Briony, she's nearly white! Look at her, she looks white!'

Molly heard the words and turned from the window.

'Mum, Mum, look at her. She's beautiful. Oh, she is beautiful.'

Kerry's voice had the tired pride of many a woman before her. The midwife carried on cleaning her up, acting deaf as she heard the exclamations around her about the lightness of the child's skin. So that was what all the secrecy was for. The big wad of money she had been promised. Kerry Cavanagh had stepped way out of line if the father was a black man. Well, the child was dark enough to cause comment. Not that anyone would say a word to their faces, of course.

Molly stepped gingerly towards the bed, and as she caught sight of the child, let out a long slow breath. It was dark, but it wasn't black. It could be a Jewish child, or an Italian. She nearly smiled at the grim irony of an Irish Catholic over the moon for a child that looked like a Jew. But that's how desperate she had become.

'She's lovely, Kerry, a very beautiful child indeed.' Molly's voice came out much happier than she had expected. It was the relief. The relief of seeing a nearly white child that had done it. And the little girl was beautiful, she was one of the most beautiful children Molly had ever clapped eyes on, and when Kerry pushed the child towards her she took it instinctively.

But as she looked down on the baby's features, the child yawned, its mouth a pink hole in its dark face, and the revulsion she felt was almost tangible. So deep was her dislike for this innocent child, it took all her might and willpower not to throw it from her physically. Instead, she passed it to Briony who took the small bundle tenderly. Laying it on the bed beside its mother, she unswaddled it from its blanket and kissed the tiny hands and feet, even though they were still bloody.

'Oh, Kerry, I love her to death already. She is beautiful, wonderful. I could kiss her and eat her!'

Bernadette and Kerry laughed.

'You're bloody mad! Oh, Kerry, she is lovely though. Look at those great big eyes, she'll break a few hearts when she grows up.'

The child's deep black eyes reminded everyone of what she was and the room went quiet. Kerry pulled her baby to her naked breasts and said softly, 'Oh, Briony, I never believed I could love something so much. But I do. Oh, God help me, I do.'

Briony smiled down at her sister and put her hand on top of hers where it held the child's head.

'I told you, didn't I? And I'll tell you something else. That feeling never goes away. I know that myself. Isn't that right, Mum?' All the animosity had gone from Briony now as she looked at her mother, and Molly, feeling a great big lump in her throat, said: 'No, Bri. You never lose that feeling for your children. No matter what they do.'

Even as she spoke the words, she knew they were lies. Kerry was nothing to her now, and this grandchild was even less. The knowledge, accepted and admitted, was nevertheless true. And like most truths, the knowledge ripped her apart inside, because it hurt.

It was Christmas Day. No one had slept, but the dinner was still festive and gregarious. Molly was drinking heavily, and no one minded. The whole house was full of good will and camaraderie. Molly sat in the kitchen with Mrs Horlock, who was also full of beer, and the two women discussed the situation in the house in hushed tones.

Mrs Horlock could sympathise with Molly, even though she couldn't totally agree with her. The new child had been adopted by the whole household. Briony and Bernadette could not bear to be away from her for any length of time, and they all talked about her incessantly.

Upstairs in Kerry's room Briony looked at the baby for the thousandth time and said, 'She is the best Christmas present ever. All we need now is Eileen's little baby and we'll have a whole new generation of Cavanaghs under one roof.'

Kerry got upset, knowing that Briony was thinking of her own son who was enjoying his Christmas Day with others.

'Thanks for standing by me, Bri.' Her voice was thick with tears, the enormity of what she had done just now hitting her. Bernadette and Briony cuddled her as she wept.

'I don't know why I'm crying, I've never been so happy in me life!'

Bernadette laughed out loud.

'You're just tired, that's all. Mum always cried after a baby.'

Briony nodded in agreement.

'Mum cried because she wasn't sure how she was going to afford the new arrival. Well, Kerry ain't got no worries on that score.'

'That's the truth. Come on, Kerry, drink your glass of port.

The midwife said it will build your blood up, whatever that means!'

Bernadette held the glass to her lips and Kerry sipped the thick red liquid as she had been told.

She wiped her eyes with her fingers. 'How's you and Marcus, Bern?'

'We're all right. He's getting me a ring after Christmas. At least, we've talked about it anyway.'

Briony made a face, making Kerry laugh through her tears. 'That should please Mother, a respectable married woman in the family. Good luck to you, Bern, he's a nice bloke.'

'Give me the baby, Bri.' Briony picked up the child and placed her in her mother's arms.

'What you going to call her?'

Bernadette cried: 'How about Noel, as it's Christmas?'

Briony tutted loudly.

'Don't be stupid, Bernie, that's like naming her Turkey.'

They all laughed.

'How about Christine then, the feminine of Christopher? Bearer of Christ? It is Christmas after all, the birthday of Christ himself. Christine.' She tried the name again. 'That's a nice name.'

Kerry shook her head.

'No, I know what I'm going to call her.'

Briony and Bernie stared at her.

'Well, bleeding tell us then!'

Kerry smiled down at her daughter and said, 'Liselle. It was Evander's mother's name. It's all I can give her of her father.'

Briony nodded.

'It's a beautiful name for a beautiful girl. Look at that hair! It's already long and curly.' She poked her face down at the child. 'Lissy, Lissy Cavanagh, can you hear us, eh? We're all talking about you. You're the only little girl in England, in the world in fact, with three mums!'

They all laughed again.

'Lissy! Her name's Liselle.' Kerry's voice was indignant.

'Oh, come on, Kel. It's a bit of a gobful, ain't it?'

Bernie agreed. She stroked the little girl's hair and said, 'Lissy is nice, it suits her. It's soft somehow. She'll be Lissy to me, I think.'

Kerry grinned.

'Oh, all right! Lissy it is. I wonder how Eileen will get on when her time comes?'

Briony shrugged.

'She'll be all right. I hope she has a boy, then we'll have one of each! You're still coming tomorrow, aren't you, Bern? Only I was worried about driving down on me own in this weather.'

'Marcus will drive us, he's coming later anyway. By the way, have you opened your presents? I mean other than this big present here!'

They both shook their heads and Bernadette ran from the room to get all their presents from under the tree.

Liselle snuffled into her mother's breast and, looking down at her, Kerry felt a rush of protective love.

'I'm glad Mum came. I didn't think she would. Did she take much persuading?'

Briony shook her head, saying lightly, 'Nah, in fact I got the impression she was glad to be asked, you know?'

Kerry grinned.

'Love her, I bet she was relieved all the hag was over.'

Briony got off the bed and walked to the window. 'Look at that weather. I'm looking forward to seeing Eileen tomorrow, I hope the weather don't stop us.'

Kerry pushed herself painfully up on the pillows. 'I shouldn't think it'll deter you, Briony. I like it to snow at Christmas. It's fitting somehow.'

Briony agreed, glad the conversation had veered away from their mother.

Bernadette came in with her arms full of presents. Kerry gave the baby to her and she and Briony began opening theirs.

Briony picked up a small present wrapped in gold paper. She opened it carefully, a deep abhorrence of wasting anything stopped her tearing the paper apart. Inside was a small velvet box. She opened the lid and gasped.

Lying on plush red velvet was a choker. It was a large diamond-studded B with either side a thick black ribbon with which to tie it around her neck.

Kerry and Bernadette both gasped along with her.

'Bloody hell, Bri, that's some present! Who's it from?'

Briony shook her head. 'I don't know, Kerry.'

Bernadette smiled then, taking a small envelope from her skirt pocket, gave it to Briony.

'Marcus was asked to deliver it, here's the card that went with it.'

Ripping open the envelope, Briony pulled out the card. It had a silhouette of a woman against a gold background. Opening it, she read: 'Happy Christmas, Briony. I saw this and I had to buy it for you. Because you are a B, in the nicest sense of the word. Be happy, Tommy.'

Briony's eyes burned with tears. He hadn't forgotten her, and even if they weren't together, as she wanted, he was saying he still cared about her. If he still cared enough to do this, there was hope for them yet.

Briony fingered the beautiful choker with wonder. What with the birth of Liselle, and the present from Tommy, a present that said though they were no longer a couple he still thought of her, still admired her, this was a better Christmas than she could ever have anticipated.

Chapter Thirty-one

'So what do you think then? It's March now, we could have the opening night for the Manor in ten days. Make it a Friday night and we can cater to the clients for the weekend. Those who want to stay on, of course.'

Mariah watched Briony from under heavy lids. 'If you want the opening then, that's fine with me. It was you who delayed it to build a swimming pool.'

Mariah had been set against the pool, the conservatory to house it had cost a small fortune on its own. That was without getting the pool dug, and the mosaic tiling which Briony insisted had to be the best. She hoped it wasn't going to be a big white elephant.

Briony smiled. 'Listen to me, Mariah, I know one thing, and that is you have to spend money to make money. Men are going to pay a small fortune to use that house, and you get what you pay for. It's a good excuse for the girls to be undressed as well. I think women walking around half-naked in a house like that doesn't really give the right impression. We can dress them in wonderful costumes. They can skinny dip, cavort all night in six foot of water, I don't care. But it adds to the value of the property and it's something different. Most large estates are having pools put in, along with tennis courts. It's a sign of wealth and also a sign of the times. It will pay for itself in six months.'

Mariah lit another cigarette and pulled on it hard. 'You do

realise there's a depression out there?' She pointed at the window.

'Depressions only affect the little people, never the big ones. And we are big people, don't ever forget that.'

Mariah shook her head. 'What about all this talk of more strikes . . .'

Briony interrupted her.

'I ain't interested in all that. Let them strike 'til the cows come home. It don't affect us, or the people we deal with. I have five cabinet ministers champing at the bloody bit to get into the Manor. I've made sure it's talked about in my houses, as I hope you have and all. The rich are like the poor, they'll always be with us, and if I can remove a portion of their wealth, and ding it in me own pocket, I will. I don't know what's got into you lately, Mariah, you're like a bear with a sore arse!'

She laughed.

'I don't know, Bri. There's trouble brewing in this country . . .'

Briony cut her off impatiently.

'Then let it brew. Once it affects my businesses, I'll take an interest. My betting boys have never done so well, so there's money somewhere. But then there's always money for a bet, even when there ain't none to feed their kids. That's my working class, Mariah. A pint of Watney's, jellied eels or pie and mash, and a bet on a Saturday night. The old woman in best bib and tucker down the local with the old man, a few gins, a good row or a good fuck, depending. Those are the people you're talking about. Christ almighty, what do you want from me? I ain't interested in those people. I give to charity, I do me bit for the orphans, and I also make sure no one on my manor goes too hungry. That is it. I ain't old JC himself, and quite frankly, I don't want to be. So drop all your bleeding hearts' speeches and let's get the bloody Manor up and running.'

Mariah nodded in agreement. 'All right, I was only saying! How's Kerry and Lissy, by the way?' Mariah's voice was genuinely interested. Lissy had captured the heart of everyone she came into contact with.

404

'Oh, she's great, my Lissy. You want to see her now. She's growing by the day. Her eyes are like dark pools. Honestly, Mariah, she's exquisite. Clever and all! She pulls her head up to look round. Now would you credit that, not four months old yet?'

'She's strong, I felt her grip last time I saw her. She'll be a beauty and all. That long black hair. I've never seen such hair on a child.'

Briony smiled widely.

'And how's Eileen faring?'

Briony's smile faded.

'She ain't right, Mariah. Due any day, too. That nun's coming tonight, Sister Mary Magdalene. I think she'll be a great help. Eileen really thinks the world of her, she can get through to her. But she's so thin! No matter what you give her to eat, she don't put on a pound. All she has is this great big belly, and her arms and legs are stick thin! She looks weird.'

Mariah nearly said 'She is weird', but stopped herself. She couldn't take to Eileen but could never tell that to Briony.

'What's the doctor said?'

Briony shrugged. 'Not a lot. Just that her nerves are not all they could be. She drinks port wine every day for her blood and eats plenty of liver, once more for her blood, and takes a lot of rest. In fact, she ain't got out of bed this last three weeks. I reckon she should be made to have a walk or something. The room stinks of her. I know that's horrible but it's a bitter smell. It's in her sweat, I think.'

Mariah grimaced.

'I've heard her talking to herself and all. That's how she was before, when it all started. She's definitely out of her tree. I don't know what's going to happen once the child comes. I'll look after it, and she'll have to go back to Sea View, I suppose. I feel like shaking her sometimes, telling her to pull herself together, but of course, I don't.'

Mariah sighed softly.

'It must be hard, Briony.'

405

'It is. Watching someone you love going down hill by the day, and unlike the doctor I don't think it's the pregnancy that's making her ill. I remember her as she was before. It's a symptom, but not the whole reason, if you know what I mean. I don't think the pregnancy's helping, but I think she wants to die. Honestly, that's the conclusion I've come to.'

Mariah got up and put her arm around her little friend's shoulders.

'You can't know that, Bri. No one wants to die.'

Briony smiled grimly.

'I know Eileen. She's weak, God love her, and too much has happened to her. She ain't like us, Mariah. She's different. Highly strung, me mum calls it. "Sensitive" the doctor calls it. I call it plain and simple nuttiness. She's as daft as a yard brush, and that's the truth of it. I only hope this nun coming will snap her out of it for a while.'

Sister Mary Magdalene cast a shadow over the house for the first few hours after her arrival. Everyone, including Briony, was watching their language, watching what they spoke about, and all were acting completely out of character. Kerry was terrified the nun would find out Liselle was illegitimate, Molly was terrified she'd find out Briony owned brothels. And Bernadette had told a rather subdued Marcus that he couldn't stay with her while the nun was under their roof. Cissy took to curtsying at her every time she laid eyes on her, Mrs Horlock avoided her like the plague, and only Eileen acted natural around her. Natural only in the fact that she was the same as she was every day, except she smiled every now and then at the young nun.

Sister Mary Magdalene, for her part, felt the different tensions in the house but was more concerned for Eileen, who looked dreadful. The doctor visited every day, she knew, and was the best money could buy, and yet Eileen looked like a dead person already. Her face was covered by thin stretched skin, and her bones protruded through it. Her stomach was huge, a great lump that made her arms and legs look painfully thin in comparison. Even her hair looked dead, no lustre or sheen on it. Her blue eyes were flat, the colour of slate. They moved in her head slowly, as if the action was painful. The nun started praying within minutes of walking into Eileen's bedroom.

Later, as she sat down to eat with Kerry, Bernadette and Briony, she said: 'This is a lovely piece of beef. I like good food. Though I suppose I shouldn't, being with the Sisters of Mercy!'

Briony smiled at her. She had a wonderfully soft voice, an Irish lilt that held authority and carried without her having to raise it.

'How do you find Eileen, Sister Mary Magdalene?'

The young nun flapped her hand at Briony.

'Sister Mary will be fine, or just plain old Mary. I was lucky, my name was already Mary. We've a nun at Sea View called Sister John the Baptist! Now that's a mouthful, and she insists on it all as well. Behind her back, I call her JB.'

Bernadette and Kerry laughed, scandalised.

Briony smiled.

'You haven't answered my question, Mary?' It felt strange to address a nun thus and Briony wasn't at all sure she liked doing it.

'Shall I tell you the truth? I think she's dying.'

Hearing the words so plain, so true, threw Briony. She dropped her fork with a loud clatter on to the parquet flooring of her dining room.

'Well, you did ask. I've never seen a person so ill-looking in all my life. God love her, she's had more than a body can cope with.'

Bernadette put down her cutlery. Kerry just sat staring at the tiny Irish nun. She was sure the sister was about to get a slap across her wimple from Briony for daring to say such a thing.

Briony stared as well. She held back her natural urge to give this chit a piece of her mind because she knew the girl was merely stating a fact, a fact Briony also knew to be true. Instead she said, 'I've thought that myself. Tell me, Mary, what can we do? What can we do to make her better?'

The little nun finished chewing her piece of beef and said

truthfully, 'All we can do is pray. Pray that the child's safely delivered. We don't want to lose them both, now do we? If she survives the birth, then I think she'll be fine. But there's not an ounce of meat on her, and worst of all she's lost the will to live. You only have to talk to her to realise that. Who's been emptying her chamber?'

Kerry looked startled at the question and said, 'I have, we all have, why?'

'She's sicking up her food, I've seen it before. Is the chamber covered with a cloth or paper?'

'Of course it is, we ain't going to walk round with a big Richard, are we!' Bernadette's voice was high and Kerry kicked her under the table.

'I thought as much. She's been emptying her stomach after every meal. That's why she's no weight on her. I only hope the child's been nourished properly.'

Briony licked dry lips. All along she had guessed at something like this.

'I make sure she drinks her milk and her port wine. I give her that myself. The doctor also prescribed a tonic, she takes that regularly. She has warm milk with honey in it before she sleeps, and one of us sleeps in the room with her so she must be keeping that down.'

The little nun nodded.

Bernadette started to cry.

'Don't you be crying now. We'll all work together to get her over the birth. I'll stay up at nights with her, as well as during the day, and we'll see she can't get rid of any more food. She'll have to keep it down if we're watching her, won't she? Then, once she's safely delivered, we'll see about getting her properly well. So she can look after her child.'

Briony nodded. 'Maybe the baby will give her the will to live again?'

The nun nodded and cut herself another slice of beef. 'I'm starving! Look at me, eating like a battalion!' She carried on eating her meal, but didn't answer Briony's last question because she didn't want to say out loud what she really thought.

It was the child that was killing Eileen Cavanagh.

Jonathan la Billière and Rupert Charles were enjoying themselves immensely. Kerry was up on stage belting out a fast
number, the club was buzzing. Everywhere people were
chatting, dancing or drinking. The air was thick with cigarette
smoke, and the atmosphere was genial. Jonathan and a young
lady called Helen were holding hands. On the left of Jonathan
was Rupert and his amour Peter Hockley, also holding hands.
More than a few people who saw them gave a second glance in
their direction. Peter was wearing make-up: his eyes were lined
with kohl and his lips stained ruby red. He had on a man's suit
and open-toed sandals with his toenails painted the same colour
as his lips. The effect was startling.

Jonathan was drunk, and quite oblivious of the stares they
were gathering. His film *The Changeling* had been a success.
He was now famous and many people gave him a second look.
Now that Hollywood was calling, this was his farewell party,
given by Rupert for his old friend. Everything had been
provided by him, including the young and attractive Helen.
Now Jonathan was out of his head, on a mixture of cocaine,
brandy and champagne that made him ignore the stares and
jibes around them.

Peter jumped from his seat, a cigarette in a gold holder
dangling from limp fingers.

'Oh, come on, let's dance!' He was an exhibitionist who loved
to shock, loved being stared at – half the reason for his garb –
and also loved to irritate. He was like the child to whom a smack
is as good as a kiss. He walked unsteadily to the dance floor
where, lurching sideways, he careered into a table full of people.
There was a loud crash. A woman shrieked as an ice bucket hit
her lap and a large man stood up. Angrily picking up Peter by
the scruff of his neck, he threw him towards Rupert, shouting,
'Take this disgusting excuse for a man home! You should be
ashamed of yourself, walking in here with this creature! I've a
good mind to call the police.'

Two bouncers appeared as if by magic and the table was

righted, the champagne replaced and the man soothed by promises of a free night at the club.

Peter laughed out loud, but his expression changed when Briony appeared. Her face was stark white, two large red spots of anger standing out on her cheekbones.

'This is it, you're finished here, Rupert. I want you out now! You can either walk out under your own steam or I'll have you all thrown out!'

Jonathan shook his head and looked at her blearily. He seemed unaware of the recent scene.

'Hello, Briony. How are you?'

She sighed heavily. Looking at her men, she said: 'Get rid of them, now.'

Rupert stood up and said loudly, 'Madam, no one speaks to me like that!'

Briony looked him up and down and said scathingly, 'Why don't you just piss off before I really lose my rag?' Her voice was low and menacing.

All around people were watching the spectacle. On stage Kerry had started another number, her voice straining to rise over the hubbub. People were muttering among themselves and Briony, seeing the ruin of a good evening, was getting more annoyed by the second.

As Rupert and Peter were ejected from the club she said to Jonathan, 'I can't believe you could still associate with those two! You're the one who told me they were on a downward slide. Now go home and sober up, man. You sicken me like this.'

Jonathan bowed low, his drink-fuddled brain unable to comprehend what had taken place around him.

When they had left, Briony apologised personally to her customers, and told the doorman that under no circumstances were Rupert and Peter ever to be allowed entry into the club again.

Briony arrived home at just after four in the morning. She was tired out. In her Hyde Park house there had been trouble. A valued customer had contracted syphilis and Briony had had to

410

tell the girl responsible. She had gone mad, saying the customer had given it to her. After what seemed an age, Briony had finally sorted out the situation. The girl's working life was suspended until a treatment of arsphenamines was working. The man in question, not a very amiable person at the best of times, was a well-known industrialist who had lost two wives through his philandering and was now eager to get into parliament. A scandal was not in his best interests but nevertheless the man raged and blasphemed until Briony felt an urge to slap his face for him. Instead she had smiled, and smoothed everything over. When she finally got home she was fed up, tired out and in need of a good night's sleep. Peter was bad enough, but the trouble at the house had made a bad evening even worse.

She poured herself a large brandy and tiptoed up the stairs to her bedroom. As she undressed, she heard a tap on the door.

'Come in.'

It was Sister Mary Magdalene.

'I'm sorry to disturb you, but I think you'd better come and look at Eileen.'

Briony sighed heavily. Pulling off her dress, she grabbed a wrapper and followed the nun from the room. In Eileen's bedroom she froze. Her sister was lying in bed wide awake. Her eyes were bright and she was smiling.

'Hello, Bri. Come and talk to me for a minute. You look all in.'

Briony smiled in wonder.

'Eileen? How come you're all bright eyed and bushy-tailed at this hour?'

Eileen shrugged.

'I feel fine. I was just thinking about when we were kids. Sit down for a while. I feel the urge to talk to you. You've been very good to me, Briony, you know that, don't you?'

She sat on the bed, her tiredness forgotten, and took her sister's hot hand in hers. Close to, in the lamplight, she could see the feverish glow to her sister's face.

'I'll go down and make us all some tea, shall I?' The nun's voice was low.

411

'Please, Mary. If you don't mind.'

'I could drink a gallon of tea. I've got a thirst on me, Bri. A real thirst.' Eileen's voice was stronger than Briony could remember for a long time.

When the nun left the room, Eileen said: 'Remember when Kerry used to put on her shows down the basements? All her rude songs! Then when the priest come she'd change to a hymn and we'd all join in?'

Briony smiled, remembering.

'Yeah. I remember. We had some good laughs.'

'I liked living in the basements. I wish we'd stayed there, Bri. We were much safer in a lot of ways. Remember how cold it used to get in winter, though? The walls would freeze up inside.'

Briony frowned. 'How could I forget?'

Eileen nodded seriously.

'Mrs Jacobs' baby froze to death one Christmas, remember that? And they had to put it outside in the snow 'til the ground was soft enough to bury it.'

Briony squeezed her sister's hand tightly.

'Don't think about things like that, Ei, just think of the nice things. The summer days when we'd all swim in the Beam river, or walk out to Rainham and go pea picking.'

'I liked the basements. It was when we left them, or when I left them, that all my troubles started . . . I don't think I was ever meant to be happy, Bri. But I was as a little kid. Dad used to make us laugh, didn't he, sometimes?'

Briony swallowed hard.

'Yeah, I suppose he did.'

'I never meant to kill him, you know. It was an accident. Here, I'll make you laugh. Do you remember Sally Connolly and her talking dog?'

Briony laughed, remembering.

'Yeah, she could make that dog do anything. It was a big bastard and all, weren't it? I can still see the day it bit her dad for smacking her one.'

Eileen grinned.

'That's right. She'd given it half her dad's dinner and he went

412

garrity, and when he smacked her, the dog went for him. It had to sleep outside after that, and anyone who walked past their house got growled at.'

'It wouldn't let her dad in unless they got Sally up to calm the dog down!'

They both laughed together, remembering happier times. Eileen grimaced and Briony was immediately concerned.

'You all right, Ei?'

She nodded. 'Yeah, the baby's moving that's all.'

'You looking forward to having it?'

Eileen wiped a hand over her face and ignored the question. 'I was thinking the other day about when Bernadette was ill that time. Do you remember? You was only small yourself. She had the whoop. I sat up all night with her because Mum was flat out herself. I sat with her little head over a bowl of hot water. I really thought she was going to die. But the next day she was all right. The doctor gave me a sweet. Said I was a good girl.'

'I was the one going out in the freezing cold to fill the kettle, how could I forget that? I was only a kid meself.'

'You was five and Bernie wasn't even two. Dad wouldn't go out any more. He said he had to sleep to get up for work. Mum was just plain knackered. I hated him for that because you know something, he wasn't working, Bri. He lied, said he had a day's work but he never. You walked in and out all night filling that bloody thing.'

Eileen's voice was sad now and Briony kissed her cheek. 'Don't get maudlin.'

'I was eight years old. That was the year of Mr Lafferty's party. That was a great day, weren't it? Two barrels of beer, and all the faggots and peas you could eat! He won a big bet, a really big bet, and blew nearly the lot on that party. The next day he lost the last of it on another bet!'

Briony grinned.

'That was Mr Lafferty all right. His daughter married a Salvation Army geezer, and he disowned her.'

'I always liked her. Mrs Lafferty was down the pop the day after the party to get enough money to feed her brood. Mum was

413

scandalised that she hadn't had the sense to raid Mr Lafferty's pockets while he was drunk and salvage a few bob!'

Sister Mary Magdalene came in with the tray of tea and Briony poured them all a cup.

Eileen drank her tea scalding hot, gulping it as if she was dying of thirst.

Putting down her empty cup she grinned, and the sight made Briony want to weep. Her face was like a living skull.

'I needed that. It's funny, you know, but I feel a lot better. Much better, in fact.'

The nun patted her hand.

'You're looking and sounding better, if I might say so.'

'Mary? While you're here can I ask you to do something for me?'

The nun nodded. 'Of course, anything.'

'When my baby's born, if anything happens to me, will you be a witness that I want Briony to have it? You would have it, wouldn't you, Bri? Don't let Mum have it. I don't want me mum bringing it up. I want you to. You and Kerry and Bernie. Promise me?'

Briony nodded.

'Of course I promise, but nothing's going to happen to you. You'll get better. You're better already. Look at you, nattering on. You're halfway there already. So don't think about anything like that. Now do you want another cup of tea?'

'Please. Mary, I was just talking to Briony about when we were kids. I helped deliver Briony, you know. I was only three, but I was the one who held her head while me mum pushed her out. The midwife was late, and me and me mum delivered her between us. After it was over me mum sat me by the fire with Briony in me arms while she burnt the rags and the newspapers. I was just coming up four, but I can remember it clearly.'

Mary smiled.

'Well, you would, something like that.'

'I loved Briony more than the others, she was like my baby after that. The others came thick and fast, a few dead ones and a few misses, as me mum called them. But Briony was special to me. I'd helped her into the world, as if I'd given birth to her meself.'

Briony felt an absurd lump in her throat hearing her sister talk. A great rush of love for Eileen washed over her.

Eileen grimaced again, and her tea spilt into the saucer. She made a grunting sound and Mary and Briony both looked at one another in alarm. Taking the cup from Eileen, Briony pulled back the covers of the bed. Lying between Eileen's legs, unmoving, was a tiny baby. She dropped the cup to the carpet with shock.

'Jesus save us! Mary, get the doctor! For goodness' sakes, get a doctor!'

Eileen lay back in the bed, a triumphant smile on her face. Briony stared down at the child. It looked like a skinned rabbit. Then it moved, its small hand making a fist, and mewled like a newborn kitten.

'It's alive! Oh, thank God, it's alive.'

Sister Mary pushed Briony out of the way and took over. It was Briony who telephoned the doctor, Kerry and Bernie were outside on the landing and Mrs Horlock and Cissy were inside helping.

Briony pushed through the door, her heart beating like mad, her face flushed.

Cissy held the little boy in her arms by the fire, and Mrs Horlock pushed down on Eileen's stomach.

'What's going on?'

Mrs H flapped a hand in front of her face and resumed her pushing.

'There's another little bugger in here or I'm a Chinaman. Come on, Eileen love, push!'

Eileen lay in bed, her face screwed up in concentration. Briony watched entranced as another head appeared. The child slipped from its mother without a sound then set up a lusty wailing as it hit the cold of the air.

'Twins! Oh, Eileen, you've got twins!'

Kerry and Bernadette burst into the room at this and both began doing a little dance.

Eileen lay back, her face wet with sweat. 'What are they?'

Mrs Horlock smiled at Eileen and said, 'They're boys. Two boys as identical as your own two hands!'

Sister Mary looked the children over and grinned. 'They're small, but they're healthy. Who would have credited that, eh? Two of the little buggers!'

Kerry, Bernie and Briony, along with the other occupants of the room, all stood open-mouthed with shock as they heard the little nun swear.

She laughed with delight, her relief at the birth being over making her excited.

'I think the Good Lord will forgive a bit of overexuberance at a time like this, eh?'

Eileen was cleaned up and both her sons placed in her arms at her request. She looked down into their tiny faces and smiled.

'My sons, my boys.' Her voice was thick with emotion.

Cissy and Mrs Horlock disappeared to make them all some breakfast. Bernadette and Kerry got dressed. Bernadette was going to fetch their mother and Kerry had to feed Liselle who had set up a wailing of her own. Briony hugged the tiny nun and hugged Eileen.

'They're beautiful boys, Eileen. And what a night! Why didn't you let on you were in labour?'

Eileen smiled and said softly, 'I wasn't sure, to be honest. Take these two for me, Bri, would you?'

She took one baby and Sister Mary the other. As they unswaddled the babies and began to wash them, Eileen gave a long sigh.

Briony smiled at the nun. 'She must be tired out, bless her.'

The nun placed a baby back against her chest and said sadly as she walked to the bed, 'I think she's been tired for a long time, Briony. She's gone.'

Briony walked to the bed, one tiny baby snuggled into her breast, and as she looked at Eileen's serene face, gave a loud cry.

The doctor arrived five minutes later, but he was too late. As Briony remarked to Sister Mary, he was fifteen years too late.

Chapter Thirty-two

Briony stared down at the two children lying side by side in their cots. Each slept on his stomach, tiny hands clenched into fists as if they were born to fight. If one moved, the other moved. Just three days old and so alike it was impossible to tell them apart. As Briony looked at them, she was filled with love. Eileen had known what she was doing when she gave these boys to her. They filled a deep gaping void in her, that had been growing bigger and bigger in the years since she had handed over her own child. Now these two motherless boys assuaged that grief.

Briony had found two wet nurses, Lily Nailor, whose own baby had died a week before, and Carol Jarret, whose child was off the breast and being cared for by her mother. Needless to say, only Lily lived in. The two boys had already become the focal point of the house, along with Liselle. It seemed that after years of being peopled only by adults, the house was now full of babies. Everywhere Briony looked was evidence of them.

Molly was prostrate with grief. Even Briony had warmed to her at this evidence of her love for Eileen. She was taking the death of her child badly, and when Sister Mary had told her of Eileen's dying wish that the twins should go to Briony, had acquiesced without a murmur. Briony felt already as if the boys were her own.

She stroked the two downy heads. They were so alike it was startling. Both had the same burnished copper hair that was already darkening, eventually to become a deep chestnut-brown, and both had deep-set blue eyes. They had nothing of their gentle mother in them, though Briony could see nothing of O'Malley in them either. She was glad. These were Cavanaghs, and would be called Cavanagh. She would see to that.

Jonathan la Billière awoke, a pain shot through his skull and he groaned. He looked at his watch, and groaned again. Sitting up in a strange bed, he was relieved to find himself alone. He had been partying with Rupert and Peter for three days solid and now he had woken thirsty, hung over, and stinking. Catching a glimpse of his reflection in a mirror opposite, he pushed his hands through his dark hair in consternation. He had deep shadows under his eyes and needed a shave badly. He lay back in the bed as he felt giddiness coming over him again. He was finished with drink, he promised himself that. He was due in Hollywood in less than a fortnight and had a lot to do before then.

He smiled at his own good fortune. *The Changeling* had shown everyone what he had always known: he was a damned good actor. The story was a melodrama about a man who comes back years later to claim his inheritance, after an evil housekeeper switches her child for the rightful heir. It was a stupid storyline, but he had made it work. He *was* the Changeling and he had given the part all he had. The film was a success, and now offers were pouring in thick and fast. He was pleased with himself, pleased at how his life was going. The boy from the South London backstreets, still alive in him, though carefully submerged these days, kicked himself each day to make sure it was all true.

He walked out on to the landing and realised he was in Peter's house. He opened a door nearby, looking for a bathroom of some description. No luck. It was as he approached another door that he heard the noise. He stood still and listened carefully.

It sounded like someone crying.

Walking towards the sound, he opened Peter's bedroom door. It was an act he was to regret all his life.

Peter was sitting on the floor naked; the whole room seemed to be covered in blood. It was even on the ceiling, great red splashes vivid against the white paint. The bed was one deep crimson stain, and on it lay a young man Jonathan could not remember seeing before. Beside him, sitting with his head in his hands, was Rupert.

Peter looked at Jonathan over his shoulder and said brokenly, 'It was only a game, a silly game . . . I never meant it.'

He started crying harder, his face a mass of make-up and tear stains.

Jonathan put his hand to his mouth to stop the tide of sickness rising up in him. The fresh smell of blood was cloying, sickly sweet on the air. Staggering from the room, he ran down the stairs. He picked up the phone and dialled Briony's number. She was the only person he could think of who would be able to sort out a mess like this.

Briony was at the house in twenty minutes. She walked through the door with her usual air of capability and common sense. The first thing she did was to give Jonathan a large scotch, then she went up and looked at the damage for herself.

Staring at Peter and Rupert, she shook her head in disgust. She didn't bother checking if the boy on the bed was still alive. It was obviously far too late. He was no more than sixteen, she saw. His hands were tied behind him, and his legs were manacled to the bed. His throat had been cut from ear to ear. When she forced herself to look closely, she found that his head had been practically severed from his body. Nowhere in Briony's wildest imaginings could she envisage a sex game resulting in this. And she knew more about the sexual wants of people than most. But this was out of her territory.

Peter was crying again. His face had two long glistening trails of mascara down it. Briony stifled an urge to let him feel some pain and scratch his eyes out.

Leaving the room, she went down to Jonathan. 'Any servants here?'

419

He shrugged. 'I have no idea.'

'I should imagine Peter has someone come in. With his lifestyle, he wouldn't want anyone living here, would he? It stands to reason.'

'What are we going to do, Briony? I didn't know who to call. If this gets out, my career will be over before it's even fucking started.' Jonathan clenched his teeth. 'Why, oh why, did I ever take up with Rupert again? I must have been mad. The two of them were getting out of hand, and this is the result. You don't know the half of it . . .'

He was nearly hysterical and Briony said, 'Oh, shut up, Jonathan, let me think.'

She paced the room for a while.

'I'm going to ring Mariah. She'll help you get away. The main thing is to remove you from here. OK?'

Jonathan nodded. 'You're so good to me, Briony! I knew you'd know what to do.'

'Go upstairs and get dressed. I have a couple of calls to make. Come on, get your arse in gear!'

She rang Mariah then picked up Peter's telephone book and dialled Lord Hockley's number. She spoke to him personally and afterwards sat smoking 'til Mariah arrived. Her driver took Jonathan home and the two women waited in silence for Lord Hockley. Both knew that this was something they could use to their advantage, though neither voiced the thought out loud. Briony, herself, was numb, Eileen's recent death still an open wound. When Lord Hockley arrived she had the grace to feel deeply sorry for the man.

She walked wordlessly up to the bedroom and opened the door. Lord Hockley, who had fought in the Boer War and had witnessed first hand the tragedy in the trenches of the Great War, took one look at the naked boy on the bed and, putting his hand to his heart, made a deep moaning sound that seemed to be pulled from his strong barrel chest.

Then, entering the room, he took the knife from beside his son and threw it at the wall. Its bone handle made a loud cracking sound as it broke under the blow. Then he began to belabour Peter, pulling him up by his short-cropped hair and slapping him across the face, the shoulders, anywhere on the boy's body he could make contact. He finished by kicking him in the chest.

'You animal! You filthy little animal! Is this what I brought you up for? This – carnage!'

Rupert watched the scene through glazed eyes.

Lord Hockley turned to Briony and said: 'And where do you fit into all this, eh? Only I've washed my hands of the blighter if you're thinking of getting money out of me. I want no more to do with him. This is the end! The finish!'

Briony said in a low voice, 'I want nothing. I was called here by a mutual friend. I thought that as this Peter was your son, you'd better sort it all out. I want nothing from you, nothing. Except for you to finish what your son started.'

She saw Hockley deflate in front of her eyes. His whole body seemed to sag.

'Come on, let's go downstairs, get out of this. It's up to you now. But if I was you I'd try and help your son, because that boy is dead and nothing is going to bring him back. He's more than likely a pick up, so I shouldn't imagine anyone's looking for him just yet.'

Briony's sensible words penetrated the man's distress. But an innate sense of justice fought with his natural instinct to protect not just his child, but his family's good name. He followed Briony down the stairs.

Mariah poured them all a drink and Hockley swallowed his straight down and held out his glass for more.

'I gave that boy everything, but even as a child . . . His mother encouraged it, you know. She's the real culprit. Should have let me send him overseas, put him in the army like his forebears, but no. Her darling boy had to be encouraged, he was artistic. Artistic, my eye! He's plain unnatural, an offence to the eyes of God. My only son, can you believe that? My only son. And look where he is now . . .'

Briony heard the sorrow in his voice and felt an urge to flee.

To get away from this house and its occupants. She had enough to think about as it was. Her Eileen was dead, and Peter Hockley was alive. It was so unfair.

'Shall I call the police then?' She hoped he would say yes. She wanted Peter Hockley to pay the proper penalty for the ending of that young life. But she knew that even if she telephoned the Chief Inspector, it would be hushed up, because Hockley was a newspaper baron and he had clout. A great deal of clout. He shook his head slowly.

'No. I will make sure everything's taken care of. By the way, who was the mutual friend you spoke of?'

Briony shook her head.

'That's for me to know, and you to find out. If you'll excuse us, Lord Hockley? It's been a long night and I have a feeling it's going to be a very long day.'

Mariah finished her drink. As they went to leave, Lord Hockley's voice stayed them.

'Why didn't you phone the police?'

Briony looked back and answered truthfully. 'Would it have made a difference? Let's face it, there's no way this is ever going to come to light is there? You might be angry with your son now but you won't want him banged up, no more than I would my child. No matter what they'd done. But I trust you remember in years to come that we kept quiet about this, Lord Hockley. That we didn't go to the other newspapers, the ones you don't control.

'Now, if you'll excuse us, we've done our bit. The rest, I'm afraid, is up to you.'

Briony was still thinking of the scene she had witnessed earlier in the day as the priest spoke his last words over Eileen. Kerry and Bernadette held Molly between them, and Briony stood away from the small group alone. Eileen's death heralded an end of an era. Never again would the five sisters be together. She heard Rosalee crying and felt the sting of tears herself. Marcus was holding Rosalee to his chest. No one was ever sure exactly how much she understood. If they cried, she cried; if they laughed, she laughed. Today she was breaking her heart. Maybe somewhere in her mind she realised what was going on. Or maybe she just felt the deep unhappiness around her.

Sister Mary Magdalene was also crying; her young face, so soft and virginal-looking, seemed out of place here.

So many people had turned out for the funeral, Briony had found it hard to believe at first. It seemed that every woman in the East End of London had gathered at The Chase graveyard to mourn her. The Chase was on the old Romford Road, surrounded by countryside. Eileen would be pleased to be laid to rest here, Briony was sure of that.

The cortège had grown longer and longer as people joined it all along the route until now there was a large silent crowd. Briony knew it was their way of lending support. Their way of looking after one of their own.

She swallowed down the hot burning tears with difficulty. She felt a soft touch and looked round to see Tommy standing beside her. Biting her lip, she held on to him, feeling the strength of him through her coat, feeling a peacefulness settle over her.

Father McNamara blessed the coffin, Briony threw in the first lump of dirt and a single white rose. All the sisters followed suit, even Rosalee. Molly had to be taken from the graveside, her wailing becoming hysterical.

As Briony stood by her sister's open grave people filed past her, murmuring condolences. Everyone knew she had taken on Eileen's boys. It was common knowledge, and proved once more that Briony Cavanagh was one of them, for all her money and her businesses. Local hard men paid their respects to her personally, looking out of place in their suits and clean shirts.

Tommy finally walked her from the graveside and over to his car. He drove her back to her house himself. In the car Briony shed the tears she had been holding back. Tommy let her cry, knowing it could only be for the good. Briony bottled up too much. She needed to let off steam. Then outside her house he took her in his arms and comforted her.

Briony, smelling the familiar smell of him, allowed herself to be held. Never had she felt so alone in all her life, and never had she been more grateful for Tommy's company.

Molly was drunk, stinking drunk. She was so drunk she could barely move in her chair. Briony got Marcus and Tommy to carry her mother up to bed. She stripped Molly with difficulty and slipped the quilt over her. As she looked down on her mother's swollen face she felt a tremor of love for her. Abel had taken his mother home earlier. Mother Jones would always come first with him, and Molly knew that and was hurt by it. Even at her daughter's funeral, his mother had taken first place. Briony felt her mother's pain as surely as if it was her own.

As she walked from the bedroom she saw Tommy standing on the landing, leaning against the wall.

'Thanks for coming, Tommy, I appreciate it.'

He smiled, his familiar little grin, and Briony felt her heart lurch.

'Would you like to see the boys?'

Tommy nodded and followed Briony into their room. He looked down at the two babies and laughed aloud. 'Oh, Briony, ain't they small?'

She nodded, placing a finger in each child's right hand.

'But they're strong. They've got a good grip. Poor Eileen. Two beautiful children and she'll never see them grow up . . .'

Her voice broke and Tommy put an arm around her shoulders. 'Who'll bring them up now? Your mum?'

Briony shook her head furiously.

'No way. I'm going to bring them up. They're my boys now. Mine. Daniel and Dennis Cavanagh. Aren't you, my lovelies?'

She bent closer to them and Tommy sighed softly. 'They're O'Malleys, Briony. Eileen was legally married, remember?'

Briony shook her head.

'No, you're wrong. These two are Cavanaghs. Eileen gave them to me. I'll be their mother, I'll bring them up, and they'll be brought up as Cavanaghs. That's an end to it. I have great plans for these two young men, Tommy. Great plans.'

'I'm sure you have, Briony.'

424

She was unaware of the undercurrent in Tommy's voice.

'They'll have everything. Liselle will be like a sister to them. She's a beauty, too. They're the next generation of Cavanaghs and all living under one roof. I'll make sure they have the world on a plate. The best education, the best of everything. I promised Eileen I'd look after them and I will.'

The bigger of the babies turned himself over and Briony picked him up tenderly.

'Look at your Uncle Tommy, Boysie.' She looked at Tommy and said: 'We call him Boysie because he's the bigger one. I don't know why but he looks like a Boysie, don't he?'

Tommy smiled and nodded agreement.

Briony kissed the child softly on his tiny rosebud lips. 'Who's their mummy's little babies then, eh? Who's my beautiful boys?'

She placed the child back in his crib tenderly and then picked up the other. Daniel snuggled into her arms naturally, used to the feel and the smell of her.

'Oh, Danny Boy.' She looked at Tommy again. 'This one is the quieter of the two. As alike as they look, they're different in many ways. Boysie is much louder. Danny Boy, well, he'll be a thinker, I reckon. He's the quiet one.'

Tommy watched her look at the child intently, practically drinking him in with her eyes.

'They're lucky to have you to look out for them.'

Briony shook her head and said truthfully, 'Oh, I'm the lucky one, Tommy. It's me who's the lucky one. I can give these boys so much. And in return it'll be like having my own boy back. Like having two Benedicts to care for. I owe it to Eileen and to myself to make sure these two little spats have the best that money can buy. And I'll see that they do.'

He touched the child's downy head and said, 'Money can't buy happiness, Briony. You more than anyone should know the truth of that.'

She pulled the child from him and said tartly, 'Well, at least I can be miserable in comfort, can't I? Which is infinitely preferable to being miserable as well as cold and hungry. Why must you always put the mockers on everything, Tommy? Why can't you just once say something I want to hear? These two little boys deserve to be happy and I want to make sure they are. And the kind of happiness I want for them takes a great deal of money.'

Tommy sighed and said in a low voice, 'Don't try and *make* them happy, Briony, let them *be* happy. I often think you don't know what real happiness is. All the years I've known you I can honestly say, hand on heart, I don't know of one time when you was ever really happy.'

Briony put the child back in the crib. Facing Tommy, she looked into his eyes. The sight of her long neck and Titian hair enflamed him, she was so beautiful, so alluring. Her eyes were like emeralds glittering in her head. Her mouth was trembling as she said, 'That, Tommy, is because I have never really been happy. Not since the day I gave up my boy. But now I have a second chance, and Eileen's boys are that chance. She wanted me to do my best for them, and I swear on her grave that I will do just that. I'll look out for them, and love them, all the days of my life.'

'That's very noble, but what about you, Bri? What about you having happiness? Don't you want to be happy, inside yourself? Don't you want to feel the same happiness you're so determined to give to these two children?'

Briony shook her head in confusion.

'But don't you see, Tommy? I *will* find that happiness now. I'll find it through them. With them. Because of them. Even today, when I've buried my Eileen, I feel a certain happiness, because I have these boys. Can't you understand that?'

Tommy shook his head.

'No. Frankly, Briony, I can't.'

She watched him walk from the room. Then, sighing heavily, she turned back to the boys.

Tommy let himself out of Briony's house. Getting into his car, he drove away from her. Inside he was in turmoil, because that last conversation had proved, as if he had not already known, that with the advent of those children he had finally lost her for good. She had not had much to give him before. Now she would have even less.

He acknowledged, bitterly, that he was jealous of Eileen's boys, two little motherless boys. He was. Because today he had decided to take Briony back, and had found that she had even less need of him than before. It was ironic that after leaving her, after convincing himself he was better off without her, he had found out too late just how wrong he had been.

He felt a burning need to cry because he had just left behind the only woman he would ever care about, the only one he would ever want or need.

It was this knowledge that hurt him more than anything. Because he, himself, had broken the bond between them, and enjoyed himself while doing it. He had broken Briony's heart and all along had been setting himself up for more misery than he had dreamt possible.

Briony had her sisters and those children. Now he was the one left with nothing. Because he wanted nothing else, and so nothing else would do.

She probably didn't even realise he was gone.

St Vincent's church was once more packed out. The new priest, Father Tierney, looked over the sea of faces and smiled. It did his heart good to see so many people here, men as well as women. It was the christening of the Cavanagh boys, as they were being called already. The highlight of the christening was seeing the film star Jonathan la Billière stand as their godfather, with Kerry as godmother to Daniel and Bernadette to Dennis. As he poured the holy water over the boys' heads they both set up a wail that could be heard outside the church. Briony and Bernadette quietened the boys as Kerry sang. The church was hushed as her voice came out low and sweet:

Swing low, sweet chariot, coming for to carry me home . . .

Everyone stood in silence as she sang. More than a few people

427

would remark on the strangeness of the song and the way she sang it. And more than a few would also remark later behind closed doors on the dark-haired little girl who had sat up bright-eyed and alert as she viewed the proceedings from Cissy Jackson's lap! She was darker than was natural, everyone tacitly agreed, but no one said it anywhere near the Cavanaghs.

Briony smiled at Jonathan and he grinned back. He was more than grateful to her for sorting out the business with Peter and Rupert. He had made a special journey back from America for this christening and the stir it had caused had been worth every mile of the journey. On that dreadful morning he had believed his whole career was over. When Briony, despite all her own troubles, had told him that it was sorted out, he had felt a deep, abiding thankfulness. He would do anything for her now. Anything.

Back at Briony's house there was plenty to eat and drink. All the remaining sisters, together with Molly, Jonathan and Mariah, were sitting in Briony's lounge chatting between themselves. Marcus came in with two bottles of expensive champagne.

'This was Jonathan's gift and I thought we'd open it now.'

Everyone took a glass and toasted the infants.

'To Danny Boy and my Boysie!' Briony's voice was filled with love.

'To the boys!'

Kerry sipped her drink and placed a crawling Liselle on the floor. Lissy, as she was now called by everyone, tried to pull herself up using Molly's skirt as an anchor.

Kerry smiled at her mother who strained to smile back. Liselle stood up uncertainly then dropped down on to her bottom with a thud. She set up a wail and Briony scooped her up off the floor and hugged her close.

'What's wrong then, Liselle Cavanagh? You'll be walking soon enough. Kerry, this child is so intelligent I don't know what to do with her! Look . . . It's as if she knows exactly what I'm saying.' She kissed Liselle's mouth and said, 'Have you been here before, madam?'

428

Liselle grabbed Briony's hair and pulled on it hard, laughing as Briony made a mock stern face.

Molly got up and walked away from the scene. No matter how often she saw the child, she still felt a deep dislike for her. The whole idea of the child's father and the fact that he had lain with her daughter disgusted her.

She smiled, though, as she looked at the twins. Now there were two boys to be proud of! Her grandsons, the light of her life. In them was held out the hope of greatness. She knew that Briony would see they got everything befitting two such handsome lads. Who knew what they might become?

Kerry watched the change in her mother as she bent over Eileen's boys and forced down the hurt she felt inside. Since the birth of the twins, Lissy had been left out in the cold. Oh, Briony still made a fuss of her, as did Bernadette. But the boys were the real focal point. They were twins for a start, so that made them special, and they were white. Wholly white. She tried to keep these thoughts from invading her mind, but still they plagued her at all hours of the day and night.

She drained her glass in one swallow and went to get herself another. She had seen the looks today, outside the church. The peering looks at Lissy as Kerry had stood, head high, with her daughter in her arms. People guessed, she knew that, but Lissy was her true love. She worshipped her daughter even while she resented the feelings the child produced in her at times. She poured herself another drink.

More Dutch courage. She found she needed it more and more as Lissy was growing up.

Briony saw Kerry toss back another drink and made a mental note to have a word with her. She was drinking a lot lately. Her eyes strayed to Marcus and Bernie. Now there was a match made in heaven if ever she saw one. They'd be married before long. She smiled as she thought of it.

Molly was still cooing over the twins and Briony smiled again. It was six months since Eileen had been laid to rest and the boys were now two fat healthy babies. The hurt of bereavement had lessened with them in the house. Briony had opened the Manor, which was going great guns, and now she smiled at Mariah as she thought how lucky she was. She had her health and she had money, plenty of it, and was making more by the day. She also had two little boys to care for, and if at times like this she thought of another little boy, it was now a bitter-sweet remembering. Danny Boy and Boysie had done a lot to assuage her guilt and hurt. But one day she would have Ben too, she was determined on that. One day he would know who she was.

Cissy came into the room, flushed and excited. 'The *Barking and Dagenham Post*'s outside. They want a picture for the paper!'

Briony laughed as they all put on their hats and coats and trooped outside to her front garden.

The photographer lined them all up, with Briony in the centre, the two boys asleep in her arms. Her face was almost obscured by a large-brimmed hat. Beside her stood her mother on one side, and Jonathan, the real reason for the photograph, on the other. The rest of the family, including Mrs Horlock and Cissy, gathered around them. Kerry, also a celebrity, stood smiling while trying to hold a struggling Lissy in her arms as the flash went off with a loud crash followed by a blinding light.

The picture was the talk of Barking for a long time, and Briony kept a framed copy on her mantelpiece for the rest of her life. Every time she looked at it she would smile sadly. The only person missing was Eileen.

Briony laughed and joked through the rest of the day. Late in the evening, though, as she sat with Jonathan, she heard the twins cry. Leaping from her seat, she bolted from the room, leaving Jonathan staring after her and Bernadette and Marcus laughing.

The pattern was already set. The twins called, and Briony came running.

BOOK THREE
1947

'Out of the crooked timber of humanity no straight thing
can ever be made'
— Immanuel Kant, 1724–1804

'He that maketh haste to be rich shall not be innocent'
— *Proverbs*, 29, xviii

'Believe me! The secret of reaping the greatest fruitfulness
and the greatest enjoyment from life is to live dangerously!'
— Friedrich Nietzsche, 1844–1900

Chapter Thirty-three

'I swear to you, Boysie, I ain't done nothing! Danny, Danny Boy, tell him for Christ's sake!'

Dickie Lawson watched as two identical faces peered at him through the gloom.

'You're a liar, Lawson. You tucked us up and we ain't having it.'

Boysie grabbed him around the throat with one large fist. Tiny Dickie Lawson looked at him with terrified eyes.

'Now I'm going to hit you, see, hit you so hard even your grandchildren will have an headache.'

Daniel stood by while Boysie began pummelling Lawson with his fists. As the man dropped to the floor, Daniel kicked him once in the stomach.

The twins looked at one another and smiled. Then, checking their suits to make sure they were still in pristine condition, walked out of the alleyway and along the Barking Road.

'Little ponce he is! I tell you now, Danny, he better have my winnings by the end of the week or I'll muller him. Mind you, after tonight I think he'll be paying us out all right. Quick smart.'

Boysie looked around him as he walked, taking in everything and anything. Convinced that people were looking at him, admiring him. He had an air of arrogance that tended to draw people's attention. Daniel on the other hand kept his eyes straight ahead. Of the two boys he was the quieter, the one who did the thinking, the one who was the planner. Unlike Boysie, who lost his temper in an instant and was just as quick to forget a fight, Daniel was unforgiving. He had to have a reason to resort to violence but when he did, he never forgave, ever.

They got into their car in Marlborough Road and made their way towards Manor Park where they lived.

Barking and Dagenham were still showing the signs of the war in great empty spaces filled with rubble. Dirty children were playing where terraced houses had once stood. The Becontree Estate was underway, new homes, shops and new churches to go up upon the rubble and ashes of the past. The spirit of the people, though hungry, homeless and drained by a war that left many of them without men or a place to call their home, was as it always had been. They'd won, and if the price they had paid was high, it was for King and country – though the wags said for a King they hardly saw and for a country that was going to the dogs!

It was the joke of London when Buckingham Palace was bombed and the King said he now felt like a Londoner. The silly old bugger should have been in the East End during the blitz, stepping across gaping holes in the road with electricity cables and gas mains open to the elements; he should have heard the screaming of the women and children as fires raged and people tried frantically to find relatives and even family pets. Suddenly even a scabby old cat was important.

Still, it was over now, the building had begun and a new breed of youth was emerging. The wide boy arrived in 1945 and was to become a role model for the children growing up. The country had undergone a change, a big change. Old values were slowly disappearing, the King and Queen were no longer just to be obeyed and worshipped from afar, the young ones wanted none of what their parents had endured. There was more work and money to be spent.

Women who had never been outside the home before had been earning good money in the war, and had enjoyed their independence. Now the ones with husbands back home were adjusting once more to being 'the wife', or 'her indoors', and the

434

widows were keeping their heads above water as best they could. It was a sad woman who didn't have a full belly once her husband was demobbed. Children were being born left, right and centre, the new generation that was to change the world. Or so they thought.

As for Danny and Boysie, they had lived through the Blitz, seen bodies dug out of mounds of steaming rubble, and witnessed all the horrors of the war from the home front. They were changed as a result. Like many young men they had an outlook on life that shocked the older generation.

It was survival of the fittest now. That was the law of the streets where Boysie and Danny were about to make their mark.

As the twins drove home they chatted.

'Shall we go up the club later? After the bit of business.'

Danny nodded as he drove. 'If you like, Boysie. We've got to see The Aunt beforehand, though. I'll drop round Auntie Bernie's so we can get spruced up first.'

'I can't wait for tonight. It's like a dream come true, ain't it? I'm so excited inside.'

Boysie's euphoria made Daniel laugh.

'Just remember, after tonight, there's no going back.'

Boysie shrugged. 'I don't want to go back, I can't wait to get started.'

Bernadette and Marcus lived two doors down from Briony in Manor Park. The road they lived in was tree-lined and contained fifteen houses, all large and rambling, all with half an acre of gardens, and all looking very well kept. Bernadette's still had the leaded lights from the original windows and the house was gabled. She lived there with Marcus and their two young daughters, Rebecca and Delia. The names were hated by the rest of the family, but as far as Bernie was concerned, they were classy. Bernie, as the years went on, had become obsessed with being classy. She opened the door to the boys herself and grinned at them widely.

'Hello, me ducks. In you come. The bathroom's free!'

Boysie grinned back at her. She was a bit of all right was

Auntie Bernie. Both boys went up for a quick wash and brush up and came downstairs to a large mug of tea.

Becky and Delia sat on the floor in front of the fire and gazed up longingly at the two big men in their front room.

Every time Bernie clapped eyes on her nephews, she felt an overwhelming feeling of love and pride. They were so handsome, and so huge! Both stood tall at six foot, both were well built. They had the same blue eyes, the same thick eyebrows, and the same brown-red hair. Boysie had a thinner face than Daniel though it was only noticeable to people who knew them exceptionally well.

In turn the two boys loved their aunts to distraction. Briony was referred to as 'The Aunt', though they called her Mum when they were with her. Bernie was next best; living so near and doting on them, it was inevitable. Then came Auntie Kerry, the singer, the famous one of the family who lived in Knightsbridge with their cousin Liselle. Then there was Auntie Rosie, or 'poor Auntie Rosie' as she was known, whom the boys had always adored uncritically. Their granny, Granny Moll, also worshipped them. In short, they felt quite at home in a family of women.

Nothing they did could ever faze 'The Aunt'; everything just washed over her. Even when they'd set fire to the house in Barking by accident, she'd eventually laughed it off as a boyish prank. When the house had been bombed in the Blitz she'd laughed about that too, moving them all to Manor Park without any fuss. The boys had missed being called up by months, their Auntie Briony keeping them from going with a mixture of backhanders and chats with influential friends. Now they were just reaching manhood, voting age, the time to strike out on their own, and were still inexorably tied to 'The Aunt', though neither realised this fact.

They always dropped in on their Auntie Bernie to clean up properly before they went home. It had always been that way. The Aunt only ever saw them looking perfect. Even as little boys they had done it. Filthy rotten, they'd drop in on Bernie and she would spruce them up. It was their mark of respect for the woman who had brought them up and whom they loved wholeheartedly.

The clock chimed six and of one mind they rose to leave. 'Thanks for the tea, Auntie Bernie.'

Bernadette kissed them both. Delia, the younger cousin at eight, held her arms up for a kiss and Boysie threw himself on the carpet, holding his leg.

'Oh . . . Oh! Help me, I got a bone in me leg, maybe two!'

Bernadette, Delia and Rebecca laughed at his antics. Bernie dragged him up.

'You are a case, Boysie. Here, let me brush your coat down.' Out in the hallway she took a clothes brush from a hook by the coatstand and brushed at his coat. Smoothing the shoulders with her hands, she said, 'There you go, son. All ready for Briony.'

The two boys kissed her on her cheek. 'Thanks, Auntie Bernie. See you tomorrow.'

Leaving their car in her drive they walked to their own house.

Briony was writing some letters when she heard the front door open. As always, she felt a rush of pleasure at the thought the boys were once more in the house.

'Hello, boys. What's to do?' she greeted them.

She had asked them this same question every day of their lives from young babies and somehow they expected it, welcomed it, and always answered in the same way.

'We're doing all right.'

Briony rolled her eyes in mock annoyance. '"We're doin' all right"? Is that what that bleeding poncey school was costing me the national debt for!'

Both boys grinned sheepishly.

'Come here and give me a big kiss.'

Standing, she hugged them, looking even smaller between the two big hulking men.

'You in for dinner?'

'Yeah. Then we're off to a club.'

'Right then, I'll let Cissy know. Pop in on old Mrs H, will you? She loves seeing you both.'

As they left the room she smiled to herself and went back to her letters again. The boys were home, the house was alive and everything was well once more.

Mrs Horlock, now in her eighties, was bedridden. She had shrunk 'til all that was left was a frail old body and a wispily covered skull. Her teeth were long gone and she sucked up stews, broths, and bread and milk noisily. Her mind, though, was still as sharp as a knife. As the two boys entered her bedroom she treated them to a gummy smile and patted her bed.

'Hello, you pair of 'andsome little gits! Come and see your old Auntie H!'

They sat either side of her on the bed and took a thin hand each.

'Hello, Auntie H. How you feeling?'

'With me bleeding hands as always! What you two been up to then? Been fighting?'

'Her shrewd eyes scanned the two of them and they smiled. 'Got me winnings have you?'

'The end of the week.' Boysie's voice was tight.

'That scut Lawson's tucked you up, ain't he? Well, listen to me. When people tuck you up and get away with it, it's like they won, see?'

'I gave him a dig. If he ain't got the brass at the end of the week, I'll slaughter him.' Boysie's voice was matter-of-fact.

'Good boy. Now there's another fight this week in Bethnal Green. I want you to put a tenner on for me. It's Jimmy Sands and Michael Derry. Put a tenner on Derry for me, he'll piss it.'

Daniel laughed.

'I'll see Tommy Lane about putting the bet on for you. Might have a monkey on him meself. Do you want us to get you a drop of the hard, Auntie H?'

The old woman cackled. 'What do you think? 'Course I do. You off out with the birds tonight, I suppose?'

'Something like that.'

'Oh, Danny Boy, the girls who get you two will be lucky!'

They kissed her and made their farewells.

Cissy was big. Over the years weight had piled on her. She

now ran the house in between carrying on relationships with different men, from American airmen of indeterminate age to the coal man who had a wife and thirteen children. She was as ugly as the day was long but her ample breasts and cheery manner helped enormously, coupled with the fact she wasn't too fussy. She would say to Briony: 'If they've got their own teeth and a bit of hair, that's good enough for me.'

To which Briony always replied. 'Cissy, they only have to be breathing to be good enough for you!'

This reply always sent Cissy into gales of laughter. She said the blackout was the best thing that had ever happened to her and Briony was inclined to agree. Like a lot of unmarried women, and a good few married ones, she had had what was termed 'a good war'.

Tonight the boys sat down to a large dinner. They started with a nice slice of home-made chicken liver pâté with hot toast. Then they devoured a large roast chicken and finished off with a slice of apple pie. They had never known anything about shortages. In Briony's house there was always plenty of butter, milk, eggs and meat, and the boys never questioned this, just took it all as their due.

Both of them held their stomachs with their hands and declared at exactly the same time, 'That was handsome, Cis.'

Cissy swelled with pride, holding back an urge to take a bite out of them.

Briony laughed.

'You two can certainly eat! Cissy, love, bring the coffee through, and a cup for yourself.'

Cissy did as she was told and they all sat chatting for a while. Both boys lit up cigarettes and Briony watched them through half-closed eyes.

'What's this I hear about you two being over Bethnal Green way, in a drinking club?' She had chosen her moment carefully and was gratified to see them start.

'Oh, I hear everything, my loves. Now listen to me. I give you a lot of freedom, but take this bit of advice. You only play with the big boys when you're big enough to win. You get my drift?'

Both boys nodded and Briony smiled at them. Relaxed now, they smiled back. Daniel and Boysie looked at one another and raised their eyebrows. They were being given permission and they both knew this.

'Listen, Mum, we want to start up our own business but we aren't really sure yet in what way. We went to the club in Bethnal Green just to feel the place out like. We're going to another tonight in Canning Town. There's a lot of money to be made with these clubs. People want a bit of life after the war. *We* want a bit of life, don't we, Boysie?'

'Too right we do!'

'Well, just as long as you know what you're doing. If you need anything, you only have to ask.'

They each grasped one of her hands.

'We know that, Mum.'

Briony nodded but her heart ached. Here they were surrounded by people who loved them. She corrected herself, women who loved them. They had been fawned over and petted since birth. Briony knew that it was a harsh world out there and wanted to protect them from it. She knew they were spoilt rotten, she knew that they had been given more than was good for them, but they were fine boys nonetheless. A bit wild at times, she had had the police round on more than one occasion. But somehow she had always got them out of it, and knew she always would. They had become her life and the habit of loving them would have been too hard to break, even if she'd wanted to.

'I set the plans for Berwick Manor in motion tomorrow. You want to see the state of it! Jesus, they wanted it for a hospital. Well, all I can say is they must have had sick pigs in there, it's like a bleeding shithouse! Still, we all had to do our bit for the war, I suppose. There's plenty of work ahead if I can get the wood. Luckily I have a friend who can get me all I want.'

'At the right price?' Boysie's voice was jocular.

'Of course. You don't have a dog...'

Both boys interrupted her.

'...and bark yourself!'

440

Cissy shook her head. 'As clever as a bag of monkeys, these two, Bri. They'll go far.'

Briony laughed and said, 'That's what worries me!'

Boysie stood up. 'We'll never leave you, Mum.'

'Nah, we know when we're well off!'

The place the boys were going to in Canning Town was a snooker hall. It was tucked away in a little turning just down from The Bridge House pub. They had dressed carefully for their evening out and both wore black suits, white shirts and black ties. Their hair was Brylcreemed back and they wore light beige camel-hair coats.

The October wind was biting as they slipped through the little doorway and entered the snooker club. It was nearly empty, as they knew it would be, and walking up to the tiny bar they ordered large whiskies. The man behind the bar surveyed them warily. He knew who they were all right, the Cavanagh twins. This was the first time he had ever seen them in his establishment and it worried him. Wherever the Cavanaghs went, trouble followed.

They were a pair of little fuckers in his opinion, but what could he do? Their aunt was Briony Cavanagh.

The twins drank their scotch and looked around them. The place was dim. Four men were playing a desultory game of snooker, watching the boys surreptitiously as they chalked their cues. Eyeing one another with unspoken questions.

At just after eight-thirty three more men walked in. The proprietor smiled at them eagerly but the snooker players kept their distance. Everyone including the twins knew who these men were. The McNees were well known in Canning Town, all over Silvertown for that matter. They were three lunatics who took protection money from little clubs such as this and played the heavy for the bigger villains who couldn't be bothered to do their own dirty work. The eldest, Seamus McNee, was hoping to become the torturer for the Rileys eventually. It was his only aim in life. They clocked the twins immediately and nodded in their direction. The twins nodded back, smiling cheerfully.

'Fancy a drink, Seamus?' Boysie's voice was loud and jocular. 'Another round here, mate, and whatever the McNees want.'

The proprietor heaved a sigh of relief. He had been worried that there was going to be trouble with them all. He set about pouring two large scotches and three pints of Guinness with whisky chasers, the McNees' trademark.

'We'll have a drink with you.' Seamus sounded like he was doing them a favour. He saw Boysie's face harden and clicked his fingers at the owner.

'Ain't you got something for us?' He held out a large meaty paw.

'Of course I have, Mr McNee, I ain't never let you down, have I?' His voice was nervous. The feeling of foreboding was back. Declan and Porrick McNee smiled at the twins in a friendly manner and Seamus rolled his eyes.

'All right, Declan? How's it going, mate?' Daniel's voice was low.

'Oh, not too bad. What one are you? I always get you two mixed up.'

Boysie laughed as he watched the owner hand over a roll of cash to Seamus.

'That's because you're as thick as fucking shit.'

Seamus turned to face them, dropping the money into a pool of beer on the bar.

'What did you say?' His voice was outraged.

The twins laughed together.

'What, you deaf as well as stupid?'

Seamus stood erect, his face growing red with temper. As he drew back his fist the twins looked at one another and stepped away from him, then together they put their hands inside their overcoats and took out sawn-off shotguns. The four men playing snooker all dropped to the floor.

Boysie took the money off the bar and laughed as he put it in his pocket.

Then he pointed the gun at Seamus McNee's legs and pulled the trigger. The explosion as the gun went off shook the small club. The owner crossed himself before running out through the

442

back of the bar and locking himself in the toilet. Declan and Porrick looked at their brother writhing on the floor in agony as if they had never in their life seen him before. Boysie and Danny laughed out loud.

'Get your brother to the hospital, lads. I think his little legs is hurting him.' Then they tossed back their drinks and walked towards the door.

Daniel stopped and looked back. 'Oh, by the way, tell Seamus we'll be picking up all your rents in future, OK? And if he causes any more bother, the next shot goes right into his head. Tara.'

Porrick, never noted for his brains at the best of times, waved and said tara back.

Outside, the twins laughed and joked with each other all the way to the car. They were high on adrenaline, both feeling the rush of pure pleasure that their violent act had produced.

The story hit the streets within hours.

The Cavanagh twins were well and truly on their way.

Briony was with Mariah, sorting out how best to get the Manor back up and running. It had always been their most lucrative house, and now the war was over and everyone was getting on with their lives, they wanted to get it back in business. Mariah had been all for refusing to let it be used as a hospital but Briony had stood firm. It was the least they could do for the war effort. She had been so patriotic that everyone had been amazed. Once the Blitz started Briony had arranged for a soup kitchen, and for clothing and soap to be supplied to bombed-out people. She had doled out money, taken people in until they found alternative shelter, and had won the hearts of even the most hardened charity worker. And if she had also been the instigator of a thriving black market, she felt that her efforts to help far outweighed any of the shady things she'd done. Now all she wanted was to get on with her old business.

The call came for her at ten minutes past ten. Mariah handed over the phone while Briony was laughing about something. Her face sobered up almost immediately and Mariah watched in amazement as she had slammed down the phone and poured herself a large Napoleon brandy.

'I'll kill those two little fuckers! By Christ, I'll kill them!'

Mariah looked at her friend and shook her head.

Briony was still a very good-looking woman even though she was well into her forties. Her figure was slim, and her face barely lined. The new fashions suited her and her spectacular hair was worn in a chic French pleat. It was only her voice that betrayed her. Until she opened her mouth, people always assumed she was from the upper classes.

'You'll never guess what the twins done tonight?'

'What?' Mariah's voice was shocked. Briony never spoke about the twins like this. Usually she spoke of them as a mixture of the Pope and God himself.

'They only shot bleeding Seamus McNee in the legs. In a snooker hall in Canning bloody Town. The stupid little gits! Wait 'til I get my hands on them. It's all over Silvertown so you can bet it'll be everywhere in the morning. And as for the Rileys, well, I just heard they're not too happy about it. The McNees worked for them.'

'Oh, for Gawd's sake!'

Briony swallowed the burning liquid and shrugged.

'Oh, sod the Rileys, they don't bleeding well scare me. It's the audacity of those two little sods. They sat in that house tonight like butter wouldn't melt! They must have been planning this . . . You wait 'til I get my hands on them.'

Mariah took a deep breath and spoke.

'Listen, Bri, me and you go back a long way, girl. Let me tell you something now. Those two boys are out of control. Look at last year when they had that fight at the fair in Victoria Park. They crippled that bloke, remember? Even as little kids they had a violent streak. This is the culmination of it. You've got to put your foot down once and for all. Stop bloody well getting them off the hook.'

Briony closed her eyes 'til they were slits and looked at the big woman in front of her. Mariah bleached her hair and still wore dresses that were too tight; she plastered the make-up on these

444

days but she looked her age: sixty-two. It suddenly occurred to
Briony that out of everyone she knew, Mariah had never been
one to sing the boys' praises. She had always pointed out their
shortcomings. Even though at heart Briony knew that what her
friend said was true, hearing her pulling her boys to pieces went
against the grain.

'So that's your opinion, is it?'

Mariah shrugged. 'For what it's worth. It's about time
someone told you the truth of it. You and your family treat them
like visiting royalty. Well, look where it's got them. They've
kneecapped a known villain in a dirty snooker club. I bet you're
really pleased about their good education now, ain't you! And
another thing while we're about it . . .'

Briony held her hand up to stem the flow.

'I think I've heard enough from you for one night, Mariah. I
never realised before that you didn't like my boys. But I think I
get the picture now, thank you very much.'

She started to pull on her fox fur coat and Mariah grabbed her
arm.

'I love those boys, Briony, but unlike you I can see their
faults. They play you, girl. They get all spruced up round
Bernie's before they darken your door, then they sit and smile –
and I tell you now, girl, they're taking the bleeding piss! Oh, I
don't dispute they love you. No . . . they worship you. But all
the same, they know what you want from them and they deliver
it. This is the proof of it. You told me tonight that they were
thinking of getting a little business. You was pleased as bloody
punch. Finally settling themselves, you said. And what is this
business? Collecting fucking rents! It's villainy they want, girl.
They want to be like the Rileys. Like . . .'

Briony pushed Mariah in her ample breasts, shouting, 'Go
on, say it! They want to be like *me* . . . me and you. Because
you're in all this up to your bloody neck too!'

'I know I am, but unlike your bloody boys, me and you don't
heavy people. We don't shoot stupid bloody thugs in dingy little
clubs. Can't you see that if you don't put a stop to their gallop,
they'll end up dead or locked up?'

Even though Briony secretly agreed with everything Mariah said, her deep-seated loyalty to her family got the upper hand.

'They're my boys and I'll deal with them.'

'Well, you do as you see fit. But don't say I didn't try and warn you!'

Briony opened the door and snarled back, 'Don't worry, I won't.'

Slamming the door behind her she stormed out of Mariah's house. She was even more annoyed with the twins now because on top of everything else they'd caused her to row with her best friend. All the way home in her car, she had a pain in her chest.

It was true what people said: the truth hurt. It hurt a lot.

Danny and Boysie came in at two-thirty. After the snooker club they had gone to The Two Puddings in Stratford and had a quiet drink. Watching the Rileys' counterparts, the Moneys.

Michael Money was the leader and Boysie and Danny had made a conscious effort to ingratiate themselves with him. He was unaware that he was next on their list. Then at ten-thirty they had gone to a drinking club in Frith Street owned by Tommy Lane. There they had gradually come down from their earlier euphoria. As they walked in at the front door of their aunt's house, the drawing-room door opened and Briony stood there waiting for them.

'Well, well, well, if it ain't Frank and Jesse James!'

Despite themselves they smiled. Only their Aunt Briony would talk to them like that.

'Get in here, you two. Now!'

They walked into the drawing room behind her. Both stood in front of the blazing fire and looked at her.

Even in her rage she was overcome by the sheer power and magnetic quality of the two men in front of her. The two viciously handsome faces were turned towards her. The boys' eyes and bodies were fiercely alert.

'I want to know what happened tonight in Silvertown.'

'I think you already know, Mum.' The way Boysie called her

'Mum' tugged at Briony's heart. They were her boys, her big boys now. Her Achilles heel.

'I know enough to realise you two must be off your fucking rockers!' Her voice filled the room. 'Shooting people in front of witnesses. Carrying sawn-off shotguns. What next? You going to go in Scotland Yard and rob their payroll? You must be stupid. You *are* stupid. The Rileys will come after you hammer and tongs. Seamus was to be their next torturer, they worked for the Rileys, all the McNees, and what do you do? You go and shoot them. Jesus wept.'

Boysie and Daniel looked at the little woman in front of them.

'We ain't scared of the Rileys, or the McNees, or the Moneys. We know what we're doing, Mum, so just calm yourself down. Gordon Bennet, anyone would think we'd done something really wrong!'

Daniel's voice was jocular and suddenly Briony saw them both as plain as day. They'd always been the same, even as children. If they wanted something, they asked, then they asked again more pointedly, and finally they demanded it. She had always seen that they got what they wanted. She'd wanted to make up to them for not having Eileen, not having a father. She'd wanted her boys to have everything. Now the upshot of all this was standing in front of her. They wanted what the Rileys and the McNees and the Moneys had, and they would get it, she had no doubts about that at all. They'd get it.

They walked towards her and kissed her, as they always did, one on each cheek, and Briony was undone. Nothing she could say now would do any good. She had to retreat or she had to fight with them, and she wouldn't fight with them. She couldn't because then she knew they'd leave her, and if they left her she'd have nothing. Nothing at all. She had to go along with them, had to accept it. Deep inside herself, though she wasn't aware of it, she was secretly proud of them. They wanted a life of villainy and, being her boys, had started at the top. At the pinnacle. If they took the Rileys out of the game they were set up for life.

'Oh, boys. You do worry me. What can I do to help you with the Rileys? Do you want me to smooth it over?'

Boysie laughed.

'The Rileys don't trash you, do they?'

Briony shook her head. 'No. Not really.'

'Well, they don't trash us either. Me and Danny Boy know what we want from life.' He walked to the window and pulled back the heavy velvet curtains.

'There's a big old world out there, Mum, and me and him, we're gonna be the kings of it. Ain't that right, Danny?'

He nodded.

'We want to make our mark in our own way. Without you, Mum. We're men now, and we're men who know what we want. And nothing and no one's gonna stop us.'

Briony knew it was a threat and finally saw what Mariah meant. They were saying: 'We'll do it with you. Here in this house. Or we'll leave and do it on our own.'

Briony went to them both and hugged them to her.

'It's also a dangerous world out there, full of people like the Rileys and the McNees and the Moneys. Don't you ever forget that, boys.'

They smiled at her then, two identical smiles with identical white teeth.

'We won't.' It was spoken in unison and Briony nodded at them. The course was set.

Chapter Thirty-four

'Come on, Mum, get up! It's after ten.'

Liselle pulled the covers back from her mother's body and sighed.

'Please, Mum, you're recording at eleven-thirty.'

'Leave me alone, Liselle, I'm tired.'

Kerry's emaciated body was curled in a ball. Liselle put her arm under her mother's head and pulled her forcibly to a sitting position. Then, half dragging and half carrying her, she pulled her from the bed, across the bedroom and into the shower. Kerry felt the cold water hitting her body and began to gasp for breath. Liselle laughed.

'That'll teach you to tie one on! I'm getting sick and tired of having to do this. Now, when you're awake come down and have something to eat and a cup of coffee. I'll drive you to the studios.'

Kerry stuck two fingers up at her daughter's retreating back and turned on the hot water. Five minutes later she emerged from the shower and wrapped herself in a towel. Then, going back into her bedroom, she opened the dressing-table drawer and took out a bottle of pills. She swallowed five without the aid of water and slipped on a dressing gown. Downstairs her daughter was waiting for her.

'You look like you've been done and left!'

Kerry smiled. 'I feel like it, love. Where's me coffee?'

She poured out the coffee and they drank in silence. Liselle studied her mother. Kerry was working late in the clubs singing, she was cutting an album, and she was also taking far too many pills. What really annoyed Liselle was that her mother looked so bloody good on her way of life. Anyone else would have been burnt out, looked terrible, but not Kerry Cavanagh. She seemed to thrive on work, work and more work. Even during the war she'd travelled all over the world singing to the troops and had come back raring to go. It was the pills that bothered Liselle, those and the vodka.

At twenty-one she was her mother's full-time minder. She wasn't sure exactly when this had come about, but it had. It seemed to Liselle that she had spent her life looking after her mother instead of the other way round. She even signed all the cheques these days because her mother was either unavailable or stoned out of her brain. Now Liselle froze off reporters, she confirmed Kerry's singing dates, checked that her clothes were all looked after, that her mother remembered to eat, hid as much drink as she could, and all in all made sure her mother was presentable for her public engagements. It was getting harder by the day. As Kerry's eyes began to glaze again she sighed mentally. At least she could sing OK on the pills. It was when she had had the drink that it got difficult, though her mother's reputation was well known in the business.

'Come on, Mum, eat a bit of scrambled egg.'

Kerry made a face.

'I wouldn't eat that crap if you paid me! I've had a bit of toast, that'll do.'

'Well, go and get dressed then, we've got to go in a minute.'

Kerry stood up.

'You're a right old bossy boots, Liselle, do you know that?' It was said in a jocular manner but it hurt Liselle nonetheless.

'Someone's got to get you sorted out. If it was left to you . . .'

Kerry sobered up immediately. 'I know. I know, love.'

Liselle watched her mother walk from the room and wished she could bite her tongue off. Her mum was a difficult charge, she really was. But Liselle loved her.

Going out to the hallway she looked in the big mirror by the phone. The face that stared back at her had deep circles under the eyes and her full lips were painted with a deep red lipstick. Her deep brown eyes were heavily made up and her thick blue-black hair pulled up on to her head. She often wondered how she had got so dark, her mother would never tell her about her father, only that she had loved him very much and he had left her. She'd daydreamed as a child that he was a Spaniard or an Italian. Her granny always said they had Basque blood in the family, maybe it had come from there? It was strange not to know your beginnings and lately it had bothered her very much. But it was pointless asking her mother or her aunts, they all clammed up as soon as it was mentioned.

She heard her mother's footsteps on the stairs and picked up the keys to the car. It would all come out in the wash as her granny always said when gossiping about someone when she didn't know the full story. It would all come out in the wash. Smiling at her mother they left the house.

Kenny Riley was so annoyed his face was coming out in red blotches. His breathing was painful and his fists ached from clenching them. He looked at his right-hand man, Michael Money, and sighed.

'I want those Cavanaghs given a lesson they'll never forget, do you get my drift? I think they're a pair of little piss-takers who need to be taught a few manners!'

Michael Money nodded. He was still reeling from the shock of the shooting himself. The fact that the twins had turned up at the pub after and had chatted to him as if nothing had happened scared him. Scared him very much. Boysie was a nutter, a temper merchant, but Danny now, he was a different ball game. He was cute, he was clever, and by Christ if he was the brains behind the two, then they'd all better watch their backs. He didn't say this to Kenny Riley though, he knew when to keep his peace. At the moment Kenny was on a short fuse and anyone who lit the match under it was guaranteed a long stay in the Mile End Hospital.

'What about their aunt, Kenny? She ain't exactly Snow White.'

Kenny clenched his teeth and said sarcastically in a high voice: 'Oh, are we frightened of women as well as children now then? Shall I run home and get me old Mum to sort it all out for me? Eh? Shall I, Micky? Or how about me and you make some jam sandwiches and go for a nice picnic in Victoria Park, and when we come back all the naughty boys might be indoors having a bath and eating their tea! Bollocks to Briony Cavanagh! Bollocks to all the Cavanaghs! Go out and get them and bring them here to me. I have a few words to say to them that might just frighten the little fuckers enough to make them leave me and mine alone.'

Michael Money nodded his head furiously and backed out of the room. As he looked around the crowded offices of Riley and Co. in Bethnal Green, at men, some too old to be villains really, some far too young, at the caches of guns and other paraphernalia garnered over the years, he felt a feeling of foreboding. Young the Cavanagh twins were, but frightened? Not a chance. Especially not Boysie. Boysie was a bona fide nutter, that was well known. Now he had the task, the frightening task, of telling them that Kenneth Riley Esquire wanted to see them. He didn't know at that time who he was the more scared of, the Rileys or the Cavanaghs.

He soon found out.

Boysie and Danny had been up since seven. They had as usual eaten a large breakfast cooked by a very subdued Cissy who had heard the news and was torn between a natural hatred of violence and shock at thinking her twins were even capable of it. But as the meal had worn on their usual bantering had won her over and she consoled herself with the fact that the boys must have been driven to such a desperate act. Finally, by the time she had washed up their plates and made them another pot of tea, the McNees were the undisputed villains of the piece in her mind.

By eight-thirty Bernadette and Granny Moll were also at the house with Auntie Rosie in tow.

Molly, to everyone's shock, was absolutely made up over

what the boys had done. Briony sat and listened in amazement as her mother hugged them and kissed them and told them they were good sensible boys who knew what they wanted and went after it. Her mother's easy acceptance of it all shocked Briony and Bernie to the core. Watching the boys' performance, and Briony was honest enough to admit it *was* a performance, she felt a grudging respect for them even though they had shot a man. Mariah was exactly right in what she had said: they did play her and their aunts and their granny. The twins were what you wanted them to be, even when you knew darned well they weren't! They still kept up the illusion of being her boys, her good boys.

Only the boys were now men, dangerous men, and the worst part of it all was that she still loved them with every ounce of her being. No matter what they did.

Rosalee was sitting on a chair and Boysie was helping her drink her tea. The gentleness of him as he wiped her chin with his clean white handkerchief and kissed her wet lips made Briony's heart ring with love. Danny brought her another cushion and placed it at the small of her back, making sure she was comfortable.

Molly watched them with Rosalee and felt her heart swell with pride. These were men to be proud of – unlike her husband who had allowed life to get the better of him, who had sold his daughters off for the price of a drink and a good meal, these two here would always look after their own. The women who got them wouldn't scratch in the dirt for a living, wouldn't have to rifle through pockets in the dark, feared of waking the drunken tyrant in the bed beside her, to salvage a few shillings of their wages. Oh, no. These were men who'd bedeck their women in finery, would provide for their children, and love and respect their women. After all, weren't they brought up by a houseful of women? Even Briony, the bastard of hell as Molly sometimes still thought of her, had made sure the boys respected women and had given them an insight and knowledge into women's lives.

453

Oh, they were good boys, good men, and if they shot the legs off that scut McNee, who really cared? He was a dirty torturer, could do things with a pair of pliers that would make the Borgias sick to their stomachs. Now her boys would become the Barons of the East End and the streets would be safe and she could carry on holding up her head with pride.

The twins, for their part, accepted their granny's adulation as they had always done: with wide smiles and plenty of hugs. Briony, watching, was impressed in spite of herself. Eileen's boys would go far all right.

It was just a case of whether they went too far.

Kenny Riley was waiting for Michael Money to arrive back with the twins. All day he had been thinking about what they had had the temerity to do. As he had looked around him at his crew, as he thought of the main men who worked for him, the earlier rage had worn off slightly and he was suddenly left wondering if maybe the Cavanaghs would indeed become a force to be reckoned with. With hindsight he remembered they were closely linked to Tommy Lane, one-time Baron and an old favourite of their aunt's. Tommy, still a bachelor for all his womanising, was not a fool, and the boys would get plenty of support there. Also there was Marcus Dowling who worked for Briony and was a hard man himself. Briony Cavanagh was a hard case too. It was said years before that she was in on the disappearance and murder of Willy Bolger, Ronnie Olds and one of his minders. She and Mariah Jurgens were both shrewd enough to woo the right people, and they not only courted villains like Tommy Lane but also befriended high court judges and members of parliament, to name but a few.

By lunchtime he was beginning to sweat and regretting his earlier impulsive behaviour. He should have had the twins gunned down and then made his peace with the families. That was the usual way of the East End. Once they were dead there was nothing anyone could do. The McNee brothers wanted vengeance, his own brothers wanted vengeance, he wanted vengeance. But it was vengeance with a bitter taste. He had seen the worry in Michael Money's face and Michael wasn't easily scared.

Neither was he, for that matter, but the motley crew outside, much depleted by the war, seemed to him all of a sudden like a Darby and Joan club. Old lags and young tearaways were all he had now. Fuck the war! It had been hard in that department. Some of the best minders had joined up and died, while less patriotic counterparts like himself had gone on the trot and sat the fighting out from pub basements and other such places, building an empire that was now there for the taking by people like the Cavanagh twins.

He lit himself a Lucky Strike and pulled on it deeply. Life was a bastard sometimes, it really was.

Michael had tracked the twins down to their aunt's house and sat just down the road from it in his Ford Deluxe station wagon, waiting for them to emerge. He loved Manor Park, it was a very desirable area. He approved of Briony Cavanagh's house, which must be worth all of twenty thousand pounds. In fact, this was the sort of life he thought he could get used to.

Michael Money was clever and he knew it. He had had no formal education to speak of, but he'd had the education of the pavements and the streets, which to his mind was all he needed. He was debating whether to make an alliance with the Cavanaghs and help wipe out the Rileys when the twins pulled out of the driveway in an Aston Martin.

Turning on his engine he decided to follow them, until he plucked up the courage to put his money where his mouth was and make a decision on whether to try and take them to Kenny or try and do a deal. He realised almost immediately they were going to Bethnal Green.

Boysie was humming in the car, enjoying the ease with which they travelled. They passed a police car and Boysie, being Boysie, waved at the occupants.

'How do you think The Aunt took last night, Boysie?' Danny's voice was worried.

455

'All right. She's a game old bird, she knows the score.'

Danny turned a corner and looked over his shoulder. 'We're being followed by Michael Money in his stupid fucking car with the wood all over it.' His voice was disgusted.

'Let him follow, he'll know the score soon enough. They all will, The Aunt included. Don't worry about her, Danny. She's shrewd and she's crooked, like us. She'll come round once today's over and all this is finished once and for all.'

Danny carried on driving while Boysie made sure he had everything they needed for the final part of their exercise.

Briony went to the house in Hyde Park where she knew she would find Mariah. As she walked into the offices behind the main part of the house, Mariah raised her head and the two women locked eyes.

'Hello, Mariah. I've ordered us coffee.' Briony's voice was normal. It was her way of saying sorry and Mariah knew this.

'Great, I could do with a cup. We had a good night last night in all the houses. I had the receipts brought over this morning and I've been going through them.'

They chatted about business until they had their coffee in front of them, then Mariah spoke.

'What happened with the boys?'

Briony smiled brightly, too brightly.

'Not a lot. They shot McNee all right, today they're going after the Rileys and the Moneys. But apart from that they're great.'

'I'm sorry, Briony.'

'What for? They're nearly twenty-one, old enough to look after themselves now. I mean to say, if you're big enough to shoot a known lunatic with a sawn-off shotgun, you're old enough for anything, ain't you?' It ended in a question and Mariah went round the desk and put her arm around her friend's shoulders.

'Do you think they can handle it?'

Briony nodded. 'Oh, they can handle it, all right. I think that's the trouble.'

'Come on, drink your coffee. Like you say, they seem to know what they're about.'

Briony sipped the coffee and put the cup back in the saucer with a clatter.

'You know what really bothers me about it all? What Eileen would have thought. She entrusted them boys to me, on her death bed. "Look after my boys", those were her words. I feel that if she could see them now, she'd be disappointed. You knew our Eileen. She hated any skulduggery. She was straight as a die. You know, I see her in them sometimes, the movement of their heads or an expression when I talk to them. She wouldn't have allowed them a free rein like I did. She would have chastised them more. Seen to it they kept up their schoolwork. I protected them from so much . . .'

She put her hand up to her brow and leant her elbow on the desk. 'I don't know what to think now. In a way I expected something like this, I think. Only not so soon. I wanted to hand the clubs over to them, the night clubs, and I wanted to expand the other businesses. I wanted them legit, you see. Now they've taken matters into their own hands and I can't do a thing. Only sit back and help them if I can.'

Mariah poured a large scotch and gave it to her. 'You did your best, girl, you can't do no more than that. Some people have it built into them. That's what I think, anyway. Look at them American boys, what's their names, who committed that murder back in the twenties? Leopold and Loeb, that's it. They were sons of millionaires and they went off the straight and narrow. All you can do now, as you say, is let them get on with it and pick up the pieces if it goes wrong.'

Boysie and Danny slowed the car down as they approached the headquarters of the Rileys. They had taken over a vacant house in Shoreditch after it had been bomb damaged and now they ran their various businesses from there. Kenneth Riley himself still lived in Bethnal Green.

Michael Money watched aghast as he saw Boysie get out of the Aston Martin in broad daylight and pull the pin from an

American issue hand grenade. As he threw it through the window of the building, Michael put his hands up to his face.

The Aston Martin sped away and Michael Money sat in shock and disbelief as the building and surrounding area was rocked by the explosion. Then he turned on his ignition and drove home to tell his brothers the news.

The King was dead, long live the Cavanaghs.

Liselle loved to hear her mother sing. As she sat in the recording studio and watched Kerry talking to the musicians, explaining what particular beat she wanted and whether any musician could have a solo, Liselle always felt proud.

She asked politely, as always, if any of the technicians wanted a coffee and then went in search of a cup for herself. The technicians always said no. She guessed, rightly, that like her mother they preferred a drop of the hard stuff but she asked anyway. It was good manners. Her mother had already topped herself up with a few large vodkas provided by her current amour, Victor Sanderson. Liselle didn't particularly like him, but he owned Badger Records now and had taken more than a shine to Kerry Cavanagh, one of his star artists.

Where her mother's love life, or more correctly sex life, was concerned, Liselle stood back. Her mother had always gravitated from man to man, never staying with any of them longer than five minutes. Her temper when in drink generally put them off. But this didn't seem to deter Victor, which was one thing in his favour with Liselle. As she walked out of the studios in Abbey Road and went over to the coffee shop opposite, she bumped into a big black man.

'I'm sorry, I didn't see you there.'

The man touched his cap and walked on. Liselle forgot about him and carried on over the road to get her coffee.

She didn't see the black man get into a large black Roadster just down the road and carry on watching her from there.

Kerry began to sing. Everything was quiet, as if a funeral was about to take place, and as she sang the opening bars of her song,

Victor Sanderson sighed with contentment.

This was talent on a grand scale.

Kerry still sang the blues with a deep throaty voice, but had emerged with a sound all of her own over the last twenty years. She was up there now among the greats and her voice was a guaranteed seller. When people thought of singers, great singers, they thought of Ella, of Billie, and of Kerry Cavanagh. Her voice had wafted through dusty dance halls and expensive night spots all through the war, and she had emerged bigger than ever. Now Victor Sanderson was going to see that she didn't go the way of Billie Holiday and her counterparts. He was going to watch her like a hawk, an investment that would make him more money than he dreamed of. On top of all that, though secondary to it, she was a great looker, and great in bed when she was sober enough. It was no hardship to him, looking out for her.

If only she could be made to go to America where her records sold like hot cakes, they would be set. But nothing he or anyone else said would get her there. She'd go to France, anywhere in Europe, but never to the States. Jonathan la Billière had tried to talk her into going over to Hollywood for a holiday, but she had flatly refused. That had fazed even Victor. Jonathan la Billière, the biggest movie star in the whole world, and Kerry had turned him down! Even a pretend romance would have hit all the papers, Victor would have made sure of it. He'd have personally written the copy! La Billière was an old family friend; they went back years apparently. Unlike most women who would have shouted this fact out straight away, he had found it out through a mutual friend. But the fact remained, Kerry would not go anywhere near America and if you wanted a fight with her, you just tried to force that issue. They had been offered a staggering fifty thousand pounds for her to appear at Madison Square Garden and she had coolly declined. Victor could have cried.

He had even tried to speak to that sister of hers, the one who ran the whorehouses, but she had politely told him to get on his bike. Oh, in nicer words than that, but that had been the general drift.

Still, he consoled himself, Kerry was being good at the moment, she was turning up at the right places at the right time and she wasn't always plastered. Her daughter played a big part in that. She watched her mother like a hawk. Between them they'd see her all right, and maybe get her overseas one day.

Dickie Lawson found the twins in Soho. It was early-evening and they were having a drink in Tommy Lane's club, The Bolthole. Dickie looked at the two of them and took a deep swallow as he plucked up courage to go over to them.

The club was small and select and it cost a fiver to get in. The people who used The Bolthole wanted to be somewhere where the police, wives, girlfriends, or even Military Police during the war, couldn't get to them. Dickie had paid over his fiver, signed himself in and now he had to walk into the lion's den.

He could have kicked himself for trying to tuck the twins up with the bets. He felt faint every time he thought about it. Everywhere he went they were being talked about. Anyone who'd shoot a McNee in the legs and blow up Kenny Riley was guaranteed to frighten Old Nick himself, let alone a small-time hustler like Dickie Lawson. Plucking up courage, he went over to them. Boysie and Danny watched him approach them in the bar mirror. He stood behind them uncertainly for a few seconds before he spoke.

'All right, lads?' His voice was strangled-sounding, as if one of the twins already had a hand around his throat.

Both of them turned around at once.

'Well, well, well, if it ain't Dickie Lawson. Come to buy us a drink and pay over our winnings, have you?' Boysie's voice was loud, jocular, and Dickie took heart.

'That's right, lads, what you having?'

He took a brown envelope out of his jacket pocket and slipped it on to the counter. Danny picked it up and opened it, counting the money.

'There's only a hundred quid in here, Dickie boy.'

He bit his lip and then licked his lips which had dried in record time with fear.

'That's what I owed you, lads . . . hundred quid.'

Boysie snapped his fingers and the barmaid sloped over and smiled at them.

'What can I get you?'

'Two very large scotches, my love, a half of bitter for me little mate, and whatever you want of course.'

The barmaid set about getting the drinks and Boysie turned back to Dickie who was now a deathly shade of white.

Danny laughed.

'What we want, Dickie, is our rents. As you probably know, poor Kenny Riley is well out of the ball game now, through explosives like. He left us everything he owned. And that, I think, includes yourself.'

Dickie, seeing the light, the crystal clear, plain as day kind of light, nodded his head furiously.

'Of course . . . Of course, lads.'

He slapped his sweaty forehead with a sweaty palm and, taking out a roll of money, paid up without a murmur.

Boysie poked Dickie in the chest none too gently.

'A word in your shell-like. We ain't your lads, see? We are Mr Cavanagh to you. Do you think you can remember that?'

Dickie was once more nodding, harder now.

'Yes, lad . . . I mean, yes, Mr Cavanagh!'

Boysie and Danny laughed out loud.

'Good lad! Now pay for the drinks like a good boy and then piss off. You're beginning to annoy us. We'll see you next week, Dickie. You won't have to look for us, we'll find you. All right?'

Half an hour later they were on their way to meet two girls, both good Catholics, both definitely virgins. Both waiting to be plucked like nice ripe gooseberries.

All in all, life couldn't be better for the Cavanagh twins.

Liselle sat in The New Yorker, Briony's latest club, with her mother and watched her get roaring drunk. She was the life and soul of the place, as usual, and eventually got up and sang a few numbers to the delight of the audience. Bessie, who now sang there with the Velvetones despite periodic threats to go home to the States, stood in the wings and smiled. Until she turned and saw the black man standing by the stage door. Then her heart began to hammer in her ears and she closed her eyes tightly.

When she opened them again the man was gone.

It was the lights playing tricks on her, that was all, but for one moment she could have sworn she saw Evander Dorsey standing there. Fatter, greyer, but Evander all the same. As Kerry called her out on stage she put a smile on her face and stepped into the lights, but the niggling thought that she had seen Evander spoilt her evening.

As they sang together, that old favourite 'Summertime', she looked at Liselle sitting at the table, drinking soda and looking dead on her feet, and felt foreboding wash over her.

That girl wasn't a child any more and soon, very soon, she'd need to be told the truth. She didn't look Negro at all, at least she didn't to the British, but in the South she would be known immediately for what she was, and Bessie knew from experience that the girl could give birth to children as black as the African slaves who were her forefathers.

Oh, the girl needed to be told all right, and Kerry wouldn't be the one to do it. Kerry had enough difficulty just getting through an average day. Someone else would have to tell her, but who?

As the song finished she bowed and held on to a rather drunken Kerry, stopping her from falling over.

It was seeing that black guy that made her think these morbid things, that was all.

A little later Liselle helped her mother from the club and got a taxi to take them home. Tired out as she was, she didn't notice the black man standing in the doorway at the side of the club. If she had, she wouldn't have realised he was the man from earlier in the day.

Evander watched his daughter get into the taxi. He walked to the Roadster once more, and the three white men sitting in it.

'Yeah, that's her all right. I had to be sure.' He lit himself a cheroot with crooked and deformed fingers. 'Tha's my girl, no mistakin'. Looks jes like my sister.'

The three white men in the car nodded.

Evander smoked his cheroot and nodded to himself as if carrying on a conversation. Only no one was interested in what he had to say. He pulled out a hip flask and took a deep draught of cheap brandy.

He laughed softly to himself. Liselle! That bitch had named her for his mama.

Chapter Thirty-five

It was two months since the twins had taken over the East End of London. Briony had adjusted to the fact that the boys were now men, that she had very little say in what they did or, worse still, how they did it. Instead, she threw herself into the re-opening of Berwick Manor. The Manor represented a lot to her, it was the pinnacle of her achievements. She had had just about everyone who was anyone in there, and wanted it like that once more. She wanted it lit up like a beacon, with all the old crowd, and some new faces.

As she stood alone looking over the place she felt a tiny thrill of anticipation. The damage wasn't too bad when you got used to it. Mainly the carpeting and the wall coverings. Most of the original mouldings were still in perfect condition. In the top bedroom, where prominent cabinet ministers had spent many a sleepless night, she found a letter wedged between the windowsill and a walnut dresser. Briony picked it up and glanced at it.

It was for a Flying Officer Byron, from his wife Juliette. She smiled as she read the endearments from her. The longing for her husband's return home. The little anecdotes about the children. It was a lovely letter written in graceful handwriting by a woman whom Briony visualised as neat in body, mind and home. She hoped that Flying Officer Byron had made it home, she really did.

She sat on the bare mattress, clutching the letter. Trying to imagine what it must be like to love a man like that. To have his children and look after his home and just dedicate your life to that one person and their progeny. It was a strange thing to her, this being married. It was something she couldn't for the life of her imagine. Bernadette had married her Marcus and overnight she'd turned into a household drudge. Oh, she enjoyed it, Briony knew and respected that. But there was no real reason for it. She had had the girls and now took care of them, Marcus and the home. Bernadette was happy just overseeing her family. Making sure meals were prepared on time, that the house ran smoothly.

Well, Cissy did all that for Briony, and before her Mrs H had done it. If she had had to stagnate in a house just waiting for a man to breeze in and out as it suited him she'd have gone mad. Stark staring mad.

She glanced down at the letter again. The sender's address was in Northumberland. She pushed the letter into her pocket. She'd mail it to this Juliette Byron, whoever she was. Maybe she'd want it back. Especially if Flying Officer Byron hadn't made it home.

She wandered out of the room and looked out of the window at the greying skies. The view from the Manor had always entranced her. From one side of the house were wide sweeping fields that in the summer glowed yellow with corn. From the front of the house the view was of Rainham marshes, and from the top window you could see right up Upminster Road North to the church with its clocktower.

She heard a noise and turned from the window. Standing at the top of the stairs was a man. In the dimness brought on by the overcast skies she couldn't make out his face. As he walked towards her she put her hand to her chest in momentary fright.

'My God! It's you.' Her voice was a whisper.

'Surprised to see me?' His voice was the same as always and Briony was transported back over the years to her first sight of a young boy in a new suit that looked too big, with a voice that had just broken properly.

'Tommy. Tommy Lane. You're the last person I expected to see.'

He smiled then, that easy smile that she remembered so well. Even though they had spoken by phone over the years, they had met only twice, by accident. Then they had been chillingly polite to one another. Now he was here, in the Manor, and she knew it was for a good reason.

'They don't call me Bad Penny Lane for nothing, you know!'

Briony smiled. 'Come down to the kitchen and I'll make us some coffee.'

They walked down the stairs in silence, both aware of the attraction still between them. The gathering storm overhead served to make the atmosphere even more charged.

Briony put the kettle on the range and turned to face him. 'Black coffee, I'm afraid, there's no milk.'

Tommy sat down at the scrubbed table and looked at her as if drinking her in. Despite herself, Briony blushed at his scrutiny and Tommy laughed out loud.

'Now I've seen everything. Briony Cavanagh blushing? That's a turn up for the book, I must say!'

She grinned.

'It's the shock of seeing you, I think, Tommy, after all this time. I take it this is a friendly visit?'

His face sobered at her words. Standing up, he went to her and put his hands on her shoulders. Looking down into the deep, green depths of her eyes, he said, 'As friendly as you want it, Briony.'

She felt the confusion in him, in herself. Suddenly she wanted Tommy Lane like she had never wanted anyone or anything before. He was here, a reminder of her past, her youth, her old life. He was like a big present, waiting to be opened. All she had to do was tear away the wrappings.

A new feeling swamped her body as the first slap of thunder trembled overhead. It started in her groin and its warmth spread gradually up into her stomach and breasts. She found, for the first time ever, that she couldn't even talk, couldn't speak to make her feelings known.

As she parted her lips, Tommy took her into his arms and kissed her hard. Bruising her mouth, he forced his tongue into her mouth, exploring her with it. Briony felt the feeling swamp her then, and she kissed him back, hard kisses, as they rubbed against one another's bodies, discovering each other for the first time in over twenty years. They finally came together up against the scrubbed pine table, Briony hooking her slim legs around his waist and grinding her hips into him as she finally felt the sensations that had always been denied to her. Never had she expected to feel this passion in her lifetime.

She ground into him, crying out into the silent kitchen. A flash of lightning lit up the kitchen and they saw each other properly then. The feeling was enveloping her now, she was dying to capture it properly, and he was carried along with the want in her, now in him. She heard him groan and her heart raced. Don't let this stop, she thought. Don't cheat me now. And it didn't. She felt the first tentative throes of orgasm, felt the hardness of Tommy inside her, and it was enough then. It was finally enough. Clutching at his hair she jerked in his arms, pulling him deeper and deeper inside her until there was nothing. No thunder, no storm, only the two of them. Together they shuddered and moaned and finally were spent. Briony felt the sweat on her brow, the dampness of her body. He held her to him, gently, firmly, and they felt the thundering of each other's hearts.

Briony kissed his face. Little kisses over his eyes, his cheeks, and on his mouth. She held his face between her tiny hands and she knew, at last she knew. The mystery of man and woman. What had driven Kerry and Bernie, and what had driven Juliette Byron to write such a letter to her absent husband. She felt a flicker of jealousy for the women who had found this out when young, when well able to follow their star. She was forty-four years old and felt like a newborn.

The kettle was screaming on the hob and the rain battering, against the windows. Pulling away from one another, Briony and Tommy smiled at one another shyly. As if they had just met. Briony looked down at the lacy scrap of underwear on the stone floor and giggled. Her cami-knickers were torn beyond repair. Tommy had his trousers around his ankles and looked ridiculous, but handsomely ridiculous. She pulled down her skirt and rebuttoned her blouse quickly with trembling hands. Taking the kettle off the range, she made the coffee, listening to his movements. Frightened that he might leave her now, and never come back.

As she turned to face him, she swallowed deeply. Then slowly, squeezing out of her eyes as if unsure what they were doing, the tears came. Hot stinging tears. Tommy went to her and took her in his arms, whispering endearments, stroking the erratic red hair that had escaped from the confines of its French pleat.

'I never knew, Tommy. I never knew you could feel like that. I've been only half alive all my life. Only half alive . . .'

Tommy held her tightly. If anyone had told him that his coming here would have brought this on he'd have laughed aloud at the very thought. But it was as if today they had reached their turning point. She had been there in front of him, his girl, his Briony. His best friend for so long. And fate had decreed that today was to be the time for them. The time for them to get together properly. As they should have done years before, when young and eager.

'I know, Bri . . . I know, my love.'

And he held her while she cried. There was time enough to tell her why he had followed her here, why he had waited to see her alone. For the time being they had one another and that was enough.

God knew, he had waited long enough for her. Even if he hadn't fully realised that himself until today.

It was Sunday and Liselle slept in till ten-thirty, secure in the knowledge that her mother had nowhere to go today and she could let her sleep. They'd go to evening Mass with Granny Moll as they did every Sunday, then out to dinner. The drinking would start about eight-thirty, and her mother would set herself up for the week.

Lying in bed listening to the sounds of the radio, Liselle sighed. She lifted one slim arm to turn the radio up slightly. The darkness of her arm against the white chest of drawers made her stare. Pulling the covers from herself, she looked down at her body. Even her nipples were black. She remembered at school, all the other girls had had tiny pink nipples, and they had all laughed at her brown ones, brown ones that were now nearly black. She frowned. Her pubic hair was jet black, tiny black spirals that seemed to grow prolifically around the tops of her legs. Yet she knew she was attractive. Men looked at her twice. It had always been that way.

She had developed earlier than her friends, having large heavy breasts by the time she was twelve. Her school friends had been envious of her, but she had shrugged it off. Her mother said all the Cavanagh girls had been early developers and she had been satisfied with that explanation. But lately, she had wondered about herself. During the war, a black airforceman had smiled at her. She had smiled back, naturally, as you did to anyone who smiled at you in a friendly manner. Her Granny Moll, seeing the exchange, had gone mad. She had gone for the man in the middle of Brick Lane, bringing the eyes of passersby on to them. Going to her granny, Liselle had pulled on her arm, shame and hurt welling up inside her.

'Granny . . . Gran, leave it be!' she'd cried.

The man had looked at her and said, 'She's your granny, girl?' His voice had been incredulous. She had nodded, humiliated. But the exchange had stayed with her, bringing all sorts of fancies into her childish heart. Now at twenty-one she remembered the long buried incident and it troubled her.

Sitting up in bed, she clasped her knees. She would ring the twins and arrange to see them. They always cheered her up.

When Kerry got up, she found Liselle's note. She went into the lounge in a green silk wrapper and poured herself a large vodka and fresh orange juice. She drank it straight down and immediately poured herself another. Then sitting down she picked up the Sunday paper and lit herself a cigarette. She was reading the *News of the World* when the telephone rang.

Leaning out of her chair, she picked it up, the smell of Mrs Harcourt cooking her some eggs making her want to gag.

'Hello.'

'Is that you, Kerry girl?'

She dropped the phone on to the beige carpet, staring at it as if it was a demon. Scrambling from the chair, she picked the receiver up once more and held it tentatively to her ear.

The line was dead.

Placing it back in its cradle she stood there staring at it, willing it to ring.

She knew that voice. That deep brown voice.

It didn't ring again. Kerry sat all day, with the bottle of vodka by her side, waiting. Still it didn't ring. She spent the rest of the day lost in a drunken world of jazz music, smoky clubs, and the arms of a big handsome man called Evander Dorsey.

Molly stood outside St Vincent's church with Rosalee. Both had on their best hats, coats and gloves, though Rosalee's gloves were grubby where she had insisted on picking privets all the way to the church. Molly pursed her lips and shook her head. Abel was asleep in bed, getting ready for his night's work at the club in Soho that Briony now owned. It was his way of getting out of going to Mass, she knew that. She saw the twins and Liselle get out of the boys' Aston Martin and her heart swelled with pride. They never missed Sunday evening Mass with their gran.

As they walked into the church and genuflected before the Cross of Christ, Molly felt as if her whole life had been worth it for this. Boysie helped Rosalee into the front pew, which was now reserved especially for them, and the others filed in beside her. All knelt and said the regulation prayers, then sat back in silence, waiting for the priest and, hopefully, Kerry to arrive. Liselle watched the back of the church anxiously every time the doors opened. Her mother had better turn up. If she didn't it meant she was too drunk, and Liselle hated her mother when she was really plastered.

Father Tierney walked down the church and everyone stood up. Boysie looked around the church as the service started, automatically making the responses in Latin as he always had.

471

Boysie and Danny liked Mass. They always had from little children. They liked the feel of the church and they respected its sanctity. They believed in God as they believed in themselves. As the Mass drew to a close and the priest asked for prayers for the sick and the dying, the twins sat happily with their gran and their aunt and cousin Liselle, and enjoyed the feeling the church always created in them.

In there, with its high ceiling and its quietness, they could really believe that there was peace on earth and all was well with man.

Well, with these two men anyway.

The twins dropped their granny off at Briony's and then took Liselle home. As they walked into the large house they heard the housekeeper, Mrs Harcourt, a widow of uncertain age, shouting.

Liselle rushed into the lounge where her mother was lying unconscious on the floor, the phone beside her.

'Oh, Miss Liselle! I can't wake her up. She's been drinking steadily since she got up, wouldn't eat a blessed thing, and now she's unconscious!'

Liselle turned on the woman, saying sharply, 'Well, shouting at her when she's like this isn't going to help, is it? Go and make a pot of coffee.'

Danny and Boysie looked at one another. Of one mind, they picked up their aunt and carried her up the stairs to her room. Plonking her down on the bed none too gently, Boysie threw a cover over her.

'She should be put away, Liselle, as much as we all love her. She ain't doing herself no favours with the drink.'

Liselle sighed heavily.

'She won't go. I've tried all that. There's a place in Surrey where they dry you out, but she goes mental if you even mention it. Sometimes I feel like buggering off out of it, I really do. Just leaving her to it. I've got no life to speak of. I just watch her day and night. Look what happened when I went out with you today. All this.'

Danny felt an enormous surge of affection for the cousin who was more like his sister. Their situation while growing up had been so similar, no father and their Aunt Briony being the main person in their lives, even Liselle's.

'Come on, she's out for the count now. Let's all go out together, we know a terrific little club!'

Boysie joined in. 'Yeah. Come on, Lissy, she'll be out 'til the morning. Even black coffee won't help her now.'

Hearing the name they had called her as a child made Liselle smile. 'All right then. I suppose you're right. She won't wake now for about twelve hours.'

'There you go then. Get dressed up and we'll be your dates tonight.'

Boysie spoke in fun but Liselle looked at him and said seriously: 'Boysie, you two are the only dates I've ever had.'

As she left the room the twins looked at one another sadly. Poor old Liselle, stuck looking after their Auntie Kerry who could sing, who could do anything as long as it was musical, yet couldn't leave the drink or the drugs alone.

As they went to leave the room Kerry stirred and opened her eyes. Looking at the twins she said: 'Evander?' Then closing her eyes she was gone again.

Boysie said, 'What did she say?'

Danny shrugged. 'Something about lavender, I don't know. Come on, let's go downstairs, this place gives me the creeps.'

Liselle got changed and walked out of the front door as if the weight of the world had been lifted from her shoulders. When her mother was unconscious, like now, at least she knew where she was, and how long she was going to be there. That in itself was a result.

Molly had kissed her grandchildren then, taking Rosalee by the arm, walked up the drive to Briony's house. Rosalee was slow and Molly had to fight an urge to drag her along. At forty, Rosalee had lasted a lot longer than they had expected. Her weight was enormous, but she waddled through life happily enough and everyone doted on her, especially the twins. As they walked through Briony's front door, Ciss, hardly able to contain herself with excitement, whispered: 'Have a guess who's here, Moll? Tommy Lane!'

Molly's mouth dropped open. 'You're kidding?'

Cissy shook her big fat face 'til her cheeks wobbled. 'I ain't. He's in there now with Briony, Bernie and Marcus, as large as life!'

Molly divested herself and Rosalee of their coats in double quick time and, taking Rosalee's hand again, went into the drawing room.

Tommy and Briony were sitting on the chesterfield by the french windows, and Bernie and Marcus were in easy chairs either side of the fireplace. Rosalee, waddling in behind her mother, looked at Briony and as always clapped her hands together and said in excitement: 'Bri, Bri.'

Briony got up from her seat. Kissing her sister, she led her to the chesterfield, placing her between herself and Tommy. He took Rosalee's hand and squeezed it.

'Hello, Rosie love.' He was genuinely pleased to see her.

Rosalee for her part smiled a huge toothless smile and said, 'Tom.'

Everyone in the room was absolutely amazed.

'Jumping Jesus Christ, did you hear that!' Molly's voice was low with shock.

As if showing off, Rosalee said once more, louder than anyone had ever heard her speak before: 'Tom.'

Marcus shouted, 'Well, I'll be buggered!'

And Briony, quick as a flash, shouted back, 'Not in here, you won't!'

Even Molly laughed then.

'Didn't I always say she could talk more than we thought, Mum, didn't I?' Briony's voice was so happy even Molly was gladdened at the sound of it.

'You did that, Briony. You did that. Now I think I'll have a drop of hot rum to celebrate. Would anyone like to join me?'

Briony felt as if her ship had indeed come in. Rosalee was more animated than she had ever seen her, she was drinking without help, and Tommy was sitting so close. She couldn't wait for night to come so she could leap into bed with him and experience again the things she had felt that afternoon.

'How's herself?' Molly's voice was confidential as she enquired after Mrs H and Bernie laughed.

'We've been up to her. She's as right as the number ten bus, Mum.'

'I'll pop up to her meself in a minute. Poor old soul she is.'

Bernie got up to replenish Marcus's glass and Tommy saw that she was now a middle-aged woman. Her figure was fuller, her waist long gone. He was sad for a second as he visualised her as she had been when he'd first known her.

As she placed the glass in her husband's hand Marcus winked at her and Tommy smiled to himself. They were happy, that much was evident. He knew that Marcus was one for the ladies, it was well known in their circles. Obviously Bernie knew nothing about it, which was good. A wife, a good wife, was worth hanging on to. Bernadette sat down and crossed her legs demurely. Her ankles were fat, and Tommy looked at them in consternation. When a woman aged, a beautiful woman, it was like the destruction of a beautiful painting.

He let his eyes roam to Briony. In the firelight, with only the lamps on, she looked exactly as she had the last time he'd seen her. Oh, the fashions had changed, but she was still the woman he had known, only now she was a real woman. In all respects she was a woman. And he intended to keep her like that. For as long as he could. He had wanted to see her about the twins, but that could wait now. He would pick the right time to talk about them.

'Did the twins go to Mass with you, Mum?'

'They did, God love them. Liselle came too, as usual.'

Briony frowned slightly. 'What, no Kerry tonight?'

Bernie sighed. 'Probably drunk out of her head. She really worries me, Bri. The other day I rang her up and she could barely talk. It's not fair on Liselle. That poor girl has to cope with everything now.'

Briony said after a few seconds' thought, 'Kerry has a lot of responsibilities, you know. I asked her to cut down on the concert dates but she didn't want to. I might go and see Victor. He manages her well, I admit, but I think he pushes her too hard at times. A friendly word might be in order there.'

Molly made a disgusting noise with her lips as she let her breath out and said nastily, 'Send the twins round to see him. They'll make sure my Kerry's not overworked.'

Briony laughed. 'If you had your way, the twins would be threatening everyone who ever drew breath! For God's sake, Mum, Kerry has always pushed herself, you know that. She's more famous these days than the bleeding Pope!'

Molly loved her daughter's fame, like she loved the twins' newfound notoriety.

'Well, all I'm saying is, she should have a bit of rest like.'

Marcus joined in. 'She should be dried out really. One of the barmen at The New Yorker said she done a bottle of vodka in an hour the other night. She won't last long drinking like that.'

'I always had a lot of time for Kerry, you know that, but if her drinking is as bad as you say, something should be done. I watched my old mum's liver give out through the drink. She went bright yellow one day, and within a week she was dead.' Tommy's voice was low.

Bernie coughed slightly and said, 'I think he's right.'

Briony nodded.

'Well, we'll have to put it to her. If she won't go we'll have no alternative but to have her committed.'

Molly felt her face stiffen. Another daughter sent to a mental home. 'Oh, she's not that bad, for goodness' sakes. She's not mad, for crying out loud, she just likes a drink.'

'Oh, Kerry likes a drink all right, a bottle at a time. When she was in France, just after the war, Bessie told me that they had to sober her up every night before her performance. I don't think it's so much the drink as the pills she drops with it.'

Molly, her own tongue loosened by drink, said, 'She's never been the same since she had that child. That's what sent her on the drink. Not the singing.'

Unbeknown to her, the twins and Liselle were in the hallway, having let themselves in with a key. They had decided to see if Briony wanted to come out with them. Molly's voice floated through the door to them and all three stiffened as they heard it. Unaware, Molly carried on.

'An illegitimate child's bad enough, but one like that? I ask you?'

Liselle was so still, she looked like a statue made of bronze. Boysie and Danny watched her fascinated.

Briony's voice broke through their grandmother's. 'Shut up, Mum. You're always the bleeding same with a drink in you! Kerry loves that girl, we all do. No matter where she came from. Now just leave it, all right. Just bloody well leave it!'

Molly stood up. 'I've every right to speak me mind where me own child's concerned.'

Bernie was trying to placate her. 'Mum ... Mum ... Sit down. Let's leave it now. It's in the past.

Briony walked over to her mother and poked her in the chest. 'Why do you always do this? A couple of bevvies and you get stroppy. The world according to Molly Cavanagh. You've never had any time for Liselle, we all know that. Well, listen to me and listen good. Our Kerry was a fucking saint to keep her, you should be proud of her. Anyone else would have got rid of her quick smart.'

All Molly's feelings burst like a cancer inside her. The strong rum toddy made her tongue run away with her. Forgetting everything, where she was and with whom, she bellowed: 'And that's what Kerry should have done! You should have made her do it. You could have talked her round. But no, not you. Not bloody Briony the marvellous wonder woman Cavanagh. You welcomed her in here with open arms. Knowing she'd slept with a bloody bl—'

Danny burst into the room and everyone stared at him. A second later the front door slammed and they heard Boysie calling Liselle's name as she ran up the drive.

'She heard you, Gran, she was listening to you! You nasty old bitch! What's she ever done to you? What's all this about? You been drinking as usual? Is that it? I'll go and help Boysie find her and you'd better be gone by the time we get back, Gran. I ain't in the mood for you tonight.'

Tommy watched the drama unfold before his eyes and sighed. But the way Daniel had spoken was like listening to Briony. Earlier that day she had said 'They're my boys', and Tommy was inclined to agree with her. Well, if they had some of their natural mother and some of Briony in them, they couldn't be all that bad. No matter what he had heard.

Briony said slowly, 'Go home, Mum. Just go home.'

Marcus got up and took Molly's arm.

'Come on. I'll take you home, love.'

Molly stared at Briony, her face troubled. 'I didn't know the child was listening, I swear. I wouldn't have hurt her for the world.'

Briony laughed bitterly.

'Of course you wouldn't. You've never wanted to hurt anyone, you. But Christ himself knows, somehow you always bleeding well manage to!'

Boysie caught up with Liselle at the bottom of the street. She was crying, really crying, and he held her to him, stroking her hair and whispering endearments.

Danny arrived a little while later and they tried to take her back to their house but Liselle refused.

'I don't ever want to see me gran again! Ever.'

Danny wiped her eyes with a clean white handkerchief and smiled crookedly.

'You know Gran. When she's had a drink she's always stroppy. Look at last Christmas when she started on poor old Mrs H, accusing her of all sorts. Forget it.'

Liselle looked up into his face and said through her teeth, 'If she'd said about you two what she's just said about me, would you forget it?'

Boysie and Danny both looked away, knowing they wouldn't.

'Whoever my father was, he seems to have made quite an impression on everyone. I wish now I'd listened to the rest of it, I might have found out just what was so very wrong with him.'

478

'Come on, girl, we'll get the car and take you home.'

Boysie and Danny had guessed that Liselle had what was termed 'a touch of the tarbrush' in her. But how could they tell her that if she didn't even guess it herself?

Chapter Thirty-six

Tommy and Briony sat up waiting for the twins to return. Bernadette had left shortly after Marcus had taken Molly and Rosalee home. Sitting in her warm lounge with the fire roaring and Tommy Lane by her side, Briony finally felt the enormity of what had taken place. Her anger against her mother grew virulent.

Tommy grasped her hand in his. 'She should have been told, Bri . . . before now.'

Briony nodded and swallowed hard. Her face white and earnest, she looked at him. 'I know that, Tommy, better than anyone. But how? How do you tell a girl something like that? Especially at this time, with all the black servicemen who were over here in the war? The feeling against them by men in particular? Black people live under a stigma. It's wrong, we know it's wrong. But not everyone's us, are they? Christ himself knows I wanted to tell her, I wanted to tell her when she was fifteen. But when she don't look black, it seemed unfair somehow. Now bloody Mouth Almighty's started a chain of events that can only lead to trouble. Oh, Tommy, sometimes I could wring my mother's bloody neck!'

'Well, the twins will see Liselle all right.'

Tommy kissed the palm of her hand. Briony smiled crookedly and touched his face with gentle fingers.

'I'm so glad you came to the Manor today, Tommy. Really I am. You know us all so well.'

He smiled at her then. She saw the lines around his eyes and mouth. The two deep grooves alongside his nose, the greying of his hair. Time raced on with no regard.

She poured herself another drink and sipped it gratefully. 'It's funny, you know, Tommy, but a long time ago when Liselle was small I had a chat with one of the black girls in one of my houses. Nice girl she was and all. Real looker. She told me that a white-looking Negro could have children as black as night. We even had a black girl once with blue eyes. I think that's when I built up a wall in me mind about poor Liselle. If you don't think about it, it goes away. Well, it doesn't go away, that much was proved here tonight. Problems don't go away, mate, they just get bigger and bigger, and for the first time ever, I don't know the answer to this one.'

'You'll find the answer. You always do.'

Briony leant against him.

'I could never share anything before, not really. Not with a man. Not with you. I honestly never thought of you really, all those years ago. I didn't wonder what your reaction would be to anything, and it wasn't because I was selfish. At least, I don't think it was. I think it was because I didn't know how to be with a man. Not really. Not properly. Henry Dumas and me dad saw to that. Today was like a whole new world to me. I really loved it. Then all this happened.'

'Look, Briony, take a bit of advice. You can't take on everything for everyone. No more than you can be everything to everyone. You need to keep a little bit of yourself for yourself. Does that make sense? You need to keep a little bit of all that love you've got back for yourself. For Briony Cavanagh.'

She nodded and sighed.

They stayed cuddled together in the firelight until the twins arrived home.

Liselle was quiet all the way back to her house. Boysie sat in the back of the car holding her to him, as if frightened she'd open the car door and run off. Daniel drove, his face hard and set. His granny had gone too far tonight. Her attitude when in drink had always left a lot to be desired, though they had laughed it off before. But this time she had really hurt someone.

Inside her house Boysie had made Liselle a strong cup of tea and they had sat with her, in their aunt's ornate lounge, and silently kept her company. No one seemed to know just what to say to her.

Finally, Liselle began to cry again. Quietly this time. She was held by the twins, both with an arm around her, both telling her not to worry, they'd sort it all out for her. And as they eyed each other over the top of her head, they both knew that that's exactly what they would do.

They'd find out who and what her father was. At least that way she'd know.

Upstairs Kerry slept the sleep of the drunk, unaware that her daughter's world had been shattered beyond repair.

Evander looked at Skip Paquale who smiled at him. Evander smiled back, but the smile, or grimace, didn't reach his bloodshot brown eyes.

He noted the other man's expensive suit, clean-cut good looks and flat, athletic stomach. Skip looked what he was, a ladies' man, from his well-cut hair and sweet-smelling skin to his hand-made shoes. He was also a hood, a small-time Mafia man earning money from the numbers and a few other lucrative ventures. He was the great-nephew of Tommy Corolla, a big mob man who had his own family. At twenty-five Skip felt he wasn't getting the action he deserved so he was making a little action of his own on the side.

That was where Evander Dorsey came in.

He had been very drunk one night, working in a seedy bar, his gnarled hands playing him up. During his break someone had put a record on the juke box. It was one of Kerry's. He had sat back on the stool listening to her voice, looking down at the deformed fingers of his hands, when a guy beside him had asked him what he was thinking about. The guy was Delroy Burton, a black spiv who owned the club Evander was playing in. For some reason he had felt a great rage against Kerry, because she was big, a big star, famous, while he, Evander, was left broken down, working in dives because of her. He had told Delroy the whole story, having more and more drinks bought for him. The next night Delroy had been waiting for him, buying him drinks and getting names, dates, places, anything about his time in England. Then he had ignored him and Evander had just been sorry that the free drinks were not coming any more and forgot about Delroy.

Then one night a few months later Delroy had come to his house. Evander lived alone since the terrible 'accident' to his hands. Hands that were numb a lot of the time where they had been hastily set in Liverpool by a little black woman called Rula Demoinge. Hands that could still play music to a degree, but had lost the suppleness and eagerness of before. Hands that were getting weaker and more gnarled as the years wore on. Delroy had come to the little shanty where he lived with two white men. Italians. The men had been introduced and one had produced a couple of bottles of Wild Turkey and a hundred dollars. All they wanted was to hear the story of Kerry Cavanagh. Evander, eyes wide at the sight of the money and the booze, had welcomed them in with open arms and told them everything, embellishing the story as drunkenness descended. Later that night they'd left him, a hundred dollars richer and drunk enough to sleep.

He hadn't seen them for six months when they once more turned up, minus Delroy, and with the intention of 'helping him out'. They had taken him from Alabama back to New York, bought him new clothes, cleaned him up, watched his drinking, and now here he was, back in London, living in a nice place in Notting Hill Gate. Evander was to be the instrument of blackmailing Kerry Cavanagh. In return he would get back some money and self-respect, both the things that had been denied him when Kevin Carter and his henchmen had stamped their booted feet on his hands. It was a sweet revenge, a just revenge on the woman who had brought him this low.

But the child had thrown him, he had to admit that. He hadn't known about no child. A good-looking girl, more like an octoroon, like the whores in New Orleans. But she was his child all right. Looked like his sister Eulalie who'd had the same whitey look about her. His mama said she was the product of a sugar farmer, poor white trash. Well, Kerry wasn't poor white trash, Kerry was loaded, and he was going to see, with the help of Skip Paquale and his boys, that a few thousand dollars came his way. It was just and fitting, it was right.

Might even get enough to buy his own place. He wouldn't be playing the piano for much longer, the rheumatism had set in and his hands were getting to be less than useless.

He sat back in the chair contemplating his good fortune in meeting Delroy and Skip. Or 'Mr Skip' as he had to call him. Mr Skip to an Eyetalian! He smiled to himself at the thought. They were no better than him, they were just immigrants. His forefather had been in the States a mighty long time, longer than Paquale and his so-called family.

He knew the drink was making him aggressive and closed his eyes, once more seeing the creamy limbs of Kerry Cavanagh. She had been one hell of a loving woman.

She had also been his downfall, and he was looking forward to paying her back.

Skip looked at the big, bloated man sitting opposite him and hid his disgust.

'We move in tomorrow. You stop your drinking now, you hear?'

Evander opened one yellowing bloodshot eye and nodded. So tomorrow was the big day?

Big deal.

He drank the last of his whisky and, getting up unsteadily, made his way to bed.

Liselle woke up and looked out of her window. It was early December and in the night it had snowed. The snow already lay thick and quiet everywhere. It was just after five-thirty. She had only dozed. In her mother's room she heard the radio playing. Liselle pulled on a dressing gown and went in to her. Kerry lay on her bed still in the crumpled green wrapper, a glass of orange juice in her hand. Liselle sighed. Taking the drink from her

485

mother she sipped it and raised her eyebrows.

Kerry laughed huskily.

'Ain't a drink to be found in the house. I take it you had a good hide up before you went to bed?'

Liselle had the grace to go red.

'It's snowing.'

Kerry laughed again.

'I know. I hate the snow meself. Always did. When we were kids, in the basements, snow could mean death. Honestly.' Her voice sobered. 'It was so cold in there anyway, damp and smelly. We woke up one morning and the whole inside of the room had a film of ice everywhere. Little babies froze to death that year. Little tiny babies. We used to have blue feet, navy blue feet, with big red sores on them.'

Liselle snapped at her, 'Stop it, Mum. For goodness' sakes!'

Kerry heaved a heavy sigh. 'I'm sorry, Lissy. It's just that I woke up thinking morbid thoughts. I have a feeling on me that something bad's going to happen. It's the snow, I think. I hate the solitude of snow. Even if you shout it somehow muffles your voice.'

Liselle shook her head.

'I think the trouble's already started.'

Kerry sat up in the bed and frowned. Liselle saw in the harsh light of day the veins beginning on her mother's cheeks from the drink. The deep hollows under her eyes that her make-up would make disappear, to leave her looking beautiful and young. Too young for this dark-haired girl to be her daughter. Yet unlike other mothers, Kerry always told people about her daughter and never, ever lied about her age.

'What do you mean, love?'

'Last night there was murders round Auntie Briony's with me gran.'

Kerry laughed then in relief.

'There's always murders where your gran's concerned! Give her a drink and you've got a loony on your hands.'

Kerry's dismissive tone annoyed Liselle and she said nastily, 'Yeah, well, last night she informed the whole world and his wife that I should have been aborted. That having an illegitimate child was bad enough, but one like me . . . That's what she said, Mum. Those were her exact words.'

Kerry scrambled up so she was kneeling. 'Did she say anything else, girl? Did you say anything about me? About you as a baby?'

'Did she mention my father, you mean? No. But if it's not too much trouble, I wouldn't mind knowing who he was. After all, he is my dad! My father. The man who made me, if you like.'

Kerry's face blanched a sickly white. Liselle tried again, calmer this time.

'I have a right to know, Mum. I'm nearly twenty-two and no one seems to tell me anything. I don't know his name, nothing about him. I wonder, you know. I always have.'

Kerry licked her lips and stared at the beautiful girl in front of her. The girl she loved but who was a permanent reminder of what she had done, what she had been too cowardly to do. How many times over the years had she wished she had got on a boat and gone to find him? As she had wanted to. But she was a coward. It was easier to rely on the strength of Briony, to stay with her family, than to trek thousands of miles to a man who might reject her, who might have told her the truth about their relationship. Who had been beaten over her. Who must hate her for her part in his eventual downfall. That's why she refused down and out to sing in the States, or even to go there. It was still an open wound.

Now here was her child, the result of her union with Evander Dorsey, asking her for the truth. Could she say to her: 'I spoke to him yesterday, he rang me up. Your father's near, only I feel inside he's here to harm us. Not here to be welcomed with open arms by his old lover and his daughter.' No, she couldn't ever tell her that.

Instead she said, 'Why don't you let me worry about things, love? Your father was a nice kind man who left us. He didn't want to but he had to. Now leave it at that, and go and make me a nice strong pot of coffee. There's a good girl.'

Kerry's voice brooked no argument, Liselle had heard that

tone many times over the years. Especially when she had asked about her father. Seething inside with anger, she flounced from the room, banging the door behind her. Kerry got up and lit herself a cigarette. Going to the window, she looked out at the white expanse of roofs and road. Blinking back tears, she smoked her cigarette in silence.

Out there somewhere was Evander Dorsey. It had been him yesterday, she would know that rich dark velvet voice anywhere. He was out there somewhere waiting for her and their child.

Boysie and Danny sat in Mrs Horlock's room with Cissy and Briony, listening to the story of Liselle's birth. They sat side by side on the bed, their sleek heads bowed as between them the three women told them the story from start to finish. When Briony got to the part about Kevin Carter's breaking Evander's fingers they both looked up and nodded, as if silently agreeing with his actions. It was the only time they moved. Mrs H watched them with shrewd rheumy eyes.

'That bloke went and we was all glad, it could only bring trouble to her, Kerry. She couldn't see that herself, not then. But then the child . . .'

Boysie shook his head.

'So Liselle is a half-chat then? Her dad was some soot piano player me Auntie Kerry was boffing . . .' He sounded disgusted. Somehow guessing something and finding out it was true were two completely different things.

Briony shook her head.

'Evander was a handsome man. If it had been today, who knows? Plenty of women have half-chats, as you call them, now. The Americans saw to that, son. But this was in the 1920s. It just wasn't done then. It just wasn't done.'

'But Auntie Kerry with a big soot!' Boysie's face was twisted with contempt.

Briony slapped his face, the crack resounding in the room. Danny stood up as if ready to fight her while Boysie rubbed at his smarting cheek.

Briony pointed at them and bellowed: 'That's my sister you're talking about. You wanted to know and we told you. Don't you get bloody lairy with me over the truth, I won't have it, you hear me? Liselle is your flesh and blood, boys. Why should anything change now? So her father was a soot. Big deal. He was a talented, handsome man as well.'

Danny stared at her and said quietly, 'If he was such a saint, why did you go to such lengths to get rid of him?'

'Because of this, the way you're acting. By Christ, I thought I'd brought you up a bit better than this. Your mother loved that little child when she was born. She doted on her. If you ain't inherited any care for people from me, I had hoped at least that my Eileen's tolerance would have rubbed off on you. You're like me mother. Everything has to be cut and dried. Well, the real world ain't like that. We never know where our heart's going to lie. You two have got to fall for someone yet, and believe me you don't know who it could be. It could be the biggest whore God ever put on this earth, but something could make you want her. That's real life, my loves.

'With my Kerry it was him. Black as night, handsome as the devil. He was like her, talented and beautiful. It was inevitable they'd fall in love. Only small-minded people like you two and me mother – and me, me as well – stopped them being together. Sometimes I look at her with the drink in her and it's like a knife twisting in me. I stopped her going to him, and the upshot's the fact that she's never known a happy day since. Not really. She kept Liselle and that's all power to her as far as I'm concerned.'

Boysie and Danny looked at Briony in shock.

'It's the thought of it, Mum . . . I mean, whoever's gonna want Liselle now?'

'Whoever gets Liselle will be a damned lucky fellow. That girl's worth fifty of others roundabout. Briony's right. Don't fall prey to small-mindedness, lads. It's a sin against God.'

Cissy's voice, normally good-humoured, was so vehement that the boys stared at her hard. Briony could have kissed her. It took good old Cissy, the funster, the woman the twins had always played pranks on and whom they loved in a haphazard, affectionate way, to put it all in perspective.

'She's still your cousin, who grew up with you, who you played with, who you always loved. She ain't changed because she has a bit of the tarbrush in her. It just makes her different to outsiders, that's all. Now, how about I make a nice pot of strong tea?'

Cissy made everything normal once more. Had taken the edge off the proceedings.

'I'll have a cup, me mouth feels like a buzzard's crutch.'

'Oh, Mrs H! You're disgusting.' Boysie's voice was overloud. Cissy left to make the tea, Briony sat on the bed and sighed.

'Don't let Liselle know about all this. Let me tell her when the time's right. Don't treat her any differently, will you? Don't hurt her more than she's been hurt, and she's gonna be hurt.'

Danny nodded.

'Don't worry, Mum, we'll look after her. And if any of this does ever get out, well then, people can bastard well answer to us!'

The phone rang while Liselle was in the shower. Kerry picked it up hesitantly.

'Hello?' It was a question.

'Hello, Kerry baby. It's me, Evander.'

She closed her eyes as the feelings enveloped her once more. It was as if the past was there in the room with her.

'Kerry? Answer me, girl. Aren't you pleased to hear from me? I've seen my daughter. I've seen you, too.'

Kerry's mouth was dry.

'What do you want, Evander? Tell me?'

'I jus' want to see you again, for old time's sake. I don't want no trouble, girl. I had enough of that the last time.'

Kerry nodded, as if he could see her. 'When . . . When do you want to see me?'

'How about this afternoon? I know you're working tonight.'

Kerry didn't question how he knew this. Instead she said: 'Where? What time?'

'I've rented a little house in Notting Hill Gate. It's number

490

sixteen Rillington Place. I'll expect you about two-thirty.'

Kerry nodded into the phone again, unable to speak properly.

Evander spoke once more, a worried tone in his voice. 'You are gonna come, girl? I'll be expecting you.'

'Yes . . . I'll be there.'

He laughed throatily. 'See you then.'

Kerry stared at the phone in terror. It was him. She had been right. And no matter how she tried to believe him when he said he was only here to see her for old time's sake, the frightened feeling inside her wouldn't go away.

Skip Paquale had sent his henchmen out for the rest of the day. Together he and Evander set up the front room of the little house ready for Kerry's visit. A tape recorder was hidden inside a box on the mahogany coffee table by the settee. They tested it three times before Skip was happy with it. Finally, placing a bottle of Wild Turkey and a bottle of vodka on the same table, with two glasses, he was satisfied.

'I'm warning you, Dorsey, don't get tanked up and ruin this or you'll be sorry. I want her right where I can really bleed her. You just reminisce with her, that's all, and find out about the girl. Get me?'

Evander nodded.

'That girl's a gold mine to us. A real gold mine. Without her we ain't gonna get a dime. Keep that in mind.'

Evander nodded again. In spite of everything, he had a sudden longing to see Kerry. Really see her. He found he was genuinely interested in the child. In his girl. Hearing Kerry's voice, after all this time, was something he had not been prepared for. He lit up one of his cheap cheroots and then his mind clouded again. Every time he looked at his hands it hurt him. Through Kerry he had lost his livelihood. His talent. He mustn't ever let himself forget that.

No one was worth the price he'd paid: years in dingy little dives, each day the crippling of his hands becoming more and more apparent. Each year the bitterness inside him growing. Until now. He was back in England once more, only this time he wasn't here to hit the big time and make a fortune. This time he was here to make blood money off the back of the woman who'd been like a Jonah to him from the day he had first laid eyes on her. She had had his child, his daughter, but that was nothing, he had to remember that. The child was his passport out of chocolate town and back into the real world where money cushioned everything. The colour of your skin, the roots you came from, even what friends you had.

With his own place he could be someone again. Evander Dorsey could once more hold his head up, could once more have a future.

Chapter Thirty-seven

Liselle heard her mother come into the house at seven-thirty. She heard footsteps heavy on the stairs and knew Kerry had been drinking. She carried out her mother's clothes for the evening. She was singing tonight at The New Yorker as she did once a week whenever she didn't have concert dates. Victor had been on the telephone twice that afternoon, demanding to know just where her mother was. She had been supposed to meet him to discuss her recording contract and some dates for a European tour. Victor was livid to be stood up, and for the first time ever Liselle felt like telling him to piss off. One day she would. One day, good little girl Liselle would tell them all to piss off, her mother included.

'Oh, baby, I've had a lovely day. Such a lovely day.'

Liselle smiled as her mother came in. It was a forced smile and she hated herself for it.

'Tonight, after the show, I have a big surprise for you.'

'Good. Now how about getting in the bath and then getting dressed? We're late as usual.'

Kerry's face dropped at her daughter's flat voice. It was because she'd been drinking. She shouldn't have drunk that vodka. But hadn't today been a celebration? Couldn't she have a celebratory drink?

She walked into the bedroom and began to run a bath, pulling off her clothes and dropping them on the floor. Well, she'd please her baby tonight. It had come to her in the taxi on her way home. Evander, her Evander, had wanted to see that she and

Liselle were all right. All her worrying about trouble to come was unnecessary. He had just wanted to see her again. And as they had talked she had seen a shadow of the younger Evander emerge. The man who had attracted her. Well, in the cab it had dawned on her. She would take her daughter to see him. It would please Liselle so once she had met him, spoken to him, heard the full story, and it would please Evander. He had been touched that she'd named her after his mother. He had told her that three times. Sitting there with him had been like going back to her youth. Their time together was short but fruitful. Her baby girl, the result. Now it had come to her how she could right the wrongs she'd done to Liselle and Evander. She had told him how she'd wanted to go to him, how she'd nearly booked the passage but how she'd chickened out. If only she had gone! If only she'd followed her star! Things might have been so different. He was the father of her child and tonight she would give them both a big present.

She'd give them each other, father and daughter.

Skip had played the tape back five times. Evander sat quietly, listening to the husky, unmistakable voice of Kerry baring her soul.

'You did good, Evander, better than good even. That bitch ain't gonna know what hit her. This should be good for two hundred thousand dollars at least. There ain't no way she'll want all this common knowledge, it'll ruin her overnight.'

Evander's mouth fell open at that statement.

'And ... Mr Skip, how much of that is mine?'

'How does twenty-five thousand grab you, black boy?'

Evander grinned. 'It grabs me OK.'

Greed was to the fore now. Listening to Kerry telling the world about their life together had been hard at first, he had felt like a snake in the grass, but the twenty-five Gs would soon put paid to that. He could buy a decent place for that. A decent place with decent acts and a good clientele. A good black clientele.

Skip's two henchmen let themselves in the house. Marty

Duval and Kelvin Tomcola were young and not too bright. Exactly what Skip wanted in his heavies.

'Let's all have a drink to celebrate our good fortune. In a couple of days we'll be on our way back home, out of this godforsaken snowhole, and richer than we dreamed. What a Christmas present! The best part of it all is, we can bleed that bitch for years and years.'

Evander frowned at the words.

Then a large glass of bourbon was placed in his hands and he drank the toast with his so-called friends. But the words stayed with him.

At just after eleven a knock came on the front door. Skip looked out of the window and was amazed to see Kerry Cavanagh and her daughter on the doorstep.

'Jesus Christ! It's the broad and the kid. They're on the doorstep!'

Pushing the two other men from the room, Skip told Evander to let them in and play the game again.

This was working out even better than he'd hoped. As he crept up the stairs to join the others he wished he had reset the tape recorder. This would have been better than ever.

Outside it was snowing again and Liselle looked at the shabby house and shivered.

'Mum, what are we doing here? What's this big surprise?'

Kerry, buoyed up with drink, pills and excitement, grinned, hugging her fur coat around her tighter.

'You'll soon see.'

Evander stood uncertainly behind the front door. This was not on the agenda, this was not supposed to happen. On the other side of that door was his child. If he met her, spoke to her, he would have to acknowledge her as such. Then he would have to cheat them both. Kerry was hard enough, but he figured she owed him. The child owed him nothing. He wished he hadn't had so much drink, or that he'd drunk more so he would be oblivious of all these feelings assailing him. Shame, guilt. And worst of all, much worse than the other two, longing. He was longing to see her now.

495

Kerry knocked again. From the landing came Skip's angry voice.

'Open the fucking door, black boy, what you waiting for? Christmas?'

The voice brought him back to earth and Evander opened the door. Kerry swept in, dragging the girl behind her, her red fox coat still glistening with flakes of snow. Her hair glossy and sleek on her head like a luxurious hat. He had to concentrate on Kerry because he was frightened to look at the girl with those deep brown eyes and that coffee-coloured skin.

Kerry, always the dramatist, held out Liselle's arm and said loudly: 'Baby, meet your father.'

Evander looked at his daughter then, full in the face. All he was aware of was the distaste he saw there, coupled with shock. Too late, he remembered he was in stockinged feet, his trousers unbuckled because they were tight, his shirt, clean on that afternoon, stained with drink and food. But it wasn't that that appalled her: it was the grey-tinged hands with their claw-like fingers.

Kerry looked at them both. Seeing Liselle's eyes riveted to Evander's distorted hands, she grasped her daughter by the shoulders and pushed her into the open doorway of the lounge. She closed the front door that was letting in a weak light from the street together with the freezing snow, and followed her daughter into the warmth.

'Yes, look at his hands. That was your Aunt Briony's work. Oh, she denied it, but she did that. Broke his fingers, every one of them, and his wrists, too. Smashed to smithereens in Briony's name. Now you know why I never told you. Was never going to tell you. Then he turned up here and I realised that you had to know. Especially after last night.'

Liselle still hadn't opened her mouth. She was staring in disgust at the man in front of her. He was fat, he was unkempt, this was not what girlish dreams were made of. This was not what she'd wanted. Deep inside herself she had known he was a black man, she admitted to herself she'd always known, but she had never really expected to have it thrust on her like this in a dingy little house in Notting Hill. It was laughable. That this man, with the huge belly and the clawed hands, could have been her reason for living! Nowhere in her wildest imaginings could she imagine him young and handsome and taking her mother, her beautiful mother, and giving her a child. Herself.

Evander looked at the girl with her silky blue-black hair and the high prominent cheekbones, her sensuous lips, and felt the enormity of what he'd done. What he had created. In the States she would have been aware of what she was from day one and would have adjusted accordingly. Brought up here, in this cold barren country, she wasn't remotely prepared for what life was going to dish out to her. Inside himself, he felt a cracking, breaking sensation. It was fear: fear of what she would think of him, fear of what was going to happen to this tall lithe creature who would draw men to her, who had such a beautiful, appealing exterior thanks to himself and his forefathers. Here in England she'd live in a no man's land, neither black nor white. Brought up white, she'd have no understanding of the black culture, of her people. Until she began to breed. Then she'd bear the legacy of her father and his father's father.

Kerry watched the two eyeing each other. Going to the table she poured out three stiff drinks. Handing one to Evander and one to Liselle, she sat on the settee, watching them warily now. It had not worked out as she had thought. It had all gone wrong. No one spoke a word for what seemed an eternity.

Kerry guzzled her drink, coughing at the unfamiliar taste of the raw cheap black market bourbon.

Evander stood silently with his drink in hand. He didn't want a drink now, when he should want one, when he should be gulping the precious liquid down to kill the pain inside him.

'Sit down, child. We need to talk.'

His voice was deep. Hearing it for the first time, Liselle was snapped out of her shock. Putting the drink on the mantelpiece untouched she strode past him, out of the room and out into the snow-filled night. Slamming the front door behind her she hurried away, slipping and sliding on the icy pavement.

497

That couldn't be her father. It couldn't. Not because he was black, but because he was so horrible. He was dirty-looking, he smelt of stale food and cheap scotch. She came from better than that, she knew she did.

She made her way back to The New Yorker in a cab. Auntie Briony would know what to do.

She always did.

The twins were in one of their 'spielers', an illegal gambling club in Stepney. The place was packed out as usual. The twins were now treated like visiting royalty wherever they went in the East End. People went out of their way to be noticed by them. If they went into a shop, the cigarettes or whatever else they bought became 'gifts'. Stallholders made a fuss of them, shopkeepers kept on the right side of them. The twins, Boysie especially, loved this. Revelled in it.

The 'spieler' was approached through a large barred door, a small peephole was opened to establish who was there, and then they were duly let in, frisked, and allowed to get to the gaming tables and the bar. Prostitutes worked the clubs, generally married women out for a bit of adventure and a few quid to supplement the housekeeping. Nothing was organised in the twins' establishments unless they organised it themselves.

The place was buzzing tonight. The twins got themselves a drink and went through to the offices. They were waiting for a young Jew named Isaiah Lipman. He was twenty-five years old and one of the best 'longshoremen' in the business. The twins wanted to cultivate him.

The Jewish community and the Irish were similar in a lot of respects. They were immigrants, they were disliked by the majority, and Jewish men seemed much like the Irish in the fact that they either succeeded beyond imagination or they were wasters. Both cultures, though, had an inbred cunning. The Lane, or Petticoat Lane as it was better known, traded on a Sunday because of the Jews. Like the Irish they kept to their religion no matter what else they might do. And it paid off for them.

Longshoring was the term used for a particular scam. It involved renting cheap premises, getting headed notepaper printed up and then opening accounts with suppliers. For the first couple of months, while the business was supposedly getting on its feet, you paid for your goods as invoiced, with cash off the hip. Ready money. Gradually building up your credibility as a customer. Then one day you ordered fantastic amounts from your suppliers on credit, as usual. Then you disappeared off the face of the earth with up to one hundred thousand pounds' worth of stock. Usually electrical appliances or good clothes. Anything that could easily be sold on. This stock then found its way on to the markets, into shops and anywhere else it could be sold.

It was a very easy operation, it was patience that was needed. That was where Isaiah came in. Danny and Boysie wanted everything yesterday.

Boysie sipped his drink. 'That was a turn up, what The Aunt told us about Liselle. I guessed though. We both did. But hearing it like, that's a different thing.'

Daniel looked at himself in the mirror on the wall behind their desk. He patted down his hair and, licking a finger, smoothed one of his eyebrows.

'Yeah . . . We'll have to watch the rhyming slang now, Boysie. Lemonade, spade. Macaroon, coon. Whistle me dog, wog. Sounds different when it's one of your family, don't it? If someone called Liselle that, I'd break their fucking necks. I'd rip their heads off with me bare hands. Yet I use those terms all the time.'

'That's because we ain't never known many blacks. I always liked Bessie, even as a kid. I liked that flowery smell of her when I was little . . . We'll have to stop saying front wheel skid and Yid, as well as a four be two, once old Isaiah becomes a part of the firm. Fuck me, we're going international, ain't we?'

Danny laughed. 'Yeah. I'm looking forward to meeting this bloke properly, though. He ain't a hardman, but he's got brains. Brains we can use to our advantage. Once we get him under our wing, we'll leave him to work on his own. He won't tuck us up.'

Boysie laughed as he left the room. 'He wouldn't dare, Danny Boy.'

Briony listened to Liselle's story with amazement tinged with annoyance. Only Kerry would pull a stunt like that! Anyone else would have done it gently, prepared the ground. But anyone else wouldn't have been under the influence of vodka and barbiturates. The way she felt now, if she saw Kerry she would be hard pressed not to slap her a ringing blow across the earhole.

'All right, love, calm down.'

'But you don't understand me! It wasn't that he was black. I knew that, I've always known that, though I couldn't admit it to myself. Now I know it's true, I don't care. It's him, the man himself. I can't believe he's my father. He smelt, Auntie Briony, of stale fags, booze and food. He was gross. He was so . . . so . . . tatty-looking. That's what hurt me, that I could have sprung from him. And his hands . . . his hands were horrible. Then Mum said *you* had had that done to him. You got someone to break his fingers. But you wouldn't do anything like that, would you?' It was a plea.

Briony sat down in her chair and sighed. Outside the office was the sound of Bessie singing, the clinking of glasses, the buzz of conversation. If only they were out there instead of in here, trying to make sense of something that happened over twenty years ago. Something that should have stayed buried.

'Listen, my love. Your father was a big handsome man when he knew your mother. Really, he was like a big black Adonis if that's possible!' She smiled to take the edge off the words. 'He was talented, really talented. Together they could have conquered the world. When I got rid of him, and I did get rid of him, make no mistake about that, it was because twenty years ago . . .' Briony swallowed hard. 'Well, you have to realise, it was in the twenties. Mixed marriages were unheard of then. It wasn't like now when lots of girls marry their black GIs. It's a different world now, love. Then it would have ruined your mother and him. A black man seen with a white woman could cause murder to be done.'

Liselle sniffed, wiping her nose with the back of her hand. 'Your father looks like he does now because I sent someone to force him to leave. Well, the bloke, Kevin Carter, went too far. He broke his hands. I never asked him to, I take oath on that, Lissy. But I suppose that having his hands destroyed stopped Evander earning his living, doing what he did so well. He was a brilliant jazz pianist once, believe me, and I truly regret my part in putting an end to his career.'

Liselle nodded, trying to take in what her aunt was saying, trying to decipher her true feelings from amongst the sadness and shock that was enveloping her. Her aunt made it all sound so nice, so romantic. Her mother wanted the brilliant black man who could play the piano. Now, all these years later, Liselle was to be saddled with a man who'd been crippled because her aunt thought that getting rid of him was the best thing at the time.

'Shall I take you home?'

Liselle shook her head. 'Can I stay with you, please? I don't want to see me mum. Not for a while.'

Briony smiled and put her arm around the girl's slim shoulders. 'You can stay as long as you like, my darlin'. You know that.'

The twins had arrived at the club just after one-thirty. Briony had sent Liselle home with Tommy to look after her. She herself was determined to find Kerry. She was not at home, Briony had been ringing in ten-minute intervals, so they made their way to Rillington Place.

The twins had listened to Briony's explanation of the night's events in silence. Boysie shook his head in disbelief. His Aunt Kerry was a fruitcake. Poor old Liselle! They knew that their own mother hadn't been all the ticket, and now by all accounts Aunt Kerry was tipping herself over the edge. Well, they were finally going to meet the soot who had caused all this hag. They hoped for his sake he wasn't here to try and cause trouble.

Briony had voiced the opinion that it seemed funny, on reflection, for a man to turn up all these years later and rent a house. A tourist went to a hotel. Suddenly, it seemed very suspicious. Getting in touch with Kerry whose number wasn't listed . . . Who did he get it from? Who else knew he was here?

'Don't worry, Mum. If necessary we'll blast off every front door in the road but we'll find the right house. Stop letting it bug you.'

Boysie caressed a Beretta he kept with him at all times. Daniel smiled as he drove. In the boot was a shotgun that could kill a marauding elephant at a hundred paces. They'd find out the score all right.

In fact, he was quite looking forward to it.

After Liselle had left the house, Kerry got up to follow her. Then three men walked into the room. Kerry, in her usual drunken state, barely noticed. But when one man, whom Evander addressed as Mr Skip, pushed her back into her seat, it dawned on her that here was big trouble.

She looked at Evander with frightened eyes. 'What's going on here? Who are this lot?'

Skip laughed out loud.

'We are your biggest nightmare. Pour the lady a drink, Marty.'

Marty did as he was bidden and Kerry took it gratefully. But as Skip explained to her what they wanted, she gradually began to feel a numb fear.

Evander listened to Skip's gloating voice, wishing himself anywhere in the world but in this dirty little room. As he watched Kerry's eyes widen with fear and the realisation of what was happening, he felt sick inside himself.

Twenty-five thousand dollars was a lot of money. But was it really worth all this? When did this get so out of hand? When did it become so dirty, and so shaming?

As Skip had played back the tape Kerry's mouth had opened and shut, like a fish out of water, gasping for life. Now she knew why he had asked her three times why she had named her child Liselle for his mother. Why he had repeatedly asked her about their life together. It was for this. Even in her drunken, drugged state she saw what a fool she'd been. She'd wanted to right wrongs when the biggest wrong was being done to her!

She started to laugh, a low chuckle at first. Then, as all became crystal clear, it turned into a full-throated belly laugh. Four pairs of eyes watched her in amazement.

'You can give this to anyone you like. The newspapers, anyone. I couldn't give a monkey's fuck!' Her voice was shrill. 'I ain't ashamed any more. I don't care. My baby knows now. She knows. Once she knew about this, it was blown wide open. You did all this for nothing . . . nothing!'

Skip gave her a stinging blow across the mouth. But still she laughed.

'Go on, beat me up! Nothing you can do to me can really hurt me, because I've been hurting all my life.'

But the laughter was gone from her voice now.

Skip, seeing his well-laid plans go awry, took her at her word. He began to lay into her with heavy fists. Evander stumbled across the room, his useless hands clawing at the man attacking Kerry. The two younger men watched with morbid fascination. Evander turned to them.

'You fools! She's famous . . . If you really hurt her, you'll all be finished.'

His voice persuaded the other two. They began pulling Skip off her, dragging him from the room as he hurled abuse at Kerry, at them and at Evander. They pulled him into the kitchen and tried to calm him down.

Evander went to Kerry. Her mouth and one eye were bleeding profusely. Her arms were crossed defensively. Pulling her into his arms, he held her close, sorry to the core for what he had brought on her.

An hour later he saw the headlights of a car coming up the road. The curtains were back. He had opened the window to let in some air. Skip, calmer now, was still in the kitchen, trying to salvage part of his plan. Marty sat in the room with them, refusing to let either Kerry or Evander leave.

Kerry's face was swollen, her lip split, one eye black and blue. Evander was still holding her to him tightly. The shock of what had happened had counteracted the vodka and even the pills. Kerry was aware that they were both in great danger. Skip came into the room, calmer now.

'Listen to me, lady. I am gonna sell those tapes to the newspapers and whether you care or not, your career will be destroyed. Everyone will know what your daughter is and what you are. I have ten black men who will sign confessions saying they've slept with you. Had disgusting, perverted sexual relationships with you. Your name will be dirt, synonymous with every kind of filth, when I've finished. Unless you pay me what I want. Do you understand what I'm telling you?'

Kerry nodded painfully. 'How much?'

'Three hundred thousand pounds. I've upped the ante because I don't like mouthy broads, especially mouthy broads who sleep with niggers.' His voice was so vehement even Evander was shocked.

'I don't have that kind of money.'

It was Skip's turn to laugh now. 'Then my advice to you, little lady, is to find someone who does.'

The car Evander had heard was the twins' Aston Martin.

As they parked in the narrow road and got out, they saw into the room of number sixteen. It was the only house still lit up.

'Wait here and keep down,' Danny ordered.

Creeping into the small front garden he looked in at the window of the lounge. The net curtains were about two inches too short for the window and he saw Kerry sitting on the settee opposite him, her face bloody. Beside her was the black man, Evander Dorsey; he was holding her hands in his. The three white men were sitting around the room watching them; one had a gun beside within easy reach of his hand. Daniel found his eyes riveted to his aunt and the man beside her. He glanced once more at the gun and went back to Boysie and Briony.

'They're in there all right, with three other men. One has a gun. Aunt Kerry's face is a mess, someone's roughed her up.'

'What?' Briony's voice was incredulous.

'That's the truth, the coon's sitting on the settee with Aunt

Kerry. Something is happening here, Mum, and I don't know what. But me and Boysie will find out in about one minute.' He motioned to Boysie with his head. 'Come on, round the back. You sit in the car and wait. We'll open the front door when everything's sorted.'

Briony bridled.

'Excuse me, Danny . . .'

'Mum, please do as we ask – there's a shooter in there. Danny and me will sort it. Now sit in the car and wait.'

He took the Beretta from his coat and checked to see it was loaded.

Briony snatched the gun from him.

'Listen to me, you two will do as I say for once. I mean it. Get around the back. I'm going in the front. I'll sort out the geek with the gun once I'm in there.'

Boysie shook his head.

'Oh, leave it out, Mum . . .'

'No! You leave it out. That's my sister in there, and something's not kosher. Don't let's argue amongst ourselves out here. They'll let me in. I'll pretend I've come because of Liselle, because she's so upset. You two come in in five minutes, right? I don't want to hear any more about it.'

With that she walked away from them and up the pathway towards the front door. She turned and motioned to them to go around the back. As they disappeared down the alleyway that separated the house from the one next-door, she put her own Beretta into the pocket of her fox fur coat and knocked loudly on the door. Inside, everyone stood stock still as the hammering on the door reverberated through the house.

Skip slid off the table and picked up the gun.

'Stay here, I'll deal with this.' Pushing the gun into the waistband of his trousers and covering it with his jacket, he went out into the cold hallway. He opened the door to a tiny redhead and breathed a sigh of relief.

'Is my sister still here? My niece came home in a terrible state. Is Kerry here . . .' Briony walked into the house without a by your leave, pushing past the man to walk into the lounge.

Kerry's face and Evander's frightened eyes told her everything.

Turning to the man who had answered the door, she said in a shocked voice: 'What the hell is going on here?'

The man walked towards her, smiling nastily. As he opened his mouth to speak, Briony moved so fast he didn't have time to think. Nobody did. In a split second she was behind him with the Beretta digging into his kidneys.

'One move, big boy, and I'll splatter your guts all over this house!' She looked at the two other hoods, still sitting in the fireside chairs. 'Take out any weapons you've got and place them on the floor in front of you.' Skip started to put his arms down and Briony pushed the gun into his back once more.

'Don't even think about it! I'll just take you with me, boy. I'll take your gun myself, thank you.'

As she spoke Daniel and Boysie walked into the room. The sight of sawn-off shotguns gave all three prisoners a sinking feeling in their guts.

Boysie and Daniel, smiling now, were looking the three Americans over.

'Imagine leaving your back door open.'

'Especially in an area like this. It's a wonder you weren't burgled. Now I think we need a few explanations, and you three are going to provide them.' Danny's voice was soft as silk.

As Skip looked at the two young men and the tiny redhead he knew he would never see the outside of this room. Shaking his head in amazement, he resigned himself to that.

One thing Skip had always had in his favour: he knew when he was beaten.

Chapter Thirty-eight

Briony listened with barely controlled emotion as Evander told the whole story. His voice was low, honest and without guile. He did not attempt to underplay his own role or justify himself, which did him some good with Briony and the twins. The East End had a saying: 'If you get a capture, hold your hand up.' When he said that Skip was related to Tommy Corolla, a Mafia don, the twins laughed out loud.

Boysie, always quick to joke, said to Skip, 'I couldn't give a fuck who your godfather was, mate, my godfather's bleeding Jonathan la Billière. You're dead as a frigging doornail, not because of what you done, but because of who you done it to. You so-called Mafia prats should find out just who you're dealing with before you start your little games over here.'

To prove his point he punched Skip in the head three times, knocking him to the ground. Boysie was losing that famous temper of his. Briony watched calmly.

'Leave it for a while, Boysie love. Let Evander finish.'

'He's a ponce, they're all ponces, that black bastard included!'

Kerry was crying softly. 'Look, leave it, please, I just want to go home now!'

Briony patted her arm and said loudly, 'What you want, Kerry, is a drink. Well, this is one time when you'll have to wait. We have to sort this thing out tonight, once and for all.'

Looking at Evander, she said, 'I take it you're sorry now, for all this?'

Evander looked at the ground. He nodded.

Briony stared at him. He was like a caricature of the man she'd known. Every time she saw his hands, she felt a flush of shame.

Making a decision, she stood up. 'Is there a phone here?'

Evander pointed to the hallway. 'Out there.'

'I'll phone up Tommy. He can take me, Kerry and Evander back to my place. You two can do what you like with these. They're pieces of shite and I don't care what happens to them.'

Going to Skip, she lifted his face towards her with one perfectly manicured finger. Looking into his eyes, she said, 'You made your big mistake when you touched my sister. No one, I don't care who they're related to, ever touches me or mine.'

Walking outside to the hall to telephone Tommy, it occurred to her that phoning him this way was just like old times.

It seemed the past was always there like a spectre, waiting to rise up and catch you unawares when you least expected it.

In the end Tommy had stayed to help dispose of the three Americans under fifty tons of concrete that was due to be poured into the footings of the new Ford plant at Dagenham. Briony drove back to her house with a frightened Evander, his few belongings, and a shocked and subdued Kerry. When they got to Briony's house, Liselle had already gone up to bed and Briony was secretly grateful for this. It was four-thirty in the morning. The three new arrivals were wide awake, and quiet. Too quiet.

Kerry helped herself to a large neat vodka and Briony poured herself and Evander large brandies. She surveyed the man in front of her for a good while.

Evander looked like a beaten man, but Briony guessed he had looked like that for a long time. It was in his eyes, his stance, in those clawed and deformed hands that had trouble holding on to the balloon-shaped glass.

Finishing her drink silently, Briony took Kerry and tucked

her up in bed. She had no fears about Evander running off, he would be easy enough to find. Kevin's overenthusiasm all those years ago would guarantee that.

She checked Kerry's face over and, satisfied it was just cuts and bruises, went back down to the room where she had left Evander. Pouring them both another drink, his in a tall tumbler this time, she sat opposite him and spoke.

'You realise those men are dead, don't you?'

Her matter-of-fact voice frightened Evander. She had changed, this Briony. He remembered her as softer, younger admittedly, but softer inside.

He nodded in answer to her question and Briony sighed loudly.

'In a way, I can see your point of view. I know you must have found it very hard over the years. I also realise that the offer of a large sum of money in your circumstances was very tempting. I did something bad once, a long time ago, and was paid a large amount of money. Once you get a stake, you can make it grow.'

'I wanted a little club of my own. Before it was too late.'

Briony nodded, as if understanding him, agreeing with him. 'But the reason you're here, Evander, is because my niece Liselle knows you exist, Liselle knows about you. No other reason. You understand me?'

He licked dry lips and nodded furiously.

'I will provide you with money, a car and decent clothes. Also a place to live. You, for your part, will make friends with your daughter, or at least try to. I want her to see you as you once were. If everything works out well, I'll give you enough to open a club. So my advice to you is, think long and hard about what I just said. The ball is in your court. I want my niece to have a few good memories to take her through her life. You will be one of them.'

To herself she thought, God knows she'll need them after these last few days.

It was the week before Christmas and the snow was piled high. It was a windowsill winter, as the wags said on the market stalls.

509

The snow cleaned up London while it lay thick, and even the bomb sites looked picturesque.

Evander was now on relatively good terms with his daughter and Kerry was relieved that the trouble was over at last.

Briony, for her part, had pushed it all from her mind, concentrating on getting Evander and Liselle at least partly reconciled. She knew that they had talked a couple of times well into the night and this pleased her immensely.

If Liselle could get some idea of her background it would make her situation easier to bear. There was a marked change in her. She seemed quieter, more controlled. Her easy laugh had disappeared and Briony mourned for the innocent girl that was gone much as she loved the woman who was emerging. Molly was still getting what she termed the 'bum's rush' from everyone, and Briony hoped this taught her a lesson. Even poor old Rosalee was overlooked in the effort to make their mother pay for what she had done.

Evander seemed to have come into his own once he had money in his pocket and at least the appearance of independence. Bessie had whooped with delight at seeing him which pleased Liselle who didn't know Briony had arranged it. Bessie made Evander out to be the best thing since sliced bread and he sat back and accepted the accolade, unaware that Briony had talked Bessie through it.

Kerry, after the trauma, was drinking more than ever and unable to function at work. Briony had had to put the hard word on Victor through the twins, and unknown to Kerry herself, she was going into the clinic in Surrey after Christmas. Satisfied she had done all she could for her family, Briony concentrated on Tommy and Mariah and the businesses. But there were two further shocks awaiting her towards Christmas 1947 and the first happened while she was out shopping.

Coming out of Fortnum and Mason into a thick blizzard, Briony stood under the canopy waiting for Boysie and the car. As she turned round she came face to face with Isabel Dumas and Benedict: a grown-up Benedict carrying a young boy in his arms. Briony knew immediately this was her grandson and the rush of blood to her head made her feel faint.

Seeing his mother's face, Benedict frowned. Then, looking at Briony fully, he wondered where he had seen her before. She looked familiar. Very familiar. He smiled at her hesitantly. Briony looked into the face so like her own and smiled back, her heart thumping in her breast like the band of the Coldstream Guards. The boy in Benedict's arms had the green eyes and red hair of his grandmother, though today Briony's hair was hidden under a large hat.

'Hello, Isabel.' Briony spoke carefully, pronouncing her words properly.

'Why, Briony. How are you?' Isabel's voice was strained and Benedict looked from one to the other in consternation.

'I don't think we've been introduced?' His voice, soft and musical, was like a dream to Briony.

'This is Miss Briony Cavanagh. Miss Cavanagh, *my* son, Benedict Dumas.'

Briony nodded to him.

'And this little scallywag is my son, Henry. Henry Dumas.'

Briony put up a gloved hand and stroked the plump cheek lightly.

The child had a toy gun. He pointed it at her and said, 'Bang!'

Briony smiled widely. The child was exquisite. Was beautiful. Was her grandchild. She felt like blurting out the truth there and then. But Isabel, seeing her expression, shook her hand quickly and hustled the others off, away from her. She watched them disappear into the snow-filled street, her heart breaking. She had seen her boy, her son, and her grandson.

She could see the twins in that child, the same shape of head, the same build. She smiled bitterly. He even had a gun.

Boysie drove up with the car and was shocked to see she had been crying.

Benedict waited until they were home before he spoke.

'Who was that Miss Cavanagh we met? I feel I know her somehow.'

511

His father choked on his cup of tea and Benedict slapped his back hard.

Isabel shook her head and said dismissively, 'Oh, she's a madam to be honest. Did a lot of charity work in the war. Couldn't ignore her after that. But she really isn't to be encouraged.'

Benedict nodded. But there was something else about the woman, something so familiar it preyed on his mind for the rest of the day.

The next shock for Briony that year was even more serious.

Molly was beside herself with annoyance, continually telling poor Rosalee exactly what she thought of Briony and her gang, as she referred to her daughters and grandchildren. Mother Jones was bad again, and Molly's time was taken up with looking after her. Unlike previous illnesses, this one was serious enough to have the doctor visit daily without being asked. Mother Jones had picked up a 'flu virus and it was really knocking her out. Molly was single-handedly taking care of the old woman who was now bedridden and incontinent of both bladder and bowels. Consequently, Molly was very busy and for this reason didn't notice Rosalee's unusual quietness. When she finally did, she was grateful for it. But Rosalee was ill herself. Unable to tell anyone exactly what was wrong with her, she just sat passively, feeling worse by the day.

'What are we doing about Gran? Is she coming here for Christmas?' Boysie, always the first to calm down after an argument, wanted to see her now, and his Auntie Rosalee for whom he had bought a beautiful brooch as a Christmas present.

Kerry shrugged. 'To be honest, Boysie, I thought she'd have been in touch by now. I sent Mother Jones a basket of fruit. Abel's really worried about her. I expected me mother on the doorstep before now, moaning about looking after her.'

Briony bit her lip thinking about this for a second. 'Tell you what, how about me and you pop round and see the old girl tonight? That way me mother can either act as if nothing's happened, or she can start her antics. Either way we gave her a chance. But I ain't begging her. No way. This last turn out was all her fault, and if she does come for Christmas she ain't drinking. Kerry's bad enough.'

Boysie laughed. 'Fair enough. Danny should be in soon, we'll all go.'

Briony looked at the big man in front of her and grinned. 'You're missing your old gran, ain't you? Big as you are.'

He smiled good-naturedly. 'She's a pain in the arse at times, but she ain't really a bad old stick. It's Christmas Eve tomorrow. We'll go tonight and see how the land lies. I want to see Auntie Rosalee anyway.'

Briony smiled again. The twins loved poor old Rosalee. Other children might have been ashamed of her, but not them. They doted on her.

They were all missing Rosalee in their own ways, herself included. It was a sad fact that her mother and Rosalee went hand in hand. In fact it was one of her mother's saving graces, the way she looked after her. Yes, they would have to go. For Rosalee's sake, if for no other reason.

Bernadette watched her husband closely.

'Why the change of clothes at lunchtime, Marcus? That shirt was clean on this morning.'

He turned from the elaborate mirror on their dressing table and chucked her under the chin.

'I've got to see an important client today. As you know, Briony has expanded her clientele and now I have to deal with some very important people. I have to look respectable.' His voice had the evasive quality she hated.

'You looked respectable this morning, Marcus.'

He rolled his eyes and sighed loudly. 'Look, Bern, I am getting a bit sick of all this questioning. I'm only changing my shirt, not having a bath to meet a fancy woman. Now will you just leave it?'

Bernadette bit back the retort that was on her lips and kept her peace. Fifteen minutes later he left the house without kissing her goodbye. That was her punishment for questioning him. Walking into her daughter's bedroom she absentmindedly smoothed the quilt on a bed and straightened up already perfectly straight pictures. The girls were too old to take up all her time now, she admitted that fact to herself. Which was why she had too much time to think. Think about Marcus, and his increasing handsomeness.

Why was it a man could father fifteen children, a hundred children, and still look untouched? Whereas a woman like herself paid the price for her children's birth in every stretch mark, in the sagging of her stomach muscles, in the spreading of waist and hips. Going into her own bedroom she picked up the shirt her husband had discarded and held it to her nose, breathing in the smell of him. His soap, his sweat, and, thank God, for once no smell of perfume. Cheap perfume. That smell had been there a lot lately.

She had known for many years that Marcus was a philanderer. He liked women and was in a job where he was surrounded by them. Beautiful women. Until now it had only bothered her periodically, knowing that as the mother of his children she held the upper hand. That was until about six months ago when she had first noticed the distinctive smell of cheap perfume. The same smell had lingered on a lot of his shirts since then. A cloying, orangey fragrance, a whore's smell. Only this whore was still in attendance six months later and that worried her.

One night stands she could cope with, they were more or less an occupational hazard with Marcus's job. But a permanent woman was a different kettle of fish. That meant commitment of some sort, it meant he was having regular conversations with her, maybe about Bernie herself and the children. It meant that Marcus was enamoured enough to see the same girl again and again. Maybe fancy himself in love with her. It meant a threat to Bernadette, her children, and their idyllic homelife.

It meant big trouble.

She put the shirt into the washing basket and sat on the bed.

514

The house was exceptionally quiet. The girls were both round at friends' houses, her cook and cleaner had the day off. Alone and troubled, she sat on the bed observing herself in the large gilt mirror opposite, finding herself sadly lacking in any attractions that might snare a wandering husband. The tears came then. Seeing her face in the mirror, screwed up with misery, only made her feel worse.

But the Cavanaghs were fighters. All the Cavanagh women were, and by Christ she had more to fight for than most.

She wiped her eyes, dragging at the lids with her fingers, enjoying the pain she caused herself.

She would fight all right.

Molly was cooking a small capon, braising it in a thick gravy so Mother Jones could just suck at it, when she heard the car pull up outside the house. She smiled to herself. So the buggers had come at last. She'd resigned herself to waiting out Christmas and maybe New Year until she saw her family. She put in a small shake of salt and tasted the bubbling gravy before she deigned to answer the knock on her front door.

Rosalee, sitting by the fire, saw her nephews and made a snorting noise with delight. Boysie and Daniel, striding past their granny, went straight to her, talking loudly as they always did, even though she wasn't in the least deaf, and making a big fuss of her.

'Hello, Auntie Rosalee, how are you, darlin'?'

Briony stepped in at the front door and nodded at her mother. 'Mum.'

Then walking to Rosalee she too made a fuss of her. Only unlike the boys she stared at her sister for a long while first.

Molly pursed her lips and went back to her cooking. Well, she mused, at least they came, even if it was just to see Rosalee.

'That smells handsome, Gran.' Boysie as always was the first to make a friendly overture.

Molly suppressed a grin and said sternly, 'Well, sit yourself down then! There's plenty to go round.'

Daniel and Boysie sat at the scrubbed table and Briony sat

515

with her sister on the fireside chairs. She lit herself a cigarette.

'How's Mother Jones?' Her voice was neutral.

Molly shook her head and said truthfully, 'I'll be surprised if she lasts the Christmas, Bri. She's bad this time, God love her. The priest is coming tonight.'

'We'll go in after the boys have eaten.'

Molly nodded and the room was quiet once more. Finally she swallowed her pride and said, 'How's Liselle and Kerry?'

Briony pulled on her cigarette. If her mother asked that, she was admitting responsibility for what she had done. It was something they all knew but no one alluded to.

'They're fine, Mum. Great in fact. Liselle's father is over here actually, visiting her.'

Briony took great pleasure in seeing her mother's face whiten. The wooden spoon clattered to the floor.

'What did you just say?'

'I said, Evander Dorsey is over for a visit, from the States. Liselle is very pleased finally to know him, as a matter of fact.'

Briony berated herself inwardly for enjoying saying all this to her mother, but God himself knew, she'd asked for what she got.

'I wouldn't be surprised if she went over for a visit next year.'

Molly stooped down to pick up the spoon. Running it under the tap, she said, 'Jesus, Mary and Joseph! Would you credit that?'

Boysie and Daniel laughed, enjoying their gran's discomfiture.

'He's a nice bloke, Gran, me and Boysie really like him.' Daniel rubbed salt into the open wound with glee.

Molly, cute enough to know that the joke was on her, kept her peace. Now they were all here in front of her, she realised just how much she had missed them all, especially the twins. 'I'm glad the child has met her father. It must be a great load off her mind. How did she take it?'

Boysie laughed out loud then. His gran was not only eating humble pie, she was chewing it in big lumps and swallowing it without water.

'Oh, better than we expected, Gran. Much better.'

Molly nodded and began dishing out broth, cutting large lumps of soda bread, hot from the oven, for the twins. She placed the food in front of them and they attacked it with relish.

'Rosalee looks rough, Mum, has she been all right?' Briony's voice was low and concerned.

Molly flapped a large hand and shook her head. 'Oh, you know what she's like. She's been off her food a couple of weeks, that's all. It's all the upheaval with Mother Jones. You know how she hates change of any kind. And she's missed you lot.' The last was a barb aimed at them all, and it met its mark because all three felt ashamed.

Molly, satisfied she'd paid them all back for their earlier jokes at her expense, felt happier.

Rosalee guessed she was being talked about, and whimpered. Her fat cheeks were white and her eyes a flat grey. Briony took one pudgy hand in hers and squeezed it gently.

Well, we're here now. I thought you might like to come for Christmas, Mum, you and Rosalee?'

Her sister whimpered and took her hand from Briony's. Holding it to her side, she rocked herself in the chair.

'Is her hand hurting, Mum? Has she knocked it?'

Molly shrugged.

'Not that I know of, but come to think of it, she's been holding it like that for a while. I looked her over last week and I can't find anything wrong there. No broken bones anyway. I think it's the snow. She hates the cold. All she wants to do is sit in front of that fire and keep as warm as toast.'

Molly bent down to her daughter and smiled widely. 'Don't you, darlin'?'

Rosalee smiled and nodded, her face devoid of any real expression.

'We'll try and come for Christmas but with Mother Jones as she is . . . Well, I can't leave her, can I?'

'I suppose not.'

Molly put the kettle on for tea and said nonchalantly, 'Will that . . . Will Liselle's father be there for Christmas like?'

517

'Yes. He will. We're all having dinner at my place.'

Briony frowned to herself. She was treading a fine line at the moment with Evander and Liselle. The girl felt that her father's disfigurement was all Briony's fault, and in reality it was. But it was all a long time ago, and in her youthful ignorance Liselle couldn't understand different circumstances and different times.

'What's he really like then? This . . . Liselle's father?'

Daniel and Boysie looked at their gran and felt sorry for her. She couldn't even bring herself to say his name.

'He's all right. Ain't he, Danny? He loves Liselle, Gran. He really does. I think it's done her good meeting him. She seems more grown-up somehow. More sure of herself.'

Molly made the tea and kept her peace. A little while later she went into Mother Jones with a small bowl of broth and some soda bread. Briony and the twins joined her.

Rosalee sat by the fire, the pins and needles in her arms beginning to fade a little now. But the pain across her chest, as if a great weight was lying across it, was still there.

Kerry wasn't singing, in fact she wasn't really doing anything except drinking. The shock of what had happened to her had affected her more than she would admit. The cuts and bruises had faded. She had told Liselle she'd had a fall, and Liselle had upset her by not questioning that, assuming her mother was drunk. The injuries had gone but the reason for them was still fresh in her mind. Evander had been trying to blackmail her. He had taken her trust and abused it. She had been a fool. A complete and utter fool.

Now, seeing him and Liselle together was like a knife inside her gut. Twisting and turning for the maximum pain. And three men were dead, she was sure of that. The twins would have taken care of them. Kerry wondered what Eileen would have thought of the two boys she had entrusted to Briony. Eileen, the sister with a goodness of spirit lacking in the others. Eileen who was too kind for this world and its harsh realities. Eileen whom they all missed, each and every day. What would she have made

518

of her boys, her babies, taking people and making them disappear?

Briony didn't even care. She didn't care what they did as long as they were all right. As long as the family survived whatever was thrown at it.

Kerry couldn't admit to herself that she was jealous of Evander now, of his need for his child and her need for him. That Liselle was picking up his ways, his expressions. Was gradually blanking her out and welcoming her father in. Even though he had tried to destroy her, destroy them both.

Briony said she wasn't ever to tell Liselle the truth of the situation. That she should only know her father as a kind man, the man he had been twenty years ago, before he was embittered by years of hardship. What about *her* years of hardship, knowing that she had a child who was destined for sorrow? Knowing that she had to live with that fact. Knowing she hadn't been woman enough to follow her star when she should have, when it would have been right to follow it.

Each day the closeness developing between Evander and Liselle made her more aware of the distance widening between herself and her child. She found it hard to forgive Evander for what he had attempted to do. She found it harder to face the fact her child now had a foot in two different worlds.

Well, she consoled herself, he was leaving for the States in the New Year. Only a few more weeks and she could wave him goodbye and get back on to her old footing with her daughter.

But deep down inside she knew the footing would never return. Liselle and Kerry were worlds apart now, divided by skin colour, and by deep-seated prejudice. But she couldn't allow that thought to surface just yet. She wasn't drunk enough to forget it immediately afterwards. She wasn't drunk enough even to admit it.

Not yet.

Chapter Thirty-nine

'That tree looks a right picture, Bri, even if I say it meself.'

Briony smiled at Cissy's happy face.

'It's not half bad, is it? How's Mrs H? Do you think we'll get her down tomorrow for a bit of dinner?'

Cissy snorted through her large nose. 'She wouldn't miss Christmas with them lads for nothing. Though I must admit, Bri, I think this'll maybe be her last one.'

Briony sighed.

'What with Mother Jones going, and she's going hard by all accounts, and Mrs H catching up with her, we're gradually shrinking, aren't we?'

Cissy nodded.

'Well, the lads have yet to marry, and Liselle. Not to mention young Becky and Delia. We'll soon swell the numbers up again! When you get old you're not frightened of death. Well, not as frightened of it as you are when you're young. Put it this way, Mrs H has had a good innings. She's ready to meet her maker. She told me that herself.'

Briony knew Cissy was talking for effect. Over the years they had become very close, like mother and daughter. Closer in fact than most family. This fact touched Briony deeply. Cissy had been a workhouse child, Mrs Horlock was the only individual to give her a pleasant word. All Cissy had known until then was the back of someone's hand and their curses.

Briony placed the last few presents under the tree, smiling wryly at the present for Evander. It was indeed a lovely tree, and it was going to be a lovely Christmas. She would make sure of that personally. It was Liselle's twenty-second birthday.

Christmas Eve had always been a magical time to Briony. Even in the days when there was no guarantee there'd be even an orange in her stocking. It was the very feel of Christmas Briony loved. The fact of being part of something the whole world was involved with. Knowing that millions of children all over the world were experiencing the same feeling of anticipation as she was. That feeling had never left her, ever. Which was why she donated so much money each year to the welfare organisations. Boots for Children was all well and good, she always gave to that particular charity, but her favourite was the Catholic Church's annual Christmas present rout. Where every child, no matter what its religion, got a present, a few sweets and a piece of fruit. The thought of all those happy faces cheered her.

She had bought Rosalee a brightly coloured coat as she did every year. A thick warm wool coat that would please her immensely. She caressed the silver wrapping paper, looking forward to seeing Rosalee tear it to pieces.

It was going to be a good Christmas.

Evander was feeling closer to his daughter by the day. After a particularly difficult beginning they were finally getting to respect and trust each other. He knew she found it hard to look at his hands, and could understand that. He still found it hard to look at them himself. They were now next to useless. His piano playing was laboured and he found it painful. But he also found it extremely difficult to stop playing, which was the bug bear. The music was in him day and night. Hearing a beat or a few notes brought back his longing, and this made him either resentful of whoever was playing, or depressed because he knew he'd never play like that again.

He also found it hard to face Kerry. If only he could make it right with her, he would be happy. But Kerry was finding it hard to forgive him, and in the same circumstances he would have felt the same.

Liselle watched the changing expressions on her father's face.

Father. The word seemed strange to her, alien. Yet she knew it was the truth. This man with the deep brown voice and the claw-like hands had been the reason for her existence. It was so hard to visualise him as a young man, with handsome good looks, a way with women, and her mother's heart held firmly into his then perfect hands. Now she knew, it didn't really affect her any more.

She had known she was different since childhood, had guessed she was part-coloured. Admitting it had taken a burden from her. A great burden. Over the years she had been asked out numerous times. But she had always put the man off. Perhaps because deep inside she didn't want the heartache she knew the relationship might bring. Her only wish now was that she was a little darker so there could be no mistake about her parentage. This lightness, this illusion of whiteness she gave out, would always cause her the most trouble. With white people anyway. She knew now that Bessie and the band had always known about her, not just because of Evander but because they had known half-castes all their life. Only their half-castes in America were from black women and white men. Her mother, as usual, had done it the other way round.

This thought made her smile. She felt an enormous respect for her mother now because she had kept her child against the opposition of her own mother and family. Kerry, as weak as she could be, was strong enough to brave the world for her. For that alone, she deserved every ounce of respect Liselle had inside her and she would get it.

She had felt the estrangement between her mother and father and was sorry, desperately sorry, because she had seen her mother's happiness at bringing them together. But something had happened to change that, and Liselle would dearly love to know what it was.

She sipped her cold coffee and grimaced. Evander smiled at her. He looked at her all the time, and far from embarrassing her, she quite enjoyed it. It was the look of a man who really knew her for what she was.

'Why is my mother so against you now?' Her voice was low,

with the same huskiness as his. Evander thought hard. Should he tell her?

'I think I've a right to know.'

It could have been Kerry, all those years before. Wanting to be told about his family, his mother, his life.

'Listen, child. Your mother and I . . . Well, all I can say is I did something bad to her. Real bad. If I tell you, then you might look at me differently.'

'I need to know. My mother has been there for me all my life. I know she drinks, and she can be selfish at times, but I really need to know everything. Everything to do with the three of us. It's the only way I can ever really be myself.'

Evander nodded, seeing the logic of what she said. She was wise, this child of his. She had the same candour as her mother, and just a hint of his own mother, a woman who had brooked no nonsense from her big sons and even bigger, more aggressive, husband.

'It's a long story. It began when I got back to the States.'

He told her quietly and calmly about the life he'd had there, leaving out some of the least savoury parts but not ducking the truth either. He told it like it was. Until Liselle, in her imagination, could smell the dirt, feel the heat. Could feel the decline of this once proud man as he tried to pick himself up in a country where his colour was burden enough without being crippled. She could feel the stale enclosed atmosphere of each chocolate town he drifted to, his hands growing stiffer, his piano playing more laboured. His life descending on to a plane of poverty most English people only heard about. When he got to the part where he met Skip he faltered and Liselle poured him a glass of scotch, waiting patiently while he sipped it, gathering himself together.

All the time he spoke she was silent. She watched him, his hands moving unconsciously, face paling, growing grey and bleak. Body sagging in the big plush seat, he told her everything except the part where her twin cousins disposed of the Americans. He knew instinctively that was another part of the story he should keep from her. Like the parts where he played piano in cheap brothels to whores full of syphilis and cheap whisky. Some things were best left unsaid, even if they were the truth.

When he finished, Liselle stared at him for a short while. Her face held no hint of her thoughts at all. Her mind was like a closed book to him. Just as he wondered whether she was going to get up and walk out on him, away from him forever, she moved.

Kneeling in front of him she put up her sad, beautiful face. He saw what was inside her then, all the love and the need. She put her arms around his waist voluntarily, the first daughterly embrace. She put her forehead on to the rough broken hands he held in his lap and he felt the hot salty tears running over them. Awkwardly he gathered her to him, kissing the sweet-smelling hair, feeling his child for the first time, her delicate bones pulled against his heavy body.

Looking over her head as he held her, he felt his own tears then. For his daughter, for himself, and for Kerry. His beautiful Kerry who had taken everything he had to offer without a thought for herself or what her love could bring to her door. Yet he had brought her more trouble than she deserved. More trouble than she could ever have anticipated.

Yes, most of all he cried for his Kerry, the girl she had been, and the woman she had become. He had helped shape both, and he wasn't proud of what he had created.

It had all started in that dirty room in Stepney. It ended here in a plush hotel in Mayfair.

His child knew it all, and still she wanted him.

Bernadette watched as Marcus walked out of the house in Hyde Park with the blonde. The girl, and she was only a girl, nineteen at the most, was tall and willowy, with thick heavy hair, cut in a page boy style, and startlingly long slim legs. Even wrapped up in a fur coat, Bernie knew she'd have big breasts. Bernie watched from a taxi as Marcus unlocked the passenger door of his car and the blonde caressed his arm as she spoke to him. Bernadette bit on her lip, feeling the rage building up inside her.

So this was the competition, was it? Well, it was competition she could well do without. Miss Bathing Belle 1947 was even more beautiful than she had dreamed and a tiny part of her could see what her husband was so attracted to. If she was working in the Hyde Park house she was an expensive brass. A very expensive, very young brass, but a brass all the same. She slept with men for money. Except Marcus, of course. He wouldn't pay for a woman, he wasn't the type. He was too bloody good-looking for a start.

The taxi driver rolled himself another cigarette and coughed loudly, annoying her.

'You finished here yet, love?'

Bernadette snapped at him, 'No, I bloody well ain't. I'm paying you, so just shut your trap and wait 'til I tell you where I want to go.'

The taxi driver, used to getting all sorts in his cab, just shrugged.

'All right, love, no need to get out of your tree.'

Bernie fumed silently. If she was the tall blonde the cabbie would be wetting himself with excitement. He wouldn't talk to Miss Long Legs Strawberry Blonde like that. He'd sit here 'til bleeding doomsday if she was in the cab.

Two-faced bastard! They were all two-faced bastards. Especially Marcus. Oh, especially him. The futility of her anger made her more annoyed. The snow-covered streets annoyed her. The fact that the tall blonde bitch was even breathing annoyed her.

'Take me back home. NOW!'

The girls were due in. Presents had to be wrapped. What a Christmas Eve this was turning out to be. As they drove she thought about Marcus and the girl. Sorry now she had seen the competition because she wasn't sure what to do about it. How could a woman in her forties hope to compete with that? She might be the mother of Marcus's children, might run his house, might share his bed. But she knew that as far as sex went, and she meant real sex, the kind of sex they had enjoyed those first years before the children had arrived, that was long gone. Now

526

he lay on her for a while, told her he loved her, disposed of his seed inside her, always hoping she would get pregnant and give him a son, then he was snoring gently, no doubt dreaming about the strawberry blonde with the long, oh so long, legs.

Bernadette paid the taxi man without giving him a tip. She paid him and waited for her change, enjoying the feeling of having something over him. He pushed the change into her gloved hand roughly, giving her large house a final sneering appraisal as he drove away. She knew what he was thinking. Living in that place and not even a tip on Christmas Eve! She knew it would be his Christmas story up the pub with his mates, and at home with his wife and family. The house would get bigger with each telling until everyone thought he'd dropped her off at Buckingham Palace.

She walked up her drive, depressed, deflated, and more than anything ashamed of her actions towards the cab driver. It was Christmas Eve and she should have given him a tip. But it was Christmas Eve and she was forty-two and her husband was strupping a young girl.

That was the difference.

She opened the front door of her house to pandemonium. Rebecca and Delia were fighting in the hallway. Delia, always the volatile one, had Becky's hair in her hand and was yanking it. Overcome by her day, Bernadette swiped the two of them with her large black leather handbag. She swiped them mercilessly, their tears and screams barely reaching her.

Holding the bag up menacingly, she shouted, 'Get out of my sight now, the pair of you.'

Delia opened her mouth to argue and got another painful swipe from her mother's bag.

Bernie took off her coat, hat and gloves and dumped herself into a seat. The tree was glaring at her and she felt an urge to get up and drag it from its pot and destroy it. Destroy it and everything in the house that was remotely connected with Christmas.

The dinner was nearly ready to be served and Briony and

Tommy poured drinks for the assembled family. Everyone was there, and Molly, a subdued Molly, watched the black man, as she still thought of Evander, sitting with Liselle and chatting amiably to her. She shuddered every time she looked at him. It weren't natural, she kept telling herself. But she kept her peace, knowing she was there on sufferance.

The twins chatted to Tommy and Marcus, business talk that seemed just about acceptable at the gathering as far as Molly was concerned. Kerry was drinking heavily and alone, barely bothering to answer Bernadette when she spoke to her. Delia and Becky sat on the floor like a pair of young foals, all long legs and ankle socks. Molly wished Abel was here, but he had to watch his mother. Mrs H was coming down to dinner the next day, but Molly decided she might go up for a visit before that. The drinks in this house were stingy this year. Hers was like cat's piss.

Rosalee sat beside Briony, a weak rum punch in her hand. Briony noticed she had difficulty in holding the glass and took it from her gently, holding it to her lips. Rosalee sipped it and Briony smiled at her.

'All right, Rosalee?'

'Bri . . . Bri . . .'

Her voice was lower than usual. She held her right arm to her chest, her expression pained.

Briony decided that as soon as Christmas was over she was taking her sister back to the Mile End Hospital and getting her the once over by Dr Matherson. He liked Rosalee and was good with her. She wasn't right, and Briony wondered if maybe her sister was getting her change. Maybe it was coming early? She seemed to sweat an awful lot lately, as cold as it was out, and she seemed to be bloated around the face though she was losing weight. Her arm seemed to pain her as well. There was something not right with her.

Briony kissed her face gently and Rosalee smiled, looking more like her old self.

Briony's eyes strayed to Tommy, her own personal present. Together they made one hell of a team. There was a knock at the front door and she got up to greet Mariah. Now everyone was here they could sit down to eat.

'Come in and get your coat off. We're eating soon. Have you been to the houses, is that why you're late?' Briony raised an eyebrow and Mariah laughed.

'Well, let's just say I had a quick peep! It's always a busy night and I thought I'd give the girls a bit of moral support.'

'You're coming to Midnight Mass, I take it?'

Mariah slipped off her coat and displayed a white and gold evening dress that was gaudy and tight and much too young for her. 'Of course. If Mary Magdalene was good enough for old JC, I'm sure I am.'

Briony laughed at the blasphemy, though she wouldn't have if anyone else had said it.

Bernadette was quiet and Briony found her eyes straying to her throughout dinner. She hardly ate anything, and there was a tracery of fine lines around her eyes that was more pronounced than usual. She wished Bernie would smarten herself up. It wasn't as if she had no time, everything was done for her. She could spend time on herself if she wanted to.

She watched Bernie watching her husband. Putting two and two together, she sighed. Marcus had played away from home for years. Bernie knew, she had discussed it with Briony on more than one occasion. But it had never really bothered her until now. She had always been sure she was the main recipient of his affections and that had been enough. Briony had once offered to put the hard word on him and Bernie had laughed. Marcus was too damned good-looking for his own good, she had said. It was natural women would want him, and that was OK with her as long as he stuck to the brasses and was discreet. Briony had admired her sister then. She wondered what had changed and decided to keep her eye on Bernie. If she could help, then she would.

The twins were chatting with Evander. Briony watched them. It was funny, but the more they saw of him the more they liked him. They could listen to his tales of America for hours. Probing for details about the country, about the way of life there, the cars and the clothes. The States fascinated them.

At ten the dinner was nearly over, with just dessert, coffee and brandy to be served. Briony was pleased with the way the meal had gone, but troubled by the different undercurrents. Tommy caught her eye and winked and she winked back saucily.

Bernadette saw the exchange and it depressed her beyond measure. Everyone treated her with contempt. Everyone.

It was just so unfair. She had tried to be respectable, she had tried to be good, and what had it got her? Nothing, that's what. Her husband was having sexual gymnastics with a girl young enough to be his daughter, her sister, a sister who was a madam of all things, had her old beau back. Even that drunken Kerry, Miss Golden Voice, was sitting around the table with a bloody great black man who had fathered her child. Her illegitimate child at that! Now he was treated like visiting royalty and Bernie was overlooked as usual. Overlooked and made to feel like a joke. All of them, Rosalee included, had made a hash of their lives in one way or another, were not even respectable, and here she was, the only one to be wedded lawfully, and she had all this on her plate!

The old Bernie was resurfacing with each passing second. The Bernie who was jealous of everyone – her sisters, her friends, anyone. Who wished bad on the whole world.

St Vincent's church was jam packed as it was every Christmas Eve. Most Irish men did what they called their devotion, Christmas, Easter and the Apostle Saints days, and without fail Ash Wednesday and All Souls.

In the front pew Briony held Rosalee's hand and pointed out to her, as she did every year, the wooden pieces of the nativity. Rosalee listened with the same rapt attention as she did every year. When the priest finally arrived, all the grubby altar boys were in place, some smelling suspiciously of cigarettes.

The Mass began. The twins and all the Cavanaghs took it seriously. A calm fell on to the church that was to Briony's mind a little piece of heaven on earth.

Beside her, Rosalee was gasping and Briony held her hand gently. The Mass was long as always on Christmas Eve, and the number attending Communion was great. Rosalee was asleep against Briony's arm. Rather than wake her sister, she got Tommy to take her weight while she took Communion herself.

He looked down on her, and as he did, his face blanched. Her head rolled to the side, and her eyes, half-closed, saw nothing. He realised immediately she was dead. Putting his arms around her he pulled her against his coat. He sat like that until the end of the Mass, holding back a great urge to cry for the woman who had known nothing of malice, of the world, who was still an innocent.

Just after the final blessing Father Tierney asked the congregation to listen to his last few words with serious attention. He then cleared his throat.

'In church this evening we have a woman who has been with this community since a child.' Everyone looked at Briony. 'Well, she's always been pretty free with her money, as we all know.' There was scattered laughter at this and Briony felt her face burning. 'Now this same women and her two nephews, the terrible twins as I called them when they were my altar boys . . .' He looked at the twins in a mock stern way over his pince nez glasses and there was more laughter. 'Well, the fact is, these three have donated over twenty thousand pounds to my orphans' fund.' He paused for the intake of breath he knew would be forthcoming and wasn't disappointed. 'So I wanted to thank them publicly and to make a point of acknowledging the respect I have for them all. Firstly as good Catholics, and secondly as very, very good and kind people. The Cavanaghs.'

His Irish voice rose on the last two words and the church went wild. The clapping was loud and long.

Briony and the twins sat stunned at what the priest had done. Not one of them had expected it. Father Tierney came down and made the sign of the cross in front of the altar and then shook hands with the twins and Briony, thanking them once more.

Tommy sat supporting Rosalee, his terrible secret still

untold. He waited until the church began to empty before he crooked his forefinger at Boysie and whispered the secret for the first time. He looked at Rosalee in Tommy's arms and, kneeling down, put a hand gently to her face. Then, to the amazement of the priest, he began to sob, loud sobbing that caught the attention of everyone around him. Kerry, drunk as she was, took in the news quicker than anyone else. She sat crying silently alone until Evander, still smarting over the shock he had caused to the congregation, put his arm around her and tried as best he could to console her.

Briony was stunned. She sat beside her sister while the priest held the purple stole to her and whispered the prayers for the dead.

Her Rosalee was dead.

Her Rosalee whom she had loved all her life. Had cared for, fed with frozen fingers in the basements. Had played with and crooned to. Whom she had loved as Rosalee. Just Rosalee, her sister and her friend. She was gone forever.

Poor Rosalee, people had always said. They had never realised just how rich she was.

Chapter Forty

'I don't care if it is Christmas, I don't care if Christ himself is coming here to gamble, I want me money, Davey, and I want it now.' Boysie's face was dark with anger.

Davey Mitchell was terrified, but made a good show of hiding this fact.

'Look, Boysie, I borrowed the money and you're charging me interest on it. I'll pay it, right. It'll be paid.'

Boysie clenched his fists and held them up in front of his face.

Davey felt a thrill of terror.

'Don't mug me off, Davey, don't even think about mugging me off. You borrowed a grand, now you owe two and a half. I want that by New Year's Eve or I'll hurt you. Really hurt you.'

The last was said low and Davey swallowed hard. 'You'll have it.'

He looked all injured innocence and Boysie began to breathe heavily through his nose. Davey Mitchell annoyed him beyond measure. He was so cocksure. He had borrowed a thousand pounds to open his own spieler, Boysie and Daniel had lent him the money in good faith. They knew, from whispers on the street, that the spieler was doing very well, so where was their money? The interest was rolling up by the day, but that had not deterred Davey in the least. He still gave them a load of old fanny every time they sent someone to pick up what was their money after all. Now Boysie had visited personally and he was annoyed. Deeply annoyed. Davey Mitchell had best watch that big Yid mouth of his, and that cocksure attitude, because he needed putting down a peg and the mood Boysie was in, he would be the man to do it. No trouble.

Boysie poked him in the chest, hard.

'I'd better have it, Davey, or your guts will be strewn all over fucking Bethnal Green. Right?'

Davey nodded. But he still didn't look as if he was really bothered and Boysie fought down an urge to smash him in the face.

He left the little office and walked through the games room. As he left the club and climbed into his car he took a few deep breaths to calm himself. He sat still for a couple of minutes and decided he would make arrangements with Davey after the New Year for a larger cut of his takings. He might even just take the club from him. That would teach the bloody ponce a lesson he wouldn't forget in a hurry!

Smiling grimly now, he pulled away from the kerb. His next stop was a man called Liam O'Docherty, a bookie. Liam owed them over two grand. He was a good payer usually, but that didn't deter Boysie. He would go and tell him he wanted his money, and quick.

He had to do something, and this was as good a something as anything else he could think of.

Unlike Daniel, who was still ensconced in his bedroom moping after Rosalee's death, Boysie needed excitement. He needed action. And by Christ he would find it if it killed him!

Briony and Tommy were sorting out the final arrangements for Rosalee's funeral. The coffin was chosen, the shroud was a delicate pink and white, the rosary in her hands of olive wood brought from Jerusalem and given to Briony by the priest. It had been blessed by the Pope himself.

As Briony sorted out food and other arrangements she fought an urge to scream. Every time she thought of Rosalee in that church, dead and silent, she wanted to scream. She was to be buried beside Eileen, which helped. At least they would be together. All the Cavanaghs would be together in the end.

Tommy saw Briony's haunted face and kissed her gently. Briony put her arms around him. She was exhausted from lack of sleep and he pulled her close. Oh, what would she have done without him? He had been like a rock for her. Had held her up when she thought she would just collapse, because somehow all her strength seemed to have drained out of her. That phenomenal strength that was her trademark, that made her the woman she was, seemed to have disappeared overnight until now she found it hard even to pick up a phone. Mariah had told her to take things easy, leave everything to her, and Briony was grateful. Even work had lost its usual appeal. Was not enough to take her mind off her sister's death. Rosalee had been such an integral part of her life. It was hard to imagine life without her.

The doctor said her heart had given out on her. Just given up. She had had a massive heart attack which accounted for her holding her arm; he said she had probably had pain along her arms and her chest and couldn't communicate that fact. Briony berated herself for not taking her sister to a doctor immediately. For not realising that she was really ill. For not taking enough interest in her.

Tommy had ordered strong hot coffee, and as he poured Briony out a steaming cup she once more blessed him for his support. How on earth had she done without him all these years? How could she have let him go?

It amazed her to think she could ever have contemplated living her life without him.

Davey Mitchell was in The Volunteer in Barking, drinking with two brothers called McCain. They were both men well respected in their own right as hard men, but also well liked because they were jokers. Both had a great sense of humour and they told jokes non-stop, each vying with the other to be the funnier. They worked for the twins, and were happy to do so. They had been friends of Davey Mitchell's for many years. Davey sat at the bar drinking large scotches and laughing at their jokes.

Pete McCain was telling one as usual.

'So this bloke goes in the hairdresser's and says, "I want me hair cut with a large hole on top of me head, scissor marks all around the sides, and a fringe that's five different lengths." This big poofy hairdresser says, "I can't do that, sir!" And the bloke says, "Why not? That's how you fucking cut it last time!"'

Jamie McCain busted up with laughter as did Davey, Pete McCain, and half the bar.

Davey ordered another round of drinks as Jamie McCain said, 'How about this then? This bloke is at the funeral of an eighty-year-old man, and there's loads of young girls around the grave crying. Right? So this young bloke like, he says, "What they all crying for?" And the undertaker he says, right, "Well, the old boy was a really good lover, see. All the young girls liked him." So this bloke says, "Get out of it, you're mucking me about!" And the other undertaker says, "He ain't, son, I had to give him a wank to get the coffin lid on!"'

Davey and half the bar busted up with laughter again. Maisie, the large barmaid, served them their drinks tight-lipped and Jamie grabbed her hand.

'Sorry, Maisie, that one was a bit near the mark.'

'You just remember there's ladies in here, Jamie McCain.'

Davey pushed a five-pound note over the bar and said, 'Fucking ladies? I don't see no ladies in here, love.'

Maisie snatched the money from the bar and put his change in a puddle of beer deliberately.

Davey looked at the soaking wet money and Maisie smiled at him sarcastically.

Davey poked a finger in her direction and said, 'You pick that money up and you sort it for me. Now.'

Pete and Jamie sighed loudly.

'Leave this to us, Maise. Give it a rest, Davey. You're out of order.'

He turned on Jamie and sneered. 'Don't you tell me when I'm out of order, mate. Just because you work for those pair of Cavanaghs, the nancy boys. Don't you get fucking lairy with me!'

Pete stepped towards Davey and Jamie held him back, both

536

serious now. All their laughing and joking gone.

Jamie poked a finger at Davey and said quietly, 'You're pissed so I'll forget what you just said, Davey boy. Get yourself off home.'

The bar was quiet now, people watching the proceedings with eager eyes.

Davey was very drunk and all caution was gone as he said in a high girlish voice, 'What's the matter, boys? You scared that pair of fucking paper hats the Cavanaghs will hear what I said about them? Are we scared they might get their aunties after me? Oh, they can't get all their aunties, can they? The big fucking nutty one died the other day! Good job and all. I wish they'd died with her. Fucking bits of kids telling me . . . ME . . . Davey Mitchell, what to do! I worked this town when they were still a twinkle in their father's fucking eye!'

The whole bar was silent now and Jamie shook his head. 'You must be out of your mind.'

'What, you gonna tell them what I said then? Run and tell them, go on. See if I care!'

Peter McCain pushed Davey hard in the chest. 'We won't have to, you stupid bastard, the whole fucking pub heard you! What you on, Davey, eh? A fucking death wish?'

Davey walked unsteadily to the door of the pub. Looking at all the faces around him, he laughed out loud.

'Bollocks to the Cavanaghs! They don't scare me.'

Tommy heard about Davey before the twins and it bothered him. He had wanted to speak to Briony about them for a while, but the time never seemed right. Now he knew that Davey Mitchell was dead. That was a certainty. Boysie and Daniel would not take such public humiliation. And Davey Mitchell, drunk or sober, should have known that.

But the twins had to be made aware that you didn't just kill people willy-nilly. They were far too violent for the wrong reasons. Even a small debt was called in with a violence that was astounding to the hardened men of London. A few hundred pounds and Boysie or Daniel would have arms or legs broken.

537

They had crippled someone over seventy quid. It wasn't as if there was any rhyme or reason to it. People who owed them hefty amounts of wedge were just left, then one day Boysie called the debt in. No warning, nothing. It was ludicrous. That sort of thing would be their downfall.

He would talk to them. For Briony's sake, it was the least he could do. Because if she lost those boys, it would finish her. They were her boys, her babies, no matter what they did to anyone. However big they became, to her they were her Eileen's children, and she would never see any wrong in them. No matter what they did.

Briony was heading for a fall, and deep inside Tommy knew no matter how hard he tried, he couldn't even hope to catch her.

Boysie went into the Chapel of Rest. Daniel was already there, sitting by the open coffin. His face was pale, his eyes dead. He put out a hand to his brother and Boysie grasped it, holding it tight.

'Poor old Auntie Rosalee. Look at her, Boysie. She never done no one a day's harm.'

'Nah. I know that. The Aunt's taken it really bad.' Boysie's voice was low. He looked at Rosalee in the coffin for a few seconds and then said, 'I thought I might find you here, Danny boy. I came earlier today, after I saw that slag Mitchell. I suppose you've heard?'

Danny's face darkened in anger. 'I heard.'

'So what do you say we pay him a little visit?'

Danny turned in the chair and squeezed his brother's hand 'til it hurt. Then he half smiled as he said, 'What do you think?'

The twins locked identical blue eyes for what seemed an age. Then Boysie laughed deeply.

'I thought you'd say that. Let's go.'

Mariah came to Briony's just after six. She kissed her friend gently on the cheek, nodded to Tommy, and then after she had been given a brandy, spoke what was on her mind.

'Listen, Bri, I know you've got a lot of hag at the moment but

538

I must talk to you.' She paused. 'It's about the twins.'

Briony raised an eyebrow and Tommy looked down at his drink, grateful to Mariah for doing what he should have done. He knew, he knew exactly, what she was going to say.

'What about the boys, Mariah?' Briony's voice was neutral.

'That prat Davey Mitchell slagged them off this afternoon in The Volunteer. I mean, really slagged them off. He made remarks about Rosalee as well.'

Briony frowned. 'Go on.'

Mariah took a large gulp of her drink.

'The word on the street is that the boys are after him, rooting for blood. You've got to stop them. I had a whisper today from an Old Bill at Bethnal Green. They want them, Briony. They want them badly. If they touch Mitchell, they're banged up. Over with, finished, done, and there's nothing we can do about it. All our judges and politicians will do no good. Murder isn't something they want to get involved with.'

Tommy was impressed with the way Mariah just laid it on the line for Briony. She didn't dress it up as he would have done. She just told it like it was.

Briony silently digested what Mariah said to her.

'They're out of control, Briony. I've said this to you before, you must put the hard word on them. Now. Before it's too late. If they top Mitchell, they'll put themselves away, and all the donations to charity and all the good feeling from the East End won't mean a tinker's fart.'

'What did Mitchell say about Rosalee?'

Mariah waved a hand at her and said dismissively, 'Oh, a load of old crap. He was pissed out of his head. Anyway, what does it matter? Words can't hurt her. Nothing can hurt her, Bri . . .'

Briony stood up and put down her glass. She lit herself a cigarette slowly, drawing the smoke deep into her lungs before blowing it out.

Mariah sighed heavily. 'For Christ's sake, Tommy, you tell her, will you? If she won't listen to me, she might at least listen to you.'

'Mariah's right, Briony. You have to try and stop them from

going near Mitchell. It's the talk of the streets. If they touch him they're away. Pure and simple. I was going to talk to them myself, I wasn't really sure what to do.'

Briony nodded slightly, her eyes far away as she said, 'You leave the boys to me.'

Bernadette was sitting in her kitchen eating a large slice of cake. Bernadette was a comfort eater, she knew that, and the knowledge annoyed her. She would balloon in weight if she wasn't careful. The house was as quiet as the grave. The girls were at her mother's; Mother Jones was on the mend and demanding all sorts. The girls enjoyed helping their gran, and Molly enjoyed their company. Liselle was still hardly speaking to her and this thought made Bernadette laugh.

Liselle was like something from a novel. She really thought she was it. Just because she was young and her mother was famous, she thought she was something special. Well, all she was was a half-chat!

Bernadette knew she was being vindictive and nasty, and knew she was ashamed deep down, but, oh, it did feel good. Who the hell did they think they all were anyway?

They were nothing; none of them was anyone of importance. Not Briony or Kerry or Liselle or that long-legged tart who was even at this moment with her husband – the two-timing two-faced git!

Finishing the last piece of cake, Bernadette poured herself another large whisky. She drank it straight down and the wooziness made her want to laugh. She looked bleary-eyed around her pristine kitchen and then, pulling herself from her chair, walked over to a long wooden shelf that held an assortment of teapots, her lovely teapots that she had collected over the years and which had miraculously escaped the Blitz. With one swipe of her hand she destroyed them. They smashed to the floor, their shattered pieces scattering to all corners of the large room.

Stepping through the mess carefully, she went out of the kitchen and through the hallway to her drawing room. There she took her wedding photos down and stamped on them. She looked at Marcus's face smiling up at her and ground the heel of her shoe into it with every ounce of strength she had.

A little while later she walked unsteadily up her neatly polished stairs and went into her bedroom. Then she opened Marcus's big heavy wardrobe and began pulling out his clothes.

Boysie and Daniel were shocked to see Briony walk into their gambling club in Canning Town.

'Hello, boys. Surprised to see me?'

Boysie stood up and offered her his chair. Briony sat down, her body leaden with fatigue.

'I hear you're both looking for Davey Mitchell? He mouthed off about you and a few other choice things in The Volunteer.'

Daniel lit a cigarette and passed it to his aunt. Briony took it gratefully.

'He's out of order. He needs a few lessons in good manners.'

She nodded. 'I agree totally. But not yet, boys. You're burying Rosalee tomorrow. I don't want any cloud over her funeral. Get that, the pair of you. There'll be no violence before her funeral or after it. It's a mark of respect.'

Daniel opened his mouth to speak but Briony held up her hand.

'I ain't here to argue, boy, I'm here to tell you. No violence, nothing. Let's get this funeral out of the way first.'

Both boys looked at the desk. The scratched wooden surface suddenly seemed fascinating as they digested what their aunt had said. Briony watched them both, feeling sadness at the way they had turned out, yet no real surprise. They were of her blood, they had the same wants and needs as her. They were indeed more her children than Eileen's. After what Tommy had told her tonight, she was sorry for this. Heart sorry.

It seemed they were able to terrify the very life out of people and that was wrong. That kind of violence was mindless, and totally against anything she had ever taught them. If she told them about the police being on the alert she knew they would want to take out Davey Mitchell more than ever. They would pit their considerable wits against the police, she knew that as sure as she knew who her own mother was. She also knew it would be their downfall. As Mariah said, where murder was concerned, none of their 'friends' would come near them. The carefully nurtured judges, the bent politicians, would leave them out in the cold. And Briony admitted to herself that that was how it should be.

Davey Mitchell was a fool of the first water, what he had said about Rosalee was foolish in the extreme, but it didn't warrant death. Throughout her life she had dealt with people from every walk of society, and one crucial lesson she had learnt was this: you never did anything unless it gained you something. Useless violence gained you nothing but bad feeling and hatred. She had used violence many times, over the years, but only as a last resort. That was real life. But her boys, her darling boys as she always thought of them, used their muscles and their paid muscles for all the wrong reasons.

She had known deep inside the first time they had asserted themselves that they were gone from her. She only hoped she still held enough weight with them to make them listen to her now.

'Well? Have you listened to anything I've said?'

Boysie looked from the desk to Daniel and their eyes locked. Briony watched them as she had so many times when they were children. Sometimes she thought they communicated without words. That they could see into each other's minds. They both nodded simultaneously.

'I mean it, I want no trouble to mar my Rosalee's passing. No trouble at all. If you defy me now on this, I'll never forgive either of you.'

Daniel smiled, one of his winning smiles, and took hold of her hand gently.

'We won't defy you, Mum. Don't worry. It'll all be sweet as a nut.'

Briony nodded, feeling a surge of relief go through her veins.

But to himself Danny was thinking: He'll keep. Davey boy will keep. For a few weeks anyway.

Marcus was with Davinia in one of the best 'rooms'. The house wasn't busy yet so they were taking advantage of the lull in her regular customers. As she sat on the edge of the bed and brushed her hair, he watched her. Once the Berwick was up and running properly, she would be one of the star attractions, and what an attraction she was. Five feet ten inches tall in her stockinged feet a forty-two-inch chest and a hand's span waist. Her legs were so long. He had never seen legs that length in his life. Her hair was dyed, that was the only imperfection so far as he was concerned. Her skin was flawless.

He dragged deeply on his cigarette and smiled as she faced him. Her eyes were a bright blue, with deep brown arched eyebrows that gave them a mysterious appearance. Her mouth was a perfect pout in repose and he felt a stirring inside himself once more.

Davinia, real name Sally Jenkins, looked down at him and smiled lazily.

'You're feeling very energetic tonight.'

Her voice was low, a controlled sexiness underlying all her words.

Marcus laughed. He knew every wile a whore possessed, but he had to admit Davinia was really good at her craft. It annoyed him sometimes that she played him like a john, like a customer. It wasn't that he was in love with her or anything like that. It was the principle of it. He wasn't paying her, so she should behave herself. It was that simple. But he had noticed over the years that a lot of the girls didn't know when to stop acting. Even her cries of delight had turned into practised moans of ecstasy lately. She had been with him six months, longer than any of his women in the past, and as delectable as she was, her days were numbered. But he wouldn't let on to her, not just yet anyway.

Bernadette was like some kind of automaton lately. He knew she was upset about her sister, and he also knew, but wouldn't admit it outright, that he should have been with her tonight. But Davinia was here, and he was here, and the house was quiet. He justified himself every way he could. He noticed that his earlier interest was gone and lit himself another cigarette from the butt of the previous one.

'I saw a lovely flat today. I'm thinking of renting it.'

Marcus drew on the cigarette again. This time he looked down at the gold and green bedspread.

'I can't really afford it, but it is lovely. So dinky!'

Marcus blew out a swirl of smoke and then looked at her again. She was still brushing her hair, looking at herself in the many mirrors strategically placed around the walls. He could see about twenty Davinias, from all angles.

'Is that right, Davinia? It must be expensive if you can't afford it.'

She looked at him then, fully.

'We could be together there, more often. Without all the other girls knowing about it.'

Marcus cleared his throat and looked around for the ashtray. He put his cigarette out and stood up, his body still lean and firm, even at his age.

'Listen, Davinia love, I don't want a permanent relationship, I told you that at the outset. I have a wife and two children . . .'

Davinia walked to him, her breasts wobbling seductively. She put her hands on to his shoulders and looked into his eyes.

That was when pandemonium broke out.

They both heard the screaming and shouting and looked at one another in shock and consternation. Marcus made a grab for his trousers, thinking one of the customers or the girls was getting out of order, when the bedroom door banged open.

Marcus had never felt so shocked in all his life as when he saw Bernadette standing in that room with two suitcases. She looked at him and then at Davinia. He was in the process of putting on his trousers and stood there with them half up his legs, his mouth open in astonishment.

Dropping the cases, Bernadette pulled herself straight. Looking at the two of them, she said loudly, 'You want him, darlin', you can have him. Washing and all!'

Behind her women and girls of all shapes, sizes, colours and creeds watched the show with glee.

Giving Marcus and Davinia one last look of contempt, Bernadette walked from the room, pushing through the assembled women with every ounce of dignity she could command.

The day of Rosalee's funeral dawned cold. It had begun to snow again during the night, and the streets were covered with a glistening whiteness, which hid the black greasy slush beneath. As they all stood around the graveside, Briony looked at her family and felt a chill of apprehension. She looked at her mother and Abel, both white-faced and tight-lipped. She knew Rosalee would be missed by her mother, missed dreadfully.

She looked at Kerry, flanked either side by Evander and Liselle, her face, even at this early hour, showing the signs of drunkenness. Well, Kerry was going away in the New Year whether she liked it or not. She would drink herself to death otherwise. Briony guessed shrewdly that once Evander returned to the States Kerry would be happier. It had all worked out wrong for her. The knowledge of his real reason for arriving on her doorstep had broken her. Liselle, though, seemed happier to have her father nearby. She had spoken of going out to see him in America.

She looked at Cissy's big moon face, tears still shining on her red-veined cheeks. Poor Cissy. They had been through a lot together over the years. She felt a huge surge of emotion as she looked at her friend. Then her eyes strayed to Bernadette and Marcus. A rather quiet and shocked Marcus. Briony was pleased to see them together again. Their two daughters cried quietly for their aunt and Briony studied them. Two more Cavanagh girls, with the same looks and mannerisms. It seemed that the Cavanagh looks were hard to stamp out. All her nieces and nephews had the unmistakable look of the family, even Liselle. They were strong women and men. Mustn't forget the Cavanagh men.

The twins were broken-hearted. Briony watched them with a detachment she would have thought impossible a few days before. But some of the things Tommy had told her had changed her towards them. Oh, she knew she would get over the shock of learning about their sadistic ways, their vindictive assaults. They were her boys, no matter what they did. But she would like to think she could influence them enough to see the errors of their ways. She could try to change them.

Jonathan stood with the twins, his face grave. It had been good of him to fly over from Hollywood for the funeral. He had been a good friend over the years, and would continue to be for a long time.

She stared at the coffin, seeing Rosalee in her mind's eye, smiling and clapping her hands, all those years ago in the basements, her chubby feet blue with the cold. Briony had sold herself to take them out of there, to give them all a better life, and the result was Eileen dead, Rosalee dead, and the new generation inheriting problems that were far worse than mere cold and hunger.

Was it all worth it?

It was a question she couldn't honestly answer. Not now while her heart was laden down with this unhappiness, this terrible destructive unhappiness.

Only the future could answer that question. Only hindsight could give her even a glimmer of an answer. She would wait.

She had been waiting all her life for something, her natural son for one thing. A few more years wouldn't make much difference.

BOOK FOUR
1968

'Freedom's just another word for nothing left to lose.
Nothin' ain't worth nothin', but it's free'
> – 'Me and Bobby McGee', Kris Kristofferson.

'The great nations have always acted like gangsters, and
small nations like prostitutes'
> – Stanley Kubrick

'In trouble to be troubled is to have your trouble doubled'
> – *The Further Adventures of Robinson Crusoe*, Daniel Defoe

Chapter Forty-one
1968

Delia smacked her daughter's chubby leg hard. A deep red handprint appeared in the skin as if by magic.

'You touch that once more, Faith, and I'll hammer you.'

Faith looked at her mother and, lips trembling, put back the brightly coloured ashtray on Briony's coffee table.

Briony put her arms out to the child and she climbed on to her lap, starting to cry now she had a bit of sympathy.

'Auntie Briony, you ruin her!'

Briony laughed out loud.

'What else are children for? She's only three, Delia, she doesn't really understand right and wrong yet. Give the child time!'

It was said lightly but Delia was aware of her aunt's controlled anger. She couldn't bear to see a child smacked, it completely threw her. Delia wondered how Briony would have been if she had had to live as Delia did, in a high rise flat with a man who was no good whatsoever.

She stifled this thought. They had all warned her about Jimmy Sellars and she should have listened. Now, after refusing all their offers of help, she was tied to a man whose sole occupation in life was getting stoned, listening to Hendrix, and having sex, preferably with everyone else but her. The worst of it all was she still loved him. Was, in fact, besotted by the bugger. This fact never ceased to amaze her. Knowing what he was, she still wanted him.

So much for this new permissive society.

Her old Auntie Briony was more permissive, what with her bloody 'houses' and her other nefarious businesses. She loved her Auntie Briony though, she did. Even at her advanced age, in her sixties now, Briony still looked good. Her hair did not have to be dyed, which amazed everyone; her face, lined as it was, still looked youthful. Her slim figure had not an ounce of spare fat on it. Delia looked down at her own overweight body and sighed. It wasn't fair really. Even her own mother looked better than she did, but she had had her face done. Face and breasts, at her age! It was embarrassing.

She watched Briony kiss Faith and smiled. The child was so loved by everyone. She was glad. Briony took the child's little hand in hers and kissed the fingers greedily, making Faith laugh. Then Delia saw her aunt frown. Pushing up the child's cardigan, she revealed a large purple bruise.

'How the hell did she come by that?'

Delia heard the outrage in her aunt's voice and shook her head dismissively. 'You know what children are like, she caught it in the bars of the cot.'

'It's about time you put her in a bed then, Delia! Christ, that looks painful.' Briony looked at the little girl on her lap and said sweetly, 'Is my baby hurting, my poor little Faithey?'

Faith grinned her best grin and Briony kissed her once more, hugging her tight. Delia relaxed. That had been a close one all right.

Too close for comfort.

Boysie and Daniel were visiting their gran. She still lived in Oxlow Lane and they made a point of calling in often. She was alone now, Mother Jones passing away in 1950, and Abel dying of cancer in 1966. Molly was in her eighties, and though she now lived on the bottom floor of her house, finding the stairs too difficult, was still alert, still fiercely independent, and wanting to stay in her own home no matter how often Briony tried to persuade her to come and live with her.

She made the twins a large pot of tea and sat listening to their chatter. They were still her boys. Her favourites. Their reputation was now legendary in London but every time Molly looked at them she saw her gentle daughter who had died birthing them. Her eyes misted over. More and more lately she was thinking of the people who had died. Abel, Mother Jones and even Mrs Horlock. The dead seemed more real to her than the living. Except for her grandsons. They were her whole existence rolled into two large men. They had taken over many of Briony's clubs, and had also taken over the houses. They owned everything from used car lots to large plant hire firms. They had fingers in every pie and Molly was as pleased as punch with them.

She began to doze in her chair, the fire roaring even in the late-spring sunshine.

Boysie and Danny looked at her and grinned at one another.

'Gran . . . Gran . . . Before you nod off I want to tell you me news,' Boysie said.

Molly sat upright in the chair. 'I wasn't asleep, you cheeky young bugger! I was thinking!'

Boysie laughed. 'Well, think about this then. I'm getting married.'

Even Daniel laughed at the shocked look on her face.

'What, to that Emerald bird?'

Emerald was a high-class call girl Boysie had been seeing for about a year.

He shook his head. 'Nah! I'm marrying a girl called Suzannah Rankins. Her nan used to run the bingo down at the church. Remember her?'

He was talking loud and slow and Molly slapped his arm.

'I ain't in me bleeding dotage, you know. I still have all me faculties! 'Course I remember Jessie Rankins. We was good mates. She's in a home now, poor old bitch.'

'Well, I'm marrying her granddaughter, Jessie's son's girl. Remember Jessie's son, Frankie Rankins?'

Molly looked at Danny and shook her head. 'Will you explain to this bleeding numbskull that I can hear him all right? I ain't at the end of the street.'

Danny laughed. 'All right, Gran, keep your hair on.'

'How old's this Suzannah then?'

Boysie looked shamefaced.

'Twenty-one, Gran.'

'Good bit younger than you then.' She paused. 'Bring her around on Sunday at five-fifteen, I'll tell you what I think then.'

'I'll bring him personally, Gran, all right?'

The twins climbed into their white Rolls-Royce and drove away, oblivious of the stares of the other tenants in the road. They were sponsoring a boxing tournament for under-fourteens in Wapping, and were dressed up ready to have their photos taken for the local papers. They both looked the part: neat black suits, slicked-back hair and plain grey ties, their practised smiles coming now without any effort on their part. Big, powerful men, both physically and mentally.

They thought they were untouchable.

'What time are you meeting Suzannah?'

Boysie shrugged.

'About seven. I'm seeing her mum and dad tonight, about the wedding like.'

Danny laughed. 'It seems funny, thinking of you married.'

Boysie laughed too. 'I want a family, Danny Boy, a family and a nice house and a nice wife. A decent type of bird. I've had me eye on Suzannah since she was at school. She's a good kid.'

'Yeah, the emphasis on "kid"! She'll wear you out, mate, before you know it you'll be draped in nappies and smelling of piss and sick!'

Boysie rolled his eyes in ecstasy.

'I can't bleeding wait!'

Danny punched him on the arm, none too gently.

'Well, just so you know and don't get soft.'

Boysie stopped laughing and said seriously, 'Don't worry, I won't.'

They had had a small confrontation and both knew it. Daniel wasn't happy that his brother was marrying. It was like splitting them up. But he would allow it, as long as nothing else changed. Their business partnership would stay as it was, Boysie had confirmed that.

Detective Inspector Harry Limmington looked into the face of the man sitting opposite him in the interview room.

'You're going down for a twelve stretch, my son, and I'll laugh my head off as they pass sentence.'

Larry Barker was rolling a cigarette and Limmington saw his hands shaking. He smiled to himself. He had him worried all right. Really worried. They had had him in the station for twenty-eight hours and he hadn't slept once. He had been interrogated continuously, with only a cup of coffee now and again to relieve the pressure. He was ready to crack.

'How many kids you got, Larry? Five, is it?'

He nodded. 'Yes, Mr Limmington. Five boys.'

Limmington laughed scathingly. 'Another crowd of fucking thugs growing up! What is it with you villains, why don't you have many daughters?'

Larry lit his thin roll-up with trembling hands. 'I don't know, Mr Limmington.'

Limmington stood up and smashed a closed fist on to the table. '"I don't know, Mr Limmington. Yes, Mr Limmington." I want results, boy, and I want them now! I'm losing me patience!'

With that he clubbed Barker a stinging blow across the side of the head, sending him flying off the wooden chair and on to the floor.

The young PC standing in the corner of the room kept his eyes straight ahead.

Larry was dragged up from the floor roughly and shoved back on to his seat. The lack of food and sleep, the overdose of nicotine and the blows, had all taken their toll. He was indeed broken.

'Now, Barker, you tell me all you know about the Cavanaghs and I'll take you to a nice clean cell, get you a bit of egg and bacon, and let you have a lovely long sleep.' Then he bellowed: 'So don't wind me up, boy! I know they was behind the blag, or at least a party to it in some way. I want answers and I want them now or I'll kick you from one end of this station to the other!'

Larry wiped a grubby hand across his sweating forehead, leaving a long black stripe.

'I ain't got nothing to say about the Cavanaghs, Mr Limmington. Nothing. With respect, sir, you can scare me, you *do* scare me, but not half as much as the Cavanaghs. You'll have to go somewhere else to get them grassed. I'd rather do me twelve years alive and kicking than get off with it all and be dead.'

Limmington sighed deeply. He knew now as sure as eggs was eggs that Barker wouldn't crack. But it had been worth the try.

He wanted the Cavanaghs, he wanted them desperately. The twins and that bloody dragon Briony.

They were a taint on the earth, they were scum, and he wanted them out of the ball game for good.

Kerry watched the woman warily as she put a sandwich and a glass of milk on to the table in front of her.

'Come on, Miss Cavanagh, get this down you, you'll feel much better.'

Kerry smiled half-heartedly and took a bite of the ham and tomato sandwich to placate her. Then she picked up the milk in an exaggerated gesture and sipped it, holding it up first as if toasting the woman before her – with her great muscled arms and harshly cropped hair.

'You're a card, Miss Cavanagh, and no mistake.'

The woman, Betty Bradley, shook her grey head and walked from the room. Kerry pushed the tray from her and looked once more out of the window.

She needed a drink desperately.

She could cheerfully kill for one.

But Briony, Briony the wonder woman, the marvellous sister who knew everything and was practically omnipotent, had seen fit to supply her with a large, obviously lesbian, minder. Betty Bradley watched over her day and night. It was sickening.

Kerry sagged visibly in her seat, her show of defiance leaving her drained.

She had not worked since 1949. She had not sung in public

since then, and only rarely in private. She had sunk into a world of booze and drugs after Briony, wonderful Briony, had seen fit to send her to that place where they had dried her out.

Well, they had dried her out in some ways. But not the way they wanted.

Six months later she had emerged from the beautifully kept grounds of Fairhaven in Surrey, slim, bright-eyed, and dead inside. It had shown in her performance and it had also shown in her face. She had lost it all, the need to sing, the love of music, she had lost everything that had made her special in that place, thanks to ECT.

Within a year of being home she was on every kind of drug imaginable, she was into heroin, barbiturates, hashish, anything she could lay her perfectly manicured nails on. The last doctor she had seen had told her the same as all the others: she was self-destructive.

Then why the fuck didn't they just let her destroy herself.

Suzannah Rankins was dressed in her best. She wore a short dress of white broderie anglaise, her legs in skin-tone tights and her make-up minimal. She had not worn much makeup because her dad didn't like it. Her dad didn't like anything, least of all her relationship with Boysie Cavanagh, and that was a big part of his attraction. Boysie was the main man, and when he had singled her out she had felt so special, so grown-up – yet so in awe of his fine clothes and cars and jewellery she had wanted to die of happiness. She really liked him as well. She wouldn't go so far as to say she loved him, but as good as. Now he was marrying her, and she was glad she had taken her mother's advice. If she had slept with Boysie, she knew he would only have used her. It was her virginity that attracted him, and her freshness. Well, soon she'd be married as she had always dreamt she would be, in a nice church in a big expensive dress with a rich husband beside her.

It was a dream come true all right.

Then, as Mrs Boysie Cavanagh, she could do what the hell she liked. No worrying about playing her records loud and at all hours, no worrying about what time she was in. No more hassles from her mum and dad, she would be a respectable married woman.

Briony and Tommy were visiting Mariah. She now lived in aged splendour in a small but expensive ground-floor flat in Hampstead. She was surrounded by rock musicians, models and other well-off but unconventional folk, and loved every second of it. Her face, still plastered with make-up, looked garish, the thick green eyeshadow and painted red lips emphasising each of the considerable creases on her face. She held large, loud parties, and the twins and all the children doted on her. She was especially close to Delia, Bernadette's younger daughter. Rebecca was married to an accountant and living in Brighton, an old married woman years before her time. Delia on the other hand was full of life, unconventional, and generally preferred by everyone, Bernadette and Marcus included. Bernie often wondered aloud how the hell they had got Rebecca, so prim, proper, and tight-lipped.

Molly always said Rebecca was like Eileen, she didn't need the excitement of the world like all the others, she was a respectable girl. Everyone rolled their eyes when Molly started her ramblings but her great age guaranteed she was listened to respectfully.

Briony sipped her drink and looked with pleasure around her friend's small garden. The young couple above Mariah had their windows open and the sound of heavy rock music was blaring. Mariah, to the amusement of Briony and Tommy, was tapping her foot in time.

'So how's the Berwick these days?'

Briony sipped her glass of white wine and sighed. 'The twins have done well with it. It's mainly a gambling place really, the girls are all dispersed around London and the home counties. They're raking the money in, though.'

Mariah laughed.

'Good, that's what I like to hear. As long as they don't forget their old Auntie Mariah and her ten per cent of the profits!'

Tommy laughed.

'As if they could ever forget that! Have you heard Boysie's getting married?'

'No! What, Boysie? The most eligible bachelor in town! Who to?'

Briony answered her. 'To a young, very young, lady called Suzannah Rankins. She's only twenty-one but seems like a really nice kid. The big do's in June. Boysie can't wait.'

'I bet he can't if she's that young! Horny old devil. How's Danny Boy taking it?'

'Better than we expected, to be honest. I thought there would be hell to pay. I mean, they were both confirmed bachelors, but Boysie's besotted with this little girl, and I for one am heartily pleased. He wants children, a nice house, the whole works.'

'Not before time either. Him and Danny are so close, too close at times.' Mariah nodded to herself. 'He was always a strange one, Daniel. Very deep.'

Briony put down her glass of wine with a bang on the ornamental ironwork table and said tartly, 'Well, there's no law against that, is there?'

Mariah sat up in her chair and laughed.

'You'll never change, Briony Cavanagh, not while there's a hole in your arse! Them boys are grown men, big grown men, they don't need you looking out for them, they're quite capable of looking out for themselves. And stop seeing bloody slights everywhere. It's getting harder and harder to talk to you lately! It's your bleeding age catching up with you!'

Briony shook her head and sighed. 'I'm sorry, Mariah.'

'So you blinking well should be. Now let's change the subject. How's all the other houses going along?'

Tommy launched into a long conversation with Mariah about the different houses and Briony sat quietly, watching the two of them talking, her mind troubled.

The boys were once more getting too big for themselves and it worried her. She had had word off the street that the Cavanaghs' days were numbered. They were being watched, being monitored by the tax man, and they still were flying dangerously close to the wind. They thought they were indestructible. Well, she knew from experience that no one was indestructible. No one.

The worst of it was there was absolutely nothing she could do about it.

Tommy's voice brought her back to the present. 'What? sorry, Tommy love, I was miles away.'

'We'd better make a move if we're to get to Kerry's in time for tea.'

'Oh, yes, I forgot we were due there.'

As they said their goodbyes and walked out to their car, Briony saw as if for the first time the stooping of Tommy's shoulders and the hair that was now all grey. As he held the car door open for her she wondered when he had got so old-looking, and why she hadn't noticed it before.

Doreen Rankins was beside herself with pleasure at having Boysie Cavanagh inside her house. Every time she thought of his Rolls-Royce outside her front door she felt a thrill inside her eighteen-hour girdle.

'Have another sandwich, Boysie.' She said his name timidly, shyly.

He took another cucumber sandwich and bit into it. 'Best sandwiches I've had in yonks, Mrs Rankins.'

Doreen patted her newly permed and treated hair and giggled like a schoolgirl.

'Oh, call me Doreen. We don't stand on ceremony in this house.'

Suzy raised disbelieving eyebrows at her mother's complete change of character. But Boysie had that effect on people.

'We're over the moon at your news, Boysie. Our little girl has made us very happy, hasn't she, Frank?'

Doreen looked at her large silent husband with an expression of desperation on her face.

Frank nodded. 'Oh, yes, son. We're over the moon.'

Boysie grinned and winked at Doreen saucily before taking another slice of walnut cake.

'May I be so bold as to ask for another cup of your excellent tea, Mrs . . . I mean, Doreen?'

'Of course you can. We went to Spain last year, and they have a saying there: "My casa your casa". Something like that. It means . . .'

'My house is your house.'

'Oh, Suzy, isn't he clever? Imagine knowing Spanish.'

Boysie and Suzy laughed.

He liked the old bird Doreen, she was all right. The father was a bit weird, a bit too quiet. But as long as they had no objection to the wedding, he wasn't bothered.

'We're booking St Vincent's for the wedding, Doreen, my Aunty Briony is seeing to that for me. She'll be in contact soon, so you can decide along with Suzy what you want. I hope you won't be offended, Mr Rankins, but I would like to insist from the start that I shall be paying for the wedding, and there will be no expense spared.'

Suzy watched her father's face. It looked almost pleasant now. He absolutely hated spending money. His favourite saying was: 'A penny earned is a penny saved.'

Frank Rankins leant forward in his seat and picked up his pipe.

'Please, son, call me Frank,' he said happily.

An hour later Boysie was at Suzy's front door kissing her goodbye before going off for an evening of business.

'Well, that went all right, love.'

'Oh, Boysie, I can't wait!'

He kissed her cool clean lips and grinned. 'Neither can I, love. Neither can I!'

Chapter Forty-two

Jimmy Sellars woke up feeling drained. He had been tripping for most of the previous day, but now he'd come down with a vengeance, from the feeling of paranoia to the quick 'rushes' that kept making his heart beat a violent tattoo in his chest. He could hear Delia's soft breathing beside him and Faith's low crying coming through the thin wall from the bedroom next door. It was the crying that had woken him. He gritted his teeth. The kid got on his nerves. This whole set up got on his nerves.

Leaning off the mattress that was on the floor, he picked up half a joint from the overflowing ashtray and lit it, taking the cannabis deep into his lungs and holding it there for a good while before letting it out slowly. He felt the rush hit his brain and tried to relax.

He let his eyes roam around the room, settling for split seconds on the posters and paintings all around. He looked at his favourite poster, a back view of a girl dressed in a short white tennis dress, holding a racquet in one hand. With the other she scratched a perfectly tanned buttock. She had no underwear on. Feeling himself getting hard, he allowed his usual sexual scenario to run through his head. The girl turned to face him and lifted the front of the dress, giving him the come on.

He turned over in bed and looked at Delia. Her breasts were spilling out of the covers in the early-afternoon light, the stretch marks visible, blue-grey. He felt his erection deflate and wished he was still tripping. He could handle Delia then. Sexually he couldn't bear her any more. He wondered briefly why he'd ever taken up with her. Since the birth of Faith she was a pain in the arse. Correction, he told himself, she had always been a pain in the arse. But she had been good in the sense she'd had money. She'd always had money. And with Purple Hearts going at £60 a thousand in Piccadilly, she had supplied him the capital to start his own business.

Now they lived in the council tower block, and she didn't take money from her family any more. She relied on him to keep her and the kid. That was the most annoying thing of all. All that lovely money going to waste, and that crying bastard in the other room.

He glanced at his watch. It was just after one-fifteen and that bitch was still asleep. The kid should have been fed hours ago, no wonder she was crying. Sometimes the child went to bed at five after only being up three or four hours. He elbowed Delia in her ribs none too gently and she woke with a start.

'What was that for?' Her eyes were ringed with mascara and kohl pencil, her hair a mass of backcombed knots.

'Get up and see to the fucking kid, will ya? It ain't been fed for ages.'

Delia turned on to her back and let out a long breath. 'Give us a toke first.'

Jimmy passed the roach to her and as she pulled on it she burned her fingers. Jumping up in bed, she flicked the red hot flakes off her chest.

'Serves you right, you fat bitch. Now make me a cuppa and get that kid sorted out.'

Delia got out of the bed, her large cumbersome body heavy with the LSD and cannabis of the night before. Jimmy closed his eyes so he wouldn't have to look at her.

Delia pulled on a dressing gown, none too clean, and he heard her bare feet padding out of the bedroom.

Jimmy waited, tense in the bed. He heard the short slap and the child's heartrending cry. Leaping off the mattress, he stamped into the child's bedroom. Faith was standing up in the

562

cot that was too small for her, a red handprint on her cheek. Her nose was running snot and her eyes were obliterated by tears.

He grabbed hold of Delia's hair and slapped her across the face three times, back-handed slaps that sent her head this way and that with the force of the blows. Holding her chin in one big grubby hand, he pressed his face close to hers.

'One of these days, Delia, I'm gonna tell your precious family about the way you treat that kid. I'll tell them all about your little act, good old Delia, mother of the year. Now feed the child, for fuck's sake, and let me get some peace. I've work to do this afternoon.'

She looked into the long-haired, bearded face before her and bit her lip to stop the tears.

She knew what his work was this afternoon, what it was nearly every afternoon. Hanging around the 'Dilly trying to look like he was somebody, selling a bit of this, trying a bit of that, and ending up in bed with some little tart in a cheesecloth top with no bra.

Gathering up all the spittle she could in her drug-coated mouth, she spat into his face.

Then the fight really started.

Detective Inspector Limmington was sitting in the offices of the Home Secretary. His hands were nervously picking at bits of lint, real or imagined, on his good black suit, which last saw the light at his son's funeral. His only son had died during National Service, one of those freak accidents that mean nothing to anyone but the victim's parents and the people who witness it.

A woman of indeterminate age smiled at him from behind a large desk and said, 'You can go in now.'

Harry Limmington walked through the doorway to the right of him and closed the door quietly. The large man behind the desk offered him a seat and Harry sat down, listening to him finish his telephone call.

'OK ... Yes ... OK then, I'll be there at about eight-thirty ... Yes, usual place, the Lords' Bar.'

563

He broke the connection and smiled widely at the tall, grey-haired man before him. Standing up he held out a large hand, not a gentleman's hand, more a workman's. That first impression stayed with Limmington.

'Sorry to keep you, old chap, a bit of urgent business. Now, can I offer you a drink? Coffee, tea, something stronger?'

Limmington smiled. 'Tea would be good, thanks, sir.'

The man pressed a button on his telephone and said: 'Tea please, Miss Pritchard, for two.'

Limmington wondered how often he had tea for one when he had appointments. The man in front of him, despite all his good-humoured camaraderie, looked capable of it. For that reason Limmington was glad he was on the right side of him. He'd seen him on television countless times and now he was with him, was even more aware of the power that emanated from him.

They chatted about nothing 'til the tea was served to them, a weak brew in paper-thin cups that Limmington was not sure he really wanted to hold. Then, when Miss Pritchard shut the door, the man before him grinned.

'You want the Cavanaghs, I want the Cavanaghs. I think we could help one another there.'

Limmington raised one eyebrow and sipped his tea to give himself more time before answering. All the time he was thinking, Why pick on a DI? Why me? He could smell a dead dog before it was stinking.

The man before him seemed nonplussed at his lack of response. Harry Limmington enjoyed the sensation he was creating.

'I want you to give everything you collect on them to me, me personally. I think that between us we can nail them.'

'You do?' The two words were spoken low.

The man smiled now, happy to have a response.

'I certainly do. I think you should know, though I have a shrewd idea you already do, that the Cavanaghs have ears in all departments. They know everything, or at least their aunt does,

564

before you can say knife. To catch them we will have to get up very early in the morning, very early indeed. But you look like an early riser to me.'

Limmington smiled back then. A slow smile.

'I think I get your drift, sir.'

The man rubbed those large hands together and smiled back. 'All their big friends are getting cold feet these days, you know. The Cavanaghs are making a lot of enemies and now their so-called friends want them off the streets almost as much as we do. But it has to be done diplomatically, which is where you come in.'

Harry Limmington settled back in his chair then. Even his fear of breaking the porcelain tea cups deserted him. He knew what he was here for now, and the knowledge was like balm to him. He didn't care how many big, well-heeled arses he had to save in his quest to get the Cavanaghs. He wanted them so badly he could taste it. Now it seemed they were within his reach.

Henry Dumas had expired at the select Sunnyside Nursing Home in Torquay, his wife and son with him. Albeit not so much from choice as for appearance's sake. Now Benedict and his wife sat in the lawyer's office with his mother, waiting for the final reading of the will.

Isabel, looking younger since her husband's death, sat with her hands clasped in her lap, wishing this was all already over.

Mr Otterbaum the solicitor looked at the three of them over his pince nez and took a deep breath.

'This will was made in 1951. It's short and to the point. Your husband was never a man of many words, Mrs Dumas, as I'm sure you know.'

Isabel nodded slightly, thinking, Get on with it, you silly old fool. Before it occurred to her the man was younger than she was.

'"I, Henry Dumas, being of sound mind and body, leave everything I possess to my natural son Benedict. He can see to his mother as he sees fit."'

The three people sat up straight in their chairs, outraged expressions on their faces.

· '"As his mother is Miss Briony Cavanagh, I expect he will make his own mind up about that. My wife, however, Isabel Dumas, gets nothing, her father having left her well provided for."'

Mr Otterbaum looked at them with a pained expression.

'I can only tell you what your husband put down. I can't begin to express my sorrow at the contents. It was drawn up by my father . . .'

His voice trailed off.

Isabel had closed her eyes tightly.

'The bastard! The dirty rotten stinking bastard!' The words were whirling around her head. She had not realised she had said them out loud.

Benedict looked at his wife, then his mother, with a stunned expression on his face.

'What the hell is going on here?'

Isabel grasped his hand and shook her head. Then the tears came.

An hour and a half later, Benedict had been told the true story of his birth, and such was Isabel's rage at her departed husband, she told it with the same cold callousness she knew he would have used. Benedict listened gravely to the story of a young girl giving birth at thirteen years old and felt the rainbow trout he had eaten for lunch rising up inside his stomach.

Now he knew why he had never liked his father, why he'd always felt a distaste for him. Now he knew why his father had never been to him as other fathers were to other sons. The truth of his life was laid bare and Benedict, not having the hardness or strength of his natural mother, cried.

Fenella Dumas, his wife, listened to the story with detachment. There was one thing in Fenella's favour. No matter how much Isabel disapproved of her otherwise, nothing threw her. Nothing at all.

She was quite looking forward to telling the children. Natalie especially, being a golden sixties child, would absolutely love this. Their real granny was a tart of the first water. It was like something from the *News of the World*.

566

Benedict, however, had different thoughts on the subject.

Briony, Kerry and the twins sat drinking weak coffee and talking about the wedding. It was the first time Kerry had shown a spark of interest in anything for years. She wanted to know where it was, what they were wearing, what they were going to eat. She wanted to know every detail. Her face was animated and Briony detected something of the old Kerry then, the live wire Kerry of her youth, and this spark saddened her.

Boysie sipped his coffee and took a large bite of a cheese sandwich. 'I was wondering, Auntie Kerry, would you sing for us? In the church like. I know that Suzannah would love that.'

Briony watched Kerry's face close. 'Oh, I don't know . . .'

'Come on, Kerry, we can't have a marriage and you not sing. You always sing at everything.' Briony's voice was light.

Kerry lit a cigarette and shook her head. 'I ain't sung properly for years, Bri . . . I don't even know if I still can.'

Briony gripped the arms of her chair and laughed out loud. 'I'll tell you what, let's have a go. Me and you. I'll help you. We'll practise every day, see how it goes. What do you think, boys?'

'I think Boysie's wedding won't be the same without his favourite aunt singing for him. Come on, Auntie Kerry, you can pick the number yourself. We'll get Bessie's old band, they're still going strong. Last I heard they was at Ronnie Scott's. What do you say? Bessie will be going anyway.'

Kerry began to feel a thrill of enthusiasm surging through her body.

'Well, I can give it a try. I heard a great number the other day actually . . . It was on the wireless . . .' Her voice trailed off. 'I don't know, boys, I don't know if I can still hack it.'

Boysie and Daniel grinned at her, identical grins, showing identical teeth.

''Course you can. Us Cavanaghs can do anything!'

Kerry smiled and took another deep drag on her cigarette. Some of the Cavanaghs can do anything, she thought. But not all of them.

Not me.

'Is Evander coming over for the wedding?' Her voice was light.

Boysie's face sobered instantly.

'Would you mind if he did? If you don't want him there he won't be invited. Lissy will understand.'

Kerry sighed. 'I don't mind, Boysie. You have whoever you want, my lovely, it's your day after all.'

Boysie kissed her cheek gently. She could smell his lemony aftershave and the remnants of the scotch he had drunk at lunchtime.

Her mouth watered.

One drink, that's all she needed, and she'd sing like a blasted canary. The wedding would be laden down with booze and they couldn't watch her continuously.

Not even the Cavanaghs could do that.

'Did I tell you the BBC were after your aunt to sing on one of their shows?' Briony told the boys proudly. 'Since "Miss Otis Regrets" has been used for that perfume ad, she's become quite famous again.'

Daniel shook his head.

'Why don't you go for it, Auntie Kerry? I've heard you singing to yourself and you sound OK to me. You'd probably be a guest on loads of programmes. Might even get on Simon Dee's.'

Kerry laughed nervously.

'Look at me, Danny Boy, I'm an old woman. Who'd be interested in me?'

Briony tutted loudly. But what Danny said had given her an idea.

'Be ready at nine-thirty tomorrow, Kerry. Me and you are off out for a while.'

'Where to, Bri?' Kerry's voice was suspicious.

'You'll find out in the morning. It's a surprise.'

Marcus and Bernadette listened to their daughter with shock and anger registering on their faces.

Delia played her trump card by lifting up her grubby tie dyed tee shirt and showing them the bruises on her chest and shoulders.

'He really gave me a hiding, but I took it to stop him touching the little one.'

All eyes went to Faith who sat on the settee eating an iced cake.

Marcus felt a great rage in his chest and instinctively put up his hand to stem the erratic pounding of his heart. 'You mean, he's been beating up you and the child?'

Delia nodded, her eyes big and round with self-pity.

'And you never told a bleeding soul about it?' Marcus's voice was high with disbelief. Not at his daughter's story, but at the fact she had taken it all this time without telling a soul.

'That's why I never wanted you up the flat, see? Jimmy had people there all the time, drug dealers, all sorts . . . He made me keep you away. Then, today, he really went off his head. I thought he'd surely kill me or little Faithey.'

Bernadette swallowed hard. Her maternal instincts were telling her to protect her child and her grandchild, but her womanly instincts were telling her that her Delia, whom she had loved dearly even with all her faults, was a blatant liar. It was one of her less appealing traits but she had been like it since a child. She embroidered everything, eventually believing the story she had created. Bernadette's eyes flickered to her husband who was now pacing up and down the room, his hands clenched into fists.

'If Jimmy was beating you and the child, love,' she asked, 'why didn't you ever tell us before? You stayed here for two weeks a while ago when you and him had the last bust up. Why didn't you tell us then? We never even had an inkling that anything was going on.'

Bernie watched her daughter's eyes flicker and her face colour up. Delia was floundering. She hadn't expected anyone to question her. Marcus saved her when he bellowed:

'For fuck's sake, Bern. The girl was obviously terrified of him! Can't you see that?'

Bernie held up a hand.

'All I'm saying is, she had plenty of occasions to tell us,

frightened or not frightened. I mean, think about it, Marcus! She don't exactly come from a family that scares easily, does she? What with you as her father, and Briony and the boys. This Jimmy Sellars must be some kind of prat if he thought he could get away with all she reckons!'

Delia jumped from her seat, her voice hysterical.

'That's why I never said nothing, Dad, because she always takes his side. Always. I knew she wouldn't believe me.'

She stamped across the expanse of the lounge and dragged Faith up.

'Well, if I ain't welcome here, I'll go somewhere else, but I ain't going back to that bastard to get me face smashed in.'

Marcus went to her and took the terrified child from her arms. Then, cradling Faith to his chest, he said to Bernadette: 'I don't believe you, Bernie, sometimes you bleeding well amaze me! Your daughter is standing here bruised from head to foot and your granddaughter with a black eye, and you stick up for that piece of scum! Jesus wept, woman, when you had your last face lift they must have cut into your sodding brain by accident!'

He turned to his tearful daughter. 'You stay here, my love, and you leave that ponce to me and your cousins. He won't be hitting anyone for a long time. Now, is he still at the flat?'

Delia sniffed loudly for maximum effect.

'He ain't there now, but he will be tonight. Late tonight.'

'Then me and your cousins will go and sort him out. Now you take little Faithey and get her upstairs. If you need any money for anything, see me later. All right?'

Delia nodded. Taking her daughter, she left the room, giving her mother a last smouldering glance over her shoulder.

Marcus shook his head in disgust. 'I don't believe you, Bernadette!'

She shrugged lightly. 'Obviously not. You believe her though, I take it?'

'Sodding right I do! That long-haired beatnik has raised his fists once too often. Tonight he gets his comeuppance. No one touches me or mine without they answer to me personally.'

Bernadette allowed herself a little laugh.

'I'm delighted to hear it, but listen to me, Marcus, and listen good. Our little girl is a fucker, and a lying fucker at that. Take it from me, mate, I know her better than anyone. So think long and hard before you go round and see that lad. He ain't as black as he's painted. Christ himself knows there's been times when I've wanted to hammer the cow myself!'

Marcus looked at her, disgusted.

'Where did the bruises come from then? Answer me that?'

'I ain't disputing he cracked her one, Marcus, all I'm saying is, she might just have deserved it. She could make the Archangel Gabriel get the hump when she starts her antics.'

Marcus shook his head at his wife and stormed from the room.

Bernadette sighed loudly.

She loved her daughter, she did. She loved both her children. And as big a bugger as Delia could be, she was her favourite. But Bernadette had always called a spade a spade, it was one of her few saving graces. And Delia could try the patience of a saint.

Upstairs, Delia put Faith on to her old bed and stroked the child's red hair. Jimmy had left her after the fight, telling her he wanted her out by the time he returned. He had told her she was a fat ugly bitch and he wanted nothing more to do with her. He had told her she was soapy, like a great big smelly unwashed whale. That's what had really hurt her. That and the fact he meant every word he said. He also told her that he had been seeing Olivia Sands for six months, her so-called friend. Well, he was going to get a big shock, because no one, no one at all, spoke to her like that and got away with it.

Least of all an acid head like Jimmy Sellars. And a two-timing acid head at that!

As Faith dropped off to sleep her mother stroked the fiery red hair inherited from her Auntie Briony and smiled down at her child, wincing painfully as she looked at her black eye.

She had better not touch her here, her mother would suss it immediately.

A little while later she went into the bathroom and had a long soothing bath. She eyed herself critically in the mirror opposite the bath and felt the sting of tears as she surveyed her heavy body. Since the birth of Faith she had lost the battle with her weight and it showed.

What she would do now she was back home was stick to amphetamines and lay off the cannabis. The cannabis made her hungry, but the amphetamines would kill her appetite. Before she knew it, she'd be back to her old self again.

Humming happily, she washed her hair and shaved her legs with her father's razor, blunting it.

She wished she could see Jimmy's and Olivia's faces when her father turned up that night with the twins. It really would be something to see!

The bathroom looked like a bomb had hit it when Delia finally left it. Bernadette picked up her daughter's soiled underwear, her clothes and the towels she'd used. She looked at the thick scum around the bath itself, and sighed.

Delia was home all right.

Daniel and Boysie were like raving lunatics. Every word Marcus said fired their tempers and they sat then, three big, powerful and dangerous men, planning their course of action. Marcus enjoyed the feeling of their combined wrath. It was so real, it was positively electric. And it would see that Jimmy Sellars would never again hurt his daughter or his granddaughter. Or indeed any woman. If he survived the night, he would only do so half a man, and that thought, more than anything, calmed Marcus's soul.

Ten minutes later they were driving to the high-rise flat in Plaistow where their quarry awaited them.

As they pulled into the car park that surrounded the monstrous block of flats, a crowd of youths with motorbikes and long straggly hair watched them. A white Rolls-Royce was not par for the Plaistow flats. Not by a long chalk.

Boysie and Daniel looked at them scathingly, disgusted at their clothes and their attitude. A tall boy with long blond hair and watery blue eyes looked back.

'What you looking at then?' Daniel's voice was hard. In the

dim lights from the streetlamps he saw the boy flinch in recognition.

'Nothing. Nothing, Mr Cavanagh.' All his bravado gone now he knew who they were.

'You just shut your trap and watch my motor. One little dent in it and I'll personally have each and every one of your hearts. Get that?'

They all nodded in wide-eyed fear.

The three men walked into the entrance to the flats. Both lifts were open on the ground floor and they stepped gingerly into the one that took them to the even-numbered flats. Boysie wrinkled his nose at the smell of urine, human and canine, and the stench of unwashed aluminium.

'Lovely place this, ain't it? No wonder Delia never let no one visit her here.'

Boysie pressed the button for the tenth floor and the doors shut clumsily, the machinery's cranking and groaning the only other sound in the lift itself. All three men were silent with a combined anger and lust for revenge. The lift clanged to a halt, dropping a couple of inches down as it hit the tenth floor. The doors opened and they all walked out, simultaneously letting out breath held while the lift rose through the dirty tower block. They stood in the small lobby, glancing to either side for the number of Delia's flat. Looking in at a door to the left of them, they were surprised to see a small black child of about eight playing five stones on the concrete floor. The sounds of Janis Joplin blared out of the flat opposite, where Delia had lived, and a blasting reggae number came from an open front door which was obviously the black child's home.

The little girl watched them with dark sombre eyes. No fear there, nothing except childlike curiosity.

Picking up her five jacks and a stone, she stood up and went into the hallway of her house. Crouching down on her hunkers, she watched the three men.

Daniel banged on the front door of Delia's flat.

There was no answer.

He banged on the door again, this time harder.

A young white woman of about twenty-five came out of the flat opposite. Seeing the men, she pulled the little girl into the flat and shut and bolted the front door.

Boysie moved back and then gave the door an almighty kick. It sprang open immediately.

Holding up his arms as if for applause, he led the way into the foul-smelling hallway.

At the first banging on the door, Jimmy had gone out to the hall and looked through the spyhole in the front door. As soon as he had seen who was there he had telephoned the police.

Just as he put the phone down, Boysie kicked the door in. Now Jimmy stood in the front room, with its ragged nets and brokendown settee, his head clear for once, fear making the cannabis recede inside his mind, and he waited for the good hiding that he knew was coming.

'Hello, Jimmy son, I hear you've been a very busy boy?'

Daniel's voice was low, conversational. He pulled out from under his coat a large pickaxe handle, carefully wrapped with green insulating tape, the type electricians use to bind live wires.

Jimmy's eyes were riveted to the pickaxe handle as if glued there.

'I never hardly touched her, I swear.'

Boysie laughed. 'What about little Faithey then, and her battered eye, you ponce?'

He clubbed Jimmy with a large meaty fist.

Jimmy spun with the force of the blow and landed on the settee. He held his cheekbone with a trembling hand. 'I cracked her, I admit, but I never touched that child. That was her ma, that was Delia. That's what the bloody fight was over!'

'You lying bastard!' Marcus's voice was shrill and then he began kicking Jimmy, using every ounce of force he could muster. A few minutes later, Boysie joined in with Daniel. The first crack of the pickaxe hit Jimmy Sellars on the back of his head.

Jimmy thankfully lost consciousness. He would never regain it. The last voice he heard was Janis Joplin singing his favourite song: 'Take another little piece of my heart.' He died three

574

hours later on the operating table of King George's Hospital.

The police had arrived five minutes after the three angry men had left the block of flats. Miraculously, no one had seen or heard anything. But the police hadn't expected anything else.

Limmington looked at the broken body being taken into the ambulance and gritted his teeth. He would get those Cavanaghs. He would get them, and he would put them away for good.

Chapter Forty-three

'I hope you're pleased with yourself, young lady? I hope you realise just what you bloody well caused?'

Delia's face was white and stricken. Her mouth was moving, but she couldn't seem to make any sound. Jimmy dead? Jimmy, her Jimmy, dead?

'Your father could be up on a murder charge because of you! Your father and your cousins. And do you know what really gets to me, Delia Dowling? The fact that that boy never asked for what he got. You wanted him taught a lesson. You. Now this is the upshot!'

Delia sat up in bed. 'You mean he's dead, Mum, Jimmy's really dead?'

'As a bleeding doornail, and your father and the twins were pulled in not an hour ago. I just had a call from their brief. I warn you now, girl, if anything comes of this *I'll* be up on a bleeding murder charge. Yours! Now get out of that bed, it's nearly lunchtime, and at least try and act like the grieving girlfriend, for your father's sake if not your own!'

With that Bernadette slammed from the room.

Delia lay in the bed, shocked into wakefulness. Jimmy was dead, her Jimmy. Her father had killed him. She heard a steady drumming noise and realised it was her heart beating in her ears.

Sweet, sweet Jesus, what had she caused?

Downstairs, Briony and Bernadette sat together, both worried and both furious with Delia. Faith was sitting on Briony's lap, her eye still purple and blue. She smiled at Briony with pretty even teeth. Bernadette knelt on the floor and took the child's hands into hers.

'Tell Nanny, darlin'. Tell Nanny what happened to your little face.'

Faith, at three, was a diplomat already. She licked rosebud lips and grinned, making a deep chuckle in her throat.

'No!' her little voice piped.

'Come on, sweetie, tell Nanny and she'll give you a big bar of chocolate. Just for Faithey. No one else.'

Faith's face straightened. Her eyes were bright and alert. She absentmindedly rubbed at her blackened eye, the unconscious movement of many battered children who don't feel pain as acutely as a child who is rarely smacked, let alone punched.

'A big chocolate? For me?' Her eyes opened wide as she spoke the words and Bernadette and Briony held their breaths.

'Did your daddy smack you, darlin'? Tell Nanny.'

Faith decided to tell the truth and shame the devil. Though she didn't quite put it like that to herself. She decided to say what had happened because she sensed that there was a desperate need in her granny to know. This coupled with the promise of a big bar of chocolate decided her.

'Daddy smack Mummy.' She pronounced smack 'mac'.

Bernadette nodded furiously.

'I know that, baby, but who smacked your poor eye? Was that Daddy as well?'

Faith shook her head, shy now. She pushed her face into Briony's bosom.

'No ... Daddy didn't smack you, Faithey? Who did then, darlin'? Tell Auntie Briony.'

Faith looked at Briony, then at her granny.

'Mummy smacked me.' Her lip trembled for a few seconds before she finished. 'Hard!'

Briony looked at Bernadette and their eyes were sad but alive with malice.

'I'll murder that bitch, Bri, I take oath on that.'

Briony held the tiny child to her and kissed her springy hair. 'Calm down. Nothing will be gained if you lose your rag. What we have to do is think, girl. Think long and hard.'

She bit her lip, tasting the thickness of her Max Factor lipstick.

'But I promise you this, Bernie, if they go down over that little mare, *I'll* break her neck. You won't even be in the running for that pleasure.'

Bernadette felt her sister's animosity then, and despite her own temper, and her real worry for her husband, a thin trickle of fear ran down her spine. Delia had pushed the wrong people too far this time.

Harry Limmington could not believe his luck as he sat in the canteen of Barkingside Police station.

The twins had left not only fingerprints, but also the blood-stained pickaxe handle in the boot of their Rolls-Royce. He had them right where he wanted them.

Sipping at his cup of steaming tea, he grinned to himself, a wide, pleased as punch kind of grin.

They had played right into his hands. It was a great feeling. Jimmy Sellars was the scum of the earth, a drug dealer, a lazy good for nothing who had never done an honest day's work in his life. But his death had not been in vain. No, by Christ. His death had been the big stick that Harry was going to beat the Cavanaghs' arses black and blue with. Oh, he was sure of that.

He sipped his tea again, as if it was expensive champagne. After all, this was a celebration.

Ruby Steinway was a corpulent Jew of uncertain age and temperament. He was now in Barkingside Police station with the twins and Marcus, causing his usual rumpus.

He had been their lawyer for many long years, was quick, intelligent, and best of all as bent as a two-bob clock.

Ruby waved heavily beringed hands. Diamond and rubies glittered in the fluorescent lighting.

'Listen to me, my boys, I have everything in hand. They will keep you overnight, but I should have things under control by the morning. Obviously your prints are in the flat. After all, you have visited it on many occasions.' He raised thick heavy eyebrows as he said this, and the three men smiled and nodded, understanding him immediately. 'It's just the matter of the murder weapon, and I have a feeling that that will all come right in about twelve hours. So keep your heads down, be cool and calm, and most of all,' he glanced at Daniel and Boysie, 'don't lose your tempers.'

He stood up then, his heavy briefcase banging against his short fat leg. He rubbed his thigh absentmindedly.

'I'll bid you goodnight.'

Without bothering to shake hands with them, he bowed his head once and bustled from the room.

Limmington heard about the three suspects seeing their solicitor all at the same time and hit the roof.

'You're telling me they were allowed to see their brief together? They're on a murder charge, for Christ's sake!'

The smaller man, the desk sergeant, shrugged his shoulders, and said: 'Who gives a toss? I was following orders from the Chief Constable himself, Mr Limmington. I thought you knew about it.'

Limmington bit his lip and turned away abruptly. The Chief Constable, eh? Well, the Home Secretary would have to know about that. But a little voice in the back of his mind told him that, somehow, the Home Secretary already knew.

He made his way down to the interview rooms with a stony expression on his face. He had a feeling on him that his little celebration had been premature. He had made the usual mistake most people made with the Cavanaghs.

He had counted his chickens well before they had hatched.

'Hello, Mr Limmington. Any chance of a cup of tea?'

Boysie's face was so open and ingenuous that despite himself Harry Limmington smiled. Of the twins, he had always liked Boysie. Even as a young tearaway, he'd had a way with him. Unlike his twin brother who was a different kettle of fish altogether.

'I'll arrange some tea, Boysie, don't fret. I wanted to have another word with you, on your own like.'

Boysie sat back on the wooden chair and crossed his arms over his chest, his eyebrows raised as if listening intently. Harry Limmington sat opposite him and, motioning for the young PC to leave the room, he smiled. His best smile.

'You realise that you're going down for a long time, don't you, Boysie? A long, long time. Murder is a serious charge. Now I won't beat about the bush, I'll be straight with you. I know your brother is a very strange individual. I know more about you two than you think. Now your uncle is getting on a bit, he won't do the stretch as easily as you two. More'n likely he'll die inside, in some prison hospital, without his family around him.' He paused to let this sink in.

'I think that between us we could come to some arrangement. Your cousin Delia has been sporting bruises, so has her nipper. Oh, I can find out anything if I want to. I can make it look like you and Danny boy went round there to see him friendly like and it just got out of hand. But I need your signature on a piece of paper to do that. You could save yourself, your uncle and a lot of people grief by keeping your head down, putting your hand up and carrying the can. What do you say, Boysie?'

Boysie looked at the man opposite him with a cold glare. He uncrossed his arms slowly. His voice low and even, he said, 'Why don't you get me a nice cup of tea, Mr Limmington, and then why don't you piss off? You're getting on my nerves now. Me and my brother and my uncle were nowhere near that flat and you know it. You're trying to fit us up. Well, you picked on the wrong people this time.'

Limmington opened his eyes wide as he said nastily, 'You trying to threaten me, Boysie?'

He looked around the empty room, his face showing an expression Limmington had not seen before. It was almost feral.

'What do you think? You don't scare me, mate, you don't even enter my thoughts. You're nothing, a tiny speck on the arsehole of the world. Don't sit there with your poxy newspaper advert suit and your good brown brogues and try and get one over on me or mine. You're just an Old Bill. You're dirt on the bottom of my shoes. You're nothing. Get that? Nothing. I could see you off the face of this earth if the fancy took me, so don't push me, mate. Just don't push me. Now call in your little friend and let's forget this conversation ever took place.'

Despite himself Limmington felt afraid. Boysie Cavanagh had just told him in no uncertain terms that his life could be in danger. That he was ready to extinguish him as he would a cockroach or a beetle. Harry Limmington saw for a brief second his wife Violet mourning him as she had her only son.

It was only then, in the small interview room, face to face with the least fearsome of the Cavanagh twins, that he realised, really understood, just what he had taken on.

PC Dillinger was a rather skinny man with large, obtrusive ears. He was thirty-six years old, unmarried, and had been a policeman for over ten years, never aspiring to be anything more than plain PC. He was at this moment in possession of the blood-stained pickaxe handle that was the main evidence against the Cavanaghs. It had been removed from the locked cupboard in the evidence lab by another policeman, a DC called Rushton, and had been given to him in the car park of The Oaks in Ilford half an hour earlier. He was now sitting in his black Zephyr on the London Road at The Chequers, Dagenham, waiting for someone to pick it up and dispose of it. He would be five hundred pounds better off afterwards and he had already planned exactly how he was going to spend the money.

His first stop would be Berwick Manor, where he would pick up a nice girl and play roulette. Then he would put a bit aside for his mother, and fifty pounds towards his sister's wedding.

He was startled out of his reverie by a tap on the window of the car. He got out, passed over the parcel, took the envelope with the money in and, getting back in his car, pulled away immediately. No words were exchanged.

Smiling to himself, PC Dillinger turned left and made his way towards Rainham, Berwick Manor and the good life.

Briony burnt the pickaxe handle herself, watching it until all that was left were a few cinders. Then she smiled tightly at the man in Ford's furnace room, slipped him a monkey, and walked back to her car where Jimmy Nailer drove her silently back to Manor Park and Bernadette.

Delia had not emerged from the bedroom, had neither eaten nor spoken to anyone. Bernadette had left her there, frightened of what she would do to her daughter if she spoke to her for any length of time. When Briony returned, Bernadette ran out to the hallway, beating a white-faced Cissy to the front door.

'Is everything all right, Bri?'

Briony smiled. Her first real smile of the day. 'It's OK now. Everything done. We should have them back in the morning.'

She pulled off her light coat and slung it over the banister.

'Cissy love, stop staring and make a cuppa, strong and sweet. Where's Delia, Bernie?'

Cissy rushed off to make the tea, her nervousness apparent to anyone. Bernadette followed Briony into the drawing room and stammered, 'She ain't been down. I can't go up to her, Bri, I'll muller her. I've never been so frightened or so annoyed in all me life.'

Briony nodded, understanding.

'Where's Faithey?'

'She's asleep, bless her heart. I put her down about an hour ago.'

'I'll go up to Delia. She has to know what to say. The Old Bill could be here again any time with a warrant for her arrest. They'll want to question her about the fight with Jimmy. I want her word perfect when they see her.'

Briony practically ran up Bernadette's shining staircase and burst into Delia's bedroom.

She jumped with fright as she saw her aunt at the bottom of her bed like an avenging angel.

'You've caused some trouble, my girl, but I'm pleased to say I have sorted it all out.' Briony's voice was low and hard, nothing like the usual tone she used with her niece, and Delia felt the prickle of fear getting bigger until it enveloped her whole body.

'Oh, Auntie Bri . . .'

583

Briony cut her off with a wave of her hand and sat on the bed heavily.

'Shut up, Delia, I ain't interested in explanations, not yet anyway. I want you to listen to me carefully, very carefully. The police have already been here looking for you.' She saw Delia's eyes open wide. 'Your mother sent them away with a flea in their ears, but they'll be back. She told them you was sedated with shock. They believed her, but as I say, they'll be back. Now you tell them that you had a fight with Jimmy, right. But afterwards you left the flat and you were here, with your cousins and father, all day and all night. Me, you and your mother will be the alibi. Cissy's staying here as well. She will say she served dinner here. If we all stick to the same story, they can't do a thing, get it?'

Delia nodded, her eyes wide open.

'Now listen to me, Delia, this is serious, very serious, and if the boys go down and your father too, there'll be hell to pay. Do you understand what I'm telling you? You caused all this and it's up to you to help salvage as much as we can from it.'

Delia nodded, her eyes wide and frightened. Briony knew, looking at her, that she would be the one they had to watch. She could be the fly in the otherwise perfect ointment. The evidence was gone, disposed of. That would cause a stir, but all the same, without it the police had nothing. The boys' fingerprints would be in their cousin's flat, that was only natural. So that evidence was negligible. Jimmy Sellars was a known drug dealer, anyone with a grudge could have killed him, anyone he owed money to or supplied. If they all stuck together, the three men would be home in the morning. Ruby was already working on a writ accusing the police of harassment; this would be served if they tried to carry on their investigation in the wake of the loss of evidence. Everything pertaining to the pickaxe handle was now in Ruby's possession. All the files had been lifted, everything. Tommy had seen to that. Briony herself would dispose of them when the time came.

Other than Delia, the cause of all the aggravation, it was all well under control.

She poked a slim finger at her niece.

'I know for a fact it was you who hammered Faithey, not Jimmy. That boy died because you're a trouble maker. I never thought I'd say this to you, Delia, never, but in future you give me a wide berth. You keep a distance between us because I don't know yet what I'm capable of where you're concerned. Do you understand me? The twins will be told the truth of what you done, that's only fair. You used them, and you don't ever use family. Think on that.

'You were the instigator of your own child's father's death. You was also the cause of your father and your cousins being locked up and charged with murder. I for one won't forgive that fact lightly. Neither will your mother or your father, or indeed your cousins. So take my advice, girl, get your act together, and soon. Think on what I said, and tell the police exactly what I told you. Act dumb, in shock. Tell them that Jimmy was a dealer with many enemies. He was always tucking people up. Only you can get your father out of the shit you dropped him in. Only you. Right?'

Delia nodded, her eyes fearful and full of tears.

Briony felt no compassion for her whatsoever. In fact, it wouldn't have taken much for her to give Delia a blow that would leave her ears ringing for days after.

She didn't trust her niece. That fact, on top of everything else, saddened her more than anything.

'What do you mean, the evidence has gone walkabout?' Limmington's voice was high with disbelief.

'What I say, Mr Limmington sir. The pickaxe handle is gone. The back of the Rolls-Royce has been scrubbed clean as a nun's tits, and that's that.'

'What do you mean, that's that?'

Limmington was beginning to wonder if the young man in front of him had lost a few marbles.

The young detective sighed. He had not wanted this job, knew he would have to take the flak, and it annoyed him.

'You know the pickaxe handle, sir? The one used by the Cavanaghs to murder Jimmy Sellars?'

Limmington nodded.

'Well, at some time between late last night and early this morning, it disappeared from the evidence cupboard. Along with all the records and files. It's as if it never, ever existed. We have no pickaxe, no records, we have nothing on the Cavanaghs whatsoever. Or Mr Dowling for that matter.'

'But I personally put that pickaxe into evidence myself. I ain't having this. I'm going to see the Super!'

The PC nodded imperceptibly as if expecting this. 'He's waiting for you, sir.'

Harry Limmington stormed through the building, his whole body tense with shock and disbelief. He walked into the Super's office without knocking, something he had never done in his life.

'Ah, Limmington, in you come.' Chief Superintendent Christopher Whiteside's voice was friendly and calm. 'Sit yourself down, man. Bad business this. A very bad business. I'm looking into it personally, you can be assured of that.'

Harry Limmington felt his heart sink down to somewhere in the region of his clean nylon socks.

'I placed that pickaxe into evidence myself, sir. I signed for it. I feel we can still charge the Cavanaghs with murder. I am quite willing to take the stand myself and explain their skulduggery to whoever happens to want to listen.'

Christopher Whiteside knew this was a veiled threat and grinned. The grin was similar to Boysie Cavanagh's and Limmington felt the same fear. Only this time it was tinged with disgust.

'I have in my possession a writ, a copy of a writ actually, which is to be served on yourself as a matter of fact. It states that on sixteen different occasions you have harassed the Cavanagh twins, the culmination being a charge of murder that could not be corroborated.

'Now let's look at this rationally, shall we? We have no evidence at all, we have a writ with sixteen different times you have allegedly harassed the Cavanaghs. The papers would have a field day! I have it on good authority that the *News of the World* are very interested in it already. You're a good policeman, Limmington, one of the best in fact. But if you pursue this, you're heading for a fall from a great height, in fact. Leave it. Let's just keep our eye on them and wait our chance.'

Limmington felt his body sag. It had all been for nothing. He felt physically sick.

'So you're letting them go then?' His voice was low, barely audible.

Whiteside smiled, a 'we're all boys together' smile.

'They were discharged from custody two hours ago.'

Harry turned and left the room.

He walked back to his office like a man already beaten. He picked up the telephone and dialled a number. The Home Secretary was unavailable to take his call, he was told.

Harry had a feeling he would be unavailable for a long while yet.

Boysie had gone straight to Suzannah's house, to reassure her everything was all right. Marcus and Daniel went home to Manor Park.

Bernadette and Briony were so pleased to see them the two men were overwhelmed with kisses and hugs. Cissy, bursting into tears, began to cook them a breakfast the likes of which they would never see again in their lives.

Drinking a cup of tea, they listened with troubled faces as Bernadette and Briony explained the truth about Sellars. Marcus was devastated. Daniel on the other hand was so angry Briony thought he was going to walk up the stairs and commit another murder there and then.

'She what?'

'It's true, Danny Boy.' Bernie's voice was ashamed. 'Jimmy never touched the child. He hit Delia because of her treatment of Faithey. Delia told us the whole of it last night. She wanted Jimmy taught a lesson. He'd been batting away from home, told her to get lost. She was getting her own back.'

'So you're telling me I spent the night in an Old Bill shop because that little mare wanted to get even with her bloke? I

587

nearly had a murder charge hanging round me neck, and The Aunt's been running round like a blue-arsed fly sorting it all out, and it was all because that little slut wanted Jimmy Sellars to get a good hiding. Jesus wept! We could all be doing a ten stretch now, and all because that fucking drug head wanted her boyfriend given a slap! I don't believe I'm hearing this. Where is she?'

Briony held his arm, digging her nails in with the force of her grip.

'Calm down, Danny, calm down. Losing your rag is what got you into this. If you take a bite out of her now, she'll crumble. Believe me when I say she's learnt her bloody lesson. She knows what she's done. You shouting and hollering at her ain't going to achieve anything.'

Marcus spoke for the first time.

'It's funny, you know, I always had a soft spot for Delia, more so than Rebecca. But at this minute I could cheerfully break her neck, I could. I could snap it like a twig when I think of what she's caused!'

'Calm down, Marcus. It's as Briony said. Delia isn't very stable at the moment. If you go hammering her, there's no telling what she'll do. I never thought I'd say this but that girl is trouble.'

Delia had heard the raised voices coming from below and her heart was beating a tattoo in her chest.

The worst of it all was not so much the fact that Jimmy was dead, though she was very sorry about that, but the loss of face. The being found out for what she was. And the more she thought about what she was, the more she needed something to take the edge off it. Danny and Boysie and her father were now aware that she was a liar, a troublemaker and, worst of all, a child beater. Her mother had already informed her that the child was never leaving the house with her again. Well, she wasn't too trashed about that. Faithey was a nice enough kid, but she did rather cramp Delia's style. All she had been was a way to get Jimmy Sellars, and she had done that much.

Now Jimmy was gone and Delia had blotted her copybook, she had to look for a new life.

Boysie was pleased at his reception from Suzannah who had literally thrown herself into his arms. Boysie picked her up on her front step and Doris Rankins stood at her window and nodded to herself with glee.

Her girl had picked wisely.

Boysie kissed Suzy fervently, feeling her hard little breasts squeezing against his chest.

'I knew you couldn't have done that terrible thing, Boysie. I told me mum and dad that!'

'It was all a big mistake, darlin'. Now how about me and you go for a little drive and plan that wedding of ours?'

Suzy grinned as he placed her on the ground gently.

'That would be lovely, Boysie.'

He took her to Hatton Garden where he bought her an engagement ring that was staggeringly expensive and inordinately showy.

Suzy, pleased that her man was back home and the wedding was still on, looked at it with both pride and fear.

Now she was owned by Boysie, irrevocably and forever. In fact, a little voice told her, she was owned by the whole of the Cavanagh clan.

But she swallowed the feeling down and kissed Boysie full on the lips in front of the aged jeweller. She couldn't wait to flash this ring in her friends' and relatives' faces.

Chapter Forty-four

'So where have you been then, Boysie? You just march out of here without a by your leave, and stay out all night. I wanna know where you've been? And more to the point, Boysie Cavanagh, who you've been with?'

Suzy's voice was shrill. It seemed that in the year since they had married her voice had taken on a strident quality, frighteningly similar to that of a pantomime dame.

Boysie tried unsuccessfully to put his arms around his wife's swelling belly.

'Don't you touch me, I don't know where you've been.'

Boysie gritted his teeth together and then said, as quietly as his anger would allow, 'Suzy darlin', I have been out on a bit of business. That's all. I never discuss my business dealings with you, love. The less you know, the better. Now, shut your trap and get me a bit of brekky, will you? I'm starving.'

Suzy knew by the inflection in Boysie's voice that she had pushed him as far as she could. Knowing when to retreat, she gave him a cold stare for a few seconds before she went into the kitchen and began cooking eggs and bacon. Her face was closed now, but she was still fuming.

She lived in a large imposing house, it was furnished to her taste, she had more money than she knew what to do with, and she was having a baby. Her husband, she knew, doted on her. So why wasn't she happy? Why did she cause this ruckus every time she felt like it?

Because, she told herself, you hate every second of it. You

have hated it since the novelty wore off and you got a real inkling of what your life was going to be.

She could not go out alone or with friends. She went out only with her husband, normally to clubs he owned or pubs where he was more than welcome. His aunts were frequent visitors to her house, and she was expected to visit them frequently.

Boysie watched her like a hawk. The friends who still visited were given the silent treatment by him, who said he had nothing to say to a gang of young girls.

Well, she was still a young girl, wasn't she?

She wanted a life of her own but even her music had to be turned down because Boysie couldn't stand loud noise.

Even the novelty of being treated like visiting royalty in shops and around the markets had long worn off. In fact it got on her nerves. The day before she had gone into the grocer's and he had stopped serving someone to serve her. She had seen the naked hatred on the other girl's face, as she looked at Suzy's new clothes, her packed purse, and the deferential manner bestowed on her by the shopkeeper.

Suzy had felt like screaming at her: 'You wouldn't want to be me, love. It all looks nice but it's not. My life is like a caged bird's. I can't move but there's six people asking me where I'm going, what I'm doing, and why I'm doing it.'

Even his bloody granny, Granny Moll as he still called her, was like another appendage of him. Always round the house, poking her beak in where it wasn't wanted. His Auntie Briony listened to him with rapt attention, the same as she listened to that little brat Faithey. Faithey! What a stupid name.

Suzy flung three rashers of best bacon into the frying pan. The fat was so hot it spat at her immediately, hitting her on her cheeks. The stinging sensation brought tears to her lovely china blue eyes.

She hated being pregnant, and she hated being married. Married to a man who treated her like some kind of doll, to be picked up and played with when it suited him, and then cast back into the toy cupboard until he wanted to play with her again.

She placed his breakfast in front of him ten minutes later and, pouring out two cups of tea, sat and watched her big fine husband eat the lot.

It occurred to her then, that she was beginning to hate him.

Bessie and Liselle helped Kerry dress for her television appearance. After appearing on the Music Show on BBC2, at Briony's instigation, Kerry had enjoyed a little of her former fame. Now, a year on, she was taking on quite a few engagements. Liselle was over the moon at the turn events had taken. She was now her mother's manager, which cut down the number of visits to see her father in New York but which nevertheless pleased her immensely.

'This deep green suits you, Mum, it brings out the highlights in your eyes. You'll look well on camera.'

Kerry sighed slightly.

She didn't care that much about her looks, she was more interested in getting in the green room before the show and having a quick snifter of vodka. She made the effort and smiled though.

'Thanks, darlin'. I think I'll shock quite a few people this time with my choice of song. I mean, me on the Old Grey Whistle Test! At my age.'

Her laughter was genuine.

'Listen, Mum, John Peel knows a good thing when he hears it. There's a big jazz revival that's been going on since the late-fifties. It was only a matter of time before you were remembered. You were one of the best blues and jazz singers of your day. You were singing the blues when most of the singers today weren't even thought of! I'm not surprised you're back on top again. You deserve it.'

Kerry smiled at her daughter's words. Lissy, as she still thought of her, was one hell of a daughter in some respects. Her absolute belief in her mother's talent being one of them. Liselle, no matter what, had always had a great respect and regard for her mother's voice, and now she managed her with an iron will.

No one would knock Kerry Cavanagh while her daughter was there. No one.

In some respects she reminded Kerry of Briony. She had the same single-mindedness her aunt possessed when she wanted something badly enough. Briony had kept her promise a year ago, albeit a few days late. She had taken Kerry out, dressed her from head to toe, and had arranged for Kerry to appear on the Music Show, taking her there herself and giving her two large neat vodkas to calm her nerves. Kerry had sung 'Miss Otis Regrets', clearly and hauntingly, gathering all her old fans to her once more, and quite a few new ones. Young fans who looked through old seventy-eight records on the markets to hear her old songs. In the last twelve months her life had taken on some surprising new angles, but at least she was enjoying it again.

Today, she would have two large vodkas before her performance, and the few snifters she could sneak herself. Liselle had come to terms with the fact Kerry needed a drink to sing. It was that simple. If they monitored her drinking, they could get a performance from her which pleased Kerry, Lissy, Briony and the audience. She had already guested at Ronnie Scott's and Bessie had sung with her at other venues around London.

Kerry was drinking again, but she was drinking in a constructive way that even the Harley Street doctor, bought and paid for by Briony, couldn't find fault with. As he had said himself, many people had a couple of large drinks every day. It took the edge off stressful work situations, and from otherwise claustrophobic marriages.

Kerry liked Dr Montgomery. He was her kind of doctor. She hadn't told anyone that he was the kind of guy who also administered shots of demerol for forty quid a time. After all, no one had asked her about that, had they? So why spoil a good thing?

Briony and Tommy sat in the studio with the whole of the family around them. Briony watched Boysie and his wife sitting at the end of the row. She sighed inwardly. There was trouble there, she'd lay money on that. Daniel sat beside her, his current amour Christabel – what a Godawful name that was – chattering to him nineteen to the dozen. Briony smiled grimly to herself. She wouldn't last long.

Bernadette sat with Marcus and her face, the skin stretched over the bones like parchment, was heavily made-up. Since Rosalee's death and Marcus's misbehaviour at that time, Bernie had taken an inordinate interest in her appearance. She now spent a small fortune on cosmetic surgery, and any other paraphernalia she could lay her hands on to keep her young-looking. Well, poor old Marcus was too old for his philandering now. Bernie should come down to earth with the rest of the mere mortals and start looking a little more her age.

Beside Bernie and Marcus sat Rebecca and her husband John. Briony saw the thin-lipped look of husband and wife and suppressed a smile. They even looked alike these two, with their dark hair, their almond-shaped eyes and Roman noses. Rebecca had on a fur coat even in the heat of the studio lights and Briony guessed correctly it was new. Second hand, but new to Rebecca. It was her way of showing them John was doing all right. Strangely, this fact pleased Briony. Rebecca was doing all right, and she was glad. If she wanted to go it alone, without the help of the family, all the more power to her.

Briony's eyes clouded a little as she looked at Delia. She sat with another one of the great unwashed, which was the family's terms for Delia's boyfriends. She sat quietly though. Unlike her old self, unlike the girl she was before all the trouble with Jimmy. Her pupils were dilated and Briony wondered what shit was pulsing through her system tonight. It was strange how drugs and drink seemed to play a big part in the Cavanagh women's lives. There was Kerry and her drinking and her drug taking. Now Delia. It was a crying shame really. How could they be so weak?

It amazed Briony, who could never understand that not everyone was as strong as herself, could cope with life as she did. It was one of the things everyone else knew and admitted to themselves except Briony. Because she was such a strong personality, she abhorred weakness in others.

She shifted her eyes to her mother, then grinned at Tommy who shook his head and smiled. Molly was sitting between her two grandsons, her beaver lamb coat sending out a powerful whiff of mothballs and lavender toilet water. She was a great age and a great woman, Briony accepted that fact now, all the old animosity buried. At the end was Cissy, hankie already out for when she started crying. Cissy, love her heart, cried at the drop of a hat.

The studio lights were warm and Briony settled herself into her seat. All around her were people who, young or old, had one thing in common. They wanted to hear Kerry Cavanagh sing. Briony felt so secure as she sat there, so invincible, it was like a warm invisible cloak wrapped tightly around her. They had weathered so much, this family. There was nothing more that could befall them. Or so she thought.

John Peel came out and began talking to the camera and the studio audience.

'Tonight we have a woman who has sung for nearly five decades. After a lull in her career of nearly twenty years she's back, proving that she is still one of the greats. Miss Kerry Cavanagh!'

The lights came up at the back of the stage to show Kerry and her backing group. The applause was deafening and took three minutes to settle down. When the studio was quiet, Kerry spoke to the audience in her sing-song voice.

'Thank you. Thank you one and all. Tonight I'm going to do a few of the old numbers, but first I want to sing a song I heard a few years ago which touched me deeply, and which I hope you all enjoy.'

A young man began to play an acoustic guitar, then Kerry stepped to the microphone, and taking it in her hand, she beat her foot in time for a few seconds. Then she began to sing 'Me and Bobby McGee'. The audience sat stunned, listening to the clear tones, to the breadth of her talent. Then of one mind they relaxed and enjoyed the song.

The lone guitarist was joined by two men on electric guitars, a drummer and a pianist. The blues beat picked up and Kerry belted out the chorus in a voice that was loud and clear.

Oh, freedom's just another word for nothing left to lose.
Nothing. It ain't nothing, hon, if it ain't free.

Briony sat stunned as she listened to her sister's voice, belting out the Janis Joplin number in her old inimitable style. This proved not only to Briony, but to everyone who heard Kerry, that she could indeed carry on singing 'til she dropped. She was over sixty years old yet she gave the song a new dimension, a new angle, and the band, who were all playing now as if their lives depended on it, were all feeling privileged to be in on this miraculous fact.

As she finished the number, the audience stood up and clapped the gaunt woman on stage who could still sing like an angel. The ovation was electric. John Peel came out and clapped with them. The place went wild. Even the cameramen were clapping.

Briony looked at Cissy and was not surprised to see she was crying.

Happier than she had been for a long time, Briony sat back in her seat and grasped Tommy's hand. She squeezed it tightly. He leant towards her and brushed her cheek with his lips.

'She can sing, Bri, no one can take that away from her, love.'

And Briony nodded at him furiously. Tommy was right. No one could ever take that away from her. Not even Kerry herself, and Christ himself knew she had tried.

Briony was humming the tune to herself all the next day. It seemed to her as if it was imprinted on her memory. She had heard it many times, but it had just sounded like a noise to her, a record for the young. Now it was a song for everyone.

Briony was humming it as she walked out of her house to her car. She felt light of spirit and light of foot. She felt quite youthful herself. This thought made her laugh. Tommy had gone to the dog track with Boysie, Daniel and Marcus, a pastime that was both recreational and profitable seeing as the twins owned it. She was driving over to see Kerry and Liselle. At least, that was what she'd planned until she saw the man standing on her drive.

The sun was in her eyes and she blinked furiously, walking over to the dark-coated figure. He seemed familiar to her somehow even though she couldn't see his face. As she approached him, her heart stopped dead in her chest.

The man saw the reaction his presence caused and instinctively put out a hand to steady her. Briony grasped it as if she was a drowning woman, feeling the warmth of her son's hand for the first time in many years.

'Miss Briony Cavanagh.' It was a statement not a question.

Briony felt a sensation in the pit of her stomach, a burning as if she had swallowed a bottle of acid.

'Benedict.'

As soon as she uttered the word Benedict Dumas knew that it was all true. He had watched her for a year, following in her footsteps, observing her. He had hired private detectives to find out all about her business interests and still his thirst for knowledge had not been quenched. No matter how bad the news about her, how terrible she seemed, she had fascinated him. He had to know about her. Now he had to speak to her.

A mixture of contempt for her mingled with curiosity. She was his natural mother, she had borne him.

'Come inside . . . Come into the house . . .' Briony was finding it difficult to talk. He had sought her out, as she had always prayed. He had sought her out and he was here, on her doorstep, and the joy in her knew no bounds. He followed her silently into the house.

Cissy took one look at the man with Briony and her jaw dropped with shock. It was like looking at Briony. He had the same green eyes, the same shaped face, he even had a reddish tinge to his hair. This was Briony's son, come home.

Briony shut the door and gestured for Benedict to take a seat. He sat down carefully, as if he might break the chair. Briony went to the drinks cabinet and poured two large brandies.

He accepted his without a word.

They surveyed one another for long, long minutes. Both acknowledging the likeness. Both wary, and yet greatly interested in the other, and both loth to show this fact. Finally, after what seemed an age, Briony broke the silence.

'Who told you?'

'My father.'

Briony savoured the sound of his voice, as she might have a delicious pastry or a longed-for drink of cool clean water.

'Henry? Henry told you?'

Benedict shook his head. 'He died last year. He mentioned it in his will. I never knew, never had any idea . . .'

Briony heard the hurt in him then, the hurt and the unpleasant shock the knowledge had apparently given him. It was a revelation that he hadn't enjoyed, that much was evident.

'It was a long time ago. Over fifty years actually, but you'd know that of, course.'

'You were a child, a child prostitute . . .'

Briony heard the words and the effect they had on her was like a blow. Her head was reeling. The way he had said them! And then anger came to her. It spewed into her head, and came out of her mouth like molten lava.

'Listen here, Benedict Dumas, I was thirteen when you were born, thirteen years old! My father sold me to your father, it's as simple as that. It was a business arrangement. My elder sister Eileen had gone to him first, God rest her, she never got over it. She died because of Henry Dumas, she died out of her mind!

'Now you listen to me and you listen good. Your mother bought you from me. I was a kid, that's all. I didn't know what life had in store for me, I knew nothing, yet thanks to your father I knew everything! I bore you and I loved you, God help me, I loved you more than anything in the world, but circumstances were such that I had to give you up. It was another of the Dumas business deals.

'Your father was incapable of sleeping with a grown woman, he liked little girls with no breasts and no knowledge of men. He

599

bought and paid for them as other men would a grown prostitute. I'm sorry to shatter your illusions about him, but facts are facts. He shaped my life, Henry Dumas, he shaped it and left me half a woman who felt nothing for years.

'Not a day has gone by since but I've thought of you, Ben. The only child of my body. I'm sorry if I don't fit the bill, but that's another thing I can't do anything about.'

Benedict looked into her face and what he said didn't really surprise her.

'I hated Henry Dumas all my life. It's funny, but my mother's ... my adopted mother's ... father was the only man I ever cared for. Yet now I know he was nothing to me really, no blood relation at all.'

Briony was sorry for her outburst, but this big handsome well-spoken man frightened her, even while she loved to look at him and hear his voice. He frightened her because she knew he was looking down his nose at her. Knew he would be ashamed of her, *was* ashamed of her and what she was. The knowledge made her want to cry.

'Why did you come here? Why did you want to see me?'

She asked the question even though she was terrified of the answer.

'I had to know you, I had to see you and talk to you. I had to know what stock I had come from, I had to know if you were as low as I had been told . . .'

Briony laughed then, a heartrending little sound that was nearly crying.

'And am I?'

Benedict finished the brandy in one gulp and looked into the face so like his own.

'Yes, you are.'

With that he stood up and left the room.

Briony heard his footsteps as he walked to the front door, she heard the crunch of his expensive boots as he walked across the gravel of the drive and away from her.

Then the tears did come and with them the burning heat of humiliation and shame.

He was her son, her boy. She still loved him with every ounce of her being.

Benedict walked from his mother's house and down the drive in a state of terror and shock. He had seen her, spoken to her. He had sat in her house. The biggest impression she had made on him was the fact she looked the same age as him. They could have been brother and sister.

As he pulled open the door of his car and got into the driving seat, he felt his heartbeat begin to slow down. His pulse was not so erratic now and he took long deep breaths to calm himself.

She was so young.

Brother and sister.

The thoughts swirled around in his head, making him dizzy. He saw her then in his mind's eye as a young girl, a very young girl of ten or eleven. He saw his father as he had seen him in countless old photos, taking the young girl as a grown man might a woman. Taking her as his right. After all, he had paid for her. He saw the frightened face, her crinkly red hair and those huge green eyes. The scene before his eyes sickened him, and the way he had hurt her sickened him more. But, oh, he had wanted to hurt her, that girl-woman who had borne him. He had wanted to make her hurt as he had been hurting for the last year.

But hadn't she been hurting for fifty years? Over fifty years in fact. Since she had first come into contact with his father? Hadn't he wanted to hurt her because she had abandoned him, given him to Isabel and Henry Dumas, when she was his flesh and he was hers. When they were mother and son?

Hadn't he wanted to hurt her for every hurt inflicted on him by a father who couldn't stand the sight of him, who had wickedly tortured the young boy in his care because he was the product of Briony Cavanagh and for no other reason but that? Because his mother had been a young girl, a young child, and Henry's wife Isabel had bought his son from her because she wanted a baby so desperately?

And with the clarity of adulthood and hindsight Benedict realised that he himself had also been a stick to beat Henry

Dumas with. A hold over him. Something Isabel could use to get her own back for the barrenness of her marriage and her life.

Wasn't that why he had hurt the woman back in that house? No other reason but that? Because through her he had been hurting all his life?

And now through his meeting her, and what he had just done to her, he would carry on hurting, only this time the hurt would be tinged heavily with shame and guilt.

Yet, through her, now he had it all. A good education, a good marriage, two healthy children, more money than he could ever hope to spend, and a place in society that had culminated in his inheriting his grandfather's peerage. Benedict Dumas, now Lord Barkham. He smiled a twisted smile at he thought. Lord Barkham begotten by a man's twisted desire for young children.

It was a heavy burden to carry around with you day after day, and yet he knew he would have to. For his own children's sakes.

He felt an urge to run back to that house and into that woman's arms, to cry on her shoulder and hear that deep husky voice tell him everything would be fine. Instead, he started up his Daimler and drove home to Fenella and Natalie and his son Henry Dumas the second. Home to his real life, that wasn't really his life, had never been his life.

At over fifty years old he felt like an orphan, and strange as human nature can be, after the revelations of last year, that felt quite good.

Delia was in the Jack of Spades, a small club in Soho that played jazz music, served warm beer, and turned a blind eye to the smoking of cannabis. She looked at the youth with her, about nineteen, with a three-day stubble on his chin. Already she wished she had never met him.

He loved the thought that she was related to Kerry Cavanagh. The name Cavanagh haunted Delia. Jimmy Sellars had loved the fact she was related to all those people whom he admired, the twins most of all. It was just a pity Delia herself didn't garner the respect her cousins and her aunts did. Then she might be a bit happier.

She accepted the tiny piece of blotting paper from Andy and looked at it for a second before putting it on her thickly coated tongue. It had a little smiling face printed on it. The LSD was called California Sunshine and was about as good as you could get. She felt the need for the rush tonight, a deep inner need that had nothing to do with Andy, her aunts or her cousins.

This was between her and her brain.

The thought made her smile.

Everywhere she looked were Jimmy Sellars lookalikes. All smoking dope, dropping uppers and downers and acid. The smell of chemicals should be coming out of their pores by now, she reckoned. But she did miss Jimmy Boy, missed him a lot.

An hour later she was smashed out of her skull. The room had taken on rosy edges, faces were swimming before her eyes, faces that were like plasticine models. She lifted an arm and watched the strobing. Fifteen arms moved in perfect harmony together. She smiled to herself. All around her she could see a blue heat coming from the bodies. Bodies that were entwined, were moving with perfect clarity, and yet were not moving at all. Let's hear it for California Sunshine, she thought to herself then. For being out of your box and still able to think.

Andy thrust a drink into her hand and she gulped at it gratefully, feeling the warm bubbles of lager as they made their way through her body. Every nerve was alive, every pore in her body could feel. That was what she loved most about LSD. Only when tripping could she really feel that aliveness, that being present feeling that deserted her when she was straight. When real life was just a bummer. When her feelings were deadened and frustrated by lack of chemicals. Whoever invented LSD should get the peace prize, should be fêted and adored. Whoever made this synthetic feeling of happiness should be rewarded.

Such was Delia's thinking when she bumped into the guy with the long black hair and the crooked grin.

Before she knew what was happening she was out of the club, was in a car then in a flat in Ilford, with Pink Floyd on the stereo and her own voice talking above it.

She was telling him all about her life, her child, and the death of her child's father.

The man listened gently, prompting her now and then or asking her questions.

Delia, in her drugged innocence, answered everything he asked her. Truthfully. Without a shred of nervousness.

Later on he made love to her.

That bit, as far as she was concerned, was the best bit of all.

Chapter Forty-five

Tommy watched Briony as she pushed her food around her plate. He watched her closely, taking in everything about her, from her hair, piled high on her head to reveal her slender neck, hardly creased with age, to her coral-painted fingernails. Dressed as she was in a deep green three-quarter length dress with matching sandals, she looked every bit the lady to him. Her eyes were expertly made up. The fine lines around them made her look more interesting than old.

He wished with all his heart that she would tell him what was ailing her. Whatever it was it had been on her mind for over a week. She had lain beside him, pretending to sleep, but with the knowledge of someone who has spent countless nights beside her, he knew she was faking.

'Come on, Bri . . . Tell me what's up. We've never kept things from one another, have we?'

Briony looked startled. Her eyes glanced into his and he saw first the hurt, then the confusion.

'I think that whatever's on your mind, girl, should be shared. Just talking about a problem can automatically make it seem less gigantic.' He smiled as he said that.

Briony half smiled. Tommy was shrewd enough to know that whatever was wrong with her was big. Was enormous. Otherwise she would have sorted it herself.

But should she tell him?

Should she open up to him and tell him all the demons that were plaguing her day and night? About the guilt and the fear, yes, fear, because she was frightened of her son, frightened of what he thought of her. What he felt about her.

She closed her eyes and shook her head.

'I'll tell you soon, my love, I promise you.'

'Is it very bad?'

Briony heard the hurt in his voice and was sorry. 'It's bad enough. It's a family problem.' Well, that was true anyway.

'It's not about me then?'

Briony did smile now. 'No, Tommy Lane. It's not about you. It's about something that happened a long time ago and has come back to haunt me.'

Then Tommy knew.

There was only one thing in her past that could rise up and have this effect.

Her son.

Nodding his understanding, he carried on eating the excellent steak and kidney pudding cooked by Cissy.

He made a mental note to find out about Benedict Dumas. If that little bugger was causing hag, then he wanted to know about it. It wasn't until dessert that he realised the epithet 'little bugger' was completely wrong. Briony's son was only thirteen years younger than she was.

This thought stayed with him all night. Suddenly he saw again a beautiful young girl, dressed in blue velvet. And, being a gentleman, he told himself she hadn't changed a bit.

Daniel combed his hair in the hallway mirror of Boysie's house. He could hear Suzy's voice coming from the lounge and closed his eyes. She was one mouthy cow, that Suzy. If she was his old woman he'd give her an almighty slap, shut the bitch up.

'So I've got to stay in all night on me own then, is that it, Boysie Cavanagh? Is that this evening's plan then? You fuck off out and I stay here bored out of me brains?'

Boysie stared at his little wife and sighed.

'I've got a bit of business, Suzy, I'll try not to be late . . .'

She interrupted him.

'Oh, don't you worry about me, Boysie, or should I say us?

Me and the baby. *Your* baby by the way. We'll sit in here and watch telly. Like we always bleeding well do. You go out and enjoy yourself!'

Boysie picked up his jacket from the back of the settee and quickly left the room.

Suzy, though, wasn't letting him get off that lightly. She followed him. Bursting out into the hallway, she launched herself at him, nails and hair flying.

'You big gormless bastard! You walk out of this house and that's it, the finish! I mean it!'

Boysie grabbed at her wrists and held her away from him.

'Enough!' Daniel's voice was scandalised. 'I ain't never heard anything like it in my life!'

Boysie and Suzy stared at him. He had come through the front door as Suzy's mother had left. He'd been waiting in the hall for the fight to finish before showing himself. Now, however, he had listened to enough from Suzy Rankins, as he still thought of her.

'Listen here, darlin', you married a fucking man. Ever heard of one of them, have you? If you wanted a nine to fiver, love, you should have spent your time down at the Ilford Palais or some other dive full of civil servants and insurance brokers. You wanted the excitement of being Mrs Cavanagh. Well, you've had your day, darlin'. Most dogs get one, you know. So shut your fucking trap up and give us both a bit of peace!'

Suzy stood stock still, the naked hatred in her brother-in-law's face enough to stem any further words from her.

She looked at Boysie, expecting him to defend her, but he stared at her, eyes like flint. She knew that this humiliation in front of his brother would cut deep, and felt a prickle of fear then at what she had done. Her breathing was erratic in her chest. Pain constricted her windpipe, made her eyes water. Fear emanated from her in waves. Looking at her, Boysie wondered why he couldn't smell it. It was acute, almost tangible.

So great was his temper, his feeling of complete humiliation at his brother witnessing his domestic strife, he could easily have wrung her neck.

'Boysie . . .' It was a plea.

Turning from her abruptly, he walked from the house. Danny shook his head at her and poked a finger into her chest.

'You'll push him too far, girl, then you'll be sorry. But if ever I hear you carry on like that again, you'll have *me* to deal with and all. Just remember this. He raised you, darlin', when he married you, and he could cast you back down any time he wanted to.'

DC Sefton sat before DI Belling dressed in his straight gear. His long hair was tied back in a ponytail and his earring had been removed. He accepted the proffered cup of coffee and sipped the scalding liquid cautiously.

'So, Sefton, what's the buzz on the streets?'

He shrugged.

'The usual really. I've put in my report the names of the dealers, the suppliers, and also some of the addicts. Only the ones we'll get info from though. Most of them are two sandwiches short of a picnic.' He paused so Belling could give his perfunctory laugh, then continued. 'There's something I've found out though, sir, that isn't in the report. I thought I'd have a word with you about it.'

Belling nodded. 'Go on.'

'Well, sir, I've picked up a girl. Delia Dowling actually. Well, she's a known face around the clubs, she can introduce me to a lot of people. Her cousins are the Cavanagh twins and her father is Marcus Dowling.'

He heard the sharp intake of breath from Belling and was gratified.

'The thing is, while under the influence of LSD, she told me about the death of a certain Jimmy Sellars. It seems her father and the Cavanagh twins murdered him, but they all stuck together to protect them. I get the impression she's rather out of favour with the family as a consequence of this. I think, reading between the lines, she set Sellars up. It's definitely preying on her mind. Sellars is, or rather was, her child's father.'

Belling frowned.

'I know about that. Limmington is an old crony of mine, we go way back. You did right not to put it in the report, son. Do you think she might spill the beans if pushed? If we had something on her like?'

Sefton grinned. 'To be honest, I think if you gave her the edge, she'd do anything. She's one of those people who have to be in the centre of a drama. You know the type. If there ain't one, she'll create one. You get the picture. I think she'd grass up her own granny if the price or the time was right.'

'I'm telling you, Mr Cavanagh, that's what he said.'

Vince Barlet was frightened of Boysie, but he had to tell the truth, didn't he? He had to make sure that Boysie knew it wasn't anything to do with him. He wiped a dew drop from the end of his nose with a grubby fist, and seeing Boysie's disgust at his action, hastily wiped his hand on the jacket of his mohair suit.

Vince watched the changing expressions on the other man's face and sighed. Why did he always get the shit jobs?

'So what you're saying is, Vince, Pargolis is inching in on our territory. Who's the stooge?'

'That's just it, Mr Cavanagh, I don't know exactly. But I heard a word on the street that he's been seen with Mitchell, Davey Mitchell.'

There, it was out, he had said it, and Boysie Cavanagh could do what he liked with the information.

'Piss off, Vince.' This was said calmly, almost nicely, and Vince, never one to overstay his welcome, left the room in double quick time.

Boysie watched the man leave. He looked like a snotty-nosed ferret, made Boysie feel sick. Silversleeves, they called him behind his back. He was disliked, hated even, but he knew his scam and so for that reason the boys put up with him. He was a grass, but he was too frightened to grass them. He didn't have the guts.

Mitchell, now, he was a different kettle of fish altogether. He had disappeared off the face of the earth after Rosalee's funeral, which was just as well because for all the twins' promises to their aunt about not touching him, they would have decapitated the ponce on sight, such was their temper with him. Well, they'd had a few scores to settle with him, and now they had a few more. With all the trouble and aggravation at home, and now this as well, Boysie was practically enjoying the thought of getting it all out of his system.

Limmington had spoken to Belling and was feeling on top of the world.

If what Belling said was true, they could nick the Cavanaghs this time good and proper. It was like a dream come true. Delia Dowling was unreliable in as much as she was a drug user, but she also knew better than anyone what her family was capable of. If she could be a credible witness... He savoured the thought to himself like a pools win. It was too good to be true.

The Cavanaghs had eluded him before, he knew they batted with the big boys. Well, even the big boys got their comeuppance. Eventually, they would make a mistake and he would be waiting for them.

A young PC walked into the room and smiled at him.

'There's a lady to see you, sir, rather old, small, says she wants to talk to you about something important.'

'Who is she? Do I know her?'

'I don't think so, but she seems on the level. She reckons you'll be interested in what she has to tell you. It's about Briony Cavanagh. Her name is Heidi Thompkins.'

'Send her in.'

Limmington had a feeling he was on to something interesting. Briony Cavanagh, the madam, the aunt and foster mother of the twins.

He watched in amazement as the woman walked into his office. The stench of poverty permeated the room. She was small and dressed in a collection of outlandish garments that had obviously been given to her at some kind of hostel. After smelling cider he guessed correctly that she was an Embankment maiden – the polite euphemism for the drunken women

610

who slept under the arches. But the most surprising thing about her was her eyes. She blinked constantly. It made him feel dizzy to look at her.

Getting up, Limmington helped her into a chair and then opened the window behind him. He sat down and gave his most encouraging smile, hoping her story was not a long one.

Her voice when it came was phlegmy from years of smoking Capstan and drinking neat alcohol. She smiled hazily and Limmington found it was getting very difficult to keep his own smile tacked into place.

'I'm after a bit of money, Mr Limmington, and a friend of mine told me you might be the man to provide it.'

'With respect, Miss Thompkins, why should I provide you with any funds?' His voice came out harsher than he'd meant it to, but he wasn't in the mood for this.

Eyes blinking overtime now, she said, 'Because, mate, I can finger Briony Cavanagh on two murders committed many years ago. You see, as a girl I worked for Miss Cavanagh as a tweenie in her house in Hyde Park. Well, I was young, but I was much shrewder than they ever dreamt. Maybe you've heard of Willy Bolger? He was a pimp, and he cut and killed one of Briony's girls, Ginelle. Her and Tommy Lane caused him to top himself and on the same night they took out Ronnie Olds. I knew everything that went on. Kids do. I also know that Briony Cavanagh has a child by a Mr Henry Dumas. The kid's nurse was a friend of mine. Sally and me still keep in touch. So you see, I can tell you an awful lot, Mr Limmington.'

He was finding it hard to contain his excitement. 'How do you know she murdered anyone?'

Heidi grinned. 'Because I made it my business to find out. I saw Ginelle's body in the crate the night it was delivered to us. She was well messed up. Briony said in front of me, "Bolger's dead." Later he was supposed to have shot himself, but I don't think he did, do you?

'Then there was a lot of talk about Olds. Her and Tommy took over as Barons in the East End for a while after his murder.

611

They went to Victoria Park and topped him there. I'll stand up in court and say the lot.'

'You will?'

Heidi's eyes began their strange dance once more before she said: 'For a price. In fact, I'll say I saw the lot, Mr Limmington. I'll say whatever you want me to say. Because let's face it, they have an answer for everything. And sometimes, to catch a thief, you have to be one yourself.'

Limmington sat back in his chair and relaxed. This woman had a point. He could nail Cavanagh like Christ on the cross. This woman could be told what to say, carefully coached. She could put the Cavanagh woman away for a long time. He was disgusted with himself for the thoughts he was having, but the desire, the absolute need, to put away the twins and their aunt was stronger than his innate honesty.

'When did these murders take place?'

'In the twenties. I was a girl then. I'm younger than Cavanagh, believe it or not, but I ain't had the advantages she's had, have I? I never was a girl who would flog me arse for a price.'

The last was said with an air of righteousness that made Limmington want to say: 'Anyone who'd pay to have sex with you would have to be mentally unstable!'

But he didn't. Instead he smiled kindly.

He sat forward and grinned. 'Would you like a cup of tea, Miss Thompkins?'

'I would, and a few sandwiches and all if you can arrange it. I'm so hungry I could eat a scabby horse between two mattresses.'

Limmington felt his smile sliding once more and tried valiantly to keep it in place. 'We're fresh out of horse. Would ham and tomato be all right?'

The old woman laughed then.

'Anything, my lovely. Long as it's edible. Then me and you can get down to business.'

Isabel Dumas was knitting. She seemed to spend her life

knitting or embroidering. It seemed to her she would be lost without something in her hands. Her grand-daughter Natalie was due at five, and she wanted to get the back of the cashmere jumper finished by then.

She glanced at the clock and sighed. It was just after one. Her eyes turned to the telephone and she itched to pick it up and ring Benedict, but didn't. The atmosphere was strained between them these days. The past was always there. Always.

She heard the tap on her door and called out: 'Come in, Catriona.'

A woman of uncertain years entered the room and bobbed a small curtsy.

'There's a lady to see you, mam, says to give you her card.'

Isabel took the small white card and as she looked at it she blanched.

'Show the woman in, Catriona.' The maid walked from the room, puzzled. The lady was very well dressed but her speech was at odds with her appearance. She sounded a low sort.

'Hello, Isabel.'

She looked at Briony and was half pleased to see her. The effect of age, she mused. Faces from the past were welcome. Only she couldn't welcome Briony, she couldn't.

'What do you want?'

Briony shook her head as Isabel barked out the words.

'What do you think?'

Walking towards the other woman, Briony was amazed at her changed appearance. Gone was the bigness she remembered, and the nut brown hair. Gone was every reminder of youth. Briony guessed shrewdly that Isabel had been old long before she needed to be. Had worn her years like a banner demanding respect.

'Ben won't see you, Briony,' Isabel declared.

The voice was cold, without emotion. Briony felt a second's sorrow for this woman who had lived a second-hand life. Who was still trying to hang on to the remnants because they were all she had left. Knowing this, Briony felt the awkwardness lift from her. Felt almost light. She had the edge, after all these years she had the edge, and it was a good feeling.

Sitting down in the chair opposite, she said, 'I've already seen him.'

She saw Isabel's mouth drop open. She also saw fear, naked and unadulterated, in the heavily powdered face before her.

'He came to me a while ago. He was very upset.'

Isabel sagged in her chair.

'How was he, when you saw him?' she capitulated.

Briony sighed. 'Unhappy, very unhappy. That bastard Henry saw to that.'

Isabel nodded.

'He was a difficult man, Briony. As you yourself know. I often wonder, sitting here, what I would have done had I been a girl today? It would have been so much easier. But then, you married and that was it.'

Briony spoke what was really on her mind. 'Ben came to my house, and it was difficult. He seemed set on disliking me, and yet so curious to see me. Understandable, I suppose. I wondered if you had said anything?'

Isabel shook her head.

'Not a word. I didn't even know he had visited you. He doesn't speak to me now. He hasn't for a long while. The children are beginning to notice. Fenella, his wife, understands. She's a good girl. She was all for telling the children the truth, but thank God Benedict stopped her.'

Briony grinned mirthlessly. The last few words, spoken so offhandedly, made her see red. Is that all this woman thought of her? Of what had happened?

'Oh, yes, thank God! We mustn't let them know the stock they come from, must we? We mustn't hurt them by letting them know they were the product of a sick man and a child, we mustn't ever let on about that, eh? That their father's mother is only thirteen years older than him? We must never let on about that.

'It seems to me, Isabel, that your hiding of the truth over the years is what's caused all this. Your fear of everyone knowing the truth about your husband and your life. You stole my son

614

from me really, you stole him with kindness and love. I respected you so I let you take him, and you were quick to do that, weren't you? If I remember rightly, he was taken from the house almost as soon as the birth was over. Then you had no more need of me, did you? You couldn't wait to take him away from me, in case I tainted him somehow.

'Well, the taint's there, whether you like it or not. I gave birth to him and now he knows the truth. Any unhappiness is because you thought your elaborate charade would last forever. Well, it didn't.'

Briony felt the anger spewing from her and was loth to stop it. She had wanted to say these words so many times over the years. How many times had she lain in bed, going through this scenario in her mind? Except in her mind's eye she had walked in and taken her child with her. Only her child was now a grown man, with children of his own, and all this had come too late. Far too late for any of them.

'I loved him, Briony, more than you know. I worshipped that boy. Anything I did, I did for him.'

Briony shook her head slowly.

'You loved him? I loved him as well you know, and what you did wasn't for him really, Isabel. Be honest. It was all done for yourself.'

Briony realised then that this visit had been a waste of her time and Isabel's. She'd gathered her bag up from the floor ready to leave when Isabel put a hand on to her arm. It was a wrinkled hand, but the strength in it was surprising.

'Listen, Briony, let's try and make something good come out of all this. Through you I could get my son back . . . You could make him understand . . .' Her voice was so low, desperate.

Briony shook the hand off roughly.

'Through you I lost him, through you I'll never have him. What makes you think I would help you now? My God, you've got a nerve, woman. You've got some neck! I wanted to see you one last time, because I know that after today we'll never see one another again. And do you know something? I'm glad, heartily glad, because you disgust me, Isabel Dumas. You lived a lie, here in your ivory tower. Well, now the lies come home to roost and I'm glad I'm not the only one hurting.'

Daniel listened to all that Vince had said with a face like flint. Boysie finished the story and Daniel nodded slowly.

'You know what this means, don't you, Boysie? It means we have to take them all out of the ball game. And I can tell you now, mate, with me hand on me heart, that slag Mitchell is mine. All mine.'

Boysie nodded.

'I think we'd better start making a few enquiries around the place. We have to find out their stamping ground. Then we can plan our attack.'

'We'll take them all out together, Boysie. It'll be a regular blood bath. I ain't having that cunt Pargolis mugging me off. Not him nor that prat Mitchell. I could kill someone now this minute, I'm so incensed.'

Daniel clenched his hands into large fists. The knuckles whitened with the pressure.

'First things first, Danny Boy. I'll get on the blower to Vince. That little ponce will grass us everything we need within the next few hours. Then we can plan properly.'

Danny stood up and lit himself a Dunhill cigarette. 'I think we should call a few of the team leaders in. If Pargolis has been putting his boat around the place, I think we should know why we ain't had it reported back to us. Maybe he's bought himself a few little friends, eh . . . Maybe he wants to come and live in our fucking house and all! I know, how about we just make out a will leaving everything to him? The ponce, the bloody Greek ponce! He wants what we've got, does he? He wants my life's work? Well, let's see how far he gets with no fucking legs!'

'Calm down, Danny Boy, for Christ's sake!'

'Calm down, you say? Has that fucking Suzy eaten up the little bit of brain you had to start with, has she? Remember the old joke, Boysie. I do the thinking, and you don't! Remember that, mate. I am the main man here, me, Daniel Cavanagh. I call the long shots and I am calling them all in this night. We're gonna get tooled up and we're gonna take that bastard and his cronies out, once and for all.'

'Thanks a lot, Danny, thanks for telling me what a prick I am. I really needed that tonight.'

Daniel looked into the face so like his own, except softer, smoother, and felt ashamed.

'I'm sorry, Boysie. Honest, mate. It was temper. I'm in a temper.'

Boysie laughed.

'And I'm not, I suppose? I ain't annoyed in the least, me, am I? I'm too thick to be annoyed, me . . . You and Suzy should set up house together. It's a shame to waste two houses between ya! Both of you seem to think that mugging me off is a great pastime.'

Daniel grabbed his brother's shoulders and shook him gently. He looked into his eyes.

'I was out of order, Boysie. I couldn't function without you, bruv. Me and you, well, we're one really. We function as one. Without you I'd be nothing, mate. Nothing. There's only two things important to me in this life, you and The Aunt.'

Boysie bit his lip, then of one mind the brothers embraced.

'We'll get the fuckers, Danny Boy, me and you. We'll find them, we'll hunt them down, and we'll blow them off the face of the earth.'

Peter Pargolis stood in The Two Puddings in Stratford with a large brandy in one hand and a large woman named Cynthia Malling in the other. Cynthia was a speciality brass. She could do things with her huge breasts that defied not only most people's physical capabilities but also the imagination of even the most dedicated porn lover. Davey Mitchell had provided her for his good friend's evening entertainment.

Davey watched Pargolis as he sipped his drink fastidiously. Say what you liked about the bubbles, they were a good crew if you was in with them. He knew that Pargolis was intent on taking over some of the East End businesses of the Cavanaghs and reckoned he had a good chance of fulfilling his dream.

Davey was to get a nice little slice of the action himself, otherwise he wouldn't have bothered with the Greek.

Full of beer and good-humoured camaraderie, he looked around the small pub and saw one of the Cavanaghs' henchmen, Dicky D'Arcy, standing watching them with another man, a black man he'd never seen before. Seeing his chance to bring himself up more in the estimation of Pargolis, he began to bait D'Arcy. Mitchell's big mouth always was his downfall.

'Oi, D'Arcy! Where's the twins tonight then? At home with Mummy, are they? Fucking pair of slags... How's Boysie then? His new wife looks right fucked off. Found out the twins are stuck up each other's arses, has she?'

Pargolis and his men laughed. Cynthia didn't, she had too good a knowledge of the Cavanaghs to be seen laughing at their expense.

Dicky D'Arcy lifted two fingers at Mitchell.

'Why don't you shut your mouth and give your arse a chance, Mitchell? What's wrong? Had a large shandy, have we and can't take it?'

Mitchell was serious now. He pointed at D'Arcy with a thick tobacco-stained finger.

'You tell them two pricks that their days are numbered. They don't scare me, mate. The pavement stinks of them, it stinks. Well, soon those pavements will be ours. Tell them that from me.'

D'Arcy made a big deal out of shaking. He said in a high falsetto voice: 'What's that noise?' Then looking round the pub he said. 'I do believe I can hear my knees knocking! Get real, Mitchell, you're dead meat when Danny Cavanagh hears about tonight. Dead fucking meat!'

Turning his back on Mitchell he carried on drinking and talking as if the other man did not even exist.

Mitchell walked towards him but Pargolis held him back. 'In time, Davey, in time. Soon they'll all be singing a different tune.'

Cynthia Malling picked up her bag and hitched up her heavy breasts in one movement.

618

'Where you going?' Pargolis' voice was high.

Cynthia smiled at him nastily. 'As far away from you lot as possible, mate. That's where. If I wanted a ruck with the Cavanaghs, I wouldn't have one over the likes of you.'

With that she walked from the pub, hailed a cab and went home without a penny piece earned that night, but with the sweet knowledge her departure had been witnessed. No way was she getting involved with all that. No way.

Vince followed her from the pub, whistling through his teeth. He wanted to get back in touch with the twins before they heard the lot from D'Arcy and half the clientele of The Two Puddings.

They had promised him a pony and he wanted it.

Chapter Forty-six

'What you going through all them old records for?'

Limmington grinned and waved the DC away with his hand. 'Just idle curiosity, son, that's all.'

He watched the young man leave the room then carried on with his reading. The Cavanaghs had eluded him once. Well, this time he would sew them all up good and proper. When he went for Miss Briony Cavanagh and Mr Tommy Lane he would go armed and dangerous. With the case sewn up. And through her he would get the twins.

He felt a tingling of excitement at the thought. As they closed the doors on those two he would do a dance of happiness all over the East End.

He had heard a whisper that they were to hit Pargolis. Well, let them. Pargolis was just another carbuncle on the face of the earth. The twins could hit him and good luck to them, then Limmington would have them right where he wanted them. It seemed Davey Mitchell was back in town and shouting his mouth off in the pubs and clubs. Well, he mused, the Cavanaghs would soon put a stop to his gallop and all.

He scanned the papers in front of him. It seemed Mr Ronnie Olds was found in Victoria Park, in a marquee of all things, with his entrails in his hands. Yes, it sounded like a Cavanagh had had a hand in that. Bolger was found in a back garden with his brains splattered all over the place. Could have been suicide, of course, or it could have been the work of Miss Briony Cavanagh and Mr Tommy Lane.

He had also pulled all the newspaper cuttings on Henry Dumas. It seemed he'd been a force to be reckoned with in the twenties. He'd liked little girls and all, from what Limmington had gleaned from Heidi. If he had made Briony pregnant, then she was only thirteen at the time of the birth. A flicker of distaste appeared on his face. Shame the man was dead. He could have had a little word with him, the father of Briony Cavanagh's child, a child that was adopted by Dumas' wife Isabel. Now this Isabel was a different kettle of fish all together. A peer's daughter, if you please, and the spawn of Briony Cavanagh was now Lord Barkham, a respectable and influential businessman. Limmington wondered if he knew the stock he really came from. That was a poser. He'd have to tread warily here, but tread he would or his name wasn't Harry Limmington!

Heidi Thompkins had a point. If he couldn't make the charges stick, then he would have to play around with the evidence to suit himself. He was quite willing to do that to ensure they all got banged up once and for all. The ends justified the means in Harry Limmington's book. As far as he was concerned, all the Cavanaghs were scum.

Briony was tired out. It seemed she was always tired lately. She brushed out her hair, looking at herself critically in the mirror of her dressing table. It was a strange feeling, seeing herself. She still looked in the mirror expecting to see herself as she had been when young. But Christ knew, she felt old lately. She'd felt old since she had seen her son. Her true son. But, she admitted to herself, she'd felt a lot better since she had seen Isabel. That was something she had needed to do for many a long year, and she had enjoyed it in a funny sort of way. Isabel had been the cause of great sadness, Isabel and Henry.

She smiled ruefully. Now she had a grandson named Henry Dumas. Strange the way life snuck up on you, without you even realising it. Strange and disturbing. She wondered how Henry had felt seeing her image before him day after day, because Benedict was her double, like the spit out of her mouth as an

East Ender would say. It must have galled him, seeing Benedict and knowing there was nothing he could do. She guessed, correctly, he had made the boy's life difficult. Well, she'd expected that. Henry hated to be bested and Isabel had certainly done that much. It would not have made for a good relationship between them. But then, that's exactly what Isabel had wanted, wasn't it?

Yet who had taken the brunt of it all? Briony herself. Her son now felt a rage towards her that would not be assuaged by anything she could do. It was this fact, this terrible fact, that had brought on the tiredness, the feeling of lethargy.

All her life she had hoped and prayed to be reunited with him. Now her hopes were dashed, she had nothing else to look forward to. Her eyes stung with unshed tears, and she dragged the brush through her hair, pulling it 'til her scalp ached.

The bedroom door opened and Tommy came in. Briony watched him in the mirror. He seemed so chirpy today. How she wished at that moment she could tap his energy and channel some of it into herself.

'Come on, Bri, get your finger out. It's not like you to be a lieabed!'

Something in his voice, in his words, said so lovingly and kindly, sent her over the edge. The tears sprang from her eyes and blurred her vision. Her shoulders shuddered with sobs.

Tommy realised she was crying and rushed to her. Pulling her round to face him, he held her to him, raining kisses on her face and neck.

'Come on, darlin', for goodness' sake. Tell me what's ailing you?'

Briony leant against his shoulder, breathing in his smell and feeling the strength of his body. She needed his strength today, oh, she needed it. Only Tommy could make her feel right. It had always been that way since they were children.

Slowly, haltingly, the story came out. Tommy stroked her back gently and listened to her silently, feeling rage at Benedict engulf him, rage at the unfairness of life. That she should have been taken like that, sold like that, and now all these years later have to pay for something she'd had no control over! 'Life's a bastard' was one of his mother's expressions and it fitted this situation perfectly. Life was indeed a bastard sometimes.

Picking her up, Tommy carried her to the big bed and placed her on it gently. Then he lay beside her and murmured to her. They spoke of the trouble in hushed tones as lovers do. Tommy brought out all her grief and bore it himself. He listened to her anguish, to her heartfelt sadness at the unfairness of life. Then, when her sobs were fading, he kissed her long and hard, gradually undressing her with practised fingers.

Briony watched him above her, his hair all grey now, no sign of the shiny blackness of yesteryear, but that was how she still saw him in her mind's eye.

Together they spanned the years, making love like youngsters, with a sharp abandon, a poignancy, that only the knowledge of age can bring about.

Tommy, for his part, saw the girl in the blue velvet dress, with her startling red hair and green eyes. The girl he had met every afternoon on a park bench. Today Briony was that girl again, though she had always stayed young to him.

They made a long slow loving that crept into the afternoon, and afterwards they held one another tightly, whispering of the old days, laughing at their shared memories of people long gone now and times well past.

They spoke only of the good times. It was a healing, and they both knew that.

Briony slept for a while in his arms, to wake later in the day refreshed and without a shadow of the tiredness she had felt earlier. She awoke to see Tommy looking at her with love and tenderness in his eyes, and suddenly that was enough for her.

Jimmy Granger checked his shotgun.

'So we go in now then?'

Daniel looked at him. 'That's about the strength of it, yeah. But remember, *I* want that slag Mitchell, *I* waste him first. You all got that?'

624

He scanned the faces of the men in the car and each of them nodded once.

Boysie laughed low.

'Then I take out Pargolis. You lot just look and listen, keep your eyes peeled on the people in the pub. If any of Pargolis' blokes try anything, blow them away. That goes for anyone drinking in the pub too. If you think they're a threat, just blow them away, simple as that.'

Boysie was repeating himself with nerves and excitement. Two minutes later Daniel gave the signal and they all got out of the Rolls-Royce. Six large men, with shotguns underneath their coats and murder on their minds.

Inside The Two Puddings, Davey Mitchell was holding court, telling jokes to Pargolis who laughed a little too loudly. The manager of the pub was surreptitiously watching the door, all the while serving drinks and holding conversations with the punters. The pub was only half full, the atmosphere charged. Conversations were loud and in some cases aggressive. The clientele was a mixture of workmen and local bully boys, young up and coming villains who wanted a bit of the reflected limelight being seen with the likes of the Cavanaghs or Pargolis could give them.

As Daniel and Boysie walked into the pub, their four minders fanned out in the bar area itself, having been let in by the barmaid as arranged.

One look at Daniel and Boysie and the pub went quiet. Unnaturally quiet. Men moved towards the sides, out of range of the shotguns, drinks still firmly in their hands, excitement heightened by alcohol. This was news, this was big news and they were to witness it.

'Hello, Davey, not like you to be quiet. Normally your mouth's going like the clappers.' Daniel's voice was friendly, conversational. He placed his shotgun on the end of the bar, facing away from Pargolis, Davey, and the three men with them.

Davey swallowed hard, his eyes riveted to the gun. Pargolis

watched everything in shock. His head was reeling at the sight of the twins.

'Don't worry, Davey boy, I ain't gonna shoot you, son.'

Walking towards him, Daniel opened his coat and brought out a long-handled eighteen-inch blade. It was more like a machete than a knife. At a signal from Daniel, two of his men pinned Davey Mitchell to the bar by his arms.

'Look, let's talk about this . . .' Pargolis' voice was a croak. This was not supposed to happen. This was what they were going to do to the twins. This was wrong, all wrong. He had been buying the twins' men, been setting the scene himself. He was Peter Pargolis, he was a big man.

Boysie laughed out loud, as if reading Pargolis' thoughts.

'That's the trouble with you bubbles, you talk too much, like your friend here. Never heard of the early bird then, I take it? You have to get up before your clothes are on, mate, to get one over on us.'

'Danny . . . Danny Boy, don't do this thing . . . Let's try and talk about it at least . . .' Mitchell was stuttering with fright. The bright blade was catching the light as Daniel held it up, bringing it slowly towards his mouth.

'I'm going to shut you up, Davey, I'm going to shut you up permanently, like I should have when you shot your trap off when me auntie died . . . Remember that, do you, you ponce!'

Pushing the blade lengthways into Mitchell's open mouth he pushed with all his might, slicing through the soft skin of his cheeks and jowl. The scream was loud and frightened, the man's voice gradually trailing off as Daniel pushed upwards, bringing the blade out once more and then upwards again, pushing the tip through the roof of his mouth and up into his brain.

Daniel nodded to the minders and as they let go of his arms, Davey Mitchell dropped to the floor. Finally Daniel dragged the blade free and stood with blood dripping on to the floor as he wiped it off on Davey Mitchell's good suit.

Pargolis watched the scene in morbid fascination. Then he saw Boysie walking towards him with the shotgun poised, aimed at his stomach, and knew, totally and irrevocably, that he would never see his wife or his children again.

Briony was woken by the loud knocking on her front door. Tommy got up and looked out of the bedroom window, half asleep.

'Who is it, Tommy love?'

'It's the Old Bill.'

She sat upright in the bed then, her face pale with shock. 'The Old Bill? What on earth could they want?'

She leapt from the bed and pulled on her dressing gown. She could hear the flapping of Cissy's slippers as she went to open the front door and, charging out on to the landing, she collided with Daniel.

'It's the police, Danny Boy. What have you been up to?' He smiled good-naturedly and shrugged.

'I ain't done nothing, Mum, I swear.' He smiled down at her and she watched as he belted up his dressing gown and walked nonchalantly down the stairs.

Briony and Tommy followed him. Briony had a sick feeling on her that grew as she saw the number of policemen in her hallway. 'What is going on here, please? Why are you here at this time of the morning?'

Her voice was surprisingly steady. She glared at the gaunt detective in his old, well-worn raincoat.

Limmington smiled, and took off his hat in a courtly gesture.

'Miss Cavanagh, I'm sorry to get you out of bed. It's your nephew we're after.' He turned to Daniel who was watching him with a closed expression on his face.

'Daniel O'Malley, I arrest you for the murder of one David Mitchell. You are not obliged to say anything, but anything you do say will be taken down and may be used in evidence against you. Do you understand what I have just said?'

'Yeah, I understand, and me name's Cavanagh, mate. Get it right.'

Limmington looked at the big, handsome man before him and couldn't restrain a smile. He'd said he'd get them, he had promised himself that. But in the end the two Cavanagh boys had simply taken themselves out of circulation. They couldn't hope to get away with this night's work. No matter how many high-powered friends they possessed. He had witness statements, and he had fingerprints, bloody fingerprints from the knife blade. Daniel had given it to one of his men to dispose of. He should have done it immediately instead of leaving it in the back of his car. He had them all bang to rights. Soon he'd be visiting this house a second time, and then he would arrest the woman in front of him, standing with her hand held to her mouth and those deep green eyes wide with innocence. Well, she would have a murder charge on her and all.

Handcuffing an unprotesting Daniel, he took him out to the waiting car and they made their way back to the station. Briony watched the policemen leave. They had obviously been expecting a fight and they were disappointed.

Tommy took hold of her hand and held it tightly. Then, picking up the phone, he dialled. He would find out the score of last night's work, see what he could do, if he could salvage anything.

It was two-thirty. By three o'clock he told Briony everything.

Suzy watched in disbelief as her husband was dragged, protesting from the house. Unlike Daniel, Boysie was not coming quietly. He was making a racket that woke up the whole street, and caused more than a few curtains to twitch. Looking at the large imposing house opposite his own, the owners two respectable doctors, Boysie shouted at the window: 'Had your fucking look, have you? You nosy pair of bastards!'

Then, dragging his arms away from the policemen restraining him, he took a swing at the young uniformed man nearest him and caught him a stunning blow on the temple. The boy went down and Boysie kicked him in the head with slippered feet.

Standing in his drive, he looked around at the twenty other policemen. Fists clenched, he was ready for a fight.

'Come on then, come on, you ponces. I dare you to come and take me.'

Then he laughed out loud, head back, teeth exposed.

'Come on then, what's the matter? Your mummies told you not to play with the naughty boys, did they?'

DI Canningfield shook his head in amazement. This boy was a lunatic. He should be put away where he belonged.

Boysie walked slowly down his drive, arms still up, fists still clenched.

'Come on then... What's the fucking matter with you? You've got an audience, ain't you? Show the public what hard nuts you are.'

Then he was running down the road, the police in hot pursuit. As he approached the end of it, he saw the road block. They had come prepared.

He swerved away and ran down a neighbour's drive. She watched in fascination as he scaled her side entrance. He ran the hundred and fifty feet of her back garden, stepping through her ornamental pond, his trousers heavy now with water and dirt. He launched himself at her back fence, repeating the run through the garden backing on to it. He burst from this over a large wooden back gate and out into the street parallel to his own. As he ran full pelt down the street, he bounded out on to the main road, the men behind him shouting and hollering for him to stop.

Laughing once more, he catapulted himself on to the main road, where he was hit full on by a police car.

Boysie was seen by the policeman following him to rise about fifteen feet into the air before landing with a sickening thud on the pavement on the other side of the road. His head was bent to the right in a grotesquely unnatural position.

As the police all surrounded him he looked up at them. He opened his mouth to speak and a trickle of blood slid slowly down from his nose and into his open mouth.

He mouthed the word 'Bastards' before a shuddering passed through his body and he died. A young PC watched his legs twitching in the final throes of death and put his hand over his mouth to swallow the sickness engulfing him.

The DI pushed his way through the men and, smiling to

himself, kicked Boysie Cavanagh as hard as he could in the stomach, lifting him off the pavement with the force of the blow.

The young PC watched his superior, silent and nauseated.

'That's one piece of shite removed from the face of the earth. Timpkins, get an ambulance.'

With that, the man walked back to the squad car and lit himself a cigarette.

Boysie Cavanagh lay on the cold pavement, dead but with a twisted smile on his face. It seemed even in death the Cavanaghs had got one over on them.

Daniel had not said a word since he had been told the news of his brother's death.

Limmington, against all his instincts, actually felt sorry for him. Knowing how close they were, how they were together continually and had stuck by each other through thick and thin, he couldn't help but feel sympathy for the large man before him.

'Drink your tea, son . . . Come on. It'll do you good.'

Daniel looked at the tea and then at the old man before him. Picking up the paper cup, he stared at the hot liquid for a few seconds before he flung the entire contents into Limmington's face. Limmington put up his hands instinctively, then Daniel was up and fighting. He grabbed hold of Limmington's jacket, raining punches on the man's face and head.

It was all over in seconds. The officer in the room raised the alarm and then five men were holding Daniel down, kneeling on him to contain him. His face was pressed against the coldness of the floor. Then, to the absolute amazement of the other men in the room, he began to cry, big bubbles of snot mingling with tears that seemed inexhaustible. His shoulders shuddered violently as he sobbed, mouthing his brother's name over and over.

The enormity of death hit him with the force of a twenty-pound hammer. His Boysie, his other half, was gone. Gone, never to return. They had been together since birth, had shared, had planned, had dreamed together, with never any real

630

thought for anyone but the other. It was all gone, Boysie was gone. Daniel wished he could have died with him.

Limmington straightened his clothes and knelt on the floor. He pushed back Daniel's hair from his face and, taking a hankie from his pocket, wiped his face and nose.

'Come on, son, calm yourself down. We're very, very sorry.'

PC Dawson looked at Limmington and felt an enormous surge of respect.

'Don't bother putting this in any of the statements. He reacted as any of us would have under the same circumstances. I'll ring for the quack, get him a shot. He ain't in any condition to be questioned. What we have to say to him will keep.'

With that he stood up and left the room, his jacket still crumpled up and his eye beginning to swell.

Outside Briony and Tommy sat in the waiting room. Briony was cold inside. It was a strange feeling. As if something inside her had died along with Boysie.

Tommy held her gently, his arm around her shoulders protectively, his own face grey and mottled.

All Briony could see in her mind's eye was two little scraps of humanity lying in the bed with their gentle mother. A mother who would have loved them to distraction, and done a damn' sight better job of raising them than the woman to whom she had entrusted them.

Briony had identified Boysie's remains, his wife being, in no condition to do the job herself. She had stood and stared down at the lifeless body of the man who had been a son to her. Who had been cared for and loved, oh yes, loved. She had always done that, even when they were at their worst.

But she had never really had any control over them, she knew that now. They had always gone their own way, their combined personalities and resources making that inevitable.

Now the upshot was one dead, one arrested for a bloody and senseless murder. Even with her own past, her own way of life, she could not find it in herself to condone, or indeed even understand, an act of such callousness and absolute lunacy as the twins had committed that night. They had barbarically

631

murdered in cold blood, in front of witnesses, two men who were well known, albeit well disliked. To do something like that in public you had to be either mentally unstable or a lunatic of the first order. The twins, it seemed, had been both these things. Now Daniel at least would have to pay the price. She couldn't hope to help him out of this.

Even if she had wanted to.

It was this that saddened her more than anything: she didn't want to help Daniel. She guessed, shrewdly, that it had been his big idea to kill them in The Two Puddings in Stratford, in front of everyone. It had his mark of showmanship about it. Oh, that was Daniel's way all right. It had been a calculated move by him, to guarantee total autonomy in the East End. To guarantee they would never be challenged again. Well, Boysie, God love him, was dead, Daniel had seen to that. Now Daniel would have to take the can.

It amazed her how they had even dreamt they could get away with it. It was 1969, not the days of the Wild West. Daniel's exceptional brain should have made him aware of that, but he had a kink in his nature, brought about by God knows what, that made him think they were invincible. And they had been, until that final act of folly.

She pushed her face into Tommy's coat, savouring the feel of him.

Limmington watched them as he passed through the front of the station. He mistook Briony's demeanour for sorrow at their getting caught; sorrow at losing her boys. He couldn't have been more wrong if he had tried.

It was sorrow all right, but sorrow tinged with guilt and wonderment. Like many a parent before her, she was wondering just where the hell she had gone wrong.

Liselle looked at the headline on the front page of the *Daily Mirror* and felt a tightness in her chest: BLOODBATH IN EAST END. She saw a picture of the twins with an airbrushed rip so the photograph was in two ragged pieces. Her eyes scanned the page.

Last night in Stratford two local businessmen were murdered in cold blood. Mr Peter Pargolis was shot twice with a sawn-off shotgun, in the stomach and the legs, and fatally wounded.

David Mitchell was slaughtered with a long-bladed knife.

The Cavanagh twins, Daniel and Dennis, were arrested for the two murders late last night after a major police operation. Dennis Cavanagh, better known as 'Boysie', died while attempting to evade police capture.

Liselle closed her eyes tightly. She had heard nothing from her Aunt Briony about this, nothing at all. This fact hurt her, while at the same time she wondered uneasily how her mother would be affected by this catastrophe and the newspaper coverage of the family.

Liselle leafed through the paper with trembling hands. Sure enough, there were pictures of her mother, herself and all the family, taken by the local *Barking and Dagenham Post* over the years.

Emblazoned across the top of the centre pages was a large headline reading: GOODNIGHT LADY.

Underneath was the story of Briony's houses in London and Essex. A picture of Berwick Manor showed Briony and Kerry standing in the doorway, smiling. Liselle began to read again, taking in every word, her eyes seeking for her own name and her mother's.

The Cavanaghs were born in Barking where their mother Eileen died shortly after their birth and they were given over to the care of her sister, Briony Cavanagh. Briony was a celebrated madam who ran many establishments with her friend and associate Mariah Jurgens. Her career began nearly fifty years ago, her first house bought when she was just fifteen years old. She is a well-known figure around London's East End, and is generally described as a fair and generous woman. Many of the people we interviewed, including her parish priest, had nothing but good to say about the Cavanagh family, the twins included.

Kerry Cavanagh, sister of Eileen and Briony, is a well-known jazz singer who recently enjoyed a revival of her career when her recording of 'Miss Otis Regrets' was chosen to accompany a prestigious perfume advertisement.

Less widely known is the fact that Kerry gave birth to an illegitimate child forty-three years ago, the father being the black pianist Evander Dorsey, who now owns the celebrated Jazz Club in New York.

Liselle put her hands to her face. She wept as she looked at the photograph of Boysie, then, pulling herself together as best she could, she went to the telephone to ring her Auntie Bernadette. That's where the family would be gathering. That's where she and her mother would be expected to go.

As always, the Cavanaghs felt better when they were all together. It was as if their strength could ward off any trouble.

Only this time, it seemed to Liselle, the trouble was just too big, and too public.

Delia was lying in bed, her eyes red-rimmed from crying. The knock at her front door made her heart stop in her chest. She was straight, completely straight, which was why her mind was going over and over the events of her cousin's death. She was reminded of Jimmy. It brought it all back.

She went to the front door and opened it, peering out through the gap allowed by her security chain. It was her mother. Taking the chain off she opened the door wide, allowing her mother in.

Bernadette walked in the tiny flat and her face screwed up with distaste at the stench. She hadn't brought Delia up to live like this! To live like a bloody hippy! She bit back the words that were in her mouth and said instead: 'You've heard about your cousins, I take it?'

Delia nodded, biting down on her lip to stop the tears.

'Oh, stop the act, Delia, I ain't in the mood!' Bernadette's voice was harsh and Delia felt the full force of her anger.

'You've been knocking off a bloke called Dave, ain't you?'

Delia watched her mother warily as she walked through to her tiny lounge. She watched her mother's eyes scan the dirty room and felt a prickle of shame. The place was filthy.

'What if I have?' There was defiance in her tone now, brought on by humiliation at her mother's obvious disgust for her living conditions.

'Well, your dad had a call about him. As if we ain't got enough bloody trouble on our plates as it is! It seems he's an Old Bill, CID. That was clever of you, wasn't it? But then, you always found trouble, Delia, didn't you? Well, let me tell you something, girl, if my sister ever finds out about the conversations you had with him about Jimmy's murder, there'll be another one done. Do you get my drift?'

Delia watched her mother's eyes. They scanned her face with no glimmer of maternal sorrow at what her daughter, her beautiful talented daughter, had been reduced to. Gone was the loving smile that told Delia she would put up with her no matter what. Instead there was open animosity, and it frightened Delia.

'I . . . I've not said a word, Mum . . . I swear!'

Bernadette poked her daughter in her ample breasts.

'Shall I tell you something, Delia? You was always my baby. You. Not Becky, poor Becky, who was always second best. Remember how we all used to laugh at her, at her posh ways and her posh voice? We all knew Becky would chase respectability, and deep inside I was glad. But you, miss, you was my baby, the favourite. Not any more. Not after the turn out with Jimmy and little Faithey. You don't care a penny piece for that little girl, I'm bringing her up for you. Your dad's her dad, he dotes on her. She don't even bother to ask where you are any more. And I *will* look after her, I promise you that, young lady.

'But I want to get something clear here today. If you cause any more trouble to this family, Briony won't be in it, mate. *I'll* break your bleeding neck, snap it with me bare hands, I take oath on that. Because you're a slut, a mouthy, dirty little slut! And I'm ashamed to admit I bore you.'

Delia stared at the floor, unable to meet her mother's eyes. 'You'd better take in what I'm telling you, girl, this is your last chance with me, I mean it. You get rid of that bloke. I don't care if you destroy yourself, that's up to you, but this family's got enough on its plate without you causing more hag.'

With that, Bernadette made to leave. Delia's voice stayed her.

'I'm sorry, Mum. Truly, I'm sorry about everything, about Jimmy, about Faithey . . .'

Bernadette turned at the door and looked back at her. They stared into one another's eyes for long moments before Bernadette answered.

'Save your sorry for when you really mean it. Sorry's an easy word to say, but that don't automatically get you forgiveness. That's like respect. You have to earn it. And judging by the way you live, it'll take you bloody years!'

With that she left the little flat and shut the door behind her. As she walked down the stinking staircase, strewn with used condoms and old chippy papers, dirty syringes and circulars, she held her breath. Then she walked out into the weak sunshine and breathed in deep gulps of fresh air to cleanse her herself.

Chapter Forty-seven

Briony looked around the room with keen eyes. Since the shock of Boysie's death had worn off, her survival instinct had come to the fore. She wasn't interested in Daniel any more, felt he had had all the help she could give him. She was more interested in protecting the rest of the family. Her mother for a start.

Molly sat hunched in a seat by the fire, a large hot rum in her hand. Every so often she wiped away a tear with a crumpled tissue, shaking her head as if in wonderment. Every so often she would read the newspaper accounts of her grandsons' lives. Even with one of them dead and the other locked away awaiting trial for murder, she still enjoyed reading about them.

Bernadette was white-faced and quiet. Her two nephews had been a big part of her life. She would miss them genuinely and acutely. Briony loved Bernie for this fact.

Delia was not there, conspicuous by her absence, as was Suzy, Boysie's wife, who was too busy selling her story to anyone who would pay for it: MY LIFE WITH GANGLAND MURDERER.

Scheming little bitch! She'd better not bother to attend Boysie's funeral because, baby or no baby, Briony would take great pleasure in slapping her face for her.

Kerry sat alone on a small stool, hands around a glass of vodka, her face bereft of make-up and expression. Liselle sat beside her, kneeling on the floor, sad and quiet.

The men, Marcus and Tommy, were closeted in Bernadette's kitchen. The daily woman and the cook had not turned up for work, which surprised no one. Photographers and reporters were camped outside on the pavement like vultures.

Mariah had turned up dressed in her loudest clothes and plastered with make-up and had stood out on Bernadette's drive for a full twenty minutes while they took photos and she answered questions.

'No,' she had said, 'I can't believe any of the things the papers are saying about the twins. They were hard-working businessmen who gave a great deal of money to charity.'

One reporter had asked cheekily if it was true she had been a celebrated prostitute in her day. Mariah had answered him just as cheekily.

'If you've got five crisp new twenty-pound notes, son, you can find out!'

This had gone out on the nine o'clock news to the merriment of the whole East End population.

The Cavanagh trial was going to be big business for the newspapers and television. The twins had somehow captured the imagination of the whole country, and the newspaper headline GOODNIGHT LADY was everywhere Briony looked. Her past was dragged up and embroidered so she looked like some kind of monster. Even Joshua O'Malley had been found and had sold his story to the *News of the World*, saying how his sons were brought up by Briony Cavanagh because she had threatened to kill him unless he gave them over to her. This had caused another sensation. Briony was made to look like Lucrezia Borgia.

The photograph taken outside St Vincent's on the day of the twins' christening all those years ago appeared regularly in the papers, Jonathan la Billière, herself and all the family smiling out at the world. Who would have thought then that those two innocent little children would one day cause all this?

The worst thought of all, though, was the thought of Benedict reading it all. Reading about her being a madam, a whoremaster. The papers made her sound so hard, so evil, even though many of her girls had in fact come forward to say that she had looked after them extremely well. That story did not appear. It wasn't what the papers wanted to hear.

Stories about Berwick Manor before the war, when it had been frequented by politicians and other well-known people, were appearing in the papers every day. Hints of scandals involving government ministers and diplomats were given prominence. Most of the stories held a grain of truth, but they were written primarily to shock, to sell newspapers. They were written for people who wanted to believe it all; wanted to believe that the rich, the famous, and the people in charge of their country ran around naked with young girls beside a warm swimming pool. One paper had even hinted at an international scandal involving the Russians, like the Profumo scandal earlier in the decade.

There was an awful lot Briony could have said, but she didn't. It would help no one.

Daniel was being treated like visiting royalty in Wormwood Scrubs. Even the screws deferred to him, made conversation with him, and called him 'Mr Cavanagh'. He had a man to do his slopping out, a man to deliver his meals to him, he even had his own cell.

This treatment soothed him. He was on remand and once the trial was over, was convinced he would be a free man.

He felt a shadow pass over his face and looked up from the letter he was reading.

A tall man stood before him. He was thin to the point of emaciation.

'I wondered if you fancied a bit of company?' The voice was high, a thin falsetto.

Daniel looked at the man for a few seconds, unable to believe the utter neck of the obviously homosexual individual before him.

'If I was so hard up for company, mate, that I had to resort to you, I'd fucking top meself!' He got up from his bed angrily as the man ran from the cell in blind panic.

Back in his own cell Bernard Campion, better known as Gloria, sat on his bunk shaking. His cell mate and long-time confidante Ian Snelling, known as Pearl to his friends, shook his head in annoyance.

'I told you not to go, didn't I?'

'Well, you can't blame a girl for trying!'

Gloria sat daydreaming of what it would have been like to have had the protection of Daniel Cavanagh. In this place it was as good as money in the bank.

Daniel couldn't calm himself after Gloria's visit and put the letter to one side.

A bloody shirtlifter coming on to him! The more he thought about it, the more it annoyed him.

Lying there in the six by eight cell, the silly encounter began to grow out of proportion in his mind. He began to see it as an affront to him as a man of means and position. He was Daniel Cavanagh. He and his brother were the undisputed Kings of London, the Big Boys. They were the two most feared individuals since Jack the Ripper, and that long streak of paralysed piss thought he would make out with him! The more he thought about it, the bigger the insult became in his mind.

Finally, he got up and walked from his cell. He marched along the landing kicking open cell doors and looking for the tall thin man who had not only invaded his personal space, but had also insulted his very manhood.

He found Gloria and Pearl sitting on their bunks. Gloria's face shone hopefully at the sight of him, convinced he had changed his mind about the offer. This was soon proved wrong as Daniel dragged the screaming man from the cell and began to belabour him with a long leather belt, used with the buckle end for maximum effect.

Men came out of their cells to watch the drama being enacted. It broke up the day, added a charge to the sameness of their existence.

Later on the screws reported that Bernard Campion had been taken to the prison hospital after falling down the stairs from the top landing.

Such was life on remand at Wormwood Scrubs. It suited Daniel Cavanagh right down to the ground. It was just what he needed after his brother's death and his own arrest. Somewhere

640

he could still be the main man. Could sit out his time given the respect he deserved and expected, until such time as he was let loose on the world once more.

Limmington had taken the statements made by Heidi Thompkins to the Home Secretary himself. He wanted this done properly, without any mistakes whatsoever. The Home Secretary gave him the go ahead to arrest Briony Cavanagh and Thomas Lane for two murders. Heidi Thompkins was going to swear in a court of law that she was at the house where Bolger died and that she saw Briony Cavanagh and Thomas Lane put the gun to his head. She was going to swear also that she had been present when they had discussed the murder of Ronald Olds, how Tommy Lane had ripped his belly open with a double-bladed boning knife. As long as he kept her away from the Cavanaghs, off the drink, and promised her a good few pounds, she was as sweet as a nut.

Limmington stood now, in full view of the photographers and reporters, outside Bernadette Dowling's house, the warrant for their arrest clutched firmly in his hand.

Cissy, with eyes red and swollen from crying, let him in. He walked into the drawing room with two officers, and was amazed by the number of people he saw.

Briony stood up and greeted him with a nod. 'What can I do for you, Mr Limmington?'

He was struck by the sadness in her husky voice. In the wake of her nephew's death she seemed to have aged considerably, and looking at her, so tiny, so diminished in her grief, he felt a moment's shame at what he was about to do.

Willy Bolger had been nothing but a dealer in porn and child prostitution, not exactly a pillar of the community. But Limmington's deep-rooted desire to take this women off the streets overrode the moment of compunction.

'Miss Briony Cavanagh and Mr Thomas Lane, I have a warrant here for your arrests . . .'

Briony's eyes widened. She heard Tommy's voice as if from a distance.

641

'What the bleeding hell are you arresting *us* for?'

'For the murders of William Bolger and Ronald Olds.'

Tommy laughed outright. 'Fuck me, couldn't you go back no further? Why don't you chuck in the murder of Abel and all while you're about it!'

Limmington smiled. 'If you'd both like to accompany me to the station?'

Tommy shot out his arm and grabbed him.

Two DCs grabbed him in his turn, expertly forcing his arms behind his back.

Briony sighed.

'Come on, Tommy, we'll be home before the day's over.' She looked at Limmington with hooded eyes.

'I've never heard so much old bollocks in all my life. You're living in a fantasy world, Mr Limmington, and you'll find out soon enough what happens to people who annoy me. I'll sue you and the police force for every last halfpenny you possess. I hope for your sake you're ready to take us on, because I can tell you now, we'll have cast-iron alibis.'

Limmington watched her warily as she went out to the hallway for her coat.

'I have everything I need, Miss Cavanagh.'

Briony faced him and smiled.

'Shall I tell you something, Mr Limmington? A lot of people have tried to get one over on me, an awful lot. But I'm still here.'

Limmington smiled back.

'Yes, but for how much longer?'

Before Briony could answer, Molly was shouting her head off.

'You fuckers of hell! You dirty bastards! My grandson's not cold and you're haunting the rest of me family.'

Bernadette took her mother in her arms and gave her a kiss.

'We'll be home before you can say knife!'

Limmington watched the scene and said in a low voice: 'Would that be double-bladed boning knife by any chance?'

James McQuiddan was supposed to be the best as far as

barristers went. Or so Briony had been told. She sat in chambers with Tommy as the man argued their case for bail.

McQuiddan was enormous. Even the man's hands were huge, and he had an undeniably menacing presence.

The Judge, Mr Justice Melrose Deakins, listened to McQuiddan's lightly accented Scottish voice attentively.

'Your Honour, we have here two people of the highest repute. And yet today they stand accused of two murders committed over forty years ago.

'One of the so-called murder victims is in fact on public record as having committed suicide. How can you *not* grant these two people bail? Briony Cavanagh is an esteemed member of her community, she has been an active charity fundraiser, a businesswoman widely respected. Thomas Lane is similarly regarded. Neither has ever been in trouble with the police. How my learned friend here can oppose bail . . .'

'Mr McQuiddan, I have listened to you with interest, and all I can say to you is, Miss Cavanagh and Mr Lane, pillars of the community, fundraising charity workers and otherwise exemplary citizens notwithstanding, are here charged with murder, not traffic offences. Murder is a heinous crime, and not one to be taken lightly. In view of the gravity of the charges, I have no alternative but to refuse them bail.'

Briony's face dropped, and Tommy closed his eyes tightly.

McQuiddan shook his head dramatically and stood up once more, his black robes billowing around him.

'Your Honour, I really must protest . . .'

Mr Justice Deakins held up one scrawny hand for silence. 'I think we have heard quite enough protesting from you for one day, Mr McQuiddan.'

Outside, when the news was broken, DI Limmington smiled and chalked the first round up to himself.

Briony walked into Holloway Prison in a daze. She had been so sure she was going to get bail, the decision of the judge had shocked her to the core. As she sat in the prison van between two policewomen she felt a plummeting inside herself. The bang of the steel doors behind her as she entered through the side door of the prison reverberated in her head.

The elder of the policewomen helped her down from the van. 'Come on, love.'

Briony smiled woodenly. She would not show them that she was frightened. If they put her away for a long time . . .

She swallowed down the terror and walked unsteadily through to the prisoners' reception. This room was dark, a window letting in the minimum of light due to its reinforced glass. She felt a pair of arms divest her roughly of her fur coat. Without it and her handbag she felt suddenly very vulnerable. This couldn't be happening to her. This was all some kind of mistake.

A woman called Marilyn, a prison officer for twenty years, grinned at her nastily.

'Come on, darlin', let's get you stripped, washed, suited and booted. Then we'll escort you to your cell. You're sharing with two bitches who should suit you right down to the ground.'

Briony drew herself up to her full height, five foot, and said coldly: 'Let's get something straight here, shall we? I am not your darling. In fact, the thought of it makes me feel physically sick. You may be big and you may be ugly, but it'll take more than that to put the frighteners on me.'

Marilyn looked down at the tiny old woman – and she was old, there was no mistaking that – and felt a great rage.

'No one talks to me like that!'

Briony, her old self back to the fore now the shock had worn off, said scathingly. 'Up yours, darlin'. I've dealt with bullies all my life, one more won't make much difference. Now then.' She looked at the assembled screws. 'Let's get this over with, shall we? Where do I shower?'

A younger officer called Tracy took her arm.

'I'll take you through to the showers just as soon as we've signed you in.'

Marilyn catalogued Briony's possessions in silence, the diamond rings and necklace patently annoying her. As Briony walked away with Tracy in tow she said to the other girl: 'That one needs knocking down a peg.'

'And you're the woman to do it, I suppose?'

Marilyn stared at the girl and nodded, a twisted smile on her face.

Briony had showered, been disinfected, and was now dressed in a skirt and blouse, her wet hair plastered to her head. Devoid of make-up she still looked good, which surprised Tracy. As she was walked across the landing to A wing, Briony took in everything around her. She was put in a cell on the top landing, and as the door opened a stench of stale cigarette smoke and urine hit her full in the face. She hesitated a few seconds at the door. Tracy, feeling the woman's discomfort, pushed her gently over the threshold.

'In you go, love. We eat tea at five-thirty, you'll be out for that.'

Briony stood in the cell as the door banged behind her and, taking a deep breath, stared at the two faces before her.

A tall black girl, no more than nineteen, stood up and held out her hand.

'Hello, love. My name's Letitia and this here is Marla.' Marla was small, plump and blonde, in her forties.

'Sit down, we've been expecting you. Would you like a roll?'

Letitia's face was open and friendly. Briony nodded and sitting on the bottom bunk, accepted a thin rolled cigarette.

'Tracy will bring you round a cuppa in a minute. Everything's been taken care of, Belinda has seen to that. You'll see her at teatime. It's only a sandwich but force it down, you won't get nothing else 'til the morning.'

Briony allowed Marla to light her cigarette and tried desperately to relax.

The walls of the cell were too close, the place stank, and nice as the two women were being to her, Briony would rather be anywhere in the world than here, in a small cell in Holloway prison.

Marla smiled, sensing her thoughts.

'Listen, love, it's a shock the first time. I know that from experience. But I'll give you a bit of advice. When you walk out of this cell, walk like you own the fucking place. You're a name, a big name. Your reputation's preceded you. There's plenty of little tarts in here who'd love to be the one to do you up. Get my drift?'

Briony took a deep pull on the match-thin roll-up.

'I know what you're saying, Marla, and don't worry about me. I can more than take care of myself.'

Something in the little woman's demeanour, her tone of voice, even the way she held her head, told both women she was speaking the truth.

Marla grinned.

'Get the feel of the place. It stinks, it's full of arseholes, but you get quite attached to it, as hard as that may be to believe. I'm waiting to go off to an open. Cookham Wood will do me lovely!'

Briony relaxed. 'What you in for?'

'Clipping. Prostitution and fraud. Me usual. Now our Letitia here is in for the big M like yourself, so you two should get on well!'

Letitia laughed.

'I'm on remand, there ain't no one proved I done it yet!'

Briony smiled. These two women, whom she would normally have avoided like the plague, had made her welcome in their own way and she was inordinately grateful.

'Who are you accused of topping?'

Letitia grinned.

'My pimp. His name was Delroy Lafayette, believe it or not.'

Briony took another drag on her cigarette. 'With a name like that, he deserved to be murdered!'

Letitia and Marla screamed with laughter.

'You'll fit in here lovely, Miss Cavanagh. Just lovely.'

Briony laughed, her old self.

Tracy, outside on the landing bringing them three cups of tea, heard the sound with approval. Briony Cavanagh was settling in. If she could laugh she could do her time, whatever it was going to be. Mariah Jurgens had slipped her a quick grand

646

through a mutual friend to see that Briony had whatever she wanted while she was a guest, and Tracy had every intention of seeing that she carried out her part of the bargain to the last letter. Putting a packet of Strands on to the tray with the tea, she entered the cell.

Belinda, or Big Belinda as she was called, watched out for the new arrival as they were let out of their cells at teatime. She stood leaning nonchalantly on the top landing, her keen eyes scanning the faces around her. She saw a mass of red hair between Letitia and Marla and walked towards them slowly. Belinda was in for aggravated burglary. She was big and fat, and had the most beautiful face Briony had ever seen on a woman.

As Belinda pushed her way through to Briony, people moved instinctively out of her way.

She smiled and held out a soft pudgy hand. 'Belinda Crane, pleased to meet you.'

Briony shook the proffered hand and grinned.

The four women walked down to the canteen together, Briony aware of the glances she was gathering from the other inmates. As they entered the canteen she saw a girl being dragged from the queue by her hair, then her face was slammed into the side of one of the wooden tables. No one took any notice. The prison officers in the room looked the other way.

Belinda smiled and said. 'That's Mary Molinero, she's in for drowning her baby.'

Briony watched as the girl crawled to a chair and pulled herself on to it, her face bleeding and her sobs audible.

'She gets fucking tortured over it. She held its face in boiling water. Can you understand people like that?'

Briony shook her head.

Belinda carried on talking as if the scene had never happened.

'Mariah Jurgens has seen to it that you got a good reception committee, and I'm part and parcel of it. I run this wing. If you want to take on any of the action, just say and I'll cut you in immediately. But you're only on remand at the moment and you might get a court date any time, so I'd wait 'til you're sentenced before going in for the big scams. There ain't no one gonna say a dicky bird to you, your reputation's guaranteed that, plus I've put the word out. There's some right fucking nutters in here, cut their own granny up for the price of a packet of fags! So watch your back all the same, we all have to do that.'

Briony took a mug of tea and a plate of spam sandwiches to a back table. From there they had a grand view of the whole canteen. The noise was deafening. Briony drank in everything around her, and now the enormity of what had happened had begun to wear off, she realised she had to assert herself.

'Belinda, let me eat me sandwich. I want to think, all right?'

Belinda nodded, looking askance at the two other women at the table. Briony bit into the dry as dust sandwich and made a face. What Belinda had said had worried her. 'Wait until you're sentenced.' It was as if everyone had already found her guilty. She took a sip of the hot sweet tea and that made her feel better. It was the stewed tea of her childhood. A reminder of home. She felt a lump rise in her throat as she thought of what she had come to. Hastily swallowing it down she said: 'Who is Mariah working through? That Tracy the screw?'

Belinda nodded.

'Then tell her I want a message out of here today. I want to see my brief, and quick.'

Belinda nodded once more. The sheer force of the little woman's attitude and her commanding presence hit home.

Gradually conversation started up between them and they chatted amicably until the bell rang for them to go back to their cells. It was as they walked up the stairs to their landing that the trouble started. Marilyn, the most hated screw in Holloway, stood arms akimbo in front of Briony. The buzz of conversation on the landing died out in seconds. Blank faces were swiftly averted. Briony felt the hair on the back of her neck rise as she looked into the hard face before her. Other screws were standing with the inmates, waiting to see the result of this confrontation.

'I don't like you, lady.' Marilyn's voice dripped venom.

Briony raised her head slightly to look her in the face.

'You got the "lady" right, anyway. Now get out of my way.'

Even Belinda moved back as Marilyn's arm came up. Briony grabbed at her uniform front and, jerking it as hard as she could, swung her body and turned, sending Marilyn careering down the iron stairs. Briony walked down after her slowly. Then, kneeling on the floor, she said in a whisper: 'I don't like you, fat girl, I don't like you at all. You push me too far and I'll see you dead. That's a promise.'

Standing up, she tidied her hair and walked sedately back up the stairs and on to the landing. The buzz of conversation started up again as soon as she was safely inside her cell.

The prison was as quiet as it was ever going to be. The hollow sounds of people coughing, and others moaning in their sleep, could still be heard.

Briony lay in her bunk, her face white and strained. She had to get out of here, she had to get away!

Today had been a nightmare. There was so much contained violence around her. And yet she was in here as Miss Briony Cavanagh, aunt of the twins, lover of Tommy Lane. She had her creds. Even her sister being a famous singer was thrilling to the average inmate, and her notoriety thanks to the papers had guaranteed her a place in the prison hierarchy that would be her protection. But Briony wanted none of it. She wanted to be at home in her bed, with Tommy beside her.

Before she slept, she saw Benedict's face. He would have heard everything by now. It would go out on the evening news. What would he be thinking?

Please God, she prayed, please dear God in heaven, help me.

Tommy awoke to the sound of shouting. He rubbed his eyes wearily, stifling a yawn.

'Shut up!' His cell mate Timmy Carlton punched his pillow in temper. 'I can't stand that bleeding racket any longer, first thing in the morning I'm going to drown that ponce in his own slop bucket!'

Tommy laughed softly.

'He's only a kid, Timmy. He's scared.'

'He'll be scared in the morning. I'll give him something to shout about mate!'

'Oh, stop being such an arsehole and give me a fag.'

Timmy took a tin from under his pillow and gave Tommy a roll-up.

Tommy lit it in the dark, saying, 'Can't you get these any thinner? It's like smoking a match!'

'Smoke it will ya! Gordon Bennett, Tommy, a fag's a fag. If you hadn't given all your Strands to that little ponce shouting his head off we'd be quids in!'

Tommy grinned.

'Timmy and Tommy, we sound like a bloody double act.'

Timmy took a deep drag on his own cigarette and said seriously, 'Ain't you trashed at all, Tommy? I mean you could get the big one.'

Tommy shook his head in the dimness. 'I ain't worried, Timmy, as long as my old woman gets a result. That's all I'm worried about.'

Timmy scratched his short cropped hair.

'I remember her from years ago. A right looker she was.'

'She still is as a matter of fact, Timmy.'

Timmy laughed. 'My old woman looks like the back of a bus, but she's a good sort. Always visits like, brings the kids to see me. I like seeing the kids. But they took their toll on old Gabby. She's half the size of a house these days. Used to be a right nice bit of stuff and all.'

Tommy laughed again. 'You've got some kids and all ain't you? How many at the last count?'

'Nine. Five boys and four girls. My eldest girl Susan is doing ever so well. Works in an office up West. The boys take after me, got one in the 'Ville for malicious wounding, one on the island for armed robbery and the other three won't go to school for love nor money. When I get out I'm gonna take the buggers in hand. Give me girls any day of the week. You ain't got any kids have you?'

'Nah. I'd have liked them though. But me and Briony, well the time was never right.'

Timmy kept quiet.

'Sometimes, like now, I wish I had a boy of me own like.'

Timmy heard the yearning in his friend's voice and made a noise in the back of his throat.

'Let me tell you, mate, they're nothing but bleeding hag.'

Tommy turned over in his bunk to sleep. 'Goodnight, Timmy.'

As Timmy began to snore softly, Tommy thought about his life with Briony. He had forfeited children for her. He had given up a lot. The question in his mind was, was it all worth it? As the sun came up, bringing a few rays of light through the window of his cell he grinned to himself. He didn't have to answer that question. Every time he looked at her, he had his answer. He'd gladly do any amount of time for her, he loved her deeply and abidingly.

The young man started shouting again in his sleep. His fear of prison made his nightmares terrifying.

Tommy closed his eyes tightly and tried to sleep. He was getting too old for all this.

Chapter Forty-eight

Briony and Mariah hugged each other tightly.

'Oh, Briony, how are you, love?'

Briony sat down at a table in the visiting room and shrugged. She had been in Holloway a week, and this was her friend's first visit.

'It's not too bad in here once you get used to it, Mariah. But I wouldn't say no if someone asked me to leave, know what I mean?'

Mariah laughed delightedly.

'I knew you wouldn't let all this get you down.' Her face sobered as she said, 'We tried everything to get you out for Boysie's funeral, you know.'

Briony nodded.

'Listen, Mariah. I want you to do something for me. I want you to pull in a few favours . . .'

Mariah grinned and cut her off.

'I know what you're going to say and I'm here to tell you it's all in hand. Today, while we speak, more than one person is going to get a big shock. The main person being that slag Heidi! Imagine that little bitch turning out to be the fly in the ointment, eh? I can't believe it. Well, she's at a safe house in North London and she's getting a little visit today that should make her change her statement quick smart. Also a few of our more illustrious customers are getting the bad news. Before I forget, Jonathan's coming to see you tomorrow. He's in a right state. Well, it can only look good for you. He's still news because of his knighthood in the New Year's honours. So don't you worry, by hook or by crook you'll be out of here soon.'

Briony laughed out loud.

'I should have known you'd have it all in hand!'

Mariah grabbed her friend's arm and said softly, 'We go back a long way, Bri.'

Briony nodded sadly.

'We're the old breed, Mariah. In here, in just a week I've been offered more drugs than I'd know what to do with. I'm in with women me and you wouldn't piss on if they burst into flames in front of us, and I've met young girls who make Ma Baker look like Little Red Riding Hood!'

'But you're holding your own, I take it?' Mariah's voice was low now, worried.

'Oh, I'm holding me own all right, never fear about that, and I've you to thank for me reception commitee! Now how's my Tommy? What's the news? How're the family?'

Mariah settled back in the uncomfortable chair and regaled Briony with all the news.

Both women were happier now, knowing that something was being done.

Peter Hockley was in a state of nervous prostration. Standing in front of him was a woman, a frightening woman, and in her hand he had photographs of him in full drag together with a young friend called Percy Parkinson.

Bernadette smiled as she spoke.

'My sister is going to make a full statement about an event in the twenties when you and a Mr Rupert Charles were responsible for a young man losing his life during an orgy. These photographs of you and your current amour will more than lend credibility to the story. Mr Jonathan la Billière is also willing to say he was there when your father paid a vast sum of money to hush everything up. Briony says, if she goes down, everyone goes with her.'

Peter's voice came out a low throaty croak.

'But what can *I* do?'

Bernadette put the photographs on the desk and said in friendly fashion: 'You can keep these, I have plenty of copies. Now, what do I want you to do? I want you to go and see your cousin, the Lord Chief Justice, who happens to be closely related to the Home Secretary through marriage. A brother-in-law isn't he? What a coincidence. I want you to tell him that these photos are going in the *Daily Mirror*, and the *News of the World*, the *People*. In fact, anywhere I can get them that will do you all the most damage. Do you get my drift, Peter old chap!'

He felt the sting of tears. He was himself, nowadays, the Member of Parliament for Rochford East and Shadow Defence Secretary, yet these few photos could blight his life and bring disgrace on his family. Briony Cavanagh was willing to bring up all the old trouble that he had so conveniently forgotten after his father had bought him out of the biggest scrape of his life.

He watched the woman walk to the door. As she turned she said as an afterthought: 'Before I forget, you've got forty-eight hours.'

With that parting shot, Bernadette left the room, leaving Peter with his photos and his conscience. And a clear picture of a young man bound and gagged and with his throat slit like an animal's.

Heidi, scrubbed now from head to foot and wearing a tweed skirt and a scratchy sweater, looked in shock at the woman before her. Mariah looked so out of place in this little room with its electric fire and nylon curtains. She looked too big and far too outrageous to be in a place so conservative.

Mariah spoke again.

'So what you're telling me is you came for a bit of trouble like, is that it? You thought you'd quickly make a couple of bob and fuck off? But you didn't have what Limmington wanted so he made a point of doctoring your statement to suit him?'

Heidi nodded fearfully.

'That's about the strength of it, yeah. I was so hard up, Mariah. I had nothing . . .'

She put up her hand for silence.

655

'Don't give me all your old fanny. You could have come to me or Briony, we'd have seen you all right, we always see our old girls all right. Well, you're going to tell a lot of people about Limmington's skulduggery, and you're going to be well paid for doing it.'

Heidi's eyebrows shot up with interest.

'Yeah, that's right. You're going to get a good drink. Enough to keep you pissed for the rest of your natural. But one stipulation. You disappear once it's all over.'

'Oh, don't worry, I will. All this is getting on my tits now.'

Mariah looked down at her own ample breasts, straining to escape from a lurex dress, and grinned.

'Not half as much as it's getting on mine!'

Sir Geoffrey Dance, the old man of the House, and a very respectable businessman, was biting his perfectly manicured nails, a habit he had given up in the throes of adolescence. His six daughters and his wife stared out from a photograph on his desk. In his hand he held another photograph. It had been taken three Christmases ago at Berwick Manor at a Christmas theme party, with all the men dressed up as Santa's gnomes. But even with the long false beard, no one could doubt it was indeed Geoffrey. On his lap sat a young girl of about seventeen, in a Santa Claus costume. On her long slim legs, which were wrapped around his waist, she wore fishnet stockings. The photograph had been taken from the side, and as he had nothing on the bottom half of his body, anyone could make anything they wanted from the photo. It was clear, from the pink buttocks on his lap, that the girl was devoid of briefs.

He felt a sinking sensation in his chest. The Manor had always been so private. They had never had a moment's worry about anything being leaked. The upstairs function room had always been a place where men like himself could go and indulge themselves in anything that took their fancy without the slightest fear of its ever coming back to haunt them. That was what the large amounts of money guaranteed, and he had paid huge sums over the years. Now with Briony Cavanagh and

656

Tommy Lane about to be brought to court, many secrets would be spilt. Not just his, but an awful lot of other people's too.

The last thought cheered him.

He looked at the photograph again and saw in the background, as plain as day, the current Chancellor of the Exchequer. This made him smile as he picked up the receiver.

He was in the shit all right, but then so were a lot of other people.

Fenella Dumas went into the den, as Benedict called the office he used when working from home. Placing a cup of coffee on his desk, she said: 'I think you should be ashamed of yourself, Ben, I do really.'

Benedict wiped a dry hand over his face and sighed heavily. 'Give it a rest now, Fen.'

Fenella sniffed through her Roman nose. 'She is your mother, whether you like it or not. I can't understand why you're so set against her. Think about it. She was a girl, just a little girl. Every time I think about your father . . .' her voice trailed off. 'I know now why your mother never left him on his own with Natalie. Your father was a twisted, perverted man, yet you're allowing yourself to be taken over by his petty mindedness. I'll tell you something for nothing: I'd rather be related to Briony Cavanagh than Henry Dumas. There, I've said it now.

'She needs you, Benedict. That woman really needs you. You don't have to visit her in public, but you can talk to a few of our friends, try and make it a bit easier for her . . .'

He shouted at the top of his voice, 'Oh for crying out loud, Fen, leave it!'

Fenella bit on her bottom lip to stop the tears. She had lived with and loved this man for many years. they had brought up two children and she had thought she knew him, really knew him. But since the revelation about his real mother, he had gradually died inside, been eaten up with the knowledge. Now she had a man on her hands whose innate kindness and gentleness were gradually draining away, and she didn't like it, couldn't cope with it.

'I'm telling you, Benedict, this is 1969, not the bloody Dark Ages. Legally you're Henry's and Isabel's, no one can take anything away from you. Not your title or your money. But you'd have had none of that if that poor little girl who gave birth to you had decided to keep you. Think about it. Maybe she did what she did to make sure you had the best that life could give. She never came knocking on our door for anything, did she? She never tried to get money from you . . . Oh, you're making me so cross!'

Benedict had rarely heard his wife this upset. It was as if she had already taken Briony Cavanagh into her heart and home. No matter what was written about her in the papers, Fenella just ignored it. Blood meant a lot to Fen, and as far as she was concerned, Briony Cavanagh's blood ran through her children's veins so she couldn't be all bad.

He tried to smile.

'I can remember her, you know, Fen. She used to come to Regents Park where I went with my nanny every day. I can remember her hair. She still has got the same hair, crackling and so red. It was like looking in the mirror, only I couldn't see it then. But now, when I look at Nat and young Henry, I can see her in them. I can see her in me every time I look in the mirror. I can't believe she's my mother. She looks my age, for Christ's sake! She looks just like my bloody sister!'

Fenella put a slim hand on his shoulder and squeezed it.

'She is your mother, no matter how she looks. Try and see it from her point of view. Try and understand.'

Benedict laughed softly.

'I've been trying to do that since the day I found it all out. I think the worst thing of all is the fact my so-called father could have waited all that time to hurt me and Isabel. It's sick.'

Fenella sniffed loudly.

'He was a sick man. I thought we'd already established that much. He was rotten with his own hatred. Don't you go and make the same mistake.'

Benedict sat forward in his chair. 'I don't hate her, Fen, that's the trouble.'

Fenella sighed and said gently, 'Drink your coffee, Ben, before it gets cold.'

Briony lay in her bunk listening to the chatting of her cell mates. Marla was speaking in a low voice and Briony felt a deep sadness as the women spoke.

'My daughter's still in care now. I was homeless, see, so they took her off me. I was lodging with this right spiv in Canning Town. Well, he took me rent and done a moonlight, only he don't really own the drum, see. Some other geezer does, a Pakistani called Pardel. Well, he had me removed, bag and baggage. So the Welfare came and took her off me. That was nine years ago. I was picked up the next night at King's Cross for soliciting, so when we got to court, they'd made her a ward of court, saying she was in moral danger with me! I was only soliciting to get the money for a meal and a bed like. I was hardly an old hand at the game. I mean at my age, I ask you? Anyway, I just give up after that. This is about my seventh time in here. I'm hoping to get a result and go to an open to finish me sentence. They'll bring me girl if I get an open, see.'

Briony asked softly, 'How old is your daughter now?'

Marla sighed in the darkness.

'Just on twelve. She's lovely, beautiful, like her father. He was a West Indian. She's half-caste.'

'I bet she is beautiful and all. My niece Liselle is very attractive.'

'That's your sister's daughter, isn't it? The singer. You're a very famous family really, aren't you? What with Jonathan la Billière being close and your sister being a famous singer. The twins . . .'

Briony heard the jolt in Marla's voice and said, 'My boys, and they were my boys, weren't really bad. They were just . . .'

Marla's voice came out of the gloom. 'Go on?'

Briony cleared her throat and said, 'Never mind. Forget it.'

But the twins stayed with her for the rest of the night. She saw them at every age, with their ready smiles and their constant demands.

* * *

Harry Limmington was at home eating a ham sandwich and having a cup of tea while he watched 'Z Cars'. He heard a deep voice and dragged his eyes from the screen to look towards the hall of his council house.

'What did you say?' He heard his wife cry out.

A uniformed police officer pushed past her and came into the room.

'Mr Harry Limmington, I am arresting you for tampering with a witness's statement and attempting to pervert the course of justice.'

Limmington stood up in shock, his sandwich and plate falling to the floor.

'Is this some kind of joke?' His voice was incredulous.

The grey-haired man said sadly, 'No joke, mate. You've been tumbled. Get your coat and let's have this over with.'

Five minutes later Harry Limmington was sitting in the back of a panda car on his way to Barkingside police station.

Briony kissed Marla and Letitia goodbye. As she walked along the landing she was hugged by Belinda who said gruffly, 'Don't forget us lot now, will you?'

Briony laughed out loud. 'As if I could.' She followed Tracy off A wing, and as the door was locked behind her, sighed with relief.

She was leaving the place, and the thought gave her a thrill. Soon she would be outside in the filthy London air and she'd breathe it in gratefully. Soon she would be with her family, and with Tommy, her Tommy. Then she could put all this in the past.

Twenty minutes later she was dressed, had signed for her belongings and stepped outside Holloway to a blaze of photographers and newsmen. She felt an arm on hers and turned to see Bernadette.

'Come on, Bri, we've a car here for you. Let's get you home, girl. Marcus is picking up Tommy.'

They pushed their way to a waiting Rolls-Royce and,

slamming the door behind them, Briony began the journey back to her family.

'How you feeling, Bri?'

'Great, Bernie, really great. I tell you something, I have never been so pleased to see anyone in my life before! Now all I want is a bath to get the smell of that rathole off me.'

Bernadette laughed.

'The whole family is waiting at home for you.'

Briony grinned.

'I had a feeling they might be.'

Briony walked into Bernadette's house to see Cissy crying, her mother drinking, and Kerry and Liselle popping champagne corks. Jonathan had flown over for her homecoming. As she kissed his cheek, and felt the family envelop her in their love, she knew, finally and irrevocably that she had indeed come home.

Mariah came out of the drawing room to greet her and the two women hugged.

'Welcome home, Bri. We beat the fuckers! I told you we would, didn't I?'

'We did that, Mariah. Now I want a large brandy and a nice fag. Then I want to have a bath and wash me hair!'

Mariah poured her a brandy in a large balloon glass.

'Cheers, everyone.' Briony drank the burning spirit straight back. Then, sitting in a chair, she grinned.

'By Christ, it's nice to be home.' Her voice broke then and everyone stood in amazement as she cried her eyes out. Molly finally went to her daughter and cuddled her.

'Come on now, darling. Once we get your man out, Daniel, we'll all be together again.'

Briony was saved from answering as Marcus and Tommy came through the front door.

Briony was swept up into Tommy's arms and kissed hard on the mouth.

'I've missed you, Bri. Oh, but I've missed you, girl!'

661

Then, in excitement and happiness, the homecoming party started in earnest.

Briony and Tommy lay in bed together, the aftermath of energetic lovemaking leaving them both warm and pleasantly tired.

'Oh, Tommy, I've dreamt of this. Being with you again. I really thought me and you were going to go down and they would throw away the key.'

Tommy pulled her closer to him.

'I'll tell you something, Briony, I was shitting meself. But Mariah came up trumps. She put pressure on the right people. She knew who would be the most vulnerable, and the most helpful.'

'You know, Tommy, I never thought Harry Limmington would have stooped to doctoring a statement. I always had him down as straight as a die. I know it sounds crazy, but him being bent, it's upset me!'

Tommy laughed low.

'I don't believe you, Briony! He was after putting us away for the rest of our natural and you're upset because he's a little bent! I hope he gets ten years, the ugly ponce!'

She snuggled into his arms.

'I never want to go inside again, Tommy. I think I'll retire now.'

He laughed again, louder this time. 'I'll believe that when I see it.'

'Believe it, Tommy Lane. I'm too old to be banged up!'

Tommy looked down into her green eyes. 'You'll never be old to me, Bri. You'll always be the girl in the blue velvet dress.'

Briony kissed him again. 'You're an old bullshitter, Tommy Lane, but I love you.'

'And I love you, Briony, more than you know.'

They were quiet for a while, just enjoying each other's presence, then Tommy said: 'What are we going to do about Daniel?'

Briony took a deep breath.

'What can we do? There's no way we can nobble for him, is there? It's too big. Me and you were on charges so old they were practically entered in the Domesday Book! But Danny boy, they've got him bang to rights. He committed a grisly murder in a packed pub. He went too far, Tommy. He went over the top. For all we ever done, we never enjoyed any of it. To me and you it was always a means to an end. But Danny and Boysie, God love them, they enjoyed the killing. Especially Daniel.

'They made the cardinal mistake. They really thought they were above the law. We both tried to tell them over the years, and this is the upshot. I have no intention of lifting a finger to get Daniel out. I'll get him a brief and that's that.'

Tommy stroked the erratic red hair he loved so much and said truthfully, 'I'm glad.'

She sighed.

'Are you? I'm not. I wonder what my Eileen would have thought of the way those two boys turned out? She entrusted them to me and I ruined them. I made the mistake I've always made. I loved them too much.'

Tommy pulled her to him and held her close.

'You can never love anyone too much, Bri.'

But she didn't answer him.

Briony opened the front door herself. It was early afternoon and everyone had eaten lunch. The doorbell rang as she was coming out of her kitchen with a large tin of cakes freshly baked that morning by Cissy for Tommy, who still ate as often as possible. Briony put the cake tin on the hall table and opened the door with a smile on her face, expecting it to be one of the bevy of reporters camped outside her house. She sent them out tea at intervals and they always thanked her politely.

She opened the door and the smile froze on her face.

'Hello. I hope I'm not intruding?'

Briony felt a wave of heat wash over her body as the rich voice spoke to her. She stood stock still, her eyes boring into those of her son.

'Benedict?' It was a question.

The two stood looking at one another for long moments before Tommy came bowling into the entrance hall. One look at the man at the door told him everything. He saw the same green eyes, the same heart-shaped face, the same finely boned features. Even the man's hair had a red tint.

'Benedict? Bloody hell, Bri, he's like the spit out of your mouth!'

Tommy's incredulous voice broke the tension. Benedict felt himself being pulled over the threshold and into the warmth of his mother's home.

Briony stared at her son from head to toe. She had to crane her neck to look up into his face, he was so tall. As big as Tommy. The two men shook hands, Tommy grabbing her son as if frightened Benedict was going to run away.

'This is indeed a pleasure. I'll go inside and keep everyone contained.' He laughed. 'I expect you two would like to see one another for a while in private?'

Benedict smiled as the big jovial man went back into the dining room and left them alone.

'Come through to the drawing room, Benedict. We can talk there.'

He followed her. She looked amazingly youthful from behind. She had the same easy carriage that his own daughter had, along with the deep red hair and green eyes.

Inside the drawing room, Briony turned to face him.

'I hope you've come in friendship, Benedict.'

She looked so small standing there, hands clasped in front of her like a schoolgirl, her brilliant eyes lowered. He felt as if someone had pushed a knife into his chest, so great was the pain. Then over her shoulder he saw a photograph of himself in a heavy silver frame. His childish face was smiling. The photograph was faded with age.

'Sally took me to have that photograph taken, I can remember it as if it was yesterday. I realise now she worked for you as well as my family.'

Briony licked her dry lips.

'I knew everything there was to know about you, Benedict, I got it all from her. Second hand, of course, but you'll never know how much it meant to me. I never forgot you. Not a day has gone by but you've been in my mind. You have to believe that.'

'It's funny, but I do believe you. I know you loved me dearly. I'm sorry for the way I acted before . . .' His voice faltered. 'It was finding out the way I did.'

Briony dismissed it with a wave of one jewelled hand.

'What can I do for you, Benedict?'

He smiled crookedly and shrugged his shoulders. Taking all his courage into his hands, he said, 'You can start by filling me in on your life. Then, if you want, I'll tell you about my wife Fen, and my children Henry and Natalie. Your grandchildren.'

Briony felt as if her chest was burning, so intense was the moment.

Of one mind they stepped towards one another and then Briony felt herself being pulled into the arms of her son, her flesh and blood. She could smell his aftershave, and a mingled scent of leather and tobacco. For the first time ever she was being held by her son, her big handsome son whom she had thought hated her, had been disgusted by her. It was a homecoming for both of them.

'Oh, my son, my son. I've waited so long for this. A lifetime.' Her words were thick with emotion and for long minutes they held one another, the only sound the deep steady ticking of the long case clock in the corner of the room.

Eventually Briony pulled her face from his coat. Smiling, she looked up into the face that mirrored her own.

'Why? What made you come to me after all that's happened in the last few weeks?'

Benedict smiled.

'Because, Mother, you're my blood, as silly as that may sound. You're my mother. My reason for being. Your blood runs through my veins and the veins of my children.' He grinned. 'Do I sound pompous?'

Briony shook her head, unable to talk for the sheer enormity of what was happening to her.

'I knew it that day. I had known about you for so long, but I couldn't admit it to myself. Then my wife, dear Fen, pointed out to me what I had known myself all along. You are me, and I am you really. I wanted to come back that day and say I was sorry. I was paying you back for the hurt I was feeling over my father's will. Over finding it all out like that. So cold-bloodedly. I can't ever tell you how sorry I am.'

Briony grasped his hand and held it to her cheek.

'You're here now, Ben, that's enough for me.'

'I tried to help you. I put pressure on more than a few of my friends and colleagues.'

This statement pleased her enormously. She looked at him again, as if frightened he was going to disappear as quickly as he had come.

'Thank you, Benedict. Thank you.'

As they stood there Molly burst into the room, her aged eyes still piercingly sharp.

'What's going on here then?' Her voice was loud, distrustful.

Briony smiled. 'Benedict, I'd like you to meet your maternal grandmother.'

She went to her mother and, taking her arm, walked her to Benedict and said proudly: 'Mum, this is my son, Benedict Dumas.'

Molly smiled crookedly and said, 'I've got eyes in me head. You look like two peas in a bleeding pod! Come here, son, give your old granny a kiss.'

Benedict kissed her on her papery cheek, feeling her frailness as he embraced her. Then the room seemed to be full of people. He was surrounded by his family, all smiling and looking at him curiously. He saw Bernadette and Kerry; saw his own children in these women, in their jawlines, in the movement of their head.

Yes, indeed, this was his real family. He held on to his grandmother and his mother, relishing the contact with people who were a part of him.

This was his family. Whether he liked it or not, this was the stock he came from. Then they were all touching him, wanting to get to know this big son of Briony's, this extension to their large close-knit family. He was accepted immediately and at face value, something he had never experienced before in his life.

With all her troubles of the last weeks, with all her heartache over Boysie and Daniel, Briony still felt as if she led a charmed life.

The one thing she had wanted all her life, above everything, had now come about. After over fifty years of trouble, strife and heartbreak, when every family gathering had been bitter-sweet because one crucial person was always absent, always missing, the mainstay of her life was here now.

Benedict was in the fold.

Her son had come home to her.

Briony sat opposite Daniel in Wandsworth Prison. He was sitting with his legs crossed, his handsome face dour. She was listening intently to what he had to say.

'Then, once I'm out, I'm going to go after the fucking lot of them. I'm going to tear the East End apart if needs be, but I'll find them all. Every last one of them.'

Briony sighed softly. It was always the same.

'As for that cunt Limmington, I heard he just got a slapped wrist. Well, I'll fucking pay that slag out and all for my Boysie. You see if I don't.

'And did you see that ponce on Friday, did you? Telling the court how I pushed the knife into Mitchell's mouth. I know that shite, I know his name and address. I'll torture him and his fucking kids. I'll torture his kids in front of him . . .'

Briony held up her hand.

'Enough! For Christ's sake, Daniel, that's enough! You know the old saying, don't you? "If you can't do the time, don't do the crime." You made a big mistake. You thought you could do what you wanted. Well, you can't. I've got you McQuiddan and he's good, but you're going down, Danny boy. You'd best get used to that fact.'

Danny's face twitched.

'You and Tommy never went down, did you? You two got a result.'

Briony nodded. 'We were charged with a very old crime, Danny boy. I know about violence, all right. But we were violent in the 'twenties and believe me when I say you had to be violent then. You had to take what you wanted. It wasn't like today, when the working classes can get an education, can follow their stars. I had the choice between looking after myself and my family, or going under, like me Mum had to.

'You don't know the first thing about real violence. Oh, you hurt people, you shoot them. But you have no inkling of real poverty, and that's where real violence is bred. The survival of the fittest. Me and Tommy came from an era where eating regularly was a result, where keeping warm was a major occupation. You grew up with everything anyone could want. I even sent you two to Ampleforth and what for, eh? What the hell for? You even take pleasure in keeping your East End accent. I take the blame for you two – I should have knocked you down a peg when I had the chance; but being me, I loved you so much I couldn't see your faults. I made excuses for you and in reality there were none. You were just a vicious little bastard and this is the upshot. I never hurt anyone for fun, for recognition. People had to tread heavily on my toes before I retaliated and that's why I'm sitting here and you're sitting there.'

Daniel sneered at her. 'The voice of Briony Cavanagh. Shall I tell you something? We used to laugh at you and Tommy behind your backs. You was a joke to us. Me and Boysie, we had them there.' He held out his palm. 'We had them there, and would have kept them there and all. It was grasses who tucked us up and they'll pay, believe me.'

Briony shook her head in sorrow. 'Can't you see anything, Danny? Can't you see we're living in a different world now? The days when you could walk into a pub with a shooter and expect everyone to turn a blind eye are long gone. You made the mistake of making too many enemies. The big I am, were you? Well look where it's got you. I couldn't give a monkey's whether

668

you laughed at us behind our backs, because at the end of the day, Tommy Lane is worth fifty of you, a hundred. That man deserves your respect. If you'd had any sense you'd have emulated him. Fifty years on and he's still respected, still liked and what's more, still outside on the street. The way you're carrying on you won't see the light of day until the year two thousand.'

'Well, now we both know where we stand don't we?'

Briony nodded. 'We do. I blame you for my Boysie, he followed you in everything. I'll give you a last bit of advice, my son: keep your head down and do your bird. No more outbursts in court threatening all and sundry, it just makes you look a prat.'

Danny's eyes were blazing. 'You know it all, don't you? You're not sitting in the dock. You and Tommy walked out your nicks and now you're coming on to me like some kind of saint!'

Briony leant across the table and said through gritted teeth, 'I told you, Danny, we were the old style of villain. You and Boysie could never understand us. Shall I tell you something? In all honesty, I never really wanted any of it. None of it. But I made my bed, as me mother would say, and I think we can safely say I lay down in it. For over fifty years. You two never *had* to do what you did, you chose it. You decided to be what you are.'

Daniel's face was still twisted. Getting up, he said: 'I ain't listening to this shite. I'm better off in me cell. It's Saturday, and on Saturday we can listen to our radios and have a laze about. Come to think of it, that's what we do most days. But you'd know all about that, wouldn't you? So if you'll excuse me? I have better things to do.'

Briony sat stone-faced as he went to a prison officer to be taken back to his wing. People were staring at them, their last exchange having been overheard. Standing up she walked with as much dignity as she could out of the visiting room.

She had done her best.

Mr Justice Martin Panterfield stared at the man in the dock before him. He wiped his mouth with a spotlessly clean handkerchief before delivering his judgment to the packed but hushed courtroom.

'Mr Daniel O'Malley, you have been found guilty of a vicious murder. Never before have I listened to such grisly accounts of barbaric and unnecessary violence. You took a knife and cold-bloodedly executed David Mitchell in full view of a packed public house. You and your twin brother terrified the East End of London, and were involved with a number of illegal businesses. You were a wicked and callous murderer who thought you could do what you wanted. You are the frightening result of this so-called permissive society. I would be failing in my duty to the public if I did not impose the maximum penalty the law dictates.

'I hereby sentence you to life imprisonment with a recommendation you serve at least thirty years. Have you anything to say?'

Daniel stood up, hands clasped in front of him, face devoid of expression. Then he looked the judge in the eye and said clearly: 'Yes, I have, mate. The name's Cavanagh!'

The judge shook his bewigged head. Looking around the court, he said: 'Take him down.'

Molly stood up then. Her face streaming tears, she screamed: 'You dirty bastards, that's my boy. My Boy! Danny, son, Danny.' Her voice reverberated around the courtroom as Daniel was escorted from the dock by two burly policemen. On his way down to the holding cells he held up his arms in a victorious gesture and shouted:

'That's it, Gran! I'll be back, I'll be back!' His voice was lost as he disappeared below.

Limmington looked at Briony and their eyes locked. She nodded at him almost imperceptibly. It was a job well done.

Chapter Forty-nine

Suzy looked around her mother's front room, breathing in the scent of Airwick and furniture polish. She placed her hands roughly on her stomach, repressing the urge to scream. Her mother popped her head around the door and said; 'Shall I make you a drink, love? How about a cuppa?'

'I don't want anything, leave me alone.'

The woman walked into the room and tried to take her daughter's hand. Suzy shrugged her off.

'Oh for crying out loud, leave me be, woman!'

Doreen sat down on a chair and said softly, 'I know you're hurting, love, but you must try and keep yourself together; that child will take a lot of looking after – children do. I know you're upset over Boysie, God knows I am myself.' She dabbed at the corner of a heavily made-up eye with a tissue. 'I loved that boy as if he was me own, God rest him.'

Suzy raised her eyes to the ceiling, then, leaning forward awkwardly, she said through gritted teeth. 'Cut the act, Mum, there's no one here to see it but me. As for this bloody baby, I don't want it. I can't stand being pregnant, and I hate living here.' She bit her bottom lip to stem the trembling and said brokenly, 'I'm glad he's dead, I hated him. I hated everything about him.'

Doreen sat back in her chair. Then, without warning her hand shot out and she slapped Suzy a stinging blow across her face. 'You little bitch! Let words like that get out and there'll be trouble, my girl. You broke your frigging neck to get up that aisle and don't you forget it. When I think of the shame we've had to endure because of your association with them Cavanaghs, I could cheerfully throttle you, and that little child you're carrying can't be blamed. My God, I wonder at times just what you think you're playing at, madam, with your butter wouldn't melt look and that scheming brain. Let his Aunt Briony hear talk like that and you'll be singing a different tune.'

'Oh go away, Mum!'

'No I won't. You left that lovely house, all that nice furniture. Me and your Dad would have moved in there and looked after you, but no, not you. You had to come running home here like a baby.'

Suzy felt a moment's triumph as they reached the nub of her mother's annoyance. Doreen saw herself in the big detached house, bringing up her grandchild, guaranteed a good allowance and the property. Suzy had sussed that out in no time. 'You'll never live in that house, Mother, get that straight now.'

Doreen's lips moved back over her teeth, and she said, 'You're a little bitch, Suzy Rankins, a bitch. When I think of how I brought you up, gave you the best . . .'

Doreen's tirade was interrupted by the doorbell.

Suzy smiled grimly. Saved by the bell. If her mother knew how much she had been paid for her interview with the paper she'd have a fit, but there was a method in her madness. Once she was delivered of this child she would go away and make a fresh start. The name Cavanagh, which had excited her so much when she had first met Boysie, disgusted her now. She was pointed at, stared at and gossiped about every time she walked down the street.

Her heart stopped as she heard her mother's voice: 'Oh, hello, Briony, come away in. I was just making a cup of tea.'

Briony rustled into the room. 'Hello, Suzy, love.'

Suzy forced herself to look at the little woman. 'Hello, Briony.'

Doreen, overcome with awe as usual, left the two and went to make the tea.

Briony sat down on the chair Doreen had vacated and smiled. 'How you feeling?'

Suzy lit a cigarette and smiled wanly, blowing out the smoke in a large cloud around her head. 'All right I suppose.'

Briony patted her hand and the action so startled the girl she flinched. 'Calm down, Suzy! Anyone would think you had something to be frightened about.' Briony's voice was sad. 'I know you must be devastated about Boysie, we all are. He was a good boy, my Boysie. A good kind boy. I miss him so much.'

Suzy took another drag on her cigarette and kept silent.

'Have you seen the doctor about Junior?'

'I'm fine. I just wish I could get it over with.'

'I can understand that, but it will be over sooner than you think.'

Doreen bustled in with the tea and began chattering.

'I've told her she should go back to her own home, there's no room here for a baby. I've offered to go with her, like. After all, it is her house now, isn't it?' Doreen's voice was innocent and Briony closed her eyes for a few seconds.

'Yes it's her house, Doreen, but maybe it brings back too many memories, eh, Suzy?'

Suzy made herself look into the older woman's eyes and smile gratefully. 'That's right. I never want to go in there again. I can't face the neighbours, after what happened . . .'

Briony sipped her tea and nodded understandingly. 'I was wondering if you'd like to come to me until the baby arrives.'

'No! No really, I want to be here with me mum. I don't want to go anywhere else . . .' Her voice was rising in panic.

'All right, Suzy, calm down. It was only a suggestion. Everyone wants their own around them in times of upset. I can understand that. Only you are carrying all that's left of my Boysie, see. It's like my grandchild, I always thought of the twins as my own sons, as you know. Heard anything more from the reporters? I wondered if they'd asked you why you didn't attend the funeral.'

Suzy stared down at her cup, unwilling to answer the question.

673

'If you wanted money so badly, Suzy, you should have come to me. Especially with the baby coming. As long as I see the child regularly, you'll be amply provided for. I've booked you in a private clinic, that way you won't be mobbed by press when your time comes. I don't expect you want to have the child in a blaze of publicity do you?' Opening her bag, she took out a small white card. 'This is the clinic's address and phone number. Ring up and arrange your check ups with them. I'll pay the bill so don't worry about expense. They delivered Princess Margaret's children, nothing but the best for my Boysie's baby, eh?'

Standing up, she kissed Suzy's cheek softly. 'Look after yourself love, you'll see me again soon.' Suzy stared down in her cup, her eyes riveted to the tea leaves floating on the bottom.

She was never going to get away from the Cavanaghs.

Briony walked into her house with a heavy heart. She wished she could get on with Suzy, could like her. She had to if she wanted to see the child.

Tommy was on the phone in the den; she smiled as she heard him laughing. His back was to her as she stood in the doorway.

'Don't worry, love, I'll be there. Briony watches me like a hawk, but she can't watch me all the time!' He laughed again.

Briony felt as if someone had punched her in the solar plexus; all the air seemed to leave her body in a split second. She stepped out of the doorway and back into the hall. Tommy's voice drifted out to her.

'I'll see you then, all right. Yeah, you too.'

Gathering up her strength she walked into the den.

'Who was that, Tom?' Her voice was brittle, over bright. Tommy smiled at her widely. 'Hello, Bri!' He walked across the room and hugged her tightly. 'How's it go with Suzy?'

Briony disengaged herself from his embrace. 'All right. Who was that on the phone?'

Tommy flapped a hand at her.

'Oh, Fat Peter. I'm doing a bit of business with him. You're back early.'

'Yeah, I gave Bernadette a miss. I'll see her later.'

'I dropped Danny Boy a line this morning, I'll post it on me way out. He's moved to the Island tomorrow so I thought a letter might cheer him up until he gets acclimatised.' Tommy looked at his watch. 'I've got five minutes before I have to go out, fancy a quick cuppa?'

The phone rang again and Tommy rushed to answer it. 'Hello . . . Oh hello Bern, hang on she's here.' He handed the phone to Briony and, kissing her on the cheek, went out of the room, leaving Briony more unsettled than ever.

'I'll ring you back Bernadette.'

She bit her lip. Since when had he called Fat Peter love?

Bernadette was lying in her darkened bedroom with a cold flannel across her eyes. 'Oh Bri, this is torture.' She spoke through her teeth.

'Well if you have a facelift you have to expect a bit of pain, don't you?' Briony's voice held no sympathy whatsoever. 'He's cut right through your skin to the bone . . .'

'Oh shut up Bri, I feel sick as a dog!'

'Well why didn't you stay in the clinic then?' You've been home a week and you haven't stopped moaning!'

'You know why. I wouldn't leave that Marcus for longer than five minutes. You know what he's like.'

Briony didn't laugh, as usual, but said seriously, 'Is he still batting away from home then?'

'Not that I know of, but I won't give the bugger a chance. They're all the same, men – a flash of teeth, a pair of tits and they're undone.'

Briony's voice was cold. 'Not all men are like that.'

Bernadette laughed softly. 'Ain't they? Then why have you built a fortune on your houses? Most men play the field; it's just some are cleverer than others. As for my Marcus, even Pan's People on the telly have him riveted to his seat! I tell you what, if dick was brains he'd been another Magnus Pike!'

'Tommy wouldn't do it to me.'

Bernadette took the flannel off her forehead and raised herself gently on her shoulders. 'Who said anything about Tommy?'

Briony shrugged. 'No one, I'm just saying he wouldn't do it to me, that's all.'

'Well,' Bernie said grudgingly, 'he seems all right. I mean you think about it, Bri, he's no children, nothing, has he? He gave up a lot for you if you could only see it. That man's a diamond and you've never really appreciated that fact.'

'Well, I wouldn't go through all you do, no man's worth that pain.'

Bernie grinned painfully. 'In another week, I'll look the dog's gonads, as Boysie used to say. Then it'll all have been worth it.'

'Boysie also used to say that one day you'd come out of the clinic with a beard and your belly button on your forehead!'

Bernadette sighed heavily. 'I thought you was going to cheer me up! Instead you're sitting there taking the piss!'

Marcus walked into the room and saved Briony from answering. 'Cissy's just rang, your Mum's up and looking for you, Bri.'

Briony stood up and, saying goodbye to a subdued Bernadette, she walked down the stairs with Marcus. 'Can I ask you something personal, Marcus?'

'Course you can.'

'Do you still play around?'

Marcus laughed and the laugh turned into a heavy smoker's cough. 'Chance would be a fine thing! I ask you, Briony, at my age?'

Briony smiled and left the house. She was taking her mother to church and she quickened her step. She was looking forward to Mass this afternoon.

'Are you sure you're not coming, Tommy? Only your name's on the visiting order as well. This is the second visit you've missed this month.'

'Honestly, Bri, I feel rough, the ferry crossing will knacker me. You go with Delia and give Danny my best.'

'All right then. I'm picking Delia up on me way. See you later if you're in!'

676

With that she marched from the house and got into her car, wheelspinning it out of the drive. Tommy shook his head and Cissy tutted. 'You're heading for a fall trying to get one over on her, Tommy Lane.'

'Be fair, Cissy, it'll be the first time ever if I do! Did it ever occur to you that I might want a bit more out of life than what I've got? That I might want a woman who belongs with me, who has my name?'

'Well, it's not bothered you up to now has it? Christ, you and Briony have been an item for the last five decades, that's longer than most marriages!'

'Yeah well maybe it's not enough!'

'She'll go spare.'

'Well, we'll see about that won't we.'

Delia was quiet, watching the other people on the ferry. The children laughing and joking around. The women in their catalogue coats and home perms calling them to order.

'Have you seen anything of Faithey?'

Delia nodded. 'Yeah, I popped round yesterday. Me Dad's been looking after her while me Mum had her op. Honestly, Auntie Briony, my Mum's embarrassing. She looks better than I do!'

Briony looked her niece over from head to foot and said scathingly, 'Cissy looks better than you do. You could at least have made an effort. You're getting enormous again!'

Delia looked out of the ferry window, took a deep breath and said, 'That's because I'm pregnant again.'

'You're what!'

'Four months. I've got to tell me Mum.'

'Who's the father this time?'

'Ray Stockyard. He wants to marry me.'

'Oh he does, does he? And what does this Ray do? Another drug pusher is he?'

'He's unemployed. Look I ain't happy about this either, but I can't have another abortion, the doctor's already told me that.'

Briony shook her head sadly. Give her a good honest working girl any day of the week, rather than this fat individual beside her.

'I don't know what's happened to this family. Boysie's dead, Danny's banged up, and now on top of it all you're pregnant. One child with your mother because you couldn't look after her, and now this! Another poor innocent on the way. I hope you've knocked the drugs on the head, girl. If you harm that baby I'll murder you.'

They were quiet for the remainder of the journey. Briony had enough on her plate with Tommy's erratic behaviour and Suzy's attitude towards her. It seemed trouble was determined to dog her family and she was getting too old for it.

Molly and Briony were sitting by the fire. Molly was drinking her habitual hot rum toddy and Briony was nursing a scotch.

'Where's Tommy tonight?'

'He popped out, he said he won't be long.' Briony glanced at the long case clock as it chimed the hour. It was eight o'clock and he'd been gone over two hours.

'Sure he's never in these days! How's Bernadette now?'

Briony shrugged. 'Over the shock. The boyfriend's another of the great unwashed. Marcus went garrity. Honestly, Mum, I don't know what happened with all the kids.'

Molly laughed. 'Every parent says that at some time. Get the telly on, I don't want to miss Kerry.'

Briony got up and switched the television on.

Molly sighed with contentment. 'I love Morecambe and Wise. Kerry said she'd get me their autographs!'

Briony heard Tommy's key in the door twenty minutes later and went out to the hall. 'You're back then?'

Tommy laughed. 'I am! Now how about making me a scotch and soda, I could do with one.'

'Tommy, where have you been?'

Tommy slipped his coat off and grinned. 'I've been out, Briony, with a mate. Now are you going to interrogate me or are you going to let me in to watch Kerry on Morecambe and Wise?'

Briony stood her ground. 'I want to know where you've been Thomas Lane and I want to know now!'

'I just told you, Briony, I've been out! You're sounding more like a wife every day. What's it you've always said? You don't want to be married, you don't need a piece of paper to prove to the world who you are with . . . Marriage is outdated . . . So stop sounding like a harping wife and let me in to watch Kerry. I came back especially to see her.' He pushed her gently out of the way and went into the lounge.

'Hello Molly, love. Have I missed her?'

'No, Tom. She's not been on yet.'

'Good, want a refill Moll?'

Briony stood in the hallway and felt an urge to cry. She walked slowly upstairs and went into her bedroom. All her life Tommy had been there as and when she wanted him, now all of a sudden she wasn't sure of him. She felt a subtle shifting in position. It occurred to her that she needed Tommy Lane a lot more than he needed her.

It was a frightening thought.

Kerry's voice was loud. 'Will you hurry up, Briony, Liselle will be here in a minute to pick us up.'

'All right, Kerry, keep your hair on. I don't see why you want me there anyway!'

Kerry rolled her eyes at the ceiling. 'Let's not start all that again, please! You know how nervous I am when I'm doing TV. We'll be in and out in no time.'

Briony brushed her hair, looking at herself critically in the mirror.

'You look lovely Briony.' The two sisters smiled at one another.

'I don't know why you're so worried about how I look, you're the one going on telly!'

'Quick, put your hat on, I can hear Lissy sounding the horn.'

Briony pushed her hat on her head and they rushed down the stairs.

Inside the car Lissy smiled. 'You two look lovely.' She pulled out of the drive. 'That Delia's a cow isn't she? You know Bernie's taking on this child as well?'

Briony nodded. 'In fairness to Bernie, as silly as she can be, she looks after Faithey brilliantly. If Delia was my daughter I'd have got her done with the cat!'

Liselle laughed. 'Delia's all right really, she's just a bit scatty.'

Briony sighed heavily. 'I don't know where we got her from. Look at Becky, she's all right and they come from the same stable . . . Hold on, you're going towards Barking!'

'I promised Gran and Cissy I'd pick them up from Mass first.'

'You're cutting it a bit fine ain't you?'

'Stop worrying, we've all the time in the world.'

As they approached St Vincent's church, Briony looked at Kerry and said, 'What's going on here today? Look at all these cars.'

They pulled up in a space right outside the church.

'There's Tommy!' Briony got out and stared at the people outside the church, all dressed in their Sunday best. Mariah was there, her mother and sisters, nieces, Cissy, crying as usual. She saw women who had worked for her years before, bouncers from her clubs. Bessie Knight and the Velvetones. Even Jonathan La Billière was there, with his usual posse of press photographers. It was as if her whole life had risen up before her eyes.

Tommy walked towards her and grinned. 'You got here then?'

Liselle opened the boot of her Daimler and took out a posy of flowers. She gave them to Briony and kissed her on the cheek.

Briony stared down at the flowers and opened her mouth to speak but no sound came out.

'For once in your life, you're lost for words!' Taking her none too gently by the arm he led her towards the church.

Briony staggered along beside him, looking at the sea of faces around her, all smiling and laughing. As she walked into the lobby of the church, Benedict was waiting for her. He held out an arm.

'I'm going to give you away, Mother.'

Tommy brought a black velvet box from his pocket, took out the choker he had bought her years before and tied it gently around her throat.

'I hope you're not going to say "I won't", Bri. This little lot was murder to arrange and cost a small fortune.' She looked up into his face and saw the uncertainty there. She shook her head.

'I can't wait to become Mrs Thomas Lane. Let's do it!' She walked proudly down the aisle on her son's arm, her face glowing with happiness.

At sixty-five years old she finally understood what life was all about.

Tommy kissed her gently on the lips. 'I love you Bri.'

Briony snuggled into him in the warmth of the bed. 'I love you, too, only I never realised how much.'

He cupped her breast gently and Briony slapped his hand away. 'Do you mind Tommy Lane? I'm a respectable married woman now!'

Tommy laughed out loud. 'I was really scared you know, Briony. I thought, if she knocks me back now, in front of everyone . . .'

Briony looked up into his face. 'I thought you had someone else, I did.'

'I know, I let you think it and all. Be fair, Bri, you've never let me look after you really, have you? And I wanted to. I admit that over the years I stepped in to help you, but without you knowing about it. You're a hard woman to love, Bri, you are so self possessed, so strong! It's like living with a bloke at times!'

Briony kissed his chest. 'After all the trouble with the boys, my Boysie dying, Danny going away, I realised that I needed you more than anything. No matter what's happened in the past, we have had each other. If that's what marriage is, then I want it.'

Tommy kissed her again.

'How did you arrange it all without me guessing?'

'You can thank Mariah, Cissy and the whole family for that. It was hard I can tell you.'

681

'Well, I'm glad you did. I think it was the nicest thing that ever happened to me.'

Tommy pulled her tightly to him and said, 'Come here, wife!'

Briony started laughing. 'You've called me a few things over the years, but I never thought to hear you call me that!'

They both laughed.

'You realise one thing though, Thomas Lane: you got me by default!'

'How'd you make that out?'

'I was in shock!'

'You'll be in shock in a minute if you don't stop rabbiting. Now get your nightdress off!'

'Respectable married women sleep with their nighties on!'

Tommy laughed throatily. 'Not in this bleeding house they don't.'

Chapter Fifty
1970

Kerry stood waiting to be announced, feeling the euphoria induced by vodka fighting with her nervousness. She could hear the muted sounds of conversation coming from the audience. She felt Liselle take hold of her and squeezed her daughter's hand gently.

'All right, Mum?'

Kerry nodded, unable to form any words. It was always like this until she walked out into the lights, to the sound of the music. Then something took her over. Something came down over her mind and wiped away the nervousness, the fear, leaving a feeling of peace and a desire just to make the audience enjoy themselves, enjoy her. Tonight, though, it was more acute than it had ever been. She had travelled a long way to do this show and she was glad, in a funny sort of way, to be doing it now after all the events of the last year. It seemed right somehow. Right and fitting.

It was Briony who had told her to go, who had made her realise that they were getting too old to nurse grudges for any length of time. They were old and wise enough, surely, to chase their own ghosts?

Which was what Kerry was going to do tonight.

The ghost was Evander Dorsey, and after all those years, all the trouble with him and through him, she was going to sing in his club in America. CBS Television was out there waiting for her, she was going to be seen from coast to coast. 'Kerry Cavanagh the Legend' they called her these days. The twins had given her career a bigger boost than she had ever dreamed possible. After Daniel's trial her records had been recut and she had been inundated with offers to sing, star in shows, be interviewed. It had frightened her. But Briony, dear Briony, and Bernadette had told her, 'Use whatever you can, girl. If you're making a bigger comeback as a result of Boysie's death and Daniel's misfortune, then at least we can all be glad that some good came from it all.' So she had taken up the offers, she had gone on the talk shows and the music shows, she had toured the country and sang in just about every auditorium there was in Britain.

Now she was on New York's east side, in Evander's Jazz Club. There was a packed audience waiting for her, and Evander himself was going to introduce her.

In the week since she had arrived they had regained a little more of their old footing. It was inevitable when they shared a common bond, their child.

Kerry heard her cue and swallowed nervously. Her throat was dry, her eyes felt hot.

Liselle kissed her on the cheek and smiled widely. 'Go on, Mum, get out there and show them what a Cavanagh can do!'

Kerry heard Evander's voice, that deep brown voice that she had loved so much all those years ago. And as she listened, her ears tuned to it, her mind chased down the years until she could picture the handsome lover he had been.

Evander stood on stage, dressed in a dinner suit, looking dapper and confident. The hands that clutched the microphone were wearing black silk gloves.

'Ladies and gentlemen, I give you the woman they call The Living Legend, the woman who can sing like an angel, and the woman I have respected, deeply and sincerely, for far more years than either of us cares to remember!'

He swept out his arm in a dramatic gesture: 'Miss Kerry Cavanagh.'

The place went wild.

Kerry walked out on to the stage, a tall slim figure dressed in a silver evening dress cut high on the hip to expose a long shapely leg, her black hair piled high on her head, her stage make-up making her look younger, softer, than she really was.

There was an audible gasp from the audience. Kerry took the microphone from Evander and as he made to leave the stage, grabbed his arm, holding him there with her.

'First, I would like to thank you for your welcome. New York has been very kind to me.' She smiled as she waited for the cheering and the cat calling to die down. 'Secondly, I would like to thank this big handsome man standing beside me. He gave me something precious, something that has made my life complete. He gave me the gift of a child, our child, Liselle.'

She looked to the side of the stage and gestured for Liselle to join them both on stage.

She walked out into the bright lights, her eyes misting over, her heart full to bursting. She stood between her mother and father as the audience clapped, and the band played the first few bars of Kerry's opening number.

Then Evander kissed her gently on the lips and, taking Liselle's hand, walked proudly from the stage.

Kerry laughed, that deep, husky laugh so like Briony's, and said, 'Now for some singin'! This is a song I have loved for many years and I sing it tonight for all my family, both here in the States and at home in England.'

The band played louder, the lights were dimmed and her voice was husky as she began to sing the first number of her set.

'I love you so much, it hurts me.
Darling, that's why I'm so blue.
I'm so afraid to go to bed at night,
afraid of losing you . . .'

Liselle and Evander stood watching Kerry. She took the audience and held them in her hands. Then she gave them everything she had, and a little bit more.

As Evander watched her, he realised the quality of the woman who had borne his child, whom he had taken down, and whom

685

he now watched with a mixture of love and deep respect.

She was indeed a living legend, and he felt deeply honoured to be allowed once more to be a part of her life.

Briony lay in the dark, Tommy's breathing beside her regular and even. She envied him his capacity to sleep. She put a hand to her heart, reassured by the regular beating that seemed to be keeping time with Tommy's breathing.

Her heart bothered her sometimes. The twins were in her mind tonight. She had thought Daniel getting put away for so long would have made her ill, but instead it gave her a feeling of peace.

He had pushed his luck and his violent streak too far. He had had to pay the price. Thirty years. She would likely be dead by the time he got out.

Tommy turned over in his sleep and she felt his arm creep around her waist, holding her gently. Her husband. It still seemed strange to call him that. He snuffled into the pillows, sounding ridiculous and so normal she felt the sting of tears once more.

'Oh, Eileen,' she whispered into the darkness. 'You gave me the gift of your children, and I tried to do the best I could by them. I really tried.'

She saw Henry Dumas in her mind's eye, with his ridiculous large moustaches. Through him she had been given the most important thing in her life: her son. And later Henry had inadvertently brought them together again, brought them close. This thought pleased her more than anything because she liked to think that somewhere Henry Dumas was spinning in his grave, distraught with the knowledge the two of them had come together again through his folly.

'Henry, you bastard,' she whispered once more into the blackness of her bedroom, 'I bested you in the end. You were the cause of every unhappiness that befell me and mine, but I am the victor. With all my troubles the victor.'

With that she closed her eyes and thought of the twins as boys, her boys. How she would always think of them.

Boysie's daughter Deidre, born fatherless and in a blaze of publicity, was asleep in the next room.

Suzy was quite happy for her to stay with Briony and Tommy at weekends. It was her way of trying to make amends for the way she'd acted after Boysie's death. Briony put up with Suzy so she could see the child.

A new generation was growing. Faithey and Deidre were both fatherless, both cursed with mothers who were no good at all. It seemed that they needed Briony and Bernadette and even Kerry to look out for them.

Molly wouldn't last much longer, Boysie's death and Daniel's prison sentence had finished her. She had lost the will to live now, had become old overnight, really old and decrepit. Briony snuggled against Tommy's back.

Age was creeping up on them all, but while they had the children they had life and a reason for living.

She wondered how Kerry was getting on in America and smiled then, a genuine smile. At least some good had come out of all the troubles of the last few years. Kerry was back on top. She was still drinking, but at her age, what could anyone really do? At least she was enjoying her life. She was a big star again. Briony hoped she took America by storm, and being a Cavanagh, that was probably exactly what she would do.

A Cavanagh. Even Daniel had insisted, right at the last, that he was a Cavanagh. She would write to him tomorrow. His mind was deteriorating rapidly, but the prison psychiatrist said that was delayed shock at his twin's death. He was being sent to Broadmoor next week, so instead of the monthly trek to Parkhurst, on the Isle of Wight, they would have to go to Berkshire. Daniel still thought he was somebody of renown, but then, she supposed, in prison he was. They would never release him. He had already attacked two other prisoners for imagined slights. The psychiatrist said he was a psychopath. She had felt like saying to him: 'Tell me something I don't know.'

She felt her eyes getting heavy with sleep and was glad. Finally, Briony slept, only to be woken a few hours later by Deidre crying. Briony settled her on her lap and rocked her to sleep, happy now she had a child in her arms. Deidre made up for the loss of the two babies she had loved too much. She was to see Benedict the next day.

He visited regularly. She hoped that he would one day bring his children with him. But it was something they had not discussed yet. They were still feeling the way, building the love and trust between themselves.

She rocked the little girl gently, crooning softly to her. Briony kissed the downy forehead and said softly: 'Who knows what the future holds, my lovely? For me, for you, for any of us.'

The child was the living image of Boysie, she was wholly his daughter.

Yes, the Cavanagh genes were very strong. Too strong, perhaps? Who knew?

Briony carried on rocking the child, making plans for her in her mind. As always, Briony's mind was on the future. A future, she knew from experience, which would be shaped by the past.

EPILOGUE
1989

'Therefore my age is as a lusty winter, frosty, but kindly'
– *As You Like It*, William Shakespeare

'Do you think we should wake her?'

The blonde nurse nodded and smiled. 'I think she'd be very cross if we didn't. She's been looking forward to seeing you all day.'

The man came into the room and the others followed. He went to the bed and gently shook the woman beneath the covers. She opened one eye, to show a flash of vivid green, then the other eye opened quickly.

'Is it that time already?' Her voice had the querulousness of great age and the man laughed.

'We're all here, Gran.' As he spoke a boy in his late teens looked over his shoulder and grinned.

'Come on, Granny, it's not like you to be a lieabed.' The words brought a stinging sensation of tears to her rheumy eyes. That was an expression of Tommy's.

'Come here, me lovelies, and give me a kiss.'

One by one they kissed her. Faithey first, her own two children following. Then Deidre with that startling red hair so like her own. She had a young man with her, Briony noticed, and smiled at him. Then came Becky, her children and grandchildren. Then came Delia with her son Daniel, a fine strong boy, nothing like his mother at all. Though he had a look of Marcus, his grandfather, about him. Briony swallowed heavily. Bernie's dying had been a great blow; she had died five days after Marcus had had his coronary. Briony wondered if Bernie still didn't trust him, she'd followed him so fast. It seemed all the old people were disappearing, but that was how it should be. Though she didn't particularly want to leave them all, not yet.

Then Liselle was kissing her heartily. Briony squeezed her hard. Nearing seventy, Liselle was still as sprightly as a girl. She had inherited the Jazz Club on her father's death ten years before; Kerry had sung there the night she died. It was hard to believe at times that her Aunt Briony was the only one of the sisters left.

'Let Lissy sit down, will you, she's getting on.'

This was said seriously and Lissy smiled at the people in the room. Briony always forgot her own age.

Then came Natalie, Briony's grandchild, and her two boys. A pair of buggers if ever there was, Briony thought. They kissed their granny with real affection. They thought she was absolutely great. They loved bragging about her and being a part of her. Briony grabbed their cheeks tightly in her jewelled hands.

'You two need watching, my lads! You've too much of the Cavanagh in you.'

Everyone laughed.

Then came her favourite, the one she had least expected to steal her heart. He stood with his father, smiling at her. Benedict's face glowed as his son wrapped his granny in a long embrace and kissed her. He had a deep love for his granny, and his two daughters and his son all stood round the bed waiting their turn.

It always amazed Briony that a man called Henry Dumas could kiss her like that and she feel nothing but love. The love she bore her grandson. The name was exorcised for her, it meant nothing but happiness now.

She swept Henry's children into her sweet-smelling embrace and said, 'Next year, we'll all go away together. I thought we might get a big house out in the country and have a holiday there.' She saw them all smiling around her, none of them wanting to say what they were really thinking. So Briony, being Briony, said it for them:

'I know what you're all thinking – that I might not be here

next year. The thought had crossed my mind. But let's look at it like this.' She paused, eyes bright. 'There's a fifty-fifty chance I'll be dead . . .' She paused again and looked around her, at her family, at her blood, and then she said craftily: 'But there's also a fifty-fifty chance I just could still be here, alive and kicking!'

'You will be, Bri, God willing.' Tommy's face came down on hers and he kissed her gently on her lips .

'Me and you, Tommy Lane, we seem to go on and on!'

MARTINA COLE
THE LADYKILLER

HE'S EVERY WOMAN'S WORST NIGHTMARE

George Markham has a nasty little hobby. He pursues it in secret, behind closed doors. But now George's little hobby is becoming an obsession, one that erupts into an orgy of vicious sexual depravity.

Patrick Kelly is a hard man – the most feared in London. His one soft spot is his daughter, Mandy. And when she falls victim to the sadistic rapist nicknamed the Grantley Ripper, Kelly wants revenge – with or without police help.

The DI in charge of the case is Kate Burrows. It's a tough job and one that's already cost Kate her marriage. She feels for Kelly – she's a parent herself – but her growing involvement with a known villain is putting her career at risk...

As the forces of law and order and London's underworld converge in a mammoth manhunt, Kate fears she'll lose everything she's ever cared about to...the ladykiller.

CLAUDIA CRAWFORD

NICE GIRLS

THE DELICIOUSLY SEXY NOVEL FOR ANY WOMAN WHO EVER FELL FOR MR WRONG

Once upon a time, in swinging sixties' London, there were three nice girls, Georgina, Mona and Amy. Into their lives came Nick Albert, handsome, witty and utterly faithless, swearing each was his greatest love then leaving them with nothing – apart from a friendship with each other cemented by their vow to forget Nick forever.

But years later one of them breaks the sacred pact and the other two determine that, even if Nick Albert is *still* the most desirable man they've ever met, it's time he learnt the price of love betrayed...

Sassy, sexy and as sinfully delightful as its hero, NICE GIRLS is a novel no nice girl will be able to resist...

'Hilarious first novel' *Weekend Telegraph*

FICTION/GENERAL   0 7472 4170 8

More Thrilling Fiction from Headline:

TELL ME NO SECRETS

THE TERRIFYING PSYCHOLOGICAL THRILLER
JOY FIELDING
BESTSELLING AUTHOR OF *SEE JANE RUN*

'People who annoy me have a way of... disappearing'

Jess Koster thinks she has conquered the crippling panic attacks that
have plagued her since the unexplained disappearance of her mother,
eight years ago. But they are back with a vengeance. And not without
reason. Being a chief prosecutor in the State's Attorney's office
exposes Jess to some decidedly lowlife types. Like Rick Ferguson,
about to be tried for rape – until his victim goes missing. Another
inexplicable disappearance.

If only Jess didn't feel so alone. Her father is about to re-marry; her
sister is busy being the perfect wife and mother; her ex-husband has a
new girlfriend. And besides, he's Rick Ferguson's defence lawyer...

Battling with a legal system that all too often judges women by
appalling double standards; living under the constant threat of
physical danger; fighting to overcome the emotional legacy of her
mother's disappearance, Jess is in danger of going under. And it looks
as though someone is determined that she should disappear, too...

'Joy Fielding tightens suspense like a noose round your neck and
keeps one shattering surprise for the very last page. Whew!' *Annabel*

'The story she has to tell this time is a corker that runs rings round
Mary Higgins Clark. Don't even think of starting this anywhere near
bedtime' *Kirkus Reviews*

Don't miss Joy Fielding's *See Jane Run* ('Compulsive reading'
Company), also from Headline Feature

FICTION/GENERAL   0 7472 4163 5

A selection of bestsellers from Headline

THE CHANGING ROOM	Margaret Bard	£5.99 ☐
BACKSTREET CHILD	Harry Bowling	£5.99 ☐
A HIDDEN BEAUTY	Tessa Barclay	£5.99 ☐
A HANDFUL OF HAPPINESS	Evelyn Hood	£5.99 ☐
THE SCENT OF MAY	Sue Sully	£5.99 ☐
HEARTSEASE	T R Wilson	£5.99 ☐
NOBODY'S DARLING	Josephine Cox	£5.99 ☐
A CHILD OF SECRETS	Mary Mackie	£5.99 ☐
WHITECHAPEL GIRL	Gilda O'Neill	£5.99 ☐
BID TIME RETURN	Donna Baker	£5.99 ☐
THE LADIES OF BEVERLEY HILLS	Sharleen Cooper Cohen	£5.99 ☐
THE OLD GIRL NETWORK	Catherine Alliott	£4.99 ☐

All Headline books are available at your local bookshop or newsagent, or can be ordered direct from the publisher. Just tick the titles you want and fill in the form below. Prices and availability subject to change without notice.

Headline Book Publishing, Cash Sales Department, Bookpoint, 39 Milton Park, Abingdon, OXON, OX14 4TD, UK. If you have a credit card you may order by telephone – 0235 400400.

Please enclose a cheque or postal order made payable to Bookpoint Ltd to the value of the cover price and allow the following for postage and packing:
UK & BFPO: £1.00 for the first book, 50p for the second book and 30p for each additional book ordered up to a maximum charge of £3.00.
OVERSEAS & EIRE: £2.00 for the first book, £1.00 for the second book and 50p for each additional book.

Name ....

Address ....

....

....

If you would prefer to pay by credit card, please complete:
Please debit my Visa/Access/Diner's Card/American Express (delete as applicable) card no:

Signature .... Expiry Date ....

Dangerous
Lady

Martina Cole

HEADLINE

First published in 1992
by HEADLINE BOOK PUBLISHING

20 19 18 17 16 15 14 13 12 11

ISBN 0 7472 3932 0

Typeset by Keyboard Services, Luton

Printed and bound in Great Britain by
Cox & Wyman Ltd, Reading, Berkshire

HEADLINE BOOK PUBLISHING
A division of Hodder Headline PLC
338 Euston Road
London NW1 3BH

To my parents

Book One

LONDON, NOTTING HILL

If possible honestly, if not,
somehow,
make money – Horace, 65–8 BC

Am I my brother's keeper? – *Genesis*, iv, 9

Chapter One

'You took your bloody time!'

Dr Martin O'Reilly stared down into the child's face and sighed.

'I had to see another patient. Now where's your ma?'

'In bed, of course.'

The little boy went back to sit on the stairs with his seven brothers. They ranged in age from three to fourteen. The doctor lit a cigar. He stood in the hallway puffing on it for a few seconds to make sure it was fully alight. The smell of the Ryans en masse was enough to turn the strongest of stomachs, though the slum stench was in his blood now, he reckoned. It permeated his clothes and skin. He started to pick his way up the stairs, careful not to tread on any little fingers. The children shuffled left and right on their bottoms to let him pass. He was also careful not to touch the wall. The smell he could combat with his cigar, but the roaches – he would never get used to them. How the buggers ran up the walls he would never know. They defied gravity.

On the landing he pushed open the first bedroom door, and there in front of him was Sarah Ryan. She was lying on a large double bed, her belly huge and swollen. He smiled at her, his heart breaking. Sarah Ryan was thirty-four years old. Her faded blonde hair was scraped back from her face into a bun, her skin was pale and dry. If her eyes had not been so bright and alert, she could have been mistaken for a corpse. He could remember coming to this house fifteen years earlier to deliver her first child. A fine-looking woman she had been then. Now her body was fat and

3

scarred from constant childbearing, and her face wrinkled prematurely from habitual frowning.

'It's well on then?' His voice was gentle.

Sarah tried to hitch herself up in the bed. The old newspapers that had been placed underneath her crackled at the movement. 'Yeah. It's good of you to come, Martin. I told the little sods to get their dad, but as usual he ain't nowhere to be seen.'

She gripped her belly as another pain shot through her. 'Oh, it's dying to be born this one.' She smiled faintly. Then her eyes stretched wide as she saw the doctor take a syringe out of his bag.

'You ain't sticking that thing in me! We had all this out the last time. I ain't having any bloody injections. This is me thirteenth child and I never had one with any of them. Not even the stillborns. I ain't starting now.'

'Come on, Sarah. This will ease you.'

She put up her hand to stem his protests. 'I'm sorry but them things hurt like hell, whereas giving birth . . . it's nothing. Nothing . . .'

Martin put the needle on the small bedside table and, sighing heavily, pulled back the blankets covering her legs. His expert hands felt around her sides and then he slipped two fingers inside her vagina. When he had finished he pulled the blankets back over her.

'I think this one's breech.'

Sarah shrugged.

'First one if it is. I ain't done so bad. Ben was saying the other day that soon they would drop out as I walked down to the shops!'

She laughed and the doctor laughed with her.

'That would do me out of a job. Now you relax for a minute, I won't be long. I want one of the boys to run an errand for me. ' He left the room, shutting the door quietly behind him.

'She had it then?' This from eight-year-old Leslie who had let him in earlier.

'No, she hasn't had it yet. Be patient, you young bugger.'

The doctor turned to the eldest boy, Michael. At nearly

4

fifteen he was already over six feet tall and towered over the little Irish doctor in front of him.

'Michael, go and get old Mother Jenkins. I'm going to need help with this one.'

The boy stared down at the doctor for a few seconds. 'Me muvver's gonna be all right, ain't she?' His voice was deep and concerned.

The doctor nodded. 'Of course.'

The boy still did not move.

'She's never had old Mother Jenkins before.'

The doctor stared up at the boy impatiently. 'Look, Michael, I can't stand around here all day talking to you. Your ma's bad, but if we can get this baby born she'll be all right. The sooner you get Mrs Jenkins the better. Time's short.'

Michael turned slowly away from the doctor and placing one hand on the banister and the other on the wall he slid down, jumping over the younger boys' heads. As he landed heavily on the linoleum, the doctor called to him: 'Tell her I'll be paying the ten shillings or she won't come.'

Michael waved to let the doctor know he had heard, then, opening the front door, he rushed out.

The doctor looked down on to the younger children's heads and his teeth clamped down even harder on his cigar. Michael's foray down the stairs had caused the cockroaches to fall from the walls. The youngest child, Benny, not only had them crawling in his clothes, but one adventurous roach was slowly making its way across his face. Martin watched the child flick it gently away and made a mental note to see the landlord about getting the house stoved. It would never get rid of the damned things permanently but at least it would give the Ryans a breathing space.

'Now then, I want a couple of you to go and find your father.' Geoffrey, Anthony and Leslie all stood up. The doctor pointed at them in turn. 'You, Geoffrey, try the Latimer Arms. You, Anthony, go up the Roundhouse. And you . . .'

Leslie nodded, his eyes fixed on the floor.

'. . . go to the Kensington Park Hotel. If you can't find

5

him in any of those places then try the Bramley Arms. If by any chance you do find your da, tell him that he is needed at home. Can you all remember that?'

The three heads nodded and they went on their way. Martin went back into the bedroom with Sarah.

'Sure they're good boys you've got there.'

Her voice sounded sceptical. 'I don't know about that, Doctor. They're a bit wild at times. It's the old man. He takes the belt to them for nicking one minute, and then the next he's sending them out to do it. The poor little sods can't win.'

She doubled up as another pain hit her.

'Relax now, Sarah.' He pushed a few stray hairs from her face. It was getting dark so he pulled the curtains and put on the overhead light. He lit himself another cigar from the butt of the previous one. Then, with it firmly clamped between his teeth, he examined her again. When he had finished he had a worried look on his face. He visibly relaxed as he heard a voice in the hallway. A few seconds later Matilda Jenkins had pushed open the bedroom door. She stood at the end of Sarah's bed, all eighteen stone of her.

'All right, Doctor?' This was a form of address, not a question.

'All right, Sarah? The bloody stairs knacker me these days. But them boys!' She flapped her hand at Sarah. 'Talk about scatter them. One look at me coming up 'em and they run like mad!' Her deep booming laugh reverberated around the bedroom. The doctor was paying her the ten shillings, she could afford to be friendly.

'It's a big woman you are, Matilda, to be sure. Now get yourself back down the stairs and heat me up lots of water. I want to sterilise me things. This little fellow's breech.'

Matilda nodded her head vigorously.

'Righto, Doc. I'll send around the neighbours, get them to put their kettles on. We might even get a cuppa out of them!'

As she stamped from the room, Sarah glared at the doctor.

6

'What's she doing here? I ain't got ten shillings, and if I did have I'd give it to the kids. They ain't eaten since yesterday, and until that man of mine comes home, they won't eat at all! Knowing him, he's shacked up with some old sort somewhere and won't be home till the morning!'

She was near to tears.

'Calm down now, Sarah. I'm paying her.' He grasped one of her hands. 'Now be quiet, woman. I can't cope with this on me own. So you whisht now, and save your strength.'

Sarah lay back against the pillows, her face drenched with sweat. Her lips were cracked and dry. Turning awkwardly towards the bedside table, she picked up a glass of water and sipped the warm liquid gratefully. A little while later Matilda bought up a bucket of steaming water. The doctor set about sterilising his things, including a large pair of scissors.

By nine in the evening Sarah was in great distress, as was the child within her. Twice the doctor had tried to push his arm inside her to turn the child and each time he had failed. He wiped his hands on a towel he had brought with him.

This child had to be born, and soon, or he would lose the pair of them. Blast Benjamin Ryan! It was always the same. He gave her a child every year, but was never there when it came into the world.

The little boys kept their vigil on the stairs. All were tired and hungry. Michael, waiting at the top, was silently cursing his father as he looked at his younger brothers' little faces. Benny was sucking the arm of his jumper.

Suddenly there was a loud banging on the front door. Six-year-old Garry answered it, only to be knocked flying as two policemen came crashing in. Michael took one look at them and, swearing under his breath, ran into his mother's bedroom. Cries could be heard from the stairs as the policemen tried to make their way up to the landing, the remaining boys making it as difficult as possible for them in the hope that their brother would get away.

Michael had opened the bedroom window and was half in and half out as the policemen burst into the room.

Then the lights went out.

'Who turned off the lights, you little bastards?'

'No one turned off the bleeding lights. The electric's gone.' Sarah's voice was faint. The policemen turned on their torches.

'Bring those over here. This woman is in danger of her life.' The urgency in the doctor's voice brought both men to the bed. The boy was long gone, they both knew that. Sarah was writhing in agony, tears on her cheeks.

'You lot want slaughtering. My boy ain't done nothing.'

Matilda Jenkins broke in, 'Look, has anyone got a shilling for the meter?'

'I have.' The smaller of the two policemen fished some change out of his pocket. Leaving his colleague to help the doctor, he walked from the room and carefully made his way down the stairs. Stepping through the children as gently as he could, he went to the cupboard under the stairs and, locating the meter, put a shilling in. He put in another, and turned off his torch as he stepped out of the cupboard. Seven pairs of eyes were looking at him with open hostility, even the youngest's who was not yet four. The man looked at the boys as if seeing them for the first time. At the heads close-cropped to combat the lice and the holey jumpers with elbows poking through. He stood for a while staring at them. He felt for the first time in his life what it must be like to be one of them and was overwhelmed with a feeling of sadness and futility. Taking out his wallet, he pulled out a ten shilling note and offered it to Geoffrey, the second eldest.

'Get yourself over to Messer's and get some fish and chips.'

'We don't want old Bill's money!'

'Hark at the hard man! Well, clever clogs, your little brothers are starving, so go and do what I tell you.'

He pushed the money into Geoffrey's hands. All the boy's instincts told him to throw the money back at the policeman, their natural enemy, but his little brothers' faces changed his mind. They had not eaten for nearly two days. Sullenly, he pushed past the man, who held on to his arm.

'Tell that brother of yours that we'll catch him in the end so he might as well give himself up.'

Geoffrey pulled his arm roughly away. Then, looking at the man as if he was so much dirt, he let himself out of the front door. The constable walked back up the stairs, shaking his head.

In the bedroom, Sarah was fighting to get the child born. The other policeman was holding her down, while the doctor was cutting her down below. As he cut she gave an almighty push and ripped open to her behind. The child slipped into the world, still in its birth sac. The doctor punched this open and looked at the little blue face inside. He cleaned its nose and gently blew into its mouth while he pressed tenderly on its tiny ribcage. The baby coughed and gave a little cry. Then, taking a deep breath, began to bawl its head off. Quick as a flash the doctor had cut the cord, passed the child to Matilda Jenkins, and was stitching away at Sarah as if his own life depended on it.

She lay against the pillows, her whole body numb. She swore to herself that this was going to be the last child.

'Your first girl, Sarah.' Matilda's voice was kind.

She sat up in the bed, dumbstruck, her face aglow as if lit from the inside. She grinned, showing all her large yellowing teeth.

'You're joking! I thought it was another boy! A *girl*! Is it really a girl?'

Even the policemen smiled at her. She was genuinely amazed.

'Oh, let me have her. Let me hold her! A daughter at last, thank Gawd!'

Matilda placed the child in her arms. The baby was now cleaned up and Sarah looked down into the bluest eyes she had ever seen.

'She's a beauty, Sarah.'

She stared down at her daughter in wonderment. This was her thirteenth child, but her first girl. All tiredness was forgotten as she gazed at her daughter. Then she looked around her at the other smiling faces, and remembered why the policemen were there. The elder of the two had been coming to the house for nigh on fifteen years. Ben had even been at it all through the war.

'What's my Mickey supposed to have done now?' Her voice was flat.

'He's been running for a bookie again, Sarah. I've warned him twice now. This time I'm going to nick him. So you tell him to come and see me.'

She looked back at her daughter. The doctor had finished, and, after removing the old newspapers from under Sarah, covered her up. She looked back at the policeman.

'I'll tell him, Frank, but he's like the old man. He goes his own way.' Her voice was low.

Matilda Jenkins opened the bedroom door and called the rest of the boys in. They all trooped in, eating their fish and chips, and clustered around the bed. Benny could not see anything so pulled on the doctor's coat.

'What do you want, child?'

Benny looked up with his little monkey face. His mouth was full of food.

'Is it Hovis, then?'

'Hovis?' The doctor's voice was puzzled. 'What are you on about, boy?'

'Hovis . . . you know, brown bread. Well, is it?'

The doctor looked around him for enlightenment.

'Brown bread? Are you delirious, child?'

'He means is it dead? Brown bread . . . dead. Get it?'

This was spoken by Anthony, and his tone indicated that if anyone was stupid it was not his little brother.

'Brown bread, bejasus! No, it's not. It's very much alive. Now eat your chips, you little heathen. Brown bread indeed!'

The policemen laughed.

'How long you been in London, Doc?' the elder asked. 'Twenty years? And you still don't know the lingo.' They thought this highly amusing. 'We'd better be off, Sar. Don't forget to tell Michael when he gets in.'

'I won't forget, Frank. I'll tell him, but he won't come. You know that.'

'Well, try and persuade him. Good luck with the new arrival. See you all.' The two men left.

Sarah looked at her sons' faces and smiled.

'It's a girl!'

All the boys grinned at her.

'A daughter for me old age.' She hugged the child to her. 'I'm going to call her Maura. Maura Ryan. I like that.'

'Shall I go and get Mickey, Mum? I saved him some chips.'

'Yeah, Geoff. Tell him the coast is clear.'

The doctor stopped packing away his instruments and looked at Sarah sternly.

'You knew where he was all along?'

She grinned at him. 'Course I did. He's in the Anderson shelter at number 119. He always hides there.'

Seeing the funny side of what Sarah said, Martin O'Reilly threw back his head and laughed out loud. Seven mouths stopped chewing as the boys stared at him.

'What a night! Your little girl certainly picked her time to arrive. She saved young Michael's bacon tonight, that's a fact.'

Sarah chuckled with him. 'She did that all right!'

Pat Johnstone, Sarah's best friend and next-door neighbour, came into the bedroom with a tray of tea. She ushered all the boys out and poured Sarah a strong cup.

'Here you are, girl. Get your laughing gear around that. What about you, Doc? Fancy a cuppa?'

'That would be grand. I'm parched.'

Pat poured the doctor out a cup of tea and placed it on the bedside table. Then she sat on the bed next to Sarah. She looked at the baby and gasped with surprise.

'Oh, my Gawd! She's a cracker, ain't she?' Her naturally loud voice seemed to bounce off the walls. 'Gis' a little hold, Sar.'

Sarah passed the child to her and took a deep drink of her tea. 'This is just what I needed, Pat.'

'Is that right the filth came in looking for your Mickey and the electric went? I nearly wet meself laughing when Mrs Jenkins told me, I thought it was so funny.'

11

Sarah rolled her eyes to the ceiling. 'Oh, please, Pat. Don't remind me!'

The doctor finished putting his things away and drank his tea. 'That was lovely. It just hit the right spot. Now I'll be off, Sarah. Don't get out of bed until I tell you that it's safe. I've had to put in a lot of stitches. If you start to bleed, send one of the lads around for me, OK?'

'I will, Martin. And thanks for everything.'

'That's all right. I'll see you in the morning. 'Bye now.'

He went out of the bedroom and down the stairs to the hallway where Matilda Jenkins was waiting for him with her hand out. He slipped a ten shilling note into her palm.

'Thanks, Matilda. 'Bye.'

''Bye, Doctor O'Reilly.'

She closed the front door behind him. He walked down the flight of stairs that led to the road and looked at his car, a Rover 90. It was his pride and joy. There was not a windscreen wiper to be seen. He should have known this would happen in Lancaster Road.

'Little buggers!'

He got into his car and drove off. On 2 May 1950 he had brought Maura Ryan into the world.

Chapter Two

1953

Sarah Ryan glanced around her kitchen. A feeling of satisfaction swept over her. It looked beautiful. Taking a deep breath she sighed with contentment. She had not felt this happy for years. The table was laden with food. Turkey, ham, a large joint of beef, all carefully prepared and waiting to go into the oven. The kitchen was filled with the aroma of mince pies and sausage rolls cooking to a golden crispness in the oven.

She was startled out of her reverie by a loud crash from above. Her mouth set in a grim line, she went to the kitchen door. Opening it wide, she shouted as loud as she could: 'I'm warning you lot, one more noise and I'll come up there and scalp the arses off yer!'

She stood listening for a few minutes, trying not to smile. Then, assured that the children were all in their beds, she went back to her preparations, humming a little tune. Her last task was to lay thick strips of bacon across the turkey. Finally she stepped back from the table to admire her handiwork. Then, picking up the poker from the hearth, she banged it three times against the back of the fireplace. A few seconds later the banging was answered by two sharp thuds. Going to the sink she filled the kettle with water and placed it on the gas. As the kettle came to the boil she heard the back door open and popped her head into the scullery to see her friend Pat Johnstone kicking snow off her shoes.

'Get yourself in, Pat, I've got the kettle on.'

'Oh, Sar, it's brass monkey weather out there tonight!'

Coming into the kitchen, Pat dropped into an easy chair by the fire. She looked around the kitchen, impressed.

13

'By Christ, you're well set up this year.'

Her voice held a hint of jealousy. Sarah poured the steaming water into the tea pot and smiled at her friend.

'Michael brought the lot in this morning. I couldn't believe it meself when I saw it! There's sweets and biscuits as well as nuts and fruit. He's a good boy.'

Pat nodded her head, reckoning up the cost of everything in her mind. She realised that what was being said about Michael must be true. You couldn't buy all this working at Lyons bakery or the Black Cat factory. Crime certainly did pay by the looks of it.

'And there's presents for all the kids,' Sarah chatted on happily, unaware of the animosity she was creating. Pouring the tea into two thick white mugs, she gave one to her friend. With a tea cloth around her hand she opened up the oven and took out the mince pies and sausage rolls, placing them on the top of the stove to cool as she put the turkey in to cook. Her movements were quick and confident. She straightened up, wiping her forehead with the bottom of her apron, and then went to the dresser to open the drawer. Taking out a package, she passed it to Pat.

'I nearly forgot! Happy Christmas.'

Pat Johnstone took the package and placed it on her lap. She looked at Sarah's face with troubled eyes.

'I didn't get you nothing, Sar . . . I ain't got the money.'

Sarah dismissed this. 'Oh, shut your face and open it.'

Slowly Pat tore the brown paper apart. Then her hand went to her mouth. Her voice shook as she tried to speak.

'Oh, Sar! Oh, it's lovely . . .'

Sarah patted her friend's shoulder gently.

'I knew you'd like it!'

Pat pulled the white blouse out of the wrapper and held it to her cheek, rubbing the soft material against her skin.

'It feels like silk!'

'It *is* silk. As soon as I saw it, I knew it was for you.'

All the terrible things she had thought earlier rose up in Pat's mind. Jealousy of her friend had been steadily mounting in the last few months. It had started the day three months previously when Michael paid to have the house

14

stoved. Sulphur candles had been burning for days, leaving the house free of vermin, then the whole place had been painted from top to bottom. Like most of the women in the street, Pat Johnstone had been angered by it all. By Lancaster Road standards, the Ryans had gone too far up in the world, making them aliens. If it wasn't for the fact that Michael Ryan was now a force to be reckoned with, the other families would have tried to force them out.

All this flickered through her mind in a split second and she felt ashamed. She had gone to school with Sarah, and they had helped one another over the years. Now Sarah was remembering her friend and Pat felt she didn't deserve it.

'It's absolutely gorgeous, Sar.'

Satisfied that her friend was happy, Sarah sat opposite her and took a quarter bottle of Black and White whisky from the mantelpiece. She poured two generous measures into their cups of tea.

'This'll keep the cold out, Pat. God himself knows we need it in this weather.'

Picking up her mug, Pat toasted her friend. 'Merry Christmas to you, Sarah . . . and many more.'

Settling themselves into their chairs, warmed by the whisky, the two women began the serious business of the day: gossiping.

Michael Ryan walked down the Bayswater Road. He walked, as always, as if he owned it – head held high, even in the driving snow. At eighteen, Michael was magnificent. Over six foot two, he was built like an athlete, his dark brown overcoat emphasising the spread of his shoulders. He still had thick black unruly hair, which he now wore cut in a DA. His eyes, deep-set and a striking blue, seemed to drink in everything around him. The only softness about his rugged face was in his lips. They were full and sensuous like a woman's, though at times they gave him a hint of cruelty. Women and men were drawn to Michael Ryan, and he knew it. He used it to his advantage as he used everything.

Now he watched the women lounging against the railings

of Hyde Park. Even in the snow on Christmas Eve the streetwalkers were out.

A few of the younger girls, new to their beat, looked at him with interest. One opened her coat to reveal a scantily clad body. Michael looked her up and down, his lips curling with contempt. He wouldn't touch a tom with a barge pole. An older woman, seeing the exchange, laughed out loud.

'Cover yourself up, girl. Before you get frostbite of the fanny!'

The other women laughed, glad of some light relief. Michael carried on walking. He didn't really mind the prostitutes. In fact, he admired them. To his mind theirs was a business, like any other. Supply and demand. What he didn't like was the way some of them looked at him as a potential John. He liked to think that people put him above that kind of thing. He crossed the road, dodging the traffic skilfully. The snow was easing up and last-minute shoppers were everywhere. The Portobello Road had been packed.

He walked into the warmth of the Bramley Arms. Pushing his way among the men he went to the bar, nodding a greeting here and there. Over the last year he had worked hard to create an image for himself and it was paying off. People were deferential towards him. He snapped his fingers at the barmaid and ordered a brandy. He didn't particularly like brandy, but it was a part of his image. It set him above other people. The men at the bar moved to give him room.

He sipped his drink. Ranging around the crowded bar, his eyes settled on a group by the window. He picked up his drink and made his way over to them. One of the men glanced at him, giving a double take as he realised who it was.

Tommy Blue felt a knot of fear somewhere in his bowels. The four other men at the table with him sensed his panic and stopped talking to look at the newcomer. Seeing Michael Ryan smiling at them, they seemed to crowd together, hunching in their seats. Enjoying the terror he was creating, Michael drank his brandy in one gulp. Then,

16

wiping his hand across his mouth, he placed his glass gently on the table.

'I've been looking for you, Tommy.'

His voice was quiet.

Tommy Blue felt his heart sinking. He tried to smile, his lips trembling.

'I think me and you had better have a little walk.'

Looking around the table at the other men, Michael pointed at Tommy.

'I'll be waiting outside for you.'

Turning, he pushed his way to the door. Outside he leant against the wall of the pub. He bit on his lip, the feeling of excitement in his breast causing his heart beat to pound in his ears.

A group of Salvation Army singers were making their way along the road. Pulling a pack of Strands from his pocket, Michael lit one. The strains of 'Onward Christian Soldiers' gradually grew closer. He pulled hard on the cigarette. He would give Tommy Blue five minutes before going in after him.

Inside the Bramley Arms, Tommy was rooted to his seat.

'How much do you owe, Tom?' This from Dustbin Daley, a totter from Shepherd's Bush.

'Forty-five quid.' Tommy's voice was low.

One of his companions whistled.

'I'd better get out there . . . otherwise he'll come in after me.' Getting up unsteadily, Tommy made his way to the door.

Dustbin Daley shook his head. 'He must be bloody mad.'

The others agreed with him. Their earlier high spirits were gone now, out of the door with Tommy Blue.

Tommy shivered as the cold hit him. He was wearing a thin jacket, torn in places, and a thick multi-coloured scarf.

Michael threw his cigarette on the slush-filled pavement and ground it out with his boot. Pushing himself from the wall he grabbed Tommy's jacket and pulled him along the road. The Salvationists were alongside them. A young girl pushed a tin in their direction. She smiled at Michael as she rattled it.

'Merry Christmas, sir.' Her eyes held open admiration.

Pulling his coat open, he pushed his hand into his trouser pocket, and taking out two half crowns dropped them into the tin. The girl flushed with pleasure.

'Thank you, sir. Merry Christmas.'

Nodding at her, Michael resumed piloting Tommy Blue along the pavement. The tambourines and the singing faded into the distance. The two men walked in silence for five minutes. Tommy Blue could not feel the cold now. He couldn't feel anything. Fear had completely taken over. Tommy Blue was on automatic pilot. All he could do was wait. The beer he had been drinking steadily all day was now weighing heavily on his stomach.

Michael slowed down in Treadgold Street. The laundry here was known affectionately as the bagwash. Michael himself had brought his mother's laundry here on many occasions. Now it was deserted, shut up for the Christmas holidays. Taking a key from inside his coat Michael opened the double doors of the building and pushed Tommy inside. Pulling the doors shut behind him, he turned on the lights. Tommy stood immobile.

Taking out his pack of Strands, Michael lit one slowly. He pulled deeply on the cigarette and blew the smoke into Tommy's face.

'You've made me very cross.' As usual Michael's voice was quiet.

Tommy's face seemed to come to life. He blinked his eyes rapidly.

'Look, Mickey, I . . . I tried to get the money. I swear it!'

'Shut up, Tommy. You're beginning to annoy me.'

Dropping the cigarette he grabbed Tommy's scarf, forcing him backwards until he was against one of the huge machines. Bringing his right fist back over his shoulder he punched Tommy in the face with considerable force. Tommy's nose seemed to collapse underneath the blow. Michael let him drop on to the filthy floor. Groaning, Tommy curled himself up into a ball, his hands covering his head. Michael kicked him in the back, the force of the blow sending Tommy across the dirt-strewn floor. Picking up one

18

of the large wooden podgers the women used to push down the bagwashes, Michael prodded Tommy on the shoulder.

'Hold out your arm.' Michael's voice held no emotion whatsoever. Tommy was blubbering.

'Please . . . please, Mickey, I'm begging you.' He looked up at Michael, his face bloody and awash with tears. 'Don't do this . . . I swear I'll ge-get the money somehow.'

Kicking him in the legs, Michael brought the podger down on Tommy's shoulders.

'If you don't put your arm out, I'll break your bastard back for you. Now put your arm out!'

Michael's voice echoed around the laundry. Slowly Tommy placed his arm on the floor, his whole body jerking with fear. Twice the 'podger' smashed down on his elbow, shattering the bone. Tommy screamed with pain. He was struggling to keep conscious as red-hot waves of nausea washed over him. He threw up on the floor, beer mixed with bile steaming in the cold.

'Get up, Tommy.' Michael's voice was quiet again.

Slowly he dragged himself to his feet, his arm hanging awkwardly against his side, the sleeve of his jacket gradually staining crimson. Droplets of blood ran over his fingers and dripped on to the floor. He leant against the machine, crying quietly.

'You've got seven days, Tommy, that's all, to find the money. Now piss off.'

Michael watched Tommy stagger from the laundry. He checked himself over to make sure there was no blood on his clothes. Then, whistling to himself, he washed the podger clean and put it back where he'd found it, against the far wall. Then, still whistling, he turned off the lights and locked up.

Joe the Fish listened avidly to everything Michael said to him, nodding his head now and again and every so often muttering, 'Good . . . good.' When Michael had finished, Joe smiled at him. 'The arm was good and broken?'

'Yeah. Smashed to smithereens!'

Joe the Fish sighed. He had a distaste for violence, but in

his business it was a necessity. He looked at Michael Ryan sitting opposite him. He liked the boy, could see himself in Michael. The boy had the same urge to better himself. That had been Joe's ambition as a young man. Like Michael he had started out as a 'breaker' – a heavy – until he had built up his own business. Now he was a respected member of the community. He owned shops, clubs and market stalls, from Petticoat Lane to the Portobello Road. His most lucrative business, though, was the bets. Joe had been a bookie for over twenty years, gradually moving into loan sharking. He had realised as soon as he had employed Michael that he had found himself a kindred spirit. Michael was innately honest. If he said the punter had paid him fifty quid, Joe knew that was what had been paid. Most of the breakers kept a portion for themselves, knowing that the unlucky punter would eventually pay that portion once again. Michael Ryan, though, had his own set of principles. He might beat a man up so badly he needed hospital treatment, yet Joe knew that in Michael's mind, keeping any money back would be tantamount to stealing. Joe liked him. He liked the way Michael looked at his home. He liked the respect that Michael afforded him.

He coughed and spat some phlegm into the fire, hearing it sizzle as it hit the coals.

'From January I want you to take over the "breaking" side of the business. I'll inform all the men that they're to take their orders from you.'

Michael stared at Joe. Then a wide grin broke out across his face and he shook his head in amazement.

'Thanks, Joe! Bloody hell!'

Joe, like most people, felt happy to see Michael grin. It was as if a blinding sun had emerged from behind a black cloud. Michael had the gift of making people *want* to please him, as if by giving him pleasure they were somehow indebted to him. Joe felt a rush of warmth go through him. He would enjoy working with this boy, teaching him the ropes. He let his eyes travel over Michael's body. He certainly was a fine-looking boy.

Michael watched Joe's eyes and a thrill of anticipation

went through him. Joe the Fish was fifty years old. He had never married or had an association with any woman as far as Michael knew. What he did know was that Joe liked to be surrounded by young men. In the last few months he had consciously ingratiated himself with Joe, flattered him, let Joe think that he was grateful to him for giving him the breaker's job. He stared into Joe's face and smiled at him, his deep blue eyes seemingly full of gratitude and admiration. He watched Joe heave his bulk out of the chair. A flicker of repugnance crossed Michael's features, to be quickly replaced by the dazzling smile he knew caused Joe so much happiness.

Opening one of the drawers in his desk, Joe took out a small box. He walked around the desk and gave it to Michael.

'Just a little token of my appreciation.' Joe's voice was low and husky. Leaning against the desk he watched Michael's face as he opened the box. When he heard the deep intake of breath, Joe relaxed. He would not rush the boy, he had to let him come to him.

Michael stared at the tie pin glinting up from the red velvet lining. It was gold, in the shape of a large M, encrusted with diamonds. Looking up into Joe's face, Michael felt a moment of terror at what he had to do. Then, seeing the softness in Joe's eyes, he swallowed heavily. It was now or never.

Placing his hand on the top of Joe's thigh, he gently brushed his knuckles against the man's groin. Joe stared down at the large, rough hand gently rubbing against him. Closing his eyes momentarily, he felt a rush of ecstasy pulsing through his body. He opened his eyes and stared down into Michael's face. In the firelight, he looked like a dark angel. His blue eyes held an amber glow that caused Joe's heart to somersault inside his breast.

Dropping heavily on to his knees, he placed his hands on Michael's thighs, rubbing and kneading them, his breath coming heavily. Watching him, Michael smiled to himself. He thought Joe looked ridiculous, and noticed that he had a film of sweat above his lips which he licked at nervously.

21

As he felt Joe begin fumbling with his trousers Michael stifled an urge to slam his fist into Joe's head. He couldn't go back now, not after all the planning and scheming of the last few months. Joe was his ticket out of Notting Hill, his passport into the world of real villainy. Gritting his teeth he lay back in the chair and forced himself to relax. Outside, in the muffled stillness of the snow, Michael heard a lone voice singing 'Silent Night'. Looking down at the top of Joe's balding pate, Michael listened to the haunting childish voice and could have cried.

Sarah was basting the turkey when she heard Benjamin come in. The front door was slammed as loudly as possible, causing Sarah to wince. Putting the turkey back into the oven, she sat back in her chair. Benjamin stumbled into the kitchen, his hair and clothes still laden with snow. He grinned his wide toothless grin at her and made his way unsteadily across the room to her side.

'Hello, Sarah, my darling!'

As usual when drunk, he spoke to her as if she was at the other end of the street.

'Will you keep your voice down! You'll have all the bloody kids up!'

Benjamin stared down at his wife, blinking his eyes as he swayed unsteadily before her. The more he tried to concentrate, the more blurred she seemed to become. Finally seeing two Sarahs, he staggered into the seat vacated by Pat Johnstone not an hour ago. Lifting up one of his legs he broke wind loudly, causing Sarah to purse her lips. He sat in the chair smiling amiably at her, his clothes beginning to steam with the heat of the fire.

Wordlessly she pulled herself from her chair and swiftly began making him some ham sandwiches. She looked at the clock and noticed it was twenty-past one – everyone was in now except Michael. Placing the sandwiches on a plate, she gave them to her husband. She was bone tired. She had been working since seven in the morning.

Going through the scullery she pulled on an old coat and went out into the tiny back garden. Squatting down, she took a plate from the top of a large glass bowl. The snow had drifted up the sides and on to the plate. Carefully she wiped it clean. Then, touching the green mass inside the bowl softly, she smiled. The younger children loved jelly. That was one good thing about the snow, it kept everything nice and fresh. Replacing the plate, she stood up and went back inside the house, banging her slippers on the step to get rid of the snow.

Back inside the kitchen she heard her husband snoring loudly. He was sprawled in his chair, his long legs out-stretched, his hand holding the plate of sandwiches away from his body. Taking the plate gently from him she placed it in the sink, then checked the turkey one last time, turned the gas down as low as it would go and made her way up to bed.

As she undressed in the bedroom she saw her daughter had climbed into their big double bed. This was Maura's first real Christmas. Slipping into the bed Sarah looked down on the white-blonde head and felt the familiar tight-ening in her guts. The child stirred and burrowed deeper into the bed. Placing her thumb in her mouth, she sucked on it furiously for a few seconds before settling down once more into a deep sleep. If Benjamin had given her nothing else in their life together he had given her this child, and for that Sarah would forgive him anything.

Michael woke up and glanced at his watch. It was three-fifteen. Shaking his head to clear the fustiness he noticed a fat arm around his waist. In the dying firelight he looked down on the sleeping face of Joe the Fish. Somewhere inside himself he felt disgust at the events of the previous few hours. He was acutely aware of everything that had gone on in front of the then roaring fire. Mixed with his revulsion was also a tiny feeling of excitement. He now had Joe the Fish in his grasp, as he had sworn to himself that he would. A cruel smile played at the corners of his mouth. He would play Joe like a musical instrument. He would slowly become the focal point of his life. Then, when Joe had served his purpose, he would dispose of him. Michael knew what he had to do. He had been planning it long enough.

Gently, he brought his face down on to Joe's and kissed him on his lips. Joe's watery eyes opened and he smiled, displaying discoloured teeth.

'I've got to get going, Joe.'

Yawning lazily, the older man stretched his plump arms above his head.

'All right, Michael love.. Try and get around tomorrow. I'm always alone on Christmas Day.' His voice sounded sad.

'I will. Don't worry.'

Joe watched Michael dressing in the firelight, his heart bursting in his breast. In his mind's eye he relived their love-making of a few hours before and the picture of Michael lying underneath him as he penetrated him rose in his mind. He couldn't quite believe he had found himself such a beautiful animal. As Michael slipped on his overcoat Joe felt a wave of loneliness wash over him.

'See you tomorrow then.' Michael's voice was gentle and caressing. He favoured Joe with one of his blinding grins. Pulling himself up from the floor he stood before the dying fire, his short fat legs and large stomach making Michael feel sick inside.

'Haven't you forgotten something?' Joe's voice sounded like a young girl's – high and breathless with anticipation. Michael frowned at him, bewildered. Then seeing Joe's lips pucker, he walked over to the fireplace and embraced him. Joe pushed his tongue into Michael's mouth, kissing him with an energy that startled him. Breaking away gently, Michael smiled at him and quietly left the room.

The picture of Joe's doughy white body seemed to be imprinted on his mind. As he walked out into the silent white world Michael was glad of the freezing cold that seemed to cut down into his lungs. A light snow was falling and he raised his face to allow the soft flakes to fall on his skin, willing it to wash away the disgust he felt inside.

The street lights gave the pavements a glittering glow as if thousands of diamonds were lining his path. Picking up speed, Michael began to smile. He shook his head and shrugged in the stillness of the night. The worst was over now. He knew what he had let himself in for and he was glad. Let the fat old queen use his body. It had put food on his mother's table. It had bought the kids clothes. It would eventually bring him untold riches. Never would he allow himself to feel bad about it again.

He looked up into the black sky and waved his fist at the stars. This was a new beginning for the Ryans. He was going to pick them up out of the gutter and establish them in the monied world where he knew they belonged. Shoving his hands into the pockets of his overcoat he felt the little box that contained the tie pin. He grinned. As soon as the shops opened after the holidays he was going to go out and buy himself a tie!

When Michael saw the happy faces on Christmas Day, the food that seemed inexhaustible and the merriment his gifts had brought, he finally came to terms with himself. Anything, however bad, was worth all this. After a large, noisy Christmas dinner, Michael sat with his sister Maura asleep on his lap. As he looked down at her sleeping face, sucking contentedly on her thumb, he swore that he would commit murder if it kept his family as happy as they were now.

It was a promise he was to keep many times.

Chapter Three

1955

Garry and Benny Ryan were playing on the bombsite that was once Testerton Street. The day before they had noticed while coming home from school that an enormous mound of sand had been left there. That meant one of two things – the remaining houses were either being patched up or demolished to make way for pre-fabs. Either way they knew that their playground was going to disappear. Both boys had been up and out by six-thirty. If they timed it just right they could scavenge for a few hours before going to the Royalty in Ladbroke Grove for the Saturday morning minors.

They had played in the mound of sand for over an hour. Benny, at nine, was already a true Ryan. Big for his age, he towered over Garry who was eleven. Garry had a long thin body, giving him a waif-like appearance. He was the only Ryan to wear glasses, which he was forever pushing higher on his nose, the thick lenses giving him an owlish appearance. Where Benny was dark-haired with the characteristic Ryan dark blue eyes and full-lipped mouth, Garry was the opposite. He had light brown hair and a feral quality about him that made people do what he wanted. Garry was the acknowledged genius of the family, forever reading. His room was strewn with books and papers. He also fancied himself as an inventor – a pastime that had his mother caught between maternal pride and an almost uncontrollable urge to murder him.

The June sunshine gave their play an added vigour. All around them the world had come to life. The hum of the traffic was getting louder and every so often the rattling of a train set the dirt trembling. To the right of the mound of sand stood what remained of the houses in Testerton Street. The bomb had been a direct hit and only the last few dwellings had still been standing afterwards. These had no fronts left. Their rooms were great gaping caverns that miraculously still had wallpaper and broken furniture inside.

The two boys knew every inch of these houses. From the roof rafter of the most stable hung their 'bundle' swing. Now summer was here the swing would become a focal point for the children around and about. Boys would come from as far away as Shepherd's Bush and Bayswater to play on it between fighting rival gangs. Providing the work didn't start too soon, it would be a good summer.

Scrambling down from the mound of sand, Garry began walking towards the houses, his hands and knees stained orange. Seeing his brother walking away Benny followed hastily, rubbing off the damp sand from his hands on his shorts. He caught up with Garry, puffing for breath.

'What we gonna do then?' As always he waited for Garry to decide what games were to be played.

Garry looked up at his brother, his thin face already grimy. 'We's gonna look for bombs and things. Lee's hid some gunpowder he swiped from under the Arches and I'm gonna pinch it off him.'

Benny looked worried for a second. Lee at thirteen was already as big as Roy, who was seventeen, nearly six feet tall, and was also bad-tempered.

'Lee'll smash us up!'

Garry smiled and pushed his glasses higher up his nose. 'He's got to catch us first!'

Benny laughed nervously. Lee would catch them, he always did, but he kept his own counsel because when Garry got mad he sent him home. Then he'd have to play with his sister! He followed Garry into the end house. The stairs were still sound and both boys made their way up to the top floor. Standing dangerously close to the crumbling edge, the two looked out across London. Over the last few years the landscape had changed. From their vantage point they could see the whole of their world. In the distance Garry saw that the fairground had arrived at Wormwood Scrubs Park. He poked Benny in the ribs and pointed to it, a thrill of expectation going through them both.

'I'm gonna get Mickey to give us some money! We'll go there later and see what rides they've got!'

In his excitement Benny jumped backwards and tripped over a lump of wood. As he landed on the floor boards he gasped, 'Here, Gal, look at this lot!'

Garry was already staring at what lay beneath his brother's large feet.

'Where'd you reckon they come from?'

Garry shook his head. Kneeling down on the floor, he picked up an empty cartridge case. There were over a dozen in all.

'I reckon someone nicked them and then left them here!'

Pushing his glasses up on to the bridge of his nose, Garry snapped: 'Trust you to state the bloody obvious. These have been hidden here by a little firm, and I think I know whose it was!'

Benny pulled himself up from the floor with difficulty. Both his hands were stinging where he'd skinned them.

'Who d'you reckon hid them then?'

'I bet it was that gang from Elgin Avenue.' Garry's voice was triumphant.

'Come on, let's nick them quick. Before anyone comes.'

Both boys began stuffing the empty cases down their shirts. Then they ran down the stairs as fast as they could. As they ran out of the house into the sunshine they both skidded to a halt. Lee, Leslie and Roy were walking towards them. Garry looked at Benny, his face troubled.

'Whatever you do, don't tell them about this lot.' He patted his shirt. Benny's hands were smarting and he rubbed them gently on his shirt. Tears were already forming in his eyes.

Roy noticed the two boys and called to them. 'What you two standing there for? What you done?'

Garry as usual did the talking. 'We ain't done nothing. We thought you was looking for us, that's all.'

29

'What would we want with you two?' Roy's voice sounded incredulous. 'We get enough of you at home. Now sod off, the pair of you.'

Neither boy needed to be told twice. They ran off as fast as their legs would carry them. When they reached the safety of the pile of sand they sat on top of it and watched their brothers. The three older boys stood by the opening of the houses. They were all smoking.

'Did you smell them? I reckons they've been to the baths in Silchester Road. They've all got that smelly stuff on their hair.' Benny's voice was disgusted. In his mind anyone who could have a bath without being told to needed treatment. He himself had a bath every fortnight, a sixpenny one with soap and towels supplied. He hated it. If his mother didn't stand outside waiting for him he'd spend the money on something important, like caps for his gun and comics.

A little while later three girls arrived on the scene, two blondes and a redhead. Garry laughed.

'Dirty bleeders! That's why they've been to the baths. They're going snogging!'

They watched the three girls pair off with their brothers and go off in different directions. Even more disgusted, Benny stood up.

'Come on, let's go home. I'm hungry.'

Silently the two boys made their way home.

It was three in the afternoon when Roy brought Janine into his house. It was the first time he had brought a girl home and both he and Janine were nervous. Grasping her hand in the hallway, he smiled at her.

'Everything's gonna be all right.'

He looked down into her green eyes and as always had the urge to kiss her. She had milk-white skin and long thick red hair. To Roy's mind Janine was class. She was also very tall – five foot eight inches. In a way he was glad that she was 'in trouble'. It would give them the push they needed to come out into the open.

He led her by the hand into his mother's kitchen. As usual Sarah was cooking. Even on days like this with the

30

sun cracking the pavements Sarah still cooked. With nine children to feed, preparing a meal was a major event. She looked at Roy and Janine, her surprise showing on her face. Roy stood awkwardly in the kitchen and, still grasping Janine's hand, smiled at his mother.

'Mum, I'd like you to meet Janine . . . Janine Grierson.'

The girl stretched out her free hand and nodded her head. 'Pleased to meet you, I'm sure.'

Her voice was very low and refined. Wiping her hand on her apron, Sarah took the girl's hand and shook it gently.

'And you, love. Well, sit yourselves down. I've made some ginger beer. Would you like a glass?'

Without waiting for an answer, she went to the scullery and took the large jug from the table out there. She needed time to think. Grierson? Grierson? Where did she know that name from? She carried the jug back into the kitchen. Roy had sat Janine at the kitchen table and was standing beside her. Then, like a bolt out of the blue, it came to Sarah. This was Janine Grierson. Her heart sank in her chest. Her father owned the butcher's in the Portobello Road. He had also owned the house next door to Christie's round in Rillington Place. What on earth was Janine doing with her Roy? Not that she didn't think her son was good enough for her, oh no! But Eliza Grierson had great plans for her only daughter, Sarah knew that much.

Forcing a smile on to her face she poured out two glasses of ginger beer. As she placed them on the table, Roy spoke up. 'Janine's pregnant, Mum. And I'm the father.'

Outside in the garden, Maura was watching Garry and Benny working. Benny was holding the cartridges steady while Garry filled them with the gunpowder. After watching a particularly thrilling Lone Ranger at the Saturday morning minors, Garry had experienced a renewed interest in the making of bombs. He pushed the wadding carefully into the cartridge before taking it from Benny and placing it on the garden wall. He stepped back to admire his handiwork. That was the last one.

Maura sat on the wooden crate. Her long blonde hair

seemed to come alive in the sunlight which gave it golden highlights. Her aquamarine eyes carefully watched every movement her brothers made. At five, Maura knew that if she wanted to be a part of their games she had to sit and watch quietly, otherwise they would sneak out of the garden leaving her alone.

She saw Garry give Benny a large hammer. Then Garry carefully took one of the filled cartridges and placed it on the grass. He had to press it down a couple of times to stop it falling over. Then he nodded at Benny who took the hammer and brought it back over his head, ready to smash it down on to the cartridge at a sign from his brother. Garry pushed his glasses higher on his nose and raising his hand as if he was starting a race, brought it down heavily to his side . . .

Inside the house Janine was crying quietly as Sarah spoke. 'It's nothing against you, lass, but think of your father. He'll go stark staring mad when he hears. Baby or no baby, there's no way he'll allow you to marry Roy. I know it.' Her voice had a finality about it that made Roy's blood run cold in his veins. He opened his mouth to answer. Both women were looking at him expectantly. They saw his eyes open wide until they seemed about to start from his head.

'Benny! Benny . . . don't you bloody dare!' His voice was so loud both women jumped in their seats. A split second later an almighty bang erupted from the garden, followed by Maura's frenzied screaming. The three adults seemed to be catapulted from their seats as they ran out into the back yard.

Maura had seen the hammer descend on to the cartridge just as she heard Roy's voice come from the house. The impact of the hammer hitting the brass casing of the cartridge had caused a flash of blue light followed by an enormous bang. As if in slow motion she had seen Benny travel backwards through the air, landing heavily on his back among the rubbish that littered the end of the garden.

32

That's when she started to scream. Through her tears she saw Garry scaling the wall as he made a run for it.

Roy ran to where Benny was lying, his heart pounding in his ears. This time Garry had really done it. He had finally killed somebody. Picking Benny up gently he cradled his head in his lap, conscious of his mother standing in the garden, her hand over her mouth as if terrified of what she might find. Benny was soot-blackened all over. The smell of burnt powder seemed to hang around him in a cloud. Looking down into his brother's face, Roy felt the tears come into his eyes.

'Benny . . . Benny!' Roy's anguished voice carried up into the pale blue sky. Janine, stunned, had gone to the little girl sitting on the crate. Instinctively she pulled the child to her breast, stroking the long blonde hair.

Roy clutched Benny to him, cuddling the dirty head to his breast. Opening his eyes Benny looked up into his brother's tearstained face.

'What happened?' His childish voice broke into everyone's shocked thoughts. 'One minute I was hammerin'. The next I was blown up!'

Benny looked around him, a bewildered expression on his face. 'Where's Garry gone?'

Picking him up, Roy felt the terror slowly leave his own body. 'When that little bastard gets home, I'm gonna murder him. If it's the last thing I do in this life . . .'

Maura clung to Janine, enjoying the flowery smell of her. Her cries had subsided to little hiccups. Sarah let Roy carry Benny into the house, and as she looked at Janine comforting her only daughter, the ice in her heart melted. Going to the girl, she put her arm around her shoulders.

'That Garry will be the death of me. Well, if you think you could stand the strain of being part of this family, you're welcome.

Janine's white face made Sarah's natural good nature come to the fore. Pushing the girl's heavy red hair back from her face, she said, 'I'm warning you, though . . . excitement like this is an everyday occurrence!'

'Oh, Mrs Ryan, my father is going to go mad.'

Sarah waved her hand at the girl, her voice sounding more confident than she actually felt.

'He'll get over it, love. He'll get over it.'

James Grierson was stalking around his house in a fit of temper so acute he could almost taste it. Unlike his wife, who had taken herself off to bed like one of the heroines in the penny dramas, he, James Grierson, was going to *do* something. What exactly he wasn't sure, but he would think of something. Stamping up the stairs he went into the bedroom he shared with Eliza.

'How could a daughter of mine take up with that bloody scum? A filthy, stinking Ryan!' He clenched his fists and raised them to the ceiling. 'I could throttle the bitch. My God, my mother used to say: "Show me the company you keep and I'll tell you what you are." Never was a truer word said!'

Eliza closed her eyes and groaned. Since Janine had told them that morning that she was pregnant, her whole world had fallen apart. Only a week ago, she had stood in their butcher's shop and completely demolished the reputation of young Carrie Davidson for the same thing: having to get married. She could hear herself talking to anyone who would listen about the shameless hussy. Now it had happened to her daughter and she didn't like it, she didn't like it one bit. Eliza Grierson was known as a gossip of Olympian standards. She prided herself on her ability to sift through the most innocent conversations and turn them into major scandals. She knew that this trouble with her daughter would be all the more enjoyed because it was a reflection on herself. She groaned again and pushed a pillow over her head. If it had been anyone but a Ryan . . . She felt tears of frustration stinging her eyes. She could cheerfully throttle Janine herself!

A loud banging at the front door stopped both of them in their tracks. Pulling back the curtain, James Grierson looked down into his garden and groaned. It was not a very good day today, and he had a terrible feeling that it was going to get worse.

Michael and Geoffrey stood in the Griersons' front garden. Like everything of Eliza Grierson's, the garden was what she described as 'classy'. It was also immaculate, as were the curtains at the windows and the shiny brass knocker on the door. This was opened by a rather subdued James who said gruffly: 'You'd better come in.'

Michael and Geoffrey walked into the spacious hallway as if they owned the house. Opening the parlour door, James ushered them inside.

'What do you want?' His voice was clipped.

Michael sat himself down in an armchair and looked around the room slowly. Geoffrey sat on the rather hard horsehair settee.

Taking a packet of Strands from his pocket Michael gave one to Geoffrey and after offering the pack to James, who refused, laboriously set about lighting the cigarettes. He knew that his slowness was annoying James Grierson. It was a calculated move. Drawing the smoke into his lungs he put his head back against the chair and blew two large smoke rings. Then, looking at James, he smiled.

'I understand, Mr Grierson, that my brother Roy has been shunting your daughter.'

Geoffrey watched the red flush creep up James Grierson's neck and continue until it reached his receding hairline. Stamping across the room, the man made as if to grab Michael's shirt. Grabbing Grierson's hand in a vice-like grip, Michael laughed.

'Naughty, naughty.'

Then pushing the older man from him, he sat forward in the chair. James was sent sprawling across his own parlour carpet, a blinding anger building inside him.

Michael pointed at him, the cigarette smoke curling around his finger.

'In three weeks' time, Mr Grierson, my brother is gonna marry your daughter, with or without your permission. Personally I would advise you to give them your blessing, what with the baby and all. A new little Ryan . . . a Ryan that your daughter is carrying inside her.'

Slowly James Grierson pulled himself up from the floor.

Geoffrey put out his hand to help but was ignored. Waving his hand away, the older man slumped down on the chair opposite Michael.

Staring at him, Michael underwent one of his lightning changes of mood. From anger and animosity he turned in a split second to a benevolent caring brother only here to see justice done. His rugged face softened. All irritation seemingly forgotten, he leant forward in his chair and smiled at James Grierson – one of his most stunning smiles that seemed to wipe the cruelty from his face at a stroke. He began to speak in a man to man voice.

'Listen, James . . . may I call you James?' The man nodded, not at all happy with this bewildering change in his antagonist.

'The way I see it is this. Your daughter has been made pregnant by my brother.' He opened his arms out wide in a gesture of helplessness. 'They love one another, they want to marry. It's not as if Roy's had it on his toes, is it? He's quite willing to do the right thing by the girl. I know you've had a shock. No man likes to think of his daughter . . . well, you know what I mean. But, the only thing left to do is to get them married. I hope you will change your attitude, soften towards them?' His voice was now redolent with an underlying threat that was not wasted on James Grierson. Michael Ryan was offering him a face saver and he knew it. He was being told in no uncertain terms that he could come out of all this as the loving, caring father who would do anything to keep his daughter's reputation; who welcomed her choice of husband with open arms; who would not bow down in the face of adversity, but would rise up and conquer it.

For the first time in his life James Grierson felt a grudging respect for a Ryan. He knew he was being manipulated but, he asked himself, what was the alternative? He had heard stories about Michael Ryan. That he was as queer as a nine bob note. That he had taken over Joe the Fish's businesses and made a name for himself among the villains. At nineteen Michael Ryan was already becoming a neighbourhood legend. 'Cruel but fair' was the local opinion. Could he really let his only child become a part of this family? Even as the question formed in his mind he knew it was useless. If he went against this young man sitting opposite him, he would in effect dig his own grave. The course was already set. Janine was marrying Roy Ryan whether he liked it or not. What he had to do now was stretch out and take the hand of friendship being offered to him. He sighed heavily and his voice came out in a nervous croak.

'You're right, of course. If they really care for one another . . .'

He swallowed deeply as Michael Ryan took his hand and shook it, the animal strength of the handshake reminding him acutely of exactly what he had done. His lovely Janine had brought him this low, had brought Michael Ryan into his home. He could have wept.

Three weeks later, on the first Saturday of July, James Grierson gave away his only daughter to Roy Ryan. It wasn't until after the reception, once home in his bed, that he finally gave way to the tears that had been building up inside him since Michael's visit. He felt he had taken his only child like a lamb to the slaughter.

It would be twenty years before he discovered how right he had been.

Chapter Four

1957

Michael was fuming, his blue eyes dark with anger. He rubbed one hand across his face and stared stonily at Joe.

'Look, Michael, you had no right to borrow any money behind my back. This is *my* business.' Joe the Fish pushed a pudgy finger into his chest.

Making a fist Michael smashed it down on the desk in front of him, causing their empty coffee cups to rattle in their saucers.

'So it's your business now, is it?' Michael's voice was bitter. 'I suppose this is *your* office as well? Don't let's worry about the money *I've* brought in . . .

Joe sighed loudly. He interrupted Michael as if he was talking to a little child.

'Oh, for Christ's sake, Michael. No one's disputing that you've done well. What's annoyed me is the fact that you borrowed out five grand without even bothering to mention it to me.' Joe's voice was cajoling. In his heart he was frightened of Michael, frightened of his phenomenal temper. 'Come on, son . . . try and see it from my point of view.'

Michael picked up his pack of Strands from the desk and lit one. He sat at the desk, his head hanging forward on his chest, taking quick drags on his cigarette. Joe was conscious that Michael's hands were shaking. He knew he was trying to calm himself down.

Joe sat in the chair opposite and placed his elbows on the desk. Michael was such a difficult boy. He gravitated from extreme happiness to a difficult and dangerous depression in the space of seconds.

Normally Joe would have let Michael have his head, he was a good businessman, but this latest flouting of the rules had angered him. He had loaned five thousand pounds to Phillip Wreck, one of the most notorious villains in Paddington, and in Joe's mind Michael had more chance of getting the Pope's inside leg measurement than he had of getting that money back.

Michael stubbed out his cigarette, grinding it into the ashtray with such force Joe thought it would surely break. Snapping his head up he looked at Joe, his mouth clamped closed. In the quiet room Joe could hear his laboured breathing.

'I'm warning you, Joe . . . I'm warning you now . . . don't fight me on this. I know exactly what I'm doing. I'll get that money back. I'll get it and the interest on it, you just wait and see.'

There were tears in Michael's eyes. He's just like a child, Joe thought, it's as if I've taken his toys away from him. The difference being that when Michael was like this he was liable to explode into a raging temper at any moment.

Joe felt the familiar fingers of fear touching him. It was Michael's very unpredictability that drew Joe to him. Twice Michael had lashed out at him and hurt him, only to be contrite and loving in the next breath. Although Joe had never tried to analyse their relationship, inside himself he knew that it was the boy's vicious streak that attracted him.

'All right, Michael, I'll let it go this time. But in future, you come to me.'

Michael's face broke into one of his winning smiles and Joe felt himself relax.

As Michael looked at the man sitting opposite, his fat ugly face grinning like a Cheshire cat's, he felt an impulse to smash his fist into his teeth. Instead he carried on smiling. Joe didn't know it but his days were numbered. Soon he would be out of the way and he, Michael, could get on with his life.

Joe got out of his chair and walked around the desk. Standing behind Michael he began rubbing his taut muscular shoulders. Feeling the solid flesh beneath his fingers he felt himself harden, completely unaware that Michael was planning his demise.

Roy was in the butcher's shop in the Portobello Road. His father-in-law had given up trying to explain to him the different cuts of meat. Roy had been working for him since three weeks after his wedding, and he hated it. He felt like a kept man. He couldn't do the job, he knew it and his father-in-law knew it, but it was all part of the grand master plan: How To Keep Your Daughter At Home. They lived with Mr and Mrs Grierson. They ate with Mr and Mrs Grierson. And they watched from the sidelines as Mr and Mrs Grierson between them brought up the baby, Carla. It had been a few months before Roy realised he had married what his mother would have called 'a lazy bitch'. Janine was quite content to let her mother take over the baby, the cooking, everything. That left her free to play at being married which consisted of getting herself done up to the nines and visiting her friends all day, now and again taking the baby, all nice and clean, out in her pram. Playing at being mother of the year.

Roy winced as he thought of her. What had happened to the girl he had fallen in love with? The spirited young woman who had been as eager for life as he was? Admittedly they were only nineteen, but surely, he reasoned, there must be more to married life than this? If he mentioned moving out of her parents' house, she dissolved into tears. Last night had been the last straw. He had told her there was a flat going in Westbourne Park and she had had hysterics.

'How am I gonna cope with a baby on me own?'

That's when he had lost his temper. 'Well, we won't find that out until you try, will we? God Almighty, Janine, you've never once looked after the bloody kid for a whole day since it was born!'

After that her mother, Eliza, had come into the bedroom and led Janine out, taking her into her own bedroom. Then this morning she had told him that Janine was 'delicate' and needed her mother to look after her. He was frankly

41

bewildered by it all. He wanted them to have their own little place, where Janine looked after the baby all day and cooked his meal in the evening. What he had was a pampered, spoilt brat whose only interest in life was lipstick and what was on at the pictures. She never looked at the child unless she had to. Even his mother had noticed it. She had asked him a few Saturdays ago if everything was all right between them. He had felt like telling her everything but just couldn't. He wouldn't even know where to begin.

'Hello, Bruv.' Roy was brought out of his reverie by Michael's voice.

'Hello, Mickey!' He hadn't been so pleased to see someone in all his life.

'Fancy skiving off for a few hours? I've got a bit of business I want to talk to you about.'

Roy wiped his bloody hands on his apron. 'I'll be with you in a tick.' He walked through to the back of the shop and called out to his father-in-law. James Grierson came down the stairs that led to the flat above the shop.

'What's all this row about?' His voice was loud and agitated. 'Can't you even look after the bloody shop? Want me to hold your hand now, I suppose.' Roy was conscious that Michael could hear every word and groaned inside.

'I've got to shoot off for a couple of hours.'

'You what!' Grierson's voice was incredulous. 'This is a bloody business here, not a bloody knocking shop where you pick your own hours . . .'

His voice faltered as he saw Michael slip through the doorway. Grierson paled.

'Who do you think you're talking to?' Michael's voice was icy. He pointed at Grierson. 'I'm talking to you. You had enough bunny just now . . . so answer me. Who d'you think you're talking to?'

As Michael stepped towards him, Grierson stepped backwards, his hands coming up to defend himself if the visitor lashed out.

Michael snapped at Roy: 'Get your coat.' Then walking to where Grierson was cowering against the wall, he grabbed him around the throat. 'Now, I don't know what's going down here, but I know this much – if you *ever* talk to my brother like that again, I'll rip your nuts off and ram them down your throat. Do you understand what I'm saying?'

Grierson was nodding his head furiously when Roy came back with his coat. Pulling Mickey away gently, he led him through the front of the shop and out into the street. He was ashamed that Michael had heard his father-in-law speak to him like that. He was ashamed that he himself let him.

'Come on, Roy, we're going to the KPH. I think we'd better have a talk.'

They walked in silence. The bright October day belied the cold wind. Roy noticed that everywhere they walked people acknowledged Michael. It was as if he was their sovereign and they his subjects. Depending on how influential people were, Mickey either nodded at them or gave them a hearty greeting. Roy was impressed. Michael's name was becoming synonymous with those of the Krays and the Richardsons, two of the most influential young gangs of that time. Roy knew that Michael kept up a friendship with them. An uneasy alliance. It seemed that once people met him they decided they were better off having him as a friend than an enemy.

They walked into the red warmth of the Kensington Park Hotel. Michael ordered them both hot whiskies and they settled down in the lounge bar.

Michael took his cigarettes from his overcoat pocket, and then slipped the coat from his shoulders. Folding it up carefully, he laid it across a chair. All his movements were performed with a natural grace. Roy shrugged off his own coat while still sitting, letting it fall over the back of his chair. Adjusting his trouser crease fastidiously Michael sat down again, settling himself into the over-upholstered chair. Then, pulling a large white ashtray towards him so it would be within easy reach, he lit a cigarette. Throwing the packet across the table at Roy, he finally spoke.

43

'How long has he been talking to you like that?' His voice was quiet.

Roy hung his head. 'I know it sounds bad, Mickey, but he is my father-in-law . . .'

'I couldn't give a fuck if he was the Immaculate Conception! There's something wrong, ain't there? The Roy I knew would never take that from anyone, not in a million years.' He lowered his voice. 'Come on, Bruv. What's the SP?'

The barman brought over their hot toddies and Roy was glad of the few seconds' reprieve. He could feel Michael's eyes boring into him. When they were settled again, Roy spoke.

'I don't know, Mickey. Since Carla was born it's as if I don't exist any more. Janine and her mum and dad act like she never got married. I feel like a lodger in the house. I eat their food, I sleep in their bed, I shag their daughter now and again.' All the bitterness of the last two years seemed to boil over and come tumbling out. 'And I mean, now and again. Every three weeks when they go and visit her bloody granny in Bethnal Green. She says she can't do it while Mummy's in the house. Then old man Grierson treats me like the village idiot. I'm not a butcher, Mickey. I hate looking at the meat, I hate touching it . . .' His voice trailed off.

'So what are you gonna do?'

Roy shrugged and took a gulp of his drink. 'I dunno.'

'You don't know? So that's it then, is it?' Michael was getting annoyed. 'Why don't you give her a right-hander? Show her who's boss. Tell her old man to go and stuff his bloody butcher's shop up his Jacksey. I knew she spelt trouble . . . I bloody knew it!'

'All right . . . All right, Mickey. Keep your hair on.'

'Why don't you come and work for me? That's what I wanted to talk to you about.' He saw a gleam of hope appear in Roy's eyes.

'I'd jump at the chance, you know that.'

Michael laughed. Roy was like a bloody kid at times. He looked at his brother's open face, and made a mental note

44

to tell his mother what was going down with him. He knew that she was worried.

'That's settled then.' He looked at his watch. 'From two-twenty-five today you are a working member of the Ryan dynasty.' They both laughed. Anthony and Geoffrey worked for Michael already. Now he had Roy.

'What's the pay, Mickey?' Roy sounded uncertain.

'Bloody good, that's what.'

'I wouldn't ask, but what with the baby and everything . . .'

'No worries, I'll start you on thirty quid a week. That's a bit more than the others, so keep stumm about it.' Michael tapped his nose with his forefinger.

Roy was amazed. He was going to go and get Janine and the baby and if necessary drag her to the flat in Westbourne Park. This was gonna be a new start. Mickey was right. Maybe she needed a right-hander. And if his father-in-law stuck his oar in, he would get one and all!

He drank his whisky down and felt the warm glow through his body. It was partly the alcohol and partly the knowledge that he was finally going to do something about his life. The worry he had been feeling about Janine was replaced by elation. He would take a leaf out of Mickey's book. Hit first, ask questions later.

Michael watched his brother's face and guessed immediately what was going through his mind. He motioned to the barman to refill their glasses, a feeling of satisfaction running through him. He had a soft spot for Roy, the same as he did for Benny. They were both too nice for their own good. He was going to toughen Roy up. Make him into someone. Then, when Joe the Fish was out of the way, the businesses would be run exclusively by Ryans. He raised up his steaming glass to his brother.

'To the Ryans!'

'The Ryans!'

Geoffrey and Anthony were sitting at the end of Penzance Gardens, where it met Princedale Road. It was nearly two-fifteen in the morning. They sat in a black Humber Snipe.

Both were freezing and both were nervous, especially Geoffrey. At twenty-one he was two years older than Anthony. They were identical to look at. Both had the Ryan dark hair and firm chin. Anthony had more of Michael's ruggedness whereas Geoffrey had softer features, almost effeminate.

Anthony spoke. His voice in the darkness caused Geoffrey to jump. 'How much longer have we got to wait?'

'How the hell do I know? What do you think I am? The Oracle or something?'

'Very funny. You get on my wick, do you know that?' Anthony's usual animosity was coming to the fore. Anthony Ryan was known in his family as able to pick a fight with his own fingernails. The only person he was even remotely respectful to was Mickey. 'You think because you've read a few crappy books you know it all.'

Geoffrey rolled his eyes up towards the roof of the car. 'Do me a favour, Ant . . . Save all your hag for what we've got to do tonight. I ain't in the mood.'

They were silent again. Anthony was frustrated because he wasn't as quick-brained as Geoffrey so always came off worse in an argument. It didn't deter him though. He tried a different tack.

'I saw that sort you've been knocking about with last night. I'd give her one meself.' Knowing that it would annoy Geoffrey, Anthony braced himself for the ensuing argument. Instead, Geoffrey put his hand over his brother's mouth. They listened. Footsteps were approaching the car. They sat tense and nervous. Anthony's hard features looked as if they had been carved from stone. His fists were clenched tight on the steering wheel.

The man who was walking towards them stepped into the light of a streetlamp. It was Joe the Fish. He was walking unsteadily along the road, obviously the worse for drink. Geoffrey nodded and Anthony started the car. He did not put on the headlights. Reversing back a little, they waited until Joe began crossing the intersection between Penzance Gardens and Princedale Road. Pushing his foot down on the accelerator, Anthony thrust the car forward.

Hearing a loud noise through his drunken haze, Joe turned in time to see the car coming at him. He raised his arm as if to protect himself as the car hit him full on. His body flew into the air and landed on the bonnet. His head crashed against the windscreen. Anthony slammed his foot on the brake. As the car screeched to a halt, Joe's body slid from the bonnet on to the road. Anthony ran the car over him one more time before speeding off. The whole operation had taken less than three minutes. A woman who had been up getting herself a glass of water heard the commotion and ran out into the street. She took one look at Joe's face and began to scream. Lights began to go on all over Princedale Road.

Anthony and Geoffrey drove the car from Holland Park to Moscow Road in Bayswater. The streets were deserted. Parking the car they left it there and walked around to Porchester Terrace, throwing the keys to the Humber Snipe down a drainhole. In Porchester Terrace they picked up a blue Mark 1 Zephyr and drove sedately home to Lancaster Road. It was just three o'clock.

Inside a private house in Beauchamp Place, Knightsbridge, Michael picked up his cards and studied them carefully. He was on a winning streak tonight. He had three aces and two kings. Joe had left an hour earlier. He had been given a lift to the Bayswater Road by a mutual friend, Derek O'Connor. If everything had gone according to plan then Joe was well and truly out of the picture, and he, Michael, had the perfect alibi. He smiled smugly to himself as he raised the bet by fifty pounds. If Geoffrey and Anthony had bungled the job tonight, he would personally batter their brains out.

Sarah heard a loud banging on her front door. She glanced at the clock on the bedside table. It was five o'clock in the morning. Sleepily she dragged herself out of bed. Benjamin was snoring his head off as usual, so it wasn't the police after him – that would make a change. She yawned, went down the stairs and opened the front door.

Two men stood there and she recognised at once that they were CID.

'Is Michael at home, love?'

Blinking her eyes rapidly to try and clear her head, Sarah said, 'Come inside and I'll go and look.'

The two men walked into the hallway.

She went upstairs and looked into Michael's room. The bed hadn't been slept in. As she walked back on to the landing, Geoffrey came out of his room.

'Who's that downstairs, Mum?'

'The old Bill. They're looking for Michael. What's going on?'

She knew her sons and would bet her last pound that Geoffrey had been awake waiting for something like this.

'You go back to bed, Mum. I'll sort out the filth.'

Both turned as they heard a door opening. Maura Ryan came out of her room, clutching a raggy doll. Sarah went to her, picking her up in her arms. Geoffrey went down the stairs.

'Mickey ain't in.'

'Well, where is he then?' This from the older of the policemen.

'He's up West. At a house in Knightsbridge. What do you want him for?' Geoffrey yawned in their faces, stretching his arms over his head and finishing by scratching his belly lazily. The younger policeman noticed that his pyjamas were hardly creased. Geoffrey Ryan hadn't been in bed. The trouble would be proving it.

'Somebody tried to murder Joe the Fish earlier.'

Geoffrey felt as if someone had thrown a bucket of cold water over him. 'What do you mean, tried to murder him?'

'Exactly what I say. And knowing how close Mickey is to him, I thought we had better let him know.' The older officer was trying to goad him.

Unlike Anthony, Geoffrey could keep a lid on his temper. Deliberately misconstruing the policeman's words, he shook his head sadly and said, 'Mickey's like a son to that man. This will come as a great shock to him. What exactly happened?' He had to know what was going on.

48

Half of his mind was saying silent prayers. He'd been sure Joe was dead when they left him.

'Someone tried to run him over a few hours ago. He's fighting for his life in St Charles's Hospital. The hospital said to try and get his next-of-kin. We assumed that was Michael Ryan. Two men couldn't get any closer than those two have been over the last couple of years, could they?' The policeman raised his eyebrows and his colleague laughed.

Geoffrey was saved from answering by his mother's voice. She had been carrying Maura down the stairs and had heard the policeman's remark.

'What are you trying to say? I know you lot with your dirty insinuendos.' She hitched her daughter up on to her shoulder, holding her steady with her free hand. The other was gripping the banister rail, her knuckles white and bony. 'My Michael is a decent clean-living individual. Now I'll thank you two to get out of my house.'

Hiding a grin, Geoffrey took the heavy child from her as she came to the bottom of the stairs. Maura sat in his arms, an alert expression on her face. At seven she was already wise to the likes of the police. Sarah pushed angrily at the two policemen. She looked so tiny beside the two men, yet so ferocious, that Geoffrey laughed out loud.

'That's it, Muvver. Tell the bastards to sling their hooks.'

Opening the front door, Sarah let the men out. She was fuming. How dare they say that of her Michael! Her temper was caused by the fact that she had a terrible suspicion that what they said was true. Slamming the door on them, she turned her anger on her son.

'Well, don't stand there like a gormless eejit! Go and get dressed and find Mickey!'

Placing Maura carefully on the floor, Geoffrey ran up the stairs. Maura followed her mother into the kitchen, curling up on one of the easy chairs by the fire.

'Can I have a standing up egg, Mum?'

Sarah nodded. 'Of course you can have a boiled egg if that's what you want.'

She filled the kettle, her mind racing. If Joe the Fish died

49

then it would be a murder charge for somebody. But who? Michael? She pushed the thought from her head. Whatever she thought about her boys, there was one thing she knew: they were not murderers. They were just tearaways. High-spirited tearaways. Or, at least, she hoped that's all they were. Putting the kettle on the gas, she went to her daughter and hugged her tightly.

Joe was lying in the hospital bed. Nurse Walton looked down at his battered face. She shook her head and turned to see the policeman by the bed grimacing at her. She blinked and sighed.

'Who would do such a thing?' Her voice sounded very young.

PC Blenkinsop pushed out his narrow chest and tried to look like an all-knowing, sophisticated officer.

'You'd be surprised. It's a wicked life out on the street these days. He might look like an old man who's been run over a few times to you, but to me . . .' he puffed his chest out even further '. . . he's a vicious criminal.'

Nurse Walton looked suitably impressed. 'Just wait until I tell my mum!'

PC Blenkinsop looked as if he was readjusting his shoulders inside his tunic top. He thrust out his chin and smiled.

Joe groaned and immediately had the attention of both of them. 'Mickey . . . Mickey.'

PC Blenkinsop was writing down Joe's words with a flourish of his pencil. Licking it, he waited expectantly.

Michael stood in the entrance to the ward. He had known that a policeman would be in attendance. Squaring his shoulders, he walked down the ward towards Joe's bed. He could see the young PC and the nurse through the inadequate screens. Putting a sober expression on his face, he went to the bed.

PC Blenkinsop noted Nurse Walton's reaction to Michael Ryan and it annoyed him. He thrust out his lip like a petulant schoolboy.

'And who might you be?' He stood up and seemed to roll on the balls of his feet. Michael gave him a scathing glance.

He picked up Joe's hand which was heavily bandaged. He turned to the nurse and smiled sadly at her.

'How bad is he?' His voice sounded wretched. Nurse Walton stared into his dark blue eyes and was immediately filled with pity for him.

'He's very bad. The doctor says he'll be surprised if he lasts out the day.' If she had known Michael, she would have noticed the glimmer of relief that came into his eyes.

'Has he said anything at all?'

The PC interrupted. 'He has been calling for a . . .' he glanced importantly at his notebook '. . . Mickey.'

Michael nodded. 'That's me.'

The young nurse brought Michael a chair and he sat beside Joe, holding the old man's hand and stroking it every now and again. The PC watched him. So this was Michael Ryan. He couldn't wait to get back to the station and brag about how he'd seen him.

The nurse brought Michael a cup of tea and he thanked her, giving her one of his radiant smiles. PC Blenkinsop could have cried. She didn't even know he was there now.

Shortly before seven in the evening Joe opened his eyes and immediately recognised Michael. He passed his tongue over his cracked lips and tried to speak. Michael could see by the look in his eyes that he knew who had ordered his accident. Agitated, Joe tried to lift his head off the pillow.

'Mickey . . . Mickey . . . you . . .' Then his head fell back and he died.

Michael closed his eyes, a feeling of euphoria surging through him. He had got away with it! Then, as could happen with him, he felt a deep despondency replace his feeling of elation. Tears welled up in his eyes, spilling over on to his cheeks. In his own funny way he would miss Joe who had been his passport into the real world. For that he would always be grateful to him. He would give Joe the Fish the best send-off anyone had ever seen.

PC Blenkinsop looked embarrassed. Later on in the station canteen he had everyone hanging on his words.

'Yeah, I'm telling you. It was quite touching. Michael

51

Ryan cried like a baby. Well, it was to be expected really. After all, the old boy died calling out his name.'

At Joe's funeral a week later, the police noted that all the gang bosses stopped to pay their respects to Michael Ryan. He was well and truly established now. That, together with the fact that Joe had willed him everything he possessed, made Michael Ryan a very happy man.

Chapter Five

Sister Rosario looked at the pinched face of Maura Ryan and her heart went out to the child. She had noticed her being teased mercilessly all through the dinner hour, no doubt due to the fact that her brother Benjamin had been expelled the day before. The nun realised that now the child had no one to protect her, some of the other children were making up for lost time. She watched Margaret Lacey lean forward across her desk and pull hard on one of Maura Ryan's long blonde plaits. Sister Rosario didn't like Margaret Lacey. She didn't like any of the Laceys, with their carroty red hair and green malicious eyes. And this Margaret Lacey was the most brazen strap of a child she had ever come across. The nun leapt from her seat, causing her chair to fly backwards. The noise brought thirty pairs of eyes to rest on her.

'Margaret Lacey, come out here at once!' Her voice reverberated around the classroom. Margaret, her face pale with fright, slowly edged her way from behind her desk and began to walk to the front of the class. Sister Rosario was without doubt the hardest nun in the school. No amount of tears could shake her. Margaret stood before her, trembling. Tapping a ruler across the palm of her hand, Sister Rosario stared at the child for a few seconds. She knew from thirty years' experience that bullies were a breed apart. Most were inherent cowards who picked only on people whom they knew were frightened of them.

The nun's countenance and dark brown close-set eyes challenged the child before her.

'Did I see you pull Maura Ryan's plait?'

Margaret's big green eyes seemed to have taken possession of the whole of her face. Her tiny pink mouth was trembling. Already, tears were beginning to glisten in her eyes.

'N . . . N . . . No, Miss . . . I mean, Sister.'

In her fright she had begun to stutter. This caused some of the other children to titter, quickly putting their hands over their mouths to stifle the sound.

Margaret Lacey was the class bully and the children enjoyed seeing her get, for once, what she doled out so often.

'Are you calling me a liar?' The nun's eyes had narrowed.

'No, Sister!' Margaret's voice was stronger now. Whoever heard of calling a nun a liar? It was unthinkable. Her own mother would kill her if she knew. Her eyes were now riveted on the ruler in the nun's hand. She knew that it was liable to come swishing down on her hands and legs at any moment.

Sister Rosario was enjoying Margaret's discomfiture. Running her tongue across her teeth she glared down at the object of her annoyance. Her white wimple covered nearly all her head, revealing only wrinkled yellowing skin that, combined with her dark eyes, had earned her the epithet 'Lizard Features'.

'So . . . you admit to pulling Maura Ryan's plait then?'

Maura watched Sister Rosario completely demoralise Margaret Lacey. She sat in her chair, her face scarlet. She did not thank this nun for making her the centre of attention. She knew that whatever Margaret got she would make sure Maura got it back one hundredfold.

'Yes, Sister . . . I pulled Maura's plait.' This was said so low as to be virtually inaudible.

'Speak up, child.'

'Yes, Sister. I pulled Maura Ryan's plait.' The high piping little voice was trembling with fear.

Smiling smugly at the class, Sister Rosario lifted the ruler. 'Hold out your hand then.'

The thin little hand come out. Margaret closed her eyes tightly as the ruler came down hard six times across her palm. Against her will, hot scalding tears burst from her eyes and down her cheeks. She held her injured hand to her breast as if frightened it might drop off, and at a nod from Sister Rosario made her way back to her desk, rubbing at her injured palm with the thumb of her good hand.

Sister Rosario's beady eyes scanned the classroom for about twenty seconds before she said, 'Let that be a warning to any would-be bullies in this class. Next time it will be twelve strokes of the ruler and your name read out at mass.'

Thirty faces looked scandalised at the thought of having their name read out by Father McCormack. Picking up her chair, the nun turned to her blackboard and began writing on it.

Seizing her opportunity, Margaret leant forward across her desk and whispered to Maura.

'You're dead, Ryan. Come hometime I'm gonna kill you.'

Maura closed her eyes, a knot of fear already forming in her stomach. Everyone was frightened of Margaret Lacey, even some of the boys. Which was surprising really because she was so small. But small or not, she could fight and that was all that counted. Maura sat back in her chair and looked out of the window to the side of her. A group of younger children were playing rounders. The voice of Miss Norman, the games teacher, drifted in at the window now and again. Always encouraging, never reprimanding. As Maura watched the dust motes flying through the air in the rays of the June sun she wished that she was outside with the younger children. That she was anywhere away from Margaret Lacey and her cronies who would without doubt be waiting for her as she left the school. Why was it that time always flew when you didn't want it to? The minutes sped by until the bell that heralded hometime.

Slowly Maura went to get her coat, hoping against hope that if she took long enough Margaret would get fed up and go home. She walked slowly from the school, across the playground and out of the gates into Latimer Road. Sure enough, Margaret was waiting for her, about twenty yards past the school gates. She had three of her cronies with her: Jennifer Howard, Betty Leeds and Vanessa Rouse. Maura began walking towards them like a condemned man on his way to the gallows. Prickles of sweat had broken out along her backbone. She bit down hard on her lip as she watched the four girls.

She saw that Jennifer and Vanessa were laughing at her and something inside her stirred. In all her ten years she had always had one or other of her brothers watching out for her. Now here for the first time she was fighting her own battle. And fight it she would! She swallowed deeply. She could hear her heart crashing in her ears. She decided then and there that she was not going to stand for it. She had eight brothers and had had to fight or argue with every one of them at some time or another. Holding her head high, she walked faster, swinging her schoolbag menacingly.

The four girls looked at each other, puzzled. This wasn't supposed to happen! First they were going to make her squirm, then Margaret was going to hit her . . . Betty Leeds began to hop from one foot to another, a sure sign of agitation. Vanessa and Jennifer stepped back behind Margaret. Maura stopped in front of them, still swinging her school bag. She gave a loud sniff.

'Well?' The insolent way she said it made the other girls gasp with astonishment. Margaret Lacey soon found her tongue.

'I'll "well" you, you ugly bitch you! I'm gonna smash your face in!'

The other girls smiled. This was more like it.

'Well then, don't just stand there talking about it . . . do it!'

All eyes were glued to the swinging schoolbag. Margaret was silent for a few seconds. She could feel the others losing their nerve. If she didn't do something, and soon, they would desert her. She spat on to the pavement casually.

'I will when I'm good and ready!'

Margaret Lacey was getting more worried by the second. She had thought she'd give Maura's long blonde hair a few good tugs, a scratch or two on her face, and then home to tea, basking in the other girls' admiration. Now she wasn't sure what to do. She might even get hit herself! She decided on a delaying tactic. Kneeling down on the dusty pavement, she made as if to tie her shoelaces.

The next thing she knew, she was lying sprawled across the pavement. Maura's schoolbag had hit her straight in the side of the head. Next, her long red hair was pulled so hard she felt as if it was going to come out by the roots. Finally, she felt a kick on the knee that brought a shocked cry to her throat. She lay on the pavement staring up at Maura Ryan, amazed. Her three friends had already run off. As soon as Maura's schoolbag had hit Margaret in the head, they had made their escape, frightened in case Maura decided on a repeat performance on one of them!

Maura just stood there stunned, staring at Margaret lying at her feet. She had done that! She had knocked Margaret Lacey down! She could feel her chest swelling with the joy of it. She had actually defended herself against Margaret Lacey, the school bully, and she had won. She had done it alone without one of her brothers to defend her!

Seeing Margaret begin to pull herself up, Maura's natural kindness came to the fore. This would be all over the school tomorrow. She tentatively held out her hand to help Margaret up. The smaller girl looked at her long and hard before accepting it. Maura pulled her to her feet and began to brush down Margaret's uniform, which was covered in grey dust. This was all done in silence, except for the occasional sniff. Maura saw the small swelling on Margaret's grubby knee and felt ashamed of herself. She had kicked her very hard and Margaret *was* smaller than her. In silent agreement they walked together down Latimer Road, into Bramley Road and then through to Lancaster Road where both girls lived. They stopped outside Margaret's house first and stood looking at one another.

Margaret sniffed loudly and said, 'Come in if you want. Me mum's at work.'

It was the hand of friendship. Maura shrugged nonchalantly. 'All right then.'

They walked up the steps that led to the front door. Margaret's house was the same as Maura's except it had been made into flats. Margaret's family lived on the top floor. Being large town houses they were three storeys high with large basements. As many as five families lived in them. As they made their way up the stairs the smell of cooking and urine seemed to overpower them. Margaret's flat had no lock on the door. There was no need for one, there was nothing to steal.

'You take off your things and I'll make us sommme bread and marmite.'

'Ooh, lovely. I love marmite.'

As Margaret made the sandwiches and a pot of weak tea, Maura glanced around her. The room was filthy, clothes and newspapers strewn everywhere. Unlike her own home that was stoved regularly, cockroaches were on everything. A particularly adventurous one with large quivering antennae was being slowly buried in the rancid margarine. Maura shuddered inwardly. The last few years her mother had been waging a war on all vermin, including bed bugs. Money was now plentiful in her home, thanks to Michael's employing her brothers in his business, while the majority of the people in Lancaster Road were still no better off than they had been before the war. Margaret's mother worked at the new Black Cat cigarette factory out in Harlow and her father still worked in Lyons bakery. Maura watched with distaste as Margaret flicked the cockroach out of the margarine with the breadknife. It landed on the floor where it lay on its back, its numerous legs doing cycling motions as it tried to right itself. Wrinkling her nose Margaret stepped on it, the crunching noise sounding like a gunshot in the hot evening air.

'I hate them bloody things.'

'So do I.' Maura's voice sounded small.

Soon the girls were eating their sandwiches and drinking weak tea. Neither of them mentioned what had taken place outside the school and neither of them would. From outside, the sounds of a game of cricket floated into the hot airless room. Finishing her tea, Maura got up to go.

Margaret offered Maura her little finger with a shy smile. Maura linked it with her own, vowing that the two girls would be best friends for always – through thick and thin. This was the female way of becoming blood brothers – unlike the boys they did not cut each other's thumbs.

Margaret walked Maura down the stairs to the street. 'I'll be here in the morning to walk to school. OK?'

Margaret nodded her head vigorously. 'See you then, Maura.'

''Bye.' Maura walked towards her own house. She felt lighthearted and gay. What had started out as a bad day had suddenly become brighter.

In the road a gang of boys with a makeshift cricket bat stopped their game to look at her. Already the news was travelling fast. Dinny O'Brien, one of Garry's friends, smiled at her.

'That right you podgered Margaret Lacey, Maws?'

She nodded, feeling herself blush.

'We're friends now, Dinny.'

He looked away, disgusted. Trust girls! In Dinny's code, if you beat someone in a fight you made their life misery for as long as possible. You did not become friends with them.

Maura hurried home. As she let herself in at the front door her mother's voice came booming out of the kitchen.

'Is that you, Maura!'

'Yes, Mum.'

She went into the kitchen where Sarah was standing, hands on hips, her face like thunder.

'Where have you been, you bloody little sod? I've been out of my mind with worry about you.'

Maura chewed on her lip, staring at her mother. She very rarely got told off and when she did it upset her.

'Well? Answer me, you little cow.' Sarah's face was haggard.

'I went to me friend's house and had a bit of tea.' Her enormous blue eyes had tears glistening on their lashes. Sarah saw her daughter's face crumple and her heart melted. Pulling the child into her arms, she hugged her close.

'I'm sorry, love, but you gave me such a fright. It's not like you to stay out like that. You're normally the first one home. I was worried.'

'I'm sorry, Mum, I won't do it again, I promise.' She tried to smile at her mother, genuinely sorry to have vexed her.

'I sent Benny, Garry and Lee out looking for you.' As if her words had conjured them up, all three burst into the kitchen.

'Mum . . . Mum!' They were all talking at once. 'Have a guess what!'

'One at a time . . . One at a time.' She held up her hands for silence then pointed at Garry, the most honest of the three.

'Right then, Garry, you tell me what happened.'

He pointed at Maura who was beginning to panic.

'It's her.'

'What about her?' Sarah looked at Maura, a frown on her face.

'She's been and gone and smashed Margaret Lacey's face in!'

Sarah's eyes widened. 'She's what!'

The tone of her voice frightened Maura. She pulled on her mother's flowery apron.

'I had to, Mum. She was gonna kill me 'cos Sister Rosario gave her the ruler for pulling me plaits.' She looked into her mother's face, pleading for understanding.

'Am I hearing right? You . . .' she pointed at Maura '. . . had a fight with Margaret Lacey.' She screwed up her eyes as if she was having difficulty seeing her child.

Maura was gabbling with fright. 'I hit her with me bag but we're friends now, Mum. That's where I was earlier when you were looking for me.'

Sarah shook her head slowly as if to clear it. So this one had gone too, another fighter in the family.

'Go on, all of you . . . out in the street to play. Your dad will be in soon and I haven't got a bit of food on.' She pushed the children towards the kitchen door. She wanted them all away from her.

The three boys ran out. Maura stood for a second looking at her mother. 'I'm sorry, Mum . . . honestly.'

Sarah's voice was tired. 'Get yourself outside, Maws. Go on now.'

When she had gone, Sarah poured herself out a large mug of thick black tea. She spooned four heaped spoonsful of sugar into it and some condensed milk and sat at the kitchen table. She sipped her tea and her body seemed to sag in the chair. Her mind was racing, though.

Leslie, aged twenty, was doing three years for robbery. Anthony, aged twenty-two, was with him, doing five years for robbery and malicious wounding. Michael was like the local Mafia, everyone was frightened of him. He now had all the older boys working for him. Over the years she had forced these thoughts from her mind, telling herself that her sons were the product of their father. And now this! Her only daughter, the apple of her eye, had been brawling in the street. It just wasn't fair. Her mother used to say that what was bred in the bone came out in the blood, and she had been right.

Oh, Sarah had plenty of money these days and the house was lovely. After the lean years, she had been only too happy to take the money her sons thrust on her. She had never questioned where it came from, though she knew deep inside. But if their lifestyles affected her daughter, she would murder the lot of them. Maura was going to have the chances that she herself had never had. One of her children would achieve something in this world. She was determined on that.

Outside in the summer evening, Maura was the centre of attention.

'Well done, Maws.' This from Garry, who was very fond of his sister.

'I hit her with me bag, that's what done it.'

They all looked across the road as they heard their father call. Maura's eyes lit up and she skipped across the road to meet him. Benjamin Ryan had had a skinful, that much was evident. He was flushed around his ample face and neck. Under one arm he had a large box of crisps and a bottle of

Tizer. He passed the box to Lee who had followed Maura over the street and picked his daughter up in his arms. The old man, as they called him, worshipped his daughter and they all knew this and accepted it. In their own way they all felt the same. Maura rubbed her face against his cheek and felt his stubble scratching against her smooth skin. She breathed in his familiar odour of best bitter and Woodbines and snuggled against him, safe and secure.

'How's me best girl then?'

'All right, Dad. Had a win?'

He laughed at her cheek.

'How do you know I've had a win?' He asked the question in a mock stern voice.

'The box of crisps and Tizer for a start, and your beery breath.'

Benjamin looked at his sons, a theatrical scowl on his face. 'Hear that, boys? Typical woman! She'll drink the Tizer and eat the crisps, and still complain where they come from!'

Benny laughed with Maura, but Garry and Lee just smiled wanly. The memory of empty bellies because their father had gambled away all the National Assistance was still fresh in their minds. They all walked up the steps and into the house.

Sarah had started the evening meal. She completely ignored her husband until he fell asleep in his chair, whereupon she woke him up and berated him all the way up the stairs, their shouting and swearing affecting the children not one iota. Half an hour later they sat down to their tea. Maura was once more in high spirits. As they sat chatting around the table there was a loud knock on the front door. Garry answered it and came back into the kitchen with two policemen.

'Go and wake your dad up.' Sarah's voice was heavy.

The elder of the two policemen smiled at Sarah but she dropped her eyes and tried to busy herself at the sink. Every nerve in her body was jangling. Every time the police visited her house she felt a heavy sickness inside her. Maura and Benny carried on eating.

Benjamin Ryan shuffled into the kitchen in his trousers and string vest, his braces hanging down the sides of his legs.

'What the fuck do you want?' His voice was menacing.

The older policeman looked at the children, a question in his eyes.

'Never you mind them, they'll hear what you got to say sooner or later. Now spit it out, man. I ain't got all day.'

'Very well. We've got some bad news for you, concerning your son Anthony.'

'What about my Antney? Escaped, has he?' Benjamin's voice sounded hopeful.

'No, not exactly. I'm sorry to tell you, Mr Ryan, that your son is dead.'

'He's *what*!' Sarah's hand went to her chest and she struggled to find breath. Lee went to her and folded her in his arms. The younger children were pale and silent.

'He was stabbed to death this morning in Pentonville prison. In the showers. We're doing everything possible to find the people responsible.'

Sarah's sobbing was building to a crescendo. The younger policeman was watching her, fascinated.

'Jesus H. Christ!' Benjamin was trying to clear his drink-fuddled brain. 'Who would want to kill my Antney? Everyone liked him . . .'

The younger policeman dragged his eyes from Sarah and looked at Benjamin.

'Well, someone didn't. You don't stab your mates.'

Benjamin went for him. 'Why, you dirty little bastard!'

The other officer intervened, all formality forgotten now.

'Calm down, Benny. And you, Brown, shut your bloody big gob!' He pushed Benjamin back against the kitchen wall. 'Look, Ben, we've been questioning Leslie all morning and he won't say a dicky bird, but we think he knows who done it.'

Benjamin pushed the man away. 'Of course he won't tell you. He ain't a grass.'

'Grass or no, Ben, this person has killed his brother.'

'And that person will pay. Thanks for coming, Bill, but you can go now. I need to speak to me wife.'

His tone held dismissal and the two officers left the house. Benjamin pointed at Lee.

'Go up West to Mickey's and tell him what's happened. Tell him, Geoffrey and Roy to get their arses home – now.' Lee nodded. Still holding his mother, he walked her to his father. As Benjamin tried to comfort her, Sarah pushed him violently away.

'Don't you dare touch me! You've brought us to this, you conniving old bastard.'

Getting up from her seat, Maura ran to her mother. The two held on to each other tightly. Benjamin looked frightened by his wife's attitude. The hatred in her voice had shocked him.

'Garry, nip round and get the quack for your mother.'

The boy ran from the room, frightened. His mother's wailing, following him down the front steps, seemed to spur him on. Maura, tears running down her face, was frightened out of her wits. Anthony was dead . . . her brother Anthony who had alternately teased and comforted her was lying somewhere dead, never to come home again. Fighting Margaret Lacey seemed so futile now. Why was it that bad things always happened when you were feeling happy?

The voices had been going on all evening. Maura could not sleep. She slipped out of bed, where her mother was snoring softly. The doctor had been in and given her some sleeping pills. He had tried to give her an injection but it had only made her more hysterical. Pulling the cover up over her mother's shoulders, Maura crept from the room and down the stairs.

The front room door was slightly open and she pressed her face to the crack. Her eldest brother Mickey was walking up and down the room talking, his face set in a dark scowl. Maura loved Mickey. He was her favourite brother. She thought he was the handsomest of them all. All the boys were dark, with deep-set blue eyes, but Mickey was magnificent. He had something that attracted people to him – men as well as women. Maura adored him. He was like a god to her. Now, though, she was seeing a Mickey that she didn't know. His teeth were gritted together and he had dark circles under his eyes. He looked ferocious.

'I swear I'll kill the bastards! So help me God, I'll kill them.'

'Calm down, Mickey. Calm down.' This from Geoffrey.

'Calm down, you say? When them bastards have stabbed our brother to death?'

Geoffrey took a long drink of his whisky.

'Calm down and think clearly, that's what I'm saying. Think with your head and not your heart.'

Michael stopped abruptly in his pacing and punched the wall.

'I'd rather have given the bastards the cab ranks than see Antney dead.'

Geoffrey sighed.

'Well, it's done now, Bruv. What we've got to decide is how we retaliate.'

'We'll blow the fuckers off the face of the earth, that's what we'll do!'

'I was thinking along those lines.' Everyone in the room stared at Gerry Jackson, one of Mickey's closest friends, and he coloured slightly.

'What I thought was, right, they've got a rank in Ilford, ain't they? In the High Street.'

All heads nodded in agreement.

'Well, on Saturday night, Lee here and a few of his mates can go up the Ilford Palais, right? Later on in the evening they go into the Greek bastard's cab rank, ask for a cab to say . . . Wanstead. Anywhere, just so they can get a good look in. If he's there, one of them can trot off and let us know, then we can poodle round and petrol bomb the place. We can sit round Green Lanes waiting for word. It must be someone they won't recognise. That would teach the saucy gits a lesson.'

Mickey nodded his head.

'Yeah, that sounds dawdy, Gerry, I'll have some of that.

Meantime, me and Geoff and Roy, who'll be the main suspects, can be causing a disturbance somewhere else.'

'Brilliant! That's it then.'

Maura, listening to all this, was frightened. Her brothers were planning to blow someone up! She had heard people talk about her brothers. Tearaways and out of control, had become the prevalent opinion in Lancaster Road. Yet she realised that people were always nice to their faces, especially Mickey's. A couple of Saturdays previously, she had walked with him along the Portobello Road. They had stopped to get some fruit for her, and the stall-holder had insisted that it was a gift, refusing Michael's money as if it was the norm to give his produce away for free. Now she knew why people acted like they did. It was because her brothers blew people up.

She started to hop from one foot to the other. She was scared. Anthony was dead and her brothers were going to blow someone up. Suddenly, the door opened and Roy was standing in front of her.

She saw his face go pale.

'What's this then? Can't you sleep, Princess?' His voice was very loud. He picked her up and carried her into the front room. It was heavy with cigarette smoke and she coughed. Michael held out his arms to her and she shrank away from him, clinging to Roy. This Mickey frightened her. This was not her brother who cuddled her and bought her things . . . this was a man who blew people up. She looked fearfully into his face. He was so hurt by her attitude he was nearly in tears. With all that had happened with Anthony, he was near the end of his tether. Suddenly sensing this, Maura slipped out of Roy's arms and ran to him, big dry sobs bursting from her throat and bouncing off the walls.

He scooped her up into his arms and holding her tightly, rubbed his face into her soft, sweet-smelling hair.

She cried hard, wracking sobs distorting her voice. 'I want Antney to come home . . . I want Antney to come home! Blow the bad man up, Mickey. Blow the bad man up!'

He looked at the other men in the room, his eyes resting on his father. Through her tears Maura heard someone mutter, 'Jesus Christ!'

Michael held her until her sobs subsided. Holding her away from him so he could look into her face, he spoke to her. His voice sounded worried.

'Listen, Princess. You must never . . . ever . . . tell anyone what you heard here tonight. Do you understand what I'm saying? If you tell anyone, even a friend, then the police will come and take us all away. Even Dad. Do you understand me?'

She nodded at him solemnly. 'I won't tell anyone, Mickey . . . not even Mum.'

Instinctively she knew that this was what he wanted to hear. He blinked and the relief in his eyes was evident. 'Good girl. You're a good girl. Now, let Dad put you back to bed.' He kissed her on the forehead and lips tenderly, then placed her on the floor. 'Good night, Princess.'

She took her father's outstretched hand and began to walk from the room. At the door she looked back over her shoulder at Mickey, her face serene. In her white nightdress she looked like a golden angel. She opened her mouth and spoke.

'I meant what I said, Mickey . . . get them that done in Antney.' With that she carried on walking with her father. Benjamin looked at her sadly. His little girl was learning the realities of life. He just wished she could have been spared them a little longer.

On 20 July 1960 they buried Anthony Ryan. The funeral cortège went slowly past Wormwood Scrubs prison, up past the wagon works and on to Saint Mary's Roman Catholic Cemetery at the top of Scrubs Lane. There were five cars from the funeral parlour following the coffin. Behind these were two dozen other cars containing friends and relatives. A police car containing Leslie, handcuffed but in his best suit, was last in the line.

In the first car Sarah sat dry-eyed, staring out at the passing roads. As they had passed by Du Cane Road, where the entrance to Wormwood Scrubs prison was, she had been reminded of how many times she had been there, visiting either her husband or one of the older boys. Her husband had been proud of how he had lived his life. 'I'm a ducker and diver.' How many times had she heard him tell someone that? Well, the result of his way of living was upon them today. Her lovely boy dead. She felt the hot tears bunch in her throat.

Looking into her troubled face, Benjamin placed his hand gently on her arm. She smacked it away. She blamed him for all this. He had encouraged the boys to be villains. Even when they had been little more than babies he had started to corrupt them. If they had been beaten in a fight, he would give them a good hiding and send them back out to do the job properly.

'None of my boys are Nancys,' had been one of his favourite expressions, coupled with, 'All my boys are hard.' He had dragged them to dog tracks, pubs, bare knuckle fights. He had taught them how to pick a lock, steal a car, to shoplift . . . The list was endless.

What had he done? she asked herself. She felt an urge to fell him to the floor of the car, strike his face and hurt him as she was hurting inside. Her big manly husband – at this moment she hated him. She crossed her arms across her breasts and hugged herself. Her gaze lighted on her only daughter and her face softened. This one he could not touch. A beauty was her Maura. Sarah's pride in her daughter knew no bounds. With her white-blond hair and dark blue eyes, she was exquisite. Now Maura's hair was hanging in long waves, unaccustomed to being out of plaits, her eyes sad and shining with unshed tears. Sarah knew that the child was bewildered by all that had happened. She leant across the car and grasped Maura's hand, forcing herself to give her daughter a little wink. The cars stopped and everyone got out, standing around in little groups, talking in hushed voices.

Sarah's seven remaining sons carried Anthony's coffin to the graveside. The main mass and requiem mass had already been said in the RC Church in Notting Hill. Now all that was left was to bury her boy. The youngest, Benny, although only thirteen, walked with his brothers, carrying the coffin. Michael had placed Maura, dressed in white, at the front of the coffin. She led them slowly through the graveyard to the burial site.

Father McCormack was standing silently by the yawning hole. The sun was high in the sky and beating down on the mourners' heads. In the yew trees nearby, birds sang and the hum of traffic and smell of exhaust fumes carried on the air. Outside the cemetery walls were carts carrying totters from Shepherd's Bush. The rag and bone men were grim-faced and silent. Benjamin Ryan's eldest brother was leading them. Their horses had the old-fashioned black plumes rising up from their harnesses. The carts had been washed down and polished for the day's event. Paddy Ryan wiped a tear from his eye as he watched his brother's son being lowered into the ground.

Bees were quietly going about their business, bumbling from flower to flower, the hot summer day bringing them out in force. The priest's voice droned on. The police had once again handcuffed Leslie. Funeral or no funeral they were not taking any chances. Maura was holding Michael's hand tightly, her face pale and troubled.

The policeman to whom Leslie was handcuffed was impressed by the turn-out. The Krays, Richardsons, and many more villains had come to pay their last respects. It showed the respect accorded to Michael Ryan.

Mickey stared stonily into the grave. Anthony's oak coffin had a large brass crucifix on the lid. The INRI above Jesus's head was glinting in the sunlight. In his mind's eye Michael could see Anthony's face inside it, staring upwards at darkness for the rest of eternity. He clenched his teeth together before he lost control and cried out. He prayed for the first time in years to the Holy Spirit to come and take his brother's soul. To care for him and protect him. He prayed to the Immaculate Conception and Holy Saint Anthony, the patron saint of miracles. He prayed to every saint and martyr he could remember from his years of Catholic schooling. Somehow, today, there being a God was important.

Out of the corner of his eye, he saw a movement. He turned his head. Being so tall he was head and shoulders above most of the mourners. To the left of him, standing about ten yards from the small crowd around the graveside, was a man. Michael stiffened. Feeling the change in him, Maura looked up into his face. She noticed that he was staring across the graveyard. She followed his gaze, through a small gap in the mourners opposite her, and saw the object of Michael's scrutiny.

The man was dark – not dark like her brothers but swarthy. His thick black curly hair seemed to grow around his head like a crown, leaving his forehead exposed where it had receded. He reminded her of the mad professor in her comics. The sun was behind him and she could see the glare that shone on his bald pate. Instinctively she knew that this was Stavros, the Greek man that her brothers had been constantly talking about since Anthony's death. The man was smiling slightly.

She looked from him to Michael and realised that her brother was going to go over to the man. He was pulling back his shoulders in his arrogant way. Holding Michael's hand tightly, she pulled on it. He looked down at her. When they both looked back a split second later the man was gone, but his face was stamped on Maura's memory. Then she felt the hot, scalding tears come into her eyes, spilling down her face and entering her mouth, their saltiness exploding on her tongue. From far off she heard shrieking. It was a few seconds before she realised that it was coming from her.

Michael picked her up in his arms and held her tightly to him, murmuring endearments into her hair and stroking her back until she was spent. After what seemed an age all that could be heard were little hiccups. Even the hardest of the men there was sobered by her outburst. Reggie Kray, always a lover of children, had tears in his eyes as he watched Michael comfort the girl. Like most Londoners from working-class backgrounds, family was important to them all. You looked after your own, no matter what.

A little while later, still holding Maura in his arms,

Michael threw his handful of dirt on to the coffin. When the service was finished, he put her down gently by their mother and, picking up a shovel, filled in Anthony's grave, helped by Geoffrey and Roy.

One of the rag and bone men's wives, Lilly McNamara, had been asked to sing while this was being done. She was noted throughout Kensington and the surrounding areas as a fine singer. In the hush, broken only by the scraping of the shovels in the dirt and the soft thuds as it landed on the coffin, she sang 'Amazing Grace'. To outsiders it would have looked incongruous: men in black zoot suits, all with fashionable elephant's trunk hair styles, filling in a grave, surrounded by more men and women dressed in black. The women's hats and bright make-up made them look like exotic birds. To the Ryans and their like, Anthony had been given a magnificent send-off.

Sarah stood dignified and erect as her sons buried their brother. She would not cry here; she would wait until after the wake, when she was alone. In the scorching heat she had felt as if she would pass out; now she wished she had. It would have saved her having to watch this grisly ritual, the burying of her son's remains. She closed her eyes, her hand on her daughter's soft and springy hair.

When the singing was over and Anthony buried, the mourners went to the family and paid their respects. Diana Dors, the secret object of the young policeman's desire, hugged Michael long and hard. She was a firm favourite of everybody there, a kind, loving, generous woman who never in all her life judged anyone. Freddie Mills and his boyfriend Michael Holiday each clasped Michael to them. Freddie Mills had been Michael's boyhood hero. It had been worship of him that had aroused Michael's interest in boxing. Nowadays he met him socially, as an equal. A few days before Anthony's death they had been together at the Lancaster Road Baths watching local semi-professional boxers.

It did not escape Sarah's notice that Michael was treated as the head of the family and her husband relegated to second position. That was how it should be. After all,

Michael was the main provider. He made sure that she had ample money. More than enough in fact. She did not feel overawed by the company at her son's funeral. She had known Violet Kray for many years. The Richardson boys had been visitors to her house for a long time. Many of the mourners were young men who had grown up with her sons. Petty criminals most of them, but good boys all the same.

Roy's wife looked depressed as usual. Sarah knew that it was not the funeral that had put the sad look on her daughter-in-law's face, but something quite different. Janine and Roy had problems, she was sure of that. Neither of them looked happy these days. Their daughter, Carla, nearly five now, looked as if she hadn't been washed for days. Sarah made a mental note to go and see Janine. Even in her grief she could still look out for her remaining children.

Finally, they began to make their way back to the cars. Sarah noticed Roy trying to take Janine's hand and being shrugged off. She frowned. As if there wasn't enough unhappiness in the family, they had to bring their petty squabbles into the cemetery with them.

Benny was staring at the mound of dirt that covered his brother. Benjamin walked back to get him, his old face looking more haggard and careworn than usual. He had been drinking steadily since the early morning.

'Come on, son.' His voice was slurred but gentle.

Benny was staring intently at a large worm wriggling on the pile of damp earth. In his mind's eye he saw it boring its way into the earth, down, down, until it reached his brother's face. Covering his own face with his hands, he was overtaken by silent sobs that made his shoulders shake. He was as tall as his father, and as Benjamin took his namesake into his arms, he felt the strength of him.

Sarah was watching them. She realised for the first time how Benjamin must be feeling. After all, Anthony had been his son too. A feeling she had not known in over a decade slipped through her body. All animosity towards her husband dissolved and a spark of affection for him seemed to light up inside her, as it had in the old days.

She couldn't blame him entirely for what had happened. Children would go their own way in the end. In the environment they lived in it was inevitable that kids would turn to crime. All she could really blame him for was not working hard enough to get them out of it. She sighed heavily. How could he? He had never had the chance.

All this flashed through her head in an instant. She looked around the cemetery. The brilliant sunshine seemed to be mocking her. It was too nice a day to be burying a young life. It should have been cold and raining as befitted a funeral. She saw the flowers gently swaying in the light breeze, the lichen-covered gravestones that hid their contents from the world, and was overcome with sadness. The birds were still singing as she made her way slowly to the cars. Her body seemed to have shrunk since Anthony's death, giving her the appearance of an old woman. She was only forty-four.

Back at the house everyone was drinking. Maura pushed her way through the adults and stationed herself in the front room next to the table piled high with food. Presently she was joined by Margaret Lacey. This had been arranged the day before. That morning Margaret had complained of a bad bout of sickness. Her mother, anxious to get to work, had given her the day off school. Now she was up and dressed and holding her new best friend's hand. She could not even imagine what it must be like to have a brother who had been murdered. Her mum and dad had talked of nothing else for days. According to them it was a wonder something like this had not happened before. Margaret, though, wisely kept this bit of information to herself.

Mickey came up, and, taking the two girls by the hand, led them out of the house and into the back garden. He could not bear to be away from Maura today. She was so innocent and trusting. With his guilt over Anthony, he felt that at least she loved him and didn't blame him for the death. No one would dare say that it was his fault outright, but he knew what was going on in everyone else's mind.

He sat in an old deck chair and the two girls sat on the

ground, each leaning against one of his legs. He was already half drunk. The sun was so hot it was impossible to open his eyes without being blinded. Eventually he dozed. Maura and Margaret sat by him for hours. The friendship of a lifetime was bonded that day. Maura and Margaret became a pair, the friendship only to end with the death of one of them.

That night in bed Maura had her first nightmare. It was of the man in the cemetery coming after her with her mother's bread knife. She was to have the same dream intermittently for the rest of her life.

Chapter Six

Carla Ryan opened her eyes. The sun was streaming in at the windows of her room. She lay for a few moments watching the patterns it made on the ceiling. A cool breeze drifted over her thin little body. She rubbed her arm, where she had a large bruise above the elbow. Her mother had picked her up bodily the night before and dragged her into her room where she had then thrown her on to her bed. She had bumped her arm on the little bedside cabinet. The pain had made her lose her breath for a few seconds. Lifting up her pink nightdress her mother had then smacked her behind as hard as she could, afterwards putting her face next to Carla's and telling her that she had had enough. Her mother's breath had been sour as it always was when she had been drinking.

What exactly her mother had had enough of Carla was not sure. All she had done the night before was make herself a sugar sandwich. She had asked her mother for something to eat over and over again, until finally she had decided to get it herself. She supposed it was the sugar all over the table and floor that had made her mother cross.

She sat herself up in bed and swung her little legs over the side. She yawned and her long brown hair fell over her face as she stretched her arms out. She winced as her bad arm was stretched. This was going to be a sore one, she reflected. Like the one she'd had on her leg a few weeks previously. Slipping off the bed she crept across her room, opening the door as silently as possible.

She looked through the crack into the hallway. Opposite her bedroom was the kitchen. She waited a few seconds for any sounds that might tell her that her mother was in there but out of her range of sight. Nothing. She walked across the hall and into the kitchen. The sugar she had spilt everywhere the night before was sticking to her bare feet. She was hungry again. She was always hungry. Sneaking across the kitchen she made herself some bread and margarine.

She was kneeling on a kitchen chair, her long hair trailing in the margarine, when she heard the steps. The heavy thudding steps that meant her mother was getting up. She froze. Her heart was fluttering in her chest. Her breathing came rapidly. Remembering the night before she threw her knife from her hand as if it was red hot, then tried to push the sticky mass of bread and margarine underneath the bread wrapper. In her haste she was clumsy and only succeeded in pushing the loaf of Dinkum bread and the sandwich off the table and on to the floor, already sticky from the sugar.

Tears of frustration stung her eyes. She felt her mother's presence before she turned and faced her, her little grubby hands clenching and unclenching with nerves. Janine looked at her coldly. Her daughter's face was exquisite even when she was terrified. Her eyes were a startling violet colour that made her look incredibly strong-minded. Coupled with her dark brown hair and high cheekbones, she looked like a miniature woman. Janine watched her daughter sweep her hair away from her face with a gesture that was more fitting to a sexy movie star than a four-year-old girl. Her long neck and strong pointed chin were shown to advantage by the gesture.

Janine chewed her lip, staring spitefully at her child. She knew that if she didn't speak Carla would get more and more nervous, eventually breaking the heavy silence herself. She noticed the black bruise on her arm and a wicked light glowed in the back of her eyes. She would have to keep the child's arms covered, because Roy would go crazy if he thought his little angel had been whipped. She gritted her teeth and, aping the child's earlier movement, theatrically swept her own thick red hair off her face. She looked like a sleek, tawny cat about to pounce on its prey. Carla stared back at her, every nerve in her body tensed and waiting. As her mother swept back her hair in a parody of her own action she dropped her eyes. Everything she did annoyed her mother. How she sat, how she stood, how she ate, how she spoke. Every movement was ridiculed and parodied.

She wished her father was home but he was very rarely around much these days, and when he was her mother fought with him. Carla would curl up on his lap and hold her hands over her ears desperately trying to block out their arguing. She loved her father and missed him when he was away. She thought of him as a big tree, with strong branches that enabled her to climb him, which she did when he was home. With Roy holding her by the arms she walked up his body until, reaching his shoulders, she flipped over and landed on her feet, screeching with laughter. She wished he was here now. Her mother daren't touch her when her father was at home. The tension in the kitchen had reached its peak and, stuttering in fright, the child spoke.

'Where's me dad?' As soon as she spoke the words she flinched inside. Why had she mentioned him? She closed her eyes tightly. Somewhere inside her was a weak hope that she had not spoken. She heard her mother's slippers crunching across the sugar-strewn floor. She squeezed her eyes shut as tightly as possible. As she felt her hair being yanked, she screamed. The pain was searing through her scalp. Shaking her like a rag doll, Janine began to shout.

'You want your dad, do you? You little slut! He's out whoring as usual. Shacked up with some woman somewhere. He don't care about you.'

Carla was trying to drag her mother's fingers from her hair. Crying now, and frightened, she screamed back at her mother, 'Please, Mum . . . Please . . . Let go of me hair . . . You're hurting me!'

Sarah heard the screams from the entrance hall of the flats. Grabbing Maura's hand she ran up the stairs and banged on the front door with her fists, demanding to be let in. Janine heard the banging and shouting and went cold

77

with fright. She threw Carla from her and looked around her wild-eyed, like an animal seeking an escape route. The state of the kitchen registered inside her mind somewhere. Carla lay sobbing where she had landed, holding her poor injured head in both hands. Her granny's banging on the door was like music to her ears.

She watched her mother walk out of the kitchen as if in a trance and a few seconds later Carla was nestled in her granny's arms. Little kisses were planted on her wet face, and murmured endearments and gentle strokes administered. Gradually the child calmed down. A handful of her hair was lying on the floor.

Maura watched the whole thing wide-eyed. Janine was now sitting at the kitchen table smoking a cigarette. Maura took in the dirty sugary floor and the loaf of bread now scattered everywhere, the filthy table and the stacks of dirty dishes. She dragged her eyes from it all, disgusted. She didn't like Janine. Taking the weeping Carla out of the kitchen Sarah motioned with her head for Maura to follow her, which she did gratefully. Going into Carla's room, Sarah laid the child on the bed. Maura watched as her mother checked the little girl from head to toe, shaking her head and tutting as she did it. Finally, Sarah turned to her own daughter.

'You stay here with Carla. Find some half-decent clothes and get her dressed. I'll call you if I need you . . . all right?' Her voice was thick with emotion. Maura nodded wordlessly. In the kitchen Janine sat at the table smoking yet another cigarette. Pulling herself up to her full height, Sarah glared at her.

'Now then, Janine. I think you'd better tell me exactly what's been going on here.' Her voice was determined.

Janine glanced at her and, all the hatred and animosity falling from her, began to cry. Groaning as if in physical pain, she rocked herself back and forth in her chair – her teeth bared as if she was grinning at some diabolical joke. Sarah stared at her. Where on earth was the beautiful, vital girl her son had married? How did this scruffy, dirty-looking individual come into being? The girl was only twenty-two years old. She looked at the filthy kitchen. The windows were so grimy it was difficult for the sun to penetrate them. The whole place stank. She had always understood that Janine's mother was never off the doorstep, that's why she never came herself. Say what you like about Eliza Grierson, she was a very particular housewife, so how come the flat was in this state? She shook her head in puzzlement. And just how long had Janine been beating the child? By the looks of Carla she had not had a decent meal for weeks.

Sarah blamed herself. She should have come over sooner, she should have spoken to Roy, but how did you ask a grown man about his home life? Once they left home it was up to them surely? That had been her own mother's philosophy. She was distressed, unsure how to go about sorting this situation out. Suddenly Janine spoke.

'No one ever said it would be like this!' Her voice was high. 'I hate it all . . . I hate the cooking and the cleaning and the dirt and the washing and the mending. I hate this flat – it's like a prison to me. Sometimes I don't see anyone for weeks on end. I'm so lonely.'

Sarah was nonplussed. Janine took a deep breath and all the fears and worries inside her came tumbling out like a great canker that had finally burst. 'Roy's never here. He leaves me for days on end. And Carla . . . that bloody Carla is like a permanent reminder of my bloody mistake! If it had't been for her I wouldn't be here . . . I wouldn't be here!'

She began crying again in earnest. Sarah went to her. She hesitated a few seconds before putting her arm around the girl's thin shoulders.

'What about your mother, Janine? I thought she came to see you.'

She gave a harsh bitter laugh.

'Well, you thought wrong, Mrs Ryan. My mother . . . my darling mother . . . has nothing to do with me anymore.'

'But why, Janine? Why?'

'Oh, it's a long story. She told me that if I left Roy and

went home she would forgive me having Carla and everything . . . forgive me bringing shame on them by marrying a hoodlum. That's her choice of word not mine. And as much as I hate Roy at times . . .' she began to cry again '. . . I know that if I left him, I would never be happy again. I can't live without him, Mrs Ryan! I love him so desperately yet I can't seem to make him happy. When he's here I start fights and drive him out of the house. I want him to want me and he doesn't. I know he doesn't . . .'

'Dear God, Janine. What on earth's the matter with you, girl? Look around you, for Christ's sake. Who'd want to come home to this? It's like a bloody pig sty.' Janine's declaration of love for her son had softened Sarah up. She reasoned that if she could help the girl, she could save their marriage as well as the child. 'Look at yourself. You look like the wreck of the Hesperus! No woman likes housework, but it's got to be done. At your age I already had five children living and not the hope of a decent wage coming. You've got it made if only you'd realise it.' She began rolling up the sleeves of her best dress. 'I'll tell you what we'll do. First we'll have a cup of tea. Get ourselves nice and calm. Then we'll go through this place like a dose of salts. Scrub it out from top to bottom. With the two of us working like blacks we'll have it done in no time. What do you say?' Janine nodded but Sarah could see her heart wasn't in it. She tried a different tack.

'Then you can go and get your lovely hair done while I get some food cooked. Can you imagine Roy's face when he comes home to everything nice and clean and homely? I'll take the little one home with me for a few days to give you a break. Now what do you say to that?'

Janine brightened up and Sarah smiled but deep inside she was worried. The only reason Janine had cheered up was because she was taking her child from her. She sighed. Even when your children grew up they still made demands. You were never free of them. Wearily she put on the kettle for the tea. Already she was tired, and by the looks of the flat by the time she was finished she would be exhausted.

Well, soonest done soonest mended, as her mother used to say. She made the tea.

In the bedroom Maura had dressed Carla in a fairly clean pinafore dress. All the child's socks were dirty so she had turned a pair inside out and put them on her. They looked pretty clean. She was sitting on the bed cuddling Carla when her mother came in and told her to go to the shops and get some bits and pieces. She was instructed to take Carla with her and get her a big ice cream, and one for herself also.

She was amazed at how quickly Carla seemed to get over what had happened to her. At the mention of ice cream the little girl became excited and animated, bouncing up and down on the bed. Maura felt so sorry for her. Her arms were like sticks and the purple-black bruise looked swollen and painful. Yet jumping on the bed she could almost be a normal, happy little girl. She had seen the pity in her mother's eyes and a great rage against Janine had rushed through Maura. If she was older she would go into that kitchen and tear her apart.

Instead she took the money from her mother and walked sedately down to the shops with Carla, playing with her and making her laugh. She knew that Carla was coming home with her and decided that she would take the little girl into her bed with her. After all, she was her aunt. She had a responsibility towards her.

Three hours later the little flat was sparkling clean. Janine seemed to get up some enthusiasm as her mother-in-law chatted to her, telling her about her own difficult marriage, and how it was hard when one was young and unsure of oneself. For the first time Janine felt that she had an ally, and it made all the difference to her. Sarah was consciously getting her confidence, telling her what she knew she wanted to hear.

When Janine finally opened up to her she felt the loneliness and unhappiness emanating from her. Sarah reproached herself. She should have visited her more often, should have taken more of an interest in her – and just wait until she went around to Eliza Grierson's! She'd floor that bitch with what she had to say to her! The supercilious old cow! Sarah was looking forward to it. She'd 'hoodlum' her before she was much older! Next on her agenda was that galloping big son of hers. Letting the girl get into this state, and neglect that little child. She'd annihilate him as well! When she got her hands on the bugger, that was. From what she'd gleaned from Janine he came and went like a bloody ghost, flitting in and out as it suited him. Sarah's mouth set in a grim line. He wasn't too big for a clout round the ear hole, whatever he thought.

Janine came into the kitchen dressed up for her trip to the hairdresser's. Sarah smiled at her.

'You look a picture, love. Like one of them girls on the adverts! Now get yourself off and I'll fix you something for your dinner.'

Janine smiled shyly at Sarah. She felt better than she had for months. 'Thank you, Mrs Ryan. You've been so good to me.' Her voice was trembling with emotion.

Sarah waved her hand impatiently. 'Don't you think it's about time you called me Sarah? As for thanking me . . . for what? I should have been here for you a long time ago. I'm ashamed of meself.'

Janine went to her and kissed her on the cheek.

'Thanks . . . Sarah.' She said her name timidly, as if it felt strange to address her so. Sarah just grinned at her.

'Get yourself off and I'll have a lovely meal waiting for you, OK?'

Janine nodded and left the flat, feeling lighter hearted than she had for many days. Sarah watched her go and wiped her arm across her brow. She was sweating. It had been a hot and sultry summer. In a way she was grateful to Janine. Today had been the first time since he died she had not been tortured with thoughts of her Anthony. She looked out of the now sparkling window and heaved a deep sigh. She began to cook the meal, briefly wondering how her own household was coping without her. She pictured Benjamin waiting for the food to run out of the cupboard and into the frying pan, and smiled. It would never occur to him to cook himself anything. Well, he would just have to wait. She had more pressing things on her mind.

As she prepared the vegetables, she heard the front door open. Thinking it was Maura and Carla she called out: 'I'm in here, lovelies.'

'What you doing here, Mum?' Roy was standing in the doorway, staring at the kitchen as if he was in the wrong house.

Sarah smirked at him nastily. 'Well, well. The Wandering Jew's returned to his home at last!'

She looked at his crumpled clothing, and the dark shadow on his jaw. 'Obviously your new lady love isn't looking after you very well.'

She slammed the saucepan of potatoes on to the draining board. Roy stared at her warily. There was something funny going on here.

'So, now that you're home, are you thinking of staying at all? Or are you just going to get a change of gear and go off again on your merry way?' She gripped the handle of the saucepan.

Roy looked at her, bewildered. 'Are you being funny? Where's Janine and the kid?' Too late he realised his mother's intention. The saucepan and potatoes hit him full in the chest, the water drenching him.

Sarah ran to him, slipping on the wet floor. Righting herself she slapped him across his face, a white hand print appearing as if by magic. 'I'll give you where's the kid . . . she's your daughter, Roy Ryan, and you fought hammer and tongs to marry her mother. When I think of the trouble you caused because you couldn't keep your private parts to yourself! You've driven that poor girl to distraction.'

'I've what! Now you hold up a minute, Muvver.'

Sarah screamed at him: 'No, I bloody well won't, you gormless eejit! Before that girl took up with you the most she ever did in her life was get dressed up for church. She wasn't brought up to do all this.' She gestured around the flat. 'She's been slowly going out of her mind stuck here day in day out, and do you care? Not on your bloody nellie! I'm ashamed to admit that you're my son! That poor innocent little child has taken the brunt of everything. She's got a bruise on her arm like she's been ten rounds with Dempsey . . . and it's all your fault.'

Roy's mouth was hanging open with disbelief.

'Shut your bloody gob up! You look like a mental deficient standing there gawking.'

Roy's mouth snapped shut. 'Janine won't do anything around the place.'

'Shut your trap, I said, or you'll be getting another smack off me otherwise. You're not too big for a good hiding, you know.'

Roy wanted to laugh. He towered over his mother. He had to admire her though. She stuck by her guns. Inside him there was a little nagging doubt. What his mother had said was true. He didn't try to understand Janine. Slowly bending down Sarah picked up the saucepan. It was dented on one side. She stifled an urge to brain her son with it, and instead placed it in the sink. In unspoken agreement mother and son began clearing up the debris. Potatoes had flown to all four corners of the kitchen. Water was everywhere. When it was all put right, Sarah pushed Roy into a chair. Outwardly, she looked her old formidable self. Inside, she was gloating. She was actually enjoying herself! She had not had so much fun for a long time, since before she buried Anthony.

She made a pot of tea. Putting a cup in front of Roy, she said, 'I came here this morning because I knew that something wasn't right. I sensed it at the funeral. The child looked like the orphan of the storm, and Janine looked terrible. I admit that I'm as much to blame, I should have come to visit her, but I understood her mother was never off the doorstep, so I left her to it. When I came here this morning she was pulling the child's hair out of her head.'

She watched Roy's mouth harden. 'And don't you come the old biddy with me! If *you* had done your job properly, been a decent husband, then all this could have been avoided.' She poked him in the chest. 'You are going to get yourself sorted out, my man, and you're going to start coming home at nights. I sat in many a night myself when you were all younger, waiting for that piss artist of a father of yours to come home, knowing in my heart that he was down the Bayswater Road, spending desperately needed money on old brasses. How I never got a dose of clap I'll never know! Well, I won't have any of my sons going the same way.'

Roy sat staring at her. He knew, as all the boys had always known, that she had not had the best of lives with his father, but she had never before spoken to him like this. He knew that she was trying to help him save his marriage, and in a tiny part of himself he knew that she was right. He had left Janine to fend for herself. He had chosen to ignore the fact that she took out her frustrations on Carla. But he just didn't know what to do. He was ashamed that his mother had so accurately put her finger on where he spent his nights. Since Michael had opened a hostess club in the West End, he had literally had his pick of women to spend the night with. It had been easier than coming home to fighting and arguing. To a dirty home and an unhappy wife.

But he still loved Janine. He had thought that taking her away from her mother's influence would have encouraged her to stand on her own two feet. Instead she had leant even more on him and he just couldn't take it, so had chosen the easy way out. Now he had to face not only Janine and little Carla, but his mother. He heard the front door open and braced himself, looking at his mother for support. As Janine walked into the room, Sarah stood up and smiled at her.

'You look an absolute angel, doesn't she, Roy?' She poked him in the shoulder, her bright smile belying the force she had used. Janine smiled uncertainly at him. The tension in the kitchen was like an electric current. Janine did look like an angel. Her hair was swept up off her finely boned face, emphasising her long neck. Her deep green eyes were made up expertly and there was a wistfulness in them that pierced Roy's heart. She was a cracker, he thought. She really looked the business. His mum was right, Janine was like a high-spirited thoroughbred. She needed gentle guidance. He got up from his chair and held out his arms to her. Janine hesitated for a few seconds before she slipped into them.

Sarah watched, a satisfied expression on her face. Now all she had to do was go and see Father McCormack and get him to sort out her Michael and she would be happy. Half an hour later she left the two love birds, Maura and Carla in tow. Her next stop was the Church and Father McCormack. She looked at her watch. If she hurried she would catch him as he finished six o'clock mass.

Sitting in the refectory with a glass of wine in front of her, Sarah poured out her heart to the priest.

'I feel ashamed to tell you this, Father, but Michael has bought himself another club, this time a bordello.' She sipped her wine to steady her voice. 'Men go there to . . . Well, I don't have to paint a picture, now do I?'

Father McCormack looked at her through shrewd eyes. He was sixty years old and had been the parish priest for over thirty years. His hair was grey and cut in an American crew-cut. He had heavy grey-flecked eyebrows that gave him a wise demeanour and looked on religion the way some men looked on marriage: as a necessary part of life. You made the best of it. He put his large, soft hands together.

'I see, I see.' His Irish accent was still thick even though he had left Ireland over forty years previously. 'Sure that Michael was always a difficult one. I can see why you're worrying.'

'I think that if *you* had a word with him, Father . . .' Her voice trailed off.

'Well, Sarah, I'll do my best. But your Michael was always a strong-minded fellow. He might not like the interference.'

Sarah was determined that before she left this room she would have an appointment to save her son's eternal soul! She tried a different approach.

'Oh, Father, I know what people say about my Mickey, but as you know yourself, stories get stretched in the

86

telling. All he needs is a little gentle guidance. If you were to talk to him, I'm sure he would listen to a fine man like yourself. Even when he was an altar boy, he always had a high regard for you.'

The priest raised his eyebrows. When Michael had been an altar boy he had also stolen the lead from the church roof! But he had the glimmer of a plan forming in his mind, and it would please this poor soul sitting before him. He decided to do as she asked.

'Hostess club, you say? Well, I think that a few words from me are called for, as you say.' Sarah jumped in before he could change his mind.

'If you come to my house at eleven o'clock tomorrow morning, I'll make sure that he's there.'

He smiled at her, showing tobacco-stained teeth. 'Eleven o'clock it is then. Now tell me, how are the other children? I hear that all the older boys are driving big expensive cars and living the life of Riley. They all work for Michael, I take it?'

Sarah dropped her eyes.

'Yes, Father, that's true. But if you can help to sort out Mickey, the others will follow suit, I'm sure.'

'Well, Sarah, we can only put our trust in the Lord.' He looked up at the ceiling as if expecting to see him floating there. 'As it says in the Bible, "God is no respecter of persons", Romans 2–11. Michael Ryan may be a big man on earth but in heaven he's just another of God's children.'

Sarah smiled at him. There was nothing, she thought, like a chunk of the Bible when spouted by a true believer. She left a little while later, happier than she had been for a long time. Over the years her religion had been a great comfort to her. As she had suffered one setback after another – no money, another still birth, one or other of the boys in trouble with the police – she had turned more and more to the church. Benjamin was no good at all. If she relied on him for anything, it never happened. Whether it was her housekeeping or anything, he always let her down. Michael, God love him, had been a good son in many ways.

He had looked after his younger brothers and sister, he had made sure that she always had enough money, but she had been hearing things of late that had frightened her. Anthony's death had been the last straw. She knew that her eldest son was involved in all manner of criminal activities, that he was thought of as a kind of mobster. She shuddered. She was all for a bit of ducking and diving, that's how everyone lived in her estimation, but from what she had gleaned recently about her sons, it was a completely different lifestyle they were after. She had seen the effect that Michael had on the people around and about. She herself was now treated like visiting royalty when she went anywhere.

She could, to an extent, understand Michael's craving for recognition. She was shrewd enough to understand that the way he had been treated as a child would give him the added drive and determination to better himself. But she herself drew the line at prostitution. In her mind it was the ultimate degradation, and any man who could live off the proceeds of it was the lowest of the low. She fervently hoped that Father McCormack would be able to talk some sense into her son. The robbing was bad enough though the insurance companies could afford the losses and money had no soul. But the wilful destruction of young lives was a different kettle of fish altogether. She had been shocked to read in the *News of the World* about the drugs that were available now to youngsters. What on earth was the world coming to? Young girls selling their bodies for drugs.

In the war years and after, women had sold their bodies to feed their children. That fitted in with Sarah's creed. You could do anything to feed the children, to keep the family fed or clothed. Even sell your body. But that had been for women with no man to protect them, so they had to do whatever they could and were respected for it. Sarah herself knew many women who had moonlighted down the Bayswater Road to supplement meagre war pensions or National Assistance. What Michael was doing was disgusting. He was putting them on the game, women and young girls who would otherwise never have dreamt of doing it. He was offering easy money, a far cry from the days when it was a means to an end.

She watched Maura and Carla skipping in front of her. Maura looked huge beside the tiny Carla. Dear Maura, she had taken the poor little thing under her wing. Sarah only hoped now that Janine and Roy sorted themselves out. That it wasn't too late for her to take to her daughter. Oh, the worry of having children! A Jewish woman Sarah had been friends with, before the war, used to say to her, 'When your children are young they tread on your feet. When they get older they tread on your heart!' How right she had been! The poor woman had died when she had been bombed in the blitz. A direct hit. Sarah often thought of her. Too many good people had died in the war, had suffered in one way or another. She sighed. She was dead tired. Now she had to go home and start her own cooking and cleaning. Still, she consoled herself, Father McCormack was coming in the morning and hopefully everything would right itself.

Father McCormack sat opposite Michael and appraised him. There was no doubt about it, he was a fearsome-looking individual.

From his dark expertly cut hair to his hand-made shoes he was the epitome of the new young man. His single-breasted suit was made of mohair and he flicked a trace of ash off his trousers with a perfectly manicured hand. His closely shaven face was tense and his usually sensuous mouth set in a grim line. The priest had guessed that he was well aware of the object of this visit.

Sarah had made a pot of tea and left them together in the overcrowded room. It was as if, after years of having no furniture at all, Sarah had gone mad for it. The room was filled with tables, knick-knacks, chairs, and a large horse-hair three-piece suite. Religious paintings were all over the walls. The Sacred Heart, the Last Supper and the Crucifix-ion stared down at them. Our Lady of Lourdes looked at the doorway opposite her in a gesture of supplication. On the large sideboard that covered nearly the whole of one wall statues of the Virgin and Child, as well as the holy family, stood silently. One particularly macabre statue of Saint Sebastian, arrows poking out of every limb, was given centre stage. The priest found his eyes drawn towards it and made a conscious effort to stop staring at it. He picked up his cup of tea and turned his gaze back to Michael.

'I expect you know why I'm here?'

Michael sniffed and uncrossed his legs. 'Yeah.' His voice was wary.

The priest nodded as if in understanding. 'Well, Michael, if you know then it's pointless me droning on now, isn't it?'

'Yeah.' This was said insolently. Michael's fear of priests and nuns was long gone.

Father McCormack sat forward in his chair and replaced his cup on the table. His face hardened. He spoke in a low voice. 'What I am here for today is something completely different. When your mother, good woman that she is, came to see me yesterday I was not shocked to hear what she had to say. I guessed that you were breaking the law in some way. I'm not a fool, you know. Anyway, that's all neither here nor there . . . I want to speak to you as a man of the world.'

Michael looked at him. His blue eyes were sceptical.

'What I'm after is a little donation.'

Michael sat up in the chair, stunned. 'A what!'

The priest became agitated. 'Whisht now, whisht. You'll have your mother galloping in here else. As you know, I am rather sympathetic to my countrymen. There's poor Paddies in London even now, God love them, who have been driven out of their homes by the Proddies. It's every Irishman's duty to help these poor unfortunates.'

'Look, Father, just because my name's Ryan don't mean I'm Irish.'

The priest banged his fist on the little table, causing the cups to jump in their saucers.

'Listen here, you, since nineteen-twenty the Catholics have been discriminated against in Ulster, Belfast, all the

North. They can't even get a council house out there! The bloody Protestants run the whole fecking sheebang! I collect money for the IRA so we can build up an army and fight the bastards at their own game. One day, my laddo, we'll be ready for the eejits. We forced them out of the South and we'll fight the buggers in the North. We want an Irish Free State that spans the whole of Ireland.'

The priest's eyes were alight. Michael stared at him as if he was mad. He had heard stories of Ireland from the cradle, as most Catholic children had. He could still hear his granny singing 'Kevin Barry' on Saint Patrick's Day, still remember the stories of the Easter Uprising and the Famine. How his ancestors had left the meat that Queen Victoria had sent over to them to rot in the streets rather than accept help from the English. But this was nineteen-sixty, for Christ's sake. Who gave a toss what was happening out there?

Father McCormack drank his tea. Wiping his mouth with the back of his hand he spoke again.

'I know an awful lot about you, Michael Ryan. There's nothing I can't find out if I want to. All I am asking is a little donation now and again. You'd be surprised at how many people give money to the cause. The Americans have regular collections in their bars and churches. Ireland is a poor country and needs all the help it can get.'

Michael laughed.

'Supposing I give you some money . . . now and again . . . what would you do in return?'

The priest took a handkerchief from the pocket of his black cassock and mopped his forehead.

'I would tell your mother exactly what she wanted to hear. If it came from me she would believe it. I can be a very persuasive man.'

Michael ran his tongue over his lips, and shook his head. 'What about the poor orphans and the starving blacks?' His voice was sarcastic.

'Sure, they would get a bit as well, God love them. Though I think most of the blacks are in Notting Hill.'

Michael burst out laughing.

91

'All right then, Father. You've sold me. But I'm warning you now, you've got to keep my muvver sweet.'

Father McCormack smiled.

'I will, Michael son.' He sighed heavily. 'Sure, it's a terrible world we're living in today. Money makes it so much easier. I remember this room when there was hardly a thing in it . . . except children, of course. Your mother always seemed to have plenty of those. Well, I must be off. It's been grand chatting to you, Michael. I'll expect you at the Presbytery in a few days with your donation.' He held out his hand. 'I won't give you a blessing . . . I don't think you need one!'

Michael shook his hand. 'I have a feeling I've just been conned, Father. An Irish Catholic Northern Ireland? Donations to the IRA . . .?' He smiled. 'If it was anyone else I'd kick their arse out of the door.'

The priest's face straightened and he looked meaningfully at Michael.

'Don't mock what you don't fully understand. Your religion is the mightiest in the world. Remember this? *Dominus illuminatio mea, et salus mea, quem timebo?*'

Michael translated it for him, smiling as he did so. 'The Lord is the source of my light and my safety, so whom shall I fear?'

'Would you listen to that! You remembered your Latin.'

'Yeah, I remember it all right. And I don't fear anyone, not even God. *You* remember that.'

Father McCormack digested the veiled threat gracefully. 'How could I forget? But I'll tell you one thing before I go. One day the troubles in Northern Ireland will be known all over the world, and the British will have to listen to us. When that day comes you remember my words, Michael, because we won't forget our friends, whoever they are.'

With that the priest picked up his hat and left the room.

Michael watched him leave. He felt like laughing out loud. The old boy had lost his marbles somewhere along the line. Still, if it kept his mother off his back, he didn't care. He picked up the tray of tea things and took them to the kitchen where he glanced at the clock. If he got his head down for a couple of hours he would be nice and fresh for the evening. His new club was raking the money in. After the lean war years, people wanted a bit of fun. And he would make sure that they got it!

Chapter Seven

1966

'You look nice, Maws. Where you off to?' Sarah's voice was tight.

'I'm going up Tiffany's with me mates.'

'Tiffany's? Where's that?'

Sarah's voice had taken on the tone of an interrogation. Garry answered for Maura.

'It's in Ilford. The old Allie Pallie.'

'What's she going up there for? What's wrong with the Hammersmith Palais?'

Maura sighed and tossed back her hair. 'There's nothing wrong with round here, Mum. I'm just meeting some of the girls from work, that's all.' Her voice was beginning to rise and she tried in vain to control it.

Sarah wiped her hands on her apron and stared at Maura, her face wrinkled in concern. 'Well, it's a bloody long way to go if you ask me.'

'Well, I'm *not* asking you, Mum. I'm nearly seventeen and I can do what I like.'

Sarah walked towards her daughter. Garry tried to pull her back, holding her arm gently.

'Let me tell you something, Madam. You *can't* do what you sodding well like . . .'

Her diatribe was cut off by Michael who stormed into the kitchen. The constant bickering between Maura and his mother was beginning to get on everyone's nerves.

'For Christ's sake, Muvver, give it a rest. Let the girl go out if she wants to. Anyway . . .' he put his arm around his mother's shoulders '. . . Garry's going up there tonight. He can give her a lift on the back of his scooter.'

'I'm not getting on the back of his scooter with all my new gear on!' Maura's voice was horrified.

'Just as well, 'cos I ain't going up the Palais.'

'Tiffany's.'

'Tiffany's then. I'm going to the pictures with me mates.'

Maura smiled triumphantly. 'Well, that's settled then.' She picked up her shoulder bag. 'Gawd Blimey, it's worse than living in Scotland Yard here. Where you bin? What you been doing? What did you talk about? Did he kiss you? I wouldn't mind, but I can't get a bloody boyfriend! As soon as they find out who I am they shy off.

'"You Mickey Ryan's sister?" they say. "Yes," says I, and watch them poodle off down the road. So stop worrying about me getting in the club, Muvver, I don't get the bloody chance!'

She snatched her coat off the kitchen table and stormed out of the kitchen, shouting, 'And if by any chance I do need an escort, it won't be my bloody brother. Ta rah!'

She walked out of the front door and gave it a satisfying slam behind her. In the kitchen Michael and Sarah stared at one another, shocked. Garry went to the sink and washed his hands. In the back of his mind he was cheering Maura on.

'Well, I never, Michael. Did you hear the way she carried on?'

He sighed heavily. 'I think the whole of Notting Hill heard it.'

Garry wiped his hands on a tea towel and faced his brother. 'She's got a point though, ain't she?'

Michael looked at him. It was like looking at a miniature version of himself.

'What do you mean by that?' His voice was cold.

Garry plucked up every bit of courage he had.

'Well, the way that everyone's at her. If I was her, it would drive me up the wall.'

'If you was her you'd be getting the same treatment. She's our sister, our responsibility. If we don't look after her, who will? You want to put your brain in gear before you open your trap, Garry. Our Geoff was right about you.

He said an original thought in your head would die of loneliness. After hearing the crap you just come out with, I'm inclined to agree with him.'

Garry's face was scarlet with embarrassment.

'Come on, you two, get a move on or you'll be late.' Sarah was worried. She knew that Michael was capable of attacking Garry for what he had said. In Michael's mind it was tantamount to mutiny and he would not stand for anyone disagreeing with him.

He took a comb from the pocket of his suit and stood at the sink. Looking in the mirror that was perched precariously on the windowsill, he combed back the hair that hung over his eyes. Then, turning to Garry, he pointed the long steel comb at him.

'In future, Bruv, keep your nose out of what don't concern you.'

He kissed his mother lightly on the forehead and walked out of the room. Garry was fuming inside. Sensing this, Sarah went to him.

'He don't mean it, Gal. But he's right about Maura, you know. You should all look out for your sister.'

Garry shrugged her arm off and picked up his crash helmet. 'We're not looking out for her, Mother. We're trying to own her, and that's a completely different thing.'

When he had gone Sarah carried on with her chores, but Garry's words stayed with her all evening.

Maura breathed a sigh of relief as she slammed the front door. It was getting more claustrophobic in that house by the day. If it wasn't for Margaret she would go mad. They were as close as two friends could be. They worked in the same office, they ate their lunch together, they went down the Lane on Sundays and the Roman Road on Fridays. The only cloud on the horizon was a boy called Dennis Dawson. Margaret had been seeing him for nearly a year and Maura had the feeling that they were going to get married. Still, she consoled herself, she would always have Margaret as a friend.

Tonight the two girls were meeting Dennis and one of his

mates up Tiffany's. She had nearly had heart failure at the thought of Garry going up there. That was all she needed. The only reason they were going there was because they could be pretty sure that one or other of her brothers would *not* be up there and Maura would have a bit of privacy. How she hated the way her brothers protected her, and her mother was all for it. She was beginning to dislike her mother. The last few years Sarah had practically suffocated her only daughter. Maura wished that she could meet a nice bloke and get right out of it. If she married, at least she would have a life of her own, away from prying eyes. She daydreamed sometimes about finding a little flat but knew they were just that – daydreams. There was no way she would ever be allowed to go and live alone.

She saw Margaret waiting for her outside her house and she gave her a little wave. They made a funny pair. Maura was tall, nearly five ten, and big-boned. She was what her father jokingly called 'a good eyeful', with her large breasts and wide hips. Her long blonde hair was backcombed up into a beehive, kept firmly in place with sugar and water, making her look even taller – like an amazon. Her eyes, still a startling blue, were now heavily made up, with black liner and white eye shadow, the false eyelashes giving her a startled doe look. In her short shirtwaist dress and white winklepicker shoes she was the height of fashion.

Margaret on the other hand was still under five feet tall. Her orange-red hair was worn bouffant, and her orange lipstick made her look like a small circus clown. She was very flat-chested but had big legs and a large behind. When they were younger the boys in the streets whistled the Laurel and Hardy music as they passed. Nowadays they took no notice if people stared at them, they were used to it.

'You managed to escape then?'

'Oh, don't talk to me about it, Marge.'

Margaret laughed her billy goat laugh.

'You'd better check in your bag. It might be bugged.'

'Don't even joke about it, Marge, I wouldn't put it past them.'

98

They began to walk to the bus stop.

'What's Dennis's mate like?'

'Well, he's tall and very good-looking. He's twenty-four years old.'

'What job's he got?'

Margaret shook her head. 'Dunno. Dennis did tell me but we was too busy . . . well, you know.'

'No, I don't know. And you know that. Come on, Marge, tell me. What's it like?'

Margaret pursed her bright orange lips. 'What?' Her voice was innocent.

'You know very well, Marge. A bit of the other?'

'Maura Ryan! I am not discussing my sex life at a bus stop!'

Maura burst out laughing. 'Why not? It's never stopped you before!'

Both girls laughed and pushed each other in the chest.

'Come on, tell me.' Maura's face straightened and she looked earnestly at her little friend.

'Well, I've only done it a couple of times as you know. But . . . I like it. It's nice, but a bit embarrassing. Dennis said that I'll get over that. In fact, he says I'm a natural!' The last piece of information was given with a toss of her head.

'Oh, hark at the Duchess of Duke Street.' They both laughed again. The bus pulled up and they jumped on it, going upstairs so they could smoke.

'Two to Holborn, please.' As they lit their cigarettes Maura felt the familiar annoyance wash over her. This was another bugbear. Her brothers all smoked yet when Mickey had seen his sister smoking he had snatched the cigarette from her hand, grinding it out with his heel, shouting at her that only slags smoked. He had done it in the street in front of everyone. She had thought that she was going to die of shame. Now she could only smoke when well away from them.

They got off the bus at Holborn and got a train to Mile End, from there taking another train to Ilford. They were in Tiffany's at nine forty-five. If they got in before ten it

99

cost only a pound. They went straight to the toilets and repaired their makeup and hair. As they came out of the toilet and into the bar Maura's heart stood still in her chest. Standing beside Dennis was the best-looking man she had ever seen in her life. She looked at Margaret with a question in her eyes and when she nodded felt a burst of happiness like she had never felt before.

'Hello, darlin'.' Dennis kissed Margaret on her cheek. 'Maura, this is me mate Terry. Terry, this is Maura.'

She shook the stranger's hand timidly. Terry Petherick was well over six foot. It seemed strange to Maura to look up at someone. He had dark blond hair yet his eyes were a light brown. Maura was besotted after one smile.

'Would you like a drink?' His voice was deep and it sent her pulses racing.

'Please.' Her throat was dry with nerves. 'I'll have a scotch and dry.'

She was surprised at her answer. What on earth had made her say that? She drank half of bitter normally, but somehow she couldn't say that to him. He would think her terribly unsophisticated.

'Ice?'

She nodded at him. As he took Margaret and Dennis's orders she watched him. When he went to the bar she whispered into Margaret's ear, 'He's gorgeous!'

At the bar Terry Petherick was thinking about Maura. He had been surprised at how big she was, but she was absolutely fantastic. She was incredibly sexy and didn't even realise it! As she had walked towards him he had felt a physical pain in his guts. She was like one great big present, just waiting to be unwrapped. He paid for the drinks and took them back to the others.

Maura gulped at her drink. The music seemed very loud all of a sudden. They were playing a Beatles number. 'Love Me Do' seemed to be reverberating off the walls. Maura could see Terry's lips moving but could not make out a word. She smiled and gestured that she couldn't hear him. He laughed, showing perfect white teeth, and putting his mouth to her ear, he shouted: 'Another drink?'

She looked at her glass and was amazed to find it was empty! She smiled and nodded.

When he brought her back another drink he moved close to her trying to have a conversation. 'Do you come here often?'

'No. Only in the mating season.'

The record ended just as she spoke and her voice caused people to stare at them. Terry's eyebrows went up and she felt herself blushing furiously. Why had she said that? It was a silly saying of Margaret's. Now he would think she was a tart. She could have kicked herself. She concentrated on her drink to hide her embarrassment, deciding that whisky was all right. Just like drinking ginger beer really. She noticed that it was getting very hot all of a sudden.

Terry grinned at her ruefully. 'Another?'

She was aware of the disbelief in his voice even above the din. He bought her another drink and she sipped it. A slow dance came on. Putting her glass on the bar, she went on to the dance floor with him. As it was quieter now, he began to talk to her.

'I thought I'd better dance with you in case you wanted another drink.' His voice was jocular.

'I don't drink shorts very often.'

'I thought so. Are you nervous or something?'

'Yes . . . Yes, I am.'

He smiled a funny little lopsided grin and pulled her closer. She could feel his heartbeat against her breast and it gave her a feeling of longing she had never experienced before. She closed her eyes.

'What do you do for a living?' he asked.

'I work with Marge. We're typists for a firm of accountants in Charing Cross.'

'That's right. I remember Dennis telling me now. I'm a policeman.'

He felt the change in her.

'You're a what!' Her voice sounded shocked.

'I said, I'm a policeman. What's wrong with that?' He was puzzled. Maura could hear it in his tone.

101

'Nothing! It's just that I've never met a policeman before.' God forgive me for lying, she thought.

He relaxed. 'Well, don't worry. I'm not on duty so I won't arrest you. Not tonight anyway.'

She tried to smile at him. Bobby Darren was crooning 'Dream Lover' and Maura stepped back into Terry's arms. They finished the dance in silence. When they went back to Dennis and Margaret, Maura picked up her drink and slugged it straight back. She signalled to Margaret and both girls went into the toilets.

As soon as they were in there Maura said: 'He's only an old Bill.'

'He ain't!' Margaret was stunned.

'Oh yes he is, Marge. What am I gonna do?'

Margaret put her finger to her bottom lip. Her tiny heart-shaped face was screwed up as she thought the problem over. She looked up at Maura.

'Do you like him, Maws?'

'Oh, yes, Marge. But a filth . . . Jesus!' Maura was nearly in tears.

'Then it's simple. Just don't tell him about your brothers.'

'Do you honestly think I could get away with it?'

Margaret grinned. 'It's a doddle!' Her green eyes widened as she thought of a plan. 'Look, Dennis obviously ain't said nothing to him about your family and I'll put him wise. He don't see that much of Terry anyway. You just carry on as if nothing's happened. Let's face it, your brothers are more well known on their own turf than around this way. Anyway, you're not responsible for them, are you?'

'No, Marge . . . I know that. But I would feel a bit snidey pretending that I don't know them.'

Margaret rolled her eyes at the ceiling. 'Look, pea brain, you're not denying them . . . you're just not mentioning them. There's a difference. Like in confession when I tell Father McCormack that I have sinned in a personal manner – I don't tell him I'm having it off, do I? It's just a matter of not letting on, that's all.'

Maura still wasn't convinced.

Margaret sighed. 'Well, it's up to you, Maws. But I think

he's lovely, and you can tell a mile off that he likes you. Now let's get back to them before they send a search party out looking for us.'

Later in the evening Maura was sitting in a small Chinese restaurant with Terry. What Margaret had said earlier had been going through her mind over and over again. She tried to reason with herself. Just because he was a policeman didn't mean she couldn't go out with him, surely? She shook her head to clear it. It was all the whisky she'd had. She was drunk.

'Do you come from a large family, Maura?'

'Oh, the usual, Terry. A few brothers, that's all. How about you?'

'There's only me now. I had a brother but he died.'

Maura's heart went out to him.

'Oh . . . I'm sorry. One of my brothers died. I know how you must feel.'

'We lost Joey to cancer when he was twelve. I was sixteen at the time. Funny, though, I still miss him. How did you . . .?'

Maura looked at the tablecloth.

'He got run over. I was only a kid. I don't really remember it.' Another lie, she thought. Not a day went by but she saw Anthony's face, and superimposed on it the face of Stavros, smirking slightly as he had been in the cemetery.

No one in her family had been the same since Anthony's funeral. Her mother and father had aged dramatically overnight. Michael and the boys had become harder, more violent somehow. As for herself, she just missed him. Sometimes in the middle of a celebration, Christmas or Easter, she would think of him and the knowledge of how he had been murdered would cast a shadow over everything.

The food arrived. As they served themselves from the many little dishes, Maura surveyed her companion. She could really get to like Terry and the thought frightened her. She was going to murder Margaret tomorrow, going off with Dennis and leaving them like that. Now he had to take her home whether he wanted to or not.

'Eat up, Maura.' She smiled at him and brightened up. He wouldn't have asked her out for a meal if he didn't like her, she reasoned.

'Sorry. I was miles away.'

'Maura?'

'Yes.'

'Can I see you again? I don't think I've enjoyed myself so much with a girl for ages.'

He smiled at her with that lopsided grin and she was undone. Her whole body seemed to tingle with expectation. He liked her!

'Of course you can. Whenever you want!' She popped a prawn ball into her mouth and bit on it, showering him with sweet and sour sauce.

'Oh, I'm sorry!' She leant across the table to wipe his face with her napkin and knocked his glass of wine into his lap. Mortified at what she had done she leapt out of her seat and collided with a waiter, sending the plate of egg fried rice he was carrying flying through the air. She stood in the restaurant with her hand over her mouth and tears in her eyes. Terry burst out laughing, causing all the people in the restaurant to take their eyes off Maura and begin staring at him. He laughed so hard that he had a fit of coughing which, in turn, caused big tears to roll down his face. He stood up and, throwing a handful of money on the table for the bill, led a scarlet-faced and humiliated Maura out of the restaurant and into the night air.

'Now can I trust you with my car? You won't knock my wheels off or pull my radio to pieces?' Although it was said in a jocular fashion it was too much for Maura. The whisky, the heat, the Chinese food, the humiliation, and finally the cold night air all took their toll. She threw up in the gutter.

Terry rubbed her back as she heaved. When she had finished she leant against his car, gulping in the cold air. Her forehead had small beads of sweat on it that glistened in the lamp light. Her mascara was smudged under her eyes. One of her eyelashes had come unstuck. Gently he pulled it from her eyelid. Giving her his hanky, he went back to the restaurant and came back with a glass of iced water.

She stood there dejectedly looking at him, convinced that he would never want to lay eyes on her again. She looked at the red wine stain on his trousers and felt tears pricking her eyes. She frantically blinked them away.

'Feeling better now?' His voice was gentle. He handed her the glass of water. 'Drink this down and you'll feel much better, I promise you.'

She shook her head.

'Come on, drink it.' The authority in his voice surprised her and she took the glass and drank the water. The coolness eased her throat which was burning. She handed the glass back to him and he returned it to the restaurant. She breathed deeply, trying to settle her nerves.

He came back and unlocked the car, helping her into the passenger seat. As he pulled away from the kerb, he said, 'I think you drank too much.'

'It was the whisky. I've never drunk it before. Normally I drink a half of bitter.'

She looked at his profile. He looked solid, not just physically but mentally, with an air about him that denoted an inner strength. He smiled.

'Well, if it's any consolation, it happens to us all! I can remember the first time I got drunk on Scotch. I threw up all over my mum's slippers! Never touched the bloody stuff since, so you're in good company.' He poked himself in the chest. 'I can't take my drink either.'

He felt in his jacket pocket and brought out a pack of Juicy Fruits. 'Have one of these. It will freshen your mouth up.'

She took one gratefully.

'Where do you want dropping off? I know you live in Notting Hill.'

'Do you know the Bramley Arms?' He nodded. 'Well, there will do. I live nearby.'

'I'll take you right to your door.'

'No . . . That's all right. It's my dad. You know.'

He glanced at her and grinned. 'I get it. You're supposed to be coming home with Margaret.'

'That's it. He's a bit old-fashioned.'

They chatted on until they came to the Bramley Arms. The water and the Juicy Fruit seemed to have done the trick because she felt great. And better still, the big hunk of man beside her made her feel terrific. He stopped the car and turned to face her.

'When will I see you then?'

'Whenever you like.'

He smiled at her eagerness. 'Let's see.' He put his head to one side as if he was thinking, closing one eye and giving his little grin. 'Tomorrow's Sunday. How about Monday night? I'll pick you up here at about seven-thirty. Is that all right?'

She nodded and he pulled her into his arms and kissed her, then waved his finger in her face and said: 'And no drinking whisky!'

She grinned and got out of the car.

'See you, Maura.'

''Bye.' She watched the car pull away. He wanted to see her again! She felt as if she could float up into the starry night. It was two in the morning and she walked the short distance to her home as if on a cushion of air. He wanted to see her again! She couldn't believe her luck!

She had a little nagging worry in the back of her mind about Mickey, but pushed it impatiently away. As Margaret had said, what people didn't know couldn't hurt them. Anyway, Mickey and the boys weren't really bad. They were just tearaways.

As she pushed the key into the lock of the front door she heard a row going on. She walked into the kitchen just in time to see Benny punch Garry in the face. She ran and stood between them.

'What on earth's going on?'

'Get out me way, Maws. I'm gonna kill that little runt.'

'Calm down, Benny. What's he done?'

'Calm down? You dozy cow! He's poached my fucking bird, that's what he's done. The no good dirty ponce!'

Garry pushed Maura out of the way and faced his brother. 'She ain't your bird. She can't stand you, she told me that herself.'

With that Benny launched himself at Garry. As they fought, their mother and father came into the room, followed by Leslie and Lee who separated their brothers.

'What the hell's all this row abaht?' Benjamin's voice was slurred as usual. He was still half drunk.

'That wanker's poached me bird, that's what.'

'For the last time, Benny, she ain't your bird.'

Leslie threw Garry across the kitchen where he fell against the fireplace. He pulled himself up slowly. Leslie pointed at him.

'What's her name?'

'Mandy Watkins.'

Leslie and Lee looked at one another and burst out laughing. 'Not Mandy Watkins from Bletchedon Street?'

Benny and Garry nodded warily. There was something going on here.

'What's she doing, Les, making a career out of the Ryans?' Lee and Leslie began hooting with glee.

'What do you mean?' This from a sullen Benny.

'Me and Lee's had her, and Geoffrey. Me and Lee had her at the same time. She's a dog.'

'You're lying, you . . .' Garry went for Leslie who grabbed his arms and held him tightly, pushing his arms up behind his back expertly.

'Ain't we had her, Lee?'

He nodded, still smiling, then picked up a pack of cigarettes from the table and lit one.

'I take oath that we've all had her. Christ almighty, she's had more pricks than a second-hand dart board!'

'That's enough!' Sarah's voice echoed off the kitchen walls. 'I won't have this kind of talk. If you have no respect for me, your mother, at least have some for your sister.'

All the boys looked shamefaced.

Leslie spoke. 'Sorry, Mum. We're out of order.'

'Who wants a cuppa?' Maura tried to defuse the situation. The boys all nodded but Benjamin and Sarah went back to bed. Maura put the kettle on.

'Have a good time, Sis?'

'All right, Garry, I suppose.'

As she made the tea she thought about the way her brothers had talked about Mandy Watkins. She had known Mandy all her life. The papers might talk about the swinging sixties but the nearest most girls of Maura's age got to it was in the clothes they wore. If her brothers even suspected that she had been with a boy, all hell would break loose. She put their tea on the table. Benny and Garry were bosom pals once again. Kissing all the boys, she made her way up to bed, taking her tea with her. Her last thought before she fell asleep was the reaction she would get if they knew that she had been out with a policeman. She didn't care, though. She couldn't wait until Monday!

Chapter Eight

Margaret and Maura were in Maura's bedroom, painting their nails. They had worked out a system. On the nights that Maura saw Terry, Margaret would come to the house and they would get ready there as if they were going out together. In reality, Maura was meeting Terry and Margaret, Dennis. Maura had been seeing Terry for nearly five months, and miraculously had managed to keep him a secret. Sometimes though a terrible feeling of dread came over her. She knew that she was playing with fire but couldn't help herself. She was absolutely besotted with him.

'How's you and Den these days, Marge?'

'Great! We're getting engaged.'

Maura's eyes rounded. 'You're joking?'

'Oh no I ain't! We get on so well. He's got a good job and mine ain't that bad. We're thinking of saving up a deposit for a little house.'

Maura was impressed.

'Good luck to you, Marge. Dennis is lovely, and you can see how much he thinks of you.'

'He's all right, I suppose.' Margaret was embarrassed. 'How about you and Terry? You doo-dahed yet?'

'No, we most certainly have not!' Maura's voice sounded shocked even to her own ears. 'No disrespect to you, Marge, but I want to save myself for when I get married.' Even as she spoke she knew she was being a hypocrite. She wanted to do it more than anything in life.

Margaret laughed. 'You can't fool me, Maws. You're more worried about your brothers. It's 1966, for Christ's sake. Saving yourself for marriage, my Aunt Nellie!'

Maura ignored the jibe and started to apply mascara. 'I have all me life to do that.'

'That's just it though, ain't it? You don't! Imagine still doing it at forty!' Both girls laughed. To them forty seemed positively ancient.

'I'll think about what you said, Marge. Now can we drop the subject?'

'Be a damn sight better if you dropped your drawers and got it over with!'

'Marge!' Maura's voice had lost its joviality now and she sounded annoyed.

'All right, all right, keep your hair on! I'm sorry!'

'I should bloody well think so and all! You're obsessed with it.'

Margaret glanced at her watch and jumped off the bed. 'Come on, Maws. Get a move on. It's nearly a quarter past seven.'

Both girls scrambled into their coats. It was October and the nights had turned very cold. They hurried down the stairs. Michael and Geoffrey were in the hallway. Geoffrey whistled at them.

'You two look nice. Who's the lucky lads then?' Maura thought she was going to faint with fright.

Mickey glanced at Margaret and chucked her under the chin. 'You might be little, Margie, but you poke out in all the right places.'

Sarah's voice stopped Margaret from having to answer. 'Will you leave the poor girl alone! I don't know what comes over you sometimes, Michael. You can see she's embarrassed.'

He picked Margaret up and hugged her. 'She knows I'm only joking, don't you, Margie?' Margaret smiled shyly and nodded her head. He placed her gently on the floor and turned to Maura.

'Now you, Princess, you look absolutely gorgeous!' He frowned. 'I wish you'd lay off the make-up, though.'

Maura rolled her eyes up to the ceiling. 'Everyone wears their make-up like this, Mickey. It's the fashion.' Her voice, as usual when talking to Michael, was strained.

'Well, I think it suits her.' This from Garry who had just come in the front door. 'You look a cracker, girl.'

'Thanks, Gal.' Maura smiled gratefully at him. He was the only brother who allowed her to live her own life. He worked for Michael but wasn't as subservient towards him as the other boys. And though Michael acted as if he was annoyed with Garry when he spoke out of turn, Maura also got the impression that he admired Garry for it. Geoffrey snatched the books Garry was carrying from under his arm.

Garry and Geoffrey were the only readers in the family. They shared a common bond, a love of literature. The other boys revelled in baiting them about it, but in a good-natured way.

Michael put on his best voice and said, 'And what is one reading this week?'

Garry grimaced at him.

'I've read this, Gal. It's quite good. Heavy going at first, but then you can get into it.'

'I've read it before, Geoff. I like Voltaire.'

'I like revoltaire.' Michael parodied Garry's voice.

Everyone laughed. Geoffrey looked at Michael.

'In *Candide* it says, "If we do not find anything pleasant, at least we shall find something new." A very astute man. It's for that reason people like us read, ain't it, Gal?'

'Oh, for Gawd's sake, don't start on all that crap!' Mickey's voice was full of fun. 'I've read a few books in my time, and there's one thing I've learned . . . there's a difference between education and being well read.'

'Come on, Marge, before Robin Day turns up to join in the debate!'

'You saucy cow! Where you off to and we'll give you a lift?'

'Oh . . . we're just off to get the train to Holborn.'

'We'll drop you off. Come on then, Geoff, let's make tracks.'

Maura and Margaret exchanged dismayed looks.

'That's all right, Mickey. We don't want to put you out.'

'You're not. See you all.' He kissed his mother on the

111

cheek. As he passed Garry he pretended to punch him in the arm. 'See you later, book features.'

'Tah rah, Mickey.' Garry took his books back from Geoffrey.

Inside the Mercedes, Margaret and Maura sat quietly in the back. Maura felt panic building inside her. She was meeting Terry at Holborn, and prayed her brothers would not see him there. If he came over to them she would have to introduce him, and that thought was enough to bring on near hysteria.

Michael's 280 sports car pulled out of Lancaster Road and into Bramley Street. It was already dark. As he turned the corner a police car pulled out in front of them. Slamming on the brakes, the car skidded to a halt. It was obvious to Michael and Geoffrey that the car had been waiting for them. A policeman waved Michael over to the side of the road. His face dark with temper, he parked the car.

A plainclothes policeman got leisurely out of the panda car and walked across the road to them. He looked at the tax disc on the windscreen and motioned Michael to wind down his window. 'Insurance certificate, please.' Michael already had it in his hand.

The policeman took it and studied it.

'Well, well, well. I never thought I would see a Ryan driving a new Merc with all the rent paid.'

'Well, officer, we live and learn, don't we. Now fuck off!'

'That's not very nice, Mickey. You should have a bit more respect for the boys in blue.' The voice dripped sarcasm. 'It looks like pimping in the West End is a lucrative business. Who's that in the back? A couple of new girls?'

The policeman was knocked off his feet as Michael jumped from the car.

Geoffrey was trying to drag him back by holding on to his overcoat. He could see what the police were trying to do. They wanted Mickey to lose that famous temper of his so they could legitimately nick him.

'That's my sister you're talking about, you ponce!'

112

Two uniformed policemen got out of the Panda car and joined their boss. Geoffrey got out of the car and stood in front of Michael, willing him to calm down. If Mickey went berserk here there were too many witnesses.

Michael pushed him out of the way. 'No one talks about my family like that and gets away with it. Do you hear me?'

The two uniforms stood in front of their boss to protect him. They were both terrified. It was true what they had heard: he was crazy all right. 'Mad Mickey' they called him. Since the Krays had been sent down, Mickey Ryan was the Number One. The only one left of all the big-time crooks. And unlike the Krays and the Richardsons, Michael Ryan was as cunning as a fox.

'So that's your sister in there, is it? I'm sorry, Michael. It was an easy mistake to make. I should have guessed because you don't have a lot of time for girls, do you?' He was goading again. He noticed that the veins were standing out on Michael's forehead and against his will felt a surge of apprehension. Geoffrey tried to save the situation. He grabbed Mickey's arm.

'They're trying to wind you up. Ignore them. If you blow your top, they'll nick you double quick.'

Michael's breathing was returning to normal. Geoffrey faced the plainclothes officer. 'Look, what do you want?'

The man ignored him and carried on talking to Michael. 'Can't your club run without you? I heard you had a very good doorman. Gerry Jackson, ain't it? Another brainless Mick . . .'

Michael shook his head in disbelief.

'If I'm not mistaken, you're Detective Inspector Murphy, ain't you? So you would know all about brainless Micks, wouldn't you?'

The two uniforms laughed and the Inspector was annoyed. 'I wasn't born in Ireland, Ryan.'

'Neither was I, nor any of my brothers. Neither was Gerry Jackson, by the way. Now why don't you take these two little boys home? It's way past their bedtime.' The two uniforms sobered up instantly. Michael was calm now. Maura got out of the car and went to him.

113

'Can my brothers and I go now, please?'

The uniforms were giving her the once-over. One of them smiled at her.

'Who are you smiling at?' Michael's voice was loud. The young uniform was in a quandary. He didn't want to answer Michael, but at the same time didn't want to look like a coward. He was saved from answering by the DI.

'Very attractive girl, Michael.' He smiled at Maura, feeling a little bit sorry for her. He looked at her feet. In her winkle picker shoes they looked enormous. 'Do your feet go right to the end of those?'

He tried to sound jocular. She was only a kid. He had a daughter about that age himself. Maura looked at him with the arrogance of youth.

'Do their heads go right to the top of their helmets?' She jerked her head in the uniforms' direction.

Everyone looked at her in amazement. Michael and Geoffrey burst out laughing, surprised at Maura's front, but proud of her all the same.

'Now, Mr Murphy, can we go? Or would you like to ask us some more questions? Only I don't know about you, but we're very busy people.' She was as surprised as everyone else at her outburst. But she was annoyed. What gave this man the right to speak to people like he did! She would bet her last pound that her Terry didn't carry on like that. She got back into the car with Margaret. Now the excitement had worn off she was shaking.

She heard the DI saying, 'I'm gonna have you, Ryan.'

Michael laughed softly. 'Yeah, Murphy. Of course you are.'

Without bothering to speak again Michael and Geoffrey got back in the Mercedes. The three police stood watching them. Murphy knew when he was beaten and decided to retreat on this occasion. He made a mental note to have Maura Ryan checked out. Young girl she might be, but she was as streetwise as her brothers. She had made a fool of him and he wouldn't let that go. Once the uniforms had told their version in the canteen, he would be a laughing stock.

In the car everyone was congratulating her.

'Oh, Maura, how could you?' Margaret's voice was filled with awe.

'She's a Ryan, Margie. And she showed that tonight! I thought I was going to piss myself. Murphy's face!' Michael was roaring with laughter. 'I'll tell you something though, Geoff. I'll do for that bastard one day. I take oath on that. He winds me up!'

'You get wound up too easily. They can't touch us, Bruv. They can't prove nothing!' Geoffrey stressed the last two words.

'I thought we was all gonna get nicked!' Margaret's voice was still quavery. Michael looked in the mirror and caught her eye.

'I can just see you in Holloway, Marge. Them big butch warders would all be after a little thing like you!'

'Aaow, dont!' She put her hand over her mouth.

'Don't be rotten, Mickey. Marge, he's winding you up. What on earth would they nick us for?'

'That Murphy's all talk. He couldn't nick himself shaving.'

They all laughed and joked until they got to Holborn. Maura was praying that Terry was not about. Her prayers were answered. When she and Margaret got out of the car, Michael and Geoff drove off immediately.

'Sod that, Maura, I thought we was gonners there!'

'I know Mickey's my brother, but he scares even me when he gets annoyed.'

'Don't you think he's a bit weird, Maws? I mean, one minute he's foaming at the mouth and the next . . . laughing and joking.' Michael's quicksilver temperament made Margaret nervous. Maura was annoyed.

'No, Marge, I don't actually!'

'I wasn't criticising him, Maws . . .'

'He likes you, Marge. He always makes you feel welcome when you're round our house. There's nothing wrong with Mickey. He's just . . . highly strung.'

In her heart Maura agreed with Margaret's opinion of Michael, but she would never admit it openly. Maura was more like her brothers than she cared to think about. There was a loyalty in her family that would not, and could not, be understood by outsiders.

Margaret was contrite. 'I'm sorry, Maws. Here, imagine the old Bill thinking we was old brasses!' She tried to lighten the atmosphere between them.

Maura giggled. 'Bloody cheek!'

They stood outside the station until Dennis came up.

When Margaret and he had gone, Maura thought about what had happened. Tonight she had discovered a new side to herself. She had not intended to say what she had. It just came out. She shrugged and pulled her coat tighter around her. It was getting cold. She saw Terry walking towards her and smiled at him. The familiar lurch in her breast that always heralded his approach left her breathless. She ran into his arms for a kiss.

'Hello, Princess!' Maura froze in his arms then pulled away from him.

'Do me a favour, Terry. Don't ever call me that again.' Her voice was frosty. Terry couldn't believe her attitude.

'I'm sorry, Maura. I . . .' He held out his arms in supplication. Maura could see that he was bewildered.

'Look, it's no big deal. It's just that I hate that expression, that's all.' Her voice was rising.

'All right. Keep your hair on!' He was annoyed and she knew it.

'Terry.' She drew his name out softly and slipped her arm through his.

'What?' His voice was flat and expressionless. He had really been looking forward to seeing her tonight. Then, within two minutes, she had started an argument with him. He couldn't believe it.

'I'm sorry, Terry.' Her voice was small.

He relaxed. 'Let's forget it. I've booked a table for us up West in a snazzy restaurant.' He saw her face fall again. Now what was the matter with her?

Maura was in a state of acute agitation. She couldn't go up West with him! Supposing Mickey saw her? Or one of her other brothers? Not to mention all the people who worked for them. They all knew her. Michael might come

116

into the restaurant to say hello! She felt faint just thinking about it.

'Are you all right? You've gone very white.' His voice was all concern. Maura's mind was reeling.

'I feel a bit under the weather. I haven't eaten all day. Can't we eat around here?' She knew she was clutching at straws but nothing would get her up the West End.

'But I booked the table especially. We're celebrating.'

'Celebrating what?'

'Never you mind. I'll tell you when we get to the restaurant.'

Oh, God, please help her.

'Oh, let's stay around here . . . please. I don't fancy travelling back up West.' Her voice was wheedling. He couldn't help smiling. She was some girl! Not two minutes in his company and she was biting his head off. Now she didn't want to go to an expensive restaurant in the West End. He shook his head at her.

'All right. You win as usual. What's it to be? Indian? Greek? What?'

Maura felt the tension drain out of her. She kissed him hard on the mouth.

'Greek, please. I just love taramasalata!'

She tucked her arm into his. Twenty minutes later they were sitting in a little restaurant drinking retsina.

'So what are we celebrating then?'

'I've been given a transfer. I applied for it about six months ago. Anyway, today I was told that it had been passed. From next month I will be at Vine Street! That's why I wanted to go up West tonight. Get the feel of the place.' He grinned at her.

Maura felt herself smile in response. She felt the muscles in her face moving. 'What exactly will you be doing up there?'

'It's hard to explain really. There's a lot of illegal gambling up there, always has been, as well as prostitution and drugs.'

The waiter placed two moussakas in front of them.

'Anyway, some firms – that's gangs to you – are using the

117

hostess clubs as a front for many other things. Guns, blackmail . . . the list is endless. Well, I'll be a very small cog in the wheel that's trying to stamp it all out.'

'I see.' Maura was finding it increasingly difficult to swallow.

'You don't see, but never mind, love. You'll never have to worry about it. Or are you a closet villain?' She laughed with him, amazed that she was still able to function normally while her insides were doing the Twist!

'How about a toast to your new job?'

'I'll drink to that, Maura.'

They clinked glasses and Terry chattered on.

'It's so exciting. Do you know that there's men running clubs up there who would murder somebody like you or me would have a cup of tea? It's unbelievable, I tell you.'

She stared into her glass of wine. What was she worried about anyway? Michael wasn't involved with anything like that. And drugs? Never!

But a little nagging voice at the back of her mind kept reminding her of the way he had blown up the taxi rank after Anthony died. A little voice was whispering: 'They all work for Michael now.'

She pushed the thoughts firmly from her mind, forcing herself to concentrate on what Terry was saying. All the while icy fingers were touching the back of her neck – ghostly reminders of the past. Later on, when they left the restaurant arm in arm, she shivered. Terry pulled her closer to him.

'I want you, Maura.'

'I want you too, Terry.' And she was surprised because she meant it. At this moment she wanted him more than she had ever wanted anything in her life.

'Really?' His voice was husky with longing.

'Yes . . . really.'

'Oh, Maura, you don't know how much I wanted to hear you say that.' He clasped her hand and pulled her to his car. 'Come on, before you change your mind.'

'Where are we going?'

'You'll find out.'

She felt the thrill of sexual anticipation sweep over her body, wiping everything from her mind except Terry, herself, and their need.

Inside the car he kissed her, long and hard. He fumbled in his pocket and took out a key.

'Do you see this?' Maura nodded. 'Well, it's a key to a flat in Islington. I rented it today. Not for this, Maura, I swear. But to be nearer my job. All that's in it is a bed and a camping stove, but it's home for us . . . if that's what you really want.'

Maura loved him just for those words. He wasn't trying to force her into anything.

'I want to go to your flat in Islington, Terry.'

He kissed her again and then started up the car. Tonight was his lucky night.

On the way to the flat, Terry had stopped and bought a bottle of wine. Maura sat nervously on the edge of the big double bed while he opened the bottle and brought her a glass. She took it from him. The bedroom had large bay windows covered with grubby nets. Grantbridge Street was the centre of bedsitterland. Even now, record players and radios could be heard. Occasionally a shout or a loud laugh broke the gloom. There was no light in the bedroom, only the moonlight and the subdued glare of the streetlights outside the window. Maura was glad. She drank the wine and placed the empty glass on the floor by the bed. Terry walked out to the kitchen, talking as he moved.

'It doesn't look much now, I know, but you wait until I've finished it – decorated it, I mean. Hey, why don't you help me? We could go to Camden Market together and pick out some furniture.' He walked back into the bedroom with the bottle of wine. 'What do you say?' His voice was eager.

Maura caught some of his enthusiasm. 'I'd love it.'

He refilled her glass and gave it to her.

'Look, Maura, you don't have to sleep with me, you know.' His voice was caressing. 'I'll understand if you're not ready.'

119

She looked up. In the half-light he looked boyish. She traced the contours of his face with her finger.

'I am sure, Terry. In fact, I'm positive!'

He sat on the bed beside her and kissed her gently. 'Well, as long as you're sure.'

He stood up and removed his shirt. Maura watched him, fascinated. The muscles of his arms and chest were rippling as he moved and she felt a hot flush creeping over her body. She took a deep breath and slipped off her coat. The room was not very warm and she felt goosebumps on her arms. Her dress fastened up the front and she began to undo the buttons. She could sense his eyes on her and felt a sudden bashfulness. She had never in her life undressed in front of a man – not even a doctor. She came to the last button and, plucking up all her courage, slipped the dress off her shoulders and let it drop to the floor.

Terry watched her. His throat was dry and his breathing heavy. Standing there in the moonlight in her underwear she looked magnificent. Her breasts were huge – like giant orbs in the confines of her bra, spilling over the top like overripe melons. He couldn't believe his luck. She was like a larger than life fantasy that had just come true. He dragged his eyes from her breasts to her long legs. He was surprised at how small her waist was. She was like some voluptuous painting by Titian. He could feel himself hardening.

He slipped off his trousers and went to her. Putting his arms around her back he unhooked her bra, letting her opulent breasts free. He pulled the brassiere from her body and dropped it on to the floor. Instinctively her arms crossed over her chest. He gently pulled them away, staring down at her body. He groaned.

'Oh, Maura. You're beautiful . . . You're so beautiful!'

He pressed his lips against her nipples and she jumped. She could feel them hardening under his tongue and was caught between pure ecstasy and an urge to run from the room. Her heart was hammering in her breast and her breathing was irregular. She could feel herself panting. He squeezed both her breasts together and licked and chewed on her nipples, sending delicious waves of euphoria through her. He pulled her gently on to the bed. They fell together, their arms and legs entwined. He loomed over her.

'I love you, Maura. God, I love you.'

If he never said it again, the way he had just expressed himself to her would last for the rest of her life. She felt his fingers hook into either side of her panties, and as she felt him pull them down her body she closed her eyes. It was finally happening. The mystery of man and woman was about to be unfurled before her. She bit on her lip, an exquisite agony tearing her apart. Her natural shyness was trying to overcome a new, bigger, and more intense feeling.

Unaware that she had even done it, Maura opened her legs wide. As his tongue flicked over her thighs she groaned out loud. Slowly, he pushed his forefinger inside her. She was like a juicy peach.

Terry was in a fever of excitement. Who would have dreamed she would be so fiery the first time? She was like an experienced woman, the way she moved her body and opened herself up to him. He loved everything about her – the way she looked, the way she acted – everything. He especially loved the smell of her.

Maura felt him push himself up on his arms. She opened her eyes, and as he straddled her watched his swollen member trying to push into her. Her eyes opened wide. It was too big, surely? She pushed her elbows into the bed to pull herself up, but she was too late. She felt a tearing pain as if Terry pushed against some kind of obstacle. Then she felt a wave of dizziness as he slipped right up inside her. As he moved backwards and forwards she thrust her hips up to meet him at every stroke, a jumble of feelings and emotions raging through them both. Suddenly, she felt a shuddering somewhere in her bowels. It seemed to be slowly creeping into her groin and up . . . up into her stomach. She arched her back, and as she lost control in the final throes of orgasm felt Terry biting on her breasts. She called out . . . All self-consciousness seemed to dissolve in this all-encompassing feeling. She was aware that she was wailing and moaning, but she didn't care. This feeling was too good, too exciting to let go of. She felt her legs grab Terry's thighs and was trying desperately to push him further inside her.

Above her Terry was watching her, fascinated. As he felt his own orgasm beginning to pulsate he felt her legs gripping him and drove his penis into her as hard as he could, bursting inside her like a dam.

They lay together, their bodies bathed in sweat, their hearts beating a tattoo on each other's chests. Terry kissed her gently, little tiny kisses, all over her face and neck. He licked her throat and tasted the saltiness of her.

'That was fantastic, Maura.'

She lay beneath him, shy again, amazed at her own feelings.

'Thank you, Maura. For letting me be the first. And if it lies with me, I will be your last. You're my girl now. You'll always be my girl.'

He kissed her again and was surprised to find that she was crying gently. He was immediately concerned. 'I didn't hurt you too much, did I?'

'No, you didn't hurt me. I'm crying because I'm happy. That's all.'

He gathered her into his arms and held her tightly. He had promised himself that he would not get too involved with her, but at this moment he could no more have parted from her than he could have cut his own throat.

Maura felt the heightened awareness that comes with lovemaking. That feeling of infinite perception that envelops lovers in its embrace. She was acutely aware that she had burnt her boats. That she now belonged to the man lying with her. That her family had taken a back seat in her life. But she was also aware that no matter how she felt, her family would never allow her to relegate them to second place. The fact that Terry was a policeman would be enough for Michael. He would never countenance her having an association with one. He would take it as a personal affront.

She felt Terry's hand running over her body, kneading

her breasts and shoulders, and was caught up in a feeling of presentiment. They were doomed and she knew it. She closed her eyes tightly, praying to her God to take pity on them. To help them find a way out of the morass they had jumped into. She wished fervently that they might be allowed to be together, that nothing would happen to make them part. And even as she prayed and wished, she knew, deep inside, that it was all useless. But with the foolishness of youth, she convinced herself that somehow, somewhere, there was an answer to their problem.

Finally, she abandoned herself to him once again, the moonlight playing on their bodies as they loved each other with a strength that surprised them both. Their whispering and low moans echoed around the empty flat, like ghosts that danced on the ceiling with their shadows.

Maura had never dreamt that she could feel like she felt at this moment. She had indeed burnt her boats. But she smiled while she did it.

Chapter Nine

Benjamin Ryan pushed his wife out of his way. He was drunk as usual, but today, instead of his normal boisterous drunkenness, he was in a violent, vindictive frame of mind.

Sarah watched him warily. Ever since Anthony's death her husband had suffered these fits of depression. His face was bloated and red-veined. His large nose was reddened and bulbous. His dark blue eyes, inherited by all the children, were now listless, the whites a sepia colour, like an old photograph. He looked terrible. His once black hair was grey, hanging across his face in greasy tendrils. Sarah shook her head sadly. He was grey-skinned and the weight that had once given him an air of affability had dropped off him, leaving only a large beergut that hung offensively over his trousers. He stalked across the bedroom to her. Sarah put her hands up to her face through years of habit. The chances were that she was going to get a good hiding. She braced herself for the blows.

'I want some money, Sar . . . I'm warning you.'

His breath was sour and she tried to turn her face away from him. He grasped her chin with his hand and pulled her face towards him. He grinned at her, showing yellowing teeth. 'What's the matter then? Turning your face away from me these days?' He squeezed her chin in his large hand, causing her to flinch. 'That's right, my lovely . . . You be scared of me, because if you don't give me some of the money you've got stashed, I'm gonna beat you all around this room. Now where is it?'

Sarah was trying desperately to pull herself away from him. He pulled his right arm back and punched her in the stomach. He used such force she fell to her knees, winded.

He grabbed her hair, forcing her head up to look at him. 'That's just a taster, Sarah.'

She nursed her injured stomach with her arm, feeling sick. She stared at her husband, and gathering all her strength she spat at him. She saw his lips draw back over his teeth.

'You old trout! I'll bloody murder you for that.'

As his fist was raised to begin his beating she screamed, holding her arms over her head. His first punch hit her on her wrist, causing her to cry out in pain. Somewhere above the din she heard the bedroom door opening, then she felt Benjamin being pulled away from her bodily. It was Garry and Lee.

Lee felt a rush of emotion he had never known before. Seeing his mother kneeling there while his father beat her caused him to lose control. He was aware that he was punching and kicking his father. He could feel the surge of adrenaline as his arms and legs came into contact with Benjamin's body. He could easily kill this man who had fathered him. Eventually Garry pulled him away, forcing him to sit on the big double bed. His breathing was loud and noisy. The effort he had used on his father had exhausted him. He felt his mother's arm go around his shoulder. He grasped her rough workworn hand. His knuckles were bleeding.

Benjamin was too drunk to feel anything. He lay on the bedroom floor staring up at a picture of Our Lady's Ascension into Heaven. Her pale blue and gold gown was swimming before his eyes. He could taste blood in his mouth. Running his tongue around his gums, he found that one of his few remaining teeth was loose. Garry looked at his father with a feeling of disgust coupled with distress. The older man's woeful face was like an open book. All the setbacks, troubles, humiliations and causes for discontent were there for anyone who wanted to look. Only nobody ever wanted to. Even his own sons regarded him as an object of derision, tempered with a love that came more from duty than any feeling of filial affection. Garry sighed.

'Help him up, son. We'll put him to bed to sleep the

worst of it off.' Sarah's voice was flat, resigned. Before the boys had grown up, she would have endured the beating; years of experience had taught her that it was preferable to giving him the money.

Garry and Lee, calmer now, put their father to bed. Benjamin was pliable. He allowed his sons to strip him and bundle him under the covers. Within minutes he was asleep. The three went down the stairs together. In the kitchen Lee examined his mother's arms and face. She shrugged him off.

'I'm all right, Lee. Give it a rest now, for Gawd's sake.' She made one of her endless cups of tea.

Garry took his and went back upstairs to his room. He placed the tea on his dressing table and went back to what he had been doing before his mother's scream. He was making a car bomb. The main work had already been done in one of Michael's lock-ups. He was now perfecting the detonator. He took his glasses off the bed where he had left them earlier and slipped them on.

Garry's years of being the inventor of the family had paid off. Michael had taken his expertise and channelled it to his own advantage. Garry made everything, from molotov cocktails to delayed-action devices for robberies or personal revenge attacks. His natural misanthropy and lack of interest in possessions gave him the perfect temperament for an explosives manufacturer. In Garry's mind there was no black or white, just fuzzy grey areas that he could interpret to his own advantage. Like Michael, he was a psychopath. He could champion causes with a fervour that amazed those around him. He could also see two sides to an argument, could balance the debate in his mind or that of whoever happened to be interested. But there was another side to him that even his own brothers did not realise. He would not stand for anyone or anything getting in *his* way. He had no real feelings about anyone, except his sister Maura. He was incapable of deep feelings or emotion. If Garry had a girl friend, she was his property. He would be jealous and moody. The girl always seemed to think this was because he felt deeply for her, but Garry felt the same way about his car or his record player. It was *his*. Until the time came when he tired of it.

The bedroom door opened and Lee came in. 'Mickey just phoned and said that we're all to meet him at the club tonight. Nine-thirty, OK?'

'All right, Lee. Thanks.' Garry carried on with what he was doing. Lee walked out of the room. The earlier trouble with their father was now forgotten. In the Ryan code, if you didn't mention it then it had never happened. When Benjamin had slept off his drink and emerged once again into their world he would be treated with the usual haphazard affection.

Garry had finished his detonator and smiled to himself happily. He began clearing away. His room was so tidy, Garry would know if anyone had been in while he was out. He had everything strategically placed.

Like all the rooms in the house, this also had a religious print on the wall and a small crucifix over the bedroom door. Garry's religious painting was of Jesus's entrance into Jerusalem on Palm Sunday. Jesus sat on a donkey, the marks of the stigmata on his outstretched hands, his face as always serene with a hint of sadness. Around him were crowds of people holding their palm leaves, expressions of ecstasy on their faces. The print was in beautiful pastel shades of blue and pink. Picking up the detonator, Garry went to the picture. Holding the device under the Donkey of Christ, he laughed softly.

'Bang fucking bang!'

Jesus still sat there, the yellows and golds of his halo shadowed by Garry's body, still serene and still sad.

Mickey, Geoffrey and Roy sat in the offices above their club, Le Buxom, in Dean Street. All three were wearing the usual dark suit, brilliant white shirt and thin black tie. It was their uniform. Michael's tie had a grey stripe going through it horizontally. It was his way of being just that little bit different. He lit a cigarette and blew the smoke out noisily.

'So what else have you found out then?' He stared at Geoffrey.

'Plenty. He's a bit of a rogue, is old Hanley. He likes the gee gees for a start, and he's not averse to a bit of skirt now and again either. Both expensive pastimes for old Bill. He usually goes round to the wives of convicted criminals offering them a bit of consolation.'

Mickey laughed. 'In return for a bit of the other, I suppose.'

'Exactly. He now owes us about three hundred quid. He was betting quite heavily in our South London shops. I tipped the lads the wink to give him as much tick as he wanted, which they did. Now we have him right where we want him. By the short and curlies.'

'Good work, Geoff. Arrange for him to come and see me next week. Another face would be to our advantage. Especially a prat like Hanley.'

'How about we give him a free night here, before you see him? Let him have his leg over with one of the girls for nix. That should soften him up before you give him the bad news.'

'Yeah, I think that's what we'll do, Roy. Bent filth are ten a penny these days. What we want are the ones who can do us the most good. Hanley's at Vine Street, from what I understand. He's the one who liaises with all the other nicks. We'll cultivate him, I think.'

Geoffrey and Roy nodded in agreement.

'Now about the loan sharking. I had a visitor today . . . do you remember old Moses Mabele?'

Roy nodded. 'The old West Indian bloke who lived in our street?'

'That's him. His wife Verbeena was mates with Muvver. Used to help her out now and again with money. Old Moses used to work in the Docks.'

'Yeah. What about them?' Geoffrey's voice was puzzled.

'Well, they moved Plaistow way. They got one of the old Dockers' Mansions – he was working in the East India Docks. Anyway, to cut a long story short, Moses popped off a bit sudden like . . .'

'What's this got to do with us?'

'Well, if you'd listen, you might learn something, Roy. Now where was I?'

'Moses had popped off.'

'Thanks, Geoffrey. Moses popped off a bit sharpish and Verbeena couldn't afford to bury him like. So she went to one of our "borrowers" – no prizes for guessing who that was.'

Geoffrey groaned. 'Not George Denellan!'

Mickey smirked. 'The one and only. Anyway, the rub is she couldn't pay it back quick enough and Georgie boy sent round some heavies . . .'

'You're joking!'

'I wish I was, Roy. I bunged her a couple of ton for her trouble and told her the debt was scrubbed. What I want you two to do is go and see Denellan. Put him straight about a few things. She's an old lady, for Christ's sake. I want at least an arm broken. He's got to learn that he works for me, not the government. You don't belt old dears. In fact, you don't lend money to old dears, period, not without querying it with one of us first. He takes too much on himself and he's beginning to aggravate me.'

'I'll go, Mickey. I don't like Denellan anyway, he's a ponce.'

'All right then, Roy, you can sort him out. What an advert for us, eh? Beating up old ladies!'

They all laughed.

Geoffrey got up and poured them all a drink. 'What's happening with that Smithson, Mickey?'

Michael took the glass off him and sipped the brandy. 'Our Garry's made him a little surprise present. He should be getting it some time over the weekend.'

'You're definitely trouncing him then?'

'Yep. I don't like doing it, Geoff, but that saucy bugger's asked for it.' He poked his finger in the air. 'Nobody tucks me up and gets away with it. It'll be a lesson to all the blokes who work for us.'

'How much exactly did he poach?'

'Nigh on two grand.'

Roy whistled softly. 'That much?'

'It's not so much the money as the principle of the thing. One bloke owed us a monkey. He paid three oners over, and then the last two hundred plus the fifty quid interest. Next thing he knows he's got three blokes waiting for him as he leaves for work. They'd trashed his motor.' Mickey laughed softly. 'The poor bastard is informed that he still owes three hundred smackers. Anyway, he paid it . . . but he came to see our Lee and he told me about it and that's how we uncovered the little bastard's game. Fuck me! It ain't as if we don't pay him enough. For a bloke who came out of the South London slums he's done bloody well. Do you know, his kids go to private school? Straight up.'

'That don't surprise me, Mickey, he always fancied himself. He still brags in pubs about how he worked for the Richardsons.'

Michael snorted. 'Don't talk to me about him. He's history now.'

The three men were quiet for a few moments. Geoffrey got up from his chair. 'Shall I bring the other lot up then? See what's happening with their teams?'

'Yeah. Hang on, what's the time?'

'Eleven-thirty-five.'

'I bet you a tenner Benny's sitting in the club watching the stripper. She comes on at half-past.'

They all laughed.

'He's sex mad. Most of the girls don't have to "go case" with the punters, they can go home with Benny!'

Still laughing, Geoffrey made his way down the stairs to the club's foyer.

Gerry Jackson, the doorman, nodded at him. 'We're pretty full tonight, mostly Americans. Must be a convention on somewhere.'

'Plenty of money then?'

Gerry nodded. 'The touts reckon that the streets are full of them. I bet a few get rolled, don't you?'

'Bound to, ain't they? Stupid bastards. They flash their money about like it's going out of fashion. Someone's got to stomp them, it stands to reason.'

Geoffrey walked into the club itself. The air was thick

131

with cigarette smoke and cheap perfume. At the bar area seats lined each wall to either side. They were plush red velvet, well upholstered and fixed to the wall. On them sprawled women and girls of every shape and colour. On entering the club, punters were able to see the merchandise and if a particular girl took their fancy, she accompanied them to their table. The hostesses were only allowed to drink champagne – which they tipped on to the carpet when the punter wasn't looking. With a different stripper on every twenty minutes this was not difficult. At the moment a tall blonde of about thirty was dancing semi-naked to 'Pretty Flamingo'. She bent over almost double and her long bleached blonde hair touched the floor. She swayed her buttocks suggestively before hooking her fingers into her sequinned panties and slowly pulling them down her legs.

Geoffrey smiled. Sure enough there was Benny, sitting on the edge of his seat, his tongue poking out of his mouth as he watched the girl in a state of hypnotic fascination. Stepping out of her panties, the stripper stood up and turned to face the audience. Her pubic hair was black, in stark contrast to the whiteness of her hair. She raised her arms above her head and once more set the tassels on her small breasts spinning.

The music ended and she nonchalantly picked up her discarded clothes and walked from the stage. She would strip in six or seven different clubs during the course of the evening. She passed by Benny and Geoffrey saw him squeeze her buttocks. The girl smacked his hand away and glared at him, shouting at the top of her voice, 'When you're old enough, Little Boy!'

Benny laughed good-naturedly. Geoffrey called him and he walked over, his moon face wreathed in smiles.

'You never give up, Ben, do you?'

Benny grinned. 'Old slag! She's got a face like a carpenter's nailbag. Let's face it, I don't want to *marry* her, just fuck her.'

'Well, she obviously don't want to fuck you.'

Benny tapped his nose with his finger and winked lewdly.

'She will. It's just a matter of wearing her down! She'll come round in the end.'

Geoffrey laughed. 'You'll wear your dick out if you're not careful. Where's the others?'

'In the back bar as usual. You know they don't like sitting with the peasants!'

'Get upstairs, you ponce. Mickey's waiting for you. I'll go and get the others.'

He walked across the dance floor. All round the walls were large photographs of women in various stages of undress. Geoffrey stopped at a table where a small bald-headed man was sitting with two girls. He smiled at the girls warmly and shook the man's hand.

'How is everything, sir?' His voice was solicitous.

The small man grinned, showing expensive-looking teeth. 'Just fine, son. These here two ladies is just about as fine as you could get.' His voice had a southern drawl. The two girls giggled. Geoffrey noticed that one of them was high.

'I'm glad to hear it, sir. We like all our guests to enjoy themselves.' He nodded at the man and moved away from the table, his eyes taking in everything that was going on around him. One of the hostesses, a young lady who called herself Shirelle, had her head buried in a man's lap. Geoffrey sighed with annoyance and, pulling back a curtain at the end of the dance floor, walked into the back bar.

'What on earth's going on here?' His voice was loud. Two hostesses were sitting at a table. Geoffrey recognised them as Liverpool twins who Denise, the head girl, had taken on a few days previously. They were tiny little things with wide brown eyes and mousy blonde hair. They were not particularly pretty but their attraction was that they only worked together. They had little half-formed breasts and were no more than fifteen. From what he had gleaned they had been toms for quite a while. Looking at them, it was obvious they had been roughed up.

Garry spoke. 'We caught these two "doing a dolly".'

Geoffrey was stunned. 'You're joking!'

'Oh no I ain't! Me and Lee were walking across the dance floor to come in here and I saw them, as plain as day. One

133

of them slipped her arms around the bloke and kissed him on the mouth. While she was doing it she lifted his wallet and passed it to the other one. They've obviously done it before because it was all over in a split second. In fact, if I'd have blinked I'd have missed it. The slags!'

Both girls looked at Geoffrey with frightened eyes. In Soho you could be striped up for less. No clubs liked their punters rolled. It brought them to the attention of the police – the last thing a hostess club needed.

'Where's the wallet now?'

'I've got it, Geoff. It's got over three hundred quid in it.'

He gave a low whistle.

'Look, Lee, go back in there and tell the punter that the girls had to go somewhere. I noticed as I passed through that Monique and Cynthia are still up in the meat seats. Bring them to him. They're good girls. Pretend to find the wallet under the table. Make a big thing out of it. Oh, you know what to do.'

'What about these two?' Garry nodded at the girls.

'Sling them out. Give them a slap, Garry, but don't go too far. All right.'

Garry nodded at him.

'When you've finished, get your arses upstairs. Mickey's waiting for you.'

He stormed out of the back bar and went to where Denise was standing. She was nearly fifty years old and weighed in at seventeen stone. Her face was heavily made up and she wore too much rhinestone jewellery. She had been a prostitute for over thirty years. Her bright orange hair was piled up high on her head, and somehow she had squeezed her enormous bulk into a lurex two-piece. Her huge pendulous breasts spilled over the top. She smelt of gin and Parma violets.

'I want a word with you, Denise. Garry and Lee just caught those scouse birds "doing a dolly".'

'Look, sonny, I ain't got eyes up me arse, you know. There's over thirty brasses in here. I can't watch them all.'

'Well, my advice to you, Denise, is to get some eyes put up there then! And in the back of your head. That slag

Shirelle was giving a punter a blow job earlier. Now either get your act together or you get another job! This is my last warning.'

He stormed off before she could answer him. Shrugging her ample shoulders, she cursed him in her head.

One of the girls on the meat seats had heard the exchange. She shouted to Denise: 'What's the matter then? You been a naughty girl?' All the other girls laughed.

Denise curled her lips back from her broken teeth. 'Oh, go fry your shite!'

The girl made a face at her and called out, 'She's a silver-tongued bastard, ain't she, girls?'

Denise picked up her Sobranie cigarette from an ashtray and pulled on it, stifling an urge to put it out on the other girl's face.

She'd murder that bloody Shirelle!

Detective Inspector Murphy was driving home to his house in Putney. Since his run-in with Maura Ryan he had been doing some snooping and what he had found out had given him food for thought. She was as clean as a whistle, never even been cautioned, but she had an Achilles heel and he had found out what it was. Tomorrow morning a certain young DC was going to get a shock. He smiled to himself. He quite liked young Petherick as well! He began to whistle a little tune. He would teach Maura Ryan a lesson she shouldn't forget. If there was one thing he hated, it was mouthy young women.

Maura got out of bed and began to get dressed. Terry lay for a while watching her. She was the sexiest girl he had ever known. The secret of her allure was the fact that she was completely unaware of it. She sat on the edge of the bed and smoothed her stockings up her legs. He pulled her backwards and kissed her, fondling her breasts.

'Is it my imagination or are your boobs getting bigger?'

Maura pulled away from him. 'Don't be so rude!' She pursed her lips. 'Come on, Tel, get dressed. You've got to run me home.'

135

He got off the bed and stretched himself lazily. 'I wish you didn't have to go.' His voice was childlike.

'Well, I have. And soon. So hurry up.' She picked up a pillow and threw it at him. He caught it and threw it back, knowing it would cause a pillow fight. Five minutes later they lay semi-naked on the bed, both trying to catch their breath.

'I love you, Terry.' Maura's voice was low.

'And I love you, Maura. More than you think.'

She smiled at him. She hoped that what he said was true, because tomorrow she was going to find out whether she was indeed pregnant. She bit her lip. There was going to be murder, she could feel it in her bones.

Michael arranged to see Lee on his own. His brother stood in front of him, his face pale. As far as he knew he had done nothing wrong.

'That right you give the old man a hammering today?'

Lee swallowed noisily. 'He was belting the old woman.'

Michael smiled one of his radiant smiles that seemed to light him up from inside. 'You did good, Lee. Remember this . . . you always look after the womenfolk. You never, ever let anyone hurt them, no matter who they are. I'm proud of you, Lee.'

Lee smiled with relief.

'I'll bung the old man a few bob tomorrow. He'll be as sweet as a nut. Now get yourself off home.'

Lee left the little office with his heart singing. He could hear the first few bars of 'Jailhouse Rock' and hurried down into the club. The girl who stripped to this particular record was a six foot amazon with olive skin, jet black hair, large brown eyes, and the biggest tits he had ever seen in his life! He settled down next to Benny, who being a thoughtful kind of boy had saved him a seat!

Chapter Ten

'Detective Constable Petherick, the big boss wants to see you.'

The WPC who gave Terry the message was grinning all over her face. He looked across his desk at Detective Sergeant Jones and made a little face. Far from being amused DS Jones just stared at him sadly and shook his head.

'You must have been barmy, lad, if you thought you could get away with it.'

Terry looked at him nonplussed. 'What are you on about?' His voice was genuinely bewildered.

Jones picked up some papers from in front of him and pretended to sort through them. 'Get yourself into the office, son. The Chief Inspector doesn't like to be kept waiting.'

Terry stood up. The WPC who had spoken to him was standing with one of her cronies and laughing. He had a sneaking feeling that the object of their amusement was himself. He racked his brains trying to think what he had done wrong. As far as he knew all the reports he had typed up were fine. He'd had two 'collars' in the last few weeks, and neither of them had been in any way abnormal. There was nothing that he could think of that would merit being seen by the Chief Inspector. He made his way across the crowded office to the glass partition that served as the Chief's office when he was down 'below' with his men and tapped on the door.

The Chief Inspector was deep in conversation with DI Dobin when he motioned with his hand for Terry to enter. He walked into the office tentatively, shutting the door quietly behind him. The two men stopped talking as he entered and the Chief told him to sit down. Both the Chief and the DI regarded him stonily. Terry sat down opposite the Chief. He could feel sweat coming out of every pore in his body. He wiped the palms of his hands on the front of his trousers. As far as he knew he had not done anything wrong. He was trying frantically to think of any slip-up he could have made when the Chief Inspector spoke.

'Well, Petherick. This is a nice kettle of fish, I must say.' His voice was hard. Never had Terry been reprimanded before, not even when he had inadvertently written down a suspect's numberplate wrongly and it had led the inquiry team to go to the house of a respected judge.

He cleared his throat. 'I'm sorry, sir. I'm not with you.'

'I've been wondering the same thing myself, young man.'

Terry watched his superior. He was not loved by his men but he was respected, which in Terry's mind was a much better thing. Chief Inspector Harris was an ample man who ran his squad along the lines of an army platoon. Indeed, he had been a colonel in the Lancers. He still sported large handlebar moustaches that had earned him the nickname 'Flying Officer Kite'. He was a large, extremely corpulent individual, much given to brightly coloured clothes that made him look like a confidence trickster. But for all that he was shrewd. Very shrewd indeed.

'I am sorry, sir. I really don't have any idea what you're talking about.'

The Chief looked up at DI Dobin, a smirk on his chubby red face.

'Hear that, Dobin? The cheeky young bugger's begging me pardon.'

Dobin nodded. Personally he thought that the Chief was an arsehole. He would not have given Murphy houseroom, but the Chief *was* the Chief, and if he saw fit to listen to Murphy . . . Dobin mentally shrugged. What could he do? He felt sorry for the boy. He was getting caught up in one of Murphy's little vendettas. Dobin had heard the chat in the canteen about how Maura Ryan had wiped the floor with him verbally. He had laughed, along with most of the

138

others. Now it seemed Murphy had done a bit of digging and had uncovered poor Petherick's association with the girl. He was to be Murphy's sacrificial lamb.

Most of the plainclothes police had had associations with villains' female relations. There was nothing like a twelve stretch to bring the Casanovas out of the woodwork, especially if the villain's wife was a nice-looking sort, and the majority of them were. He felt sorry for the boy in front of him.

'Seen much of your girlfriend, Petherick?' The Chief's voice dripped with sarcasm and innuendo.

'I saw her last night, sir.' Dobin closed his eyes. He couldn't look! The Chief linked his fingers together and leant on his desk.

'How long have you been seeing this Miss "Ryan"?' He stressed the 'Ryan' and suddenly Terry had a terrible sick feeling in the pit of his stomach. His mind was screaming 'No' but it was all becoming frighteningly clear.

Ryan . . . Ryan . . . Ryan . . . seemed to be swimming around in his head, like a rogue shark waiting to pounce on him.

He licked his lips.

'I have been seeing her for about nine months, sir.'

'Nine months. How thrilling for you. Taken you home to meet Mummy and Daddy and the boys, has she? Especially her brother Michael . . . I bet he just loved you, didn't he?'

'No, sir, she has not.' He stared at the men defiantly. He was in a kind of Limbo now. The officers in front of him had already tried and convicted him in their minds and he was quietly furious.

The Chief's voice rose a few octaves at the tone of Terry's voice.

'Well, young fellow me lad, you have a decision to make. I suppose you realise that her family between them have done more time than bloody Big Ben?'

'NO! No, sir . . . I didn't.'

The Chief's voice seemed to thunder from him. Terry and Dobin were aware that everyone outside had gone quiet and were listening to all that was taking place.

'Don't you take the piss out of me, sonny. I was doing this job when you were just a drunken twinkle in your father's eye!'

Suddenly it was all too much for Terry. The énormity of what he had found out, coupled with the humiliation of being bawled out in full earshot of his colleagues, took its toll. He lost his temper. He stood up and, putting his hands on the desk in front of him, palms flat, shouted in the Chief Inspector's face.

'I'm not taking the piss out of you . . . you can't take the piss out of shit! Surely *you* know that? You seem to know everything else. As for Maura Ryan, it never occurred to me to run her through Interpol. Let's face it, if every bit of skirt that got pulled around this place was checked out for credibility, there wouldn't be any time to catch criminals. And another thing: Maura Ryan is a decent law-abiding girl who never mentioned her family. Now, I might add, I bloody well know why!'

He stood staring at his boss, flecks of spittle at the corners of his mouth. Somewhere in the distance he heard the sound of clapping. He guessed, rightly, that it was his partner, Jones. Obviously the whole of their slanging match had been witnessed. He felt his heart sink. He had just thrown away his career, all that he had worked for. He felt an insane urge to bang his head repeatedly on the desk in front of him.

DI Dobin was having trouble keeping his face straight. He wished he had the nerve to clap the boy. It was about time someone gave the sanctimonious old bastard a taste of his own medicine. Then, to the amazement of everyone, the Chief Inspector actually smiled. His large moustaches seemed to crawl upwards towards his eyelids and he was showing small, even white teeth.

'Good lad! The fact that you lost your rag shows me that you're not guilty of anything. You must understand that the last thing we need here is a bent copper. I know they exist, but please God not in my division.'

He sat back in his chair, placing his fingers together and resting his elbows on the arms of his chair. He stared at

Terry for a while before he continued speaking. Then his voice was low and adamant.

'It's either her or the force. You realise that, don't you? I can't have one of my men running around with the sister of the biggest villain London's ever known. It would cast doubt, not only on your integrity but on the integrity of your colleagues. You can understand that, surely?'

All the fight had left Terry and he dropped into his chair, defeated. He nodded. Dobin handed him a cigarette and he took it gratefully. Taking his matches from his pocket he lit up, aware that his hands were shaking.

Dobin spoke for the first time. His gravelly voice was quiet. 'Has she ever asked you about your work, Terry?'

'Never, sir. In fact, she hated me even mentioning it. Now I know why. It's all falling into place. Why I could never pick her up from her house . . . never phone her there . . . Oh, lots of things.'

The Chief was sorry for the boy.

'Well, lad, I'll give you twenty-four hours to make your choice. I hope you decide to stay with us.' He held out his hand to show that the meeting was over. Terry shook hands with both men and left the office. In the main office, the hubbub of conversation had begun again. A few of his friends smiled at him and patted his back. WPC Lomax, who had brought him his summons, winked at him saucily. Terry ignored everyone and went to his desk. He picked up his jacket.

'I'm going home, Jonesy. I don't feel very well.'

'Go home, lad, and come in tomorrow. He's given you an ultimatum then, has he?'

'Yeah.' Terry's voice was tired. He needed time to think. Away from this place.

'Well, if it's any consolation, son, I think you have the makings of a good copper. Don't throw away a perfectly good career for a piece of skirt. They're never worth it.' Jones's wife had been one of an army of long-suffering women who, faced with the loneliness of being a policeman's wife, had got herself an alternative wage packet.

141

Jonesy still carried a torch for her though he would never admit it.

'Thanks for the vote of confidence. God knows I need it at the moment.'

'That slag Murphy had told everyone before he saw the old man. Never could stomach the bastard. There was talk once . . . a few years ago now . . . that he was in on the Train Robbery. Nothing was ever proven against him, mind, but he's had a hard job living it down, I can tell you. What's this Maura Ryan like?'

'She is one of the sweetest girls you are ever likely to meet. I just can't believe that she is in any way related to that shower.'

'Well, you know what they say, son. You can pick your friends, but not your relatives. I reckon the bloke who said that had never been in the police force.'

Terry tried to smile. 'See you tomorrow.' He slipped on his jacket and left the building. He sat outside in his car for ten minutes before pulling away, his mind screaming one question: Why?

Margaret and Maura walked into the little chemist's. They had both had the day off work and had spent the morning walking aimlessly around the shops. It was twenty minutes before they plucked up the courage to enter the chemist's shop, standing outside waiting for it to empty of people. Now they were finally inside, Maura felt as if she wanted to scream. An Asian man stood behind the counter.

'I . . . I would like the result of my test, please.'

The little man smiled, showing decaying teeth. 'Surely you would, madam. And the name?' He spoke with the inbred politeness particular to the Pakistani race.

'Miss . . . I mean, Mrs Ryan.'

He grinned at her. Oh, they were all Mrs in this country, he thought. Even those who were not. He went into the back of the shop and looked through the test results that had arrived that morning. He walked back into the shop and looked at Maura pityingly before he said, 'I am pleased to tell you that the test was positive.'

It was the standard reply that was hardly ever what the woman wanted to hear. 'You are three months pregnant.'

Maura's face dropped. Under normal circumstances she and Margaret would have had a laugh at this man's expense. Mimicked his voice to each other and remarked on his rotten teeth, saying he had a mouth full of dogends, the standard expression for tooth decay. Now she very much doubted if she would ever laugh again. She had a terrible feeling, as if her head was filling up with hot air. She felt much too hot, and prickles of warmth crept up her back to her neck. She was having trouble breathing. She put her hand up to pull her blouse away from her throat . . . As she fainted away on to the floor the last thing she heard was Marge's voice, coming from somewhere in the distance, high and croaky.

'Oh my Gawd! The bleeding shock's killed her! She's dropped down dead!'

Maura woke up on a little couch in the back of the chemist's shop. As she opened her eyes and took a deep breath she vaguely wondered how on earth the two tiny people looking at her anxiously had managed to carry her in there. Margaret's face had tears and mascara running down it.

'Oh, Maws, you gave me such a fright . . . I thought you'd copped it.'

The little chemist pointed at a cup of hot sweet tea beside her. 'Come along, madam. Be drinking it up, it will make you feel much better. It's the best thing for shock. And it's a terrible shock you had, I am thinking.' He looked at the two girls closely.

Maura pushed herself upright on the little couch and picked up the cup of tea. Her dress had somehow risen up over her thighs and she noticed the chemist staring at her legs. Hastily she tried to pull her dress back down, spilling her tea as she did so.

'I am having a friend who can help ladies like yourself . . . young ladies who cannot tell their mummies and daddies what has befallen them. I will write his name and address down and give it to you. Tell the man that Mr Patel sent you. It will cost you only eighty-five pounds. That is very cheap price.'

He hurried back into the shop. The two girls stared at his retreating back. Maura felt as if she was trapped in some kind of nightmare that would never end. She glanced around the room. It was chock-a-block with boxes and packs of shampoo, disinfectant, bleach, and all manner of weird-looking instruments. The only nice thing about it was that it smelt lovely . . . of pine-scented bath cubes and perfume.

The little man rushed back in with a piece of paper. 'This man is very very good, madam. A very nice man indeed.'

Maura took the piece of paper, because she didn't know what else to do, and placed it in her shoulderbag.

The man kept chattering on until finally Maura put down the tea and stood up. She felt absolutely terrible and as if he read her mind he pointed to a small door in the corner of the room. Entering the tiny toilet, Maura retched for what seemed like ages, the dank and musty smell of the carpet tiles mingled with the overpowering smell of urine seeming to spur her on. Cold droplets of perspiration were standing out on her forehead and she wiped them away with the back of her hand. She staggered out to the smell of the pine bath cubes.

'Come on, Maws, we better make a move.' Margaret took her arm and, thanking the little man, they left the shop. They walked for a while in silence before Margaret said: 'You should have seen that skinny little sod trying to lift you on to that couch . . . If I hadn't have been so worried, I'd have pissed myself laughing!'

Maura, seeing in her mind's eye the incongruousness of the situation, started to laugh. Margaret laughed with her, and soon the two girls began to scream with laughter. Passersby paused to stare at them, smiling themselves and thinking it must be a great joke. Maura's laughter was tinged with hysteria. They held on to one another, screeching, until Maura's laughter turned to deep racking sobs.

'What am I gonna do, Marge?'

Margaret led her into a small coffee shop and sat her

down. She ordered a pot of coffee from a fat bored waitress and went back to her friend. When she was seated Maura repeated her question.

'What the hell am I gonna do? There's gonna be murders committed over this.'

'There's not a lot you *can* do, Maws, except tell everyone. People are funny like that. Remember Gina Blenkinsop? She got in the club by some bloke who had it on his toes. Well, she had her baby and now her mum and dad absolutely dote on the poor little thing.'

Maura snapped at her friend, 'Oh, yeah? I can just see Mickey, can't you? Holding the baby at the christening . . . every villain in London on one side of the Church and the best part of Vine Street nick on the other. Use your bloody head, Marge. This baby will be as welcome as a pork chop in a synagogue.'

The waitress brought over their pot of coffee. She laid out the cups and saucers and the two girls sat quietly until she had finished. When she went Margaret tried again. 'I still can't understand why you never went on the pill.'

Maura sipped her coffee and banged the cup back in the saucer.

'Oh, don't be so bloody ridiculous! How could I go to O'Reilly? He would have been straight round my mother's!'

Margaret swallowed her temper. Maura was in one of her moods and in fairness, Marge admitted, she would be the same if the boot was on the other foot. She took a deep breath.

'I told you to go to that doctor in Hampstead where I go. He'll give you slimming pills . . . anything you want, as long as you can pay.'

Maura screwed up her eyes and stared at Margaret. Her weight was a touchy subject. 'Are you being bleeding funny?'

'Of course not! Anyway, slimming pills would be a bit of a waste of time now, don't you think?'

She looked meaningfully at Maura's waist. The look brought Maura back to reality and she wailed: 'Oh, Marge, what am I gonna do!' Her voice held a plaintive note. She put her hands on her belly. She had a little life in there, and somewhere inside her she was pleased. She loved children. Her brother's daughter Carla had always been like a little sister to her. She had never resented the amount of time she spent at the house. Maura was aware that Janine did not really like her only child, but it had never mattered because Carla was doted on by herself and her brothers. Now she had a child growing in her own body and knew that it would be hated, despised, because its father was a policeman. The biggest cloud on her horizon was not Terry's reaction but Mickey's. He would want to kill Terry stone dead just for sleeping with his sister, and when he found out that Terry was a policeman . . . she felt sick with fright. He would kill Terry, then herself – in that order. He would take it as a personal affront. She closed her eyes tightly to block out her brother's image.

'I tell you what I'm going to do, Marge. I'm going to go and see Terry and tell him everything. About the baby . . . the boys . . . everything. He loves me, I know he does. We could go away together somewhere. I know that he'll stand by me. He's got to!' Her voice was full of panic. Margaret wondered who she was trying to convince with her talk about going away.

'I hope he stands by you, Maws.' Her voice sounded sceptical.

Maura wailed, 'Oh, don't put the mockers on me, Marge! As if I haven't got enough troubles.'

Margaret stretched her hand across the table and held on to Maura's. Squeezing it tightly, she smiled at her best friend. They had come a long way together since the fight outside their school. She just wished that she had as much faith in Terry Petherick. She liked him well enough, but couldn't see him standing by Maura, somehow. She might not have any qualifications but she was cute enough to realise that Terry Petherick would not want relations like the Ryans in his job. She said a quick Hail Mary, as she used to when she was a child, and prayed that Maura would not come unstuck. Though another part of her mind said: She already has.

Terry was sitting in his flat in Islington. The chair he was sitting on had been a present from Maura. They had been strolling through Camden Market when they had seen it. It was large, high-backed, and upholstered in green leather. They had homed in on it together, both of the same mind. Instead of a settee they would have the chair, then they could cuddle up in it together. Something they had since done many times. They had bartered with the stall owner for it, laughing and joking until a compromise had been reached. For the grand total of six pounds they had got their 'loveseat'. Maura had then bought some material, a riot of green and blue brocade, and had made the curtains for the windows. He remembered thinking as he watched her sewing them: She's a natural homemaker.

Over the months they had been together he had fallen deeply in love with her. Her smile, her cheeky quips, her long legs and incredible breasts . . . Now he had to decide whether that love was strong enough. All day a little voice had been nagging at him, telling him that if he really loved her he would have thrown in his job there and then . . . Oh, he had defended her, but not vehemently enough to tell his boss where to stick his job, and logic told him that's what he would have done if he really, really loved her.

He stood up and went to the window. It was cold outside and a solitary little boy was kicking a football around the road. He turned abruptly from the window and walked into the bedroom. He stared at the bed. Maura had really abandoned herself there. She had shocked him at times with the intensity of her loving. She wasn't a girl who would give herself lightly, he knew that. Was that why he was feeling such a bastard? Because deep inside he knew that there was no competition really. Maura Ryan was an also-ran.

He went back into the small living room and opened the bottle of Teacher's he had bought on the way home from work. What he needed was a stiff drink. He poured himself a large Scotch. He needed something to numb his mind for what he was thinking of doing. He checked himself. What

147

he was *going* to do. He had decided then, and not even realised it.

He took a large gulp of his Scotch, grateful for the burning sensation it created in his throat. All his life he had had one ambition: to be a policeman. He had studied long and hard with that one thought in mind. Now he had to choose between the job he loved and the woman he loved, and the woman had lost. He had to admit that to himself . . . Oh God!

If she had been anyone's sister but Michael Ryan's! The thought of Michael brought his heart leaping into his mouth. He took another long pull of his whisky and sat back in the armchair. Everyone knew about Michael Ryan and his brothers – they were notorious. There was talk of their being involved not just with drugs and whores, but arms too. Not just the odd sawn-off either, but high velocity rifles, rocket launchers, and anything else that the British Army wouldn't miss. Jesus Christ, how did he ever get personally involved with all this! He was starting to sweat. He had before him the awesome task of giving Michael Ryan's baby sister the Big E. He put the glass he was holding to his forehead. The enormity of it all was breaking into his consciousnes.

All day he had been worried about Maura . . . Her reaction. How to let her down gently. In his worried state he had concentrated wholly on Maura. Now the thought of her brother invaded his mind. He rolled the glass along his skin, savouring the coldness as he became unbearably hot.

He sat back in the chair. Everything in the room seemed to be mocking him. Even the TV set in the corner. Once again the dreadful feeling of foreboding pervaded his being. Michael Ryan would not like his sister being with a policeman, he would lay money on that.

He closed his eyes again. In his mind he could see Michael standing over him, threatening him with bodily harm. Suddenly he tensed. He could hear the scraping noise of a key going into a lock. His whole body was taut. In his mind's eye he could see Michael Ryan letting himself into his flat. He sat in the chair paralysed with fright, the knuckles of his hand white as he clutched the glass. He heard the door swing open with its familiar creaking groan. Every nerve in his body was jangling. For the first time he knew the smell of fear. It seemed to rise up into his nostrils, an overpowering aroma of hot sticky stale sweat. Supposing Ryan had taken the key off Maura? They could have been seen out together. A hundred different thoughts whirled around in his head, leaving him breathless and dizzy . . .

Instead of Michael's heavy footfall, he heard the familiar clatter of Maura's heels as she stepped into the hall on to the worn linoleum. He collapsed into the chair like a rag doll. A thin trickle of sweat slipped down his forehead, over his eyebrow and down on to his cheek. A feeling of euphoria swept over him. It was Maura . . . Maura . . . Her name bounced around inside his head like a crazy pattern in a child's kaleidoscope. She walked into the lounge and smiled at him.

'You all right? You look as if you've seen a ghost.'

He stood up awkwardly. Placing his glass on the small coffee table he went to her. Maura was in the process of putting her key back into her bag. Reaching out, he took it from her gently and slipped it into his trouser pocket. Maura looked at him.

'What did you do that for?' Her big luminous eyes held a hint of fear. He tried to smile and succeeded only in grimacing.

As he looked at her he didn't see her lovely trusting face. Terry saw only Michael Ryan. A very angry Michael Ryan.

'I think that we're getting a bit too serious, love.' It sounded lame even to his own ears. 'I think we should cool it for a while. We're both young . . .' His voice trailed off. He felt so bad he could not meet her eyes. Maura just stood there thunderstruck.

'I beg your pardon?' Her voice sounded small and hurt.

Terry still could not bring himself to look at her so he walked back over to the window.

'It's quite simple really, Maura . . . I don't want to get

149

involved right now. I want to be free. Go out with other women. I don't want to get tied down just yet.'

'I see.' Her voice·was flat. Pride had taken over. 'And just when did you come to this earth-shattering conclusion, may I ask? Only I was under the impression that you was my bloke . . . My chap, if you like that expression better. Now I find that I was just a screw.' She stormed across the room to him, pulling him around to face her with considerable strength. 'Let me tell you something, Terry bloody "I want to see other women" Petherick! I'm . . .'

She stopped herself there and then. How could she tell him about the baby? Her eyes darted around the room, looking for a chance of escape. It was all going wrong. All the words she had practised on her way over here dried up inside her head. The picture she had built up in her mind of Terry taking her in his arms and whispering that they would always be together, no matter what, faded in front of her eyes like chalk paintings in the rain. He was dumping her. He had had his bit of fun and now she was ancient history.

The fight left her as quickly as it had come. The urge to rip his face open with her nails dissolved along with all her dreams and hopes. She felt the hot salty tears come and forced them away. If she had to go, she would go with dignity. She glanced around the room. She had experienced so much pleasure in this little flat, the result of which was inside her at this very moment. Should she tell him? Should she scream it out into his face? Make him take the responsibility? Even as the words formed in her mind she knew that she would never say them to him. She would never tell him about the child. Having him on sufferance would be far worse than not having him at all. She bent down wearily and picked her bag up off the floor. She had not even realised that she had dropped it. She turned to leave and his voice stayed her.

'Believe me, Maws, I am really sorry about this.'

His voice sounded so sincere. She laughed bitterly. He had the knack of sounding sincere. Last night in bed he had told her that he loved her, and had sounded sincere. The lying, two-faced bastard!

Without facing him, she said: 'Terry.'

'Yes?' His heart was breaking.

Gathering up every ounce of strength and hatred she could muster she turned to face him, launching herself at him with arms flying. She felt his skin tear beneath her nails. Felt the pure rush of pleasure as she made him hurt, as she was hurting. As quickly as the attack began, it stopped. The sudden urge of energy left her drained.

'You can fuck off, Petherick!' She saw his hand go up to his face. Four deep grooves on his cheek were bleeding simultaneously. She smiled at him, a nasty evil smile, and pointed her finger at him. Her long scarlet-painted nails made him flinch.

'I never thought I would ever say this to you. You're a dirty rotten swine. You took me and you used me. I trusted you, Terry.' Her voice broke. 'But I tell you something now, boy. The day will come when you will want me . . . when you will need me. You'll live to regret this day, because if you live to one hundred years old you'll never find anyone to love you like I do.'

With that she turned away from him and left the flat, slamming the front door behind her.

Terry watched her leave. In his heart he knew that what she said was true. She deserved much better than the treatment he had given her. She was his first love, the first woman to meet him on an equal plane, and he had destroyed her with a few simple words. He was not surprised to feel that he was crying. The tears were running into the scratches on his face, making them sting. He had a terrible feeling that although he had destroyed Maura, somewhere along the line he had also destroyed himself. He saw droplets of blood falling on to his shirt, their deep crimson colour spreading over the material.

Suddenly he couldn't let her go. He ran to the window. Pulling back the net curtain, he looked out on to the street. She was on the other side of the road, her head tucked into her coat. He knew that she too was crying. Fumbling with the ancient catch on the window he finally opened it and leant out, calling her at the top of his voice.

'Maura . . . Maura . . . come back!'

His voice carried to her on the wind.

He knew that she could hear him, saw her hesitate before walking away faster, her white-blonde head tucked even further into the collar of her coat. He watched her until she turned the corner, the hum of the traffic grating on his ears.

Pulling his head back inside, he closed the window. The once friendly little room looked alien now, and hostile. Everywhere he looked was Maura Ryan . . . He could see her flitting about, putting up the curtains, making sandwiches or curled up with him on their special armchair. He could breathe in her perfume and taste her musky body. She was everywhere around him. He sat in the chair.

He was still sitting there thinking about her when he passed out much later in the evening. He had drunk the whole bottle of Scotch.

Maura was devastated. If someone had told her that Terry would dump her like that she would have laughed at them. 'I want to see other women.' Those words kept echoing in her head. They would stay with her for the rest of her life. Anything he could have said, even that he hated her, would not have had the profound effect that those few words had. Well, let him see other women! She hoped to God that he caught a terrible disease from them.

She passed the Angel and made her way along the Pentonville Road. The fact remained that she was still pregnant. She had an urge to go and drown herself but dismissed it. It was getting dark and she wandered aimlessly, trying to figure out what on earth to do. All around her were couples, holding hands, laughing, kissing. She pushed her hands further into her pockets and carried on walking, letting her legs carry her wherever they wanted to go. Terry's face was fresh in her mind, his softness and his tenderness welcome memories to her in the cold evening wind.

She found herself at Kings Cross Station and was surprised at how far she had walked. A black cab came along the road and she hailed it, telling the driver to take her to

Notting Hill. She sat in the back, huddled into a corner of the seat, staring listlessly out of the window at the rapidly moving landscape. A lone tear rolled down her face and she wiped it away impatiently. She was done with crying, she had more important things to think about.

The cab driver looked over his shoulder at her and asked cheerfully, 'Whereabouts in Notting Hill, love?'

'Lancaster Road, please.' She wouldn't go home just yet. She would go to Margaret's. Margaret would know what to do. She rested her head on the window, her breath coming in little gasps that barely managed to create steam on the glass surface. She felt so lonely, so frightened. Her bottom lip quivered as she tried to stop the tears of frustration and rage. She loved him so much!

'You all right, love?' The driver's voice was concerned.

She sat up in her seat and saw him watching her in the mirror above his windscreen.

She gave him a small childish smile. 'No, actually, I'm not.'

He had a broad good-natured face. 'You listen to me, girl. If it's boyfriend trouble that's put that frown on your boat, remember this. Us blokes ain't worth it!' He laughed at his own wit.

Maura looked back out of the window, then forced a large smile on to her face. 'Don't I bloody know it!'

Chapter Eleven

Michael Ryan was in the Valbonne nightclub in Kingly Street having a quick drink with his boyfriend, Jonny Fenwick. It was a well-known fact that Michael Ryan was a 'brown hatter'. Not that anyone would call him that to his face. Far from taking anything away from his street credibility it enhanced it, because queers were known to be nasty bastards. They had a cruel twist to their nature and the best thing to do was to keep on the good side of them. There was no queer bashing when Michael Ryan hit the streets. He also took a woman now and again which further puzzled his friends and adversaries alike. It was proof of his ever changing habits. He treated his friends like he treated his lovers. He could go one way or the other.

At the moment Michael was besotted by Jonny Fenwick's youth. He was a beautiful boy with thick blond curly hair and large, wide-spaced grey eyes. Mickey had put him up in a flat and paid him an allowance. He was Jonny Ryan now. Michael owned him, lock, stock and barrel. Jonny loved it, and loved being seen with Michael. Tonight, though, he was in a dilemma. He had heard a bit of gossip today concerning Michael's sister and was not sure whether to tell him or not. He certainly didn't want any comebacks off Michael if what he said turned out to be false. But Michael was in fine fettle tonight, full of laughter and jokes, and Jonny decided to risk it. Not only that, but that bitch Tommy was looking at him all gooey-eyed and Michael was loving it, so Jonny would use it as an excuse to get him away from the bar *and* Tommy! He tapped Michael's arm.

'What, mate?' Michael's voice was warm.

'It's a bit private, Mickey. I heard a bit of news today . . .
I don't want to talk about it here.' He looked meaningfully
at Tommy and pursed his lips. Michael nodded.

'Come and sit down then.'

He picked up their drinks and led Jonny over to an empty
table away from listening ears. Jonny sat down and crossed
his legs, placing his hands one on top of the other on his
knee. He leant towards Michael theatrically.

'It's about a member of your family. But first I want your
solemn promise that you won't go ape shit in here.'

Michael's eyes narrowed. 'I won't lose my temper. Now
tell me what you heard.'

Jonny flicked his hair out of his eyes with a girlish gesture
and said, 'I asked you to promise me, Michael.'

He gritted his teeth. 'For fuck's sake, Jonny, spit it out. I
ain't got all night.'

Jonny licked his lips nervously. He wasn't at all sure
that he was doing the right thing now. Michael spoke
of his little sister as a mixture of the Virgin Mary and
the Queen. Either way, she was completely beyond
reproach.

'It's about your sister . . . She's got herself a boyfriend.'

Michael relaxed. 'Is that all? Who?'

Jonny took a sip of his gin and tonic before answering.
'It's a policeman from Vine Street.'

Michael looked as if he had been hit by a bus.

'A what!'

'Keep your voice down! Do you want the whole world to
know? He's a young Detective Constable. Remember my
friend little Mo, the fat queen from Kensington?' Michael
nodded. 'Well, apparently he has a few friends at Vine
Street, though myself I'd call them customers. Anyway,
one of them told him. It seems a bigwig there . . . some
bloke called Murphy . . . pulled the rug out from under him
today. Told his Chief Inspector that he was seeing her . . .
your sister. Apparently there was a big to-do about it.
Anyway, little Mo rang me. And being a good boy, I
thought you ought to know.'

Michael was staring at Jonny without seeing him. His

face was dark with fury. The conniving little bitch! She'd been knocking about with a filth right under his nose. He felt a blinding compulsion to wring her neck.

'Phone this little Mo and find out who his customers are. Names, ranks, the works. Tell him from me that if he decides to become coy I'll break his fucking neck.'

Jonny nodded. 'All right, Mickey. First thing in the morning.'

Michael was in the throes of a violent rage. Maura had never even brought a fellow home. A small rational thought broke into his reverie. It said to him, Well, she wouldn't, would she? Of course not. She had a bit more sense than to bring an old Bill straight into her family of criminals. He could easily walk out of this club and smash her to a pulp. At least one good thing had come of it. He had the means to blackmail a few of the shirtlifters on the force. He consoled himself with that thought.

'Look, Jon, I have to get around to me own club now. I'll see you later on tonight.'

Jonny smiled his best smile. He had been the teller of very bad news and now he was scared. Michael was capable of taking the whole thing out on him.

'All right, Mickey love.' He fluttered his eyelashes as a woman might. Watching him, Michael experienced one of his lightning changes of mood. He laughed softly, guessing what was going through the boy's mind. Wagging his finger in Jonny's face, he said: 'Behave yourself, you!'

To which Jonny answered seriously, 'I don't have much choice do I?'

Michael squeezed his shoulder affectionately and left the club.

As he made his way to Dean Street he thought about what Jonny had told him. The doorman of the Pink Pussycat hailed him and he waved back halfheartedly. His arrogant, strutting walk and dark countenance were familiar features around Soho. Unlike most of his contemporaries Michael didn't feel the need to be surrounded by minders. His immense size, coupled with the fact that he was known to carry a piece, was warning enough for any would-be assassins. Since Michael had taken over as the Baron of the West End he had not had one serious threat. He was, to all intents and purposes, the business – the highest accolade that a villain could be awarded. As he walked to his club he was hailed by touts, prostitutes, bouncers and pimps. He crossed Shaftesbury Avenue into Dean Street itself and slowed his pace. If Maura was knocking about with a filth he would kill her. He hadn't fought tooth and nail since he was seventeen to have his little baby sister blow it all wide open for him. He gritted his teeth in temper. He had worshipped her, would have given her the earth if she had asked for it. But he wouldn't allow her to have this bloke. Never! He would find out everything he could about this copper and then he would nip it in the bud. He stormed into Le Buxom at ten-fifteen.

The club was just picking up. A few stray punters were having a drink. They were 'weekend warriors' – the nickname given to men who saved up their meagre earnings as civil servants or bank clerks and came up West once a month for drink, sex and excitement. An experienced tom could tell them a mile off from their off-the-peg suits to their Freeman, Hardy and Willis shoes. The older women gravitated to them, secure in the knowledge that it would be an easy lay. These men were too scared of their wives and the police ever to cause any trouble. They were seldom rough, and because they had to make their money stretch were hardly choosy. The only bugbear for the club was the fact that they only ever bought one bottle of champagne, making it last all night, until the final stripper had departed. A weekend warrior was the only sort of punter who provided the women with an opportunity actually to drink the stuff.

Michael looked around the club. It was half empty. He noticed Benny sitting at a table with one of the younger girls, a pretty little piece known affectionately as Pussy. Despite his anger Michael smiled. Benny had a permanent hard on. As soon as a new hostess arrived, Benny was there, cock standing to attention. There was a long-standing joke in all the rival clubs that without Benny, Le Buxom would have gone bankrupt years ago. Michael stood by the meat seats. For once the girls there were subdued. He had that effect on people. The girls rarely spoke to him unless he addressed them personally. The stench of cheap perfume was overpowering. Michael nodded to them and made his way out into the foyer and upstairs to the offices.

Geoffrey, Leslie and Garry were already in there having a drink. He greeted them and poured himself a large brandy. Sitting behind his desk, he looked directly at Garry. If anyone knew Maura's whereabouts it would be him.

'Do you know if our Maura's got a boyfriend?'

Garry looked at his brother in bewilderment. 'What if she has? It's none of our business.'

Michael was out of his seat and round the desk, knocking Leslie flying out of his chair as he pushed past him to get to Garry. He grabbed him by his shirt front, pulling him up out of the chair with considerable strength.

'"None of our business" you say . . . I heard a whisper on the street tonight that our sister is knocking about with a filth!' He threw Garry back into his seat. His temper was seething. If he didn't get some kind of answer soon he would explode.

Leslie stared at Garry, who was gasping for breath. There was no doubt about it . . . Mickey was an awesome bastard. There was no one to touch him. Mickey was the business. Well the business.

'Who told you all this then, Mick?' Geoffrey tried unsuccessfully to defuse the situation.

'Never you mind who bloody well told me! It's enough that I've heard. I want you two –' he pointed at Leslie and Garry – 'to find out how true it is.'

Geoffrey tried again. 'It's not definite then? What I mean is . . .'

Michael screwed up his face and bellowed at his brother, 'Oh, for fuck's sake, Geoffrey . . . I don't want a government White Paper on it all. I just want the facts! Now do what I fucking well told you to do!'

Leslie and Garry scrambled from the room. When Michael was in one of his tempers, you did not argue with him.

Geoffrey poured himself a brandy. When Michael was like this, it was best not to rock the boat in any way.

Michael swallowed his own brandy in a gulp and grimaced. 'So what do you think, Geoffrey?' His voice was once again steady.

'Who told you?'

'Jonny actually.' He sounded wary.

'In that case . . . no way. Not our Maws.' His voice was dismissive. He did not like Jonny. He did not like the fact that Michael was homosexual, though he would never say it outright.

Michael guessed, rightly, exactly what had gone through Geoffrey's mind.

'I know you don't like Jonny. That's tough. But I'll tell you this much – for all his faults he ain't a liar. And there's one thing that seems to have escaped your notice . . . most people don't even know we have a sister.'

Geoffrey digested this bit of logic, watching Michael sitting at his desk chewing his thumbnail. Geoffrey knew from experience that Michael could sit like that for hours. Sighing, he poured himself another drink. He hoped for Maura's sake that what they had heard wasn't true.

Downstairs, Leslie and Garry had told Benny what had happened. He was still sitting with Pussy, except now the night had lost some of its enchantment. Sensing that she had lost his attention, the girl stroked his thigh, pouting at him prettily. He smiled at her with a crafty little grin guaranteed to melt the hardest of hearts.

'Pussy.' His voice was caressing.

'Yes?' She looked into his eyes. Their blue depths mirrored her features.

'Let's go, shall we?'

'All right then.' They stood up together. Benny wanted out of here before Michael decided to rope him in on everything. There were many things he would do for his eldest brother, but even he drew the line at a witch hunt on his only sister. Gathering up their things, they left the club. Hailing a cab outside, Benny jumped in, pulling Pussy in after him. There was a little hotel just off Leicester Square where he could hole up with her for the night. And that's what he intended to do. The thought of ringing home and warning his sister crossed his mind, but he soon dismissed it. He didn't want any part of this whatsoever.

The girl snuggled up to him in the back of the taxi, and for the first time in his life Benny wondered if he would be able to get it up.

The way he was feeling, he would need Charles Atlas to lift it for him.

Garry and Leslie got out of their car. They were going to see another policeman. This was their second visit in two hours. The first had been to a young PC who had been as bewildered as they were. They had left no wiser to their sister's antics than they had been before. It had cost them twenty quid to keep him quiet, but it was worth it. He was going to keep his ear to the ground. The man they were going to see now was a sergeant in Notting Dale police station. He had been on the Ryans' payroll for about five years. Well, now he could earn his money.

They knocked on his front door. It was nearly twelve-thirty. The small terraced house was in darkness. A light came on upstairs and Sergeant Potter's grizzled head appeared from a window.

'Who the bloody hell is it?'

He peered myopically down at them.

'It's Leslie Ryan. I wanna see you, Sarge.' Leslie's voice was a theatrical whisper.

Grunting and moaning, the old man retreated back inside the room. Leslie and Garry heard him clumping down his stairs. The hall light went on and the door was opened.

'What the hell are you playing at? Coming round here at this time of night?'

Garry and Leslie walked into the hallway.

'We've got a few questions, and we want you to give us the answers.'

The old man looked at them maliciously. He had a sneaking suspicion that he knew what they were going to ask. 'Would the questions be about your sister by any chance?'

'That's right, Sarge. What do you know about her then?' Garry sounded menacing and the man realised that he had forgotten for a moment just who he was dealing with. He licked his lips.

He started talking in a self-righteous tone of voice. 'Now you listen to me . . . I didn't know anything until today, I take oath on that. A friend of mine who's now at Vine Street gave me a ring at Notting Dale. He told me that there had been a bit of malarkey with one of the plainclothes there. He got hauled over the coals because he was knock – I mean, seeing your sister.'

He was fiddling with the cord of his plaid dressing gown, his short stubby fingers tobacco-stained. Leslie and Garry stood quietly staring at him.

The man began to babble. 'Honestly, boys, I didn't think you would be interested in it. I mean . . . I assumed you knew about it all.' He was getting desperate.

'What's the bloke's name?'

'The bloke who rang me or your sister's fancy man? Sorry, I mean boyfriend.'

Garry closed his eyes wearily. He spoke slowly and deliberately. 'Who was the man who rang you up?'

'Oh, it was an old friend.'

'Listen, you!' Garry pushed him across the hallway. 'I just want his name, not his fucking life story. Now who is he?'

The old man had fallen back on the stairs and sat there watching the two boys. Upstairs he could hear his wife getting out of bed. Her high-pitched, nasal voice floated down the stairs. 'Who's that down there, Albert? Sounds like an 'erd of bloody elephants from up here.'

He groaned. That was all he needed, his wife awake and sticking her oar in where it wasn't wanted.

'No one, dear. It's police business. You go back to sleep.'

162

'Well, just you tell them to keep their great big galloping feet off of my clean floor.'

'I will.'

Leslie had an urge to laugh and stifled it. 'The name of your informant?'

'It was a bloke called Jones . . . He's a DS at Vine Street.'

'Is he reliable? I mean, if he said something was true, would that be the case?'

'Oh, yeah. He's a rare one, old Jonesy. If he told me he had seen old Nick himself I'd believe him. He's not a spinner.'

Garry snorted. 'That makes a change in the police force. I thought you needed a degree in being a lying bastard before they would have you?'

Albert pursed his lips. Even though he was on the take, he still took a pride in being a policeman.

'What was the bloke's name who's been seeing my sister?'

'Petherick. Detective Constable Terence Petherick.'

'That's all we wanted to know. You can go back to bed with old vinegar tits now.'

As they left the house, Leslie slipped the old man a ten pound note.

'Listen, Sarge, we want his address. If you can get it there'll be a pony in it for you, all right?'

'OK, son.' All his animosity was forgotten now. He could do a lot with twenty-five quid. Anyway, he reasoned, they'd get their information one way or the other so he might as well feather his nest while he had the chance. 'I'll keep me ear to the ground. Don't you worry.' He closed the door behind them.

His wife's voice came once more from above him. 'Al . . . bert!' She had the knack of singing his name out in such a way that her voice carried for about three miles.

'Oh, shut your row, you stupid old bitch!'

His wife sat in her bed, her face a mask of Pond's cold cream and abject disbelief. Her curlers were placed strategically around her head like a crash helmet. She hitched up her ample chest, her mouth settling to a grim line. A malevolent gleam in her eye, she pulled the covers off her. Swinging her legs out of bed, she placed her feet in her carpet slippers, stood up and picked up the heavy chamber pot from underneath the bed. She walked out of the bedroom on to the landing. As her husband reached the top of the stairs she flung the contents into his face . . . that would teach him to answer her back!

She clumped back into her bedroom leaving her husband clutching a soggy ten pound note in his hand. He spat. Only his Gladys would have the nerve to empty an 'Edgar Allen' all over him. Sod them bloody Ryans! If they hadn't got him out of bed none of this would have happened.

Garry and Leslie drove back to Dean Street. It was just on one o'clock. They arrived at the club at one-thirty-five. The balloon went up at one-forty.

Maura was lying in bed wide awake. It was nearly two-thirty in the morning and she was no nearer sleep than she had been at nine o'clock when she had got into bed. Her mind was turning in circles, her thoughts drifting away on different tangents as she tried to see a way out of her predicament. There was none. She had talked everything over with Margaret, but neither girl could find a solution to her problem. A problem that was getting bigger in Maura's mind with every passing second.

She was in a quandary. If she told her family who the father was there would be murder. Especially if she told them he had dumped her. As much as Terry had hurt her, she wasn't going to be the cause of his getting beaten to death. And if she knew Mickey that would be the outcome. She placed her hands on her belly. There was a tiny little person in there, a completely new life waiting for her to bring it into the world. She turned over in the bed again. The blankets and sheets were tangled around her.

How could he have dismissed her like that? She was still reeling from the shock. She had thought he would have been over the moon once the news had sunk in. She had seen him picking her up in his arms and kissing all her fears away. Telling her that he loved her. That they would go away and get married, away from her brothers, to Scotland or somewhere. Now, in bed, in the dark, she could see her plans for what they were: childish fantasies. Terry had no more need of her than he had of his car. When it was old hat, you traded it in for a newer model.

She felt the familiar sting of tears. Well, he wouldn't hear about this child from her. She wouldn't lower herself. If he didn't want her then he didn't want his child either. But what was she going to do about the baby? She couldn't see herself as one of these unmarried mothers, brazenly having their babies and sod the neighbours. If it had been anyone else, her brothers would have been round the boy's house, given him a good hiding, and then the wedding would have been arranged, quick smart. But this was a situation that could not be resolved so easily. Even if Terry wanted to marry her, Michael would move heaven and earth to stop the marriage taking place.

She was hot again so she pushed off the blankets. In her short nylon nighty she looked far more seductive than she felt. Her long smooth legs were spreadeagled on the blankets, her arms were hugging her breasts. She had combed out her long hair before getting into bed and it fanned around her head giving her an ethereal appearance, like a saucy angel.

She rolled her head from side to side on her pillow. Oh, why was she being plagued like this! It was bad enough being pregnant without all this added worry. She turned herself over again in the bed. This time she was facing the window. She stared out into the darkness, only the light of the streetlights to illuminate her room. Earlier she had prayed – to the Immaculate Conception and Saint Jude, the patron saint of no hope! Above her bed was the Sacred Heart, a large golden vessel pulsing outside Christ's body. He had looked benevolently down on her for years. She began to pray to him again. In the half-light she could see his golden heart glinting. She began to murmur the Eucharistic prayer.

'"Father, you are holy indeed, and all creation rightly gives you praise."'

As she prayed she heard a car drive into Lancaster Road. She saw the car's headlights cast long shadows over her bedroom ceiling as the engine died down and guessed, rightly, that her brothers were home. She heard them coming into the house and carried on praying.

'"All life, all holiness comes from you . . ."'

They were coming up the stairs. She could hear the thud of their shoes.

'"Through your son, Jesus Christ our Lord."'

Her bedroom door was thrown open and the light turned on. She pulled herself up in the bed and put her hand over her eyes to shield them from the sudden glare. Michael and Geoffrey stood at the end of her bed like avenging angels.

She squinted at them. 'What's going on?'

'I was just gonna ask you the same thing.'

'I don't know what you're on about, Mickey. I ain't done nothing!' Her voice was full of fear.

With one bound he was across the room. He grabbed her hair, yanking her head back. 'You bloody tart! You've been knocking about with a filth, ain't ya?'

'No . . . Mickey, I swear!' She was screaming with fear.

'Don't lie to me, you slag.'

He pushed his face closer to hers. She could smell his breath as he shouted at her, 'Lover boy got an ultimatum today, Maura. Either his bit of skirt or his job. I understand the job won.'

Maura's head was reeling. That was why he had dumped her! That was why he had taken the key from her. He knew who she was!

'He was called into the Chief's office. Told what a naughty family you'd got. I'm the fucking laughing stock of the Metropolitan Police Force over you. Every villain from here to Liverpool will be laughing up their sleeves at me. I could bleeding well murder you!'

Maura was not listening to him. All she could think of was the fact that Terry had known about her when she had gone to him. It was the name Ryan that had created the rift between them. Somewhere deep down inside her a grain of contempt was forming. It was her family that he objected to, not her. Even though it proved that it was not anything she had done that had caused their rift, instead of pleasing her she felt a disdain for him that was so strong she could actually taste it. The gutless bastard! The dirty gutless bastard . . .

He didn't even have the nerve to tell her why he was dumping her. He'd said he wanted to see other women when in reality he meant: I am frightened of your brothers. He had destroyed her and didn't have the decency to tell her truthfully why. She was carrying his child inside her. The fruit of their so-called love. If he walked into her room now, Michael wouldn't be in it. She would rip him to shreds, Terry Gutless Petherick would be a dead man, and it wouldn't be her brothers who killed him.

Michael and Geoffrey were watching her, fascinated by the changing expressions on her face.

'Leave me alone, you!' she screamed at Michael at the top of her voice, all fear of him leaving her at the thought of what Terry had done to her. Michael brought back his fist. As he went to slam it into her body, Sarah's voice stayed him.

'Oi! What the bloody hell's going on in here? It's a wonder you ain't woken up the whole bleeding street.' She took in the picture before her and ran to her son. Raising herself up on her toes she grabbed hold of Michael's hair, shaking him like a dog with its prey.

'Don't you dare raise your hand to your sister, you great gormless bastard! Leave go of her hair before you pull it all out.' She pummelled Michael's chest with her fists. It said a lot for his feelings for her mother that he didn't strike her, but instead threw Maura back against the pillows.

'Go back to bed, Mum, and let me sort this out.'

'No, I bleeding well won't!' She looked at her husband

167

who had followed her into the room. 'Tell him to leave her alone.'

She pulled her daughter into her arms.

Benjamin, as usual, was half drunk. He looked at everyone in the room with his drunken leer and, finding it difficult to concentrate, waved his hands at his wife. 'Leave Mickey alone. He knows what he's about.'

Sarah lost her temper.

'That's right, Ben, do what you always do. Pass the bloody buck. This time to your son. You drunken bastard! Get out of me sight.'

She turned her gaze on Mickey.

'Now you tell me what's going on here. Your father might be scared of you but I ain't. I'll never be frightened of something that came out of me own body, so just you remember that. Come on, I'm waiting. What's going on?'

Geoffrey answered for him. 'She's been seeing an old Bill.'

Maura's little sob was the only other sound. Sarah stroked her daughter's hair gently and sat herself on the bed.

'So what? Why should that worry you lot? Who the hell do you think you are . . . the Krays? You're nothing, do you hear me. Nothing!

'Out on the street you might be hard men, but in here . . .' she gestured around the room with her free hand. '. . . you're just my boys. That's all. And I never thought I would see the day when you raised your hand to your own sister.'

Sarah was aware that she was speaking for effect. She knew enough about her boys to know that they were greatly feared. She had found guns hidden in the coal house and had sat beside her sons in courtrooms. She had even read about them in the papers. The *News of the World* had had a big spread a few weeks earlier about the hostess clubs in Soho, and one of the clubs mentioned was owned by this great handsome son of hers. A son she was finding it increasingly difficult to love these days. And now on top of everything she had this – her only daughter, her pride and joy, being attacked in her own home. Just because she was seeing a policeman. A decent man more than likely. Yet she knew that her daughter's lovelife was doomed.

She looked down into Maura's tearstained face. 'Is it true, Maws?'

Maura couldn't lie to her mother so she nodded.

Benjamin, more alert now, said, 'Oh my God!'

Sarah turned on him like a mad dog.

'I'll give you "Oh my God", because your daughter's decent. By Christ, it's a wonder we haven't got a whore on our hands, being brought up with you lot. You're all whoremasters, the lot of you!' Her voice was thick with tears. 'I can't hold me head up in the street because everyone knows about you all . . . everyone knows my sons are glorified pimps.' She turned on Michael. 'Well, my lad, I hope you get your just deserts in this life. That you pay for all that you've done. For the innocent lives you've ruined and for the death of my Anthony. I've always blamed you for that.' She wagged her head at him. 'If he hadn't been working for you he would be at home with me now.

'I also happen to know that you're a queer, Michael Ryan. And I hear that they're very good to their mothers. So perhaps you could make me a happy woman now by getting out of this house and not coming back. It's high time you left anyway, at thirty-one. Go and live with your boyfriend, and take that little snipe with you!' She pointed at Geoffrey. 'Yes, you. You always walked in his footsteps, tried to emulate everything he did. Well, you can follow him out of this house tonight. Go on. Get out, the pair of you.'

Michael was staring at his mother as if she had grown another head right in front of his eyes. He worshipped her, lived for her. If she turned her back on him he had nothing. He stepped towards her, his voice wheedling.

'Mum? Don't be silly, Mum . . . I don't want to leave you.'

Sarah cut him off. 'It's a fine thing we bred between us, Benjamin. A cruel, sadistic mummy's boy.' She put up her arm to push him away. 'Get out of my sight, Mickey. You're making me stomach turn. While you kept your violence outside this house I could ignore it, but to see you attacking your own sister . . . and her no more than a child. That's finished you as far as I'm concerned. Now just get out.'

She turned her back to him and pulled Maura tightly to her breast. Michael stood there, dazed. Geoffrey went to him, taking him gently by the arm and leading him from the room. Neither looked at their father who stood staring at his wife as if she was a stranger. He had never heard her say so much in one go, in all their years of marriage. He heard the front door slam. Turning slowly from his wife, he went back to their room.

Maura and Sarah cried together.

'Oh, Mum . . . poor Mickey!' Even after what had happened Maura could still find it in her heart to feel sorry for him. She knew that her mother was the most important thing in his life. For her to say all that to him, and for him to stand and take it, spoke volumes. Anyone else would have been dead.

'Don't waste any pity on him, Maws. He's no better than a wild animal. The thought of him with another man makes me sick to me guts.'

Sarah made herself comfortable on the bed and smoothed back her daughter's hair from her face. She loved Maura. She admitted to herself that she had been overprotective towards her, had allowed Michael and the other boys to run her life. But when she had walked in this room and seen Michael attacking her, something inside her had snapped. Garry had been right all along. What she had done was try and take over Maura's life, and this had been the outcome. Her daughter had found herself a man, a decent man more than likely, and the boys wanted to tear it apart.

She said softly, 'Who's the lucky man then?'

Maura sniffed and wiped her eyes with the back of her

hand. 'That's the ironic part about it, Mum. As from today I'm not seeing him any more. He packed me in.'

Sarah smiled to herself. 'Listen, child, you will meet a lot of fellows and think that you love them. It's human nature, part of growing up. Don't make the same mistake as I did and marry the first man that comes along. I've regretted marrying your father all my life. You get yourself a decent man with a decent profession. Let me sort out Mickey and the rest of them.'

Maura cried harder. 'You don't understand, Mum. Terry . . . he was the one for me. I really loved him. When he finished with me today, I wanted to die.'

Sarah did smile now. Maura sounded so young and naive. 'That'll pass. And in a few months someone else will be "the one". It's all part and parcel of growing up.'

Sarah's patronising tone made Maura angry. Rising up on her elbow she shouted, 'In a few months' time I'll be out here!' She gestured with her free hand.

Maura had a sneaking feeling of triumph when she saw the shock on her mother's face.

'Oh no, Maws! Never that. Is that why Michael . . . ?'

Maura collapsed back on to the pillows. 'No, Mum. He doesn't know. I only found out myself today.' Her voice broke. 'I was gonna tell him . . . tell Terry everything. About the baby, Mickey . . . But before I got the chance he dumped me. Said he didn't want to get tied down. Wanted to see other women.' Her face screwed up into a mask of tragedy. 'Oh, Mum! What am I gonna do!'

Sarah was stunned. She sat on the bed staring at her daughter, the word 'pregnant' echoing inside her head. It made her squirm inside. She had become pregnant at fifteen. Her father had gone round to Benjamin's house and given him the 'hiding of his life', as he had boasted afterwards. Then the marriage had been arranged. Her life had been ruined because of a furtive, fumbling, sexual exploration up a dark alleyway. Well, that was not going to happen to her daughter. No, by Christ! Her only daughter would get a decent crack at life. She personally would see to that. She made a decision. 'You're going to get rid of it.'

'What!' Maura thought she was hearing things.

'I said, you're getting rid of it!'

'But, Mum!' Maura's voice was shocked. 'I can't do that. It's a sin!'

Sarah's thin-lipped mouth set in a grim line.

'It's a pity you didn't think of that when your knees were pointing at the ceiling. That was a sin as well! No, I've made up my mind. The child must go.' Seeing her daughter's sad face, her voice softened.

'Believe me, Maws, you will thank me for this some day. Could you imagine the trouble this would cause with Michael? His sister pregnant by a policeman – of all things – who'd dumped her? There'd be murder done.'

Maura felt numb inside. 'That's why he dumped me, Mum . . . because of who I am. A Ryan. He never told me that – Mickey did. That's how he found out about it all.'

Sarah kissed Maura's forehead lightly. Suddenly she felt weary, old. 'Get yourself off to sleep now. We'll make our plans in the morning.'

When her mother had settled her down and left the room Maura lay for a while in the darkness. Everything had gone wrong for her. Now she was not only pregnant, she was the cause of Michael and Geoffrey being thrown out of the house. She felt the useless tears run from her eyes and thought, I'll never sleep again. But she did. Only to be plagued by the old nightmare . . .

Downstairs Sarah had made herself a pot of tea and was on the second cup. There would be no sleep for her tonight, that much she was sure of. She finished her tea and settled herself into her chair. Closing her eyes, she began to pray to our Lady of Perpetual Succour.

'"Most holy Virgin Mary, who, to inspire me with boundless confidence, has been pleased to take that sweetest of name, Mother of Perpetual Succour . . ."' Sarah's lips were barely moving in the dimness of the kitchen. '". . . I beseech thee to aid me at all times . . ."'

Chapter Twelve

It had finally been agreed between Maura and her mother to use the address given to her by the little chemist. Old Mother Jenkins would normally have been the one chosen to perform the operation but her encroaching senility, coupled with the fact she couldn't keep her mouth shut, had made Sarah chary of even approaching her. Though abortions were sometimes performed in the local hospital, the fact that the Ryans were a well-known family had put the damper on that idea as well. So it was that at three and a half months pregnant Maura finally went to the little flat in Peckham, accompanied by her mother. It was a high rise block, and Mr Patel lived on the tenth floor. Sarah had already visited the flat to arrange things. After the long journey up in the lift, she knocked on the front door.

Both women had been silent throughout their journey from Notting Hill. Maura felt sick with nerves. There was a part of her that was rebelling against all that was happening to her. Whenever these thoughts entered her head she reminded herself what Mickey would do if he knew, and the knowledge that he would commit a murder generally brought her back to her senses.

The door was opened by an Asian woman. She wore a canary yellow sari and smiled at them constantly, as if trying to make up for her lack of English with courteousness. Maura and Sarah found themselves nodding their heads at her like marionettes.

She showed them into the lounge. Maura had never seen so many colours in one room in all her life. There were greens and blues and reds of every shade imaginable; the walls had brightly coloured carpets hanging on them like paintings. Maura caught her mother's eye and felt an irresistible urge to laugh. She wasn't sure who was the most nervous.

A small untidy Asian man came into the room. 'How are you doing, madams?' He shook their hands and smiled at them so that the whole marionette game began again. 'If you plis follow me?' He led them through a small door into the kitchen.

The place stank of stale curry and there was a nasty undersmell that Maura couldn't pinpoint. It could have been blood. She wasn't sure. Whatever it was, it caught in her throat, burning it. The kitchen was small and in the middle was a large formica-covered table. It was yellow with a small black pattern going through it. Maura stared at the table fearfully. To the right of her was a work surface and an array of stainless steel tools upon it. She was beginning to sweat. She felt her mother pull her coat and slipped it off her shoulders, letting it fall into her mother's arms.

'Please would you make sure your bladder is empty?'

'Er . . . I . . . it is.' Maura was stammering with fright.

'Good. Please be removing your undergarments and get on to the table.'

'What? You're going to do it in here?'

The man looked at her, puzzled. 'But of course.'

'Come on, Maws. Slip off your drawers.'

Burning with embarrassment, Maura slipped off her panties. With her mother's help she climbed on to the table. It wobbled under her weight and Maura had an awful vision of the whole lot collapsing underneath her. She closed her eyes for a second. On the ceiling above her she could see the naked light bulb. Years of cooking had left the flex with a coating of grease and fly droppings. She closed her eyes again. She must have been mad to come here.

'Mum . . . Mum! I've changed me mind.' Her voice was urgent.

'There now . . . there now. Quieten yourself. It will all be over soon.'

174

Maura pulled herself up with difficulty and Sarah forced her to lie down again.

'For goodness' sakes, Maura! Will you behave yourself?'

She was a child again, in the dentist's or the doctor's. Only this time it wasn't a filling she was having done, or a few stitches in a cut, it was to be the slaughter of her unborn child.

'Money, please.' The little Asian man had his hand out-stretched.

Sarah took an envelope out of her bag and handed it to him. He ripped it open and took the money out. He counted it. Then putting the money back into the envelope, he pushed the lot into the pocket of his cardigan. He used such force he pushed the garment out of shape.

Sarah, watching him, was aware that his fingernails were filthy. She forced herself to look at her daughter. Maura was now gripping the sides of the table. Her long hair was hanging over the edge, nearly touching the floor.

Mr Patel smiled at his wife. He was happy now. He had the money, even if this silly girl changed her mind.

'Put your ankles together and let your legs drop open.'

Maura did as she was told, fear taking over. Mr Patel stood at the end of the table staring at the opened body for a long while. He was sweating. The palms of his hands were damp and he wiped them on his grubby cardigan. He parted her pubic hair with his finger. Sarah saw him lick his lips and turned her head away in disgust, the bile rising up inside her. The man picked up one of his instruments and slipped it inside Maura. She felt the cold intrusion into her body and stiffened.

'Relax, madam, it will soon be over.'

Maura felt the stinging pain as the steel tip probed for the neck of the womb. When she felt the hard aching agony as he opened the cervix, she gasped. Picking up the curette, a long piece of metal with a strange-looking loop on the end, he began the scraping.

Sarah could hear the animal-like grunts coming from her daughter, could see large beads of sweat appearing on her forehead.

The man worked fast, scraping into the depths of her body. Sarah heard him mutter something in his native language as Maura tried desperately to sit up.

'Oh, Mum . . . please . . . the pain! I can't stand the pain!' Maura's voice was drenched with agony. Then she shrieked like a dog caught in a trap. The woman tried to clamp her hand over Maura's gaping mouth. Tears were rolling down her cheeks and into her ears. She could feel the wetness as she rolled her head from side to side on the hardness of the table. Pushing harder now, the man carried on his scraping. Sarah and the woman held Maura's shoulders to stop her rolling off the table. Sarah felt as if she was caught in some kind of nightmare.

'Just relax, Maws . . . relax.' Someone in the next flat turned their radio louder to drown out the screams. The strains of 'I wanna hold your hand' filled the little kitchen.

Maura tried to close her legs and Mr Patel forced them apart with his shoulders. 'Goodness gracious, woman. Will you keep still?'

'Mum . . . Stop him, Mum . . . I can't stand it. Please!'

Maura felt herself urinating. A bubble seemed to have burst inside her. Then she felt the hotness of the urine and blood. The man yanked out the instruments and shouted to his wife in their native tongue. Mrs Patel went to the sink and, tipping the dirty cups out of the washing up bowl, brought it over to the table. Somehow, between them, the couple managed to get Maura to squat over the bowl.

She felt a lump slowly leave her body, looked down through her sweatdamp hair and saw a baby, about four inches long, lying in mucus and blood at the bottom of the dayglo orange washing up bowl. It was perfect. Her shoulders began to shake uncontrollably. She felt the hysteria rising up inside her like a tidal wave. That was her baby. She began to cry, harder now, a high piercing crying that was tinged with mania.

Snot was hanging from her nose in long fat lines that dripped into the bowl and mixed with the blood and urine. She could see her white thighs smeared with blood on either side of her baby's orange coffin. She fainted, dropping forward on to the table, sending the washing up bowl and its grisly contents all over the kitchen floor. Sarah stared at the tiny foetus, her grandchild, and felt shame crawl over her body. It began in her legs and crept up her body to her heart. What had she done? Dear Lord, what on earth had she done?

Mrs Patel shook her arm and somehow Sarah was snapped back to life. She dragged her eyes from the tiny corpse and began to help the couple to clear up.

When Maura woke later her panties were back on and she could feel a sanitary towel between her legs. She felt dreadful. She noticed that she was lying on a strange bed in a strange room. She gazed around her, dazed. Then she remembered where she was, the scraping of the cold steel inside her, and felt the familiar panic return. The image of her baby rose up before her and she began to cry again.

Sarah, hearing that her daughter was awake, went into the room. She gathered her into her arms, her own heart breaking. Now she knew why her church outlawed abortion. Why it was considered a sin. She had been the instigator of a horrific deed. She had brought all this pain and suffering on to her daughter. She kissed Maura's head softly.

'It's all over, my love.' She helped her daughter to sit up.

'Oh, Mum, I do feel rough.'

Her stomach felt as if it had been ripped open. She had just had an abortion without any anaesthesia whatsoever. Although neither of them knew it, Maura would never be the same girl after what had happened that afternoon.

Half an hour later she and Sarah were in a taxi, on their way back to Notting Hill. Both sat in silence until, once again tucked up in her own bed, Maura said: 'I wish I'd had the guts to have kept it, Mum. Every time I think of it lying there . . .' Her voice broke. Sobbing, she turned her face into her pillows.

Sarah left the room. She could not face her daughter. She

went down the stairs and into her front room where she poured herself a large whisky. She would not forget this day's work in a hurry.

Later in the evening, when she went to her daughter, Maura was asleep with the tears she had cried still glistening on her long lashes. Sarah pulled the blankets up around her daughter's shoulders, praying that her child would find some comfort in her rest, would wake up restored a little. She knew that it would be a long time before either of them felt their old selves again. If indeed they would ever feel anything again.

It was not until the next morning that Sarah found out why her daughter had slept so peacefully and for so long. Finding that she could not wake Maura, Sarah pulled the blankets from her, disturbed by her daughter's whiteness. A mass of deep red blood had seeped from her, till it covered nearly all her lower body and soaked the sheets and bedding. Maura Ryan was haemorrhaging her life's blood away.

Sarah's screams finally brought her friend Pat Johnstone running into the house. She took one look at the scene before her and phoned for an ambulance. The two women sat together as Maura was operated on, united in grief and worry.

Pat Johnstone had known immediately what had happened and she swore to her friend that the knowledge would go to her grave with her. After phoning the ambulance she had phoned Michael, not knowing what else to do. Now she held her friend's hand.

Sarah sat in limbo, waiting for the operation to be over. She would wish to her dying day that she had not taken her daughter to that little flat in Peckham, that she had let her have the baby in St Charles's hospital where they were fighting so valiantly to save her life. She closed her eyes tightly to blot out the troubling visions that kept disturbing her . . .

She heard the swish of the swing doors that led to the operating theatre and turned in the direction of the noise. It was the surgeon. His gown was covered in blood and his face strained. For one awful moment Sarah thought that her daughter had died. Then he spoke.

'Mrs Ryan, your daughter is over the worst now.'

Sarah heard her own voice. 'Thank God! Oh, thank God.'

'I wouldn't be so quick to thank him if I were you, Mrs Ryan. Your daughter was very badly smashed up inside. We've had to remove her ovaries. An infection had set in and I'm afraid she was in no fit state to fight it. Whoever the person was who operated on your daughter, they should be facing a life sentence.' He shook his head slowly. 'By rights she should be dead. As it is she will never have a child . . . another child. She still hasn't regained consciousness yet. But as I said before, the worst of it is over. Though how she will react mentally, I really couldn't say.'

'Thank you, Doctor. Thank you.' Sarah's voice was low and full of shame.

'Whoever it was who did this to your daughter should be put away. I have never, in all my years, seen anything like it. It was as if they had used a battering ram inside her. I'm afraid I must insist that you give me the address. I won't tell the police anything about your daughter. I feel she has been punished enough. But I cannot allow this ever to happen again.'

Sarah nodded. Opening her bag she gave the surgeon the piece of paper the chemist had given Maura. He took it. Patting Sarah's shoulder, he said, 'I know that sometimes the easy way out looks inviting. But it never works out, you know. In the end it pays to do things properly. Your daughter's being taken to Intensive Care if you would like to see her.' He walked off with the paper clutched in his hand.

When Sarah and Pat got to the Intensive Care Unit Michael was already there. He had just arrived in the hospital. Seeing him, Sarah forgot all the harsh words and ran into his outstretched arms. Michael held his mother to him, tears in his eyes. While all the staff looked at the big handsome man comforting his mother, Terry Petherick was being beaten mercilessly by two hired thugs. It would be three months before he came out of hospital and nearly a year before he went back to work.

Sitting his mother down, Michael asked one of the nurses to get her a cup of tea. He wiped her eyes with his handkerchief and then went into the little ward to see his sister. He stared down at her, shocked by what he saw. The years seemed to have been piled on her overnight. Her high cheekbones stood out starkly against her white skin; her cheeks had sunk into her face, leaving deep hollows. As he looked down at her he made a solemn vow to himself. No matter what she did, or what happened, he would always be there for her. He knew that if it had not been for him, she would not be lying there. That Petherick would not have dumped her. Now she was hurting and it was his fault. If it was left to him she would never know hurt again. Petherick was being paid out for his part in it, even as he stood there. Paid muscle was beating him to a pulp. And that was as it should be. As he had told Benny, you looked after your womenfolk.

He took her hand gently in his and Maura regained consciousness. She opened her eyes and looked up into Michael's face. She ran her tongue across cracked lips, trying to speak. He put his head nearer to her face and what she said caused him to sob into her shoulder.·

'My poor baby, Mickey. My poor innocent baby.'

He gently enfolded her in his arms, their tears mingling together. If it cost him his life, she would never know sadness again.

A week later the surgeon, Mr Bernard Frobisher, was told by the police that the address he had given them had been firebombed three days previously. The tenants of the flat, Mr Ahman Patel, his wife Homina and eldest daughter Naimah, had been killed.

The police thought it was probably a racial attack; they had no idea who could have done it. Mr Frobisher wisely kept his opinion to himself. He had no intention of putting his own family in jeopardy. Especially not for a back-street abortionist.

Chapter Thirteen

Maura had been out of hospital six weeks and the whole family agreed that she was a changed girl. She had a brittleness that sat uneasily on her now slim shoulders. She had lost so much weight that Benny playfully nicknamed her 'Beanpole'. With her height and new svelteness she looked like a fashion model. Except for her breasts. Somehow, although they had shrunk with the rest of her body, they were still large enough to make her feel 'top heavy'. She had smiled at Benny's jokes about her body, but deep inside felt she had paid a high price for her newfound slimness.

She was sitting by her bedroom window looking out at the children playing in the street. She remembered when she had played the same games with Margaret. Tin Pan Alley, Hopscotch, Five Jacks. She longed for that safe world now, when the only worry she'd had was what time she had to be in by. Maura's profile, as she looked down on the children, showed the extent of the change in her. Her nose was more sharply defined, a Roman nose, her cheekbones looked as if they had been carved from ivory. Her dark blue eyes were deeper set. Earlier, she had creamed her face and hands, still unaware of how lovely she really was. Although she saw herself in the glass, she never really took any notice. It was as if the day she had left the hospital, Maura Ryan as was had ceased to exist. Now a beautiful outer shell, inside she felt nothing. Nothing at all. Until today. Today she had the beginnings of a plan forming in her mind, and she needed Michael's help to fulfil it.

She smiled as one of the children below her screamed and pointed to something on the pavement. She guessed, rightly, that it was some kind of insect. It brought back a memory from her subconscious. She could smell the dampness of the scullery, that cold dampness that seemed to seep into the bones. Anthony had locked her in there when she was a small child. Turning out the light, leaving her in the darkness. She had been far too small to reach the light switch. She had stood in the dank world he had created, knowing that the army of cockroaches was scrambling beneath her feet. She shuddered as she thought of it. The fear and panic it had created rose up inside her again, as it had on that day. She had imagined they were running up her legs, into her knickers. Until she had felt the hot wetness as the urine had run down her chubby legs, soaking her socks and shoes. That's when the screams had been forced from her throat, high piercing screams that had brought her mother and father and Michael . . . a very angry Michael who had taken off his belt and laid into Anthony until his screams had matched her own.

Again the image of her baby in the washing up bowl filled her head. She forced the picture away, shaking her head as if it would help to make it disappear. She did not blame anyone but herself for what had happened in that tiny flat. She told herself that at least twenty times a day. Not her mother or Michael. Not anyone but herself. And Terry.

She blamed him with all her heart and soul. From the moment she had seen the body of her child, their child, lying in that dirty bowl, hatred for him had entered her body. A seed had been planted that day, and Maura had nurtured it and cultivated it, until now it had grown tall, like a bedraggled beanstalk in a fairy tale. She had read about his beating in the *Daily Mirror* and felt nothing for him. No pity. No sorrow. Nothing. She was as empty where he was concerned as she was about herself. As the seed of contempt had grown inside her, it had strangled the memory of every nice thing he had ever said or done, until she had forgotten his goodness. Forgotten the fun they had had and the closeness they had shared. She knew that if he had not dumped her that day, she would have had the baby. Somehow she would have found a solution to her problems. She chose to forget her fear of Michael. Her fear of having a baby alone. In Terry Petherick she had found the perfect scapegoat. She knew that the police knew exactly who had ordered his beating but like so many things that happened thanks to the Ryan family, they could not prove it. She smiled to herself. Well, if everything went as she planned, she would soon be a real member of the Ryans. An active working member . . .

She hoped that Terry was in agony. That he was so badly hurt no one would ever look at his handsome face again. That was her prayer. The only good thing to come out of the whole sorry business was that Michael was back in her mother's good books. Although he had not come back home to live, he still visited frequently. It seemed that the day he had moved out had started the ball rolling for them all. Geoffrey, Leslie, Lee and Garry had all moved out. Only Benny and herself remained at home. Lee and Garry shared a flat off the Edgware Road; Geoffrey had bought himself a flat near Michael's, in Knightsbridge. The house was quiet now, unlike the old days when they were all young and it was noisy from early morning to late at night. In a funny way she missed the hustle and bustle of her younger days.

She was roused from her reverie by a tap on the bedroom door.

Michael walked in carrying a large box of chocolates. She gazed at him affectionately. There was no doubt about it, he was one hell of a good-looking man.

'You keep buying me chocolates, Mickey, and I don't eat them.'

'No . . . but I do!' He grinned at her mischievously, and then, throwing himself across the bed, rolled off on to the floor, rolled again sideways and was kneeling in front of her, offering the box of chocolates in a gesture of supplication. Arms outstretched, eyes raised to the ceiling, like a Japanese Geisha girl.

'And all because the lady loves Milk Tray!'

Maura burst out laughing. 'I wouldn't mind but they're Black Magic.'

'That's right, laugh at me after I risk like and limb for you.'

He sat back on his heels and looked at her. 'How are you feeling?' His voice was gentle.

Maura sighed. 'I feel OK. Though I would feel a damn' sight better if everyone stopped asking me that, I just want to forget it.' She slumped into her chair, her face closed again. She stared at him warily. 'Actually, Mickey, there is something I want to ask you.'

He shrugged. 'Ask away, Princess. Anything you want, you can have.'

'Honestly, Mickey? Anything?'

He put his hand on his heart. 'I give you my word, as they say on the telly.'

Maura leant forward in her chair and grinned at him. 'I want you to give me a job!'

Michael stared, his face a study in dismay. 'I don't know about that, Maws.'

'You promised me, Mickey.' Her voice was hard and shrewish. 'You promised me anything. Anything!'

'Yeah. But I never expected this.'

'Look, Mickey.' Her voice was wheedling now, cajoling. 'I have been thinking about this for a while now . . . I want to take over the ice cream and hot dogs.'

'You!' He sounded as if he had been poleaxed.

'Why not? I worked them often enough as a kid.'

He pushed her back into her seat. 'You don't understand, Princess.'

She pushed herself forward again, her voice desperate. 'Oh, but I do understand, Mickey. That's just where you're wrong. I know exactly how to run them. A bloody kid could do that. If you're worried that I ain't got the bottle then you can stop. I have got it, Mickey. More than you would think. I've spent the best part of my life listening to you lot plan and scheme. I could piss it, Mickey, if you gave me the chance.'

'Look, Maws, it's a dangerous business for a bloke. Let alone a bird.'

'I know that, Michael, but I'm your sister. Not some

184

nonsense bird out to make a few bob. I could do that on me back like your hostesses. I know that if you give me the chance, I could make a go of it. At first I would be respected because I'm your little sister, but I guarantee you that within a few months I'd be respected for myself.'

'But you don't understand, Maws . . .'

'I do! That's just what I'm trying to tell you if you'd listen to me. I know that if someone puts a van on one of our pitches, licence or no licence, they get warned off. Or you try to buy them out, depending. If they won't play your game, you petrol bomb them. They soon get the message. If you happen to know the person and like them, and the pitch isn't major, you arrange for a little percentage. Christ Almighty, Mickey, we're all from the same stable. If you can't trust me, who can you trust?'

Michael digested this bit of logic.

'I don't know, Maws.' She sensed that he was thawing towards her, and pressed home her advantage.

'I swear to you, Mickey, that I will make you proud of me. I'll run those pitches better than they have ever been run before!'

Seeing her face, so full of hope and anticipation, Michael couldn't deny her. After all she had been through, the pain and heartache, it seemed small compensation. He grinned. 'All right. You win.'

Maura threw herself into his arms, pulling them both to the floor. She kissed him full on the mouth.

'Oh, Mickey, thanks. Thanks! I'll work like a nigger for you, I promise. You won't regret it.'

I've got the ice cream and hot dogs, she thought, thrilled at the implications. If Terry Goody Two Shoes Petherick wanted to catch criminals . . . let him try to catch her!

'I promise you, Mickey, you will never regret this.'

And he didn't.

Maura walked across the Yard towards the small crowd of men. They were all staring at her. Some watched her with hostility, others with curiosity. She was their boss, and like most workforces they were waiting to see the outcome of a

185

new regime. They were all aware that she was Michael Ryan's sister. Just seventeen years old. Most were amazed at the sheer size of her. She was taller than most of the men there. She smiled at them all, hiding her nervousness behind a façade of friendliness.

'Right, I expect you all know me, and over the next few weeks I hope to get to know you. I'm new at this business, I admit, and I will be open to any friendly advice you may wish to give me. But I must stress this one fact . . . at the end of the day it's my decision that counts. Now if any of you gentlemen find that hard to accept, I suggest you see me after I've finished the rotas. OK?'

She scanned the sea of faces before her, looking for any hint of trouble. Everyone looked neutral. Not bad for starters, she thought.

'Now if the runners would all stand aside, I would like to see the actual drivers and workers.'

Most of the younger men in the crowd broke away and made a smaller gang by themselves. The runners were the young men who kept a look out for the police. They stood at strategic points near the vans watching not only for beat policemen but also panda cars. They also eyed up any competition that came on to their patch, reporting all back to the drivers – the mainstay of the business. It was not unusual to see an ice cream van wheelspin away, dragging a runner into the service hatch as it went, especially on the police patches: Westminster, the Houses of Parliament, Knightsbridge, outside Harrods, and Baker Street where Madame Tussaud's brought so many tourists.

The drivers and servers stood quietly. They employed and paid their own runners, the Ryans only paid these men. Eventually, if the runners proved any good, they were given new pitches as and when they came up. It was a close-knit community that these men lived in. If they were caught, and hauled into Bow Street court, they gave 'moody' names and Michael paid their fines. It was an arrangement that suited everyone. In the summer, especially, there was an awful lot of money to be made. And as with any lucrative business, many people who wanted a piece of the action.

Maura coughed to clear her throat. 'I think that for the time being, we stick to the usual rota. So you can all go to your usual pitch today. I will be looking over the takings and popping along to see you now and then.' She smiled again. 'I hope you will all bear with me on this.'

The men nodded at her, happier now they knew where they were to be stationed. Most knew their pitches like the back of their hands. They knew every road, alleyway, and escape route on their own particular manor.

'Off you go then. If you have any trouble, ring me. If I'm not here, someone will find me.'

She turned away and walked to the caravan that served as her office. Michael was watching her from the window. He had been listening to her address the men and was impressed. Against his better judgement, he began to think that she might just be able to do the job after all.

The men all gravitated to their vans. Most were subdued. None had ever worked for a woman before. All had lived on the fringes of crime, were petty burglars, car thieves or 'kiters' – people who bought stolen cheque books and then used them to buy goods that could be sold off to fences. Maura's advent into their masculine world was a shock. But she was Michael Ryan's sister and so they would afford her a trial period. If she didn't work out, and they were all sure she would not, Michael, being a businessman first and foremost, would 'out' her and they could all get back to normal!

Maura walked into the caravan feeling sick with apprehension. It had gone much better than expected. Michael laughed and shook his head slowly. 'Sure you want all this hag, Princess?'

'Yes, Michael, I'm sure. Now, if you don't mind, I have some books to look over.'

'Oh, well. Pardon me for breathing.'

Maura laughed. 'Have a quick coffee before you go. There's still a few things I'm not sure of.'

'Okey doke. But I'll say this much to you now, Maws, you did well out there. They're the scum of the earth but they're good workers. But for Gawd's sake, watch them! If they kiss your hand, count your fingers. And if any get a bit too saucy, you let me know. Most off them would put their granny on the streets if they thought she could pull in a few bob. Start as you mean to go on, love. Be fair but hard. That's the only law they know. Show that you're stronger than them and you've got friends for life. Show a chink of weakness and . . . well, to put it bluntly, you're fucked.'

'I'll remember that, Mickey. Now about these books?'

'You sort out the books, Maws. I know sod all about it. I told Benny to get his arse down here this morning and show you what he'd been doing. All I ever did was pick up the overall total. How Benny got to it, I don't know. So you'll have to sort that lot out yourself.'

'Well, Benny should be here soon. I'll ask him.'

'You do that. Now one last thing, Maws. In the drawer of your desk, on the right hand side, is a gun.'

'A gun?'

'Yes, a gun. I told you this was a dangerous business. But don't worry, I've left one of my best boys outside. No one will bother you while he's there. But just in case, that's where the gun is. If the filth come snooping about, tell them that they're paid up to next month. If they see you here they might try it on. On no account get rid of that firearm. Right?'

Maura nodded. She looked troubled and Michael laughed. 'Still think you can hack it?'

She straightened in her seat. 'Yes, I bloody well can. Now do you want a coffee or not?'

As she went to put the kettle on she had a fleeting feeling of being involved in something way over her head. She pushed the thought and the feeling firmly from her mind. This was her inauguration into the world of the Ryans. This was to be her career and she would make her name synonymous with villainy. Her brother Michael wouldn't be in it once she got started!

Danny Forster had been a runner for nearly two years. He worked for 'Big Bill' McEwan, a large extrovert Scotsman. He was standing at Baker Street tube station, watching for roving policemen and panda cars. It was a bright spring day and the tourists were just arriving in force. He saw a strange van parking just down the road from him. It was a Milano Bros ice cream van. He frowned. Within minutes they were open for business. He walked quickly past the van. Inside were four men. He could not see any runners so he assumed that two of the men were breakers. He walked slowly back to Madame Tussaud's and told the Scotsman what he had seen.

Big Bill McEwan was not known for his quiet temperament. He was once described by a judge as 'a most obnoxious individual who should not be walking the streets with innocent people'. Big Bill had taken this as a compliment. He saw himself as different from the average person and was gratified that someone educated, as the judge so obviously was, should agree with him. Getting his considerable bulk out of the ice cream van he meandered down to the rival camp. When he arrived he realised that he had been expected.

'This is my patch. I want you lot to piss off – and sharpish!' His large stomach, hanging over his trousers, quivered as he spoke.

A very good-looking Italian smiled at him, displaying perfect teeth.

'We have a licence. Legally we are allowed to be here. I think it is yourself who is maybe . . . how you say? . . . in the wrong.'

Big Bill stared at the man through small piggy eyes. He decided that the Italian was probably a simpleton. Everyone in the 'creaming' business knew who he was. That's why he got to work 'The Sword', one of the best pitches in London.

'Are you going to fuck off or not?' His voice brooked no argument. By now a crowd had gathered to watch the exchange. Tourists and Londoners alike sensed that a battle was taking place and stood waiting to see who would be the victor.

'No . . .'

Before the Italian could finish his sentence, Big Bill was

189

already walking away and hauling himself back into his van, a bright pink and yellow affair with 'Dingle Dells Ice Cream' written in green letters along the sides. Without speaking to his server he started up the van and reversed out of his parking place. The server was still trying frantically to get a lid on the hotplate, which was covered in chopped onions and half-cooked hamburgers. He turned off the gas and the ice cream valves. He was not taking any chances.

Big Bill drove his ice cream van straight at the Milano Bros vehicle. The four men inside stood rooted to the spot as they realised his intention. He hit the back of their van so hard a box of flakes that had been standing on one of his own back shelves shot forward into the front seat, crumbling its contents all over Big Bill's trousers.

He reversed back again and once more rammed the Italians' van. They were hanging on to anything they could grab. Then, pulling his van up beside the driver's window, Big Bill shouted at the four men: 'I'll be back tomorrow with shooters and anything else it takes to shift you. This is your one and only warning.'

Then he drove away at a leisurely pace. The Hot Dog War of 1967 had started.

Maura listened to all that Big Bill had to say. In the few weeks she had been doing the job she had begged for, she had gained an insight into the world of the 'creamers'.

'So what are you going to do, Mrs?'

Maura sighed. If he called her 'Mrs' once more she would strangle him.

'Well, Bill, I'm not sure exactly what action I'll take yet, but I promise you that I'll have it sorted in the next twenty-four hours, OK?'

'You'd bloody well better have, Mrs. I've lost an awful lot of money today.'

Maura cut him off. 'I'm quite well aware of that, Bill. Now you shoot off home and leave this to me.' He turned to go and she called him back.

'One more thing. My name is either Maura or Miss

Ryan. I don't care which you use. But, please, don't call me Mrs.' She smiled at him icily.

'Fair enough, Mrs. I'll let you know what I decide to call you.'

Maura mentally chalked one up to Big Bill.

Left alone she pondered what he had told her. This was the chance she had been waiting for. If she could successfully pull this off alone, without any help from her brothers, she would be set. She called in her minder, a large black man called Tony Dooley after his grandfather, an Irishman who had taken a West Indian woman as his wife. Tony stood in front of Maura as she outlined her plan. When she had finished, he smiled. Maura took the gun from the drawer and placed it in her shoulder bag. It was time to go and see the Milano Brothers.

George Milano surveyed the young girl before him. He let his gaze roam over her body. He decided she had good tits. He was disappointed that Michael Ryan could make such a bad decision. He had always understood that Michael was an astute businessman. He had respected him. Then this! It had hit the street that he had given his little sister the ice cream and hot dog business. Now she sat here, in his office, making veiled threats. It was laughable! He smiled at her.

'Listen, Miss Ryan, I appreciate you coming here today to speak to me, but I'm afraid that you are wasting your time. I have legitimate licences for all those vans of mine. My advice to you is to go and see your big brother . . . or has he given control of the rest of his businesses to your mother?' He spoke in a sarcastic manner, causing Maura to grit her teeth.

'So you won't listen to what I have to say?' Her voice was soft. He shook his head, still smiling that maddening smile. Maura stood up. She noticed him looking at her legs.

'Very well, Mr Milano. We shall have to come to some other arrangement.'

She left the office with Tony Dooley following her, her head held high. Milano might have won the first battle but she was determined to win the actual war. She went from the Milano Brothers' offices in Aldgate East to Brixton where she had a meet with one of Tony Dooley's brothers. Two hours later she left the meeting smiling.

Back in the caravan she had a telephone call from Michael. She assured him that it was all under control. All he had to do was wait. Tony made her a cup of coffee and they sat together companionably. News came in all day of different pitches that had been encroached on. Maura told each driver the same thing. To go home and come back the next day.

Geoffrey was annoyed and Michael knew it. 'She can't cope with all this on her own!'

'Let's just see how she gets on, Geoff. I think she might surprise us.'

'What if she gets hurt? Have you thought of that?'

Michael laughed. 'She won't. Why do you think I gave her Tony Dooley? Just leave her be, Geoff. If she cocks it up we can easily take over. If she gets a result, she's proved herself a worthy asset. Now let's forget it.'

Geoffrey was livid with Michael. How could a young girl like Maura be expected to cope with the likes of the Milano Brothers? 'Have you any idea how she's going to sort it all out?'

Michael lost his temper. Sometimes Geoffrey was like an old woman!

'No, I ain't! Now for fuck's sake give it a rest. She asked for twenty-four hours and she's gonna get it, all right?'

'All right . . . all right. Keep your hair on!'

They sat together in silence. Michael hoped that Maura did not let him down. He was well aware of the stir her appointment as head of the creamers had created on the street. He had been a laughing stock, not only among rival villains but among his own workforce. Not that anyone would ever say it to his face. In their world women were either wives or mistresses. They were not thought capable of running a 'moody' business, unless they were brasses; then they sold the only asset they had, their bodies, and nine times out of ten a man was behind that – either a pimp or a boyfriend. He crossed his fingers as he thought about what he had done. A lot lay on Maura's performance in the next twenty-four hours. He just hoped that he had not underestimated her.

George Milano was forty-five years old. His wife was twenty-two. She had flown over from Palermo two years earlier, a week before he married her. She had already given him two sons, and was lying beneath him passively as he puffed and panted on top of her when the telephone by the bed rang. George glanced at the clock. It was two o'clock in the morning. Not letting his stroke falter, he answered the phone, still pumping away at her. She watched his face, a detached expression in her eyes. She had been quick to learn that if she lay quietly he was soon finished. Even though she felt nothing for this fat old man on top of her, it annoyed her female pride that he answered the phone while he made love to her.

'Yeah?' His voice was breathy and stilted.

'Is that George Milano?' It was Maura Ryan's voice! He was so shocked he nearly missed his stroke.

'What do you want?'

'I just thought I'd let you know that your yard was blown up five minutes ago. I happened to be there when it went up.' The line went dead.

As did George's erection. He lay on top of his young wife with his mouth hanging open, the telephone receiver still in his hand.

Magdalena Milano brought up her long slender arms and, putting a finger under her husband's chin, pushed his mouth closed. She had to endure his nightly assaults, she accepted that, but she did not have to look at his false teeth and his yellow tongue.

The action spurred him back to life. He leapt from the bed, his flaccid penis lost in the roll of fat that was his stomach. Screaming abuse in Italian, he began to dress himself. Magdalena rolled over and closed her eyes, grateful to whoever was on the phone for cutting her husband's sexual appetite short. When he left the house five minutes later she was asleep.

By the time George got to his yard in Aldgate East the worst of the fires had been put out. He saw a police car and went straight to the officers standing by it.

'I know who did this thing! It was the Ryans! They rang me up to tell me . . .' His voice trailed off. Sitting in the police car was Maura Ryan.

She looked at him innocently. 'I beg your pardon?'

Suddenly George Milano realised exactly what he was up against. His vision of usurping the Ryans' position in London was replaced by one of his body floating in the Thames. He heard the two officers laughing. Turning from their grinning faces he went to what had once been his yard. Nearly all his vans were destroyed. As Maura watched the man's shoulders slump inside his suit she felt a moment of pity for him. She had just ruined his business. Then her heart hardened as she reminded herself that if he had had his way the boot would be on the other foot. She got out of the police car. Her brother owned most of the officers in this area. She went to George Milano and put her hand on his shoulder.

'I did try to warn you, Mr Milano.'

He nodded imperceptibly. 'I know that.'

'I'm not sorry for what happened here tonight, but I am sorry it had to come to this.'

He nodded again. She left him. Getting into her car with Tony Dooley, she went to her own yard. She would stay there for the rest of the night with Tony and a couple of his friends. If there were going to be any comebacks she would sort that out herself as well.

Tony bought the *Daily Mirror* at five-thirty. The explosion in the Milanos' yard had made the middle pages. It said that following the ramming of rival ice cream vans in Baker Street, a well-known Italian ice cream merchant's yard had been firebombed. The police believed it was the work of another Italian family. The Italians were known to be the main distributors of ice cream in London and the surrounding areas. The story went on to describe George

194

Milano's father's rise to riches. From an ice cream barrow-boy in the late eighteen hundreds, he had built up the Milano Brothers business empire . . .

Maura, Tony and the other men laughed. They had done it!

Michael took the call from George Milano at nine-fifteen. 'Hello. Michael Ryan here.'

'Hello, Michael. It is George . . . George Milano. How are you?'

'I'm fine, Georgie. Which is more than I can say for you, ain't it?'

'I did not realise your sister had your protection . . .' His voice sounded desperate. Michael cut him off.

'My sister has my protection, Georgie, but only when she asks for it. Whoever done that bit of business last night works for *her*, Georgie, not me. It's her you've got to pacify.'

The line went quiet.

'I know what you was thinking, Georgie. Chatter always gets back to the person being chattered about. I know what the word was on the street. That I was a nutter for allowing my sister to take over the creamers. But it paid off, didn't it? She pissed all over your fireworks, didn't she? Well, I'll tell you again. If you wanna bargain, you do it with her.'

He replaced the telephone in its cradle, then laughed out loud. He looked at Geoffrey, and, pointing to the newspaper on his desk, said, 'She's a fucking girl ain't she?'

At six-thirty that morning Maura's workforce turned up for work. They greeted her warmly. She had not only their respect but their friendship. To Maura this was an added bonus. As she watched them sorting out their vans and stocking up, she felt a sudden pride in what she had done. They drove from the site with her watching. Then, as if all of one mind, they began to play their jingles. The noise was deafening. The Dingly Dell music was a clanging rendition of the old music hall favourite: 'How much is that doggy in the window?'

195

Maura laughed out loud as she placed her hands over her ears to blot out the noise. All that day she found herself humming the tune. It was a turning point in her life. Within eighteen months she ran every site in London. Thanks to her own natural friendliness, coupled with a ruthless use of pickaxe handles and muscle men, Maura Ryan was well and truly on her way.

Book Two

Pecunia non olet
(Money has no smell) – Emperor Vespasian, AD 9–79

I fear the Greeks,
even when they bring gifts – Virgil 70–19 BC

Chapter Fourteen

1975

Roy walked into the Lotus House Restaurant in Dagenham. It was three-thirty in the morning, 1 December 1975. He walked up to the tiny bar in the corner of the restaurant and banged on the counter. He frowned. Mr Wong was usually there to greet him, offer him a complimentary drink and pay him his money. Instinctively, Roy's hand went into his jacket, to the gun that he kept there. With his free hand he banged once more on the counter.

'Oi, anyone at home!'

He sensed rather than heard two men step from the shadows of the dimly lit room. He turned to face them.

'Mr Ryan? Mr Roy Ryan?' A short swarthy man stood there smiling at him – an oily smile that dripped from his face. Looking at him, Roy knew that if he got close enough the man would stink of garlic. His hand tightened on his gun. 'You have no need of your firearm tonight, Mr Ryan. I am intending to be very nice to you. Very friendly. I am a very generous man.'

He snapped his fingers at the large muscular young man beside him.

'Dimitri, get Mr Ryan and myself a drink.' As the younger man walked to the bar, the smaller one offered Roy a seat.

'Who are you?' His voice was careful and controlled.

'I am Mr Dopolis. You may laugh if you want.' He paused to allow Roy to chuckle. Roy ignored him. 'Normally you English hoot with laughter when you hear it.' He shrugged. 'Unfortunately, that was my father's name and his father's before him.' He smiled again. 'I could not have changed it.' His voice was conversational, as if they were old friends.

'Look, Mr Dopolpolis, or whatever your name is, what do you want and how do you know who I am?'

Mr Dopolis shook his head sadly.

'You young men! Always in a hurry!'

He snapped his fingers again and the boy brought over their drinks.

'Please, Mr Ryan. Sit down and have a drink with me.'

Roy sat down opposite the man. Up close he realised that his first thought had been correct. Dopolis *did* stink of garlic.

'Drink your whisky, Mr Ryan. We are going to have a little chat.'

Dimitri stood between the two of them and Roy noticed that he was carrying a gun. In his padded leather jacket it would have been virtually undetectable by anyone else. However, Roy was unnerved to observe that it was no ordinary handgun the youth was carrying. He would bet his last pound that the thigh-length leather the boy was wearing had a special 'long pocket' fitted inside it. That meant only one thing. Young Dimitri was carrying a sawn-off shotgun.

He glanced at the door, weighing up his chances of escape. Mr Dopolis laughed out loud, bringing Roy's head round to face him again.

'I know what you are thinking, young man.' Dopolis held his hand up as if to stop Roy leaving. 'You are free to go when you have heard what I have to say. You won't need *your* gun. Not tonight anyway.'

The man's voice was cold and calculating, as if he took great pains to pronounce his words properly.

Roy leant back in his chair nonchalantly and took a long sip of the Chivas Regal Dimitri had placed in front of him. He was well aware that he was not Brain of Britain. Roy had never overestimated himself. He could work the bookies, the hostess clubs, the minding. He was also first in line for any armed robberies that were in the offing. Roy was the eternal heavy. That's why he was in the Lotus House now. He was collecting the 'rents', the protection money. What he did not know was that Dopolis had picked him out for these very qualities. He wanted a message taken to Michael Ryan and Roy seemed to be the perfect messenger boy.

'I want you to tell your brother something for me, Roy. May I call you Roy?' He did not wait for an answer, but carried on as if taking everything he said for granted. 'I want you to tell Michael that although he has run the West End satisfactorily for many years, people are getting . . . how shall we say? . . . upset at the way he has gradually taken over East London and even parts of Essex!'

He laughed as if it was all a big misunderstanding. 'He collects the "rents" on the restaurants and bookies, not to mention the pubs and the clubs. He owns all the cab ranks. He even has the monopoly on the ice cream and hot dogs. Not forgetting that he gets a percentage of any blags that take place on the manor. Now I ask you, is that fair? My friends and I would like to know what is left for us? We want to earn a living as well. We have all joined forces, so to speak. We have only one avenue left for making money – drugs – and the blacks have always had the edge where they're concerned.'

His voice became low and conspiratorial, as if Roy was his dearest and oldest friend. 'You must tell your brother what we have been discussing. Tell him that myself and many others have joined forces. We will fight him if needs be. Tell him that we want the East End. The pubs, the clubs, the restaurants. Everything. He must make do with the West End, North London and South of the water. Surely that is enough for him? Tell him that he has my word we will not interfere with him.'

Roy burst out laughing. He sat and literally roared with laughter. Great bursting gales of merriment that rendered him incapable of talking. This man was some kind of nutter. He had to be. Everyone in the East End who was employed in a 'fringe' business, whether it was a jellied eel or a market stall, worked indirectly for Mickey. Even the blaggers, and they were getting more and more as the years went on, came and saw Mickey or one of his intermediaries before nipping into their local Tescos waving their sawn-offs at everyone. Now this little Greek twat wanted him to take a threatening message to Michael. He bubbled over with laughter again, forgetting the youth with his shotgun, forgetting everything except the crazy man before him.

Dopolis stared at him icily.

'You can laugh, Mr Ryan, but I am afraid that I and my friends are very serious. Very serious indeed. As you will soon find out.'

Roy wiped his eyes with his handkerchief. 'Listen, Cocker, Mickey has not, as you put it, muscled in on the East End. We fought for this shitheap and we won it fair and square.'

The little man sat straighter in his chair. 'Your brother –' he pointed at Roy – 'firebombed a taxi rank belonging to my cousin Stavros. Only two days after your brother's funeral my cousin was crippled for life. He was so badly hurt he could not control his armies.' Dopolis's face was red with temper and he had flecks of spittle at the corners of his lips.

Roy interrupted him rudely.

'Armies! What fucking armies? He couldn't control a bumper car. He had my brother murdered!' Roy was losing his own temper now. The last shred of fear dissolved in the face of Dopolis's argument. Anthony's death was still an open wound with all the Ryans.

Dopolis forced himself to remain calm. He smiled. 'That famous Irish temper of yours . . . it will be your downfall one of these days. Remember this – when you are in a temper you do not think straight. Michael should have worked out an agreement with my cousin. Something that would have been satisfactory to both parties. If he had done that your brother would be alive today.'

'Bollocks!' Roy stood up. 'Let me tell you something, Mr Oppodopolis or whatever your fucking name is . . . Mickey will rip your ears off and shove them up your arse. And he'll smile while he's doing it. So do yourself a favour and piss off. I'm a very busy man.'

He pushed Dimitri out of the way. 'As for your Action Man, if you're gonna use your weapon, do it now. You've been standing there like the orphan of the storm . . . you big prat!'

The boy looked at Dopolis who shook his head slowly. Roy walked through the service door into the kitchen of the restaurant.

Mr Wong was sitting in there with his wife and daughter clutching him, frightened. His son was standing behind his father. He had recent bruises around his face. They all stared at him pathetically. Roy's blood was up now and taking his gun from its holster he stormed back into the restaurant. These people paid protection money. The least he could do was protect them. The restaurant was empty. He walked back to the kitchen.

'What happened?'

All four started talking at once, the mother and daughter in Cantonese. Roy put his hands over his ears and shouted: 'SHUT UP!' at the top of his voice. They all stopped speaking abruptly. Roy pointed to the son, Hap Ki, who spoke reasonable English, and said: 'You tell me what happened.'

'I tell you, Mr Ryan. The man took monry we had for you. In future, he say, you pay monry to us. Get bugger! I say we pay Mr Ryan. We always pay Mr Ryan. Nor anymore they say. If we no give monry, then place burned to ground by weekend. Still we not pay. My father tell them that Mr Ryan good friend and will protect us . . . So they start to bash me in face.' He pointed to his swollen eye. 'So my father gave them monry. We can't pay you now.'

Roy nodded. 'Never mind about that now. Look, I'll be back at the weekend as usual. If they come to see you before I get back here, phone me at this number.' He took a small card out of his jacket pocket. 'Now don't worry. This will all be sorted out in a few days.' He nodded to the women and walked out of the kitchen. He put his gun back in its holster. Then taking a serviette from the counter, carefully picked up the glass that Dopolis had used. Now, he thought, we'll see how good our friends at the Met are.

He left the restaurant and went to his car. Tessa, his Doberman, was lying on the back seat asleep. She shot into action as he unlocked his car, barking and growling. Roy spoke to her gently until she calmed down. She had been lying asleep on more than sixteen thousand pounds. As the dog settled back down Roy smiled to himself. He collected over sixty-four thousand a month. There was no way Michael was going to let that go, especially not to a relative of Stavros, the man who'd murdered Anthony. Roy started up the car. That Dopolis had to be some kind of head banger.

Michael Ryan was pacing up and down his office, a sure sign he was agitated. He pulled on his cigarette and blew the smoke out noisily from between his lips.

'Did he look familiar like? Have you ever seen him about?'

Roy shook his head.

'Nah, never seen him in my life before. He was a saucy fucker, though. The big bastard, Dimitri, was carrying a sawn-off, I'm certain of it. They'd collected old Wong's rent before I got there so they were definitely waiting for me.'

'What exactly did he say about Stavros?'

'Just that he was his cousin, that we had bombed him out and while he was hurt . . .' Roy laughed again '. . . he couldn't control his "armies". Armies, I ask you! Then he went on about you having the whole of London. Oh, Mickey, I tell you. He was a right prat.'

Geoffrey got up from his seat and glanced at his watch. 'How about we let Roy get home and get some shut-eye? It's nearly half-past four.' He looked at Roy. 'I expect you're dying to get home. The baby's due any day, isn't it?'

Roy nodded, a big grin on his face.

Michael rubbed his eyes with his fingers and leant against the wall of the office.

'I'm sorry, Roy. You get off home, mate. Tell Janine that

she's got to phone the old woman as soon as she comes into labour. The old Dutch is like a cat on a hot tin roof over this baby.'

Roy laughed.

'If you could see the bloody stuff that they've got for it. Cots and cribs and bleeding layettes. It's enough to drive a man to drink, I tell ya!'

Michael smiled. 'You love it, mate. Is Carla going home when the baby's born?'

Roy's face dropped.

'I don't think so, Mickey. Maura's house is nearer her college and that.'

There was an embarrassed silence. It was a well-known fact that Janine could not stand her daughter around her. Carla gravitated between her grandmother's house and Maura's. Geoffrey coughed loudly.

'Anyway, mate, we'll see you later on. Give Janine our best.'

'I will, Geoff.' He got up to go. Michael took a package off his desk and passed it to Roy.

'One last thing, would you drop this off at Black Tony's house? Tell him it's a pound bag and I want the money for it by Saturday latest. Give it the big'un while you're there. He's been getting a bit lairy lately.'

Roy took the package.

'Okey doke. See you later then.'

When he had left, Geoffrey poured out two brandies. Giving one to Michael, he sat himself in the easy chair opposite the desk. Michael sat at the desk rolling the brandy in his glass.

'So, Mickey. What do you think? Trouble?'

Mickey sipped his drink. 'With a capital T, Bruv.'

He tossed back the rest of the brandy and stood up. 'Let's get off home, Geoffrey, I'm knackered. I can't think when I feel like this.'

Geoffrey gulped his own drink down. By the time he had pulled on his overcoat, Michael had already turned off the lights and made his way down the stairs. Outside the club they stood on the pavement, both gulping in the cool night air. Michael touched Geoffrey's shoulder before getting into his car and driving off.

As Geoffrey watched Michael's Mercedes pulling away he was aware of a feeling of annoyance. He walked slowly to where his own car was parked. He knew in his heart that Michael wanted Maura's opinion on the night's aggravation and he resented it. Over the last few years she had gradually moved up in the firm, until now, at only twenty-five, she practically ran the lot with Mickey. She was his right hand, as he never tired of telling anyone who would listen. She was the only person who could openly disagree with him and get away with it. This fact alone had earned her the respect not only of all her brothers but of the entire workforce, every man Jack of them. She had also masterminded a bank robbery that still had the police baffled eighteen months after the event. Geoffrey was beginning to hate her. Marvellous Fucking Maura . . . the Woman of the Century. He unlocked his car and sat in it for a few minutes, staring out into the night. His whole life had been built around Michael, and he was realising more and more each day that his brother did not really need him. It was a frightening thought. Without Michael, Geoffrey was nothing and he knew it. He started the car up. As he pulled away he turned on his radio. The soothing sound of the Carpenters filled the car. Geoffrey smiled to himself. Maura was like most women . . . give them enough rope and they generally hanged themselves. Eventually she would foul her nest and Michael would give her the bad news. All he had to do was wait.

He relaxed his grip on the steering wheel and allowed the strains of 'We've Only Just Begun' to wash over him.

Michael had driven from the club to Maura's house in Rainham, Essex. He had to see her about the events of the night. Maura had something that he would never have in a million years: she had a calculating nature. She never let her emotions interfere with her work. Michael respected this trait in her. Where he would lose his temper,

Maura would calmly sort out a crisis. Her favourite expression was, 'Think with your head, not your heart.'

He looked at the house. It was in darkness. He got out of his car. When Maura had bought this house he had laughed at her. It was a large Georgian monstrosity that had seemed to be falling down. Now, a year laer, it was beautiful. She had put in new windows, new doors, and the large overgrown frontage was now an in-and-out driveway. She had bought the place for pennies and if she sold it she would more than double her investment. In Michael's eyes this was another of Maura's clever schemes. Something that, until she had looked into and studied, he would never have dreamt of investing in.

He crunched across the pea-shingled drive up to the large double front door. He rang the bell. About five minutes later a bedraggled Carla opened the front door to him, her face lighting up as she smiled.

'Hello, Uncle Mickey. Auntie Maura's just getting dressed!' Michael playfully slapped her behind. 'Don't you let Maws catch you calling her "Auntie"! She'll skin you alive!' They walked into the lounge.

'Don't worry, I won't.' Her voice was full of fun.

In fact, Carla was one big bundle of fun and laughter. She was a natural mimic, and had the gift of making people laugh. It always amazed Michael that her own mother had so little time for her. Still, he reflected, she had Maura and his mother. They more than made up for Janine's indifference.

'Shall I make a pot of tea?'

'Yeah. There's a good girl.'

He watched her as she left the room. At twenty she was a lovely girl. She still had reddish-brown hair and freckles, but now had the grace that her mother had always had. She walked like a cat, with a long-legged stride. As she was now, in a shortie nightdress, her legs looked impossibly long. Michael sat himself on the Chesterfield and waited for Maura. When she walked into the lounge she looked as if she had never even been asleep. Her blonde hair was now cut in a bob and it was immaculate. She wore a pink silk robe that barely covered her full breasts, and high-heeled mules. She grinned at her brother.

'So what brings you here at daybreak?'

'There's been some trouble, Maws.'

'I guessed as much. Ah, here's Carla with some tea!'

She took the tray and placed it on the Edwardian table to the left of the sofa. As she poured the tea Carla kept up a stream of chatter.

Michael smiled and answered Carla's seemingly endless supply of questions, relaxing back into his seat. Maura had good taste. The room was decorated in a mixture of peach tones and pinks. The carpets and heavy drapes were a deep burgundy. It was a cosy room. Even though it was full of expensive furniture it was a room that looked lived in, from the magazines on the coffee table to the Jacobean bookcase full of every title imaginable. Dickens and Trollope rubbed shoulders with Harold Robbins and Len Deighton. Maura's tastes in reading were as extreme as everything else in her life.

Carla did not think it at all strange that her uncle should get them out of bed at six in the morning. It was like everything else in her life with them. The unexpected was the norm around here and you had better get used to it or you were liable to go up the wall!

Michael and Maura allowed Carla to chatter to them. She was like the family mascot. Loved by them all, as if the rejection she had experienced when her mother had literally handed her over to Sarah, had made her their communal property. In their own ways, they tried to make up to her for what her mother had done. Though with Maura, Michael guessed, it went deeper. Carla was the child she had had aborted from her body. She was funding Carla through college. Maura made sure that Carla had everything, from decent clothes to a small car.

Carla finished telling them about her latest boyfriend and glanced at the ormolu clock on the mantelpiece of the Louis XVI fireplace.

She squealed: 'Oh, no, it's nearly seven o'clock! I'd

better get a move on. I've got to leave at eight!' She flitted from the room, all legs and hair. Michael laughed.

'She's a nice kid, Maws.' Even though Maura was only five years older than Carla, no one ever alluded to that fact. It was as if Maura had always been a woman. In Michael's eyes anyway she had never been any different. She had been a little sister for a long time, then she had become the mainstay of his life. There had never been an inbetween. Maura had never seemed to have that coltish look that Carla had. That magical illusion that was the turning point from adolescent to woman. Maura had become a woman overnight and had been one ever since. Maura Ryan had been a woman from the age of seventeen.

'She's a good kid, Mickey, as well as a nice one. I miss her when she's at Mother's.'

'I bet you do. She's company in this great big rattling drum of yours.'

Maura laughed. 'You leave my house out of it. You're just gutted that you didn't buy it. Now what's all this about? What's happened?'

Michael explained to her. She sat curled up on the seat beside him, chain smoking as she listened. She did not interrupt him once. When he had finished, she smiled.

'So it's Stavros's cousin is it?'

He smiled too.

'Well, we'll give the fat little bastard a run for his money!'

Michael grinned at her. Maura had said the words that he wanted to hear.

'That's exactly what I thought! Listen, Maws, I want you to think over what I've said. Get a few ideas together and then meet me later at the club. I'll get off home now or Jonny will think that I've been topped by someone. I'll see you later then.'

'All right, Mickey. What about the glass that Roy nicked? Shall I have it sent over to the Met? They might come up with a name . . . a legitimate name and address.'

Michael slapped his hand on his forehead. 'Bugger me, Maws. That went right out of me mind. I've left it in the club.'

'Never mind, Mick. Just you get home and get a bit of sleep. I'll sort all that out.'

When Michael left, Maura went to her kitchen and made herself some tea and toast. The more she thought about what Michael had said, the more impossible it seemed. Who would wait over fifteen years to regain a territory? This bloke might be Stavros's cousin, but his story did not ring true.

Carla breezed into the kitchen and pinched a slice of toast from Maura's plate. 'I'll be late tonight, Maws. All right?'

'All right, love. Drive carefully.'

'I will.'

Then she was gone. As always when Carla left the house, it felt empty. She seemed to breathe life into it. Still pondering what Michael had said, Maura went up for a shower. She had a busy day ahead.

Chapter Fifteen

Maura walked into Le Buxom at ten-thirty-five. The hostesses were, as always, pleased to see her, unlike some of the men who worked for the Ryans who were wary of Maura. She was regarded as a hard-hearted bitch by the majority of them. Though if any one of them got hurt during the course of their work, it was Maura who saw to it that their wives were amply provided for. She half guessed what was said about her and made a conscious effort to keep the myth alive. Maura was happy enough with their respect, she did not want their love. She wanted to be known as a hard bitch. It suited her. The only people she could not con into disliking her were the hostesses.

They loved her. She always made sure that the girls with children got a good bonus around Christmas time, which was much appreciated. Also, most hostess clubs left the girl to sort out her hostess fee with the punter. Maura had a rule that the hostess fee, which was twenty-five pounds, went on the overall bill. Then, if there was a row over it, which was what frequently happened in the clubs, the bouncer would ensure that the hostess fee also was paid. A girl who had sat all night with a punter and talked him into buying champagne at two hundred pounds a bottle and cigarettes in packs of fifty that cost three times their retail price, could help run up a bill of over seven hundred pounds. If there was a fight over the payment she was hardly likely to be going on to a hotel with the punter. Therefore all she had for her efforts was the hostess fee. At least in Maura's club they could guarantee that. It was not unusual for a customer to be taken to the back bar where he was punched and threatened until the bill was paid.

Consequently, Le Buxom was known as the place to work. Maura offered them a degree of protection that had gradually wiped out pimping on her girls. For that they respected and loved her. They also kept their ears to the ground and let her in on anything that they heard. If they got any kind of venereal disease they were out, that was Maura's main stipulation, along with drugs and drinking. She had seen the effect that these things had on the prostitutes. It made them violent and aggressive. All prostitutes looked on one another as rivals. Hostess clubs were alive with gossip and back biting and trouble. Whores would rip one another apart, yet defend a sworn enemy to the police; would show a young 'greenie' the ropes, then try and muscle in on her punter. They lied, cheated and stole from one another.

All clubs had 'head girls', older, over the hill prostitutes who were as hard as nails. They were employed to keep order among the girls and liaise between them and the punters. In some clubs, if the head girl was offered a 'drink' – a percentage of the girls' 'case' fees – they would book these girls before their allotted time. (Hostesses generally lived by the rule that first into work was the first to be booked at a table.) So if a girl was offering a 'drink' she would be more likely to get a generous punter, either Arab or Chinese, both races known to be well heeled and unafraid of large fixed bills.

This form of hostessing had been gradually stamped out in Maura's club and the girls were grateful for it. Maura's club had waiting lists of girls who wanted to work for her. She ran her club like she ran her cab ranks and her hot dog stalls – fair and square. She was always on the right side of the police and had never had so much as a parking ticket herself. She was a very different person to the naive young girl that Terry Petherick had known. She was frightened of no one. Even the large, hard-faced prostitutes, known lesbians and violent streetwalkers, held no terror for her. She walked the streets of Soho without a trace of fear. She had established her reputation long ago.

Tonight, an ex-hostess had brought in her baby and every woman in the club was clustered around the tiny bundle. Punters were left sitting alone while the child was duly praised and cuddled. The girl, Jenny Randle, had left the club a year earlier to marry one of her regular customers, a banker from Chiswick. She was radiantly happy. Maura took the baby into her arms and breathed in the smell of Johnson's baby powder and urine. The baby was wrapped in a white shawl and all that was visible was a tiny heart-shaped face, still red and wrinkled. The child opened its eyes and yawned, its tiny little rosebud mouth making a perfect 'O'. Maura felt the familiar longing rising inside her, and was embarrassed to find tears in her eyes. That was all she needed in front of the hostesses! Proof that she was soft.

'Oh, Jenny, she's beautiful . . . Gorgeous.'

'Thanks, Miss Ryan. I'm so happy.'

Michael walked down the stairs and into the club. All he saw was twenty-odd women huddled together at the entrance to the meat seats.

'What's going on here? A bloody union meeting?' His voice was annoyed. At his words the girls broke away from Maura. Michael was astonished to see her standing there, in a hundred-pound suit, holding a baby! As he looked into her face he saw the naked longing there, as did most of the hostesses, and suddenly he could not be cross with her. Maura treated the girls as if they were valued employees. Sometimes it drove him mad. She listened to their stupid quarrels, helped them when they were in trouble, financial or otherwise, arranged abortions for them, even paid for their baby-sitters if the woman was having a hard time getting 'case'. He admitted, grudgingly, that the club ran smoothly, but this was the ultimate piss take. It was like a secretary going into her office with new offspring. The bird was a brass, for Christ's sake. Next thing they'd be having Tupperware parties. Maura smiled at him.

'Jenny's new baby, Michael. Isn't she lovely?'

213

All the hostesses were on their guard, waiting for his reaction. Maura gave him a penetrating look that begged for his co-operation in front of the girls. He smiled to himself. She had so much front! Only Maura would expect him, Michael Ryan, the most feared man in London, to make a fuss of an old tom's baby. With all the aggravation they had at the moment with that nutty Greek, Maura expected him to act like the benevolent uncle! He took out his wallet, and pulling out a couple of ten pound notes thrust them at Jenny. He smiled his most winning smile that secretly melted all the women's hearts.

'Get the baby something from us, Jenny.'

She took the proffered money and grinned at him.

'Thank you, Mr Ryan. I will.'

Feeling embarrassed, he left the women to carry on their inspection of the tiny scrap of humanity and went upstairs to his office.

Maura grinned at the hostesses who were all smiling at each other. It was at times like this that they were made aware of how lucky they were to have Maura Ryan's championship. She treated them as real people, not just whores. Even though they sold their bodies for a living, a fact that automatically made them second class citizens to the legitimate section of the female community, Maura made them feel like honest working girls. Like real people, doing a respectable job.

She handed the tiny baby back to Jenny and pulled down the jacket of her pale gold silk suit.

'She's a diamond, Jenny. You're very lucky. Now then, you lot!' She made her voice jocular. 'There's some lonely-looking punters sitting at the tables! Back to work!'

The girls who had left men sitting alone went meekly back to their tables, glad of the change in their nightly routine. Jenny's baby had been a little light relief.

Maura, leaving the other girls still cooing over the baby, followed Michael upstairs. In the office she put her finger to her lips and laughed.

'Not one word, Michael Ryan!'

214

He sat behind his desk, scowling at her.

'Well, Maws! What next? National Insurance stamps and baby showers?'

'Oh, shut up, you old bastard! What you seem to forget is that those women down there . . .' she pointed a perfectly manicured finger to the floor '. . . bring us in an awful lot of money. Jenny was one of the best hostesses in the West End. She brought thousands into this club.' Maura started to giggle. 'Not to mention a few highly respectable customers. If you remember rightly she worked the New Rockingham club before we poached her . . . *and* she brought her customers with her. So there!' She poked her tongue out at him saucily.

Michael ran his hands through his thick dark hair. There was a little glint of malevolence in his dark blue eyes. 'Have you by any chance thought over the problems of last night? Or was you out visiting the waifs and strays at Routen House?'

Maura walked behind her brother and slipped her arms around his neck. She kissed his cheek lightly, breathing in the smell of Old Spice aftershave.

'I love you when you're angry, Mickey. And Routen House was closed down years ago. They don't have workhouses no more. They have to go to the Salvation Army.'

Michael grabbed her hands and squeezed them. He laughed. 'You've got an answer for everything. And that Carla's getting just like you. Another trappy bird in the family is all I need!'

Maura pulled away from him and got herself a drink. She needed one. Holding Jenny's baby had unnerved her more than she liked to admit to herself. As she had clasped it to her breast she had felt a squeezing sensation in the pit of her stomach, similar to the feeling that preceded driving fast over a large hill. Her tummy had turned over. What she would not give to have a child of her own! She sipped her whisky.

'Well, down to business. What do you think about all that last night, Princess?'

Maura settled herself in the chair opposite her brother.

215

She crossed her silk-clad legs and leant her right arm on the desk, staring at Michael.

'Well, it sounds to me like the bloke wants us to split territories. Let's face it, we've got our fingers in a lot of pies, haven't we? I sent the glass over to the fingerprint boys this morning.' She shook her head. 'I don't know, Mickey. They make me laugh. They want their money for their little flutters and bits of skirt, then when you want them to return the favour, their arsehole goes. Well, I made a few go this morning, I can tell you! We should have a result late tonight. Realistically, Mickey, until this Dopolis makes his next move, or we find out something about him, we can't do much anyway.

'As for the protection money, he obviously knew that Wong's was Roy's last call, so taking the old boy's rent was just a token thing. A little bit of defiance. Roy had over sixteen grand in his motor. Even though he had Tessa in the car, if this Dopolis had wanted the money he could have got it. If what Roy said was right, and the young bloke had a sawn-off.' She shrugged. 'Well, they could have taken the lot, couldn't they? No, I think we had better wait until this Dopolis gets in touch. Then I bet if we offer him a little bit of action, he'll be as happy as Larry. The fact that he's Stavros's cousin does put the mockers on it a bit . . . it means we all hold grudges. But for Christ's sake, Bruv, who would be mug enough to take us lot on?' She waved her hand dismissively. 'We'll just wait and see, I ain't too trashed about it all.

'Now then, what about those houses out in Essex? Have you thought about them at all?'

Michael nodded. 'If you think they're worth it, it's up to you.'

He was digesting all that Maura had said. It made sense.

'Well, the thing is, Mickey, they're all knockdown rebuilds. And I've got a smashing little firm of NHBC housebuilders who would love the work. We'll make a fortune, Mickey. There's no doubt about it. Property is the business to be in these days.'

'Like all the old "tut" you've bought around the old docks?'

Maura smiled tolerantly.

'You crack me up, Maura. Imagine buying a load of old warehouses and Dockers' Mansions! . . .'

'Those old Dockers' Mansions will be worth a fortune one day, boy. You mark my words.'

'Oh, yeah, Maws! I can just see everyone dying to live in a two up two down, with a carzey in the garden and a tin bath in the front room. I bet you'll have queues of people just dying to buy them!'

Maura laughed. She sat back in her chair. She had never regained the weight she had lost after the abortion and was fashionably thin. In her gold silk suit and matching shoes and shirt she looked as if she had just stepped from the pag s of a fashion magazine. Her white-blonde hair was freshly washed and framed her face like a platinum halo. Her bright blue eyes were expertly made up. She was, Michael reflected, a very beautiful and sophisticated woman. Yet she had never, to his knowledge, had a boyfriend. Not since the policeman. Michael guessed, rightly, that she still held a torch for him. Though they had never, ever discussed it. It was the only taboo subject between them. They discussed everything under the sun, except Terry Petherick.

'Do you remember Auntie Nellie's house, Mickey? I used to love staying there when I was a kid. I remember one New Year . . . the old man was in the 'ville, I think, and Mum dropped me off there for a couple of nights.' Maura closed her eyes as she remembered it all. 'I was only about six or seven, and as the clock chimed in the New Year Uncle Bertie opened the front door. It was foggy that night. I can see it so clearly. All of a sudden all the ships' hooters began to blast. It was as if all the boats were going to sail straight into their little front room. The noise was deafening. Uncle Bertie gave me a hot toddy to help me sleep . . . I loved that little house.'

Michael grimaced at her comically. 'Turn it up, Maws! You'll have me crying in a minute!'

'You rotten sod! You've got no soul, that's your trouble! For your information, Michael Ryan, those old places will be worth the National Debt in a few years. There's talk of them building a marina there, everything.'

'On the old docklands?' His voice was sceptical.

'On the old docklands.'

'Well, I still can't see it, Maws.'

She sobered as she looked at him. 'Property is the money making scheme of the future. I'm telling you, Mickey. Houses don't eat nothing and they make you a fortune. You buy them cheap and you sit on them until the prices rise.

'There's so much building going on in London at the moment, soon there'll not be any building land left except what can be reclaimed from the old dock areas: Wapping, Woolwich, all up the Thames.' She smiled. 'You just wait and see.'

'Do you know something, Maws?'

She looked at him, puzzled. 'No. What?'

'You are one clever bird. If you had been a bloke you could have taken over the world.' His voice held genuine admiration.

'Well, I've got you and the whole of London. That's all I want, Mickey.'

'You'll always have me darling.' Michael's voice was soft. Maura smiled at him. As long as she had Mickey she didn't need a husband, a lover – anything. As she looked into his dark blue eyes she was aware of how much he had changed over the years. At forty years old he was still a handsome man but his body was more bulky now than it had been. He was beginning to run to fat. Yet he was still good-looking enough to gather glances wherever he went, from men as well as women. His dark hair was touched with grey. His face still had the high cheekbones and deepset eyes of his youth, except now he had the crow's feet and lines that denoted middle age. Like most handsome men, his age suited him. Unlike women who tried to keep young for as long as was physically possible, men like Michael wore their age with a panache that made it look like a desirable attribute. Maura poured them both out a whisky.

'Before I forget, Mickey. I had Mahoney on the blower

218

today. He wants some more hardware, mainly M16 rifles. He said that Father McCormack would get them to Eire as usual. Don't ask me how. Probably by boat. He wants them by the end of the month and I said that was fine . . . provided he paid the money up front. I don't really like dealing with them, Mickey. But as you say – if we don't, someone else will.'

He nodded. Father McCormack's predictions in Sarah's front room all those years ago had proved startlingly accurate. Now they dealt with many aspects of the Irish Republican Army's operations. Not only arms, but also providing safe houses and, when possible, safe conduct for its soldiers.

'How much are they willing to spend?'

'A lot. The arms from Libya have dried up since the Arabs started fighting amongst themselves, but the money from America is astronomical now. They can't spend it quick enough. Shall I get in touch with Dixon then?'

Michael sighed. 'Yeah. Use Billy Bootnose as a go-between. I don't want you or me seen with them.'

'I will do. While you were sleeping the day away, Michael, I – ' she poked herself in the chest '– have been sorting out the monthly accounts . . . as well as sorting out the fingerprint men!' She laughed. 'We've had a few big bets placed at the bookies, but no harm's been done. The club's doing all right. Considering it's nearly Christmas, the hot dogs are bringing in a small fortune. Especially on the new sites we took over.'

'You bought them out then?'

'Oh, yeah!' Her voice was indignant. 'It was all done legally and above board.'

'Except Roy had an axe in his hand when you went to negotiate!'

Maura made a little moue with her lips.

'Well, I think that did help. But I gave them a good price, Mickey. Well above the pitches' value. The cab ranks are booming, thanks to the cold weather and armfuls of Christmas presents. All in all, life is good. Once we sort the Greek prat out, we'll be laughing!'

'Thanks for sorting all that for me, Maws. What's the SP on the family front?'

She frowned. 'Not too good actually, Mickey. I had word today that Benny and Garry have been getting lairy in pubs and clubs all over town. Shouting their mouths off about you, me, and anything they can think of.'

'That don't sound like our Garry, Maws!'

'I know, but it's the truth. They haven't been working, Mickey. Sammy Goldbaum said he hadn't seen either of them for days. He's been running the ranks himself. I think we should give him a drink for that. I thought we could slip him a monkey as a Christmas box.'

Michael slammed his fist on to the desk.

'All right, do that. Fucking marvellous, ain't it! A pissing front wheel skid running me businesses, and me own brothers, who get paid a hefty portion, are doing fuck all! Well, I've just about had it this time. If they don't pull their socks up, they're out on their arses. I can't afford to have lazy bastards on my team.'

'I know what you're saying, Mickey, and I'll get Geoffrey to have a word with them. By the way, have you heard from any of the boys today?'

He shook his head. 'No. Why?'

'Oh, nothing. It's just that I haven't seen hide nor hair of any of them, that's all.'

She yawned.

'You get yourself off home, Maws.'

'I might just do that, Mickey. I'm shattered. Not surprising considering I was woken out of my sleep this morning. Six o'clock this morning, to be precise.'

Michael laughed.

'I'll wait here for the bloke from the Met. As you say, we can't do anything until Dopolis makes a move or we find out more about him. We've got to find out exactly what we're dealing with.'

Maura walked around the desk and kissed his forehead. 'See you tomorrow, Mickey. Goodnight.'

'Goodnight, Princess.'

Maura left him and made her way to her car. As she

drove home she hoped that Carla would be in when she arrived. She worried about her, especially with Janine having another baby. Though Carla seemed happy enough about the impending birth, Maura was worried that the baby would further push her out of her parents' life. It was this overshadowing worry that made Maura shelve thoughts of the trouble with Dopolis. She wasn't to find out for a few days that he was a very dangerous man indeed.

Chapter Sixteen

Benny sat at the kitchen table eating an enormous breakfast. He insisted that his mother made him two eggs, five pieces of bacon, black pudding, mushrooms, and three giant sausages every morning. He ate this with five pieces of toast and washed it down with a whole pot of tea. He wiped the last of the toast around his plate and popped it into his mouth. He sat back in his chair replete, holding his stomach with both hands.

'That was handsome, Muvver.'

Sarah laughed. He was the last child to live at home and she was dreading the day when he, too, flew the nest.

'I don't know where you put it all, Benny.' She picked up his empty plate and placed it in the sink.

'I think I'll have a quick fag and then be on me way. It's about time I showed my boatrace at the betting office.' His voice sounded worried. Sarah turned to face him. Benny was her baby. She was aware of all his faults and still she loved him.

'Michael won't put up with you skiving off, you know. Or Maura.' Sarah's voice was tight when she spoke about her daughter. She could never get used to the fact that Maura ran the businesses with Michael. It bothered her more than she cared to admit. In Sarah's mind women married and had children. She admitted to herself, grudgingly, that Maura could not do that. But she still felt that no woman should live or work in what was to her a man's world. The shady life of Soho and hostess clubs was, to her, the lowest in the world, filled with the dregs of humanity.

Benny lit his Benson and Hedges cigarette and finished

his cup of tea. He glanced at the old kitchen clock. It was nearly eight-thirty.

'I'm off then, Muvver. I'll see you tonight, about sixish.' He got up from the table and kissed his mother lightly on the cheek. Sarah smiled at him and said what she said to him every day.

'You be careful now, Benny. And do what our Michael tells you.'

'I will. See you.' He went from the house. Sarah carried on with her washing up. She'd had a bad feeling on her since she had got out of bed – like a dragging pain in her side. She wiped her hands and turned on her radio. Jimmy Young would be on soon and she liked him. She began her day's work. Janine would be around at about ten and they were going to plan the Christmas celebrations.

She now looked on Janine as her daughter and Maura as a distant relative. Sarah would never admit to herself or anyone that she actively disliked Maura these days, it seemed blasphemous somehow. She did not like Carla living with her either. She wished she could get Janine and Carla to become close, but she had resigned herself long ago to the fact that Janine would never like her child. That she could not stand being in the same room as her.

She sighed. Children were a bind really. You loved them but they never seemed to be out of your life. Wherever they were they demanded your time and energy. She consoled herself with the fact that at least there would be a new baby soon. If she waited on the other boys to make her a grandmother she would be disappointed. None of them seemed to want to settle down, Michael for obvious reasons. She knew he had a man living with him. She closed her eyes and shuddered. As for Geoffrey and the rest of the boys – they gravitated from woman to woman. Now here was Janine, in her thirties, having another baby – though she had a sneaking suspicion that if Janine had been able to get rid of this child she would have.

Sarah began to wipe the kitchen table with a damp cloth. She'd better get a move on. She wanted to get the house sorted before Benjamin decided to get out of bed. He was another one. At fifty-nine he was like a man of ninety, shuffling about the house waiting for the Bramley Arms to open. She carried on cleaning, unaware that before the day was out there would be trouble the like of which she had never even dreamed of.

It was eleven o'clock and Michael and Maura were in the small offices above Le Buxom. The glass had been sent back late the night before from West End Central police station. The prints on the glass were not known to them. Whoever it was had no criminal record. Michael and Maura were no nearer to finding out exactly who Dopolis was and what he dealt in than they'd been at the beginning.

'Well, we've had our people out on the street but this Dopolis is an unknown face. I don't know, Maura. The more I think about what went down in old Wong's, the more shirty I get.'

The phone rang and Maura answered it. While she took the call Michael lit himself a cigarette. There was something funny about all this and he could not put his finger on it. No one was an unknown quantity. There had to be someone who knew them, or of them. Yet this Dopolis seemed to have appeared out of thin air.

Maura put down the phone and stared at Michael. 'That bloody Benny has gone on the missing list again. He ain't turned up for work.'

Michael groaned.

'What about Garry the boy wonder? 'as he turned up?'

'Funnily enough, he has. And according to Sammy Goldbaum, he was surprised that Benny hadn't turned in.'

'If I know Benny, Maws, he's got himself a new bird and he can't keep away. Well, I'm gonna dock the sod's pay this week. See how far he gets with the women then!' He laughed. 'As much as he annoys me, I have to laugh at him. He'd travel miles for a new conquest. He's like one of them wolves. He sniffs the air and can smell a bitch on heat from ten miles away.'

'Sex and food . . . that's our Benny. His two main occupations. Well, all joking aside, Mickey, he's got to be

225

taught a lesson this time. He's twenty-nine, for Christ's sake, and he follows his dick like a teenager.' She pointed across the desk at Michael. 'You've got to put the hard word on him. He'll listen to you.'

'All right. When he finally turns up. Now, any more business before I shoot off home?'

Maura shook her head. 'I did the main work yesterday. There's just the usual today. Where's Geoffrey, by the way? I ain't seen him.'

Michael chewed his bottom lip and Maura, seeing this, sat back in her chair. She looked annoyed.

'Not again!'

'I'm afraid so, Maws. He thinks that I give you too much of my time. I had another row with him this morning.'

Maura lit herself a cigarette. She was fuming. 'What's it this time then?'

'He thinks you should be doing the cabs, not him.'

Maura pulled on her cigarette and stared at her brother. Geoffrey was beginning to get on her nerves. Although he was brought into everything that they did, was informed of every transaction that was made and was generally thought of as the main brother after Michael, he still kept up a petty coldness towards Maura. He acted as if she was just there to be humoured. At first Maura had accepted this. Now, nearly eight years later, he was getting on her nerves. Geoffrey could not be made to see that she was an asset to the businesses. That she was trying her hardest to make them more or less legal. Whatever she did he poured cold water on it. If she told him to do something, he nodded and smiled and then did exactly the opposite. What Geoffrey did not realise was that Michael was getting fed up with it all as well.

'Look, Mickey, can't you have a word with him?' Her voice was desperate. 'I understand that he feels put out, but if he would only try and work with me, instead of against me . . . I'll tell you something now that I was going to keep to myself. He goes through all the files.'

Michael's eyebrows rose and Maura laughed. 'Honestly,

Mickey. He comes in here in the middle of the night and checks over all that I've done.'

Michael grinned. 'Sometimes I think he's a few sandwiches short of a picnic. Still, do me a favour and swallow. I've got enough on me plate at the moment, without you two going ten rounds.'

'You will have a word with him though?'

'Oh yeah, yeah, yeah.' He stood up, exasperated. 'Fucking real, ain't it? What with him and Benny, it's a wonder we ever get anything done!

'Well, I'm off, Princess. Unless there's anything else?'

'No, nothing, Mickey.'

'I'll be off then. See you.' He kissed her cheek. Maura watched him pull on his overcoat.

'See you later then, Mickey.'

She sat at the desk chewing on her pen. Outside the window she could hear the steady hum of traffic. It had been a bitter cold morning, but inside the office it was baking. She slipped off the suede shoes and wriggled her toes. In her plain green suit and white silk blouse, she looked very young and carefree. Like an office clerk. It always amazed people when they met her that she was Maura Ryan. Her name always preceded her, and though they were prepared for her height and magnificent bosom, they were always unprepared for her looks. They soon found, though, that behind her pretty face was an analytical brain that could pick up and dissect whatever was being said to her. She sat for a while thinking about Geoffrey. She had tried so hard to work with him and he would not play along. The jangling of the telephone broke into her thoughts.

'Hello.'

'Hello, Maws!' Margaret's nasal tones were instantly recognisable.

'Hello, Marge! I was going to ring you tonight. How's the kids?'

'Oh, they're all right, Maws. Looking forward to Christmas. The twins have got their Nativity play next week, that's why I was ringing you. They want you to come down and see them both in it. Can you make it?'

'Tell them it's a date. I wouldn't miss it for the world. I'll bring Carla. She should be on her holidays from college by then. How's baby Dennis?'

Marge groaned. 'He's in his playpen now, but about ten minutes ago he flushed the toilet roll down the loo. Honestly, Maws, he's worse than the girls ever were. You need eyes in the back of your head!'

Both women laughed.

'I must see them soon. I really miss them.'

'Well, don't come and spoil them. The girls are already too big for their boots.'

Maura's voice was cynical. 'Marge, girls can never be too big for their boots – or anyone else's come to that! Now, have you spotted any more houses?'

'Funnily enough, I have. Three. Two in Southend and one in Shoebury. They all have knockdown rebuilds on them.'

'Great. I'll have a look when I come over to see you.'

'How's your house coming along?'

'It's finished, Marge. You and Den must come to dinner one night. You'll love it.'

'Oh, I bet it's gorgeous. You're lucky, Maws.'

Maura went on the defensive. 'Luck don't enter into it, Marge. I work bloody hard for what I've got.'

Marge's placating voice came over the line. 'I know, I know. I didn't mean it like that and you know it. I meant lucky to have a good job, a nice home, and a lovely bank account! Especially the lovely bank account. Me and Den seem to spend the money before the poor bugger's even earned it!' Margaret was laughing.

'Listen, Marge, I'd swap everything I've got for a nice bloke and a couple of kids.'

'I know that, Maws. I wish you would meet someone.'

'Oh, Margie, get real, will you? Blokes my age want to settle down, have some babies. I can't give that to anyone so it's not worth the aggro. I mean, I can't see me being allowed to adopt, can you? No, Marge, I accepted that a long time ago. I'll have to make do with me wheeling and dealing!'

'Well, you certainly seem to have a flair for it.'

'Long may it last, Margie! Look, I've got to go. I'll give you a bell and let you know when I'll be over, all right?'

'Okey doke. See you.'

She hung up.

Maura lit herself another cigarette. What she wouldn't give to be Marge! She smiled to herself at the thought of little Dennis and his tricks. He was a case . . .

Geoffrey burst into the office.

'Where's Mickey?'

'He left a while ago. What's wrong?'

'We had a call at the cab rank in Manor Park. Some nutty bastard reckons there's bombs in all the ranks we've got. I've phoned around and had the places cleared, sent all the drivers home.'

'You what!' Maura stubbed her cigarette out. 'On the strength of one bloody crank call!'

Geoffrey lost his temper.

'It was a crank all right . . . a crank called Dopolis. Can't you see this is the start? The prat wants war!'

Maura sat back in her chair, her face a study in disbelief. She stared at Geoffrey blankly for a moment then she shot into action. 'Get all the boys together at my warehouse in Wapping. Tell them me and Mickey will meet them there.'

Geoffrey stood looking at her. He curled his lip in contempt.

'I ain't your fucking messenger boy!'

Maura closed her eyes and said, through gritted teeth, 'It's bad enough we have this crisis with a nutty Greek. The last thing we want is to be arguing amongst ourselves. Now will you do as I ask . . . please?'

Geoffrey turned on his heel and stamped from the room. Maura turned her attention to the telephone and dialled Michael's number.

'Is that you, Jonny?'

'Oh, hello, Maura. Mickey's not . . .'

'Shut up and listen to me. Mickey will be home at any moment. You tell him that I am on my way over. Do not open the door to anyone except Michael or myself. Do you understand?'

The urgency in her voice communicated itself to him.

'What's going on!' His voice was high and frightened.

Maura slammed the phone down on him. She was in no mood to console that little faggot. She took a deep breath to control her heartbeat which was hammering in her ears, feeling a wave of apprehension wash over her. Slipping her shoes back on, she quickly left the office.

Michael and Maura walked into the club at eleven o'clock. It was a freezing night and a fine covering of snow was glistening in the light from the doorway. A surge of hot air hit them as they entered the club. Gerry Jackson took their damp coats from them.

'Brass monkey weather, ain't it?'

Michael nodded. 'Any news from Benny?' Everyone else had turned up at the warehouse meeting. Benny was the only exception. No one seemed to know where he was.

Gerry Jackson smiled.

'If I know your Benny, he's shacked up with some old bird somewhere!'

'Maybe, Gerry. Tell Geoff to come straight up when he gets here, OK? And get one of the hostesses out on reception.' Michael gave Gerry a small green address book. 'Tell them to try all these numbers. They'll get a ton if he's located. All right?'

Gerry took the battered address book. 'Will do. Shall I have some coffee sent up?'

Maura rubbed her hands together. 'That'll be just the thing, Gerry. How's Anne and the boys?'

He smiled sheepishly. 'She's pregnant again.'

'So I heard. I reckon she'll be like my mum. She won't get a girl for years!'

Gerry rolled his eyes at the ceiling.

'Oh, don't dare say that, Maura! We've got five boys already.'

Maura smiled at him. 'You shouldn't have married a good Catholic girl then.'

She followed Michael upstairs to the offices. As she entered behind him the telephone rang. Maura picked it up, hoping that it was Benny.

'May I speak to Michael Ryan, please?'

'Who's calling?'

'Tell him it's concerning his younger brother.'

Maura handed the phone to Michael and gently picked up the extension. She listened to a man's voice.

'Mr Ryan, I imagine you are missing one brother by now. Correct?'

Maura looked at Michael's set face and implored him with her eyes not to lose his temper.

'I have not missed my brother at all actually . . . Mr Dopolis. This is Mr Dopolis, I take it?'

The man laughed gently. 'How very astute of you, Mr Ryan.'

'Well, it wouldn't take a fucking contender for Mastermind to sus that much out, would it?'

'I hear from your voice that you are worried. I notice that you English always resort to bad language when you are in a tight corner . . . But I promise you that if it rests with me, no harm will come to your brother whatsoever.'

The words were spoken sincerely, but with a small underlying threat.

'Well, Mr Dopolis, what have you got my brother for? The rents and rates are fuck all to do with him.'

'I understand that, Mr Ryan. We want to use him to bargain with you. I know that you are a . . . how shall we say? . . . temperamental fellow. I want you to realise that we mean business. I knew that you would guess that the bomb threat was a hoax. I was just showing you my power, if you like. I know, for example, that you had a meeting at the warehouse today. I know everything that you do.' His voice was smug. He was obviously enjoying himself. 'Perhaps we could meet at your warehouse tomorrow?'

Maura and Michael were astounded. How could he have got that kind of information?

'When do you want to meet?'

'Tomorrow at six-thirty. It will be nice and dark by then.

Also, I want you to have plenty of time to think over my terms. I must stress to you here and now, Mr Ryan, that I am open to negotiation, providing it is in my favour . . .'

'And just what are your terms?' Michael was having trouble controlling his temper.

'Firstly, I want the East End of London for myself and my family. We have a few legitimate businesses there but it is not enough for us. We are not happy being such little fish. We are willing to make you a payment of half a million pounds for all your businesses there. A reasonable offer, I think.' He waited a few seconds before continuing.

'Secondly, I want your word that there will not be a gang war. Very sordid in this day and age, don't you think? We are both reasonable men. And, lastly, I will give you my word that we will never, ever, try and muscle in on the West End. That would remain wholly your domain.'

Michael chuckled, a grating phlegmy chuckle that should have warned Dopolis that he was not really amused.

'You don't want much, do you, cocker?'

The man's voice went cold.

'I want what I am entitled to, Mr Ryan. My cousin Stavros was willing to negotiate with you but you were young and hot-headed. You did not have the wisdom to talk things out. Sadly, you lost your brother and my cousin was crippled for life. I do not want a repeat of all that. But I am warning you now, I will fight if necessary. I have taken your young brother as a token, to show you that I know all that you do. I could have picked you all off one by one, your sister included, and have had the lot. The East and the West. But I am not a greedy man. No one can have everything. It just causes greed and envy, Mr Ryan.'

Michael listened to the man's voice as if fascinated by it. His eyes held the malevolent gleam that heralded one of his tempers.

'Yeah, well, the only thing you're causing right now, Mr Dopolis, is my blood pressure to rise! If anything should happen to my brother, either accidentally or deliberately, you will pay. Believe me, mate, that is a solemn promise.'

'Nothing will happen to your brother, Mr Ryan. Provided

you do what I ask of you. I will see you tomorrow at six-thirty.'

The line went dead.

As Michael and Maura replaced their receivers, Gerry Jackson came into the office with a tray of coffee.

'Any news, Mickey?'

'Tell the hostess who's ringing around not to bother. We've found him.'

'Where?'

Before Michael could answer, Maura spoke.

'We'll tell you later, Gerry, OK? Now if you don't mind I want to speak to Michael alone.'

Offended, Gerry placed the tray on the desk and walked out. Michael was annoyed.

'Here, hold up, Maws. Gerry is like family. You can't just dismiss him like that.'

Maura walked to the desk and began to pour the coffee. 'Mickey, that Dopolis just said that he knew where we all were today, right? He also said that he could have picked us off one by one, right? Now doesn't that tell you anything?' Her voice was peeved.

'Obviously someone in the firm is grassing.'

'Precisely.'

Michael banged his fist on the desk, causing the coffee to slop over the rim of the cups.

'Listen, you, Gerry would no more grass me than he would cut his own throat! You're out of order, Maura.'

She banged her own fist on the desk.

'Look, Mickey, I don't want to argue with you. All I'm thinking of is the fact that these people have got our Benny and I ain't taking any chances where his safety is concerned. We must play this one very close to our chests.'

Michael sighed and ran his hands through his hair. He looked old suddenly.

'Maybe you're right, Maws.'

She went to him and put her arms around his waist. 'We'll beat the buggers at their own game. With all the feelers we've got out in the street, something's bound to come up. It always does.'

233

'And what about his "terms", as he put it?'

'What about them?'

'Well, what are we going to do?'

'We play along with him, Mickey. To be honest, I wouldn't care if we let the East End go. It's pennies and halfpennies to what we can make once the building begins in London.'

Michael clenched his fists. 'Docklands . . . docklands, always the bloody docklands! Your brother is being held captive by a fucking nutter and that's all that you can think about. It's like a cancer with you!'

Maura was stunned. She looked up into Michael's face and what she saw there made her flinch. He was really worried about Dopolis.

She lost her temper again, this time deciding to tell him what she had been putting off for months.

'Can't you see further than that big hooter of yours? Sometimes you bloody well amaze me, Mickey. We are paper millionaires. We should take his money and get Benny back. Whoever controls the West End, controls the whole of London. It's always worked like that. Let the silly old bastard have it if he wants it so bad. He'll only be working for us anyway. Think about it, Mickey. We'll still get a pull off any blags that go down. We'll just be shifting the aggro, that's all. Then once the building starts, we'll be laughing all the way to the bank. Legally.'

'I ain't so sure about that . . .'

Maura clenched her fists. This was like a gift from the gods if he could only see it! She had wanted to lease out the East End anyway. Get rid of it. Now she had the perfect opportunity.

'Mickey, all that talk about luxury flats and the marina is true. I know for a fact that certain people have been buying up the place. They've been collecting money to fund the project for years. Oh, for God's sake, Michael. Do you want to be a hoodlum all your life? Well, do you? Answer me!' She pushed him in the chest.

Michael grabbed her hand and pushed her away from him. 'Why not? I ain't done too badly, and neither have you.'

234

Maura had tears in her eyes. If only he could be made to see. 'So you want to duck and dive all your life, is that it? This is a chance for us to be somebody in our own right. A legitimate way to spend our cash. I know that to the likes of you and me, living in the old dock areas would be anathema. We grew up in post-war slums, no better or worse than Tobacco Road or the Isle of Dogs. To us, you ain't made it unless your address has West One on it. But things are changing, Mickey . . . this country is going building mad at the moment. Everywhere you look, new housing estates are going up. People are even buying their council houses. We're cultivating a nation of home owners, and you can't see it! Soon all the sites will be played out, except for the old dock areas. And I want to be in on it. I want that *and* the West End.' Her voice trailed off. She could have cried her eyes out, but her pride stopped her.

Michael poured them both a large brandy. He passed Maura her glass and shook his head slowly. 'All right, Maws, you win. I'll take the half a mil. When Benny's back home I want to see all you've got on this docklands scam. I just hope that Dopolis hasn't roughed Benny up. For his sake . . . As you say, indirectly Dopolis would be working for us anyway.'

Maura put her glass on the filing cabinet beside her and ran into his arms.

'Oh, Mickey, Mickey . . . you little darling! I promise you won't regret it. I'll get on to our solicitor now and get him to draw up an agreement to take to the Greek bastard's meet. We'll show them! Just you wait and see. The name Ryan will be known the length and breadth of England. Just like Wimpey's!'

Michael laughed at her.

'What about Fitzpatrick's? Let's at least keep this thing Irish.'

Maura did a little dance of happiness. Michael smiled at her. She was right. They should let the East End go. Get Benny back safely. His dad had always said it was hard to own the two. That's what had happened to the Krays. He would let Dopolis have it, take his money, then pay

235

him back one hundredfold for poaching his little brother. Dopolis would be made painfully aware of the fact that he worked for the Ryans.

He took a cigarette from his pocket and lit it. A thought had occurred to him. The only outsider to know about the meet today was Jonny. He made a mental note to have a word with his boyfriend. He was sick to death of him anyway. This had given him just the push he needed to out Jonny.

Michael drank his brandy and the two of them made their plans. When Geoffrey arrived the excitement was over. He realised that he had been too late. Again.

Downstairs, Roy, Leslie, Lee and Garry watched the strippers. When they were finally called upstairs into the office they were all glad to hear that their brother had been located, especially Garry. As Michael gave them their orders none of them realised that the real trouble was only just beginning. That events were being put into motion that would smash their world apart.

Chapter Seventeen

Benny watched as the man came into the room. It was the same man who had brought him some food earlier in the day. Benny smiled painfully, trying to get some response. In the fight that had occurred during Benny's kidnapping, he had lost two teeth and acquired a large black eye. The man was also sporting a black eye so Benny thought that evened things up. The man ignored Benny's smile and picked up the empty plate and cup. He checked that the handcuff which held Benny's right hand to the bed post was secure. Then he left the room, banging the door behind him.

Benny tried to get comfortable on the bed. The muscles in his right shoulder were screaming. He reckoned that he had been in the room twenty-four hours. He could smell the urine that was in a bucket by his bed. He had just enough space to kneel up and urinate into the bucket. As yet he had not been allowed to open his bowels. Not that he fancied going in front of an audience, and he had a sneaking suspicion that was what would happen. He rubbed his shoulder with his free hand.

The room he was in was some kind of office, he was sure of that. It had the hollow feel that was peculiar to portakabins and the like. It was definitely not a house that he was being kept in. He felt the giant swelling above his eye and grinned – he had given them a run for their money. If they had not had the element of surprise he would have won the fight hands down. Now all he had to do was wait. He had been told briefly by his captors that he was being held until an agreement had been reached with Michael. He wasn't too worried about it. He knew that he was worth more to his captors alive than dead. He just hoped that someone had had the savvy to tell his mum that he was not coming home for a few days. She would be worried.

He tried to settle himself back against the bedpost. His round boyish face had a dark stubble around the jaw; he looked terrible. He ran his tongue over his teeth. He wished they would let him have a wash and brush up. He hated this dirty feeling. The bed was filthy and it stank. It was also damp. In the corner of the room was a paraffin heater which gave out a sickly smell as well as a sticky cloying heat.

He decided then and there that when he got home he would find out the names of the people who had held him here and would personally give each one a good hiding. This place was a dump. He wouldn't keep his dog, Driver, in conditions like this . . .

It never occurred to Benny that he was in any danger or that there was a good chance that he would never leave the room alive.

Maura and Michael walked into the warehouse at six-fifteen. Geoffrey, Roy and Leslie were already there. Garry and Lee arrived at six-twenty. Geoffrey had put up a set of spotlights. From outside the warehouse still looked empty. Dopolis arrived, accompanied by two big men, at six-thirty-five.

The two men with him were, Michael guessed, just brawn merchants. He also noted, as did his brothers, that they were both armed. Dopolis looked like a dark-skinned dwarf standing between them. The Greek nodded to them all, giving a half bow towards Maura.

It was freezing inside the warehouse. It seemed colder in there than it did outside. The snow was coming down harder and had decided to settle. In the bright glare from the spotlights they looked like characters rehearsing for a play. Dopolis was the first to speak. He cleared his throat theatrically. Dopolis had a taste for drama that spilled over into everything he did.

238

'I am so glad that we could have this little chat. I hope that you have thought over my proposition.'

'Where's Benny?' Michael's voice was flat.

Dopolis laughed and Maura saw the tendons stand out in Michael's neck. She touched his arm lightly to remind him that he was not to lose his temper.

'Surely, Mr Ryan, you do not think that I would be so foolish as to bring him here? I must first find out how the land lies.'

Garry was staring at the three men in front of him. He stifled an urge to open his coat and blow them away with his shotgun. He could feel the sweat slippery on his palms.

Maura could sense the mounting tension. Her voice seemed to echo around the building. 'We have decided that we like your offer, Mr Dopolis.'

The three Greeks stared at her in amazement. Surely Michael Ryan was not going to allow a woman to negotiate for him?

'Young lady,' Dopolis's voice was gentle, 'I have come here to do serious business.'

Maura's voice was brisk. 'I am well aware of that fact, Mr Dopolis. My brother has every faith in me as I am sure you will soon realise.' She smiled. 'Now, shall we get down to business?'

Mr Dopolis was nonplussed. That much was clear to everyone watching. Never in his wildest imaginings had he envisaged discussing business with a woman. He had heard that Maura Ryan was a very astute business woman but nevertheless, he was a Greek and Greeks did not allow their women to interfere in men's business. It crossed his mind that this may be Michael Ryan's idea of an insult. Women were for pleasure or for childbearing as far as he was concerned. Maura could read the expressions on his face as if they were written on his forehead in indelible ink.

She began to talk in her best no-nonsense voice.

'You have offered to buy out our holdings in the East End for half a million pounds. We shall accept that offer

239

with good grace. But only with the proviso that you work, indirectly of course, for us.

'We would only expect to be consulted on major issues. Everything else would be down to yourself. We shall keep our interests in the warehouses and the property . . .'

Dopolis seemed to have gathered his wits together.

'My dear girl, the half a million includes all this.' He gestured around the warehouse with his arms. 'I have a pressing need for these old warehouses myself. I want –' he paused for effect, 'everything you own from Dagenham to Tower Bridge. I want everything you have in Katherine Dock, East Dock. Around London Dock. I want all you possess on the Wapping Road, in Whitechapel and Shoreditch. I want Bethnal Green. In short, I want it all.'

Maura, Michael and Geoffrey were flabbergasted. Dopolis smiled coldly. 'Do not insult me by trying to negotiate with me. I have given you my terms. I would never work for you!' He spat out the words like bullets from a gun. 'I want it *all*, do you hear me? Every little bit, lock, stock and barrel. And if we can't settle this amicably then we will fight you. *I* will fight you to the death.'

He put a pudgy hand to his breast. 'I came here for an answer to my terms, that's all. Nothing else.'

'What about Benny?' This from Leslie, who was dying to start a fight.

'What about him?' Dopolis shrugged. 'He is my bargaining point. While I have him, I also have you.'

Michael stepped towards him, causing Dopolis to retreat; a fleeting expression of fear crossed his sallow face.

Michael pointed at him. 'You can't just demand, mate.'

'Oh, Mr Ryan, that's where you're wrong. While I have your brother I can demand all I want. And I will tell you something, Mr Ryan . . . I have a man behind me who is so big that he would scare even you. Yes, even you! I am a trusted friend of this man and I can tell you now that he has much money and arms to fight you with. I know you are a force to be reckoned with but I have at my disposal a larger, more dangerous force. Do you understand what I am saying?'

Dopolis had a demonic look on his ugly face. In his temper he had spoken so forcefully that long strands of spit hung from his lower lip.

'Listen, mate.' Michael went to him. As he walked he clicked his fingers and Geoffrey, Roy, Leslie, Garry and Lee brought out their shotguns from beneath their coats. Maura stepped back from them. Despite herself she was getting frightened. She had never thought it would get this far.

Michael picked Dopolis up by his camel hair overcoat, lifting him off the ground as if he weighed nothing at all. 'You are beginning to get on my wick. Comprendez? Or whatever it is you bubbles say.' He threw Dopolis on to the filthy floor and turned to the minders. He could see they were frightened. 'Don't even think about getting your little pop-pops out. You'd never walk out of here. So just button your mutton while I tell your short-arse little mate here the score.' He went to where Dopolis was sprawling on the cold floor, his face like thunder. Grabbing him by the lapels of his coat, Michael dragged him upright and pushed his face down to his.

'You tell your Mr Big that if my brother ain't home by ten o'clock tonight, I am coming after him. If as much as one hair is harmed on Benny's pretty little head, I will kill you all. Slowly and painfully.'

He punched the Greek to the ground again. Dopolis watched as Michael took a length of lead piping from his pocket. He tried to scramble away. Michael brought the piping down on his legs.

'You want everything, do you? All that I've got? Don't want much do you, you wanker?' He brought the lead down on Dopolis's elbow and a powerful crack echoed around the warehouse. The two minders were staring, fascinated, at Michael Ryan in action. Leslie and Lee giggled as they heard Dopolis try to stifle a scream.

'Well, you'll get nothing, mate. Not a brass razoo, as the Aussies say. You've got more chance of getting a dose of clap off the fucking Pope than you've got of getting a job off me cleaning out toilets. You made a fatal mistake, Mr

241

Dopolis. You were stupid enough to annoy me. I want me little brother and then I'm coming after you and your Mr Fucking Big. So you had better start saying your prayers, OK?'

He smashed the lead piping into the man's face, felt Dopolis's nose collapse and smiled. The Greek was a bloody mess.

He looked to where the two minders were standing and said calmly, 'Pick him up and take him home. He's annoying me.'

The two men stood paralysed with fear. They had never seen a look the like of which was on Michael Ryan's face now. He had enjoyed every second.

Mickey shouted at them: 'PICK HIM UP AND PISS OFF!'

They did as they were told, their movements jerky and awkward in their fright. Carrying Dopolis between them, his legs hanging uselessly, they began to drag him from the warehouse. Michael called to them, and then standing in front of them pushed his finger into Dopolis's broken nose. The bone and gristle were open to the freezing air.

'This is just for starters. You wait until I really lose me rag. I want me brother. And I want him tonight.' He jerked his head at the two men and they dragged Dopolis from the warehouse as fast as they possibly could. Michael pulled a handkerchief from his pocket and wiped the blood from his finger.

'Coo, Mickey . . . you scared me.'

'Listen, Princess, I might rant and rave but I would never hurt me own.'

'What about if they grassed you up?' This from Leslie, who always asked the wrong thing at the wrong time.

Michael stared at him nastily. 'Why? Are you thinking of trying it?'

Leslie blanched. He dropped his gun in fright and Michael laughed.

'No . . . No, Mickey. Not me. N-never!'

'I was only joking, you nonce.'

Michael was on a high. He was always the same after a

bout of violence. 'Well, Maws, it seems your ideas about the docks are spot on.'

Geoffrey nodded. 'This Mr Big, whoever he is, must want all this. It's got to be something to do with all this chat about redevelopment. Why else would anyone want this heap of shit?'

Michael shrugged.

'Once our Benny's home we'll rip this town apart. No one can hide from us. Not for long anyway. This has taught me one thing, though. If we're going to keep any sort of order we must rent out the East End in little pieces. Geoffrey, I want you to keep your ear to the ground. See if any old wags are out and about looking for a bit of action. I'm getting sick of the lot of it. What's it the Yanks call it?' He laughed out loud. 'A conglomerate. That's what we'll become – a conglomerate! Take a leaf out of the big knobs' books. Get loads of little firms to do the shitty work. Only there won't be any golden handshakes floating around!'

Maura was unnerved by how quickly Michael could forget what had just taken place. It was as if Dopolis had never existed. As if he had not been beaten to a pulp. She shuddered, and Lee put his arm around her.

'You cold, Maws?'

Michael carried on talking. 'I should have listened to you ages ago, Princess. We're going legal at last. Should please Mother anyway. Let's get back to the club. This place gives me the heebie jeebies.'

Ten minutes later they were all on their way to Dean Street. Maura and Michael travelled together and he talked to her all the time, not seeming to notice how quiet she was. They parked the Mercedes in Old Compton Street. For some reason Dean Street was cordoned off. There were people milling around everywhere. Maura and Michael saw that Geoffrey and the others had arrived before them. Maura walked up to Geoffrey. His skin looked grey in the twilight. She noticed police were everywhere. She heard the high screeching of an ambulance as it travelled along Shaftesbury Avenue. A large crowd had gathered, mainly

243

bouncers and hostesses, a few punters and sightseers mixed in with them.

She felt Michael's breath on her neck as he spoke to Geoffrey. 'What's going on here?'

'It's the club, Michael. It was firebombed.' Geoffrey's voice was dead. As if he could not really comprehend what had happened.

'What!' Michael and Maura spoke in unison.

'I said it's been firebombed.'

'Is anyone hurt, Geoff?'

He shook his head. 'I don't know, Maura.'

She pushed her way through the crowd and stared at what had once been the entrance to Le Buxom. The wind was picking up and little flakes of snow were stinging her face. She could smell the burning.

Then her heart seemed to explode inside her chest. She felt her hands clench into fists and a breathlessness as if she had run for miles. Walking towards her, from the entrance of the club, was Terry Petherick. Even in the freezing cold she felt a wave of heat sweep through her body. He still had the same long-legged stride. The same dirty blond hair. The same lopsided grin. She was aware of her rapid heartbeat crashing through her body. For the first time in eight years she was seeing the man she hated. Only she did not hate him. She realised that she loved him . . . loved him with every ounce of her being.

The sights and sounds around her were blocked from her mind. All she was aware of was a feeling of being alive. Really alive. For the first time since she'd had the abortion she felt an overpowering urge to throw herself into his arms. Beg him to forgive her for what she had done to their child. He was getting closer to her. She could feel the heat creeping along her flesh . . .

'Hello, Maura. Long time no see.' His words were a vocal caress and she felt herself tremble. Her throat was dry and she knew that if she tried to speak to him she would begin to cry. The tears were already there, hot and aching behind her eyes. She bit down hard on her lip.

Terry Petherick was looking at her with his penetrating

stare. He thought of the Maura he had known, the vulnerable young girl, and felt ashamed of what he had done to her. Through her sophisticated hair style and expensive clothes he could still see the girl she had been. The young woman he had made love to and whom he had nearly died for. She was still there, inside the new shell, looking at him through the blue stillness of her eyes. They would never change. When he had been beaten up he had lain in the hospital bed thinking about her. He had never held any grudge about what had happened to him. He had felt at the time that he deserved it. He deserved to feel the pain. He still felt that, especially now, looking at the face that had haunted him for eight long years.

Michael's voice broke into their private thoughts and snapped them both back to reality.

'Well, well, well. If it ain't the Casanova of Vine Street.'

Maura felt a flush come over her face and neck.

'Hello, Mr Ryan. I suppose you know that your club was firebombed?' Terry's voice was quiet and controlled. 'Your doorman, Gerry Jackson, was badly hurt, and a young lass, a young blonde girl called . . .' he looked at his notebook '. . . Sheree. No one seemed to know her surname.'

'Well, anything you want to ask you talk to my brother Geoffrey. He's over there.' Michael pointed to where Geoffrey was standing with Lee and Garry and Leslie. 'I want to get my sister home. This ain't no place for her. Especially now.'

'Quite.' Terry's voice was smooth. Maura noticed that he still had his baby soft skin. She wanted to reach up and touch his face. Feel his flesh beneath her fingers again. She closed her eyes and felt Michael's arm go around her.

'Come on, Maws. There's nothing we can do here.'

She wanted to throw Michael from her. She couldn't walk away from Terry now. Not when she had found him again. She felt Michael pulling her gently away and still she watched Terry, turning her head as Michael steered her through the crowd back to the car. And she knew in her heart that Terry felt the same as she did. It was written in his eyes and face. Suddenly all the noise and bustle around her became real once more. She came back to earth with a jolt that made her want to cry out in anguish.

'Come on, Princess. In the car, love.' Michael's voice was caressing, like a lover's. Only this time it was not enough for her.

In the space of a few minutes all the old longings had come back to haunt her. Long suppressed sights and sounds were rushing back. The little flat in Islington. Their favourite restaurant. The smell of his body as he slipped his maleness inside her. It was like a strong heady potion that had miraculously brought her back to life.

'Come on, Maws. Get in the car.'

She opened the door and sat in the car obediently. Leslie and Lee were already in the back, Garry squeezed in with them. For Maura the whole day's events had been wiped out by that one chance meeting.

Michael got into the driving seat and put the key in the ignition. He started up the car and pulled away. When they were driving along Shaftesbury Avenue, he spoke.

'I suppose you all realise what's happened, don't you?' Nobody answered him. 'The bombing of the club had already been arranged, well in advance. From five minutes after me belting Dopolis, the word had been sent out. It was a foregone conclusion. Whoever threw the petrol bomb was ready and waiting for word.'

Gradually, what Michael was saying penetrated Maura's brain.

'Benny ain't coming home, is he, Mickey?' Garry sounded as if he was going to cry.

'I doubt that very much, Gal. I doubt that very much indeed.'

'The dirty bastards! The filthy rotten dirty bastards . . .' Leslie and Lee were both in shock.

'Well, I have an idea where some of Dopolis's information came from. And that's where we're all going now.'

They drove on in silence. Everyone was thinking about Benny. Michael gripped the steering wheel. Mr Big had better watch out. He was coming to get him.

The enormity of what had happened hit Maura like a bucket of icy water. Benny was probably dead already . . . She felt the shaking in her hands and legs that was caused by shock. As she looked out of the window of the car she saw that they were in Knightsbridge. Harrods had its Christmas decorations that brought people from miles around. Everywhere she looked were lights and Christmas messages, in the shops and the restaurants. And Benny was dead. Or about to die. She closed her eyes and saw his face. Then Terry's face.

Garry was sitting hunched up in the back, racking his brains like Michael, trying to come up with a name. Someone who would have the guts to take on Michael Ryan. Someone who held a grudge . . .

Michael parked the car outside his flat. They all followed him inside. Maura realised that Roy was missing and asked Mickey where he was. He put his key into the lock of his front door.

'I sent him home, Maws. He's the only family man among us. After what happened at the club, I sent him home.'

She nodded as he opened the door. They all followed him into his lounge.

Jonny was sitting on the couch. He was wearing his straight gear: grey polo-necked sweater and black Staprest trousers. He was very white. His blond curly hair had been freshly washed. It was still damp. He stared up at Michael and smiled. Maura noticed that he was a bundle of nerves.

'Get us all a stiff drink, Jonny . . . now!' Michael sounded ferocious. Jonny leapt out of his seat to do his bidding. He was shaking so much he nearly dropped the decanter of whisky. Everyone sat down on Michael's deep green Habitat settee. Jonny brought them all a drink. Michael stood at the fireplace and, as Jonny handed him his drink, said: 'How much did they pay you?'

Jonny tried to bluff his way out of it. He knew that his life depended on it.

'I don't know what you're talking about, Mickey!'

Michael threw the contents of his glass into Jonny's face. Then, grabbing his blond curls, cried: 'Tell me, Jonny. Answer my question.'

'I swear to you, I don't know what you're talking about. Please!'

Michael brought his knee up into Jonny's groin, using such force that the boy's whole body was lifted from the ground. Michael let him drop on to the carpet in front of him. Then, taking out the lead piping he had used on Dopolis, he waved it in Jonny's face.

'You can make this hard for yourself or easy, Jonny. Either way you will answer my questions. Now, I ask you again, how much did they pay you?'

Jonny lay on the floor, heaving. His hands were holding his testicles, which felt as if they had been forced from their protective sac. He was in agony. Michael had dropped his glass and Jonny had a fleeting image of him smashing it into his face. Michael kicked the glass at him as if he had read the boy's mind.

Jonny hunched his shoulders up and held his testicles tighter. 'Five . . . five gr-grand.'

Michael laughed a bitter laugh.

'Five lousy grand? You let my brother die for five lousy grand? I'd have given you that if you'd asked me. You fucking scum queen!'

He brought the lead piping down on Jonny, busting his head open with the first blow.

Maura jumped from her seat and grabbed Michael's arm.

'Not here, Mickey. Don't kill him here. Find out who approached him. Then let them have him.' She poked her head in her brothers' direction. They were all sitting on Michael's giant settee watching him.

Maura stared down into Jonny's face.

'Who bought you off, Jonny? You may as well tell me. You're a dead man anyway. If you don't start talking, I'll let Michael and Garry torture you. I mean it, Jonny.'

He was crying, his tears mingling with the blood that was dripping down his face from his head.

248

'Maura . . . I . . . I swear I didn't mean any . . . harm. He made me do it! He said . . . you . . . was all finished. That I'd better get away . . .'

'Who was it, Jonny? Tell me who it was.'

'It . . . was . . . Sam. Sammy Goldbaum.'

Michael spat in Jonny's face.

'Not Sammy. Never! You poxy little shit stabber . . .'

'I swear to you, Mickey. Please believe me.' Jonny was crying hard now. 'I loved you, Mickey. I did. I'm so sorry . . .'

Michael kicked him in the legs. 'Yeah, you loved me all right. You ponce! You loved me so much you done a deal for money. Five shitty grand you sold me and my brother for. Wanker!'

He nodded his head and Garry and Leslie picked Jonny up from the floor between them. They did not need to be told that Jonny was not to come home. They would enjoy putting him away, for Benny's sake.

Jonny screamed out in fear. 'Please, Mickey! Please . . .' Tears were rolling down his face and mingling with blood and the mucus from his nose. 'I only told him things because I thought you wouldn't be there any more to protect me. I'm begging you, Mickey . . . please!'

Michael raised the lead piping above his head and smashed it down with all his might across Jonny's head. Jonny was suddenly quiet. He would never utter another word.

Garry, Leslie and Lee carried him from the flat.

Michael sat on his giant sofa and put his head in his hands. 'Benny's dead, Maws. Because that slag sold him for a lousy five grand. I want Goldbaum next. Sammy, my friend. Well, from now on, it's family always.' He wiped his streaming eyes.

'Come on, Mickey. Me and you will sort out Sammy together.'

They left the flat. As they got into the car, Maura heard the high piping voices of a group of carol singers. They were singing for charity outside the restaurants in Beauchamp Place. Maura could have wept herself. This had been one of the worst days of her life. Instead she lit them both a cigarette and braced herself for the night ahead. She knew that tonight she was going to commit a murder, and instead of being frightened felt a deadness in all her limbs. Thoughts of Terry Petherick were a luxury she could not afford. She had come too far with Mickey ever to be able to live a normal life again. Together they would pay back everyone responsible for Benny's death. The familiar hardness crept back into her deep blue eyes and she put away her childish dreams forever.

Terry was like the expensive present that all poor children wanted but could never hope to attain. She had felt for a few moments the agonising pleasure that he had always created in her, and she would have to make do with that for the rest of her life. She would think about it in her lonely bed when all this was over, but tonight they had a job to do.

As Michael's Mercedes sped through the streets of London Maura saw in her mind's eye the little baby in the washing up bowl and finally laid that ghost to rest.

She opened the window of the car and let the cold night air whip at her face. Benny was dead, love his heart. Big lovable Benny was dead. Her mother and father would be devastated.

As they drove past the Giorgiou used car lot in Bethnal Green, they were completely unaware that Benny was lying not twenty yards from where their car stopped at the junction with Roman Road. He had died at seven-ten precisely.

250

Chapter Eighteen

Sammy Goldbaum was sitting at his kitchen table, looking around the familiar room, breathing in the same old smells: gefilte fish and kanadelach soup. His wife Noola made the best Matzo balls he had ever tasted. On the wall to the right of his chair was a photograph of his three daughters. The eldest, Rebekka, had his large bulbous nose – the only one to inherit his Jewish legacy. The other two, Beatrice and Ruth, both had the blonde prettiness of his wife. He wiped his forehead again with a large handkerchief. He had been sweating profusely since he had heard the news. He was aware that Michael would be coming for him and so he waited, patiently but feeling very frightened.

His wife Noola sat opposite him. She was more than worried by the look of her husband. He looked terrible. You did not live with a man for over thirty years without knowing his every thought and action.

'Tell me, Sammy, what is ailing you? You sit there like a statue, staring into space. Is it the police you are frightened of? Have you got into trouble again?'

'Noola!' Sammy's deep voice was exasperated. 'Keep your nose out of my affairs. Always you must know everything. I tell you, Noola, it's not always healthy to know too much. Go to bed. God knows, you could do with the beauty sleep.'

He tried to smile at her but it did not quite work. She reached across the table and gripped his arm.

'Sammy, in all the years we've been married I've always stood by you. I've lied to the police. Even to the Rabbi, may God forgive me. But I did it for love. Now I see you scared out of your wits. You've sent the girls over

251

to my mother's house for the night, and all you can say to me is: "Go to bed, Noola." Do you think I am a fool?'

He shook his head. Trust her to begin one of her arguments, tonight of all nights. She had been a good wife to him, an exemplary wife. Over the years he had grown to love her more than he had thought possible.

'No, Noola, my darling. I would never think that you were a fool. But I tell you, you should have gone to your mother's with the girls. It could be very dangerous here tonight.'

'But why, Sammy? Tell me why?' Her voice was desperate. He looked into her faded eyes. Her grey hair was, as usual, rolled up in enormous curlers with a bright green chiffon scarf tied around them. Suddenly he saw her as she had been thirty-five years ago: a small thin young Jewish girl, with a trim figure and a bubbling, overpowering personality. She had made him laugh. Being a big man, he had wanted to protect the tiny scrap that was to become his wife; instead she had taken him over. But he had never once resented her for it. She would always be quicker than he to see the point of a debate or the way out of any trouble. He had begun to rely on her early in their marriage and it had never changed. Until tonight. No one could help him now. No one at all.

He took a deep breath. She deserved to know the truth.

'I sold out Michael Ryan, Noola.'

Noola's hand flew to her mouth. Her grey eyes screwed up into tiny slits until they finally closed, as if trying to blot out what her husband had said to her. She took her hand from her mouth and put it to her heart as if trying to stop its beat.

'Oh my God, Sammy! He will kill you.' Her voice cracked with emotion.

'I know that, Noola. I am waiting for him now. That's why I sent the girls away. I am sure he would not hurt them or you. But I think it would be better for all concerned if I was alone when he came.'

252

'But why, Sammy? Why?' Her voice was stronger now, truculent. 'He has always been a good friend to you, looked after you.'

Sammy wiped his forehead again.

'I know that. You think I don't know that?'

Noola sat back in her chair and stared at her husband. It all became as plain as day to her.

'God help you, Sammy Goldbaum. You've been gambling again. That's it, isn't it?'

He nodded his head.

'So, like Judas Iscariot, you betrayed your friend. Your very good friend.'

'I did not think that anyone would get hurt.' His voice was self-righteous. 'I swear, Noola. Then tonight I heard on the radio that his club, Le Buxom, had been fire-bombed. And I realised I had caused a lot of trouble. Now all I can do is sit and wait for my punishment. It is pointless trying to get away from him.'

Noola got up from her seat and went to her husband. She kissed his hot dry lips and sweaty forehead and she went to bed. She knew that she would never see her husband alive again. She took three Mogadon sleeping tablets, and when Maura and Michael arrived was out cold. As Sammy said, sometimes it was best not to know anything.

Janine looked at her husband Roy. He was eating his breakfast and it seemed to her that every mouthful was a trial to him. 'What's going on, Roy? I've already heard on the news about the bombing.'

He stopped chewing and glanced at his heavily pregnant wife. Then, putting down his knife and fork, he got up from the table and went to her, pulling her into his arms.

'Bombed!' He tried to make his voice light. 'It was a gas leak. You know what it's like if anything happens in Soho. The press always has a field day.'

'But a young girl died, and Gerry Jackson is seriously ill.'

'I know that, love. It was burns. Honestly, Jan, it was a gas leak from the building next door.' He caressed her swollen belly. 'You just worry about Junior here. I'll take care of everything else.'

'If it's trouble, Roy, I want to know.'

He turned her back towards the cooker and patted her behind. 'You just worry about making me a nice cup of Rosie Lee. Then I'd better be off.'

Janine filled the kettle and plugged it in. Then she turned the radio up. It was the eight-thirty news. The announcer's voice crackled around the kitchen as if unaccustomed to being listened to in this household.

'The bombing of the West End nightclub, Le Buxom, was this morning said to be a terrorist attack. The owner of the nightclub, Mr Michael Ryan, has been seen over the years with various IRA sympathisers. Mr Ryan is a known gangland figure, though attempts to bring charges against him have always failed. He was not available for comment this morning. Mr Heath . . .'

The voice droned on and Roy carried on eating his breakfast. Janine placed his cup of tea in front of him. She did not know what to do. She felt the baby kick and her hands went to her swollen belly protectively. She thought of ringing Carla and dismissed it. She would wait for him to leave then she would phone her mother-in-law.

Sarah Ryan looked terrible. She had not slept all night. Her straggly grey hair had escaped from its usual bun and her round open face looked more wrinkled than usual. Her body had grown fatter over the years and now everything about her seemed to sag – her breasts, her stomach, even the folds of skin under her neck. She had always looked older than her years, but in the last twenty-four hours had become positively decrepit-looking. She was just fifty-nine. Her eyes, though, were alert and filled with a bright intelligence that seemed to glow out of her wrinkled face. She was worried out of her mind about her youngest son. She had not seen him for over forty-eight hours, not since he had devoured one of his Olympian breakfasts. She knew that something had happened to him. She had tried unsuccessfully to contact Michael and Maura. Both were nowhere to be found. Carla had told her that she had not seen Maura for a couple of days. She had not seemed too bothered about it, but Sarah knew that her nervousness had communicated itself to the girl and now she too was worried.

Since the news about the bombing of the nightclub she had had a sick feeling in her guts. She had spoken to Roy late the night before but he was closemouthed about everything she had asked him. Protecting himself and the others, she guessed. She poured out a large mug of tea and took it up to her husband, who as usual had drunk himself into a stupor and gone to bed. She placed the tea on the bedside table and shook him roughly, the sour smell of his breath adding to her feeling of nausea.

'What? What do you want?'

She stared down at his sunken face. He had not shaved for nearly a week. He looked what he was . . . like dirty Irish scum. She had to stifle an overpowering urge to throw the mug of steaming hot tea into his face.

'Benjamin . . . he still hasn't come home.' She tried to get some response. Benjamin opened his eyes and stared around him blearily.

'Oh, piss off, Sar. Benny's a grown man. He's probably out shagging. You know what he's like.'

He sat up in the bed and looked at the clock. It was just after nine.

'Jumping Jesus Christ! What you woke me up for?'

Sarah sat on the bed and gripped his arm. 'I think something terrible's happened. Michael's club was bombed last night.'

'What!'

'It was on the news. Roy said it was a gas leak but the man on the news said it was a terrorist attack.'

She watched the different expressions flicker over Benjamin's face and sighed. In his state he would have difficulty even working out what day it was, let alone following all this. It had always been the same. She could never rely on him to be of help in any way, shape or form. It was beyond him. For the first time in years she needed him and he was going to let her down. She heard the telephone ringing in the hallway and rushed off to answer it, hoping against hope that it was young Benny. It was Janine. Sarah felt the hope seep from her body as she heard her daughter-in-law's voice.

'Can you come over to me, Sarah? Please.'

'Yes, Janine, I'll come to you. Give me an hour.'

When she replaced the receiver she rang Carla. By ten-thirty the three women were closeted together in Janine's house. For once the atmosphere between mother and daughter was forged by a common bond. They were all frightened, but as yet did not really know what exactly they were frightened of.

Mr Desmond Buckingham Gooch walked his dog across Hampstead Heath every morning. He rose at five precisely and breakfasted on a soft boiled egg and one slice of toast. He then walked his dog Victory across the Heath. He was there by six o'clock every morning, come rain or shine. His neighbours called him 'Colonel Blimp', though never to his face. Victory was a cocker spaniel, a splendid animal, though scatty. She never came when he called her and completely disregarded his orders, and he loved her with all his heart. She was his sole companion.

This morning she had stopped by a litter bin attached to a lamp post. He called her in his most commanding voice. She ignored him as usual and stayed exactly where she was. She began to whine. She got up to her hind legs and tried to scratch the metal bin. The lamp post was giving out an eerie light. It was just becoming day in the cold twilight world of a winter's morning. A fine covering of snow had settled during the night and in the gloomy light of the breaking dawn the lamp post seemed to be radiating a burnt orange glow that barely illuminated itself. For a few seconds Desmond Buckingham Gooch felt a prickle of fear. Then, his natural common sense coming to the fore, he walked purposefully to the bin. Victory could probably smell one of those damned hamburgers that young people these days seemed to live on. If he had his way he would bring back the days of powdered egg and rationing. Youngsters today had it too easy, far too easy in his opinion. He looked into the bin.

A head stared up at him, covered with a layer of early morning frost. He staggered backwards, his hand going instinctively to his chest. He felt the vomit in his mouth, his boiled egg and toast mixed with bile burning his tongue and gums. He threw up on to the pavement. Taking deep breaths, he dragged Victory roughly away from the bin and put on her lead, then he half pulled and half kicked his beloved dog back to his flat. Inside his hallway he leant against the front door, trying to calm his heartbeat. He made his way into his bedroom and, sitting on his bed, opened his bedside cabinet and took out the pills the doctor had given him for his heart. He placed one under his tongue with a trembling hand. Victory sat staring at him, her bright red coat glistening with snow. When he felt the life coming back to his limbs, he picked up the phone by his bed and called the police.

The news of the finding of the head did not hit the streets until twelve-thirty.

It was Benny Ryan's.

Mrs Carmen De'Sousa, a West Indian woman, was coming home from a nightshift at Ford's in Dagenham. She walked slowly up Lower Mardyke Avenue towards her block of maisonettes. She had had a bad night. Their union representative had wanted to call them all out. She shook her head in its large woolly hat. This country amazed her.

She heard the rubbery screech of car tyres as somebody attempted a wheelspin in the frosty morning. She ignored it. Cars came and went at all hours of the day and night. You became immune to the sound, as you became immune to the noise of radios, record players and ghetto blasters. If you were sensible on the Mardyke Estate, you kept your nose out of other people's business.

She started to walk up the steps that led to her landing, gripping the rail that ran parallel with the steps. It was very icy, the snow had settled, and all around her the world was blanketed in a white layer that made even the Mardyke Estate look pleasant. As she reached the top step she stopped. She could hear a faint mewling. She walked past the entrance to her landing and began to walk down the flight of steps that led to the garages that ran the whole length of the block of maisonettes. No one in their right mind kept their cars there these days. They were full of junk, old furniture, old bikes, mattresses and general rubbish.

She heard the soft mewling again and called out in the darkness, 'Marley? Id that you, boy?'

She reached the bottom of the steps and felt rather than saw that there was something lying sprawled out in front of her. She squinted and peered at the ground. The lights had been broken down here for over five years. She felt in the pocket of her heavy blanket coat and took out a box of Swan Vestas. She lit one and held it in front of her. It was to be an action she would regret all her life.

Lying on the floor in front of her was the body of a young man. A young blond man. She stared at the body for what seemed ages, a scream stuck in her throat. Then the match burnt her fingers and pain spurred her into action. She began to scream and wail at the top of her voice. Within five minutes nearly every resident from her block of maisonettes was with her.

Jonny's body had been found.

Denise and Carol McBridge walked to the bus stop together. Both girls worked at Van Den Bergh and Jurgen's in West Thurrock. Their bus came at five minutes to seven. Two stops later they alighted and made their way from the London Road to the dirt track that had always been used as a short cut to their factory. As usual they were joking around, barely able to see in the winter half-light. Carol tripped over something and swore softly. It was a large rolled-up canvas. Nothing unusual about that. This was a known dumping ground. What was unusual was what was poking out of the bottom end of it. On closer

258

inspection, the girls found that it was a pair of feet. Rather large feet. As if of one mind they scrambled over the bundle and ran as fast as they could to work, fear giving their feet wings.

Sammy Goldbaum's body had been found.

Denise's and Carol's manager was very good. He gave them the rest of the week off on full pay.

Maura sat in the interview room at Vine Street police station. She lit another cigarette and pulled on it hard. She was frightened, very frightened. But outwardly she looked as if she did not have a care in the world.

The WPC who had been assigned to stay with her looked her over critically. She approved of the pale grey suit Maura wore. It was plain but, with the single strand of pearls and the pearl earrings, it looked what it was: exclusive and expensive. WPC Cotter approved of everything about Maura Ryan, from her shiny white-blonde hair to her crocodile skin shoes and bag. It was common knowledge that this was the woman who had nearly ruined DS Petherick's career. It was an old story that had been embellished over the years until now it was part of Vine Street folklore.

DI Dobin came into the room. He smiled at Maura and she smiled back. She had been here for hours and they still had not charged her. She had called her brief and he was on his way from Cambridge. All she had to do was keep a clear head. They had nothing on her.

She forced the events of the night before from her mind. Sammy Goldbaum had deserved everything he got. Sammy was to become another blank spot in Maura's mind, along with everything else she had ever done that was decidedly wrong. DI Dobin and the WPC and everyone who touched Maura's life in some way, however trivial, were never in any way aware that she was like a time bomb: a dangerous time bomb that would eventually explode. Her outer veneer of calm and friendliness hid a mass of emotions and feelings that would one day spew out like a festering cancer.

'Am I going to be charged with anything?' Her voice was calm and controlled.

DI Dobin cleared his throat. Against his will he had taken a liking to this girl. Which was more than could be said of his feelings for her elder brother. The sad part was they both had perfect alibis and not even an outstanding parking ticket between them.

'I am afraid, Miss Ryan, that I have some bad news for you.'

Maura's face remained neutral. She took a long drag on her cigarette.

'Oh? And what's that?' She braced herself for what she knew was coming.

'A head was found earlier today in a litter bin in East Heath Road, just off Hampstead Heath. It was your brother Benjamin's.'

He watched her face blanch. The corner of her mouth began to twitch upwards. It was the only outward sign that she felt anything.

'Now, Miss Ryan, I ask you again – have you anything to tell me about the death of Jonny Fenwick or Samuel Goldbaum?'

Maura stared at him blankly. She put out her cigarette and immediately lit another. She shook her head. DI Dobin watched the tears begin to gather in her lovely eyes. He could see what had attracted young Petherick to her. Even with her height and her woman's body, she still had a naivete about her that made men want to protect her.

He knew as sure as eggs was eggs that if this lovely creature sitting in front of him had not actually committed the murders herself, she, along with her brother Michael, had ordered them. And he also knew that they would walk out of this police station because there was no evidence to go on. Michael had been with a 'friend', a young barrister who had already been in and given a sworn statement, and this young woman had been with Timothy Repton, a well-known actor who starred in a twice-weekly soap opera called 'Crossways'. Mr Repton had also been in and given a sworn statement. Both the witnesses to their whereabouts were beyond reproach and both were, in DI Dobin's opinion, lying bastards.

It was always the same with the Ryans. They were more slippery than a greased eel. Also, the Chief Super had been running around like a blue-arsed fly. He had received word from a big wig somewhere along the line, and now the Ryans were to be 'courteously' escorted off the premises. He sighed.

'Well, Miss Ryan, thank you very much for your time. You can go now.'

Maura stood up. She slipped her crocodile skin clutch bag underneath her arm and held out her free hand. Dobin shook it gently.

'Is my brother being released?'

'Yes, Miss Ryan, he's waiting for you at the reception desk.'

'Thank you. Thank you very much. Have you any idea who could have hurt . . . murdered my brother Benny?' Her voice was low.

'No, Miss. But rest assured we will do all that we can. As we will to investigate the bombing of your brother's club.'

Maura bowed her head and followed him from the room. Unlike her, Michael was making himself heard. Maura could hear him before she saw him.

As she turned the corner and walked to him, he pointed at her. 'Don't you worry, girl. These bastards will pay for this day's work. My little brother's dead and *you* arrest *me*!' His voice was indignant. 'And my little sister! My club's been bombed and you lot don't give a toss about it. I'm a taxpayer and I want me rights!'

The Chief Superintendent was nearly in tears. 'Please, Mr Ryan. We must follow every lead.'

'Why ain't you out looking for the real criminals, eh? The rapists and the child molesters. Why ain't you out looking for whoever murdered my little brother?'

Maura slipped her arm into his. 'Come on, Michael. Calm down, love. Let's just get out of here.' She led him

261

out into the afternoon air. 'Please, Mickey, let's get home. I think I'm going to be sick.'

Michael put his arms around her and cuddled her to him. 'Don't worry, Dopolis will pay for what he's done, darlin', and he'll pay bloody dearly.'

At this moment Maura did not want anyone to pay for anything. She just wanted to run away from it all. Instead she smiled wanly. The worst was yet to come. They had to face their mother.

Sarah had been sitting in the darkness of her front room for hours. When the police brought her the news about Benny she had walked into the room, pulled the heavy curtains and sat in the chair by the fire. She felt nothing. Nothing at all. But she would. Oh, she knew that much. She would. It was like Anthony all over again. She had made Benjamin go with the policeman to identify young Benny's remains. Let him do some of the dirty work for a change.

In the flickering firelight her religious statues looked lifelike. Getting out of the seat, she went to the large sideboard that held them all. She opened one of the drawers and took out her wooden rosary. She went back to her seat. Kissing the Cross of Christ, she began to pray.

She could hear Carla's sobs coming from the bedroom above her, but did not really care. It would do the child good to find out just what her Auntie Maura and Uncle Michael had caused. It might take some of the shine off them for her. She had already refused to see Geoffrey. He had arrived just after the police and she had told him to bugger off out of it. She did not want to see any of her children except Maura and Michael. Oh, she wanted to see them all right! She wanted to throw them out of her house and her life. They were filthy . . . putrid.

She heard the click of the front room door opening and glanced towards it. In the light from the hall she could make out Maura and Michael's silhouettttes. She said nothing. They walked into the room quietly, shutting the door behind them. Sarah carried on praying.

'"Hail Mary, full of grace, the Lord is with thee. Blessed art thou amongst sinners and blessed is the fruit of thy womb, Jesus . . ."'

Michael watched his mother. She was so short that her feet did not touch the floor properly as she sat on the large horsehair chair. The room had its own distinctive cloying stuffiness, a sickly sweet smell of lavender polish and dusty velvet.

'Mum? Shall I turn the light on?'

'"Holy Mary Mother of God, pray for us sinners, now and at the hour of our death, Amen."

'"Hail Mary, full of grace . . ."'

'Come on, Michael. Let's leave her.'

Maura's voice sounded something in Sarah's head. It was as if her daughter's voice triggered an explosion. Sarah's voice came to them from the semi-darkness.

'So you want to leave, Maura Ryan, do you?' Her voice was low, conversational. As if they were having a friendly chat about the weather. 'Did you know that your brother's head was found this morning? In a litter bin, of all places.' She was amazed to hear herself laugh. 'Yes, a litter bin. Just the place to put rubbish, isn't it? In a dustbin. Where will they put you two, I wonder, when you're dead? Down in the sewers, I expect, with the rest of the shit and the effluent. Oh, yes. That will very likely be where you two will end up. In the filth and stink of the sewers!'

'Mum! For God's sake.' Michael's voice was shocked.

'Don't you "God" me, Michael Ryan. Because I'm finished with you, do you hear me? I am finished with you . . . I should never have forgiven you over my Anthony.'

Maura listened to their mother's voice. She knew that what Sarah was saying would break Michael's heart.

'And what about me, Mum? What about me?'

Maura's voice was hard. Sarah felt its iciness and shivered in her seat.

'You filthy whore! I know all about you, Maura Ryan. You and him.' She poked her head towards Michael. 'Do you know what people say? That you two sleep together. Did you know that? Only I know that's not true

263

because he's as queer as a fish and you're a neuter. You're not capable of sleeping with any man, Maura Ryan.'

Maura felt a hot flush creep over her body. She went to the lightswitch and flipped it. The room was filled with the glaring brightness of a one hundred watt bulb.

Maura walked to her mother, her lovely face twisted into a mask of hatred.

'So I'm a neuter, am I? And whose bloody fault was that? Yours! Call yourself a mother? *You* took me to the abortionist. And *you* held me down on the bloody table while that Paki bastard ripped my baby from inside me. You turned us all into what we are, Mother. Even poor Benny. Another Mummy's boy, still at home at twenty-nine years old! You made it impossible for any of your children to lead a normal life. You drove your husband to drink and your kids into being neuters.

'I may end up in the gutter or the sewers. Who knows? But at least if I go there I'll have finally told you what I think of you. You're a nasty vindictive old bitch! You're even jealous of me and Carla, ain't you? Go on . . . admit it!'

Sarah stared at her daughter, mesmerised. Of all the things she had envisaged at this meeting with Maura and Michael, this was not one of them. She had expected silence as she read them the riot act. Not this.

'Sitting in the bloody dark saying the Rosary! You old hypocrite. Well, let me tell you something. Your old darling Father McCormack is an active IRA member. That's how we all got involved. When you sent him to talk some sense into Michael, the priest dragged him into it all. He was laughing at you, you stupid old cow!'

'No! I won't have you say that about the priest. You're a dirty liar!'

'SHUT YOUR BLOODY MOUTH UP!' Maura's voice bounced off the walls. 'Do you hear me? Shut up for once in your life. We may not be pillars of the church but we ain't got anything on our conscience where you're concerned, Mother. Everything you ever had come from Mickey, later on from me and the other boys. You had nothing . . . NOTHING!'

Maura ran to where the religious statues stood bearing witness to their fight. Picking up the statue of Saint Sebastian, she threw it to the ground.

'Not even the money to buy this shower of shite!'

She stopped abruptly, gasping for breath. She saw her mother sitting in the chair. She looked like a very old woman. All the fight left Maura and she went to Michael.

'Come on, Mickey. Let's go.'

'Mum . . . You didn't mean what you said, did you, Maws? Mum, look at me.'

Sarah sighed heavily.

'Get him out of me sight, Maura, and take yourself with him. You both disgust me.'

Maura turned round to face the woman she had alternately loved and hated all her life.

'Not half as much as you disgust me, Mother.'

As Maura spoke, Michael seemed to snap out of his reverie. 'I worshipped you, Mother.' His voice was dangerously low. 'All my life it's been, "Michael, get me this, son." Or help with that. But you never really cared about me, did you? I was just a pair of hands as far as you were concerned.'

His eyes were moist and Maura felt her heart breaking as she watched him confront the most important person in his life. 'I helped you with the kids as they came along. I fetched and carried while you had your long . . . painfully long . . . pregnancies. Then as soon as you were delivered of yet another child, you allowed the old man back into your bed, didn't you? Even after the dead babies you were both back at it like a pair of dogs copulating.

'You wonder why I turned out like I did? Well, I'll tell you why. I never wanted a woman and all that it entailed. I never wanted an emotional leech sucking out my entrails like you did to all us. Anthony's dead, and our Benny – and I'd give anything to be with them! Away from this house and this family and *you* . . . especially you.

'Come on, Maws. Let's leave her to her prayers and her religious mania. It's all she's fit for.'

Sarah felt as if she had been stabbed to the heart. She'd

never realised just how much she had come to rely on Michael's unquestioning support.

She sat still in her chair, trying to control her breathing. As Michael pulled Maura from the room they came face to face with Carla. She was standing in the hallway, her lovely face twisted in pain, arms hugging her slim body.

'Get your stuff together, Carla, we're leaving.'

She shook her head. Her long red-brown hair swirled about her face.

'I'm not going anywhere with you, Maura. I'm staying here with Nana.'

'I said, get your stuff together.' Maura's voice brooked no argument.

'No. I'm not going.'

Maura sighed. 'You do what you like, Carla. You know where I am when you want me.'

Carla curled her lips in contempt. 'I'll never want you. Never! You're nothing but murderers.'

Maura brought her hand back and slapped Carla a stinging blow across her face.

'You stay here with your precious Nana then . . . I don't give a toss any more. You can do what you like. Come on, Mickey. Let's go.'

As they left the house Benny's Alsatian, Driver, ran from the kitchen down the front steps. He leapt about in the snow, ecstatic to be out in the air.

Michael opened the door to his Mercedes and the dog jumped into the front seats then dived over into the back. He sat there with his tongue hanging out, his heavy tail thumping the seat as it wagged.

'I'll take him home with me, Mickey.'

They got into the car and Michael pulled away from the kerb with a heavy heart.

Inside the house Sarah and Carla held on to each other tightly.

Michael finally spoke as they drove along the Bayswater Road. 'When we get to your drum, Maws, we've got to round up the boys. The old Bill ain't got nothing on us but we have to plan our next moves cautiously.'

Maura did not answer him. He took one hand off the steering wheel and patted her leg.

'Listen, Maws, I ain't learnt much in this life but I have learnt this. When you hit a major setback you put it behind you as quick as possible. Benny's dead. Nothing will ever bring him back again. What we do now is decide when and how we retaliate.'

Maura nodded her head wearily. Her mum was right. Mickey was mad . . . and she had a sneaky feeling that she was as well.

Driver put his head on Maura's shoulder. She could feel his hot dog breath on her cheek and lifted her arm and caressed the dog's soft fur. Benny had loved his dog as he had loved his life – wholeheartedly. She realised with a curious insight that Benny had probably not even realised he was in danger. That fact would never have occurred to him.

She closed her eyes tightly and instead of the tears she had been expecting, began to laugh. A slight giggle at first that gradually built up into a deep rollicking belly laugh. A laugh that made her shoulders shake and her tummy hurt. Somewhere in the distance, far off, she heard the dog begin to whine, and for some reason this just made her laugh harder.

Michael stopped the car and pulled her towards him. She could smell the dank dampness of the material of his coat. Then the tears came at last. She saw Terry Petherick, Anthony and Benny, as clear as a photograph in her mind. Then she saw her mother's face, old and wrinkled . . . a feeling of panic welled up in her and for a few minutes she thought she really had gone mad.

How had this happened to her? And, more importantly, how had she allowed it to happen? Both questions were to remain unanswered for many years, but as she sat in the car with Michael and Driver that night, she realised for the first time just how lonely and unhappy she really was.

'All right, Maws. All right, my love. I'll look after you. Don't you worry.' Michael's voice was soft and husky.

She did not want Michael to look after her. She wanted Terry Petherick to put his arms around her and whisper his words of love, as he had done before. Long ago. Before she had become bad. But, like many other bad things in her life, she forced the thoughts away. Where they waited patiently for the day they would all creep out into the open and torture her, like the long forgotten nightmares of her childhood.

Chapter Nineteen

'Merry Christmas, Auntie Maura!'

Margaret's twin daughters jumped on to the little bed where Maura was sleeping. She opened her eyes, not sure for a few seconds where she was. Then seeing the two bright faces, she tried to smile.

She was at Margaret's. She sat up in bed and hugged Patricia and Penelope. The sleeping tablets she had taken the night before made her feel groggy. She yawned. 'Merry Christmas, my lovelies.'

'Thank you for our Christmas presents, Auntie Maura. They were lovely.'

The two identical little faces beamed at her and she felt the familiar tightening in her guts. What she wouldn't give to be the mother of these two! She hugged them both to her tightly.

Margaret came into the bedroom carrying a tray. Maura could smell eggs and bacon.

'Oh, Marge. Don't be silly. I can get up.'

Margaret pursed her lips and shook her head. 'Oh no you won't, Maws. Oi, you two! Dad's got your breakfast waiting for you downstairs.'

The two girls got off the bed, their bright ginger hair telling anyone who looked at them who their mother was.

Patricia, the elder of the two by five minutes, grimaced. 'Oh, can't we stay up here, Mum?' Her voice had the whine that made Margaret feel like murdering her.

'N.O. spells no. Now hop it, the pair of you.'

The two girls ran from the room.

'Honest, Marge, I couldn't eat a thing.'

The greasy smell of the bacon and eggs was beginning to make her feel sick.

'You *will* bloody eat it. After all you've been through this last few weeks!' Margaret's voice was scandalised. 'You'll end up ill if you're not careful. Smoke, smoke, smoke! Drink, drink. And then sleeping pills to blot out the world.'

'Oh, give it a rest, Marge, for Christ's sake.'

Margaret put the tray across Maura's legs as if to trap her in the bed.

'No I won't give it a rest! You're my best friend and I feel that it's down to me to tell you a few home truths.'

'Such as?' Maura's voice was sarcastic.

'For a start, you look old and haggard. You're drinking too much. It's impossible to get a civil word out of you. You're moody, sarcastic, and to be honest, Maws, you're beginning to get on my tits!'

Maura closed her eyes and yawned again.

'Margie, just in case it's escaped your notice, I recently had a brother murdered. He was spread all over London like a paper chase. His left foot and various other parts of his anatomy are still unaccounted for. I had a big fight with my mother and Carla who are under the impression that me and Mickey were to blame for Benny's murder. I was arrested by the police and kept for over three hours on suspicion of *two* other murders. And you have the nerve to sit there and tell me that I am not my old self!' Maura's voice rose. 'It's enough to make the Queen feel depressed.'

Margaret sighed. She loved Maura wholeheartedly. 'Look, Maws, all I'm trying to say is, pull yourself together. If not for my sake then for the kids. I can't stand them seeing you like this. Last night you was so pissed Dennis had to carry you up to bed.'

'I know. Marge, I'm sorry. It's just that with all that's happened, I feel responsible . . .'

'That's crap and you know it! I can swallow a lot, Maws, but not self-pity. That's a luxury none of us can afford.'

Maura looked at Margaret as if for the first time. Since

having the kids she had become huge. In her pink candle-wick dressing gown she looked like a little pink Buddha. Her red hair was pinned up untidily and her face had the harassed look that seems to be worn only by mothers of young children. It was only her eyes, the deep sea-green eyes, that still held the image of the girl she had been. They were as sparkling and mischievous as ever.

Cutting off a small piece of bacon, Margaret held it to Maura's mouth. Reluctantly she ate it. Slowly Margaret fed her the whole breakfast. When the last piece of food had been eaten she placed a mug of tea in Maura's hands. Then, picking up the tray, she made her way out of the room. As she opened the bedroom door, holding the tray against her side with one hand, she looked back over her shoulder at Maura.

'You can't plan and scheme on an empty stomach, you know!'

'And just what do you mean by that?'

Marge smiled at her cheekily.

'I'm not as silly as I look, you know, Maura Ryan. So I'll thank you not to act as if I am.' She lowered her voice. 'What I know and what I've guessed will go to my grave with me. Now, you need your wits about you at this time, and I intend to see that you have them.'

She walked from the room and let the door slam shut behind her.

Maura leant back against the pillows and sighed. Good old Marge. The only real friend she had. She sat up in bed, and, putting the tea on the night table, picked up her packet of cigarettes. She lit one, drawing the smoke into her lungs. Margaret was right. She did need her wits about her. If only Carla would talk to her she would feel better. Every time she tried to get through to her, the phone was slammed down. She had even tried ringing Carla's friends. But nothing. She had not answered any of Maura's messages. Maura could imagine her mother, in her element, poison-ing Carla against her. Oh, she had guessed her mother's game all right . . .

She took another pull on the cigarette and felt a wave of

nausea sweep over her. The combination of fried food, cigarette smoke and acute hangover was suddenly too much for her stomach. With her hand pressed tightly to her mouth, she ran from the bedroom into the bathroom. Dropping her cigarette into the toilet pan she retched. She heaved until she thought her insides were going to come up. A cold sweat broke out all over her body. She leaned against the wall, trying to gather her wits about her. Turning on the shower, she slipped her nightie over her head and stood underneath the shower head. She shivered as ice cold water ran over her body, making her teeth chatter. Still she stood there, trying to bring some kind of life back into her limbs.

After a few minutes she felt the delicious sensation of warmth that only cold water can bring. She felt the tightening of her skin as the blood vessels beneath the surface tried desperately to pump warm blood around her aching body. Her nipples were rock hard and as she turned the water on to hot she savoured the exquisite sensation of the heat gradually invading her bones. She put her face up to let the water cleanse her from head to toe. Gradually she felt the life begin to come back to her. For the first time in days she actually felt something that was real and tangible.

Then the tears came. A torrent of salty rivulets that mixed with the heavy water from the shower and ran away, down her breasts, over her empty stomach, on to her feet and into the shower tray.

In her mind she saw the loathing on her mother's face. The handsome carefree face of Benny, the young boy who had always been in some kind of prank. She saw the face of Terry Petherick, as it had been the night of the club bombing. She had known then that he still cared for her, that if she had not been Maura Ryan they would have married. She would have been like Margie, juggling the bills, looking after the kids and just being loved. As Dennis loved Marge, even with her large mauve and silver stretch-marks and empty breasts. And she, Maura, would have loved it. Every second of it.

272

Instead she had more money than she knew what to do with. She ran a business that was more crooked than the Government of Cuba, and had a brother who was at this time almost totally dependent on her. As for the younger boys, they blamed *her* for Benny's death. Not Michael but her. They believed that if she had not wanted her dock properties so badly, and had given them to Dopolis, Benny would still be alive. And she had to be honest and admit to herself that they were right. She cried harder. Whoever said that money made you happy was a liar. A dirty rotten stinking liar! She would give every penny she had at this moment to be just plain ordinary Mrs Terry Petherick. He was the only man she had ever wanted and he was the only man she would ever want, even if she lived to be a hundred. If only she had kept that little baby! If she had nothing else now she would have had that. She would never have taken over the ice cream and hot dogs. She would never have become the person she was now. The person who had watched her brother murder an old man, Sammy Goldbaum, who had been waiting patiently for them to arrive. He had walked so meekly to the car. And now she had his blood on her hands and could never escape from any of it.

She had always thought that if she ever came face to face with Terry Petherick she would spit in his eye. Instead she had felt an urge to tell him all that happened to her. About the baby and her life with Michael . . . everything. She had wanted it to be like it had been once before. When she was young and free. She was still young, but too much had happened over the years ever to allow her to be the girl that she once had been.

She turned off the tap and stood in the confined space of the shower cubicle. The sudden silence was startling and broke her out of her reverie. Her tears were gone now and all they had left in their wake was a heavy tiredness. Stepping from the shower, she wrapped a large towel around her body. As she dried her hair she thought about what she was going to do next. Then she made a decision. All that she could do now was go forward into the future.

No matter how exciting the past may have been you could never recapture it. What Margaret had said earlier was right. Self-pity was a destructive force. She would have to make herself stronger. Much stronger. What she really needed was to get laid!

She smiled to herself. That was what Marge had been telling her for years! She shrugged aggressively, as if throwing off all her previous worries and cares. She wiped the steam from the mirror on the wall opposite the shower and stared at her face. Her hair hung in limp, damp strands around her face which was puffy from crying. She smiled to herself. She was going to pick herself up and slowly mend all the broken pieces. She and Michael could take on the world. She had absolutely no one else now. She had lost them all, one by one. But she knew that she would always have Michael and Margie. Good old Margie.

She remembered that it was Christmas Day. Back at her own house she had the mother-of-pearl jewellery box that she had bought for Carla . . . She forced the thought from her mind. Let the ungrateful little bitch stay with her mother! Maura did not need her. She did not need anyone.

She ran her hands through her hair, feeling the silky softness of it. Letting the towel fall from her body, she ran her hands down her neck and over her breasts, travelling down her tight stomach to her pubic hair, enjoying the sensation. Picking up her nightie from the floor she put it back on, then went back into the bedroom where her overnight bag was. She felt a lot better. Much better, in fact. As she plugged in her hair dryer she was actually humming a little tune. Margie was right. Self-pity was a bummer. All that she could do now was go forward.

When she finally went downstairs she had her make-up on and her hair done to perfection. She was wearing a dress that would have cost Marge two months' housekeeping and was gratified to hear the long low whistle that came from Dennis.

'If I wasn't so happy with my old Margie I'd be after you myself, Maws!'

Marge laughed. 'Listen here, Dennis Dawson. You couldn't pull a ligament these days, let alone a beauty like Maura. Especially not since you lost your hair.' She smiled at Maura. 'All he's got these days is six hairs and a nit!'

Maura laughed with her. Dennis had lost his hair early, and Maura knew that it was a sore point with him.

'Come out here and have a cuppa. You look much better.'

Maura followed her out into her little kitchen. 'I feel a lot better, Marge. Thanks for letting me come.'

Margaret plugged in the electric kettle. 'What you on about, you silly cow? This is your home for as long as you want to be here.' She opened her arms wide and Maura walked into them. Margaret's tiny plump body held on to Maura's tall thin frame. Maura got upset again at the show of emotion.

'If you knew what I'd done, Marge!'

'Shhh.' Margaret stepped back from Maura and raised her finger to her lips. 'Look, Maws, I know that you and Michael ain't strictly kosher. I've always known and I don't care. You're me mate and that's all I'm interested in.'

Maura looked at her and frowned. 'Sometimes, Marge, I don't think that I'm all the ticket. I get so moody and I think really weird things.'

'Maws love, you've been through an awful lot, you know. Just let yourself heal naturally. Benny's death would make anyone feel rotten. It was horrific. You need time to get over it, that's all.'

'Maybe you're right, Marge.'

She wanted to tell Margaret what Mickey had done to Sammy Goldbaum and Jonny Fenwick. She wanted to tell her that she had helped him. She was experiencing that feeling again – as if she was on the outside of her body looking in. She had always known that Michael enjoyed inflicting pain on people. And until the night with Jonny Fenwick and Sammy Goldbaum it had not bothered her.

'Maura!' Margaret's voice broke into her thoughts. 'Mickey's on the phone for you.'

Maura stared around the kitchen blankly. Margaret looked at her curiously. 'You all right, girl?'

Maura nodded and walked out of the kitchen into the lounge. The twins were watching *Mary Poppins* on television and baby Dennis was now sitting on his dad's lap. Maura's mind registered the fact that the Christmas tree was falling to one side where the kids had been playing underneath it. She walked out into the hallway and picked up the receiver lying on the telephone table.

'Mickey? It's me.'

'Oh, darling. You'll never guess what?'

His voice was bubbling over with excitement.

'What?' Maura's voice was flat.

'I just had a visit from Sammy Goldbaum's daughter. You know her . . . the one with the big hooter?'

'Rebekka.'

'Yeah, that's it. Rebekka. Anyway, she said she had come to see me on Christmas Day to show that she bore me no ill will. Not that I give a toss anyway. Those front wheels are like the eye ties, full of crap. Anyway, the bottom line is she brought me some documents that belonged to Sammy. I've just been through them, and have a guess what I found along with a load of old betting slips?'

'What?'

'The name of the property developer we've been looking for. The mastermind behind Dopolis.'

'But Sammy said he had no idea who he was . . .'

'I don't think Sammy realised just what he had. You see, I found an old cutting from a newspaper. The *Daily Mirror* in fact. It was from the racing section and it had a picture of Dopolis. And get this bit, Maws. He's in the Royal Enclosure at Ascot! Now what, I asked myself, was he doing in there? Then I realised that he was standing with none other than William Templeton! That's when it hit me. He's the Mr Big that Dopolis was talking about.'

Maura was stunned. 'But he's a peer of the Realm!'

Mickey laughed. 'I know. Saucy bastard! I bet he's even in You Know Who . . . or whatever that book's called.'

Maura laughed despite herself. 'It's *Who's Who*, you wally. Christ Almighty, Mickey, if you're right . . .'

'I know I'm right. I've got a gut feeling about it. Look, can you get over to me now?'

'I can't, Mickey. I promised Marge and Den I'd have Christmas dinner with them.'

'All right then, Princess. But get your arse over here as soon as you can. All right?'

'All right, Mickey. Merry Christmas.' Her voice was sad.

Michael's voice lost its excitement. 'I know it's been a bad time, the last few weeks, but I promise you, Maws – I'll make it up to you somehow. Merry Christmas, my darling.'

Maura put the phone down gently. The implications of what Mickey had just said were phenomenal. She went back into the lounge and started to play with the children. She held them to the floor and tickled them till they screamed with laughter. Marge and Dennis watched her with amused expressions on their faces. This was more like it. This was the old Maura.

It wasn't until she was sitting at the dining table eating her enormous Christmas dinner that the excitement hit her. Lord William Templeton . . . Suddenly she could not wait to get started on him. Together Michael and she would eat him alive.

She picked up a bright blue cracker and pointed it at Patricia. 'Come on, Patty. Let's see who wins the paper hat!'

Lord Templeton was also sitting at his dinner table in his large rambling house in Kent. The house dated back to the fifteenth century and over the large inglenook fireplace was a painting of one of his ancestors. It had been executed by Holbein, one of Henry VIII's favourite painters.

There was an old story in his family that it was this ancestor who had actually ordered the death of Sir Thomas More. William liked to think that the story was true.

At forty-five, he was a somewhat jaded man. Over the years he had used his vast wealth to engage in many pastimes, both sexual and otherwise. He had hunted big game in South Africa and had smoked hashish in Turkey. He had travelled to the Himalayas and had seen the Manta Rays leap from the sea in the Maldives. He had experimented with drugs, and did not think there was any country in the world that he had not visited. He had married once, when he was very young, a large voluptuous woman, years older than himself. She had left him after one year, taking with her a large amount of money and his good wishes. She had taught him much: that there was no pleasure without pain; that a man, especially a rich man, needs to use his wealth wisely. He had never, as far as he knew, fathered a child. Unlike most men, William Templeton did not have the urge to reproduce. He rather liked his solitary life. If he wanted a woman they were easy enough to find.

He picked at his expertly cooked Christmas dinner. At this moment he was a very worried man. He was regretting getting involved with the Greek, Dopolis. For a start it had not achieved his objective – the warehouses that the Ryans owned in the old docklands. Dopolis had turned out to be a penny ante type villain. Not at all the hard man he had said he was. The Ryans had completely obliterated him. If only he had had the sense to keep his eye on the proceedings, then the young boy, Benjamin, would never have died. He shuddered. He had been impressed with Dopolis at first. Had admired his plan of action. How was he to know it was all going to backfire?

He pushed his plate away from him. He had no appetite. Dopolis should never have ordered the boy's killing, and such a horrible death . . . Now he would have to be very careful. The only avenue left to him was to get someone harder than Michael Ryan and from what he could gauge that would be a very tall order indeed.

278

His manservant, a rather pinched-faced man called Rankin, cleared the table in front of him. Templeton sat back in his large comfortable chair. His dining table could easily seat twenty-four people. Normally he would have accepted an invitation from a friend for the Christmas festivities, but this year, after all the trouble with Dopolis, he had a hankering for his own company and his own hearth. He conceded that he had made a fatal mistake with the Greek. He toyed with the idea of going to see Michael Ryan and offering him a good price for the warehouses, but pushed the idea away as quickly as it occurred to him.

Some of his best friends had done a stint in Ford Open Prison; in the circles he moved in it was inevitable that you would eventually meet someone who had either embezzled money from the bank that they had worked for or been involved with some kind of fraud. But that was a fact of life. This Ryan, though, was a rough type and his sister wasn't much better apparently. He lit up a Cuban cigar and poured himself a large Remy Martin into the glass that Rankin had left conveniently by his elbow. No, he had made a tragic mistake. What he had to do now was try and recoup his losses. But he was sure of one thing. He *would* get those warehouses. He would get all the Ryans' properties along the Thames.

He smiled to himself. As usual he was absolutely amazed by his own intelligence. He thought of himself as the epitome of the upper class male. God in heaven, he was a cousin to the Queen! Only by marriage, he admitted, but it was a close enough connection to get Nigel Dempster practically wetting himself with excitement every time he appeared in public. He relaxed. There was nothing whatsoever to tie him in with Dopolis.

He sat in his chair, smoking his cigar and drinking his brandy, planning his next move. When the building finally started in the old docklands, every foot would be worth a small fortune. He sat all evening scheming how he would get the Ryans' properties.

Luckily for him he was not aware that Maura and

Michael Ryan were also planning and scheming along the same lines – how they were going to get *his* properties, and his co-operation.

Maura and Michael were now certain that William Templeton was their man. An old friend of Michael's who worked on one of the gutter papers had run his name through the newspaper's computer and supplied them with every piece of gossip ever written about him, as well as some facts that had never been published. And their friends in the IRA had been very helpful. Their final recourse had been to some paid 'informers' in the Foreign Office who had supplied information that had shocked even Michael. It seemed that Templeton was a major shareholder in an arms factory that had been supplying anyone with the readies for years. Templeton was certainly no angel, that much was apparent. And that he was protected by the old boy network was more than obvious. Though as Maura had pointed out, there had to be more people involved with him, and with all his businesses. His main buyers were North African countries; Iran, Iraq, Libya – the list was endless. He also supplied Romania and the Czechs. All in all, Templeton seemed like their kind of guy!

Michael was jubilant! The only cloud on their horizon was Dopolis. Although they now had just about everything they wanted to know about him, plans for his demise were put on hold for the time being. He was the bait with which they were going to lure William Templeton. As Michael had playfully remarked to Maura, 'Let him get over his injuries first. He can pay for Benny when he's better!'

Sarah Ryan had still not acknowledged either of them. This had cut Michael deeply. His mother had been his life. But the estrangement from her had brought brother and sister closer together. They spent every available minute in each other's company. Maura now needed Michael more than ever. When she was with him he could convince her that Sammy Goldbaum's and Jonny Fenwick's deaths were just the paying of a debt. While she was with him she could accept that. Away from him, she was frightened and lonely. Every day that passed was making her more bitter and confused. They had spent the days since Christmas following up their leads on Templeton, and decided they would pay him a visit on New Year's Day. Until then they would bide their time.

On the 29 December 1975 Roy's son was born. He rang the news through to Michael at seven in the evening. Maura and Michael arrived at St Mary's Hospital at eight-thirty. After looking at the new baby fleetingly, Michael and the rest of the boys took Roy out to celebrate, all feeling the loss of Benny more than ever.

Maura was left with Janine. She noticed that her mother was nowhere to be seen.

She held the baby, Benny Anthony, in her arms. 'He's beautiful, Janine. I hope you realise just how lucky you are?'

Janine smiled wearily. 'I'm a bit sore, Maws, but he was worth it.'

Maura nodded. She was staring at the baby so intently that Janine felt a prickle of fear.

'I nearly had a baby once, Janine. A long time ago.' Maura's voice was sad. For the first time ever Janine pitied her.

'I know, Maura. Roy told me.'

She held the baby tighter to her chest.

'It was a lovely gesture, naming the baby after Benny and Anthony. It brings them back somehow.' She kissed the baby's downy head. 'I think that if they'd at least let us bury Benny, half the battle would be over. I can't stand to think of him on ice.'

'Please, Maura. Don't talk about it.' Janine was nearly in tears.

Maura's sing-song voice as she spoke about her brother made Janine feel frightened. She had always been a little in awe of Maura. Now she was terrified.

Maura smiled radiantly at her.

'I'm sorry, Jan. I'm getting a bit morbid!' She kissed the

baby's head again and squeezed him to her breast. It took all Janine's willpower not to snatch her baby away. Janine was sensitive and felt things very deeply. She did not want this woman anywhere near her child.

Roy had said recently that he did not think that Maura was right in the head. Looking at her now, Janine was sure that she was capable of anything. She had a terrible feeling that Maura would even kill a baby if it would get her what she wanted. Janine shivered.

'You cold?'

'No, Maura, just tired. It takes a lot out of you, having a baby.'

'Like shitting a football, is how Marge described it!'

Janine pursued her lips. She had never understood the Ryans' use of bad language. They swore in much the same way as her mother said 'God bless you'.

Janine took all her courage into her hands and decided to approach Maura with an idea that had been floating around inside her head for months.

'Maura?'

'What?' She was rocking the baby in her arms, completely engrossed in his little face. He was looking up at her with the dark blue Ryan eyes.

Janine picked at her bedsheet, watching her sister-in-law warily.

'It's about Roy.'

Maura laughed gently. 'He's like a dog with three lamp posts! I've never seen him like this. All the boys are ribbing him terrible. You'd think this was the first baby ever born!'

'I know . . . I know.' Janine was finding it difficult to find the appropriate words.

Maura sensed that there was something going on and looked Janine in the face.

'What's on your mind? Come on, spit it out. I'm not really an ogre, whatever my Mum might say.' Her voice was bitter.

'I was wondering if you would help Roy set up a little business . . .'

Her voice trailed off as she saw the look of shock on Maura's face.

'You what! Roy work outside the family? You must be joking.'

Janine started to cry. 'Oh, Maura, I'm so frightened.' She put her face into her hands. 'I feel like a policeman's wife, wondering if he's going to come home. Then after what happened to Benny . . .'

Maura pulled her hands away from her face. 'You're just overwrought, that's all. Having a baby makes you go funny.'

'NO! It's not that!' Janine lost all caution. 'I don't want to be left a widow, bringing up the baby on my own. I want us to be a normal family. A real family. Roy's not meant to be a thug.'

Maura put the baby into the cot by the bed. Her face was set. She loomed over Janine and began to speak to her in a low and menacing voice.

'Shall I tell you something, Janine? In case it had escaped your notice. Roy, as much as I love him, is as thick as two short planks. He can barely count over fifty. He still reads *Marvel* comics, for Christ's sake! The best he could ever have expected out of life was a job on the council or with the Water Board. Either way, you'd not be spending the kind of hefty wedge you're used to now. Your father tried to turn him into a butcher and look where that got him. If Roy knew what you'd said here tonight he'd give you a well-deserved slap. Now about the other load of shit you was spouting . . .'

She pushed Janine back against the pillows hard and poked her in the chest. 'You want to be a real family, do you? You dumped your daughter on my mother if you remember rightly, love. If push ever comes to shove, you can dump your new arrival on her and all, can't you? Don't you ever try and bullshit me again. DO YOU HEAR ME?'

Maura's loud voice made the baby whimper in his cot. 'I'm going to forget what you've said in here tonight, Janine, because I know that having a baby can make you a bit distraught. I'm warning you, though, if I ever get wind that you've said this to anyone else, I'll come and sort you out myself. Get it?'

Janine nodded, her lips trembling. She realised that she had just made an enemy for life.

Maura watched her closely. Then she smiled a soft little smile that did not reach her eyes. Picking up her bag from the floor, she opened it, took out a blue velvet box and handed it to Janine.

'Well, open it then.' She snapped.

Janine was shaking so badly that Maura had to place her own hands on top of hers to help her open the box. Inside was a gold and platinum identity bracelet.

'I'll have his name put on it for you.'

Janine swallowed heavily. She did not want it. 'Tha . . . thanks. It's lovely. Beautiful.' A stray tear slid down her face. Maura wiped it away gently with her fingers.

'Cheer up, love. You just had a lovely little boy. You should be laughing, not crying.'

Janine forced a smile she did not think she had in her. 'As you say . . . it's my hormones or something.'

Maura laughed. 'That's the ticket. Now, I'm off to the Crown and Two Chairmen. If that lot are left on their own with Roy, he'll end up legless.' She put her bag under her arm and kissed Janine on the cheek.

'I heard a little saying the other day, Janine. It might give you something to think about. It was on a wall in some public toilets and Mickey read it. It said: "Life is like a shit sandwich. The more bread you've got, the less shit you have to eat." I'd think about that if I was you.'

With one last glance at the baby, Maura left the room. Janine was convinced that she was fuming inside and she was right. She sat in the bed staring at the identity bracelet. The tears came in a red hot rush. She felt like a trapped animal.

Her mother-in-law had been right. They would never let Roy go.

A while later a nurse came in and gave her a little talking to. And Janine sat in the bed silently as she was told all about 'the baby blues'. She was still crying when the nurse finally gave up and left her.

Maura drove to the Crown and Two Chairmen feeling better than she had for weeks. It had taken Janine's smugness and petty strivings for respectability to bring her out of her depression.

She was honest with herself, though. Holding the new baby had brought back all her maternal feelings and she had resented the fact that the baby was Janine's. Had she but known, Janine could not have picked a worse time to ask Maura for a favour.

Chapter Twenty

Maura walked into the Crown and Two Chairmen pub in Dean Street. As usual it was packed. She pushed her way through the throng of people and finally located the boys in the corner. Roy was already very drunk. The air was thick with cigarette smoke and camaraderie. Leslie saw Maura first and raised himself from his seat unsteadily. He was as drunk as a lord. Maura smiled at him.

'Hello, Mawsh.' His voice was slurred.

'Sit down, Les, before you fall down.' She looked around the table. Her six remaining brothers were all sitting, looking like clones of one another, all in different states of inebriation. Only Michael was even remotely sober. He stood up and offered her his seat.

'Sit down, Maws, and I'll get you a drink. What'll it be? Scotch?'

Maura sat down and nodded at him. He went to the bar.

'Well, you lot seem to be enjoying yourselves.' She made her voice sound jovial. Five pairs of eyes stared at her blankly. Maura felt for the first time the impact of their combined wariness and it hurt her. Only Geoffrey looked different and she realised that he looked smug. Smug and very, very sure of himself. Maura mentally chalked one up to him.

'Well, Roy, you got a son at last.'

He nodded at her, a silly grin on his drunken face. Maura began to search in her bag for her cigarettes. It was obvious that she was not welcome. In her present state of mind she was not sure if it was over Benny or because it was a boys' night out. Michael came back with a tray of drinks and she

287

took the double Scotch he gave her and drank it straight down.

'That bad, Maws?' Michael's voice was soft.

'No. Actually it's worse. If you boys will excuse me, I have got some work to do in the club. OK?'

She picked up her bag and left as quickly as possible. Outside in the freezing night she breathed a deep sigh. It was still snowy, though most of it had turned to slush and black ice. She walked carefully up Dean Street to Le Buxom. The main damage to the club had been in the foyer. The little reception desk where Sheree Davidson had been sitting on the night of the bombing had taken most of the blast from the petrol bomb. The damage to the club had turned out to be minimal. Mainly cosmetic. But as Maura walked inside she was acutely aware of the fact that Sheree would never again walk in there with her tall stories and deep braying laugh. She had been popular with both punters and the other hostesses. She had left two children, who were now in the care of the courts. Their father, or fathers, no one was sure, were nowhere to be found. If indeed Sheree ever knew who they were.

As for Gerry Jackson, he had been taken to a Burns Unit in Billericay. His wife had already been made an interim payment of two thousand pounds to get her over Christmas and the New Year. She would receive a substantial weekly amount until it was decided by the doctors what would happen to Gerry. If he never worked again he would be more than amply provided for.

The club was once more up and running. It had been reopened less than a week after the 'trouble'. As Maura walked into the familiar blast of warm air she could hear 'My Eyes Adored You'. Her mind registered that Louise Barton was doing her act. Maura looked at her watch. It was nearly eleven and she was surprised that it was so late. She slipped off her fur coat and locked it in the little cloakroom just inside the entrance to the club.

Picking her bag up off the floor she went over to the meat seats and started her night's work. A new girl called Monique, for once a real Frenchwoman and not a phony, had started a few weeks previously. She was a very very beautiful girl, very intelligent, and not at all the usual class of tom. There was just one thing that had puzzled Maura: she would take literally any punter. And another of the girls had told Maura that she would 'go case' for as little as fifty pounds. The minimum that her girls usually worked for was one hundred pounds plus their hostess fee. That told Maura one thing: Monique either had a violent pimp who insisted on a night 'quota', or she had a drugs problem.

Maura guessed it was the latter, and if it was, then it would not be long before they were busted. The busts were well staged. They were told at least a week in advance when one was going to occur so they could put off any well-known citizens, such as judges or more rarely politicians. The police had no qualms about arresting any of the girls that were taking, or happened to possess, drugs. It gave the so-called raid credibility. But Maura did not work like that. She would not, like some club owners, employ 'stooges' to give their busts a veneer of realism.

Monique was sitting with two black girls. They were chatting together amicably, which was unusual in itself. There was a fierce rivalry between the black and white toms, but Monique seemed to be liked by everyone. Maura went to where they were sitting, and smiled.

'Hello.' She nodded at the three girls. 'I wonder, Monique, could I see you upstairs for a few minutes?' Maura's voice was friendly. The other girls would assume that Maura had a 'homebird', a regular punter who had arranged to pay for the girl over the phone. That entailed stumping up for two bottles of champagne, fifty cigarettes, and a small administration fee. The girl would then be cabbed to the man's address.

Monique stood up and Maura noticed that she was very bright-eyed. Her pupils were dilated. She followed Maura upstairs to the office. Maura turned on the lights and, walking to the window, shut the venetian blinds. She turned back to face Monique and, smiling still, offered her a chair. The girl sat down. Instead of walking around the desk and sitting in her own chair, Maura stood in front of Monique, leaning on the edge of the desk.

'Monique, hold out your arms, please.'

'But why?'

Maura cleared her throat. She hated this. 'Would you please hold out your arms? You know why.'

Monique had long black hair and dark hazel eyes. In the bright light of the office Maura was surprised at how hard-faced she really was. In the muted light of the club she looked much younger. Maura had thought she was in her twenties. Looking at her now, though, she put her much nearer forty.

'Please, Monique. Don't make this any harder than it already is.'

Monique held out her arms. Maura checked them for track marks. There was nothing.

Monique looked at her triumphantly. 'You see, Miss Ryan. Nothing.'

Maura smiled apologetically. 'Take your stockings off, please.'

Monique's face dropped. 'I beg your . . . how you say?'

Maura finished her sentence for her. 'Pardon. I beg your pardon. Now, if you don't mind, take your stockings off. I want a quick shufti at your calves and your shins, OK?'

Monique's eyes glittered with malevolence. She reminded Maura of a cornered rat.

'Take your stockings off, Monique. Either you do as I ask or I'll call one of the bouncers up here to have them forcibly removed. It's your choice.' She saw Monique's eyes go to the beaded bag on her lap. 'And don't even think about trying to shiv me, darling. It would only end in tears. And they wouldn't be mine.'

Maura's voice was as hard as concrete now. Monique surveyed her, weighing up the pros and cons. After a few seconds she dragged her tight black velour dress over her thighs. Slowly she began to undo the suspender belt. Monique rolled the stocking down to below her knee and held her leg out for inspection. Maura grinned. She was used to every ploy in the book. She took off the black patent leather shoe that Monique was wearing and pulled the stocking off completely. The bottom of her leg was a mass of needle marks. Even between her toes. Maura threw the stocking back at her and sighed.

'You're a bloody mug to yourself. You know that, don't you, Monique?'

The woman shrugged. She began to put her stocking back on.

Maura carried on talking. 'I know for a fact that you can speak German, Arabic, and even a smattering of Japanese. You're not a fool. Why do you take drugs?'

Monique slipped her shoe back on and took the cigarette that Maura offered her. Maura offered her a light. Monique puffed on the cigarette.

'You people make me laugh. Oh, don't look so . . . how you say? . . . shocked. I come here night after night and I sleep with strange men. Some of them are very nice men. Very kind. Some, they are rough and they want to hurt you.'

She saw Maura's face change and laughed. 'You are a very funny girl. You do not want me in your club because I take drugs. Well, let me tell you, I have been a prostitute since I was seventeen. Over twenty years. I have to have something to give me a bit of happiness and I find it in drugs. I have slept with thousands of different men and while I work for people like you, I make you very much money. How many of my men have refused to pay their bills, eh? None. I can sweet talk any man I want. So please don't lecture me!

'I will leave your club. It's shit anyway since the bomb was thrown in here. All the girls are nervous.' She stood up and put her cigarette out in the ashtray on the desk. 'I will say one thing before I go. Who is worse, eh? Me because I sell my body, or you for earning good money off that fact?'

'I give all the girls a good deal here. I offer them a degree of protection that they would not get anywhere else in London.' Maura's voice was defensive.

Monique laughed. 'True. True. But you are still a pimp in my eyes *and* theirs.' She gave her Gallic shrug. 'Goodbye.'

Monique walked from the room and Maura suddenly felt flat. It seemed that she was not 'Miss Popular' these days. Even her own brothers were wary of her. Except for Michael, of course.

She laid her arms on the top of the desk and rested her head on them. What she would really like to do now was walk out of this office, out of this club, and in to her car. Then she would like to drive and drive and drive until she arrived somewhere where no one knew her and she could be exactly what she really was – a twenty-five-year-old girl. Not woman . . . girl.

She was startled to hear the door opening. It was another of the hostesses, a very young girl by the name of Candy. Whether or not that was her real name was debatable. She was carrying a cup of coffee. Maura sat up in her chair and tried to smile at her.

'I thought you looked as if you could do with this, Miss Ryan.' She placed the coffee on Maura's desk. Maura could smell the aroma of whisky. As if reading her mind, Candy smiled.

'It's an Irish coffee. A very strong Irish coffee.'

Maura smiled, her first real smile for days. 'Thanks, Candy.'

Candy sat in the chair vacated by Monique. She was a natural blonde, her hair lighter than Maura's which was unusual as Maura's was nearly white. Candy's was a silver blond and she had the most amazing brown eyes. It was a startling combination. A few weeks earlier, all the hostesses had put in five pounds each and Candy had shown every one of them her pubic hair. It was exactly the same colour as the hair on her head. She had stopped all the arguments about herself, and made herself nearly a hundred pounds richer.

The girl hitched up her strapless dress. The movement seemed to accentuate her childishness.

'You look right done in, Miss Ryan.'

'I feel it actually, Candy.'

The girl sniffed loudly. 'I wanted to see you about something personal.'

Maura sipped the steaming and fragrant coffee and lifted her eyebrows in an invitation for the girl to continue.

'A bloke was hanging around outside the club earlier.'

'What was he – a pimp?' Maura sounded bored. This was the last thing she wanted even to think about. Let alone *do* something about.

Candy shook her head. 'Oh, no. He was nothing like that. He was a policeman.'

'A what!'

'An old Bill. You know, lily law.' Candy laughed.

'What was he asking about? The night of the bombing? What?' Her voice was anxious.

Candy relaxed into her seat. 'No, nothing like that, Miss Ryan. He was asking about you.'

Maura's mouth dropped open. 'Me?'

'Yes, you. He gave me this to give to you.' Candy took a slip of paper from between her boobs. 'He asked me if you would be in tonight. I said I didn't know and then he offered me twenty quid to deliver that to you. So I did. I hope I haven't done anything wrong?'

Maura's eyes were devouring the words on the piece of paper. 'No . . . No, Candy. You were right to take the message.'

She got up from her desk and, picking up her bag, slipped the note inside. Then she took out her purse and gave Candy three twenty-pound notes.

'Oh no, Miss Ryan, I couldn't. The bloke gave me a score.'

Maura pushed the notes into the girl's hand. 'You take it, Candy. You did very well tonight.'

Candy took the proffered money and smiled craftily. 'Well, if you're sure . . .'

Maura laughed out loud. She could feel the adrenaline pulsing through her body.

Candy stood up too and Maura did something that would make her a friend for life. She hugged the girl.

'Candy, can I trust you never to tell anyone about this?'

She put her hand gently on Maura's arm. 'Look, Miss Ryan, I don't know what was in that note. I didn't read it. And I'm not a grass. You've been good to me and if I can repay you somehow, I will.'

'Thanks, Candy. I appreciate it.'

Candy smiled and went back downstairs. She liked Maura Ryan. Whatever anyone said about her, she looked after the girls. And Candy, being honest in her own way, admitted that she would not get very far without her. It would be back to a pimp and either Park Lane or, when her looks went, King's Cross. At least at Le Buxom she had the chance to get herself a little stake. And for that she would be eternally grateful.

When Candy left the room Maura snatched the note from her bag. It was from Terry Petherrick! She could not believe it! She read it again.

'IF EVER YOU NEED ME, CALL THIS NUMBER. LOVE, TERRY.'

Underneath was his phone number. Maura was ecstatic. He *did* still want her. Otherwise why would he bother to send her a note? She hugged the scrap of paper to her. Terry had put himself on the line to get this message to her. It crossed her mind that it was some kind of frame up but she had felt the attraction between them. And if nothing could ever come of it, at least she would always have the satisfaction of knowing that he had still wanted her, whatever she had done, because he must know everything that had transpired over the last few weeks. She sat back in her seat and drank the now stone cold coffee. The whisky bit into her taste buds and suddenly she realised that she was starving. She'd pack up here for the night and go home. Home to her own house. Not Michael's flat.

She felt as if she was on a high. Monique, the reaction of her brothers to her in the Crown and Two Chairmen pub, Benny, Sammy, Jonny, Janine – all was wiped from her mind for a few precious moments as she thought about Terry. She wrote a note to Michael saying she would see him in the morning and, humming to herself, got her stuff ready to go home.

She sat on the edge of her desk and stared at the telephone. She glanced at her watch. It was twelve-fifteen. Was it too late to ring? She opened up the slip of paper and stared at the words. 'Love, Terry' seemed to leap off the paper. Love . . . She picked up the phone and dialled the number. Her mouth was dry and she felt lightheaded. Supposing he was asleep or had company? Her heart dropped a little at that thought. Then, before she knew it, she could hear his voice.

'Hello? Who is this? Is that you, Maura?'

His voice was soft and as he said her name she could hear the yearning that she was experiencing herself.

She swallowed heavily.

'Terry.'

She heard the relief in his voice. 'It *is* you.'

The line went quiet as each tried to think what to say.

'I want to see you, Maura.' Terry sounded unsure of himself. 'I mean, if you want to see me, of course.'

'I was just going home. To my house. I just got the message.'

'Can I come to your house, Maura?' His voice was pleading.

'I'll give you the address.' She could barely talk.

'I know the address. I'll meet you there soon!' His voice had a jubilant ring to it that made her heart lurch in her chest.

She laughed. The ice had broken into a thousand pieces. 'Of course. You're a policeman – you would know my address.'

'Naturally.' She could practically see his little lopsided grin, could hear it in his voice.

'See you soon then.' She replaced the receiver and shivered with delight. She was hungry again. Only this time it wasn't for food.

Terry Petherick was staring at the telephone in his hand. She had rung! He wasn't wrong. She still wanted him as much as he still wanted her! He picked up his car keys and jacket and literally ran from his flat. He leapt into his car, a Ford Escort, and began the journey to Rainham. To Maura's house.

He had found himself driving to Dean Street earlier that evening, hoping for a glimpse of Maura. That was all. He had experienced an all-consuming passion for weeks just to look at her. Ever since he had seen her the night of the bombing, it had been like stepping back through a doorway, into another world. There had been women over the years but never any who affected him like Maura Ryan.

Every warning bell in his body was clanging and jangling at this moment, but he did not care. All he was really sure of was the fact that he had to see her. Touch her. Feel her. Even knowing what she had done – that she had been an accessory to murder. The attraction that had been between them from the start was still there like a shining beacon. He put his foot on the accelerator and whizzed through the icy streets towards her and all that she promised. For once in his life he was acting on impulse, and he was loving every moment of it. He felt alive. Really alive. And it felt good.

Maura pulled into her drive and sat in the car for a few minutes. She could feel her own nervousness and savoured every second of it. She looked at the large house sitting in ghostly darkness and for the very first time was glad to be home . . . and glad that Carla was not there. She had never been with a man since Terry, had gradually suppressed all her feelings, both sexual and romantic, concentrating on her work and Carla. And now her senses were filling her up, overflowing from her body, like the bursting of a great dam.

She got out of her car and went into her house. Her daily woman, Mrs MacMullen, had been in and as usual had left the central heating on low. The house was warm and inviting. Maura ran up the stairs like a young schoolgirl getting ready for her first date. She threw off her clothes and stepped into the shower, scrubbing her body until it glowed pink.

When she finally heard Terry's car she was in her lounge in a white silk dressing gown, sipping a glass of red wine. As she heard his footsteps crunch on the gravelled driveway she felt an intense euphoria flood her body. He had come. He had really come for her. She went into her hall and opened the front door.

She noticed that he was breathing as heavily as she. And then, without a word spoken, she was being kissed. And it was all so natural, as it should have been. How it once had been. He was kissing her face, her eyes, her neck. Taking his hand, she led him slowly up the stairs and into her bedroom.

They faced one another in the soft light from bedside lamps. She stared deeply into his eyes and saw mirrored in them her own feelings of love and desire. She began to unbutton his shirt and as she pulled it from him saw the broad shoulders, the tightly muscled arms, and felt new again, as she had the first time they had made love. He opened his trousers and showed her he was hard. She traced the outline of his erection with her fingers, softly and tantalisingly. She was feeling the woman heat between her legs and the tightening of her nipples. He was naked and she watched him, fascinated, as he stood before her, proud and strong. He opened the cord of her dressing gown and she stood, quivering with excitement and longing.

She saw his eyes roaming over her body and wanted him then, more than she had ever wanted anyone or anything in her life. He pushed her backwards gently on to the bed and kissed her body, little biting kisses that were hurtful and so erotic. He tasted the muskiness of her and felt the heady delight that he had thought was gone forever. He pushed her legs up to her shoulders until she was full open to him – like a ripe pink peach. She watched him enter her with one deep thrust, and she groaned like an animal. Together they moved in perfect unison.

She matched his strokes with hard thrusts of her hips

against him. She could feel the mounting excitement as she reached her orgasm and heard herself moaning and panting, begging him to thrust deeper. She could feel the droplets of sweat from his body dripping on to hers and gripped him with her legs, drawing him inside her, deeper and deeper, until she thought that she would die of pleasure. Their slippery bodies thrashed wildly as they reached orgasm. She could feel his hand squeezing her breast so hard that she cried out.

Then they lay, spent and replete, their hearts thudding against each other's chests. They lay tangled together for long quiet minutes, savouring the familiar feel of one another after so long an absence. Finally Terry leant on his elbow and kissed her gently on her swollen lips, and she looked at his face – the face that had alternately haunted and drawn her for nearly nine years – and smiled.

'It's been so long.' Her voice was so low as to be virtually inaudible.

'Too long, Maura. Much too long.'

They lay together until their bodies became still and the passion that had encompassed them had drained away. He kissed her again, staring down at her as if he wanted to devour her. His eyes drank in every feature and his brain filed them away, never to be forgotten. And she did the same, lying there. They were both aware that it was only a temporary love affair. That in the cold light of day they would have to part, each going back to their different world which neither would ever be able to leave. But this was never said. What they had at this moment was enough for them. And if they had to part, they would at least have had this night.

Terry gathered her to him and locked her into his embrace. 'I never meant to hurt you, you know. I swear.'

Maura spoke softly. 'I know, Terry.' She should tell him about the baby now. It was the perfect opening. But she could not. She would never, ever tell him about it. A lone tear slipped from her eye as she looked at him and he licked it away with his tongue. She would not tell him about their child as he would not talk about what Michael had had done to him. It was like a silent agreement, an unspoken treaty. So they lay together, speaking the love words that came so naturally to their lips. And then they loved again. Not the wild thrashings of before but a long, slow, leisurely loving that left them both breathless and satiated. Then all too soon it was the morning and they could delay their parting no longer.

'Come on. I'll make you some breakfast.' She pulled on her dressing gown and went to the kitchen. The birds were singing in the early morning light and Maura wished that the day would never come. That they could keep the night forever. She heard him whistling as he showered and felt an urge to cry out. Against God. Against fate. And against injustice.

She took a loaf of bread from her freezer and made toast. She had just finished scrambling the eggs when he came into the kitchen, his hair still wet from the shower. She gave him a cup of coffee and placed his breakfast in front of him.

'You never cooked me breakfast before.'

'I was never allowed to stay out all night in those days.' She made her voice light.

He smiled. 'What are we going to do, Maura?' The words were like a physical blow. They both knew that there was nothing they could do.

She sat at the table opposite him.

'What happened last night was beautiful, Terry, but we must accept it for what it was – a beautiful interlude from our lives. Our real lives. Tomorrow is a new year . . . 1976 . . . and you will go back to your policing while I will go back to being Maura Ryan.' She smiled sadly. 'Please don't let's spoil it with might have beens and halfhearted promises. We live in different worlds, you and I. Worlds that can never be united.' Her voice broke.

Terry knew that she was right, and he loved her all the more for her honesty. Too much had happened over the years. And she was more of a woman in his eyes for what she had just said than any so-called Earth Mother would ever be.

They ate breakfast together, both acutely aware of the sky gradually becoming lighter outside the kitchen window. They chatted about nothing, little inconsequential things that stopped them thinking or talking about the big things. The real things. The real world. Finally Terry got up from his chair, and Maura knew that the parting had come.

'Can't we meet sometimes, Maura?'

She shook her head sadly. 'No, Terry. It's best we leave things as they are. There's no future for us.'

'Will you come to the door with me?' She could hear the tears in his voice. She shook her head.

'No. You go. I'll sit here. I don't want to see you driving away from me.'

'Oh, Maws.' He was kneeling in front of her, holding her so tight she could barely breathe. 'I can't go, Maura. I can't leave you like this.'

She kissed the top of his head. 'Go. Go on. Don't make this harder than it already is.' She cupped his face in her hands for the last time.

'I love you, Terry Petherick. God help me, I'll always love you.'

'I know. I love you too.'

She pushed him away from her. She had read so many times the phrase 'their hearts were breaking', and now she found out that it was true. Your heart could break and it was an intense physical pain that made you want to scream out, a deep roaring scream, from the depths of your body.

She sat at the table and it was as if her senses had been magnified a thousand million times. She heard his footfalls on the thick carpet. The sound of the front door closing behind him was like a deafening crash. And finally she heard his car start up. Then she listened to it driving away.

Away from her . . . and back to his real life.

It was over. The night was finished and real life had begun again. But she would carry the memory of it with her to her grave. She cried, a loud, noisy cry that was all the more wrenching because it sounded so lonely.

Terry drove home to his flat in Hampstead. He drove slowly, not in the reckless way he had driven the night before. Leaving Maura had been the hardest thing he had ever done in his life, but he knew that she was right. That she was stronger than him. Much stronger. And he guessed, correctly, that she was much lonelier. But whatever she was, he loved her.

Chapter Twenty-one

It was the third of January and Maura and Michael were driving to Lord Templeton's office. Maura still had the glow of lovemaking on her, despite the tears afterwards. In the last few days she had somehow resigned herself to being without Terry, to being without any man, though the thrill of the sexual encounter was still vivid in her mind and body. Michael was discussing what had happened between Maura and Janine.

'Calm down, Maws, for Christ's sake. After what happened to Benny, you can't blame her for getting a bit shirty. Janine's what's known as a shitter. And there's plenty of them about, believe me.'

'It's not that, Mickey. But the fact that Roy was a Ryan is what attracted her in the first place. She was after a bit of rough and then she came unstuck. Look at how she dumped Carla! Now Roy, who's turned out to be a bloody good provider, is in a bit of schtuck, she wants him to become a bloody bank clerk or something! It's laughable.'

'Then laugh! I know that our Roy would no more leave this firm that he would cut his own throat. Stick him back in the bookies, that should shut Madam up for a while.' He grinned. 'I wonder what she'll say when she finds our Roy wants us to be godparents? That should go down about as well as a pork chop in a synagogue!'

Maura laughed, a harsh bitter laugh.

'What a start to the New Year. Benny dead. Mother treating us as if we've contracted bubonic plague, the old man permanently pissed . . .'

'Stop talking crap, Maura.' Michael's voice was sharp as glass. 'What happened to Benny was an occupational

303

hazard. It could have been any of us. You, me, any of us. That's the chance we take in our line of . . .'

He paused as if looking for a word. Maura finished the sentence for him.

'Business!'

He grinned. 'That's it, Maws! Business. All we can do now is go on from here. We can't bring Benny back no more than we could Antney. Concentrate on Templeton. He's the goose that's gonna lay our golden eggs. Only he don't know that yet!' He laughed again.

'You were dead right about the docklands, I can see that now, Maws. He offered Dopolis the East End bait. What Lord Willy was after was the warehouses and the old Dockers' Mansions.

'I know this much, girl. He's gonna need muscle. Plenty of muscle. And we have that in abundance. That's our strength.'

She nodded absently.

'I'm telling you, Maura, 1976 is going to be *our* year.'

She looked out at the cold, dirty London streets and sighed. 'I hope so. God, I hope so.'

Lord Templeton stepped out of his limousine. His chauffeur held the door open for him and Templeton walked past him as if he was invisible, as he did every day. He walked with his confident stride up the flight of steps that led into the main reception area of his building in Park Lane. His liveried doorman saluted him and he acknowledged the man with a minute nod of his head. His personal secretary, David Manners, followed him, practically running to keep up. He had a detailed list of Templeton's appointments for the day.

Templeton strode purposefully into the large reception area and, just for a second, his step faltered. Standing beside his personal lift were Michael and Maura Ryan. Swallowing deeply, he glanced around him. The staff milling about were staring at him curiously. Pulling himself together, he plastered a broad smile on to his face and carried on walking to his lift.

He concentrated his attention on Maura. He was surprised at how lovely she was. She looked like a deb in her light beige Chanel suit with its black piping. Her hair, freshly washed, glistened in the artificial light. He took in everything about her from the kidskin boots to the silk scarf wrapped carelessly across her shoulders and held there with a gold and diamond tiger brooch. Against his will he was impressed. She was exquisite.

As for the man standing beside her, he was probably the most outstandingly handsome man Templeton was ever likely to see. Michael also was dressed in impeccable taste. Templeton felt that sickening feeling that precedes a fall from a high place. Never in all his life had he been intimidated. Now that he was experiencing it, he decided he did not like it one bit. He carried on walking towards them, and with every step that took him closer felt more scared, more nervous.

Maura smiled as he approached them and held out her hand. 'So pleased to meet you at last, Lord William. My brother and I have been so looking forward to it.' Her voice held no trace of its usual cockney accent.

Her words reassured Templeton slightly and he smiled back at her, showing perfect white teeth.

'Delighted, my dear. If I had known how lovely you were, I would have made sure we met much sooner.'

He turned his attention to Michael, amazed at just how big he was – almost a foot taller than himself. Michael shook his hand without speaking, his hard eyes telling Templeton exactly how the land lay.

His lift door opened and he ushered them both inside, waving David Manners away imperiously.

'I'll send for you, David, when I need you.'

Manners nodded. There was something funny going on here, he knew that much.

The old man who worked the lift gave Maura an appraising stare.

They made their brief journey in silence. Maura watched Templeton's face. She knew that he was frightened but had to admit to herself that for all that she liked the look of him.

305

He was angular-looking: pointed nose, pointed cheekbones, and even pointed ears. He had a mass of sandy brown hair that, she guessed, was difficult to tame. It seemed to give him a slight air of vulnerability. He had very deep brown eyes, and thin sparse eyebrows like most sandy-haired people. It was his mouth that attracted her. It was not very big for a man, but it was strong. It could have been due to his very angular jawline. Whatever it was, she liked it. She only hoped they could all come out of this place today with a degree of accord.

The lift doors opened and they all stepped out into a wealth of mahogany. The walls were panelled, the only furniture a large mahogany desk and two leather-covered wing chairs. Behind the desk sat a young woman, the standard secretary to a rich man. She was very attractive in a subdued way. Maura could picture her unpinning her luxuriant black hair one day and turning into a femme fatale. She put her hand to her mouth to stop herself giggling. She had to try and control the weird things that kept invading her mind.

By the secretary's desk were two large double doors. Templeton opened these and led them into his office. Michael looked around him contemptuously. Like the room outside this also was a shrine to wood. Once more it had panelled walls, but in here they were adorned with a few well-chosen and, Michael guessed, very expensive sporting paintings. He was not aware that the largest, of a beautiful dark horse, was in fact a Stubbs. The floor was covered in the same deep grey carpet as the ante room. There was another, much larger mahogany desk. Along the right- and left-hand walls were two large Chesterfields, black and gleaming, as if just taken from their protective wrappings and never yet sat upon. In front of the desk were two more wing armchairs. Maura sat in one and Michael in the other.

Templeton went to the double doors and told his secretary to bring in some refreshments. He then walked nervously to his own chair behind the desk. As he reached it he stumbled and had to grab the desk to right himself.

Eventually he sat down. His chair was much higher than the two opposite; an American designer had once told him that it would give him a psychological advantage. Obviously the designer had never met anyone like the Ryans. He put his hands together as if in prayer.

'What can I do for you?' He was embarrassed to find that his voice sounded cracked and high. It was Maura who answered him.

'I think you already know the answer to that, Lord William.' She made his name sound ridiculous. Her voice had hardened now they were alone and once again he was reminded of how dangerous these people were. He was saved from answering by his secretary who came in wheeling a trolley, also mahogany. Michael was beginning to wonder if the man was a wood fetishist. The trolley held not only coffee and tea but also toast, muffins, jam and honey.

'Would you like me to serve, sir?' The girl smiled, watching Michael from the corner of her eye.

'Just leave it, Marie.' Templeton's voice was brisk. The girl nodded and slowly left the room, shutting the double doors behind her.

Maura pulled off her kidskin gloves and placed them on the floor with her bag.

'Fancy a cuppa, Mickey?'

Michael nodded and Maura poured three cups of tea, as if they were at a tea party. She handed one to Michael who spoke for the first time, his voice as rough as concrete.

'Well, this is nice, I must say. My little brother Benny used to love a cup of Rosie in the mornings. Said it made him crap.' He looked directly at Templeton, causing the hairs on the back of his neck to rise.

'Crapped regular did our Benny. Seven o'clock every morning. Did he crap himself while he was being murdered? I understand you know all about it.' Michael's voice was matter-of-fact.

William Templeton felt sick. The cup of tea that Maura had handed to him was rattling in its saucer. He was shaking from head to foot. Maura put down her own cup and, going to him, removed the cup and saucer from his grasp.

'What do you want?'

Michael sipped his tea and said: 'What we want is a little bastard called Dopolis. I think that you know where we can find him. I want to question him personally about my brother's death.' He smiled at Templeton. 'The police are looking for Benny's murderer as well, you know. Why don't you give them a ring? Ask them about me, Michael Ryan. Ask them about my temper.' He was talking in a conversational way, and somehow it made his words more frightening. 'My temper's a legend in London, ain't it, Maws?' She nodded. 'I once rammed a Rolls-Royce because I thought the driver had given me a dirty look. Wrote off a brand new Merc doing it. But, you see, my temper is atrocious.' He leant towards Templeton. 'It's just like the wrath of God. Only in London, I *am* God.'

'I had nothing to do with your brother's death. I swear it!' Templeton was aware that he was babbling.

'Then you won't mind telling us where Dopolis is, will you?'

'I have no idea.'

Maura shook her head as if looking at a naughty child. 'I don't think you realise what you're dealing with here. We . . .' she gestured with her hand towards Michael '. . . are like terminal cancer. We'll get you in the end, so you might as well save yourself unnecessary grief. You've already made us very angry and that's dangerous. Now, I'll give you one last chance. Where can we find Dopolis?'

Templeton was rooted to his chair. His eyes darted around the room as if looking for some kind of divine intervention from behind the panelling. He had thought he was dealing with illiterate fools. But no. The so-called fools had tracked him down and cornered him on his own territory. All he could do now was extricate himself as best he could.

'He lives in Surrey.' He scribbled the address on to the pad in front of him and practically threw it across the table at Michael. Please God, he prayed, make them go away now. If you do this for me, I swear that I will be a good man from now on. Like many a man before him, he was praying as a last resort.

Michael picked up the scrap of paper and stood up. 'Right then, I'm off. I'll leave you in my sister's capable hands. She can explain to you all about the partnership.'

'Partnership?' Templeton was flabbergasted.

Michael laughed. 'Catches on quick, does old Willy. The partnership between us. Me, her, and lastly you.' He pointed towards Templeton. 'Oh, and before I forget, I'll be calling you Willy. Lord William's a bit too much of a gobful, ain't it? You, though, will call me Mr Ryan. If – but only if, mind – I get to like you, I might let you call me Mickey.' He laughed again. 'Give you something to look forward to, won't it?

'There's just one last thing before I go. Don't get Harry Dash – that's flash to you – with my sister here. Whatever she says, you do it. Get that?'

Templeton stared at him.

Michael shouted: 'I said, GET IT?'

'Yes!'

'There's a good boy. Well, cheery bye, or whatever you big nobs say.'

Kissing Maura on the cheek, he left the room. Templeton stared at the doorway as if he had never seen it before.

Maura poured herself another cup of tea. 'Right then, shall we get down to business?'

She felt a bit sorry for the man in front of her. After her night with Terry and the hurt she felt at their parting, she found room in her heart for pity. She took a deep breath and started on what had long been her favourite subject: docklands.

'We know you were really after our properties in Tobacco Dock and similar areas. I happen to know you also have properties there. The idea is that we pool resources. I realise that you have more of an insider's knowledge of what's going on there. Between us we could sew that place up. Once the work starts, we can guarantee the labour and that there will be no delays of any kind. We "own" just about every major contractor in the South East. If push ever came to shove we could stop work there from ever beginning, and I know you wouldn't want that to happen. We're willing to let our brother's death go as far as you are concerned. Dopolis will pay for that. You can either come in with us or sink. It's your choice.'

She picked up her cup and drank her tea. William Templeton was dumbfounded. He was being threatened by a woman! And a working-class woman at that. And these yobs wanted to go into partnership with *him*! If it wasn't so scary he would laugh. He was all for cads and bounders – as long as one kept to one's own class. But to be associated with Michael Ryan! It was unbelievable.

Dopolis had turned out to be a bigger mistake than he had first thought. Now he would *have* to get involved with the Ryans, whether he liked it or not. His idea of getting the Greek to start a gang war seemed stupid now that he had met the real McCoy. He admitted to himself that he had been a damn' fool. His belief that the working class was a bunch of mindless dunderheads had proved fatally wrong. It seemed he was the dunderhead at this moment.

'Well, what's it to be? I haven't got all day.'

Templeton grimaced. 'I don't really seem to have much choice, do I?'

Maura smiled at him. A real smile that made her look very young and very pretty.

'Believe me, Lord William, when I say that you saw the nice side of Michael today. Unless you'd lived our kind of life, you could not hope for one minute to be able to understand us. I would ask you, though, to treat us with the same respect as you would any business associates. You will find that you deal mainly with me. I run the property side of our businesses. What I'm hoping to learn from you is the redevelopment business. It is my fervent wish that my family should find a good respectable outlet to channel money into.'

Grudgingly, Templeton admitted that he could like this girl. She was at least sincere. He shrugged his shoulders at the inevitable. He knew that he had to deal with the Ryans whether he liked it or not. There was no way out. He was caught up in a spider's web, and like the fly knew he would eventually give up struggling.

'The development business is not really respectable, Miss Ryan. In fact, it can be very dirty.'

Maura interrupted him, laughing.

'I think you misunderstand me, Lord William! What I mean by respectable is that, although it may be illegal and at times dirty, it is socially acceptable. Like adultery. If you want my honest opinion, I think you and your kind are the biggest bunch of hypocrites I have ever had the misfortune to come across.' She took a cigarette from the packet she had placed in front of her and lit it, blowing the smoke across the desk into his face.

'You frown on Mr Working Class for having a little flutter. Yet the Stock Exchange gambles daily with millions of pounds. Banks do it, and building societies. And let's face it, it's not even their money they're using. But there you are. The double standard prevails. One set of rules for the Hooray Henrys and another for Mr Joe Public. Well, let me tell you something. I may not have a family tree like yours, or be that articulate in my grammar, but there's one thing I *have* got going for me – I have money. Plenty of it. And with the kind of money I have, every door can be opened. Even the Royal Enclosure at Ascot. That's how we found you out. You broke the golden rule of villainy, Lord William. You let the world in on what you were doing. A fatal mistake.'

A light seemed to go on behind Templeton's eyes and Maura could not help grinning at him.

'Let me guess. You couldn't resist showing off to him, am I right? Well, that little faux pas on your part led us straight to your door. Whereas me and my brothers – Michael especially – our faces are slapped across the *News of the World* at least once a month, but they can't prove anything. It's all supposition. Now you,' she pointed at him with her cigarette, 'are going to be our Mr Legit. I want you to tell me exactly what's going to happen to the old docks.'

Templeton stared at Maura for a few seconds. He knew that all she had said was right.

'Maura . . . may I call you Maura?'

'Of course.'

'I think that you and I could do business together. I have a feeling we could even be friends.'

She smiled at him and breathed a sigh of relief. She made a conscious decision to prove to him that she was as good as, if not better than, anyone he had done business with before.

'Seeing as we have you by the bollocks, as my brother would term it, I don't see why we can't be friends. Now, about the docks.'

She was being deliberately crude. She wanted his friendship, but she also wanted his co-operation and until she was certain she had that, she would continue to remind him just who he was dealing with.

Templeton pressed the button of the intercom on his desk.

'Yes, sir?' The sweet voice of Marie crackled into the room.

'Hold all my calls and bring in some fresh tea.'

'But, sir! You have an appointment in ten minutes to see the Secretary of State for the Environment!'

'Then you'll just have to tell him that I am in an urgent meeting.' He cut off the connection.

Maura raised her eyebrows at him and he was amazed to hear himself laugh. He had taken rather a fancy to the girl. Opening a drawer in his desk, he brought out a folder. He opened it and took out some papers and a map. He passed this to Maura. While she studied it, Marie brought in some more tea and removed the large trolley. Her face was set in a frown. This time she banged the door shut behind her.

'Well, Maura, I will tell you all that I know. This,' he swept his hand across the papers in front of him, 'has been discussed behind closed doors for some time. As you so astutely pointed out, there's a lot of money to be made there. In 1967 the East India Dock closed. In '68 the London Docks. In '69 Katherine Dock, and in '70 Surrey

Docks. All we are waiting for is the eventual closure of Millwall, and the Royal Victoria and Albert. That is when it will all start to happen.'

'So the other docks will eventually close?' Maura kept her voice neutral. In fact, she was flabbergasted.

'Oh, yes. Within the next five years. That's why no money's going in there. The more rundown and depressed the area gets, the more we can justify reclaiming the land. Job creation etcetera.' He smiled at her. 'I am afraid that we live in a world where the masses are spoonfed bullshit, if you will forgive the expression. The average man on the street buys the *Sun* to look at a pair of breasts. In reality, he's reading Tory propaganda. Whoever is in office at the time all this begins, be it Tory, Labour or, God help us, Screaming Lord Sutch, will be jumping on the bandwagon. Funding it, giving out grants. "We'll give you money to make money" . . . that's every government's policy. Personally, I think it will be the Conservatives, but I'm not worried either way. This has been sewn up for a long time. Now, drink your tea while it's hot and I'll explain to you more fully. I think you will find it fascinating.'

She and William Templeton smiled at one another. Maura shook her head slowly and said, 'And they have the nerve to call *us* villains!'

In 1976 the Docklands Joint Committee published the London Dockland Strategic Plan. The Ryans and Lord Templeton were on their way.

Book Three

THE DOWNFALL

It is a strange desire to seek power and to lose liberty –
Francis Bacon, 1561–1626

What will you give me, and I will deliver him unto you?
And they covenanted with him for thirty pieces of silver –
Matthew, xxvi, 15

Book Three

THE DOWNFALL

Chapter Twenty-two

12 February 1985

Geoffrey Ryan parked outside Le Buxom. It was not yet nine o'clock in the morning. He picked up his briefcase from the passenger seat of his dark blue BMW, locked up his car and went into the club. The cleaners all greeted him. In 1980, a restaurant had been opened in what had been the basement. This meant that the club was open nearly twenty-four hours of the day. He went down there to discuss the day's menu with Peter Petrillo, the head chef, who had finished a ten-year stretch in Parkhurst then been given the job by Michael Ryan.

Geoffrey looked over the menu briefly and nodded his head, as he did every day. Then he ordered coffee and went up to his offices. He lit a cigarette and, settling himself into his chair, began his work for the day, going over the figures for the clubs and wine bars – a new acquisition of Maura's to cash in on the yuppie boom. When he opened a drawer to get his calculator, he saw it was missing: Michael had been in and taken it again. Putting his cigarette out, he pulled himself from his seat and made his way to Michael's office next door.

Although Geoffrey had the largest office, most of the business was done by Michael and Maura from the smaller office. He knew deep inside that they had given him the larger office to placate him. Also, the smaller office was always referred to as Michael's office when in reality it was Michael's and Maura's.

He frowned as he walked through the door. He never came in here unless he absolutely had to. The room was empty. He looked on the large desk for his calculator,

317

moving papers and files haphazardly. As he turned away he noticed that the small filing cabinet was unlocked, the keys still in the lock but the top drawer slightly open. He shook his head. Walking to it he pushed the drawer shut and was about to lock it when he stopped dead. Biting his lip he pulled the drawer back open. This was the one place he and the others were barred from. Only Michael and Maura had access to it. Now by some twist of fate it was open to him and he was torn between a desire to know what was in there that was so private and fear that he'd be caught looking. He decided to take his chances. Checking the corridor outside, he shut the door quietly and went back to the filing cabinet. He pulled out one of the files and began to read it. After a few minutes he forgot his fear of Michael and Maura, and took the file back to his office. A deep rage grew inside him as he realised just what he had stumbled across.

Maura and Leslie were in Brixton. They pulled up outside a block of flats. Leslie got out of the car and opened the door to let Maura out. Having locked the car, he followed her up the filthy stairs that led into the block of flats. They were low rise flats, only two storeys. Maura walked along the balcony until she came to No. 28. She knocked on the front door, which was opened by a little girl of about eight. The child was half caste and, Maura noticed, extremely thin and emaciated.

'We're looking for Jackie Traverna's house. Is this it?' Maura's voice was friendly and kind.

'Yeah. But she's in bed.'

'I think she will see me. Just take me to her, my love.' Maura's voice sounded false, even to her own ears. She had lost the knack of talking to children.

The child shrugged her skinny shoulders. As if to say, who cares? Maura followed her up a dark narrow hallway and into a small bedroom. The place was messy, the bedroom entirely taken up by a large double bed, though Maura guessed that when Jackie was on her feet she kept it clean and tidy. In the giant bed lay Jackie herself. Her coffee-coloured skin was shining with a film of sweat.

Maura gasped when she saw her. 'Leslie! Get in here.'

He ran in the room thinking that Maura had come across some kind of trouble.

'Fucking hell!' His voice was shocked.

In the bed lay Jackie, recognisable only by her wiry Afro hair. Her face was so swollen she looked as if she had been attacked by bees. On each of her cheeks was a large stripe which went from the corner of her mouth to rise up until it disappeared into her hairline. Jackie looked up with sad eyes.

'Maura.' Her voice was muffled.

'All right, Jackie. All right, mate. Who did this? Was it Rubens . . . Danny Rubens?'

Jackie nodded her head, fear in her eyes.

'Don't you worry now. I'm going to see you're looked after.'

'Thanks. Can't . . . speak.' The woman could barely move.

'I know. I know. I'll be back later. All right?'

She smiled at Jackie, but inside she was fuming. 'Come on, Leslie. Get your arse in gear.'

Once they were back inside the car, Maura lit herself a cigarette and said, 'Pick up Lee and Garry. We're going to pay Rubens a little visit.'

Geoffrey had been reading the file for about an hour. He was still reading it when Michael came into his office. Geoffrey looked up at him, the hurt in his eyes almost a tangible thing. Michael saw the green folder and tried to play for time.

'Any more coffee going, Geoff?'

Geoffrey ignored him. Picking up the folder, he threw it across the desk.

'Thanks a lot, Bruv.' His voice was flat.

Michael sighed. 'For Christ's sake, Geoff. You're not my keeper, you know.'

Geoffrey lit another cigarette, his hands trembling.

319

'That's just it, though, ain't it, Mickey? I ain't nothing.'

'Look, Geoff, you know what they say. What you don't know, don't hurt you.'

Geoffrey pulled on his cigarette and let out the smoke through his nose, looking like a belligerent bull.

'You've mugged me off, ain't you?'

Mickey laughed. 'Come on, Geoff. I would have told you eventually. Why are you making such a big deal?'

Michael's voice was getting tight. He did not feel like all this today.

'I'll tell you why I'm making such a big deal, shall I? I've just read this crap.' He pointed to the green folder. 'And I realise just what I am in this firm. I run the clubs, sort of. I run the wine bars, sort of. I watch over the bookies and the cab ranks. While you and Maura — marvellous fucking Maura – do the *real* work.'

'Leave her out of this.' Michael's voice was hard and low.

Geoffrey stubbed out his cigarette. 'No, I won't leave her out of all this. She's the cause of it all. Since the day she came into this firm you've pushed me out.'

Geoffrey's voice was high and he knew it sounded hysterical, but he did not care. He had to get this thing sorted out, once and for all.

'You're talking crap and you know it, Geoffrey. Now give it a rest, for fuck's sake.'

Geoffrey began shouting, all caution gone now. 'No, I will not give it a rest! I read, by accident, that you are about to embark on the biggest gold robbery this country's ever known, and you have the nerve to stand there and tell me I would have been told eventually! And when was that gonna be? When it was in the papers or on the news? Just what kind of cunt do you take me for? What else has been going on behind my back, eh? Well, answer me then.'

Geoffrey had risen from his seat and stood in front of Michael who was a good three inches taller and at least two stone heavier. Both knew that if it came to blows, Michael would win hands down. Geoffrey did not care.

Michael tried once more to pacify him. 'Keep your voice

down, Geoff. There's no need to let everyone know, is there?'

'I bet everyone *does* bloody know! Everyone except me, that is.' He prodded his chest. '*I've* stood by you through thick and thin, from day one. But since that fucking leech Maura came on the scene, I've been pushed out. It's been you and Maura . . . Maura and Michael . . . the dynamic duo. Batman and Robin's got nothing on you two. She was shagging an old Bill and yet you treat her like visiting royalty.'

Michael's hand went up to Geoffrey's throat. He slipped his other hand around his brother's neck and squeezed.

'Let's get the violins out, shall we? Geoffrey's little heart is broken! You ponce! You disgust me.'

He hurled Geoffrey away from him and went to the window, running his hands through his hair.

Turning back, he thrust out a finger. 'I'll tell you why Maura has taken your so-called place, shall I? Because she's got more bollocks than you will ever have! You've been like a bloody albatross hanging around my neck all my life. I've had to carry you ever since we were kids.' Michael wiped his hand across his face, agitated and annoyed. 'If you'd been left to your own devices, you'd have been banged up years ago. And *you're* jealous of your own bloody sister because she has what it takes. She sussed all this out.' He gestured around him wildly. 'You couldn't organise the proverbial piss up, mate. You could never have figured half of what she has. You fucking wind me up! You always have done.'

He pointed at Geoffrey again, his face contorted with temper. 'Shall I tell you something? You're working here because Maura suggested it. If it had been left to me, I'd have had Gerry Jackson running this show, mate. I'd have dumped you years ago. But, no, Maura said: "Family first." I swallowed, but deep down in my heart I didn't give a toss.

'Now if you don't like it, you can piss off. But I tell you this now. If you ever . . . ever . . . speak about her like that again, I'll bury you. Now do me a favour and fuck off before I really lose me rag.'

321

Geoffrey stared at Michael, dumbstruck. He could feel the waves of resentment coming out of every pore in Michael's body. He realised something he had known secretly for years, something he had never dared admit to himself before: he irritated Mickey. And yet he would have died for him. He was the only brother left who was not married or living with a girl. Even Michael had a regular boyfriend. He had lived his life for Michael.

He straightened himself up slowly and, picking up his jacket and car keys, walked from the office. As he came down the stairs into the foyer he realised that the cleaners had all stopped work. They had been listening to everything. He could feel his face burning with humiliation. He left the club and got into his car as if in a daze. That Michael could have spoken like that to him! He felt sick with the realisation of what had just happened. And with the fact that nothing could ever be the same between them again.

Maura and the three boys were at Danny Rubens's gaff, a terraced house in Tulse Hill. Lee banged on the front door hard. It was opened by a young girl who looked about seventeen. Though knowing Rubens's taste, Maura thought she was probably about fifteen, top whack.

'Is Danny about?' They pushed past the girl into the house.

'He ain't up yet. He don't get up before twelve.'

Garry smiled at her. 'Well, it'll be a nice change for him then, won't it?' They all began to walk up the stairs.

'Who is it, Estelle?' A deep brown voice bellowed the words down the stairs. The four walked in its direction.

Maura and her brothers noticed that the house was very well decorated and very clean. Inside Danny's bedroom, Maura smiled at him.

'Well, well. You are a big boy, aren't you?' Danny Rubens was lying in bed naked. He pulled the duvet over himself. He was still half stoned from the previous evening but alert enough to know he had invited big trouble to his house.

'Shut the door, Garry. We don't want everyone hearing Danny's screams.'

Danny's big black face was sweating and his eyes were like dark brown pools in his head. His head was shaved and Maura could see a vein pulsing, just below his right eyebrow. He was scared, very scared, and that was just what she wanted. Danny Rubens had taken to body building while doing a three-year stretch for aggravated assault. He was enormous and that usually gave him the edge.

'What you want?'

Maura laughed. 'Cut the coon talk, Rubens, you've never been out of London in your life.'

Garry, Leslie and Lee guffawed at this. They knew how to play the game. Maura pulled the duvet from his body, leaving him naked and exposed.

'I'm here about a girl of mine – Jackie Traverna.'

'Ain't never heard of her.'

Maura opened her bag and lit one of her cigarettes. Every action was watched closely by Rubens. She puffed on her cigarette until the end glowed.

'I've been hearing stories about you, Rubens.' Maura pointed to her brothers. 'Hold him.'

Leslie and Lee went to the bed and, after a struggle, held Danny Rubens down on it. Maura gestured to Garry. 'Hold his legs open for me.'

She drew the cigarette smoke into her lungs and watched impassively as Rubens tried to fight his way out of the situation. Finally he was lying spreadeagled on the bed. 'Now I want you to tell me why you striped up one of my girls.'

Rubens was absolutely terrified. His eyes were stretched to their utmost, showing all the yellow whiteness.

'I tell you, sis, I ain't never done no harm to no black chick.'

Garry punched him in the face.

'If you ain't never heard of her, how do you know what colour she is?'

'I guessed, man. I guessed.'

'Oh, shut up, you black ponce.' This was Leslie. 'Let my

323

sister speak.' His voice was slow and bored-sounding. Rubens thought he would wet himself with fright.

'I have heard, Mr Rubens,' Maura stressed the Mr, 'that you have some rather big ambitions. One being to become the Pimp Extraordinaire of the West End. I also hear that you are after some of my girls.'

She sat on the bed and opened her bag. Rubens was holding his head off the bed, straining his neck to see what was going on. He was naked and vulnerable and did not like it.

Maura took a snub nosed .38 special from her handbag. Rubens's eyes were now like flying saucers.

'What you want with that!' He was nearly crying.

'My sister is going to blow your balls off, Danny. One by one.'

Leslie's voice was jocular.

Maura held the gun against Rubens's genitals. He could feel the hard coldness of the steel against his skin. She rubbed it gently along the length of his penis and under his testicles. Rubbed it slowly, dreamily, as if she was enjoying it. Then she took another long drag of her cigarette. Rubens, who had been 'The Daddy' while he was in Durham jail, who had been working the streets nearly all his adult life and who could instil fear into most people, burst into tears. They ran from his eyes and down his face. Great bubbles of snot billowed out of his nose and his gigantic shoulders heaved.

'Please . . . don't shoot my cock off!' He sounded like a small boy.

Garry, Leslie and Lee were laughing again.

Maura put her cigarette butt on Rubens's stomach. He felt the burning through his tears. Maura left the cigarette on his tight belly, so the embers would scorch the skin slowly and painfully. He was howling in pain.

'Where's your Stanley knife, Danny?' Maura's voice was soft and gentle, as if they were lovers on a picnic.

'I swear . . . I swear to you I ain't got no Stanley knife.'

'Pain is a terrible thing, isn't it? Jackie Traverna was in

324

pain, Danny, she was in such terrible pain.' Her voice hardened. 'Now it's your turn.' She nodded at Leslie who took a Stanley knife from the pocket of his jacket. He held it glinting over the man's face.

'What's it to be, Danny boy? Cheek or cock? It's up to you. But make your mind up quickly or I might just do both.'

Danny was staring at Leslie's face and knew he was not joking. He saw, even through his fear and his tears, that he had met with a will much stronger than his own.

'Please, man. Please.' His voice was just a croaky whisper.

'Face it is then!' Leslie grinned and pulled the Stanley knife from Danny's eye down to his mouth. He cut deeply and confidently. The blood came out slowly, as if not sure what it wanted to do as the layers of skin gradually unfolded. By the time he had repeated the action on the other side of the man's face, the blood was pumping out with each of his heartbeats. They all stood up as if of one mind. As his hands were released, Danny brought them up to his face. When he took them away, his palms were stained with deep crimson blood.

He screamed loudly, painfully, like a hare caught in a trap.

'Don't ever get ambitious for anything or anyone that belongs to me, Danny. Next time you might not be so lucky.'

'Oh, God, I'm bleeding! Help me somebody!' The white satin sheets on his bed were slowly being dyed red.

'Come on, boys. We've got a lot of work to do.'

As they left the room the young girl Estelle ran inside. When they left the house, her screams were even louder than Danny's.

Geoffrey was sitting in his flat. He had poured himself a large Scotch and was sitting on the sofa remembering every detail of his life with Michael. One memory stood out like a shining beacon. He gulped his Scotch as he remembered a day almost forty years earlier.

He had been just coming up eight, Michael nearly ten. It was during the war, and their father had dropped them both through a hole in the remains of a bombed out house. Mickey, as usual, had no fear. He just put his torch on and shone it around the debris-strewn cellar. The occupants of the house were lying around like lumps of bloody red meat. The stench had been unbearable. Geoffrey could still remember the way he'd felt that day, rooted to the spot with fear. His father's voice had been coming from above, urging them to hurry up. Looting bombed houses was a serious criminal offence.

Michael dragged the body of a little girl off a tin petty cash box. She had been blown across it in the blast. He then passed this up to their father and quickly began collecting up anything that was useful, edible or saleable. He had gone about his work silently and quickly, calling softly to Geoffrey to help him move the body of a man. He had known it was a man by the clothes. The face had completely gone.

Geoffrey had found it impossible to move. Michael had gone to him and punched him in the stomach, winding him, urging him to hurry up and help him. Between them they dragged the man's heavy body on to the floor. Geoffrey had been crying by this time. Michael had stripped the man of his wallet and watch. Then he had gone to the woman who had been grotesquely thrown to the floor. Her legs were wide open and her arms and neck lay in positions that would have been impossible had she been alive. Michael took her brooch and her wedding ring. Geoffrey had heard the crunching click of her bone as he had broken her bent finger to remove it. Then their father had pulled them both out of the hole. He could still feel the sting of his father's belt later that night as he had been strapped for 'being a baby'.

From that day on he had tried to emulate his brother. He had joined him in beating people, robbing the bombsites, everything. In all truth, Geoffrey admitted to himself, he had hated every minute of it. And it dawned on him now that Michael knew this, had always known it, and that's

326

why he despised him. In Maura, Michael had found a kindred spirit. Another loner. Another warped version of their father. He finished his glass of Scotch and sat back in his seat.

He couldn't join Mickey now, that much was obvious, but he would sure as hell beat him. And that bitch of a sister! He had the knowledge and he would sit and wait, and then one day he would use it. He saw once more the looks that had been on the cleaners' faces, and felt an urge to murder the pair of them.

Still, as his old dad used to say when they were small: 'Don't get mad. Get even.' That's just what he intended to do.

Maura and Michael were eating a late dinner in The Greek Revolution in Beauchamp Place. They had been discussing their day. They made a stunning pair. Even at thirty-five Maura was still as young-looking as ever. She dressed down, never wearing clothes that were in fashion but choosing plain and expensive classics, as only the very rich can. Her blonde hair was longer now, cut into a long bob. It hung just below her jawline, framing her finely boned face. With her lightness, and Michael's dark good looks, they were the perfect foil for one another.

Even in his fifties, Michael was still a very attractive man. He dressed conservatively but well, sticking as he had always done to greys and blacks. Occasionally he wore something he termed 'ostentatious', but those times were few and far between.

'Well, I think Geoffrey's probably over his tantrum by now.' Maura sounded worried.

'Quite frankly, Maws, I don't give a shit. He winds me up.'

Maura was quiet for a moment. She had felt the tension building up between them for months. It truly amazed her that Michael, who was usually so perceptive about everything, failed to notice what was in front of his eyes. Geoffrey was jealous of her and she knew it. But now he was also jealous of Michael, and she had a gut feeling that Geoffrey could turn out to be quite dangerous.

Michael wiped his pitta bread around the plate, picking up the last of the tsatsiki, and popped the bread into his mouth. 'So, tell me. What are you going to do for Jackie Traverna?'

'Oh, I don't know, Michael. The poor bitch is in a terrible state. Give her some money, I suppose.'

Michael laughed. 'You're like a fucking social worker! I'd better keep a close eye on you, girl. Next thing I know you'll be giving all our cash away to the starving millions!'

Maura smiled, knowing that Michael was deliberately steering the conversation away from Geoffrey.

'Before I forget, Maws. Willy Templeton wants in on the gold plan. I said yeah. What do you reckon?'

'Why not?' She shrugged. 'He seems to be in on everything else.'

She picked up a prawn and pulled its head off. 'If that's what you want, Mickey. I'm easy.'

'He's doing a great job down at St Martin's Wharf. It's a funny thing, Maws, but having a lord on your side certainly helps matters along. Don't you think?'

His voice was cold and calculating.

'Of course it helps. It's like going to parties with famous people. Everyone's a starfucker at heart. Stars included. They love us because we're rough diamonds. Personally, I don't give a monkey's either way. I like Willy, though.'

And she did. She liked him very much and it was strange, because she knew that without him Benny would still be alive. Even knowing that, she still could not help liking and admiring him. He was what she had learned to term an 'educated villain'. Through William Templeton she had met many more like him – rich, educated men who pulled off brilliant scams. Scams that were never allowed to get into the newspapers or come to prosecution because the firms involved would lose their credibility on the Stock Market with disastrous economic and political results. Instead the wrongdoers were given enormous golden handshakes and a big party as a leaving present. And their pictures appeared in the papers with the sob story: 'Ill health brings the head of So and So corporation's career to an end.' 'I want to spend more time with my wife and family' was another favourite excuse. It was not only the big businessmen who were involved in these things, but politicians, judges . . . just about every profession had its fair share of con men. Gradually, through William Templeton, Maura and Michael were finding out exactly who they were. And they were learning a whole new ballgame.

The waiter brought their main course, kleftiko, and refilled their wine glasses. When he left them, Maura spoke.

'I want an early start tomorrow. I've finally sorted out the last few wrinkles in the gold plan. If everything looks OK to you, we can begin to set it all up.'

'I'll drink to that, Maws.' Michael picked up his glass of Chablis.

'Cheers.'

They touched glasses. If you did not know them you would think they were planning a party, not the biggest bullion robbery England had ever known.

While they were sitting in the restaurant, Danny Rubens was lying in hospital. He had been sedated heavily, but one of the nurses was intrigued. Because, although he was in a deep, drug-induced sleep, his hand was still holding on tightly to his genitals.

Chapter Twenty-three

14 February 1985

Maura knocked on the door of Geoffrey's flat. He lived not far from Michael in Knightsbridge. She had been there only twice before. Even though they had worked together and were brother and sister, they had an accepted and unspoken agreement: I don't like you, so keep your distance. Up till now Maura had respected this.

Geoffrey opened the door. He seemed surprised to see her standing there. He looked terrible. He had not shaved for a couple of days, and being so dark-haired now had dark stubble around his jaw. Maura was shocked to see that it was tinged with grey.

He and Michael had been so alike all their lives, Geoffrey was like a watered-down version of his brother. He looked great, he was handsome, but when people saw Michael they seemed to overlook Geoffrey afterwards. Today he looked old and ill and Maura felt sorry for him. The lines around his eyes, so sexy on Michael, made Geoffrey look jaded and debauched. His dark hair, normally washed and gleaming, was greasy and lank. She watched him look her over from head to toe. It was a sneering look as if she was so much dirt.

'And what do you want?' His voice was belligerent. His face was close to hers and she could smell the sourness of the vast amount of Scotch he had been consuming since his fight with Michael.

'May I come in?' Her voice was neutral.

He held the door open and watched her pass. For the first time in her life she was a bit frightened of him. He slammed the door shut behind her and walked into his lounge. Maura followed, unsure if she was doing the right thing. The room was in a state of chaos. The curtains were still pulled even though it was nearly lunchtime. She went to his oak bookcase and studied the titles for something to do. Her mind was trying to think of a way to defuse the situation.

Geoffrey pulled open the heavy curtains and the weak February sunshine lit the room. She carried on looking at the books, waiting for him to open the conversation. Give her some kind of inkling of how to go about pacifying him over what had happened.

'Thinking of taking up reading? How about *Crime and Punishment*? You can borrow it if you like.' His voice was sarcastic.

She faced him.

'Why didn't you turn in for work yesterday?' She tried to sound ignorant of what had taken place between the two brothers, but as soon as she spoke knew she had said the wrong thing.

Geoffrey laughed.

'Are you telling me that Big Brother didn't tell you all about our little fight? Mickey even tells you when he gives his boyfriend one up the jacksey. I'm sure a good row with his brother would have been worth mentioning.'

Maura stared at Geoffrey for a few seconds before answering him. She decided to come clean with him. It was obvious that he was not going to make this easy.

'Look, Geoff, he did tell me about it. And he really is cut up about it. You took it too much to heart . . .'

Geoffrey sat in a chair and began to laugh at her.

'Oh, get stuffed, Maura. Cut up? He'd be more cut up if that mangy old dog of Benny's died. He don't give a toss about me, and from now on I ain't gonna give a toss about him.'

'But where will you work? What will you do?' She went to him and knelt in front of his chair.

'Oh, don't you worry, I'll still be working for you all.' He stressed the you. 'But I tell you now, and you can tell Mickey this if you like, I'll not be at his beck and call twenty-four hours a day. When I've done my stint of work

I'm off. And I won't do any "heavy" work. If you or him want anyone roughed up or threatened, then you'll have to get one of the others to do it.'

'That's fair enough, Geoff. I was thinking, how about you take over the docklands? I think you and Willy would work well together, and me and Mickey . . . well, we have other irons in the fire.'

Geoffrey grinned, a horrible smelly grin that made her feel sick.

'So little sister has come to pour oil on troubled waters? You're offering me the docklands because you think that it will make me toe the line. Be a good boy.'

'No, Geoffrey. You could have had it before.'

He cut her off, his voice low and serious. 'Do you realise that I am over fifty years old? I have never married or even lived with a woman. I just worked that business with Michael. And then you came and you took it all from me. You inveigled your way into his pocket and you've been resident there ever since.' He was looking at her with a hatred that was tangible. Maura sat back on her heels and stared into a wrinkled, hate-filled face. In the grey sunlight he looked like a gargoyle come to life. But he had hurt her. Hurt and annoyed her.

'Do you know your trouble, Geoffrey? You don't know how to live a life. You act like a leech sucking everyone else's glory. You lived in Mickey's shadow, mate. You didn't have to, it was your own choice. You could have married if you'd wanted to, but you didn't. Not because of Michael, but because you knew deep in your boots that you weren't fit to mate with anyone. Mother called me and Michael neuters years ago, and maybe she was right, but I think that you're one as well.'

'You bitch! How dare you come here spouting your crap?'

Maura stood up and smoothed out the creases in her skirt. Slowly and deliberately, she leaned towards him. 'Just because you've read a few books don't make you Magnus fucking Magnusson you know. You're full of old shit, mate. You want to put down Herman Hesse and

Tolstoy and go out of this flat and get yourself a bird. A real bird, not one of the high-heeled call girls you normally knock around with. A real woman, with a mind of her own.

'You make me sick, Geoff. You're always moaning about something. Everything in your life is analysed and picked over until you find a slight to *you* somewhere in it. Whether it's a chance remark or a frigging so-called conspiracy, like the folder you read the other day. You're paranoid, that's your trouble. Now if you want to come back to work tomorrow, go to the offices at St Martin's Wharf. If not, then that's up to you.'

She started to walk from the room. His voice stayed her. 'I hate you, Maura. I hate you so much I can taste it in my mouth. It's like gall. Mother said to me once you weren't like a normal woman. You didn't have the normal feelings any woman has. And now I know it's true. You even killed your own baby.'

She turned on him like a tiger. Her voice bitter, she said, 'That's Mother's opinion, is it? Well, next time you two are chatting about me ask her this. Ask her who held me down on the table that day when a dirty old man scraped my baby away. Ask her that. And while you're about it, ask her why she accepts money from Michael every week, yet won't even acknowledge his existence. Ask her why she drove poor Carla into marrying that bloody Malcolm. Why she kept her and never tried to reunite her with her mother. I know what everyone thinks about Janine but I'll tell you this much . . . once Mother got Carla into her house and had another little girl to dress up and take to mass, she would never *let* her go back home. You an' Mother are like two peas in a pod. You're both manipulators but neither of you could ever manipulate me or Michael. That's what gets up your noses!'

Before he could speak again she had left the flat, slamming the door behind her.

Geoffrey sat in the chair for a while, thinking. All his instincts told him to forget Maura and Michael forever. But his devious brain told him that if he did not work for them he could not gather his information. And he would gather it. And he would use it. He would swallow his pride and go into work in the morning. But he would be biding his time . . .

Maura drove to Jackie Traverna's house. She was fuming inside. Geoffrey was a pain in the neck. He always had been, and she had a feeling he always would be. She parked her Mercedes Sports outside Jackie's block of flats. Locking it carefully, she went up the small flight of stairs.

As she walked along the landing towads Jackie's flat she was aware of the attention she commanded. Women were standing on the landing chatting, children of all colours and creeds were playing both on the landing and on the concrete forecourt of the flats. Everywhere was the flaking paint and crumbling brickwork that denoted the conditions of poverty these people lived in. The women who were chatting looked at her burgundy Jasper Conran dress and quite obviously real fur coat, and were quiet and hostile. Maura had to turn her body sideways to pass them.

In their crumpled velour tracksuits and shapeless dresses they looked like old women, yet Maura could see from the tight skin on their faces that they were much younger than her. If her life had been different she could quite easily have been one of them. Then her mind rebelled against that thought.

No. She would never have allowed herself to look like these women. Most of them had given up hope at a very early age. No matter what had happened to her, she knew she would always have kept her self-respect.

Jackie's front door was ajar and she walked inside, hesitantly. If those women who had looked at her with naked envy knew that she carried a gun in her bag, they might have had different feelings.

'Jackie? Jackie love?' Her voice was soft. She heard a noise from the bedroom and went inside. Jackie was lying on the bed. Her face had lost some of its puffiness and she looked better. Not much better but better than she had on Maura's last visit.

'Oh, Maura . . .' Jackie tried to speak.

335

Maura sat on her bed. 'I just popped by to see you, Jackie. Shall I make you a cup of tea?'

Jackie's deep brown eyes opened in surprise. Maura Ryan making her tea? It was like expecting the Queen to wash your kitchen floor.

Maura smiled at her, guessing her thoughts. She found the kitchen and made a pot of tea. The room was tiny but relatively tidy. She noticed that there was hardly anything in the cupboards. Leaving the tea to draw she walked back out on to the landing. The women were still there and Maura guessed that they had been discussing her arrival. She strode purposefully towards them.

'Do any of you happen to be friends with Jackie Traverna?'

A fat woman with long straggly brown hair answered her. 'I am. Why?' Her voice was hard and flat.

'I suppose you know that she's had an accident.'

The fat woman sighed loudly. 'I've been taking her Debbie to school for her. Why?'

'If I gave you the money, would you get her in some shopping?' Maura saw the women exchange looks. 'I'll pay you to do it, of course.'

The fat woman shrugged. 'All right.'

She followed Maura back into the flat. Maura was gratified at the friendly way in which she went into Jackie's room. Maura picked her bag up from where she had placed it on the bed. Opening it, she took out five twenty-pound notes. 'Do you have a freezer, Jackie?' The woman nodded her head.

'Good. There's a hundred pounds there and I want you to fill her freezer and cupboards up. I'll give you a score for your trouble. OK?'

The fat woman stared at the money in astonishment. Then she took it from Maura. She guessed from Maura's voice that she was not Social Services or Probation. When the woman went she would find out about her from Jackie.

When the neighbour was gone, Maura poured Jackie and herself out some tea. Taking it into the bedroom, she placed Jackie's cup into her hands. She had managed to pull herself up in the bed and Maura could see the purple bruises on her arms and shoulders. Damn Danny Rubens!

Opening her bag again, she lit two cigarettes and gave one to Jackie. Maura studied her face. She had about thirty stitches in each cheek and would carry the scars for the rest of her life. She pulled out a building society book and gave it to the woman.

'Inside there is five thousand pounds, Jackie. I want you to use it for a holiday or whatever. When you're feeling better I want you to take over the job of head girl at the Crackerjack, our new club.'

It took Maura a minute to realise that Jackie was crying. She took the tea from her and placed it on the floor by the bed. Then she put an arm around her shoulders.

'Hey . . . hey. Calm down, Jackie.'

She spoke with difficulty. 'You've been so good. I was so worried. I thought I'd end up at King's Cross with the pervies.'

Maura looked into her eyes. 'No way. You're a good girl, Jackie. And the head girl's job is a bloody good earner. You'll be fine. Absolutely fine.'

She picked Jackie's tea up from the floor and passed it to her. 'Now you drink this while I get you and me an ashtray!'

When the fat woman got back from shopping she was amazed to find the 'rich bird', as she had termed Maura in her head, washing the kitchen floor. When Maura left a little later she was sure she had pushed up Jackie Traverna's street credibility a hundredfold, and only wished Jackie had not had to go through all that pain and suffering to achieve it.

When Maura got to her own house a bunch of white roses had been left in the glass porch. Intrigued, she opened the card. It said: 'Happy Valentine's Day. Mickey.'

She smiled to herself, but deep inside a little voice was asking her why she never got flowers from any 'real' men. Men who were not related to her. Inside the front door was a pile of letters. Picking them up, she went through to her kitchen. She placed the roses on the draining board and flicked through the letters. Bills and circulars. Then she noticed a thick cream-coloured envelope. Opening it, she brought out a beautiful card. It had real velvet flowers on it, arranged in a basket made of gold thread. This was definitely not a Woolworth's special. She smiled. Michael again. She opened the card and nearly died of shock.

'Will you be my Valentine? Have Dinner with me to-night. 7.30 at the Savoy. Willy.'

For a few sweet seconds she felt that powerful excitement that a new love affair can bring. Then she glanced at her watch. It was past five now! She ran up the stairs to get ready. She was gonna knock his eyes out!

William Templeton sat at his table. He sneaked a glance at his watch. It was twenty to eight. She wasn't coming. He felt his heart sink. Maybe he should have rung her. Then she could have cold-shouldered him over the phone and that would have been the end of it. But he had seen that card in Harrods and had felt a foolish urge to buy it for her. He almost laughed. At his age? On the wrong side of fifty . . .

He had that terrible feeling people get when they have been stood up. That feeling that makes them think that everyone knows what's happened to them. That everyone is smiling at them behind their hands. He felt a shadow fall across him as he stared at the menu for the hundredth time and waved his hand imperiously.

'I'm not ready to order yet, thank you.'

'I should hope not. The least I'd expect is that you would wait for me to arrive!'

His eyes lifted and she was standing there, looking lovelier than he had ever seen her before. She had on a grey fitted dress of watered silk. As with all her clothes, it was perfectly plain. But with her breasts and slim waist, she did not need any of the frippery that most women wore. In her ears she had perfect pearl earrings and around her neck a small single strand of the same grade. Her pale white skin brought them to shining life. Her silky white-blonde hair looked immaculate, as always. William took pleasure in the admiring glances that were coming their way.

He stood up awkwardly. 'I thought you weren't going to come.'

Maura sat down and smiled at the waiter who held her chair.

'Well, I didn't get your card until after five o'clock so I had to rush a bit.'

'You look exquisite, my dear, like a very beautiful painting. Now then, some champagne, I think.' He smiled. 'Real champagne, not the dishwater that's served in your clubs!'

Maura laughed. Really laughed, for the first time in years. It felt good to be pursued. Wanted. And this man certainly wanted her . . . She relaxed back into her chair and let good feelings wash over her.

Chapter Twenty-four

19 March 1985

'Where did you get the number plates from?' Michael was keyed up.

Leslie grinned. 'I got the numbers from a motorway service station car park. I had the actual plates made up by Jimmy Charlton. He owes us a favour.'

'Good. Are the Range Rovers ready to go? And the bikes?'

Leslie nodded. 'Yep. They've been serviced and valeted. They're as clean as a nun's knickers.'

Garry grinned. 'I've sorted out all the guns. They're cleaned and ready to go.'

'Good. Very good. You realise this is a big undertaking, don't you? This ain't like a normal blag. Every filth in the country is going to be looking for that gold. It will be the biggest chance of promotion since Ronnie Biggs had it on his toes.'

'Well, they ain't caught him yet.' Maura's voice was jocular. Everyone laughed except Mickey.

'There's still time for that. Whatever happens, don't get too cocky, lads. Just keep to the ground rules I laid down and we'll be OK.'

Maura stood up and looked around at her brothers' faces. 'What about the hole?'

'All done. Ready and waiting.' This from Lee.

'Then all that's left is to sort out the alibis. I'll leave that to you lot. Whatever it is, make sure it's tighter than a duck's behind. OK?'

Everyone nodded.

'See you in the morning then.' Michael smiled at the faces around him. 'Unless there's any questions?'

'I've got a question.'

'It would be you, wouldn't it, brain box?' Maura's voice was light.

The chances were that if Garry asked a question it would be a good one.

He adjusted his glasses. 'What happens to the filth?'

Michael and Maura had been half expecting someone to ask this.

Michael answered. 'I wasn't going to tell you till the morning. But as you ask . . .'

He paused for effect and swept his gaze around all his brothers.

'You waste them. Every one of them. The fewer people to identify us, the better.'

Roy coughed. 'What about the old Bill though, Mickey? They're in on it, ain't they?'

'Yep. Right up to their shitty little necks. All the more reason to get rid of them. People get jumpy.' He shrugged his shoulders as if to finish his sentence.

'Righty ho. Now who fancies a few pints?'

The four younger brothers all got up from their seats.

'No pissing it up tonight!' Michael's voice was stern. 'And, Garry, contact lenses tomorrow.'

'Don't worry, Mickey. Everything will be fine. As sweet as a nut.'

When the boys left, Maura turned to Michael. 'I ain't happy about knocking everyone off, Mickey.'

Michael sighed heavily. In his dark handmade suit and pristine white shirt he looked like a banker. Which was exactly the impression he wanted to create. In the small portakabin they both looked out of place.

'Look, Maws, you can never leave anything to chance.' He went to her and put his arm around her shoulder, pulling her so close she could feel his breath fan her face. 'You just let me do all the worrying now. You've done your bit.'

'Once the killing starts, Mickey, we lose the protection of all our plants. You realise that, don't you?'

'Yeah, I realise that, Maws. But that Tory MP, the one soliciting in King's Cross . . . well, he's gonna be our scapegoat. The day after tomorrow the pictures we've got of him will be on their way to the gutter press. That should take most people's minds off the actual robbery for a while. Until the main shock wears off anyway.'

Maura was quiet and he took it as a sign of acquiescence. 'Come on, girl, let's get off home. We're all a bit jumpy.'

Driving home Maura was more than jumpy. She was positively terror-stricken. As she drove into her driveway she saw that all the lights were on and her heart lifted a little. Carla was here. She jumped out of the car with delight. That meant that little Joey was with her as well. She let herself into the house.

'Auntie Maura! Auntie Maura!' Four-year-old Joey ran towards her, his chubby arms outstretched.

Maura picked him up in a big hug.

'Hello, Tiger.'

She saw Carla watching them from the kitchen doorway. As always when she saw her she was overwhelmed with a feeling of love and affection. Carla looked like a young Janine, with her red-brown hair and slim figure, except Carla had something more – she had a womanly aura that Janine had never had.

'I've just made some dinner. You couldn't have timed it better.'

'What brought you here? I didn't expect you until the weekend. Not that I mind. You could move in if you wanted to, you know that.' Maura sounded almost her old self. She could kiss Carla for taking her mind off what was happening tomorrow.

Carla went quiet. Her face closed up in the way that Maura knew so well. Something wasn't right.

'What's happened?'

Carla ran her hands through her long hair in her old familiar gesture.

'Come and have dinner, Maws. I'll tell you while we eat.'

Maura followed her into the kitchen. She was frowning now. Joey was holding her tightly around the neck. In the kitchen she could smell a chicken casserole, and realised that she was in fact quite hungry. She sat at the large kitchen table and watched Carla while she worked. This was Carla all over. She would not tell Maura anything until she was good and ready. She guessed that the trouble was with Malcolm, Carla's husband. After Benny's death and Carla's rejection of Maura and Michael, they had not seen her for nearly a year. Then one day Maura had come home to find Carla sitting on her doorstep. She had had a big row with her Nana, as she called Maura's mother. Maura had immediately installed her back in her own room and all had been forgiven between them.

Then, six years ago, Carla had married Malcolm Spencer. He had been two years older than Carla at twenty-six, and for Maura at least it had been loathing on first sight. He was an architect, he was middle-class, and he was the most pompous ass that Maura had ever come across. But Carla had loved him, so she had swallowed her own reservations and countenanced the match. When Joey had been born she had nearly liked the man who was married to the most important girl in her life. She could see how pleased he was with his son and it had made him seem human somehow. Until the christening.

This had been a strained affair as her mother was there, naturally. Sarah had studiously ignored her eldest son and only daughter. That was bad enough, but then Malcolm had upset everyone there. Carla was holding the baby next to the font, everyone standing respectfully around. Carla had handed the infant to the priest and had lost her grip, only slightly. The priest had instantly taken a firm hold on the child and no harm was done. It was the kind of thing that in most families would have been considered an excuse for a joke. Brought up every now and then in family gatherings with a bit added on.

Instead, Malcolm had snatched the child from his wife, causing Carla to lose her own balance. Maura and all her brothers had stood tight-lipped until the service was finally over. There had been no enjoyment after that. Everyone had just stood patiently waiting for it to end. After the service, outside the church, there had been murder. Michael had told Malcolm in no uncertain terms that if he ever as much raised his voice to his niece, or dragged her over again, he would bury him underneath the new motorway currently being built.

Maura was sure that the incident had finally shown Malcolm what he had inadvertently married into. Since then there had been a strained truce between all parties concerned. Now here was Carla and little Joey and she would bet her last pound there was something seriously up.

She played with Joey, who had recently learnt to sing 'The Wheels on the Bus', until such time as Carla finished preparing the meal. Finally, they were all seated and eating the chicken casserole. Carla had also made duchesse potatoes and broccoli and Maura was enjoying it until Carla started telling her what had happened.

Carla and Joey were supposed to be going to the zoo with his playgroup. When Carla had driven him there, with a packed lunch and his mackintosh because the spring weather had been so uncertain, she had been told that one of the minibus drivers was ill so the trip had been cancelled. Joey was heartbroken and had refused to stay at the playgroup. So Carla had put him back in the car and instead of going to the zoo as planned, decided to take him home with her and catch up on some household chores. She guessed that Malcolm would not be too happy as he worked from home the days that Joey went to the playgroup, especially today as they were not due to come home until five o'clock.

When she had reached her house she had noticed a pink Fiesta in the drive. She had parked her own car outside on the road, thinking that someone from Malcolm's work had come round to see him. Getting Joey out of the car, she had gone around the side of the house and in the back door, reasoning that if she opened the porch door, and then the front door, she would more than likely disturb Malcolm and his guest. Inside the kitchen she pulled off Joey's coat and wellingtons and made him a drink of orange. He sat at the table drinking it, for once quiet and still.

Putting on the kettle Carla decided to ask Malcolm and his visitor if they wanted a cup of tea. She left the kitchen, crossed the large entrance hall and went to the door of the room that was Malcolm's office when he was home. She tapped on it and walked inside. Her mind registered the fact that the heavy brocade curtains were drawn. She had not noticed this from the front of the house as this room backed on to the rear garden. Although the room was quite dark she could see well enough. She could see that Malcolm was sitting on his office chair, and that sitting on top of him, with her blouse open exposing her breasts and her skirt pulled up to her waist, showing anyone who cared to look that she was knickerless, was Miss Bradley-Hume, Malcolm's secretary. They were unaware of her for a few seconds and Carla stood rooted to the spot watching the rise and fall of Miss Bradley-Hume's buttocks. Then Malcolm had put his head forward to kiss the woman and had seen Carla standing there. In his fright he stood upright, dropping the prim and proper Miss Bradley-Hume on to the floor. Carla was mainly aware of the fact that Miss Bradley-Hume had large, rather baggy breasts.

Then she had the woman's long mousy hair and was pulling her by it across the carpet. She could see the woman trying to free herself, clawing at Carla's hands that had her hair in a vice-like grip. Malcolm was staring at Carla absolutely shell shocked.

Giving Miss Bradley-Hume a hard kick in her stomach, she turned her attention to her husband. Seeing him standing as he was with his underpants and jeans (his designer jeans that he thought made him look so macho) around his ankles, she was finally convinced that she had married a complete and utter fool. His little skinny legs with their sparse hairs looked like a chicken's. She noticed that his member, which had never been that big to begin with, had now shrunk into a small wrinkled sausage and she had the urge to laugh. If only he could see himself! Mr Important!

Miss Bradley-Hume had picked herself up off the floor and retrieved her knickers, which were on the drawing board. She stood now, fully attired, in front of Carla.

'This is not what it looks like.' Her refined twang sent shivers of diabolical hatred through Carla's body.

'Get out of my house, you slut. You fucking filthy dirty slut!'

Miss Bradley-Hume's long horsey face dropped with shock. Carla laughed, her eyes wild.

'Oh, have I shocked you with a naughty word? Fuck . . . don't you like that word? Well, that's what you were doing, you upper-class whore. You were fucking my husband. Fucking, fucking, fucking . . .'

Malcolm shuffled across to her as quickly as his trousers would allow. She felt the stinging blow as he slapped her across the face. Then she was calm. She watched Malcolm pull up his ridiculous jeans.

'Get out of *my* house now. Both of you.'

Miss Bradley-Hume went quickly. The change in Carla's voice was enough to send her running to her car. On her way out of the door she knocked Joey to the floor. His shocked crying penetrated Carla's rage. Going to him, she picked him up.

'All right, baby. It's nothing. Just a little accident, that's all.'

She turned back to her husband. 'I meant what I said, Malcolm. I want you out of *my* home.'

He tried to bluff his way out, his domineering personality coming to the fore.

'I will not leave this house. You're overwrought. I admit I've been a naughty boy . . .'

'Naughty boy!' Carla's voice was incredulous. 'You're a fucking cretin, Malcolm, that's what you are. And you're getting out of this house, or I'll get my uncles to move you for me!'

It was the first time she had ever threatened him with anything, let alone her uncles. Malcolm was aware that his hold over Carla was not as tight as usual. He tried a different tack.

'Will you stop using that F Word! You really are showing your working-class lineage today, aren't you?'

Carla was patting Joey's back. His sobs were quieting now as he listened to his parents' quarrel.

'I am going to Maura's, Malcolm, and when I get back from there in a few days I want you out.' Her words had a finality about them that frightened him.

'Oh, baby, I know what I've done is wrong. But she was asking for it.' His voice was wheedling. Cajoling. He needed her.

Carla laughed harshly. 'I should think she *was* asking for it. No one else but you would fuck something so ugly. Only you. We're finished, Malcolm. Finished.'

'What about Joey? I'm his father!' Malcolm was self-righteous now.

'If you do what I tell you, and get out of my life and *my* house, I may let you see him from time to time.' She was enjoying herself. Now that the initial shock had worn off, she realised that she finally had a bona fide reason to get rid of him.

'Carla, please. For all the love we've shared . . .'

'Drop dead, Malcolm.' Her voice was flat and hard. 'Come on, Joey, let's go to Auntie Maura's, shall we?'

She went from the room, across the large entrance hall and finally out of the house. Settling Joey into his car seat, she went back into the house and collected her bag and a few things. As she left for the last time Malcolm tried again.

'Please, Carla.' His voice was desperate now.

Standing on the driveway, she placed the middle finger of her right hand in the air then, gathering as much air into her lungs as possible, shouted at him: 'Rotate on it gently, arsehole!'

Then, getting into the car, she drove to Maura's.

Maura listened to Carla in amazement. She could not help picturing her dragging the woman across the carpet by her hair.

'Oh, Carla love, I'm so sorry. It must have been terrible.'

Carla smiled sheepishly.

'Stop spitting the meat out, Joey.' She looked back at Maura. 'Actually, Maws, I enjoyed every minute of it! I think I finally saw him as you all see him.'

'We've never seen him with his cacks down!'

Both women laughed. 'You know what I mean. He's a prat, Maws. A prize prat.'

Maura was serious. 'But you did love him, didn't you?'

Carla looked at little Joey. 'Yeah. I did love him in the beginning. But not any more.'

Maura carried on eating. The food was tasteless now. She was consumed with a feeling of hatred for Malcolm that made her want to go and kill him.

'Can you imagine Nana's face when she finds out I've left my lawful husband?'

Maura was cavalier. 'Oh, sod her, Carla. Let her think what she likes. You can stay here with me until we get you sorted out.'

Carla put her hand gently over Maura's.

'I know that. I'm like a bad penny, ain't I? Always turning up. My mum didn't want me. Nor my dad. And now even my husband's done the dirty on me. Maybe I do something wrong.'

'Don't be so silly!' Maura's voice was sharp. 'I'll tell you something, shall I? Once, a long time ago, I was in a similar state to you. I went to Marge's. Well, she said something that I'll never forget. She said that self-pity was a luxury none of us could afford. Those weren't her exact words, but that was what she meant. You must pick yourself up, brush yourself down . . .'

'And start all over again.' Carla sang the last sentence and they both laughed again.

'Yeah, well. That's about the strength of it.'

'In a funny way I feel free. Like I've been let out of prison after a long stretch.'

'That's good, Carla. Try and keep that feeling. It will help you over the next few weeks. And there's one other good thing. My mother won't ring you here so you can put off talking to her for as long as you want.'

Joey upset his beaker of milk and both women jumped

up to get a cloth. Even though Carla's being there was because of trouble, Maura was glad to have her and Joey anyway. It took her mind off what was going to happen the next day. And she could not rule out the fact that it would give her a cast-iron alibi if, by any chance, the police did decide to interview her.

Chapter Twenty-five

It was 4am on 20 March 1985. Maura and Michael were sitting in a portakabin in a yard owned by Michael's friend, Jim Dickenson. Jim was an old lag. Throughout his life he had been put into prison for various offences, ranging from bank robbery (he got only eight years because his gun was not loaded) to extortion. He had tried to blackmail a high-powered executive who was a transvestite. On leaving jail he had approached Michael. They were friends from the Notting Hill days of Joe the Fish. He was a big powerful man and Michael had set him up in a plant hire business in Cranford. He had bought the business as a going concern and it had been put into Jim Dickenson's name. To all intents and purposes, Michael Ryan had nothing whatsoever to do with it.

The yard consisted of over four acres of land, surrounded by ten-foot fence panels and guarded by three Dobermans and a Rottweiler. This morning, though, it was empty of any life other than Michael and Maura. The dogs were shut into a pen kept especially for them. Their barking and howling was already getting on Maura's nerves.

Michael glanced at his watch. It was four minutes past the hour.

'Another ten minutes, Maws, and it will all be over.'

Maura lit yet another cigarette and tried to concentrate her mind on Carla and Joey.

Roy and Gerry were waiting at the roundabout on the Bath Road. Both were on 650cc Kawasaki motorbikes. They were dressed in black from head to foot. Gerry could feel the sweat pouring from his forehead. He was frightened, really frightened. He wished he had the guts just to start the engine and go . . . go anywhere away from here.

Roy was thinking about Janine, and Benny who was nearly ten. Where his wife had completely disowned Carla, she tried to possess the boy. He closed his eyes, trying to concentrate on the job in hand. If they went wrong now, that would be the end of them. Banged up good and proper. He felt the loose feeling in his bowels and hoped that he would not have to empty them at the roadside. He reassured himself with the fact that this robbery had been planned down to the minutest detail. What he would not give for a fag! Just to be doing something other than waiting for the lights of the articulated lorry. He could sense the nervousness of Gerry Jackson and it made him feel worse. He breathed deeply, trying to control his heartbeats.

Garry, Leslie and Lee were in a dark blue Range Rover. All three were already wearing black balaclavas with just slits for eyeholes. Garry kept up a stream of low chatter. Leslie and Lee just grunted replies. All were nervous. Garry caressed the shotgun that he was holding. At four minutes past four they all started counting down.

There were just ten minutes until the off.

Davie Muldoon drove the container lorry with its cargo of gold towards Heathrow airport. His mind was miles away on an argument that he'd had with his wife the night before. She was a pain in the bloody neck. First she informs him that her mother's coming, yet again. Then she drops the real bombshell. She's pregnant again. Four bloody kids in five years.

She looked like something from a Hammer horror film already. She tipped the scales at just over sixteen stone! When he had first met her she had been eight stone with the best set of bristols he had ever seen. Nowadays, what with the rolls of fat and the stretch marks, it was like mounting Red Rum. But true to form she went by her old ruse. Attack was the best form of defence. Before he could comment on the fact that they could barely meet the mortgage payments as it was, without another baby to feed and clothe, she had started on about his drinking. Well, if she had a good look in the mirror she might get an inkling as to why he drank so much.

He needed at least eight pints of Hurlimans even to consider kissing the ugly bitch. He shook his head sadly as he drove along. He had been well and truly caught there. All his mates had warned him: 'Look at the mother and see the daughter, twenty years on.' He was well gutted.

The house looked like a council tip. She never cleaned up. Last night she had stood before him in all her glory. With her bleached yellow hair with the roots grown out nearly two inches she looked like a candidate for the black and white minstrel show. He grinned to himself. Her out-size nightdress had been stained with everything from baby puke to tea. Even her teeth were going rotten in her head. She said it was because of having the kids so quick, but he had already made a shrewd guess that not cleaning them was also a large contributory factor. The dirty bitch! He shuddered. She was only twenty-four! What would she be like in another five years?

Joey Granger had been watching the changing expressions on his friend's face with fascination. He also had an idea what had put them there. He had met Davie's wife Leona only once and that had been enough. She had reminded him of a Rottweiler in drag. Poor old Davie, he had to be the most easy-going bloke in the world. Which was probably why she got away with so much. If she had been his wife he would have given her a good slap a long time ago.

'Light me a fag, Joey?' Davie's voice was soft.

'We're not really supposed to, you know.'

'Of course I know, but it's never stopped us before!'

Joey lit two cigarettes and passed one to Davie.

'I hate these big pulls, they make me nervous.'

Joey laughed lightly.

'Smoke your fag and calm down. There's more old Bill out there than on the Masonic Lodge's annual Beano!'

Davie smiled despite himself.

353

In front of the articulated lorry was a white Granada. Inside were Detective Inspector Tomlinson and three younger men, DS Milton, DC Johns and DC Llewelyn. DC Johns was what was commonly termed a chatterbox.

'So, sir, if no one knows that this gold is going to Heathrow, why so many police?' His voice was very young and very naive and DI Tomlinson was sorry for him. Just for a second though. He had too much else on his mind.

'DC Johns?' His voice was stern.

'Yes, sir?'

'Shut your bloody trap for five minutes, and give your arse a chance!'

Llewelyn and Milton laughed softly. Johns sat silent and embarrassed. How were you to find out anything if you never asked? he reasoned.

Tomlinson was nervous, very nervous, and the younger men put it down to the seriousness of what they were doing. In fact, he was more aware of what was going on than they were or even than the Bank of England was. He had always had a passion for the horses. Over the last few years it had become an expensive passion. A passion that Michael Ryan had encouraged wholeheartedly. At this moment he could not make his mortgage payments, his car payments or, God help him, his maintenance. He was also into Michael Ryan for so much money he felt faint if he thought about the actual amount. It was his job to see that these three imbeciles bodged their job. Then he was home and dry, with all his debts paid.

The guns were still locked in the special armouries built into the dashboard in the front and the armrest in the back. He had the keys, and would take as long as he could before arming the three young cowboys in the car with him. He sneaked a look at his watch. Four minutes till the off. He was surprised to find that he was not even sweating.

Behind the articulated lorry was another unmarked car. This time it was a Sierra. A dirty brown-coloured Sierra 1600E.

Inside were DI Becton and another three young plain-clothes, DS Bronte, DS Marker and WDC Williams. Becton was annoyed. He did not like the thought of a WDC in this thing at all. He also held the magic keys that would arm what were in effect little more than children. Becton, too, had to make sure that his end of the operation went wrong.

After twenty years in the police force he had finally been found out. He was married with three teenage children, a lovely wife Jeanette whom he honestly loved with all his heart, and a nice detached house in Chiswick, nearly paid for. He had only one problem and it was a big one. He had discovered many years ago that he had a penchant for very young boys. Up until now it had never interfered with what he termed his 'real life', his family and his career. Then a week ago he had been sent certain pictures of himself through the post in a plain brown envelope. There was no mistaking that it was him in the pictures. They were in glorious colour. They were also very explicit.

He had been standing in the hallway, clutching the pictures to his chest, when Jeanette had walked out there. She had looked as pretty as a picture in the early morning light, not at all like the mother of three teenaged children or like the wife of a sexual pervert, because when he had seen himself in those pictures he had realised exactly what he was. And the thought of her knowing and his children knowing had nearly brought on a heart attack.

He had telephoned the number enclosed with the picture and now sat in this car, with two young men and a lovely young lady, waiting to do something that would be a blot on their career files all their life. He glanced in the mirror and saw the meatwagon full of uniforms driving behind him. He looked at the clock on the dashboard of the Sierra. Three minutes to the off. He was trembling.

As the meatwagon passed them, Gerry and Roy started up their bikes. Gerry's took three good kicks before it roared into life. They pulled their visors down on their helmets and nodded to one another, then they roared off behind the

355

meatwagon. It was about two hundred yards from the roundabout. Inside the meatwagon were ten armed officers, most of them dozing. Only two were alert. One was the driver, DS Raymond Paine, and the other the controller of the radio, DS Martin Fuller. Both were unaware that they were going to be blown off the road within seconds. Outside the window, Paine could hear the dull drone of the police helicopter that was following them above. He yawned. He hated these special assignments.

Roy had already cocked his .357 Magnum. He drove parallel with the meatwagon and with one shot completely disabled the vehicle. The back tyre blew out with a ferocious bang that woke up all the sleeping officers. They woke up just in time to feel the van mounting the grass verge at the side of the road and then turn over twice before it finally came to rest on its right side, on the opposite side of the carriageway.

'Jesus Christ! Did you see that?'
Up above in the helicopter Officer Watts and Officer Harper had seen in the dim light a bright blue flash.
'Calling all units in the vicinity of the roundabout on the Bath Road. We have reason to believe a robbery is in progress . . .'

As the helicopter message came over the radio in Becton's car, WDC Williams answered the call. Becton and the two young men were already out of the car and going to the aid of their colleagues. WDC Williams was aware in the pandemonium that Becton had not unlocked the small arms cache. She punched the dashboard in frustration. There had been the definite sound of a shot, officers were undoubtedly injured, and they did not have so much as a lolly stick between them. It was pathetic!
She picked up the radio handset and began to call for the fire brigade and ambulances.

* * *

DI Tomlinson had done his job properly. At least from the Ryans' point of view. As soon as the shot had been fired he had pulled the white Granada on to the side of the road. The articulated lorry had had to swerve to avoid him. It had wheezed to a stop, only to find its way immediately blocked by a Range Rover that seemed to appear from thin air.

'It's a robbery!' DC Johns' voice was incredulous.

Before they had even had time to answer him, two sawn-off shotguns had been pointed at the windows of the car. Within seconds, the doors had been opened and they were all lying on the damp road with their hands handcuffed behind their backs.

Davie and Joey were sitting in the articulated lorry, dumbstruck. Then a big man in a black balaclava motioned with a large gun for them to open their doors. Before the trip they had been told not to open the specially constructed doors even if Jesus himself appeared and asked for a lift. This was all forgotten in their panic. They opened the doors and jumped from the cab.

Davie watched his lorry being driven away by two masked men.

Garry, Leslie and Lee jumped into the Range Rover and as they screeched off saw that the police helicopter was hovering just above their heads. Leaning dangerously out of the front window, Garry, always the most adventurous of the boys, opened fire on it with his M16 rifle. He had brought it with him deliberately for this job. In the distance, on the M4, they could hear the wailing of the police and ambulance sirens. Garry's hair caught fire beneath his balaclava as the helicopter exploded. Leslie dragged him back inside the window, then helped him to put his hair out. They were laughing hysterically now. It was all over.

Back at the yard, Maura and Michael were in a state of nervous agitation. It was four-twenty-five. As if of one mind, they both left the portakabin and stood in the yard. Just to the right of them was an enormous black hole. It was twenty-five feet deep and almost forty long. It had been dug vertically as if it was a sloping runway, which in effect it was. It was fifteen feet wide. Brother and sister walked across the gravel and opened the large iron gates.

'Mickey, I'm so scared.' Maura's voice was barely a croak.

'Ain't we all, darling?'

He smiled at her in the darkness. She could not see it but she could hear it in his voice.

Fifteen minutes later the articulated lorry drove through the gates followed by the Range Rover. The bikes had been left at the scene of the robbery.

Roy drove the lorry straight into the hole. Getting out, he and Gerry scrambled up the sloping floor.

On either side of the hole were gigantic mounds of dirt. The hole itself had been dug by a large drag line crane. It had taken nearly five hours.

Leslie, Lee, Garry and Roy all got into giant Caterpillar 'dozers. In less than an hour, they had filled the hole back in. The lorry was gone. It had disappeared off the face of the earth. It would sit under the ground for a few years until it was safe to try and shift the gold. Michael watched his brothers parking different types of plant over the burial place. It was covered with everything from dumper trucks, low loaders for cranes and the caterpillar 'dozers.

At the scene of the robbery, pandemonium was breaking out. Becton and Tomlinson were both receiving the sharp edge of Chief Superintendent Liversey's tongue. He was absolutely fuming.

'The bloody lorry has disappeared off the face of the earth. You two didn't even have the sense to arm your men!' He was spitting with temper as he spoke. 'How the hell am I supposed to explain this one away? That's what I'd like to know. If I didn't know better I'd think you were communists! You bloody fools!'

He was interrupted by an ambulanceman. 'Excuse me,

sir, but there were no fatalities. I thought you would like to know. Only one major casualty and that was a gunshot wound. I gather that in the course of the van crashing, one of the men in the back inadvertently shot the fellow sitting opposite.'

'What about the helicopter pilots?'

'Burnt to death, I'm afraid.'

'Then how can you say there were no fatalities? You're all bloody fools!'

Liversey stomped away from the men. He knew this much – heads were going to roll over this and he had a feeling that his would be one of them. He would have been even more galled if he'd known that the articulated lorry that had been carrying nearly twenty million in gold bullion was buried, with the engine still hot, not two miles away.

At eight o'clock that morning, Jim Dickenson opened his yard. By eight-fifteen it was a hive of activity. He loved his plant hire firm. He loved Michael Ryan for letting him have it. By five that afternoon the newly filled-in hole was just part of the usual landscape. Not one of the men who worked there even guessed that they were walking and driving over twenty million pounds' worth of gold. Yet the robbery was to be their only topic of conversation for ages.

At six-fifteen, Maura and Michael were driving along the M4 back into London. Leslie and Garry had driven off earlier, as had Roy. Lee was to dump the Range Rover in Langley, Slough, where he had left his car. Everyone agreed it had been a good night's work. Gerry Jackson had left earlier than everyone else as he had to open the main betting shop in Wandsworth. After all, life had to go on.

Maura walked into her house in Rainham at nearly nine in the morning. She was tired out. Little Joey was there to greet her and she kissed and cuddled him for a while before going up to bed. She noticed that Carla did not enquire where she had been all night. After a warm bath, she slipped naked into her bed. The coolness of the sheets was reassuring to her somehow. She had managed to talk Michael out of a killing spree, but he had still allowed Garry to shoot at the helicopter. She burrowed into her pillow. She had heard on the news that the men had been burnt to death. Both were married with children. The radio announcer's voice had been so matter-of-fact about it.

She turned over again in bed and attempted once more to get comfortable and empty her mind of all the bad things. She had too many bad things filed away. She heard Joey's joyful laughter float up the stairs and into her bedroom and the thought of the helicopter pilots' children rose up in front of her. They were small and helpless in her mind's eye. And faceless. Like her own baby which still wandered into her thinking sometimes, especially when she was down like now. The robbery itself bothered her not one iota. It was the killing. She did not think for a moment that what she had told Leslie to do to Danny Rubens counted. He was scum. He had cut up one of the girls who worked for them and he had paid the price. She could not look on the police as her brothers did, as the enemy. An omnipotent force that had to be thwarted at every turn. She did not really care about the police much, one way or the other.

Except for Terry Petherick . . . She sat up in bed and rearranged her pillows, sinking back into their coolness. If she started to think about him then she would never get any sleep. She heard the bedroom door creak open.

'Are you asleep?'

Carla's voice was soft.

'No, love. Come on in.'

Carla walked into the bedroom with a glass of brandy. She went to Maura and put it on the bedside table. 'I thought you could possibly do with this. I left Joey watching a Postman Pat video, so I have a few minutes to myself.'

Maura sat up in the bed. She knew that Carla was offering her an opening, if she wanted to talk to her. And she did want to talk; she wanted to tell her how unhappy she was about all that had happened in the last twenty-four hours. But she couldn't. She picked up the glass of brandy and sipped it. Carla tried again.

360

'William Templeton rang last night. He wants you to call him as soon as you can. I forgot to tell you.'

'Thanks. I'll ring him later.'

'I was listening to the news just now. It seems that two of the policemen who were guarding some gold that got stolen were shot dead about half an hour ago. The police think that the raiders may have thought they could identify them.'

She watched Maura's face closely and was not surprised to see her blanch.

'A Vecton I think it was, and a Tomlinson.' Her voice trailed off as she watched Maura's features. Her aunt's mouth was moving but she seemed unable to speak.

Maura's mind was whirling. Not Vecton . . . Becton and Tomlinson. The two who were being blackmailed. She put the brandy on the bedside table and, pushing Carla away roughly, jumped out of the bed.

She practically ran to the wardrobes that covered one entire wall. They were mirrored and Maura could see the reflection of her breasts, bouncing as she ran to them. Pulling one of the doors open she started to dress herself, dragging the clothes on to her body in her haste. She pulled on a pair of jeans and a cashmere sweater, and then, pushing her bare feet into some leather moccasins, ran out of the room and down the stairs, Carla following her.

'For goodness' sake, Maura. What's up?' Carla's voice was troubled. She knew that Maura was upset over what she had said. She felt responsible.

'Nothing. I just have to see Michael, that's all.' She picked up her car keys and ran from the house to her car.

Carla went into the lounge where Joey was sitting in front of the television set, watching Postman Pat and Jess. She sat on the sofa and stared at the screen, wishing that she had kept her mouth shut.

Michael was asleep when he heard the pounding on his door. He immediately thought it was the police, and jumped out of his bed naked. Then he heard Maura calling through the letterbox.

361

'It's me. Let me in now!'

Thinking that something had happened he rushed to the front door and let her in. As he opened up she almost fell into his hall. Her hair was dishevelled, her face streaked with mascara. He shut the door quickly and tried to grasp hold of her. She pushed him away roughly.

'You bastard! You rotten stinking bastard!'

Michael's mouth dropped open with shock. 'What? What have I done?'

'You had those two policemen shot after you promised me . . .'

Michael yawned. 'Oh, is that all? I thought it was something important.'

His voice was low and full of sleep.

Maura stared at him in astonishment. Is that all? she thought. That is the extent of his morality.

'I thought something had happened. Something terrible.' He walked into his bedroom and pulled on a dressing gown. She followed him and, as he turned to face her, tying the belt, launched herself at him, hair and nails flying. Her right hand dug into his face and she felt the skin tear as she scratched him deeply.

'You rotten bastard! You stinking lousy bastard!'

Within seconds he had grabbed her arms and thrown her on the bed. He held her there, with her arms pinned to her sides, while she fought him like a wildcat. Using every ounce of her strength she tried to get away from him, so she could carry on her fighting. She could hear herself spitting obscenities at him, all the bad things that she had carefully locked away over the years bubbling out of her body. Spewing out from between her lips. And still Michael held her down on the bed, his face placid and closed. Finally, after what seemed to Maura to be an eternity but was only about five minutes, the tears came. Hot gushing tears that soaked her face and hair in seconds with their salty residue. She felt the fight leave her body as if it had been exorcised.

Then Michael had her in his arms. He was stroking her hair and murmuring calming words and phrases. And Maura was aware that she was letting him. She needed him.

His arms were circling her like steel bands and she knew she would forgive him anything. Had, in fact, already forgiven him for what he had done. It was herself, Maura Ryan, she would never forgive.

Michael held her until she was calm again and her crying just little hiccups. Then, pushing her away from him so he could see into her face, he spoke.

'Listen, Maws. Those police were on the take. One was a child molester. He hung around the train stations looking for little rent boys. Now I'm queer, Maws. Or gay, whatever you want to call it. But most gay men would no more touch them little boys than they would cut their own arms off. That's pervert country, Maws, where all the nice Mr Respectables in their city suits and briefcases get a quick blow job off some poor little bugger, before going home to the wife and kids and their dinner.' His voice was low and sure and hypnotic.

'As for the other one, he was more bent than a nine bob note. His wife suffered because he was a violent wife-beater. And when he began to take his temper out on the kids, she went on the trot and divorced him. He still had an injunction order out on him, to stop him going around her house and belting her.' He watched her face for any sign that she was weakening. He did not like this Maura. A frightened, beaten Maura. She sniffed loudly and looked into his eyes.

'What . . . what . . . about the heli-helicopter pilots?' She still could not control the little heaving sobs.

'They were nothing to do with you, Maws. That was down to me and the others. All you did was help us plan it. Don't go to pieces on me, Maws. Not you. Think of them as you would a scumbag like Danny Rubens. It's Us and Them, girl, and up until now you've lived by that rule. Don't go soft on me now. You've run this firm with me for years. You've been the mainstay of it. But I could do without you, Maws, if you really wanted out.'

His soft voice had an underlying threat in it that did not go unnoticed. She swallowed deeply.

'I don't want out, Mickey.' And she didn't. It was all that she knew.

He smiled. One of his best smiles that seemed to light his face up from within.

'That's my girl.' He enfolded her in his arms again and she relaxed against him. Michael was right. In all the years she had worked for him and with him it had never seemed to bother her before. But deep, deep down in the bottom of her being she knew that the killing had always bothered her. She still woke up at nights with her body bathed in sweat, thinking about Sammy Goldbaum. She opened the little filing cabinet in her brain and once more filed all the bad things away. Until the next time she broke down.

Michael held her close and stared at the wall over her shoulder. Of all the things he had expected to come from the gold robbery, this was not one of them. He had only seen her like this once before, after Benny's death, when Sammy and Jonny had been put away. Well, he would do now what he had done then. Keep her by him. Watch over her. And hopefully snap her out of it. He kissed the top of her white-blonde head. He did love her. He loved her very much.

The Gold Bullion Robbery hit every front page, as did the killing of the policemen. Everyone was blamed from the IRA to an Italian terrorist organisation, the latter in the *Sun*'s leader, three days after the robbery. The *Guardian* called for a Government Inquiry into how such a top secret operation could have been leaked to a person or persons unknown.

The police kept a low profile. They had their suspicions as usual, but no solid evidence of any kind. Chief Superintendent Liversey was given early retirement, as were two prominent members of the board at the Bank of England. If the police had held an Internal Inquiry they might have been given to wonder how so many high-ranking officers could afford holidays in the Seychelles and the Bahamas.

The robbery was finally knocked off the front pages

by a Member of Parliament. He had been secretly photographed propositioning a prostitute who worked King's Cross 'rough trade'. As usual the British public much preferred to read about a good sex scandal rather than a robbery with violence and murder. The *Daily Mirror* called for another Government Inquiry, this time into the sex lives of prominent Tory MPs. The particular MP involved remained a favourite of Michael Ryan's for some time.

Geoffrey Ryan wrote out all he had read about the robbery in the green folder. He then placed it with the file he was gathering on Maura and Michael. One day, though he did not know when that day would be, he would use it against them.

Chapter Twenty-six

12 October 1986

Michael Ryan walked along the Embankment. He turned up his coat collar to try and warm himself. People were hurrying by. A man walked up behind him and fell into step with him.

'Mr Ryan, you're very late.' He had the soft Southern Irish drawl.

'I know. I was caught up in some last-minute work. You know how it is.'

The man, although a full head shorter than Michael, was very powerfully built. His small dark eyes continuously scanned the crowds of people as if on the look out for something or someone.

'We need to know if you can deliver, Mr Ryan. We have been waiting this last two weeks for word. That's why I arranged this meet today. Every Garda from Belfast to Liverpool is looking for me. It's only for yourself that I came out of me hiding.'

Michael took a deep breath. He was as good looking as ever and more than one woman gave him an admiring glance as they passed.

'Look, Mr O'Loughlin, these things take time. Especially now. As you just said yourself, everyone is looking for you, and the people you are likely to be dealing with as well. Christ Almighty, I'm taking as big a chance as you are! All I can tell you is what I have been telling you for days. I am doing the best that I can. Everyone is shitting hot bricks at the moment.'

Patrick O'Loughlin's face hardened and he grabbed Michael's arm.

'Look here, Ryan, you have more than enough police and judges in your pocket. Rumour has it that you have more than your fair share of politicians as well. All I want is a few passports, that's all. Jesus knows, we have enough guns and Semtex to rearm the bloody British Army. But it's not guns or Semtex we're after these days. It's passports.'

'Give me another couple of days. I have a big job going on in St Martin's Wharf. I have Germans, Micks, the lot on it. I'll get you passports and perfect watertight covers. Now let's leave it there, shall we? I'll be in touch in a few days. OK?'

'I don't seem to have much choice, do I?'

O'Loughlin nodded at Michael and, turning away from him, disappeared back into the crowd. As he walked away from Michael two men approached on either side of him. Too late he realised their intent. As his hand went inside his jacket for his weapon, he felt a gun being pushed into his side.

'If you try anything, Pat, I'll drop you here in the street.'

Then he was bundled into a waiting Daimler at the kerbside. As he was relieved of his gun one of the men spoke to him.

'You've been grassed, Pat, me old mate. Well and truly grassed.'

Pat O'Loughlin sat back in the seat with a show of careless indifference. Inside he was like a seething cauldron. He stared out at the passing buildings. Michael Ryan had double crossed him. Only he could have fingered him. Involuntarily he clenched his fists. Michael Ryan would pay.

Maura got out of bed still half asleep. The low buzzing of her alarm had woken her too early, or at least that was how it felt. She stood by her bed and stretched. Pulling on a robe she went downstairs to her kitchen, picking up her mail and the daily paper as she went through her hall.

She made a pot of tea and, lighting one of the sixty cigarettes she would smoke that day, unfolded the paper. Staring out at her from the front page of the *Daily Mail* was Patrick O'Loughlin. She studied the picture, stunned. Then she looked at the headlines: IRA KILLER ARRESTED. Forcing her mind to work, she read the story.

'Due to information received, Patrick O'Loughlin, wanted for the bombing of a military base in Surrey where four soldiers died, was picked up by the police as he walked on the Embankment yesterday. He is also an escaped prisoner. He was given four life sentences for sectarian killings in Belfast. The man he was seen with yesterday is still being sought by the police . . .'

Maura's mind was racing. O'Loughlin had met Mickey yesterday and any policeman worth his salt would have recognised Michael Ryan. The ones who were not in their pay tried to make their careers by nicking him. She pulled deeply on her cigarette, got up from her seat and went to the telephone on the kitchen wall. She rang Michael's number. It was answered almost immediately by his boyfriend.

'Get Mickey, now!'

'But he's in the shower . . .'

'Well, get him out then!' Her voice was harsh.

Richard Salter pursed his lips. He did not like Maura and she did not like him. Placing the receiver on the small coffee table he went into the bathroom. Michael waved him away, soap running down his body as he washed his hair.

'Mickey love, your sister's on the phone. She says she must speak to you now.'

Michael stood under the water for a couple of seconds to get rid of most of the soap. Then pulling a towel from the rail he put it around his waist, knocking Richard flying as he hurried out of the bathroom. He picked up the phone, dripping water everywhere.

'What is it, Maws?'

Richard watched as Michael's face changed from undisguised shock to seething rage. He ran back to the kitchen to finish making the breakfast. Whatever that sister of his was saying had certainly given Michael the hump! Still, he reflected as he scrambled eggs, at least *he* had not done anything wrong.

Ten minutes later, as he placed breakfast on the table, he heard the front door slam. Michael had gone without even kissing him goodbye! Richard sat at the table with his face set in a frown. Damm that bloody bitch! He looked at Michael's fluffy scrambled eggs and, smiling, picked it up and scraped it on to his own plate. Waste not, want not, that was his motto.

Michael got into his car, his mind working overtime. As he made his way through the busy morning traffic his rage subsided. Maura had said that they had to think this thing through calmly, and she was right. He had a niggling suspicion in the back of his mind about who had grassed him up. His face set into a hard frown. From what Maura had told him the paper had more or less said that whoever had been with O'Loughlin had been responsible for his being picked up. Joe Public didn't know who that was but the IRA did. And that could mean big trouble. He had been dealing with them for years.

He carried on driving out of London towards Essex. He could not understand why Maura lived in that great big house out in the sticks. He pulled into her drive and got out of the car. She already had the front door open. He kissed her on the cheek. She put her finger to her lips and he followed her through the house to her kitchen, where her daily woman, Mrs MacMullen, was pulling on her coat.

'You'll be paid for today, Mrs Mac, but I need the house to myself.'

'Oh, that's all right, lovie. I don't mind.' She smiled at the pair of them and walked out of the kitchen. They both stood silently until they heard the front door slam.

'She let herself in while I was in the shower. Sorry about that. Coffee?'

Michael nodded.

'Look, Maws, whoever fingered me was very close to

home. The only ones who knew about the meet were me, you and Geoffrey.'

Maura shrugged, not taking in what he was saying. 'It could have been someone from O'Loughlin's end.'

Michael sat at the table. 'Why would one of the Micks want to set me up?'

She turned to face him. 'Well, it certainly wasn't me!' Her voice was cold.

'I know that, Princess. That leaves only one other person . . .'

When Maura realised what he was saying she began to shake her head in disbelief.

'No. Not Geoffrey. For Christ's sake, Mickey, he's our brother.'

She poured out the coffee with trembling hands.

'I think that Geoffrey has tucked me up, Maws. It's a gut feeling. He ain't been right for a long time now. Whoever grassed to the old Bill knew exactly where we were meeting, everything. I only knew an hour before-hand myself. You know I have the phones swept once a month. They're cleaner than the Russian Embassy's. No, whoever it was, was close to home. There's no doubt about that.'

'It could have come from O'Loughlin's end.' Her voice was sad. Even as she spoke she knew that Michael was right. She sat down heavily, as if very weary. 'So, Mickey, what are you going to do?'

He sipped his tea. 'What do you think? I can't let this go.'

Maura bit on her thumbnail. 'You don't know for sure yet, Mickey.'

'Listen, Maws, there's a few things that have been bothering me for a while. He asked to be put back into the clubs, didn't he? He didn't want to work with William any more. Right?'

Maura nodded her head slowly.

'Well, the takings went right down. I asked him about it and he said that all the clubs were in the same boat. Then I find out that the New Rockingham Club and the

371

Pink Pussycat have nearly doubled their takings. So I know that he has his hand in the till. He was also seen with Old Billy Bootnose, a known nark. Richard saw them.'

Maura flapped her hand at him. 'I'm sorry, Mickey. For all Geoff's faults he ain't a grass. As for your Richard . . .'

Michael bellowed at her, 'Oh, Maws, grow up for fuck's sake! It's staring us in the face. Richard works in and around London, picking up garbage for the gossip columns. There ain't nothing that he don't know or can't find out. You might not like him but that don't alter the facts. Geoff is selling us out. Not just me. I bet you any money you like, it's you as well.'

'So what's the next step?' Her voice was small.

'Let's just say he won't be going home to dinner with that snot-nosed bird he's got himself.'

Maura gave Michael a level stare, then shook her head, 'No, Mickey. You can't! Not your own flesh and blood. For me, Mickey. For Mum. Don't do it.'

Michael placed his big hand over her smaller soft one and squeezed it.

'I can't let this go, Maws.' His voice was quiet now. Final. Maura looked at him wildly, trying to think of a solution to the problem.

'Mickey, please. I'll sort this out.' She forced conviction into her voice. 'I'll get rid of him to another country. He can go to Spain, look after our holdings there. I'll sort it out with him, I swear. He'll toe the line. He must know that you've tumbled him. I'll be responsible for him.'

'All right. All right.' Michael's voice was annoyed. 'You've got twenty-four hours to get rid of him. If he's still around after that, then he's dead. You can tell him that from me. Now I have got to go and square it all with Kelly. You can bet your life they all think it was me fingered O'Loughlin.'

He stood up abruptly and Maura was reminded just how big and dangerous he could be. He kissed her on the forehead and left the house. She sat for a few minutes letting all he had said sink in. Then, lighting another cigarette, she went to the phone and called Geoffrey. Her heart was so heavy, she felt physically sick at the turn of events. If Geoffrey refused to leave the country he was a dead man.

Michael drove to Le Buxom. Although they had offices all over London, the club would always be his favourite place. He had built an empire from these tiny offices and always felt safe here. He had never enjoyed working on the building projects, always feeling more at home with the seedier businesses. To all intents and purposes they were legitimate, valid excuses for spending money. They paid tax, they paid VAT. But deep in Michael's heart it would always be the clubs, the betting offices and the robberies that were his forte. Unlike Maura, he had never lost touch with his poverty-stricken roots. He only had to close his eyes to see once more the cockroaches, the bare floors, and his mother's ever-swollen belly.

Michael wanted money that would astound the senses, money that would be a never ending pit to draw from. He wanted to be like the educated villains he had met through Templeton. He wanted to wear his riches like a cloak, he wanted to be able to buy anyone and anything that he desired. And with the gold heist and the docklands' holdings he would be able to do that. He knew that they had pulled off one of the biggest scams in the history of English crime. That the police were no nearer solving the case of the stolen gold than they were to solving the murders of Jack the Ripper. He had been secretly pleased with himself. Now Geoffrey was going to ruin that.

He had an insight into himself that would have amazed and confused his sister. He knew in his heart that Geoffrey was his Achilles heel. If he ever got caught or called in for questioning, he knew that it would be because of Geoffrey. None of the other boys would ever dream of trying to implicate him or Maura. But Geoffrey would.

In 1980 Garry had been identified at the scene of a

robbery. He had appeared at the Old Bailey, accused of armed robbery. Michael had retained the best barrister in London, Douglas Denby QC. Garry had walked free, but Michael knew that if he could have been persuaded to chat to the police about his eldest brother, the boy would never even have had to go to court. Yet Michael had not been worried. He knew that even if Garry got fifteen years, he still would not open his mouth to anyone. Not so Geoffrey. Geoffrey reminded him of a snake, fooling its quarry into a false sense of security, before pouncing on it and destroying it. He had a viper in his camp and his sister could not see it. And the sad part was, Geoffrey wanted to destroy her more than he did Michael.

He parked his car. After carefully scanning the road for anything suspicious, he got out and went into the club. Gerry Jackson was there.

'Hello, Mickey!' Michael heard the pleasure in his friend's voice and was gratified. Gerry was wearing his toupee. On the night of the club bombing his hair had been burnt off and it had never grown back. During the day Gerry wore his hairpiece. He had also lost an ear, and part of his face and neck was still raised and mauve all these years later. Michael cared for Gerry as much as he did his younger brothers.

'All right, Gerry? Anyone been asking for me?' He kept his voice light.

Gerry shook his head.

'The Irish looks better. Is it a new one?' Gerry laughed at the reference to his wig. He was very good-natured despite his ferocious looks.

'Yeah. Cost me nearly two hundred quid. Real hair, see.' He took the toupee off his head and handed it to Michael who took it from him. He did not know what else to do.

'Yeah. It's lovely.' They both laughed together. For the first time in years Michael remembered them as children, playing together. Gerry's dad had been killed in the war and his mum had worked the Bayswater Road.

She had brought up her six children on the proceeds of the game and National Assistance. She lived out in Enfield now, a respectable old lady who doted on her grandchildren.

Michael had a terrible feeling of foreboding as he stood with Gerry. He threw the wig back to his friend and, smiling, went up to the offices.

It took him a while to get through to Kelly. When he finally did he was not surprised to find that he was treated with the utmost suspicion.

'Look, Kelly, I was set up. I take oath on that.'

Kelly's thick Northern Irish accent crackled over the wire. 'Pat O'Loughlin was a bad man to cross, Ryan. Once they ship him back to the Maze he'll be back in the driving seat. You're a dead man.'

Kelly's voice was matter-of-fact, as if he was discussing the weather.

Michael was having difficulty in controlling his temper. The famous temper that could instil fear into the most hardened of criminals.

'I told you, it was a set up. What more do you want from me? I've been associated with your bloody organisation for nearly thirty years, mate. I was giving contributions before you was even born.'

If he told them about Geoffrey they would never trust him again, and then his brother would be dead and his mother would be heartbroken.

Kelly broke into his racing thoughts.

'We think, Mr Ryan, that you have done a deal. An hour ago Sean Murphy and Liam McNamara were picked up at another of your so-called safe houses. You're a dead man, Ryan.'

The phone went dead.

Michael sat staring at it in amazement. Murphy and McNamara! He put the phone back in its cradle. A cold sweat had broken out on his forehead. He got up from his chair and went to the drinks cabinet in the corner of the room. He poured himself a large brandy and drank it straight back. Geoffrey had done him up like a kipper.

Well, he would wipe Geoffrey Ryan off the face of the earth. Sod Maura, and sod his bloody mother! He would get the word out that Geoffrey had grassed the Irishman up. That way, if the IRA got to him first, all well and good. If not, then Michael himself would blast the bastard through his guts. He could do without the Irish anyway. He phoned Maura's house. He had to let her know what was going on.

Templeton answered the phone.

'Willy?'

'Why, hello, Michael.' His voice was warm.

'Is Maws there?'

'No. She's gone to your mother's to see Geoffrey. Can I help? I said I would man the phones for her. I wanted to take her out to lunch, but you know your sister. Business first!' His tone was jocular and friendly.

Michael forced himself to laugh.

'If she comes back before I see her, will you give her a message for me? Tell her that I *must*, absolutely must, get rid of the employee we were discussing. Tell her that Kelly insisted. Got that?'

'Yes. Don't worry, I've written it down.'

'See you later then, Willy.'

''Bye, Mickey.'

So Maura had swallowed her pride and gone to their mother's house. Obviously that was where she'd tracked the little bastard down to. He must think he was safe there. The slag!

Michael pulled on his coat and left the club. It was now early afternoon and the traffic was thick. He finally drove into Lancaster Road, seething with anger. Geoffrey had tucked him up and Geoffrey would pay. He would try and get his brother to leave his mother's house, but if he wouldn't then he would drag the bastard out if need be. Fuck his mother! Fuck the lot of them! He wasn't going under for the toe rag. In his temper Michael did not notice the black Granada Scorpio that was parked opposite.

* * *

376

Maura had finally located Geoffrey at their mother's house. Garry had answered the telephone and she had told him not to say she had called. She had a feeling that if Geoffrey knew, he would try and get away. She had to see him before Michael did. She told Garry to keep him there until she arrived. She had parked her car in Bletchedon Street and walked around to her mother's house, in case Geoffrey had been scanning the road from the window. As she had walked up the familiar steps her heart had been hammering dangerously. She had not been to this house in over ten years. Not since the fight after Benny had been murdered. She shuddered. She did not want to see her mother and open all the old wounds, but she had to. She only hoped Geoffrey would realise that she was trying to help him.

She plucked up her courage and knocked on the door. She could hear the dull taps of her mother's shoes across the linoleum and guessed that she had come from the kitchen. The door opened and the two women came face to face for the first time in eleven years.

Maura was shocked at the sight before her. Her mother was nothing more than a fat little old lady. Her face was wrinkled up like a walnut and her hair, still in the scraped bun of old, was completely grey. Only the eyes were as she remembered them, alive with malice and triumph.

Maura realised her mother thought that she had come to beg some kind of forgiveness. Well, that was all right with her. She would play any kind of game she had to today. She knew, though, that seeing her mother meant nothing to her now.

'Hello, Mum.' She was amazed to find that her voice was normal.

Sarah's eyes swept her from head to foot. Maura was wearing a black trouser suit with a white cashmere jumper underneath. She could practically hear her mother counting up the cost in her head.

'What do you want?' Sarah's voice was flat. It was obvious to Maura that she was going to make it as hard as possible for her.

377

Maura walked into the house without being asked. She had to push past her mother, and was made aware of just how tiny she was.

'Is our Geoffrey here?'

As Maura spoke she walked through to the kitchen. Sarah followed her. Her mettle was up but she kept silent. There was something funny going on here. Geoffrey was like a scalded cat. Every time the phone rang or someone knocked, he nearly had a seizure. Well, she had a feeling that her daughter held the key to a mystery and for that reason, and that reason only, would stomach her presence in her house.

Maura entered the kitchen. Geoffrey and Garry were sitting at the kitchen table. Garry smiled at her, but Geoffrey looked as if he had been struck by a thunderbolt.

'Hello, Geoffrey.' She looked straight at him. The kitchen looked and felt familiar. It had not changed one iota in the last ten years.

'Can I speak to you? Alone, please.'

She saw Geoffrey's eyes go to his mother who was standing behind her. Maura nodded at Garry. Getting up from the table, he went to where his mother was standing.

'Come on, Muvver. Let's leave the lovebirds alone for a minute.'

Sarah pushed at him roughly. 'Get your bleeding hands off me! What's going on here?'

Maura turned to her mother and, grabbing her shoulders, bundled her none too gently out of the kitchen door.

'Let go of me, you bloody lanky bitch!'

'Garry, take her into the front room. Her statues are probably lonely.' Maura's voice was sarcastic. She looked closely into her mother's face. 'Keep your nose out, Mum. It doesn't concern you.'

She shut the kitchen door firmly, blocking out her mother's raised voice. She could hear Garry trying to pacify her. Geoffrey was watching her warily. Maura could feel the fear emanating from him.

'Michael knows everything.'

378

Geoffrey dropped his gaze.

'Let's face it, Geoff, it wouldn't take long to sniff out something so putrid, would it? I've come to help you, though looking at you, I don't know why I bothered. You've got twenty-four hours to get out of the country.'

Geoffrey's head shot up. There was a peculiar light in his eyes, as scared as he was.

'I ain't going nowhere. You don't scare me.'

Maura laughed out loud. 'Oh, but I do. I scare you shitless, and so does Michael. And the mood I left him in, he'd scare the devil.'

As she spoke, she heard four loud bangs, then Geoffrey began to laugh hysterically.

Michael screeched to a halt outside his mother's house. Fiona Dalgleesh was walking her young son to the shops and was startled by the squealing of wheels. She grabbed her son's hand. Bloody lunatic drivers! She saw a large, good-looking man get out of the offending car. It was about fifteen feet away. Then, in the weak October sunshine, she saw a distinct gleam. She looked across the road to where a black car was parked and opened her eyes wide with shock. A man was sitting in the passenger seat of the car, and he had a gun! Without thinking she threw her son to the pavement and lay on top of him. A piercing cry escaped from her lips.

Michael got out of the car still seething with rage. He heard the girl scream and looked in her direction. He saw her throw herself on top of a little boy. It was the last thing he was to see. A moment later a bullet entered the side of his head and splattered his brains all over the pavement.

The girl saw him crumple and fall, a bewildered expression on his face. The man with the gun then got out of his car and shot the victim three more times. Even in her shock and fear, Fiona Dalgleesh knew that those shots were unnecessary. The big, good-looking man was already dead.

As the car drove away, the road became once more

quiet and residential. Only Michael's blood, running along the pavement in crimson rivulets, showed that anything was wrong.

When Maura and Garry heard the shots they both rushed from the house. Sarah followed them. Geoffrey stayed in the kitchen alone.

Suddenly the street was full of people, emerging from all the houses like ghouls. Maura ran down the steps to the pavement. She raised Michael's head and cradled it in her arms, too shocked even to cry.

Geoffrey, her mother, her brothers . . . everything was wiped from her mind. When the police and ambulance arrived they had had forcibly to pull Maura from her brother's body. Her white cashmere jumper was stained with blood and particles of brain and skull. Garry stood beside her, silent and shocked. Sarah had taken one look at her eldest son lying sprawled across her daughter's lap and walked back into her house. She felt nothing.

Maura and Garry were taken to hospital suffering from shock. Maura had to be sedated. The next morning she left the hospital with William Templeton. The newspapers were in attendance. All the nationals had pictures of Maura with Templeton's arms around her. She was aware, even in her grief, that he had burnt his boats for her and she was grateful to him. He took her to her house and kept the world away from her.

She refused to speak to anyone, not even Carla or Marge or her brothers. Roy took over the reins of the business and though nothing was ever said, all the brothers wondered what had happened with Geoffrey and why, as the eldest after Michael, he had not taken over the businesses himself.

Maura had three separate interviews with the police. She told each of them the same thing. She had no idea who had been behind her brother's murder.

But she did know and she concentrated all her energy into that fact. After two weeks of seclusion Maura felt ready to face the world again. She emerged from her grief, tougher and harder than ever before. She had hatred inside her now, a great big sour-smelling hatred. And she was going to use it to her advantage. Michael was dead, but the Ryans would go on. She owed him that much.

Chapter Twenty-seven

Maura walked into the club at nine-thirty, exactly fourteen days after Michael was murdered. Gerry Jackson went to her and put his hand on her shoulder gently.

'If you need me, Maura, just call.'

She nodded at him and walked up the stairs into the offices. The music in the club was loud and harsh. She could hear the chatter of the customers and the clink of glasses above the din.

Roy was obviously shocked to see her.

'Maws?'

'I had to get back into the world, mate. Thanks for taking over everything. I promise you won't lose by it.'

He got up from the desk, embarrassed to be caught sitting in what had been Michael's seat.

Maura waved him back. 'You don't have to move, Roy.'

He sat down again. He was shocked at the change in her. She looked old. The years had piled on her in the short time since Mickey's death. She also had a steely glint in her eyes that had not been there before. If he did not know better he would think it was Michael come back in female form.

'I've kept everything going here as best I can, like. I know that's what Mickey would have wanted.'

Maura could hear the sadness and loss in his voice. Going to where he sat, she slipped her arms around his neck.

'I miss him, Roy. It's like a physical pain at times. As if a crucial part of me is missing.'

'I know, Maws. I know.' He held her hands in his own, surprised at the gentleness in her. 'We'll find out who set him up, Maws. Don't you worry, girl.'

She sighed. She knew exactly who had set him up. She straightened up, running her hands through her hair.

'What's been happening here?'

'Oh, nothing for you to worry about, Maws.' Although she could not see Roy's face, she knew that something was up by the sound of his voice. She walked around to face him and sat opposite him on the chair by the desk.

'What's up?' Her voice was hard.

'Look, I'll tell you about it another time. You're in no fit state . . .'

'Cut the crap, Roy. I'm a big girl now, in case you haven't noticed. I also run this firm. I have done for nearly twenty years.' Her voice softened at the look on his face. 'You have no need to try and protect me, Roy. I can do that myself.'

'We've had aggro out on the streets. Every firm with dreams of the big time has been showing its face.'

Maura sighed heavily.

'I should have guessed that the tombrobbers would be out in force.'

'Look, Maws, it's nothing I can't handle.'

She picked up the pack of Benson and Hedges from the desk and lit one.

'I want to know what's been going on, and I want to know NOW!'

Roy just sat staring at her. Maura knew that he wanted to help her, that he wanted to do what Michael would have done. But he would never be Michael in a million years. *She* was the nearest thing to Michael Ryan. In fact, she felt as if he had entered her body and was looking out of her eyes, so strongly did she feel his presence at this moment.

'Look, Roy, I need to get back to normal. I know you all loved him, but me and Mickey . . . it was special.' Her voice was low and charged with emotion.

Roy felt choked. He looked into her ravaged face, so skilfully made up, and knew that all that she said was true. Maura and Michael had been closer than any two people he had ever known. He spoke and his words had the effect of a bomb blast on her, so great was her rage when she heard them.

'A black crew have been muscling in on the hot dogs. Yardies. They swooped on three prime sites the night Mickey died.'

Maura's voice when she finally spoke was dripping with malevolence.

'Yardies? YARDIES? I ain't trashed at the Scotland Yardies so a bunch of bloody coons won't give me any grief. I'll sort the buggers out myself. Get Gerry from downstairs and get on the phone to the other boys. We're going to have a sort out on the street. Starting with the bloody "macaroons". Now tell me *everything* that's been going on since Mickey died.'

Roy began to speak, glad in his heart that Maura had come to take over the reins. He had not done a very good job, he knew. He had wanted to but had no idea how everything was run. Maura, Mickey and Geoffrey had always been the thinkers of the family. The rest of the boys had been the heavies. He had been impressed with Maura's acumen in the past, now he was impressed by her dogged determination to sort out all the trouble that Michael's passing had created.

Barrington Dennison was thirty years old. He stood five foot ten and, as a body builder, his shoulders and arms were huge. His biceps measured over twenty-eight inches. Barrington Dennison was proud of his physique and proud to be black. His hair, which was grown into long, fat, spiralling dreadlocks, was tied in a pony tail with a piece of spearmint green leather. The leather was the same shade as his tracksuit.

He walked with a strutting cockiness away from his BMW car. In Brixton, where he was born, the letters stood for 'Black Man's Wheels'. His current girlfriend, an eighteen-year-old blonde, was sitting in the car, smoking a joint. She was waiting for Barrington to conclude his business.

Barrington was a Yardie. He told everyone who asked

that he was one. He loved it. Within hours of the news of
Michael Ryan's death hitting the streets, he had taken over
three sites that he had been after for a long time, believing,
as many people did, that with Michael's death the streets
were once more open territory. He also dealt in grass and
ecstasy. And lately crack.

He looked at his watch, a brand new Rolex. It was just on
eleven-fifteen and time for a pull. A 'pull' was the term
used for clearing the tills on the pitches. This was done
every few hours. That way, if the pitch was robbed,
whoever did it would not get too big a 'wallet'.

He was unaware as he walked towards the busy pitch that
he was being watched.

Maura called to him: 'Are you Barrington Dennison?'
Her voice was friendly and soft.

Barrington glanced in the direction of the voice and
saw a good-looking white woman standing by a Mercedes
Sports. He smiled at her and was pleased to see her smiling
back. 'Yo, Momma. You wantin' me, baby?'

He walked over to her, his strut even more emphasised
as he realised that all the people on the hot dog pitch were
watching him. A rich white bitch could only do his street
credibility good. He stood in front of her, pleased as punch
that he was in full view of the people on his pitch. He
watched her lick her lips.

He grinned at her, showing perfect white teeth.

'I have something for you, Barrington.' Her voice was
caressing.

She was opening her bag, a large leather shoulderbag.

'Do I know you? You sure look familiar.' He stopped
talking as he saw her take a length of lead piping from the
enormous white leather bag. He heard her laugh.

'I'm Maura Ryan, you big, fat, bastard.'

As his mind registered her words he was held from
behind. He could feel himself being dragged on to the dirty
pavement, and for a second wondered if he could still be
seen. Then he was being held by two large white men, and
suddenly he was frightened. It had all happened too fast for

his brain to react. They had got him exactly where they wanted him. He could have wept.

He saw Maura Ryan raise the piping over her head and bring it down with considerable force on his knees. The piping was twelve inches long and three inches thick. It shattered his kneecaps. He screamed. Then he felt the piping come down again and shrieked again. White hot pain was flashing behind his eyes, coming in sickening waves. He felt the arms that held him loosen their grip. Then Maura was kneeling beside him. She pulled his head up by its dreadlocks and stared into his face.

'Don't ever get ambitions again, prick. Do you hear me? Next time I'll leave you in the same state I left Danny Rubens in. Michael Ryan is dead, but I am alive and kicking and don't you ever forget that. You pass the message on to your Yardie friends.'

Barrington nodded through his agony.

Maura and the men stood up and he watched through a haze of pain as they approached the pitch. It was deserted. The two young black boys working it had run off. They had no intentions of getting involved with that type of violence. Maura and Roy secured it and left.

As Maura went to her Mercedes she passed Barrington Dennison again. She looked at his twisted legs and pain-ravaged face, and felt herself begin to buzz with excitement. She had handled that exactly as Michael would have done. He would be proud of her!

When they arrived at the other pitches, they were already deserted. Bad news travels fast on the streets.

Barrington's girlfriend was so stoned she did not even realise that anything out of the ordinary had happened until the ambulance arrived. She had been too busy listening to Bob Marley singing 'Redemption Song'.

Back at the club, Maura and the boys discussed the measures they would have to take to re-establish their superiority in London. Within a week it was done. Maura had proved herself a shrewd woman and slipped on Michael's mantle easily. When she was sure she was firmly

387

entrenched, she turned her attention to the Irish problem and her brother Geoffrey.

Kelly was waiting for Maura in a small bedsit in Kilburn. The owner of the house was a sympathiser. There were many of them in London.

Kelly heard a car drive into the deserted street and glanced at his watch. It was just after two-fifteen. This must be Maura Ryan. He got up from his seat and went to the window. Pulling back a grubby net curtain, he watched her as she locked up her car and walked into the house. The front door was already open. He could hear her soft steps on the stairs.

He carried on looking out of the window to make certain there was no one else about. He was still not sure exactly what kind of meet this was going to be. The death of Michael Ryan must have hit her badly; he knew himself how close they had been. For his own part, Kelly had always liked and respected Maura, and enjoyed doing business with her. In the IRA there was no discrimination; women were blooded along with the men. He had met women in the cause who were much, much harder and shrewder than many of the men. He knew women who would not think twice about blowing up a school bus or shooting a pregnant woman, something that most of the so-called hard men would baulk at. But above everything else he trusted Maura Ryan, and it was for that reason, and that reason only, that he had agreed to meet her tonight.

He turned from the window as she tapped lightly on the door of the room, and let her in.

'Hello, Kelly.' Her voice was neutral.

'Maura. Please take a seat.'

As always, he was courteous. It came naturally to him where women were concerned.

Maura sat on the tiny PVC sofa and took the glass of Bushmills that Kelly offered her. He sat opposite her and smiled. He was quick to notice in the light of the naked light bulb that she smiled with her mouth but not her eyes. She was obviously still grieving. As she opened her black bag to

388

get her cigarettes, Kelly felt a small twinge of uneasiness. Maura sensed it.

'Don't worry, Kelly, this isn't revenge time. I know exactly what happened and I want to explain it to you.'

He picked up a book of matches from the small coffee table between them and lit her cigarettte for her.

'Go ahead. I'm listening.'

Maura pulled on the cigarette and blew the smoke out through her nose.

Kelly grimaced. He could stomach many things from women, but smoking was not one of them.

Maura breathed in deeply. When she spoke her words were hesitant and sad.

'It wasn't Mickey who grassed up O'Loughlin and the others.'

'Well, who was it then?' His voice was brisk.

Maura took a gulp of the Bushmills, its peaty tang giving her courage.

'It was my brother Geoffrey.'

Kelly digested this bit of information.

'Mickey was good to you over the years.' Her voice was full of the pain of losing him.

'Listen, Maura.' Kelly's voice was gentle. 'There was one thing Michael could never understand. In London, the Ryans are big. You own the majority of the police force. You run the main clubs. Your businesses include gambling, drinking, sex, all the things that are big money spinners. You're also involved in the building and construction games. But, you see, to us and the likes of us, you're small fry really. We're an international organisation, known and feared all over the world. We're given money by Gadaffi, Baader Meinhof, the PLO. The list is endless. All we ever gave you was our trust. And that trust was broken.'

Maura was angry. 'For God's sake, Kelly, why do you think that I'm here tonight? I want to clear Michael's name. He'd been paying into your cause since 1960. He helped you over the years more than he had to. He hid people. Got arms, Semtex. He gathered information on Members of

Parliament and members of the armed forces. People whom you then blew up and killed or maimed.'

Kelly interrupted her.

'I'm not disputing all that. Michael was a good business asset over the years. Holy Jesus, we never wanted to harm him but it was the logical step to take after what happened.

'What exactly do you want here tonight? Tell me that, Maura. Michael's death is done, over with. I'm sorry we got the wrong man though that can soon be remedied. But I think that you came here tonight to ask for something. Not just to tell me that your brother Geoffrey is for the chop.'

'What I want is us all back on our old footing.'

Kelly laughed. Really laughed.

'Sure, you're a funny lass. Three of our best men are on their way to the Maze and you want us to forget all about it! Are you demented, woman?' He laughed again, wiping his eyes with the back of his hand.

Maura lit another cigarette from the butt of the previous one. She looked solemn and annoyed.

'I'm glad to think that you had such a high regard for Michael.' Her voice dripped sarcasm. 'That he was so indispensable to you. But you see, Kelly, Michael meant everything to me. Everything. His death was not a "logical step" in my eyes. It was a brutal killing that was unnecessary. If you had waited and let us inform you of the circumstances, it could have been avoided.'

Kelly was sorry for his laughter. In his first flush of joviality he had forgotten that he was talking about this woman's kin. In the IRA you had no allegiance to family or friends. Only to the cause.

'I'm sorry. Sorry to the heart for laughing. But you do understand what I was saying?' He looked into her sad white face and was sad himself. There were many women like her who had lost their loved ones to the cause. Husbands and sons who would never be coming home again, or were rotting in the bloody Maze. He tried again.

'You realise that Geoffrey is a dead man now, don't you?'

She nodded.

'Look, Maura, I'll tell you what I'll try to do, but I can't promise anything. I'll talk to a few people for you . . . explain the situation like . . . put them straight. The fact that you sacrificed Geoffrey should tell them that you're trying to re-establish your old footing. But that's all I can do. I can't personally guarantee anything. You must understand that.'

It was all she had expected. She had at least seen the back of Geoffrey. That was her main reason for coming here. She smiled at Kelly wistfully.

'Well, I for one won't hold a grudge. I remember when my brother Benny was murdered, Michael said it was an occupational hazard. He said it could have been any one of us, and he was right. It's the price we pay for the life we lead, I suppose.'

'It's the same with us, Maura. Sure, isn't that fecking Geoffrey the foolish one? Biting the hand that feeds him. Well, in a family the size of yours, there has to be one bad apple. It's the law of averages.'

Maura shrugged.

'I suppose so. Still, he won't be around much longer.'

Kelly smiled and poured them both out another drink.

'I can guarantee that. Now drink up. You look as if you need it.'

Chapter Twenty-eight

November 1986

Michael's body was being lowered into the ground. It was a freezing cold day. A fine rain had been falling all morning and overhead dark clouds were gathering for the storm that would erupt later in the afternoon. Maura was not crying. Her eyes scanned the crowd of people; over a hundred had turned out for Michael's funeral. She noticed that the hostesses were out in force. Some of them had stopped working over twenty years previously but stood now with their younger counterparts, in their smart coats and brightly made-up faces, looking genuinely sad. It pleased Maura to see them there. They remembered the strong, vibrant Michael of his youth.

Her eyes wandered to Geoffrey who was standing to the right of the grave. Maura could see he was crying, tears streaming down his face. He stood beside their mother, who was stony-faced and dry-eyed. Maura felt an urge to walk around the open grave and throw him in on top of the brother he had helped to murder. If it had not been for him, no one need be here today. Michael would be in his office as he always was, bright and early, no matter what time he had got to bed the night before. She only hoped that wherever Michael was he would see Geoffrey's death. She smiled to herself. It was to be the typical IRA assassination for informers. Kneecapped first and then a single shot to the back of the head. Ten days after the funeral, Kelly had said.

Geoffrey raised his gaze from his brother's coffin and locked eyes with his sister. He thought for one moment that she was smiling at him and smiled back at her tremulously. Then, when she dropped her eyes, he realised that the breach with Maura would never be healed. Geoffrey knew that he had opened up a can of worms that was going to be the finish of him. All his years of planning and watching and listening had been to no avail. When he had set the ball rolling for Michael's death he had regretted it almost immediately. He would give his own life now to have him back.

Maura stared into the gaping hole. Michael was down there in a wooden box and he would never be coming home. She hated Geoffrey with a vengeance now. If she had let Michael finish him when he had wanted to, maybe it could all have been avoided. If someone had told her a month ago that she would be the instigator of one of her own brothers' deaths, she would have protested vehemently. Now she could not wait for it to happen.

She saw that people were watching Geoffrey pityingly as he cried and that only made her anger more intense. She was disgusted. She turned her face away and buried it in William Templeton's coat. He held her tightly to him, murmuring into her hair.

'It's all right. Everything will be all right.'

Sarah Ryan was watching her daughter. She noticed that Carla was as usual close by her. Sarah herself had Geoffrey on the left of her and her grandson Benny on her right. She reached out her arm and placed it across her grandson's shoulders. He shrugged her off. At almost eleven years of age he thought that he was too old to be cuddled, thought that he was a man. He wished he had been allowed to stand with his father and his uncles. He had loved his Uncle Michael, and although he did not know it, was the double of him as a child. He had the same features, expressions, everything. He also had the same quirk to his nature that Michael had had. Sarah and Janine both doted on him and did not realise that he was turning into a greater misogynist by the day.

Sarah concentrated on her only daughter. She wished that she was burying *her* today. As bad as Michael had been she had preferred him to her daughter. In Sarah's mind men were a violent breed. It was a fact of life. While women should be strong but never violent.

She'd watched women brawling in the street – 'old shawlies' as the olden day Irish women had been called. Her own mother had been known as the most argumentative woman in Shepherd's Bush. But Sarah could never condone her daughter's way of life. She could not see what should have been staring her in the face: that Michael and Maura were as one, twins born years apart. She could not see that her daughter had loved her brother wholly and desperately. She could not see that Maura had been slowly dying inside since she was sixteen and had experienced the pain of rejection by Terry Petherick and the agony of having her baby scraped from her body. That all the pain and hurt had had to come out at some time. In some way Sarah herself had pushed the memory of the abortion into the back of her mind. If she ever did think about it she soothed her own guilt by telling herself that a child from her daughter's body should never have been allowed to walk the earth.

Terry Petherick and two other policemen were sitting in an unmarked car by the funeral cortège, jotting down the names and car numbers of everyone at the funeral that they recognised or were unsure of. From another car a police photographer was taking photos. In spite of everything, all the policemen were impressed by the number of influential people who had turned up to pay their last respects. It showed them also that Michael Ryan had had a lot of pull to get such a turn out.

The Shakespeare Set, also known as the Dear and Dahling Brigade, were all there: so-called respectable actors and actresses who lived on the fringes of the London gangster scene. There was the usual smattering of over the hill models, hoping to get their faces into the nationals once more and then sell their 'my nights of love with gangland murderer' story to the *News of the World*. Even though Michael Ryan was the best-known shirtlifter in the South East! Even after his death the sycophants and hangers-on were still after a little bit of reflected glory.

Terry Petherick smiled to himself. He had noticed a few back-benchers looking solemn and nervous. I wonder how much they owe? he thought to himself, and carried on scanning the mourners. A good few boxers and sports promoters were there along with some big name gangsters from Liverpool and Birmingham. They had travelled down to show their faces and offer their condolences, and also to see how the land lay. Whether there would be an opening for them now. See if the Ryan family was as strong as before. Terry counted three QCs and two judges, one of whom had been drummed out of his profession because of a penchant for rent boys and child pornography. Quite a little cache, he mused. There were the usual blaggers, mainly small-time, in catalogue suits and nervous twitches, who would relive Michael's funeral for years as the highlight of their criminal career. Give them a bit of pull if they ever got banged up again.

Then Terry saw that the funeral was now over and people were making their way to their cars. That's when he saw Maura. He felt the familiar tightening in his guts that she caused whenever he laid eyes on her. She was as lovely as ever and he relived in his mind the last night they had spent together. He was still unmarried, and it was because of this tall, stately, and utterly unscrupulous woman. He wound down the window of the car and the damp cold whipped at his face. He knew that she had seen him.

Maura was walking towards her funeral car when she saw the face of the man she had alternately loved and hated watching her. William had his arm round her waist and felt her body stiffen. He held her tighter but she pulled away from him and walked to Terry's car.

'Bloody hell! They won't do nothing to us, will they?'

Terry could have laughed at the fear in the young PC's voice, but was too busy watching Maura approach him. She spoke and her husky voice sent his pulses racing.

'Hello, Terry. It's been a long time.'

'Hello, Maura. Too long.' They stared at each other as if devouring one another with their eyes. The policemen and William Templeton were well aware of the spark that was flaring between them.

'I'm sorry about your brother's death.'

As Terry spoke, Garry and Leslie came over to the car, accompanied by a drunken Lee. They were all incensed at the police and press being there. Outside the graveyard was a film crew who were recording all the famous people who had turned up. Michael dead was as newsworthy as he had been alive.

Garry leaned in at Terry's open window.

'Why don't you fuck off? Mickey's dead and you lot still won't leave him alone.'

Leslie and Lee stood aggressively behind him. The atmosphere was charged with malice.

'Leave it, Garry!' Maura's voice was clipped and as hard as steel.

He faced her angrily.

'They're plainclothes filth, Maws.'

'Just shut it. I won't have any aggravation today. Now get moving. People are beginning to stare at us.'

Her voice dripped ice and Garry, Leslie and Lee were nonplussed for a moment. Lee, who was well away, did not grasp the warning in her voice. He lurched towards the car, belching loudly.

'You wankers!'

Maura grabbed his arm. Her hand was like a steel band. She spoke through gritted teeth.

'Garry, you'd better take him away from me before I get really annoyed.' She shoved Lee towards Garry and Leslie. 'I'll deal with you lot later. Now, take him and get out of my sight.'

The two men took Lee away from the car hurriedly. Maura was watching the people around her. She knew that the confrontation had not gone unnoticed. She nodded her head to Terry and walked to her own car. She was fuming inside at Lee and Garry but her own brain was telling her that she had been a fool to stop and talk to

Terry in the first place. But she could not help herself. Seeing him sitting there had brought it all back, the longing and the wanting that she had suppressed for nearly all her adult life.

Sarah had witnessed Maura's talk with the police and had taken a long hard look at Terry Petherick.

He sat in the car watching Maura walk away from him. The other two policemen were terrified.

'I thought we was all gonners there, sir.'

Terry dragged his eyes from Maura's retreating back and looked at the younger man.

'No. You were quite safe, son. Even the Ryans wouldn't murder in broad daylight.'

His friend, DS Cranmer, walked over from the other police car. Opening the back door of Terry's Sierra, he got inside. 'I see your old bird stopped for a chat then?'

Terry laughed. 'Get stuffed, Cranmer.'

As Cranmer chatted on Terry was wondering if he would ever live it down. It was the first thing any new officer was told when he came to Vine Street. And the funny thing was, nearly all of them were impressed by it. He shook his head at the double standards in his world.

Maura reached her waiting car amid condolences and offers of help for the future. She noticed that William had disappeared somewhere in the crowd. When she finally stepped into her car Roy was waiting inside for her as she had asked him. She settled herself and tapped on the glass screen that separated them from the driver.

He spoke to her over a microphone.

'Yes, madam.'

'Could you please take me to the Bramley Arms? We will not be going back to the house just yet.'

The driver nodded and started up the limousine, leaving St Mary's RC cemetery behind. When they arrived at the Bramley Arms a few minutes later they got out of the car and went straight into the back bar.

On the table was a bottle of Remy Martin and two

glasses. Maura slipped off her black coat and gloves. Sitting at the table, she poured out two stiff drinks.

Roy sat beside her. He accepted the proffered drink and waited for her to speak.

Maura gulped at the brandy. Getting out her ever-present cigarettes she lit one, drawing the smoke deep into her lungs. Roy noticed that her hands were trembling.

'Did you notice Anthony's and Benny's graves? They look tatty. Remind me to get on to the cemetery officials.'

Roy nodded at her. He could see that she was wound up to fever pitch.

Maura looked into Roy's open face. She realised how like Michael he looked. How all the boys looked like Michael. She felt an urge to cry. Really cry. She gulped at her drink again. Seeing Terry had re-opened old wounds.

'I wanted to talk to you, Roy, as the next in line in age.'

He looked shocked. 'What about our Geoff?'

Maura took a deep breath and slowly and precisely told Roy everything, glad of something to take her mind off Terry Petherick. Glad to be able to share her problem with someone . . . to be planning ahead. When she finished telling him he was white-faced and tight-lipped.

'He tucked Mickey up? That's what you're telling me, ain't it?'

Maura nodded.

'I'll kill him, Maws! I'll kill the bastard!' He raised himself out of his seat as if he was going to do it immediately. Maura grabbed his arm.

'Don't worry. As I told you just now Kelly's going to sort it out. He owes Michael that much.'

Roy sat back in his seat and wiped his hand over his face. 'I knew that something wasn't right, Maws, but I could never find out what it was. To think that Geoffrey's been waiting and planning this for years. The dirty sod!'

'Well, the only people who know about it, Roy, are you and me. And it's got to stay that way. Especially now with Mickey dying. We're going to be in the frontline.'

Roy nodded slowly.

'Why did you never tell me this before?'

Maura sighed heavily. 'When Mickey was alive we thought we had it all under control. Geoff was working for us. The friction that had occurred over the years seemed to have died down. Oh, there's lots of reasons. I never wanted Geoffrey dead. Never. Not until Michael was murdered. Christ, I even tried to save him!' Her voice broke.

Roy poured out another stiff brandy and put the glass into her hands. She took a large swallow to steady her nerves.

'So what's going to happen with the businesses now?'

'Firstly I'm going to hand over the docklands to Willy and the accountants. Willy's a partner and he's trustworthy. Then I'm going to extend all our other operations. I'm going to try and get rid of the gold bullion as well. Michael and I had a contact in the Channel Islands. He can offload the majority of it. But I'll need a number two, Roy, and that's why I am asking you. What do you say?'

'You know the answer to that, Maws.' He took her hand gently in his. 'I'll do whatever you say. I know you're the brainy one. Janine's always calling me a thicko.' He grinned.

Maura was annoyed.

'Listen, Roy, you might not have a degree but you're cute enough. Janine should watch her trap. She's got too bloody much of it.'

'Don't worry, Maws. She don't get it all her own way. She just thinks she does.' He raised his thick black eyebrows and smiled. Maura found herself smiling with him.

Roy picked up his glass. 'Well then, girl. Here's to us!'

'To the Ryans!'

They both drank deeply, then Maura stood up unsteadily. 'We'd better get to the wake. Good grief, I'm pissed!'

'On a day like today, Maws, it's the only way to be.'

They laughed softly together. Except Maura's laughter was tinged with hysteria.

* * *

Back at Michael's flat the atmosphere was tense. Michael's boyfriend Richard was red-eyed and nervous. He had taken the death badly. About forty people had been invited back to the flat, mostly family and close friends. When Maura and Roy arrived, the first person she saw was Gerry Jackson. She went to him, the brandy making her more open than she usually was.

'You'll miss him more than anyone, Gerry. You went back a long time.'

He nodded sadly.

'Yeah, Maws. I will. You know that me mum's here? She always liked Mickey. Say hello to her for me. It would mean a lot to her.'

'I will, Gerry. She's a good woman.'

'I remember once when we was all small . . . you weren't even born then . . . me and Mickey was only about twelve. Just after the war. Well, me mum was on the "bash" then, down the Bayswater Road. I'm not ashamed of it. She fed and clothed the lot of us from her earnings. Anyway, me and Mickey was out playing and this gang of older boys came into Kensington Gardens and started taunting me about me mum. They were about sixteen and I was scared, Maws. Bloody terrified! And then Mickey started to punch the biggest one. He went garrity. And the other boys, they were frightened, see. Because even then Michael had something about him that scared people.'

His voice was low and charged with emotion. 'Did you know that he sent my old mum a ton every Christmas? Never forgot her once. A nice card and a hundred quid. I loved that man, Maura. Loved the bones of him. Whatever people might say about him.'

Maura was touched by his devotion. 'He loved you, Gerry. I know he did.'

Gerry brought out a large white handkerchief and blew his nose. His scarred face and missing ear were more noticeable than usual.

'He loved *you*, Maws. Loved you to death.'

She felt the large ball of tears in her throat and hurriedly excused herself. She made her way to the kitchen and got herself a drink. The kitchen worktops were piled with alcohol of every kind. Michael's boyfriend followed her in there. Looking at his white face, Maura felt sorry for him. She had never liked Richard, had never liked any of Michael's boyfriends, but seeing the grief on the man's face, she was sorry for him.

'I'll miss him, Maura. I know that people frowned on us but we loved each other in our own way.' She could see the tears shining in his eyes and suddenly wanted to escape from the flat. Run away somewhere where Michael was unknown. She fought down the feeling of panic. She was drunk, that's what was wrong with her. From the lounge she heard her father's voice starting to sing.

She patted Richard's shoulder and walked back into the lounge, holding on to her glass of brandy tightly. Her father was singing an old Irish ballad and it sounded funny with his cockney accent. She leaned against the wall and listened to the words of 'The Wild Colonial Boy'.

Maura studied her father's shrunken form. Thanks to her mother's dominance, she had hardly seen him over the years, and, looking at him as he sang, she was suddenly lonely for him. For his cuddles and his kind words. Everyone in the packed room, full of cigarette smoke and perfume, stood silently while he sang an ode to his dead boys.

Maura, along with many people in that room, blinked away tears. She decided that Michael would have approved of his father singing. Would have enjoyed it, had he been here. She sipped at her drink.

When Benjamin finished singing everyone called for another and Maura's voice was the loudest. Drinking his beer and clearing his throat, Benjamin began singing once more.

Down in the valley, the valley so blue,
Hang your head over . . .

Maura listened to the sad words and felt the grief inside her gradually ebbing away.

> Send it by letter, send it by mail,
> Send it by care of the Birmingham jail . . .

She knew the songs back to front. They were songs that had been sung at countless funerals over the years. Then her Auntie Nellie, an old lady now, began to sing a song that had all the older people joining in. It was an old Irish rebel song and it made Maura feel sick.

The people they were singing about had murdered the man they had all come to bury, if only they knew it.

> Oh, I am a merry ploughboy,
> And I plough the fields by day,
> But I'm leaving home tomorrow morn
> To join the IRA.

Maura looked at Geoffrey, standing by their mother, and knew by his face that he was thinking the same thing as herself. Well, the same people would be getting rid of him soon and she thanked God for it.

She swallowed back the rest of the brandy, then made a decision. She was going to get Willy Templeton and she was going to take him to her house. Then she was going to have mad and passionate sex. It was the only way, to her mind, to end a day like today.

She lurched away from the wall and went to find him.

Chapter Twenty-nine

Maura had been teaching Roy the ropes slowly over the last few months, until now, in January, he was finally getting an understanding of all the different aspects of the businesses. She had handed the docklands over to William Templeton. All she had to do there now was turn up for monthly meetings. She had found herself concentrating more and more on the family businesses as time went on – the clubs, betting shops, and the newer borderline businesses, such as the Mortgage and Investment Corporation that Michael had set up in 1984. Today she was trying to explain all this to Roy, as she wanted him to come in and take a large amount of the donkey work from her.

'The rub is, Roy, we give mortgages through our own lending company. Now the company itself has no actual investors, so we sell our clients to other companies, such as the Bank of Kuwait, etcetera. It's pretty simple really. That way we make a quick profit, and if the client gets into difficulties with their payments, then *they* can foreclose. That way *we* never have to take anyone to court. It's all out of our hands.'

'Sounds simple enough.' Roy's voice was worried and Maura guessed that he had not really grasped what she was saying. 'It is. That's the beauty of it. We advertise in the local papers, offering everything from small personal loans to remortgages. You'd be surprised at the number of people out there who want to "unlock their capital", as the advertisers put it. We offer from five to a hundred grand, secured against their properties. Even bought council houses. Literally anything. Our main aim, though, is to get the first-time buyers. We're already renting office space with a series of estate agents. That way, when people see the property they want, we're there waiting for the poor buggers. It's a doddle, Roy. You'll soon pick it up, mate.'

Roy frowned as he listened to her speak.

'And this is legal, Maws?'

His voice was sceptical and she laughed. 'Yeah, it's legal, all right. Hard as that is to believe.'

'What if they can't afford the place they want?'

'That's easily remedied. You can borrow three times your earnings, so if a youngster comes in and he earns, say, twelve grand a year, for argument's sake, then the borrower will tell him to bring in some "moody" pay slips, say one for a week when he did a load of overtime, so it looks like he earns sixteen grand a year. So instead of giving him a mortgage for thirty-six grand he gets one for forty-eight grand. I know it sounds bent, but believe me, Roy, banks and building societies do it all the time.'

'I see.'

Maura lit a cigarette and continued. 'Now about the council estates. I've extended the areas for the tally men. And that's another misnomer. The way that the law works, you can lend people money providing they buy goods from you. You can't under any circumstances offer them money straight off. What the tally men do is, they knock on someone's door and then offer them a continental quilt set at, say, two quid a week. The quilt set costs a score so you know that you have five weeks to get them to borrow off you.

'After a few weeks, the tally man then offers them a loan of maybe fifty quid, to be paid back at a fiver a week. The person takes up the offer and they get the money on the spot. They then pay back eighty quid. A clear profit of thirty quid. I know it doesn't sound much like that, but when you consider we make about three thousand loans a week it soon mounts up. Then they're offered a ton. The tally man holds out the hundred pounds and nine times out of ten the temptation is too strong. They go for it.'

'But what if they can't afford to pay the money back, Maws?'

'Then we send the big boys round. Some of the larger council estates are into us for a small fortune. And before you ask, it's perfectly legal. Getting into debt is now socially acceptable. You want that TV or video, you get it on the never-never. Big stores offer credit, everyone offers credit, it's like a public service these days. Even the social security has jumped on the band wagon. They borrow money now as well!'

Roy grinned but his big moon face was bewildered by it all. 'Can I take these files home and study them?'

'Of course you can. The sooner you learn the better.'

He picked up the files and put them into his briefcase.

'The bloke from Jersey is just about ready to shift the gold.'

'Don't you think that it's a bit quick, Maws? Michael was looking at leaving it for five or six years.'

'Well, Michael ain't here now, is he? I make the decisions and I want shot of it. The bloke's popping over at the weekend. I want you at the meet with me, OK?'

'Sure, Maws. Whatever you say.'

She went to the coffee percolator and replenished their cups. Passing one to Roy, she smiled at him sadly.

'Have you seen anything of Mother?'

Roy sipped the lukewarm liquid and shrugged.

'She was pretty cut up about Geoffrey.'

'I guessed as much.'

'Why didn't you go to the funeral, Maws?'

'Because I'm not a hypocrite, that's why. I would have spat on his grave.'

'Have the old Bill been in touch?'

Maura shook her head vigorously, sending her hair rioting around her face.

'Not so much as a hello, kiss me arse or anything. And that's just how I like it!'

'But don't you think that's strange?'

'Not really. They know that we do business with the Irish. They probably think he double crossed them or something. To be honest, I don't give a damn. If they had anything they'd be battering the door down, but I'm too wily for the old Bill. I have more plants in the police stations in London than there are in the Royal Botanical Gardens! If they walked in here now they'd find nothing. Nothing that they could nick me for. Me and Mickey only ever made one mistake and that was Geoffrey. Only you and I know the score now. Without one of us talking they ain't got nothing. So relax.'

'Well, you ain't got any worries where I'm concerned.'

'I know that, Bruv. That's why I'm trusting you with all this.'

Roy smiled at her, pleased to be so well thought of.

'Right then, Roy.' Maura checked her watch. 'I've got a meet with a firm of "blaggers" from Liverpool. I'd better get on me way. It's ten-thirty now. If I don't leave soon I'll catch the lunchtime traffic.'

Roy stood up and stretched. 'Okey doke. Sure you don't want me to come with you?'

'No, thanks. I've been dealing with this little firm for about eight years now. They're kosher. See you later, mate.'

Roy left the house and Maura lit herself another cigarette. Roy was working out all right. He couldn't express himself very well, but he was shrewd enough. He was getting the hang of everything. She had given Leslie the betting shops for a while. He was doing a good job. Garry and Lee were finally getting their act together. They had got a bit lairy after Michael's funeral but she had nipped that in the bud. All in all, considering what had happened, things were going quite well.

She finished her cigarette and got ready for the meet with Tommy Rifkind. It would be the first with him since Michael's death. He had come to the funeral to pay his respects, but now Maura had to deal with him alone. For a few seconds she wondered if it was all worth it. But as usual she pushed the thought away. The least she could do was carry on, for Michael's sake. He had built this little empire up from nothing, from being a bookie's runner at barely ten to a breaker in his teens. She owed her brother this. As she owed him everything. And if he was watching over her, as she sometimes fancied that he was, she hoped that he was pleased with how she was carrying on without him.

When Maura got to the club in Dean Street, Tommy Rifkind was already inside waiting for her. She showed him up to her office immediately. Like herself he was a busy person. He had his number two with him, Joss Campion, a six feet six inch rugby player with the ugliest face Maura had ever seen. Tommy, on the other hand, was five foot eight with a slim, lithe build. He also had the darkest brown eyes that Maura had ever seen on a light skinned man. Michael had always said that he had a touch of the tarbrush in him. Inside the office the men sat down and Maura smiled at them.

'Sorry to keep you. Get yourselves comfortable and I'll organise some coffee.'

A little while later they were all drinking hot coffee laced with brandy, Tommy's favourite. Joss Campion had poured his into his saucer and after blowing on the hot liquid loudly was now slurping it from the saucer. He was completely unaware of all the noise he was making. Maura had to bite her lip as Tommy rolled his eyes at her.

'Joss, would you rather I put the saucer on the floor for you?'

Joss hung his enormous head like a child.

'Sorry.'

'I apologise, Maura. Joss's mother never quite managed to get him completely house trained, you see.'

She laughed. 'That's all right. My brother Benny was much the same.'

'I'm glad you understand. My wife won't have him in the house.' Tommy smiled. 'Well, Maura, down to business. I have a little proposition to put to you.' She nodded. 'I've acquired some information on a bank in South London. The pull from it will be around two hundred thousand.

As usual we'll give you twenty per cent, on the usual terms.'

Maura licked her lips as she thought.

'How many cars would you want?'

'Two. One a high-powered vehicle, the other a non-descript Volvo estate. You know the type of thing, a family car.'

Maura nodded. 'OK. I'll put the word out on the street. I can supply "shooters" if you need them.' Tommy shook his head. 'In that case, all I'll need is the times and the date. And I do ask that you keep the violence to a minimum. It's not just you, Tommy. I tell all "blaggers" the same thing.'

He smiled.

'This will be as sweet as a nut, as you cockneys say. You'll be given the information seven days before the off.'

'Great. That was short and sweet!'

'I try to please. By the way, I'm so sorry about Geoffrey, Maura. So soon after Michael.' He opened his arms in a gesture of helplessness.

'Yeah, well. These things happen. I'm in full control now and nothing has changed really. I'll run the streets as they've always been run. I won't take any nonsense.'

Tommy was quite aware of the underlying threat and nodded as if he was answering a question.

'I respect that, Maura, and you have nothing to worry about from me and mine.'

She laughed heartily, but when she spoke, her voice was icy cold.

'I know.'

Tommy felt a prickle of fear on the back of his neck. In Liverpool he was the Daddy. What he said invariably went. He prided himself on not being frightened of any man, yet this tall, beautiful and intelligent woman sitting opposite scared the life out of him.

He had never wondered, like many people, why Maura was not married. There were rumours that she was a lesbian, but he knew different. It was simply that the man

410

who would take her on, her and all that she entailed, had not been born yet.

He cleared his throat.

'Did you receive the wreaths I sent?'

'Yes. Michael would have appreciated it. He always liked you, Tommy.'

'I expect you miss him.'

'Oh, yeah, I miss him.' She stood up abruptly to let him know that the meeting was over. She held out her hand and he shook it gently.

'I'll be in touch then.'

'OK.'

Joss smiled at Maura as he left and she forced herself to smile back. When they had left the office she lit herself a cigarette and, opening the drawer in her desk, took out a photo of Michael and herself. They had been having a drink in the club downstairs and Leslie had snapped them laughing together. It turned out to be a beautiful photograph and she had had it enlarged. She sat staring at Michael's handsome face. Oh, she missed him all right. Desperately.

Sarah Ryan sat at her kitchen table sipping a cup of steaming hot tea. In front of her, spread out on the table, were the papers from a file she had found in Geoffrey's old bedroom. He must have hidden them there at some point before he died. She knew that she had been meant to find them. Written in them, in Geoffrey's large bold script, was all the information he had gathered about Michael and Maura over the years. As Sarah read them a seething rage gathered inside her. Now she knew why Geoffrey was dead. Four sons she had buried, Anthony when he was no more than a baby. What was she to do with the information in front of her? She could take it to the police now and get it over with, but it incriminated all her sons, both living and dead. She had heard through the grapevine that Roy was now Maura's number two, whatever that meant. Janine had told her all about it a few days ago. She sighed. If she did take this little

411

lot to the police, the whole family would be put behind bars.

She picked up the papers and took them upstairs to her bedroom. She hid them in her wardrobe. She would leave it for a while until she had thought it all through.

She looked out of her bedroom window and down on to the street. She saw Margaret walking along with her mother. If only Maura had turned out like her, Sarah would be a happy woman. If only she had not met up with that bloody policeman, that Terry Petherick. If she had got herself pregnant by anyone else, it would all have blown over. Then a thought struck her. That's who she could take the papers to if the day ever came when she decided to make them known to someone. She smiled to herself nastily. That would keep it in the family, so to speak. If she was going to expose her daughter, then that's who she would expose her to!

She clasped her hands together in a gesture of prayer and whispered: 'Oh, Jesus in Heaven, in the Kingdom of goodness and light, help me to make the right decision.'

There was one thing that Sarah was sure of: Maura was capable of anything, even capable of hurting her own mother if she had to . . .

Janine was sitting drinking coffee with Roy. The years had not been kind to her. She looked much older than forty-eight and her face held a permanent frown. Benny Anthony burst into the kitchen.

'Hello, Dad!' He was surprised to find his father at home and it showed in his voice.

'Hello, son.' Roy's voice was warm. 'No school then?'

'Nah. There's a teachers' strike on.'

Janine butted in to their conversation.

'Get upstairs and do some of your homework. Your dad's busy.'

Benny's face dropped.

'Oh, Mum!' He was whining. 'I hardly ever see me dad.'

Janine's voice rose in a screech. 'You do what I tell you!'

Roy cut her off. 'For crying out loud, Janine! Keep your hair on.'

She leapt from her seat. 'Oh, that's right! Shout at me in front of Benny. Go on, Roy. Turn him into an animal like you and that stinking sister of yours.'

He sighed. 'You're beginning to sound like a broken record. Do you know that? The same old shit is dug up and pulled out, day after day.'

Janine was standing in front of him. Her face was a mask of hatred.

'You won't get your claws into him.' She pointed to where Benny was standing watching the fight between his parents. 'Oh, no. Not you or that whore of a sister of yours. She's already turned my Carla against me. I'll see you both dead first!' She ended on another screech.

'Calm yourself down, you dozy bitch. You're frightening the boy.'

Janine began to laugh.

'Me! Me frighten him? That's a laugh. His father's working for the biggest whoremonger and murderess in London and you accuse *me* of frightening the boy! Are you sleeping with her, Roy? I heard that Mickey was.'

He got up from his seat and slapped her across the kitchen. She fell to the floor, a large red mark already appearing on her face. She put her hand to her cheek silently, afraid now of a Roy she did not know.

'You stinking bitch! That's the last time you badmouth me or my family. Do you hear me? How the hell have I stood you all these years, with your miserable face and your slutty ways? Well, you've ballsed yourself right up now because I'm going. I'm gonna leave you to pickle in your own juices, Janine, and I'm taking the boy with me.

'As for our Carla . . . you dumped her, darling. You dumped her on me mother. So where you got your information from I don't know. And Carla left my mother's because my mother is like you. She wants to own people and Carla won't be owned. Neither will I from now on.'

Janine slowly pulled herself up from the floor.

'You'll take my son nowhere, Roy. I mean it. I'll go to the police . . . I swear it, Roy. I'll do for you.'

He stared at her, disgusted.

'You would and all, wouldn't you?' His voice was quiet.

'Yes, I would. You'll never turn my son into a Ryan. Not in a million years. I'd see you dead first.'

Roy picked up his briefcase and walked to his son. 'Don't worry. I'll be back to see you in a few days.'

Benny was crying and threw himself at his father. 'Oh, please don't go, Dad! Don't leave me here with Mum and Nanny Ryan. I hate them . . . I hate them!'

Roy pulled the boy close and looked at his wife. 'See what you've caused, you bitch. SEE WHAT YOU'VE CAUSED!'

Janine was staring at her son as if he had grown another head. Then, forcing herself to move, she went to him and tried to pull him from his father's arms.

'No, Dad. Please! Don't leave me here with her. I want to go with you. Please, Dad. Please don't leave me here.'

As Janine tried to pull her son away from his father, Roy turned and punched her as hard as he could in the face.

'Get your bloody hands off him!' Roy was shouting again.

Janine had been knocked backwards by the force of the blow, grabbing the edge of the kitchen table to save herself from falling. Her nose was bleeding profusely and she could feel her eye beginning to swell.

'Son.' Roy shook the hysterical boy. 'I promise you that I'm not going to go anywhere. I'm gonna stay.'

Janine opened her mouth and Roy pointed at her. 'One more word out of you and I'll commit a fucking murder. Yours! I'm staying here. This is MY house! Get it? I can't leave this boy here alone with you, he hates you as much as I do. You're nothing but a silly, vindictive bitch. You move to the spare room as from tonight, and if I ever get wind that you've tried to take this boy away from me, or this house, I'll bury you.

'I should have put a stop to your gallop years ago, with

414

your sluttish ways and your delusions of grandeur. I'm sick to death of you! So now you know.'

Roy held his son tightly. He should have put his foot down years ago. Instead he had let her have it all her own way, just to keep the peace. Well, no more.

'Come on, son. We'll go and get a McDonald's, shall we?'

Roy knew that Benny lived for McDonald's. At this moment he would have given his son anything to stop the racking sobs that were shaking his body.

He put his arm across his son's shoulders and walked from the room. Janine's face hardened. If it took her the rest of her life she would get even with him for this.

In the car, Roy let Benny's sobs subside before he spoke to him.

'I'm sorry that I hit your mum, son. I lost me temper.'

'I ha . . . hate her. I hate . . . her and Nanny Ryan.'

Roy sighed. What a state of affairs! That would teach him to break his usual habits. He had gone home for a quick coffee and five minutes' peace. Instead he had opened up a complete hornets' nest. His son hated not only his mother but his grandmother as well.

Benny sniffed and wiped his nose on his sleeve. 'I do, Dad. They never leave me alone. You're never there so you don't see them. They're both at me all the time.'

'Well, I can promise you this much, son. I'll be there for you in the future.'

Benny tried to smile. 'When I grow up, I want to be just like you, Dad.'

Roy bit his lip. Good job Janine couldn't hear him. He grinned.

'We'll see, son. We'll see.'

Chapter Thirty

'I'm telling you, Sarah, that's what happened.' Janine wiped her eyes with the back of her hand. 'He walked out with little Benny and they didn't come in till late.'

'And Roy actually raised his hand to you?'

'Yeah. Look at my face. Then when they finally came in he said that if I didn't toe the line he would take Benny and move into Maura's.' Janine was crying again.

Sarah put her arm around her shoulders. 'He didn't mean it, love.'

Janine pushed her away. 'Oh yes he did! I know he did.' She put her face into her hands. 'I have to get my Benny away from him otherwise Maura will get her claws into him and that will be that. Benny already thinks that the sun shines out of her . . .'

'Listen, Janine. For all Maura's faults, and God knows there are many, she wouldn't harm the child.'

'Not now maybe. But in the years to come, she will. She'll have him in the family business. And I couldn't stand that, Sarah. Not my Benny. My baby. He's eleven now, but what about when he's seventeen or eighteen? That's not far away, is it? First he'll go on the protection rackets. Then she'll have him in the betting shops. Then the hostess clubs. Where will it all end? I don't want my son shot like yours. Can't you see that? I don't want to be taken to the morgue to identify my son's remains.'

'Calm yourself down, Janine, that's not going to happen.'

'How do you know? You've already buried four sons!'

Sarah was silent as she digested the logic of Janine's argument. And she had to admit to herself that the girl was right. If little Benny went the same way as his father and uncles . . . And aunt. Oh, yes, she mustn't forget his aunt . . . that is what would happen.

The other boys were all living with girls. Only Leslie had married his. They would all have children, the Lord willing, and what would be the end result? They would eventually take over where their fathers left off.

'Listen, Janine. I promise you now that that will never happen to Benny. Not if I have anything to do with it.'

She made another of her famous pots of tea and finally, after calming Janine down, sent her back to her own house. Alone, Sarah thought about what Janine had said. It was odds on that Benny would eventually go into the so-called 'business'. All the grandchildren would, unless Maura and the others were stopped.

Her husband had had control of the boys when they were younger. He had taught them how to lie, cheat and steal. How to be 'hard men'. Now look where it had got them. Four of her sons had been brutally murdered. Not a day went by but she thought of them all. Even Michael, as a small boy. In her mind's eye she saw him when he was a child, when Benjamin used to take him to the bombed-out houses.

She looked around her kitchen. It was nice. Nice and clean and modern. A far cry from the days of cockroaches and squalor, when they had coats on the bed to keep them warm and only a thin stew to fill up their ever-empty bellies. Oh, they had come a long way since then, and in her own fashion she had been proud of Michael's determination to lift himself out of the slums. Until the killing had started. When Anthony had died, she had died a little bit herself. And Benny's death, her lovely, good-natured Benny who was always in trouble of some kind but always laughing . . . his death had broken her more than any of them. Then Michael, then Geoffrey. She could never allow that to happen to any of her children again. Or her grandchildren.

She got up from the table and glanced at the clock. It was just on one. She had plenty of time. Benjamin was drinking in the Kensington Park Hotel and would not be back for hours. She went to the phone in her hall and dialled the number she had taken down after Michael's funeral. She had got the number from Directory Inquiries, and now she knew why. She had taken it down for just such an occasion as this. It was the number of Vine Street Police Station.

'Good afternoon, Vine Street.' The clipped impersonal voice crackled in her ears.

'Can I speak to Detective Inspector Terry Petherick, please?' Sarah's voice was quavery and nervous.

'Who's calling?'

'I . . . I would rather not say. I . . . I have some information for him.'

'Hold the line, madam, and I'll see if he can take your call.'

The line went silent, and Sarah was beginning to wonder if she was doing the right thing when a deep male voice asked how he could help her.

Terry Petherick was putting on his sports jacket, ready to go to lunch. His friend and colleague Cranmer called to him as he was leaving the office.

'Hang on, Tel. There's a call for you. Some woman. She won't leave her name.'

Cranmer held the phone out. Terry walked across the crowded office, his heart beating fast. Surely it could not be Maura? The sensible part of his brain pooh-poohed such an idea but the illogical part hoped and prayed that it was her.

'Hello, Petherick here.'

'This is Sarah Ryan.' The second name was barely audible.

'Who?'

'Maura Ryan's mother.'

It was a Ryan but not the one he wanted.

'What can I do for you?'

'I want to see you, in private like. I have some information. You must keep this secret, though. Some of your men are on my daughter's payroll.'

419

Terry frowned.

'That's a very serious allegation.'

Sarah swallowed deeply and closed her eyes.

'I have certain papers in my possession that I think you would be interested in.'

'I see. So you want to meet me, is that it?'

'Yes, that's it. But you mustn't let anyone know what you're doing. Believe me when I tell you these papers could incriminate a lot of people. Do you know Regent's Park?'

'Of course.'

'I'll meet you there Saturday. In the Zoological Gardens, outside the cafeteria, at three.' Sarah replaced the receiver before he could answer. She was sweating profusely.

Terry stared at the telephone.

'Who was it?'

'Mind your own business, Cranmer!' He tried to make his voice jocular. 'I'm off for my lunch. See you later.'

As Terry left the police station and went to his car he was intrigued. What could Sarah Ryan, the well-known matriarch of the Ryan family, want with him? He knew that Geoffrey Ryan's murder was not even really under investigation. How they managed to get away with all they did was a mystery in itself . . . or was it? He had often thought that one or two of his colleagues were on the take. Not just because they had plenty of money, though that was one sign, but because the Ryans always seemed to be one step ahead of the police. He knew from experience that knowing someone was guilty was one thing, proving it a different thing altogether. He was sure that the Ryans had inside information. Well, he would know when he met Sarah Ryan . . .

If only he was meeting Maura! But she had come a long, long way since the last time they had met. She was into the Ryan businesses up to her pretty little neck. They were further apart now than ever before. The word on the street was that Maura had taken over from Mickey with all guns blazing.

Suddenly he was not very hungry. All he really wanted

was something that he had tasted many years ago. Like Adam and Eve, he preferred forbidden fruit.

Sarah put down the telephone and went back to her kitchen. Her heart was beating a tattoo inside her body. She had started the ball rolling, and she was glad. She would end her daughter's reign of terror. As she set about making her husband a meal, she thought again about what Janine had said and hardened her resolve. She would sacrifice her sons and her daughter if it saved at least one person from being destroyed. And if little Benny was to be saved, then she was the only one to do it.

It wasn't until much later that she remembered that the reading of Michael's will was to take place the next day, Friday.

Sarah sat in the solicitor's office with her husband. She sat well away from her only daughter and four remaining sons, as if they carried a fatal disease.

The solicitor, Derek Hattersley, was more nervous than the people in front of him. He kept having to blow his nose. This was a very difficult will. In his experience each member of a family regarded himself as the rightful chief beneficiary. He cleared his throat and began to speak.

'I must tell you all beforehand that the bulk of Mr Ryan's estate goes to just one person. He had, however, made some very substantial bequests to you all.' He smiled, trying to bring a note of lightness to the occasion. The only person to smile back was Benjamin Ryan and Derek Hattersley was aware that the man was slightly drunk.

'I'll start then.' He cleared his throat again noisily and began to read. '"I, Michael David Ryan, being of sound mind, leave everything I own, other than the few bequests I have detailed, to my sister, Maura Ryan."'

Derek Hattersley glanced around the assembled family and was surprised to find that not one person had changed expression. All were as blank-faced as they had been when they arrived. But he reminded himself that these

421

people were also criminals. They would not be the type to show their emotions anyway. He took a deep breath. If they wanted to fight about it, they could do it amongst themselves. He would not get involved.

'"I leave her all my properties and holdings. I also leave her two thirds of the monies in my bank account. The rest is to be shared between my mother and father and my brothers. I leave twenty thousand pounds each to my niece Carla Ryan and my nephew Benjamin Anthony Ryan. This is to be put in trust for Benjamin Anthony until he is twenty-one. Carla Ryan may have access to her money immediately. I also leave fifteen thousand pounds to my great-nephew Joseph Michael Spencer, also to be held in trust until he is twenty-one, and twenty thousand pounds to Gerry Jackson my closest friend."' Derek Hattersley blew his nose again and looked at the people in his office.

'Mr Ryan was adamant that the will be as short as possible and in his own words. He wrote the will himself and I drafted it for him. He also left two letters to be given out on this day. I have no knowledge whatsoever of their contents.' He relaxed, feeling he had extricated himself from any tricky situation that might arise. 'The letters are addressed to his mother and his sister.' He nodded at each woman as he spoke.

Still nobody said a word. Then Sarah asked in a shaky voice, 'Where's my letter?'

'I have it here, Mrs Ryan.' He passed the long white envelope to her, and Sarah stared at her dead son's small close-knit writing.

'I want my share of his money to go to the police widows' fund.'

Roy was stunned.

'You can't do that!'

'Oh yes I can, Roy Ryan. I want none of his blood money.' She picked up her handbag and, jerking her head at her husband to follow, left the office.

Derek Hattersley blew his nose again. It was now red and shiny. He passed Maura's letter to her and she thanked him politely.

422

'If you would be so kind as to sign some documents . . .'

'Certainly.' Maura smiled at him.

Twenty minutes later they all left the office.

'Well, that's that then, Maws. Mickey's last will and testament.'

'Yeah, Garry. It's the final parting, ain't it?'

Leslie put his arm around her. 'Cheer up, girl. Mickey wouldn't want you moping.'

Maura tried to laugh. Leslie trying to be tactful was not a very pretty sight.

'Let's all go and have a good drink!' This from Lee.

'Sounds good to me. What about you, Maws?'

'All right then, Roy. Let's go back to the club. There we can drink for free!'

Sarah and Benjamin were in the back of a black cab. Benjamin was annoyed.

'You've got too bloody much of it, Sarah. They're you'r own flesh and blood, yet thanks to you I hardly ever see them nowadays.'

She crossed her arms over her chest.

'You should think yourself lucky! They're nothing but bloody criminals. Mind you, that shouldn't worry you, should it?' Her voice was sarcastic. 'You're no better. I've been on this earth for seventy years, and I've spent over fifty of them years with you. Fifteen I was when you got me pregnant, Benjamin Ryan. Fifteen! And I stuck by you, no matter what you did. I stuck by you. And for what? What? To bring a crowd of bloody hooligans into the world, that's all.'

She looked out of the taxi window at the passing people, all living lives that did not touch hers.

Benjamin scowled, his leathery old face more wrinkled than usual.

'You make me laugh with all your "holy joeing". When you was fifteen, Sarah Ryan, you was what would be termed today "a right little raver"!'

'I was not!' Sarah's voice was incredulous.

The London cabbie was listening avidly to the old

423

people in the back of his taxi and had difficulty in keeping his face straight.

'Were so!' Benjamin's voice had the truculent note that grated on Sarah's nerves.

'Oi, mate!'

'Yeah.' The cabbie's voice was full of laughter.

'Do you know the Bramley Arms?'

'You hum it, son, and I'll play it.'

Benjamin scowled deeply at the cabbie. 'None of your sauce. Just drop me off there. You can dump her where you like.' He pointed at Sarah with his thumb, leaving her silent and tight-lipped all the way back to Notting Hill.

Once back inside her house Sarah made herself a pot of tea. Taking it into the lounge, as she now called her front room, she poured herself out a cup. Then sitting in her chair by the fire, she opened Michael's letter. Trust Benjamin not to be interested in his eldest son's last communication. All he was interested in was the money the boy left. She began to read.

Dear Mum,

I am writing this letter to you because I feel that there are many things that have to be said. I know that my life was not what you wanted for me, but it was the path that I chose and I do not regret one day. The only regret I have is that I loved you, Mum, and it hurt me when we fell out with one another. I understood how you felt about Benny, as I loved him as well. If you are reading this then I am with him and Anthony, and gone from your world. I want you to know that I will miss you more than anyone.

I want to ask you something, Mum. I want you to look out for our Maura. She needs you. She always has done. Since that trouble with the policeman, she has been hurting inside. I know this is true, Mum, because I have watched her. I have done all that I can for her. I now ask you to try and take her back into the arms that held her as a baby. Maura needs

424

her mother. Please tell Dad that I loved him very
much.

I will always love you, Mum, no matter what.

Michael

Sarah felt the scalding tears behind her eyelids and squeezed
her eyes tightly shut to block them out. The letter in front of
her was from the old Michael, the young tearaway, not the
hard, embittered, bloodthirsty man that he became. She saw
him as he had been the night that Maura was born, tall and
strong and with his whole life in front of him.

'Oh, God. Oh, son.' She put her hand to her mouth and
held it there tightly. Now the tears did break through, like
a damn bursting.

'My beautiful son. Oh, God help me, I loved him so
much.'

In the club Maura and her brothers were getting drunk.
Good and drunk. Maura could feel the first waves of
euphoria coursing through her veins, knowing that it would
soon turn to maudlin sentiment.

It was a 'Michael' day. He was in the forefront of
everyone's mind. Gerry Jackson had joined them and Lee
was acting as bartender. Sitting in the meat seats they all
drank steadily and seriously, as if by the sheer act of
getting drunk they would all feel the pain of Michael's
death less.

'I can remember when Mickey was working for Joe the
Fish. Handsome bleeder he was then and all.'

'That's a long time ago, Gerry.' Roy's voice was unsteady.

Gerry gulped at his gin and tonic. 'Your old mum used
to be really hard up them days. Everyone was. All the
birds was after him but he never spent his money on
them. Took it straight home to his muvver. Do you know,
Maura, that he bought your communion dress from the
proceeds of a robbery?'

'No, Gerry.' She smiled at him, glad to be talking about
her brother.

'Oh, yeah. I remember it as clear as day. Me and him ripped off a betting shop. He was a crafty sod! Even then he was streets ahead of everyone. Joe the Fish tried to keep him in line but he couldn't. He was "ducking and diving" all the time he worked for the old git.' Gerry's voice was hard now. 'I hated that old bastard.'

'Well, Mickey didn't, did he?' Leslie was well and truly drunk otherwise he would have chosen his words more carefully. 'Mickey was knocking him off, weren't he?'

Garry turned on him. 'Shut your bloody gob!'

'Well, Mickey was queer. Mickey was as queer as a nine bob note. As for Joe the Fish . . . that's where he got the bloody nickname! From "queer as a fish" . . .'

Leslie didn't finish because Garry punched him in the face, knocking him off his chair.

'You just shut your bloody trap up!'

'All right. Calm down.' Lee tried to pour oil on troubled waters.

'Bollocks, you! You're always sticking up for him.' Garry was belligerent when he was sober. Drunk he would fight his own finger nails.

'Shut up.' Maura's voice was low. She could not get up the enthusiasm to stop the argument.

'Look, Garry, we're here to honour Michael's name. So sit down and wrap up. If you can't take your drink, you shouldn't get drunk.'

Roy's voice was stern and authoritative. Everyone stared at him in awe. Leslie pulled himself from the floor and slumped back into his seat. Maura, through her drink-hazed mind, realised that Roy had really begun to get confidence in himself. He would be a good number two.

'When you gonna read your letter, Maws?' This from Lee, trying to change the subject.

'When I feel up to it.' She got up from her seat and made her way out to the reception area. Picking up the phone, she rang Willy at his office on St Martin's Wharf. He answered himself, which was a godsend as Maura was aware that she was having difficulty forming her words.

'Ish that you, Willy?'

426

'Hello, Maura.' His tone was cool. She had been seeing him less and less since the night of Michael's funeral and he didn't like it one bit. In spite of himself he thought a lot of her and it galled him that she could take him or leave him as the fancy took her.

'I'm pissed.'

'What do you want me for? I'm very busy . . .'

'I've just been to the reading of Michael's will and I'm lonely and depressed.' And drunk, she thought.

'Really? So you want to see me, I take it?'

'Yeah . . . What I need at this moment is a good hard shag!'

William smiled. She certainly had a way with words. But if he went running now she would just carry on using him. On the other hand, he had finished most of his business for today and she did sound lonely and desolate. He couldn't bring himself to say 'desperate' but that's what he really meant, and deep inside he wanted Maura on any terms.

'Where can I meet you?'

'Come and get me from the club. I'll be waiting for you.'

She replaced the receiver and went back to the meat seats. The men were all friends again, talking about Michael, each trying to outdo the others with funny anecdotes. Maura sat back in her seat and picked up her replenished glass. She raised it in a silent toast to her brother.

Her last thought before she passed out was that Michael would have approved of this drinking session in his honour. When William turned up an hour later he had practically to carry her to his car.

He took her home, silently annoyed at the condition she was in. She lay across the back seat of his car snoring softly, her large breasts straining against the thin silk blouse she was wearing. He had to admit that even drunk and dishevelled she was still the sexiest woman he had ever known.

* * *

427

Maura woke at eleven-thirty that evening with a violent headache. She noticed that she was naked in her own bed. Slowly the events of earlier in the day came into her mind. She turned over in bed and felt someone lying beside her. It was William. She could feel that her body had been roughly mauled and guessed that he had taken advantage of her drunken state. Well, she had asked for it really. She lifted herself up gently and felt the waves of sickness assail her. She stepped gingerly from the bed, placing one foot firmly on the floor before attempting to walk in the semi-darkness to the bathroom. She could hear William's loud snores coming from the bed.

In the bathroom she looked into the mirror above the wash basin. She looked terrible. Her make-up was all over her face and her eyes were more lined than usual. She looked old. Older than her thirty-six years. She washed her face, splashing the cold liquid over her face and neck to try and bring some life back to her brain. Then she remembered the letter.

She pulled on an old bathrobe that was hanging behind the bathroom door and went down to the lounge. Her bag was on the coffee table where Willy had obviously left it. Picking it up, she turned on one of the lamps by her reading chair. She settled herself down with her feet tucked up underneath her, opened the bag and took out the white envelope. She stared at Michael's closely written script for a while before she carefully ripped open the envelope and took out a single page of writing.

Hello, Maws,
If you're reading this then I'm brown bread! [He had drawn a little smiley to let her know that it was a joke.] You will already know I have left everything to you. You deserve it. It amounts to well over a million pounds. The docklands will bring in much more eventually. You have it all now. Everything.
    I am writing this letter as I wanted to tell you

some things that I may never have told you while I lived.

Firstly, I am heartily sorry for what happened all those years ago. I know that you loved that old Bill with all your heart and I ballsed it all up for you. I have tried to repay you for that, Maura.

Secondly, I think that you should try and marry old Templeton. If you did you would become a lady. Though you always have been in my eyes.

I love you more than you would ever think. Don't end up like me, Maws, with no home life to speak of. I admit that is the price I pay for being a homosexual.

Thirdly, try and make it up with Mother. You were very close once, and I think that deep down you both miss one another. Try and heal the breach, that's all I ask of you.

Lastly, I don't trust our Geoffrey as far as I can chuck him. He's not kosher, Maws. Put our Roy in as your number two. He's got more savvy than people give him credit for. Also try and keep an eye on the old man. Whatever happens with Mother, you was always his favourite and I know from talking to the boys that he misses you very much.

Well, that's about it, my darling. Keep this letter private as I don't want everyone knowing that I am really as soft as shit! [Another smiley.]

Look after the boys for me, and look after yourself. There's a codicil to my will that I asked old Hattersley to keep private. I have left my flat and personal belongings to Richard. We have a good relationship and I want to leave him provided for.

I also left fifty grand to Save the Children. That is not to be made public in any way. I have a feeling, Maws, that I will never make 'Old Bones', as Auntie Nellie used to say, so I write new letters every year to be on the safe side.

Look after yourself, Maws.

Your loving brother,

Michael

429

P.S. Hattersley is as bent as a two bob clock. I have left some papers for you that he will be holding until you have read this letter. Go and see him on the sly. It's stocks, bonds and other papers. There's also the number of my Swiss bank. They will be notified on my death that you are the new executor.

Maura stared at the letter. Trust Michael to cover all his bets. Only he would leave letters that were updated every year. She looked at the date at the top. It was written on 5 August 1986, before all the trouble with Geoffrey. She sighed. Fifty grand to Save the Children. Her eyes were misty. When they had seen pictures of the starving children on the news he had not said a word about it. Yet it had moved him enough for him to leave them fifty grand. That was the kind of gesture he would make. The papers always had him as a shady, murdering villain, and that was just how he liked it.

He knew about Geoffrey, had always known. If only she had let Michael sack him when he had wanted to maybe all this would have been avoided. She closed her eyes to stop the tears. She had done enough crying and it would not bring him back.

She opened her eyes and saw William standing in the doorway.

'My dear girl, you look absolutely scrumptious.'

She put the letter into her bag and smiled at him, a hard cynical smile that did not reach her eyes. She let her gaze roam over his body.

'You took advantage of me earlier, didn't you?' Her voice was low and husky. He nodded. 'Well, now I'm going to take advantage of you!'

William laughed, trying to imitate a cockney accent. 'Does that mean I'm gonna get a good hard shag?'

Maura placed her bag on the floor and stood up. 'Only if you're a very good boy.'

As they went back to bed together Maura prayed that William would be enough to take her mind off her troubles. Even as she thought it she knew it wouldn't happen. There was only one person who could do that, and he was as far from her grasp as the Milky Way.

Chapter Thirty-one

Saturday was cold and bleak, with a flurry of snow in the air. While Maura and William were eating a leisurely late lunch together, Sarah was sitting on a bench waiting for Terry Petherick. He arrived just after three. He smiled at her as she sat stony-faced and silent. Looking at him, she was reminded that he had fathered her first grandchild and was made aware of just how beautiful that child would have been.

'Mrs Ryan?'

Sarah nodded and he sat down beside her.

'It's cold today, isn't it?'

She nodded again.

'Would you rather we went and got a cup of coffee? Had our little chat in the warm?'

'Yes. That would be better. I'm frozen to the marrow.'

Terry took her arm and led her into the cafeteria. Sitting in the warm drinking a cup of hot sweet tea, Sarah was plagued by doubts. She knew that what she was about to do would cause no end of trouble, not only for Maura but all her children.

She took a deep breath. 'If I give you the information, could you make it easier on my sons?'

'The information is mostly about Maura, I take it?'

Sarah nodded her head.

'Well, I could try. It really depends on what kind of information you give to me.'

Looking at Sarah, Terry felt like a snake in the grass. She was an old woman. She was Maura's mother. If things had worked out differently, she could have been his mother-in-law. He sipped his coffee. Her sons had

433

beaten him nearly to death. He wondered if she knew that.

'I know many things about my daughter. My son Geoffrey, he kept names, dates, papers, that sort of thing. Going back years. I think that it was Maura who had him . . .' Her voice trailed off.

'Is that why you wanted to see me?'

Sarah gazed deeply into his eyes.

'You knew my daughter before . . . Well, before she went into the business with Michael.'

'You know about that then?'

'I knew everything. Maura was pregnant.'

Terry's eyes opened wide.

'That's impossible!'

'No, son. She was pregnant all right. That's why Michael had you so badly beaten. I took her to a back-street abortionist. She nearly died from what that bastard did to her. She was ill for a long time. It was because of the abortion that they sterilised her.' Sarah had no idea why she was telling him all this. Perhaps in her own way she wanted to make some sort of allowance for her daughter's actions. Give him some of the blame.

'I never knew. I swear to you that I never knew.'

'Oh, I know that, son. Maura told me that herself. She had gone to your flat to tell you when you finished with her. By then Michael had found out about the two of you, and the rest's history.'

Terry was reeling. Maura pregnant by him!

Sarah sipped her tea and began to talk again. Telling him everything.

'She changed then. I'm not saying it was all your fault but when she came out of the hospital she was hard. As the years went on she seemed to get harder. As if she was taking all her hurt out on the world. Whatever she may be now, before that happened to her she was a good girl. A kind girl.'

'I don't know if this will make any difference, Mrs Ryan, but I loved her.'

'I believe you did.'

'I just can't take it all in. If I had known, I would have stood by her.'

Sarah shook her head.

'You wouldn't have, son. Michael would never have let you. Even if you had left the police force, he would have hated you until the day you died. That's why I wanted to see you. In a way you're caught up in this as well. I want my grandchildren to grow up away from the taint of the Ryan name. I want them to be factory workers, road sweepers, anything! Anything but villains.'

'I understand. But you must realise that once you start something like this, it can't be stopped. There'll be no going back.'

'I know that. I've made up me mind. My children have got to be put right. Only I can do that. I made them, now I must destroy them. It's simple really. I want your help. If needs be, I'll go in the witness box.'

'No! That won't be necessary.'

'Listen, you, if you're worried that something might happen to me – don't be. I'm seventy years old and in all those years I've never been frightened of anything that came out of me own body.'

Sarah opened her bag and took out the file of papers that Geoffrey had left. She handed them to Terry.

'These are all that Geoffrey left. My phone number is on the outside of the file. Get in touch whenever you need me. The only thing I ask is, please try and help my boys. I know they must go away but the main one you should be after is Maura.'

She got up from her chair. Holding out her hand, she shook his. Then, nodding at him, she left.

Terry sat alone, thinking about all that had been said. Maura pregnant with his baby. He saw her as she had been that first night they had made love. Her willingness to learn from him. Her trusting eyes and soft body. He felt the burning of tears in his throat. She had been so soft then. He realised that having an abortion must have destroyed her. She loved children, they had discussed them enough times. Then he thought of the last night he had spent with her. That coming together of adults. The frenzied thrashing of their bodies. The cool musky smell of her. And she had not told him even then about the baby.

Neither of them had married. Both were put on this earth for one another, and one another only. He knew that now. He put his head into his hands.

A voice broke into his thoughts. 'Are you all right?' A short dumpy waitress stood beside him.

'Yes, thank you.'

She looked concerned about him. 'You look terrible.'

Terry stood up and threw three pound coins on to the table.

'It's nothing. Just a bit of bad news, that's all.'

He walked out into the freezing air, putting the file that Sarah had given him under his arm. He would read it later. At the moment all he wanted to do was walk and think.

Maura and William had gone back to bed. They were snuggled up together. Maura smiled at him, her first real smile for days. At last she had found someone to care for her. And he did care for her, she knew that. She would put all the bad behind her and just concentrate on the good.

She was still quite young and Michael's letter had shown her that time could run out quickly. She thought fleetingly of Terry Petherick, as she always did when she was feeling solemn. Terry Petherick was standing in Regent's Park thinking about her at the same moment.

Both began to make plans. And although Maura did not know it, both her plans and his would one day merge with explosive consequences.

Terry was in a quandary. A week had passed since Sarah had given him the papers. He had no doubt that what Geoffrey had recorded was true. The names and dates coincided perfectly. What was worrying him was that not only were most of his colleagues on Maura's payroll, but a few of the higher ups too. His Chief Inspector for one. Armed with all this information, he was not sure who to confide in. This wasn't a case of a few bent coppers. This was more a case of a few honest men against a veritable army of policemen on the take! Whatever happened, it would burst wide open not only his friends but the whole of London's police force.

He now had documented evidence that Maura and Michael Ryan were behind the bullion robbery of '85. Geoffrey Ryan had even procured the route map that had been used. Terry was in no doubt that it was probably full of prints. He even knew who was warehousing the gold. All well and good, except how in all honesty could he break this news without letting on that the police were also involved right up to their shitty little necks?

He could have cried. In the last seven days he had looked at his friends with new eyes. Had listened to their accounts of arrests made and known deep in his heart that they were deliberately looking the other way where the Ryans were concerned. No wonder Mickey and Maura had got away with so much. They owned not only Vine Street but West End Central as well. He couldn't believe it. They had 'tags' in Brixton, Kilburn, Barking. In fact, there was not one station where they didn't have an 'ear' on the payroll.

Now he, Terry Petherick, had all the information he needed to put them away. Even the full co-operation of their mother. And his hands were tied because when the Ryan ship finally went down it would take the police force with it. It was bloody laughable! As for this Templeton . . . he was up to his neck in skulduggery of one sort' or another and his family connections had kept him out of jail for years! Terry wasn't up against a few big villains, he was up against the whole bloody establishment.

He picked up the phone on his desk and dialled the number of the Special Investigations team. He would give the lot over to them. Let them have the honour of sorting it all out. He was sick to the stomach with the lot of it.

While the phone rang he doodled on his pad. It wasn't till later in the day he saw that he had drawn a heart with a dagger in it.

Superintendent Marsh was sitting staring out at the city skyline. It was dark and the lights were shining like beacons across the Thames. He had been sitting like that for nearly three hours. The information that the young DI had brought in had completely destroyed his equilibrium. He had been waiting for something like this for ten years. Now it was dropped, literally, into his lap he wasn't sure exactly what to do with it. He was waiting for his superior, who thankfully was not on the bent list, to come and talk with him. If all this information was true, and he had a sneaking suspicion that it was, all hell would be let loose and the West End police would be running on a skeleton crew. He shook his head at the enormity of what he was about to unleash, the sad part being that DI Petherick had unwittingly dug his own grave. If this hit the tabloids, no one would work with him ever again. Policemen were like doctors. They never shit on their own, no matter who the patients might be.

Terry was called at home at midnight. He was told to get dressed and meet Marsh at twelve-forty-five. As he got in his car he realised that he had started something that would have repercussions for years to come. Maura Ryan would finally be put away, but he wasn't sure it was a fair price to pay for all the trouble it was going to cause. He was even less sure an hour later when he found out exactly what was to happen.

He was sitting in a small back room in a terraced house in Wimbledon. Superintendent Marsh had been talking steadily for nearly an hour. While Marsh paused to light his cigar, Terry jumped in.

'What you're trying to say is that the people in authority will be getting off scot free?'

Marsh inhaled smoke into his lungs and coughed. Holding his hand across his mouth, he tried to explain.

'Look, son, I know how it must seem. The thing is, some of these men have been with the force for twenty years. They will retire quietly . . .'

'And get their pensions and their early retirement bonuses!' Terry's voice was disgusted. 'I can't believe my ears, Marsh. I bring you evidence of corruption on a bigger scale than anyone could ever dream of and you have the gall to sit there and tell me that the majority will be walking away completely exonerated.'

Marsh nodded.

'I know how you feel, son.'

'No, you don't! You have no idea what I am feeling at this moment. I am bitter and disgusted. These people have been collecting money from known criminals for years and they are not going to be brought to account. Whereas the little fish like Dobin will be crucified for them.'

'Listen, son . . .'

'Stop calling me fucking SON!' Terry smashed his fist on to the table in front of him. 'We're creeping around in the middle of the night like burglars. I can't believe this is happening. You tell me that bent coppers are going to walk out of their jobs without even a slap on the wrist. We are carrying on like guilty criminals, meeting in dingy little houses in the middle of the night, and the actual scumbags that we're here on account of are walking away from it all. It's not bloody on, mate.'

'Listen, Petherick. If this hits the streets we're fucked. If you want it plain then I'll give it to you plain. Can you imagine the outrage this would cause if it ever hit the tabloids? Have you thought? Our street credibility would be lower than a fucking gas meter bandit's! Think about it. We'd never live this thing down. The only way we can even begin to sort this out is internally.

'They know that they've been collared. They're leaving the force. That's all that we can do! When you get older you'll realise the sense in what I'm saying. Else all the toe rags they've put away, the rapists, muggers, murderers, would be screaming for retrials as soon as their arresting officers were nicked. We're talking too many people to let this ever get out. I know that what they're getting seems a small price to pay for their misdeeds, but believe me the other way would cost us more.'

Terry was stunned.

'What about Maura Ryan? Or is she to walk away too?'

'Don't you worry about her, we have her bang to rights.'

'Of course, let's get our priorities right, shall we? Get the real villains. Well, let me tell you something, Marsh, I think that Maura Ryan, as bad as she and her family are, is as nothing compared to the filth you're letting off so lightly. In my book a bent copper is worse than any villain.'

Marsh walked around the table and put his hand on Terry's shoulder.

'I know . . . I feel the same. I'm following orders the same as you. But the sheer magnitude of what you found out is what's stopping us making this public. Can't you see that? The force would be crucified in hours. Top men in key jobs on the take? Come on, son. It's too much.'

Terry listened to Marsh and had to agree with what he was saying. It just seemed unfair to him that so many people would walk away without so much as a stain on their character when, by rights, they should have been made to take the consequences of their actions.

'I'm still not happy. Even if this does cause trouble, surely it would be worth it? Joe Public isn't as stupid as you seem to think. I for one would much rather see justice being done than take part in something that I know is wrong.'

Marsh puffed on his cigar. His shiny bald head had a fine layer of perspiration over it. This young man was beginning to get on his nerves. The last thing the force needed at this time was a cop as honest as this one. Terry Petherick wanted to stir up a hornets' nest, and there was no way he would ever be allowed to get away with it.

'Look, go home. Sleep on it. Once you've had a chance

to think about this logically you'll see it from our perspective.'

Terry got up slowly from his chair and looked into Marsh's eyes.

'Now I know why we're nicknamed the "filth".'

When Terry had left, Marsh sat back down at the table. If only everything was as easy as Petherick seemed to think it was. The nice policeman gets the naughty villains. Only in this world, most of the police were villains! Marsh let out a long drawn-out sigh. It was his job to keep Petherick's mouth shut. And that was just what he intended to do.

Terry drove home in a temper. The streets were deserted and he had an urge to drive to Fleet Street and shout his mouth off about the lot of it. He knew he wouldn't, though. He hadn't come this far in his career to blow it now. He realised that for the second time in his life he'd had to make an important decision between the force and Maura Ryan. And that for the second time the force had won.

Chapter Thirty-two

Janine put Roy's breakfast in front of him. He began to eat. She poured herself a cup of coffee, walked out of the kitchen into the lounge and laced it with vodka. As she turned from the drinks cabinet she jumped. Standing in the doorway watching her was Roy.

'I thought you were eating your breakfast.'

He finished chewing his mouthful of food and pointed to the cup Janine had in her hand.

'Bit early even for you, ain't it?'

Janine dropped her eyes. She felt herself blushing. 'It's my life, Roy . . .'

'Well, in future, if I ain't here, you get Benny a cab to school. I don't want you wrapping your car round a lamp post with my son in it. Pissed out of your nut!'

Janine's voice rose. 'I'm not pissed!'

Roy sniffed and wiped his nose with the back of his hand. 'Not yet. You just do what I tell you. Get it?'

Janine stared at him, her face twisted with anger.

Roy bellowed at her: 'I SAID . . . GET IT?'

'Yes. I get it. I'm not deaf, you know.'

'No, darlin', not deaf. Just half pissed as usual.'

Roy walked back to the kitchen to finish his breakfast. Standing on the bottom stair in the hall watching him was Benny.

'You dropping me off at school, Dad?'

Roy nodded.

'Great. Mum's driving is getting worse.'

'In future, son, you do not get in any car with your mother, right?'

Benny shrugged his shoulders.

443

'Suits me, Dad.'

Janine, listening to all they said, swallowed her coffee and vodka down in two gulps and refilled her cup. Sitting on the settee she sipped the neat spirit. Slowly the tears came. Roy had taken everything away from her over the years, her self-respect and now her child. The tears came, tears of self-pity. A little while later she heard them leave the house. Benny had not even bothered to say goodbye to her.

Roy and Maura were driving out to Essex. She had an appointment with a goldsmith, Lenny Isaacs. Roy pulled up at some traffic lights and looked across at her.

'You're in a good mood today, Maws.'

She smiled at him. 'Yeah, I am actually.'

'What's brought all this fun and laughter on?'

'Nothing, you cheeky bugger. You better go, the lights have changed!'

'Oh, shit!'

A van behind started blowing its horn.

'All right. All right, I'm going. So what's the secret then, Maws. A bloke?'

'Maybe.' Maura thought of William Templeton.

'It *is* a bloke!' Roy's voice showed his surprise.

'Listen, dickhead, I'm in a good mood because I just am. That's all.'

'Women's bloody logic amazes me!'

Maura laughed at him.

'Talking of women, what's the score with Janine?'

Roy scowled.

'I thought we were talking about women. Not the monster from the black lagoon.'

'Nasty, nasty.' Maura grinned.

'Listen, Maws, Janine is getting on my nerves. She drinks like a fish.'

'Janine? She was always a teetotaller.' Maura sounded sceptical.

'Not any more. The marriage is going down the pan. Correction, *is* down the pan. We haven't slept together for

444

over four years. If it wasn't for Benny I'd have had it on me toes ages ago.'

'How long has she been drinking?'

'The last year or so, I think. But the last few months she's been drinking quite heavily.'

'She always was a funny bird. I never liked her, I admit that. But all the same, she is your wife.'

'I tell you now, Maws, if it wasn't for Mother I'd dump the bitch. But Mother thinks the sun shines out of her arse.'

'That's a fact. Well, Roy, you know your own mind. Myself, though, I'd get shot of her, whatever the old woman thinks. Let's face it, you're the one who's got to live with her, not Mother.'

Roy nodded.

'What's the score with this Isaacs bloke?'

'Apparently he knows the big boys in Jersey. Reckons he can get rid of the gold over there, and gradually it will be put out on the market again. That means that the market will be flooded and the price of gold will drop, but by then we'll have made a mint, if you'll excuse the pun, and some prat will be running all over Europe counting the gold reserves. Eventually some bright spark will suss out that the missing bullion is being sold legally and it will all be hushed up. As usual. So if you want to buy any gold in the next few years, stick to South African Krugerrands!'

Roy burst out laughing.

'You're bloody mad!'

'I know . . . I know. I'm happy mad, though, that makes a difference!'

'I hope this Isaacs bloke ain't going to waffle all day. Front wheels never seem to know when to shut up. Sammy Goldbaum used to chew my ears off!'

At the mention of Sammy's name Maura felt herself go cold. She hadn't thought about him for a long time.

'Here! You all right, girl? You've gone pale.'

Maura lit a cigarette.

'Yes, I'm OK. Just felt a bit funny for a second.'

Roy realised that he shouldn't have mentioned Sammy Goldbaum. He could have kicked himself.

'I tell you what, Maws, before we go on this meet, what do you say we find a nice little pub and have a bite to eat and a drink?'

Maura knew Roy was trying to make amends and smiled at him. 'That would be great.'

Terry Petherick was called in to see Marsh. He took the seat offered to him and waited silently for his boss to tell him what was going down.

Marsh lit himself a cigar, his only extravagance. Blowing smoke across his desk, he began: 'Have you thought over what we were talking about?'

Terry nodded.

'I take it you are more amenable today?'

Terry nodded again.

'Good . . . good. We've decided that the collaring of the Ryans will be given to you. I'm sure you already know that whoever gets them has his career made. Unless, of course, you get knobbled by them first.'

Terry stared at him. He could see nothing to laugh about.

'We know that you're as straight as a die, and in view of all the information you've gathered we feel it is only fair . . .'

Terry interrupted him.

'All right. Cut the crap. What exactly's going down?'

Marsh had an overwhelming urge to put his cigar out in Petherick's face. Who the hell did this little shit think he was? Instead he took a deep breath and tried to control his temper.

'Yesterday Maura and Roy Ryan had a meet with a goldsmith . . . Lenny Isaacs. I had her tailed. Obviously they're going to be shifting the bullion soon. That's when we're going to pounce. Once she's nicked for that we can pile on the other charges as and when we feel like it. As I told you the other night, we have her bang to rights. We swoop when they make the exchange. It's as simple as that.

'About the other business . . . the Complaints Investigation Bureau are dealing with it internally. We're not going to approach anyone until the Ryans have been collared.

That way they won't get any warnings. You and I will be working together closely on this one. You mustn't mention it to anyone. I'll see you in a few days when I have more to tell you.'

'Sarah Ryan asked me if it was possible to get the boys lighter sentences?'

Marsh smiled nastily. 'Well, there's no harm in asking, I suppose.'

When Terry had left the office Marsh sat for a while smoking his cigar. It would not do to tell Petherick that none of the Ryans could be allowed to go to prison. The Ryans were going to be wiped out. They had bought themselves too many friends in the force to be allowed to live. They had to be shut up, and shut up permanently. As Petherick would be finding out all too soon . . .

Sarah was making Benjamin's dinner. He had come in from the pub and gone straight up to bed. Said he felt tired today. Sarah was annoyed. Felt drunk more like. As she was peeling the potatoes she heard a crash from above her head and looked up at the ceiling. Nothing. She listened again. Then putting down the potato peeler, made her way up the stairs to their bedroom.

Benjamin Ryan was lying on the floor clutching his chest. One look at his face, grey and drawn, told Sarah he was very ill. She went to him and tried to lift his head from the floor.

'Benjamin!'

He opened his eyes. Sarah noticed the blue tinge around his lips.

'It's me chest, Sar. Get me a doctor. I've gotta pain in me chest . . .'

Sarah ran down the stairs and phoned an ambulance. Then she rang Janine and told her to tell the boys what had happened. Slamming down the phone, she went back upstairs and sat on the floor with her husband until the ambulance arrived.

Sarah sat in the Cardiac Care Unit with her husband until he lost consciousness. She was praying over him all day. At seven in the evening Maura and Roy turned up, both pale and worried. Janine had not thought to try and contact the other boys. Roy took his tiny mother into his arms.

'What happened, Mum?' His voice was gentle.

'It was terrible. He collapsed in the bedroom. I found him on the floor.'

'Do they know what caused it?'

'Yes. He had a coronary. He's never been ill in his life.'

'We would have been here sooner but we was out all day. You should have rung one of the other boys, not Janine. They'll be here soon.'

He was going to murder that drunken bitch when he got home. His father ill in hospital and she'd left a message at the club for him to call! Not even telling Gerry Jackson what it was all about.

'I was too scared to call anyone. I didn't want to leave your father. Look at him. He looks terrible.'

She sounded so old that Maura and Roy were suddenly reminded of the fact that their parents could die soon. That their father could be dying now.

Roy sat his mother in the chair by the bed then looked at his father's wasted body.

'I'm going to find a doctor, Maws. Look after Muvver. I'll find out what's going on.'

Maura automatically put her arm around the woman she had hardly spoken to for years. Both forgot their animosity in the light of Benjamin's illness. They were just a mother and daughter, united in their grief.

'Everything will be all right , Mum . . . I promise you.' Sarah held Maura's hand in her own.

'Oh, Maws, he's so ill. What will I do without him?'

'Don't you worry, Mum, he'll be all right.' Maura's voice sounded much more confident than she felt.

Leslie, Garry and Lee turned up a little while later. All were sober, looking worried about their father.

Maura and Sarah stood by Benjamin's bed, the two women supporting each other as best they could. The boys were outside the room, quiet and nervous. It was too soon after Michael's and Geoffrey's deaths to face another one.

Though they had all treated Benjamin with scant respect and only haphazard affection over the years, now he lay ill they were all reminded of the fact that he was their father. Even a bad parent was entitled to respect on his death bed.

Carla rushed into the hospital at ten-thirty. Her long red-brown hair was blown all over the place and she had on an old coat. Even untidy, she looked lovely. She went straight to Roy. Her father held her while she cried. She was the living image of Janine, and for a second he remembered the vital woman he had married.

'How's Grandad Ryan? I was out all day with Joey. I only got the message when I came home.'

'He's very ill, Carla. But they think he could pull through.'

'Come on, Carla. Sit here beside me.'

Garry's voice was soft. Carla was like the family mascot. She sat down in the chair and he gave her a cup of coffee. Inside the room Maura and Sarah stood either side of Benjamin's bed. At ten-forty-two he opened his eyes and looked at them.

'Me two best girls. I suppose I've missed the pub?'

Looking at their anxious faces, he tried to grin.

Sarah and Maura laughed through their tears.

'Yes, Dad, you missed the pub.'

'Remember what I've always said . . . when I die, I want me ashes put in the Bramley Arms.' He closed his eyes.

Maura and Sarah finished the sentence for him: 'So you'll always be there for opening time.'

It was a saying of his they had heard all their lives.

'That's it, girls. I think I'll have another sleep now.'

He closed his eyes. When he was asleep the two women hugged one another.

'I reckon he'll be all right now, Mum.'

The nurse who was in the room and heard the exchange smiled at them.

'Why don't you all get home and get some rest? He's stable now.'

'Come on, Mum. I'll run you home.'

'No, I can't stay in that house on me own. I've never spent a night there alone since before the war.'

Maura could hear the fear in her mother's voice. 'I'll stay there with you. Don't worry. Come on, let's get you home.'

Both women kissed Benjamin and left the room.

Maura drove Sarah home a little later, amazed at the way events had brought them together as Michael had wanted.

'Sleep in my bed with me, Maws.'

'All right then, Mum.' They went up to the bedroom, both quiet and sad.

As they undressed they were both aware of the truce that had been drawn up between them. Maura knew that for the first time in years her mother needed her. She was sorry that it had taken her father's near death to achieve it.

Sarah got into her bed and watched Maura folding her clothes. She looked at her daughter's unblemished body and beautiful profile. She would have been a fit mate for that Terry Petherick. He was one of the few men she had seen who towered over her daughter. Maura took off her bra and Sarah looked at her large firm breasts and pulled her eyes away quickly, feeling that spark of jealousy many women feel when they see their daughters' strong, taut bodies. Maura slipped into the bed beside her mother, feeling strange at the turn of events. She had rung William earlier and told him what had happened, and that she was staying the night with her mother. She knew he was miffed as he wanted her with him.

They were now a real couple, making plans with each other. She had decided to give herself to him as he wanted her too. Seriously and for always.

'I'm frightened, Maws.' Sarah's voice sounded hopelessly old and tired. Maura patted her hand.

'He'll be fine, Mum.'

'I was eighteen when I married your father. My father, God rest him, had gone around to Ben's house and given him the hiding of his life. Then he had arranged the wedding. That was over fifty years ago now. And Michael had been that child. My first born son. 1935 that was. Then I had child after child. Your father. He used to joke that he only had to walk past me to get me pregnant. You were me last one. Me daughter for me old age. I never really loved your father, you know, but when you spend all that time with someone, it's hard to imagine being without them. Even when they're a waster, like your father.'

'I can understand that, Mum. It's a long time.'

'It's good of you to stay with me, Maws. I know we haven't exactly seen eye to eye.'

'Look, forget that, Mum,' Maura interrupted her mother. 'We're together now. That's all that matters. That's what families are all about. Pulling together in the bad times and sharing the good.'

Not that we ever did that, Maura thought to herself.

Sarah stared into Maura's face. In the light of the bedside lamp, she looked very young and Sarah was reminded that she was the tool that was going to destroy her daughter. Whatever happened she was going to have to do that. Maura smiled at her sadly.

'Do you remember when I was a kid and I used to sleep with you when the old man was in prison? We used to have chats. That's what you always used to call them . . . chats. I wish we could turn the clock back to those days. Be like we were then.'

'So do I. But nothing can ever be the same as it was.' Sarah sounded as if she was holding back tears and Maura assumed they were for her father. She never dreamt they could be for her.

'I wish I had kept my baby, Mum. I still think about it sometimes.' Maura's voice was wistful.

'I wish you'd kept it and all. I wish I'd never taken you to that flat in Peckham.'

'That's all water under the bridge now, Mum. I went of my own accord.'

'No, Maws, it was me. I was scared that you'd be tied to someone you didn't love, like I was. Then, when I met Terry . . .'

'You met him? When?' Maura's voice was sharp, and Sarah realised her mistake.

451

'Oh, it was at the funeral. Michael's funeral. I spoke to him there.'

Maura relaxed. 'Oh, then. Yeah, our Garry had a go at him.'

Sarah swallowed deeply.

'I know. I was watching. Along with many other people.'

They were quiet for a while, both occupied with their own thoughts. Then Maura spoke softly.

'Look, Mum, let's just concentrate on getting me dad out of hospital and back home. Everything else is done. Over with.'

She nearly told her mother about William Templeton but stopped herself. She knew that her mother didn't really like him.

'Mum?' Maura's voice was quiet.

'Yes.'

'You don't regret having all us kids, do you?' Suddenly it was important that she knew the answer.

Sarah was silent for a while before answering.

'Of course not, Maws.'

As she spoke, she asked God to forgive her for lying.

Chapter Thirty-three

February 1987

Leslie and Garry were collecting the protection money. As they pulled up outside a Greek restaurant in Ilford, Garry noticed a blue Granada parked a few cars away from them.

'Les . . . see that blue Granny? I'm sure it's been following us.'

Leslie looked at the car.

'I haven't noticed it.'

Garry got out and walked to the Granada. He tapped on the window. As it opened he leant down and looked into the car.

'What you doin' here?'

The blond man inside looked puzzled.

'I beg your pardon?'

'I said . . . what you doin' here?'

'I've come to have a meal in the restaurant. Why?'

'Nothing.'

Garry walked away from the car, still not sure what was going on. He got back in his own car beside Leslie.

'Let's sit here a minute and see if that bloke goes in the restaurant.' Sure enough, the man got out of his car and locked it up. Then he went into the restaurant.

'You wait here, Les.'

'OK.'

Garry went into the restaurant. The man from the Granada was studying a menu. Leslie walked through to the kitchen, picked up the envelope with the 'rent' in and walked back out again. As he passed the man's table he said, 'Have a nice meal.'

The blond man watched him leave. After a quick moussaka and a brandy, he paid his bill and left. He drove to the nearest phone box. He had to let Marsh know that Garry Ryan had tumbled him.

Maura and William were visiting Benjamin. He had been home from the hospital for ten days and was not taking kindly to his new regime. No drinking, no smoking, no fats.

'Seems bloody silly living if you can't enjoy yourself.'

William smiled.

'Really, Mr Ryan, once you get used to the changes they won't seem so bad.'

'I dunno about that. It's easy for you to say, ain't it? You ain't been told you can't enjoy yourself no more.'

William shook his head. Benjamin Ryan was not only ignorant but stubborn. He had absolutely refused to conform to any advice that the doctors had given him.

'Nuffink but a load of bleeding foreigners. Can't understand half of wot they're waffling about. Bloody macaroons, eye ties and sodding krauts telling *me* wot to do!'

Maura laughed.

'Oh, Dad, Doctor Hummelbrunner isn't German. He's Austrian.'

'All the bleeding same if you asks me.'

'Leave him, Maura. I'll make sure he follows the doctor's orders. Now shut your trap, Benjamin Ryan, when we've got visitors. Would you like another cup of tea, Lord William?'

'I really wish you wouldn't call me that, Mrs Ryan. Willy will be quite adequate.'

Sarah smiled uneasily. She didn't like having a lord in her house. It made her uncomfortable. Where her daughter was concerned, there seemed to be nothing but trouble. Sarah had read about this Templeton in Geoffrey's papers. He was a villain. Only in Sarah's eyes he was worse than her children, because he had been given a good start in life which was more than her brood had ever had. It wasn't right . . .

454

Sarah was beginning to regret her newfound friendship with her daughter. She should have kept it as it was. Kept her away from the house. The trouble being she was the apple of her father's eye. She waited every day for that Petherick to call her about the papers she had given him and up till now she had heard nothing. She was beginning to wonder if she had done the right thing.

'You all right, Mum?'

Sarah looked at Maura.

'Tired, Maws, that's all. I think you two had better make a move in a minute. I want to settle your father for a nap.'

'Okey doke. I've got to meet Leslie and Garry anyway.'

William Templeton got up and placed his cup and saucer on the coffee table.

Maura went to the bed that had been put in the lounge and kissed her father goodbye.

'Take it easy, Dad, and do what Mum tells you.'

'I will, girl. See you tomorrow then.'

'Goodbye, Mr Ryan.'

'Tata, son. See you again.' He winked at William. 'Bring me a medicinal brandy next time.'

'Oh, Dad. Give it a rest, will you!'

When Maura and William had left Sarah settled Benjamin for his nap. 'Our Maura's done well for herself there, Sar. Looks like he's got a couple of bob.'

'Well, money isn't everything and I don't think our Maura's exactly hard up.'

Benjamin caught hold of her hand. 'I never give you much, did I, gel?'

She looked into his rheumy eyes.

'Well, you did your best. Now try and get yourself off to sleep. I'll call you at nine o'clock for your tablets and we'll watch a bit of telly. How's that?'

'All right, love.'

Sarah collected the used cups together and carried them out to the kitchen. As she filled the sink with hot water she looked around her, remembering the cockroaches, the empty bellies, and the years of hardship she had

455

experienced within these walls. And she remembered Maura with her long blond hair flying behind her as she played out in the street . . . Leslie's permanently running nose. 'Silversleeves' the others had called him . . . She could almost hear Mickey's voice floating up from the basement . . .

She turned off the tap and began to wash up. In her mind's eye she could see Geoffrey on the day Maura had made her first Holy Communion. Geoffrey had been so proud of her. All the boys had been scrubbed up and taken to the church. Garry and Lee had been irritating her all that morning. Geoffrey had thumped the pair of them. She had felt so proud of them that day. She had walked, head high, with her nine children all clean and shining.

She smiled to herself. If only you had an idea what was in store for your children! All those years ago she had thought Maura would grow up, marry, and give her grandchildren. Instead, she had grown up and done the complete opposite. First thing in the morning she would phone that Petherick and see what was going on. If she had to wait much longer she'd have a heart attack herself! Once Maura was arrested she would be able to breathe freely. Whatever happened, she had to get her away from the boys. Benjamin's heart attack had shown her that they weren't getting any younger. If she was to sort her family out before she herself died, she had to do it now.

Maura and William were in Le Buxom by ten o'clock. Gerry Jackson had been in the act of throwing out a prominent Member of Parliament who had a penchant for trying to dance with the strippers when Roy had arrived. Recognising the man, Roy had taken him down to the restaurant to try and sober him up before the place got packed. He left him with one of the waitresses and went back into the club.

'That old bastard gets worse, Gerry.'

He nodded.

'He gets on my bloody nerves. He'll be on telly tomorrow

or the next day telling everyone to listen to their consciences and vote for the Tory Party.'

'Mickey had the right idea, you know. He used to keep records on all the prominent citizens and use them to his advantage.'

'Yeah, I know. The West End's full of bloody Arabs at the moment. That'll cause hag, it always does. They won't go near the black birds and so the blondes will be "going case" two or three times a night, which means permanent bitching. By the way, that coon Rubber was in here earlier, selling coke. I slung him out but I thought I'd let you know. All the hostesses are as high as kites.'

'Thanks for telling me, Ger. That's all we need. Well, keep your eye on them. I don't want them fighting with the punters. They can do what they like to one another.'

Roy went back up to the offices to see Maura.

'All right, Roy?'

'Yeah, not too bad. We've got the Right Honourable Dickhead in again tonight and that bloody Rubber's been in and sold the hostesses coke. Other than that, everything's fine!'

Maura laughed.

'Send Leslie round to have a word with him. I heard through the grapevine he got a good hiding outside the Pink Pussycat last week for selling bad stuff. Tell Leslie to make it plain that this is his last warning. I don't want this place raided for drugs.'

'Okey doke. Leslie and Garry are due in shortly anyway. Actually, Garry rang in earlier. Reckons he was being followed by a bloke in a blue Granada.'

Maura rolled her eyes to the ceiling and took a deep breath. 'I don't believe him! He is so paranoid it's a joke!'

William Templeton looked at her, puzzled, 'What do you mean?'

'Oh, Will, it would take all night to explain it.'

Roy started to chuckle.

'He thinks that he's being followed all the time. We all wind him up about it. He's really paranoid.'

'Has he always been like this?'

'Since he was a kid. He told me once that when he gets really wound up he hears voices!' Roy laughed.

'Good God!'

Maura put her hand over her mouth to stifle her giggles. 'No, not God . . . more like the devil!'

William smiled but in fact he was disturbed.

'What did you say to him?'

'Not a lot, Maws, just the usual. That I'd phone around the Bill shops and see if they had any information. I'll tell him later it was just a mistake on his part.'

'Good. Humour him. That's the best way.'

'If you want to shoot off, Maws, I'll pick up the rents. I'm staying on here for a while anyway.'

'Thanks, Roy. That would be great. Once Les has been sent to sort out Rubber, would you ask him to pick up some parcels for me? The addresses are on this piece of paper.

'We're meeting Isaacs again on Sunday night to complete the deal, so I want you, the boys and Gerry Jackson with me. Tooled up. Sawn-offs, not handguns. OK?'

'What time?'

'We'll meet here at about five-thirty. Right then, Will, let's get going.'

He stood up.

'Would you like to go out to eat?'

'Why not?'

'See you's later then.'

When Maura and William left, Roy started going through the papers. Sunday was two days away, and he was going to wish that he had listened to Garry's story. Although none of them knew it, the net was closing.

Lennie Isaacs was sitting in his hotel room, shaking like a leaf. Terry Petherick and Superintendent Marsh were sitting opposite him.

'I swear on my mother's grave, I don't know what you're talking about!'

Terry flicked the ash from his cigarette onto the carpet.

'Listen, Lennie, we know everything. We know about

the gold, about the robbery, and we also know about you. So why don't you save yourself some trouble and just tell us what we want to hear?'

Lennie was biting his lip. His short stubby fingers were trembling and he was trying as hard as he could to stop himself crying.

Marsh looked at him pityingly.

'I can promise you, Lennie, that the Ryans will not know where we got our information from. All we want to know is when the meet will be. We'll do the rest.'

'I'm sorry. I know nothing. I'm over here on holiday.'

Terry lost his temper.

'Cut the crap, Isaacs! You're over here to buy illegal gold. How about we pull you in now? Leak your name to the papers. Say that you're helping us with our enquiries. Then leave you on remand in funky Brixton where you can sit and wait for the Ryans to waste you!'

Lennie paled.

'You wouldn't do that to me!'

Terry smiled.

'Just try us and see.'

Lennie looked down at his hands. Terry could see his shiny pate through his thinning hair.

'It's on Sunday. We all meet on Sunday. You realise that I'm a dead man?'

Marsh stopped chewing his thumbnail and said, 'We'll see about that, Lennie. Don't worry. Now tell us nice and slowly what's supposed to be going down.'

Lennie cleared his throat and took a sip of his wine. 'We're meeting at a place called Fenn Farm.'

'We know all about Fenn Farm. What we're more interested in is times.'

'Seven-thirty on Sunday evening.'

Terry looked at Marsh.

'That only gives us thirty-six hours.'

'Don't worry, Petherick. We'll be more than ready for them.'

Lennie Isaacs wiped a stray tear from his eye. Maura Ryan would have his nuts for this. He was already dead.

Maura had just put a chicken in the oven and was preparing the vegetables for Sunday lunch. She wanted to eat at twelve so she and William could have the afternoon free. When she had finished scraping the carrots, the telephone rang. It was Margaret.

'Hello, Marge.' Maura's voice was warm.

'Hiya! I thought I'd give you a quick ring and see how you was getting on.'

'Terrific. I was just starting the dinner actually.'

Margaret's voice was incredulous. 'Maura Ryan cooking! Now I've heard everything!'

'Ha, ha, Marge!'

'This William must be some guy. If he can domesticate you, he must be the business.'

'He has not domesticated me . . . I often cook.'

'Pull the other one, Maws, it plays "Hard Day's Night"! Seriously, I'm just pleased you're so happy. It's about time.'

'Oh, Marge, it's great! I wish to God I'd got myself in a relationship years ago. I don't think I'm in love exactly . . . but I just want to be with him all the time. In fact, I *am* with him all the time.'

'I can remember when me and Den were like that!'

'Come off it, Marge, you and Den are still like love-birds. You two even embarrass your own kids with all your kissing and cuddling.'

'Don't talk to me about my kids . . .'

Margaret's voice was sad.

'Why, what's happened?'

'It's Penny. She's got herself a bloke.'

'What's wrong with that? You can't keep them tied to your apron strings forever.'

'It's not that, Maws. He's a bloody Sikh.'

'You're joking!'

'I wish I was. He even wears a turban. Mind you, I had to laugh. Little Dennis saw them together in the High Street and went up and asked him when his head was gonna get better. That's how we found out. Penny and him had a big fight about it and when I tried to sort it all out, Dennis dropped the bombshell.'

Maura was laughing so hard she had an ache in her ribs.

'I wish *I* could see the funny side of it all.'

'You bloody hypocrite, Marge! You're the one who brought them up with liberal ideas. Everyone's the same, no matter what colour they are or what religion. Now poor old Penny's got herself a coloured bloke, you're doing your nut!'

'Well, I never thought they'd want to go out with one, did I?'

Maura was still chuckling.

'What's big Den got to say?'

'Oh, him! He's about as much good as an ashtray on a motorbike. "Leave her alone, Marge. Let her find her own way . . ." I said, "You won't be saying that when she's walking round with a red spot on her forehead and a gold lamé sari."'

'Oh, Marge, stop it. You're making me guts ache. Can you see her in a sari with all that ginger hair of hers?'

'Oh, I don't know what to do.'

'Well, if you want my advice, I wouldn't protest too much. Remember what we were like at that age. The more people try and tell you what to do, the more you're inclined to go against them!'

'Yeah. I've thought of that.'

'Let her get it out of her system.'

Maura heard William get out of bed. 'I've gotta go, Marge. I'll try and get over to you tomorrow. Say about lunchtime, how's that?'

'All right, Maws. I'll make us a nice quiche.'

'How about a curry? You'd better start practising Indian cookery.'

'Piss off, Maura!'

'And you! 'Bye, Marge.'

Maura put the phone down and leant against the wall, laughing. Poor old Marge!

'What are you laughing about?'

Maura went to William and kissed him.

461

'I'll tell you all about it later. I've started the dinner, we're eating early today. I thought we could go out this afternoon for a walk or something. I have to leave at four to meet Roy and the others.'

William looked down into Maura's bright blue eyes.

'Tell you what. Scrub the walk, we'll go back to bed. How's that?'

Maura kissed his mouth hard.

'I was kinda hoping you'd say that!'

Terry and Marsh were in the Special Operations room at Scotland Yard, going over the final details with a hand-picked bunch of men. Marsh had recruited them from the SPG. All had licences to use firearms.

'So we swoop at precisely seven-forty-five. That gives them fifteen minutes to negotiate with Isaacs. We've put a man with him so he doesn't lose his nerve. He'll introduce him to Maura Ryan as his partner. You all understand what you are to do?'

All the men nodded.

'Good.'

Terry stood up and faced them.

'The main aim is to bring the Ryans in. All of them. This is going to be one of the biggest busts this country has ever seen. Nothing is to go wrong. You only fire if it is absolutely necessary and then you aim only to wound if possible.'

The men nodded and looked at one another. Unknown to Terry they had all been told to open fire immediately they entered the barn. Not one person was to be allowed to leave that place alive, Lennie Isaacs included. No one knew why this young DI was being kept in the dark. They were just following orders.

4.00

Sarah was sitting with Benjamin watching a Doris Day film on TV. She was trying to knit and finding it increasingly difficult to concentrate. She had left message after message for that young man Petherick and he had not been in touch. She was worried that one of the people who worked for Maura had found out what she had done. If Maura knew she would kill her, she knew that. For all her talk of never being frightened of anything that came out of her own body, she was increasingly nervous. Today for some reason she had had a terrible feeling of foreboding. It had been weighing down on her like a lump of concrete in her breast since she had got out of bed this morning. She put her knitting down and rubbed her eyes.

'How about a nice cuppa, Sar?'

Benjamin spoke without taking his eyes off the television. Sarah stood up, glad of something to do. She made her way out to her kitchen and put the kettle on. She had been going to visit the boys' graves today. Mainly Anthony's, Benny's and Geoffrey's, she only ever paid Mickey's a flying visit. But for some reason she did not want to leave the house.

As she set about making the tea, a deep coldness came over her and she had to sit down at the kitchen table. She had only felt like this twice in her life before and that was when Benny had died and Geoffrey had gone missing. She had had a feeling similiar to this the day the police had reported to her George's body had been found. She closed her eyes to blot out the picture of him in the mortuary. He had been shot in the back of the head and the bullet had come out just under his jawline He had had a surprised expression on his face. Now she had that feeling again. She was convinced that something was going to happen today. Something bad.

When she finally took the tray of tea in to Benjamin he was asleep. She turned the sound down on the TV and sat and drank her own tea. Waiting for a knock on the door or the phone to ring.

4.30

Maura was driving to Le Buxom to meet the boys. She had not felt so happy for a long time. William had tried to persuade her to let Roy deal with the business today and she had been very tempted to stay in bed with him. After all these years she was finally having a relationship with a man, and loving every second of it. She only wished she had let herself go before now. She found herself smiling at complete strangers at traffic lights and laughed to herself. If this was love she was enjoying every moment of it. She decided that she would pass more of the business over to Roy. He was doing so well now. She wished he could get rid of Janine but knew that concern for Benny kept him with her.

She could understand that. If she had become a mother she knew she would have done anything for the good of her children. She wished again she had kept her baby. It would have been grown up now with a life of its own.

She pushed the thought from her mind. She was happy today and nothing was going to interfere with that! She turned her thoughts to Marge, determined that nothing was going to spoil her happiness. All she wanted to do was get the meet over and get back to William.

She was humming a little tune as she pulled into Dean Street.

4.45

Lennie Isaacs had dosed himself up with brandy. The policeman assigned to keep him from bolting was Detective Sergeant Paul Johnson. He had been given his orders two hours ago. Once the shooting started he was to push his gun into Isaacs' side and blast him. There was something definitely fishy about all this but as his old dad used to say: 'Ours is not to reason why.' If it got him a promotion he didn't give a toss. The likes of Lennie Isaacs were scum anyway. He'd be doing a public service.

Lennie sat in the barn. It was freezing and he shoved his hands into the pocket of his sheepskin. He was praying for the first time in thirty years. DS Johnson sat opposite staring at him. Lennie wished to Christ the copper wasn't such a big bastard. He would have tried to make an escape. The trouble was he had never been the hero type. More the 'I'll scratch your back' class of villain. He hadn't

464

slept all night and had been jittery all day. Maura Ryan, whether she was nicked or not, would make sure he disappeared. Oh, God in heaven, help him, for fuck's sake!

Chapter Thirty-four

4.50

Fenn Farm was derelict. It had not been worked for years. Maura had bought it for a song at an auction a few years previously and was going to sell it eventually, subject to planning permission for a housing estate. Green belt land was not classed as sacrosanct any more. If you had the money and the contacts you could build just about anywhere you wanted to. Arable land that was worth only a few hundred pounds an acre could become, overnight, prime building land worth millions. This was the Thatcher era, when anything that was commercially viable and cost the government nothing was encouraged wholeheartedly. Even building estates on old power stations was acceptable, provided you filled the land in with plenty of concrete first. Then the people who bought the houses were given lists of trees they could plant, trees with very shallow roots that would not disturb the sludge and radioactive waste lying beneath the houses. It was a developer's dream, and Maura Ryan had had the foresight to cash in when land was still at nominal prices. The days when the working-class men dreamt of winning fifty thousand pounds on the pools were long over. You could not buy a flat for that amount now, let alone live for the rest of your life on it. England was the epitome of the consumer society.

Today Terry Petherick was watching from the sidelines as the farm was being set up ready for the arrival of the Ryans. Everywhere he looked there were men with high velocity rifles, all taking up position in and around the barn. The light was fast fading, and Terry was reminded of an old World War Two movie, seeing the men dressed in black

467

spiriting around with faces covered in camouflage make up and guns glinting in the half-light. He fingered his own gun and prayed that he would not have to use it. Especially not on Maura Ryan.

He was sitting on an oil drum watching the activity around him when a man standing near him answered a call on his walkie talkie. Terry had not been issued with one and until this moment had not thought it strange. When he heard what was being said on the man's radio, it became crystal clear to him just why he had been overlooked in that department.

The voice crackled over the radio and into Terry's brain. 'Remember, not one Ryan is to leave the farm alive. You cut them down as they arrive.'

'Understood. Over and out.'

The man began to walk towards the barn door, and Terry realised through his reeling thoughts that the man had not noticed him. In the twilight and with the camouflage make up he was indistinguishable. He sat for a while on the oil drum, letting what he had heard sink in.

Maura and her brothers were going to die. They were being led here, to this farm, like lambs to the slaughter. And it was his fault. He had taken the files to his superiors and then had listened to their excuses as to why none of the judges and policemen on the Ryans' payroll would be brought to justice. Now it was revealed to him with shocking clarity why the Ryans had to die. While they held knowledge that could rock the country, they were dead men. And women. He must not forget Maura, the mastermind behind it all. It was she who was the biggest target: Maura who was the fly in an otherwise perfect ointment. He could have kicked himself. Here he was, with his ideals about justice – good and bad, law and order – and there was no such thing. Not in this country, or indeed the world.

He looked at his watch. The luminous dial showed that it was just five o'clock. Looking around him surreptitiously, he began to move slowly towards one of the last remaining cars outside the farm. He was praying that the keys were still in it.

He slipped behind the wheel of the Sierra Estate and felt a surge of thankfulness that was almost sexual. The keys were in the ignition. He swallowed deeply, feeling the momentary hesitation that always precedes an act of wrong doing. Only what he was doing was not wrong. He had sworn an oath to uphold the law in this country, and as far as he was concerned that was just what he was doing. Stopping the wanton murder of a whole family. No matter what they had done, nothing warranted what was to happen at this farm tonight. He had two hours before the Ryans were supposed to arrive and he would try and stop them if it was the last thing he did.

He started the car up and drove cautiously away from the farm house and the barn. He drove as if he was supposed to be driving the car away, neither too fast nor too slow. He remembered that on their way to the farm today he had seen a phone box in the lane about a hundred yards from the farm's exit. He drove there, his breath barely entering his lungs in his state of nervous tension. If somebody tried to stop him, he would use his gun. Whatever happened, Maura Ryan was not going to die, not in a barn on a cold February evening, mown down like a dog.

5.05

'Right then. Is everyone happy with what they are to do?'

Roy, Leslie, Garry and Lee nodded at Maura.

'Good. We'll have a quick coffee and then make tracks. It'll take over an hour to get there.'

'I still think we're being watched.' Garry's voice was low.

Maura sighed.

'Oh, for Christ's sake, Gal. If we were being watched, one of our plants would have let us know before now. You're so paranoid lately.'

'I'm telling you now, that bloke I saw in the blue Granny was definitely waiting for us.'

'Give it a rest, Garry. You're like an old woman sometimes.'

469

Garry looked at Roy. 'Well, when we're all fucking nicked, don't say I never warned you.'

Lee laughed, then said in a girlish voice, 'All right then, Garry. I promise you with all my heart.'

Garry looked at him, frowning.

'I'm glad you think it's funny. I hope you find it as amusing when you're sitting in Parkhurst or Durham doing a twelve stretch.'

Leslie pulled on his cigarette.

'Only twelve years? I'd have thought we warranted at least a thirty.' He looked at Lee. 'Remind me to nail someone's leg to a table. We can't have the Krays outdoing us at the last moment.'

Everyone laughed but Garry would not be silenced.

'Yeah. And the Krays are still inside, remember that. In fact if you –' he pointed at Leslie viciously – 'get put on the "Island", you might get banged in a cell with one of them. Reggie, that is.'

Lee grinned.

'Not you though, Garry, you'll be put in Broadmoor with Ronnie. That's where all the nutters go.'

'Oh, shut up, for Christ's sake. No one's going any-where.' Maura was getting annoyed.

Garry flicked his hair from his eyes. 'Well, there's one thing I can guarantee. You won't be in Cookham Wood with the other long-timers like Hindley. You'll be top security, girl. We'll all be A grade. Like terrorists.'

Before Maura could retort, Lee spoke. His voice was soft as silk. 'Have you been reading that book again? *How to Win Friends and Influence People*?'

Everyone laughed.

'Oh, piss off, the lot of you! The last book you's read was *Fluff and Nip*.'

Then the phone rang and Maura picked it up, chuckling as she did so.

Terry went into the phone box and dialled directory enquiries. He asked them for the number of Le Buxom. When they gave it to him, he dialled the operator for a

470

reverse charge call. He did not have a single coin on him. He stood in the cold with bated breath as the operator tried to connect him. Le Buxom was the only place he could think of where someone would know the whereabouts of Maura Ryan.

He was literally praying as he heard the distant clicking and whirring of the telephone exchange.

Maura picked up the phone. 'Hello?' Her voice was calm and happy.

'I have a reverse charge call from a call box in Essex. Will you accept the charges?'

The operator's clipped tones were bored and efficient.

Who on earth could be ringing her from a call box? Maura racked her brains.

'Of course.'

'You're through, caller.'

'Hello, can I speak to Maura Ryan?'

She felt her heart stop dead in her chest. She would know that voice anywhere. All around her the boys were good-naturedly ragging Garry as they drank their coffee. In Maura's head there was only one sound: Terry Petherick's voice.

'Is there anyone there?' He sounded desperate. 'I must speak to Maura Ryan or someone who can contact her.'

'This is Maura Ryan.' She was amazed at how calm her voice sounded.

'Maura, this is Terry . . . Terry Petherick. Please don't put the phone down.'

'What do you want?' Even as she spoke so normally she could feel the almost adolescent longing and excitement he had always created in her.

'You mustn't go near Fenn Farm. The Special Investigations Branch are waiting for you. They're armed and ready.'

'What!' The sound of her voice silenced her brothers. They all looked at her.

'I know it sounds crazy, but believe me, Maura, you're in big trouble. We know everything about you. Everything.' He stressed the last word.

'But how?' She sounded very young in panic.

'Look, can we meet? I can't stand here explaining it all. They're looking for me . . . or will be when they realise I've gone.'

'What are you talking about?' Maura's voice was scared.

'Look, Maura, is there anywhere we can meet? It must be somewhere the police don't know about. Have you a secret hideaway?'

Maura was thinking out loud. 'Marge's house . . . Carla's . . .' Then it struck her. 'Do you know Mickey's old place?'

'Yes. I know it.'

'I'll meet you there.'

'OK.' Terry put the phone down and went to the car.

'What's happened, Maws?'

'You were right, Garry. The old Bill have tumbled us. Isaacs must have grassed.'

Garry stood up from his seat and threw his coffee cup at the wall.

'I knew it! I bloody knew it! You wouldn't listen, would you?'

'Calm down. Calm down. Shouting and hollering ain't gonna help us.'

Roy looked at his sister.

'What's the score?'

'I'm not sure yet. I want you all to lie low for a while. I'm meeting somebody who knows what's going on. Fenn Farm is well and truly out of the question. I'll be at Mickey's old flat. I want you all to ring in there from wherever you decide to go. All right?'

'Who was that on the dog and bone?'

'Just a friend, Les. A good friend.'

'Well, I'm off to Muvver's. Who wants to come?'

Leslie nodded at Lee. 'I'll go with you. At least she'll guarantee some decent grub with an alibi.'

'Well, wherever you all go, don't forget to ring me at Michael's.'

'What about Richard? He might not like you just turning up at his drum.'

Maura picked up her bag and scowled at Lee.

'Fuck Richard!'

'No, thanks. He's not my type.'

Maura laughed despite herself. 'Come on, you lot. Let's get a move on.'

Richard was asleep in bed with a Filipino man he'd picked up the night before. They had only emerged from the bedroom once to have some sandwiches before they went back to bed for another session. Richard was cuddling into the man's back when he heard the hammering on his front door. He hoped it was not that bitch Denzil again. Since Michael had died he had practically haunted him. Richard's most oft repeated statement was: 'Straight I may not be . . . choosy I most definitely am!' And he had not sunk as low as Denzil. Not yet anyway.

He walked naked into the hallway.

'Who is it?' His voice was high and cracked.

'It's me. Maura Ryan.'

'Oh!' Richard opened the front door and let her in. Since Michael's death he had added a mortice lock to the door which was why Maura's key was not enough to gain her access.

'I never expected you!'

Maura could hear the surprise in his voice.

'Well, you've got me, Richy baby. Until I say otherwise.'

She walked into the lounge and threw her bag on the sofa. Going to the drinks cabinet, she poured herself a large Remy Martin.

Richard was in a quandary. He most definitely did not want Maura Ryan in his flat. And it *was* his flat. Michael had left it to him. But he was not brave enough to ask her to leave. He just stood in the doorway watching her. She was wearing a deep red trouser suit that perfectly complemented her white-blonde hair. Her large breasts were just covered by a white silk shirt. Richard could see that she was braless. He had envied her her breasts from the first time they had met. He had also been jealous of the way Michael worshipped her. The fact that he knew

473

she did not like him had not helped matters very much either.

He heard a stirring in the bedroom and felt faint with fright. He had completely forgotten about his Filipino friend! He saw Maura's puzzled expression and tried to smile.

'It's a friend of mine.' As he spoke the man came out of the bedroom and Maura could not help but stare at him. He was tiny and slim, like most Filipinos, but he had the largest organ Maura had ever seen in her life. It was like a baseball bat. She made a conscious effort not to let her mouth fall open with shock.

'This is my friend, his name's Weykok.' Richard's voice trailed off as Maura began to guffaw with laughter.

'Well, it would be, wouldn't it?'

Weykok stood with his thin bony shoulders pulled back, as if trying to emphasise his enormous member. He seemed to enjoy the stir that he was creating. Richard turned to him and bundled him back into the bedroom. Maura sat on the sofa laughing her head off. She had needed something to lighten the situation and it had come in the shape of a man called Weykok.

Richard came back into the lounge; he was wearing a silk dressing-gown. 'He's leaving now.'

As he spoke the little man came into the room, fully dressed. He held out a tiny hand.

'Money, please.'

Maura saw Richard flush. Enjoying herself, she said innocently, 'Does he charge by the inch or the centimetre? After all, we're in the common market now.'

She started to laugh again and Weykok laughed with her good-naturedly. Maura went to her bag and opened it.

'Have him on me, Richard. How much?'

Weykok seemed to understand this as he said politely, 'Eighty-five pounds, madam, please.'

Maura pulled out two fifty-pound notes and gave them to him, saying, 'Keep the change.'

The little man bowed to her, and after a mumbled conversation with Richard in the hallway, left the flat.

'Well, Richard, I'm afraid I'll be invading your space for a while. Let's try and get on, shall we?' Her voice was friendly.

'Are you in some kind of trouble, Maura?' Richard was serious.

'Sort of.'

'In that case I'll do all I can to help. Not for you but for Michael. I know that's what he would have wanted me to do.'

He said the words simply and with an innate sincerity that made her feel guilty for her earlier jokes at his expense. She was reminded that she needed him. Needed him badly.

'Someone will be coming here soon to see me.'

She saw his face fall and hastily reassured him. 'Don't worry, Richard, there'll be no violence or anything like that.'

She saw him relax and for a second felt sorry for him. She sat back down on the sofa and patted the seat beside her.

'Come and sit here, Richard. We need to talk.'

Terry Petherick was in Dagenham. He parked the car he was using in the car park of the Ship and Shovel public house. Leaving it there, he went out on to the A13 and flagged down a passing mini cab.

'Bloody hell! You in the TA?'

As Terry sat beside the minicab driver, he remembered that he was still blacked up.

'Yes, actually. I've been on manoeuvres and my car broke down.'

'Oh, I see.' The man's voice was gravelly as if he needed to clear his throat. 'Where you want droppin' off?'

'Could you take me to Knightsbridge, please?'

'Yeah. Course, I was in the TA, you know. Went to Germany once . . .'

Terry closed his eyes. This was all he needed, a 'weekend warrior' for a cab driver.

* * *

Maura was chatting to Richard, trying to make friends with him. She knew that she needed him, desperately. She could not help noticing that all around the room were pictures of Michael and Richard, laughing and with their arms around one another. It was only Richard's association with her brother, and his fear of her, that was keeping him from throwing her out, she knew that.

'I needed somewhere to meet someone important. Where no one would think of looking for me. I know this is a cheek, Richard, but it was the only place I could think of.'

He shrugged.

'Well, it's yours for as long as you want to use it. Now, can I make you something? Tea? Coffee?'

Maura smiled. 'Coffee would be great.'

She looked at the large cuckoo clock on the wall. It was nearly a quarter to seven. She bit her lip. Where was Terry?

Roy was sitting at home with little Benny. He was nervous and worried. He would ring in to Maura at seven. Give her a chance to sort herself out. He looked at Janine. She was lying on the couch half drunk. He suddenly felt a tightening sensation in his bowels. For the first time in years he was scared.

Sarah was watching the three boys surreptitiously. They had all turned up together to visit their father, but they were not right somehow. They were all taut as bowstrings, as if waiting for something to happen. Garry got out of his chair.

'Can I use your phone, Mum?'

'Of course you can.'

He went out into the hallway and rang Maura. While he was doing it, Leslie and Lee kept Sarah in the front room chatting. Both were nervous under the plaster gaze of the holy family and the various saints that stood around the room. It seemed every time they visited her a new statue had been added to the collection.

Sarah sat with them while they chatted to her and Benjamin, but still had the bad feeling in her side. The

476

dragging feeling that seemed to be increasing as the day wore on.

At six-thirty Marsh realised that Terry Petherick had gone missing. Busy as he was getting everything set up, he had not given him a thought till then. Although Terry did not know it, he was going to be silenced along with the Ryans. Oh, they would not kill him. Not unless they had to . . . He was going to be named as the person who had shot Maura Ryan on her entry into the barn.

Now Marsh knew that somehow Terry had cottoned on to what was going to happen and had driven one of the unmarked cars out of the farmyard. He was fuming. There had been two cars outside, both to be driven away before the Ryans were due to arrive. In the commotion, as everyone got ready and set up the barn for the meeting, Terry had just got into one of them and driven off. God knew where. Personally Marsh hoped it was not to the newspapers. While Maura Ryan was alive and kicking they dared not touch her. She could open her mouth about things that would smash open the Metropolitan Police force and West Midlands Serious Crime Squad, and she also knew things about docklands and other prime areas of development that could bring down the government. He shivered. She had them literally by the bollocks.

Now there was another thing that he knew for definite. Maura Ryan was not coming anywhere near this barn or even this county. Terry Petherick had jumped fences today. In either camp, whether it was the police's or the Ryans', Petherick was a dangerous man.

Terry knocked on the door of Michael's flat and Maura let him in almost immediately. They stood in the hallway staring at one another for long moments, both drinking in the other as if they were dying of thirst.

Maura was the first to speak.

'Come through, Terry.'

He followed her into the lounge.

'This is Richard, an old friend of my brother Michael's. He lives here now.'

Terry held out his hand and Richard shook it.

'I'll make some more coffee, shall I?'

'I could certainly do with some.'

Richard smiled at Terry and went to the kitchen.

'Sit down.'

They sat on the sofa together, nearly touching, and Maura felt the heady sensation of being close to him for the first time in years. She savoured it for a few moments to try and commit it to memory. Terry was doing exactly the same.

Finally Maura spoke. 'So, what's going on?'

'You're not going to like what I have to tell you, Maura.'

'I know that, Terry. But I still have to know the score.'

He took a deep breath.

'Your brother Geoffrey kept a file on you and Michael.' He watched her large blue eyes open wider. 'When he died it came into your mother's possession. It had details of the gold bullion robbery, even the route map – which incidentally had your prints all over it. It had the names of every high-ranking official in the government, police and law courts, how much you paid them and what you paid them for. Maura, it had everything.'

She was absolutely dumbstruck.

'Your mother rang me and asked me to meet her. I did.' He swallowed deeply. 'She gave the file to me and I passed it on to the SIB.'

Maura shook her head in disbelief. 'The Special Investigations Branch? I see.' Her voice was small. 'So between my mother and yourself, I was well and truly . . .'

'No, Maura. No. I know how it sounds but we wanted to help you.'

Even as he spoke he knew it sounded lame.

'Come off it, Terry! I'm not as daft as you seem to think. You and my mother wanted me put away. Neither of you thought about all the so-called "goody two-shoes" wankers on my payroll. It never occurred to either of you that *they* were abusing *their* positions. Oh, no! You two just wanted

478

me sent down, out of harm's way. Well, let me tell you something. If it hadn't have been me and Michael buying them bastards off it would have been someone else. This bloody country is rotten to the core, mate. Everything has its price, whether it's a small backhander to get a bit of planning permission or a large donation to the appropriate political party for a development. Like docklands . . . .'

'I know now that what you're saying is right.'

'Oh, shut up! Shut up!' Maura was shouting now and Richard was listening to everything that was being said.

'You was always an idealist, Terry . . . like some sort of bloody knight errant. Always wanted to get the bad guys, didn't you? Well, let me ask you something. What's happening to the people we've been buying off? I bet they aren't being given a twelve-gun send-off, are they? Are they? Of course not. They'll walk away as they always have done with an OBE or a golden handshake. No one must ever know that Sir Godly Goodly, who just happened to go to Cambridge with most of the other scum from the higher echelons of British Society, is on the fucking take!'

Her mouth was flecked with spittle and she ran her hand through her hair in agitation. 'Why aren't they after the real criminals? The rich and pampered criminals. Why must we take the fall for them? You answer me that.'

Terry stared at her, knowing that all she said was true. He was aware from the day that Marsh had told him what was going to happen to the men on Maura's payroll, that it was unfair. That the Ryans were going to carry the can for them so that Joe Public never knew what was really going on. He felt a fool. He had betrayed her. After all he had done to her in the past, he had betrayed her again because he'd thought that what he was doing was right. And now he knew that there was no such thing as 'right' and 'wrong' any more. Was it right that judges could sit on a bench and put away men for being a danger to society at large and then acquit other men who were a much bigger danger, just because they were being paid to do so? Was it right for the top police who were financing their gambling or other hobbies to be retired when in reality they should be doing

479

time? No, it was wrong. Maura Ryan was a criminal but she had never pretended to be anything else. She did not shield herself with the mantle of a good education and a law degree. If what she did was wrong, at least she did it without pretending to benefit the nation.

Richard walked into the room with a tray of coffee and sandwiches. He placed it on the coffee table and spoke. 'I couldn't help hearing your conversation.'

Maura and Terry both looked at him as if they didn't know who he was. They'd forgotten him.

'I work for the papers. You know that, Maura. From what I've just heard, I think that while you have access to journalists you're safe as houses.' He looked from one to the other. 'Think about it. Maura knows all the people who are on her payroll. While you're alive, Maura, the police dare not touch you.'

'They were going to kill them all. Every one of them. At Fenn Farm tonight.' Terry's voice was flat.

'If you'll forgive me, I guessed as much for myself. What you must do, Maura, is leave the country. Go somewhere where they can't get to you.'

'They would!'

'No, let me finish. You must write down everything you know about the people who are on your payroll then you must leave it with someone, to be opened only on your death. That way you will live a very long time, believe me.'

Maura and Terry stared at him. As fantastic as it sounded, it held the ring of truth.

'I know plenty of journos who'd commit murder for a story like this. It's got everything a journalist needs.'

'He's got a point, you know.' Terry's voice was excited.

Richard spoke again. 'Honestly, Maura, I know what I'm talking about. Look at Profumo. Christ, that still gets dragged up every so often. People like to think that the rich people who run big businesses and the people in government are in cahoots with shadier people. It makes them feel better about their own lives. There's nothing the British like more than to tear someone apart, preferably someone they created or voted in in the first place. The gutter press makes its money doing it, whether it's the Westland affair, the Profumo scandal or a judge who's into pornography. As long as it's someone with plenty of money or a high profile, the British Public loves it.'

The more Richard spoke, the more sense he made to Maura.

'But where could I go?'

'Anywhere you wanted to, really. While you're alive and kicking and able to open your mouth, you and your brothers are as safe as houses.'

She slumped back on to the settee. 'Let me think about it. I can't concentrate . . .'

'Drink your coffee and have a sandwich. We'll think of something, don't you worry.'

Maura was beginning to understand what Michael had seen in Richard. He wasn't just a pretty face.

Chapter Thirty-five

Marsh was worried. Very worried. It seemed that Maura Ryan had gone on the missing list. From information he had received, it seemed the only person at her house was William Templeton. Lord Templeton. Three of her brothers were at their mother's and the other brother, Roy, was at his own house in Chigwell. Maura Ryan had not appeared at any of her clubs or other businesses. He had put a call out to watch for her car but didn't hold out much hope there. He was dealing with a dangerous lady, a woman with the means of destroying numerous people, himself included. And to top it all, she now had the championship of Terry Petherick!

He sighed and lit one of his cigars, looking up as the door of his office opened.

It was Superintendent Ackland of the Special Investigations Branch. Ackland was notorious in the force for his violent and disruptive personality. He was one of those men who should by rights have chosen a life of crime. Brought up in the Gorbals, he had an animal cunning and an empathy with the criminal mind that was out of place in the world of the police. Or so Marsh had thought until he had read the names of seemingly respectable men on Maura Ryan's payroll.

Like many Scotsmen, James Ackland was quite small, with a muscular body and the high forehead and erratic hair of his ancestors. He had tiny blue eyes that seemed to be permanently on the move, darting around his head as if he was frightened that by the act of relaxing his gaze he would miss something important. Even after twenty years in London, his Scottish accent was as pronounced as ever.

'You've read the files, I take it?' Marsh's voice was low.

'Aye. I have that.' Ackland laughed. 'Well, there's one thing for sure . . . she's a canny lass. The way I see it, there's not a lot we can do to her. Or her family, come to that.'

His face seemed to straighten, as if wiped clean with a blackboard rubber. 'But I'll think of something. Though myself, I think the people on the take should be brought to book. But you know and I know they won't be.'

Marsh nodded and puffed on his cigar.

Ackland picked his rather bulbous nose, making Marsh feel sick.

'The only way out is to annihilate the bitch. Usual code of conduct, of course. We find her, then we have what the papers euphemistically call a "shoot out". It's odds on that she's carrying a firearm. Christ, man, from what I read in the file, I wouldn't be surprised if she was carrying a tactical nuclear missile!'

His voice was jocular again. 'I don't like covering up for people, especially people who should know better, but there you are. We're all under orders.'

Ackland helped himself from the bottle of Famous Grouse that Marsh had on his desk, pouring the dregs from a coffee cup into a waste paper basket and filling it nearly full.

'We have to find her first.' Marsh's voice sounded as if that would be an impossible task.

Ackland sniffed. 'No one can hide forever, Marsh.'

Maura was writing furiously. She was making a document which, if it got into the wrong hands, would bring the country to its knees. Her brain was working overtime, remembering every little detail she could about the people she had dealt with. Unknown to her there were people named in her account who had not appeared in Geoffrey's. She was concentrating on the 'biggies', as Richard had called the cabinet ministers and the Bank officials. She also listed every large developer and industry chairman who had at one time or another dealt with either herself or Michael.

Terry watched her as she worked, reading each page as she finished it and realising with each word just how corrupt and evil the established order had become.

William Templeton was worried. Very worried. Like Marsh he was wondering where on earth Maura had got to. He glanced at his watch. It was nearly two in the morning and still no word. He looked around Maura's lounge at the family pictures that abounded. On top of the television cabinet were photographs of Carla. From a small child to a grown woman, her life was lovingly documented. On the occasional tables were photos of Maura and her brothers, mainly Michael.

He got up from his chair and went to the kitchen to make himself yet another coffee. As he poured hot water over the coffee granules there was a knock on the door. Banging the kettle down on the worktop he answered it, his heart in his mouth.

A man was standing outside the porch. He was holding a police badge in his hand. Slowly, William opened the door.

'Sorry to disturb you at this time of night, sir.' The man had a pronounced Scottish accent. 'I am Superintendent Ackland of the Special Investigations Branch. Could I please talk to you for a moment?'

The man smiled and William saw that he had tobacco-stained teeth. He held the door open and gestured for the man to come inside.

Please God, don't let her be dead. William was convinced that it was bad news of some kind. It was not until Ackland told him that he was going to be arrested and charged with certain offences, including conspiracy to murder and armed robbery, that he realised just how bad.

'Do you realise who I am?' His voice was outraged.

'Aye, I do. But you see, Lord William, I couldn't care less if you were the Prince Regent himself. If you don't do what I tell you, I'll drag you to the polis station so fast you'll burn a hole in the pavement! Outside this house is an army of policemen, with guns, just waiting for a word from me.

485

You're going to be the bait that tempts the big fish. The big fish being Maura Ryan.'

'I have no idea where she is.'

'Maybe not, but it's odds on you'll be able to find out. Now, shall we have a nice cup of tea and a chat?'

Ackland's voice was friendly and for some reason this worried William more than anything.

Maura was in deep trouble and he guessed that he was going to be asked to double cross her. This Scottish lout had as good as already said that. What was worrying William was the fact that, as much as he cared about Maura, his own skin would always come first. It always had.

At two-thirty Maura took a rest from her writing to have a cup of coffee. Richard had produced a photocopier that he kept for when he worked from home. He was busy in the bedroom copying all that Maura had written so far. Richard had wanted to be a 'real' journalist all his adult life. He realised that in his hands he had the scoop of the century and that he could never use it. As he read what Maura had written his eyes goggled. He would bet his last pound that the Secretary of State for the Environment was probably sitting at home and sweating like a pig. He must have been told all that was going on. The same could be said for the Home Secretary.

As he read, Richard had the beginnings of a plan forming in his mind.

In the lounge Terry and Maura drank their coffee in silence.

'What do you think the outcome will be?' she asked.

Terry shook his head.

'I really don't know, Maura. I feel responsible for it all.'

'That's not surprising, is it? Considering you are! You and my mother.' Her voice was bitter.

'I don't blame you for being upset with me but I am trying to help you now. Surely that says something?' Terry was desperate to reassure her of his backing.

'You're trying to help me now because the people that

you worked for . . . the people that you revered and tried to emulate . . . turned out to be more bent than I am. *That's* why you're trying to help now. You said yourself that you knew before you even went to Fenn Farm that the so-called "biggies" who were on the take would walk. I don't need you, Terry Petherick. I never needed you.'

'You did need me once, Maura.' His voice was quiet and earnest.

She lit a cigarette and looked into his face.

'Oh, yeah? And when was that?'

'When you were pregnant. When you had the abortion. When you were lying in hospital desperately ill. Your mother told me all about it.'

He sounded calm and caring.

Maura snorted. 'So, mouth almighty told you that as well, did she? What else did she tell you? Did she tell you that she once accused me of sleeping with Michael? Did she tell you that? Did she tell you that for all our faults, real and imagined, she took the money that was sent to her every week?' She was quiet for a few seconds. Then, her voice low, she spoke again.

'I never needed you then, Terry, so don't flatter yourself. I was young and naive and the only mistake I made, as I see it, was getting involved with someone like you. Even then you wanted to change the world. Michael told me what happened to you. We had enough plants in the force, even then. You were pulled over the carpet for your association with Michael Ryan's sister and you dumped me. You had a choice, me or the force, and your precious police force won. Then, when my mother gave you Geoffrey's papers, you couldn't wait to run to your superiors with them. Terry Petherick, the Vine Street Marvel, uncovers the biggest case of corruption this century. Only you didn't realise then that what you actually had was something the government and the police would rather hush up than expose. You struck out, mate.'

'I've lost everything. My job . . .'

'Oh, sod your job!' Maura was shouting. 'I don't give a toss about you or your stupid job!'

'Whatever you think now, Maura, I loved you. But we were so young then. What about the night we spent together after Benny died? You told me then that you still loved me.' He pointed at her. 'You told me to go the next morning. It was your decision.'

He felt an urge to weep. He had inadvertently brought her nothing but grief from the day they met.

'I sent you away because I wanted to.'

'Oh no you didn't! I won't have you saying that. You sent me away because you were in too deep with Michael. It was for that reason and that reason only.'

Maura watched his handsome face and admitted the truth of what he was saying to herself.

'Shall I tell you something? Shall I tell you the real truth of my life?'

'Yes. Please tell me.'

'When I met you in 1966, I felt something I had never felt before. Or since.' She stared at a spot on the carpet, afraid to look at his face. 'I wanted you so badly I could taste it. Do you remember when you told me you were a policeman? I nearly had a heart attack!'

She laughed solftly. 'I sneaked around for months to meet you, lying to my mother and father and my brothers. Then, when I got pregnant and went to your flat to tell you, you finished with me. I had that baby scraped out of me by a dirty little Paki. I can still smell that flat sometimes. I can still see the baby lying in the bottom of a washing up bowl. Perfectly formed and dead.

'And do you know what the ironic part of it is? I never wanted to be anything other than a wife and mother. I know that the feminists would crucify me if they heard me speaking like this but it was all I ever wanted: a husband, a home, and children. A houseful of children. Then when I had the abortion and it went wrong, I came out of the hospital and all that had been taken away from me. I had nothing to give to a husband or a lover. I was empty inside. I nearly died, you know. And for a long time that's exactly what I prayed for. Then I had the idea of working for Michael. He never really wanted me to work in the family business but I forced him. I knew that he felt responsible for what had happened to me and I used that to get the ice cream and hot dogs from him. After that, I gradually took over from poor Geoffrey.

'If I hadn't gone into the business then, Geoffrey and Michael would have stayed together as a team. Though Michael never really had a lot of time for him, I must admit that. And somehow, all that happened over the years built up and built up . . . until this. I'm the most wanted woman in England now and all I ever wanted was to be Mrs Average. That child would be twenty-one now. Grown up and going out into the world. Instead it was flushed down a toilet in a multi-storey tower block in Peckham, and I'm being hunted by armed police . . .'

Her voice trailed away and Terry knew that silent tears were falling from her eyes. For the first time he realised just how much he had really hurt this woman. He asked himself for the hundredth time since Mrs Ryan had told him about the abortion, whether he would have stayed with her had he known. And being an honest person he knew that he could not answer that question so many years later. All he was sure of was that he had wrecked Maura's life. That she had always been inside him somewhere, like a piece of a puzzle that was gradually being put together.

He put an arm around her hesitantly, afraid that she would push him away, but she didn't. Instead she held on to him tightly, pulling his body against her own as if trying to crawl under his skin. And he held her while she cried and was not surprised to feel his own tears fall as they both healed a breach that spanned twenty years.

Richard had heard what had been said and being a tactful person coughed loudly before he went into the lounge. Maura and Terry pulled away from one another and Richard acted as if he could not see they were both very upset. Instead he smiled brightly and sat on the floor in front of them.

'I have the most amazing idea. I think that you'll love it.'

Maura wiped her eyes, grateful for the intervention. He

489

was going up more in her estimation with every hour that passed.

'What is it?'

'I've been reading what you've written down and I think that you have more than enough to do a deal.'

'What kind of deal?' Maura's voice was more alert now.

'I think that if our friend here . . .' he pointed at Terry . . . 'goes to see his superiors with a copy of what you have written, and tells them that there are numerous other copies in the hands of unscrupulous people, then they'll be more than ready to come across.'

'They'll never do a deal.'

'How can you be so sure, Terry? I think that the Secretary of State for the Environment will have the last say on what happens. After all, there are some pretty heavy heads on the chopping block.'

'But who will we give the copies to?'

'Let me worry about that, Maura.'

'I know one person who would be glad to help us.'

'And who's that?'

Maura looked at Terry. 'Patrick Kelly.'

'What, the IRA man?' Terry's voice was shocked.

'Yeah. He's an old friend of mine. We go back years. Plus he owes me one.' She thought of Michael as she spoke.

'Wouldn't he use it, though?'

'Only to his own advantage. The British Government are in closer contact with the Irish than people think. They trade information with each other when necessary. The government know who the real leaders behind SinnFein are. Gerry Adams is just the media go-between. The real leaders are never mentioned.'

'Rich and important men, I suppose?'

'No, Terry, not all of them. I know that the IRA get a bad press but the majority of them are fighting for a cause that they believe in. Like any society they have all sorts, from the lower end of the scale to the top of it. Kelly is at the top of the scale and I know I can trust him.'

'So that's one person. Can you think of any more?' Richard was loving every second of this now. It was the most exciting night of his life. For the first time he was involved in something that was really important, and even though he would never be able to boast about it, he would know inside that he had been a part of it. Had helped to mastermind it.

Maura frowned. 'The only other person I can think of is Derek Lane.'

'But no one knows where he is.' Terry's voice was puzzled.

Maura couldn't help laughing. 'Terry, Derek Lane and people like him are easy to find if you have the right connections. Michael and I were in partnership with him out in Spain. He owns the monopoly on the timeshares out there. I have the full partnership with him now that Michael's dead. I could fly out to Marbella and explain the situation to him.'

Terry was flabbergasted. Even though he knew that Maura and Michael were heavyweights as far as the British gangland scene were concerned, he never dreamt for a second that they were in league with people like Derek Lane. Yet he should have guessed. After all, they were birds of a feather really. Derek Lane had gone on the trot in 1977 and not been seen or heard from since. He was wanted for countless murders and other serious crimes. He had been the Birmingham equivalent of Michael Ryan, only unlike Michael had not tried to work within the law as well as outside it. In the end England had got too hot for him and he had disappeared.

'Well, that's two good people. They'll do for the moment. Now then, Terry, are you willing to be negotiator? Will you go and see Marsh?' It was the least he could do for Maura.

'Yes. I'll go.'

Richard smiled.

'Good! Now all we have to do is work out what terms we want and everything will be underway.'

Maura laughed softly. 'You're really enjoying this, aren't you, Richard?'

He nodded his head at her. 'Yes, actually, I am. Now who wants more coffee?'

* * *

Roy heard the phone ring through a fitful sleep. He sat up in the chair, not sure for a moment exactly where he was. He looked at the clock on the mantelpiece. Four-fifteen. The television showed an old black and white film. He dragged himself over to the phone.

'Yeah?'

'Roy? Roy Ryan?'

The clipped voice was familiar.

'Yeah. Who's this?'

'It's Jackson. DI Jackson.'

'Well, what do you want?' Roy had never liked Jackson.

'William Templeton was brought in earlier and he's shouting his mouth off about your sister and other things. I thought you ought to know.'

The line went dead and Roy stared at it for a few moments, letting the words sink in. Then he dialled Michael's flat.

Maura answered.

'Maws? I just had a call from Jackson. Willy's been nicked and he's telling them anything they want to know.'

'OK, Roy. Thanks.'

'What's happening, Maws?'

'At the moment you're as safe as you possibly can be. After eight o'clock this morning, everything will be fine, I promise you.'

'But what . . .'

'Roy, I'm sorry, mate, but I have to go. Get some sleep. I promise that you'll be fine. Tell the other boys for me.' She put the phone down, leaving Roy for the second time in five minutes with a dead phone in his hand.

'They've dragged in William Templeton.' Maura's voice was flat. She had hardly thought about him since the trouble had started and yet, not twenty-four hours ago, she had been making love to him.

'Does he know much?' Terry was concerned.

'No. Nothing that they don't already know. If I know

492

Willy, he'll be trying to save his own neck. They must have picked him up from my house.'

'Well, let's forget him then and concentrate on what the terms are going to be. We haven't got long now.' Maura stretched and both men watched the rise and fall of her breasts. She yawned loudly.

'Right. Where were we?'

Chapter Thirty-six

Marsh and Ackland were already sick to death of William Templeton and the Home Secretary had been on the phone twice in the last hour. Like everyone else he wanted this 'little business', as he put it, cleared up once and for all. Marsh had wondered fleetingly whether the Home Secretary had been up all night as well, because by the annoyed note in his voice Marsh got the impression that the man was tired. Sick and tired, by the sounds of it. As they all were.

The phone on his desk rang and he answered it.

'What!' He had lost any remnants of civility at about four in the morning. Now, at eight-fifteen, he had had just about enough.

'Detective Sergeant Petherick is here to see you, sir. I told him that you were not to be disturbed but he insisted that you would see him.'

The WPC's voice was petrified. She had already been bawled out twice by Marsh already, and she had only come on duty at seven o'clock.

'Send him up, girl! Send the bugger up!'

Marsh slammed the phone into its cradle.

'It's Petherick . . . the little scumbag!'

William Templeton stared at the two policemen. Marsh snapped at him, 'Go into the other office, you. And keep your mouth shut!'

William walked through the connecting door and sat down. He was tired and hungry and scared. From what he could gather, they knew all about him and his royal connections were not going to help him at all. He sat in the uncomfortable chair and put his head in his hands.

Terry walked into Marsh's office with his head held high

and a confident stride. Under his arm was a blue cardboard folder. He could feel Ackland measuring him up.

'Well, well, well . . . if it isn't the laughing policeman.' Marsh's voice dripped sarcasm.

Terry sat in the chair vacated by Templeton.

'It seems to me that I'm the only policeman in England who actually has something to laugh at. I know for a fact that you don't.'

Marsh screwed up his eyes. This was not the man he had seen previously. This was a man with a secret, an important secret, and one who knew how to use it.

'What happened to you? Where did you go?'

Terry looked at Ackland.

'I can't tell you that. What I can tell you is, Maura Ryan is willing to do a deal.'

'A what?' Marsh's voice bounced off the plasterboard walls.

'A deal.' Terry threw the folder on to the desk. 'In there is information. More than was in Geoffrey Ryan's file, I might add. There are copies of this information with numerous different people. I am here to talk business with you, gentlemen. And the Home Secretary, if he hasn't already been informed.'

Terry relaxed into his chair. He was enjoying this which was the last thing he'd expected. He watched Ackland pick up the file and flick through the papers.

'And what kind of a deal were you looking for?' Ackland's voice was resigned, as if he had expected something like this.

'Maura Ryan wants to be left alone. She and her brothers. She wants to keep her holdings in docklands, which are perfectly legal, and to run her clubs as before.'

'And what will she give us in return?'

Terry smiled at Ackland. 'In return she won't open her mouth about any of this.' He pointed to the file that Ackland was holding. 'And she will return the gold bullion that went missing in eighty-five. She also gives you her word that she will only deal with legitimate operations in all her future business investments.'

'And you honestly think she'll get away with this?.' Marsh was practically foaming at the mouth.

Terry nodded. 'Yeah, I do.'

'Your career is finished, my boy!'

Terry laughed. 'Oh, shut up, Marsh, for God's sake. You sound like something from "Dixon of Dock Green". This whole place . . .' he waved his arm '. . . is rotten, mate. Rotten to the bloody core. Of course my career is over. It was over before it began. Because if you read those files carefully, Maura's and Geoffrey's, the only people to get any kind of real promotion were those on the bloody take!'

Ackland sighed.

'So you know where Maura Ryan is, I take it?'

'Yeah, I know. And I'll never tell you, so you'd better think again if you're going to try and kick it out of me.'

Terry stood up. 'I'm warning you both now. Copies of those files have been faxed to two other countries. They were sent hours ago to reliable people. If so much as one hair of Maura Ryan's head is harmed they go straight to the tabloids. The Ryans own a bit more than you think. They own journalists and newspaper editors, with more than a few television newspeople thrown in. Not just in England but in the States and in Europe. Maura Ryan is willing to retire gracefully and just carry on with her legitimate holdings. Think about it carefully, gentlemen. She is not a woman to cross, believe me.'

Ackland raised his hand to silence Marsh who looked as if he was going to have a coronary at any moment.

'I'll have to speak to my superiors before anything can be decided.'

'Fair enough.' Terry glanced at his watch. 'I'll be in contact in four hours. At twelve-thirty.'

'You won't get away with this, Petherick. I'll get you personally.' Marsh's voice dripped with venom.

Terry leant on the desk, both palms flat, and looked into Marsh's sharp-featured face.

'You'll get me, will you? Funny how you don't want to get the others, the ones on the take. The big developers and the MPs and the Chief Super that you work for. Does he know that he's been tumbled yet? That his holidays in Kenya and the Maldives are over? That his little scams have all been found out? Does he know that the Ryans even have the name of the prostitute he visits every Wednesday night? The one who ties him up and spanks him?

'Don't say you're getting me, Marsh! Go and get some real villains for once in your life.'

Terry straightened his back and stared defiantly at the silent and grim-faced man before him. 'One last thing. Would you tell the Chief Super that I have a bit of news that might interest him?'

'What's that?' Marsh spat the words out.

'Tell him that the girl he sees every Wednesday, Samantha Golding, was diagnosed as having Aids. Tell him the Ryans even knew that before him. Before any of you. And don't you dare act the outraged policeman with me! You were willing to take part in the murder of an entire family. If you had done you would have kidded yourself it was for your country. Well, you know and I know it would not have been. It would just have saved a load of fat bastards' arses. If you loved your country so much you should have pissed off to the Falklands, Marsh. And from what's in that file,' he pointed to the folder Ackland was holding, 'that was another complete cover up and shambles!

'Now, I'm leaving. I'll be back in touch at half-past twelve.'

He stormed out of the office, leaving a white-faced Marsh and a quiet and subdued Ackland.

'You asked for that, Marsh. I have to take my hat off to the man. What he said was true.'

Marsh was in such a monumental temper he forgot his fear of Ackland. He picked up his cigar and said, 'Oh, fuck off, you Scottish turd!'

In the office next door William Templeton began to laugh.

Terry did not go back to Michael's flat. It had been arranged that he would go back to his own place, in case he was followed.

498

He drove there on a high. At least he had told Marsh exactly what he thought of him. Inside his flat he made himself some coffee and sat reading the paper. He had lost the urge to sleep, was in the state of overtiredness that seems to make a person more alert and mentally agile.

He sat at the table and thought about Maura. Nothing he did would get her out of his mind for even five minutes. Once again the words on the page in front of him were replaced by a vision of her face. She was flying to Marbella today. Although he had told Marsh that the file had been faxed through to two different countries, it was not true. Maura was going to take copies to the people concerned herself. She was flying to Marbella at five-thirty from Gatwick.

He sipped his coffee. He had lost everything now. His job, his way of life. And he had sacrificed it all for Maura Ryan. He looked around his kitchen, and then, as if he had been jolted from his chair, went to the phone. He knew what he had to do.

Sarah was enjoying having the three boys home. The feeling of foreboding that had plagued her the whole day before lifted off her as she cooked breakfast for them. She prepared what had long been known in the family as a 'Benny Special': two eggs, five slices of bacon, black pudding, tomatoes, beans, mushrooms, and even fried liver sausage, along with huge amounts of toast and a good strong pot of tea to wash it down with. She had felt sorry for Benjamin, eating his poached egg while they wolfed down his favourite meal, but consoled herself with the fact that he would thank her for it one day.

Just after breakfast the phone rang and Garry ran to answer it. Sarah was not sure what was said but the boys all looked a lot happier. She left them all in the kitchen while she gave Benjamin a blanket bath. He still couldn't get out of bed.

As she washed her husband's face, he grabbed her arm gently. 'All right, Sar?'

'Yeah, why?' She looked at him, puzzled.

'You're enjoying having the boys home again, ain't you?'

She smiled. 'Yeah. I miss them all.'

'I never gave you much, did I, girl? Except the back of my hand. It makes you think, you know, being stuck in bed.'

Sarah looked down at her husband's rapidly wasting body. Just for a split second she saw the eighteen-year-old boy who had whistled at her one bright summer evening in 1934. He had been tall, dark and handsome, wearing a bowler hat that night which had somehow set him apart from his contemporaries. Sarah felt an enormous lump in her throat for the man he had been.

'I know I never tell you very often, Sar, but you was always my girl. You know that, don't you? I always loved you.'

She nodded at him. It was one of those rare moments that occur in everyone's life. One of those times when there really isn't anything to say.

Ackland had spoken to the Home Secretary at length, and was now waiting for Terry Petherick to ring through to his office. Marsh had already left, as had William Templeton. Whereas Marsh had been disgusted by the turn of events, Templeton had been relieved – though Ackland was quick to guess that Templeton knew he had lost Maura Ryan's friendship.

He sighed heavily as he waited for Terry to call. The file that Petherick had left was, even at this moment, winging its way across London to be studied and talked over with the Secretary of State for the Environment amongst others. Ackland, unlike Marsh, knew when he was beaten and deep in his heart was glad that Maura Ryan had eventually outwitted them. His own conscience said to him: Why should she be a scapegoat for the real criminals?

He was glad when the phone finally rang. Lack of sleep was catching up with him.

Maura picked up the phone at twelve-forty. It was Terry and she knew even before he spoke what had happened.

She could feel his euphoria coming over the telephone line.

'They've agreed! Agreed to everything!'

'Oh, thank God!'

Maura took her first really deep breath for what seemed like days.

'They didn't argue about any of it?'

'No, Maws, not a thing. It's perfectly acceptable. Tell Richard he did a good job. We all did a good job.'

'What about my brothers?'

'Fine. Everything's Hunkydory.'

'Thanks for all your help, Terry. I promise you won't lose by it.'

Maura's voice was humble and sounded strange to Terry's ears.

'So you're off to warmer climes then?'

'Yeah. I suppose we won't see each other again.'

'Well . . . you never know what's going to happen, do you? I'd better let you go. You have a lot to do before you fly out.'

'Goodbye then, Terry. And thanks again.'

'You're welcome.' His voice was soft. 'Goodbye, Maura.'

He put down the phone and Maura stood in Michael's flat feeling more desolate and alone than she had ever done before. She had beaten the police and the establishment and yet she felt nothing. Nothing except an overwhelming loneliness.

Richard came into the room.

'We won then?' He sounded happy.

'Yeah. We won.'

He was sad to hear Maura's flat and broken voice. 'You'd better get a move on, you know. You have to be at Gatwick by three-thirty.'

'I know.'

Richard put his arm around her. She was much taller than him and he had to look up into her face.

'Michael used to say to me when I was down: "Ricky, remember that today is the first day of the rest of your life." I know it's an old cliché, but it's also a very true one.'

'Oh, Richard. What would I have done without you?'

She kissed him full on the mouth then said, 'I'd better phone Roy, tell him the good news.'

Maura sat on the Monarch Flight to Gibraltar. It was five-twenty-nine and the plane was due to take off at any time. She was sitting in a window seat. The seat next to her was unoccupied and she was glad – she was not up to making conversation with strangers. Plus she was shattered. She had been awake for nearly twenty-eight hours.

She closed her eyes, willing the plane to take off. Terry Petherick came straight to mind . . . She admitted to herself that she still had all the old feelings for him. The feelings that had assailed her on and off for over twenty years. When she had spoken to him on the telephone and he had said goodbye, she had felt as if her heart had been ripped from her chest. What was it about the man? Why did he make her feel like this? Even when she had learned that William, who was supposed to love her, had been willing to trade her to the police, she had not felt the intensity of feeling as when she had heard that single word from Terry: 'Goodbye.'

When she had told him the night before about the baby and what had happened, she had hoped, deep down, that it would bring them closer together. And it had, for a little while. But only for a little while. She supposed he thought that by doing the negotiating for her with the police he had repaid any debt that he owed her. She bit her lip.

In the seat in front of her were two little boys, both excited to be going on holiday. The bigger of the two, a boy of about ten with light brown hair and mischievous brown eyes, kept looking through the gap in the seats at her. As they jumped around in excitement Maura knew that she would not have a lot of peace on the flight.

She closed her eyes tighter, willing the plane to take off so she could at least have a cigarette. She felt someone sit down in the seat beside her and pretended she was asleep. She was too overwrought to start making small talk with anyone.

502

'Maura Ryan, I arrest you.'

Her eyes flew open and she looked at the man beside her, dumbstruck.

'But . . . but . . .' Her voice was locked inside her throat.

'I hope you're pleased to see me?' Terry's voice was deep and husky. He was smiling that little lopsided grin that had captured her heart so many years before.

'But I don't understand. When I spoke to you . . .'

'I was still trying to get on this flight then. They held the place for me, you know. One of the last perks of being a policeman. My final abuse of my position.'

He smiled at her again. 'I don't know if you want me, Maura. But I want you more than ever. I think deep in my heart I've always known that one day I would come and claim you as my own.'

She was still staring at him in absolute amazement. Terry was frightened now. If she pushed him away this time it would be for good and he did not think he could live with that.

The plane began to taxi down the runway, building up speed. As its nose left the tarmac, Maura smiled at him.

'Oh, Terry. I'm so glad you came. So very, very glad.'

He kissed her then, a long lingering kiss that was witnessed by the two boys in the seat in front. It was their giggling that broke them apart.

'Do you mind?' Terry's voice was jocular and the two little faces disappeared from sight.

He looked at Maura's radiant face and thanked God she still wanted him.

'So you're arresting me, are you?' Her voice was full of love.

He nodded at her, drinking in every feature and contour of her face.

'Yes, I'm arresting you . . . and I'm afraid that you're going to get a life sentence. The whole of it to be spent with me.'

Maura looked at him seriously. 'I'll still be running the clubs and . . .'

Terry put his finger to her lips.

'I don't care, Maura. All I want from now on is you.'
They smiled at one another as the plane gradually flew higher into the sky.

MARTINA COLE
GOODNIGHT LADY

SHE KNOWS EVERYONE'S SECRETS...

The infamous Briony Cavanagh: quite a beauty in her day,
and powerful, too. In the sixties, she ran a string of the
most notorious brothels in the East End. Patronised by
peers and politicians – even royalty, some said. Only Briony
knew what went on behind those thick velvet curtains, those
discreet closed doors, and Briony never opened her mouth
– unless she stood to benefit.

Only Briony knew the hard and painful road she'd travelled
to get there. From an impoverished childhood that ended
abruptly with shocking betrayal, she had schemed and
manipulated, determined to be mistress of her own fate.

But her flourishing business brought her into contact with
the darker side of life at the violent heart of London's
gangland. Along with her material success came risk and
danger. And the Goodnight Lady had her own secret place,
a place in her heart that was always shadowed with loss...

Don't miss Martina Cole's bestsellers, *The Ladykiller*
and *Dangerous Lady*, also from Headline:
'Move over Jackie [Collins]!' *Daily Mirror*
'Sheer escapism...gripping...will definitely keep you guessing
to the end' *Company*
'Graphic realism combined with dramatic flair make this a winner'
Netta Martin, *Annabel*

FICTION/GENERAL   0 7472 4429 4

A selection of bestsellers
from Headline

THE CHANGING ROOM	Margaret Bard	£5.99 ☐
BACKSTREET CHILD	Harry Bowling	£5.99 ☐
A HIDDEN BEAUTY	Tessa Barclay	£5.99 ☐
A HANDFUL OF HAPPINESS	Evelyn Hood	£5.99 ☐
THE SCENT OF MAY	Sue Sully	£5.99 ☐
HEARTSEASE	T R Wilson	£5.99 ☐
NOBODY'S DARLING	Josephine Cox	£5.99 ☐
A CHILD OF SECRETS	Mary Mackie	£5.99 ☐
WHITECHAPEL GIRL	Gilda O'Neill	£5.99 ☐
BID TIME RETURN	Donna Baker	£5.99 ☐
THE LADIES OF BEVERLEY HILLS	Sharleen Cooper Cohen	£5.99 ☐
THE OLD GIRL NETWORK	Catherine Alliott	£4.99 ☐

All Headline books are available at your local bookshop or newsagent, or can be ordered direct from the publisher. Just tick the titles you want and fill in the form below. Prices and availability subject to change without notice.

Headline Book Publishing, Cash Sales Department, Bookpoint, 39 Milton Park, Abingdon, OXON, OX14 4TD, UK. If you have a credit card you may order by telephone – 0235 400400.

Please enclose a cheque or postal order made payable to Bookpoint Ltd to the value of the cover price and allow the following for postage and packing:
UK & BFPO: £1.00 for the first book, 50p for the second book and 30p for each additional book ordered up to a maximum charge of £3.00.
OVERSEAS & EIRE: £2.00 for the first book, £1.00 for the second book and 50p for each additional book.

Name ....

Address ....

....

....

If you would prefer to pay by credit card, please complete:
Please debit my Visa/Access/Diner's Card/American Express (delete as applicable) card no:

Signature .... Expiry Date ....

Martina Cole was born in Avely in Essex and brought up as part of a large, close-knit family, living in and around Dagenham and Rainham for most of her life. She has been writing since childhood, and was encouraged by her English teacher to try to earn a living from it – advice she didn't take until she was twenty-five, though for years she wrote romantic fiction in exercise books for a friend.

Her first novel, *Dangerous Lady*, available from Headline, was a major bestseller and was warmly praised:

'Move over Jackie (Collins)!' *Daily Mirror*

'All the ingredients to be a huge hit' *Today*

'A major new talent . . . a roaring success . . . a powerful tale of gangland London' *Best*

Also by Martina Cole

Dangerous Lady

The Ladykiller

Martina Cole

HEADLINE

First published in 1993
by HEADLINE BOOK PUBLISHING

10 9 8

ISBN 0 7472 4085 X

Typeset by Keyboard Services, Luton

Printed and bound in Great Britain by
Cox & Wyman Ltd, Reading, Berkshire

HEADLINE BOOK PUBLISHING
A division of Hodder Headline PLC
338 Euston Road
London NW1 3BH

I dedicate this book to
Les and Christopher

I would like to thank my agent, Darley Anderson, for his faith, his trust and most of all his friendship.

Many thanks to Sergeant Steven Bolger of the Windermere Police Department, Florida, for all his help while I researched this book.

And a little thanks to Julie, for typing and typing and typing.

And a special thanks to my husband and son, they know what for.

BOOK ONE

'Of all the griefs that harass the distress'd
Sure the most bitter is a scornful jest;
Fate never wounds more deep the gen'rous heart,
Than when a blockhead's insult points the dart'
     – Samuel Johnson, 1709–84

'I have chosen thee in the furnace of affliction'
       – Isaiah, 48, x

'Blood is compulsory, they're all blood you see'
     – Tom Stoppard, *Rosenkrantz*
      and Guildenstern Are Dead

Prologue

'All I asked you to do was take off your muddy shoes. For Christ's sake, George, are you thick or something? Can't you even take in the most simple thing?'

Elaine Markham looked at her husband's expressionless face and fought down an urge to slam her fist into it. She could feel herself gritting her teeth and made a conscious effort to relax. Once more her eyes went to the wet mud all over her kitchen floor.

Sighing heavily, she took out the floor cloth from underneath the kitchen sink, slammed the cupboard door shut and began to fill a plastic bowl with water. George Markham watched his wife as she sprinkled some Flash into the water. Sitting down on one of the kitchen chairs, he began to remove his gardening shoes, careful not to let any more mud or dirt fall on the pristine floor.

Elaine turned from the sink with the bowl of water and shrieked at him: 'Can't you do that on a piece of newspaper? Are you so stupid you can't even think of doing a simple thing like that?'

George stared at his wife for a few seconds, chewing on his bottom lip.

'I'm sorry, Elaine.' His voice was low and bewildered. The sound of it made his wife screw her eyes up tight.

Pulling off his shoes, George went to the kitchen door and dropped them outside. Shutting the door carefully, he turned back to his wife.

'Give me that, Elaine. I'll clean up the mess.' He smiled at her sadly, causing her breathing to become laboured. She shook her head in irritation.

'No. You'll only make it worse. By God, George, no wonder you can't get on at work. It's a wonder they even allow you to go there every day.' She put the bowl of steaming water on the floor and knelt down. As she began washing the floor she was still complaining.

'Honestly, you're enough to drive a person up the bloody wall. You can't do anything . . . *anything* . . . without ballsing it up in some way. Look at last week . . .'

George watched his wife's ample buttocks moving under her apron as she worked and talked. The rolls of fat around her hips were shuddering alarmingly as she scrubbed at the floor. In his mind's eye, he saw himself getting up from his seat and kicking her as hard as he could in the rump, sending her and the bowl of water flying. The fantasy made him smile to himself.

'What are you grinning at?' He brought himself back to the present with difficulty and focused on Elaine's face. She was staring at him over her shoulder, her bright green eye-shadow and ruby red lips lurid in the glare from the strip light.

'Nothing . . . Nothing, love.' He sounded confused.

'Just piss off, George. Out of my sight.'

He continued to stare at his wife. He watched as her strong arms and hands wrung out the floor cloth, her fingers squeezing until every last drop of water was gone. He wished he was squeezing Elaine's neck. Instead he went towards the back door.

'Where are you going now?' Her voice was high and querulous.

George stared at her.

'I still have some things to do in the shed.'

Elaine rolled her eyes to the ceiling.

'Well, why on earth did you come in in the first place? Messing up the floor, causing all this.' She spread her arms in a gesture of wonderment.

'I just wanted a cup of tea. But I can see that you're busy . . .'

He made a hasty exit from the kitchen and pulled on his

4

gardening shoes again outside the back door. Elaine stared at the closed door for a few seconds. As always after she had 'been at' George, as she termed it to herself, she felt guilty. Guilty and flat. He was just so useless. Over the years, his placid acceptance of their way of life had driven her mad. Sighing, she carried on washing the floor.

Inside his shed, George bolted the wooden door and leant against it for a few moments, the sweat cold on his forehead. Licking his lips, he closed his eyes and began to breathe deeply.

One of these days Elaine was going to get a shock. She was going to open her mouth once too often. He could feel the hammering of his heart against his ribs and placed his hand over it as if to quell the movement.

He turned from the door and walked to the opposite end of his shed. Pulling a pile of gardening magazines from an old school desk, he opened the top. Inside the desk were a couple of scruffy jumpers – his gardening jumpers. Taking these out, he smiled. Underneath them were his books. His *real* books, with real women in them. Women who did not nag and chide and want. Women who just lay passively and smiled. Whatever you might do to them.

He picked up the top book. On the cover was a young girl of about twenty. Her arms were tied behind her back and she had a leather collar around her neck. Her long golden blonde hair lay across her shoulders and partially obscured her breasts. A man's hand was pulling her head backwards, his hairy maleness messing up the girl's lovely locks. She was smiling.

George stared at the picture for a while. His small, even teeth just showed beneath his lips in a slight smile. Licking his lips again, he sat in his chair. He opened the magazine slowly as if for the first time, wanting to savour the pleasure of every picture.

He looked at the girl in front of him, a different girl this time. Oriental-looking, with tiny pointed breasts and a curtain of black hair. She was on all fours; the leather strap

5

around her neck was attached to her feet. If she struggled against it, you could see that she would choke to death. A man was behind her. He wore a black leather mask and was about to plunge his erect penis into the girl's anus. Her back was arched and she was looking at the camera, a smile of beatific pleasure plastered across her face.

George sighed with contentment. He slowly looked through the magazine, pausing here and there to hold the book away from him, to see the pictures from a different angle. He could feel the familiar sense of excitement building up inside. He pushed his hand into the crease of the chair. He felt around for a second, then his hand found what he was looking for. He drew out an army knife, then, placing the magazine carefully across his knees, he pulled the knife out from its cover. It was a large knife with a seven-inch serrated blade. He turned it around in the sunshine that was streaming through the window, watching it glinting. He looked down at the girl in the centrefold of the magazine. Her face was looking up at him in a mixture of agony and ecstasy as a hooded man ejaculated into her face, the semen running down her chin and on to her breasts.

Carefully and precisely, George began to dismember her. He drew the knife across her throat, slitting the paper. Then he began to tear at her breasts and vagina. All the time she watched him. Smiling at him. Encouraging him. He could feel his erection building, could feel the cold sweat under his arms and across his back. He began to hack at the magazine, pushing the knife into the paper. He heard the rush in his ears as if he was swimming underwater and then the graceful, almost euphoric waves of the orgasm as it reached its crescendo.

George lay back in the comfortable old chair, his breathing coming in small gasps, his heartbeat gradually returning to normal. He closed his eyes and gradually the sounds and sights of the day came back to him.

He could hear his neighbour's strimmer outside his shed. Could hear the children next door playing in their paddling pool. Their high-pitched baby laughter drifted into his consciousness. A bead of salty sweat dripped into his eyes and he blinked it away. He shook his head slowly and looked down at his lap. That was when he saw the blood.

He blinked rapidly for a few seconds. The girl was covered in blood. The body that he had slashed to pieces was slowly being stained crimson. George stared.

He pushed the magazine from him, every nerve in his body vibrating with shock.

He had cut himself! He stared down at the gash on his thigh. It was pumping blood everywhere. He jumped from his seat in a panic. The knife had slit his jeans and pierced his own flesh!

He must tell Elaine. Get her to take him to the hospital. He went to the shed door in a blind panic.

Then he remembered the books.

Holding the injured leg with one hand, he gathered the magazines from the floor. He thrust them into the child's desk with the others. Bundling the jumpers on top, he shut the lid. He could feel the blood running down his leg.

He picked up the pile of gardening magazines and threw them on top of the desk. Blood was everywhere now.

Pulling the bolt from across the top of the shed door he burst out into the sunlight. The sound of splashing and shrieking coming over the larch lap fence assaulted his ears. George ran up the path to the back door and thrust it open.

Elaine was preparing the vegetables for dinner. She turned towards him in dismay. He stood before her, covered in blood.

'I – I've cut myself, Elaine.' He was nearly crying.

'Oh my God, George!' She grabbed a tea towel and wound it round his leg, pulling it tight. 'Come on. I'll drive you to the hospital.'

George lay in a cubicle of the Accident and Emergency department of Grangely Hospital. He felt sick. A young nurse was trying to remove his trousers.

'Please, Mr Markham. I must take them off.' Her voice was young and husky.

'No! No, you mustn't. Cut the trouser leg off or something.'

George and the nurse stared at one another. Then both looked towards the curtain as it was pulled back. The young nurse breathed a sigh of relief. It was the Charge Nurse, Joey Denellan.

'What's the matter, Nurse?' His voice held the false jocularity peculiar to male nurses.

'Mr Markham won't let me remove his trousers.'

The man smiled at George. 'Bit of a shy one, are you? Well, never mind. I'll do it for you.'

The nurse left and before George could protest the young man was pulling off his jeans. George tried to grab the waistband but the boy was too strong. They were off.

George swallowed deeply and turned his head away from the boy's face.

Joey Denellan stared at the wounded leg with an expert eye. Deep, but it had not affected any main arteries. His eyes flicked over the man before him and stopped dead. No wonder the old boy was so against Jenny pulling his trousers off. The stains were very recent and still sticky. What had he been up to that could have got him such a large gash in his leg? He shrugged. Theirs was not to reason why.

'What kind of knife was it?' Joey was careful to keep his voice light.

'Oh, a Swiss army knife.' George's voice was small and the younger man felt sorry for him.

'Well, it will need a few stitches in, but don't worry. You didn't sever anything important. Would you like me to see if I can find you some clean pants?'

George heard the 'man to man' inflection in the other's voice. He nodded. 'Please. I . . .'

'Righty ho then. I'll be back in a minute. The doctor will be here soon, OK?'

'Thank you. Thank you very much. Would you . . . keep my wife away, please?'

George's eyes were pleading and Joey nodded slowly.

8

'OK. Don't worry.' He walked from the cubicle and went out to the reception area.

'Mrs Markham?' He looked around the assembled people and was not surprised to see the fat woman with the dyed red hair and bright green track suit stand up and walk towards him. He had somehow known that this would be the poor bloke's wife.

'Is he all right? My God, only George could cut himself while sitting in a bloody shed. Honestly, Doctor . . .'

'Nurse. I'm a nurse.'

As Elaine went to speak again he interrupted her.

'We're going to stitch your husband after the doctor has seen him. If you would like to get yourself a coffee or something, there's a machine at the end of that corridor.' He pointed to the swing doors to the right.

Elaine knew when she was being shut up and her eyes took on the steely glint usually reserved for George. Turning away, she walked towards the swing doors and pushed them open with such force they crashed against the walls.

Joey Denellan watched her. No wonder the poor old sod looked so downtrodden. Being married to her must be like being married to Attila the Hun. Still Joey was puzzled. How did the old boy get the gash on his leg? What had she said? In a garden shed. How did that account for the semen, which it definitely was, in his underpants? He heard someone call him.

'Joey, an RTA on the M25.'

'How many involved?' He walked towards the reception desk.

'Four. Estimated time of arrival seven minutes.'

'OK. Call Crash.'

Joey began to make arrangements to receive the casualties from the road accident. George Markham was pushed from his mind.

'Are you coming, George?' Peter Renshaw's deep booming voice seemed to bounce off the walls of the office and hit George in the face.

9

'Coming where?' He peered at Renshaw.

'To the do, Georgie. The bloody leaving do – for Jonesy.'

'Oh, yes. Jonesy's leaving do. Of course, of course. Yes, I'll be going.'

'Good on you. Got him a strippergram, the lot! Tell you what, Georgie, it will be a great do. Bl-oody great!'

Peter Renshaw had a habit of stressing some words by chopping them in two to get his point across. It drove George up the wall.

Renshaw was a salesman for the clothing company for which George worked. He towered over George in height and it was obvious he liked this. Peter Renshaw was in his early thirties and from what everyone could gather, he earned a lot of money. He was the number one salesman. He liked George for some strange reason and always made sure he was invited to any dos that were on the agenda.

'I arranged the strippergram meself, Georgie boy. Biggest set of Bristols this side of the water. Can't wait to see old Jonesy's face.'

George smiled.

Old Jonesy . . . Howard Jones was younger than George himself. About forty-five was Howard Jones. George was fifty-one. He shuddered inwardly. Fifty-one. His life was nearly over. Peter Renshaw's voice was still booming on.

'It's all arranged. The Pig and Whistle first. Twenty quid whip-round by the way. Then on to that new nightclub – what's it called? The Platinum Blonde, that's it. Watch all the little birds stru-tting their stuff. Be a right laugh!'

George carried on smiling.

'Well, I'll let you get on then. Got a hot piece of pussy down in accounts who's just dy-ing for it. See you Friday then?'

George nodded. 'Yes. See you on Friday, Peter.'

He watched the man walk from his office. Old Jonesy . . . He supposed they called him Old Markham. He looked at his watch. It was five thirty-five. He got out of his chair and, putting on his jacket, made his way out of the building.

Kortone Separates was a thriving firm, even in the recession. George worked in the book-keeping department of accounts.

He left the small corridor and went to the stairway that led to the car park. He never used the lifts. As he walked down the stairs he saw Miss Pearson kneeling on the floor picking up some papers. She was young, only about eighteen, and had worked for Kortone's for a year. George had never spoken to her. She had left three buttons undone and from the landing above her George could see the swelling of her bosom as she stretched out her arms to gather the papers.

He stared down at her. The creamy flesh was firm and inviting. The girl looked up at him. He saw the heavily made-up face and forced himself to move down the stairs. He bent down and retrieved some papers, handing them to her silently.

'Thank you, Mr Markham.'

She knew his name! George felt an enormous surge of pleasure over this little fact.

'You're welcome.' He stood up and looked down at her again. Then the door above opened and Peter Renshaw's voice boomed down to them.

'There you are! I've been looking everywhere for you. You sly old fox, George. Might have known you'd be where the pretty girls are!'

Miss Pearson looked at Peter and gave a broad smile. George watched her face closely.

'Oh, Peter.' Her voice was husky and breathless. 'I waited for you but . . .'

George was aware of Peter Renshaw's footsteps on the stairs, bringing him closer. He quickly picked up the rest of the papers from the floor and handed them to Miss Pearson.

George walked away from them, certain that he would not be noticed. He was right. Neither of them said a word to him. He walked out of the building and unlocked his car, an A-reg Orion. He sat in the driving seat, waiting.

The couple finally left the building and walked towards Peter's car, Renshaw's arm draped across the girl's shoulder,

11

one hand squeezing her breast. Miss Pearson giggled and pushed it away.

Another slut. Another whore. What had Peter said? Dying for it? George closed his eyes and savoured the picture his words had conjured up.

He visualised Miss Pearson, her body open to him, her legs sprawled apart, tied to the legs of a bed. Her hands tied behind her back, her heavily made-up face smiling at him as he approached her. She was begging for it. Begging and pleading with him . . .

'Mr Markham?' George's eyes flew open.

'Are you all right? You look very white.'

George stared at the man looking in at the window of his car. It was the car park attendant.

'Yes, thank you.' George smiled timidly. 'I felt a bit tired, that's all.'

The man made a salute and straightened up.

George watched him walk away, his heart hammering in his ears. He tried to get the picture back in his mind but it was no good. Trembling, he started up his car and drove into Grantley town centre. The books he had ordered were due in today. He smiled, enjoying the late summer sunshine and the exquisite feeling of anticipation.

It crossed his mind briefly that his 'hobby' was now becoming an obsession, but he thrust the thought aside. His leg was still sore and he rubbed it absentmindedly as he drove.

It was the end of September 1989.

Chapter One

Elaine Markham looked at her husband as he watched the television. His shiny balding head was nodding up and down as if he was agreeing with everything that the newscaster said.

'Oh, for Christ's sake, George! Stop agreeing with the TV.'

He turned in his chair to face her, a hurt expression on his face. Elaine closed her eyes. She could feel her hands clenching into fists and made herself relax.

'Shall I make you a cup of Ovaltine, dear?' George asked in his soft voice.

'Yes, you do that.'

George went out to the impossibly clean kitchen and set about making the bedtime drinks. He put on the pan of milk and then, opening one of the kitchen cabinets, took out Elaine's sleeping pills. Carefully grinding one between two spoons, he placed the powder in the cup with the sugar. Smiling, he poured steaming milk into the cup and stirred it vigorously. Then, removing two more of the sleeping pills, he took the Ovaltine and the pills into Elaine.

'Here you are, dear. I brought your pills in for you as well.' She took the drink and pills from him.

'Thanks, George. Look, I know I go on at times . . .' Her voice trailed off.

'I don't take the slightest bit of notice, Elaine. I know that I – well, that I irritate you is the word, I suppose?'

George smiled at her, the sad smile that always made her want to rip him to shreds.

She put the sleeping pills into her mouth and washed them down with the Ovaltine, burning her lips.

George was still smiling.

'This tastes bitter.'

He raised his eyebrows and took a sip of his own drink.

'Well, mine is fine, dear. Maybe it's the aftertaste of the pills?'

'Could be. I think I'll take my drink up with me.' She pulled herself from her seat with difficulty.

'Night, Elaine. Sleep well.'

She stared at her husband.

'If I slept well, George, I wouldn't be taking sleeping tablets.'

'It's just an expression, dear. That's all.'

Was it her imagination or was George different lately? Although she could not pinpoint what had changed, she had the distinct feeling that the balance between them was shifting slightly. Looking at her husband now, she would swear on a stack of bibles that he was laughing at her.

'Good night then, dear,' he said again.

She tried to smile at her husband.

'Yes. Good night, George.'

She walked from the room and his gaze followed her. As she made her way up the stairs to their room, the feeling of uneasiness came over her once more. It was the beginning of December and George had been 'wrong' somehow for the last couple of months. Nothing she could put her finger on exactly, but subtle little differences. He had taken to going out in the evenings for walks, for instance. He was only gone an hour or so but . . .

She pulled off the candlewick dressing gown and sat on the edge of the bed. He had never once, in twenty-seven years of marriage, gone out walking anywhere. In fact, it was his pet hate.

She took off her sheepskin-lined slippers and rubbed at the corn on her foot. Her legs were fat like the rest of her and were disfigured by varicose veins. She stared at them and shrugged.

She sat against the pillows, picked up her latest Mills and

Boon and read while the pills took effect and she finished her Ovaltine.

The words were becoming blurred. She blinked her eyes, trying to focus. The pills were working quicker and quicker lately.

Finally she gave up. Turning off the bedside lamp, she settled down to sleep.

Ten minutes later, George popped his head around the bedroom door and grunted in satisfaction as he heard his wife's heavy snores.

George slipped out of the house. He had on his heaviest overcoat as the night air was cold and damp. In the street light he looked no different from anyone else who walked the streets late at night. He pulled on the cheesecutter hat he had recently purchased and began his prowling.

He felt a freedom he had not experienced for twenty years in this new pastime. He walked the length and breadth of Grantley. Silently and diligently he walked. Tonight he had decided to walk by the flats that were on the other side of town. Taking a deep breath, he began his lonely trek.

As he walked, he kept a vigilant eye out for open curtains and movement. He walked to the end of Bychester Terrace and turned right. Peabody Street took him on to a dirt road that led round the perimeter of Grantley. No busy traffic, only a lone car containing a courting couple here and there. George was outside the flats in Beacham Rise within fifteen minutes.

Stationing himself under a large cherry tree opposite the small block he waited. It was eleven-fifteen before he saw anything, and as usual it was the woman who lived on the second floor. The flats were what was termed 'low rise', only three storeys high. George had been here many times in the last eight weeks and it was always the woman on the second floor who provided his show. Where he was standing, under the cherry tree, was a small hill, part of the council landscaping plan, which gave him the perfect vantage point

15

to see into the woman's flat. Taking the small opera glasses from his pocket, he watched.

Leonora Davidson yawned cavernously. She stretched her hands above her head and pulled up her thick black hair. She was dead tired. She would have to stop all the overtime, it was killing her.

She unbuttoned her blouse slowly, letting it fall from her rounded shoulders on to the floor. She unhooked her bra and let her breasts fall free, rubbing them furiously as the itching started. Lifting one breast with her hand, she looked into the mirror of her dressing table. A thick red line marked the tender flesh. She sighed. She would have to get herself some decent bras.

She cupped her breasts in her hands and pushed them up, as if weighing them. She had definitely put on weight. Then she unzipped her skirt and let it fall to the floor. Stepping out of it, she kicked it away from her.

Leonora looked at her body in the mirror. Not bad for her age. A bit saggy these days but everyone lost the war with gravity eventually. She automatically held her stomach in, then let it out. Sod it! There was no one to admire her any more. Why bother?

Yawning again, wider this time, she went to her dressing stool and picked up her nightie, a wincyette affair that kept her warm if nothing else. After one last stretch, she turned out the light and climbed into bed.

George stood under the cherry tree entranced. When the light went off in the bedroom, he mumbled a curse under his breath and pushed the opera glasses back into his overcoat pocket. He was sweating. Taking a handkerchief out of his trouser pocket, he mopped his forehead.

Stupid bitch! What he would not give to be in that flat now. He would show her what it was all about, by Christ! Standing around naked. Inviting people to look at her. The slut! In his heightened excitement George was unaware of the two youths who had been watching him watching her.

16

'What you doin'?' The voice caused him to swivel around on the balls of his feet.

'I . . . I beg your pardon?' His voice squeaked with surprise. Two youths stood there, one wearing a long leather coat and with straggly brown hair. The other was wearing a large sheepskin and was what George knew was called a skinhead.

'You heard, you old ponce. What was you doin' watching Mrs Davidson getting undressed? You a nonce?'

The boy in the leather coat stepped towards him, a menacing look on his face.

'Got any money?' This from the skinhead. George smelt a distinct odour of glue and vomit.

He stared at them, nonplussed.

The youth in the leather coat lurched towards him and he stepped back nimbly.

'If you two don't go away I will call for assistance.'

The leather-coated boy mimicked him.

'"If you two don't go away I will call for assistance." Well, we—' he pointed to his friend and himself '—might just call the filth ourselves. You're a fucking peeping Tom, ain't ya? So just give us your dosh and you can go. Quietly.'

The skinhead heaved and George watched in revulsion as a stream of vomit ejaculated from the boy's mouth. It landed just by his shoes, splashing them. The odour wafted into his nostrils as the sick steamed in the freezing night air.

The leather-coated boy laughed uproariously at his friend, who was now hanging on to the cherry tree for support.

Fumbling inside his coat, George pulled out two five-pound notes and handed them to the boy. Leather coat took them from him and pushed them into the pocket of his jeans.

'Come on, Trev. Let's trounce the bastard.'

Trevor was not capable of letting go of the cherry tree and so the leather-coated boy launched himself at George alone. He held up his arms in self-defence as the first blows hit him in the face and head. He could feel himself being pushed down to the ground and the knowledge that he would end up lying in the skinhead's vomit was all that kept him upright. He felt the cold sting as the boy's fist came into contact with his face. Then he was rolling down the small hill, the leather-coated boy kicking him.

'Oi! What's all the racket about out there?' A man's deep voice echoed across the road and the boy looked up in its direction. A light was on on the third floor and a large man in a string vest was leaning out of a window, shaking his fist. Lights were going on all over the flats. George heard the two boys stumbling away while he lay on the cold ground, gasping for air.

Leonora Davidson heard the shouting and leapt from her bed. She pulled on her dressing gown and slippers and looked out of her bedroom window. She saw the body of a man lying at the bottom of the small rise, underneath the lamp post. She could see the two youths running away. One of them, in a leather coat, was dragging his friend along. She gritted her teeth. No one was safe these days. It was obvious the poor man had been mugged! She walked from her flat, picking up her door keys as she went, and ran down to where a small crowd had gathered around the injured man.

'What happened, Fred?' Her breath steamed in the cold night air. She shivered.

'Little buggers want slaughtering. Mugged this poor old bastard as he walked by!'

George still lay on the ground, quite enjoying all the attention.

'Oh, you poor thing.' Leonora's voice was filled with pity. 'I called the police. They'll be here in a minute.'

George's ears flapped at the word 'police'. He was up off the ground and brushing himself down in record time.

'Really, there's no need for the police. They'll never catch them anyway. And I'm in a hurry.'

He began to walk away from the small gathering.

'But if you saw them you could give a description like.' Fred's voice was cajoling.

George was shaking his bald head. He was aware that he had lost his hat somewhere along the line. He looked around for it frantically.

Leonora walked over to him.

'You've had a terrible shock. Shall I make you a nice cup of tea?'

George could not believe what she was saying. She was inviting him into her home. If it had not been for her he would not be in this condition. The stupid whore!

'It's perfectly all right. I just want to get home.'

His voice held its usual meekness and he saw her smile at him pityingly.

A police car sped around the corner of the flats and screeched to a halt by the little crowd. George put his hand over his face in dismay. This was all he needed.

'All right, all right. Calm down. What happened?'

Everyone started talking at once.

Sergeant Harris's voice boomed out and George guessed it would wake up any of the residents who were not already up.

Sergeant Harris looked at Leonora.

'What happened, love?'

'This poor man was mugged. Right here.' She pointed to George who was trying to creep away.

The sergeant looked at him, bewildered.

'Where are you going?'

'I . . . I really must get home. My wife will be worried . . .'

Harris smiled at him. In shock, he thought to himself.

'Come on, sir. Come to the station and we can get this all sorted out in no time.'

'NO!' George was amazed at the sound of his own voice. 'I . . . I . . . Oh, leave me alone!'

Harris stared at him stonily. 'We're only trying to help, sir.'

'You know you won't catch them. I just want to go home and forget about it.'

He began to walk away as quickly as he could.

The small crowd stared after his retreating back. Sergeant

Harris nodded at PC Downes and they got back into their Panda car and followed him.

'Get in, sir. The least we can do is give you a lift.'

George got into the car, his heart in his boots.

'Well I never, Fred! That poor man was in shock, I reckon.'

'You're right there, Leonora love. Poor old git. Not safe to walk the sodding streets these days . . .'

'That's the truth, Fred. I even get worried in me flat, with all the doors locked. You hear so much about rape and violence, it makes your blood run cold. Then to see that poor old man getting beaten up like that . . .' She left the sentence unfinished.

Sergeant Harris kept up a stream of chatter all the way to George's house.

'Look, sir. If you change your mind just pop into the station.'

'I will, Officer. At the moment all I want is to get home. This is the house.'

The Panda car pulled up outside George's home and he made a hasty retreat. Once inside he pulled off his overcoat and hung it on the banister, then went up to the bathroom. His face was slightly swollen but not too much. He breathed a sigh of relief.

He went back downstairs and checked his overcoat. It was covered in vomit. He cursed silently and set about cleaning it.

Fifty minutes later, there was no evidence of his escapade whatsoever. He made himself a cup of tea, and carrying it into the front room went to the lead light cupboard that housed the brandy and poured a generous measure into the cup. He sat on the settee and drank it gratefully.

When he had finished he felt better, and getting up from the sofa went up to his wife's room and popped his head around the door. Her snoring was loud and heavy. He smiled to himself. Three Mogadons to knock the old bag out, but it was worth it.

20

Sneaking downstairs, he went to the hall cupboard. Opening it, he pulled up the carpet and folded it back. Then, using the screwdriver he left there for this express purpose, he prised up one of the floorboards. There, staring up at him, was his Mandy!

He picked up the video almost lovingly, afterwards replacing the floorboard and the carpet. He took the video into the lounge. Pouring himself another measure of Three Barrels brandy into his dirty cup, he watched the film. As he did, he felt the tension and pain of the last few hours leave his body. As Mandy was assaulted over and over by a motley crew of degenerates, George Markham finally relaxed.

Visions of Mrs Davidson cupping her breasts kept coming into his thoughts. Her furious rubbing of them. He watched Mandy take a man's penis into her semen-smeared mouth and suddenly her face was Mrs Davidson's, the man was him. He felt his breathing getting heavier.

One thing good had come out of the evening: at least he knew her name now.

The next day, George did not go to work. His face was swollen and he told Elaine that he had an abscess on his tooth. She dutifully rang his office and then left to go to her own job.

She worked in a large supermarket in Grantley town. She was a 'checkout girl' and hated it.

Left alone, George had an idea.

Dressing himself meticulously, he got into his car and drove to London. As he admired the Essex countryside (even in the cold and wet it looked magnificent) George made his plans. After the fiasco of the night before, he decided that he should get himself kitted out properly.

He turned on Essex Radio and sang along to the Carpenters as he drove. Lighthearted and gay, he made his way to London's West End.

George walked nervously into the shop in Soho. It was his first time in a sex shop; he'd always sent for his books and videos by post. But once inside he felt strangely at ease.

Behind the counter was a man of about his age who smiled

at him as he browsed around the shop. The only disappointment was that the books and videos were tame. Tame and boring. He picked up a leather mask and took it to the counter.

'Eighty-five quid, please, guv.'

George meticulously counted out the money. It would be his Christmas present to himself. He felt almost jovial.

'You into bondage?'

George nodded shyly. 'Yes.' He smiled his secret smile that just showed his teeth. 'Yes, I am.'

'Was you after the hard porn like? Only if you was, I think I can help you . . .'

George picked up the carrier bag with the mask in and smiled again. Wider this time.

'I've got snuff movies here for two hundred quid a throw.'

George was perplexed. 'Snuff movies?'

The man saw his confusion and pulled him to one side to explain.

'Look, they're films with birds in . . . getting the business like. But they ain't pretend, see? It's really happening to them. That's why they're called "snuff" or "stuff" movies.'

The man could see that George was still unsure. He sighed. He had been in this game for thirty years, man and boy. He knew a nonce when he saw one, and he would swear on his grand-daughter's head that this bloke was one. A prize nonce.

'Look, it's the Yanks who thought them up. They kidnap some bird. Tie her up. Rape her and all that, you know . . . And her screams and moans are real, get it? Real. It's true. I've got a new lot in and they are well dawdy, I can tell you. There's one where the bird is actually dead and they still fuck the arse off her. Going like hot cakes they are.'

George's eyes were gleaming.

'How much did you say they were?'

'Two hundred smackers, mate. And cheap at the price, I can tell yer.'

'Can I pay by Barclaycard? Only I haven't got any more cash, you see.'

22

'Course you can, guv. We take everything here. Even American Express. Just as long as you have some other form of identification, we're cooking with gas.'

The man smiled and George smiled back. He felt as if he had found a true friend.

'If I was to give you a ring every now and then to see what was in stock, so to speak . . .'

The man patted his shoulder.

'Course you can, my old cocker. I'll save you anything a bit near the mark. How's that?' The man knew a policeman from thirty paces and was patting himself on the back. This bloke was a right pratt.

'Oh, thank you so much. Where I live . . .' He spread his hands helplessly.

'I know what you mean. People don't understand us real men, do they?'

The shopkeeper was busy taking the credit card from George before he had time to change his mind.

'No, they don't.'

He left ten minutes later, with his mask and his new film, both in a plain brown carrier bag clutched in his sweaty hand.

Looking around him at the faces and sounds of Soho, George Markham felt as if he had finally come home.

When Elaine opened the front door after her day at work, George had the dinner on and a pot of tea waiting for her.

'Sit yourself down, my love, you must be tired out. I've made us a nice bit of steak and chips.'

Elaine stared at her husband as if she had never seen him before. He seemed almost happy.

'Thank you, George. I must say I'm glad you bothered to cook. I didn't feel like it one bit.'

He chucked her under the chin as he placed a cup of steaming tea in front of her.

'For you, my precious, anything!'

He grinned at her, and Elaine grinned back.

There was definitely something odd here. The last time George had chucked her under the chin had been over twenty years ago, when they had still been happy. She sipped her tea and tried to shake off her suspicions. That had been before they'd had to move. Before everything had started going wrong.

Elaine drank her tea, watching George as he cooked.

She shook her head. There was no doubt about it: he was happy.

But why?

Chapter Two

George sat at his desk, blind to the ledgers in front of him. All
he could see was the movie that he had purchased from the sex
shop in Soho. Ever since he had watched it, he'd had a sense of
unreality. Sometimes it frightened him, like the night before
when he had been sitting with Elaine watching a programme
about Giant Pandas. He had sat, sipping his tea, watching the
film – and then he had just gone. Gone away in his mind to the
other film. He was *in* the other film. He was the star. He was in
complete control.

He had been brought back to reality by Elaine's voice. It
could crack glass and sour milk, all in one fell swoop. But his
aberration had scared him. Because lately he could not control
his thoughts at all. They ran away with him any time of the day
or night.

He shook himself mentally and told himself to get on with
the job in hand. He stared once more at the sales ledger in front
of him.

'Mr Markham, have you five minutes to spare?'

The voice of Josephine Denham broke into his thoughts.
He turned in his seat to see her standing in the doorway,
smiling at him.

'Of course, Mrs Denham.' His voice was soft and polite.

Josephine Denham turned and walked back to her office.
George Markham gave her the creeps and she did not know
why. He was always polite. Chillingly polite. He never took
days off for no reason, he always kept himself to himself, never
took long lunches or tried to engage her in banter, like some of
the other male employees. All in all he was a model worker. Yet
she had to admit to herself there was something about his soft,

pudgy body and watery grey eyes that gave her the willies. She sat at her desk and observed the little man in front of her.

'Please, take a seat.'

She watched George take the material of his trousers between his thumb and forefinger and pull it up before sitting down. Even this action irritated her. She saw his funny little smile, that just showed his teeth, and felt even more annoyed. George on the other hand was surreptitiously looking at Josephine's enormous breasts. He could see the rise and fall of every breath she took.

As far as he was concerned, Josephine Denham had a chest of Olympian standards.

She saw his smile widen, and forced herself to grin back.

'I am sorry to have to call you in, George. You've always been a good worker . . .'

He was more alert now. The smile had gone.

'I'm afraid that in these difficult times . . . with the recession . . . well, we're going to have to let some of the staff go. You will be paid redundancy money, of course.'

George felt as if someone had burst his own private bubble of happiness.

'I see.' But he didn't see. He didn't see at all. He had been with this firm for fifteen years.

'How many will be going?'

Josephine Denham took a deep breath. He may as well know now as later.

'Five. Johnson, Mathers, Davids and Pelham. Not forgetting your good self, of course.'

George stared at her. His expressionless face seemed to be drinking her in. She shuddered.

'I see.' So all the older men were to go. The young so-called dynamos were all staying. George felt an urge to leap from his chair and slap the supercilious bitch with her painted face, her dyed blonde hair, her fat, wobbling breasts. The dirty stinking slut! The dirty whore! He hoped she died screaming of cancer. He hoped they sliced her breasts inch by inch. He hoped . . .

26

'Are you all right, Mr Markham?' Josephine Denham was nervous. He had sat staring at her for over five minutes. No expression on his face, nothing. He knew and she knew that he was finished. No other firm would take him at fifty-one. He just did not have what it took. He had no charisma, no personality. George Markham had nothing going for him at all.

'I really am dreadfully sorry, George.' She said his name timidly. Unsure of herself.

He looked at her before turning towards the door. 'You will be.'

His voice was muffled and Josephine could not hear him. 'Sorry, I didn't quite . . .'

George turned to face her and smiled again.

'I said, you will be.'

Was he being sarcastic? She watched as he shuffled from her office, his shoulders even more rounded and dejected-looking than when he had come in.

She breathed a sigh of relief. At least she had got that out of the way.

She picked up her cigarettes and lit one. For some unknown reason she was shaking. She grinned to herself. Imagine being nervous of a little runt like George Markham!

But her uneasiness stayed with her all day.

George went back to his desk and sat silent and still until lunchtime. His mind was whirling underneath his calm exterior. He got into the little pub, the Fox Revived, at five past twelve and ordered himself a large brandy.

The barmaid was about forty-five with long bleached blonde hair and enormous false eyelashes. Her tiny, empty breasts were visible through her cheesecloth top. George looked at her in disgust.

Another slut. They were all fucking sluts. He put his hand to his mouth, shocked at even thinking such a word.

'That'll be one pound ninety, please.' The barmaid's voice had a nasal twang as she tried to speak in a refined manner.

'Thank you very much, dear. Please have one yourself.'

She answered his tiny smile with a wide one of her own, showing big tobacco-stained teeth.

George handed her the five-pound note and waited for his change. Then, taking his drink, he went to a small corner table and sipped his brandy.

Elaine would go stark staring mad when he told her. It would be another thing to hold against him. Oh, Elaine was good at collecting grudges. She collected grudges like other women collected hats or shoes. She still hadn't forgiven him for that other business. She never mentioned it, oh no, but he knew that it was there between them, like a silent ghost. He took a gulp of his drink, the rawness of the cheap brandy burning his throat.

It was not his fault. He had hardly known what was happening. One minute they had been smiling and laughing and the next the girl had been screaming. Oh, that scream! It had gone right through his skull and into his brain. The silly little bitch. Surely she had known what was going to happen?

'Hello there, Georgie boy!'

Peter Renshaw stood in front of him, positively beaming with good humour and camaraderie. George felt his heart sink to his boots. This was all he needed, that bloody numbskull Renshaw twittering on.

'Hello, Peter. Can I get you a drink?'

'No. It's my shout, Georgie. Not every day I see you in my little love nest!'

George watched him click his fingers at the blonde monstrosity behind the bar and wink at her.

'Vivienne, my cherub. Bring me a G and T with ice and a slice, and whatever my good friend here is drinking. Oh, and not forgetting one for your lovely self.'

George watched the woman preening as she smiled her assent. Peter sat down beside George and whispered: 'She's been round the turf a few times, but she can warm a man's cockles when the fancy takes her.'

George wrinkled his nose in disgust and Peter laughed.

'Listen, Georgie boy, a bit of advice, man to man.' He nudged George in the ribs. 'You don't look at the mantelpiece when you're stoking the fire. Know what I mean?'

George smiled for lack of anything else to do. He wished that Renshaw would have a massive heart attack and die if that was what it took to keep him quiet.

'If you say so, Peter.'

'Pete! Pete, for God's sake, Georgie boy. No one calls me Peter, not even my old mum, God bless her.'

Vivienne brought their drinks to the table and George saw her tickle Peter's neck with her fingers as she walked away. Bloody dirty filthy slag!

'What you staring at, Georgie? Fancy a quick bonk with her, do you?' Leaning back in his seat, Peter went to call the woman back.

George, mortified at what Peter meant to do, dragged the man's head round by grabbing the collar of his sheepskin coat.

'NO! Peter . . . I mean, Pete.' He calmed his voice. 'I was just thinking, that's all. I had a bit of bad news today.'

'So they told you then?'

George looked at him, perplexed.

'Told me what?' Peter could not detect the edge to George's voice.

'That they was "outing" you. It's been common knowledge for months.'

George was dumbstruck. So everyone knew? Everyone but him. Everyone had been looking at him and laughing at him. Oh, yes, laughing at him. Laughing up their bloody sleeves at him!

Peter watched the amazed expression on George's face turn to one of virulent anger. It shocked even him. He'd thought that George had known. Everyone else had. Sorry now, he put his hand on George's arm.

'Hey, I'm sorry, old man. Christ, I thought you knew. I really thought you knew.'

George took a deep breath.

'No, Pete. I didn't know. I really didn't.'

George's voice was his own once more. Quiet and polite. 'I never even guessed.'

'Come on, Georgie boy. Best thing that could happen really. I mean, what are you – fifty-eight? Fifty-nine?'

'I'm fifty-one, Peter. Fifty-one.'

'Oh. Well, never mind anyway. Get an early pension. Live a little. See the kids.'

'I have no children, Peter. Elaine and I never . . .'

'Oh.'

Peter was finding it increasingly difficult to find things to say. He himself had a wife, four children and a string of mistresses and one-night stands the length and breadth of the country. People like George amazed and intrigued him. How could you live fifty-one years and have nothing to look forward to? He saw himself in years to come, when he was a bit long in the tooth for affairs and fumbling encounters, living with his wife and watching his grandchildren grow up. With hundreds of happy memories to see him through the twilight years.

'Come on, Georgie boy, drink up. Think of the great leaving do we'll have for you! There, that'll cheer you up.' He snapped his fingers at the barmaid again. 'Another round here, Viv, if you please.'

The pub was beginning to fill up and George watched Peter greet friends and acquaintances. He nodded hello at different introductions and all the time his mind was in a turmoil.

What the hell was Elaine going to say?

Elaine sat in the canteen at work and stirred her coffee listlessly.

George was not right, yet she had to admit he had been a lot better to live with these last few weeks. He had been lighthearted. Like before all the trouble.

She pushed the unpleasant thoughts from her mind. George had paid his debt to society. He had a clean slate. They had built themselves a new life of sorts. After twenty years, maybe it was time to let go of the past.

'Oh, Elaine, I hate Fridays, don't you?'

Margaret Forrester sat down at Elaine's table and slipped off her shoes.

'My feet will end up in the *Guinness Book Of Records* one of these days. The most swollen feet in the world.'

Elaine laughed at her friend.

'Why do you insist on wearing those heels? Get yourself a pair of comfortable flats.'

'No. My legs are me only vanity. I won't let them go till I have to.'

Elaine shook her head. 'Shall I get you a coffee?'

'Oh, yes please, Elaine. And a bowl of cold water if they've got one.'

Elaine got her friend a coffee and they sat together chatting.

'So where you off to on holiday then?'

Elaine shrugged.

'Probably Bournemouth again.'

'Oh, sod off, Elaine. No one goes to Bournemouth these days unless they go in a wheelchair. Why don't you come to Spain with me and the girls? Sun, sand, sea, sex . . .'

Margaret did a little dance in her chair.

'I can't wait to get there! Last year we was in this hotel, right on the seafront, and next door was only a bloody parrot sanctuary. All bloody night the sodding things screeched. And you know Caroline from frozen foods? She threw all our shoes at them one night. Pissed out of our heads we was. We had to go and ask for them back the next day. It was a scream!'

Elaine smiled.

'I don't know, Margaret. George . . .'

'Oh, balls to George! It's only a hundred and twenty quid for the fortnight, full board. I know it's in March and it's not that hot. But, oh dear me, do we have a good time! Please come.'

For the first time in her life Elaine felt a surge of pleasure in doing the unexpected. George was quite capable of looking after himself.

Margaret put her hand on Elaine's arm.

'Come on, girl. Let your hair down before it's too late.'

Elaine ran her tongue slowly over her teeth, then bit her lip. Margaret could see the indecision on her friend's face.

'All right then . . . I'll go!'

Elaine began to laugh in excitement.

'We'll go and book it after work. That way you can't change your mind.'

'George will have a fit when I tell him.'

31

'Let him! My old man did the first time, but as I said to him: "You only live once".'

'That's the truth.'

Elaine bit her lip again. This time in excitement. Two whole weeks without George! Bliss . . .

Elaine heard the front door shut and squared her shoulders as if waiting to begin a fight. But George wouldn't fight. George never fought about anything.

He would give her his wounded soldier look, his baffled schoolboy look, or his 'What have I done to deserve this?' look. She carried on mashing the potatoes. George entered the kitchen. Summoning every resource she had, Elaine put a smile on her face and looked at her husband.

'Hello, George. Sit yourself down, the meal's nearly ready.'

She saw George's right eyebrow rise and forced herself to carry on mashing.

He sat in his usual seat at the table. The white Formica table that they had bought from MFI aeons ago. When white Formica tables had been important to them.

'Have a good day?' She was determined to be friendly.

Oh yes, Elaine, George thought, I had a great day. I was called into Mrs Denham's office and all but kicked out of the firm on my arse. He put the back of his hand over his mouth. He must stop swearing to himself. One day he would forget and swear at Elaine.

'Not bad, love. You?' His voice was low and flat.

She put the mashed potato on the plates next to the pork chops. George watched her as she patted it into shape with her fingers. Then she began to ladle out the peas.

'I had quite a good day actually, George.'

He allowed himself another lift of the eyebrow. Well, well, well. That was a turn up for the book. Elaine enjoying herself at work . . . If she was to be believed, she ran the whole store single-handed from her till.

'That's good, dear.'

Elaine was pouring the gravy and had to stifle an urge to pour it over George's bald head.

32

'That's nice, dear. That's good, dear. Hell's bells, George! I'm your wife. You don't have to be polite to your own wife.'

George could see the confusion in her face as she looked at him. Elaine was such a difficult woman. He could just imagine the reaction if he told her that she bored the arse off him. That her voice went through his head like a marauding migraine. That he wished she were dead so he could claim the insurance money.

Elaine put his dinner in front of him.

She was still talking, but George was on the special auto pilot he reserved for Elaine's chatter about work.

'Anyway, when they asked me . . . I mean, one of the girls had dropped out you see . . . I thought: Why not? I'd love to go to Spain.'

George was in the process of eating a piece of tough pork chop when he realised what she was saying.

'Spain? Did you say Spain?' Elaine heard the incredulity in his voice and it annoyed her. What did he think then? That she was not the Spain sort?

'Yes, I said Spain, George. You know, where the Spanish people live.'

'And you're going? You . . . to Spain?'

Elaine put down her knife and fork, balancing them on the side of her plate.

'Just what's that supposed to mean?'

George opened his mouth to answer but Elaine was in full flood by then.

'I suppose you think of Spain as full of page three girls and blond Adonises? Well, let me tell you, George, the girls at work have a bloody good time there, mate. A bloody good time. And just for once in my life—' she poked herself in the chest with her thumb '—I am going to join in with the real world. I am going to have fun. Have a laugh. I'm not too old to enjoy myself.

'Let's face it, if I waited for you to show me a good time, I'd be six feet under.'

George watched her face as she spoke. Her features were

33

bunched like a screwed-up handkerchief and for one dreadful moment he imagined her topless on the beach.

Then he started to laugh. He laughed until the tears ran from his eyes and he had an attack of coughing. He laughed while Elaine slapped him on the back to stop him choking. Finally he was too weak to laugh any more and slowly his breathing returned to normal.

She was staring down at him, bewildered.

'I am sorry, Elaine. Sorry for laughing. It's just that you gave me a shock. I mean, you've never wanted to go before, have you? And now out of the blue . . . You go, Elaine. You go and enjoy yourself. I can just see you with a lovely tan. It will do you the world of good.'

She was nonplussed. She had a sneaking feeling that George was taking the piss.

He read her mind and spoke again.

'I laughed because after all these years you can still surprise me.'

Elaine relaxed.

'Shall I open a bottle of wine, dear? To celebrate?'

'Yes, George. Do that. You do that.'

She sat back at the table and resumed her meal. She was too hard on George, that was the trouble. He was pleased that she was going off to enjoy herself. He didn't begrudge her a little time away from him. She made up her mind to be more friendly, try and understand him a bit better. A short while later they clinked glasses.

'To Spain, my dear.'

'To Spain.'

They finished their meal in peace, and George left Elaine finishing the bottle of wine while he went for a walk.

George walked the streets for twenty minutes, his hands deep in his pockets and his head burrowed into the neck of his overcoat. He liked the winter months, liked the anonymity the dark nights created. He made his way to Motherwell Street and walked slowly along the lines of houses.

How the hell was he going to break the news to Elaine about

34

his redundancy? From what he could gather from Renshaw, he would be out on his ear in February. He shuddered. He had calmed her tonight but that wouldn't last long. He closed his eyes briefly, pondering his problem. His redundancy would only make her more convinced that he was an all round loser.

Geraldine O'Leary smiled at herself in her mirror. Still not satisfied with her make up, she applied more fuchsia pink lipstick. Opening her mouth wide, she spread it liberally then rubbed her lips together. She smiled at herself again, satisfied. Picking up her hairbrush, she began to pull it through her long brown hair, the electricity crackling as she did so.

Mick O'Leary watched his wife from the bed. Even after twelve years she could still excite him. At thirty-four she was the mother of his three children and did not look much older than the day he'd married her. He gazed at her as she slipped on her bra and pants. Their eyes met and they smiled, an intimate smile.

'I wish you wouldn't go tonight, Gerry.'

'I don't want to go, Mick. But if I stay home I'll regret it next week, you know that. Fifteen quid is fifteen quid. And Christmas will be here soon . . .' Her voice trailed off.

Mick sighed. Getting off the bed, he pulled on his trousers.

'I suppose you're right. You're not wearing that blouse, are you?'

Geraldine looked down at the blouse she was buttoning up. 'Why? What's wrong with it?'

'You can see your bra through it.'

'Oh, Mick! You're crazy . . .'

'Well, I don't like the thought of men looking at my wife.'

'Women come in the wine bar as well, you know.' She pursed her lips at him and he laughed.

'Not as good-looking as you though, girl.'

Geraldine smiled and slipped on a black skirt. Then she stepped into her high-heeled shoes and sprayed herself liberally with perfume.

Checking her make up one last time, she left the bedroom with her husband and they went downstairs.

Sophie, Donald and Grania, aged three, five and ten respectively, looked up as they came into the lounge.

'See you all later, and be good for Daddy.'

Sophie, in pink pyjamas, put out her arms for a cuddle and Geraldine picked her up, smelling the babyness of her and cuddling the little girl to her chest.

'You be good, madam.' She looked over at her husband who had sat down and picked up the TV section of the paper.

'Don't let her play you up. Eight o'clock is bedtime for the three of you.'

Grania and Donald groaned.

'I mean it. Or no sweets tomorrow.'

She placed Sophie on the couch with her brother and sister and pulled on her coat. As she buttoned it up she gave her orders.

'There's some chicken left in the fridge, Mick, if you fancy a sandwich, and I got you in some beers. Oh, and before I forget, I've left my Avon order by the phone. The girl will be calling around tonight.'

'You just get yourself off, Gerry. I'll sort out this end. See you later, love.'

She kissed him on the mouth.

'Be careful, Gerry, and don't take any lip. Right?'

Geraldine looked down at her husband's face and grinned. 'Right. 'Bye, kids.'

She kissed them all in turn and went from the house. The cold wind hit her in the face as she shut her front door and began walking the half mile to the wine bar where she worked. As she walked, she made Christmas lists in her head. She had already got most of the stuff for the two eldest. Grania had a bike which was at this minute hidden in her mother-in-law's shed and Donald had an Atari game. She was deliberating whether to get Sophie a kiddies' kitchen set or a doll's pram when she turned into Vauxhall Drive.

She instinctively pulled her coat tighter around her. She hated this bit. The road was wide and pitted, banked on the left hand side by woods. She had played in the woods many times as a child and knew every inch of them. Yet still they gave her the creeps. It was so dark, and only a couple of the houses were now lived in. The others had been demolished to make way for a new development that had never been built. Many years ago this had been the 'good' end of town. Now it flanked the woods on one side and the council estate on the other and the large Victorian dwellings were gradually being razed to the ground.

Her heels clattered on the uneven pavement as she walked and the sound comforted her. She could see the end of the road ahead and relaxed.

Silly cow! she chided herself. Frightened of shadows!

She began to walk faster, the lights at the end of the road like beacons drawing her towards them.

George had been standing in the entrance of the woods for about fifteen minutes. He looked at the luminous dial on his watch. Here she came. Right on time. It was a quarter past seven.

He swallowed and flexed fingers that were now encased in white cotton gloves.

As Geraldine passed him he stepped out from his hiding place and grabbed her hair. The long brown hair that was her best feature.

As she opened her mouth to scream, George grabbed her under the jaw and began dragging her into the woods. As she kicked out to free herself she lost one of her shoes. She was terrified.

George was puffing and panting; she was bigger than he'd thought. He dragged her along with difficulty, her muffled cries annoying him. He still had a good hold on her hair and jaw. Pulling her sideways with all his strength, he threw her down.

Geraldine hit the ground with such force it winded her. She lay in the dirt, stunned for a moment. But only a moment. George saw her pull herself to her hands and knees, and as she tried to rise he kicked her as hard as he could in the stomach, sending her reeling back on to the ground.

Geraldine was holding her stomach with both hands when

she saw the man kneeling beside her. Gathering up every ounce of strength she had left she rolled away from him, trying to get to her feet.

George watched the woman rolling away again and tutted. She was getting on his nerves now. Picking up a piece of wood which lay close to hand he brought it back over his head and slammed it down on her skull. He watched her crumple and sighed with relief. He sat quietly beside her for a few moments until he got his breath back and his heart stopped hammering in his ears. Then, pulling out his handkerchief, he wiped his forehead clean of sweat.

Happier now, he looked at the woman. She was lying on her back with her head turned away from him and he smiled to himself. Good! He didn't want her watching him. Going to her, he began to unbutton her coat. George decided he liked her coat and opened it up gently. Then, humming to himself, he began to pull off her skirt. No tights on, and in this weather as well! He tutted to himself again. Her limbs felt heavy as he undid her blouse and laid it back neatly with her coat. Still humming, he looked down at her bra. In the dimness he could just make out a piece of plastic. He fiddled about with it for a second and then her breasts seemed to burst out of it into his hands. She had been wearing a front fastening bra – she must have known what was going to happen! George caressed her breasts. He was feeling a deep tenderness towards the woman now. Then he used the knife to cut off her panties.

While he carried out his ministrations he felt the excitement building up within him. And such was his feeling of ecstatic happiness as he pulled her legs open, he had to stifle the cry that had gathered in his throat.

This was what she wanted. This was what they all wanted.

It was when George lay across her, spent and replete, that he found out why she had not moved at all during his little 'game'.

The lump of wood, so convenient, had contained a six-inch nail. It had been forced through her skull and into her brain.

George looked at her and tutted once more.

It was her own fault. All her own fault. Women always

caused trouble. They were just so bloody stupid . . . Stupid fucking bitches! Bringing his fist back he smashed it into her face as hard as he could.

Mick O'Leary looked at the policewoman's face in disbelief. He had been up all night and thought that maybe his mind was playing tricks on him.

'What did you say?'

The WPC had never felt so bad in all her life. She saw the three children huddled together on the settee. Their father's fear had communicated itself to them. She could have cried herself.

'Your wife was found an hour ago, Mr O'Leary. She's been murdered.'

The WPC watched the man's face crumple before her eyes, and put her arm around his shoulders.

'Not my Gerry . . . Not my lovely Gerry. Please tell me that it's not true? Please?'

Mick O'Leary's voice broke as he spoke the last word and he put his hands to his face, the tears bursting through his fingers like a dam.

'Dad! Don't cry, Daddy!'

Ten-year-old Grania pulled her younger brother and sister into her arms. She had never seen her daddy cry before.

'I want my mum. When's my mummy coming home?'

At the same moment as Mick O'Leary was being told that his world had been ripped apart, George Markham was cooking his wife a nice breakfast.

Elaine walked into the kitchen, the smell of eggs and bacon making her mouth water.

'Oh, George, I would have done that.'

He actually laughed.

'I wanted to do it for you, my love. I do love you, you know Elaine.'

'Do you, George?'

For some unknown reason his saying that he loved her depressed her more than anything else he could have done.

George held out her chair for her and she sat down at the table.

'Eat that up, my dear.'

Elaine stared at the eggs, bacon and tomatoes, and her appetite came back.

George watched her eat.

That's why you're so fat, Elaine, he thought, because you're a greedy bitch.

'Now then, my dear, what's it to be? Tea or coffee?' His voice was as polite as ever.

But George had a secret. A very important and exciting secret that he would not tell to a living soul.

He ate his own breakfast. For some reason he had a ravenous appetite this morning.

Chapter Three

Elaine sat at her till in the supermarket. Every customer who had passed through the large glass doors today had had only one thing on their minds: the rape and murder of Geraldine O'Leary. Since the body had been found, Grantley had been buzzing with news, views and assumptions. While tills crashed around her and people packed their shopping Elaine chatted to a customer, a woman who had known the victim.

'It makes me go all funny, just thinking about it.' The woman paused to force a large packet of cornflakes into her shopping bag.

'I mean, poor Gerry, she had three of the most gorgeous children you're ever likely to see. And she was happily married.' She nodded her head sagely. 'And how many can say that in this day and age?'

'You're right there. So who found her then?'

The woman rearranged her silk scarf. In the heat of the supermarket it was beginning to make her head itch.

'It was a young kid. He was on his way to deliver the papers. Well, he used the cut through from Vauxhall Drive and there she was . . . dead as a bleeding doornail!' She shook her head again.

'I bet this will just be the start. You mark my words. This is just the start.'

Elain grimaced and totalled her till.

'Seventeen pounds and eighty-five pence, please.'

The woman opened her purse and took out a twenty-pound note. 'Bleeding daylight robbery, if you ask me. I ain't even got the makings of a dinner here!'

Elaine smiled in sympathy but her mind was still with Geraldine O'Leary. Poor woman, to die like that. She shuddered.

Giving the woman her change, she went on to the next customer.

The whole of Grantley was appalled and shocked at the rape and murder. Every woman knew that it could easily have been her and they were all frightened.

Frightened and excited. Because nothing like this had ever happened in Grantley before.

Detective Inspector Kate Burrows looked down at the body and winced.

Detective Sergeant Willis watched her surreptitiously, smiling slightly as he watched her blanch.

Who, he wondered, in their right mind, would give a female copper a rape and murder? Women were too emotional for this type of thing.

He looked Kate up and down on the sly. Not a bad-looking bird for her age. Bit flat-chested to his mind, but she had good legs and nice eyes. Deep brown eyes that matched her hair exactly.

Willis dragged his mind back to the present as the pathologist spoke again.

'The nail entered the head here.' He pointed to Geraldine's temple. 'On the left-hand side, where it entered the brain. I would say that death was instantaneous. We found traces of semen on her thighs and breasts, which is unusual in these cases. Only a small amount was inside the vagina.'

The man rubbed his eyes with the forefinger and thumb of his right hand.

'The blow to the face was administered after she had died. As you can see, he crushed the nose. She has several broken ribs. I would hazard a guess that she had been kicked. Kicked very hard as one of the ribs broke and punctured a lung.'

He shook his head. 'A very brutal attack. Very calculated. She has scratches and particles of dirt on her knees. My guess is that she put up a fairly good fight.'

'Any skin under the nails? Anything else for us to go on?' Kate's voice was low and subdued.

He shook his head. 'Nothing, I'm afraid. Of course we can get a DNA reading from the semen . . .' His voice trailed off. He shrugged. 'Maybe some traces of hair or fibre will turn up off her clothes. I'll let you know.' The pathologist began combing Geraldine's pubic hair slowly and carefully, his mind back on his job. Kate turned away from the woman's rapidly greying body.

'Thanks.'

She walked from the mortuary and Willis followed her. Neither spoke until they were back in the canteen at Grantley Police station sipping cups of coffee.

'Look, don't let it get to you, love. These things happen.'

Kate stared at the younger man, frowning in concentration. She took a deep breath.

'How dare you?' Her voice was low and filled with rage. Willis was shocked. 'How dare you patronise me like that? Just who the hell do you think you are? "These things happen"! Is that what you honestly believe?'

Her voice was incredulous. 'Do you think that Mrs Geraldine O'Leary is standing in heaven thinking: These things happen. Do you think her husband and children are just shrugging their shoulders thinking: These things happen!'

Her voice was beginning to rise and Willis looked around him in embarrassment.

'These things don't just happen, boy.' She stressed the last word. 'Out there somewhere is a murdering rapist. Do you understand the enormity of that? Do you? Well, DO YOU?'

Willis sat rigid in his seat, crimson with shame. Everyone in the room had gone quiet and was sitting watching them.

'It means that for the majority of women normal living will now be curtailed at four-thirty when it gets dark. It means that women who live alone or whose husbands work nights will be sitting uneasily in their own homes. It means that even locked in a car driving along they will not feel safe. It means that parents with young daughters will be sick with apprehension

43

until they return from school, work, wherever they may have been. The list is bloody endless! How dare you sit there and tell me these things happen?

'And one last thing, while we're getting ourselves sorted out. I am a Detective Inspector. I am your boss. So in future you address me as such. In the six months I have been here there has been a general lack of respect, and as from today your lackadaisical attitude stops.'

Getting up from her seat, Kate stormed from the canteen, leaving a hush behind her.

Willis sighed heavily and one of his friends, DS Spencer, went to his table.

'So the vixen's got claws, has she? Flash bitch! If she'd spoken to me like that I'd have punched her in the mouth.'

A female voice from a nearby table said, 'Very macho, Spencer. Sure you ain't the rapist? I hear the victim had a broken nose.'

'Get stuffed!' Spencer went back to his cronies and sat down.

'Bloody women. Whoever it was who let them in the force in the first place wants psychiatric help. As for that Burrows . . . Uppity cow!'

'She's been put in charge of the murder and rape, so you'd best get used to it.'

Spencer looked at the speaker. 'Well, let's see how well she does, shall we? Personally she gets on my wick.'

'Maybe that's what's wrong with you, Spencer. She *won't* be getting on your wick.'

Everyone laughed.

Spencer picked up his cup of tea and with his free hand shoved his middle finger under the other man's nose.

'Spin on it, Fisher.'

Fisher grinned.

'Only if you ask me nicely!' He fluttered his eyelashes suggestively.

Spencer drank his tea down. Bloody women. It would take a rape to bring out their true colours. He wouldn't mind but the silly bitch O'Leary had probably been asking for it.

44

Kate Burrows sat in her office and tried to calm down. She admitted that she had been hard on Willis, but he got on her nerves. Most of the plain clothes at Grantley CID got on her nerves. She rubbed her hand over her face. She had been on the receiving end of discrimination since she had joined the force, it was an occupational hazard. But this lot here . . .

She turned her attention to the file in front of her. She wanted every bit of information imprinted on her brain. As in most of the cases she worked on, she wanted to be more knowledgeable than her male counterparts. She began to read.

A little while later there was a tap on her door.

'Come in.'

The door opened and Willis walked into the room.

'Yes?' Her voice was clipped.

Willis nodded. 'Ma'am, Superintendent Ratchette would like to see you, if you're not too busy.'

'Thank you, Willis.'

She watched him turn and walk meekly from the room. Mentally, Kate licked her finger and chalked one up to herself.

'You wanted to see me, sir?'

Superintendent Ratchette smiled at her as she entered his office.

'Sit down, Kate. I suppose you know that we have had the nationals on to us already?'

She grimaced. 'I didn't know, but I guessed it wouldn't take long.'

'Well, as usual they're making a nuisance of themselves. We must try and contain this as much as possible. Hopefully this is just a one-off thing. It's all we need, especially with Christmas not two weeks away.' Superintendent Ratchette's voice was tired and Kate felt sorry for him.

'Well, at the moment, sir, there's not that much to go on. We're hoping that forensic will show something up. I've already arranged the door-to-door, it's within a mile radius. The usual thing. Every male from fourteen to sixty-five will be interviewed – their make of car checked, where they work, where they were between six-thirty p.m. and seven a.m. Oh, and before I forget, I've made DS Dawkins the office manager. She's good.'

Superintendent Ratchette raised a bushy grey eyebrow. 'I bet that went down well, didn't it?'

'Not really.' Kate laughed ruefully. 'Two women on a big case. Makes male CID eyes red just thinking about it!'

Ratchette laughed out loud. He liked Kate Burrows.

'Well, whatever you think, Kate, it's your case. If you could just keep me informed of any developments, as and when they occur?'

'Of course, sir. But I don't like the feel of this one. Geraldine O'Leary worked at Rudys wine bar, but from what I can gather she was not a woman who encouraged men, although she was good-looking and would obviously attract them. We're checking out all the customers anyway. Most are local men. Her husband was baby sitting last night and a woman called Conroy called around at seven-thirty to collect an Avon order and stayed chatting till gone eight when Geraldine O'Leary's mother came round to drop off some Christmas presents. There's no way it's the husband. His alibi is watertight.'

Ratchette nodded at her.

'Looks like you've got your work cut out for you.'

Kate stifled a yawn. It had been a long day and it still wasn't over.

'I have a feeling this is going to be a tough one, sir, a very tough one.'

George walked into his house and was grateful for the warmth of the central heating. He was freezing. Under his arm he had the local paper. He could hear Elaine clattering around as she cooked. Taking off his overcoat, he hung it up in the hall cupboard and silently entered the kitchen.

Elaine turned from the sink and jumped.

'Oh, George! You gave me a start. I didn't hear you come in!'

46

She waved her hand in front of her face as if cooling herself down.

He smiled.

'Sorry, dear.' He sat at the table and looked at the paper. He smiled wider. Across the front page in large black letters was one word: MURDER.

Settling himself into his chair, George began to read. This morning the body of a woman had been found in Grantley Woods. She had been raped and murdered . . . He felt the familiar excitement flow through his veins. The victim was a Mrs Geraldine O'Leary, a thirty-two-year-old mother of three.

The poor children! The poor, poor children. Shaking his head, he began to read again.

Elaine placed a cup of tea by his hand and he looked up at her.

'Isn't it terrible, George? That poor woman. Those poor little children losing their mother like that, and just before Christmas as well.' George was surprised at the emotion in Elaine's voice.

'It's all we've talked about at work. I mean, no woman's safe, is she?'

George tutted and shook his head. 'You be careful, Elaine.' He pointed a finger at her. 'Promise me you'll get a taxi home from work? I don't want you standing at bus stops in the dark.'

She stared at her husband and then smiled.

'Oh, George! You old silly.'

Despite herself Elaine felt an enormous surge of pleasure at his concern. Getting taxis home from work! Well, she would, because as George said it wasn't safe for her to be standing at bus stops in the dark.

She started to dish up the dinner.

Later in the evening, the sex murder was reported on Thames News. Elaine shook her head sadly. But George smiled. His secret smile that just showed his teeth.

Kate finally arrived home at eleven-fifteen. She pulled into her drive and decided that she just couldn't be bothered to park the car in the garage. She was too tired. Getting out of the car she locked it, stifling a large yawn.

The front door was opened as she approached it and a woman of indeterminate age practically pulled her into the hallway.

'Get yourself in now, love, you must be frozen. I've got your dinner in the oven keeping warm.'

Kate smiled to herself. Her mother still thought she was eighteen.

'Where's Lizzy?'

'Oh, she's in the bath, she'll be down soon. I heard about the terrible goings on today. Scandalous, bloody scandalous! Was it the husband?'

Kate followed her mother through the lounge and into the kitchen, where on a small breakfast bar her knife and fork were laid out. She sat on the stool gratefully and accepted a cup of steaming coffee.

'It wasn't the husband, Mum.'

Evelyn O'Dowd wasn't listening which did not disturb Kate. Her mother never listened to anyone or anything.

'It's usually the husband or some other relative . . .'

Evelyn opened the oven and Kate felt her mouth water as the tantalising aroma of a good beef casserole wafted towards her.

'Be careful of that plate now, it's roasting.'

'Thanks, Mum, this is just what I needed.'

'I've made soda bread to go with it.'

Evelyn O'Dowd was tiny and thin, like a little bird. She had black eyes that darted continually and never settled on anything. She wore black all the time which accentuated her thinness. She still looked after her forty-year-old daughter as if she was ten. Kate loved her.

As she broke off a piece of bread her mother sat opposite her with a cup of coffee and the ever present cigarette. Taking a large draw on it, she blew smoke across the breakfast bar and smiled.

'What a feather this one will be in your cap – when you

finally solve it, of course. Which you will, I'm sure of that.' It was said with absolute certainty.

'Well, we're doing the best we can, it's early days yet, Mum.'

Kate ate the food with an enthusiasm that pleased her mother no end.

'If only your father could have lived to see you, he'd have died of happiness!'

Kate grinned to herself. Her mother's Irish sayings were not only unintelligible most of the time, they were often highly amusing – though Evelyn didn't always think so.

Declan O'Dowd had been a London docker and had made sure his two children received a good education. Kate's elder brother now lived in Australia to where he had emigrated to twenty years before. He was a civil engineer and had a wife and five children whom Kate and her mother had never seen in the flesh. Kate had made her career in the police force. Declan O'Dowd had died a happy man shortly after she had passed out from Hendon.

Kate's mother had come to live with her shortly after Lizzy, her daughter, had been born. Danny Burrows, Kate's husband, had left her when Lizzy was three months old. He showed up periodically over the years, turned everyone's world upside down and then disappeared again. Kate was secretly dreading this Christmas because he was due on one of his flying visits. Lizzy adored her father, which made it hard for Kate to keep everything on an even keel.

She heard her daughter patter into the room in her slippers.

'Hello, Mum. I heard about the murder. Me and Gran watched it on the news.'

'Hello, baby, come and give us a kiss.'

Lizzy went to her mother and put her arms around her. At sixteen she was exquisite. Sometimes the beauty of her own daughter made Kate frightened. Lizzy had the O'Dowd darkness, like her mother and grandmother, but she also had porcelain white skin and startling violet eyes. She looked sixteen going on twenty-five. Unlike her mother she was full-chested, already a thirty-six B and still growing by the looks of her. She was as tall as her mother but far more graceful. One thing she had not inherited from Kate was brains. Though shrewd enough in her own way, she was no scholar, had no interest in anything academic. She worked now in the local Boots, filling shelves and waiting for the magical day they trained her for the tills. That was the height of her ambition and Kate accepted this.

'How was your day then, love?'

'Not bad, Mum, the usual. With the Christmas rush, we just don't stop. I never even had my coffee break today. Mr Williams the manager said I was doing very well indeed, though.'

She put on a very posh voice for the last part and Kate and Evelyn laughed. Kate broke off some more soda bread and mopped up the gravy on her plate.

'Shall I run you a nice bath, Mum? I got some bath crystals from the Body Shop last week. It's the aromatherapy range. They're lavender and supposed to make you relax.'

'That would be gorgeous. Today has been pretty hectic.'

Lizzy went from the room and Kate and her mother smiled at one another.

'Sure, she's a good girl, Katie. That fellow's been ringing her again. I think it's love.'

Kate lit herself a cigarette from her mother's pack and pushed her plate away from her.

'Well, she's young, the boys are bound to be after her.'

'True, Katie, but I worry about her. I don't think she realises the effect she has on them, you know.'

'That's part of her charm, I think. We'll keep an eye on her.'

'That we will. Now you smoke your fag while I clear this lot away. You'll need all the sleep you can get, I'm thinking.'

Kate grinned again. Her mother was not happy unless she was looking after someone. Over the last sixteen years, Kate did not know what she would have done without her.

Going up to the bathroom a little while later, she lay in the steaming and fragrant water. She had been working for sixteen hours non-stop. She had seen a woman practically dismembered on a mortuary slab, had set up an incident room, and had organised over thirty policemen and women for the door to door inquiry. She had at her fingertips information about anyone and everyone.

Yet her mother still made her feel like a child. And after a day like this, it felt good.

George lay in bed with Elaine. He listened to her deep snores and smiled into the darkness. Every time he thought of Geraldine O'Leary he felt great.

Once more he replayed in his mind what he had done. He took himself through the act step by step, congratulating himself on his cleverness.

Then he frowned.

Into his mind's eye came pictures of his mother. He wiped his hand across his face in the darkness as if that would erase them. He saw his mother as she had been when he was a child. Her bright red hair, naturally red not dyed like Elaine's, was shining in the sunlight. Her sea green eyes were sparkling mischievously, and George could see himself smiling back at her. He could see the room: the cast-iron fireplace with the dried flowers in the hearth, the Victorian prints on the flock wallpaper and the black leather Chesterfield. He could also see the pipe and the bag and the china bowl.

George tried to shut out the images but they were too strong. He lay in bed and watched.

'Come to Mummy, Georgie boy.' Her voice was a caress. She held out her arms to the little boy in front of her. In the distance Georgie could hear the sounds of the anti-aircraft fire. He stood silently in front of her.

She spoke again, her voice harder this time.

'I said, come to Mummy, Georgie.'

The little boy looked at the doorway and his mother laughed.

'Come in, kids!' Her voice was loud.

George looked at the doorway with frightened eyes. He watched his elder sister and brother come into the room.

'Lie on the floor, Georgie boy.'

The child shook his head and began to edge his way

backwards. He watched his mother's red-lipsticked mouth twist into an ugly shape.

'Don't annoy Mummy, Georgie. Just lie on the floor.'

The child watched the others make a semicircle around him. His elder brother Joseph was so close he could smell the odour of bull's eyes coming from him.

He closed his eyes at the inevitable. She had already given them the sweets. They would want this over with as quickly as possible. He felt the familiar sensation of ice water in his bowels as the older children pulled him to the ground. He felt a surge of hatred for his mother as his shorts and underpants were pulled off. He felt the contained violence from the others as they held him, face down on the floor.

He began to cry. Slowly at first, then violently, painfully, as his mother began pushing the rubber piping into his rectum. He tried to fight but it was useless. He felt the warmth of the soapy water hitting his bowels and then he felt the sick, wrenching feeling as they emptied. He winced as she ripped the rubber tubing from inside him. Then it was all over.

He lay on the floor looking up into his mother's smiling face. The sweat was standing out on his forehead, and he felt the waves of nausea washing over him.

Then he saw his mother's heavily made-up face approaching his own, felt the coolness of her lips as they sucked at his mouth.

'That feels better, doesn't it, Georgie boy?'

Lying on the floor of the parlour, weak and sick, he nodded at her. Fighting back the words.

Then his mother picked him up in her arms tenderly and took him to his bed. He felt the coolness of the sheets that smelt of Lux soap flakes and then the red pain in his behind.

He saw her smile again.

'You're Mummy's little soldier, what are you?'

The child watched her through tear-filled lashes and sighed, sending a shudder through his thin little body.

'I'm Mummy's little soldier.'

Then he was pulled up from the bed and held against her ample bosom while she rained kisses all over his face and neck.

George watched it all as if it was a film. He closed his eyes to shut out the sight. But his mother just would not go away.

She never went away.

It was Saturday and George was alone in the house. After carefully washing up the breakfast things and putting them away, he made himself a pot of tea. While it brewed on the kitchen table he walked down the garden to his shed and brought back his scrapbooks.

Sitting at the kitchen table, he settled himself down and opened the first book. He felt the anticipation course through his veins as he looked at the familiar pictures and smiled.

Soon he would have his own album of death with pictures of his victims instead of Peter Sutcliffe's. He had already started it.

George took a sip of his tea and began to read, though he knew the words off by heart. After a while he glanced at his watch. It was nearly lunchtime. He had hours yet until Elaine came home from work. He decided to watch his video. He clenched his fists tightly with sheer elation at his good luck.

No Elaine. No noise. No company.

Putting the scrapbooks back in the shed, he locked up the house, closed the front room curtains, unplugged the phone and put on his new film.

As the pictures flickered before him, George finally relaxed.

The girl on the video looked just like Geraldine O'Leary and the most violent of the men looked just like him.

This was what they wanted. This was what they all wanted. Walking around, covered in make up and perfume. Even the very young girls. He knew all about them.

In his agitation George started to blink rapidly.

He had seen films of school girls. The real life ones were as bad. Learning to be sluts, every last one of them. Oh, he had watched them, walking to school. He began to nod his head. Bare-legged, some of them. With bouncing bosoms, emphasised by their school uniforms. Oh, he knew all about women. Dying for it, the majority of them. Just dying for it.

53

Well, he would show a few of them before he was much older. Oh, yes. He would show them.

The girl on the television screen was dead.

George cleared his mind. This was the best bit.

He smiled.

Detective Sergeant Amanda Dawkins brought Kate a cup of coffee.

'Thanks. I could do with this.'

The other woman smiled. 'You look beat.'

Kate nodded. 'I feel terrible. I didn't have a very good night and today isn't much better.'

Amanda sat down opposite her.

'Well, we're gradually collating all the door-to-door info. The thing with this type of inquiry is that everyone with a grudge against their neighbour tries to implicate them.'

'I know. The thing is that for every five hundred screwball accusations, there are normally one or two that are worth following up.'

'Drink your coffee, ma'am. Before it gets cold.'

She grinned.

'Call me Kate. I only threw my weight around yesterday because I am getting heartsick of this lot.'

She waved her arm in the direction of the male CID staff.

'Bloody load of know-alls they are. Well, I'm going to make myself felt and heard from now on. I tried the friendly, tactful approach and it didn't work.'

Amanda grinned, showing crooked white teeth.

'This lot have never had a woman in charge of them before. It's galling for them, to say the least.'

Kate sipped her coffee.

'Shall I tell you something, Amanda?'

The girl nodded, a slight frown on her face at the other's tone of voice.

'I don't give a toss what they think. If they give me any more hag, they're off the case. I would appreciate it if you would be so kind as to set the rumour flying. Know what I mean?'

Amanda giggled.

'I know exactly what you mean, ma'am.'

'Kate.'

'Sorry, Kate.'

'That's better. Now then, let's get this show on the road because I have a feeling that this murder was only for starters. Whoever did it is getting ready for the main performance, and I want to find him before he does any more harm.'

Kate's serious intention communicated itself to the younger woman. Amanda nodded at her boss, glad that she was going to be working with her and not one of the male officers.

DS Spencer was watching the two women. He sighed. Nudging his friend DS Willis, he poked his head in their direction, a frown on his ruddy face.

'Looks like the Dolly Sisters are getting better acquainted.' His voice was disgusted.

Willis shook his head in exasperation.

'Oh, give it a rest, for Christ's sake. She's in charge and that's that. Let's just put all our combined experience together and find the bloody nutter who's on the loose.'

Spencer's face closed up.

'Oh, yeah, of course. I suppose your experience with shoplifters and vandals will be invaluable, won't it?'

Willis coloured slightly. He had not been a DS for long and this was his first big case. No one else had mentioned this fact except Spencer. But what more could he expect from the man? He was the most ignorant, bigoted and self-opinionated officer in the whole of the division.

'Well, thanks for the little reminder, Spencer. All this new empathy policing should be just up your street, I reckon. Since we're obviously looking for a complete and utter pratt, we can all just follow your line of thinking, can't we?'

Spencer looked as if he had been slapped across the face. 'You cheeky little bastard!'

Willis grinned. 'And you're a miserable old bastard. Know your trouble, Spencer? You never got further than DS, did you? Well, if you listened to yourself sometimes, you might find out why.'

Willis walked away, leaving Spencer open-mouthed with

astonishment and rage. But against his will a phrase sprung to mind which he could not ignore: The truth hurts.

How many times had he said that to other people?

Too many.

He forced his mind back to the case, looking at the blown-up photograph of Geraldine O'Leary on the wall.

It was one of the pictures taken in the morgue. Her greying face with the splintered nose was pinned up beside another smaller photograph taken a few months previously by her husband. In it Geraldine was laughing, her eyes crinkled at the corners. She looked what she was: a beautiful young wife.

Spencer shrugged. Willis was right about one thing. The man who murdered her had to be caught, and fast. Before he struck again.

Chapter Four

1948

The two small boys walked fast. Driving rain was pelting into their faces. The smaller of the two had red-rimmed eyes and had obviously been crying. A large clap of thunder boomed overhead, followed by a flash of lightning that lit up the sky.

'Come on, George, for Christ's sake.' The bigger boy began to drag his brother along by his coat sleeve. As they turned into a small cul-de-sac George tried to pull away.

'I'm not going in there. I mean it.'

Joseph sighed loudly and faced his brother. He did not like the job he had been given. In his heart of hearts he couldn't blame Georgie for running off, but their mother's word was law. He looked into the terrified little face before him.

'Look, Georgie, the sooner you get in there, the sooner it will be over. Now come on.'

He resumed dragging him along the pavement until they came to the house they both lived in. In the dark stormy light it looked sinister. The brickwork was stained black and the front door, even with its polished brass knocker, looked dingy. Joseph pulled his brother up the garden path and banged the knocker hard. The door was opened almost immediately by a mousy-haired girl of fifteen. She looked at her youngest brother with tenderness.

'She's a bit quieter now, George. Hurry up out of your wet things.'

They walked into the hallway and he pulled off his wet coat slowly. His heart was hammering in his chest. The house always seemed to smell of cabbage; the odour hung on the air, making him feel sick. It mingled with the smell of beeswax polish, and the heaviness of it burned his quivering nose.

'Is he gone?' Joseph's voice was a whisper.

The girl shook her head.

'You go on upstairs, I'll take Georgie in.' The brother and sister looked into each other's eyes. Joseph turned away, unable to face his sister any longer. He forced himself to smile at the little boy beside him.

'I'll wait upstairs for you. Micky Finnigan gave me some comics yesterday. You can read them after me if you like.'

Georgie nodded and swallowed deeply. His grey eyes seemed to have taken possession of his whole face.

'Pull your socks up, Georgie.' He did as he was told. Clumsily he dragged the thick woollen garments up his shins. The three stood stock still as they heard a movement from the front room. Then Joseph ran lightly up the stairs as if the devil was after him. George felt his hands begin to tremble as the front room door opened and a harsh light fell across him.

'So you're back home, are you?' His mother's voice was hard and low. She held the door open for him and at a little push from his sister he walked through. His mother's fist hit him in the back of his head and sent him careering into the room.

'Mum . . . Mum! Don't hit him, Mum!'

Nancy Markham turned to her daughter. 'Get upstairs now, before I give you more of the same.'

George lay on the cold lino, terrified. He watched as his mother knelt beside him and pushed her face close to his.

'Run away from your mummy, would you, Georgie boy?' She entwined her fingers in his hair and pulled his head towards her.

'Where was you running off to this time?'

The child's trembling communicated itself to her. She brought her red-stained lips back over her teeth and then, closing her eyes, began to lay into him. His skinny little body was unable to cushion the ferocious punching and he lay with his hands covering his head.

Upstairs Joseph lay listening to the muffled sounds of his

58

brother's beating. His mother's foul-mouthed shouting reaching a crescendo.

Nancy stood up, her breathing laboured. 'Now you go and apologise, Georgie boy.'

The child was sobbing, every so often gulping large draughts of air into his aching lungs. His nose had a thin trickle of blood running from it. He stood up unsteadily, grabbing the table for support.

'You heard me, boy!' She slapped the child hard across the face. He stumbled from the front room and through the connecting door to the kitchen.

He felt his mother stand close behind him and looked into the big man's face.

'Don't you worry, Bert, I've given him such a larruping he won't be so quick with his tongue in the future.'

The man looked at George with tiny dark eyes. The boy could smell the rancid odour of stale sweat and swallowed down the urge to vomit. The man's belly was quivering as he moved to make himself more comfortable in his seat. His string vest was stained with tea and food. George tried to concentrate on the man's red-veined, bloated face.

'He ain't saying much, Nance. What's the matter, you little bastard? Cat got your tongue?'

George bit on his lip for a second.

'I'm very sorry . . . I'm sorry.'

Nancy Markham put her face so close to her son's he could smell her breath. 'You know what else to say, Georgie boy.'

He swallowed and took another deep breath. 'I'm sorry . . . Dad.' The last word was barely audible.

'Speak up, lad.'

'I'm . . . sorry, Dad.'

The man saw the hatred in the child's eyes. It was unmistakable. For one second he felt frightened, then pulling himself together he grinned, showing tobacco-stained teeth. This little runt was no more than five stone! He screwed up his eyes and made himself look as ferocious as possible, wanting to intimidate the child.

'You remember to call me that, boy.' He poked his finger

at George. Then he looked at Nancy and bellowed: 'Where's me fucking tea, woman? Get this little shit out of me sight and get yourself sorted!'

Nancy pushed George out of her way and stood in front of the man.

'Don't you talk to me like that, Bert Higgins . . .'

He pulled his enormous bulk from the chair and brought his fist back.

'You want a right-hander, Nance, or what? You might be able to sort out little kids but don't ever think you can order me around!'

George watched his mother's face as she battled with herself as to whether to carry on fighting or whether to retreat. As usual her fighting temper came to the fore and George bolted from the room as her hand went to the teapot on the table and she flung it at Bert.

George took the stairs two at a time, his injuries forgotten in the panic to get away from them. He rushed into the bedroom he shared with Joseph, straight for his sister's arms. He began to sob again as he heard the crashing from below. Edith caressed the short-cropped head, wincing every time a loud crash thundered up from below. She saw Joseph lying on the bed staring at the ceiling and felt a sense of futility.

'Oh, please God, make them kill one another. Please make them both die.'

Her anguished voice was muffled with tears. Since Bert Higgins had moved into the house eighteen months earlier their lives had been even more disrupted than usual. Nancy had found in him a bully who was even more violent than she was. They had been alternately loved to death or beaten within an inch of their lives ever since they could remember. But since the advent of Bert, things had gradually grown worse. Their mother had never been stable; now she was positively deranged. Her main outlet for her frustrations was George. Edith did her best to keep him from her mother's rages but lately it was getting more and more difficult. Bert drank, her mother drank, and the children, mainly George, took the brunt of it. Edith had been given the task of cleaning the house. Nancy Markham had pretensions to respectability, even blind drunk.

All three stood rooted to the spot as they heard their mother running across the front room and out into the hall. Her heavy footfalls on the stairs were followed by Bert's.

'Talk to me like that, would you, you slut? You bloody big fat slut!'

'Take your filthy hands off of me, Bert Higgins, I'm warning you now.'

They listened to the scuffle on the stairs and then heard a thud and all went quiet. The three looked at each other in consternation.

'Nancy? Nance?' Bert's voice was low and filled with fear.

Edith pushed George from her and ran from the room.

'Oh my God!' She ran down the stairs and pushed Bert roughly away. Her mother was lying sprawled on the stairs, her head bleeding profusely from the temple.

'I never meant it, she fell and hit her head.'

Edith ignored the man and examined her mother. It was a flesh wound. As she peered at it, Nancy's eyes opened and she pushed the girl away from her.

'Get away out of it, you.' Joseph and George stood at the top of the stairs dumbstruck.

Nancy put her hand to her head and brought the fingers away blood-stained.

'You bastard! I'm bleeding.'

'Look, Nancy, I'm sorry. Honestly, darlin', I wouldn't hurt you for the world, you know that. I could cut me hands off.'

Edith walked slowly up the stairs. She knew she wasn't needed any more. It was the same thing over and over again. No worries about Georgie who would be bruised for a week or ten days, and who would get another hiding between times. No concern for Joseph who was getting iller and iller with his nerves each week. Not a thought for Edith who had to keep everyone together. Let's just worry about Mummy and her bloody head. A bloody head she asked for, to all intents and purposes.

'Come on, you two.' She pushed the two boys into the bedroom and closed the door.

A while later the three heard Bert and their mother enter their own bedroom and the squeaking of the bed springs and loud groans that heralded their making up.

Chapter Five

23 December 1989

Mandy Kelly pulled her coat tighter across her breasts. It was freezing. Her toes in her flat-heeled boots had already gone numb. She would murder Kevin when he finally arrived. She looked at her watch again. It was eight-fifteen, he was a quarter of an hour late. She stood by the light of the phone box and stamped her feet. She wouldn't mind but he had her car, and if she got a taxi her father would guess immediately what had happened and then all hell would break loose. Plus it was Saturday night and they were supposed to be going out to eat with her father and his new girl friend. Well, she had to be honest, she wasn't worried about missing that so much, but her father would be upset. Sod Kevin! He always did this to her.

She pushed her hands deeper into the pockets of her sheepskin. The cold night air was burning her lungs with every breath she took. The street was deserted except for the occasional car. Everyone was either putting the finishing touches to their trees after a hectic day's shopping, or ensconced somewhere warm with a drink or a meal. The world was at the quiet empty stage that seemed to suspend the laws of time until Christmas Day came. She pulled her long blonde hair from inside the collar of her sheepskin. The air was damp and her hair was lank around her face.

Oh God, it was so cold.

She watched a dark blue Orion drive past her slowly and stared after it uneasily. She was sure that it had driven past once before. She shrugged. No need to worry, Kevin would be here soon. She smiled to herself. Her orange lipstick was smudged where she kept rubbing her lips together. Her father would be waiting for them, they were supposed to leave at nine. If Kevin didn't hurry up she wouldn't even have time to change.

She carried on watching the road, hoping against hope that Kevin would drive along in her white Mercedes sports and take her home.

Sometimes she wondered what exactly it was Kevin liked about her. Whether it was the fact that her father was Patrick Kelly, or whether it was her car, or whether it was in fact her he liked. She tried not to dwell on thoughts like these as they upset her. Like her father's girl friends who were getting younger and younger by the month. She looked at her watch again. Eight twenty-five. Oh, sod Kevin! She wasn't going to stand here all night.

She went into the phone box and picked up the phone. It was dead.

That was all she needed. Pulling her coat tighter around her she began to walk down the road, still keeping her eye out for Kevin and her car. The car that she never got the chance to drive any more.

She saw a set of headlights coming towards her and her heart leapt into her mouth. Please let it be Kevin!

It was the dark blue Orion and it stopped beside her.

'Come on, Kevin. Have one more drink.'

'Nah. I'd better get going. Mandy will be doing her nut.'

Jonny Barker laughed out loud and looked at the crowd of men around him.

'He's well and truly pussy whipped, ain't he, boys?'

Everyone laughed, none more so than Kevin Cosgrove himself. 'Nah, I've got to, lads. I'm half an hour late as it is.'

Garry Aldridge clapped Kevin on the back. He was as drunk as a lord.

'I'll tell you sommick, mate, since that murder I won't let my bird go nowhere unless she's in a cab or a crowd.'

Kevin looked at his friend's open face and for the first time worried about Mandy. She was a pain in the arse in a lot of respects, but he would not like anything to happen to her. Not just because he cared about her, though that was part of it, but because her father was what was known as a Bad Man. A very Bad Man indeed.

Putting his pint of lager on the bar, he said his goodbyes and made his way hastily to the car.

Opening the door, he climbed into the luxurious smell of leather and musk perfume. Mandy's perfume.

He loved this car. He envied Mandy her father's money, but admired her more because she still went to work. She was a beautician. In a few months her father was going to buy her her own shop.

He drove into Portaby Road and scanned the kerb looking for Mandy. She was nowhere to be seen. He had arranged to meet her here because it was quiet, and there would not be much chance of anyone who knew her father seeing her standing around waiting. If Patrick Kelly knew that his daughter did not really have the use of her own car he would go mad. He had bought her a car every year since she had passed her test at seventeen. Always a brand new car and always a very expensive one. Kevin knew for a fact that this Mercedes had cost well over forty thousand pounds. That was why he loved driving it. He loved the feel of being in something that was pure class. He turned around at the bottom of Portaby Road and began to drive back up it slowly. Mandy was definitely not here.

Kevin gripped the steering wheel tightly. That meant only one thing: she had gone home without him and without her car. He felt his heart sink as he began to drive to the outskirts of Grantley where Patrick Kelly lived with Mandy in a large rambling house.

Kelly would be furious. Though Kevin would never admit it outright to her or to anyone else for that matter, he admitted it to himself: Patrick Kelly frightened him out of his skin. He frightened anyone who had even half a brain.

Kevin drove slowly. All the excitement he usually felt at driving the car was gone now. It had been replaced by fear.

Bugger that bloody Mandy! Why didn't she just wait like he'd told her?

Patrick Kelly poured himself a brandy in a large snifter and sat back in his chair. He looked at his new girl friend Tiffany and hid the glimmer of annoyance that swept through his features as he watched her, watching herself, in the full length mirror opposite her chair.

Tiffany was nineteen, three years younger than his daughter, and she was built like Jayne Mansfield. Kelly liked his women voluptuous. He allowed himself a slight smile. Tiffany would not even know who Jayne Mansfield was. She was what he commonly termed as thick as two short planks. But that was all right because he didn't particularly want to talk to her. Just go to bed with her.

The large Christmas tree in the corner twinkled with lights and he glanced at it for a few seconds, then his eyes strayed once more to the photograph of his late wife, Renée, on the mantelpiece. Suddenly he was engulfed in sadness. He shrugged silently inside his Armani suit. A memory of another Christmas came to his mind, he could see Renée holding Mandy in her arms in their little bedsit, the bathroom was full of steam and the smell of camphor. Mandy, just turned one, had croup and both he and Renée had sat in the damp little bathroom all night with her.

He missed Renée, missed her every day of his life. They had worked together to build up their businesses, she was the real brains behind the repo business, not him. He had always been the muscle, the hard man. He had collected outstanding debts from villains, men who had done a robbery and then tried to 'tuck up' the other men with them.

Kelly had a knack of finding people, of making people tell him their whereabouts – he still had it to this day, despite his large house, his hand-made suits and his aura of semi-respectability. Deep down in his boots he knew that he was

66

still an East End urchin, still got a thrill from his illegal dealings. Even though these days he mixed with the highest in the land for one reason or another, he knew that inside, he would always be Patrick Kelly from the East End. The years of living in coldwater bedsits, rat-infested tenements and watching his mother work herself into the ground would never be far from his thoughts, and as far as he was concerned, that was how it should be. He was honest enough to admit to himself that it was his dead wife's business acumen that he could thank for his respectable way of life these days. It had been Renée who had somehow managed to get them their first respectable client. Without her, he would still be pretty well off, but the chances were he'd have been sent down by a judge years before. He had learnt from her, and now he missed her. He had respected her, loved her and built a life with her for their only child.

Suddenly, Tiffany annoyed him more than ever. He did not want her sitting there, with her tight dress and professionally tanned legs, he wanted Renée. With her blonde hair swept up as it had always been and her tiny frame encased in a nice black dress that screamed of class, to him anyway. She had dressed quietly, had a quiet demeanor that he had loved. He looked at the tree again and felt the sting of tears. Christmas was always an emotional time. It was a time to think of absent loved ones, a bitter-sweet remembering. Ten years he had mourned her, taking on the responsibility for his daughter, a daughter who had all her mother's zest for life, even if she had taken up with that geek of a boyfriend. He looked like he was a bit Stoke on Trent, but Mandy had assured him he was straight as a die. Patrick still had his doubts.

The silence was beginning to get on his nerves: Tiffany was a girl of few words. Even in bed she lay back with a serious expression while he did the business, then she got up silently and washed herself over the bidet before getting back into bed and going straight to sleep. It was like shagging a blow-up doll. The only time she showed any emotion was when she was admiring herself in the mirror. The telephone jangled into the stillness of the room and Kelly jumped in his chair. He went to the table and picked the phone up thinking it might be Mandy.

It was Bill Doon.

'Pat, I've been to see the bloke and he's skint. He's blown the bloody lot on the horses. His wife never even managed to get a bit out of him for Christmas, the ponce.'

'What did you do, Bill?'

'That's why I'm ringing you, shall I give him a hiding or what?'

Patrick closed his eyes for a second and then gritted his teeth.

'Now you work for me don't you, Bill?' His voice low and patient as if he was talking to a child.

'Yeah.' Bill's voice was puzzled.

'And I pay you a good piece of wedge to collect outstanding debts for me don't I?'

'Yeah.'

'Then go and break his fucking arms. Jesus wept, I might as well go and do the fucking job meself.'

'All right, Pat, keep your hair on. He's got six kids sitting in that flat with him.'

'Then take him out of the flat, you pratt, and as it's Christmas you can give him a dig near a casualty department, how's that?' He slammed the phone down. After a couple of seconds he picked it up again and pressed 4. The phone was answered by Kelly's right-hand man, Willy Gabney.

'What do you want, Pat?'

'I want you to make up a goodie bag, Willy, and drop it round Bob Mason's place. He won't be home for Christmas.'

'Okey doke. Mandy back yet?'

'Not a bleeding sign of her. That ponce Kevin's probably still tarting himself up!'

He put down the phone and poured himself another large brandy. The ormolu clock on the mantelpiece showed ten to nine. Where the hell was Mandy? He had booked the table for nine thirty.

Kelly sat back in his chair and fingered a piece of paper in his breast pocket. It was the deeds to a small hairdressing salon and beauty parlour, his gift to his daughter for Christmas. He allowed himself a small smile.

Mandy would be over the moon.

He sipped his brandy in the silence once more. Tiffany, he noticed, was still watching herself in the mirror.

George Markham was smiling at the girl in his car. Her eye was already beginning to swell where he had punched her. It was her own fault for trying to fight him. Here he was trying his hardest to be friendly and nice and all she could do was sulk! He had driven to a piece of wasteground and now they were both watching each other warily.

Mandy was terrified. Since the man had stopped and asked directions, everything had gone wrong. She had walked to his car and the next thing she had known she was being dragged bodily into the car. She had kicked and screamed and no one had come to help her. She could feel a throbbing above her right eye, and it hurt her ribs every time she took a breath. As he had dragged her across his lap by her hair she had scraped her knees and thighs on the metal of the car. They had driven away fast and she had attempted to open the door and jump but he had held on to her hair, making it impossible. She would have landed under the wheels of the car.

Oh, please, please. Someone, anyone, help her!

George liked the look of her, he decided. The only thing he did not like was the orange lipstick. He hated orange lipstick. Mandy saw him scowl at her and her heart lurched. She inched her way round, her arm behind her back. She was going to open the car door and run for it. Run as hard as she could.

George read her mind.

Taking a length of rope from the glove compartment, he grabbed her hands.

Mandy began to fight, her long false nails flying dangerously close to his face. Sighing heavily, George punched her with all his might. He hit her on the cheekbone and heard the high cracking sound as it broke beneath his knuckles.

69

The girl slumped back on to the seat dazed, the red hot pain in her face making her quiet and subdued. The man was mad. Suddenly Mandy knew that with stunning clarity. If she didn't play along he would kill her. Maybe he would kill her anyway. She lay back in the seat crying quietly. Wishing her dad was here. George tied her hands together as if she was going to say her prayers.

'Please let me go.' Her voice was low and surprisingly gentle and childlike.

George felt magnanimous, even happy at the humility of the request. She learnt fast, he would say that much for her. Rubbing his hands together, he leaned over her and took a carrier bag off the back seat. He pulled out the black leather mask he had purchased in the sex shop.

Mandy was in a state of fear so acute she was rooted to the seat. Her eyes opened wide as she saw the man putting the mask on. He even turned on the interior light of the car, and pulled the mirror above the windscreen towards him so he could fit the mask on properly.

It crossed George's mind that she had seen his face clearly already, but he could hardly drive around Grantley with the mask on, could he? He felt the fear coming from the girl and was gratified. It was all working out even better than he'd expected.

Getting out of the car, he slipped off his 'good' overcoat, as Elaine called his Burberry. Folding it carefully, he laid it across the back seat. It was freezing cold and George shivered. Then he walked round to the passenger side and, opening the door, dragged Mandy out. Pulling her along by her coat, George led her to an old shed that had been standing empty for years. He opened the door and pushed her inside.

Mandy landed on the dirty floor, and was in too much pain to care. She watched as the man took two candles from his suit pocket and lit them.

George smiled. That was better. Going to Mandy, he untied her hands.

'Take off your coat.'

She lay on the floor staring up at him. A thin line of blood was seeping from her nose and rolling down the side of her face.

'I said, take off your fucking coat!'

George put his hand over his mouth. But the swearing seemed to do the trick because she pulled herself up slowly.

He felt the stirring of excitement and then grabbed the front of her sheepskin and tore it from her body. As he dragged it from her arms she seemed to spin over and George heard a heavy thud as she landed back on the floor.

He shook his head. Another one! Out in this weather in a little jumper and skirt. Still, at least she had the sense to wear tights. Thick tights.

He could see the fear in her eyes and he grinned.

Mandy watched the man lay her coat on the dirt floor. She tried to gather her wits about her and glanced around the shed. There were no windows, only the door, and he was wedging a piece of wood under that. Lying about on the floor were numerous pieces of wood and metal. Just to the right of her was a crowbar. She would await her opportunity and then make a grab for it. She swivelled her eyes back to George. Her face was so sore, she was having difficulty swallowing. She watched as the man came back to her.

'Lie on the coat, dear, or you'll get a cold.'

His voice was muffled inside the mask and he could feel the warmth of his breath against the leather.

George liked wearing the mask, it made him feel different. He had wanted one of these masks since he'd read Donald Neilson had worn one to murder Lesley Whittle.

Mandy dragged herself on to her sheepskin. Her whole body was aching now. Especially her face and knees. She looked down at her legs and saw the blood seeping through the holes in her tights. She felt panic welling up inside her and fought it down. She had to keep a clear head. She had to get hold of that crowbar. She pushed her hair from her face and George watched her through the mask's eyeholes. It was a very feminine gesture, a graceful gesture, and George felt an enormous lump in his throat as he looked at her.

His mother had possessed a grace of movement just like that, a feline quality that had set her apart from other women. He smiled into the mask with tenderness.

'What's your name, dear?'

Mandy didn't reply. Just stared at the mask.

George tutted to himself. She was getting difficult again. Women were always the same. You tried to be nice to them, to help them even, but were they grateful? Were they?

He began to breathe heavily and the mask grew even hotter. He was beginning to sweat now and it was all her fault. He kicked her on the leg, a savage kick that brought the tears back into her eyes.

'I asked you your name, you little slut!'

'It's Mandy . . . Mandy Kelly.'

Her name was Mandy! His favourite name! The name of the girl in his video . . . Mandy.

He watched her tiny pointed breasts that poked through her jumper as if surprised to be there and felt an aching in his loins.

He knelt in front of her.

He wished he did not have to wear gloves. He clenched and unclenched his hands in anticipation.

Then she kicked him. He felt the sting as her boot came into contact with his chest. In a split second, she had rolled away from him, across the dirt floor, eyeing a lump of metal!

The dirty stinking bitch was trying to grab a weapon! But George beat her to it. He jumped up and ran to her. As her hand curled around the crowbar he stamped on it with his heel. She screamed, loudly and piercingly.

George picked up the crowbar and before he knew what was happening he had broken open her head. He threw down the crowbar. It made a dull and hollow thud as it hit the dirt floor.

Now look what you made me do, he thought.

It was all her own fault. They were all the bloody same. Troublemakers the lot of them.

Dragging the girl's body back to the sheepskin, he dumped her on to it and arranged her limbs so that she was

72

open to him. He was sweating like a pig now, even in the extreme cold. It was the mask.

George sat back on his heels and looked at her for a long moment.

Then he began to take off her clothes.

'Well, I'm starving.' Tiffany's voice was like a spoilt child's.

Patrick Kelly turned from the telephone and bellowed at her: 'Then fuck off, love. Go on. FUCK OFF!'

Slamming the phone back in its cradle, Patrick Kelly stormed over to where Tiffany was sitting. Kevin saw her flinch. Kelly picked her up bodily and half dragged, half ran her from the room. He threw her from him as they entered the large hall.

'Get your coat. Get a cab. Get out of my sight, Tiffany, or I'll punch your stupid face in.'

She rubbed her arm.

'Oh, come on, Pat. You know I didn't mean it.' Her voice was low and pleading and Kelly felt a moment's pity for the girl.

He breathed out heavily, suddenly feeling deflated. Where the hell was Mandy? It was gone eleven now. He picked up the phone in the hall and dialled a number.

'Jimmy? Drive the car around the front. Tiffany's going home.'

Kelly saw her lips tighten. He replaced the receiver.

'So when will I be seeing you then?' Tiffany was slightly mollified by the fact he was sending her home in one of his cars and not a taxi.

'You won't, love. Not now. Not ever.' His voice was low and hard.

'I beg your pardon?'

'You heard. Here's Jimmy with the car. Get your coat and go.'

She watched him walk back into the lounge and shut the door. Bloody cheek! No one, but no one, dumped her without a by your leave. She had a good mind to give him a piece of her mind.

Luckily for Tiffany, she didn't have one.

Kevin sat in the armchair. Neither man said a word as they heard the crunch of the wheels on the gravelled drive. Kelly poured himself another drink. He did not bother to offer one to Kevin.

'Well then, I've tried all her mates. All me relatives. Everyone. Are you sure she ain't got another bloke who she could be out with?'

Kevin bridled despite himself.

'Of course I am. She's not that sort of girl.'

Kelly nodded at him as if agreeing.

'One thing I want to get straight in me mind. Why did you have her car? And if you had it, how was she going to get home?'

Kevin's heart was beating a tattoo in his chest. He had been waiting for these questions all night.

He licked his lips nervously.

'Well.' He cleared his throat. 'She said to me to use her car today to pick up some things like I said I would . . .' His voice trailed off.

Kelly walked to his chair and stared down at him.

'Yeah? Go on.'

'I arranged to pick her up from the phone box in Portaby Road. Only when I got there – I was a bit late like – she wasn't there.' Kevin could see Kelly's slate grey eyes hardening by the second. 'So I come here, thinking she'd got a cab or something.'

'What time was you supposed to pick her up then?'

'Eight o'clock.'

'And what time did you finally get there?'

'About twenty to nine.' Kevin's voice was so low Kelly couldn't hear it.

'What time? Speak up, lad, for Christ's sake.'

'About twenty to nine.'

Kelly's face screwed up in abject disbelief.

'What do you want for Christmas, son? A Rolex or fucking Big Ben hung round your neck, eh? You left my baby

74

standing outside a phone box for forty minutes in this weather!'

Throwing the brandy glass to the floor Patrick Kelly delivered a stinging blow to the younger man's ear, knocking him off the chair.

'You ponce! You little ponce! My Mandy could be fucking dead because of you. Start saying your prayers, boy, because if I don't locate my baby soon, you'll be dead. Do you hear me!'

Kevin wiped his running nose with the back of his hand. He was absolutely terrified.

'Y-Y-Yes. I'm sorry . . .'

'You're sorry, are you? You've been driving round in my Mandy's car for weeks. Oh, I know all about it, sonny boy. I've had you watched. Now I don't doubt you've heard some stories about me. About my businesses up West, and the heavies that work for me. Well, you take all you've heard and times it by ten and you'll get a little inkling of what you are so desperate to marry into. I make the Godfather look like Little Red Riding Hood. You remember that, boy, because if anything, anything at all, has happened to my little girl, you'll be deader than an Egyptian mummy!'

Kelly's face was contorted with rage. He had the same sick feeling inside him he had had the day Renée had died. It was like history repeating itself.

She had been killed driving home from her mother's in West Ham. She had been over two hours late and he had known deep in his heart that something had happened. Her Mini that she loved so much she had named it Jason had been hit by a lorry on the A13, outside the Henry Ford public house. But his Mandy wouldn't be in a car accident, because this pratt in front of him had her bloody car!

He went to the phone and picked it up. He dialled a number and turned back to face Kevin, who had pulled himself off the floor and was now sitting back in the armchair crying.

'Bloody real, ain't it? Patrick Kelly, the most feared man in London, phoning the Old Bill!'

75

Kate was at home putting the finishing touches to the Christmas tree with Lizzy. As her daughter put the old fairy on the top, she remembered when Lizzy had made it. She had been only five at the time and every year since, the pieces of cardboard and tattered lace had graced the top of the tree.

'That looks lovely.'

Lizzy stepped back to admire her handiwork. 'Not bad. I'm really looking forward to Christmas this year, Mum.'

'So am I, love.'

As she spoke there was a loud banging on her front door. Lizzy ran from the room and a few seconds later there was a loud squealing. Kate closed her eyes briefly. The wandering hero had returned, as per usual. Her mother walked from the kitchen and looked at Kate, her eyebrows raised.

'It's himself?'

'It is.'

'Well, it makes her happy anyway.'

Kate plastered a smile on her face as her daughter tugged her father into the room. Kate was aware of the chaos of the room and grinned, this time genuinely. Gone were the days when she took trouble for Danny.

'Hello, Dan, long time no see.'

He looked great, as usual. He was tall, blond and deeply tanned. Kate wondered, not for the first time, why men looked better as they got older. He was hugging his daughter to him with real affection.

'Hello, Kate old girl.'

'Not so much of the old, Dan, if you don't mind.'

They looked at each other over their daughter's head.

'Oh, Mum, Dad's laden down with gear. Presents for all of us.'

Kate saw the question in Dan's eyes and sighed inwardly. He had his suitcase with him which meant he wanted to stay 'for a while'. Over the years he had done this to her a few times. It meant that the current recipient of his affections had either caught him out with her best friend or just caught him out in general.

76

Evelyn walked into the room and Dan immediately embraced her, lifting her off the floor as he kissed her.

'Evelyn, you never change!' For once he was being truthful. She looked the same at seventy as she had at sixty.

Evelyn waited until he put her down and then said, 'Neither do you, Dan.' They looked at each other, the animosity between them almost tangible. 'I see you've got your case with you this time?'

It was a question and Dan avoided her eyes, turning instead to his daughter.

'I thought I'd spend some time with my girl. Now how about a cup of tea for a cold traveller?'

Lizzy skipped from the room to the kitchen, her grandmother following her. Dan looked at Kate. His deep blue eyes were sparkling.

'You look great.'

'So do you. How's things?'

She picked up a couple of Christmas tree decorations and began to hang them precariously from the branches.

'All right, I suppose. Look, Kate, can I stay, just for the holidays?' His tone was wistful and Kate, with her back to him, afforded herself a little smile.

'Of course you can, Dan, provided you don't mind the settee?'

'I'm quite used to it now, Kate.'

'I'm sure you are.'

The silence between them was heavy. Kate made herself relax. She put up with Dan's invasions for Lizzy's sake, knowing that the girl enjoyed them. Dan was a wastrel, a lazy good for nothing – and his daughter adored every bone in his body.

Kate had never attempted to put her daughter wise about her father. Instead she allowed him to come into their lives when it suited him and then gritted her teeth and smiled until he breezed out again. Kate could even sympathise with Lizzy; once upon a time he had had the same effect on her. She was living for the day when Lizzy found out her father's shortcomings herself. Then she would pick up the pieces and breathe a sigh of relief.

Lizzy came back in the room with a mug of steaming tea. Dan had ensconced himself on the sofa and Kate watched from the easy chair as Lizzy gave him the mug, careful not to let one drop fall on to her father's natty outfit. She would bet her last pound that every bit of money he had was already spent. His presents would be large and as expensive as possible. Now he wanted somewhere to recuperate and relax that did not cost anything. Kate knew he was mugging her off and it annoyed her.

'So how's Anthea?'

'Oh, she's fine, fine. Got her boys home for Christmas, so I thought I'd come and see my poppet.' He ruffled Lizzy's hair as he spoke and she smiled at him.

Kate felt an urge to be sick but fought it down bravely. 'When's she expecting you back?' It came out sweetly but Dan and Evelyn, who had walked into the room, both knew it was a loaded question. He was saved from answering by Lizzy.

'Oh, Mum! He's only just got here and you want to know when he's going?'

The phone rang and Kate went out to the hall to answer it, glad of the respite.

'Hello, DI Burrows speaking.'

'Kate? Ratchette here. Bit of bother, I'm afraid. Could you sort it out for me, please?'

'What's up, sir?'

'It seems that one of the town's leading citizens has mislaid his daughter.'

'Who?'

'Patrick Kelly.' Ratchette's voice was flat. 'I've had the Chief Constable on to me. It seems the girl went missing at eight this evening. The boyfriend was supposed to pick her up from Portaby Road and when he got there she was nowhere to be seen. She's not a girl to go off without telling anyone apparently, so the Chief Constable himself wants the matter thoroughly investigated.'

Kate could hear the annoyance in Ratchette's voice.

'I'll go and see him, don't worry. It's probably nothing. How old is the girl, by the way?'

'Twenty-two. I think she had a row with the boyfriend and is holed up at a friend's but the boy's too frightened to tell the father.'

Kate laughed softly.

'Well, you can't really blame him for that, can you? Patrick Kelly isn't exactly a calm and caring individual.'

'No, Kate, he's not. But he's very friendly with the Chief Constable. At least, that's how it seems to me anyway.'

'Don't worry, I'll sort it out.'

'Thanks, Kate. Give the girls my best, won't you?'

'Of course. I'll let you know what happens, sir.'

The line went dead in her hand.

She walked into the living room and smiled her best smile.

'I've got to go in, I'm afraid. A girl's gone missing.'

'Oh no . . . Who?' Lizzy's face was concerned.

'No one you know. Look, I'll be as quick as I can, all right?'

'Mum's on the murder-rape, Dad, she's in charge.'

'Really, Kate?'

'Yes. Look, you lot catch up and I'll be back soon.'

She went from the room and pulled on her coat quickly. Evelyn followed her out with Lizzy.

'I hope the girl turns up, Mum.'

'I think she will, love, don't worry.'

'You make sure you ring me as you're coming home and I'll have something hot for you when you come in. Wrap up now, it's bitter cold out there.'

'Mum, I'm forty years old, you know.' This was said playfully.

'You don't look that old, Mum. You only look about thirty-eight.'

'Thanks a million, Lizzy, I feel much better!'

'You don't mind Dad staying really, do you?'

Kate looked into the lovely face and felt a twinge of guilt. 'No, of course not.'

Lizzy kissed her and went back into the living room. Kate and her mother looked at each other for a few seconds.

'She's growing up at last, Kate.'

'So it would seem. See you later, Mum.' She kissed the tiny woman in front of her.

Evelyn held her daughter's arm. 'You be careful out there now, with a maniac on the loose. I'll sort out his lordship if he starts his antics.'

''Bye, Mum.'

Picking up her car keys Kate went out into the cold night air. She felt a strange sense of relief to be out in her car. As she pulled away her mind was once more full of the investigation. They were nowhere near solving the case. It had not been planned but was a spontaneous act. Geraldine O'Leary had been murdered by a random killer. Those were the worst kind of cases. In almost eighty-five per cent of murders the killer was known to the victim, the percentage was even higher in rape cases. She honestly believed that whoever had murdered Geraldine O'Leary had not known who their victim was going to be. But even knowing this brought her no nearer to solving the case; quite the opposite in fact, it made everything harder, much harder. The door to door had not been much use, though there were a few leads they were following up. A sighting of a dark coloured car in Vauxhall Drive at about six fifty-five. They did not know the make, only that it was a saloon. It was like looking for the proverbial needle in a haystack. She turned right at the crossroads that led to the outskirts of Grantley and Patrick Kelly's house. She did not need to find out his address. In Grantley, everyone knew where Patrick Kelly lived.

Especially the police.

Kate felt a flicker of annoyance, even though this call had got her out of the house and away from Dan. If Frederick Flowers was so worried on Patrick Kelly's behalf, why the hell didn't he come out here and investigate the matter himself? Normally a person had to be missing for over twenty-four hours before the police were interested, especially when it was a grown woman. It was different with children, but this Mandy Kelly was twenty-two, for Christ's sake. She pulled into the sweeping gravelled drive and stopped in front of the large Georgian house, set in three acres of parkland. It was lit up like Battersea Power Station. Seems that massage parlours and repossessions paid well and earned friends in high places as well. Kelly's electric bill came to more than her mortgage by the looks of things.

The entire house was floodlit and even the trees had lights in them. You'd have no chance of creeping up to Patrick Kelly's door without being seen. Nursing her resentment she walked up to the front door and rang the bell.

One of the first things Kate noticed was that the house was decorated in superb taste. Not what she expected at all. She looked around, impressed despite herself. Obviously Kelly's money ran to interior designers. She followed Kelly into the drawing room and took a seat on the chesterfield. The room was beautiful, with the original ceiling roses and cornices; the walls were lined with books, everything from leather-bound volumes to garish paperbacks. It was predominantly silver grey with dusky pink carpets and curtains. It was a room designed by a woman, Kate was certain. It had a woman's feel for colour and space. Men tended to put things in the first place available and just leave them there. Women thought a room out, knew how a room would look at its best. Women, Kate had observed, took time with details. Small details that could make a room like this.

Despite its immense size, it was a homely room and obviously well lived in. A sleek black cat lay asleep before the fire. Her eyes rested on Kevin Cosgrove, who sat whitefaced and subdued. Kate guessed, rightly, that he was the boyfriend, and that he had been having a hard time from Kelly.

She took the scotch Kelly offered and sipped it gratefully. This was the last thing she had wanted tonight. Even with Dan, the long lost father's return, this was still not what she needed. The scotch was good and she savoured it for a second before she looked at Kelly directly.

'What makes you think that your daughter's gone missing? She could be at a friend's, anything.'

Patrick stared at Kate as if seeing her for the first time.

'What did you say your name was?'

'Detective Inspector Burrows.'

Kelly put his tongue between his lips and stared at her for a long moment as if committing her to memory. The action and the tone of voice were not lost on Kate and she felt her temper rising. He was trying to tell her she was here at Flowers's express command and she had better take this seriously. Kate fought down the urge to confront him. Instead she broke his gaze by putting her drink on the small occasional table beside her and rooting around in her bag for her notebook and cigarettes. It was going to be a long evening.

As she put a cigarette in her mouth, Kevin Cosgrove gave her a light, his hands shaking. Kate put her hand over his and held her cigarette to the flame. His eyes held a warning and he shook his head imperceptibly.

Kate breathed in the cigarette smoke and sat back, crossing her legs.

Kelly watched her from his chair and approved of her. She had a bit of spunk and he liked that. Providing she didn't 'come it' with him, she was a woman he'd want in his corner if the time came. He looked into her eyes as she spoke.

'Why are you so worried about your daughter, Mr Kelly?' As she spoke, Kate realised that the man really was worried. This was not an over-anxious father throwing his weight around, this was a genuinely worried man.

'This pratt here was supposed to pick my daughter up at eight.' He flicked his head at Kevin, who kept his eyes firmly on the carpet. 'He had her motor, her car. He went to pick her up and she wasn't there. I've rung her mates, her aunt, the fucking manageress of the shop where she works, I've rung everyone in Grantley and I can't find her. This is no girlish prank, Ms Burrows. My baby is definitely on the missing list. Now then, what are you going to do about it?'

Kate took another drag on her cigarette and met the dark blue eyes full on.

'Has Mandy ever gone missing like this before?'

Kelly shook his head. 'Nope. Never. Me and Mandy are like that.' He crossed two of his fingers together. He licked his lips and took a large gulp of brandy.

Kate pushed her hair off her face and watched Kelly. He was handsome all right. In other circumstances she would have given him a second glance. This was the first time she had seen him in person. Oh, she'd seen pictures of him, everyone had. But in the flesh, he had a presence. He was a man who was all there, was alive. He crackled with energy and vitality. Now, seeing his concern for his daughter, Kate felt a stirring of pity for him.

'Have you and Mandy had an argument, Kevin?' She looked at the boy; his face was ashen and he still stared at the carpet as he shook his head dismally. With one bound, Kelly was out of his chair and had dragged the unfortunate boy from his seat. Holding him up by the hair he pushed him towards Kate and shouted.

'Tell her anything she wants to know, boy, I'm warning you. If Mandy turns up here and her story differs from yours I'll snap your bastard neck for you.'

Kate jumped up and separated the two men.

'Mr Kelly please! This is not doing anyone any good. Now calm down, will you? Can't you see you're frightening the life out of him? How can you expect him to tell you the truth when he's so obviously terrified of you?'

Her words crept into Patrick's brain. It was after eleven now and Mandy had still not been in touch. He could feel a panic inside him like the day Renée died. When she hadn't been home at five thirty, he had known, deep in his gut, that she'd never walk in again. He felt the same now. He forced down the panic and went back to his seat. His haunted expression tore at Kate's heart. If it was her Lizzy, so soon after the murder of Geraldine O'Leary . . . she shuddered.

Kevin Cosgrove was crying silently. Kate led him back to his chair and, without asking, poured them all another drink. Patrick took the glass from her and drained it, his handsome face haggard.

'You don't know my Mandy, she wouldn't stay out without letting me know. No way.' The last was said with the finality of a father who knows his child.

Kate glanced at the clock on the mantelpiece; it was nearly eleven thirty.

Patrick saw her looking and exploded again.

'Want to get home, do you? Am I boring you or something?'

As he opened his mouth to speak again, Kate held up her hand for silence.

'No Mr Kelly, you're not boring me, you're annoying me. Until you calm down and speak rationally, we will get nowhere. Now, if you don't mind, I'm going to ask you some simple questions. If you could just bring yourself to answer them, we might start getting somewhere.'

Kelly's eyes were like slits. The cheeky mare, she was talking to him as if he was a naughty little kid. He felt a surge of annoyance and something else as well. Admiration. She was not intimidated by him and he was glad. If his Mandy had gone missing, then this woman would find her. The cold fear that had engulfed his body for the last two hours gradually let go its hold.

'I'm sorry Ms Burrows.' He emphasised the Ms.

Kate looked at him and smiled slightly. 'That's all right, Mr Kelly. I have a daughter too. I can imagine what you're going through.'

'Can you?' It was a question they both knew she could not answer.

'Right, Kevin, what were your exact arrangements with Mandy?'

As Kate questioned the boy, Kelly watched her from his seat. Even in his agitated state he could see she was an attractive woman. What he really liked about her though, was her sass. He did like a woman with a bit of spunk in her. Mandy's mother had had that. She was as quiet as a church mouse till you set her off, then you'd better watch out. This Ms Burrows was interesting. She was taking his mind off his child for a few minutes and for that, he was grateful.

84

Kate felt his attention and shrugged it off. She wanted to get her job done and get back home. This house was too fraught for her liking.

'Listen you.' Caroline's voice had a smile in it. 'I am not having it off in an old shed.'

Barry laughed with her.

'Well, there's one thing for certain, girl. My wife and your husband ain't gonna let us use their beds, so it's the back of the motor, or the shed. I've got a sleeping bag in me boot. We'll be as snug as two bugs in a rug!'

Caroline screeched with laughter again.

'What's the time?'

Barry stared bleary-eyed at his watch.

'Half-past twelve.'

'My old man ain't expecting me in till after two. He thinks I'm doing an extra shift.'

'So what's it to be then? Out here in the motor or in the shed?'

'You've done this before, ain't you?'

Barry nodded.

'Yeah. I've got a sleeping bag, a bottle of wine and a couple of plastic glasses. All waiting for you, my darling.'

'Oh . . . go on then. But you're sure no one comes round this way at night, ain't ya?'

'Yes! Now help me lug all the stuff in.'

They got out of the car. Caroline carried the wine and the glasses. Barry carried a large sleeping bag. Caroline pushed open the shed door. As she walked in she stumbled over something and screamed with fright.

'Here, hold up, girl. You'll have the Old Bill here if you're not careful.'

Dumping the sleeping bag on to the floor, Barry flicked his lighter into life.

He heard the real scream that came from Caroline this time and was hard pressed not to follow it with one of his own.

On the floor in a pool of blood lay a young girl. She was nearly naked.

The lighter burnt his fingers and he pulled his thumb off the fuel button. In the darkness Caroline began to panic and Barry pulled her from the shed. He held her to him tightly.

'Calm down . . . Calm down!'

He could hear her teeth chattering and guessed she was in shock.

He took her back to his car, turned the engine on and put on the heater. Then, taking his torch from the glove compartment, he went back to the shed. His mind was in a turmoil. He stepped gingerly inside and shone the torch on to the girl's body. Her head was stuck to the floor where the blood had dried on to her hair and the dirt. He knelt down beside the body and put his fingers to the main artery in her neck.

She was alive! Surely not?'

He felt again with trembling fingers. He was positive there was a faint heartbeat. He jumped up quickly and, opening the sleeping bag, covered her with it. Must keep her warm. Must keep her warm. Don't move her. Bless her little heart. Let her live, God. Oh, let her live!

Running from the shed, he jumped into his car and drove as fast as he could to a phone box.

Within fifteen minutes Mandy Kelly was on her way to Grantley Hospital and Caroline and Barry were explaining their embarrassing story to the police, who promised that neither of their spouses would be informed of the circumstances that heralded the finding of the girl.

In the pocket of the sheepskin the police found a purse. It contained Mandy Kelly's credit cards.

A positive ID had been established.

Kate was listening to Kelly talk about his wife and daughter. Kevin had gone upstairs to lie down and, without his presence, Kelly seemed to relax a little. Kate knew that he was blaming the boy for whatever had happened to Mandy. Kate still thought there was a good chance Mandy would turn up any minute. She'd probably had an argument with Kevin and stormed off, possibly because he'd taken her car again.

Kate could not begin to comprehend the wealth that enabled a man to give his daughter a fifty thousand pound car for her twenty-first birthday. She thought of the sovereign earrings she had bought Lizzy for Christmas, the struggle she had had to find the money for them, and shook her head. The funny thing was that Kelly, back to his old self now, was an interesting and articulate man. He spoke of his wife and child with a love that was almost tangible. He was telling her a story now about his first months of fatherhood.

'Anyway, there I was, all on me own with Mandy, a baby like.' He smiled. 'Well, she wanted her dinner. She was crying her eyes out. Do you remember those big glass bottles in the sixties? I picked one up out of the hot water to check it on me arm and I dropped it. It shattered all over the kitchen floor. Well, that was it then. We only had the one bottle and I was beginning to panic when I saw the sauce bottle on the table. I put Mandy in her pram, she slept in a pram then, because we couldn't afford a cot, see. And I washed out the sauce bottle and sterilised it with boiling water, then I made a feed up and put the teat on the top and fed her.'

Kate laughed with him, picturing the scene in her mind.

'Well, Renée came home like, laden down with the shopping, took one look and went through the roof.'

It was the sort of thing she could see him doing. He was resourceful. She had been on the point of leaving when he had persuaded her to have another drink. She had guessed that he was frightened of being alone at this time, that he needed another human being. She had stayed out of pity and now she was glad. He was a good talker, a great storyteller and even though she knew what he was capable of, she liked him. She trusted him, too, though why this should be so after his earlier performance she had no idea. Kelly was a hard man, but he had an Achilles heel. Mandy Kelly.

Already, Kate felt as if she knew the girl. And if all her father said was true, she was most definitely not a girl to go off without letting him know. Kelly was the kind of father who would demand to know his daughter's whereabouts. It was as much a part of him as his swearing.

'I'm sorry about carrying on earlier, but I've been out of me mind.' His voice was low. Kate knew it had taken a lot for him to give her an apology.

'I understand, Mr Kelly.'

As if of one mind, they both looked at the clock; it was just after half past twelve.

'Where the hell can she be? When she walks in, I'll slap her from one end of this room to the other, I take oath on that. I've never raised me hand to her before but I will tonight, by Christ.'

Kate put her hand over his. 'Calm down, hitting her won't solve anything.'

'No, but it might make me feel better.'

The phone rang and Kelly rushed to answer it.

'Mandy?'

Kate saw his face dissolve from hope to fear in the space of seconds. He held the phone out towards her and said, 'It's for you.'

'Burrows here.'

Patrick Kelly watched her face blanch and in that moment he knew that something had happened to his only child. He clenched his fists so tightly the nails dug into the skin of his palms, drawing blood.

Kate put down the phone and looked at him fully.

'We've found your daughter, Mr Kelly. It seems she's been attacked.'

Kelly stared at the woman in front of him, confusion and pain flitting across his face.

'Attacked? My Mandy?'

His voice sounded like a little boy's, full of hurt and disbelief.

Kate nodded. 'She's in Grantley Hospital and they're operating on her. She's in a bad way.'

Patrick Kelly felt the wetness in his eyes and did not care. He felt as if his world had just come to an end. He swallowed hard. When he finally spoke it was in a low croak.

'Is she gonna die?'

Kate put her hand on his arm gently.

'I think we'd better go to the hospital, don't you?'

As she sat beside him on the way, Kate felt that she had received an insight into Patrick Kelly. He had his Achilles heel, just like everyone else.

All her problems seemed small in comparison to what the man beside her was going through.

They drove in silence.

George was still sitting in his lounge. It was just past one. He could hear the regular thud-thud of the music from a party a few houses down. He took a long drink of his Ovaltine. It was stone cold and he grimaced.

Elaine had gone to bed earlier and he had told her he was feeling overtired. She knew that when he got like that he could not sleep. She had been happy to leave him downstairs.

He smiled to himself ruefully, laid his head back on the chair and savoured once more the events of earlier in the evening.

She was a very silly girl. Well, he had shown her. Oh, yes, he had shown her all right. The little slut! Hanging around at night, in deserted streets. Well, he had put a stop to her gallop. Oh, yes. It might just make a few of the women of Grantley sit up and take notice of him.

They'd all be talking about him again tomorrow. Oh, he knew what would be said. Elaine, the hungry hippo, would fill him in on all the local gossip. He smiled to himself at the comparision.

In his mind's eye he saw the girl as she had been when he had left her. Legs akimbo. He grinned. He knew all her secret places now. She had seen his face. That was a mistake, he realised it now. He should have put on the mask first.

He wondered vaguely if the girl had been found yet. Mandy . . . He liked that name very much.

The party was in full swing now and George could hear one of the records blaring out.

He liked people to enjoy themselves.

As the strains of 'Blue Velvet' wafted towards him he smiled again. In his mind he saw all the young girls dancing

89

with men. He pictured tight dresses and straining busts against white silk.

Oh, they were all the same. Every last one of them.

It would be Christmas Day soon. He was glad, because he needed a holiday. It had been a hectic few months.

As they reached the hospital Kelly asked Kate to tell him all she knew. She explained that Mandy had been found with horrific head injuries and that they were operating on her. She did not elaborate. It was not the right time.

Together, they walked into Grantley Casualty Department and Kate explained who they were to the receptionist. Like most hospital receptionists, this one was a breed apart. She pulled her glasses down an almost non-existent nose and surveyed Kelly and Kate over the top of them. Her thin hair was scraped back from her face in a bun so tight her eyes had taken on a Chinese appearance. Kate could see her in a kaftan and clogs and had to stifle a bubble of laughter.

'Name of patient again please.'

'Mandy Kelly. I am Detective Insp . . .'

The woman held up a chubby finger in reproof. 'One question at a time please.'

Patrick watched the performance with a darkening face. The woman was tapping Mandy's name laboriously into her computer.

'And how was she brought here?'

'I beg your pardon?' Kate was losing patience now.

'How was she brought here? By ambulance, in a car . . .'

Kelly pushed Kate out of the way. He peered into the glasses that separated him from the receptionist.

'She came by fucking bus. There was her, with her head smashed in. Two ambulance men and a fucking dirty great stretcher. Even you couldn't have missed them walking through here. Now shut your trap and tell me where my daughter is or you'll be going in to see the doctor yourself!'

The woman's mouth puckered into a small O and a nurse, hearing the exchange, hurried out from the cubicle area.

'Mr Kelly?'

90

Patrick nodded. Kate could see the tension in his shoulders and back. It was as if someone had stuffed a metal pole inside his coat to hold him up.

'Where's my daughter? I want to see my daughter.'

'She's still in theatre. If you'd like to follow me, I'll take you to the waiting room.'

Kelly and Kate followed the young girl.

'How is she?'

'I'm sorry Mr Kelly, I really don't know, a doctor will see you soon.'

Kate followed Kelly up two flights of stairs and into a tiny waiting room off the ITU. She thanked the nurse, who offered to bring them coffee.

'I knew this had happened, I knew it. I had a feeling in me bones.'

Kate didn't answer. Amanda Dawkins walked into the tiny room and Kate motioned with her head that they should go outside, closing the door quietly on Kelly.

'How is she?'

'Bad, Kate. Really bad. Half her head's gone. It's obvious it's the same man who attacked Geraldine O'Leary. She's been raped. Buggered as well I think. She's in a terrible state. Even the doctors were amazed at how she's hanging on to life.'

Kate pursed her lips. Kelly would go berserk if anything happened to his daughter. He was wound up like a watch spring now. She nodded at Amanda.

'Look, do me a favour. Keep everyone away from Kelly for a while. I'll stay with him. Get someone out to interview Kevin Cosgrove. He's at Kelly's house. OK?'

'Will do. Anything else?'

'Not until we know more.'

As Amanda walked away Kate called after her. 'There is one more thing: ring my house and leave a message on the answerphone. Tell them I'll be there as soon as possible, OK?'

Amanda nodded and Kate went back in to Kelly.

'What's happening?' His voice was flat, dead.

91

'Nothing at the moment.'

'Is Flowers here?'

Kate was startled.

'Of course not.'

Kelly got up and began pacing the room. 'Then get him here, tell him I personally request his presence. You can also find out who's the quack on my daughter's case and then find out who's the best quack for her kind of complaint. I don't care who the man is or how much he costs, just get him.'

Kate felt her mettle rise again. All her sympathy for Kelly evaporated out of the little window and she pulled herself up to her full height.

'With respect, Mr Kelly, I am not a secretary. If you want Frederick Flowers, or another doctor, I suggest you get them yourself.'

Kelly looked at her with a stunned expression on his face. He was used to people jumping when he told them to jump. He was used to pure unadulterated agreement with everything he said and did. He stared into Kate's face and she could see the battle raging inside him. His hand clenched into a fist and Kate knew it was taking all his willpower not to slap her a stinging blow.

What she'd said was tantamount to mutiny.

He bit his lip, his chest heaving. He pointed a finger at her, waving it up and down in front of her face.

'If I don't do something I'll explode, and if I explode here you will never see the like again as long as you live. I just *can't* sit here and wait. I have to do *something*.'

It was said simply and sincerely and Kate felt the power of him then, knew the depth of fear inside him and felt petty. Petty and nasty and childish. The man was trying to cope with his grief as best he could. He needed to be moving, doing, as if the act of movement would take away his fears. Would at least postpone them. If he was doing something he wouldn't feel so useless. Kate swallowed hard.

'I'll arrange for a phone for you.'

As she walked past him he grabbed her arm. She looked first at his hand, the fingers digging into her arm, and then up into his face. She saw the terrible knowledge in his eyes and then he crumpled. It was as if someone had punctured him – he just crumpled before her eyes and instinctively she put her arm around him. He clung to her.

'If she dies I have nothing, nothing.'

She steered him back to the chair and he put his head into his hands. Harsh racking sobs burst from inside his chest, exploding as they hit the air.

The nurse walked in with the coffee and Kate took the tray and hustled her out.

She gave him his coffee and lit a cigarette for him, placing it between his lips.

'It's the bastard who murdered that barmaid, ain't it?'

Kate knew it had taken a lot for him to admit his real fears. She nodded. 'We think so.'

'Has she been raped?'

Kate nodded again.

He sipped his coffee and a calm descended on him. He knew the worst now. Nothing else could be this bad.

'You realise he's a dead man don't you? Even if she lives. He's a dead man.'

Kate sipped her own coffee.

There was nothing to be said.

Chapter Six

Patrick Kelly drove home from the hospital at eight in the morning. He looked terrible and he knew it. His mouth tasted foul from instant coffee and cheap cigarettes. And he was fuming.

His daughter was lying between life and death, raped and beaten nearly to death. He felt the tightening around his heart and for one horrible second thought he was going to have a heart attack. He tried to control his breathing.

When he had seen her, his baby, lying in intensive care, full of tubes and drips and bandages, he had felt a red rage behind his eyes the like of which he had never experienced. Some piece of filth had taken his child – his child! – and forced himself on her.

She had been buggered, that was the worst of it all. His child had been buggered by some piece of scum.

Well, that piece of scum had better start saying his prayers, because Kelly was going to find him – find him and rip him to shreds.

He screeched to a halt in his driveway and as he ran towards it the front door was opened by Willy Gabney. Without speaking to the man, he rushed through the entrance lobby, the large tiled hall, and up the curved staircase, taking the steps three at a time. By the time he got to the bedroom where Kevin Cosgrove lay asleep, his chest and lungs were burning with every breath.

He threw open the bedroom door and it crashed against a bureau, sending an antique jug and bowl crashing to the floor. Before Kevin had even opened his eyes properly, Patrick Kelly was on him. Dragging the boy by the hair he pulled him from the bed, shaking him like a terrier with a bone. He began to rain punches on Kevin's body, kicking him and screaming at him at the top of his voice.

Kevin curled himself up into a tight ball, taking all that Patrick Kelly doled out to him. Frightened out of his life, he felt the savageness of the attack but was powerless to put a stop to it. Dragging him up by his shoulders, Patrick Kelly drew his head back and brought his forehead down on to Kevin's face with all his might. The force of the blow stunned them both. Kelly let Kevin drop to the floor, the boy's whimpering barely penetrating his rage.

Gabney, who had followed his boss up the stairs, stood in the doorway, his face neutral. The violence of the attack affected him not one iota. He was only surprised that Kelly had acted out the whole thing himself. It was precisely what Gabney himself was paid to do.

Kelly stared at the crumpled figure on the floor below him. He pointed, his finger shaking.

'My Mandy was raped and half murdered last night, you fucking ponce! Some piece of shite buggered my baby! Do you hear what I'm telling you, wanker?'

Kevin stared up, bemused. Mandy, raped?

Kelly brought back his leg and kicked Kevin in the knees as hard as he could.

'She's in a coma. She could be a vegetable because of you. But I promise you this, dickhead, whatever happens to my baby, happens to you! Remember that. Keep it stamped in your mind.'

He was so exhausted by his exertions he could barely talk, every few seconds gasping for breath. 'You're dead meat, boy. Dead meat.'

He leant against the dressing table until his breathing returned to normal. Then he nodded at Williamson. 'Get all the lads here NOW. I don't care if it is Christmas Eve, I don't care if they're at their mother's death bed, get them here pronto!'

Gabney hurried away. When Patrick Kelly was annoyed, it was best to do exactly what he said.

Kelly stared down at the crumpled heap on the floor. Crimson stains were appearing as if by magic on the Axminster carpet. Gathering up the spittle in his mouth, he bent over the prostrate form and spat into his face.

'Get up, Cosgrove, and piss off out of my house. You get yourself a sherbet dab and all, because my Mandy's car stays here. Get it?'

Kate had been busy all day with the new development. There was no doubt in anyone's mind that it was the same man who had murdered Geraldine O'Leary. She had been shocked to see the severity of the beating the girl had taken. All the fingers of one hand were broken, as if stamped on, and a large chunk of her head had been literally hacked from the skull. Even the doctors agreed that the girl should by rights be dead. But she was a fighter, like her father.

In spite of everything Kate knew about Patrick Kelly, she still could not help liking him. He was arrogant, self-opinionated and a bit of a male chauvinist. That much was evident even to an inexperienced observer. He had obviously ruled his daughter's life. A life that she was hanging on to by a thread. But after he had calmed down, she had seen another side to him. Inside the hospital she had witnessed the depth of his grief. Even with his bombast and his violent temper, Kate had felt an affinity with him. Anyone who had to witness the destruction of a child would feel the same.

She remembered when, years before, Lizzy had gone missing for an afternoon. Everyone had told her not to worry, that she was probably playing and had forgotten the time and Kate had felt the same rage inside her. Being a policewoman, she knew exactly what could have befallen her daughter. She had seen it enough times. She had wanted to slap the supercilious smiles off the faces around her. Lizzy had been found in the local woods setting up camp with a boy from two streets away. Kate had given her the one and only good hiding of her life. Not so much because she had gone missing but because of the fear she had caused her mother. Kate had sensed that same feeling in Kelly in the night.

She had stayed with him until Mandy had come out of theatre. During the long vigil he had talked again about his daughter and his dead wife. As if the very action of talking about her would somehow keep Mandy alive. It was this gentleness that attracted Kate to him. His more sinister reputation was overshadowed by his grief for his child.

Kelly had come up the hard way and Kate wondered if events in his childhood had made him what he was. Socialisation, the social workers called it. Kate had her own opinion. She thought that Kelly was a man who would have made something of himself whatever class he was born in: he had an inbred cunning, a need to achieve by whatever means he could. And she sensed that he wanted those achievements not so much for himself but for his wife and his child. He had worked to give Mandy everything, a fifty thousand pound car and a hairdressing salon and beauty parlour. She would love to be able to hand those to Lizzy on a plate. Wouldn't all parents? No, Patrick Kelly's reputation as a hard man was only true to an extent. Deep inside he was no different to anyone else; he just earned his money in unconventional ways.

When he had finally been able to see his daughter Kate had felt his anguish. It was obvious that Mandy was not going to live; she was so badly brain damaged, it would be kinder to let her die. But she was hanging on and Kate knew that Kelly would find it very difficult to accept that she was going to die. He felt pure willpower could pull her through.

Kate sighed. When she had finally left him to go home and grab a quick shower and a change of clothes before coming to work, she had felt as if she was abandoning him. As she'd walked from the ITU, she'd felt his eyes burning into her back. Now, at her desk, she admitted to herself that she found Patrick Kelly attractive. He was one hell of a good-looking man. She chastised herself. Your trouble, Kate Burrows, is you haven't had a man for too long. You should get yourself laid. Do you the world of good.

She smiled.

She had only ever had one man in her life and she was divorced from him. Shows how much Kelly affected me, she thought. I haven't thought about sex for years.

No, that was a lie. She'd thought about it, just never done anything about it.

She was glad when DS Spencer broke into her thoughts.

'So, Ma'am, what's the next step?'

Kate sighed.

'Well, as far as I can see, we just keep interviewing. I want you to find out if any of the door-to-door had a dark-coloured Orion car. One was reported seen on the waste ground last night.'

Spencer looked at the ceiling.

'Look, Ma'am, the man who reported that was not exactly a reliable witness . . . know what I mean . . .'

Kate chewed the inside of her mouth for a few seconds before answering.

'I am well aware that the man is a tinker, a pike, a gypo – whatever you want to call him, Spencer. I am also aware that they are camped not five hundred yards from the waste ground itself. Whether the man was drugged, drunk or both is not the issue here, Spencer. I want every lead followed up. And you can tell Willis that I'll be down to interview Fred Barkis myself in about . . .' she glanced at her watch . . . 'fifteen minutes, OK?'

'Yes, Ma'am.' Spencer failed to keep the irritation out of his voice.

Kate studied the file in front of her. Fred Barkis was a known flasher. He had also acquired a dark green Mark One Cortina, and a dark car had been reported by three different people cruising around by Vauxhall Drive on the night that Geraldine O'Leary died.

Kate stared at the wall opposite her and tapped her pen on her chin. Fred Barkis was harmless, she would lay money on it. For a start he was not violent-natured. All her years of policing had proved to her that the most mild-mannered men could be animals beneath the skin, but by the same token she had also learnt that ninety-five per cent of policing was working from hunches. And she had a hunch that Fred Barkis was not the man they were after. Still, he had to be eliminated.

That was the trouble with Spencer and his ilk, she had seen it so many times: get a suspect and dress up the evidence to suit yourself. Well, she had never worked like that and she was not going to start now. How many times had she seen witnesses' statements that had been doctored? Too many. She could understand that at times the job could be stressful – like now, when they had one woman dead and another fighting for her life and literally nothing to go on – but that did not excuse using a 'live one', as a pressured suspect was called. Barkis fit the bill, but in reality they could not tie him in to both cases and they now knew from the DNA samples that they were looking for one man. Anyway, Barkis had given samples of blood, urine and semen without a murmur. No, he was not their man, he was a common or garden sex pest which was a far cry from a fully fledged sex murderer.

The most annoying thing was that the local paper had nicknamed the rapist the 'Grantley Ripper'. Whoever he was, he was local, Kate was sure of that, very sure; and she was also sure that when he read his 'nickname' he would feel pleased. The criminal psychologist had already begun his profile of the man, and certain things shone through. He was a misogynist. He also had a job or a home life that allowed him free rein to roam the streets.

The misogynist part of it Kate had already worked out for herself; the ferocity of the attacks had told her as much. There seemed to be no motive of any kind; there rarely was in such cases. He was a sick man.

What they had to try and find out now was something that tied the two attacks together in some way. Kate frowned. Could he have a job that had brought him into contact with the two women? But one worked in a wine bar and one in a beauty salon. No matter how hard she thought she could not tie them together.

Even as all the evidence was being collated, there was nothing. Not one single thing that gave even a hint of who or what the murderer was. He had worn gloves on both occasions. The fibres from the body of Geraldine O'Leary had belonged to a family of wool that was used in literally hundreds of thousands of jumpers, coats, and other garments.

Kate felt the steel band of a headache tighten over her eyes and rubbed them with her finger and thumb, pressing on the closed lids as if the action would conjure up something she or one of the other officers had missed.

Finally she stood up and made her way to the interview room. Alongside the photos of Geraldine O'Leary there were now two more. In one Mandy Kelly was smiling, long blonde hair framing her tiny heart-shaped face. In the other she was lying in a hospital bed, her lovely hair shaved from her head. Deep gouges showed up in burgundy and black where her skull had been smashed. Both eyes were swollen and her nose was broken beyond recognition. Kate sighed. All around her the incident room was a hive of activity. Amanda Dawkins had tapped into the DVLC's computer and was finding out the name and address of every person in Grantley and the surrounding areas who owned either a dark green saloon car or a dark blue Orion.

The tapping of the typewriters and the constant buzz of voices in the smoke-filled room had not given Kate the headache, it was the stress of this case.

Picking up a file from Amanda's desk, she walked from the room.

Patrick Kelly lit a Dunhill cigarette with his gold lighter and exhaled noisily. By the time he had showered and changed, six men had arrived at his house. Now they were sitting in his morning room, uneasily awaiting their orders.

Kelly looked at the lighter for a long moment. Mandy had given it to him for his forty-second birthday. Every time he thought of Mandy he felt panic rise in his breast. If she died . . . Oh God in heaven! If she died he had nothing. Nothing in the world.

For the first time, his thirst for money had become a

secondary thing. He realised he would cheerfully give up everything he possessed to have his daughter back as she had been the last time he had seen her.

Happy and smiling and alive. Bursting with youth and vitality . . .

He heard a discreet cough and snapped his eyes from the lighter in his hands to the assembled men.

'I suppose you all know what's happened?'

At his words they started to murmur condolences. Kelly held up his hand for silence.

'I want this bastard caught, and I want him caught as fast as possible. I would not wish what has happened to me and mine on my worst enemy.' He paused while he pulled himself together. 'As you are all aware, the Chief Constable is a very dear and treasured friend of mine. He has assured me on the phone today that any information I want is open to me.

'I don't have a lot of faith in the Old Bill's methods of catching criminals. After all, they've never caught me, have they? I want all of you to drop everything you are doing and find this cretin. And find him fast! I want him dead. As soon as is possible, I want him dead.

'Now, later on today I am having some files delivered here. They will contain the name of every nonce in the South East of England. I want you lot—' Kelly gestured to the men with a sweep of his arm '—to get yourself up individual armies. I don't care how much it costs, or who the men are, as long as they are reliable. I want every shirt lifter and pervert rousted and trounced as soon as possible.'

He looked around as his words sunk in.

'At the moment a skirt is on the case, a DI Burrows – a very nice woman by the way. You *do not* give her any grief, right? But you give as much grief as you like to the other officers! I want them questioned one by one, and anything that they even think is a bit dodgy you find it out, then take it from there. The wedge for the bloke who finds the wanker is two hundred and fifty thousand pounds, tax free. Now, any questions?'

The six men stared at Kelly with a mixture of sorrow at

102

what had happened to his daughter and joy at the prospect of a quarter of a million pounds.

No one spoke and he nodded at them.

'Okay, lads. Report here with whatever you get. If you find him then I want him first, right? Now then, let's all have a drink while we get our heads together.'

Kelly walked through to his bar and a fleeting picture of Kate Burrows came into his mind. She was a fighter – he liked people who stood up to him. He allowed himself a brief smile. He wouldn't give her any grief. He thought there was a good chance she would find the bloke before he did. She was a good-looking piece as well, even in his trouble he had noticed that. No, he wouldn't hurt Kate Burrows. He had a feeling that they were going to see more of each other. She'd sat with him through the worst hours of his life. He felt that he owed her something for that at least.

Once his Mandy was home from hospital and he could concentrate better, he'd make a point of seeing Kate, thanking her.

He would not allow himself to admit that Mandy might not come home.

It was like tempting fate.

Dan sat with his mother-in-law and smiled to himself. Even though he knew that Evelyn couldn't stand him, he still had a grudging respect for her. Looking round the warm kitchen, he felt, not for the first time, that he had been a fool to leave Kate. That he had dumped her with a small baby sometimes gave his conscience a nasty twinge. Since then he had had his fill of women. They liked him. He knew that, and relied on it to keep a roof over his head and a pretty good standard of living. At forty-six, though, it was beginning to pall. Anthea had not been very nice to him at their final parting. In fact she had pointed out his age in rather a derogatory fashion. She could talk, the bitch! She was on the wrong side of fifty, not that she'd ever admit it. Still, the jibe had stung.

What really hurt, though, was the fact that she was holidaying in the Canaries for Christmas and he should have been with her. Instead he had had to throw himself on Kate's mercy. Good old Kate. He knew he was all right with her because of Lizzy. She would do anything for their daughter. He grinned ruefully. Even put up with him. What was worrying him, though, was what he was going to do after the holidays. For the first time he was not going from one home to another.

Evelyn took the turkey out of the oven and basted it. The smell was absolutely delicious. Suddenly Dan knew without a moment's doubt that the only course he had left to him was to stay in this house. Somehow he had to get Kate back on his side. She had wanted him for years after he had left. He had seen the naked longing in her face when he had turned up, ostensibly to visit his daughter. He had slipped back into her bed and then, when the time was right, slipped back out of it. He knew that she would not put up with that these days. She had told him once that he was her Achilles heel, but not any more. He would enjoy the chase all the more. Before she knew it she would be eating out of his hand. At least he hoped so anyway.

Kate had changed over the years. She had made a life for herself, had a good career in the police force. She wasn't waiting there open-armed any more, but she would still put up with him for Lizzy's sake and on that he could build.

He looked at Evelyn and closed his eyes. He'd have to get around her as well.

His mother-in-law put the kettle on for one of her endless cups of coffee.

'You're quiet, Dan.'

'Just thinking, Eve, that's all.'

'Well, don't strain yourself, son.'

He grinned.

'I was thinking about Lizzy, actually.'

He watched Evelyn's face light up with interest. Her grand-daughter was the reason for her existence.

'What about her?'

He had her interest and crossed his fingers. 'I feel bad you know, Eve, that I never really saw her grow up.'

She snorted. 'Well, you wouldn't, would you? Always skedaddling off somewhere. You were a fool, you know, Dan. My Kate was a good wife and mother. I watched her die inside when you first left her.'

She pulled two mugs from their hooks on the wall and slammed them on to the worktop. 'She worked like a frigging Trojan to give that child a decent upbringing. You never even gave a few pounds here and there to help her out.'

Danny's face was a mask of regret. This was not how he wanted the conversation to go. He wanted an ally, he didn't want recriminations.

'When I came here she was in a terrible state, but she got back to work and she's done very well for herself, so you leave her alone, Daniel Burrows. I can see through you as if you was made of glass, my boy, always could.

'Now, let's have a coffee before that child gets in. It's cold enough to cut the legs from you out there.'

Danny had the grace to redden. Evelyn knew him so very well. But ever the optimist he decided to wait a while then try again. There wasn't a woman alive he couldn't charm if he put his mind to it. He was absolutely certain of that.

'Merry Christmas, George!'

Elaine smiled at him. Since booking her holiday and going out two nights a week with the girls from work, even life with him had begun to be bearable.

'Merry Christmas, dear.' He dutifully kissed his wife's cheek.

George waited for Elaine to go back to her cooking before he curled his lip with contempt. The house stank of Christmas. Of turkey and mince pies.

'Joseph and Lily will be here soon. Lily's bringing one of her sherry trifles with her. I hope your mother won't be a nuisance this year . . .'

George felt his heart sink down to his boots. It was the same every year. His elder brother Joseph and his wife came for dinner. The brothers rang each other every New Year and Easter, and every Christmas Joseph and Lily came to dinner.

105

Other than that, they had nothing to do with each other. George wished he had the guts to pick up the phone and tell them to go to hell. He wouldn't though. He never did.

He started fidgeting with his knife and fork. He didn't want any breakfast now. The thought of seeing his mother had made him feel ill.

He saw her once a year, at Christmas. She lived with Joseph and Lily. Or, more precisely, they lived with her. Joseph might have worked all his life and bought his own house, but from the day his mother had moved in with them, it had become hers. She ruled the roost.

The only good thing about Elaine was the fact that she gave his mother short shrift. When she was told that Mother wanted to live with them, she had put her foot down firmly. Refusing even to discuss the situation. It was the one and only time in his life that George had been glad he had married her.

Elaine brought his scrambled eggs to him and he smiled his thanks. He noticed that she looked nice. He looked at her for a long moment and, noticing his look, she laughed. Picking up her own breakfast, she walked to the table and sat down.

'So you finally noticed, then!'

George stared at her, more puzzled than ever.

'I've lost a stone, George. I'm down to eleven and a half now. If I carry on like this I shall be about nine and a half for my holidays!' She laughed gaily.

'Well, you certainly look much better, dear.'

'Thanks. Haven't you noticed that I've been dieting at all?'

Her voice was half happy and half sad. George realised that she had been waiting for him to notice before mentioning it.

'Well, I had an idea, but I didn't like to ask outright . . .' He was stumbling for the right words and Elaine dropped her eyes.

After all their years of marriage, there was not an ounce of closeness between them. Since her first night out with the girls, she had discovered a whole new world. A world where George did not exist for her. A world where she could forget about him, just for a while.

Joseph Markham was at screaming point. Lily had gone into one of her painfully long silences, interspersed with black looks that she threw across the car at him at every set of traffic lights. Behind, Nancy Markham stared at the back of their heads. Her heavily lipsticked mouth was set in a grim line.

Nancy Markham was big. Her body, which in her young days could bring a grown man to his knees on first sight of it, bulged over the back seat of the car. Her dyed hair, now a vivid burgundy, was shampooed and set like a bloody halo around her face that now sported numerous chins. The only thing about her that were still young-looking and alert were her eyes.

They were still a startling green colour, except that the once pristine whites were now bloodshot and tinged with yellow. She held her large handbag across her chest like a weapon, her fat pudgy hands gripping the handles so tightly her knuckles were a livid white.

'Mind that lorry!' Nancy's voice, naturally loud, was now set at a depth that could melt concrete.

'Mother, the lorry is on the other side of the road. Please, let me drive. I have been doing it for over forty years . . .'

Nancy Markham interrupted him as if he had not spoken a word. 'You're like your father, God rest him. Always in a hurry, never taking his time. You'll have a heart attack and die, you mark my words. Be careful of the motorbike!'

Her voice rose on the last few words. Joseph took a deep breath to stem the beating of his heart. If he had a heart attack it would be because of the woman sitting in the back seat!

She had driven his father to his and she would drive Joseph into having one. He knew that as surely as he knew that she would outlive the lot of them. Look at her! Eighty-one and still going strong. He shook his head as he drove. Please God George would take the brunt of her today, give him and Lily a bit of peace for a few hours. His own two children would not come near his house unless they absolutely had to, thanks to their grandmother's presence.

107

Nancy's voice broke into his thoughts again.

'Did you see that maniac? My God!' She swept her arms out in a gesture of hopelessness and knocked Lily's Lady Diana hat over her eyes. 'He must have been driving at two hundred miles an hour.'

Lily straightened her hat and turned to face her mother-in-law.

'Cars can't go that fast, Nancy. We're only doing forty-five, so all the others look fast to us.'

Joseph was aware that his wife was talking between gritted teeth.

'Joseph! Slow the car down. Forty-five miles an hour. Oy! If God had wanted us to travel that fast he'd have given us legs like a cheetah!'

Joseph carried on driving. He knew that his mother played up her Jewish ancestry to annoy Lily. Sometimes her performance as the Jewish mama was so good he felt like videoing her in action and sending it to BT to use on their adverts. It was a far cry from when he was a child and her Jewishness could never be mentioned, even in passing. Their given name had been Markowitz, but his father had anglicised it shortly after his marriage. In the East End of London then, Jews were classed lower than the Irish. At least the Irish were Catholics. Now, though, his mother revelled in her Jewish ancestry, not because of any love for her religion but because she knew it annoyed Lily who was a Christian Scientist.

He saw the signs for Grantley and heaved a sigh of relief. Soon they would be at George's.

Kate got in just in time for Christmas dinner. She took off her coat in the hall and listened to the sound of laughter coming from the kitchen. Dan must be on top form today. He was a born raconteur. Kate could see him in her mind's eye sitting up at the breakfast bar, with Lizzy hanging on every word, looking for all the world as if he was in an expensive restaurant.

She shook herself. For all his faults Dan loved his

daughter, she was sure of that much. But sometimes, seeing him brought it all back. All the pain and heartache he had caused her. Especially today, when she felt low, when she had so much going on with the murder inquiry and had to be lighthearted and gay because it was Christmas.

She walked into the warmth of the lounge and through the door to the kitchen. Dan's back was to her but Lizzy and her mother were facing her. Both were laughing out loud. Seeing her daughter, in her best dress, her dark hair brushed to a shine, eyes alight with happiness, brought a lump to Kate's throat. If she ever had to go through what Patrick Kelly had, she would die, she thought.

'Come away in, Katie, I've got your dinner nice and warm here.' Evelyn was off her chair and going to the oven.

'I'll do it, Mum, you sit back down.'

Evelyn waved a hand at her. 'You sit yourself down, young lady, and have a glass of the excellent wine Dan brought. I've nearly finished me own dinner anyway.'

Kate sat beside Dan and he smiled at her.

'Merry Christmas, Kate.'

His voice was low and while Evelyn was getting the dinner from the oven he brushed her lips with his. Lizzy giggled. Kate was stunned. She expected a lot from Dan, none of it good, but that was the last thing she had anticipated. And the worse part of all was she had felt a shiver inside her as he had done it. She forced a smile on her face and grinned at her daughter.

'Merry Christmas, love.'

'Merry Christmas, Mum. How was it today?' Her face was concerned.

'Oh, not too bad, we're getting there.' She deliberately kept her voice light. Dan had unnerved her and she had a sneaking suspicion he had guessed the fact. He was looking at her now, a smile playing around his lips.

Evelyn put a large dinner in front of her and Kate felt her appetite return.

'Oh, Mum, that looks great. I'm starving.'

'Dad was just telling us about when he was in Egypt.'

Kate took a mouthful of turkey and nodded.

Evelyn sat back at the table and winked at her daughter. Kate noticed the flushed cheeks and guessed she had been on the whiskey, or 'Holy Water' as her mother referred to it. Dan poured Kate a glass of wine and she sipped it.

'Tell Mum about the Valley of the Kings, Dad.'

'Your mother's not interested in all that.'

'Oh, but I am, Dan. You carry on with your story.'

Dan was where he wanted to be. He had an attentive audience and he loved it. He would try and impress Kate with his worldliness. She might deal with rapists and murderers and the lowest of the low, but he was an adventurer, a traveller, and that beat policing hands down!

'Well, we got to Luxor. It was something else, you know, the Nile. I mean, it was just a thrill to be there. To be walking along the banks. Well, you get a boat and cross over to the Valley of the Kings . . .'

'And Queens.' Kate spoke through a mouthful of food.

'Well, yes, and the Valley of the Queens. We went into Tutankhamen's burial chamber. You would have loved it, Lizzy. The paintings on the ceilings . . .'

Kate let Dan go on. She felt like asking him why he hadn't taken her with him; Lizzy would have loved it and Anthea's boys had gone, she knew that for a fact. While Dan was describing the delights of Egypt, Kate drank her wine and carried on eating. She had heard it all before. Oh, not Egypt, but other places – all described in detail in the same sing-song voice. Kate closed her eyes and berated herself.

Dan's kiss had affected her more than she liked to admit. She had been without a man for far too long, that was her trouble. There were plenty of men at work who had asked her out over the years, but they had nearly all been married. The few who had been divorced only wanted to talk about cases, with a bit of sex thrown in, and that had never appealed to Kate. One thing she had learnt in the police force: male police officers could be the biggest whores going but a policewoman, especially one in a senior position, had to be above reproach.

110

'What's the matter, Mum?' Lizzy's voice was concerned.

'Oh, just thinking, poppet. That's all.'

Dan put his arm around her shoulders and hugged her to him. 'You leave that old job behind you now, Kate. You've got your family around you.'

She pushed his arm from her shoulders and looked into his face.

'I've always had my family, Dan, thank you very much.'

The atmosphere at the table turned chilly. Kate carried on eating her dinner.

'She's always like this, Dad, with the big cases.' Lizzy's voice was placating and Kate felt mean for what she had done.

'I think she does a grand job. How's the young girl who was attacked?' asked Evelyn.

'In a very bad way, Mum. She took an awful beating.'

'I've seen Mandy Kelly about. She's really pretty, with long blonde hair. Her dad's a right one, always in trouble with the police.'

'No he is not!' Kate's voice came out louder than she intended and she bit her lip.

'He's been under suspicion but he's never actually been charged with anything. He's never even had a parking ticket, young lady, so just you get your facts right!' Her voice was jocular now and Lizzy relaxed.

'Well, Joanie's mum said he owns massage parlours and places like that.'

'And massage parlours and places like that are perfectly legal, love.'

'More's the bloody pity.' Evelyn's voice was disgusted.

'Well, that's the law for you. He's done nothing wrong!'

'I think men who live off women like that should be shot.' Dan's voice was low and hard.

Kate felt an urge to laugh.

'There's other ways for men to live off women than by putting them on the game, you should know that, Dan.' Kate sipped her wine so she wouldn't have to look at his face.

Dan pushed his chair away from the table and went into

111

the lounge. Kate saw Lizzy bite her lip, her face a mass of
confusion. But Dan was back almost immediately with a
packet of cigarettes. 'Let's open our presents shall we?'

'Oh yes, let's. We've been waiting for you, mum.'

Kate placed her knife and fork on her plate and followed
everyone into the lounge.

Dan gave Lizzy a large package which she opened slowly,
taking off the paper carefully. Everything in their house was
saved. Kate knew it was annoying Dan, who would have
ripped the paper off regardless, and allowed herself a tiny
smile from her seat by the fire. She heard Lizzy's intake of
breath as she took out a sheepskin flying jacket. It was the
latest fashion, and for some unknown reason this annoyed
Kate even more. Trust Dan to know exactly what a sixteen-
year-old girl would want for Christmas! Lizzy threw herself
into her father's arms and hugged him.

'Oh, Dad, it's great, just what I wanted! Wait till Joanie
sees this!'

Evelyn passed over Kate's present and once more the slow
ritual of opening began. Kate sat back in the chair watching
her daughter with glee. As Lizzy took out the tiny box Kate
caught her daughter's eye.

'Is it what I think, Mum?'

'Open it and see.'

Lizzy reverently opened the box and squealed with
delight. She threw her arms around her mother.

'Oh, thank you! Thank you! I thought they'd be too
expensive!' She held up the sovereign earrings for all to see.

'Come on, love, now open mine.'

Evelyn pushed a package into her hands and Lizzy opened
it excitedly.

'Oh, Gran!'

Evelyn laughed as Lizzy brought out a pair of Reebok
bumpers.

'I knew you wanted them so I thought I'd get them.'

'Oh, Mum!' Kate knew they cost over eighty pounds and
shook her head at her mother. 'You shouldn't have spent that
much!'

'You only live once and money's for the spending, I'm thinking.'

'Hear, hear.' Dan's voice was wistful. 'Now then, you two, here's your presents.' He gave Kate and Evelyn small packages.

'Oh, you shouldn't have, Dan, I never got you anything.'

Kate opened her present to find a bottle of Joy, her favourite perfume. Evelyn had a bottle of Chanel Number 5.

'Now isn't that grand? I've never had a bottle of real French perfume before. Thanks, Dan.'

'You're welcome. All women should be cosseted at some time, Eve, that's my motto.'

Kate felt an urge to ask him how many he had cosseted over the years, but bit it back and instead smiled at him.

'Thanks, Dan, it's lovely.'

'Still your favourite, I hope?'

'Yes, it's still my favourite.'

Kate watched as Lizzy shoved a present into her father's hands. Then she went to the kitchen and poured herself out a glass of wine.

She stared at the perfume in her hands and sighed.

Oh Dan, she thought, why did you have to do this?

It brought back too many memories and she wasn't fit to cope with them today. She had too much on her mind. She didn't need to be reminded of how lonely she was.

Not today.

George watched his mother demolish a dinner large enough for two men. He smiled to himself. She could certainly put her food away. Gone were the days when her figure was the most important thing in her life.

'Pass me the salt, someone.'

Nancy held out her hand and Joseph thrust the salt cellar into it. She belched loudly, holding her hand to her chest as if forcing the wind out. Lily and Elaine both pursed their lips in disgust.

'Better out than in, eh, Georgie boy?'

'Yes, Mother.' He smiled at her.

Nancy poked her finger at him, a nasty light in her eyes. 'Don't eat too much stuffing now, you know it gives you constipation.'

George blanched.

'Really, Nancy! We don't want to discuss George's digestion at the dinner table!' Elaine's voice was high. She could never understand her mother-in-law's preoccupation with George's bowels.

Nancy swivelled her huge bulk in her seat to see Elaine better.

'George is a martyr to constipation. When he was a child it plagued him. Why, the hospital showed me how to give him enemas. Before that I had to give him what was called in those days a "manual". I had to push my fingers . . .'

'Oh, for God's sake! We're eating!' Lilian pushed her plate away from her roughly. 'Can we just for once . . . for one year at least . . . give George's bloody bowels a rest!'

Nancy sniffed loudly and turned back to her food. 'You know your trouble, Lilian?' She shovelled a large forkful of vegetables into her mouth. 'You're too namby-pamby for your own good. Eighty-one years I've lived because I've always watched my bowels. They are the most important part of the body. They get rid of all the bad . . .'

'Please, Mother.' Joseph's voice was strained. 'As Lily says, let's leave talk of bowels till later on, shall we? Now then, George, how's work going?' Joseph beamed across the table at his brother.

'Fine.' Oh, yes, Joseph, my work's going so well they're going to kick me out soon. I can't afford a nice Daimler Sovereign like you. But you know that, don't you? That's why you ask me the same question every time I see you. Why Lily goes on and on about your large detached house. Well, it was your large detached house that lumbered you with Mother, wasn't it?

'George? Lily's talking to you.' Elaine's voice broke into his thoughts.

'He was always the same, Elaine, even as a child. Always in a world of his own. Always a dreamer, was my Georgie.

114

That's why he never got on like the others. Look at Edith, out in America. Her Joss is a surgeon. Living the life of Riley them two. Off to the Bahamas every few months. It does a mother's heart good to know that at least some of her children did well.'

Her voice was reproaching George with every word she spoke.

'Edith always enjoyed travelling, Mother. Do you remember when she ran off to Brighton with the travelling salesman?'

Elaine felt the tension she had created and was actually enjoying it. Edith's foray down to Brighton was never mentioned. Neither was the child she gave up for adoption a year afterwards.

Nancy pushed her plate away from her, her heavily powdered face looking more wrinkled than ever with the deepness of her frown.

'Only you, Elaine, would bring up something to break my heart. Joseph, George, help me into the lounge. I want to be alone.'

'I'm sure Elaine didn't mean anything by it, Mother.'

'Shut up, George, and help an old woman to a comfortable seat.'

George and Joseph both rushed to their mother's side, helping her heave her bulk from the chair. She leant on their arms as she slowly trekked from the kitchen to the lounge. Elaine and Lilian watched the three leave the kitchen. As soon as the door shut behind them Lilian whispered: 'The woman is like a waking nightmare.'

'I heard that, Lily! I may be old but I'm not deaf!'

Nancy's voice seemed to drill through the wooden kitchen door.

Elaine put her hand over her mouth to stifle a high laugh.

'She has ears like an elephant, Elaine, you don't know what it's like.'

'I can imagine, thank you very much, and before you ask the answer's no. Both George and I work and she can't be left on her own all day.'

Lily sighed.

It was worth a try, even if you already knew the answer.

In the lounge George and Joseph had set their mother on the settee, packing cushions all around her.

'Joseph, you go back to your dinner. I want to speak to George in private.'

Joseph left the room as quickly as possible. He was nearly sixty years old. He had his own prosperous business. Yet his mother could reduce him to an eight year old in a few sentences. When Joseph left, Nancy patted a tiny expanse of seat beside her.

'Sit with your mama, Georgie boy.'

He sat beside her warily.

Nancy looked into her son's face for a few moments.

'The years haven't been kind to you, my boy, have they? No. You know this yourself.'

George could smell her perfume. It was lily of the valley. The scent brought back his childhood. The terraced house in Bow, the war, his father's death, his mother's endless stream of men friends. His 'uncles' as he had had to call them. George could not remember his father and knew that there was something not right about his death.

After the war his mother had packed up what was left of their home and moved them all to East Ham where she had made a niche for herself.

Nancy Markham had been a formidable person all her life. She ruled her children. When she said do something, you did it or took the consequences. Like Edith's baby. She had wanted to keep the child. It had broken her heart when she had had to give him up. But, as always, Mother knew best.

Nancy was still talking, her voice low and caressing as she enumerated every failure in his life.

George knew that his mother did not like him, though she swore that she loved him. As he watched her ruby red lips opening and shutting he had a vision of himself getting up from the settee, going out to the hall and getting his Swiss army knife from beneath the floor boards in the hall cupboard. He could see the fear in his mother's face as she realised that he was going to plunge it into her fat body. Over and over again. Slashing and ripping at her fat breasts and overhanging stomach . . .

'George boy, you're sweating! Are you feeling all right?'

He smiled at her. His secret smile. 'Yes, Mother, I'm fine. Absolutely fine. Never felt better, in fact.'

For the first time ever, Nancy Markham felt as if her son had the upper hand. And like Elaine before her, she didn't like it one bit.

Patrick Kelly sat at his daughter's bedside in Grantley Hospital. The bruising on her face was beginning to fade, but still she lay in a deep coma. The doctors had opened a little window in her skull because her brain had swollen so much they had to relieve the pressure on it.

He held on to her hand. Christmas had no meaning for him now. The big dinner he had planned, and the present giving, were all far from his mind.

Earlier in the day he had attended mass in the hospital chapel. It was the first time in over twenty years. He'd prayed to God to save his daughter. Make her be as she was before she was attacked. Even as he prayed he knew he was a hypocrite.

While he sat in the chapel, paid muscle was looking for the perpetrator of the horrific deed. He gritted his teeth.

If it took him the rest of his life and every penny of his considerable fortune, he would find the bastard. And when he did, when he confronted him, he would exact his payment, which was death. A long slow death.

Putting Mandy's hand to his mouth, he kissed it softly.

Chapter Seven

Christmas 1948

George lay in bed staring up at the ceiling. He pulled the blankets over his shoulders and rubbed his frozen ears with his hands, breathing into his palms every so often to warm them. His whole body was numb with cold. The sash windows had iced up inside, reflecting weird murals on the walls with the breaking dawn. He poked his head out of the blankets once more as he heard a noise from his mother's room. He let his breath out slowly, carefully, watching it spiral like cigarette smoke in the cold dimness. He strained his ears to listen. Nothing. Gradually he relaxed. Then he heard the dull thud of footsteps on the linoleum. He squeezed his eyes shut as hard as he could. Maybe it was Mother going to the toilet? Or Edith? But the footsteps stopped outside his door.

He hunched himself lower down in the bed. The inadequate bedding barely covered him – one sheet, one blanket, and an old overcoat.

He closed his eyes and tried to feign unconsciousness, his mouth quivering with apprehension. He listened as the door creaked open slowly and someone came into the room. George's nose quivered as he smelt the heavy mustiness of the man. It was a mixture of sweat and beer. He was terrified. The man moved towards the bed purposefully, treading only on the boards he knew would not creak.

'Georgie? You awake?'

The child lay there unmoving. His heart was beating so loud and fast surely the man could hear it?

He closed his eyes even tighter, then felt the warm breath on his neck. George's head was tucked beneath the blanket and overcoat, and he instinctively brought his knees up to his chest until he was in a foetal position.

A large warm hand entered the bed and George felt the roughness of the skin as it began slowly to caress his buttocks. Then the bed was sinking with the weight of the man, and against his will the child was rolling into his heavy stomach.

At least he was warm.

Then the blankets were pulled over both their heads and George was being dragged down, down, into the fantasy world that was his only escape from this life.

Later the man crept from the bed, and George could finally sleep the sleep of the exhausted. His eyelashes still glistening with the silent tears, he lay there in the warm space the man vacated.

He slept then.

Bert Higgins slipped back into bed with Nancy Markham and was just settling himself when she spoke.

'How was Georgie tonight, Bert?'

He froze beside her.

'Oh, I know all about your little visits to him in the middle of the night.'

Nancy was enjoying the fear she was creating. She finally had something over him and she liked that. She liked that very much.

She laughed derisively.

'I can just imagine what your friends would say if they knew you liked little boys, Bert.'

He turned over in bed and grabbed her throat with an iron hand.

'What you going to do about it, Nance?'

She laughed again, no trace of fear in her voice.

'Who, me? I'm not going to do anything, Bert. You know me – each to his own. The only thing I want from you is more money.'

Bert let go of her and lit the candle by the bed. He lay on his back, staring at the ceiling.

'You mean . . . you're not going to stop me?'

His voice was incredulous.

'Why should I? Providing we can come to a financial arrangement, I'm not bothered about it.'

Bert smiled in the candlelight.

'You'd do anything for money, wouldn't you?'

Nancy lit a cigarette and blew the smoke out. Then she turned to him full on.

'That's about the strength of it, yes.'

'Fair enough then, Nance. How much?'

'An extra fiver a week should do it.'

Bert considered this for a few minutes.

'I can go to three quid.'

'It's five or the deal's off.'

'All right then. But what about us?'

Nancy stubbed out her cigarette, then blew out the candle.

'Us? We carry on as usual. Good night.'

'Good night, Nancy.'

She was asleep in minutes. Bert, though, lay awake for a while pondering the situation. Nancy Markham had sold her son to him for a measly five pounds a week.

George came home to find Bert slumped on the settee, snoring loudly. When Bert turned over on the settee to make himself more comfortable, George smiled to himself. A little smile that barely showed his teeth.

He could smell the alcohol fumes with every breath Bert took and guessed, rightly, that he had passed out at some point in the evening. That's why his mother had left him there.

George walked closer and stared down at the man. He had spilt a glass of whisky over himself. The smell was strong and the glass still beside him. It was trapped between his body and the back of the settee.

George picked up the bottle of Black and White whisky

and gently poured the last of it along the back of the settee. He was feeling acutely excited.

He placed the bottle back on the table and then picked up a box of matches. With shaking hands, he lit one. He stood watching the burning match in fascination until it got down to his finger tips. Then the burning sensation made him throw it from him. He watched, sucking his finger, as it ignited the whisky. In the semi-darkness he saw a tiny blue flame slowly lick its way along the back of the settee, gathering momentum as it went. A sticky burning smell emanated from it. George watched as Bert, still snoring heavily, began to breathe in the black smoke.

It wasn't until Bert's clothes caught fire that George felt a shiver of apprehension. He watched as the trouser material began to curl up and melt, his excitement growing stronger as Bert did nothing to help himself.

Then all at once the settee was a fireball. It just seemed to burst into big red and yellow flames that snaked over the arms and on to the floor.

George stepped back towards the door, the heat from the flames touching his aching face.

Then he heard an almighty roar. The flames were standing up and coming towards him.

He backed out quickly into the hallway, his woollen socks making him slip and slide in his haste. The terrible agonising roar came from the flames again. The man was stumbling round the room in panic. George saw Bert grab the brocade curtains and watched in fascination as the flames began to creep up them as well. Suddenly, everywhere was pandemonium. Edith was behind him and her screams brought George back to himself. He watched as she pulled the tablecloth off the kitchen table and ran back into the front room and tried to put out the flames on Bert with it. He was lying on the floor and Edith was patting at the flames.

'Go and get some help, George, for goodness' sake. Hurry UP!'

He snapped into action and collided with Joseph who came careering down the stairs at the noise.

'Bloody hell!' Joseph's voice was incredulous.

Then he was out of the front door and running up the garden path in his pyjamas. George turned back to the scene in the front room.

Edith's nightdress was burning, the hem was beginning to glow blue, and he ran into the room and pulled on his sister's arm.

'Your nightie! Edie, your nightie!' She allowed him to stamp it out with his woollen socks.

'What the hell's going on here?'

Nancy's voice was loud. She stood in the doorway blinking rapidly.

The room was blazing now and Edith pushed George towards the door.

'Mum . . . help me pull him outside. For God's sake, the whole place is gonna go up.'

Nancy threw George out of the front door. He stood in the rain, his feet beginning to freeze, while Nancy and Edith dragged Bert's bulk from the house. Thick black smoke was coming from the front door and the smell of burning was everywhere. Little flakes of grey ash were trying to rise up with the smoke but the rain was forcing them down on to the pavement and eventually into the sewers.

Lights were now on all over the little cul-de-sac and people were coming from their houses in fear and excitement. George felt Mrs Marshall put a heavy coat around his shoulders and pull him from the garden. Her slender arms were gentle as she propelled him towards her own house. He watched the proceedings from her lovely warm front room. He stared out of the lead light window and across the road with a feeling of unreality.

The clamour of the fire engines made him start. The firemen were clearing everyone away from the burning house. Bert was taken from the garden on a stretcher, a blanket covering his face.

George was elated. Bert was dead. He was dead. Bert Higgins was dead. He turned to Mrs Marshall and she mistook the light in the boy's eyes for unshed tears. She pulled him into her sweet-smelling embrace and kissed the top of his head gently.

'Poor little mite, aren't you?'

He had never felt so powerful. He had rid the world of Bert Higgins.

Mrs Marshall put him from her and looked into his face. 'Shall I make you some nice sweet tea?' She placed him gently on her settee and went out to her kitchen.

Joseph walked into the room and sat beside George. His face was ashen.

'Mum's gone to the hospital with Bert. Edith's gone with her. We're to stay here until they come back.'

George slipped his hand into his brother's, and Joseph squeezed it tightly.

'Mrs Marshall's making some tea, Joseph, do you want some?'

The next day George and Joseph raked through the ruined house. They managed to salvage quite a bit of stuff and piled it carefully in the front garden. Edith and Nancy came home from the hospital in the afternoon.

Nancy went straight into Mrs Marshall's, Edith came for the boys.

'Bert's dead. Mum was sedated and I had to stay there with her. Are you two all right?'

'Where are we going to go?'

Edith shrugged.

'I don't know. But don't worry, things will turn out all right, they always do somehow.' Her voice was tired and George felt a great sadness for her.

'Mrs Marshall made us eggs and bacon this morning. She might make you some if you ask her nicely.'

Edith smiled at him wanly.

'I'm not very hungry.'

George shrugged and resumed his searching.

'Do they know how the fire started, Edie?'

'Well, as far as I can gather, they think Bert fell asleep with a lighted cigarette. I know he was a pig, but to die like that . . . His face was twisted up in torment, it was terrible.

124

Skin was burnt off the bone in some places. He died in agony, Joey, mortal agony.'

Joseph put his arm around his sister.

George had heard everything and smiled to himself. Then he began to giggle out loud.

He ran out into the road, and holding out his arms began to spin round and round like a whirling dervish, until he fell, dizzy and exhilarated, on to the pavement.

He lay there in the wet, his mind reeling. He had a secret.

Edith knelt beside him and he smiled up at her. His secret smile that just showed his teeth.

Chapter Eight

Kate went for a bath at seven thirty. She put plenty of bubble bath in the water and lay back, letting the hot water seep into her bones. Her long hair was pinned on top of her head and her face scrubbed free of make up. She closed her eyes tightly. She was really feeling this case.

Earlier Lizzy had tried on all her finery and Kate had watched her twirling around the tiny lounge and suddenly felt as if a hand had gripped her heart. Supposing this man, this murderer, took her daughter and did to her what he had done to Mandy Kelly and Geraldine O'Leary? She pushed the thoughts from her mind. Nothing was going to happen to Lizzy. Kate would make sure of that. With luck Mandy Kelly would recover. She was a fighter, that much was evident.

Kate pushed her shoulders under the water. Her skin had erupted in goose pimples and it wasn't because of the cold. She closed her eyes again. She had fought hammer and tongs to get Christmas Day off, and all Lizzy had time for was her father.

Dan did look well, though. After dinner one of Lizzy's friends had come round. Joanie of the acne and the braying laugh. Kate chastised herself. What on earth was the matter with her? Poor Joanie was a nice girl. But the worshipful look she had given Dan had annoyed her. It wasn't fair the way Dan affected women . . .

She heard the bathroom door open and smiled. Lizzy with a nice glass of wine, or better still a cup of coffee. She opened one eye and sat up in the bath with shock, water going everywhere.

'What do you want?' Her voice was a loud whisper.

She crossed her arms across her breasts.

'I brought you a glass of wine and a cigarette, that's all, Kate. Don't worry, I'm not going to rape you.' Dan's voice was normal and she felt a fool. He placed a glass of wine in her hand and, wiping her free hand on a towel, as if she was a child, he gave her the lit cigarette.

'You looked done in so I thought I'd try and help you relax.'

Kate settled back in the water, glad now of the concealing bubbles. Dan sat on the toilet seat and laughed.

'I don't know why you're going all modest. I do know what you look like undressed, remember.'

'What are the others doing?' She was having difficulty keeping her voice light.

'They're watching James Bond, my dear. I taped it for them last night. How's the case going?'

His voice was conversational and friendly. Kate was taken back, over the years, to when they had bathed together. When it had been good between them, before Lizzy had been born.

'Not very well, actually. We haven't even got a suspect.'

'I admire you, you know, Kate. The way you've built yourself a career.'

'It's called working, Dan, you should try it some time.'

He smiled, showing his perfect teeth.

'Put the claws away, Kate. I know what you think of me but I've changed, you know. I realised a long time ago that I needed to grow up, and believe me when I say I'm working on it.'

Kate took a gulp of the wine and a long draw on her cigarette. This close, Dan made her feel uncomfortable. He slipped to the floor and knelt by the side of the bath.

'What are you doing?' Kate's voice was suspicious. Her hands were full and she didn't trust Danny Burrows one bit.

'I'm not doing anything. I was just going to wash your back, that's all.'

'I don't want my back washed, thank you very much. Now if you don't mind, Dan, I want to get out.'

She sat up again in the water, looking around for somewhere to dump the cigarette and wine. Dan took them from her.

'Look, Kate, all I'm trying to do is make myself useful, that's all. While I'm here . . .'

She didn't let him finish. 'While you're here, Dan, I'd appreciate it if you left me alone. We don't lock doors in this house and I'd hate to have to start now.'

'Can't you even try and be friendly?'

His blue eyes were puzzled and for a few seconds Kate felt sorry for him. Dan honestly didn't know what was going on. To him, if you wanted something you took it. He never realised how much he had hurt her in the past. How many times had she taken him back over the years, only to come home from work to find he had gone again? No note, nothing. Just her mother's pitying face. Too many times having to tell Lizzy that Daddy had gone again. That he worked away, a long, long way away, that's why he didn't write very often or call.

As he traced his fingers along her arm, she felt a response inside her. She still wanted Dan sexually, she admitted that, but she'd deny herself that satisfaction before she let him scramble her brains all over again.

'You're the only woman I ever really loved, you know, Kate. Whatever you might think of me, that at least is the truth.'

She stood up and pulled a towel from the rail, wrapping it around herself. The funny thing was, she knew it was true. Dan chased excitement. A new woman to him was as necessary as water to everyone else. If she had been able to accept that, then they would never have parted. But Kate wanted someone one hundred percent. And that sort of commitment was beyond Danny Burrows.

'Leave me alone, Dan. I mean it. You had your chance and you blew it. I have no intentions of going through all that rigmarole again. I stopped wanting you a long time ago. Now, if you don't mind, I want to get myself sorted out.'

He gave her one of his winning smiles.

'Well, you can't blame me for trying, Katie, you're still a very attractive woman.'

You should know about attractive women, Dan. Christ himself knows you've had enough of them.

After he'd left she felt flat and cheated, because she hadn't been with a man since Dan had left her for the last time, five years earlier.

Though he didn't know it, he was the only man she had ever slept with in her whole life.

She picked up the wine from the windowsill where he had placed it, and drained the glass. Her hands were shaking, and it wasn't with fright.

Sometimes, when they'd had a bad domestic, there would be a woman battered black and blue. The man would have a restraining order placed on him, the woman would be taken to hospital. Then Kate would hear that the woman had gone back to her husband, wanted the charges dropped, and the others would say what a fool the wife was. But Kate had sympathised. Some were like the little girl with the curl. When they were good they were very, very good, but when they were bad they were bastards. There were other ways of battering women too, ways that did not involve physical violence, and Kate sometimes thought that the mental battering was worse.

Unless, of course, you were dealing with the Grantley rapist. With a husband or boyfriend at least you had an inkling of what you were up against.

With him, you were on your own.

Kate's thoughts strayed to Patrick Kelly, keeping a lonely vigil by his daughter's hospital bed. She dried between her legs and felt the stirrings there. Kelly brought out feelings she had forced down for years. She closed her eyes to stop the pictures that were invading her brain. She was tired and lonely and Patrick Kelly had affected her for all the right

130

reasons – he was an attractive man. Dan, on the other hand, affected her for all the wrong reasons. Namely, because he was here now, and she knew exactly how their lovemaking would be.

She hoped that Kelly's daughter pulled through, she really did. He had such faith in himself, he had such a strong belief that Mandy would open her eyes and look at him as though she had just had a nap. Kate wanted that for him too.

Of course, Patrick Kelly kept invading her thoughts because of his daughter's terrible predicament. She forced that thought into her head and held on to it. It was just pity.

But she knew she was lying to herself.

She fancied Patrick Kelly with all her heart and soul. He was the first man she had fancied for over five years.

She heard Dan's voice coming up from the lounge and Lizzy's laughter. After all, he had given her Lizzy. For that reason alone she would forgive him an awful lot. But their days of bedding down together were over.

Patrick Kelly looked at his watch. It was just after seven. He realised that he had not eaten for over twenty-four hours. Putting his daughter's hand gently back on the bed, he walked from the intensive care unit. In the small waiting room he lit a cigarette and took a hip flask from the pocket of his jacket. The brandy burnt his empty belly. He was unshaven and unkempt.

The young PC who had been staying at the hospital, in case Mandy awoke and said anything, came into the room.

Patrick watched him as he sat down. He was only a kid. Twenty at the most.

'The nurses are turning her and that.'

His voice was apologetic. Patrick felt an enormous surge of sympathy for the boy. Christmas night and he was stuck here waiting for a half-dead girl to say a couple of words when he would much rather be at a party or something.

He offered the boy his hip flask.

'Go on, son, have a shot.'

The PC took the flask and had a few sips, coughing as the liquid hit the back of his throat.

'Merry Christmas, son.' Patrick's voice was sad and flat.

'She'll pull through, sir. It's amazing what they can do now.'

The boy was talking for effect. They both knew that.

Suddenly they heard the frenzied high-pitched bleeping of the monitors attached to Mandy. They stamped on their cigarettes and ran from the room.

Mandy's bed was surrounded by nurses and doctors. The sister pulled Patrick away from the scene as they tried to save his daughter's life.

Finally, everything was quiet and all that could be heard was the low buzzing sound of the heart monitor. Then that was unplugged and all there was was a deathly silence.

'I want to use the toilet again. George, Joseph, help me to the toilet.'

They helped their mother heave her huge bulk from the settee. This was the sixth time they had toileted her since she had been in the house.

As they walked her from the room Elaine glanced at the clock. Eight thirty. They would be leaving soon, thank God.

'So how's Betty these days, Lily?'

'Fine. She's a buyer for a big fashion store as you know. She's doing very well. Of course, we don't see as much of her as we'd like . . .' She left the sentence unfinished but even without the words being said, Elaine knew why. Nancy was hated by her grandchildren.

Nancy sat on the toilet. Her two sons stood outside the door, puffing and panting. Getting Nancy Markham up the stairs was a major event. Both the men were aware that she could walk perfectly well, yet like everything in their lives that had to do with their mother, they studiously avoided mentioning it.

George could see the blue tinge around Joseph's mouth. His mother would put him into an early grave.

'I'm ready!' Nancy's voice broke through the air like a thunderbolt. The two men opened the bathroom door. The smell of faeces was overpowering.

'You can wipe, George. Joseph did it last time, and made a bloody awful job of it.' She held a warning finger up. 'Do it properly or there will be hell to pay!'

Nancy stood, forcing all her considerable weight on to her sons' arms, before deliberately letting herself drop to her knees. Joseph and George were dragged to the ground with her.

'Fuck this!' Joseph's voice reverberated around the tiny bathroom. George looked at his brother, amazed.

Joseph had sworn in front of their mother!

Nancy had been on all fours on the floor. Before she had time to think what she was doing she was standing up of her own accord and staring down at her eldest son, hands on ample hips.

'What did you just say?'

George pulled himself from the floor and sat on the edge of the bath, giggling nervously. He was enjoying himself. Joseph lay on the floor. His arm was killing him where his mother's weight had nearly wrenched it out of its socket.

'What's going on up there? What's all the crashing about?'

Elaine's voice, which could outshout Nancy Markham's on her better days, carried up the stairs and into the bathroom. George heard the thud of her slippers coming upstairs.

'I said, what did you say Joseph Markowitz? Answer me!'

Elaine stared into the bathroom in bewilderment. She saw her mother-in-law prod Joseph's thigh with her foot.

'I'm sorry, Mother. It just slipped out.'

Nancy, realising that she was standing up of her own accord, held her chest, her eyes rolling up into her head.

'Oh, George, help me. I'm going to faint . . .'

As she crashed to the floor once more, Joseph did a roll that would have made a paratrooper proud; Elaine watched the whole charade with wide eyes.

'Listen here, George Markham, this is the last time! Do

you hear me?' Elaine's voice had risen fifteen decibels louder than usual.

'Next year, we are going away for Christmas. Now pick your bloody mother up and get her out of my house. I've had enough!'

Nancy's and Joseph's mouths both opened simultaneously, but snapped shut as they looked at George. He was still sitting on the edge of the bath and laughing his head off, tears running down his face, which he wiped now and then with the back of his hand.

Lily, who had come up to see what all the noise was about, stared around her in amazement. Her mother had warned her about marrying into the Markham family and she had been right.

They were funny. Not funny ha-ha, but funny peculiar.

When Kate received the call saying that Mandy Kelly had died, she drove straight to the hospital. Now she had two murders to contend with. When she saw Patrick Kelly, she was shocked. That he had taken the death badly was hardly surprising, but he looked positively old. Old and haggard.

She went to him. He was still holding his daughter's body in his arms and the doctors and nurses could not persuade him to leave the bedside. The body had to be put on ice, and soon. Kate motioned for everyone to move away and went to him.

'I'm really very sorry, Mr Kelly. I can assure you that we shall do all that we can to find the man responsible.'

Her gentle voice broke in on him. He looked at her with red-rimmed eyes.

'She was only twenty-two, just a baby. Just a kid, that's all. I'd bought her a shop, you know.' His voice caught and he sniffed loudly. 'A lovely little shop. She would have done well and all, she wasn't a silly girl. She had a good brain, did my Mandy.' He bit his lip hard. 'What will I do without her?' The plaintive note in his voice went straight to Kate's heart.

'She was all I had.'

Kate put her arm around his shoulders and he cried into her jacket. She stroked his hair. Patrick Kelly was a Repoman. The best in the business, it was said. He would repossess anything, from a car, to a crane, to a large yacht. He had been nicknamed 'The Snatchman' by friends and enemies alike. That his business was not strictly legal Kate was aware, he owned sex shops, massage parlours and many other businesses. Yet, as he was now, broken hearted, Kate felt an enormous affection for him. Whatever he may be, he had been a loving father and husband and at this moment in time, Kate envied his wife the love he had borne her.

'Come on, Mr Kelly, let's get you home, shall we? There's nothing you can do here now.'

She pulled him away from his daughter's body. As he let go of Mandy he slipped his arm around Kate's waist and she held him tightly while he cried, his shoulders heaving beneath his expensive crumpled suit.

When he was spent she walked him from the room, motioning with her head to DS Willis, who had met her at the hospital, to finish off there. She would take Patrick Kelly home.

Willis watched her leave and felt a spark of respect for his boss. Patrick Kelly was notorious, a villain and a thug, yet DI Kate Burrows had him eating out of her hand. One of the advantages of being a female, he supposed.

Outside the hospital, Kelly's driver was waiting for him in his Rolls-Royce Corniche. Kate helped Patrick into the back, relieved that she did not have to drive him home. As she went to shut the door, his voice stayed her.

'Please, come home with me . . . I need to talk to someone.'

His voice was wretched, and Kate hesitated only a moment before climbing into the car beside him. Maybe he would inadvertently give her some clues. People often did, without even realising that what they said had a bearing on the case in hand.

He grabbed her hand and held on to it tightly. Kate looked

135

at his strong profile as they drove to his house. He was staring out of the window at the cold deserted streets, his hard chiselled face set, despite his grief. His dark hair, though untidy, looked manly and strong to Kate. Like Patrick Kelly did. He glanced at her; his violet blue eyes held a depth of gratitude that she knew he would never be able to convey in words.

She squeezed back.

Lizzy sat with her father and grandmother watching the end of the James Bond film. As the credits began to roll she stretched in her chair.

'That was great! I love Sean Connery. Can I have a glass of Babycham, Gran?'

Evelyn looked at her.

'Oh, all right then, but just one mind!'

'Thanks, Gran.' She skipped across the room to the drinks cabinet.

Dan watched her, a smile on his face. She had really grown up since the last time he had seen her. She had the long-legged coltish look peculiar to sixteen-year-old girls. Her breasts were heavy though; she took after his side of the family in that respect. But facially she was all her mother. She was just like Kate had been when they had first met. From the long silky dark hair to the perfect white teeth. She even had Kate's distinctive nose.

She walked back to her seat with her drink and sipped it. 'Mmmm, lovely.'

'It's a shame your mother had to go out tonight.'

Lizzy shrugged. 'It's her job. Mum really has to work hard to keep us all, doesn't she, Gran?'

'That she does, child.

'Oh, I know that, but it doesn't seem fair, her having to shoot off on Christmas night.' Dan kept his voice deliberately light.

'You get used to it after a while, Dad. I can't remember the last birthday when she was home early enough for the party! Still, Gran's always here.'

136

Dan nodded and sipped at his brandy.

Evelyn stood up. 'Who fancies a turkey sandwich?'

Both Dan and Lizzy nodded assent and she went to the kitchen. Dan squeezed his daughter's hand. 'You're a good girl you know, Liz. A lot of girls would hate a mother who was never there when they wanted her.'

She bit her lip and thought hard. 'She's there when I really want her, Dad. Don't you worry about that. When's Anthea back?'

The question took him by surprise.

'Oh . . . Anthea and I are not really together any more.'

Lizzy took a large gulp of her Babycham and put the glass on the little coffee table.

'I'm glad, Dad. I never liked her very much.'

'You didn't really know her.' His voice was strained.

'No, but when I used to ring up, she'd be very off-hand with me. I felt as if I was intruding or something.'

'That was just Anthea's way. She didn't mean anything. How do you get on with your mother's . . . er . . . friends?'

'Boyfriends, you mean? She never has any. I know she gets asked out on dates, but she never goes. My friend's dad wanted to go out with her, and she said no.'

'Your friend's dad!' Dan's voice was scandalised.

'Oh, don't worry, her mum's been dead for ages. Oh, that sounds terrible, but you know what I mean.'

'Yeah, I know what you mean.'

They smiled at one another.

'Oh, Dad, it's great to have you here like this.'

'It's great to be here, love.'

If it rested with him, he'd be here for a long time to come. He was convinced that his Katie still held a torch for him, and he'd do everything he could to get that torch blazing again.

The first part of the plan was getting his mother-in-law on his side. He'd start working on that straight away.

Kate and Patrick sat on the large settee in Patrick's lounge; both were drinking coffee. Patrick had been talking about himself for over an hour and Kate let him.

All the stories about him, true and imagined, had not prepared her for the almost brutal attractiveness that he had in abundance. His dark brown hair, just beginning to grey at the temples, gave him a distinguished air and softened his rugged features. Dark-skinned and full lipped, he had eyes that were a deep penetrating blue, and from the way he moved Kate could see that he had looked after himself well over the years. Only a slight paunch belied his age. He was a very attractive man. Too attractive, in fact, for his own good. And Kate had a sneaking suspicion that under other circumstances he would deliberately make her aware of the fact.

Patrick Kelly loved women. But he had only really loved two with all his heart and soul. His wife, Renée, and his daughter, Mandy. Mandy who was lying now in a mortuary, waiting to be dissected by the pathologist's scalpel.

Kate closed her eyes. Patrick's voice was a low drone in her ears. All this unhappiness and confusion pouring out of him like a dam.

Patrick rose from his seat and picked up a bottle of brandy. He brought it back together with two Waterford crystal glasses. Like everything else in the house, they were of the best quality, but as he poured out two generous measures, Kate was made aware that money meant very little when you had no one to share it with.

'My old mum used to take in washing, you know. Me dad had had it on his toes years before, leaving me and my four sisters. My mother worked like a black to give us a decent life, but she was held back, like we all were then, by lack of education and decent jobs.

'I found my old man a few years ago. He'd only gone as far as North London. He'd shacked up with some old bird who was on the game. She kept him in the style he had rapidly grown accustomed to. He'd been a good-looking bloke in his day. I went to see him and told him I was his son, like. He just smiled and asked me if I had any money. He never even asked after my mum or my sisters. Not even casually.

'But I told him. I told him Mum died of a massive stroke,

that she'd been riddled with rheumatism from years of washing other people's dirty clothes, but he wasn't even interested . . .'

Kate saw him drop his head on to his chest.

'All those years my old mum had been waiting for him to come home, and he never even thought about her.'

'What did you do?' Kate's voice was low.

'I smacked him. Punched him all around his little bedsit. An old man, and I kicked him in . . . me own father. Then, as I left, I gave him fifty quid. Threw it on the bed. I told him that was all he would ever get from me. I can still see him crawling over the bed. His face was bleeding but he grabbed that money like a dog with a bone. I hated him then.

'I came home and I looked at my Mandy and I patted myself on the back. Oh, yes, I thought, my child will never know pain like that. But she ended up knowing a worse pain than I could ever have given her. A much worse pain.'

He sniffed loudly. 'Well, whoever this pervert is, I'm gonna catch him. I've already got blokes sniffing about, and when I do find him . . .' He left the sentence unfinished.

'You're much better off letting us find him, Mr Kelly.'

Patrick laughed at her. A hard bitter sound.

'You must be smoking, as the youngsters say. Do you honestly think I'll let the social workers and the bleeding hearts get their poncey hands on him? Do you? Do you think I'll allow him to go to some nice top security hospital, where he can roam the grounds freely and have a television and video in his room? Where he can con his way out in a couple of years and end up working in a children's home or something?

'No way, darlin'. I intend to see he pays dearly for the death of my girl and for that other woman. She had three little kids, for fuck's sake. Be honest, do you really think he is entitled to a life while my child is rotting underground? No way.'

Kate hung her head because part of her grudgingly agreed with what Kelly was saying. It was all right being high-principled, saying if you resorted to violence you were only bringing yourself down to an animal's level. But what Patrick Kelly said struck a chord with her. She had a daughter of her own. But on the other hand, she'd dedicated her life to the idea that justice should only be done through the proper channels.

She would find the Grantley rapist and when she did she would put him away. That was the law, and that's what she was paid to do. She could understand his temper, his wish to destroy the man, it was natural for him to feel like that. But although she might sympathise, she would never agree.

You could not fight violence with violence. This man, whoever he was, was sick. Sick in the mind. He needed to be taken away from society. And when she found him – not if, when – he would be put away for good.

There were always two sides to any coin. When Kelly calmed down he would see that much for himself.

At least, she hoped so. She could hear Kelly's deep breathing and she sighed gently, reminding herself that he had lost his most precious possession.

'What's the time?' Kelly asked finally.

'A quarter to twelve.'

He looked at her sadly. 'I'm sorry. I've kept you from your own family, tonight of all nights.'

'Don't be sorry, Mr Kelly.'

His face was close to her and Kate felt an absurd fluttering sensation inside her. As if she had just run a long race and was breathless. 'I am working, you know.'

Patrick Kelly stared into Kate's brown eyes. The sadness there gave them an added beauty. He felt as if the whole mystery of woman was hiding in their depths.

Kate was in Grantley police station by one fifteen. Kelly had put his car at her disposal and she had let the driver take her to Grantley Hospital, where she had picked up her own car. The less people knew about her and Patrick Kelly the better. Yet, she reasoned with herself, what was there to know? She had comforted him in his hour of need, that was all. But Kate knew that it was more than that. On her side at least. She

140

pushed the thought from her mind, annoyed with herself. He was a bereaved man, that was all.

Inside the incident room Amanda, Willis and Superintendent Ratchette were all working.

'I've been with Kelly, he's pretty cut up. I never thought I would ever say this, but I feel sorry for the man.'

'Well, Kate, we have no new developments, except that the car, the dark blue Orion that was seen on the waste ground, was also seen driving near Portaby Road earlier in the evening. A woman walking her dog said it made a U-turn near her and that's why she remembered it. First thing in the morning we're going to be interviewing these people.'

'Right. I'll see to it.'

Ratchette raised an eyebrow. 'Let one of the youngsters do their share. It's Boxing Day. You've earned your rest.'

Kate shook her head violently. 'No, I'll do it, sir. I want this bastard caught.'

Willis and Dawkins both looked at her curiously. She hardly ever swore.

'Amanda, would you get me a coffee, please? Black with lots of sugar. Willis, you can start filling me in on what's been happening here today.'

He picked up the file he had been working on and brought it over to Kate.

Ratchette watched her closely. She'd been drinking, that much was evident, but there was something else . . . something he could not quite put his finger on. Well, it would all come out in the wash as his wife was fond of saying.

Chapter Nine

George and Elaine had taken their Boxing Day constitutional in Grantley Woods. As they drove past Vauxhall Drive, George smiled to himself. He wondered fleetingly what Elaine would do if she knew that he was the 'Grantley Ripper'.

At the moment though all she was interested in was her holiday with the girls, and her two nights out a week. George knew that she was a bit nonplussed at his eagerness for her to have her own social life. She thought it was an act of selflessness on his part. She could not have been more wrong.

On the nights that Elaine went out with her friends, he went out on the prowl. He liked the word. Prowler, prowling, prowl. It was similar to prowess, another of his favourites. While Elaine was out gallivanting, he could do his prowling in peace and watch his videos without interruption. He had talked her into ringing him when she wanted to come home so that he could pick her up, make sure she was safe.

He grinned to himself. All he really wanted to know was when she would be arriving so he could clear away. Her absences had done wonders for their marriage. Now, when they were in, they managed a sort of truce. He didn't annoy her and she shut her almighty trap. He wished she had done it years ago.

Bugger Elaine! He grinned again. No chance. She wouldn't even let him have what she termed normal sex.

'George, what are you thinking about?'

Elaine watched him sceptically. She hated his long silences. He parked the car outside their house and smiled at her.

143

'I was just thinking how lucky I am to have a wife like you.'

Elaine leant back in the car seat to get a better look at him. 'Really, George?'

'Really. You've been a good wife, Elaine.'

'Oh. Well, thanks.'

They got out of the car and George noted that she did not return the compliment.

Elaine walked up the garden path and he followed her. As she opened the front door the phone began to ring and she rushed to answer it.

George slipped off his Burberry and hung it up in the hall cupboard.

'It's your sister Edith from America!'

George took the phone.

'Hello, Edith!' There was genuine affection in his voice. He had always been close to her. Both had taken the brunt of their mother's tongue and had a natural affinity.

'Hello, Georgie. I just had to ring you – Merry Christmas!'

'And to you, dear, and Joss. How are the children?'

Elaine smiled at George's happiness. God knew the man had little enough from his family, and she had always liked Edith herself. She had the same manner as George, a sad kind of demeanour that on a woman was attractive while on a man like George it was annoying. Elaine went into the kitchen and made two Irish coffees. What the hell? It was Christmas. When George had finished on the phone he came in to her, beaming.

'She sends you her love and wants us to go over and stay with them.'

Edith asked them over every year. Elaine bit her lip for a second, her round face thoughtful.

'Let's go over next year, shall we, George? We could easily afford it, and you and Edith have always been close. It would be a great holiday for us.'

George caught her excitement. 'Yes, let's. Oh, Elaine, let's.' He looked into her eager face and almost loved her.

'Right then, George, I'll see to it after the holidays! Now, I'm going in to watch the film. Are you coming?'

144

'In a little while, my love. I'll drink my coffee out here, I think, make some plans.'

'Okey doke.' She left the kitchen, beaming.

George sat at the white Formica table and smiled. Then he remembered the redundancy. He clenched his fists. Elaine still did not know that he was going to lose his job. The redundancy money would be quite a bit but that was not the same as having a wage coming in.

He brightened. He could take the redundancy money and put it in a separate account! Then he felt discouraged again. Where could he go all day? No, Elaine would find out. She always found out. There was nothing for it but to tell her the truth.

They would go out to Florida and see Edith, though. He was determined on that.

He remembered Edith as she had been when a girl. She had been exquisite. Not too tall, and she had developed early. She had the same mousy brown hair as George himself, except on her it looked right. It had a slight curl in it that made her look soft somehow. She had porcelain white skin that showed the blue veins perfectly, especially on the swell of her breasts. She had fine grey eyes that were heavy lidded, giving her a sensual look, a tiny rosebud mouth and soft round pink cheeks. His mother had always hated Edith.

Then one day she had gone away. Only George knew that she had run off to Brighton with a salesman, but his mother had guessed as much and beaten her daughter's whereabouts out of him with a belt. He had told on his sister, poor Edith. The scene when Nancy had turned up at the Shangri-La guest house must have been terrible. As always his mother had had the upper hand. Edith had been pregnant and alone, the salesman abandoning her when she had told him her condition.

How his mother had made her pay! Oh, how. She had taken a delight in reproaching Edith at every opportunity. The mother who swore to everyone that she loved her children!

Edith had lost weight while other pregnant women

145

bloomed. She had looked like a spectre; all the fight and vitality were gradually sucked from her. Then, when she had finally gone into labour, Edith had been left to birth alone in her bedroom with only their mother's reprimanding voice to help her along. George had sat outside and listened.

'All children come into the world in pain, Edith, but none as painfully as a bastard child.'

He clenched his teeth. He had only been thirteen then, but had wanted to burst into the room and strike his mother to the ground. The groans and cries of his sister had broken his heart. He sat up all night and into the next day until he heard a soft mewling sound like a kitten and knew that the child had been safely delivered after all that pain.

Edith had loved the boy. Loved him with all her heart and soul, thinking in her ignorance that her mother would allow her to keep him because adoption had never been mentioned. Believing in her heart of hearts that Nancy would soften towards her and the child once it arrived and made a niche in her heart. But it was not to be. When the boy was two months old they had come to take him away. A big woman from an adoption agency, with hard steely blue eyes and cherries in her hat, and a smaller woman, kinder, with watery eyes and a big grey folder. Edith had screamed, pleaded and begged on her knees but her mother would not relent. She had enjoyed it.

In the end, the big woman with the cherries in her hat had dragged the now screaming child from his mother's arms, pulling poor Edith along with her for a few steps until she had dropped sobbing on to the linoleum. Then it was all over. Edith's son was gone from the house and from her life. And she had been left bereft, broken-hearted. The next day George had seen his mother forcing her to drink a cup of cold tea full of Epsom salts to help her get rid of the milk in her breasts. He had finally hated Nancy on that day. When Edith had met Joss Campbell a few years later he had been so glad for her, because Joss was older than Edith and was more than a match for Nancy. When his mother had told him, as she always told any man interested in Edith, about the bastard

146

child, he had just smiled. Smiled and said he would have her under any circumstances. George had loved Joss for that one sentence alone.

Yes, he would go and see Edith. Even if it took every penny of his redundancy money. He was fifty-one now and Edith fifty-five. Life was drawing on, and he wanted to see her before it was too late.

He drank his now cold coffee and was grateful for the whisky that Elaine had put in it.

Somewhere in the world was a man, a thirty-eight-year-old man, who was probably married with children of his own. Who, because of his grandmother's warped mind, would never know the kind and gentle woman who had borne him.

George washed up his cup and saucer carefully and placed them in the plastic drainer. Then he joined Elaine to watch the film. But thoughts of Edith stayed with him all that evening.

Kate glanced at her watch. It was five forty-five. She had been interviewing people since nine that morning and was tired. She sat in her car and turned the heater on while she wrote her comments on a piece of paper. The man she had just interviewed, a Mr Liam Groves, had not been too happy to be interviewed on Boxing Day. He was not at all impressed by her explanation that it was just to eliminate him from their inquiries. In fact, he had told her in no uncertain terms to go forth and multiply. Only not in the biblical words!

She finished her notes and looked at the list of suspects. Peter Bordez, Geoffrey Carter, John Cranmer . . . the list still had over fifty names on it. She decided to call it a day.

Placing the file on the passenger seat, she started up her car. The little Fiat pulled away quickly and Kate put on the radio. 'I saw Momma kissing Santa Claus' blared out. Frowning, she turned it off. She was not into Christmas this year. Maybe next year she would be able to enjoy it.

Dan had taken Lizzy and her mother to a pantomime of all things. Which left her free, on Boxing Day, to get on with her work. She gripped the steering wheel until her knuckles were white. She scanned the houses in the streets, looking at the Christmas trees in gaily lit windows, the decorations that were hanging from ceilings. She knew that behind a similar door somewhere, the Grantley Ripper was sitting by his fireside, stuffed full of Christmas goodies. He could have children sitting at his feet. His wife might even be sparing a thought for the murdered women's families, never guessing that the man she was married to had been the perpetrator.

Kate wished she was at the pantomime. Wished that she was laughing and joking and shouting out 'Behind you' and 'Oh no you don't' to the dame on the stage of the theatre. She wished she was anywhere but Grantley at this moment.

Dan was doing his utmost to be helpful and she appreciated it. At least this Christmas she didn't have to feel guilty because Lizzy didn't have either of her parents with her. Oh, her mother was good, she worshipped her grandchild, but sometimes Kate felt a twinge of guilt at the amount of time she herself spent away from Lizzy. It was a joke really, because if she was one of the male officers then she would not have given it a second thought. But being a woman, she had to juggle her home life and her police work with expert precision. She consoled herself with the fact that her daughter understood. And Lizzy, bless her, really did.

She knew how important Kate's job was. How it kept the roof over their heads as well as helping the community. How many times had Kate snuck into a school hall, late for some school event, her male driver beside her cringing with embarrassment at the childish antics on stage. But she knew that Lizzy appreciated her turning up, and that her reputation as a DI had not suffered because of her being a mother. On the contrary, male CID officers admired her. Well, if she was honest with herself, only the older ones.

She was finished today, though. She'd had enough. This inquiry was getting to her. What she wouldn't give for a nice warm lap to rest her head in. She didn't go as far as to say a nice warm man to slip into bed with, but that was not far from her mind. Dan's arrival had aroused all her dormant sexuality. Sex with him had always been good. It had been wonderful in fact. The trouble was, Dan liked it so much he tended to spread it around and that was no good to Kate. No good at all.

She stopped at the crossroads that took her towards her house and, instead of going right, as she normally would, went left towards the outskirts of Grantley. To the large eighteenth-century house that belonged to Patrick Kelly.

She decided that she would drop in and see how he was.

Patrick Kelly sat on his daughter's bed. She was all around him. The bedroom smelled of her musky perfume; on the floor by the bed was her diary. On the dressing table inside the large bay window all her cosmetics and lotions stood vacantly, as if they knew they would never be used again. There, all alone, stood a large framed photograph of himself, Renée and Mandy. They were all laughing. It had been taken in Marbella, just before Renée's death. Now they were both gone. He turned his head at a slight tap on the door. It was Willy.

'That detective bird's downstairs, I shoved her in the drawing room.'

'Thanks, Willy, I'm just coming. Get cook to make up a tray of coffee will you?'

The man nodded and left the room. Standing up slowly, Patrick walked from the room. He walked down the staircase, his shoulders bowed as if by a great weight, and Kate saw him pull himself erect. He walked towards her with his hands outstretched, and she clasped them warmly before she thought about what she was doing.

'Ms Burrows. Very nice to see you.'

Kate smiled. 'I was passing and I thought I'd just pop in and see how you were.'

Both knew it was a lie. No one was 'just passing' Patrick Kelly's house.

'That was very kind of you. I've ordered some coffee.'

Kate followed him into the morning room. A roaring fire was in the grate and the room was pleasantly warm. It was like going back a hundred years. Kelly sat on the settee beside her and smiled sadly.

'Actually, I'm glad of the company. My sister's no good at times like this. I've told her I'll see her at the funeral, though I suppose it won't be for a while. But I need company. My friends, or people I call friends, aren't really close. I never realised until now that in fact I have very few people I can trust. Only my daughter, and my wife when she was alive.'

Kate looked into his haggard face, so different from Dan's blond smoothness.

'I see so much unhappiness in my work, it's hard sometimes just to switch off.'

They sat together on the settee.

'What about your family? Won't they be wondering where you are on Boxing Day?'

'My daughter's sixteen, and today my ex-husband has taken her and my mother to a pantomime.' She saw the flicker of pain cross his face as she spoke of Lizzy and guessed that he was thinking of his own daughter. She hurried on, 'So I have a couple of hours to myself.'

Patrick Kelly heard the underlying loneliness in her voice and knew instinctively that they were two of a kind. Loners who worked and worked, and at the end of the day had nothing except their families. And when the families were no more, they had nothing at all to show for their efforts.

'Have you eaten today?'

Kate shook her head. 'Not since this morning.'

'Then why not have lunch with me? I could do with the company and Mrs Manners has still got enough turkey to feed the third world and the poor Albanians. Unless you have to get back of course.'

'That sounds lovely. I'd love to have lunch with you, Mr Kelly.'

'Patrick . . . The name's Patrick. Right then, I'll go and sort it out.'

Kate felt inordinately pleased at his offer, even though she was astute enough to know that it came from a desire for any company, rather than hers specifically. She was still thrilled to be there.

She self-consciously fiddled with her hair, tidied up her

clothes. She wished she had worn her new suit, but she consoled herself that at the moment he didn't care what she looked like.

Willy brought in the coffee and smiled at her. Kate smiled back but inside she shuddered. The man looked like something from a bad nightmare. Half of one ear was missing, and his nose had obviously been broken more than a few times. He grinned at her from a toothless mouth.

'Shall I pour for you, love?'

Kate shook her head.

'I'll do it, thank you.'

Willy looked relieved and left the room.

Patrick Kelly returned. Lunch would be ready in twenty minutes. Leaving Kate with her coffee, he slipped into the library to use the phone.

Dimitrios Brunos, a London Greek, was one of the best 'minders' in the West End. He was also one of the most violent.

'Mr Kelly, how are you?' His voice was solicitous.

'Listen to me carefully and pass on what I say to all the others. My Mandy is dead and I'm upping the ante. There's half a mil' for whoever finds the ponce, right?'

Patrick heard a sharp intake of breath and smiled grimly. That should get some results.

'Also, I'll be looking for the slag personally, so I reckon between us we should find him. Whoever gives me his name gets the money, OK?'

'Yes. Please accept my most sincere condolences. Your daughter was a . . .'

'Yeah, yeah. All right, Dimitrios. I ain't got that far myself yet. Just let the others know the score.'

Patrick put down the receiver and closed his eyes tightly. He was going to hound the slag into the ground. He would find him and pay him out if it was the last thing he ever did. Pulling himself upright, he squared his shoulders. First thing tomorrow he was going to phone the Chief Constable to request copies of everything the Old Bill found out. Patrick intended to get to the suspects first.

151

He went back in to Kate and sat beside her. Even though she was an Old Bill, a filth, he trusted her somehow. She had the same quietness and serenity his Renée had had.

Patrick liked her.

George and Elaine had opened a bottle of wine. She was tipsy and they were watching a comedy film on TV. The curtains were pulled and the lamplight gave a cosy glow to the room. In fairness, George thought, Elaine was an exemplary housewife. Never in all their years together had he lacked an ironed shirt or clean underwear. His suits always went to the cleaner's on time, and his meals were always cooked for him. Admittedly, Elaine's cooking often left a lot to be desired, but she was at least conscientious. A good woman.

His mother, whatever her faults – and they were legion – had been the same in the housewifely stakes. Hate her or love her, the children were always well fed. She made sure they were the best dressed, the cleanest, the brainiest. Her house was the best furnished and kept spic and span. She had been proud of her Nottingham lace curtains, her wooden beds . . .

George jumped.

Elaine had placed her arm around his neck. He looked at her from the corner of his eye. She was resting her head on his shoulder.

Oh God!

'Give us a kiss, George.' Her voice was low and slurred.

He concentrated on the television screen. Bette Midler and Danny De Vito were fighting it out. *Ruthless People* the film was called. Ruthless People? He was the ruthless one. Hadn't he proved it?

'Come on, George, give us a kiss.' Elaine pulled his face round and planted a wet, sticky mouth on his own.

George kissed her. He didn't know what else to do. For the first time in over sixteen years, Elaine showed some signs of interest in him! He shuddered.

'I've had a lovely day, George. A lovely day. And next year

we will finally have a good year. Three hundred and sixty-five days of happiness. I'm going on holiday with you, to Florida to see our Edith. And I'm going to Spain with the girls.' Elaine was having trouble forming the words now and George guessed that if he kept quiet she would fall asleep. He put his arm around her with difficulty and held her close to him. She snuggled into him and closed her eyes.

Please God make her go to sleep.

His prayer was answered. Within moments the wine, the heat and the excitement of the day caught up with her and she began to snore softly into his thick cable-knit cardigan.

George breathed a sigh of relief.

He would do many things to keep her happy, but sex was not one of them.

Picking up the remote control, he turned the TV on to video. Mandy appeared on the screen. He had set the video up earlier in the evening while Elaine was making supper. He had been waiting for her to go to bed. Now he turned the sound down and watched the action on the screen. The element of risk gave it an added excitement.

So Mandy went through her nightly ritual and Elaine snored and George was happy, his finger poised over the TV button on the remote control.

In a funny way he wished that Elaine would open her eyes, but she was blind drunk and slept. And George just sat and watched.

Kate had enjoyed her late lunch with Patrick Kelly very much. They had opened up to each other. Now she sat with her own family and listened to their account of the pantomime.

'Oh, Mum, it was really funny. You should have seen the dame! He was hilarious. Joanie was there with her brothers. They sat with us and we had the greatest time.'

'Considering you didn't really want to go.' Evelyn's voice was jocular. '"I'm too old for pantomimes, I'm an adult." And when we got there she was shouting louder than anyone!'

153

'I'm sorry I missed it.'

'Dad was really funny, he made jokes all through it. I wish you could have been there, Mum.'

'So do I, Lizzy. It sounds great.'

'Oh, it was. Dad's gone up for a bath.' Lizzy looked at the kitchen clock and squealed. 'Oh my God, if I don't get a move on I'm going to be late.'

'Where you off to then?'

'Oh, me and Joanie are going to a party tonight.' She twisted her hair around her fingers. 'I'm sure I mentioned it.'

'You never said anything to me.'

'Or me.' Evelyn's voice was low.

'Well, it's been arranged absolutely ages and Joanie is coming round for me at seven-thirty. I really must go, Mum.'

Kate and Evelyn exchanged glances.

'Well, I don't remember you telling us anything about it. Where is this party?'

'It's near Joanie's house, in the next street. I don't know the number.'

'I see.'

'Oh, Mum, don't say it like that. I must go! I want to go.' Lizzy's voice was high and near to tears.

'No one has said you can't go . . . yet.'

Dan walked into the kitchen in his dressing gown.

'What's all this racket then?'

Lizzy ran to him and he put his arm around her.

'I want to go to a party and Mum won't let me. Everyone will be there.'

'Your mother never said you can't go, Lizzy. That's not fair.'

'Oh, Gran, I want to go so much. And between you, you'll talk me out of it!'

'We will not! All your mother wants to know is where it is and who'll be there!'

'I'll take her and pick her up, how's that?'

Everyone looked at Dan. Lizzy kissed him on the cheek.

'That's settled then, I'll go and get ready. Blimey, Mum,

sometimes your job really goes to your head. I'm not a suspect, you know!'

Her voice was happy once more and Kate watched her run from the room.

'Thanks, Dan. Thanks a bundle.'

He opened his arms wide. 'What have I done? All I said was I'd take her and pick her up. There's no harm in that, Kate.' He counted off on his fingers. 'First, we'll know where it is. And secondly, we'll be able to sort out a reasonable time for getting her home. Third, I'll have a quick look at who's there. I can't see there's any problem.'

He walked from the room and Kate felt an urge to jump on his back and tear his hair out. Not five minutes in the house and he was already countermanding her. Lizzy would be allowed to get away with blue murder while her father was around, it was always the same, then when he swanned off again, it would be left to Kate to pick up the pieces and get back some kind of equilibrium.

She sighed heavily.

'He's right, you know, Kate. She's not a child any more.'

'Oh, Mum, don't you jump on the bandwagon. She's so grown up that she shouted herself hoarse through a bloody pantomime not two hours ago. I saw a girl not much older than her battered and dying in a hospital bed, not twenty-four hours since. There's a bloody maniac on the loose and you tell me that she's grown up!'

Evelyn put her hand on her daughter's arm. 'That's not all that's bothering you, is it? Now is it? It's Dan taking the reins from your hands that's brought all this on. Well, listen to me and listen good. It won't last – it never does. But you can't stop that child from living a normal life. She'll be with Joanie and her other friends, Dan's picking her up. So swallow your pride and don't make an enemy of your own child.'

'I'll be glad when he goes. And first thing in the New Year he will be going. That, Mum, is a promise!'

'He only wants to see the child enjoy herself with her friends.'

Kate sighed noisily.

'Don't you start taking his side, Mum. It's bad enough Lizzy thinks the sun shines out of his . . .'

'Kate!' Evelyn stopped her flow of words. 'You should listen to yourself, young lady.'

She sat at the breakfast bar and lit herself a cigarette. It wasn't the time to remind her mother that she was forty. Her lovely afternoon had been spoiled. She would have let Lizzy go to the party eventually, she rarely denied the girl anything. But to have the decision taken out of her hands like that was irritating and downright unfair.

But Kate knew when enough was enough so she kept her peace.

Dan dropped Joanie and Lizzy off at a respectable-looking semi-detached house and after a quick kiss on his daughter's cheek drove away, pleased with the way he had handled everything. It would do Kate good to realise that he could be responsible too.

Lizzy went into the party with Joanie and was immediately surrounded by a crowd of boys. She was wearing a short black skirt and a tiny scrap of a top that emphasised her heavy breasts. Joanie stood by her side as she laughed and chatted with the guys. She was a different girl to the one her mother and grandmother knew.

'So come on then, has anyone got any puff?'

A tall thin boy with straggly hair passed her a joint and Lizzy took it from him, inhaling the fragrant mixture deeply.

'Mmm, smells like Sensimelle!' She took a large draw and held the smoke in her lungs for about ten seconds before letting it out.

Her breasts quivered and gathered the attention of every male in the vicinity.

'I have been dying for a toke all day. Where's Angela and Marianne?'

'They won't be here till later. They're trying to score a few Es over in Grays.'

Lizzy's eyes lit up. 'Oh, great. I have to be home for half-past one! There's plenty of time for fun yet.'

Everyone burst out laughing and Joanie smiled uneasily. Since they had got in with this crowd, she had not felt very happy. They were too forward for her, but Lizzy loved them. She thrived on all the attention and excitement. Joanie tagged along with her, as she always had done.

An hour later Lizzy was against the wall in the back garden with an eighteen-year-old boy named Joey Meeson. He had pulled the band of material that passed for a skirt up around her waist and was tugging at the top of her tights.

'Not here!' Her voice was scandalised.

Joey looked down at her and grinned.

'You really must learn to get into the swing of things, Lizzy.'

She pulled her skirt down and blinked rapidly. The cannabis and the vodka she had consumed were making her feel light-headed.

'Is it true that your mum's a filth?'

Lizzy giggled. 'You could call her that. She's a Detective Inspector.'

'Really? That's wild.'

'Actually, she's all right.'

'What would she say if she knew what we'd been doing tonight?' His voice was genuinely interested.

'Probably go ape shit.'

They both laughed and then Joey kissed her again. Softer this time. 'Talking of shit, how about I skin up again? This time in the bedroom?' His voice was low and husky and Lizzy was lost. He was the best-looking boy she had ever seen in her life.

'That would be fine.'

'Come on then.' He pulled her by the hand through the crowded kitchen and hall and over the bodies on the stairs.

Inside the bedroom, Lizzy found out what Joey's idea of a good time was.

And Joey found out that Lizzy, the daughter of a policewoman, was not as innocent as he had first thought.

Chapter Ten

New Year's Eve

'Are you sure you're going to be all right on your own, George?' Elaine's voice was concerned but deep inside she hoped he would not decide to go to the party. The last few days he had been getting on her nerves. George fit and well could get you down, but George ill was a nightmare.

'You go to the party, dear, and give everyone my best. I'm really much too ill to go tonight.'

She breathed a sigh of relief.

'Well, if you're sure?'

George smiled wanly. 'You go and have a good time. I've got a good book, a flask of soup and my tablets.'

She kissed him on the cheek.

'See you then. I might be late.' She giggled.

George nodded. In her new dress, a fitted emerald green sparkly affair with huge padded shoulders, George thought she looked like a cross between a Christmas tree and an American footballer. 'You look lovely, Elaine. You'll have all the men wanting to dance with you.'

'Oh, George. You old silly!' Elaine giggled again, a schoolgirl going on her first date. She dropped her clutch bag and George frowned as she strained to pick it up. Not an American footballer – a sumo wrestler. God, she was bad enough in her shell suits.

A taxi hooted outside and Elaine rushed from the room, leaving a scent of Estée Lauder and face powder.

''Bye, George.'

He listened to the thud of her feet on the stairs and the satisfying slam of the front door as it crashed behind her.

She was gone.

He was alone.

Hallelujah!

George lay with bated breath until he heard the taxi turn at the end of the street, then jumped from the bed.

'Look, Mr Kelly, it's New Year's Eve. We always get lots of punters in on New Year's Eve. She's a good kid . . .'

Kelly stared hard at the woman in front of him. Violet Mapping had been running this massage parlour for five years. She was one of the hardest toms he had ever met in his life, and he had met a few, but she had one vice: she was a dyke and liked the young girls. But this young girl was not working in his massage parlour until she was qualified.

'Listen, Vi, get the girl a certificate and she can work here till the cows come home. Till then, no way.'

'Oh, Mr Kelly, you know and I know that that piece of paper is a bloody con.'

'I don't care what you know, Violet. Once she's done a course in massage and has her certificate she can work here. Until then, no.'

Violet saw the man's face harden and decided it was better to give way on this occasion. Everyone knew about Mandy, it was common knowledge on the streets. It was best not to annoy him now.

She sighed.

'If you say so, Mr Kelly.'

'Good girl, Vi, you know it makes sense. Now then, if you get any weird ones in I want you to cop the names and addresses – the lot. Then I want you to pass them on to me.'

Violet snorted with laughter.

'They're all fucking weird, that's why they come here!'

Kelly shook his head in annoyance.

'You know what I mean. If one wants something a bit outlandish like, or gets violent with the girls, I want to know. OK? You're one of the best "lifters" in the game, Vi. You can lift a wallet better than anyone I've ever known. Only after you've lifted it, Violet, you put it back, comprenez?'

160

She narrowed her hard blue eyes.

'I give up lifting years ago, Mr Kelly, you should know that.'

The two eyed each other for a few seconds.

'Just make sure the wallet goes back into the pocket, Vi, or there'll be hell to pay. Now get back on reception. By the way, before I forget, how old is that little black bird out there?'

Violet pulled her mouth down at the corners and shrugged her skinny shoulders.

'I dunno.'

Patrick Kelly stood up.

'You don't know? Well, judging by the looks of her I'd put her at about fifteen, Vi, so get rid of her. Fuck me, I pay you to run this gaff. I might as well run the bastard place meself!'

'All right, all right, no need to get your knickers in a twist. I'll sort it, OK?'

'Good.'

'I'm sorry about your Mandy, Pat, heart sorry. We all are.' Her voice was soft now. She had been working for, and fighting with, Patrick Kelly for years. He was a good boss. Fair but hard. His daughter had been his life. Everyone knew that.

He dropped his eyes.

'Thanks, Vi.'

'Right then, face ache, I'd better go and give my little friend the bad news.' Her voice was once more loud and aggressive.

'You do that, girl, and once she's got her certificate, she can work her little arse off.'

'I'll get her a bent one off Vinny Marcenello.'

'You get it where you like, love, but she don't work till she's got it. I mean that, Vi.'

'I know that, don't I!' Her voice was shrill again. She walked from the office.

Kelly carried on looking over the books but his heart wasn't in it. Finally he got up from his desk and walked out

161

into the foyer of the massage parlour. All around the walls were plushly upholstered seats. Girls and women of every colour, creed, shape and size were sprawled all over them. They all sat up straight as Patrick walked among them.

He nodded at them absentmindedly. Then turning to the left he walked through a door to the back of the parlour. That was where the cubicles were. He walked silently along the thickly carpeted floor until he came to the last cubicle. He listened.

A childish voice wafted from behind the thin curtain.

'Do you require any extras, sir?'

'How much will it rush me?'

'Well, hand relief is fifteen quid, a blow job's twenty, and the full bifta is forty-five quid.'

Patrick heard the man laugh.

'Gis the full bifta, girl.'

Patrick shook his head and turned to walk back to the foyer. For some reason the childish voice had upset him. He knew the girl. She was only seventeen and looked about twelve. She was blonde, like his Mandy, except unlike Mandy she had never had a chance in life. He walked out of the tiny corridor, through the foyer and out to his car.

Don't start getting soft now, boy, he told himself. Tomming is the oldest profession in the world. If they didn't work for you they'd only work for someone else.

He climbed into the back of his Rolls and tapped on the window. Willy's voice came over the intercom.

'Where to, Pat?'

'Forest Gate this time. I want to see how Juliet's getting on.'

The car purred away and Kelly relaxed in his seat.

Yet the childish voice was still repeating in his head.

'Stop the car!'

'Do what?' The car screeched to a halt in the middle of the road. Patrick Kelly jumped out and ran back into the massage parlour.

'Oi, Vi. In the office quick sharp.'

Violet followed him in.

'Yeah? What?' Her voice was belligerent once more.

'That little blonde bird, what's her name?'

'Marlene?'

'Yeah, Marlene. Well, she's giving the punter the full bifta.'

'So what?'

'Well, I want it stopped. From now on there's no full sex in here, right. The Old Bill can't touch us if the girls don't cock their legs over.'

Violet looked at Patrick as if he had gone mad.

'You feeling all the bleeding ticket? We won't get any girls working here if we do something like that. Gordon Bennett, if you had the choice between a mouthful of spunk or a prattfull, what would you rather have?'

Kelly's face screwed up. 'Don't be so disgusting, Vi!'

She opened her arms wide.

'I'm only stating facts, mate. We won't get a tom in here with them rules, and you know it. Our clientele will go down quicker than free beer on a beano!'

Kelly felt sick.

'Why don't you go home and have a nice rest, Pat? It's all the worry you've had, it's turned your head.'

He felt a fool.

'Maybe you're right, Vi.'

'Listen.' Violet's voice was soft. 'We ain't social workers, mate, we're in business. Them girls out there are gonna flash their clout no matter what anyone does. It's the only thing they know how to do. So leave them to it.'

'Oh, I don't know, Vi, there's some fucking nonces about. Look what happened to my Mandy.'

'Well, let me tell you something. Them perverts, they pick on the nice innocent girls. They don't want no tom. They like a struggle. Same as them posh blokes what come here – they all want to be caned. I'm telling you, Pat, we go out the back, into the garden and cut a swish from that bleeding forsythia bush, then come back in and beat the buggers' arses black

163

and blue. Now if they didn't pay us they'd only pay the Paki down the road.'

Kelly nodded at her. He was very tired all of a sudden. 'Maybe you're right, Vi.'

As he walked back out into the foyer, the girls automatically straightened again as he passed them. Out on the pavement, an elderly woman with a small sausage dog gave him a filthy look. He sighed again.

That put the tin lid on it as far as Patrick Kelly was concerned. The old bird thought *he* was a nonce. The Rolls was parked outside once more and he climbed in.

'Forest Gate, guv?'

'No. Home, I think, Willy.'

'Okey doke.'

Kelly watched the people in the cold grey streets. It was New Year's Eve and he had arranged to spend it with Kate.

He settled into the seat once more. Sod the toms. He had enough on his mind.

'Oh, Mum! Why must I always have you and Dad on my back? All the girls in my class are going. I'll be the only one who doesn't! I'll never live it down!'

Louise Butler stamped her foot.

Her mother Doreen grinned. She had a mind of her own did Louise. She glanced at her husband.

'What do you think, Ron, shall we let her go?'

Louise breathed a sigh of relief. If her mum was asking her dad then she was going. Mum had more or less said yes. Before her father answered she had thrown herself into her mother's arms.

'Thanks, Mum. Oh, thanks.'

'Hurry up and get changed then. I'll run you over there.' Ron's voice was jovial.

Louise looked at him with a mock stern expression.

'I am ready, if you don't mind!'

They all laughed. In her designer tracksuit of vivid mauve and gold, her Reebok bumpers and man's leather flying jacket, she looked the complete opposite of her parents' idea of dressed up. But she was a hardcore acid fan, from her backcombed sixties hair style to the sovereign earrings in her ears.

'Well, I've been reading about these waves.'

'It's raves, Dad. Raves.'

'Waves, raves . . . whatever. You be careful. Don't take no drugs or anything now, will you?'

Louise rolled her violet eyes.

'As if I would. I'm not stupid, you know.'

'We worry about you, love, that's all.'

'I know that, Mum. Come on, Dad, or we'll be late. Don't take me right to the party, drop me off at Sam's. We want to make our way there together, OK?'

'Oh, all right then.'

After kissing her mother, Louise followed her father from the house. Five minutes later she was outside Sam's.

'Now where is this rave again?'

'Just up the road from here at Woodham Woods. About seven miles away. Stop worrying, Dad, we'll be fine.'

'Well, you remember that I want you in by one at the latest.'

'OK. See you later, Dad.'

She kissed her father and got out of the car. She watched him drive off before walking up the path to Sam's house. She rang the bell.

'Hello, Mrs Jensen, is Sam here?'

'No, dear. She left about ten minutes ago. With Georgina, Tracey and Patricia. I think it was them, anyway, she's got so many friends. Well, they came round for her in a blue car . . .'

'Oh. All right then. Sorry to have bothered you.'

Louise walked up the path, her heart dragging in the dirt. That bloody bitch Sam had gone ahead knowing that Louise was coming round. The two-faced cow! Well, she would have to go home and get her dad to run her to the rave. But if he did he would see that it was in an old barn, and not at all legal, and then he would make her come home.

What was she going to do?

She smiled to herself. She would thumb a ride. Might even get a lift off some blokes. That would show Sam and her lot, wouldn't it?

She pulled her long dark hair from inside her flying jacket and began to walk to the outskirts of Grantley.

She'd show them.

Lizzy was dressed and ready to go. She took one last look at herself in the wardrobe mirror before she pulled on the sheepskin that her father had bought her for Christmas. Licking her lips to gloss them, she walked to her mother's bedroom.

'Oh, Mum, you look scrumptious.'

Kate smoothed down the deep red pure new wool dress that hugged her figure, and smiled at her daughter.

'Thanks, love.' She looked at herself in the mirror, knowing that she looked good. Her hair had been washed in a coconut shampoo and gleamed under the light. She was sporting a pair of gold hoop earrings, and her face was skilfully made up.

'Now what time will you be back from Joanie's tomorrow?'

'About lunchtime, I suppose. Don't worry about me, you just enjoy yourself.'

'I will.' Kate looked into her daughter's eyes. 'You look beautiful you know, Liz. Show me what you're wearing.'

'Oh, I just shoved on my black suit. After all, the party is at Joanie's house.' She pouted her red-lipsticked lips and Kate laughed. Joanie's family were what Lizzy would call 'lame'.

'I hope you enjoy yourself.'

'Oh, I will, Mum. You just concentrate on yourself.'

Lizzy eyed her mother critically. 'Wear the red lipstick, it will look better with that dress than the coral. You're dark enough to get away with it.'

Kate laughed. 'Okey doke.' She began to tissue off her lipstick.

'What's Dad going to do tonight?'

166

Kate shrugged. 'I've no idea, love. Gran's off to Doris's. I should imagine your father's going out as well.'

'Well, didn't you even ask him?'

Kate stopped in her tracks as she applied red lipstick. 'Why should I do that?' She locked eyes with her daughter in the mirror. 'We're divorced, Lizzy, my life's my own, and your father's life is his own.'

Lizzy looked sad. 'I wish you two could get it together.'

Kate turned and held her daughter's face in her hands. 'I wished that for a long time, Lizzy, but your father has a different approach to life.' She was stumbling for the right words. She wanted to make Dan sound as good as possible and after some of the stunts he'd played on her in the past that was difficult.

'Your father is his own man, he lives his own life. And so do I.'

Lizzy stared at her mother and Kate could see her trying to comprehend what was being said.

'I'd better go or I'll be late.'

'Hang on a sec and I'll drop you at Joanie's.'

'It's OK, I called a cab. You go to your party, Mum, just forget about me for once! I'm a big girl now.'

'Well, Happy New Year then.'

Kate kissed her.

'Happy New Year, Mum.'

She rushed from the room at the sound of the taxi honking and Kate watched her go with a pang of regret. Picking up her handbag from the bed, she walked slowly from the room.

'You look a picture Katie.'

Evelyn was dressed up to the nines. She had on a bright green crimplene suit and a dark green hat. Her feet were encased in fur-lined ankle boots and she had a large brown handbag at her side.

'Will you drop me round Doris's?'

'Course I will. Are many people going?'

'About twenty I think. This'll be the first New Year we haven't seen in together, just the three of us.'

'I know that, but Lizzy's right, she is growing up however much we don't like it.'

'Where's your party again?'

'Oh, just one of the guys from the station. It's at his house.' Kate hated lying, but she wasn't ready to tell anyone about her feelings for Patrick.

'Where's Dan?'

'He's in the front room, you go and see him and I'll get me coat.'

Kate went into the front room. Dan was sitting on the settee watching television. He looked at her as she came in. She watched, with some satisfaction, the widening of his eyes. He gave a low whistle. 'You look lovely, Kate, really lovely.' He sounded sincere.

'Thanks, Dan. Did you see Lizzy before she went?'

'Yeah.' He ran his hands through his thick hair, a familiar gesture. 'Why don't you let me take you out, Kate?' His voice was small. 'You look much too good for a bunch of old policemen.'

'Haven't you made any arrangements?' She raised her eyebrows.

'Well, no. I was going to take you out – you never go out on New Year's Eve.' The petulant note was back in his voice.

'Well, I do now.' She heard her mother's feet on the stairs and smiled.

'Happy New Year.'

'Happy New Year, Kate.'

He watched her go from the room and felt an urge to drag her back. For the first time ever Kate was in charge and Dan was not sure how to act. In the past it had been her coming to him. There was a man involved this time or his name was not Danny Burrows. Kate was dressed for a date, not a party. He would make it his business to find out who it was.

As the front door closed he pulled himself from the sofa and watched her drive away. Then, when she turned the corner, he went out to the hall and picked up the phone. He dialled and after a few rings a female voice answered.

Dan had a motto in life: Always have a back-up plan.

168

* * *

In the car Evelyn kept up a stream of chatter.

'You really do look lovely, you know. It's a long time since I saw you looking so well. If I didn't know better I'd think there was a man on the horizon.'

'Oh, don't be silly, Mum. If there was a man on the horizon, you'd be the first to know.'

'Well, maybe the man himself don't know yet.'

'What on earth are you talking about?'

Evelyn smiled vaguely. 'Oh, nothing, nothing. Stop here, Kate.'

She pulled over to the kerb and turned off the engine. 'Happy New Year, Mum.'

'Happy New Year, love. And listen – if for some reason you want to spend the night with a friend, maybe you'll want to drink and then you won't be able to drive . . . you know . . . don't worry about Lizzy because I'll be home soon, should anything come up.'

She got out of the car and walked up Doris's path, her back ramrod straight.

Kate started the car and smiled to herself. Her mother was shrewd.

She began to drive to the outskirts of Grantley. She was looking forward to seeing Patrick Kelly.

George was wrapped up warm. Although he was not as ill as he had made out to Elaine, he still felt a bit under the weather. George always liked to look after himself. He was obsessed with his health. He had the car heater on and the whirring as it blew out hot air was beginning to annoy him. He snapped on the radio.

The sound of Mozart's Horn Concerto filled the car and he relaxed. That was more like it. He drove out of Grantley and along the road that led to the village of Woodham. He often drove out this way first; there was a small lay-by that was usually filled with cars with courting couples in them. Their steamed up windows excited George.

He put his foot on the accelerator and dipped his

169

headlights. He felt free, free and happy. Later on he would drive back into Grantley and go and watch the flats. He began to hum along with the music. His usually dead grey eyes were sparkling. His bushy black brows, liberally sprinkled with grey, moved up and down in time to the music. His cheesecutter hat hid the balding patch on his head.

Then he saw her. In front of him were two other cars, which was unusual for this road. Normally it was dead. But it was New Year's Eve, and all the roads were busy tonight. George had no idea about the rave that was just beginning in Woodham Woods.

The girl had her thumb out. He saw the car in front of him slow down and slowed with it. The girl walked towards the car and it pulled away quickly, leaving her standing with her hands on her hips by the side of the road. George drove past her and into the first lay-by. Taking the carrier bag from the back seat he slipped on the mask. He felt the adrenaline begin to course through his veins, and smiled. Adjusting the holes so that he could see properly, he turned around in the road and drove back towards her.

His heart nearly stopped. A car was parked up beside her. George drove past and felt a terrible anger replace his elation.

The slut! He drove along the road, and turned again.

Louise stared into the dark interior of the XR3. There were three boys in the back and two in the front. They were obviously drunk.

'Come on, darlin'. Jump in the motor, we'll be there in no time.'

Louise was not sure.

One of the boys in the back wound down his window and spat on to the roadside.

'Look, hurry up, will ya? I'm fucking freezing me bollocks off!'

The blond youth who was driving leant across the front seat. 'Look, get in.'

Louise was frightened.

'No . . . No, it's all right. I'll walk.'

'Let the silly bitch walk then. Come on, I want a drink.'

'You stupid cow!'

The car screeched away and Louise watched its tail lights disappear into the distance.

They were drunk, or drugged, maybe both. She did not like walking along the dark road, but she was not getting into a car with five blokes! No way.

She pulled her leather flying jacket tighter around her. No, she would walk and find Sam and the others. She began to hurry, sorry now that she had not gone home, because all of a sudden the thought of missing out on a rave didn't seem that bad. But if she had missed this one, she would be the laughing stock of her class. She wished she was sixteen. She wished she was at hairdressing college. She wished she was at home in bed!

Another car came up behind her and she heard it slow down. Oh, please don't let it be another car full of drunks! Let it be some dreamy boy of about seventeen with his hair cut in 'curtains' and some really nice gear, then she could show off to Sam and the others!

She turned as the car drew to a halt.

The passenger door opened and she walked hesitantly towards it. The dirt path she was on was flanked on the left by a steep bank. The bank sloped down about ten feet, into a large ploughed field. Bending, she looked into the car.

As soon as her mind registered what it had seen she jumped away from the car door, a scream issuing from her that cut through the night air.

Inside the car was a man in a black leather mask.

Nowhere in her wildest nightmares had she ever imagined anything like this! She stumbled backwards. Too late she remembered about the steep bank behind her and stepped into thin air. Landing with a thud on the dirty slope, her brand new Reeboks scrabbled in the dirt a couple of times before she finally pulled herself up.

There in front of her was the masked man! She dodged around him and ran into the road as he made a grab for her. In his hands she saw something glint and realised it was a knife.

171

She felt her bowels loosen as she realised fully what was happening. She was dazzled by a set of headlights as a Volkswagen Golf swerved to avoid her, music blaring out of the open windows. She stood helplessly in the road as it shot past. With it went her hopes.

The man was standing on the grass verge watching her. On the other side of the road was another field. She bit her lip, weighing up in her confused mind where to run. It was dark, so dark and lonely.

She backed away from the man slowly, trying desperately to think of an escape. She saw him begin to walk towards her. In the distance she heard another car, and putting up her arms began to run towards it, waving and shouting.

Terry Miller had dropped a tab of Ecstasy at six that evening. He was buzzing, really buzzing. Beside him his brother Charlie was tripping out of his head. They had driven around for over an hour trying to find the rave that every one was going on about. Inside the car the sounds of Technotronic screamed out so loudly that they could hardly hear themselves think. When Terry saw the girl in his headlights he snorted with laughter.

'Look, Charlie, she must be well stoned!'

He grinned, trying to clear his mind.

'Look at the geezer with her. Wild, man. Look at his headgear.'

They drove past the two figures and Terry sounded his horn that played the first few bars of the Star Spangled Banner.

'Wicked! Did you see that bloke, man. Really wicked.'

Louise Butler watched her potential saviours drive away, their horn blaring out into the dark night. She began to cry. Looking around her as if she thought someone was going to run out of the field behind her and save her, she saw that the man was much nearer.

Turning, she began to run. Before she had taken five steps she hit the chain link fencing that was invisible in the darkness. She felt the fence give a little and then it literally threw her back into the arms of the man with the mask.

As his arms tightened around her all the fight left her body. Fear took over and she went limp. Her shoulders were racked with sobs.

Oh please, please God, help me!

George half carried, half dragged her back to the car. Inside the mask he was smiling. His secret smile that just exposed his teeth.

Kate had had one glass of wine with dinner and was now enjoying an armagnac. Patrick smiled across the table at her. It was the second time that Kate had had dinner at his house, and he was finding that he liked her being around. She took his mind off Mandy, and that was strange considering she was on his daughter's case.

He had no illusions about the police. He had been dealing with them on and off all his life. But Kate was the first plain clothes police officer he had ever dealt with on a personal basis. Oh, he had greased a few of the Old Bill's palms over the years, such as the Chief Constable's, but they were both in the Masons. Kate was the first member of the Force he had met socially because he wanted to. Because he enjoyed her company.

She looked good enough to eat tonight. Red suited her. Her dark hair shone in the light from the candles. She looked softer somehow. More appealing. After all his empty-headed bimbos, he found he liked having a woman around him who demanded a bit of respect.

In fairness to the young girls who had come and gone over the years, he had deliberately picked well-stacked, dim-witted types whose only claim to fame was the fact that they were a good lay. He had not wanted to have to trouble himself making conversation. What on earth did a man on the wrong side of forty have to say to an eighteen year old? Nothing, that's what.

But Kate, she was a different kettle of fish altogether. They discussed everything under the sun. And she wasn't one of those pushy birds either, who wore their intelligence like a pair of boxing gloves, willing to punch a point home. Oh, no. Kate would listen to his opinions then give hers, quietly and fairly. He liked her. He knew that she was not making much headway with finding the nonce, but in fairness neither was he. The bloke was obviously a chancer. Kate had explained all that to him. He never left any clues. But she would not give up. One day he would make a mistake, then she would have him.

Only what Kate didn't know was that when that break came, Patrick would also be after the bloke. And when he was finished with him there would be nothing left. Nothing recognisable anyway.

'So you don't have anything to go on, really?' he asked.

Kate shook her head and he watched her hair ripple with the movement.

'We're gradually eliminating people from the inquiry but it takes time. We're still interviewing all men with dark-coloured Orions. We should be finished with that in the next ten days. I myself will be interviewing from tomorrow along with Spencer and Willis.'

'I see.' His voice was gentle.

'We will get him, Patrick, eventually. Normally when a murder is committed, or a rape, the person is known to us.' Kate smiled ruefully. 'I think I've said all this before!'

'You have. Come on, let's change the subject.' He nearly burst out laughing and Kate looked at him quizzically.

'I nearly said, "How's work"! My head's up my Khyber these days. Come on, let's adjourn to the drawing room, shall we?' His voice mimicked that of an aristocrat and Kate laughed. He was a character.

In the drawing room they sat together on the large settee. Patrick had brought the brandy decanter and two glasses.

'This is a lovely house – eighteenth-century, isn't it?'

Patrick nodded.

'Yeah, I picked it up for a song about twelve years ago. Seventy grand I paid for it, and that was the national debt then I can tell you. It was a ruin.' He waved his hand. 'Cost me nigh on that again to restore it back to its original beauty, but it was worth it. Renée loved it and so did Mandy. Now though – well, it's empty without them. What's a house without a woman in it?'

Kate instinctively grasped his hand.

He stared into the dark depths of her eyes. She really was lovely, with a mature quality he had grown unused to in a woman.

Suddenly he wanted her wholeheartedly. He wanted to feel her arms around him. He wanted her to love him. He wanted, needed, a woman's loving. A woman's, not a girl's. A real woman's loving.

Kate read the expression in his eyes and parted her full lips to speak. Then he kissed her – a long slow kiss that set her tingling right down to her toes. And Kate kissed him back, caught up in feelings that had nothing to do with background or career or anything except pure sensation.

He wanted her. She could feel the want and the need in him. She felt him pushing her backwards on the overstuffed settee and she let him. She lay back gladly.

This was what she had been waiting for since she had first met him though she had never admitted it to herself until now. Dan was not even in the running any more. She wanted Patrick Kelly.

She felt his big rough hand running along her body outside her new dress. Felt the tingle as he found the skin of her thighs. Then everything was forgotten except the moment. He pulled away from her and looked into her face, his expression soft and serious at the same time.

'Will you stay the night, Kate?' His voice was husky. She loved him for having the consideration to stop now. For wanting to make sure she knew what she was doing.

She nodded.

Picking her up as if she were a doll, he placed her on to unsteady feet.

She followed him up the large curved staircase and decided that even if this was for one night only, she would be happy. Even one night with Patrick Kelly was better than none at all.

175

Inside the bedroom she stared around her in awe at the sheer scale and opulence of the room.

Patrick was slowly taking off his clothes and Kate felt scared for a moment. She was not a young girl any more. She was forty years old.

Patrick walked to her and pulled her red wool dress over her head, exposing her tiny naked breasts that had never really needed a brassiere, and her lower body, encased in black tights. As she pulled her head free she looked at his face fearfully.

He smiled.

'You're lovely, Kate. Really lovely.'

And she believed that she was, then.

He pulled her to the bed. Finally naked, they gazed at one another in the muted light from the lamps placed either side of the bed.

In all her years with Dan she had never had this abandoned feeling. Had never felt the exquisite excitement that she felt at this moment. Had never experienced a hunger the like of which was eating at her now.

In the back of her mind she knew that the situation should never have got this far. The man was a villain. Patrick Kelly was a bad one, a robber, a violent repoman. 'The Snatchman' was his nickname. But at this moment Kate could not have cared less if he was a mass murderer.

She wanted him.

She had him.

She kissed him.

She would worry later. Much later.

Patrick Kelly kissed her back, then caressed her breasts, biting the nipples gently, pulling them up with his lips, until they were like tiny pyramids in his mouth. The wetness of his tongue as it slipped over them made Kate arch her back with delight.

Kelly was an experienced lover and Kate was glad. It had been so long for her she was like a dam waiting to burst. She felt his hand move gently down her body, caressing her thighs, then she felt the heat and the moistness as he slipped a

176

finger inside her. She groaned. She could feel Patrick's erection digging into the side of her leg, his excitement making her more breathless by the second. He played with her tiny button, running his thumb over it lightly, until she tried to pull his hand away. Her whole body was trembling. She opened her legs wider, feeling her juices trickling out on to his fingers. Then he was moving down her body, his dark head moving slowly away from her and as he moved he kissed her skin, the little biting kisses that she was beginning to love so much.

When his mouth engulfed her sex she held in a long breath. She was going to come. She felt the waves begin to wash over her, and as each wave began, Patrick licked and sucked her, gently pushing a finger inside her simultaneously. Kate had never experienced such ecstasy in her life.

When, finally, the tremors stopped, she looked down the bed at his smiling shiny face.

'Oh, Patrick . . .'

She watched him climb from the bed and put on his dressing gown. His member was still swollen and purple.

'Where are you going?' Kate's voice was husky and bewildered.

'There's only one thing to do after an experience like that.'

'What's that?'

'That is to go down to my wine cellar and get a bottle of nice cold vintage champagne. After a couple of glasses I think you'll be ready for round two.'

He kissed her on the mouth and she tasted herself on his lips. As he walked from the room she hugged herself. Already, she wanted him to hurry back.

Patrick walked down the stairs in a daze. She was so juicy. He had never experienced anything like it before. It was as if he had opened her up in some way. It had taken all his willpower not to plunge himself inside her there and then.

But instinctively he knew that she needed gentle loving, the hard, penetrating loving would come later. Tonight she needed a long soft loving, and he was the man to give it to her.

He could not believe his luck. Who'd have thought she'd

be so sexy? He got the champagne and two glasses and went back up the stairs. He smiled to himself as he realised he was practically running. It was a long time since he had been like this.

Too long.

Louise Butler was sobbing hard. In fact she was getting on George's nerves.

'Shut up!' His voice cut into her, sending shivers through her body.

'I . . . I want to go . . . go . . . home. Please.' She drew the last word out on a whine.

George gritted his teeth. The mask was hot again. His white cotton gloves stood out like beacons on the steering wheel. He glanced at her. She had drawn her lips back over her teeth while she cried, rocking herself backwards and forwards in the seat. Long strands of snot were hanging from her nose.

George shuddered.

Trust a woman to make a mountain out of a molehill! Anyone would think he was going to murder her. He was completely oblivious of the Swiss army knife clutched hotly in his hand, which caught the moonlight as he steered the car and drew Louise's eyes like a magnet.

He was the Grantley Ripper. He was the man everyone was talking about. He was going to kill her. She knew that as surely as she knew she would never get to the rave in Woodham Woods.

She cried harder, feeling a wave of sickness wash over her.

George drove to a large quarry near Woodham. He parked the car by the side of the deserted road and dragged Louise out of the passenger seat. The ground was hard beneath her feet and she stumbled, falling heavily on to the frosty ground. George dragged her upright by her hair.

'You are annoying me, young lady.'

He pulled her through a hole in the fencing. In the distance Louise could hear the music from the rave and every now and then a shrill cry broke the night. She was crying desperately, all the fight had left her body. She could only wait and see what was going to happen.

George pulled her towards a large hole that was blacker than the night around it. Giving her a final shove, he pushed her inside. Louise cried out as she felt her body tumbling down into the blackness. She felt her legs being pushed up over her head and heard the crack as her ankle hit a lump of granite. Her tracksuit and flying jacket dragged on the ground as she slid and bumped down into the blackness. She lay at the bottom, winded and in pain. She heard the man in the mask sliding down slowly and knew she should try and make a run for it but her ankle was already swelling inside her Reebok. Her hands and face were skinned from the descent, the gravel sticking to the skin and stinging.

She lay there in the pitch black. She had a pain in her chest that was not due to the fall, it was fear. Pure, naked fear.

George scrambled down to her. The mask was hot and he loved it. Loved the feel of it and the smell of it. He also loved the fear that was emanating from this girl. Thumbing lifts! My God, asking for trouble, just asking for it. Well, she had got it now, by Christ. She had well and truly got it now.

George felt the rage roar in his head. A red hot rage that made his hands tremble. Pulling a torch from his pocket he played the beam across her prostrate form. He frowned. She was unconscious. He sighed heavily, then taking back his heavily booted foot he kicked her in the chest, sending her skidding across the gravel. Still she did not move.

George sighed again. The mask was making his head itch.

Still she did not move.

George knelt on the gravel, and taking the knife more firmly in his hand he stabbed her in the stomach. As the knife entered her she seemed to try to double up, but it was only a reflex action. George was puzzled. He pulled the heavy leather of her flying jacket from her arm and tried to find a pulse. There was none. She was dead. George was fuming. How dare she die on him? How dare she just die like that! He pushed the knife into her calf, through the thin material of her shellsuit and the soft plump skin, hitting the bone.

George sat on his haunches, biting his lip inside the mask. He pulled it off and felt the cold air bite into his hot skin, his scanty hair standing up and waving gently in the breeze. George spat into the dirt and pulled the knife out of the girl's leg, then he began to undress her.

He carefully pulled down the bottom of her tracksuit and cut off her panties. He opened the flying jacket and folded it then unzipped the tracksuit top. He was surprised to find that she was very big-breasted. He cut the white lycra bra so that her breasts sprang free.

He had placed the torch on a small mound of dirt and the light shone on to Louise Butler's cold and lifeless skin.

George cheered up. He glanced at his watch. He had hours before he had to get home. He began to hum.

In the distance the rave had really got underway. The music was blaring and the partygoers were dancing. It was New Year's Eve. Everyone was waiting for twelve o'clock, for 1990 to begin.

Everyone except Louise Butler.

'Happy New Year, Kate.' Patrick's voice was soft.

'Happy New Year, Patrick. I hope it's a good one for you, I really do.'

He smiled sadly. 'Well, I've got to be honest, girl, I ain't looking forward to it.'

Kate felt a great sadness for the man lying beside her. While they had made love she knew that, for a short time anyway, he had forgotten the events of the previous week. It had crossed her mind that he was using her, but wasn't she using him? He was only the second man she had ever slept with. In forty years, she had had two men. In this day and age it was laughable! Only she wasn't laughing.

Kate had surprised herself with the intensity of her response. She had never known any other man but Dan, but after tonight she was more than aware of what she had been missing all these years. Dan made love like he did everything else: with only himself in mind. Patrick Kelly, whom Dan would look on as an ill-educated lout, had actually spent time on her enjoyment. Oh, and she had enjoyed it! More than she had ever thought possible. The earth-shattering orgasms that she had read about were not a con, they were there just waiting for her to experience them. She snuggled into Patrick's hard body, enjoying the feel of him.

'I bet this would go down like a lead balloon if it was known in Grantley police station. The DI knocking off a local villain!' His voice was jocular and Kate found herself laughing with him.

'Knocking off? Thank you very much, Mr Kelly!'

Patrick held her tightly.

'That's just a figure of speech. You're a good woman, Kate.'

She put her face to his and kissed him. Let the outside world hang. At this moment all she was interested in was him. She would worry about the rights and wrongs of the situation in the morning. As she felt his hands travel across her body, she closed her eyes and with them her mind.

'Oh, Happy New Year!'

Elaine had been kissed until her lips were sore and her lipstick just a faded memory. She had not enjoyed herself so much in all her married life. Normally when they were invited to a party George never wanted to go. Elaine had therefore always declined. Since her newfound freedom, however, she had decided that she would get as much out of life as she could. With or if possible without George. And tonight had been her watershed. She had been danced off her feet and had loved every second of it.

She looked around the crowded room for her best friend, Margaret Forrester, and smiled as she saw her sitting on her husband's lap. Elaine wished she could have a marriage like that. Where everything was just plain and simple, laughing and joking the norm. Her face fell as she thought about her life with George. Still, they were going to Florida and she was going to Spain, so at least this year she had something to look forward to. And this party looked as if it could go on for hours yet!

'Would you like to dance?' Elaine turned to face the man who had spoken. He was about fifty-five and fat, but jolly with it. She had already danced with him three times. Someone had put on a Roy Orbison album and she slipped into the man's arms to the strains of 'Crying'. She loved Roy Orbison, and she loved all the attention.

'I'm ever so sorry, but I've forgotten your name.'

The man grinned, showing pristine but ill-fitting dentures. 'It's Hector . . . Hector Henderson. And you're the lovely Elaine.'

She felt a tingle going down her spine that could have been romance or could just as well have been the drink. Whatever it was, she liked it.

George was pushed from her mind as they took to the tiny space allocated for dancing in Margaret Forrester's front room.

Joey Meeson watched as Lizzy danced, her body undulating to the thumping rhythm of the acid house music. About an hour earlier they had each dropped an Ecstasy tab. He could feel himself 'coming up' now. Everything around him had taken on a rosy hue and he felt excitement in his guts. Lizzy's hair was flying around her head as she danced faster and faster. Since he had been going with her he had been having a great time. No one would think her mother was an Old Bill. Lizzy wanted to try everything and she did it in style.

Joanie also watched her. Joanie was cold and fed up. She glanced at her watch and sighed. She was supposed to be sleeping at Lizzy's house tonight and Lizzy was supposed to be staying over at hers. That meant they had to stay out all night whether she liked it or not. Lately Lizzy was getting on her nerves. All she was interested in was getting out and getting laid.

A black boy with extensions on his hair walked over to her and asked her to dance. Joanie bucked up. Maybe tonight wouldn't be such a cop-out after all . . .

Lizzy went over to Joey and put her hand on his arm.

'Enjoying yourself, Liz?'

'Oh, it's great. Really great. Look at the lights!'

To Lizzy, with her heightened awareness, the lights were a swimming halo of blues and red.

'How about we go to my car for a while?'

Lizzy giggled. 'OK.'

She was so far gone that Joey had to help her walk across the field to where he had parked. As they made their way through the throng of people, boys and girls laughed and joked with them. One boy, dressed like a refugee from Woodstock, was spinning around in circles. His hair was braided with flowers and he smoked a large joint. Lizzy and Joey laughed at him. The further they got from the rave the more bodies they had to step over. Some were making out; others were just tripping out of their skulls, lost in their own world.

Joey opened the Sierra and they both got in the back. He kissed her hard, pushing his tongue down her throat.

'Happy New Year, Lizzy.'

She looked up, trying to focus on his brown eyes.

'Happy New Year, Joey.' He slipped his hand up her top and she giggled.

'One moment, please, I've got a New Year's present for you.'

'What's that?' Joey was smiling in the darkness.

Then he felt his trousers being undone and her dark head slipped down on to his lap.

'Oh, Lizzy. Happy New Year.'

She was wild all right, and he loved it.

George decided to bury the girl's body in the gravel. Let them look for this one. Let the police earn their bloody money for once. He covered her over and ran the torch around the dirt, checking that he had not left any incriminating clues. Then he walked backwards, scraping the gravel with the side of his boot. He was certainly not going to do their job for them. Oh, no.

He scrambled up the side of the quarry to his car. The heavy thump of acid house music was everywhere. George frowned as he put his mask neatly in the brown carrier bag before driving home.

The youngsters today were like animals. What sort of parents would allow their daughter out until this time of night? There was no decency in the world any more. The family was a thing of the past. In this self-righteous mood he drove home.

Well, he would make them all sit up and take notice. 1990 was going to be his year. He would make all the parents and husbands in Grantley frightened. Then they might take a bit more care instead of allowing young girls to roam the streets like common prostitutes!

A man had to be in charge. It was a man's duty. And George Markham had never shirked his duty.

He was back home, showered, changed and in bed by eleven forty-five. Elaine tripped in at four-thirty and George was well and truly asleep. She felt a moment's remorse as she looked down at his sleeping face. Then she thought of Hector and smiled. Hector Henderson. She said the name to herself a few times, enjoying the feeling it created. A good strong name. Hector Henderson. He had given her his phone number!

She giggled into her pillow, clenching her fists in excitement. She would ring him in the week.

Finally, Elaine slept.

Chapter Eleven

'How long has she been missing?'

'Since last night. Her mother's going out of her mind with worry, and I can't say I blame her, can you? They've tried all her friends. Her father had dropped her off at her best friend's house . . .'

Kate listened attentively to Amanda Dawkins.

'And she's never stayed out before? Has she got a boyfriend?'

'No to both questions, Kate. The girl seems to be the perfect daughter. Always rang if she was going to be late, always let them know exactly where she was. I get the impression from this friend, Samantha Jewson, that Louise was looked down on because of it. I think this Samantha fancies herself as a bit of a girl, know what I mean?'

'Well, we'll get the cars to keep an eye out for her, but I have an awful feeling in my gut that she is not coming home. Not alive, anyway.

'Listen, let the papers know about it, ask if any of the readers can remember seeing her. After she was at Samantha Jewson's house, she seems to have disappeared. Someone must have seen her. What's happening with the door-to-door? Anything suspicious in that department?'

'Not really, there are eighty uniforms on the job. Each has been allocated a certain number of streets, but like everything else it takes time. We had a couple of suspicious characters but their alibis are watertight. Oh, before I forget, we've received all the names of sex pests, perverts and fully fledged rapists. We're trying to locate each and every one of them. Most of the uniforms and CID from all over the county are offering to work in their spare time.'

'We could do with them as well. Right then, I think the best thing we can do now is try and calm Louise Butler's parents. If she was at a rave, how come we haven't had anything from the patrol cars about it?'

Amanda breathed out heavily.

'There were no patrol cars there.'

Kate looked aghast.

'You're joking! On the news this morning it said that over eight hundred kids turned up!'

'I know. There's more than one red face in the mobile division this morning, believe me. The old man was like a raving lunatic, apparently.'

'And can you blame him? Jesus wept! If we're not careful we'll have the heavy mob down here offering to hold our hands!'

'Well, I'd better get in to see Ratchette. Do me a favour would you? Find me a decent cup of coffee.'

Amanda nodded.

Kate made her way to the Superintendent's office, her mind whirling. No mobile units at a rave? It was bloody laughable. The barn where it was held was owned by a local farmer, John Ellis, and if Kate knew anything about it, he had known exactly what was going on. He would sell his own mother for a profit. She knocked on Ratchette's door.

'Hello, sir.'

'Ah, Kate. Bad business this. What do you think?'

'In all honesty, sir, I don't think Louise Butler's coming home. It's just a case of looking for the body really. Once we ascertain her movements, we'll know more. Someone somewhere must have seen her.'

'True. Now listen carefully. I've had the big boys on to me today. They're sending a Chief Inspector over to work with you. I must stress that it's to work *with* you, OK? He's a good man, you've probably heard of him. Caitlin.'

Kate groaned. Oh, please, not Kenneth Caitlin!

Ratchette saw her face and snapped at her: 'Look, Kate, whether you like it or not, the man's coming. You are a

Detective Inspector, I am a Superintendent. You take your orders from me and I take mine from the Chief Constable. Just try and work with him. Whatever his reputation, he gets results.'

Kate looked at the floor. Her heart had sunk down into her shoes.

'All right?' Ratchette's voice was still hard.

'Yes, sir.'

'Good. Now before he arrives, have you any thoughts on this that you want to talk to me about?'

'Actually, yes. In 1984 at Enderby in Leicester two young girls were raped and murdered. There was nothing to go on at all. The police took blood samples from just about every male in the vicinity. The only thing we've got here is the DNA of the murderer. I think, if nothing else, we should try and eliminate as many men as possible by DNA testing in the area.'

Ratchette's wrinkled face was incredulous.

'You're joking. Do you know how much that would cost?'

'A little over half a million pounds. I know it will be expensive, but for Christ's sake we're dealing with a maniac.'

'You realise that some men won't allow us to take their blood?'

'Then they will immediately be under suspicion.'

Ratchette shook his head.

'I don't know, Kate. This is something I shall have to discuss with the Chief Constable. It's already going out on this month's Crimewatch. Hopefully someone will have their memory jogged. The man isn't invisible, he must have been seen.'

'Well, up till now, sir, he's done a pretty good job of eluding us.'

'Leave it with me. Caitlin will be here in about an hour. Make him welcome, won't you?'

The fact that the Superintendent could not look her in the eye was not lost on Kate.

'Of course, sir. Now if there's nothing else?'

When he didn't answer, she rose from her seat and walked

from the room, giving the door a satisfying slam as she closed it. Bloody Caitlin! Bloody hell!

Elaine had a hangover and the shrill ringing of the telephone made her head ache even more. She heard George pick it up.

They did not get many phone calls and any other time she would have rushed out into the hall to see who it was. Today though she just wanted to curl up and die. Her mouth felt as dry as a bone and her eyes were closed against the intrusive light. She wished George would hurry up with her cup of tea.

'Hello?' His voice was quiet. Who could be ringing them? The only people to phone were Joseph and Lily, and now and again a friend of Elaine's from work.

'Hello? Mr Markham?' The voice was rough and coarse.

'Speaking.' George was bewildered.

'This is Anthony Jones from Sexplosion in Soho. You asked me to give you a ring like.'

George felt his heart begin to beat a tattoo against his ribs. He dropped his voice.

'I said I would ring you. How did you get my number?'

He heard the man laugh.

'You paid by Barclaycard, remember? I got your address from your driving licence – you gave it as further proof of your identity. I got your number from inquiries like. Listen, mate, I wouldn't drop you in it. If your wife had answered I would have given her a load of old cods. Said I was selling double glazing or something. So calm down, for Gawd's sake.'

'What do you want?'

'What do you think? I've got some new films in and they are *hot*.'

Despite his fear, George felt a tiny shiver of excitement.

'These are from Thailand, and you know what those chinky birds are like, don't ya?' The man chuckled and the action caused him to start coughing. George held the phone away from his ear as the man's phlegmy voice carried on: 'This new film makes the last one I sold you look like Noddy and Big Ears in Toytown!'

'How much?'

'Three hundred smackers.'

The man was aware that George was a bit too quiet at the other end of the phone and hurried on, 'But to you, two-fifty, being as how you're a regular customer like.'

'Well . . .'

'They won't last long, mate, these type never do.'

George was in a quandary. He wanted the film desperately, but he had already had to hide one Barclaycard statement. He racked his brains.

'Look, mate, if it's too much . . .' The other man's voice was placating and wistful. Suddenly George was frightened that the man would think him mean.

'I'll take it!'

'When can you get in?'

'First thing tomorrow.'

'See you then.'

The phone went dead. George replaced the receiver and went back to the kitchen. He reboiled the kettle for Elaine's tea.

The phone call had frightened him. George felt exposed. He poured the water into the teapot. He would get the film. He would draw the money out of the bank this time. Elaine might notice it was gone but then again she might not. He would cross that bridge when he came to it. Chinese women . . . He liked Chinese women. They knew their place all right.

'GEORGE!' He winced as Elaine's voice drilled through him.

'Who was that on the phone?'

George poured out her tea and took it in to her.

'Just a friend from work. Peter Renshaw. He wished you all the best, dear.'

Elaine took the tea.

'Oh. Do I know him then?'

'I don't think so, dear. But I often chat about you to him. Would you like a biscuit with your tea?'

'I'd love one, but with my diet and that . . .' She grinned at him, a girlish look on her face.

189

George grinned back. If she was waiting for him to say that she didn't need to diet she had a long wait.

Elaine felt the grin slip from her face. Her head was still pounding. She sipped her tea.

Imagine old George getting a phone call from a friend. Wonders would never cease.

Patrick Kelly was in his main offices in Barking. Normally on New Year's Day he would be at home with Mandy. Mrs Manners would cook a large early dinner and they would sit and chat about the coming year. Now all he had to look forward to was burying her. And in a funny sort of way he *was* looking forward to that. At least then he would know that she was not lying on ice in a bloody mortuary. He lit himself a cigarette with his gold lighter. He grasped it tightly in his hand. On the front of it was the inscription: *To Dad, Love Mandy – xxxx* It was all he had of her now.

A sharp knock at the door brought him back to earth.

'Come in.'

Two large men entered. They were brothers, Marcus and David Tully. There was only ten months between them and they looked like twins. Both had skinhead haircuts and both wore identical grey tracksuits that hugged their large beer bellies. Both wore large chunky gold jewellery. Marcus, the elder, was the first to speak.

'So where to, guv?'

'I want you two to make your way up North, to Huddersfield. There's a brand new Jag and a few bits of plant up there that need to be repossessed as quickly as possible. Take shooters with you, I think you'll need them. The bloke don't want to give them back, that's how come we got involved. There's good bunce for you both as soon as the stuff's delivered back here. OK?'

The two men nodded.

'You'll need to take a couple of drivers with you. Take young Sonny and Declan, they're pretty good, and that new bloke . . . What's his name? Dodson. Here's the address, and I'll see you sometime tomorrow with the stuff.'

'What's the plant then?'

'Two large earthmovers. The details are outside on the duty rosta. Select numbering, the works. The Jag has got private plates on it.'

'Okey doke, guv. See yer tomorrer then.'

'Try not to use the guns this time. Just frighten the bloke.'

'We'll only use them to wound, guv. We know what we're doing.'

'Be careful, that's all I ask. Now get on your way.'

The two men left the office. Patrick shook his head. They were two of the biggest lunatics he had ever met, and he had met a few in his time. Still, they got the difficult jobs done and that was the main thing.

He pressed the button on his intercom.

'Bring me in a cuppa, Debbie, will you?'

'All right, Mr Kelly.'

He carried on working until Debbie brought him in a cup of tea. She smiled at him, placing the cup on his desk in such a way that he got a glimpse of a fairly considerable pair of breasts.

'Thanks, love.'

'Anything else?' It was a loaded question and Kelly knew it.

No, thank you.' He smiled at her crestfallen countenance. Before he had met Kate Burrows, she had been on his list of 'things to do'. He had put her down as Tiffany's successor. Now he just wished she would leave him alone.

'Off you go then, Debbie.'

She stamped from the room. Physically she had a lot more to offer than Kate, but for some unknown reason he really fancied the policewoman. There was something about her. When he was with her, buried inside her, Mandy, Renée and everything else was gone from his mind.

For that he was supremely thankful.

Kate heard Caitlin before she saw him. Since the news had spread about him working on the case, the whole of the station had been in a state of excitement. She groaned inwardly. He was like something from a *Boy's Own* comic. A real macho man. She stayed seated until the excitement wore off. Caitlin's loud Irish accent boomed over everyone's heads.

'Sure Jesus, would you let a man get some air here!'

Everyone was greeting him. He was a living legend. Poor old Fabian and Spilsbury weren't even in the running where Caitlin was concerned. He made Sherlock Holmes look amateurish! Kate saw his bulky form moving towards her desk. She had worked with him once before, when she had been a Detective Sergeant. After she had been introduced to him he had sent her to get him a cup of coffee, but not before patting her behind. He had solved the case with a male DS and a DC. Or that was how it had looked on the final report. Kate fixed a smile on her face.

'Katie! How are you?' His voice sounded genuinely pleased to see her. She stood up and held out her hand.

'Chief Inspector Caitlin.'

He looked old. Kate was shocked. The man looked positively ancient. His head was nearly bald, his full mouth had that loose-lipped look peculiar to ageing men, and his startling green eyes were now watery-looking. The lids were wrinkled above them like old venetian blinds.

'You don't look a day older than the last time I worked with you.' The Irish burr was more pronounced than she remembered. 'I've been hearing great things about you, great things.'

Kate smiled.

Caitlin pulled up a chair and sat down opposite her.

'As we'll be working together, I thought we could share a desk. Make it more personal.'

Kate felt the smile freeze on her face. The smell of Teacher's and cheap cigars wafted across the confined space and she cringed inwardly.

Caitlin settled himself in the chair.

'Now what's this I hear about this madman driving an Irish Ford?'

Kate's heavy brows knitted together.

'I'm sorry? An Irish Ford?'

'An O'Ryan . . . Orion.'

Kate burst out laughing, causing many pairs of eyes to focus on her. Caitlin laughed with her. He leant across the desk in a confidential manner, scanning the room shrewdly. He tapped his nose.

'You can call me Kenny.' He nodded at her and Kate realised with growing dismay that the man was drunk. She forced the smile back on to her face.

'Whatever you say. Now shall I fill you in on all that I have?'

Caitlin leaned back in his chair. Opening his coat, he took out his handkerchief and blew his nose loudly.

'You do that, Katie. The sooner this bastard's caught the better.'

Well, they agreed on that much anyway. Taking a deep breath, Kate started to talk.

Chapter Twelve

2 January

George had left for work at his usual time of eight fifteen. By ten thirty-five he was walking into Sexplosion. Anthony Jones was behind the counter and George smiled at him tremulously. The shopkeeper gave a large toothy grin.

'Hello, cocker! Happy New Year.' He was full of good-humoured camaraderie.

'Happy New Year. Er, I have the necessary.'

'Good, good.' Tony Jones lifted the serving hatch and invited George through to the back of the shop. He looked around him hesitantly before walking through. There were quite a few customers even this early in the morning. Tony Jones shouted to a dark-haired boy of about eighteen.

'Emmanuel, watch the shop, I've got some business to attend to.' In the back of the shop he whispered to George: 'He's as queer as a nine-bob note, but he's a good little worker. Right then, look at this!'

He rubbed his hands together in anticipation and pressed the play button on a video that stood on a small table. On the television screen above it a young Chinese girl appeared. Her face was a mask of fear.

'Sit yourself down, mate, I'll make us a cuppa.' George sat down and watched the flickering images in front of him. In the dirty little office, he felt the first stirrings of excitement.

An hour later he left with the film tucked firmly under his arm, and a phone number and address in his pocket. He got into his car and began to drive aimlessly around London. It was a dark overcast day; the people milling around all looked grey. Grey and dirty.

George found himself in Paddington and smiled. He rooted around in his coat pocket until he found the address that Tony Jones had given him. He parked his car off Warwick Avenue and, locking it up, began his search. He walked along the Harrow Road until he found the small turning he wanted. He walked into Chippenham Road, scanning the house numbers. When he arrived at the right house he checked the number carefully against his piece of paper. He walked to the front door and looked at the array of bells there.

All the bells had little cards above them.

Flat one: Suzie, French model.

Flat two: Sexy Sadie, full correction.

Flat three: Imogen, Swedish masseuse.

Flat four: Carol, schoolgirl temptress.

Flat five: Beatrice, for naughty boys.

He wanted flat six: Sure enough there it was.

Flat six: Tippy – submission my speciality.

George rang the bell.

'Yeah, what?' George was startled. Hardly a submissive voice! He cleared his throat noisily.

'Er . . . Tony sent me. Tony Jones.'

Suddenly the voice changed.

'Oh, I'm so sorry, sir. You caught me offguard there.' George heard a throaty laugh. 'Bit early for me, love, but come up anyway.'

There was a whirring noise and the door clicked. George opened it cautiously. His cheesecutter hat and Burberry overcoat gave him the look of a working class spiv. His hard little grey eyes were moist with anticipation. He had drawn out three hundred pounds earlier. Two hundred and fifty had gone on the video that was now tucked away securely in his car. He still had fifty left. He'd decided to treat himself. If all that Tony Jones said was true, this Tippy was just what he needed.

He wrinkled his nose in distaste at the acrid smell of the place. The narrow hallway was littered with old newspapers and circulars. It was dark and dingy. George pressed the lightswitch on the wall by the stairs and a muted light came from above. He began to mount the uncarpeted stairs. The wallpaper was long gone from the walls, and here and there in places were rust-coloured stains that looked like blood. He began to hurry.

Inside her room, Tippy, real name Bertha Knott, was hurrying around trying to tidy up. The night before had been a hectic one with seven punters. One after the other. It was always the same in the holiday season. She picked up her discarded clothes and threw them into a small bureau, scratched and marked by years of neglect. She practically threw the overflowing ashtray and empty vodka bottle into the tiny kitchenette, the cigarette butts flying across the worksurface and into the sink. Bollocks! Sod that bloody Tony Jones! Imagine sending her a punter at this time of day. No brass worth her salt was even up before twelve-thirty!

She heard the timid knock on her door and sighed. She hoped this bloke wasn't too rough. She was sore as it was. She pulled the grubby negligee around her bony body and opened the door, a wide professional smile on her face.

George looked at the woman, dismayed. She was absolutely horrible. She had dyed black hair that looked like cotton wool dipped in liquid boot polish, her face was thin and feral-looking, and through the flimsy see-through negligee George could see that under her arms was enough hair to make a pair of identical wigs.

'Come in then, cocker.' Her voice was jovial. 'Would you like a cuppa or a drink?' George walked into the room. He watched the woman's scrawny buttocks disappear behind a curtain and looked around him, heartsore. The room was filthy, the large double bed taking up most of the space. It had black sheets on it, and George was not sure if that was their original colour or just the result of years of use. The cord carpet on the floor was covered in cigarette burns. Around the iron fireplace there were hundreds of them. Obviously the men who had used this room over the years had tried to flick their cigarettes into the hearth from the bed, and the majority had missed. One large overstuffed chair stood under the window covered in items of apparel: stockings, suspenders and other types of underwear.

Tippy came back with two relatively clean glasses full of vodka and tonic. George took his for want of something else to do. Tippy placed hers on the old bureau. Picking up the underwear from the chair, she dumped it on the floor.

'You have a sit down, luv, and I'll go and get myself ready. Sorry about the mess but you caught me on the hop like. I'll only be ten minutes. She disappeared through a door that George had not noticed before and called over her shoulder, 'Take your coat off and get comfy.'

He stood with the drink in his hand, deciding whether or not to make a run for it. Elaine's houseproud ways got on his nerves but he would rather them than this dirty cat's way of living. He walked to the chair and looked through the grubby net curtain. The street below was busy. George watched the people rushing about their business and just for a second he wondered what he was doing here. It was a disappointment. George did not class his pastimes as dirty in any sense. He had never thought that prostitutes and squalor went hand in hand. He had always imagined them as they were depicted in the media – beautiful young girls who loved their job and lived like queens. Reality was different and George did not like reality.

He had just turned from the window, intent on leaving, when the woman walked back into the room. She looked completely different! She saw George's mouth drop open and smiled. She had her hair in two pigtails. Her eyes were made up with heavy black eyeliner, her mouth was a deep red rosebud. She had discarded the dirty wrapper she had been wearing and had on long silky black stockings and suspenders, a black peephole bra and crutchless panties. An overpowering smell of Freesia perfume hung around her like a cloud. She grinned at George.

'Now this is more like it, isn't it?' Her voice had taken on a husky, girlish tone and he was gratified. All his earlier thoughts flew from his head. She looked like the women of his younger days who had adorned the packs of nude playing cards. Who had gazed up at him from his adolescent girlie mags. In short, she looked like a whore.

Her high-heeled shoes showed off her long thin legs to advantage. Her breasts were tiny and pert, the pink aureoles just hardening in the cold air of the room.

'You haven't taken off your coat. Shall Tippy take it off for you?' She slipped it from his shoulders, folding it up and placing it carefully on the chair. George faced her, his eyes shining once more.

Tippy pouted.

'Tippy wants her money first. Twenty quid for the works, anal sex is an extra tenner.'

George nodded, and handed over the notes.

'Good. Well, I'm ready when you are, lover boy.'

She watched George pulling off his clothes and grinned again. They were all the same. Stupid buggers. She gritted her teeth. Oh, please, let him be a quick finisher. She wasn't in the mood for a long day's screwing.

She lay down on the dirty bed. Even through her perfume she could still detect the sour smell of the sheets. As George loomed over her, she was planning in her mind when to take the sheets to the launderette, and whether or not to pay for a service wash. She hoped he noticed the Durex she had strategically placed in the top of one of her stockings. He looked greener than the proverbial grass to her. Maybe she should have told him fifty quid. He looked as if he could afford it.

Well, she consoled herself, his type normally came back, and she liked that. If she got another regular customer it would keep her off the streets for a bit. King's Cross was not what it had been in her day. What with the runaways and the young druggies . . .

Tippy felt George bite her nipple painfully and suppressed a cry.

Another bloody nasty bastard. She sighed heavily. Here I go again. She pulled herself up on the bed and, kneeling in such a way that George could see her breasts to their best advantage, took his phallus into her mouth.

After a couple of minutes an idea occurred to her. She lifted her head and looked into the man's face.

'For another tenner, you can tie me up if you like.'

She got off the bed and, opening the bureau, took out a set of handcuffs and some leather-look rope.

George nodded and Tippy brought them to the bed and handed them to him.

As George tied her up she thought: Oh, well, in for a penny.

Even Tippy was amazed when she heard George actually humming while he worked. Finally, with the prostitute spreadeagled on the bed, her arms and legs stretched wide, he was happy.

This was submission. She would not fight him, she would just lie there and accept whatever he did.

Getting off the bed, he went to his coat. He took his white cotton gloves from the pocket and slipped them on. Tippy watched him, half bored already. But when she saw what he was taking out of the inside pocket of the overcoat, she felt faint with fright. It was a large knife in a leather holder. As he pulled it slowly free it caught the weak January sunshine and Tippy strained against the bonds that held her.

''Ere, what you doing with that?'

George walked to the bed and smiled. 'Don't worry, I won't hurt you, my dear.'

Kneeling over her lower body, his belly hanging on to her knees, he began gently to cut off her panties.

Tippy was breathing heavily, her face white under the black eyeliner and heavy foundation.

Her mind was reeling. The bloke was a fucking nutter and she had let him tie her up!

'Look, you're not gonna hurt me, are you? Promise.'

'I promise. Now shut up!'

George's voice had taken on a harsh inflection. Tippy shut up.

Suddenly, the mild-mannered little man didn't look green

any more – he looked positively dangerous. Especially with that smile of his, that smile that just showed his teeth. Tippy closed her eyes tightly.

Just wait until she saw that Tony Jones. The ponce! Sending her a candidate for Broadmoor. Tippy lay back and prepared herself for the worst afternoon of her life.

'So, sir, what do you think?'

Kenneth Caitlin lit himself a cigar, blowing the smoke out in huge puffs that swirled around his bald head.

'From what I can see, Katie, this man is either very careful or has been very lucky. Very lucky indeed. There's nothing at the scenes of the crimes. Nothing on the bodies, except of course as you pointed out his genetic fingerprint. There is absolutely nothing else to go on at all.' He grinned at her. 'This is just up my street, by Christ. I'll find the bastard though.' He poked his finger at her. 'You just watch.'

Kate's voice was sarcastic. 'So what do you suggest we do now?'

'Well, the uniforms are out in force looking for the Butler girl. I think she's dead though. This man has never hidden the bodies before, has he? So obviously if he's hidden this one, he's playing a whole new ball game. But I'll tell you something now, Katie. They all bugger themselves up in the end. Look at the Yorkshire Ripper.'

Kate was annoyed. Caitlin was getting on her nerves.

'The Yorkshire Ripper killed thirteen women, sir, and was finally caught during a routine inquiry. Otherwise there's no knowing just how many more he would have killed. What we have here is a chancer. The psychological profile is of a man who hates women, that much we already know. A man who has a job that could possibly have brought him into contact with the victims, though I don't think so myself. If the women knew him, there would be someone else who knows him as well in the same capacity. The psychologist also says he's likely to be married. That narrows the field down a bit, if it's correct. He also has a knowledge of the area so is obviously a local man. Other than the dark-coloured car seen

201

at the scene of the second murder, and a dark green car seen at the first, we have nothing whatsoever to go on.'

Caitlin watched her. Women were always so emotional. They took their cases personally.

'Well, I'm appearing on Crimewatch this week. Maybe something will come of that. Someone who's not from the area could have been driving through and seen something.'

'Yeah, and pigs might fly.' Kate's voice was bitter.

Caitlin took another puff on his cigar.

'Pigs can fly already, or so the druggies think when they see the police helicopters.'

Kate closed her eyes. The man thought everything was a big joke. She stood and picked up her jacket from the back of her chair.

'Where you off to?'

'I'm going to see how the search is going on.'

'Leave that to the uniforms, they'll let us know soon enough if they find something. It's bitter cold out.'

As Kate opened her mouth to answer, the phone on her desk rang. She picked it up.

'I'll be straight down.'

Caitlin heard the excitement in her voice.

'Who was that?'

'I think we may have a breakthrough. Come on.'

Geoffrey Winbush walked hesitantly into Grantley police station. The desk sergeant smiled at him.

'What can I do for you, son?'

'It's about the disappearance of Louise Butler. I think I may be able to help like. I think I saw her.'

The desk sergeant was all business now. Opening the security door, he led the boy through to an interview room.

'What's your name and address, son?'

'Geoffrey Winbush, 122 Tenerby Road.'

The sergeant wrote it all down.

'Well, sit yourself down. There'll be someone to see you in a minute.'

Leaving the boy sitting at the table, he went back to his

202

desk and phoned up to Kate. Sergeant Mathers hoped that the boy could shed some light on the case.

Kate walked into the interview room followed by Caitlin. Her first thought was that the witness was a good-looking boy. He was blond with deep-set brown eyes which looked troubled at this moment, and he was well dressed. He looked about twenty. His shoulders were wide and even though he was sitting, Kate saw he was a large boy. She smiled at him.

'I'm Detective Inspector Burrows and this is Chief Inspector Caitlin. I understand you have some information about Louise Butler?'

Kate sat opposite him and Caitlin leant against the wall of the room, his cigar smouldering in his mouth.

The boy looked at them nervously.

'Well, I didn't know her personally but the other night like, I think it was her that we seen on the Woodham Road.'

'We?' This from Caitlin.

The boy nodded.

'Yeah, me and me mates. We was going to the rave – me, me brother Ricky, and three others: Tommy Rigby, Dean Chalmers and Mick Thomas.'

He swallowed heavily and Kate felt sorry for him.

'Go on.'

'Well, as we was driving along, we saw this bird, walking by the roadside. She was on her own like. Anyway, I stopped and offered her a lift. But she wouldn't get in. I'm sure it was her though.'

'Why wouldn't she get in? Did she say she was waiting for someone? Did she mention what she was doing on that road on her own?'

'No, nothing. Mick Thomas was pissed out of his head. He slagged her off.' His voice broke. 'We all did. We left her there, on that road. We left her there to die. We drove on to the rave and left her walking, thumbing a lift.'

'Thumbing a lift? Was she definitely thumbing a lift?'

The boy nodded.

Caitlin's voice made him jump as he bellowed across the room: 'You left a young girl to walk along a dark road at night? You slagged her off, as you put it, and left her there? Have you any sisters, young man?'

'Yes, sir, two.'

Caitlin had the cigar clamped between his teeth. He removed it before saying venomously, 'Well, I hope if they're ever in Louise Butler's position, they're treated better than you treated that girl. Now then, names and addresses of the other boys. Pronto. I can't be bothered to waste me breath on yer.'

Kate closed her eyes. Caitlin was right, of course. The boys should never have left her there. But by the same token, the girl should have had more sense than to walk along a road like that in the dark. But that bloody Caitlin, he had to throw his weight around. He had to make himself heard.

And the worst of it all was, Kate was the one who had to listen to the old sod!

She smiled at the white-faced boy.

'Shall I get us some coffee and then you can make your statement?'

'Please.' He began to cry. 'We never thought that she'd be murdered. We'd had a drink . . .'

'So you were drunk-driving on top of everything else? And how the thunder do you know she was murdered? We have no body that I know of.'

The boy looked at Kate beseechingly. She got up from her seat and manhandled Caitlin from the room. Outside she whispered, 'Don't you think he feels bad enough without you on his back?'

Caitlin shrugged his shoulders and buttoned up his wrinkled suit jacket. He blew cigar smoke in her face.

'No, actually, Katie . . . I don't. I think he's an arsehole.'

With that, he went back inside the interview room and she clenched her fists.

If he called her Katie once more she would be getting arrested herself. For grievous bodily harm.

She went to organise the coffee.

Kate pulled into her drive. She was tired. Winbush hadn't

really been any help. Caitlin had put the fear of Christ up him and, consequently, he had been loath to say too much. Kate had arranged to go to his house and see him herself. The trouble with Caitlin was he still behaved as if it was the old days, when everyone wanted to help out the police. He should come back down to earth with everyone else. Since the West Midlands business and now all this about false evidence everywhere you looked, the police popularity poll was down to minus two.

She let herself into her house. The smell of meat assailed her nostrils and she followed the smell into the kitchen. Her mother was turning lamb chops under the grill.

'Hello, Kate, get yourself seated and I'll make you a coffee.'

Dan got up from the breakfast bar. 'I'll do it, Eve, would you like one?'

Evelyn shook her head.

'Oh, by the way, Katie, you had a call. Said his name was Pat and could you call him back.'

Kate felt her heart freeze in her chest. She could feel Dan's eyes boring into her face.

'Thanks, Mum.' She lit a cigarette for something to do. Patrick calling here. She felt herself go hot all over.

'So who's this Pat then?' Kate detected a hint of jealousy in Dan's voice.

'None of your business, Dan, actually.' He stared at her and Kate dropped her eyes. 'He's a friend of mine if you must know.'

'I see. Where did you meet him then?'

Evelyn watched the two of them with a little smile on her face. Dan's questions were annoying Kate and if he wasn't careful he just might end up on the receiving end of her tongue. She placed the chops under the grill once more and the only sound in the kitchen was the lamb fat spitting.

'I said, where did you meet him?' Dan's voice rose.

Kate put down her coffee cup and looked at her ex-husband.

'What the bloody hell has that got to do with you?'

'It's got a lot to do with me. My daughter . . .'

'Oh of course, your daughter. Well it's a pity you didn't think of your daughter when you were whoring your way around the world, isn't it? The poor little mare wasn't even in the running then was she? WAS SHE?'

Dan stared at Kate in bewilderment. He realised that he'd opened up a can of worms.

'All I'm saying is, Kate . . .'

'You know your trouble, Dan? You don't know when you're well off. I don't like to remind you of this, but if it wasn't for me, you'd be in a bedsit somewhere now, living off the DHSS. I allow you to stay in my home because of Lizzy, but I warn you now, Dan, if you try and interfere in my life, I'll have you out the front door so fast you'll burn a hole in the carpet. Do I make myself clear?'

Dan's face was scarlet and for a fleeting second Kate felt ashamed of herself.

'Perfectly.'

He went from the kitchen quietly.

Kate let her breath out and put her head in her hands.

'He asked for that, Katie. Don't you go feeling bad now.'

'Oh Mum. I shouldn't have said it. I shouldn't have said any of it. But he annoys me so much.'

'Let me get you another coffee. Who is this Pat, by the way, or am I going to get my head bitten off as well?'

'He's a man I met during the course of my work.'

'Is that the one you spent the New Year with?'

Kate looked at her mother sharply and seeing the mischievous look on her face she grinned.

'It is actually.'

Evelyn held out her arms wide. 'You're a grown woman, Kate, you do whatever you want. Personally I think it's about time you had a bit of life.'

Kate smiled. She felt it was about time too, but Patrick Kelly was dangerous for her. For her career. He was a danger to everything, but knowing that, admitting it to herself did no good. She wanted him desperately. He gave her so much pleasure when she was with him and she had been lonely for so long. So very, very long. After the New Year, she could no more give him up now than she could cut off her own hands.

She had only been mad at Dan, because he had brought up Patrick's name when she wanted him to be a secret.

But it wouldn't be a secret for long.

She lit another cigarette. What would she do when the secret was out?

She would cross that bridge when she came to it. Everything people said about Kelly was supposition, nothing against him had ever been proved and in this country you were innocent until proven guilty. The thought had a hollow ring to it.

Kate felt she was tumbling headlong into something that she was not strong enough to fight.

But fight it she would.

If the time came.

Chapter Thirteen

Sexplosion was just getting busy when Tony Jones saw Tippy walk through the door. He smiled at her.

'Bloody hell, girl, you don't half look rough.'

Tippy's face was drawn and white.

'I want to talk to you Tony, *now*!'

He was puzzled. 'All right, girl, come through to my office.'

He looked around the shop for Emmanuel, who was trying to pick up an elderly man in a smart business suit.

'Emmanuel, get behind this bloody counter now! Come through, Tippy love.' He opened the serving hatch and she limped through.

In the dingy back room, the tom sat down on the ramshackle chair. Tony watched her warily. There was something wrong here. He hoped she didn't have AIDS or something. She did look ill, and Tippy looked rough at the best of times. All the birds who worked the submission trade did.

'Got any booze, Tone?'

He opened a small cupboard in an old sideboard and took out of a bottle of Gordon's gin.

'I ain't got nothing to go with it. Will you drink it straight?'

Tippy nodded. 'I'd drink of a cup of cold piss at this moment in time, Tony, if it blotted out the world. I've never felt so bad in all my life.'

Tony poured her out a generous measure into a half pint glass. 'Here you are, girl, get your laughing gear around that.'

Tippy took a long drink. Tony noticed that her hands were

shaking. He bit his bottom lip in consternation.

'Look, I ain't being funny, love, but I ain't got all day.'

She looked at him with hooded eyes.

'That punter you sent me yesterday . . . he was weird, Tone, really weird.'

Tony relaxed. Was that all?

'They're all weird, girl . . .'

She interrupted him.

'No, not normal weird. He was a nutter, Tony. A bloody nutter.'

Tony pictured mild-mannered George. He liked a bit of old bluey, and admittedly they were a bit near the mark, but that aside he seemed a nice, quiet, polite man.

'You're just feeling low, Tippy. All brasses feel like that at holiday times . . .'

She laughed scornfully.

'Listen, Tone, I've been on the game for eighteen years, woman and girl, and I've had some strange ones in my time, but never anyone like this. Look . . .'

She stood up and lifted her skirt. She heard Tony's intake of breath.

'Stone me, Tip, he done that?'

She nodded, big tears welling in her eyes. 'They're all over me. On me tits, arse, the lot.'

Tony stared at the criss-cross cuts all over Tippy's thighs. Some were superficial and some looked deep. All were scabbed over. Purple and black bruises abounded.

'I've been pissing blood all night, Tony. He shoved something up inside me.' Her voice broke. 'He tied me up and he had a knife. He kept holding it at me throat and threatening me . . .'

She began to cry in earnest and Tony, for the first time in his life, felt emotion for a working girl. He took her in his arms and cuddled her.

'All right, Tippy. Calm down, love.'

'How am I gonna work while I'm like this, Tone? I'll be out of action for weeks. And supposing he comes back? He knows where I live, he knows I won't go to the Old Bill.' Her face was grimy with tears and Tony set her gently on the chair.

'Listen, Tippy, I'll give you enough to tide you over. And I'll have a talk with the bloke, all right? Make sure he leaves you alone in future. OK?'

'Promise.'

'I promise. Now how about I take you to a doctor I know in Swiss Cottage. Payment on the nose and no questions asked. How's that?'

Tippy nodded, wiping her streaming face with her hands.

'I'll just go and tell Emmanuel to mind the shop and we'll be on our way.'

Tony Jones walked from the room. Who would have thought it? A polite little bloke like that with a tiger in his tank? Tony shook his head in wonderment. He'd have to sort George out in a delicate way. He didn't want to lose a regular customer. He'd just warn him off Tippy by saying she'd got herself a big coon for a boyfriend. There was nothing like a big coon or a dose of clap to get rid of a punter.

He shook his head again. Poor old Tippy. She'd be scarred for life.

Terry Miller picked up the *Grantley Times*. He had just made himself a cup of coffee and sat in his mum's kitchen smoking a cigarette. There were six Miller children, ranging in age from nineteen to seven. Terry was eighteen and his brother Charlie nineteen. To sit in relative peace and quiet in the Miller house was a very rare occurrence and Terry was enjoying it. That was until he saw what was on the front page.

It was a picture of Louise Butler and Terry recognised her at once as the girl who had run out in front of his car on the night of the rave. The girl who was being chased by the bloke in the weird headgear. He had had to swerve to avoid them. He read the article and frowned. They believed she had been murdered by the Grantley Ripper although as yet no body had turned up. He ran his hands through his hair. Should he go to the police?

If he went to them he would have to admit that he left her there. That he was high as a kite on Ecstasy and had thought they were larking about!

He screwed up the paper and threw it on the kitchen table.

He knew what he would do. He would talk it over with Charlie when he got in from work.

Terry relaxed a bit now that he had made a decision. Charlie would know what to do. He always did.

The search for Louise Butler had been going on for over two days. Police had covered every piece of waste ground, undergrowth, field, wood. Even the quarry.

Nothing.

Kate Burrows and Kenneth Caitlin were getting worried. If something didn't break, and soon, they would be back to square one. Frogmen had dragged the local river. Every shed and garage and outbuilding had been searched. Louise Butler had disappeared off the face of the earth.

Every sex pest and rapist had been interviewed and their whereabouts checked out.

Still nothing.

The Grantley Ripper looked set for a long reign of terror.

Kate sat in her office staring at the files in front of her. She rubbed her eyes with her finger and thumb of her right hand. She was bone tired. Caitlin was off at the BBC studios, he was appearing on Crimewatch later in the evening. He had walked in and taken over and the marvel man had come up with nothing. Kate looked around her at the busy incident room.

Phones were ringing, computer screens were displaying information, and still there was nothing to go on. She thought again of the Leicester murders. If they could get even some of the men in Grantley to take the blood test they would be halfway home. Because if only three thousand of the potential five thousand male suspects took the test, that was three thousand they could eliminate. There was also the chance that the man himself would go for the test. If they sent haematologists around local firms and offices then men would be honour bound to take the blood test when they saw their colleagues taking it. A subtle form of coercion.

But no one in authority would even countenance the idea. Money. It all came down to bloody money.

Kate chewed on her bottom lip. There must be something she had missed.

Even Geoffrey Winbush's statement only told them that Louise had been on the Woodham Road. Surely someone else must have seen her? She was a good-looking girl, dressed in a purple and gold track suit and man's flying jacket. She would not be easy to miss. Eight hundred youngsters had been at that rave. Someone must have noticed her.

Kate stared back at the files in front of her.

The people who owned dark-coloured Orions were still being interviewed. Nothing yet. There were only a few names left on the list from the DVLC. Maybe the man had lived in Grantley at one time and now lived somewhere else? That idea had occurred to her before now, but a gut feeling told her that he was still living locally. And if he was, the best way to catch him was through blood testing. Back to square one.

Her phone rang and she picked it up.

'Hello. DI Kate Burrows here.'

'Hello, Kate.'

She felt her heart miss a beat. It was Patrick Kelly. 'Are we still on for tonight?'

'Oh, yes, of course. I can't promise what time I'll be there, I'll have to ring you as I'm leaving work. We're pretty snowed under . . .'

'Nothing yet then?' His voice was flat.

'No, nothing concrete.'

'I'll see you later then. 'Bye.'

''Bye.' Kate replaced the receiver and smiled. She was getting to like Patrick Kelly. Getting to like him a lot. Yet the sensible part of her was telling her to grow up. She was a policewoman and he was a . . .

213

He was a what?

He was a nice man, that's what he was, and when she left this station her life was her own!

She picked up the file and began to read again. She was being paid to find this murderer, and find him she would!

Charlie Miller came in from work at six-fifteen. The house was, as usual, in pandemonium by then. All the children were in, and their Irish ancestry made loud arguing the norm. Like most children from big families, they had learnt to outshout one another at an early age. Charlie went straight up to the room that he shared with Terry and put on a Fine Young Cannibals tape. He was in the middle of getting undressed as his brother walked in with the paper.

'All right, Tel?'

He shook his head and sat on the bottom of the bunk beds.

'No, actually, I ain't.'

Charlie frowned and stopped in the middle of taking off his shirt. Terry did look bad. He sat beside him.

'What's the matter, bruv? You got aggravation?' His voice was low. Even though there was only a year between the two boys, Charlie looked on Terry as his little brother.

'It's about that bird who went missing . . . Louise Butler. Look.'

He opened the paper and Charlie glanced at it. Terry watched his brother's face.

'It's that bird from the other night! The one with the weird bloke in the mask!'

Terry nodded.

'I reckon we should go to the police. Tell them we saw her.'

Charlie shook his head vigorously.

'Not on your bleeding nelly, mate. I ain't going nowhere near them. And neither are you!'

'But, Charlie . . .'

He pulled off his shirt and threw it into the corner of the tiny room.

'No buts, Tel . . . Leave it!'

Terry knew by the sound of his brother's voice that he had

214

to do as he was told. Charlie didn't like people disagreeing with him.

Terry ground his teeth in consternation. The girl was missing. She could still be alive.

Charlie looked at his brother and sighed. Terry was such a soft touch. He pulled off his work jeans and threw them on to the little pile in the corner. He hunkered down and looked into his brother's face.

'Listen, Tel, I'm sorry about that bird and all. It's that Ripper bloke they're all going on about. But for all that, I ain't putting my . . . or your . . . face in the frame. Get it?'

Terry nodded.

'Good. Now don't let me hear any more about it. Besides, we was out of our nuts. What the hell could we tell them that would do any good?'

With that, Charlie picked up his deodorant and shampoo and went to have his bath, leaving Terry sitting on the bed, his mind in a turmoil. Fine Young Cannibals were singing, 'Jonny, we love you, won't you please come home' and the words made Terry feel like crying. He wished Louise Butler would come back home and be safe, then he could stop thinking about her.

Turning off the tape, he lay on the bottom bunk and crossed his arms under his head.

They had nearly run her over. If the Grantley Ripper had got her, as the papers seemed to think, he wished now that they had. At least her end would have been short and quick.

Elaine and George were sitting in their lounge watching South East at Six when the story of Louise Butler's disappearance came on the air. As her photograph appeared on the screen, Elaine shook her head.

'Oh, George, isn't it terrible?'

Louise was in her school uniform and looked very young. Quite unlike the girl of the previous Saturday.

'Yes, dear. That's all they've talked about at work, you know.'

'Same with us. Her mother uses my supermarket. How must she be feeling? It must be like a nightmare. This is the third one, isn't it? I was reading in the *Sun* today that the other girl, what's her name, her father is a London gangster!'

'Mandy Kelly.'

'That's it, Mandy Kelly. Imagine you remembering her name like that.'

George felt a tightening around his heart. It was fear.

'Oh, it stuck in my mind, that's all.'

Was Elaine looking at him oddly?

'Would you like a nice cuppa, dear?'

Before she could answer there was a loud banging on the front door.

'Goodness me, who on earth can that be?' Elaine's voice was high. People knocking at the door was a very unusual event in this household. She stood up quickly to answer it.

George remained seated. He was still trying to recover from his earlier slip. He looked even more surprised when Elaine walked into the lounge with two men.

'George, this is Detective Sergeant Willis and PC Hemmings. They want to have a word with you.' Elaine's voice was quavering.

'Can I make you two gentlemen a cup of tea or coffee?'

Willis smiled. 'Tea would be lovely, madam.'

George sat in his seat, stunned.

They knew it was him! They had come for him!

'Please sit down. Would you like fresh tea, George?'

He could feel his head moving up and down of its own accord. He was aware of Elaine leaving the room. His eyes were glued to the two men now sitting on his couch. He could feel his breathing quicken and strove desperately to control it.

'I'm sorry to trouble you, sir, but we are questioning everyone in Grantley with a dark blue saloon car. It's just so we can eliminate people from our inquiries.'

Eliminate. Eliminate. Eliminate. They didn't know. They *didn't* know. George smiled.

Outside the lounge door Elaine relaxed as well. Walking to the kitchen, she filled the electric kettle, her heart hammering in her chest.

George would never do anything like that. What had made her think that he would? She was too hard on him.

It was just the shock of seeing two policemen on her doorstep. It was like the other time. The terrible time. Then a thought occurred to her. Would they bring that up now? All these years later?

She set about making a pot of tea.

George would never do anything like that again. Never. Not in a million years.

In the lounge, Willis and Hemmings were listening to George's account of where he had been on the nights of the murders and the disappearance.

'I was in bed with terrible 'flu'. My wife can vouch for that, officers. May I ask you a question?'

'Certainly.'

'If one of you is a police constable, surely he should be in uniform?'

Willis smiled.

'On these kind of cases, sir, we try to be as informal as possible. We recruit uniformed officers into plain clothes so that people like yourself, who are being eliminated, won't feel under pressure. From neighbours etcetera.'

'How very thoughtful of you.'

Elaine came into the room with the tea. Her big-boned body felt clumsy and she placed the tray on the coffee table with a loud clatter.

Willis watched her surreptitiously. She was a bundle of nerves. She began to pour the tea and when she had finally finished and sat down felt as if she had run the London Marathon. She tried to calm herself.

Willis spoke directly to her.

'Now, madam, on the second of December, 1989, which was a Saturday, I understand that your husband was home with you all evening?'

Elaine nodded.

217

'He very rarely goes out in the evenings.'

'I see. Now on the twenty-third of December, which was a Saturday, he was home with you then, as well?'

'Yes.'

'And on New Year's Eve, you were home together?'

'Yes. No. Actually, he was in bed with very bad 'flu'. I went to a party at my friend's alone. George was much too ill to leave the house.'

Elaine was aware that she was babbling.

Willis and Hemmings were both staring at her. Even her red hair seemed to be trembling.

Willis smiled and closed his notebook.

'That will be all. I am very sorry to bother you, but I'm sure you understand.'

'Of course.' George was more his old self now. He could feel a giggle in his throat, just waiting to explode. They were fools. Utter fools. He swallowed hard. The giggle was nearly at the roof of his mouth.

'Would you gentlemen like another cup of tea?'

Hemmings was about to say yes when Willis declined. George smiled at the younger man. Hemmings smiled back. Elaine watched them. Was it her imagination or was George laughing at them all? More and more lately she had the feeling that George was different somehow. Now all this. Eliminating him from their inquiries.

'Have you found the other girl yet? The one who's missing?'

'Louise Butler? No, not yet. We're hoping against hope that she's gone off with a friend or a boyfriend and will get in touch with her parents. But every day that goes by makes it less likely.'

George tutted. 'How terrible. This man, whoever he is, must be very clever. I mean, three women murdered and no clues. That's if the other young lady has been murdered, of course.'

'He'll make a mistake, sir. They always do.'

'Quite.' George smiled. They always did, did they? Well, not this one, Mr Clever Clogs policeman. Not this one.

'He must be some kind of animal.' Elaine's voice was low and throaty. 'Those poor girls. No woman's safe any more.'

Hemmings nodded at Elaine, thinking, Well, you are. Any man who'd try and attack you would have to be mad!

Willis stood up and held out his hand to George who shook it warmly.

'Thanks for all your help, sir.'

'You're welcome. Any time.'

Hemmings nodded and Elaine pulled herself from her chair and saw them to the door.

'Thanks for the tea, madam.'

'That's OK. Goodbye.'

She closed the front door and leant against it, her heart beating fast once more. What was wrong with her? Why did she feel so worried?

George walked out into the hall.

'All right, dear? You look dreadful.'

'I'm fine, George. But it was like before. You know . . .' Her voice trailed off.

He put his arm around her.

'Now then, Elaine, there's nothing to worry about. It was all a terrible misunderstanding. Anyway that was a long time ago and I paid my debt to society.'

He led her back into the lounge and steered her to her chair. 'Now you stop worrying, my love. Just because I have a dark blue saloon car . . . well, does that make me a murderer?'

She shook her head.

'Of course not, George. I'm sorry.'

'There now, you're chasing ghosts again, Elaine. It's always been there between us, hasn't it?'

George's voice was soft.

She couldn't look at him in the face. After twenty years this was the first time George had ever referred to what had happened. And he was right, it had always been between them. Because it had always been in the back of her mind, from the moment she got up in the morning until she went to

219

bed at night. Even then, sometimes, it strayed into her dreams.

'I'm sorry, Elaine. Really I am. I wish with all my heart that I could go back and change that time, but I can't, I just can't.'

George watched Elaine's guilty expression and felt the laughter threatening again.

'I know that, George. It was just seeing them, standing on the doorstep like that.'

'I know, my love, I understand. I know that you've never forgiven me for what happened, and I don't blame you, darling. I appreciate the way you stood by me. Really I do.' He took her plump hand in his and repressed a shudder. 'I love you, Elaine, I always have.'

She wiped her eyes with the back of her hand, knowing in her heart that it was an excuse to curtail the physical contact with him.

'I'm just an old silly, George. I'll make another cuppa.'

George moved so she could get out of the chair. He watched the material of her shell suit strain to the limit as she bent over the coffee table and picked up the tray of cups and saucers. She must have gone off her diet over Christmas.

When she left the room he sat back in his seat and grinned. They were all bloody fools! Every last one of them. And he was cleverer than a bag of monkeys, as his mother used to say, and would outwit them all. Starting with that fat bitch out in the kitchen.

Elaine was making the tea. She felt an urge to smash the teapot against the wall. The night of Mandy Kelly's murder George had been out on one of his walks. She pushed the thought from her mind. The other night she'd been in with him. On New Year's Eve he had been ill. Very ill. She was just paranoid, that's what was wrong with her. She wished the time would go faster until her holiday in Spain so she could go away, leave George and just enjoy herself. She poured the water over the tea bags and felt the tears again.

For all George's faults he was not a murderer. He was not a killer.

She had to believe that.

She had to.

Roll on Friday. She was seeing Hector Henderson, and more and more as the days went on found that she needed him, his simplicity and his jolliness. Most of all his kindness.

Willis and Hemmings discussed George and Elaine on their way to the next address.

'He seemed OK, but that woman! She was a bundle of nerves.'

Willis shrugged.

'We affect some people like that. Make them nervous. People like her never have the Old Bill round, see. When they do, it throws them like. He was a nice bloke though. Very polite and well spoken.'

Hemmings nodded.

'I wish a few more people were like them. Afford us a bit of respect now and again. I went round a house the other week – the kid had been caught shoplifting and the father wanted to fight me. Like it was all my fault.'

Willis grinned.

'I know what you mean. Everyone's on our case these days.'

'Don't I blinking know it!'

Evelyn and Dan sat at the breakfast bar. Evelyn lit herself a cigarette.

'I think you should find yourself somewhere, Dan. After all you've been here over a fortnight. Kate's a kind woman but I think there's a chance you just might wear out that welcome of yours.' She sipped her coffee and watched him over the rim of the cup.

'Has she said anything? I mean, about me going?'

Evelyn took a deep breath. 'Let's just say I think she's had enough.'

Dan picked up her pack of cigarettes and lit himself one. Evelyn snatched the packet from his hand and put it in the pocket of her apron.

'Surely things aren't that bad? You've got the money for your own cigarettes, haven't you?'

Dan raised his eyebrows and tried to decide whether or not to confide in her. Anthea had always paid the bills. They had lived a life of pleasure. Dan had not had a proper job for over ten years. Oh, he talked about deals and the market, but it was all for effect.

Dan realised with growing dismay that at forty-six he was qualified for nothing. It was a frightening prospect.

'Listen to me, Dan, I'm only trying to help you. Kate can't abide wasters, you know that as well as I do. You were an insurance salesman once, why can't you go back to that? They must be crying out for men like you. Good-looking eejits who could charm the birds off the trees.'

Dan, for once, had the grace to look away. How could he explain to the old woman sitting opposite him that he wore a five thousand pound watch? His suits were the best that money, Anthea's money, could buy. That he had not had to think about paying a bill or buying food for God knows how long. How could he explain that Kate was his last chance? Because Kate, for all her faults real and imagined, was the only person ever to take him at face value.

He glanced at his Rolex and closed his eyes. Then, taking a deep breath, he began to talk, the words tumbling out of him as he finally admitted the truth.

'Look, Eve, I'm the wrong side of forty. I don't know if I could even get a job as a junior salesman. What would I be looking at? Ten grand a year? Fifteen top whack. That wouldn't even pay for my clothes . . .'

The self-pitying tone of his voice was not lost on Evelyn and she snapped at him.

'If you could hear yourself! Like a big ninny sitting there bemoaning your fate. If you'd let your heart rule your head instead of your winkle, you wouldn't be in this state!'

Dan stared at her in shock.

'Oh, I've seen plenty like you in me life, Danny Burrows, only the majority of them were women. What you've got to do now is get yourself together. Get a life, as Lizzy is always

222

saying. Take your jewellery and pawn it, get yourself a place to live, and then get yourself a job. It's what everyone has to do at some time – it's called taking responsibility for yourself.

'Do you know, all those years I watched my Kate yearn for you, it used to amaze me. How could such an intelligent and articulate woman want a bloody waster like you? You're no good to man or beast. By Christ, Dan, how you've lasted as long as you have amazes me on its own!'

The atmosphere in the tiny kitchen was charged. Dan felt an urge to take back his fist and slam it into the old woman's teeth. But he knew he wouldn't, because he was too much of a coward. Anthea knew it, which was why she did what she did to him. She told him what to wear and eat, when to sleep or make love to her. In short, she had called the shots and Dan had let her. In all the years he had not had one really happy day because Anthea was always the boss. What she said went. They travelled extensively, but he had to pander to her every whim. If she decided that they had had enough of sightseeing or whatever, then they had had enough. The woman sitting in front of him was right, he had to take responsibility for himself. Because there was no Anthea to do it for him now.

'I know what you're saying is right, Eve, but I'm not sure I'm man enough to do what you suggest.'

She slipped the cigarettes from her pocket and gave him one. 'Listen, Dan, Kate's sick of seeing you on that settee. Get yourself somewhere to live and gain her respect again. Get a job, sort out your life. If you really want her back, that's the only way to get her.'

'What about the man she's been seeing?'

'What man?' Evelyn sounded puzzled.

'Oh, come on, Eve. There's a man in the pipeline or my name's not Danny Burrows.'

'Well, if there is it's the first one I ever knew of.'

God forgive me for lying, she thought. She knew as sure as eggs was eggs that Kate, bless her, had finally caught herself a man. A mysterious man, she admitted, because she couldn't

223

get anything out of her daughter about him, but a man all the same.

'You get yourself fixed with somewhere to live and then start your campaign to get Kate. Life has a funny way of sorting itself out. I've learnt that much over the years.'

He smiled at her. A genuine smile. Danny had never liked Kate's mother because he had always known she didn't like him. That she could see through him as if he was glass.

'Thanks, Eve. It's meant a lot to me to have us talk like this.'

Evelyn grasped his hand and smiled.

'I'm only trying to help you, son.'

She had the grace to look down at her wedding ring, a worn gold band. She couldn't look him in the face any more. All she really wanted was to see him out of the house.

For all their chatting about him and Kate and Mystery Man, he had not mentioned his daughter once.

That was typical of bloody Danny Burrows.

Lizzy pushed her fingers through her long hair and yawned. Joey lay beside her smiling. Both were naked. Lizzy looked around the room and blinked.

'This place is a right dump.'

Joey laughed out loud. 'Of course it is, it's a squat.'

The walls were daubed with splashes of paint, and here and there large eyes were drawn, with daggers sticking out of them.

'Who did the decorating, Joey?'

'Oh, some bloke called Nipper. He fancies himself as a gutter poet and artist.'

'Well, my advice to him would be, don't give up the day job.'

The sour smell of the sheets was wafting up to her nose and she grimaced. 'Why don't you skin up?'

'All right then.'

Joey sat cross-legged on the bed and proceeded to build a joint. Lizzy watched him languidly. She liked Joey a lot. He was exciting. He knew all the places to go and all the people to know. She had bunked off work all this week, Joanie had rung in and said she had 'flu', and every day had been spent like this. Lazing around in someone's flat or car, just getting right out of it. Her mother was becoming suspicious at the amount of time she spent in her room, but Lizzie had told her everyone liked to be on their own at times.

Her mother was a pain in the ass. Always wanting to know where she was and what she was doing. Who she was with and what they had done. Her gran wasn't much better. Lizzy's butter-wouldn't-melt-in-her-mouth image had kept her in good stead the last few years, but soon she wanted to break away. Go her own way and enjoy life. If her father got himself a place she'd go and live with him.

She was like him in a lot of ways. He liked the good life, lived to enjoy himself. Her mother lived life in a vacuum. Waiting for things to happen instead of making them happen. That was the secret.

Joey lit the joint and drew on it deeply, passing it to Lizzy. She took the smoke down deep into her lungs and held it there for a while before letting it out slowly.

'That's the way to do it.' She sounded like Mr Punch and Joey grinned at her.

He had never met anyone like her before. Lizzy Burrows was game for anything and everything. He watched her sit up and flick the ash on to the floor. She was not in the least self-conscious of her body. He grabbed a breast and squeezed it. His rough hand had dirt under the nails. Lizzy pushed it away. All she wanted now was to get really stoned and lie back on the mattress thinking good thoughts. She did this all the time at home, listening to Sinead O'Connor or Pink Floyd.

She passed the joint back to Joey and lay back. He took a toke on it and, putting his mouth over hers, breathed the smoke down into her lungs. She laughed and kissed him back. From one of the other rooms came the harsh sounds of Guns'N'Roses, the heavy guitar making the walls vibrate.

'Oh, shit! Stud's back already. Come on, let's get dressed and shoot off.'

Lizzy pulled the dirty sheet over her breasts and laughed. 'Why?'

'Because Stud's like an accident waiting to happen, that's why.'

'Oh, fuck off, Joey! I'm just nicely stoned. I don't want to move yet.'

Joey sighed and scratched his greasy head.

'Look, how about we go and score a bit of Wiz or something?'

'All right, but only if we can come back here. Deal?'

'You've got a deal. Now get dressed before all the bikers come in here.' Joey was genuinely worried. The bikers were a good crowd but could get a bit out of hand. He didn't fancy Lizzy's chances much if they decided they all wanted a bit of the action. It wouldn't be the first time.

Lizzy pulled on her underwear and jeans. As she was pulling her tee-shirt over her head the door opened.

A large man with a long ginger beard and straggly blond hair stood there. He had a beer belly that hung over the top of his filthy jeans. His sweat shirt had a death's head printed on it.

'Hello, Joey, who's this?' The voice was deep and had a drawl to it that Lizzy didn't like.

'This is Lizzy . . . Lizzy Burrows. Lizzy, JoJo Downey. He runs the squat.'

Lizzy picked up Joey's fear from his voice.

'Hello.' Her voice was small.

JoJo frowned at them both through little squinting eyes, then his face broke out into a toothless smile and he grinned at them. This was more frightening than his frown.

'Come and have a drink with us, you two.' The music was once more blaring out and Lizzy slipped on her boots and followed Joey and JoJo from the room. In the lounge she saw about fifteen people, mostly men. Two girls sat with them. Both had dyed black hair and wore the female biker battledress, the uniform black leather miniskirt, black lycra top and short bumfreezer denim jacket. They had on the heavy black mascara and purple lipstick of female bikers. Both smiled at Lizzy and she smiled back. It was easier now that she was dressed.

'Sit down, love, and have a drink.' JoJo motioned to the girls on the brokendown couch to move over, and they hastily made way for Lizzy. She sat between them. Joey sat on the floor with the others. His joint was taken from his hand by a man in his forties with a studded leather jacket flung across his lap.

It was when Lizzy was sipping her cider that she realised what the man with the leather jacket was doing. He was burning something in a small crucible, watching it bubble. Then, placing it gently on the jacket, he took a syringe from off the floor and began to draw the liquid up into it. He caught Lizzy's eye as she watched and winked at her.

The music was turned down at the request of a fat man who was actually trying to sleep through all the noise. Lizzy saw that Joey was once more skinning up and quailed inside. All she wanted to do was get out of here. Get out and never come back.

But Joey was relaxed again. The two girls either side of Lizzy were both chatting together about their children. As they spoke a little girl of about two stumbled into the room. Her nappy was so wet it was falling down her legs. The girl on the right of Lizzy held out her arms and the child tottered towards her. The heavily sodden nappy slipped down her legs and she just stepped out of it, much to the amusement of the assembled people. The stench of urine was added to the other rancid smells of the room. Lizzy looked over the child's head to where the man on the floor was jacking up. The needle slipped into his blue-veined arm and he closed his eyes while he felt the first rush. He opened his eyes and looked straight at her.

'Wanna go?'

Lizzy shook her head.

'Well, stop fucking staring at me then!'

She bit her lip and the man laughed.

The joint that Joey had rolled was passed to her and she

drew on it gratefully. The girl beside her took it and puffed over the child's head.

Joey smiled at Lizzy and she relaxed. The cannabis was working at last. Someone got up and put on a Pink Floyd album. 'Great Gig in the Sky' filled the room, the woman's haunting voice soothing Lizzy. This was better, this was music she knew, and somehow the room didn't feel so menacing. The man on the floor who had jacked up grinned at her and she found herself grinning back. Then JoJo offered her a tab of LSD. She took the proffered tiny scrap of blotting paper and wiped it on to her tongue. Joey did the same. An hour later she was floating somewhere between reality and the fifth dimension. She was having a great time. Somehow more children seemed to have arrived from the bedrooms in the flat. The music, although still loud, was not blaring and someone had even made sandwiches, which were being passed around along with a cider and vodka mixture. Joey was now lying tripping out of his head on the floor.

Then there was a loud knocking on the door.

One of the girls got up to answer it and two well-dressed women came into the room.

JoJo stood up and took them out to the kitchen. Joey watched from his vantage point on the floor as they did the deal. Three thousand tabs of Ecstasy were handed over for a thick wad of notes.

Joey relaxed, happy in the knowledge that for the next few weeks at least, the place wouldn't run dry of drugs. It was just as the two women were leaving that the pandemonium started. Police seemed to be crawling everywhere.

Lizzy was so far gone by this time that she just smiled at them as they took her out to the meat wagon.

Kate and Caitlin were both going over 'suspect' evidence. This involved taking apart any statements made by known offenders and seeing if they could pinpoint a flaw somewhere along the line. As yet they had got precisely nowhere.

Caitlin yawned loudly.

'There's nothing here, Katie, you know that and I know

that. This man, whoever he is, isn't your normal nutter. He's one of the new breed.'

Kate smiled despite herself. 'New breed?'

'Sure isn't that what I just said? I've noticed over the years that the violent attacks are changing subtly. If you go back to the 'fifties and 'sixties, there were a few killers around like this one. But their attacks, bad as they were – well, they weren't as violent as now. Look at this man we have here. He batters the girls to death. Now most rapists get off on their domination of the woman. The struggling, the fear, the knowledge that they are committing the worst violation a woman can experience. This chappie here, though, he seems to want them still. As still as death, in fact. It's almost if he wants the ultimate submission. As if the woman's acquiescing, if you like. Giving him permission.'

Kate stared at Caitlin's ruddy face and nodded. 'I think I understand you. But even knowing that, we're still as far from finding him as we are from the Holy Grail.' Her voice was flat.

'Oh, we'll find him, don't you fret. It's just when. That's the bastard of it all. When. He'll make a mistake. They always do.'

The phone on their desk rang and Kate picked it up. Caitlin watched her face register astonishment.

'I'll be right there.'

'What is it, Katie? Another one?' Caitlin's voice held disbelief.

'Oh, no, it's not another murder. But it could bloody well end up as one.'

Picking up her bag she rushed from the incident room, leaving him staring after her.

Chapter Fourteen

Kate slammed into her house, banging the front door behind her. Dan and Evelyn heard her stamping up the stairs and both followed her. They found her in Lizzy's bedroom, systematically tearing the room apart.

'What the hell's going on here, Kate?' Dan's voice was incredulous.

She was pulling underwear from a drawer and searching every piece as she picked it up.

'Lizzy is at this moment in Grantley police station on a charge of possession of cannabis.' Her voice was thick with fury.

'What!' Evelyn held her hand to her heart. 'Are you sure?'

'Oh, I'm sure all right. I know what my own daughter looks like.'

She pulled the drawer from its hole and examined the underneath. There, taped to the bottom, was a small plastic bag of amphetamines. Kate ripped it off and shoved it in the pocket of her jacket.

'Look, Kate, relax for a second and tell us what happened. There must be some mistake.'

'There's no mistake, Dan. I thought that as well, until I saw her. I was called from the incident room by the desk sergeant who recognised her. She was in a squat in Tillingdon Place. Yes, Tillingdon Place, the biggest dump in Grantley, and she was tripping out of her head.'

'No.' Evelyn felt sick inside.

'Yes, Mum. Now will you two just get out? I must find out what she's got, what's going on. I got the duty doctor to give her a blood test, for my eyes only. I could break her bloody neck!'

'Listen, Kate, maybe someone took her there and gave her the drugs . . .'

'Oh, don't you think I thought of that? Well, don't you?' She rounded on Dan. 'I went into the cell and she told me to fuck off out of it. Those were her exact words. She was shouting and swearing at everyone. I have never been so humiliated in all my life. Miss Goody Two Shoes hasn't been to work for a week apparently. I went round to Joanie's and she told me everything. Lizzy wasn't at Joanie's on New Year's Eve, she was at that bloody rave! She's nothing but a lying, scheming little bitch!'

She burst into tears. Evelyn went to her and put her arm around her shoulders.

'I'll make us all a cup of coffee, shall I? Dry your eyes, Katie, crying won't solve anything.'

'I did everything I possibly could for that girl. We treated her well, tried to bring her up decently. Why has she done this to us? To herself? It's as if I never knew her.'

Evelyn kissed the top of her head.

'Sure there's plenty of people must have said the same thing after a visit from you, love. You bring your children up, you do your best, but in the end they go their own way.'

'I could cheerfully kill her, Mum, for this. From what I can gather from Joanie, she's been taking drugs since her last year at school. No wonder she didn't want to stay on and make something of herself.' Kate clenched her fists. 'If she was here now I'd tear her apart. What a foolish, foolish girl!'

Dan walked from the room, his head reeling.

Lizzy on drugs? His Lizzy? He sat at the top of the stairs as the news sank in. A little while later Kate's sobs had subsided and Evelyn pushed past him to make her daughter a coffee. Inside the bedroom Kate began once more to search the room. She had just found Lizzy's birth control pills when Dan came back in.

'Look, Dan, she's on the pill. Another first for Madam Lizzy. When she gets home I'm going to slaughter her.'

'It's because of you, Kate. You were never there for her. You should have dedicated yourself to bringing up your child . . .'

Dan's trite speech was what she needed to bring herself down from her temper. She turned to face him. Her voice was deadly calm as she spoke.

'You *dare* to tell me what I should have done, Danny Burrows? You dare to tell me about my child?' She poked herself in the chest. 'Yes, my child. Never yours, Dan. You were never here for her. My mother and I brought her up and she brought herself this low. Where that girl is concerned I have nothing on my conscience. Nothing.'

But Kate knew that no matter how many times she told herself that, she would always blame herself. Always.

She began to pull all her daughter's clothes from the wardrobe, searching the pockets as she went.

'Look at you, you'd think you were at a suspect's house instead of your daughter's bedroom. You haven't even tried to hear her side of it.' Dan's voice was disgusted. He turned and walked from the room.

Kate followed him on to the landing and shouted: 'You're another one. You can take your stuff and get out. I've had enough of freeloaders. She's like you, Dan, that's the trouble. She looks like an angel and she's a slut . . .'

She heard him slam the front room door and went back into the bedroom. The Paddington Bear wallpaper that had been on the walls for years was mocking her. On a shelf over the bed were Lizzy's dolls from childhood. Picking up the Tiny Tears she grasped it to herself, cuddling the cold plastic head to her face.

Oh, Lizzy, Lizzy, when did it all start to go wrong? How could she not have noticed what was going on under her nose? What had come over her child?

She licked the salty tears from her lips and, taking a tissue from the box by the bed, blew her nose loudly.

Placing the doll on her lap she pulled the legs off. Kate knew everywhere there was to look for drugs. It was her job, after all.

Patrick answered the door himself and smiled in delight as he saw Kate on his doorstep.

'Hello, love. Come in.'

She stepped into the hallway.

As Patrick walked her through to the lounge he frowned. She did not look like a happy woman. When she was seated on the sofa with a glass of brandy, he spoke.

'What's up, Kate? You look terrible. Is it something about the case?'

She sipped the brandy. 'No. Nothing to do with that.'

Then it all tumbled out. Patrick sat beside her, unsure if what he was hearing was true. When she had finished, he sighed heavily.

'Sounds to me like your daughter needs a good kick up the arse, if you'll pardon the expression.'

'I'm sorry to bring my troubles here but I really didn't know where else to go.'

Patrick grasped her hand. 'Listen, Kate, if ever you need me, I'll be there. All right?' He meant it. Seeing her like this made her more human somehow. It was gratifying to know that she could feel the same as him. That she had the same troubles, worries and hopes that he had. It made her more a person and less a policewoman.

Kate ran her hands through her long hair and sniffed. 'It was just the way she acted when I went in the cell. You know, as if I was the enemy or something.'

'At the moment, Kate love, you are the enemy. She probably feels ashamed of herself.'

'I know what you're saying, but she was drugged out of her head, Patrick. She was nicked in a filthy squat with a load of known druggies. The boy who took her there was called Joey something or other. He already has a record as long as my arm and he's only eighteen. I tried to kid myself that someone took her and dragged her there, you know the scenario. But after talking to her best friend, I realise that my daughter is nothing but a little slut.'

234

Patrick slapped her knee sharply. 'Hey, hey, you listen to me now, Katie, that's your child you're talking about. I wouldn't care if my Mandy was flashing her clout on the Old Kent Road if it meant having her back! You're being too hard on her. She's sixteen. Christ Almighty, didn't you ever do anything wrong at sixteen?

'Kids today have too many choices in front of them. Drugs are part and parcel of their everyday life. That's why they go to these raves. In our youth, the 'sixties and early 'seventies, we had the same thing, only we were the generation who were going to change the world. Remember Sergeant Pepper and all the other drug music? What you've got to do now is try and build some bridges with her. Try and get her back on an even keel.'

Kate stared up into his face. What he was saying made sense in some respects but she would never, ever forgive Lizzy for the charade of the last eighteen months. She had thought her daughter was pure and good, and she had been gratified by that. Seeing the lowest of the low on a daily basis made you glad your child was normal. Was safe. Was secure. To find out that she was a drug user was like finding out your twin was a murderer. It was unbelievable. To see that child lying in a cell out of her head on drugs was like having a knife twisted somewhere in your bowels.

Kelly watched the changing expressions on her face and guessed what she was thinking.

'I feel I've failed Lizzy, Pat. Failed her dreadfully. I put my work before everything. I could have got a nine to five job but I never wanted one. I wanted to be a policewoman. I suppose you, of all people find that hard to believe.'

Patrick shrugged. 'Look Katie, your job is your business, I admit that until I met you I didn't have a lot of time for the police. But that's history. I am a hundred per cent legal these days.'

'All the same though, Pat, what I'm doing with you is not really any different to what Lizzy did with the drugs. We both want something we shouldn't really have.'

Patrick stared into Kate's eyes, his expression soft.

'Drugs destroy people, Kate. I don't. I resent you implying that. I've never intentionally hurt a woman in my life. If you feel that you are in any way compromising yourself with me, then I think we should both say our goodbyes now, before it becomes even harder.'

Kate returned his gaze. He was offering her an out and she respected him for that. While another part of her, the female part of her, resented the way he was willing just to end what they had.

'I'll miss you though, Kate, you've kept me together body and soul since I lost Mandy. I've come to rely on you very much. I'd even go so far as to say I'm falling in love. But what you said has a ring of truth. All I can say in my defence is that I have nothing now in my life that I would need to hide from you.'

'What about the future?'

He smiled. 'Who knows what the future has in store for us?

Kate looked away from him and concentrated on the ormolu clock on the mantelpiece, its ticking the only other sound in the room. She bit her lip. So much had happened in the last few months. Her life would never be the same again. Her relationship with Lizzy was over. It would be different now between them. Lizzy would need a firm hand after this. All the trust was gone. The one person whom Kate had always seen as constant and good had been shown up in a dark light. It scared her. How could you not know that about your child? On the other hand, the man she had been wary of seeing, who had a bad reputation, who in her right mind she should never have got involved with, had turned out to be a good man underneath. A good and kind man, whose reputation was only believed by the people who didn't really know him.

'I don't want to finish with you, Kate.'

His voice was soft and low.

'I don't want to stop seeing you either, Pat.'

She wasn't sure she could stop now, even if she wanted to.

'When is she home?'

'Tomorrow, I could have taken her tonight, you know,

being a DI. But I didn't trust myself, Pat, I thought I might harm her if she was with me while I felt like this.'

'Why did you come to me?' It was a low whisper.

'Because I trust you, I suppose.'

He smiled and pulled her to her feet. 'Come on.'

'Where are we going?'

'I'm going to run you a nice bath, Katie, and I'm going to soap your body personally, every nook and cranny. Then I am going to lay you on my bed and stroke every care and worry from your mind. Then when madam gets home tomorrow, you'll be in a fit frame of mind to see her and get this sorted out once and for all.'

He pulled Kate to the bottom of the staircase and she dragged her hand from his.

'Oh Pat, what am I going to do? What with the case and everything, and now all this with Lizzy . . .' Her voice trailed off and Patrick took her hand once more.

'Just you bear in mind that you've got me now, Kate, and you'll have me for as long as you want me. I'm here for you whenever you need someone.'

It was said simply and sincerely and Kate followed him up the stairs gladly. For the first time in years she had someone she could rely on. It was a heady feeling.

'After the bath, we can have a good old chat. That's what you really need, you know. Someone who's not too close to the source of the problem.'

Kate followed him up the stairs. She had left Dan packing and her mother had retired to her bedroom. Kate had felt she could not stay in that house a moment longer. She had found cannabis as well as amphetamines in her daughter's room. What Patrick said made sense. She needed a real shoulder to cry on.

It was not until much later, after her bath and with Patrick snoring softly beside her, that she realised the implications of her visit to Patrick Kelly.

The irony of it all was not lost on her. But she leant up on her elbow and looked down into his face and knew the truth of it.

She was falling hopelessly in love with the man. And it felt good. Very, very good.

She pictured Lizzy as a small child. Her white socks and sandals pristine on her little feet. Her Holly Hobby dress ironed to crisp perfection. Her long dark hair brushed like burnished jet. It was her first day at school. Kate had been so proud of her. What had happened to make her daughter take drugs? When had Lizzy grown away from her?

She felt the anguished tears of motherhood blur her vision and blinked them away. She was done with crying. Patrick was right, she must build bridges now with Lizzy. Try and make some good come out of all this badness.

Patrick turned over and his arm settled across her stomach. It felt good, it felt right. She felt safe.

Kissing the dark head beside her, she settled down. Not to sleep, that was a long way away, but to think and plan. The initial shock and fury were gradually disappearing; now she needed a plan of action and would concentrate her energies on that.

Somewhere, at some time, she had missed some vital step with Lizzy. It was up to her to rectify that as best she could. And rectify it she would.

Snuggling into Patrick, she closed her eyes and let the memories drift in front of her closed lids.

The only thing she forgot to wonder was how Lizzy was going to feel about everything.

It was a mistake she would soon regret.

Kate felt the eyes of the desk sergeant boring into the back of her head as she signed the papers for her daughter's release. She made her way to the cells with a heavy heart. The fact that Lizzy had been nicked was the talk of the station, she knew that. She passed Amanda Dawkins who smiled at her sympathetically. Kate looked away. As the cell was unlocked she held her breath. Lizzy was sitting cross-legged on a mattress on the floor. Her make up was smeared over her face and her hair was a mass of tangles. She looked defiantly into her mother's face as the door opened.

'So you've come then?'

Kate swallowed deeply. 'Get up, Lizzy.'

The girl pulled herself from the mattress and stood with one hand on her hip, in an aggressive pose. The duty officer shook his head in wonder. If she was his daughter he'd give her a smack she wouldn't forget in a hurry.

'Come on, get your things, we're going home.' Kate's voice was low. She turned to the duty officer, a man called Higgins. He was nearly fifty and Kate could see the pity in his eyes.

'Has she eaten?'

'Not a thing, love, but we made her drink the orange juice. It brings them down you know, the Vitamin C.'

'Yeah, I know. Come on, let's get out of here.'

'I want Dad to come and get me.' This was said through gritted teeth.

'He can't come so you'll have to make do with me. Now come on, Liz, I'm not in the mood for games.'

Lizzy sneered, then sat back down again. 'I'll just have to wait for Dad then, won't I?'

'You're coming home with me now, Lizzy.'

She grinned annoyingly. 'I'm going to do whatever I want, Mum. I'm through with you and Gran always telling me what you want, what you expect me to be . . .'

Kate felt herself reddening. She tried desperately to control her voice.

'We can talk about this at home, Lizzy. This is neither the time nor the place.'

'Really? Funny that, because you seem to spend enough time here. I'd have thought this was the place for you, Mum, more than anywhere else.'

'I'm telling you for the last time, Liz, get up and let's go home. We can talk this through, make some sense out of it.'

Lizzy laughed out loud, her mouth wide with mirth. 'That's about right for you, isn't it? Let's analyse everything. Let's find the hidden meaning in everything. Oh, fuck off, Mum. You sound like a bad play!'

Kate spoke between clenched teeth to the duty officer. 'Would you leave us alone, please?'

The man had been so embarrassed he had been pretending to study the graffiti on the cell walls. He rushed from the cell, shutting the door behind him. He liked Kate Burrows a lot. She was a nice woman, a good DI; to see her shamed like that was terrible.

Mother and daughter stared at one another and Kate was aware that it was now a battle of nerves between them. For some reason Lizzy was enjoying this. She was not contrite or sorry or any of the things she should have been. In fact, it seemed as if she was actually enjoying it. Where, oh where, was the daughter of two days ago? Where was the girl with the ready smile and the laughing face? It was as if she was seeing a stranger, a stranger with her daughter's face and body. A body that had been well used, judging by the diary she had found.

'What's all this really about, Lizzy? Come on, tell me.'

She stood up and walked to the back of the cell. Her hair was in her eyes and she brushed it away impatiently.

'I want Dad.'

'Well, your dad isn't here, I am. And if necessary, Lizzy, I am going to take you out of here by force.'

She laughed again.

'I'd like to see you try!'

It was said in a tone of such contempt that Kate felt something inside her break. She walked across the room and, grabbing her daughter's long hair, yanked her towards the cell door. It took every bit of strength that she possessed.

Lizzy, though, was not having any of it. She brought her fist round and punched her mother in the shoulder. Kate felt the blow, and swinging Lizzy round to face her, slapped her hard across the face, sending the girl flying to the corner of the cell.

Both were breathing heavily.

'Get up, Lizzy, now, before I really lose my rag! Get up, I said!' The last sentence echoed around the small cell.

Kate walked towards her daughter and Lizzy scrambled to her feet.

'You are coming home with me now, and if you so much as

open that foul mouth of yours, I'll beat you within an inch of your life.'

Something in her mother's voice told Lizzy that she meant it. Kate grabbed the shoulder of her daughter's tee-shirt and dragged her to the cell door. She banged on it with her free hand and it was opened by Higgins. Kate then marched the girl along the cell row, through the desk sergeant's office and out of the building to the car park. She threw Lizzy in the car. Getting into the driver's seat, she started the engine.

'You'd better have a good reason for all this, Lizzy, because I want to know exactly what's going on with you.'

With that she drove out of the station and home. Neither of them said a word more.

Evelyn desperately wanted to clean up Lizzy's room for her but Kate had forbidden her to touch it. She sat on the bed looking at the utter chaos around her. Pictures of Lizzy as a child were everywhere. She shook her head. If anyone had told her that her granddaughter was on drugs she would have laughed in their face.

'Not my Lizzy,' she would have said. But now the truth was facing her and it was like gall. That beautiful girl was ruining her life, was breaking her family apart – for drugs.

From what Kate had told her Lizzy had been on amphetamines for a couple of years. She shook her head. Standing up, she looked around the familiar room. How many times had she come to tuck Lizzy in when she had been small? Kissed the soft skin of her face? Brushed the long hair till it gleamed?

She walked to the window and looked out into the dull afternoon light. That was when she saw the diary. It was a girl's diary, with birds and flowers painted on a pale green silk background. Evelyn opened it up idly and began to read.

She was still reading when Kate and Lizzy arrived. Kate had to pull the girl from the car and practically drag her up the garden path to the house. Opening the door, she pushed her daughter inside.

Lizzy walked into the front room and through to the

kitchen where she began to make herself a cup of coffee as if nothing had happened. Kate pulled her coat off and put it on the banisters. She followed her daughter through to the kitchen.

'Right then, I want to know everything that's been happening. I want to know where you got the drugs, who from, and who you took them with.'

Lizzy poured milk into her cup.

'That, Mother, is none of your business.'

Kate pushed her hands through her hair.

'I'm not going to argue all day, Lizzy, I mean it. I want some answers and I want them now.'

Lizzy faced her mother and crossed her arms over her breasts. 'That's you all over that is. "I want some answers and I want them now." Who the hell do you think you're talking to? I'm your daughter not a bloody suspect.'

'That, madam, is just where you're wrong. As far as I'm concerned at this particular moment in time you're both those things. You are suspected of dealing in drugs, Lizzy. You were at a known dealer's house, so where exactly does that leave you? I found drugs in your bedroom. I also found your diary. So I know I'm not dealing with Snow White here.'

Lizzy turned to the kettle and poured boiling water into the mug.

'I don't need this at the moment, Mum, I've had a terrible night. Maybe later I might feel like discussing it.'

Kate watched in amazement as Lizzy stirred her coffee. Her long fingers gripped the spoon so tightly her knuckles were white. Kate looked at the womanly figure in the jeans and tee-shirt. She wasn't even wearing a bra. The tee-shirt was stained and crumpled. Her hair was like rats tails and she just stood there making herself a cup of coffee. Not for the first time in the last twenty-four hours Kate wondered what on earth had happened to her child.

Evelyn had been in the front room listening to the exchange. Now she walked into the kitchen as Lizzy sat at the breakfast bar and threw the diary in front of her.

'I have seen a lot of things in my life, Elizabeth Burrows, but I never thought to see this. I felt sick to my stomach reading that filth.' Evelyn's voice was hard and cold.

Lizzy picked up the diary and looked at her grandmother.

'You shouldn't have read it, Gran.' Her voice was small. Her grandmother was important to her.

'Don't you call me Gran! Don't you ever call me that again. That you could do those things with boys and then write about them . . . It's disgusting!'

'It's real life, remember that? You must have been young once.' Lizzy felt her voice rising and tried desperately to control it. 'My life is my own now, I'm nearly seventeen years old. If I want to sleep with boys I like, then that's my business. *Mine*. Not yours or Mum's or anyone's. Mine!'

Evelyn gave her a look of contempt. 'That's all you're interested in, isn't it? You know, it's funny but over the years I can always remember you saying: me, my, mine. I want, I think, I, I, I. Never a real thought for anyone else. We all fell in with what you wanted, we all bent over backwards to do what you wanted. Never a thought for ourselves. You're nothing but a conniving, scheming, little bitch!'

'Mum!'

'Oh, don't "Mum" me, Kate. That diary says it all. I make you feel suffocated, do I, with my loving? My cuddling annoys you. Well, don't worry, Lizzy, because I never want to touch you again as long as I live.'

With that Evelyn walked from the room, her shoulders stooped.

Lizzy put her head in her hands.

'Why did this have to happen? Why did you have to let her read that?' She threw the diary on to the breakfast bar and Kate could hear the tears in her voice.

'I think you should ask yourself why you wrote it, Lizzy, and why you did those things? That's the important issue here now, not what we think.'

Tears were pouring down the girl's face and every maternal instinct in Kate's body told her to comfort her

243

child. But the descriptions in the diary were there in the forefront of her mind and they stopped her. To picture your daughter with two boys in the back of a transit van is not exactly conducive to maternal solicitude. It caused a wide gap, a void that Kate was sure would always be between them.

'Why can't you just let me live my life how I want to?'

'Because you're set on a course of self-destruction, that's why, Lizzy.'

'I didn't mean the things I said about you and Gran in the diary. I was just a bit stoned at the time and it all poured out . . . I love Gran, I always have.'

Kate sat opposite her and sighed.

'It's not just what you wrote that hurts us, Lizzy, it's the way you've been living a lie all this time.'

'I had to live a lie! If you knew what I was doing you'd have moved heaven and earth to stop me. It's my life, Mum, my life.'

Kate lit a cigarette. Lizzy leant across the table and took one from her packet.

'Yes, I smoke as well. You know everything else, you might as well know that.'

Kate shook out her match and Lizzy took the box from her hand. The touch of her daughter's warm skin on her own was like an electric shock.

She watched Lizzy light her cigarette. Her fingers were stained with dirt, her nail varnish chipped. Her lips were cracked and dry. She looked like a girl who had been tripping all night. She also looked very young and unsure of herself, but Kate knew that was just an illusion. How many times had she pulled in young girls over the years? 'Tarts' was how she had described them in her own mind. Little tarts with too much make up and too much to say for themselves. Now, here was the truth of her life in front of her. Her daughter had been sleeping with boys, and men since she was fourteen. Kate couldn't even justify it by saying it was a boy Lizzy loved, whom her daughter had been with for a long time and so sex was a natural progression. From what she had read in the diary, it seemed any boy with a pleasing face and the latest clothes was in for a good time. Kate closed her eyes tightly.

'Where's Dad?'

'He's gone, Lizzy. I don't know where.'

'Figures. You never cared about him anyway.'

'Listen, you! I let him stay here because of you. If it had been left to me I would have put him out on the street long ago. Turning up here as and when it suited him. I thought you needed a father, even a lousy father. A father who loved you was better than no father at all.'

Lizzy laughed softly.

'I never had a father. I never really had a mother either, did I?'

Kate took a long pull on her cigarette and sighed.

What the hell had happened to her life?

Evelyn lay on her bed and stared at the ceiling. The shock of what she had read was just wearing off. In place of her anger was sorrow. Sorrow for her daughter. Not for her granddaughter, but for Kate. She had battled against all the odds to give that girl everything she could possibly want. Evelyn had watched Kate over the years putting her own life on hold for Lizzy, and for what? What?

She admitted to herself that she had been partly to blame. She had spoiled the child rotten. But what else could she have done? Who would have thought that that bright articulate girl would turn out like this? That the little girl who had sat on her granny's knee and smiled and laughed, would grow up to give herself to anyone and everyone who asked her? Hadn't she tried to instil morals into the girl? Not for the first time she missed her husband dreadfully. He would have known what to do. She wiped her eyes with the back of her hand.

Lizzy had never known the love of a father, a real father. Kate used to wait in the hallway, sitting patiently on the stairs, listening for her father's boots to clump up the tiny pathway. Then, as he opened the door, she'd be picked up in

245

a big hug. Kate had known the security of love, as a child and as an adult. It was the advent of Dan that had changed her. When he had left her with a tiny baby, she had hardened her heart somehow. Oh, she loved Lizzy with all her being, Evelyn knew that, but she had also channelled her energy into her work. On reflection, Evelyn wondered now if this was such a good thing. If Kate had maybe married again and given Lizzy a father figure . . .

She shook herself mentally. 'What's bred in the bone comes out in the blood.' How many times had she said that to people? Lizzy was like her father. She used people for her own ends. Dan had been the same. He was still the same. He had packed his bags and disappeared, as he always had, at the first sign of trouble. He said he couldn't cope with aggravation. Those were his exact words. Well, he generally caused any aggravation that was floating around, but he would never admit it.

She heard the bedroom door open and put her hands over her eyes to shield the glare from the landing light.

'I've brought you a cup of coffee, Mum.'

Kate set the cup down on the dresser by the bed.

'How are you feeling?'

Evelyn had closed her eyes. She felt the springs in the bed shift as Kate sat beside her. They clasped hands.

'I don't know how I feel, to tell you the truth. Now the shock's wearing off, I keep trying to make excuses for her.'

She heard Kate sigh.

'I know what you mean.'

'Oh, Katie, that we would ever see the day . . .' Her voice broke.

'I know. Believe me, I know what you're feeling. The worst of it all to me is that I never guessed anything. Me a policewoman, a DI, never saw what was in front of my face.'

'That's because you trusted her.' Evelyn's voice was so filled with despair that Kate felt rage again. Rage at her daughter, not just for what she had done but for all the unhappiness she had caused her grandmother. Evelyn was of a different era, a different breed. She had been a virgin when she married, had stayed faithful all her married life. Even when she had been widowed young, she had never wanted another man. Kate had envied her mother her nice clean life. Now Lizzy had taken all that her grandmother held dear and dragged it through the dirt.

For that Kate would find it hard to forgive her.

The two women sat together in silent despair. Then the phone rang.

Kate answered it and went back in to her mother.

'Frederick Flowers wants to see me. No prizes for guessing why.' Her voice was trembling now.

The Chief Constable had been quite nice, Kate conceded. He had asked her what was happening and she told him as truthfully as possible. The possession charge had been dropped because her daughter had only had a small amount on her. Not enough to be a dealer, only enough for what the police termed 'personal use'.

Kate drove home in a stupor. She knew that this would be a black cloud hanging over her for the rest of her working life. But that wasn't the issue here. The real crux of the matter was finding out why her daughter felt the need to take drugs. Why she lied and cheated. What the hell was going on in the child's mind.

She pulled into her drive and sat looking at the house. It was early evening and the day had been too long. Far too long and far too fraught. She rubbed the back of her neck with a gloved hand. She had to walk into work tomorrow and face her colleagues. It was the talking point of the station, she would lay money on that.

Groaning slightly, she got out of the car. Inside the house, all was quiet. Kate went to the kitchen and turned on the light. She put the kettle on for a cup of coffee. Preparing three cups she went upstairs to her mother's room. She opened the door slightly and listened. All she could hear were soft snores. She shut the door gently then went to her daughter's room.

She opened the door and went inside. Lizzy lay in bed,

with just her head showing. Kate tiptoed to her and looked down. Her long dark hair fanned out across the pillow. In the light from the streetlamp Kate could see the long dark lashes against her daughter's cheek bones. Lizzy really was lovely. She had so much going for her, why had she felt the urge to destroy herself? Because as far as Kate was concerned, that was all people who took drugs wanted to do.

She felt a tear squeeze itself from the corner of her eye. Turning away, she looked at the familiar little room: the dolls, the make up scattered over the dressing table, the books, haphazardly placed on their shelf. She had attempted to clean up at least.

Then Kate saw the piece of paper. Walking the few steps to the dressing table, she picked it up. Words registered in her mind, but she just could not comprehend them. She read the piece of paper again and again.

Sorry, Mum . . . Sorry, Mum. Tell Gran I love her . . . Tell Gran . . .

She dragged her eyes from the paper to the bed and the deathly whiteness of Lizzy's skin made her spring into action. She dragged back the covers and stared. Even in the dim light she could see the blood. Somewhere in her mind she registered the fact it was still pumping.

Picking up a hand towel from a nearby chair, she wrapped both of Lizzy's wrists tightly. Her fingers were suddenly stiff, she couldn't control them. The hammering of her heart in her ears was like a drum beating.

She ran into her bedroom to phone an ambulance. She registered the blood on the white telephone. It was Lizzy's blood. Lizzy's. She answered the telephonist's questions calmly and rationally, she had no idea how. It was the policewoman in her taking over.

Please hurry. Oh God, please hurry. She was not sure whether she was speaking out loud. She put down the phone and rushed back in to Lizzy.

Oh God, please let her be all right. I'll do anything you want if you let her be all right. I'll go to mass every day of my life . . .

248

Like many another before, she was trying to bargain with God for her child's life.

Then, somewhere in the stillness, she heard the ambulance siren.

It wasn't until she was stumbling from the room that she saw her mother. Evelyn stood in her bedroom doorway, her face ashen.

Kate couldn't look at her. She went in the ambulance with Lizzy.

Of all the things she had expected from life, the events of the last twenty-four hours had not been remotely near them. If someone had told her what was going to happen she would have laughed in their face.

Now, in the middle of the biggest case she had ever worked on, she had problems of a much larger scale and Kate was aware that her life would never be the same again.

Kate sat in the hospital waiting room. The young doctor was smiling at her. She noticed that his hair had scissor marks in it, as if it had just been dry cut. He had a day's growth of beard covering a weak chin.

'Well, we've stitched her, Mrs Burrows. The cuts were quite deep, but not really life threatening as such. She cut lengthwise along the arm and missed the main arteries. She was unconscious because she had taken some sleeping pills. But she's awake now, though groggy.'

'Can I see her?'

'Of course. She'll stay here tonight and the psychiatrist will see her tomorrow.'

'Psychiatrist?' Kate's voice was small.

'It's standard procedure after a suicide attempt. Don't worry, everything will be all right.'

Kate swallowed the trite remark. He was only trying to make her feel better.

She stood up and stubbed out her cigarette. It had in fact gone out minutes before but she hadn't noticed.

'Can I go and see her then?'

249

'Of course. Try not to keep her too long. Sleep's the best thing for her now. Sleep is a great healer.'

Kate felt an urge to tell him to get stuffed. But she didn't. Instead she gave him a tight smile.

'Thank you.' Slipping past him she went into her daughter's ward. Lizzy had the curtains pulled around her bed and Kate stepped towards them gingerly.

She saw Lizzy's eyes open and tried hard to smile.

'I'm sorry, Mum. I really am sorry.'

'Oh, Lizzy!' All the pain and anguish inside her rose like a tidal wave and enveloped her.

Mother and daughter cried together.

'Everything will be all right, Lizzy, I promise you. We'll work this out, I swear. We'll work this out.'

'Oh, Mum, I wish Gran hadn't seen my diary.'

Kate could hear the little hiccoughing sounds in her voice.

'We'll make it right between us. You just concentrate on getting better.'

A nurse rustled into the tiny space. Kate could smell Pears soap and the smell brought back memories of when she had been younger. When Lizzy had been a baby.

'I think you'd best get yourself off home now. She really does need her sleep.'

Kate nodded. Kissing Lizzy on the lips, she pushed back her hair from her face and tried valiantly to smile.

'I'll be here in the morning, OK?'

Lizzy nodded and closed her eyes. Kate walked from the ward. As she pushed open the swing doors to the corridor, Patrick walked towards her.

'Oh, Kate, I'm so sorry.' He put out his arms and she walked into them. Feeling the strength of him, the security he offered. He pulled her to him, stroking her hair and kissing her forehead. At the display of sympathy she was undone. She sobbed into his cashmere overcoat, smelling the peculiar odour of him, Old Spice and cigar smoke.

As he accompanied her out of the hospital and towards his

car, it did not occur to Kate to ask how he knew where she was. How he knew what had happened.

She was just glad to see him.

Chapter Fifteen

Evelyn heard a car pull up and poked her head through the heavy curtains of the front room. She sniffed loudly. It was a big expensive car, must be someone for one of the neighbours. Then as she looked she saw Kate getting out of the back. She frowned. Too much had happened today for anything else really to surprise her. She saw the man emerge from the car and as they both turned towards the house she quickly shut the curtain.

She sat back on the settee until she heard Kate's key in the lock. She couldn't summon up her usual boisterous welcome for her daughter. She heard Kate speaking then a man's voice, a deep, dark brown voice. Wiping her eyes once more with a sodden hanky, Evelyn waited for them to come into the room.

Patrick helped Kate with her coat then shrugged off his overcoat. He slung them on the banister in a casual manner. Somehow this little act pleased Kate. Her home was not very grand and she knew it. But Patrick was acting as if he lived her kind of life, which indeed he had once. Only, from his beginnings, Kate's home would probably have been something to aspire to.

Patrick followed her into the front room, his eyes taking in her home. He noticed everything, from the good but worn carpets to the books that abounded in the room. It looked comfortable and warm. He saw a tiny woman sitting on the settee, dressed all in black. She had a remarkable face, one that denoted a quick intellect and a kind heart. He warmed to her immediately.

'Mum, this is a friend of mine, Patrick Kelly. He

brought me home from the hospital.'

Evelyn inclined her head. She noted the breadth of his shoulders, the long legs and dark good looks, and decided Kate had better taste than she'd given her credit for. Then the name registered. It was the man they had been talking about at Christmas dinner. Evelyn pushed the thoughts from her mind. With a name like Kelly, he must have some Irish in him so he couldn't be all bad.

'How do you do?'

Patrick smiled at her, and she found herself smiling back.

'The child?' She stared into her daughter's drawn face.

'She's fine, Mum, or at least as fine as she could be in the circumstances. The cuts weren't deep enough to really harm her. I found her just in time. She's to see a psychiatrist in the morning.'

Patrick sat on a chair by the fire and Kate turned to him. 'Can I get you a drink? I've got some scotch somewhere.' She went to the drinks cabinet and opened the door. She poured out three large whiskys.

When everyone had their drink Kate sat beside her mother. Patrick looked at them. They were like two peas in a pod, both with the same high cheekbones and widow's peak. Both had a slightly Roman nose. Individually, all their features were beautiful, but altogether they just missed being wholly lovely. Instead they had what was termed attractive faces. Women who looked better as they got older. Kate certainly looked all right to him.

Evelyn broke the silence.

'So she's to see a head man, is she? Well, I think it's for the best, Kate. There's something drastically wrong with the child.'

She nodded, her eyes on the floor. Patrick's heart went out to her.

'You're the man who lost your daughter, aren't you?' Evelyn asked.

'Yes.'

'Tragic to lose a child like that.'

254

He looked into the old woman's face, saw the sympathy there and the understanding.

'My son went to Australia, you know. I've not seen him for twenty years. It's like he died. I hear from him regularly but it's not the same as holding them to you. Watching them grow and turn into whatever they become. He's a big grown man now and all I have are photographs to chart his years. It's not like seeing for yourself.'

Her little speech touched Patrick to the core. He felt the empathy between them. Knew that she had warmed to him, that she wanted to ease his grief, and for a dangerous few seconds he thought he would cry. He swallowed the lump that had come to his throat and downed his whisky.

'Are your family Irish, Mr Kelly?' Evelyn had to keep talking, had to stop thinking about Lizzy.

'Yes. My father was a Dublin man and my mother was from Cork. I was born in Glasnevin. I came over here when I was two.'

'Jesus save us, I know Glasnevin well! Is your mother still alive?'

Patrick shook his head. 'No, I'm afraid not. She was a wonderful woman.'

'I bet you have some great memories of her?'

He smiled again.

'Yes, I do.'

He saw his mother in his mind's eye, her arms red to the elbows from doing other people's washing and ironing, her knees permanently swollen from scrubbing floors. But he also saw the tiny smile she had, that serene look when she came home from six o'clock mass every morning. Her pressing a shilling in his hand every birthday, no matter how hard up they were. Oranges at Christmas and a small toy. Oh, he had fond memories all right.

Kate watched her mother and Patrick as if in a trance. She could see that if the circumstances of their meeting had been happier they would have had a good drink of her mother's secret stash of Bushmill's and reminisced all night. She was glad Patrick was here. He was like a big dependable rock, taking both their troubled minds off Lizzy. But her daughter had to be helped and that was what scared Kate.

Getting up she went to the cabinet to replenish their glasses and found that the Bell's bottle was nearly empty. Seeing this Evelyn got up from her seat and said, 'I'll go and get me Bushmill's.'

She went from the room and Patrick smiled at Kate. 'Try and relax. Lizzy's in the best place for her at the moment. Tomorrow's time enough to worry.'

'I feel so bloody useless. How could all that have gone on under my nose?'

Patrick grasped her hand and pulled her to him.

She stared into his eyes.

'Look, Kate, you're not the only person this has happened to. Every parent says this at some time. I remember when I found out Mandy was sleeping with that geek Kevin, I felt like throttling the pair of them. But it's something that's happened and you can't make it unhappen. No matter how much you might want to. I told you, build some bridges now. Let some good come out of this.'

Oh, he sounded so right, but deep inside Kate she felt she had failed Lizzy somehow.

Evelyn bustled back into the room with her Irish whiskey. 'I call this my Holy Water, it's as good as a tonic. My cousin from Coleraine sends it to me, may God bless her and keep her. It's the mountain water that gives it the taste. You know her name's actually Katie Daly. It's true.'

Patrick laughed.

'Katie Daly' had been one of his mother's favourite songs. It was about a girl who made poteen, an illegal Irish whiskey, and the troops who came to arrest her.

Evelyn poured everyone out a generous measure. Kate sipped the liquid and felt the burn as it hit her throat. 'Tomorrow, when she sees the head man, I'll go with you, Kate, and we'll try and sort this business out. We'll make it all right, you'll see.'

'But to cut her wrists like that, Mum. She was more worried about you reading the diary than anything else.'

'And so she should have been, the ungrateful little villain!'

Patrick sipped his drink. This was getting personal.

'I think I better go soon, I know you have a lot to talk about.'

Kate nodded. The driver was sitting outside waiting and suddenly she remembered him.

'Oh, your poor Willy must be freezing!'

'I beg your pardon, Kate Burrows?'

Despite herself she laughed at her mother's scandalised face.

'That's his driver, Mum. Willy's his name. He's waiting outside for Patrick.'

'Oh I see. Well, bring him in. We don't stand on ceremony in this house.'

Patrick drank up quickly. Somehow he didn't think Kate's mother was quite ready for Willy yet.

'No, I've intruded long enough. I just wanted to make sure that Kate got home OK.' He stood up and the two women stood with him. He shook Evelyn's hand. 'It was a pleasure to meet you, Mrs . . .'

'O'Dowd. Evelyn O'Dowd.'

He smiled at her again. 'Mrs O'Dowd, I hope we meet again, in more pleasant circumstances.'

'So do I, son.'

Kate went out to the hall with him and Patrick kissed her gently. 'You stop worrying now, Kate, and if you need anything, anything at all, you just ring me. OK?'

Kate nodded, too full of unshed tears to answer.

She watched him walk down the path and get into his Rolls-Royce. When the car was out of sight she shut the door and went back into the warmth of the lounge.

'Well, you're a dark horse and no mistake.'

'Oh, Mum, he's just a friend.'

Kate sat down and picked up her drink again.

'Just a friend is he? Well, if you want my advice, I'd say make him more than a friend, if you get my meaning. Men like that don't grow on trees.'

'He owns massage parlours, Mum.'

Evelyn O'Dowd had her own set of principles, which she changed and updated depending on the situation.

'Well, we can't all be policemen can we? He's a good kind man by the looks of him. You take my advice and grab him quick, then you can show him what he's doing wrong.'

Kate sipped her drink.

'If the Chief Constable knew that I was seeing Patrick, all hell would break loose.'

Kate didn't know that the Chief Constable knew all about her and Kelly. Patrick Kelly and Frederick Flowers went back a long way. They were much closer than anyone knew – except the two of them, and they certainly wouldn't be telling anyone.

Evelyn bridled in her chair.

'Well, in that case you just refer him to me, young lady. What you do when you're out of that station is none of his business.'

If Kate hadn't had so much on her mind she would have laughed at her mother's scandalised voice.

'It's not like that, Mum, and you know it. Patrick's a nice man, you're right there, but he is also just on the verge of being a criminal.'

'I'm on the verge of being one meself, child, if I had the name of that person who gave Lizzy the drugs I'd scalp the face off them.'

Both women were silent.

'Listen to me, Katie. If you like this man, and you're happy seeing him, then you do what you want. No matter what your Chief Constable or Dan, or me or Lizzy or even King Street Charlie feels. You only live once. Live your life how you want. Before you know it you'll be old. Old as me. And when you get to my age you get a different perspective on life. Suddenly, every day seems just that little bit shorter. You feel the ache coming in your bones. You know that the best, most fruitful part of your life is over. I read once that when people get old and go senile, they go back to a time in their life when they were useful. To when they had young

258

children, and a husband coming home from work. Meals to prepare. Maybe a little job as well. I could understand them wanting to escape back to a time when they were "needed". Maybe because my days of being needed are nearly over.'

Kate slipped off her chair and knelt in front of her mother.

'I'll always need you, Mam.' At the word mam, Evelyn pulled her daughter into her arms, memories flooding back to her. Kate and her brother had both called her mam as children.

'Well, Kate, I'll be here for you for as long as you want me. The same for Lizzy, God love her. I could cheerfully cut the legs from her, but I'll always love her. Mary Ann that she is.'

Doctor Plumfield surveyed Kate and Evelyn as they sat in front of him. Kate had asked for another day of leave to try and get her family affairs sorted out. It had been granted grudgingly and she knew she was on thin ice as far as her superiors were concerned. Sympathetic they may be, but at the end of the day she was a DI and should put her work first. Particularly a murder investigation.

Lizzy's attempted suicide had been whispered around the station by now, she was sure.

Plumfield was young, and Kate thought he looked more like a social worker than a psychiatrist. He wore a pair of faded blue jeans and a rugby shirt. His hair was thinning on top but he had a small ponytail at the back. His fingers were tobacco-stained as he fiddled with a biro.

He sat back in his chair and sighed. Kate felt like a little girl who has been caught cheating in her exams.

'Your daughter, Mrs Burrows, is a very confused and unhappy girl.'

She listened attentively, all the while thinking, Tell me something I don't know.

Plumfield continued talking in a nasal voice and she decided that he must be a demon to live with. He did not address people as equals but spoke down to them.

'Lizzy has manifested signs of severe depression, and I feel that her drug taking and other behavioural patterns need close attention. To a child, Mrs Burrows, a slap is as good as a cuddle. After all, they are both forms of attention.'

'So you think that Lizzy needs more attention?'

Plumfield held up his hand. 'I am still talking, Mrs Burrows.'

Kate rolled her eyes to the ceiling. This man just could not be real!

'I can see you are used to being in charge.' He pointed a finger at her. 'You are not at the station now.'

He smiled to take the edge off his words and suddenly it hit Kate: he was a Bill hater. Kate had come across them all her working life, from the solicitors who tried to get off known offenders to the social workers who stood up in courts of law and gave character references for people who should have been locked up once and for all.

He was going to lay all the blame at her door.

Kate bit her lip and let the man speak.

'Your daughter –' this was said like an accusation '– has agreed to go into a psychiatric hospital for a while, where we can assess her properly. She will travel there later this afternoon from here. She'll be in Warley Hospital.'

Evelyn watched his loose-lipped face and felt her mettle rise. 'Excuse me, Doctor Plumtree . . .'

'It's Plumfield.'

'Doctor Plumfield then. I think you've got an awful cheek! This is my grand-daughter that you're talking about. Now I don't like your attitude, young man. Just tell us when she's going, what's going to happen to her, and how long we can expect her to be there.'

Doctor Plumfield shook his head as if he was dealing with two recalcitrant children. Kate put her hand on her mother's arm.

'Your daughter will be there as long as it takes to help her, Mrs Burrows. She is rebelling against something. What, we're not sure of yet.' He looked at Kate as he said this and the message was quite clear to her. 'This destructive behaviour needs to be looked at. If you wish to see her you may do so, but I must stress that you should try not to upset her in any way.'

Kate stood up.

'Thank you very much, Doctor Plumfield. Before we go – will you be treating her at Warley?'

'No, I won't.'

Kate smiled then.

'Well, at least we have that to be thankful for. Come on, Mum, let's go and see Lizzy.'

They left Doctor Plumfield sitting shaking his head. As they walked through the hospital to Lizzy's ward, Evelyn kept up a stream of abuse.

'The cheek of that one! To try and insinuate that we had done something wrong. I'd have liked to have cut the face off of him with a few choice words. And what's Lizzy been saying to him, I'd like to know?'

As always when she was very angry, Evelyn's voice was a thick Irish brogue.

Kate let it all go in one ear and out the other.

They finally arrived at Lizzy's ward. She was sitting up in bed listening to the radio on the headphones. Her face was washed and her hair brushed. In the hospital gown she seemed very young. She looked at her mother and grandmother and smiled tremulously. Pulling the headphones from her ears she put out her arms, and Kate hugged her.

'Oh, Mum . . . Gran . . . I'm so glad you're here!'

Evelyn pushed Kate gently out of the way and hugged her grand-daughter. Lizzy began to cry.

'Now, now, whist now. Everything's going to be all right.'

Kate sat on the bed and watched them.

'They want me to go to a mental hospital, Mum.'

'How do you feel about that?'

Lizzy shook her head. 'I don't know. They seem to think that I'm a bit touched . . .'

Evelyn broke in, 'Now don't call it that. All you need is a bit of a rest, time to sort out your thoughts.'

'I don't know what's wrong with me, though!'

Lizzy was on the verge of hysteria. Kate grasped her daughter's hand.

'Well, they'll find that out in Warley. A sui— . . . what you did, is a very frightening thing, Liz. You must try and find out why you did it.'

'I know why I did it! It was because of Nan reading the diary, that's all.'

'Why did you take the drugs?'

'Oh, everyone takes drugs nowadays. I'm not an addict, Mum. I don't take heroin or anything like that.'

'But from what I read in the diary you take them often, every day. Amphetamines, cannabis, Ecstasy. What I can't understand is how this all went on under my nose.'

Lizzy lay back in the bed. 'Sometimes, Mum, when I was stoned, I would come and chat to you when you got in. You never even guessed because the amphetamines just make you chatty. They make you high, happy.'

'And you're not happy without them?'

Lizzy stared down at the bandages on her wrists.

'Not very often.'

'But why?' Kate's voice rose and the girl in the next bed stared at them all.

'I just don't know, Mum. I don't know. I think about death all the time.'

Kate stared at the white-tiled floor. How could a sixteen-year-old girl think about death? Her life was just starting.

'Where's Dad?'

'I don't know.'

'He hasn't even tried to find out how I am, has he?' Her voice was flat.

'He'll be in touch, Lizzy, he thinks the world of you.'

'Yeah, of course he does.' Her voice was bitter and Kate and Evelyn exchanged worried glances.

Life had a funny way of catching up with you, thought Kate. Just when you thought you had it all figured out, it threw you a curve like this.

Doctor Plumfield was right about one thing. Lizzy should go to Warley Hospital.

She needed help, professional help, and Kate was honest enough to admit that it couldn't come from her or her mother.

Patrick was standing outside a house in Barking. Three of his best men were with him. It was twenty to twelve and he had arrived ten minutes earlier. This was one of the jobs that he hated. They were to evict a couple and their three children from a rented house. Patrick had been called in when the man had threatened his team with a baseball bat. In normal circumstances the men would just have forced their way in and relieved him of the weapon. But the police had been called so everything had to be done by the book. The man was watching them from a bedroom window, the bat visible.

A young PC went to the letter box and began shouting through it.

'Come on, Mr Travers, this is silly. If you come down here we can talk about it.'

He stepped away from the letter box and looked up towards the window. Mr Travers, a plasterer, who had lost his house when he had been made bankrupt, opened the window slowly. He poked out a grizzled head.

'Fuck off, the lot of you. I paid that bastard and he knows I paid him.'

The constable tried again. He lifted the letter box.

'The man you rented the house from has never paid the mortgage. It is the building society who's evicting you, Mr Travers, not your landlord. If you'll just come down we'll try and get this sorted out.'

He looked through the letter box. He could see a woman holding a young baby standing at the end of the hall. She looked haggard. Her clothes were crumpled and she had no shoes on. He noticed that her feet were filthy. She shook her head at him in a gesture of bewilderment.

'We paid him the other day. We paid him four hundred quid, a month's rent. We've been here for six months. We ain't got nowhere to go.'

Two little girls, twins, walked from one of the downstairs rooms and went to her. The constable sighed heavily. He shut the letter box and went back to the little crowd on the pavement.

'Poor bastards. This is happening more and more. Someone buys a house, gets a mortgage and then rents it out to poor gits like them. They take the four hundred a month or whatever for as long as they can, then when the place gets repossessed they've had it on their toes. Nowhere to be seen. Some of these blokes have eight or nine houses on the go. They make a fortune.'

Patrick nodded. Mortgage scams were as old as the hills. He hated these jobs.

'Let me have a go.'

The constable shrugged. 'I'm getting on to Social Services. They might find them a bed and breakfast or something.'

Patrick nodded and went up to the front door.

He bellowed through the letter box: 'My name's Patrick Kelly and I have been asked to repossess this property. I am a court bailiff. Now, Mr Travers, you have your wife and children in there with you, and they are probably frightened out of their lives. Come down and we'll try and get something sorted.'

Ben Travers stood in the bedroom. He knew who Patrick Kelly was, everyone knew who Patrick Kelly was. He was a legend in his own lifetime.

Travers looked around the squalid room. Their so-called furnished accommodation had consisted of two old beds that had come from a second-hand shop, a brokendown settee, and a gas cooker that had probably been used all through the war. He looked around the room and felt the frustration and anger building up inside him. He had come to this, with a wife and three kids to support.

Every penny he'd saved had gone to getting the key money for this house, over a thousand pounds, and then the four hundred a month rent. They'd had to get away from Louise's mother! They had lived with her for three months before they got this place, and it had been three months too long as far as he was concerned. Two years earlier he'd had a privatised council house in East Ham, a nice little business and his family. Now it had come to this, the repomen at the door for the second time. He caressed the baseball bat, then holding it down by his side slowly walked down the uncarpeted stairs.

His wife was crying quietly and he looked at her sadly.

'I'm sorry, Lou.'

'Just let them in, Ben, let's get this over with.'

He nodded and went to the front door. As he opened it Patrick Kelly walked inside. He shut the front door on all the onlookers.

'Mr Travers? I am really very sorry about this, but the eviction notice has been granted. I know that the bloke who tucked you up will get off with it scot free. By the way, do you have a name for him at all? Maybe I could find him and recoup some of your money?'

Ben Travers nodded.

'It's Micky Danby. I trusted the ponce. He was only round last week to collect the month's rent. He never told us nothing. We signed a year's lease on this place but it ain't worth the paper it's written on. What the fuck we gonna do now?'

Patrick opened his coat and took out his wallet. He pulled out three fifty-pound notes.

'Take this to tide you over. Get a B & B or something. This is my card. Leave a message with my secretary about where you are and I'll see about recouping some of your losses. Micky Danby is a pratt and I owe him a few scores meself.'

The man took the money. 'Thanks, Mr Kelly. I'll pay you back one day.' His voice was shaky.

'Give me the baseball bat and we'll get this over with.' Patrick inclined his head to the woman watching him. 'How about a nice cuppa, love, while we get this sorted out?'

The woman nodded, glad of something to do.

Patrick opened the front door and smiled at everyone. 'Everything's OK, officers, you can go now.'

'Fair enough. I've radioed in for the Social Services, they'll find them some alternative accommodation. See you, Mr Kelly.'

The PC got in his car and drove off. Patrick followed Ben Travers into his front room. It was nearly bare except for an old portable TV and a sixties-style PVC settee. He sat on it with the two little girls and gave them a big smile. He'd wait until the Social came, see what the score was. He looked at Ben Travers. He looked a big strong man.

'Working?'

'Only on the lump, here and there. The building game's fucked at the moment. They're laying down the footings for houses and then just leaving them. It's a bloody joke.'

Patrick nodded.

'Ever thought of doing this job?'

Ben Travers frowned. 'What, being a bailiff you mean?'

'Yeah, why not? It's good steady work.'

'Never thought about it.'

'Well, see one of my blokes and they'll tell you what you'll need. I'd take you on. I'm always after decent blokes with a bit of savvy.'

'I'll do that, Mr Kelly, I'll do that.'

Patrick smiled at the woman as she brought in the tea.

'Thanks, love.' He gestured around the room.

'Not worth four hundred sovs a month this.'

The woman grimaced. 'The fucking Ritz it ain't. If I could get my hands on that Micky Danby now, I'd break his sodding neck.'

Patrick looked at Ben Travers.

'Do you think she might want a job and all?' Ben Travers burst out laughing. It was a laugh he didn't think he had in him.

Patrick sipped his tea.

Since Mandy had died, he'd gone soft, he admitted that. Knowing grief as he did, he wanted to spare as many people as possible the experience. Except the Grantley Ripper. That was one man he wanted people to grieve for. When that bastard was dead, maybe he would start living a proper life, a life that he hoped would include Kate Burrows.

Kate was beginning to mean a lot to him. He thought about her constantly. The day she had come to his house to talk about her daughter's problem he had felt much closer to her. He knew that she was a DI and a bloody good one, by all accounts. He knew that they came from two different worlds, but still nothing would deter him.

When she'd said she was worried about her superiors, he'd felt like telling her that he had her superiors right where he wanted them, but he couldn't. Kate would not stand for anything like that, she was too straight. That's what he liked about her. From the first night he had met her, when she had stood up to him in his own house, he had been attracted to her. She was one of the few people who had no fear of him, even her Chief Constable would be shocked if he heard the way she argued with him sometimes.

Kate was a woman in every sense of the word, and she was a woman who would not give herself to a man lightly. When they had gone to bed together on New Year's Eve it had been like a revelation to him. Never before, not even with Renée, had he felt such a force of love in him. She confided afterwards that it was the first sexual contact she'd had in over five years. She had only ever had one man before in her life. To Patrick that statement had put her above everyone. She was clean and decent and he wanted her on any terms.

He wondered how her daughter was. How Kate was coping with the day.

He found himself thinking about her all the time.

Despite all his heartbreak, it was a pleasant feeling.

Kate and Evelyn took Lizzy to Warley themselves. They had stopped off at home and packed a case for her and then they had stayed to help her settle in. The funny thing was that Lizzy seemed glad to be going. At least everyone there seemed very nice, they had welcomed Lizzy and made her feel secure and wanted. She was sharing a room with a girl called Anita, an ex heroin addict. Anita was small and blonde and full of life; she seemed to hit it off with Lizzy straight away.

Lizzy had made Kate promise not to let on she was a policewoman. Kate had been reluctant to agree, but she saw the sense of it. In a unit where most of the people were drug abusers it would not exactly endear Lizzy to them to have a mother who was a 'filth'.

Lizzy's white, drawn features haunted her. She watched her mother and daughter talking together and felt a deep hurt, as if she had somehow been the cause of it all. She had lain awake the night before, thinking, If only I'd made Dan stay. But he had not wanted to stay. She had not made Dan go, he had practically run out of her life. Bag and baggage. Lizzy had adored her father and he had only ever let her down. Kate had prided herself on never doing so, but maybe she had failed?

As they left the hospital, Evelyn grabbed her hand to cross the road to get to the car park. Kate closed her eyes tightly. Her mother still helped her across the road. It was laughable really.

She dropped Evelyn off at home and then made her way into work. She had to see Ratchette and try and undo some of the damage that had been done there. As much as she loved Lizzy, and as much as she wanted to help her, without her job they would all be up a creek without a paddle.

Something Lizzy often forgot.

As Kate and her mother left the hospital, Dan was making his way in. It was just as well they missed each other. Kate wasn't in the right mood for him. But his presence made Lizzy happy.

Ratchette and Kate faced one another. He had offered her coffee and now the two of them sat sipping it.

'Are you sure everything's OK, Kate? If you need compassionate leave . . .'

She shook her head. 'No, I don't. Lizzy is being very well looked after and I shall be back at work tomorrow.'

'Well,' Ratchette drew the word out between his teeth, 'this is a very stressful case, Kate. As I'm sure you're aware, we need people on it who will give it one hundred percent . . .'

As she opened her mouth to speak there was a knock on the door.

'Come in.'

Caitlin bowled into the office.

'Hello there, Katie! How's your poor daughter?' He beamed at them. 'I'm glad that I caught you. When are you back? Because I've been keeping a record of everything that's been happening for you, you know, so you won't have missed anything.'

'I'll be back tomorrow.'

'That's grand, just grand. I hope everything works out with the girl.'

'Did you want anything, Kenny?' Ratchette's voice was loud.

Caitlin poked himself in the chest. 'Who me? Not at all. I just heard that Katie here was in so I came to see when she'd be back on duty, that's all. See you tomorrow then.'

He smiled at her and gave her a little wink. Then, as he was walking out the door, he slapped his forehead hard and turned back to face them. 'Have you finished here, Kate?'

She looked at Ratchette who nodded his head.

'Yes, sir.'

'Then come with me and pick up the latest reports. Very interesting they are as well.'

She put down her coffee cup and, nodding at Ratchette, followed Caitlin from the office. Once outside he linked arms with her and took her to the little pub that the station staff used. It was called the Swan and was always busy. He bought two large whiskies and, sitting Kate in the corner, drank to her daughter's health.

'Thanks, Kenny.'

He waved his hand at her. 'Sure I know what you're going through. I remember when one of my girls had an abortion, I was like a maniac for days after. You need your work at the moment to keep you sane and normal!'

'I thought you were Catholic?'

'Oh, I am, we all are, but you see she was only fourteen at the time. It was terrible, absolutely terrible. Now how's the child really?'

Kate found herself opening up to him. She told him everything.

'Them drugs is the scourge of parents. But just keep a good eye on her and keep her out of draughts. A blanket for disease, draughts are.'

Kate smiled to herself. He meant well.

'What's been happening with the case then?'

'Sweet FA to be honest, Kate. I gave Ratchette a load of old fanny just now. Hopefully, something will break soon. We're still following up on all the nonces and suspected nonces but it's a piss in the ocean, there's so many of them.'

'Thanks a lot, Kenny, for standing by me like that.'

Caitlin laughed. 'Where else am I going to get such a good-looking DI? Normally I get a big sweaty drunkard who smells like a year-old jockstrap. Anyway, one of me is enough on any case!'

Kate grinned. You found friends and allies in the most unlikely places.

'What about Louise Butler?'

'Nothing. We're treating it as a murder obviously, but if her body doesn't turn up soon . . .' He left the sentence unfinished.

Kate stood up. 'Same again?'

'That's what I like about this women's lib, it's cheaper to take a lady out these days!'

Kate went up to the bar. She glanced at the large clock on the wall. It was six thirty. She'd have a half of lager and make her way home. She was seeing Patrick at eight, and wanted to ring round and see if she could find Dan first. She had a few words to say to him which he wasn't going to like.

She was quite looking forward to it.

Chapter Sixteen

George stood in his bedroom, perplexed. His face settled into a deep frown. He knew, in fact he was absolutely sure, that his tiepin had been in the top drawer of the dressing table. Now it was nowhere to be seen. He lifted the drawer out and placed it on the bed. He began to rummage through it again.

Nothing.

He bit his cheek in consternation. There was only one place it could be. He had searched his bedroom thoroughly so he must have lost it on New Year's Eve. He began to sweat. When Elaine had left that night he had dressed quickly. He could not remember whether he had put a tie on at all, but the logical side of him said that he must have. He put the drawer back and absentmindedly tidied it.

There was only one thing for it: he would have to go back and see if it was on the body. Thank God he had had the sense to bury this one! The devil looked after his own – another of his mother's sayings that proved once more to George that she was always right.

He looked at his watch. It was six fifty-five. Elaine was off out with the girls tonight, he would go as soon as she left. He straightened the bedcover so it was nice and smooth, he hated untidiness of any kind, and walked from the bedroom. On the landing he could hear Elaine singing in the bath. 'I could have danced all night.' He grimaced. Elaine's singing was like everything else about her: terrible. As he walked down the stairs she reached a high-pitched crescendo: 'I could have danced, danced, danced . . . all night!'

George felt his shoulders disappearing into the back of his neck. Elaine's voice grated on him.

She grated on him.

At eight forty-five, George was standing over the makeshift grave of Louise Butler. He had brought his large torch with him. Setting it on the ground, he began to disinter the girl. George was puffing and panting, his gardening gloves making the removal of the stones difficult. He had not realised he had buried her so deeply. He squatted for a second to get his breath.

That's when he noticed the smell. An awful smell of rotting meat. George heaved, his face in the torchlight looking green-tinged and old. Standing up, he took his handkerchief from his pocket and tied it across his nose and mouth. Steeling himself, he began once more to pull at the stones and dirt.

He felt something soft and sighed with satisfaction. At last!

He felt along the small stones and, locating a hand, pulled it from the debris. Then he began to clear away the dirt from around the body, flicking it from the girl's face fastidiously. Leaning out of the hole, he grabbed at the torch and shone it down on the corpse.

George tutted.

After eight days of death, Louise was bloated. Her semi-naked body was twisted grotesquely in the earth. Her lovely hair was caked with dirt and the eyes that were staring at George were a milky white. Her mouth was open in a perfect O, and George cleaned the dirt out of it with his gloved finger, like a midwife with a newborn baby. He searched through the dirt as he poked it from her mouth, rubbing it between finger and thumb.

No tiepin.

He began to unearth the rest of Louise Butler, searching her meticulously, the horror gone now as self-preservation took precedence over everything. He searched everywhere, even between her legs and buttocks. Her skin was spongy and when he tried to turn the body over, it came away in his hands, ragged pieces of skin sticking to his gardening gloves.

George tutted again. This time in temper. The bloody little slut! She could get him in trouble!

He looked at his watch. It was nine thirty-seven. He had been searching for over an hour. He had been through the dirt and all over the bitch's body and the tiepin was nowhere to be seen!

Standing up, he began to brush himself down. The damp weather had made the dirt sticky and George was aware that he would have to leave soon, to be clean and ready for Elaine coming in.

Then, his temper getting the better of him, he began to kick at Louise, enjoying the feel of the soft flesh beneath his boots. He kicked at her until he was tired. His eyes were hurting and he closed them for a few seconds. When he opened them he sighed loudly.

Louise Butler's face was a pulp.

George took off his gloves and pushed them into the pocket of his coat. He bent down and, feeling a delicious tenderness take the place of his temper, arranged the remains of her hair lovingly around her face, brushing away a centipede that was trying to get back inside the warmth of her ear cavity.

Satisfied she looked all right, George picked up his torch and made his way back to his car. He had parked it about a quarter of a mile away and walked to it, dirty and bedraggled and in a daze.

Where the hell was that tiepin?

Louise Butler was fully exposed to view. Her rifled body looked milky in the moonlight.

Elaine sat in the restaurant with Hector Henderson. She smiled at him happily. Hector smiled back, displaying his erratic teeth. Elaine didn't care if they clicked now and again when he spoke, or the fact he had to hold his hand over his mouth while he pushed them back into position with his tongue. As far as Elaine was concerned, the big, fat, jolly man opposite was her own personal Rudolph Valentino.

'I hope everything's all right for you, Elaine?'

'Oh, it is, Hector, it's lovely.'

He beamed at her. His heavy face was glistening with a fine film of perspiration as he leant forward awkwardly in his chair and poured her another glass of Chianti.

'I'll be drunk!' Elaine's voice was girlish and in the subdued lighting she looked much younger than usual. She caught a glimpse of herself in the large mirror on the opposite wall and was pleased with herself. Her diet had taken off quite a few unwanted curves. She actually looked quite well. Not exactly thin, she was big-boned and knew it, but at least she didn't look so chunky.

Sitting in this restaurant, with Hector telling her all she wanted to hear, she felt quite light-hearted and gay. They had been to this restaurant twice before. It was through the Dartford tunnel and so was officially in Kent. They came here because there was no likelihood of seeing anyone that they knew. Now it had become their restaurant. Elaine loved Italian food and had practically starved herself for three days in order to enjoy a small helping of lasagne.

Hector watched Elaine tuck into her dinner. He liked a woman with an appetite. He approved of her size and shape, liked big women – he was a big man – and tonight he was going to get inside Elaine's tights if it was the last thing he did. He felt a stirring of excitement at the thought of it. Her breasts, he could see, were absolutely enormous. Being a regular subscriber to *Bra Busters*, he was automatically excited by this. He closed his eyes and savoured the picture of them loosed from their confines and lying in his open palms . . .

'Would you like a dessert, Elaine?'

She grinned girlishly again. 'I shouldn't really. My weight . . .'

Hector put up his hand to quieten her. 'You have the voluptuous figure of maturity, and that's just how I like my women.'

Elaine felt like swooning across the table. She wasn't too sure about the maturity bit, but the rest was like music to her ears. Hector took her hands in his and kissed each palm in turn.

'If only you were truly mine. But you belong to another man and I can but worship from afar instead of drinking from the fountainhead.'

Elaine listened to him with fascination.

A waiter nearby bit his lip to stop a laugh escaping. Elaine had no inkling of that though. Hector brought back the old longings she had repressed for so long. He made her feel feminine and desirable. He gave her the romance that she craved so desperately. He was, in short, her knight in shining armour.

It was then she decided to sleep with him. He could drink her fountain dry if he liked.

Kate was sitting, listening to some music, which was turned on low so as not to disturb her mother who had retired to bed at nine, an hour earlier. She was listening to Billy Paul singing 'Me and Mrs Jones', relaxing to the music and trying to think rationally about Lizzy. She had showered earlier and now sat in an old cotton dressing gown, her hair spread across her shoulders to dry naturally, her face wiped clean of makeup, shining with Ponds cold cream in the firelight. As the record ended she shifted position slightly on the settee and tucked her feet up underneath her. She needed this quiet time, without even her mother with her. She felt at times that she did not have enough time alone, except in bed. As Sad Cafe began to sing 'Every Day Hurts', she heard a knock on her front door. She glanced at the clock on the mantelpiece. It was past ten. Who could be knocking at this time? Dragging herself from her seat she went out to the hall. Through the glass of the front door she saw the unmistakable figure of Dan.

That was all she needed.

Squaring her shoulders, she opened the door. He pushed past her, his face set in a deep frown, and walked into the living room.

'Why don't you just come on in, Dan?' She kept her voice low. She didn't want her mother down here.

She went into the lounge where he was pouring himself a

brandy. This lent her anger an added edge. Who the hell did he think he was? He charged in here without a by your leave and acted like it was his house or something.

He faced her and took a deep drink of the brandy, then pointed his finger at her menacingly. She watched it stabbing the air as he spoke, adding emphasis to his words.

'What's this I hear that you're seeing a bloody wide boy? Our daughter's in hospital – a hospital for the sick in the head, I might add – and you're running round with Grantley's answer to the bloody Godfather!'

Kate suppressed a smile. So that was what really rankled. He knew she was seeing someone. I don't want you, but I'm damned if anyone else will have you.

'I'll thank you to keep your voice down, if you don't mind. My mother is in bed. As for my private life, that's why it's called a private life – it's sod all to do with you who I see, when I see them or what I do with them. Now finish your drink and go. I've had a very trying day and it's not getting any better.'

'I'm not going anywhere until I get to the bottom of this!'

Kate was exasperated. 'The bottom of what, for goodness sake? I'm a big girl now, Dan. What I do is no business of yours.'

'It is when it affects my daughter.'

This was said so low as to be virtually inaudible. Kate raised one eyebrow.

'What did you say?' Her voice was dangerously low and Dan should have heeded the warning in it.

'You heard.'

She walked towards him, and he watched the bottom of her dressing gown flapping open as she walked. She'd always had good legs.

'Listen, you, I've put up with you for Lizzy – but I warn you now, Dan, leave me alone! I mean it. You just keep out of my face.'

Dan laughed.

'My God, you're even talking like a gangster! You're warning me? You're the one who's making a slut of herself.

276

No wonder Lizzy turned out like she did, with you as an example!'

The record came to an end and the sound as Kate slapped his face was like a gunshot in the quiet of the room. Dan put down his glass. Kate could see he was trembling with temper. But she felt no fear. One thing in Dan's favour, he would never raise his hand to a woman. Oh, he might break their heart, use them, abuse their trust, but he fancied himself a gentleman so would stop short of slapping her.

'If you really cared about Lizzy, Dan, you would have seen more of her over the years. You would have tried to make her feel loved, secure and wanted. Lizzy is like she is because you drifted in and out of her life, building up her fragile hopes and then dashing them. I was to blame in as much as I let you. I let you come here and use us between women and homes. I thought it was good for her to see you.

'But I tell you, Danny boy, if she asks me anything about you from now on she won't get the nice rosy edited version, she'll get the truth. I'll tell her just what a tosser you really are!'

Dan put both palms on Kate's chest and pushed her backwards with all his strength. She landed, winded, on the settee.

His face was twisted with rage but he kept his voice low.

'And what about you then? What about marvellous Kate the Wonder Woman? You're a ball breaker, Kate, that's why I left you. You always wanted to own me. I always had to be what *you* wanted.

'Well, listen and listen good, – I always thought of you as a good woman but when I was told by an old friend you were on your back for Patrick Kelly, I finally saw you for what you really are! You'll not drag my daughter down with you. When she comes out of hospital, I'm going to ask her to come to my flat with me. And when I tell her about Patrick Kelly, I think she'll come without a backward glance.'

Kate sat up, stunned.

'I don't believe what I'm hearing.'

'And what have your superiors got to say about it, eh? I'd

277

like to know what they think about a DI running around with a bloody villain.'

Suddenly Kate had had enough.

'I think you'd better go before we both say anything else we'll regret. Lizzy is coming home to me for a short time. I've written to my brother in Australia to see if he will take her and my mother for an extended holiday. I think a change of environment and some sun will do her the world of good. What Lizzy needs now is an uncomplicated way of life, time to put all that's happened behind her. If you try and shove a spanner in the works, Dan, I'll dog you until the end of your days. I mean it. You'll not ruin that child's chance of getting well, I won't allow it.

'I'll tell you what's wrong with you, shall I? You're jealous because you think I'm having an affair, a relationship. Good old Kate, who always waited for you in the past, has now got herself a man.

'And believe me, Dan, he's more man than you'll ever be, in bed and out of it!'

The words were said in temper, in hurt, but the look on Dan's face told her the effect that they'd had on him. Dan thought he was a gifted lover, a woman's man; he lived his life for the pleasures of the flesh. Now his last hope of regaining a normal family life had turned sour on him. Kate felt a sneaking triumph at the way she had finally put him down, as he had put her down for so long.

'So you're sleeping with him then? It's true?'

All the fight seemed to have seeped out of him. In the space of a few seconds Kate saw his body sag, saw the paunch that he tried so valiantly to hold in, saw the puffiness under his eyes from too much booze and too many late nights, saw the slackness of his jaw that was finally denoting his age. Kate saw him as he really was and it was the end of the line for both of them.

Years before Dan could conquer Kate all over again with a few sweet words, a few practised caresses. He realised now, with stunning clarity, that he had played tonight's scenario all wrong.

Kate had finally and unequivocally grown up. Up and away from him. Bluster and bombast would not work now because she wasn't frightened of what he thought any more. The worst thing of all was the fact that she had never looked more beautiful or desirable to him, with her cheeks flaming and her long silky hair strewn around her shoulders.

He wanted to throw himself on top of her, felt an urge to take her there and then on the settee as he had in the past. Kate had never resisted when he'd touched her then. She would yield and abandon herself to him then everything would be fine, everything would be roses – until he felt the wanderlust again. The need for new pastures, for new faces, for a different life.

Kate heard a tap on the window and looked at him. Who could that be?

He walked across the room and peeked out of the curtain. He turned back to face her and she saw the fear in his eyes.

'Who is it? It's not someone from the hospital?' Her voice was filled with fear for Lizzy. It was nearly ten-thirty, who would be tapping on her window now?

'It's your boyfriend, come for a late night legover by the look of things.'

It took a few seconds for the words to sink in. Patrick? Here? She pulled herself from the settee and went out to the hallway. Dan pulled her back.

'Don't open the door, Kate, please. I'll do anything you want – we can get married again, anything – but please don't answer the door to him. If you do it will always be between us.'

Kate searched his blue eyes with her own dark ones. She saw the wanting in him, knew that this time she had the upper hand, what she had craved all her life with him – and it meant nothing. Patrick Kelly was nearby and he was what she wanted, for however long it might last.

Kate had never loved lightly, she had always loved one hundred per cent, and now Dan knew, looking into her eyes, that her allegiance to him had gone for good. He wasn't really surprised when she pulled her arm free and, straightening her dressing gown, walked to the front door. With those few steps she finally severed any remaining ties between them.

Patrick stood on the doorstep perplexed. He had seen the light from the front room and wondered what was keeping Kate. He was sorry now that he had come round so late, but he had felt an overwhelming urge to see her. He had been sitting in his house alone, and Mandy had invaded his thoughts as she always did when he had nothing else to occupy him, and suddenly the urge to see Kate was so strong it was almost tangible. Taking his BMW he had driven himself to her house. Now it did not seem like a very good idea.

He saw her slim form walking down the hall and felt a surge of pleasure. As she opened the door he smiled at her crookedly.

'I know it's late but I saw your lights on . . .' His voice trailed off.

Kate had never been so glad to see anyone in her life.

'Come in, it's freezing.' He followed her down the hall and into the lounge. Kate was not surprised to find it was empty. She had heard the back door close as she opened the door to Patrick. Dan was a lot of things but brave was not one of them.

'How about a drink? Tea, coffee, a brandy?' She saw Dan's glass where he had left it on the coffee table. It was still half full.

'Coffee will be fine, I'm driving myself tonight. Where's your mother?'

'She's in bed. I gave her a sleeping pill. All this with Lizzy has really hit her hard.' Kate was amazed at how normal she sounded.

'How's Lizzy?'

'Better. She seems to be thriving on being somewhere different. I know that sounds crazy but from what her doctor said, hospital can often be a stress-free environment. It gives people time to gather their thoughts, make decisions without any outside pressure. I only hope it works for Lizzy.'

She walked out to the kitchen and put the kettle on. The

only light out there was from the tube lighting under the worktops. She left the overhead lights off. Patrick followed her out and slipped off his coat. He could see her body through the thin dressing gown and felt a stirring within him. Going to her, he slipped his arms around her waist.

Turning, Kate put her arms around his neck and pulled his face down to hers. Suddenly, she wanted him desperately. He was dangerous to her, she knew that. He lived his life taking what he wanted. He was a rogue, a villain, but he was also the most exciting man she had ever come across. She could ruin her career with this association, but at this moment she did not care.

He was there, he wanted her, and, oh God, how she wanted him. After the set-to with Dan, she wanted to be held, to be loved, to feel wanted and desirable.

He undid the belt of her dressing gown and rubbed her breasts gently. Kate moaned in his ear. After tasting the delights of Patrick Kelly, you found yourself willing to run risks.

She abandoned herself to him, unaware that Dan was watching them through the kitchen window. As he saw his wife, as he still thought of Kate, put her long legs around Patrick Kelly's waist, he felt pure hatred.

And now he had something to use against her. He would go and see the Chief Constable. See what he thought about the situation. He crept away from the window.

But he was already learning one thing: the prospect of revenge was not sweet at all. It left a bitter aftertaste.

Elaine and Hector Henderson had enjoyed themselves thoroughly and she tiptoed into the house at twelve thirty. As she heaved her substantial bulk up the stairs, George spoke to her from the darkness and she screamed at the top of her considerable voice.

'Oh, George! You bloody fool! You nearly gave me a sodding heart attack!'

He clicked on the hallway light and saw a red and flustered Elaine sitting on the bottom stair, her hands over her heart.

The wild red hair that she had backcombed earlier looked as if it had been set on end by an electric shock.

'Sorry, my love. You're very late.'

'What were you doing sitting in the dark, waiting for me to come in? Are you checking up on me, George Markham?'

Elaine's voice was dangerously low. Like most guilty partners, she found attack the best form of defence.

George looked at her long and hard. Surely she didn't think he was jealous? By God, who would touch her, for Christ's sake?

'Of course I'm not checking up on you. I had one of my headaches, that's all.'

Elaine squinted at him suspiciously, her old cantankerous self battling it out with the newer, more self-confident and laidback Elaine. As she stared at her husband it suddenly occurred to her that she didn't even hate him any more. She didn't feel anything at all, and wasn't sure that wasn't worse. At least while you were hating you were feeling something.

'Shall I make you a nice hot drink, dear, and bring it up to you?'

'OK, George.' Elaine mounted the stairs. She was tired. George always made her feel tired and depressed. Thank God she had Hector.

When George brought her up a cup of Ovaltine a little while later, Elaine was sitting at the dressing table in her corset, taking off a pair of stockings. George placed the Ovaltine on the bedside table and watched her, surprised at just how much weight she had lost. Her legs were getting quite shapely! As she peeled off the stockings and waggled her toes George noticed some tiny red marks on her neck. His mouth set in a grim line. Elaine lifted her arms and unclasped her gold locket, the action causing her enormous breasts to rise up in the heavily underwired bra she wore. She moved naturally, as if after years of having her husband take no notice of her she was invisible to him. She glanced at him and jolted as she saw him watching her.

'What's the matter now, George?' Her voice was clipped and demanded no reply.

He just carried on staring. She opened the jewellery box that held her few treasures and dropped the necklace into it.

'Oh, by the way, George, here's your tiepin. I nearly hoovered it up.' She picked up a ring box from inside her underwear drawer and threw it to him. 'I don't know what possessed me to put it in my drawer. I meant to give it to you yesterday but I forgot.'

George caught the box and opened it. There was his tiepin. He grinned his widest grin. Going to Elaine, he put his arms around her and kissed the top of her head.

'Here, steady on, George.' She pushed him off in disgust but he was too happy to notice.

He had the tiepin.

It was not lost.

There were no clues.

He was free as a bird.

Kate awoke to a feeling of lazy euphoria that seemed to have started somewhere in her legs and had, during the course of the night, washed through her entire body. She could smell Patrick Kelly on her and pulled the covers back over her head and breathed in the scent of him deeply.

Emerging once more, she noticed that it was light. Her bedroom curtains were open about two inches and she saw the weak dawn and felt it was invading her privacy. She glanced at the alarm clock. Six fifteen. She could lie for a while in total silence and think about the night before. Not about Dan, he was gone from her now as surely as if he was dead, but about Patrick. Patrick Kelly . . . even his name gave her a thrill.

He was hers, or at least she felt that he was, and at this moment that was enough for her.

She had lived in a vacuum. Now, at forty, she was finally finding out what life was all about. The love side of it anyway.

If she could just get Lizzy back to her old self life would be nearly perfect. She didn't dare think completely perfect, because she knew that was too tall an order for anyone. But nearly perfect suited her right down to the ground.

The phone beside her bed rang.

'Hello?'

'Kate, this is Amanda. Louise Butler's body has turned up.'

She took a deep breath. 'Where?'

'In the old quarry. Look, I don't want to say too much over the phone. You can't miss the place, it's full of Panda cars. I'll see you soon.'

Kate put down the receiver and leapt from her bed. As she showered her mind was cleared of everything but the task ahead. As always when on a case, once she had something to work on it took priority over everything. Her mind was blank now of Patrick, Lizzy, Dan. She thought only of Louise Butler. As she walked downstairs ready for work her mother was standing at the bottom with a cup of coffee for her and a lighted cigarette.

'Five minutes won't kill you, Katie. What's up?'

She took the coffee gratefully and took a deep puff on the cigarette. Coughing hard, she gulped some more coffee down.

'Louise Butler's body has been found.'

'Heaven help the poor child! Are you fit for all this?'

'As fit as I'll ever be.'

Kate gave her back the cup and pulled on her coat, the cigarette between her teeth, the smoke curling up into her eyes making her squint. She kissed her mother and went towards the door.

'Tell Lizzy I'll get in this evening, will you? I can't promise I'll be there this afternoon, but I'll try.'

'All right, love. You get off, and drive carefully.'

Kate kissed her again and went from the house. It was a chilly morning and she pulled the collar of her coat up around her neck.

She drove to the site of the discovery with a feeling of trepidation mixed with excitement. Please God let there be some kind of clue! To Kate's mind it wasn't a lot to ask.

284

She arrived at the quarry before Caitlin and slithered down the loose-stoned rise that led to the murder scene. When she got there she wished she'd stayed in bed.

The girl's body was covered. When they pulled the canvas away Kate felt a sickening lurch in her guts.

DS Spencer watched her and rolled his eyes.

'He must have come back and dug her up!'

Spencer looked at his superior with raised eyebrows.

'Dug her up, ma'am?' His voice was sceptical. 'Looks more like an animal had her to me.'

'I can see you'd think that at first, but look at the way the dirt's been smoothed around her, the way her hair has been arranged. No, our man came back and disinterred her for some reason. Cover her up, Spencer. Where's the pathologist?'

'In the jam sandwich over there, ma'am.'

Kate walked to the large police car and climbed into the back seat. 'So what's the gen so far? Am I right in thinking that our man's been back and dug her up?'

'Well, well, you are on top form this morning, Kate! I would say that she has been recently disinterred, yes. The facial injuries were inflicted after death, I'd lay money on that one.'

Kate was stunned.

'You mean he came back, dug her up and then attacked her again?'

'Spot on. Quite a nice chap you're looking for, I don't envy you. Ah, here's Caitlin, looking a bit the worse for wear. Never was at his best first thing in the morning, was our Kenny.'

Kate watched as Caitlin slid heavily down the stony incline to Louise Butler's body.

'One other thing, Katie, the girl was stripped naked last night. He usually leaves the clothes on them, cutting off the underwear. I couldn't find any evidence of recent sexual activity, but by the marks on the skin of her buttocks I would hazard a guess they were pulled apart recently, and quite

285

savagely at that. Obviously, I'll know more after the PM. I'll have the report ready as soon as I can.

'I hate the stinkers, Kate, especially when they're young girls. She's higher than a damn pheasant at the moment. I'll be tasting formaldehyde with my dinner for days.'

Kate looked at the man beside her and bit her tongue. Nodding, she got out of the car and made her way carefully to where Caitlin was looking at the body. Higher than a damn pheasant! That was a fifteen-year-old girl he was talking about. She hoped against hope that she never became that cavalier about her job.

'Hello there, Katie darling.' Caitlin's Irish brogue drifted over to her on the cold wind. 'The fucker dug her up, the dirty bastard!'

Kate was gratified at the distress in his voice. If even hard-nosed coppers like Caitlin could still be moved, there was hope for her yet.

'Well, sir, he saved us a job, didn't he?' Spencer's nasal twang caused Kate, Caitlin and the uniforms to stare at him.

'Oh, yes, son, he did that all right.' Caitlin's voice was sarcastic. 'Shame all the perverts don't bury their victims and then dig them up later on. Save a fortune on inquiry charges that would. You stupid eejit . . . Get away out of me sight, before I give you a dig!'

Kate flicked her head at Spencer and he walked back to his police car, shamefaced. Kate felt sorry for him in a sense; she knew what he meant: at least the body had turned up, even if it was in this grisly fashion. Poor Mr and Mrs Butler.

'The pathologist thinks he attacked her again last night. Whether or not it was sexual he doesn't yet know. He thinks the face was beaten recently, but he could find no evidence of a sexual assault.'

'Probably wanked over her. That wouldn't leave anything.'

'I'm not so sure. Look at the way her hair has been arranged, the way the dirt's been smoothed around her. I think he was searching her. We know he's a nutter, and we know he's a sexual deviant.'

Kate knelt by the girl's body, repressing a shudder at the rancid smell. 'Suppose he thought he'd left some evidence on the body? What, I don't know. He could have come back, dug her up, searched her. Then when he didn't find what he wanted, or maybe even when he did, he attacked her. It's got a kind of twisted logic to it.'

Caitlin nodded. 'Sure you always was a clever girl, Katie. I think you're probably right. But this man has finally made his biggest mistake . . . He's wound me up, Kate. He's pushed me too far this time. When we find him – and we will – I'm going to beat his fucking brains in!'

Caitlin looked towards the uniforms and shouted: 'Where's the bloody undertakers? Get this child covered up and into a body bag.'

Kate stood up. In the grey light of day Caitlin looked terrible. His haggard face with its grey stubble seemed to have sagged overnight. For all his faults, and they were legion, at that moment Kate almost loved him.

'Come on, come back to the station with me and let forensic finish their work here.'

She took his arm and pulled him away gently. 'We'll go and get some hot coffee inside us.'

Both noticed she didn't mention breakfast.

Ronald Butler walked into the mortuary at Grantley Hospital, Kate beside him. The mortuary assistant pulled the white sheet from Louise's body and Ronald Butler stared down at the remains of his daughter. Kate looked away. Out of the corner of the eye she saw the man's hand go up to his mouth.

'Is this your daughter, sir?' Her voice was low. The formal identification had to be made.

He nodded and then bent double. The mortuary assistant quickly covered Louise up and both he and Kate rushed to Butler. He was now holding his chest tightly, and as he collapsed on to the floor Kate shouted: 'Get the bloody Crash team now. He's having a heart attack!'

When the assistant had run off she loosened the man's shirt and tie.

Ronald Butler was grey and a thin film of sweat shone all over his face and neck. His lips were blue. Kate knelt over his body and felt his neck for a pulse. It was barely noticeable. Entwining the fingers of both hands she pushed down hard on his chest, just to the left of his heart.

Oh, please God, let them hurry!

As if her prayers had been answered, she heard the clanging of the Crash trolley bursting through the plastic doors.

Kate carried on the heart massage until the Crash team took over and a few minutes later was gratified to hear Ronald Butler breathing relatively normally. She waited until he had been put on a trolley to be taken to the CCU. As he was being taken out of the mortuary to Cardiac Care Unit, he grasped Kate's hand.

'Would you tell my wife . . . please, tell her not to worry . . .'

'Of course I will.' Kate felt the burning inside her own chest. It was not physical pain but hatred and had been building up inside her all day.

'Louise was our life, you see. We hoped . . . we hoped she would walk back in the house. You know.' He squeezed his eyes shut to stem the tears. 'That she was still alive somewhere. Anywhere.'

Kate felt the man's agony as if it were a tangible thing. As the trolley was pushed away, she knelt down and retrieved the handbag that she had thrown to the floor as he collapsed. Standing, she went once more to Louise Butler's body and pulled the sheet away from her face.

Fifteen. Loved and wanted. Her whole life ahead of her. And now she had been reduced to a bloody pulp.

Swallowing hard, Kate left the mortuary. She had decided to be in on the post mortem and now she would go to the Pathologist's office and wait for the remains of Louise Butler to be laid on the mortuary blocks and then systematically cut to pieces.

Ronald Butler had made Kate feel the futility of all their investigations. His daughter was dead, Mandy Kelly was dead, and Geraldine O'Leary was dead. Three women raped and murdered in less than seven weeks.

They had to find him before he struck again, and they had nothing to go on. Nothing at all. Every avenue they pursued hit a dead end. Every lead went nowhere. This man was either very clever or very lucky. Or else had a mixture of the two.

She was still dwelling on it when the post mortem started. Kate had been given a small white mask to wear and when the pathologist cut Louise Butler from the breastbone to the navel she was glad of it. The stench of the gasses was appalling.

Kate watched everything through heavily lidded eyes. The burning was back in her breast. Stronger this time.

She brooded on what kind of man raped, murdered and buried a young girl, then went back and dug her up and mutilated her again?

He had to be caught.

Chapter Seventeen

Kate was feeling depressed. She'd just had the news that both Geraldine O'Leary's and Mandy Kelly's bodies could be released for burial. She decided to tell the families herself. She was not looking forward to it.

She drove towards the O'Learys' house with a feeling of trepidation. She parked just down the road and sat for a few minutes, watching the house itself. The nets were pristine white. Obviously either Mick O'Leary was a good house-keeper or he had someone helping him. Probably Geraldine's mother; Kate had met her on one occasion and had had the impression that she was a capable woman. Taking a deep breath, she got out of the car and locked it. She walked slowly to the front door and rang the bell.

The door was answered by Kathleen Peterson, Geraldine's mother, who had the youngest child, Sophie, in her arms. Kate could see Geraldine in the child: the same long, brown hair and almond-shaped, hazel eyes. She smiled.

'I don't know if you remember me? I'm Detective Inspector Burrows . . .'

'Oh, come in, love. Come in.'

The woman moved from the doorway so Kate could enter the tiny hall.

'Come through.' She walked through a doorway to her left and Kate followed her into the lounge. On the carpet toys were lying about everywhere. The television was on and Mick O'Leary was sitting in the armchair by the fire, staring at the screen. Kate was shocked at the sight of him. He was hunched in his chair like an old man, it was obvious he had not shaved for days and his clothes looked a crumpled mess.

Kathleen Peterson caught Kate's eye and shrugged her shoulders. She motioned for Kate to follow her through to the kitchenette.

Putting Sophie down on the floor, she closed the kitchen door quietly behind her. 'Sit yourself down. Would you like a coffee? Tea?

'Coffee would be fine, thanks, no sugar.'

While Kathleen put the kettle on, Kate watched the child. She stood on the floor exactly where her grandmother had left her. She watched avidly every move her granny made, her eyes darting restlessly around the kitchen to wherever Kathleen was. Kate smiled at the child, but Sophie just glanced at her and then carried on watching her granny.

When Kathleen had put the coffee in front of Kate, she sat at the small table and pulled the waiting child on to her lap. Sophie curled into her granny's bosom and popped a thumb into her mouth, shifting herself around for a few seconds before she was fully comfortable. Kathleen swept the hair back from the child's face and then looked at Kate.

'She's taken it hard, the young one. They all have.'

Kate couldn't answer.

'Have you any news about . . . about the man?'

Kate shook her head.

'I'm here about Geraldine. Her body can now be released for burial.'

The woman sipped at her own coffee and placed the cup back into the saucer with trembling hands.

'Thank God! I think that if we . . . well, if we could bury her like . . . it wouldn't seem so bad. The thought of her . . .'

'I know. Believe me, I know. Please don't distress yourself.'

'It's funny,' Kathleen's voice had taken on a confiding tone, 'I used to think that nothing really bad could happen to us. I'd see things on the news – like Suzy Lamplugh and murders and rapes – all sorts really. I'd think, How terrible, and then I'd go and cook my dinner or get ready for bingo and it would be out of my mind, you know? It's amazing how little you really care until it happens to your. To your own family. Oh, I would feel distressed for the victims and their family, but not really for any length of time . . . Now it's with me every waking moment. I feel as if she's near me sometimes, I feel her presence.'

Kate sat and let the woman unburden herself. She guessed rightly that she was the first person to cross the doorstep for weeks. After the initial shock wears off, people seem to give victims' families a wide berth. Maybe they really do think people want to be left alone, or maybe they are frightened of getting too caught up. As if that kind of bad luck is catching.

'I was shopping the other day in town and I met a girl who went to school with Geraldine. She had her children with her, two boys. Lovely little things. She said hello and we chatted for a while, and I thought after, Why couldn't it have been you? Why did it have to be my Gerry?

'I felt terrible later. Just terrible to wish on her and hers what we were going through. I mean, you can see for yourself how Mick is. He lives on tranquillisers. How could you wish that on somebody? It's wicked.

'But deep down inside I wish it had been anyone but my child. The older children are back at school but very withdrawn, and this little mite here – she doesn't know if she's coming or going. Keeps wanting to know when her mammy will be coming home. Maybe once she's buried we'll all come to terms with it a bit more. Say goodbye like. You know?'

Kate nodded, unable to swallow the large lump in the back of her throat. She took a gulp of coffee to try and right herself.

'Well, if you get in touch with the undertakers, they can collect Geraldine's remains.'

'Remains.' Kathleen smiled. 'My Gerry's gone, love, all that remains is memories. Memories and children. I used to look forward to being a granny. You know the jokes about having the children when you want, but being able to give them back? Now I have them all the time and I don't really

293

think I'm up to it. But these things are sent to try us or so they say. Would you like another coffee?'

'No thank you. I have to be on my way.'

'Have you any idea who it was who did it? I mean, my Gerry was the first of three, and people seem to think he's going to strike again. Do you think you'll catch him?'

'We'll catch him, I can promise you that.'

Kate's voice was hard and strong and Kathleen Peterson believed her.

Sophie scrambled off her granny's lap. Going to the back door she urinated on the mat, her thumb still tucked firmly in her mouth. Kate saw Kathleen's eyes roll up in dismay.

'Now, Sophie, you know that's naughty.' She looked at Kate. 'This is the latest thing with her. It's funny though, she's as dry as a bone at night. Come on, madam, let's get those wet knickers and socks off you. Though if you keep this up I'll make you wear them all day, see how you like that.'

As Kathleen went to the child, Kate stood up. 'I really must go now, Mrs Peterson. I hope everything works out all right.'

'So do I, love. So do I.'

'I'll see myself out. Goodbye.'

''Bye, lass, and thanks for coming to tell us. It's a load off of me mind.'

Kate left the kitchen and walked through the lounge. Mick O'Leary was still watching the flickering screen. He did not even know that Kate was there.

She left feeling worse than she had before.

Patrick Kelly was in the West End. He owned massage parlours the length and breadth of London and surrounding areas. Today he was in Soho, supposedly checking the books, but in effect just showing his face. It paid in this business always to be on top of everything. If the girls ever thought they could tuck you up, they would.

While he sat in the makeshift office his mind was on his daughter. The account books lay open in front of him so that if anyone came in, it looked official.

He was startled by a knock on the office door. It was opened almost immediately by a tall thin woman who strode purposefully into the room.

'All right, Pat? Everything ship shape and Bristol fashion?'

Kelly nodded. Juliette Kingsley had worked for him for years and like all his top girls – that is, the women who ran the parlours – she was a trusted friend.

'I want to ask you a favour, Pat, if you don't mind?' She sat in a chair opposite the desk and, leaning over, took a cigarette from the box on the desk.

'What is it, Ju? Trouble?'

'Sort of. Nothing to do with this place. Remember my youngest son, Owen?'

Patrick scanned his mind and came up with a picture of a tall, blond-haired, good-looking boy. Not unlike his mother.

'Yeah. What about him?'

Juliette ran her hands through her short blonde hair and Patrick was surprised to see that she was agitated.

'You know Jimmy McDougall, the pimp?'

He nodded, frowning now.

'What about him?'

'He's got my boy up the 'Dilly. I can't find him, Pat, and I'm worried out of me bleeding mind. He's only twelve, as big as he is. Well, I heard a whisper on the street that McDougall had him. I know I ain't exactly lived the life of a virgin, I don't deny it, but all my kids have done well, you know that. My eldest girl is a secretary, my eldest boy is at university, my Owen was doing well at school.

'He's my baby, Pat, my little surprise I call him. I mean, I was nearly forty-one when I had him. I can't eat, I can't sleep with worry at what he's getting into . . .'

Patrick looked at her. She looked terrible – Juliette never had looked that good. But she'd been one of the best toms in the business in her day. Bought and paid for her own house and kept her husband in the life of Riley until the ponce drank himself to death. Patrick liked her, respected her.

'I want you to have a word with McDougall for me. I know it's a cheek . . .'

He felt a rage inside him and was glad to have somewhere to channel the hatred that was slowly building up in him day by day. McDougall was a scumbag in his opinion. Anyone who lived off the earnings of young boys was a scumbag. Homosexuals bothered Kelly not one iota as long as they were consenting adults. It was the men who slept with children that disgusted him, whether they were young boys or young girls. There was a fortune to be made from youth. Extreme youth. But Kelly would have none of it.

'Don't you worry, Ju. Owen will be home within twenty-four hours. Now go and get yourself a stiff drink and let me deal with it.'

Juliette's hard face relaxed. 'Thanks, Pat. If you only knew what I've been going through.'

'I have a pretty good idea, you know, Juliette.'

'Of course. I'm sorry, Pat. What with Owen and everything . . .'

'You leave it with me, girl, and just bide your time. How long has he been gone?'

'Nearly a fortnight. I've told the school that he's been ill with 'flu'. I didn't know what else to say.'

'How did he get involved with McDougall in the first place?'

'Well, from what I can gather, a friend of his from school went on the trot about a year ago. Poor little sod had a terrible time of it at home. Didn't get on with the mum's boyfriend. You get the picture, I'm sure. Anyway, he rang my Owen up and told him what a great life he was having and Owen went to see him and I ain't seen hide nor hair of him since.'

'Well, stop worrying. If he's with McDougall he'll be home, quick smart.'

Juliette stood up and left the room.

Patrick picked up the phone and dialled. He was looking forward to sorting out McDougall.

Tony Jones was chatting with Emmanuel at Sexplosion when Patrick Kelly and three large men walked into the shop.

'All right, Jonesy?' Kelly's voice was not friendly and Tony was aware of it.

'Hello, Mr Kelly, how can I help you?'

'I want to know where I can find Jimmy McDougall. Now. This second.'

Tony Jones was squirming in his shoes. Jimmy McDougall was not a man to fall out with, but then again neither was Patrick Kelly. Of the two he decided he was more frightened of Kelly. He looked at Emmanuel.

'What are you staring at, you great big fairy? Get out the back and sort the videos or something. And keep your big trap shut about what you've heard here tonight.'

Emmanuel did not need to be told twice. He literally ran from the shop.

'What day is it today? Tuesday . . . He'll be at his safe house by King's Cross Station. I'll write down the address.'

He went to the counter and hurriedly wrote a few lines on a piece of paper. Kelly took it from him and glanced at it.

'Do you know something, Jonesy? I used to like you once but now I find you disgust me. Flogging all this crap is one thing, but to be an active participant in this kind of filth . . .' Kelly waved the paper at him and shrugged. Then, spitting on the shop floor, he turned and left, his men following

Jones breathed a deep sigh of relief. It crossed his mind to phone McDougall and warn him, but after weighing up the pros and cons of such an act in his mind, he decided against it. McDougall could do with being knocked down a few pegs and Patrick Kelly was just the man to do it.

Owen was sitting on a large settee watching a video. The glamour of his new life had already worn off. There was nothing to do but watch videos, drink alcohol and smoke cigarettes, and the novelty of all that was long gone. Plus the big man, Jimmy, who had been so friendly at first, had twice come into his room and made him do things. Things that made him feel sick. That was when he realised he was a virtual prisoner.

297

Last night he had been taken out to King's Cross Station. There, his friend Joseph had walked up to completely strange men and asked them if they wanted 'the business'. All the time this had been going on, Jimmy had stood with Owen, holding him tightly by the arm. He had never been so frightened in his life. Joseph was doing what was called 'clowning'. Picking up a punter and offering him a 'chicken'. Chicken was the term for the younger boys. If they were under the age of ten then they were termed 'spring chickens' and were worth a fortune.

Jimmy was a bit concerned about Owen's height at first, but one feel of his face, so smooth and silky, was proof to any discerning punter that he was indeed a chicken. As luck would have it, Owen had been violently sick and Jimmy had taken him home and given him a good hiding for being so stupid. In Owen's mind this was preferable to doing with one of those men what Jimmy had made him do. Now, with a black eye and bruised body, he was safe for a while. It hadn't taken him long to suss that much out.

Sylvester Stallone was stitching himself up on screen and with the resilience of a child Owen watched avidly. *First Blood* was his favourite video and Sylvester Stallone his favourite actor. He didn't like the other videos that Jimmy liked to watch. Joseph was in some of them. Joseph and Jimmy and other boys. Some of them were really young. Like the little boy Jimmy kept in the bedroom whom no one was allowed to see. He cried all the time so they had to turn the television up loud to drown him out. Then every so often Jimmy would bring back a man who would go in there with him and then the crying would be terrible for days after.

Owen had glimpsed him only once. He was about five years old, half caste with enormous brown eyes. But he had seen him in the videos that Jimmy watched. Joseph said that when they made the videos Jimmy gave them whisky and pills and it made them all laugh. But Owen didn't think he would laugh. He just wanted his mum. His mum and his old bedroom. He had only come up here for a couple of days.

Now it was two weeks and he was scared. He was sick of pizza and Kentucky Fried Chicken. He was sick of it all. Especially Joseph and Jimmy.

'You're not watching that crap again, are you?' Jimmy's loud voice brought Owen out of his reverie.

Jimmy walked over. His cumbersome body rippled with fat. He had on nothing but a pair of grubby underpants. Owen instinctively pulled the flimsy pyjama jacket he was wearing tightly around his body. He was not allowed to wear his own clothes.

Jimmy sat heavily on the brokendown settee. He patted the cushion beside him.

'Come and sit beside me, let me look at that eye. You shouldn't have annoyed me, you know, Owen. I don't like hurting my boys. I just want to look after them, that's all.' McDougall's voice had the sing-song quality that Owen was beginning to loathe, along with everything else about the man. He was aware that Jimmy was trying to talk him into doing what he wanted.

'Come on, Owen, you know it makes sense. Think of all the money you'd have if you just played along with me . . . I give Joseph ten pounds a day to spend on what he likes. And how many twelve year olds do you know on money like that, eh? Answer me that then. Over seventy quid a week I give him sometimes. And all me other boys. I've got loads of boys you know . . . all ages and sizes.' Jimmy's voice had taken on a threatening inflection. It was a veiled threat but not wasted on Owen all the same.

'Some of my bigger boys are very nasty, you know, Owen, and if they thought that someone, especially someone young and green, was taking the piss they would be very annoyed. 'Cos they love me, you see.'

Owen was half relieved and half scared when a discreet tap came on the front door. Happy because it took Jimmy away from him, and scared in case it was some of the bigger boys that he'd just been talking about. Jimmy leapt off the sofa and pulled on a reasonably clean pair of trousers from the floor. Then, smoothing his hair with his hands, he went to the front door.

Owen heard mumbled voices and then Jimmy walked back into the room with a man in a black suit. He was carrying a briefcase and he smiled at Owen. He felt his heart sink.

'The boy's in here, sir. I keep the door locked because you know what children are like. Always prying into things that don't concern them.' Jimmy spoke as if he was a benevolent father and smiled at the visitor. He smiled back and Owen felt the sickness again. The man was going in to the little boy in the bedroom.

The house where they were had once been a large, imposing residence, now it was a mismatch of flats and bedsits. It still had the communal front door and as they were on the ground floor, their front door came into their lounge. The rooms that were once the morning room and the dining room were now bedrooms. All the windows were barred, as they had been since the houses were built. Jimmy also had the basement flat. He had set-ups like this all over London. Once Owen was established and trustworthy, he would be relocated to one of the other safe houses.

He watched Jimmy unlock the bedroom and the man with the briefcase walked inside. A couple of minutes later Jimmy came out and went to the kitchenette. Owen watched him carry through a bottle of pills and a glass of whisky. Owen could hear the little boy's cries through the door and put his hands over his ears.

He wished more than ever that his mum was here. She would know what to do.

She would sort out Jimmy.

She would take him home.

Owen realised that his video had ended and the television screen was blank. He stared at it, trying to hold back the tears. If they were going to do to the little boy what Jimmy had done to him, he would be in a lot of pain.

Owen felt sick again.

Then there came another knock on the door. This time it

was loud and aggressive and Owen was convinced that it was the bigger boys that Jimmy had been talking about. He felt himself hunch into the settee.

Jimmy came out of the bedroom and called out: 'All right, all right, I'm coming. About bleeding time and all.'

He opened the door and Owen was amazed when he tried to slam it shut immediately, pushing on it with all his might. Then whoever was outside got the better of him because the door was pushed open so hard that Jimmy went sprawling on the floor and the door banged against the wall loudly.

Four large men were standing over him and one of them, a dark man in a light brown overcoat, kicked him hard in the kidneys. Then he faced the boy.

'You're Owen, aren't you?'

He nodded.

'I'm here because your mum's been worried out of her head, son. Now you come with me and I'll take you home. OK?'

Owen stood up on trembling legs. He was trying hard to pull the pyjama jacket down so it would cover his naked genitals. He saw the man in the brown overcoat frown.

'Where's your kacks, son? Go and put them on. We'll wait here for you, all right?'

Owen nodded and went to the bedroom he had been using with Joseph and Jimmy. He began to pull his clothes on as quick as possible, glad of the unfamiliar feel. He went back into the lounge and pulled on his bumpers. Jimmy was still on the floor and one of the men, a large shaven-headed character with gaps in his teeth, was grinning at him. He was holding a large screwdriver to Jimmy's throat.

'Tell them that I never hurt you, son. Tell them that, will you?'

Jimmy's voice was frightened and then Owen remembered the boy in the bedroom. It was very quiet in there now. Too quiet.

'Hey, Mister. There's another boy in there.' He pointed to the door. 'He's only a little mite. There's a man in there with him.'

301

Patrick's face seemed to harden and he opened the door. On the bed was the man in the suit and the little boy. The man had his hand over the little boy's mouth. His trousers were undone and his shirt, so nicely pressed and ironed was hanging over his flaccid penis.

'Fuck me, Mr Kelly, what's going down here?' This from one of the other large men, a hard case called Dicky Brewster. He walked into the room and punched the man in the suit as hard as he could. The little boy, realising his mouth was free, began to scream in fear. His large brown eyes were opened to their utmost and snot and tears were raining down his face into his mouth. Dicky Brewster picked up a corner of the grubby bedsheet and wiped the boy's nose and eyes gently, his great hands seeming to cover the child's whole head.

Patrick and the other men watched him, fascinated. All were shocked and appalled at what they had stumbled on. It was worse than even they had expected. Dicky wrapped the child in a blanket and picked him up, trying his hardest, in his rough-handed way, to be kind. Kelly flicked his head to the other man with him.

'Take the boys and go down to my car, Dicky. You, go with him.'

The men nodded and left the flat with the children. The little boy's sobs were subsiding now, but Patrick waited until they were gone before he walked into the bedroom. Then he began systematically to kick the suited man in the head, chest, anywhere he could. The rage inside him was white hot now and it needed to be spent. Finally, the man lay still and Patrick Kelly didn't care if he was dead. Breathing hard he went back into the lounge.

'You're a fucking piece of shite, McDougall, and I am personally going to see that you never get to ply your filthy trade in this city again.' He nodded at the man with the shaved head.

'You know what to do, Tim. Do it.'

Jimmy McDougall was terrified, and his terror gave him an added strength. He fought as hard as he could to get away from the man but Patrick Kelly kicked him in the head, a stunning blow. Then Tim pushed the screwdriver into Jimmy's ear, banging down on it hard with the palm of his hand.

Jimmy was still and silent.

Tim wiped his hands on his jeans and both he and Kelly walked from the flat.

They were disgusted.

Not at their own violence, but at what they both knew had been going on in there. It just didn't fit in with their code of right and wrong.

In Kelly's mind, a man had to do many things, such as dole out a hiding to the likes of McDougall. Anyone who lived off the proceeds of children, whether it was putting them on the streets or dealing in child pornography, was classed as a nonce or a beast. It was quite reasonable and just to maim or harm them permanently. That was right to Kelly. Just like robbing a bank was considered gainful employment. It grieved them that a rapist often got a lesser prison sentence than a bank robber. It was the old, old story. Property had more value than people. Kelly might own massage parlours and be a repoman, but he would never raise his hand to a woman or a child. The men in the car with him felt the same.

There were just some things you did not do, and these were some of them. You could break a man's arm or a leg for the payment of an overdue debt, but this was right and fair. When the man borrowed the money he knew what the penalty for not paying would be, and he generally took his punishment like a man. That was how Kelly had always lived his life. How he had survived in life. His first business had been founded on a two thousand pound loan from one of the biggest villains ever to walk the earth. Kelly had paid back the loan and the interest with it. He had showed the man the respect due to him, and now, all these years later, the man was a trusted friend.

Kelly was the old-style villain and proud of it. He had no time for the youngsters who went steaming through the trains or who took it into their heads to go and run a stolen

Range Rover through an electrical shop. Ram Raiding they called it. That was a mug's game. He blamed society for these people. He did not put himself on a par with them. He saw himself and his colleagues as businessmen. Men who did a job that had to be done. Like the job they had done tonight.

When he found the Grantley Ripper, and he would find him, he was sure of that, he would pay back his daughter's debt one hundredfold. He would exact his payment painfully and with the minimum of fuss. In Kelly's mind it was expected of him. If you didn't look out for your own then who would?

He shook his head at what the world was coming to.

Inside Kelly's car, Owen sat as still as death. Relieved to be out of the flat, but still not sure if he was out of danger. Now the relief had worn off he was wondering if he had walked into more trouble.

'We're going to take you home, son, to your mum. But first we've got to drop the little fellow off. All right?'

Owen nodded warily.

'Give me the phone, Tim.'

Kelly dialled a number and the deep voice of a Chief Inspector friend of his came on the line. He outlined the situation in as few words as possible, then smiled and switched the phone off.

'We're taking him to Charing Cross Hospital, they'll be expecting him. Come on then. Let's get our arses in gear.'

He smiled at Owen.

'When was the last time you two had a bath? You smell like a couple of paraffin lamps.'

'They look like a pair of tramps and all, guv.'

This from Dicky, who was feeling happier now they were taking the boy somewhere.

They all chatted amiably until they'd dropped the little boy off. Kelly wondered briefly what would become of him. At four or five he wasn't a runaway, more likely sold to Jimmy by his mother or father. It was surprising what people would do for a couple of ounces of heroin.

Owen was delivered to his mother's house and Juliette

304

cried her eyes out as she hugged her son to her, thanking Patrick and the other men profusely until Dicky's face was as red as a beetroot in embarrassment.

Later on, Patrick drove home and his heart felt lighter than it had since Mandy's death.

He was seeing Kate the following night and couldn't wait. He had observed Owen's happiness at the attention from his mother who had hugged and kissed and shouted and berated him in her joy to see him home in one piece. It crossed Kelly's mind that twelve, twenty, forty or eighty, everybody needed someone to care for, and to care for them. He wished he still had his Mandy.

If only they could find a clue to the villain responsible for her death.

Patrick Kelly didn't realise he had spoken that very day to the man who had George's full name, address and phone number.

Later that evening Patrick had a call from his police contact.

McDougall would live, though he would walk as if he had been on a roundabout for the rest of his life.

Kelly smiled to himself. It was a job well done.

Now all he wanted was his daughter's murderer and then he could settle down to some kind of a normal life.

Kate watched Patrick's face closely, her heart going out to him. 'I tried to get in touch with you yesterday, but I just couldn't locate you anywhere. I wanted to tell you myself.'

'I know that, Kate.' He pulled her towards him and kissed the top of her head.

'In a way I'm relieved, but in another way it makes it all seem real somehow. Sometimes I wake up in the night and I think it was all a big mistake, and if I get out of bed I'll walk into her room and she'll be there. Fast asleep, her arm draped across her eyes. That's how she slept even as a small child. But I suppose I'll get over all that eventually. The wishful thinking. I'll make the arrangements first thing in the morning. What's happening with the O'Leary family?'

'I told the mother yesterday, the husband is taking it all very badly . . .'

'I mean, how are they off for dosh? Money?'

Kate was surprised.

'I don't really know, they aren't rolling in it. They were buying their council house so I expect her death has paid off the mortgage. He's not working though, and as she worked at the wine bar for extra money for Christmas I shouldn't think he earns that much anyway. Especially with three children.'

Kate saw Patrick's jaw clench. She knew it was the motherless children that affected him the most.

'I'll send my brief round to see the mother. I'll pay for the funeral for them. I'll pay for the Butler girl's as well when the time comes.'

Kate was silent. She didn't like to say that maybe the Butlers wouldn't want him to pay for something so personal, but she knew it was a salve to him. In his mind he was making amends and actually doing something. More than anything, she knew Patrick Kelly was only happy when he was sorting out things. She knew that in his own way he was trying to take the responsibility from other people, trying to make things easier for them.

She wasn't really sure if this was a good thing. After all, he wasn't God.

'Do you want to go out, Kate?'

'Not really, Pat, but it's up to you.'

He hugged her close again. 'Good. I've had Mrs Manners make up a nice bit of dinner for us. We'll eat in and have an early night. What do you think?'

He tried to smile at her, but Kate was aware that his heart wasn't in it. But she would go along with him; she had a feeling that he needed her tonight for more than the usual reasons. Even if they didn't make love, she knew that having someone beside him through the night would mean a lot to him.

'That sounds great. I could do with an early night, I had a hard day myself.'

'Good. I'll go and make the arrangements.'

As he left the room, Kate could not help but notice the slump to his shoulders and felt a rush of love for him. She sat back in the settee and sighed. She wasn't sure if it was a good thing or a bad thing. But she knew that she liked the feeling.

George was watching Elaine. Since the night of the tiepin and his euphoric relief at finding it, the marks on his wife's neck had been bothering him. He watched her shove a Ryvita with a scraping of low fat cheese on it into her mouth. She was definitely a lot thinner and, he admitted to himself grudgingly, getting quite attractive for her age. She had toned down her eye make up, and had taken to putting kohl pencil on the inside of her bottom lashes. This small act had opened up her eyes and given them a mysterious look. He gritted his teeth.

They were all the same, women. He knew, without a shadow of a doubt, that Elaine, that slob Elaine, was having an affair. Was lifting her skirts in the back of someone's car and sitting on someone's erect . . .

'George! Are you all right?' Elaine's voice was sharp.

The picture in George's mind evaporated and he dragged himself back to reality.

'Of course I am, dear.' His voice was his usual mild and humble one.

'Well, stop staring at me, it gives me the creeps.'

George stood up from his seat and felt dizzy as a picture rose into his mind once more. This time, he was standing over Elaine with his Swiss army knife raised above his head . . .

'I think I'll go for a walk, dear, I don't feel very well. I need to clear my head.'

'But "Taggart's" on in a minute.'

'Taggart' was George's favourite programme. But tonight he had to get out of his house and away from Elaine before he exploded.

'I won't be long, dear. Tape it for me.'

Elaine turned her gaze back to the television. George knew that within seconds he would be forgotten. She would be thinking of her fancy man. He hurried from the room, grabbing his hat and coat, and left the house. As he walked down the road he pulled his gloves from his pocket and put them on. He felt a rage inside him. A blinding rage. How dare she? He didn't want her, he had not wanted her for years, but she was still his wife. His *wife*. He had married her and given her his name. He had raised her from the gutter to be his wife. But, like them all, she was a conniving cunt.

He saw Elaine again in his mind, taking off her clothes as she had been the night he had seen the marks on her neck. He saw her then in the back of a car, with a faceless man touching all her secret places. And Elaine liked it! She liked it, the slut!

George was walking faster and faster, his shoes clattering on the pavement. Elaine was like his mother. Oh, they pretended to be good women, but deep down they were whores. Like Eve, they betrayed you. You gave them your all and they took it. They took it and they smiled and they simpered – and all the time they were laughing at you. Laughing their fat ugly heads off.

George's breathing was laboured.

He stopped and looked around him. He was outside the block of council flats where he'd been mugged. He crossed the road and strode purposefully up the incline and under his tree. He watched the second floor, cursing Elaine because in his haste to get away from her he had forgotten his opera glasses.

Leonora Davidson was watching 'Taggart', unaware that not twenty yards away the Grantley Ripper was watching her bedroom window. She snuggled into her chair, a mug of coffee on a small table beside her and her cigarettes on the arm of her chair. She was content.

George watched the window for ten minutes. Nothing. He glanced at his watch. It was ten to ten.

He began to walk towards the block, his eyes scanning the street and the windows of the flats for movement.

Leonora heard a knock at her front door and tutted. 'Taggart' was just about to unmask the killer. She got up from her chair and went out into her tiny hall.

'Who is it?' Her voice was loud and impatient.

'Is that Mrs Davidson?'

Leonora frowned. She didn't know the voice.

'Who wants to know?'

'I'm the man who got mugged, you came out to help me.'
George's voice was quiet and meek.

Leonora's eyebrows went up.

'Oh, yes, I remember.'

She opened the front door, pulling back two large bolts
and taking off the chain before opening it.

George stood there smiling.

'I'm sorry to come so late but I work rather unsocial hours,
you see. I just wanted to thank you properly for all your help
that night. I really don't know what I would have done
without you.'

Upstairs, he heard a door opening and began to panic.

'May I come inside for a moment? I won't keep you long, I
promise.' He could hear footsteps on the landing above.
Whoever it was would see him. They would see his face and
know he had been here.

Leonora stepped back and George walked into her hall,
pushing the door shut behind him. He smiled at her. His
little smile that just showed his teeth. He had observed her
for weeks and knew that there was no man in the house. She
always went to bed alone.

Leonora smiled back. Now she knew who he was, she was
happier. You couldn't be too careful when you lived alone.
'Will you come through to the lounge? I was just having a
coffee, would you like one?' Her open face was like balm to
George.

'If it's no trouble . . . I don't want to put you out.'

He followed her into her lounge.

'Sit down and I'll get you your coffee. Do you take milk
and sugar?'

George nodded. 'Oh, you're watching "Taggart", I love
that programme myself. My wife's taping it for me.'

'Well, sit down, Mr . . .'

'Markham. George Markham.'

'Well, sit down, Mr Markham, I won't be a second.'

George sat down on the sofa, an old PVC affair that had obviously seen better days. He noticed that the room was clean and tidy if very old fashioned. It needed decorating. He undid his coat. He gazed at the television screen smiling to himself. Leonora came back with the coffee and gave it to him.

'So how are you now? I tell you, Mr Markham, this place is getting worse. The youngsters seem to be taking over. I don't leave the house now of a night, unless I have to. What with the muggers and the Grantley Ripper, a woman isn't safe any more.'

George sipped his coffee.

'You're absolutely right. I tell my wife that she has to be very careful. Very careful indeed.' His face clouded.

Leonora lit herself a cigarette.

'Did you go to the police station? Did they find out who did it?'

'Oh, no. It's a waste of time, the police can't catch anyone these days. Or so it seems anyway.'

Leonora nodded, not sure what to say.

'Are you divorced?'

'Yes. Ten years now.' She smiled sadly.

George watched her drink her coffee. Her hair was mousy brown and her eyes a watery blue. Around her mouth she had deep grooves. Not an attractive woman, he thought. His eyes dropped to her breasts. George liked her breasts. He had seen them many times.

He put his coffee on the table.

'May I use your toilet, please?'

'Of course. It's the second door on the right, in the hall. You have to pull the chain hard or it won't flush.'

He stood up.

'Thank you.'

He walked out to the hall and went into the kitchen. Opening the drawers slowly and quietly, he found her knives and taking out a large breadknife, he slipped it into the belt of

310

his trousers, covering it with his coat. He walked back into the lounge.

He smiled at the woman.

She smiled back.

Then he walked towards her slowly. He started to talk. 'This ornament, may I ask you where you got it?' He picked up a large vase, about sixteen inches high, made from cut glass. It was on the mantelpiece, over the gas fire. He turned back to Leonora with it in his hands.

'Oh, that was my mother's.' She leant forward in her chair that was pulled up near the fire, her hands outstretched as if to take the vase from him. As she opened her mouth to speak again, her face froze.

George lifted the vase above his head and the action pulled his coat open. Leonora saw the breadknife in his belt and the heavy vase descending towards her at the same time. She felt the scream rise in her throat, but George was too quick.

He brought the vase down with all his might on to her forehead. He was amazed that the force of the blow did not break the vase. It had not even broken the skin on her forehead, though a lump the size of an egg was slowly appearing.

She was out cold.

George sat on the sofa and watched her for a few minutes. She lay sprawled across the chair. The skirt and jumper she was wearing were both bunched up and looked uncomfortable.

George got up from his seat and placed the vase back where he had found it, arranging it precisely. Then he tidied Leonora up, pulling her skirt and jumper down so she looked more natural. Then, taking the breadknife from the belt of his trousers, he placed it by her chair. He took off his overcoat and folded it up neatly on the settee.

Satisfied with his work, he once more retrieved his knife and began the process of cutting her jumper from the neck to the navel. As usual, he laid it open tidily and began on her bra.

Leonora's arms were hanging over the sides of the chair

and her head was lying on her shoulder, slightly bent. By the time George began to hack at her skirt, she had begun to stir. He tutted and, walking out to the hall, picked up a tartan scarf from the coat rack. Going back to Leonora he pulled her head forward roughly by the hair, causing her to groan. He placed the scarf around her neck and pushed her head back.

Then he began his task. Crossing the scarf over her naked breasts, he picked up each end, wrapping the woolly material around his hands to get a good grip. He began to pull his arms outwards. He watched the tartan material stretch and stretch until eventually it cut into her neck.

George was whistling a little tune through his front teeth. All the tension was gone now. He felt himself relax.

George was back on top.

Chapter Eighteen

Elaine heard George's key in the door and glanced at the clock. It was twenty past twelve. She listened to him humming as he took off his coat and hung it up. Her nerves were jangling and she swallowed deeply as he walked into the lounge. His face was animated. The dead grey eyes seemed to be twinkling as he looked at her.

'Hello, dear, can I make you a drink? I'm having one, I'm parched.'

'Where have you been, George?' Elaine's voice was flat.

She could sense George's surprise even though his face was calm.

'Why, I've been out walking, dear, where on earth would I go?'

'So you've been walking for over three hours, have you?'

Elaine could feel his confusion. She realised that he was unaware how long he had been out of the house.

'I . . . I was just walking, that's all. I often walk, you know that.'

Elaine still sat staring at him, her eyes hard and steely. She ran her tongue over her lips before she spoke. George's eyes were glued to her, watching every nuance.

'In all the years we've been married, George Markham, I can count on one hand the times you went out walking alone. Now all of a sudden you're never in the house. I want to know where you go. And I'm warning you, George, you lie to me and there will be murder done in this house tonight.'

He stared at her for a few seconds and then he felt it: the high-pitched giggle that came from his stomach and gradually worked its way up to his throat. He tried valiantly to calm himself, swallowing heavily, but to no avail.

He burst into nervous, high-pitched laughter. Like a child who laughs out of sheer terror when being told off by his teacher. In his mind was one word: murder.

He had already committed one murder tonight. Elaine would murder the murderer. Every time he thought of it it sent him into gales of hysterical laughter. Where had the time gone? Where the hell had the time gone?

'George?' Elaine was standing now. His laughter was frightening her. 'For Christ's sake, George, calm down.'

He had dropped on to his knees, his hand holding his stomach. Tears were rolling down his face.

He was heaving with mirth. A strange sinister mirth. Elaine stood and watched him until he was quiet.

When George was finally capable of movement, he pulled his handkerchief from his pocket and blew his nose vigorously before he pulled himself on to the nearest chair. The laughter was all gone now, only fear of discovery remained. His knife-sharp brain was ticking away as he watched his wife. Did Elaine guess?

'There's something not right, George, I know it. All this walking, being gone for hours – is not like you. I have to drag you from the house normally even to go shopping.' She sat down heavily in the other chair.

'I want to know exactly what's going on.' Her voice brooked no argument, but deep inside she did not want to know. She did not want to believe what the rational part of her was dreading.

George sat quietly, twisting the handkerchief between his fingers. He needed something that would throw Elaine off the scent completely. Then it jumped into his mind and he grabbed at it like a drowning man a straw. He looked at her, gathering every ounce of sorrowfulness he could muster into his lacklustre grey eyes.

'I have a terrible problem, Elaine. I've been going out of my mind with worry about how to tell you. Something dreadful has happened.'

She felt her throat go dry. Please God in heaven, don't let George tell me . . . I don't want to know. I just don't want to know.

'I've been made redundant, Elaine.'

He watched her eyes screw up into tiny slits. 'I beg your pardon?'

'I've . . . I've been made redundant. They told me a while ago. There's five of us going in all. Streamlining, they call it. I just couldn't tell you, dear. I felt as if I had failed you again. I've been walking the streets in a daze. I'd look at you, my love, watching television, and I just couldn't tell you.'

Elaine was stunned.

'I see.'

George could hardly suppress the laughter. He was a sly old fox. He was as clever as a bag of monkeys. He could talk his way out of anything. He was the man.

'I'm so sorry, dear. I know you'll think it's another failure on my part. I always wanted to give you the best, you know I did. Things just never worked out right, no matter how hard I tried.'

Elaine sat very still. Her face was closed to George through years of habit. One tiny part of her felt that she should go to him, put her arms around him and commiserate with him. But she could not. Years of avoiding physical contact with him had made such a simple act impossible.

Poor George had received the ultimate insult. At fifty-one he was on the scrap heap. He would never work again and she, his wife, was relieved that that was all that was wrong. That he was not a murderer. That he was not a rapist. She knew she shouldn't have thought such terrible things about him, but after what had happened before . . .

She pushed the thought from her mind. She would not think about that now. She had a duty to George if nothing else.

'I'm sorry, but we'll get by somehow. I expect the redundancy money will be quite a bit. The house is paid for. I'm working. We'll get by.'

He smiled at her sadly.

315

'That's why I said at Christmas that we would go to see Edith in Florida. I knew I would have the redundancy money and I wanted you to have something to look forward to, you see. I wanted at least to have given you that. A trip to America with no expense spared. The trip of a lifetime.'

George was warming to his theme. He had killed two birds with one stone. He knew what Elaine had thought and she had been right. Oh, so right. But he, George Markham, had sneaked in and extricated himself from a very dangerous situation. Because if push ever came to shove, he would cut Elaine's throat without a second thought. Now he had told her the thing that he was most scared of and instead of the recriminations and the upset, he had her sympathy. He had told her about the redundancy. He was on top.

'I don't know whether a trip to America would be a good idea now, George, what with losing your job like that.'

'We're going, Elaine. We are going. I want to give you that. God knows, I've never made you happy and I always wanted to, you know.'

Elaine stared into his lifeless grey eyes. The faint gleam had gone now and he was once more the George she knew.

'Would you like a cup of tea?'

Elaine nodded at him.

George got up from his seat and went to the kitchen. The clock said five past one. He had better hurry and get to bed or he would be tired in the morning. He was humming again as he put the kettle on.

Dorothy Smith knocked on Leonora's door as usual. They travelled to work together. Her fat face, under a dark brown wig, was homely and friendly. When her knock was not answered, she frowned. She banged on the door again, harder this time. Still no answer.

Surely Leonora had not gone already? They had travelled to work together for over two years and they were on the ten till six shift. She looked at her watch. Nine-thirty-five. She was early, so where was Leonora? Maybe she'd popped up to the shops. She sat on the flight of stairs that led down to the first floor and ground level, her heavy bag on her knees. She smoked a cigarette and checked her watch again. Nearly ten to ten. Leonora was cutting it a bit fine, they'd be late. She ground the cigarette stub with her boot. Then she heard footsteps coming up the stairs. She stood up, a half smile on her face to greet her friend, but it was Leonora's next-door neighbour.

'Hello, love. Have you seen Leonora this morning?'

The other woman shrugged. 'No.'

'I wonder what could have happened to her? I've been waiting here for ages.'

'Maybe she overslept?'

The woman was opening her front door.

'No. I banged the door down.'

'Sure it's not her day off?'

'We always have the same days off. I don't like it. If Leonora was called away sudden like, she would have rung me. She knows I come out of me way to walk to work with her.'

The neighbour put her shopping bags down heavily in her hall and pulled the keys from the door.

'I've got a key. She gave it to me when she got locked out that time. Just in case it happened again. Cost her over forty quid to get all new locks. Bloody scandalous, I say.'

Dorothy nodded in agreement.

'Do you think we should let ourselves in like? In case she's had an accident or she's ill or something.'

'I'll knock one more time.'

Neither woman liked the thought of letting themselves into Leonora's house unless they had to.

Dorothy banged on the front door again, the sound echoing through the block of flats.

Nothing.

She opened the letter box and called through it. Then listened in case Leonora was in bed ill or something.

She straightened up.

'The telly's on.'

The neighbour slowly opened the front door. Inside, the

317

hall was quite dark. All the doors in the flat led off it and as they were closed there was no light from the windows. Dorothy switched on the light. Both sniffed and stared at one another. There was a slightly pungent smell beneath the heavier smell of lavender polish. The two women felt uneasy as they walked to Leonora's bedroom. Dorothy opened the door.

'The bed's made.' Her voice was puzzled.

Leonora's neighbour stood by the front door. She had a terrible feeling.

The door to the lounge was shut tight, and Dorothy felt a prickle of apprehension as she put her hand on the handle. She walked into the lounge.

The gas fire was on full and the television was showing a children's puppet programme. Her mind registered these facts. Her eyes, though, were on her friend.

Dorothy just stood and stared at the remains of Leonora Davidson.

Finally, after what seemed an eternity, she screamed – a high-pitched, animal scream that bounced around the tiny room, filling it with her fear and outrage.

As a parting shot, George had stuck the breadknife through Leonora's left eye socket.

Her naked legs were sprawled in front of the fire, and had been gradually singed during the course of the night. Somewhere in the back of her mind Dorothy realised that that was the funny smell.

Burnt meat.

Caitlin and Kate were elated. The killer had once again changed tack. He had gone into someone's home. That meant one thing: the victim knew him.

The door-to-door was trying to establish not only people's whereabouts, but also whether or not they had seen anybody either in or near the block of flats.

Kate's elation soon dissipated when she saw the woman's body. What kind of man would do that to another human being?

'There's semen on the mouth, breasts, and in and around the vagina. I'd hazard a guess our man went on rather a spree last night. She's been buggered, I'd lay money on that one.' The pathologist shook his head.

Caitlin was staring at the woman as if committing her to memory. She still had the breadknife jutting from her eye, like a grotesque statue. At least someone had turned off the gas fire and opened the windows.

All around people were getting on with their jobs. Scenes of Crime were taking photographs. Taking fibres from the carpet and furniture. Picking up individual hairs. Taking samples of blood from the body, the chair and the carpet. Kate saw one pop the two coffee cups into plastic bags for fingerprinting and knew immediately that would get them nowhere. He always wore gloves. Always. He was as shrewd as they come.

Caitlin pulled his gaze from Leonora's body and his eyes burned into Kate's.

'There's got to be something this time. He's not the Invisible Man, for God's sake. Someone must have seen him.'

Kate wasn't sure who he was trying to convince.

'The two women who discovered the body are both in hospital. Shock.'

'Well, I should think they are, Katie. Look at what they stumbled on. But this time we've got him. I just know it. I feel it.'

She hoped that Caitlin was right.

'Are you coming with me to watch the post mortem?'

He nodded.

'Yes. I'll be there, Katie. I want to know everything. Something is going to lead us to that bastard. I just know it.'

DS Spencer came into the tiny room and stared at Leonora's body. She was rapidly greying. He stared at her hard, like Caitlin before him.

'I expect the time of death will be difficult to determine. If the fire was on full all night it would delay rigor mortis.' Spencer's voice was smug.

'Once we get all the statements in we'll have an idea, don't you worry.'

Kate disliked Spencer, and knew that he knew that, and somehow it gave him an edge.

'You hang around here and book the body, Spencer. Sir, I'm going to see how the uniforms are doing on the door-to-door. I want to speak to a couple of the neighbours myself before I interview the two who found the body. Maybe one of them will know where her ex-husband is. From what I gather she had no children or immediate family. Do you want to come with me?'

'You go, Katie, I'll meet you at the hospital for the PM.'

'OK.'

She was glad to leave the flat. The picture of the woman's body was still in her mind.

At the first flat she visited, she was offered a cup of coffee and accepted gratefully. She needed something after the scene downstairs. The woman though, friendly as she was, knew nothing. Kate was sure of that within five minutes. She gave them a lead on the missing husband. He'd run off with Leonora's friend and was now living in Canada. Kate thanked the woman and left.

She walked to the door opposite and knocked. It was opened by a large man in a string vest. Fred Borrings brought Kate into his little flat and sat her down ceremoniously. It was obvious she had been expected.

'Now then, Miss . . .'

'DI Burrows, sir.' Kate smiled at him.

'I popped down the pub just before ten last night. You get to know all the sounds in the flats like. It becomes part of your hearing, if you get what I mean; I even know what time people pull their lavatories in the evening. I can time them.

'Anyway, I left here last night at about ten, and as I walked down the stairs I heard a door closing. It was Leonora's. I assumed she had a visitor, 'cos I remember thinking it was unusual. She very rarely had any visitors did Leonora. Very nice woman, you know, but always kept herself to herself.

320

No men calling, if you get my drift. Some of the women in these flats! My God, it's like a knocking shop. But Leonora was a good woman.'

'She never had any men friends at all?'

'No. Used to work all the time. Scared of going out at night she was, because of the muggings around this area. We seem to get all the glue sniffers here, I don't know why. Have to step over the little sods some nights to get up the stairs. They come in the lobbies to get out of the cold, I expect. Poor Leonora. Wouldn't hurt a fly.'

'You didn't actually see anyone then?'

Fred shook his head. 'Nah. I know what I heard though. I wish I'd knocked now. I do sometimes. See if she wants a packet of fags or anything from the offie. I know she don't go out at night, see. Whoever went into her house knew her. When I knocked there on me way out she'd call out to me "Who is it?" or "Is that you, Fred?" You know the kind of thing. She never opened the door without establishing who was there first.

'That's what makes me think she knew him. I've been thinking about it all morning. When I heard all the hubbub going on I went down, see. Two bloody old biddies screaming their heads off. It was me who phoned you and the ambulance. I've been thinking about it ever since. Leonora knew her attacker, my girl, I'm convinced of it.'

Kate let the man talk. What he said made sense. If she lived alone, and was not the type to socialise very much, Leonora would be aware of the dangers. Women who had no social life were always more wary of people knocking on their doors than those who got about a bit.

'Did you notice any strange cars parked outside when you went to the . . . ?'

'I went to the Hoy and Helmet. And, no, I didn't see any unusual cars parked outside. My friend gave me a lift back at about eleven fifteen and I noticed that Leonora's lights were still on. I could see them through the chinks in the curtains. It's like I said before – you get to know everything about everyone. Living on top of one another like we do.'

321

'Have you ever seen Leonora with a man? Maybe a man from work who might have given her a lift home?'

'She always went to and from work with her friend Dorothy. I've never know either of them go to work alone. They even have the same days off.'

Kate smiled to take the edge off her next sentence.

'You seem to know an awful lot about Leonora Davidson, Mr Borrings.'

He watched her grimly.

'I happened to like her, missis. I liked her a lot. There's no law against that, is there? I'm trying to help you so you can find the person responsible. That's all. You can check out my story. Plenty of people saw me in the Hoy, I use the pub a lot.'

'That won't be necessary, Mr Borrings.' It would be checked out as a matter of course but Kate was too wise to mention this. 'It's just that normally people are undecided about a lot of things that they see or hear. You know, like after a bank robbery, every witness has the robber in a different coloured sweater with different coloured hair.'

'I understand exactly what you're getting at, missis.' His voice was hard. 'But I am not like that. I don't waste words. I say what I think and I think about what I say. Be a damn sight better world if more people were like it.'

'Quite. Well, I've taken up enough of your time, Mr Borrings. Thank you very much, you've been very helpful.'

The man stood up and nodded at her but his friendliness had gone. Kate knew that he was the kind who normally overpowered people. From the little she had gleaned about Leonora Davidson, he had probably overpowered her. He was like a child who knew the right answer, jumping around in his chair, hand up in the air, quivering with excitement. Only he was the child the teacher normally overlooked.

'I'm quite willing to identify the body formally, missis. Her ex-husband's in Canada or some such place.'

'Thank you. We'll let you know if that will be necessary.'

Kate took her leave and drove off to the hospital for the post mortem.

When she got there she first went in to see Dorothy Smith. She had been given an injection of Diazepam to calm her down. When Kate sat beside her she saw that the woman had a glazed look in her eyes. She smiled and Dorothy tried to focus.

'Hello, I'm Detective Inspector Burrows. I'd like to ask you a few questions if you feel up to it?'

Dorothy nodded her head.

'Are you sure you're OK? I can come back later.'

'No. No, I'll answer you. I'll have to eventually. It may as well be now while it's all still fresh in my mind.'

'Did Leonora ever mention any men friends at all? Not just boyfriends, I mean friends in general. Maybe a man at work who was taking undue interest in her?'

Dorothy shook her head.

'Never. She didn't like men much, you see. She kept herself to herself, she was that kind of woman. I've known her for over fifteen years and if she had a man friend I'd know about it. We told each other everything.' The woman's eyes spilled over with tears.

'She was good, was Leonora, she was kind and considerate. Why would anyone want to do that to her? Why?'

Kate was powerless to answer. Instead she placed her hand on the older woman's and squeezed it gently, letting her cry.

When she quietened, Kate spoke again. 'What about Fred Borrings?'

Dorothy pulled her hand from Kate's grasp.

'He used to look out for her, that was all. I think he would have liked to have been more than friends with her, you know, but Leonora . . .' Her voice choked again. 'She didn't want anything like that. Her husband used to knock her around and she swore she'd never ever get involved again.'

Kate stared at the woman without seeing her.

Then how the hell did the man get inside her house? Maybe he was dressed as a workman, that was an old trick. Knock on a door and say you were from the gas or the electricity board and people automatically gave you entry to their homes. But surely someone would have noticed? She would have to wait and see what was said by the people interviewed. Once all the statements were collated they would have some idea to work from.

Someone must have seen something, however small. Those flats were a hive of activity. From glue sniffers to heroin addicts, that's where they congregated. Even their statements, however vague, could spark off a train of inquiry.

As the post mortem began Kate and Caitlin both had the same thought: once more the man had come and gone without being seen.

For the first time in years Kate crossed her fingers. She had a feeling that she'd need all the luck she could get.

Patrick heard about Leonora Davidson from his friend the Chief Constable. He was promised all the information they had about it within twenty-four hours. He was sitting in his drawing room contemplating the new event. However much he liked Kate – and he did like her, he liked her a lot – she was getting nowhere. Neither were the men he had employed, he had to admit. He closed his eyes and rubbed them hard.

If only he had something to go on. One little clue was all he needed. He knew that Kate was doing everything she could but this man was taking the piss now. He was sitting somewhere, laughing up his sleeve at them all, and Patrick Kelly was not a man who could stomach that. Every time he thought about it, it brought on a red hot rage.

He had picked out a white coffin for his daughter, with a deep red satin interior. The coffin was lead lined, airless and insect proof. The thought of his lovely child under the ground in the cold and the damp, with centipedes and other lifeforms crawling all over her face, in her mouth and through her long blonde hair, made him feel sick. But the man who had put her there . . . now he was a different kettle of fish altogether. Patrick Kelly would see to it that he rotted away, that he died as horrifically as he had killed.

Kelly rubbed his eyes again. The strain was beginning to

tell now. He knew he was dangerously close to exploding point. He glanced at the photograph of Mandy on the mantelpiece. It had been taken a few weeks before her death at the birthday party of one of her friends. The girl had had it enlarged and framed and sent it to him, a kindly act that had brought tears to his eyes. Whoever had taken the picture had caught Mandy with her head back, her eyes half closed, her teeth looking like perfect pearls as she laughed. It was one of those lucky photographs that occasionally get taken with a cheap snapper camera, and he loved it.

Willy tapped on the door softly before entering the room.

'It's Kevin Cosgrove, Pat, he wants to see you.' The big man's eyebrows lifted. 'Want me to smack him one and send him on his way?' Willy's voice was hopeful.

Kelly shook his head. No. Show him in.'

He felt the tightening inside his chest again. He wondered lately if he was getting some kind of heart trouble, but had dismissed the thought.

Kevin walked into the room. Even Kelly was shocked at the sight of him. He had lost weight and his usual pristine appearance was gone. His hair was unkempt and he needed a shave.

'Christ Almighty, you look like a paraffin lamp.'

Kevin stood uneasily in the doorway, his face white with fear. 'I came about Mandy's funeral, sir.'

Patrick knew that it had taken the boy a lot of courage to come to his house and in spite of himself was impressed. He knew men who were harder than granite who would not have had the front to walk into his home after what he had done to Cosgrove.

'What about her funeral?' His voice was soft.

Kevin looked around the room, fixing his eyes on a Japanese vase before answering.

'Well, I wanna go. Please.'

The last word was quiet and drawn out. A plea in itself.

He stared at the boy, battling it out in his mind.

'You can go, boy, but keep away from me and mine. I

325

mean it, Kevin, I'll always blame you for what happened to her. Always. If you hadn't've left her there alone . . .' Patrick's voice trailed off, he could feel the tightening around his heart again. 'Go on, piss off. Before I lose me rag again. And remember what I said, Kevin. Keep well away from me, son. I don't know what I'd be capable of if I saw too much of you while I was burying her.'

Kevin hung his head and turning on his heel walked from the room, closing the door behind him. Patrick stared at the door for a long time. Finally, Willy came into the room with a pot of coffee. Placing the tray on the small Edwardian table by the sofa he poured out two cups, one for Kelly and one for himself. He laced them both liberally with brandy. Kelly watched the big man's clumsy attempt at being a butler and felt amused.

'I thought you could do with a bit of a natter, Pat. I don't think it's good to be on your own all the time. You need a bit of company now and then. Cheers.' He held up his coffee cup and sipped at it, burning his mouth.

'Bloody hell, is that Mrs Manners trying to weld my lips together or what?'

Patrick laughed loudly.

Willy was a tonic sometimes without even realising it.

'Have you heard any more, Pat?'

All the formality was gone now and the serious business of the day was about to begin. Kelly had an understanding with Willy. He allowed the man a free rein when it was necessary. They went back a long way.

'No. Nothing really. I'll have all the gen on the new murder by tomorrow.'

'That little ponce had some front, didn't he? Coming round here like that. I was going to give him a right-hander just for his sauce.'

Patrick waved his hand.

'Forget him. He'll get his come-uppance one day. If God don't see to it, then I will.'

'I've been thinking, Pat . . .'

Kelly closed his eyes. That was a turn up for the book, Willy thinking.

'You know that Old Bill bird you've been knocking . . . I mean, going out with?'

Kelly nodded, on the defensive now. 'What about her?' He wasn't in the mood for a lecture from Mr Charisma today.

'Well, I heard you two nattering one day. She was saying about how they took blood samples or something for DPP or something?'

'DNA. It's DNA. DPP means Director of Public Prosecutions. Anyway, what about it?'

Willy's round face looked puzzled. 'Then what's DNA mean?'

Patrick was getting agitated. 'How the fucking hell do I know? I'm not a scientist, am I?'

'All right, all right, Pat, keep your hair on.'

'Well, what are you trying to say?'

'She was saying that they could do that here, but it would cost too much money.'

'Do what?'

'To take the bloody blood tests. Stone me, Pat, don't you listen to nothing people say?'

Looking at Willy's open face it dawned on Kelly that for once he had a good idea.

Kate had told him, one night while they were having dinner, that DNA was a genetic fingerprint. Everyone knew that much from the papers. Until now he had not really understood the full meaning of what she'd been saying.

'Do me a favour, will you? Get on to the Chief Constable and tell him I want facts on all the cases ever solved by DNA. Remember that now – DNA not DPP. We'll be here all day otherwise with files of every poor bastard the Old Bill's ever fitted up.'

'I'll do it now, Pat.' Willy stood up and went to the door.

'And, Willy.' The man turned around. 'Thanks a lot. You've been a great help, I appreciate it.'

Willy grinned.

327

'DNA . . . DNA . . .' He was still saying it as he walked out of the door, as if terrified he would forget it.

Patrick picked up his coffee and sipped it, savouring the bite from the brandy.

Maybe he could get Kate's wish granted.

Maybe then they could all get somewhere.

Caitlin and Kate had the majority of the collated statements in front of them and both were feeling down. Not even a sniff of anything out of the ordinary.

The post mortem had revealed that although Leonora Davidson had been strangled by her attacker, the cause of death was most likely 'Vagal Inhibition'. In other words she had literally died of fright.

'Well, another murder and we have nothing to go on. Bloody hell, someone must have seen something. It stands to reason.'

Caitlin nodded.

'There are clues here, it's just sorting out what could be viable. People see things and don't take in what they're seeing.' He poked the papers in front of him. 'One of these must have seen the man only they don't realise it yet. Either he's local and so they're used to seeing him, or he was walking nearby and they just passed him on the street. He *has* been seen, only he hasn't been tied in with it all yet. I think he's stopped using his car. So either he cabs it wherever he goes or it's all within walking distance.'

'He could have caught a bus.'

'There you are then, so he *has* been seen by people. If we could trace just one person who saw someone different on their bus coming home from work, whatever, we'd be in business.'

'Well, Spencer has been in touch with all the mini cab firms and he's checking out all the people who got cabs between nine and twelve on the night of Leonora's murder. So far he's come up against malice, upset, aggravation – and nothing else.

'The murders are causing strife now. One murder is

exciting, two is exciting, four means we aren't doing our job and every person interviewed now thinks their face is in the frame.'

'Sure they're all fecking eejits. Listen, I'll get Willis to go and see the bus drivers. You know, one of them might have seen something, or more precisely someone.'

Kate nodded.

'"Vagal Inhibition", I'd never heard of that before. It sounds terrible.'

'It make me sick to me stomach even to think about it. Get yourself off, Katie. I'll stay on for a while here. You get some sleep.'

She got up, smoothing down her skirt.

'You've got good legs, you know, Kate.' Before she could retort he spoke again. 'How's the girl?'

'Lizzy? She's fine. I'm going to see her actually.'

'Well, she'll soon be back on her feet, God willing. Would you get me the files under W please, before you go.'

Kate went to the filing cabinet and opened the drawer. In the back was a bottle of Teacher's. She pulled it out and took it to Caitlin who picked it up.

'This country's a terrible place, you know. An Irishman drinking Scotch whisky.' He shook his head. 'Please God I'll find a shop that sells Bushmill's one day.'

'You sound like my mother.'

'Ah, sure she's a very astute woman!'

Kate picked up her bag and jacket. 'See you in the morning, Kenneth.'

'Kenny.'

Smiling, she made her way through the room, deliberately averting her eyes from the victims' photographs on the wall. She stopped at Amanda Dawkins' desk.

'Anything?'

Amanda shook her head. 'Nothing.'

Kate sighed. 'See you tomorrow.'

'Night.'

She drove to Warley Hospital. It was early evening and the

329

traffic had just eased up so she had a straight drive. In twenty minutes she was there. As she stepped from the car and looked at the big old building she felt a lump in her throat. But Patrick was right when he said at least Lizzy was alive and kicking. If Kate had had to identify her as Ronald Butler had had to identify his daughter, she did not know what she would have to do.

With the latest murder the pressure was really on. This man had to be caught, and fast. Extremely fast. It was said that unless a murderer was apprehended within three days, the likelihood of finding the person was minimal. Which was true, but this man committed murder after murder. He had tried it, liked it, and by all the signs was now unable to stop himself.

She walked along the corridor towards Lizzy's ward. She could hear Simply Red singing 'If you don't know me by now' and she smiled slightly. At least this was not the usual hospital environment. Here Lizzy could listen to music, wear her own clothes and there were trained staff to talk to her, listen to her problems.

Bracing herself and planting a smile on her face, Kate entered the ward. Lizzy was sitting at a table with two other girls. Kate went to her and kissed the top of her head.

'Hello, Mum!' Lizzy looked great. In the week she had been in here she already had made a marked improvement.

Kate sat down at the table and nodded to the two others. A large-boned dark girl got up. 'Can I get you a coffee?'

'Thanks, no sugar.'

'I heard about the murder, Mum, it's terrible. We were just talking about it.'

Kate didn't know what to say. Lizzy had asked her not to mention she was a policewoman. Now here she was blurting it out.

A blonde girl with large green eyes and a mass of permed hair shook her head.

'You must really get stressed out in your job like. I don't know how you can look at those dead bodies, man!'

Kate grinned. The girl was impressed!

'It's not very nice, I must admit, but someone has to do it.'

'My mum's worked on lots of murders, haven't you, Mum?'

Kate felt quite embarrassed. 'Well, not lots, a few. Murder is not as common as you might think.'

'Have you any idea who the Grantley Ripper is?'

Kate looked into the girl's green eyes. 'No. To be honest we have no idea. But we're working on it.'

The dark one brought her back a cup of coffee and the two girls left. Kate sensed they knew she and Lizzy wanted to be left alone.

'They call this quality time, Mum. When you have a visitor the others have to go away.'

'Why are they in here?' Kate sipped her coffee.

'Well, the dark girl is Andrea. She tried to kill herself because she had a lot of problems. She was studying for her A levels, and everything just got on top of her. She's really nice, you know.'

'What about the little blonde?'

'She's a nurse, Mum! It's hard to tell the difference, isn't it?'

Kate laughed. 'It is! Now then, how are you?'

Lizzy sighed, lifting her fringe as she exhaled.

'I feel much better. I saw the psychiatrist again today. He's really nice, Mum. He said that I was having a personality conflict. That I tried to be one thing when I wanted to be another. He said that my behaviour was caused by insecurity. I wanted to belong but I sort of rebelled against everything.'

'Do you think he's right?'

Lizzy looked into her mother's eyes and nodded.

'I am sorry, Mum, for what I did. When I knew that Gran had read the diary, I just wanted to die. I know you love me, Mum, I love you and Gran too, but I've felt at times like I was second best, you know. Your job always took precedence over me. Dad was never really there. I know that he's a user. He uses me, I've known it for a long time, but I still love him. He's my dad.' Her eyes were pleading for understanding.

Kate nodded.

'My job came first because I needed the money, to be honest with you, Lizzy. Your father never once contributed to your keep. He left me with a mortgage, a child and a broken heart.' Kate smiled to take the edge off her words. 'I had to make some kind of life for us, I had to work. I went for promotions because it was more money. I bought the house we live in today, and I still have to pay the upkeep, your gran only gets a small pension . . .'

Kate grasped Lizzy's hand tightly across the table. 'I never meant to make you feel left out, Lizzy. You were my reason for working. I wanted you to have the best that I could provide. That's why I never had a personal life.'

'Dad's told me about your boyfriend.'

Kate felt coldness wrap itself around her heart, but when she looked at Lizzy, she saw that the girl was smiling.

'Don't look so stunned, Mum, I think it's great. I saw him once, that Patrick Kelly. He came to my school to give a donation. He's really good looking. Dark and brooding! That's my type, Mum, we have the same taste.'

Kate dropped her head on to her chest and bit her lip. After what she had read in Lizzy's diary, anyone seemed to be Lizzy's taste. Kate swallowed the thought. She had to stop making judgements or they'd never get back on an even keel.

'He's all right. I'm a bit old for a boyfriend though, don't you think? Let's say he's more of a . . . man friend.'

'As far as dad's concerned he's a boyfriend stroke lover.' He's so jealous. Honestly Mum, you should have seen him, he was practically green!' Lizzy hooted with laughter, making the others in the room look at her and smile themselves.

'What did you say to him, Liz?'

Lizzy leant across the table and in one of her old gestures, that brought a lump to Kate's throat, she pushed her heavy hair off her face and grinned, for all the world looking like a schoolgirl. This girl-woman made Kate want to weep. She blinked away the burning tears.

'I told him it wasn't any of his bloody business.'

Kate's eyes widened.

'I bet that went down well, Liz!'

Lizzy laughed out loud. 'Like a lead balloon, Mum. I told him straight though,' Lizzy was serious again now, 'I said that was the trouble with this family, everyone did what was expected of them and never what they wanted to do!'

Kate stared at Lizzy in amazement. Her daughter sounded more grown up and intelligent than she had ever done before. 'I sent him away with a flea in his ear, I can tell you.'

'Oh, Lizzy!'

'Oh Lizzy nothing. If I'm to say what I really think, like the psychiatrist says I should, then I'm afraid that please or offend, I'm gonna say it!'

She stretched her arms out wide. 'I feel great, Mum. Really great, for the first time in ages. Joanie came in this morning and we had a long chat. She told me in no uncertain terms what a complete shit I've been and I had to agree with her. But I promised her, and I'm promising you now, I'll be better. I am going to be much better.'

'Lizzy, I love you, whatever you are, whatever you do.'

She smiled.

'I know that, Mum. Now tell me, what's this Patrick Kelly like?'

'He's just a friend. When his daughter was murdered we sort of – I don't know – we sort of made a friendship, I suppose.'

'Gran says he's lovely. That's because he's Irish. Do you remember when Boy George was on Top of the Pops and Gran went, "What on earth's that on the telly?" And I said, "That's Boy George, Gran, his real name is George O'Dowd. His family's Irish." And Gran listened to him for a while and then went, "Sure he's not that bad!"'

Kate laughed. 'Yes, I remember that.'

'So come on, Mum, what's he really like?' Lizzy's little face was earnest.

'He's a very kind man. Now that's enough of that, madam. You tell me about yourself. What's been happening here?'

Lizzy began telling her about her day and Kate listened, glad to drop the subject of Patrick.

But she admitted to herself that he strayed into her thoughts often. She relived their lovemaking in her mind at odd moments. He was exciting and potentially dangerous, a lethal combination, but Kate didn't care. For the first time in her life she was being loved and she was thriving on it.

'Before I forget, Lizzy, how would you feel about going out to Australia?'

Her eyes widened. 'Really? You mean, go out to Uncle Pete?'

Kate nodded.

'Oh, Mum, that would be excellent.'

'Gran would go with you. I can't, because I can't get the time off work, but I thought you'd enjoy it. It would be a break. You'd have the sun, and see your cousins.'

Lizzy launched herself from her chair and wrapped her arms around her mother's body. Kate could feel the excitement in her.

She hugged her daughter back. Kate would have loved to have gone, but she just couldn't afford it. As it was she was going to get a bank loan to pay for Lizzy and Evelyn to go, for spending money and everything else. But she would willingly sell her soul if it meant making her daughter happy.

'Oh, Mum, you're so good to me!'

Kate kissed her soft, sweet-smelling hair.

'We'll find out when you're leaving here and then I'll book it. It'll give you something to look forward to.'

Lizzy skipped over to a small crowd by the record player and told them her good fortune. Kate felt lighter inside at seeing her daughter's happy face than she had for a long time.

At that moment Dan was sitting opposite Frederick Flowers. It was after seven and Flowers was surreptitiously trying to glance at his watch. Dan saw and it annoyed him.

'Well, what are you going to do about it?'

Dan's blond good looks had annoyed Flowers straight off. He had felt distaste for the man from the minute he had opened his mouth.

'Your ex-wife, Mr Burrows, is a senior officer. She is working on a case involving Mr Kelly's daughter.'

Dan broke in, 'But she's sleeping with the man!'

Flowers smiled annoyingly. 'I'm afraid I only have your word for that.' He stood up and held out his hand. 'I promise you I will look into your allegations personally.'

Dan stood up too and ignored the outstretched hand. He pointed a finger at the man in front of him.

'She's knocking him off, a known villain. Personally, I think that needs pretty close attention.'

Turning on his heel, Dan marched from the room. Flowers sat down and sighed.

He could just see himself ringing up Patrick Kelly and telling him to lay off Kate Burrows. Flowers and Kelly were hand in glove. They had been for a number of years.

He was surprised at Kate Burrows though, he admitted that to himself. She was a good officer, one of the best. He had not thought she would ever have got involved with Kelly. Well, that was female logic, he supposed.

But he could fully understand Kate Burrows wanting to get rid of that big handsome husband of hers. The man was a bully boy.

Getting up, he smoothed out the creases in his trousers. Home, that's where he wanted to be now. He walked from his office and closed the door, making a mental note to tell his secretary that Daniel Burrows was not to be given appointments to see him, no matter how urgent they sounded.

One set-to with him was quite enough.

Kate drove home, ate a hurried meal, bathed, changed and left the house in record time. She told her mother not to wait up for her, at which she got one of Evelyn's knowing smiles.

She drove up Patrick's drive at just before nine o'clock. Willy opened the door for her before she knocked and showed her into the lounge.

'Mr Kelly will be down shortly. Can I get you a drink?'

'I'll wait for Patrick if you don't mind.'

Willy smiled at her in his friendliest manner. He bowed and walked from the room.

Kate sat on the sofa and smiled to herself. She relaxed back into the comfort of the chair. Like everything in the house it was beautiful and practical. She was so glad that Lizzy was feeling better. It was as if a lead weight had been lifted from her. The psychiatrist had said a lot of youngsters went through what Lizzy was going through; it was part and parcel of growing up in the modern world. It was he who had suggested that a change of environment might do her good. He said that her drug taking was not habitual, she was not psychologically hooked but used drugs as a means of escape. He also remarked that Lizzy's over-active sex life was not abnormal these days. Many young girls had had eight or nine sexual partners before they were twenty. It was a real sign of the times. He was more interested in whether she had used a condom.

We live and learn, thought Kate.

Patrick walked into the room. He was wearing a deep blue dressing gown.

'Were you having a bath?'

'No, I was building a bonfire!'

Kate laughed. He came to her and kissed her. She felt his lips touch hers gently and once more sensed his animal strength. He was like a drug, dangerously addictive.

'I've had Willy open a bottle of Barolo. How about a glass?'

Kate nodded and Patrick went from the room. She sat in the chair with her hands on the arms. Another thing she admired about Patrick – there were no televisions to be seen anywhere although she knew that the big oak cabinet along the wall beside her housed a thirty-two-inch state of the art flat screen TV. Kate was not a television watcher, but a reader. That was her chosen form of relaxation. Patrick was the same. In fact, they had a lot in common. One part of her was frightened by Patrick; she knew a lot about him, and not all of it good. But when she was with him, near him, she could forgive him anything. Anything at all. She knew that she made excuses for him to herself.

He came back into the room with the bottle and two crystal glasses. He poured them both a drink and sat on the floor by Kate's chair.

'This is lovely, Kate. It's good to have a woman about the house again.'

'What about Mrs Manners?'

Patrick sipped his wine.

'Mrs Manners is a great cook and a lovely old dear, but she don't exactly turn me on, know what I mean?'

She looked down into his rugged face and felt a tightening in her stomach.

She really wanted this man.

'How's it going with the case?' His voice was sombre now.

Kate felt her good mood begin to fade.

'I take it there's still nothing to go on?'

She shook her head.

'We're doing our best, but as I said before, Pat, with someone like this, well, it's a hard slog.'

Patrick knelt in front of her and sipped his wine. 'What was this thing you was going on about before? DNA.'

'Oh, genetic fingerprinting. That's just about all we have. The trouble is no one will authorise all the money it would cost to give over five thousand men a blood test. But it's been done before, in Enderby in Leicestershire. In eighty-three, I think it was.'

'Did it work?'

Kate nodded. 'Yes, it did actually.'

Both of them were quiet and Patrick sat back on the floor. They sipped their wine in silence. It was an amiable silence. This was another thing that attracted Kate to Patrick. She could sit with him without saying a word. With Dan, if there had been a silence it was loaded. With Patrick it was natural. He stood up and took the glass from her. Pulling her from the chair he kissed her, long and hard.

'Come to bed with me, Kate, I really want you.'

She nodded slightly. Taking their glasses, they made their way up to his bedroom, where Patrick began slowly to undress her, caressing each part of her body as it became

337

exposed to him. The first time he had done this to her, she had felt as if she was going to die from pleasure. That he had a wide experience of lovemaking bothered her not one bit. Kate had never been loved like this before. He made love to her at his leisure, keeping her in a state of anticipation that was both erotic and mind blowing. He brought her to orgasm first with his mouth before he entered her, then made love to her slowly, with long hard strokes, until she felt ready to come again. She had never experienced so much pleasure and happiness from the sex act. It would be very hard to give it up now.

Chapter Nineteen

1953

George's arms were tired. He hitched up the parcels further and grasped them tighter to his chest. He stood in the queue, his feet cold and sore. He needed new shoes desperately, these were far too small and they had a large hole in the sole that he covered with cardboard. It was now soggy and uncomfortable. He watched in annoyance as the old lady in front of him made a big performance of counting her change. He felt like dragging her away from the counter and kicking her from the shop. Instead he smiled at her as she moved and placed the parcels gratefully on the counter while the bespectacled woman weighed and stamped them.

Free from his burden, his hand went into his pocket where his wages sat snugly.

He grinned to himself. His first week's wages. He would treat himself to some new shoes. His final errand of the day done, he began the long walk home. From tomorrow he could take the bus to work. Unless . . . He shook his head to clear the bad thoughts away. He walked the busy streets confidently, like a boy who knew where he was going. Over the years, he had gradually found his way all over London – north, south and east. His mother moved so often he knew just about everywhere. Now they were in Ilford and he knew the place like the back of his hand.

Finally, after an hour's walking, he came to the house in Green Lanes. He was tired. Bone tired. One good thing about his mother, she always provided a good meal. He walked round the back and let himself into the kitchen, wiping his feet fastidiously on the mat by the back door.

'You're late!' Nancy's voice was annoyed. George nodded, aware that there was no appetising smell to greet him. He glanced at the cooker in consternation.

'It's no good looking like that, Georgie boy. Until I get me housekeeping we ain't got nothing to eat. I thought we'd have chippy tonight, to celebrate like.'

George took off his jacket and hung it on the back of the door on the hanger there for that express purpose. Nancy hated sloppiness.

'Well?' It was more a statement than a question.

George slipped his hand into his pocket and took out the wage packet. It was unopened. Nancy grabbed it greedily from his hand and ripped it open. She poured the coins out into her large red-varnished hand.

'Is this all?' Her green eyes narrowed as she looked at him. 'Thirty bob?'

George nodded again. 'I need new shoes.'

Nancy laughed. 'Don't we all?' She threw two half-crowns on the table. 'That's your cut, Georgie boy. Twenty-five shillings is for your housekeeping.'

She saw his face and went on the defensive. 'Listen here, you, I kept you all your life, it's about time you paid some of it back.'

As she spoke Jed McAnulty came into the kitchen. He had obviously been asleep. He looked at the money on the table and his face lit up. Nancy saw and turned on him. 'You needn't think you're getting any of this, 'cos you're not.'

George sighed and hastily picked up the two half-crowns. He couldn't have the shoes and bus it to work. He'd have to save up. His newfound freedom dissolved around his ears while Nancy and her boyfriend fought. George walked into the front room and sat on the settee. A little while later he heard the back door slam and his mother's high heels on the concrete pathway. Jed walked into the front room.

'She's gone to get the chips.' Jed sat on the chair by the fire and ran his plastic comb through his hair. 'I don't know why you don't get yourself a little place, Georgie. Don't give that old bat your dosh.'

He was silent, staring into the fire.

'Listen to me, son, she gets a fortune doing what she does. She don't need your money, she's taking it for spite. I've never known a woman like her in me life.'

George looked at the man calmly.

'You live off her, Jed. That's where all her money goes.'

Jed bit his lip and grinned.

'Me and your mother's got an arrangement. I supply her with the means to do her job, that's all. But all that aside, son, she's got a small fortune stashed, she don't need your money.'

George knew it was true. Knew that Jed was trying to help him. But as always his loyalty to his mother came to the forefront.

'All you men – the men she meets – you all take advantage of her.'

Jed grinned again. 'Listen, boy, your mother likes her way of life. She's one of the only toms . . . I mean, working women . . . I know who loves her job.'

George closed his eyes. Jed brought men to the house for Nancy and then sat drinking downstairs while she plied her trade upstairs. The last man Nancy had had was a big Irishman who had made George part of his arrangement. Jed, in fairness, never tried anything like that on. When Nancy had mentioned it he had gone mad, saying that she was unnatural. George had quite liked Jed after that. He seemed to have taken over where Edith had left off.

'Think about what I'm saying, son. You got a good little job, try and get yourself a room somewhere.'

Neither was aware that Nancy was standing in the kitchen listening to the conversation, having forgotten her own purse, which was stuffed full of money. Money that Jed knew about but couldn't find. She had come back to the house and heard everything. Her face set in a deep frown, she went out of the back door quietly and off to the chip shop.

George lay in bed listening to the quietness. He was tired out but couldn't sleep. Jed's words were echoing in his head. If he left home and got a room he could have a life of his own. He fantasised about having a little place with nice wallpaper and a record player. He saw it in his mind as if it was real. A clean candlewick bedspread on the double bed. A stack of records by the record player and an electric fire to keep him warm. Maybe a small wardrobe with nice clothes and shoes in it. And mats either side of the bed. In one corner of the room was a comfortable chair, with his favourite books on a coffee table alongside. He was so deep in his fantasy that he didn't hear his bedroom door open. When Nancy sat on the edge of his bed he was startled.

'Georgie boy?' Her voice was low and soft.

He didn't answer.

Nancy turned on the lamp by his bed and looked down at him, her face wreathed in smiles. She took a ten-shilling note from her dressing-gown pocket and placed it on the night table.

'That's for you, Georgie. Fifteen bob a week should be enough for your housekeeping. I don't like the thought of you walking to work like that, especially in this weather.'

George stared at her warily. She raised her hand and automatically he flinched. He heard her deep throaty chuckle, then felt her cool hands on his face as she caressed him. The hands moved down his body on to his chest, moving in circular motions that made his skin prickle. Against his will he felt the erection and pulled the sheets up over his stomach. Nancy pulled them down and grinned at him.

'You wouldn't leave your mummy, Georgie boy, would you?'

Her voice was husky and George could smell her perfume as she moved nearer.

He was willing her to go away. Begging her in his mind to leave him alone, but the habits of childhood are hard to break. He associated Nancy with excitement. He felt her fingers grasp his penis, and closed his eyes tight.

Nancy stroked him. Her eyes were brilliant in the candlelight. 'Mummy loves you, Georgie boy.'

He ejaculated, his thin body jerking frenziedly.

'And Georgie loves his mummy, doesn't he?'

She kissed him on the lips, pulling him towards her. Then, turning off the lamp she left the room as quietly and unobtrusively as she entered it.

George felt the stickiness on his thighs and suddenly the dam burst. He cried – hard, shuddering sobs that were as confused as his mind. He pushed his fists into his eyes to stem the tears. Because he hated her. He hated her so much. He hated the things she had done to him, he hated the way she made him feel and hated the way she touched him. It frightened him. But most frightening of all was that, as much as he hated her, he loved her.

He loved her so much.

Nancy lay beside Jed listening to the boy's sobs, and smiled. George was all she had and no one left her. At least, not until she was finished with them.

She slept. Jed turned over and broke wind loudly, sleeping contentedly, unaware that after his conversation with George, his days were numbered.

George awoke to a cooked breakfast and bussed it to work on a full stomach. In his half-hour lunch break he bought himself some new shoes. He went home on the bus to a cooked dinner.

Nancy made a big fuss of him. It wasn't until later in the evening he found out Jed had gone. If he had been a more worldly boy he might have realised what she was doing. Instead, as usual, he was grateful for the respite in her baiting of him.

The events of the night before were forced from his mind. Until the next time.

Chapter Twenty

Chief Constable Frederick Flowers was sitting in his office reading the latest reports on the Grantley Ripper. He was not happy with what he saw. It was the beginning of February and so far the man had got away with four murders. All murders were newsworthy, he conceded that, but sex murders like these seemed to grab the public interest and the daily papers made the most of this fact. His calls were now being screened because both the *Sun* and the *Star* were after something to pin on the police force. Flowers sat back in his seat.

After twenty-two years on the force he had seen many changes. He could remember when the police were respected, admired and feared – yes, feared. Now, if you grabbed a suspect by the arm the chances were his MP would shout out from the House of Commons: 'Police brutality'. Then, when something like this happened, everyone expected an arrest within twenty-four hours.

He frowned. If they did catch the man, the bleeding hearts would get him. By the time the psychologists and the social workers and every tin pot liberal with a BSc after their name had finished, the man would be found to be unfit to stand trial and would be put away in Broadmoor with a better style of living than he had ever been accustomed to. He had seen it too many times before. At the moment though, the papers and the public were after *his* blood, so Chummy had to be caught – and quick.

Flowers picked up the reports again, but his heart wasn't really in them. He had wanted to play golf today, like he did every Wednesday, but that was a no-no. All he needed was a picture of him on the course during a major investigation and the papers would finish him overnight. He was so deep in thought when his secretary buzzed him, he actually jumped in his seat.

He pressed the button on his intercom.

'What?'

Outside, Janet rolled her eyes to the ceiling. She did not like Frederick Flowers very much and his abrupt manner got on her nerves.

'There are two men downstairs to see you, sir, a Mr Kelly and a Mr Gabney. Shall I tell the desk sergeant to send them up?'

Frederick Flowers felt his mouth go dry and a wave of nausea washed over his body. Patrick Kelly, *here*? If someone saw them and put two and two together . . .

The logical part of his brain reminded him that Kelly had never been convicted of anything, that he had every right to be in a police station. But his gut told him it was dangerous to be professionally associated with Kelly at the station. They met socially, as many police and villains did – that was part and parcel of everyday life. They were masons, they were both members of the same clubs. They both socialised regularly with the local MP. But all the same, to have him here, in his office, in front of all his staff . . . Suppose he called him Freddie?

'Sir, can I send up Mr Kelly and Mr Gabney?'

'Oh yes, yes, Janet. Show them up please.'

The worst thing was, there was no way he could refuse to see him.

Flowers opened a drawer in his desk and took out a small packet of Settlers; he popped two into his mouth and chewed them noisily while he waited for Kelly.

Why couldn't he just see him at the club as usual? What was important enough to bring him here?

By the time Janet showed the two men into his office, Flowers had calmed down, but as she shut the door behind her the sourness returned to Flowers's face.

'Have you gone mad? Coming here like this? Do you realise I have got the press practically camped out on the doorstep? Why couldn't you have seen me as usual in the club?'

Kelly looked at the tall greying man in front of him. He guessed that he and Flowers were of an age. But dissatisfaction with his life had aged Flowers. He had a large paunch that he tried to hold in with a corset and he dyed his hair. All in all, Kelly thought that Flowers was a silly, vain man and he disliked him immensely.

His voice dripped ice.

'Are you taking the piss out of me?'

Flowers blinked rapidly as Kelly stared him out.

Patrick pointed a stiff finger at Flowers and enjoyed seeing the man flinch.

'In case it escaped your notice, Freddie,' he spoke the man's Christian name with contempt, 'my daughter was murdered recently. I know the news reached you like, 'cause I can remember mentioning it to you myself on several occasions.' The sarcasm was not lost on Flowers or Willy.

Patrick sat down and his minder followed suit. Flowers returned to his seat behind his desk. He had dropped a clanger and knew it. But he was relieved. If the press got wind of who Kelly was, then the fact that his daughter was one of the victims would cover up the fact that he and the Chief Constable met socially.

'I'm sorry, Patrick, but this place is literally under siege at the moment.'

'And you've missed your golf as well? My heart's breaking for you.'

Flowers did not like the fact that Kelly had hit the nail straight on the head but he swallowed the insult. Kelly was a formidable man and knew too much about Flowers and others ever to be made an enemy.

Janet came in with the coffee and left it on the desk. She smiled at Patrick briefly before leaving. Flowers poured it with a hand that was trembling slightly. Kelly always affected him like this.

'What can I do for you?'

'I have a proposition for you, Freddie me old son.'

Flowers looked perplexed. Surely Kelly wasn't here to talk business?

'What kind of proposition?'

'It's about the murderer. I think I know how we can catch the ponce.'

Flowers put down his coffee cup.

'Do you know who he is?' He knew that Patrick Kelly had a price on the man's head. In some circles it was common knowledge.

Patrick sipped his coffee slowly.

'No, I don't know. If I did then he'd be dead, Freddie. Deader than a week-old kipper. No. I don't know who he is, but I know how we can catch him. I need your help, though.'

'In what way?' Flowers was puzzled.

'In Leicester a few years ago every man in the vicinity of a murder case was given a blood test. Which narrowed down the police's line of inquiry.'

Flowers put up his hand in a gesture of dismissal. 'It would cost too much money, Patrick. Plus there's no guarantee it would work. You don't know the whole of it. We'd have the NCCL after us, not to mention every other crackpot group. They'd say it was just an excuse to monitor people. That their DNA samples would be ready and available for investigation in every sex crime that occurred. That it was an infringement of their civil liberties. Oh, you don't know the half of it.'

Patrick finished his coffee and put his cup on the desk. 'Listen, Freddie, I couldn't give a monkey's bollock for any of this. It is going to be done, and I am going to pay for it. So just button your mutton for five minutes and listen to me. All right?'

Kelly's eyes were hard and Flowers felt the power of the man in front of him.

Patrick Kelly began to talk, slowly and deliberately. After five minutes he had Flowers in a state of fear so acute he could taste it. But after fifteen minutes he could see the sense of what Kelly was saying and relaxed. Two hours later they had reached an amicable arrangement. Patrick got up to leave.

'I had a man in here yesterday evening – Daniel Burrows.' Flowers waited a few seconds for the name to sink in before he started to talk again.

'He seems to think that I should reprimand his ex-wife because of an association with your good self.'

Flowers relaxed. There, it was out!

He watched Patrick's eyes, which were like pieces of flint. Finally, after what seemed an eternity, Kelly went from the room. Fifteen minutes later Flowers also left for the day. For the rest of the afternoon Patrick Kelly made numerous phone calls from home. By eight that evening he had spoken to the DPP, two prominent cabinet members and a host of other people. He phoned Flowers back at seven-fifteen with the result of his efforts.

The next day Kate and Caitlin were both called into Ratchette's office. Kate was surprised to see the Chief Constable in there. When everyone was seated he spoke.

'I understand, Detective Inspector Burrows, that you are of the opinion that as all we have in the way of evidence is the genetic fingerprint of the murderer, we should set about taking blood samples of all males from fourteen to seventy in this area?'

Kate looked around at the three men.

'Yes, sir. I do believe that. If nothing else it would eliminate an awful lot of people.'

'But surely the killer would not be foolish enough to take the test?'

Kate shrugged.

'That's as may be, sir. But if only some people did, at least it would narrow the field of suspects. A majority of those would be eliminated through corroborated statements. That would leave . . .'

'All right, all right, we get the picture.' Flowers's voice was impatient.

The room went quiet. Kate saw Caitlin and Ratchette look at one another briefly. She knew then that something was going on.

Flowers took out a large white handkerchief and blew his nose loudly. He made a bit of a performance out of it and Kate sensed he was playing for time.

'You fill them in on the details, Ratchette. I have to get back.' With that, he walked from the room. Kate watched him leave in amazement.

'What on earth's going on here?' Her voice was plaintive.

Ratchette smiled at her. 'You got what you wanted, Kate. You got the blood and saliva testing.'

She sat back in her seat, stunned.

'My God!'

Caitlin laughed. 'It's all set up, Katie. I've never seen anything arranged so quickly since my daughter's wedding. The testing starts on Monday the twelfth of February.'

Kate turned to him.

'How come you knew? Why was the Chief Constable in such a foul mood? Just what's going on down here?'

Ratchette answered.

'Let's just say that your idea was put to the big boys and they liked it, Kate. The Chief Constable is against the expenditure, but this man has to be caught. There's a public outcry at the moment, and now the government is putting the funds at our disposal. So make the best of it. You never know when they may pull out again.'

'But how come you knew and I didn't?'

'Let's just say it was discussed first by your superiors, shall we?'

The message in Ratchette's voice was clear enough to Kate but she still wasn't happy about it. Though she was elated that the blood testing was going to happen she was not too sure about the mysterious way it had come about. But Ratchette's tone would brook no more questions. She changed tack.

'So how many mobile units are we getting? I think that if we take the units to all the big firms, men will be forced to take the test in front of their colleagues. We could catch our man out like that.'

'First things first. We're getting eight different mobile units. We'll concentrate on the bigger firms first. There's the Ford plant and the electronics factory for starters. We'll also set one up in the town centre. Every male in the age group will be sent letters and documentation that can be produced to prove they have had the test. The sixth form colleges etcetera will be done systematically, and pensioners and the unemployed will be approached by letter to visit one of the mobile units on specified days. It's all in hand. All we have to do now is begin the groundwork. It's going out on local radio and television today, so everyone will be aware of what is happening. Firms will be asked to notify us of people who have suddenly taken holidays or sick leave. I think that we've covered just about every angle. Anyone on the electoral register who does not take the test will be immediately under suspicion, until we can cancel them out.'

'Come on, Katie, it's ten past twelve. I'll buy you a drink and a sandwich.' Caitlin stood up and winked at Ratchette.

Kate stood up and stared into her superior's face.

'Thank you, sir.'

Ratchette smiled.

'Go and get some lunch, Kate. You'll be working like a beaver now, setting all this up with us and keeping your lines of inquiry open. It's going to be a hard old slog, you realise that?'

'Yeah.'

Kate and Caitlin left the room.

Ratchette sat down. Kate Burrows obviously did not realise it but she had a powerful ally in Patrick Kelly. A very powerful ally indeed.

Kate bit into a beef and tomato sandwich, surprised at how hungry she was. She watched Caitlin chatting up the barmaid as he ordered their drinks. She chewed the sandwich slowly, savouring the rich taste. There was something wrong but she did not know what. Caitlin ambled back to the table with her vodka and tonic and his pint of Guinness with whisky chaser.

'What's going on, Kenny?' Kate rarely called him by his first name so it gave the question an edge.

Caitlin sipped his Guinness before answering.

'Look, Katie, whether you realise it or not, you've made yourself a very influential friend, and it was this friend who pushed the issue with the Chief Constable.'

Kate stopped chewing and stared at Caitlin, dumbstruck.

Everybody knew. They all knew about her and Patrick Kelly.

'Don't look so shocked, now. The police force is a very small world, you know. Look at it this way – if a new man or woman comes to a division, within twenty-four hours everyone knows their past track record, their marital status, everything. It's just one of those things. Now then, the fella you're going around with is a big man in his own way, and it was natural it would come to the attention of people. I don't think that the uniforms know, but Ratchette knew, and I knew, and now the Chief Constable knows. I gather he had a visit from your friend yesterday, and apparently he has some even bigger friends of his own. Probably how he's kept out of clink for so long.'

Kate was looking into her glass, embarrassed. Caitlin felt a twinge of sympathy for her.

'Shall I tell you something? It's a thing I've always believed. Most people in the force could have gone one way or the other. Either become a villain – and I mean villain as in bank robber and such, nothing to do with perverts or nonces – or become a policeman. You need the inbred cunning to be a villain in order to catch one. That's why so many of them get on so well.

'Myself, I've nicked men I've had a great deal of respect for. I'm not talking about gas meter bandits or kiters. I'm talking about men who have masterminded some of the biggest bank robberies in the country. I admire them, Katie, even while I've tried to find them and lock them up. Everyone has dreams of winning the pools, whatever. These men set out to steal money that makes the average person in the street drool just thinking about it.

'Kelly now, he works within the law, and sometimes just outside it, but he's first and foremost a businessman. Only he's not a kosher businessman like, say – oh, I don't know – Henry Ford or someone of that ilk. He's part of the new breed, and for myself I admire him. Anyone who can get that eejit of a Chief Constable shitting in his pants has to have something good going for him?'

Kate smiled slightly but her brain was whirling.

Kelly had gone and made the Chief Constable 'see sense'. That is exactly how he would put it when she challenged him about it. In the little time she had known Patrick she had got to understand him so well. In Patrick's mind there was no black and white. Just Patrick Kelly's opinion. And that opinion was worth more to him than the crown jewels.

'Look at it this way, Kate, he got you what you wanted and – I admit now – what I wanted. This is the most difficult case I've ever worked on in my life. We've had four horrific murders and literally nothing to go on except for the bugger's car. And the witnesses can't even agree on the colour of that! Take this opportunity and use it, girl, it's like a gift from God.'

Kate sipped her drink and bit into her sandwich again. What Caitlin said made sense, she admitted that, but she was worried all the same. If her association was common knowledge . . .

'Look, Kenny, can I ask you something?'

Caitlin took a deep draught of his Guinness and wiped his mouth with the back of his hand.

'Ask away.'

'What's being said about me and Kelly? I really want to know.'

'What do you think? "Kate Burrows is having it off with a villain." The usual.' He watched Kate turn white and could have kicked himself.

'That was a joke, Katie, a bad joke I admit, but a joke all the same. What's really being said is this. Kate Burrows has been seeing Pat Kelly. Oh, Pat Kelly says the other person, isn't he the one with the repo business? Yes, that's him, says the first person. Lucky old Kelly is the general opinion. Christ, girl, most of the senior men have tried to get into your knickers at some time or another, that's common knowledge. That you're a respectable woman and a bloody good DI is also common knowledge. *You're* making more of this than anyone. Until Kelly is convicted of something, you're as safe as houses and let's face it, Katie, he's not liable to get caught out now is he? Everything he does is more or less above board. Why don't you relax? You're too hard on yourself.'

'I've fought tooth and nail to get where I am today, Kenny. You don't know the struggle it's been.'

'I don't, no. But, if you're as worried as you say then all you have to do is stop seeing him. Meself I think you'd be a fool. They used to call you the Mother Theresa of Enfield when we worked together before. You're doing nothing wrong, child. Has he ever compromised you?'

'No.'

'Has he ever asked you anything he shouldn't, like?'

'NO!'

'Then why all the drama and fuss? Jesus Christ, you women make your own crosses you know. And believe me it's a long old journey when you have to carry it. I know. Personally, I like Kelly. He's an astute business man, a good friend, I should think and he's one handsome fucker. You do what you've got to do with him. As long as it doesn't interfere with your work, who cares? They'll be gossiping about someone else next week.'

Kate saw the sense in what Caitlin was saying. He was right. She wasn't doing anything wrong. And if Flowers hadn't said anything then there was obviously no problem.

She wanted to believe it. She had to believe it.

'You're right. I'm worrying about nothing.'

She picked up her glass and drained it.

Caitlin laughed softly and rose to get her another.

'That's the way to do it, girl.'

Kate lit a cigarette and drew the smoke deep into her lungs. She wished Patrick was with her, when he was near she had no doubts. No doubts at all. Then something occurred to her. How the hell did Kelly get them to agree to the blood testing? That's why Flowers was so annoyed with her. Everyone knew she had been rooting for it since the word go, and somehow Patrick had made it possible. Suddenly, Kate was annoyed, very annoyed and the most annoying thing was, she wasn't really sure why.

Elaine and George had finished their tea and were sitting in the lounge watching Thames news. Since George's announce ment about his redundancy, they had been living under an amicable truce. The murder of Leonora Davidson was the talk of Grantley, and Elaine was well aware that it had happened on a night when George was out walking. A hundred times a day she told herself that it was coincidence, that on the nights of the other murders he had been indoors with her – except for New Year and she was confident that he had been too ill to leave his bed then.

When the newsreader mentioned the Grantley Ripper Elaine's ears pricked up. The screen went to an outside broadcast. Grantley police station was in the background as a young girl came on the screen. Elaine was watching George's reaction as the girl spoke.

'The Grantley Ripper case. It has been announced today that the police are going to take blood and saliva samples from all males in the area in the fourteen to sixty-five age group. This means that just over five thousand men and boys will be tested.

'Wide-scale testing has been done only once before in 1983 at Enderby in Leicestershire, after two rapes and murders. The police hope that testing will eliminate as many people as possible in the hunt for the Grantley Ripper. Mobile units will be going around factories and offices, school and unemployment offices. Any man who refuses the test will be under suspicion. We shall be updating you on what happens during the course of the investigation.'

Elaine looked again at George.

'I think it's a good thing, don't you, George?'

'You're absolutely right, my dear. Best thing that could happen if you ask me.'

For the life of him he was not sure how he managed to sound so normal. He was sweating.

'I mean, George, whoever this man is, he's a maniac, a sick maniac, and should be caught and locked away as soon as possible. Hanging's too good for him. I reckon he should be tortured like he tortured those women.'

George nodded absentmindedly. His mind was racing. What was he going to do? He could not take the test. They'd be coming to his place of work. He would be forced to take it with his colleagues.

'Would you like me to make you a cuppa, George? I'm having one.'

'Yes, dear. That would be lovely.'

Elaine walked to the kitchen. Well, he seemed OK. It was her as usual. She was always down on George but couldn't seem to help it. He affected her like that.

Anyway, she reasoned, if he had had anything to worry about he would have shown it by now. George was like an open book to her. When she'd poured out the tea George walked into the kitchen and picked up his cup.

'I'm going down to the shed, dear, I want to sort out the bulbs for the spring planting. I won't be long.'

'All right then. Shall I call you when EastEnders comes on?'

'No. I won't bother tonight, I've too much to do.'

He walked from the kitchen and Elaine went into the lounge feeling a bit happier. If he was worried about anything he wouldn't be doing something so mundane as sorting out the spring bulbs.

George locked himself into his shed and put on the light. He placed a piece of material over the window and then put on the small Calor gas heater. The shed was soon warm and cosy. He sipped his tea, sitting on the old chair, and thought deeply about his predicament. He could see no way out. Finally he got up and moved the gardening catalogues from the desk, pulling out his books reverently. He finished his tea and settled himself into the chair with them on his lap.

He began idly to flick through them but tonight he felt nothing. Not even the semi-erection he usually got just from the act of having them near him. He looked through the pile and then picked out one of his favourites. He looked at the girl's face and tried to empty his mind of everything. Closing his eyes he pictured himself straddling her, his penis forcing its way into her mouth against her will. His breathing became heavier and he opened the flies of his trousers, pulling on his penis to try and force some life into it.

It was beginning to stir. Slowly he began to pull the foreskin back and forth, enjoying the sensation it created. Now he was pushing it into the girl's vagina, squeezing on her naked

356

breasts, and she was begging him to stop. Pleading with him. He rubbed at himself, faster and harder, the sensations taking away all the worry and uncertainty. He was building up to an orgasm when Elaine began banging on the shed door.

'George . . . George! There's a phone call for you. Some bloke called Tony Jones.'

He felt the icy hand of fear on the back of his neck. He pulled his hands from his trousers as quickly as he could. The small space was hot and cloying from the Calor gas heater and he felt a moment's sickness as he realised what Elaine was saying.

'Are you listening to me, George?'

'I'm just coming, dear. I think I dozed off in the chair, looking at the gardening catalogues.'

Outside in the cold and dark Elaine rolled her eyes. 'Well, hurry up, it must be costing this bloke a fortune.'

George stood up and threw the magazines into the desk. It wasn't until he was halfway up the path that he remembered that his trousers were undone. He hurriedly zipped them up and pulled his jumper down over them. Tony Jones. What the hell did he want now? He walked through the kitchen and went to the phone in the hall.

'Hello?'

'Georgie? It's me, Tony Jones.'

'What do you want?' His voice was hard.

'Calm down, I told your wife I was a friend of yours. You have got friends, I take it?'

'What do you want, Tony?'

'I've got some new films in, Georgie, and I think you'll like them.'

'I'm a bit strapped for money at the moment.'

'Well, pop in and see me and I'll do you a deal. You're a good customer, Georgie, and I'd hate to lose you.' Tony's voice was friendly now.

'I'll try and get in over the weekend.'

'You wanna see these films, mate, they're hot. The birds in them! Tits like you've never seen before . . .'

George was already picturing it in his mind and Tony knew this. He knew exactly how to sell his merchandise.

'One bird's built like a fucking Amazon and she's loving it, Georgie. For all her shouts and protests. You can see her coming as you watch.'

George was feeling hot now. He wanted the films. He wanted them now.

'I'll be in tomorrow night after work, OK?'

'You know it makes sense.'

The line went dead. George replaced the receiver.

'Bring me in the paper, George.' Elaine's voice was at full throttle and he winced inwardly. He picked up the paper from the telephone table and took it into the lounge.

'Here you are, love.'

'Who was that then?'

'Oh, a friend from work about my leaving do.'

'Leaving do? For you?' Elaine's voice was incredulous.

'Yes, Elaine. For me.'

George was annoyed now. What with everything that was happening, the last thing he needed was one of Elaine's little innuendos. Do her good to let her think he had friends. Might shut her up now and again.

'I know you find it hard to believe that people might like me, but they do!'

She was annoyed at his attitude. 'I'm sorry, George, but after fifteen years I'd have thought you might have mentioned these friends now and again.'

'When have you ever wanted to know, Elaine? Answer me that if you can. Just when have you ever wanted to know?'

With that he went back down to his shed. He was aware that he had dropped his guard with Elaine and was glad. Give her something to think about for a change. She took him for granted, always had. He locked himself into the shed and put the Calor gas fire on again.

Fifteen minutes later he was once more locked into his fantasy world.

George sat at his desk. He wished he had not bothered to come to work. The only topic of conversation was the blood testing.

Peter Renshaw was making one of his lightning appearances. George wished it was time for one of his sales visits to Yorkshire, or better still Scotland. Peter's insistence on being his friend unnerved him. But hadn't he told Elaine last night that he had friends? George pondered this for a while. He watched Renshaw monopolising the conversation, his eyes scanning the small crowd around him as if he was trying to catch them out not listening to him.

George wondered if in fact he had any friends. It was the first time in years such a thought had occurred to him. As a child he had not had many, but that was his mother's fault. She had not encouraged her children to bring friends home. George unconsciously pursed his lips. He could never remember bringing anyone home. He could not remember one true friend. He began to feel sorry for himself. No friends. Fifty-one years old and no friends. No real friends. Even Elaine had friends. Big, fat, brash till girls who dressed like tarts and spent their life in bingo halls like mutton dressed as lamb. His mother had been right about Elaine. She'd said he would rue the day he married her, and he did. But Elaine had been so sweet once. Long ago. She was the only girl who had ever shown a spark of interest in him and he had been grateful. He grimaced. Grateful to her?

Now he could have any woman he wanted. He *did* have any woman he wanted. He let his mind stray to Leonora Davidson. He didn't feel any regret. She was alone, no husband or children to worry about her. Just a lonely woman. He had done her a favour really. Lately he hadn't liked thinking about Geraldine O'Leary. Her children had been in the local paper. Beautiful children, like their mother. Elaine said they had taken her husband away to a mental hospital. That he had had a nervous breakdown. He pushed the thought from his mind. He had more pressing things to think about.

'I say, Georgie . . . I'm talking to you!' Peter Renshaw's loud voice echoed across the room. George looked at him. 'Sorted out your leaving do, old matey. Friday week at the Fox Revived. We'll all meet there straight from work. I've got a surprise for you, old chap. A bl-oody big surprise.'

George smiled at him.

Josephine Denham walked into the office. As usual she looked immaculate. She was wearing large grey-framed glasses that gave her a look of intelligence and sophistication, and was carrying a sheaf of papers.

'Can I have your attention, please?'

Everyone stared at her.

'The mobile blood unit will be here on Thursday the twenty-second of this month. The office staff will be the first for testing then the factory and warehouse staff. If we do it on a rota basis it won't affect production too much. I've been talking to the police this morning and they say that they'll be giving out questionnaires nearer the time. Anyone who is not at work that day must account for their whereabouts to me personally. I will then pass on the message to the police. If anyone is against the taking of the test please feel free to come and see me, though personally I can't see why anyone would object.'

Her eyes scanned the small sea of faces and it was evident that anyone who refused would be immediately judged guilty, by her at least. When no one answered she turned on her heel and walked from the room, her footsteps ringing on the tiled floor as she walked away.

'I'd go and see her, but it wouldn't be to tell her about the blood testing, eh, chaps? I'd give her a portion of the pork sword anytime!'

The men laughed, even George, though his mind was whirling.

What the hell was he going to do?

He looked at his watch. It was eleven thirty. He got up from his seat and began to put on his jacket.

'Where you off to, George?' This from Carstairs, a man whom George had worked with for fifteen years and barely knew.

'I'm going down the pub for some lunch actually.'

'But it's only eleven thirty!'

George never left until twelve on the dot. 'I can tell the time, you know.' With that he walked from the office.

'Well I never!' Carstairs looked at the others.

Peter Renshaw picked up his sheepskin, slipped it on and followed George out of the office. He caught up with him in the Fox Revived.

George had walked into the warmth of the pub. He knew that Peter was behind him and tried to ignore him, hoping against hope that he would take the hint and leave him alone. But not Peter Renshaw. As George ordered his drink, Peter pushed in beside him and ordered his own, paying for the two. George sighed. Picking up his glass he took it to a small window table and sat down. Renshaw followed him.

'I say, Georgie, you all right?'

He sipped his half of bitter and nodded. Renshaw, he decided, was like a virus. You just had to put up with it until it decided to go.

'Look, George, I know that this redundancy has hit you hard, but in reality it's the best thing that could have happened to you. I mean, fifteen years' loyal service. You're looking at a good twenty-five thousand, aren't you?'

George's eyes widened. 'That much?'

'Yes, I was talking to Jones. He says that as it's not a voluntary redundancy, you'll all get a golden handshake. Like they did with the dockers and the car workers. They'll be paying you off, Georgie boy.'

'Twenty-five thousand pounds?'

Peter smiled now. 'That's a lot of dosh, Georgie. I reckon you should get the next round in!'

He smiled. This time it was his secret smile. He was feeling a bit better now. He had four more weeks at work. Then he could go where he wanted. Until then he had to avoid the blood testing.

But how?

Kate's phone rang and she picked it up. She was up to her eyes in statements, had been going over the same ground over and over again. There had to be something, something trivial, that they had missed.

'Hello, Burrows here.'

361

Patrick's voice crackled over the line and Kate felt her stomach tighten.

'What happened to you last night? I tried ringing but your phone was either unplugged or you were out on the razzle.'

His voice was playful, but Kate detected a note of uneasiness as well. Carefully hidden but there nonetheless.

She closed her eyes.

'I had some work to finish. I meant to ring you today but I'm up to my eyes here. I take it you know about the blood testing?' Her voice came out harder than she'd intended.

The phone went quiet.

'Can I see you later, Kate? I think we need to talk.'

She sighed. Caitlin was supposedly reading statements but she knew that his ears were on red alert.

'I'll ring you from home. When I finally arrive there.' She replaced the receiver without saying goodbye.

She looked at Caitlin who was now watching her openly. 'What are you staring at?' She sounded childish, petulant, and knew it.

'I don't know, it's not labelled.' Caitlin's voice was like a little boy's.

'Oh, sod off, Kenny.'

Caitlin laughed, then said seriously: 'Don't you be a fool now and bite the hand that feeds you. He did you a favour, girl, if you could only see it.'

Kate dropped her eyes and made a pretence of reading another statement.

What Caitlin said held the ring of truth but her pride was hurt. Kelly had managed what she had been trying to do for months without a murmur in response.

It galled her.

Patrick stared at the receiver in his hand.

She had put the phone down on him. She had actually put the phone down on him! He couldn't believe it.

He replaced the phone in its cradle, a flicker of annoyance on his handsome face. Who the bloody hell did Kate Burrows think she was? She had stood him up last night. Now she'd put the phone down on him, apart from all that sarcasm about the

362

blood testing. He'd been under the impression that was what she wanted.

As he walked into the morning room Willy, who had been reading the paper, hastily got up from his seat.

'Comfortable were you? I hope I'm not interrupting anything?'

'Sorry, Pat, but I was just having five minutes off like.'

'Go and get the motor, Willy. If that's not too much trouble like, I'd hate to think I was overworking you . . .'

Willy rushed out, the paper rustling as he tried to fold it as he went.

Patrick smiled. His eyes strayed to the window and suddenly he was assailed with a memory of Renée. He could see her now, in his mind's eye. She'd had no qualms about slamming the phone down on him. She'd shout, 'Out there, mate,' pointing to the window, 'you might be a big man, but in this house you're only my husband. Get it?'

He laughed. She'd had so much spirit.

Maybe that's why he liked Kate so much.

Slamming the phone down on him, the cheeky cow!

Five minutes later he was in the back of the Rolls Royce on his way to his Manor Park parlour.

He grinned.

She'd actually put the phone down on him.

He couldn't believe it!

Maybelline Morgan was known for her large breasts and her larger mouth. She was now arguing violently with Violet Mapping over a customer.

'I always have him, Vi, and you bleeding well know it!'

Violet gritted her teeth. 'He didn't want you, Maybelline. He wanted the blonde girl and that's that.'

Maybelline's eyes were like pieces of flint. She wagged a deep red-varnished nail in Violet's face.

'Don't fucking push me, Vi. I need the dosh and you know it. You're not bumming me out now. I know that little bird's flashing her clout for you, that's why she's getting all the good punters.'

She pushed her finger roughly into Violet's chest. 'I'll take you out first, and then her. I'll rip you to fucking shreds . . .'

Violet knew that the argument was being listened to by the majority of the girls who were sitting outside the office door. If she didn't shut Maybelline up she would lose her authority. She grabbed at the other woman's hair, bringing her knee up into her stomach at the same time. Maybelline bent double. Still clutching her hair, Violet slammed her face into the corner of the heavy wooden desk. Maybelline dropped on to the carpeted floor, her eyebrow dripping blood.

Violet smiled at her nastily.

'Don't ever threaten me again. Now you can get your stuff and piss off.'

Maybelline pulled herself up with the help of the desk and faced Violet. Her long bony face framed by flame-coloured hair was twisted in hatred. Putting her hand into the pocket of her skirt she brought out a knife. The blade flicked into view and glinted in the fluorescent light.

Violet went white which was not lost on Maybelline. She rushed forward, slashing at her with the knife. Violet put her arms up to defend herself and felt the coldness of the steel as it bit into her skin just above the elbow, scraping on the bone with sickening ferocity. Maybelline brought the knife up and slashed at Violet again. This time she caught her on the side of the face. Both women were sticky with blood.

Violet made an effort to grab Maybelline's wrists. Using all her considerable strength, she managed to hold the other woman's arms apart.

Patrick Kelly and his minder walked into the massage parlour to a scene of pandemonium. Women and girls were clustered around the office door and Kelly could hear shouting and swearing coming from inside.

'What the hell's going on in here?'

The women parted like the Red Sea as they recognised his voice. The two men forced their way into the office.

'Bloody hell!' Patrick's voice was incredulous. Without speaking further he grabbed at Maybelline and Willy grabbed at Violet. After another struggle the women were separated. Patrick banged Maybelline's hand on the desk until she dropped the knife. Then he threw her from him and stepped on the knife. Willy let go of Violet gladly. 'What's going on here? You—' he pointed at Violet '—what the fuck has happened here?'

Maybelline answered.

'She's picking the toms, Mr Kelly, and we've all had enough. That little bird she's screwing has made over a thousand pound this week. Every decent punter that comes in gets her. Me and the other girls ain't made more than a couple of ton. If something ain't done we're going to the Paki down the road. At least he sees his girls all right.'

Patrick was dumbstruck. There was blood everywhere and the thought of HIV was not far from his mind.

'I want you two to go out to the kitchen and get cleaned up, then I want you both back in here and we'll try and sort it all out. You've got ten minutes. So get your arses in gear.'

The two women left his office and were immediately surrounded by the other girls. Willy shut the door and looked at his boss with raised eyebrows.

'I gotta be honest, Pat, that Maybelline's got a point, you know. I heard that Vi's mad about this little bird. Well, it was bound to happen, weren't it? Even the old lezzies must go funny as they get older.'

'Willy, shut up! I pay you to drive my car and do the minding. If I wanted a gossip I'd have employed Nigel Dempster, all right?'

Walking out of the office Patrick went to the kitchen. He tapped a young black girl on the shoulder.

'Do me a favour, Suzie, get a bucket and cloth and clean the office, would you, love? I'll bung you a score.'

'Yeah, all right, Mr Kelly.'

Ten minutes later Patrick was behind the desk and Maybelline and Violet were standing in front of him like recalcitrant schoolgirls.

'I'm telling you, Mr Kelly, unless we get a fair crack of the whip we'll have it on our toes. This ain't the only place to work, you know.'

'I've always looked after my girls. I resent the implication that I'm doing you down, Maybelline.'

Violet spoke. 'I was out of order, Pat. I admit it.'

Maybelline smiled at her and Kelly shook his head. These women amazed him. One minute they were at each other's throats. The next they were best friends again.

'I don't like my girls carrying weapons. If I find out you've brought a knife or anything in again, Maybelline, there'll be trouble. Big trouble. Get it?'

'Yes, Mr Kelly.'

'Now then, Violet, I want you to get your priorities right in future because if anything like this happens again, I'm gonna out the lot of you. Now fuck off the pair of you and leave me alone.'

The two women left the room.

'Pour me out a brandy, Willy, a large one.'

Willy went to the drinks cabinet and opened it. He held up an empty bottle of Remy Martin.

'Only got scotch left, I'm afraid.'

Patrick clenched his fists. 'That'll do.' He got up from the desk and went to the door. 'Violet!' His voice was so loud the girls jumped in their seats. Violet rushed from the kitchen, her face white.

'What, Mr Kelly?'

'Stop drinking my fucking booze! No wonder this place is like a madhouse. You're all either drunk or drugged!'

He slammed the office door.

He took the large scotch from Willy and drank it straight down, handing the glass back for an immediate refill. Then, sitting at the desk, he opened the drawer and took out the ledgers. If Violet was skanking off the other girls to subsidise this little bird there was a good chance she was skanking off him too.

Bloody Violet! He would have laid money on her being the most dependable of all the girls working for him. They had been friends for years.

'Willy, go out and get me a bottle of Remy Martin and give the bill to Violet. OK?'

366

Willy nodded and left the room. Patrick began to study the ledgers. The phone rang and he picked it up.

'Yeah? Kelly.'

'Pat, thank God you're there, I've been trying to trace you. You'd better get your arse over here, mate.'

'What is it, Karen?'

'Trouble, Pat. Big trouble.'

The phone went dead.

Kelly closed his eyes. If one more woman put the phone down on him today he would throw a paddy. He put the ledgers away and waited for Willy's return.

'Come on, you, we're off to Barking. Karen's been on the blower, there's hag over there.'

He walked from the office. As he passed Violet with the girls, he pointed at her.

'Don't touch me booze, and don't touch the ledgers, Vi.'

He went out to his car and began his journey to Barking. More bloody girl trouble, he supposed. Poxy toms weren't worth the hag half the time.

The trouble was bigger than he had ever expected.

As he walked through the dark-glassed door of his massage parlour in Barking, Kelly was amazed to see the girls all white-faced and quiet. He walked into the office where Karen, the head girl, was drinking a large brandy.

'Is that my brandy you're drinking?'

'Oh, shut up, Pat. Come through.'

Karen's voice was trembling and he followed her without question.

Karen took him to the cubicle area, big tears rolling down her face as she pointed to a curtained booth.

'It's in there, Pat. I can't go in. I didn't know what to do. I ain't called the Old Bill, I just didn't know what to do!'

Her voice was wretched. Willy had followed them inside and now Patrick motioned to him to open the curtain. Against his will he felt a prickle of fear.

Willy pulled the curtain open and both he and Patrick stared in amazement. Lying on the table was a girl. Her long blonde hair was nearly touching the floor and her eyes were closed. If not for the impossible angle of her neck you would think she was sleeping. She was semi-naked. Her tiny cropped top was still in place though her breasts jutted from under it where it had been pulled over them. Her lower body was exposed and her legs were wide apart.

'She's dead, Pat. I found her like it. The bloke must have walked out the front door.' Karen's voice broke again.

'What did he look like, Karen?' Patrick shook her roughly. 'Did you get a look at his boat?'

She shook her head. 'No. They all look the same to me.'

'Well, someone must have bloody seen him. Cover the poor little cow up, for Christ's sake.'

He went to the front of the parlour. All the girls were in different stages of shock.

'Did anyone see the bloke? Can anyone remember him?'

They shook their heads but an Asian girl spoke up.

'I think he was the old bloke who came in this afternoon. That's the last time I saw Gilly.'

'What time this afternoon?'

'At about one. One-thirty.'

Patrick was stumped. He looked at his watch. 'Do you mean she's been lying there dead for over five hours? She's been lying there dead, and you lot were doing the fucking business, and not one of you noticed she was gone?'

All the women stared at him.

'What did he look like?'

The Asian girl thought. 'I don't know. About forty-eight, fifty. He had a beard . . .'

'No. I had him. That's Mr Jenkins. I have him every week.' A dark-haired girl looked at Patrick timidly. 'He's ever such a nice man, Mr Kelly, very polite.'

'I'll call the Old Bill.' Patrick's voice was quiet.

It was like his Mandy all over again, only this time it was his fault. Some piece of scum had taken that girl and murdered her, and it was his fault because he owned the place. He owned every brick and every cubicle and every girl who worked here.

He went to the office and rang the police. Then he sat in the chair and waited for them to arrive.

Chapter Twenty-one

Patrick finally got to Kate's at ten thirty. He pulled up outside her house and was gratified to see that the light was on in the lounge. He told Willy to take the car home and walked up the tiny path to her front door. He rang the bell. Kate was making herself a cheese sandwich in the kitchen. She went to the door licking her fingers clean.

'I rang you at eight, but Mrs Manners said you were out. I didn't expect to see you until tomorrow.'

He walked into the hall. 'I didn't know if you'd rung or not, to be honest; I haven't been home.' He followed Kate into the lounge.

'Take your coat off. Be quiet, my mum's in bed. I'm just making a sandwich, do you want one?'

'What is it?' Kelly hadn't eaten since lunchtime.

'Cheese or cheese?'

'Cheese it is then. I'll make the tea.'

He went to the kitchen and they both worked in silence for a while.

'You upset me, you know, Pat. With what you did. But I see now that whatever way we got the testing, it can only be for the best.'

Patrick had forgotten about it. He shrugged.

'Kate, you know I'm a repoman, don't you?'

His voice was quiet and serious and it made her look at him.

'Yes, why?'

'Did you know I owned massage parlours too?'

'Yes. I knew you had a vested interest. What's all this about?'

Suddenly she was not at all sure she wanted to hear any more. What was it Caitlin had said – Patrick Kelly was one of the new breed of businessmen? He worked within the law, just. Was he going to ask her to help him with something not quite legit?

'One of my girls was murdered earlier today. I don't know if you heard it on the news? In Barking. Her neck was broken. Snapped like a twig. I feel terrible, Kate, really terrible. She was twenty-one years old.

'From what I can gather she had on average five or six punters a day. She slept with all those different men every day. Do you know, it's weird, Kate, but it never occurred to me before. Those women were like animals to me. You're sorry if people ill treat them but you forget about them quickly . . .'

Kate watched him for a second. She picked up the plates of sandwiches and took them into the lounge, then she poured the tea and took that in too.

'Come and sit down, Pat, I think you need to get all this off your chest.'

He followed Kate through into the lounge. Sitting on the settee, he sipped his tea.

'What's really wrong, Pat? Is it the girl getting murdered or the fact that she was on your premises at the time?'

Kate had hit the proverbial nail on the head and Kelly was shocked that she knew him so well after such a short time.

'A bit of both, I think, if I'm honest. You should have seen her, Kate, she could have been my Mandy lying there. I've been doing everything humanly possible to help catch this Ripper bloke and yet I've been catering to scum like him for years.'

'Well, Pat, women will always sell their bodies. From soft porn to hard porn to streetwalking, sex is one of the biggest moneyspinners in the world. The girl would maybe have done it anyway, if not for you then for someone else. Is that what you want to hear? Is that what you want me to say?'

Kate's voice was low but there was no mistaking her fury.

370

Patrick looked into her face and for the first time he saw real anger. It unnerved him.

'I heard about that girl's death today, Pat, it was on the news. I didn't know you owned the massage parlour. But shall I tell you what went through my mind as I listened to the radio? I thought, I wonder who's the man making money off this girl's back. I knew it would be a man. Funny that, isn't it? I never dreamt it was you though. The man who paid for the blood testing of five thousand men to find the pervert who killed his daughter. Will you be paying for this inquiry, by the way?' Kate lifted her eyebrows at Kelly and he had the grace to look away.

'No, I didn't think so. If you've come here for tea and sympathy and somewhere to lick your wounds I'm afraid you came to the wrong place, Pat. I have nothing for you as far as that girl's concerned. You helped murder her as if you snapped her neck yourself. Any sympathy I have is for her family. I bet that never occurred to you either, did it? That all the women who work for you are someone's daughter or someone's mother. You don't have the monopoly on grief, Pat. Try and put yourself in her parents' position. At least when you found out about Mandy's death you didn't have the added trauma of finding out she met her death while plying her trade, fucking strange men.

'What's it you just said? "Those women were like animals to me." My God, Patrick Kelly, you've got some bloody front coming here!'

Patrick stared at her.

'Have you quite finished? If I'd wanted a bloody lecture I'd have gone to a university. I came here to try and sort out my head, that's all. I never harmed that girl, I never wanted anything to happen to her, to any of them . . .'

He was floundering and he knew it. Kate had stated the plain, ugly truth and his only form of defence was attack.

'You make me laugh sometimes, Mrs Highbrow Bloody Policewoman. Well, did it ever occur to you that some of them

371

girls like their job? Did it? That if they didn't work for me they would work for someone else . . . Well, did it? DID IT?'

Kate shook her head sadly.

'I'm not seeing them though am I? I'm seeing you, Pat, and I don't care how much you rant and rave, I've nothing for you tonight. I've no sympathy for you, I'm sorry. If you want that I suggest you go and see the girl's parents. That might put it in perspective for you. Though after what happened to Mandy, I'd have thought you of all people would have understood what they're going through.'

Patrick felt the temper rising and he was honest enough to admit that it was not because of Kate's words, but because he felt ashamed. He could not admit that to her though.

'I'm bloody going. I should have known a bloody Old Bill wouldn't be any good to me when the chips were down. Your trouble is you fancy yourself as some kind of bleeding saint, Kate. Well, listen to me. I don't need you or anyone else to point out my shortcomings. I've been aware of them for years. From the time I could understand what was going on around me. Yes, I wanted a bit of tea and sympathy, the same as you did when your daughter OD'd. And thanks a lot for nothing. I tell you something now, I don't need you. I don't need anyone really, I never did and I never will.'

As soon as he said the words he was sorry. He wanted to take Kate in his arms and love her, have her love him, but he couldn't.

Kate watched him walk from the room, and heard the front door slam.

They had needed to get all this out in the open. But she was sorry it had come about like this. His dealings with the massage parlours would always have been between them; now they both knew where they stood.

That poor girl was dead. Patrick was feeling guilty, whatever he said. But where had that got her?

Kate stared at her sandwich.

She didn't feel hungry any more.

Patrick walked out of Kate's and cursed silently. He had

372

let Willy go and now he would have to phone for a taxi. He began to wander aimlessly, looking for a phone box. Like George he was finding solace in the darkness. He breathed the cold night air into his lungs and once more his mind was on Gillian Enderby. He saw her lying in the cubicle, her hair falling down over the table, nearly touching the floor. She was a sweet-looking girl. She didn't look like a prostitute, but then none of them did at first. He remembered a younger Violet – what a girl she had been!

He saw the lights of a call box and quickened his stride. Renée had never been happy about the prostitution. She would sit in for him on the repo side of the business but had flatly refused to have anything to do with the massage parlours. It was an unspoken agreement that they were never mentioned at home, even in passing.

He walked into the phone booth and after unsuccessfully trying to find a cab number rang up Willy and ordered him to pick him up. He knew better than to ask why his boss was ringing from a call box and not from Kate's.

Patrick stood outside the phone booth and stamped his feet. It was freezing. Kevin Cosgrove had supposedly been picking up Mandy from outside a phone booth. It had been vandalised, that's why she had begun to walk home. He pushed his hands deeper into the pockets of his overcoat. Gillian Enderby was at this moment on ice somewhere. Her parents were going through what he had gone through.

Later that night, as he lay in his bed, he wished that Kate was with him. He missed her. She was in her forties; she was dark when he had always had a preference for blondes; she was flat-chested and he had always liked his women to be well endowed; and to put the tin lid on it, she was a policewoman. In fact, she was the antithesis of everything he had ever said he wanted in a woman.

Yet he wanted her desperately.

Mandy and Gillian Enderby crawled once more into his troubled thoughts and finally he admitted defeat and got out of bed and went downstairs. He went to make himself a hot drink and took it back to bed after lacing it liberally with brandy.

Still he lay there, tossing and turning.

Kate, in her lonely bed, was doing exactly the same.

Willy was surprised to see Patrick up and dressed at six thirty and already on the telephone. He wondered briefly who he had got out of bed. After his own breakfast Patrick called him at seven-fifteen and said he wanted to go to an address in East Ham. It was a council maisonette. Willy saw a man answer the door and then, after a brief exchange of words, saw Patrick go inside.

Curiouser and curiouser, he thought. Then he picked up his paper and began the process of looking at the semi-naked woman on page three once again.

Patrick introduced himself to Stan Enderby and the man invited him in. Enderby was about his own age but had not had the benefit of money. He looked older than his years, from the tobacco-stained fingers, the large beer belly and receding hairline to the impossibly thin roll-up clamped to the side of his mouth.

'The wife's upstairs, Mr Kelly. Took it bad, she has. Gilly was her pride and joy, you see. We never knew that she was . . . that she did what she did.'

Patrick followed him into a tiny front room that was sparsely furnished though very clean. He sat on the chair by the window and looked down briefly at his car.

'Would you like a cup of tea, or something stronger?' Stanley held up a bottle of cheap Tesco whisky and Patrick nodded his head in assent. He waited until the man gave him his glass.

'Thank you.'

Kelly knew that Enderby was at a loss. His reputation had as usual preceded him and inhibited a natural response. He'd have welcomed blame, anger. Anything but this passivity, this pretence that he was a welcome visitor. But he knew that Enderby was scared of him. In the past he had profited from his reputation, but at this moment if Enderby had slammed the glass of whisky into his face, he would have accepted it. Would have admired him even.

'I have come to offer you my condolences, Mr Enderby. I feel a sense of responsibility for what happened to your daughter and would be most grateful if you would allow me to pay for the funeral.'

'That's more than kind, Mr Kelly. We never expected anything . . .'

As he spoke, the front room door opened and a tiny woman walked in. She was a faded blonde, and Kelly knew immediately this was Gillian's mother. They were like two peas in a pod.

'What do you want?' Her voice was aggressive.

Stanley Enderby looked at his wife in shock.

'This is Mr Kelly, Maureen.'

'Oh, shut up, Stan, for Gawd's sake.' She turned back to Patrick. 'I asked you a question, Kelly, what do you want?'

He dropped his eyes. He could see the accusation in her face. 'I came to offer my condolences, Mrs Enderby.'

'He's gonna pay for the funeral and that, ain't you, Mr Kelly?'

Stanley's voice was tight. He was not a man who could handle scenes of any kind. All his married life he had tried to avoid confrontations with his tiny but quick-tempered wife.

Maureen Enderby sneered. Her hard eyes slowly swept Patrick from his head to his toes.

'So Pat Kelly's coming around with his cheque book, is he, making everything better? I remember you when you didn't have a pot to piss in, you ponce! I remember your mother and your sisters when Gracie was moonlighting down the bleeding docks. You learnt all about whoring at an early age, didn't you? Then you came and took my girl and put her on the fucking bash and now she's dead! Well, some pervert got your girl, didn't he? I'd call it poetic justice.'

Patrick's face was white now.

'I never put your daughter on the game, Mrs Enderby. I had no knowledge of her working there. I never know any of the girls.'

Maureen rushed at him and thumped him in the chest, her face contorted with grief.

'Well, you should have then! You should have known who they were. My daughter was a drug addict. I never knew that until today . . . I never knew it. She was sleeping with men to pay for her drugs. Drugs she probably bought from you!'

Patrick shook his head violently. 'I have never, ever sold drugs. Whatever else I may have done to you, real or imagined, I have never sold drugs!'

'No, Patrick Kelly.' Maureen's voice was quiet now. 'You just sold degradation, didn't you?'

She turned to her husband.

'Get this scum out of my house, Stan. Now!'

Patrick looked at the man in front of him and shook his head as if to say: I understand.

'Take your cheque book, Mr Kelly. I want none of your dirty money. I'll bury me own according to *my* purse, not yours.'

Patrick left the maisonette and Stanley followed him out on to the landing.

'I'm sorry, Mr Kelly, but it's what happened. It's turned her head like. She'll come round. We're potless, see. I ain't worked for four years. And now we ain't got Gilly's money coming in.'

Kelly nodded. 'I'll see that you get the money, Mr Enderby.'

'I think it would be best in notes like, we ain't got a bank account.' His voice trailed off and Patrick nodded again. He went down the stairs and got into his car. Out of the two of them he preferred the girl's mother. At least her grief was genuine. Gillian Enderby's father was capitalising on his daughter's death, which hardly seemed to bother him.

But it bothered Patrick Kelly.

It bothered him a lot.

Kate had arrived at the church early and sat alone at the back, enjoying the quietness and solitude. As a Roman Catholic, Mandy Kelly's body had been left in church overnight ready

376

for the requiem mass in the morning. Her Aunt Grace was delegated to sit with the body while the soul departed for heaven. This was an old Irish tradition that was still kept alive by every new generation.

Kate knelt down and prayed for the first time in years. She had forgotten the feeling of peace and contentment an empty church could bring. She prayed for the soul of Mandy Kelly and all the murdered women and girls.

The funeral was at nine thirty, but the church had begun to fill up before nine. Kate watched from the back as various criminals and businessmen turned up. She was not too surprised when Chief Constable Frederick Flowers arrived with his wife. Or when the local MP and his wife also showed up. She did admit to a slight feeling of surprise when she noticed two prominent heads of the Serious Crime Squad. Both shook Patrick's hand and one of the men, known in the force as Mad Bill McCormack because of his unorthodox methods of obtaining arrests with a pick axe handle, actually hugged him close. To Kate it was a real education and her naivety troubled her. She was a good detective, she knew her job, but this closeness between the criminal world and the police had never before been so blatantly thrust on her. Oh, she knew that it went on, but it seemed that the days when villains and police met only under cover of darkness were over. Now they met socially.

She pushed the thoughts from her mind. It was the funeral of Patrick's only child and she should be pleased for him that so many people had turned out to pay their respects. It helped some people when their departed were shown to be popular and cared for.

She watched Patrick scanning the church and finally his eyes found hers. She smiled at him briefly. His face immediately relaxed and for those few seconds she felt once more the pull he had on her.

After the mass, as the mourners left the church and the body was taken to the grave, Patrick fell into step beside her. He held on to her arm lightly but firmly as if frightened she was going to run away. Kate glanced at him and saw the tears on his long dark lashes. She realised that he needed her, and more to the point, she needed him. She accompanied him to the graveside. As the priest began the final blessings she felt his grief as if it was a physical thing. His shoulders heaved and instinctively she grasped his hand tightly and he held on to her, pulling her to him. She knew that it was taking all his willpower not to break down there and then, in front of everybody. He was finally burying his beloved child and the full realisation of all that had happened had only just hit him.

Mandy was not coming home.

Not now, not ever.

Kate saw that she was buried beside her mother. Poor Patrick. His whole life was now buried in two small plots of land.

Kate saw Patrick's sister watching her and dropped her gaze. Finally it was all over and people began to make their way back to their cars. Patrick stood at the graveside, oblivious of the offers of condolence. Kate stayed beside him and noticed Kevin Cosgrove standing apart from all the others. He waited until the grave was quiet and walked to it. On Mandy's coffin, now lying in the ground, waiting to be covered, he threw a single white rose. Then he walked away.

'Come on, Patrick, you'd best get yourself back home now.' She pulled him gently away.

'I can't go back to that house, Kate. I can't talk to all those people.'

'You must. Come on, I'll drive back with you. You have to face people. It's just the shock of what's happened hitting you.'

Patrick's sister Grace walked with them. She was about fifty, Kate judged, and looked well on it considering she had been up all night. Her hair was perfect as were her make up and clothes. She was as fair as Patrick was dark.

'Come on, Pat. Let's get this over with. I don't believe we've met, dear. I'm Grace . . . Grace Kelly. I know what you're going to say but I'm used to it by now.

'Come on, Pat, the sooner we get this lot back, the sooner we can get shot of them. Old Auntie Ethel's pissed as a newt and if we're not careful she'll be taking bets on how many cartwheels it would take to go round the church.'

Kate saw Patrick relax. Grace Kelly was obviously a woman you listened to and nothing else. She kept up a running commentary all the way to the car.

'Look, Pat, I'll let you go with your sister. I must get back to work,' Kate said.

'I thought you were going to come to my house with me?'

'I was, but now that you have your sister, I really feel I must get back to work.'

'Will I see you tonight, Kate?' His voice was so lonely and wretched she could not have refused him even if she had wanted to.

'Yes, you'll see me tonight. You come to my house, Patrick.'

She had a feeling he was better off away from home for a few hours at least.

George walked into Sexplosion on the evening of Mandy's funeral. He was unaware of it, with more important things on his mind such as how he was going to get out of the blood testing. He had had the germ of an idea earlier in the day and now was about to sound out Tony Jones who was an integral part of it.

Tony smiled at him and took him through to the back room. George waited until the video was on before he spoke.

'Does this girl die?'

'Yeah. But they still do the business.' Tony's voice sounded bored.

'I should imagine that films like this are illegal? I mean, can't you get into trouble for stocking them?'

Tony Jones was alert now.

'You can get in trouble for buying them and all, mate.' His voice was annoyed.

George smiled.

'I appreciate that, Tony, it was just a query, that's all. Nothing to get worked up about.'

'Look, do you want the film or not?' George could hear the

aggression in the man's voice and knew that he was scared. He patted himself on the back.

'Any chance of a drink, Tony? I have a proposition to put to you . . .'

'What kind of proposition?'

'A very lucrative one.'

Tony Jones licked his lips and stared hard at George for a few seconds.

'What do you want? Beer or a short?'

George grinned. 'I think a short is in order tonight, Tony.'

He waited until they were both sitting down, sipping their drinks, before he spoke.

'I need someone to help me with something delicate. Someone who is completely trustworthy and in need of some money.'

'What for?' Tony Jones was intrigued.

'I need someone to take a blood test for me. They would have to pretend to be me, in fact.'

George saw Tony Jones' face drop. His mind was in a flutter. Blood test . . . blood test, where had he heard that? In the papers. He had read about it in the papers. George Markham came from Grantley in Essex! George Markham was the Grantley Ripper! George Markham had a half a million pound price on his head . . .

'Fucking hell!'

George felt a prickle of fear.

'You're the bastard Ripper, ain't you?'

George stared at the man and his fishy grey lifeless eyes sent a chill through Tony Jones. For the first time he was scared. He had let go his ace in his shock.

'What do you want from me?' His voice was quieter now. More controlled.

'I am willing to pay a substantial amount of money for someone to take the blood test for me. If I was caught, you see, I would have to tell the police about my accomplice in all this.'

'Accomplice? What accomplice?' Tony's voice was puzzled.

'Why, you, of course.' George smiled again. 'If you hadn't

introduced me to snuff movies, I would never have dreamt of murdering anybody.'

Tony's face blanched.

'That was nothing to do with me! I sell movies to loads of people and they don't go out murdering.' His voice was defensive. He had visions of Patrick Kelly hearing that the films that had triggered his daughter's murder had come from him. He'd had one run in with him already. He was hoping to use this knowledge to get back into his good books! Kelly would have his throat cut as soon as look at him else.

'How do you know that, Tony? How do you know that the men who buy your films aren't affected by them in the same way that I am? Death excites me, it excites a lot of people, that's why there's a demand for your films. I remember you saying they sold like hot cakes.'

He saw Tony's jaw tighten and played his trump card. 'I have left a diary of every time I visited your shop and what I bought here. I made it sound as if you were in on the whole thing. If you don't help me, Tony, and I get caught . . .' George left the sentence unfinished.

'I've a good mind to fucking kill you!'

'Oh, now don't be silly. If I died, all my personal effects would be seen, not only by my wife but by the police as well, I should think. And neither of us want that, do we now?'

Tony Jones saw his half a million pounds disappearing before his eyes. He watched George drink his whisky, taking little sips and then fastidiously wiping his mouth on his handkerchief, and a tiny spark of an idea entered his head. He was going to play George Markham back at his own game.

'How much can you pay?'

George grinned. This was more like it.

'One thousand pounds.'

Tony shook his head dismissively. 'Not enough. Two grand at least for criminal deception.'

'Criminal deception?'

'That means parading as someone else. Which is what I would be doing for you.'

'You'll do it yourself?'

'Of course. We're of an age. I'd need to know some personal things . . . the Old Bill are wily old fuckers when the fancy takes them. You find out what happens at the blood testing and let me know. I'll work it from there. I've not got a criminal record, believe it or not. Never even had a parking ticket. I'll be George Markham for two grand.'

George held out his hand but was not surprised when Tony did not shake it.

'Done.'

Tony stared at the man in front of him and thought, You will be.

George arrived home a little after eight. Elaine was sitting on the settee and called out to him as he came in the front door.

'I was getting worried about you, George.'

He took off his coat and placed it and the video he had bought in the hall cupboard. He went in to Elaine.

'Sorry I'm late, dear, we had a lot to do. I finish up in a few weeks and I have to pass over all the information to the man taking over my accounts.'

Elaine nodded.

'Come out to the kitchen, I kept your dinner warm.'

George sat at the table and as usual let Elaine chatter to him. He had noticed over the years that her chattering was a defence against the quietness that she hated. She kept up a constant stream of talk, seemingly unaware that George was not really listening.

Tonight he couldn't have listened even if he'd wanted to. He had more pressing things on his mind.

Caitlin was explaining the exact nature of the blood testing to the team in the incident room. Everyone was listening avidly as he spoke. Most were aware of the existence of genetic fingerprinting, anyone who read the papers was, but the actual task they had ahead of them was not really clear. Caitlin was hoping to enlighten them.

'The man we are looking for is blood type O, which is about fifty per cent of the population. Now this has been broken down again. Seventy-five per cent of the population is Rhesus B positive. The other twenty-five per cent being Rhesus D Negative. Well, I am pleased to say that the man we are looking for is Rhesus D. That means that we can eliminate the O group males of the Rhesus B positive blood group, thereby cutting down on the amount of men and man hours.

'At the actual blood testing, we shall be asking men for their mother's maiden name, their wife's and children's names, where they work, etcetera. We shall also take fingerprints and obviously they will sign the document saying they agreed to the blood testing and were put under no duress to take it. That should shut up the civil liberty eejits!'

People in the room began to titter. It was a bone of contention with everyone that the only lead they could follow was being criticised so much. On the one hand the public wanted the man caught and on the other they were making it as hard as possible to do it.

Caitlin lit a cigar. Clearing his throat noisily, he began to speak again.

'Now, you will all be given a set of instructions detailing exactly what you ask, where you are going, etcetera. You will be allocated men to help with any back-up inquiries and we want these carried out in as low key a way as possible. It seems that quite a few known sex offenders have been beaten up since this spate of murders and while I myself have no time for the perverts, they are not under suspicion so are entitled to our protection. Any inquiries we make must be polite and courteous. We are sitting on a potential bomb here and I don't want anyone . . .' he glanced at Spencer briefly 'especially you, buggering it up.

'Now then, most of you are thinking that the man responsible would have to be mad to agree to take the test. I think that too. But the police psychologist thinks that his ego would make him take it. That he gets his jollies as much from fooling us as from the actual attacks.' He stopped speaking and watched the sea of faces, letting all he said sink in. 'So if you get a particularly suspect individual I would like you to notify me. There's more than a few braggarts in this station alone.' He glanced once more at Spencer. 'So you know the type I'm looking for.'

Once more everyone laughed.

'Now then, are there any questions?'

Spencer's hand shot up before anyone's. Caitlin nodded at him.

'What I want to know is, are we getting more help? I mean, it's going to take ages to reinterview the new suspects . . .'

Caitlin held up a hand to silence him. 'We have more than enough man power – everyone is giving up free time from all over South East Essex. That could be social conscience but I think the double time from the Major Incident Fund is probably helping. Also the Specials come in handy at times like this for interviewing. There'll be more than enough men, don't worry about that.' He turned away from Spencer and looked at the faces before him. 'Now, any other questions?'

Before anyone could answer he turned away, saying, 'Good. Pick up your information sheets and let's get this show on the road.'

Kate smiled to herself. She had to hand it to him. He certainly knew how to run an incident room. He had answered straight off the most important question and now he wanted it all finished so the real work could begin. As much as he got on her nerves at times, Kate had to admire him. At least he got things moving.

Everyone was looking at their information sheets. It seemed that now they had a goal they were straining to get to work. It was always the same on these cases. Once a new line of inquiry opened up it renewed everyone's interest and enthusiasm.

Kate stared once more at the pictures of the dead women and girls. Her eyes lingered on Mandy Kelly and she thought of Patrick. Then she got on with the work in hand.

George came home from a particularly trying day at work.

His leaving party was the talk of the office and he had felt like screaming at them all to go away and leave him alone. Somehow even some of the men from the warehouse had been roped in and George was annoyed. He had never spoken to one of them, even in passing. The last thing he wanted was to make conversation with a crowd of working-class bullies. All they were interested in was the stripper. Oh, he knew what they were after. Pity they didn't know about him, that would shut them all up. He didn't need sluts parading around semi-naked, he could have anyone he wanted. Whenever he wanted.

He closed his eyes tightly. Elaine as usual was chattering. Sometimes he wished he had the guts to slap her silly face, slap it till it stung and her big fat ears rang.

'George, are you listening to me?' Her strident voice bored through his skull like a newly sharpened axe.

'Of course I am, dear. I always listen to you.'

'Well, what do you think about what I said then?'

'I . . . I don't really know.' George was racking his brains to try and remember one item of gossip that might have entered his consciousness since Elaine started talking at him the moment he'd entered the house.

She sighed heavily and began to baste the roast potatoes. 'You haven't heard a word I've said, have you? I tell you my manager says they're thinking of cutting down on staff.'

George interrupted her.

'But they'd never get rid of you, Elaine.'

'Who said they were getting rid of me? Do you ever listen to me, George? My manager said that I stood a good chance of being put in as supervisor on the tills. Not before time, I might add. So even though they're cutting back on staff,' she poked herself in the chest, 'I will still be employed. And at a better wage as well. And let's face it, George, now you've got the bum's rush from your job, a regular wage isn't to be sneezed at, is it?'

The last malicious twist of the knife made his breath come in shallow little gasps. So that was how she was going to play it, was it? Now the sympathy had worn off and the euphoria over the money, Elaine was going to become the one thing she'd always tried to be. The real head of the household. The major breadwinner.

George had visions of himself getting out of his chair and taking the large breadknife from the worktop and slitting Elaine's throat with it, cleanly and neatly, and laughing. Laughing his head off while he did it.

He stood up unsteadily.

'Where are you going?'

He ignored her and walked from the room, every nerve in his body taut. To George's mind this was the final insult. He walked up the stairs and went into the bedroom he shared with Elaine. There he lay on the bed and stared at the ceiling. He half expected her to come barrelling into the room demanding to know why he'd walked out on her, but she left him alone.

Down in the kitchen, it occurred to Elaine that she just might have gone too far.

George lay still until his breathing returned to normal and he watched as his whole life with Elaine floated in front of him. He saw her on their wedding day – he had been quite proud of her then. Proud that he actually had a wife. It was like a declaration to the world, as if he was shouting: 'See, someone wants me.' It had galled his mother that he had married. She wanted to keep him at home with her. Wanted to carry on 'looking after him', as she called it. She had called Elaine a red-headed whore. Well, his mother knew all about them, she had been one herself for most of her life. And in spite of everything their marriage had not been bad at first. Elaine had come to him a virgin and he had appreciated that fact. He had never tried it on with her because she was what George termed a 'good girl'. He knew that she would balk at anything other than a chaste kiss on the lips after an evening out.

Once married, though, Elaine had turned out to be quite a handful. She'd wanted sex much more often than he had. He had wanted to experiment, but Elaine wanted straight sex and no kissing. George could not keep up such a boring way of spending evenings and when she had become pregnant he had been secretly relieved.

It had been then that he had rediscovered his pornographic pastime. Before his marriage George had relied heavily on girlie magazines – or wank mags as he would call them to himself. He had built up a fantasy world of women who did whatever he bid them. He had thought that with the advent of marriage he would not need the fantasy world any more, but instead had found that he needed it more than ever.

At first, the fact that the magazines were in the house would excite him. The element of risking being caught out had always attracted George. He knew that if Elaine had found the magazines she would have blown her top and he relished that feeling. He had begun to frequent the porno movie theatres in Soho, and the bookshops that abounded there. This was in the days when the naked women had their photographs outside with strategically placed stars to just hide nipples and pubic hair. He had learned a lot from those French films, and from the blue films. That was when he had been introduced to the world of sadism and bondage.

The first time he had purchased a bondage magazine George had felt as if he had finally been let free. The pictures of the women, exquisite smiles on their faces as they were chained up and degraded, had struck a chord deep inside him. And that's when he made the terrible mistake.

He had been to an Electric Blue cinema and was travelling home on the train. They had been living in Chatham in Kent at the time. They had bought an old house and gradually decorated it and made it into a home. George saw a girl on the train. She had long red-gold hair and it had attracted his attention because it had reminded him of his mother's when she was young. The girl had noticed him looking at her and had smiled at him. A carefree smile as if she was used to being admired.

As they had neared Chatham the train had begun to empty of people until there were only the two of them. George had been thinking about the film and the girl, and when he had touched her he had only wanted to feel her hair, just the soft

387

springiness of it, that was all. But she had screamed, a loud piercing scream, and he had instinctively pushed his hand over her mouth. She had fallen sideways on the carriage seat and her jumper had risen up, showing an expanse of milky white skin. Then his other hand was pushing inside the jumper and he had felt the jutting breasts. He had experienced ecstasy then, wiping his mind clear of everything but the moment and the sensation. He had no recollection of ripping away her tights and panties, he had no recollection of beating her about the face and head, it had all been too nice. Too warm to be bad.

He had been caught as the train pulled into Chatham station. In his excitement he had not even realised what was happening.

And then there had been the police.

And the questioning.

And the arrest.

And Elaine. A heavily pregnant Elaine, who had been taken to hospital in shock when the police had knocked on the door and told her everything.

Elaine who had given birth to a stillborn son.

Elaine who had for some reason stood by him throughout the trial and had sold up and moved to Essex, so he would have a home to come home to. Elaine who had visited him in prison and written to him once a week.

Elaine who had never let him put it in the past because she hated him for it. Hated him for what he had done and for killing their child.

Elaine who had never referred to it again, except that one day a few weeks previously when the police had knocked on the door. Elaine whom he hated and loved. Oh, he loved her because she had been the mother of his child. The only thing he had ever really wanted in his life.

His son was dead. His marriage was dead.

Elaine was having an affair, he knew she was. He was so certain he could taste it. He could actually see her sometimes with a faceless man, in the back of a car. See her enormous breasts heaving with excitement. See her big fat behind being lowered on to some man's member. And it excited him. It made him want to watch them. It made him want to hide and see them doing it. It made him want to come inside his pants just thinking about it. His breathing was laboured now.

She wasn't so fussy now, was she? No more missionary position for Elaine nowadays. Not judging by the marks on her neck. He would like to put his hands around her neck and squeeze gently, till she expired.

Four women were dead. But it wasn't his fault. They had asked for it the same way that Elaine was asking for it and the girl on the train had asked for it. He had told the police that she had smiled at him, had led him on. But they didn't believe him.

They had believed her, and she was a whore. They were all whores.

And he had been locked up like a criminal! A common criminal. When all he had done was given her what she wanted. What they all wanted.

Then in the prison he had been beaten up by men who were no better than animals, and yet they put themselves above him!

But he had sat it out. He had won in the end because he had come out and had gone to Elaine and had got himself a job and had provided. He had been a good provider, until the redundancy.

What was it Peter Renshaw had said? Spend some time with the grandchildren . . .

The only time he spent time with grandchildren was when they were someone else's. George grinned to himself, thinking of Mandy Kelly, and knew that grandparents wouldn't approve of his games.

He lay on the bed and let the feelings of warmth Mandy Kelly had created wash over him. He was a bit sorry she was dead, because he had quite liked her. After all, Mandy was his favourite name.

Feeling better now, he gradually relaxed.

Downstairs Elaine was sitting at the kitchen table eating her dinner. She was seeing Hector later in the evening and she thanked God for that. Since he had come into her life she had felt as if a great weight had been lifted off her shoulders.

The great weight was George and all he entailed.

Kate was draining spaghetti while her mother put the finishing touches to the bolognaise sauce.

'Are you sure you don't mind him coming for dinner, Mum?'

Evelyn looked at her daughter. 'Now why should I mind that?' She turned off the gas under the pan and went to the breakfast bar to begin laying it. Kate put the spaghetti into a buttered Pyrex dish and went to give her a hand.

'Why is the table only set for two?'

'Because, Katie, I'm going to bingo with Doris tonight. I'll grab a bite to eat there.'

'Oh no you're not! He's making you leave your own home . . .'

Evelyn interrupted her. 'Did it ever occur to you that I might have wanted to go out more over the years, and didn't because I always had Lizzy to look after or had to wait for you coming home? No, I didn't think it had!'

Seeing the hurt look on Kate's face, Evelyn grinned at her. 'I didn't mean that really, Kate. I want you and this man to have a bit of time together, that's all. He's buried his only child today and I think he'll want you near him tonight. But for all that, if I wanted to stay in, I would. I'm going out with Doris because I want to go to bingo. I happen to like bingo so all in all this has worked out fine. Now, will you put the Parmesan on the table, please? I grated it earlier.'

Kate gave her a hug and Evelyn pulled her close. 'Don't you be hard on him now, you hear? He needs a bit of coddling tonight. Forget all the eejity talk about the blood testing and everything, he did you a favour you know.'

Kate nodded. She heard a knock at the door and went to answer it. Evelyn took off her apron and surveyed the little breakfast bar. It looked nice. She understood that Patrick's house was a huge posh affair with expensive carpets and a housekeeper and all manner of frippery! Well, as far as she was concerned her Katie's house was as good, if not better, because it had the added bonus of having herself, Katie and Lizzy living in it!

Thinking of Lizzy made her smile. She was looking forward to seeing Peter in Australia. She had been banjaxed with excitement over it, as her mother used to say.

Patrick walked into Katie's hall carrying a bottle of red wine. Kate took it from him and he slipped off his overcoat, placing it over the worn banister rail. He followed her through to the kitchen and Evelyn favoured him with one of her wide smiles.

'Come away in and sit yourself down. It's enough to cut the lugs from you out there tonight!'

Patrick grinned. He loved listening to Evelyn's voice, it was like listening to his own mother again. He missed the Southern Irish accent. It had a musical quality about it, even when spoken raucously.

Patrick took the corkscrew Kate handed to him, and opened the bottle of wine. He poured them all a glass. Evelyn took hers, and after a large gulp said, 'It must have been terrible for you today, Patrick. You just sit yourself down and get something hot inside you. Food always makes people feel better.'

Patrick looked down at his shoes.

Kate was making a salad. As she washed the vegetables, Evelyn kissed her on the cheek. 'I'm off then, Katie. Goodbye, Patrick, I'll probably see you later.'

'Let me run you round to Doris's, Mum.'

Evelyn held up her hand. 'I'm quite capable of going by shanks's pony, Kate. You get your food down you while it's hot.'

Patrick smiled at her and watched her putting on her coat, scarf, woollen hat and thermal boots. She had them all laid out in the front room. Giving them both another wave she left the house, a large leather bag clutched to her chest.

'She's a lovely woman, Kate, you're lucky to have her.'

'Don't I know it! Why don't you put some of the dishes on the breakfast bar, this salad's nearly ready.'

Patrick set about helping. As they worked they chatted amiably about little things. The distraction of doing mundane everyday tasks took the edge off his misery. It had not occurred to him until today that he had not really grieved for his child because he had not really believed she was dead. It was only the lowering of her coffin into the earth that had brought it home to him. Finally and irrevocably.

Kate placed the garlic bread and salad on the laden surface and sat opposite him.

Patrick picked up his wine glass and held it in the air. 'To us?' It was more a question than a statement.

Kate picked up her own glass and touched it against his. 'To Mandy, may she rest in peace.'

'I'll drink to that.' Patrick sipped his wine, and then putting down his glass began to help himself from the dishes. He did not feel particularly hungry, the day had taken away any appetite he had. In fact, if he had not been going to see Kate, he would have got blind drunk.

'This is the first time I've eaten Greek salad with spaghetti bolognaise, Kate.'

He shovelled a mouthful of salad in as he spoke.

'I know. But they complement each other. I think so anyway, and as we're in my house we'll eat as I think fit.'

The ice was melted completely now, and they chatted together as they ate. Nothing important or heavyweight, that type of thing could wait for the time being. Tonight was an interval. It was to be the night when Patrick's trouble and Kate's involvement in that trouble could be set aside. They were a couple of friends comforting each other.

Patrick ate. He watched as Kate sucked in a piece of spaghetti, and he smiled. He knew that when the pain was gone, he would always associate Kate with his Mandy. He would always think of them together, first Mandy and then Kate. She was the one good thing that had come out of it all. He knew that if he had been left alone tonight he would have cracked. He needed company, but the company of someone he cared about, not a casual sexual encounter. If he had gone for that he would have felt he had cheapened his daughter's life. Trying to forget her and come to terms with her burial with a stranger, would have been like an insult.

After the meal, when they had taken the remainder of the wine into the lounge, their lovemaking began quietly. Kate allowed her clothes to be removed and lay on the floor with a tapestry cushion beneath her head, watching Patrick undress.

The thrill of watching him started as a heat, deep in her loins, and gradually engulfed her whole body. She saw that he was already aroused and was glad. She wanted no foreplay tonight. She wanted something hard, and sweet, and fast.

When Patrick collapsed on top of her ten minutes later, she felt the tension slipping out of both of them and held him to her breast, stroking his hair, while their heartbeats gradually returned to normal.

'Oh, Kate, I needed that.'

She kissed him on the mouth, gently at first and then hard, pushing her tongue between his lips.

'I know that, Pat. I'm glad you came to me.'

Kissing her breasts, he rolled from her and lit them both a cigarette. He lay back on the floor beside her and placed a large glass ashtray on her stomach.

'Oh, you! That's cold.'

Patrick smiled and lay back, putting one arm under his head. 'I ain't lain on a floor like this for years, have you?'

'Oh, we do this all the time at the station. You should see us some days in the canteen!'

Patrick laughed softly.

'You're crazy sometimes.'

'It's all this screwing.'

He glanced at her profile.

'I don't call what we do "screwing", Kate. I call it making love. There's a difference, you know.'

She turned her face slightly and looked into his eyes. 'You're very romantic, Patrick. What's brought all this on?'

But she knew what had brought it on, they both did. Losing his child had made him realise that happiness was there for the taking, and when you took it you had to grab it with both hands tightly, because you never knew when it was going to be taken away again.

Taking her cigarette he placed it in the ashtray with his own and put this on the hearth. He pulled her into his arms.

'I love you, Kate. I know we haven't known each other that long, but admit it – admit you feel the bond between us?'

Kate searched his eyes. All she could see was honesty and caring. She felt an absurd lump in her throat.

'Tell me you love me, Katie, make me happy.' It was a plea. Patrick needed words of love from her tonight; he needed to resolve the feelings that had been gradually welling up inside him since he'd first laid eyes on her. He knew, without a shadow of a doubt, that if he had met her under any other circumstances he would still have wanted her. It wasn't the fact that she had been there from the first, at the worst time of his life, that attracted him to her. It was the attraction of two kindred spirits they had here, heightened by the heartbreak each had experienced.

Kate was telling herself that it was the burial of his daughter that had brought all this on, that he was unhappy and needed someone, but inside her a little voice was whispering: 'He means it. It's written in his eyes.'

She knew that if she voiced what she had felt in her heart since the first time she saw him, there would be no going back. He was a repoman, a violent repoman. He had fingers in more than enough dubious enterprises. But for all that, for all she knew about him, real and imagined, she wanted him.

He could drag her down with him in an instant. Their association would jeopardise everything she had worked for and held dear. But even knowing this, she still wanted him. She had never wanted anyone so much in all her life.

'I love you, Patrick. I think.'

Her voice was low and husky, and he laughed.

'Only think? Well, I suppose that will have to do for the time being.'

Kate ran her fingers through his thick hair and traced the contours of his face with her fingertips, gradually travelling down, over his body and along his back muscles, to his rounded behind. He even felt strong. His skin felt warm and comforting on top of hers. He covered her naturally, as if he had been made specially to fit into the contours of her body. And as they kissed the shrill jangling of the phone broke their mood.

Kate pulled herself from the floor and padded out to the hall, dragging her blouse on as she went.

Patrick lay on the carpet and lit himself another cigarette. He felt at peace with himself, something he had not thought possible on this day of all days.

Kate came back into the lounge and sat beside him, her dark nipples showing through the thin silk of the blouse.

'That was my mother. She's decided to stay the night at Doris's.' She shook her head. 'She's about as subtle as a sledgehammer!'

Patrick smiled at her.

'She's a lovely person, Kate. Reminds me of me own mum. She had the same zest for life as Evelyn. It was overwork that killed her off, bless her. My one regret is she never lived long enough for me to give her a decent life. I'd have bought her a bingo hall of her very own.'

Kate laughed, knowing that he spoke the truth.

'I would have, Kate, you can laugh.'

'That's why I'm laughing, because I know you're speaking the truth. I can just see you doing it.'

They both grinned and then Kate took the cigarette from him and took a deep draw on it.

'Do you want to stay the night?'

Patrick grabbed her thigh and squeezed it.

'I'm not that kind of boy, miss.' He fluttered his eyelashes and she laughed again.

He watched her and knew that if it weren't for her, he would never have laughed again after today. Not really laughed.

She was as good as a tonic, as his mother used to say, and he did love her. He loved her very much.

Later on, in bed, they made love and she told him she loved him again.

In the dark and warmth of the night, with the musky smell of each other permeating their bodies, it did not seem wrong any more.

They talked till the early hours about Mandy and Lizzy, both exorcising their own particular ghosts. They had so much in common for two people who were, in outsiders' eyes, so different. He agreed with her about sending Lizzy to Australia. He said that he would have done the same with Mandy. Lizzy was a girl who felt things deeply – too deeply, he said – and Kate loved him for his understanding of her situation. He seemed to have guessed that Kate felt responsible for her daughter's troubles and tried, in his own way, to allay her fears. Finally, they fell asleep together, entwined, and stayed that way till the morning.

It was over breakfast that he told her his news.

'I sold the massage parlours, Kate. All of them. I sign the contracts in five days' time, and then they are nothing to do with me any more.'

Kate's eyes widened. 'You're joking?'

'No, I'm not. Since that girl was . . . What with my Mandy and everything, I don't want anything to do with it any more.'

Kate put her hand on his and squeezed it gently. 'I'm glad, Pat.'

'It came home to me that the man who murdered my girl was like the man who murdered young Gillian Enderby – a pervert of some kind. Except my Mandy was dragged off the street and Gillian was like a baited trap, waiting to be sprung. I ain't silly enough to think that by selling the shops it won't happen again, there'll always be a demand for that type of thing, but at least now I know that I have no part in it.'

'I think Renée would have been pleased.'

Patrick smiled.

'Yeah. She would have. In a lot of ways you two are alike. Renée was small and blonde while you're tall and dark, but in your personalities you're similar. She had a brain, old Renée. She had more savvy than people gave her credit for.'

'You still miss her, don't you?'

He nodded. 'But not like before. The physical pain has gone now. When she died, I felt as if someone had chopped off one of my arms or legs. I feel like that now about Mandy. But with Renée I can remember her now without pain. It's a bitter-sweet memory.'

'I understand.'

'But I've got you now as well, and that helps me. It helps me a lot. If Renée could see me now I know she'd approve. She'd have liked you, Kate. You'd have liked her.'

Kate was not too sure about that but she kept her own counsel. Instead she poured him another coffee and smiled.

'Well, I think you did the right thing. I don't believe you would have been happy still owning those parlours, you know. Anyway, we start the blood testing in a couple of days and then we should start to get a result; if nothing else we can eliminate the large part of the male community, and that can only make our job easier.'

'Do you really think the blood testing will achieve something?'

Kate nodded. 'Yes, I do.'

Patrick sipped his coffee and then smiled back at her. He hoped so because he was footing the bill, but he would spend every penny of his considerable fortune to catch the man responsible for his daughter's death. It made no difference who got him first, himself or the police, because no matter where they locked him up, Patrick knew he could get to him. In fact, he had more chance of getting to him once he was in prison. There was more than one old lag who owed him a favour.

He did not say any of this to Kate though. Even though they were now real lovers, admitting their involvement, he saw no reason to disillusion her about his motives in helping to find the man they were after. He would cross that bridge when he came to it.

All he wanted was a name, and he would do the rest. If it lay with him Katie would never know what he had planned.

A little while later, under the shower with her, he felt a twinge of guilt at keeping her in the dark. But it soon disappeared. Knowing Kate, she would fight for the man's right to a trial by jury, lecture on his rights as a human being. He admired her so much. He smiled to himself.

'What are you laughing at?'

'You.' His voice was jocular.

'Me!'

She looked outraged so he kissed her. Some things were better left unsaid.

Chapter Twenty-two

Lizzy was packing her small case. She placed her bright green Kermit the frog slippers in last and pushed the lid down to fasten it. Her long hair was loose and trailed into her eyes. She pushed it from her face impatiently.

There, she'd done it! Picking up the case she placed it on the floor by her bed and, going to the coffee corner, made herself a large mug. She sat at the table sipping it.

Her two weeks in the hospital had been a turning point in her life. Every time she thought of cutting her wrists she felt a flush of humiliation. How could she have done that, not only to herself but to her mother and her grandmother? It was a last dramatic act, as if she was saying, 'Well, you know everything else about me, I might as well go out with a bang, not a whimper. Lay a bit of extra guilt on you all.'

Really she had done it because of her shame at her grandmother knowing about her diary.

The psychiatrist had explained to her about self-destructive behaviour. Lizzy had listened to the man, respecting his intelligence, knowing that he was trying to help her straighten herself out. And in two weeks she felt she had come a long way. One of the girls here had had a breakdown, and no one knew why. She had finally taken an overdose of aspirin and had nearly died. Her father was a respected lawyer and he had raised Cain every day his daughter had been in the ward. Finally the girl, a tiny redhead named Marietta, had admitted her father had been sexually abusing her since she was eight when her mother had died.

It was hearing this that had made Lizzy put her own life into perspective. She realised that she harboured all sorts of grudges against people. Against her mother for never being there when she really wanted her, for instance. When Kate had sneaked into school performances with her uniform on, she had wanted to die. She had wanted a mother like everyone else's. A warm human being who picked you up from school in a nice second-hand Volvo and made you your tea and spent her every waking hour with you. What she had was a woman working her way up a career ladder, with enough obstacles in her way to make Hercules balk at the task.

Deep inside Lizzy was proud of her mother. When people found out she was a detective they were impressed, and Lizzy had been jealous sometimes. She had inherited her mother's looks but not her quick brain. All in all Kate Burrows was a hard act to follow, and the worst of it all was that her mother accepted her for what she was; had never tried to force her to do anything against her wishes.

When they had spent time together, it had been good. Lizzy had loved being with her, getting the attention, but it only made it all the more lonely when her mother went back to work again, caught up in a big case. Lizzy felt then that she was shoved aside. That her mother used up all her energy on other people, other things, coming home sometimes hours after she had gone to bed. She would be half awake, waiting for the soft-footed padding of Kate's footsteps coming to her bed in the middle of the night. She would feel cool lips on her forehead and want to put her arms around the slender neck and tell her she missed her. But she never had. Her mother had smelt of Joy perfume and cigarette smoke, and the smell would bring tears to Lizzy's eyes.

She sipped the coffee again. It was only warm now, and she took the film of skin off the top with her finger and scraped it into the saucer.

Then her father had turned up periodically, upsetting the whole household with his presence. She had loved seeing him, had loved all the attention he gave her, the presents, the hugs and the cuddles. Then one morning she would get out of bed and he would be gone. Those were the days when he had come back and slept in her mum's bed. Her mother would be glowing with happiness – then off he went. He would take all the good things with him. Her mother would be hurt, Lizzy would be hurt, and her granny would be annoyed with them all.

She would hear her mother sobbing in the night and it would tear her apart. In her schoolgirl heart she would vow that if her father turned up again, she would not talk to him, would not let him use her any more. Then months later the vow would be forgotten when she would come in from school to find him ensconced in an armchair, a big smile on his handsome face, and his voice would be like a caress as he told her how she had grown, how beautiful she was, and how he was home for good now.

But it never lasted.

Then, lastly, there was her granny, the mainstay of her life. She loved that woman with every ounce of her being. But deep inside herself she had always wondered why Gran had never done anything to make her mother stay home more often. Why she had sacrificed her own life for her daughter's and grand-daughter's. And somewhere along the line Lizzy had started to think that her granny was a fool. That she was weak and foolish to spend her life looking after her grown-up daughter and grandchild. She got nothing out of it.

Lizzy had pondered these thoughts now for two weeks, and she was finally making some sense of them.

She wanted badly to go to Australia. She wanted to get away from the memory of what she had done, to herself and to her family. She wanted time to heal properly, without having to go over the same old ground, over and over again. When her mother looked at her with those big brown eyes, Lizzy could see how much she had hurt her, could see the barely concealed confusion in them, and it hurt her to know that she had put it there.

She had only been interested in how she felt, and what she wanted. She had never spared a thought for her mother and the struggle she had had trying to bring her up, buy their home, and keep them clothed and fed and warm.

It had been an illuminating time, this last two weeks. But it had also been a time of gentle healing.

She looked at the red lines on her wrists. Every time she saw them she would be reminded of what she had done. So would her mother and her grandmother.

It was best she went away to Australia, to give her mother a chance to get herself back together.

She finished the dregs of her coffee. Looking at the doorway opposite her, she felt her heart lurch. It was her father, with a bunch of flowers and that cringe-making smile he had.

She admitted to herself, for the first time, that her father actually irritated her.

The thought made her sad.

She took the flowers, dutifully admired them, and then sat and talked to him, avoiding any questions about her mother's private life. She was going home later and couldn't wait to get there.

She smiled at her father's little jokes and did not mention that she was being discharged as she knew he would insist on taking her home, there and then, and that was the last thing her mother needed now. Danny Burrows laying down the law according to him. She also noticed that his watch and gold jewellery were not in attendance. He'd obviously hocked them.

Lizzy had grown up all right.

Patrick stood with Willy, looking at the mound of dirt that was his child's grave. The flowers were still fresh and he rearranged them to cover up the earth completely. There had been over a hundred wreaths and he had sent them to Grantley Hospital to be torn apart and used in the wards. It had gratified him to see the number of people who had turned out for her. Even Mandy's teachers from school had come. And it wasn't just because of him – Mandy was a popular girl. He corrected himself. Had been a popular girl.

He heard Willy whistling between his teeth, and turned to

look at him. He was reading Renée's gravestone. He looked at Pat and smiled.

'Do you remember that time Renée locked you out the house?'

Patrick frowned.

'When was that?'

'When you was first married – you had that bedsit in Ilford.'

Patrick smiled as he remembered. It had been their first home, when he was still trying to make his mark on the world. They had both been seventeen, two children playing at grown ups.

Willy carried on, 'It was Christmas Eve and me and you had been up the Ilford Palais, remember now? You got pissed out of your head and I had to take you home. Then, when I finally got you there, Renée had bolted the door and wouldn't let you in. You ended up kipping round my mum's.'

'Yeah, I remember. And the next day when I went home she threw me Christmas dinner at me.'

Both men laughed together, basking in the shared memories.

'She was a girl, old Renée. I really thought a lot of her, Pat.'

'Well, I've lost them both now.'

He walked away from the graves with a heavy heart. Willy slipped into step beside him.

'That Kate bird reminds me of Renée sometimes. I don't mean in her looks, but she's got the same air about her like.'

Patrick nodded. 'I know what you mean.'

'Is it serious like? The relationship?' Willy's voice trailed away. He knew he was on dangerous ground, but his natural nosiness overcame any fear.

Patrick stopped on the newly cut grass of Corbets Tey Cemetery and stared at his old friend.

'It's serious enough, Marjorie Proops. Happy now you know all the scandal?'

Willy jutted his chin. 'Well, you're me mate, ain't you? I just want to know that you're all right like.'

Patrick shook his head. Making a fist, he punched the air gently by Willy's face.'

'We go back a long time. You know everything about me as I do about you. I know you just want to know how I am, and I'm all right, bearing up.'

Willy smiled. 'Well, that's all right then! Fancy coming for a beer in the Robin Hood? I ain't been in there for years. The Flying Bottle we used to call it when we was young, remember? We'd sit outside in the summer with Mandy in her pushchair and worry in case we saw someone we knew who'd tell Renée we'd taken the baby to a pub!'

Patrick nodded, smiling as he was assailed by a vivid memory.

Mandy in a white and pink organdie dress, her little fat legs wriggling with excitement every time Willy made a face at her.

For the first time it occurred to him that Willy must be feeling her loss almost as much as he was. She had been like his child as well. He had chronicled her growing up. Never missed a birthday or Christmas.

Patrick felt a lump in his throat and swallowed it down hard. He linked his arm through his minder's and Willy patted the gloved hand.

'I remember it well.'

Evelyn had made an Irish stew, a real Irish stew that was thick enough to stand the spoon up in it. She tasted it and added another dash of salt, stirring the mixture for a while. When the smell was just to her satisfaction she placed the suet dumpling on the top and put a large cover over the pan. Evelyn's Irish stews could last for anything up to a week. She added to them every day, different vegetables and different meats. The cereals and pulses gave a pungent thickness that made the final end of the stew into a thick broth.

Lizzy was home today and she wanted her to be welcomed with the smell of good hearty food.

Everything was ready. The soda bread was going in the oven the minute she heard the front door open, so they could have it nice and hot with melted butter. Her trifle was wobbling itself to death in the fridge and the little bottle of Bushmill's was snuggled into her apron pocket, where she could have a snifter without being seen.

She settled herself on the stool.

It would be grand to have Lizzy back home. There had been too much going on in the last few weeks, and Evelyn nearly admitted she was getting a bit old for it all.

Still, Kate looked better and that was good. Her child was dear to her heart and she was glad that Kate and Lizzy were finally coming to some kind of understanding of one another's ways. They were as alike as two peas physically, but temperamentally they were like chalk and cheese. She hated to admit that Lizzy had a lot of Dan's selfishness in her. But she blamed herself for that. She had doted on the child from day one.

She forced these thoughts from her mind. The child was coming home and she wanted everything to be lovely.

But she knew that what she had read in Lizzy's diary would stay with her for a long time.

She concentrated her thoughts on her son Peter and his wife Marlene. She was looking forward to seeing them. Seeing her other grandchildren for the first time. She took a deep drag on the cigarette and her thin body was racked by a fit of coughing. She'd have to knock these on the head, they'd be the end of her. She stabbed her cigarette out in the ashtray and heard the sound of Kate's key in the lock. Leaping from the stool, she put the soda bread in the oven and rushed out into the hall.

'Hello, me pets!' She hugged them both in turn, her little dark eyes darting over her grand-daughter with a critical glint in them.

She looked all right, a bit thinner, but a few good meals would remedy that.

'Hello, Gran.' Lizzy was shy all of a sudden. 'Is that an Irish stew I can smell?'

'It is, one of the best I ever made. I've done mashed swede to go with it. Now come along in and I'll get you both some.'

Fifteen minutes later they were all around the little breakfast bar enjoying the food when someone knocked on the front door. Kate stood up, wiping her mouth with a paper napkin.

'I'll get it.'

She went out to open the door. She could not help her face registering surprise when she saw who was there.

'Caitlin?'

He stood on the doorstep in his crumpled raincoat, a little smile on his face.

'I'm sorry to disturb you at home like this . . .'

'Come in. I'm sorry, I don't mean to be rude but it gave me a shock, seeing you standing there.' She took him through to the front room. 'Is it something to do with the case?' He could see the hopeful glimmer in her eyes and shook his head.

He could see the two women in the kitchen and smiled at them.

'Could I see you for a second alone, Kate?'

Something in his voice alerted her and going to the connecting door she closed it, apologising to her mother and daughter as she did so.

'What is it, Kenny?'

She had a feeling like a cold hand grabbing her neck. Something was up here, she knew it.

'It's Dan. He went to see Flowers about you and Kelly.'

Kate bit her lip. 'I see.'

'Well, Flowers wasn't interested, you know. So Dan took it one step further, Kate. He took it to the CIB.'

Kate felt as if someone had punched her in the stomach.

'I thought you ought to know. I found out through an old friend of mine, so no one at the station except me and you know about it, OK? It's not even definite that they'll investigate it, but just in case I thought you had a right to know. That ex-husband of yours is an Asshole with a capital A.'

Kate nodded. She couldn't have agreed more.

Evelyn opened the door, her face troubled.

406

'Is everything all right?'

'You must be Kate's mother. I'm Kenneth Caitlin.'

'A Kerry man by the sounds of it?'

He smiled at her and the little exchange gave Kate time to get her head together.

'Come through and have a drink, Kenny. This is my daughter Lizzy, and my mother's already introduced herself.'

'I'll be away home, Kate, I can see you're eating.'

'You'll do no such thing. Get that awful mac off and come and have a bit of stew, there's plenty.' Evelyn's voice brooked no argument. She had been intrigued by Kate's description of this man, and now she could judge for herself.

Caitlin had smelt the delicious aroma of the stew as he had walked up the garden path, and seeing the three faces smiling at him he hesitated only a second longer. Then he took off the mac and placed it on the sofa.

'If you twist my arm up me back, it does smell good!'

Kate was glad he stayed because he took over the main thrust of the conversation and she could think.

The Criminal Investigation Bureau.

Bugger Danny Burrows!

Patrick was sitting at the dining table just finishing his meal when Willy announced that he had a visitor. He wiped his mouth with an Irish linen napkin. When he heard the name of his visitor, his left eyebrow rose a fraction.

'Show him in here.' Willy nodded and left the room.

Now what would Peter Sinclair want visiting his house?

Sinclair walked into the room. He was small, wiry, and held out a perfectly manicured hand to Patrick. He stood up in greeting then offered Sinclair a seat, poured him a brandy and sat back in his own chair.

'To what do I owe this honour?'

'I had to come here, Patrick. It's about the piece of skirt you've been running around with.'

Immediately Sinclair knew he had said the wrong thing.

407

Patrick's face hardened.

'And what piece of skirt might that be?' As if he didn't know.

'Detective Inspector Kate Burrows, of course.'

'Of course.' Patrick's voice was low and the menace in it was not lost on Sinclair.

'So, Peter, how's things at the Home Office? Lively by the sound of it. Actually doing some work, are you? Well, wonders will never cease, will they?'

Sinclair took a sip of his brandy.

'You've gone too far this time, the CIB are in on this. She's compromised herself. As much as I like you, Patrick, you're a known villain . . .'

He leant forward over the table. 'To be accurate, Peter, I'm an alleged villain. My brief would have kittens if he heard you talking like that.'

Sinclair grinned. 'Come on, Patrick, let's cut the crap. You're going with a senior police officer. The CIB are having kittens.'

'The police officer you're talking about is working on my daughter's case.'

'I know that, and I'm sorry about what happened to Mandy, Patrick. But Kate Burrows is another matter altogether. She's got an ex-husband who's kicking up a stink and threatening to go to the papers about this.'

Suddenly, it was as clear as a bell why Sinclair was here. They wanted him to sort out Burrows.

'Supposing I was to talk to this Danny Burrows, make him see the error of his ways, what then?'

Sinclair smiled.

'Provided he can be made to admit he was just trying to cause his wife embarrassment, everything will be fine.'

Patrick nodded and poured himself out some more brandy. 'Would you like a cigar?'

Sinclair smiled again, happier now that he had accomplished what he came to do.

'No, thanks, but I wouldn't mind a piece of that excellent Cheddar.'

'Help yourself. I've just got to make a phone call.'

He left the room.

Caitlin was in the middle of a very funny story, about a case he had been on as a PC, when the phone rang and Kate went out to the hall to answer it.

'Kate, it's me, Patrick. I must see you.'

'I wanted to see you, actually.'

He could tell, just by the inflection in her voice, that she also had had the bad news.

'I can get to you for seven thirty in the morning, how's that?'

'I'll come to you, Pat. Lizzy's home now.'

'Fair enough. I'll see you in the morning then.'

When Kate replaced the receiver she felt a shiver of apprehension go through her body.

It was going to be a choice between Patrick and her job and she wasn't too sure who would win.

She went back to the kitchen and sat through the punch line of Caitlin's story, but her laughter had a hollow ring to it.

Kate got up the next morning with a feeling of dread. She knew the CIB's reputation. She also knew that a female officer, consorting with a criminal – even an alleged criminal as Patrick liked to call himself – was just their cup of tea. They would crucify her.

A few years before she had been witness to one of their jobs. It concerned a detective sergeant with a taste for exotic holidays and even more exotic women. He had been on the take. Kate had had to stand by with the rest of her colleagues as the man was set up and routed.

It had not been a pretty sight. She had felt sorry for him because most officers used their status for something, whether it was the odd free meal or a few pounds extra for a hobby. She was not saying that she agreed with it, just that it went on, a perk of the job. The ones the CIB should be looking out for, to her mind, were the officers who raided a flat, found a couple of weights of cannabis and stashed half of it before they made the collar. The cannabis would make its way back on to the street and the officers would pocket the money. To her that was a crime, not going to a restaurant for a nice meal on your wedding anniversary and getting a bottle of decent champagne thrown in because you knew the owner ran an after hours card club.

Some laws were just made to be broken, and when you finally realised that, you became a much better officer. Why go after the silver plate when you could get the twenty-four carat gold? She wanted the criminals, the real lawbreakers, not the flotsam and jetsam that made up the majority of collars.

It was like when police visited convicted felons and said to them, 'We're going to go back to court and you're going to admit to another thirty burglaries. It won't affect the time you're doing, they'll be classed as TIC.' Taken into consideration. Which made the figures at the end of the year look great. On paper it looked as if they had solved more crimes than they really had. Except the perpetrators of the crimes the convicted man had put his hand up for were still getting off scot free. Case closed, thank you very much.

Kate drove to Patrick's house with a heavy heart. Her job was her life. At one time, it was all she had had, except for Lizzy.

Patrick gave her a cup of coffee and told her about Sinclair.

'Caitlin had already told me about it, an old friend of his had tipped him the wink.'

He looked at her. She seemed worried, her usual happy expression was strained.

'Well, I have a solution to our problem, but I thought I'd get your say so first.'

'What is it?' Kate's voice sounded hopeful and Kelly was glad about that because he wasn't at all sure how she was going to take what he had to say.

'Well, it's your husband who's shoved a spanner in the works, isn't it?'

410

Kate nodded, taking her cigarettes from her pocket.

Patrick lit one for her and continued. 'Well, if I was to go and see him like, he might be encouraged to change his story, admit he was just trying to cause his ex-wife a bit of aggravation.'

Kate drew on the cigarette and looked into Patrick's eyes. 'You wouldn't hurt him?'

Patrick held out his arms in a gesture of denial. 'As if I would!'

Kate was tempted, sorely tempted, but a little part of her was not sure. She could be condoning an act of violence. Because for all Patrick's charade of being the big benevolent boyfriend, if he had to give Dan a slap to achieve his ends he wouldn't even give it a second thought.

'Let me think about it, Pat.'

'What's to think about? I go see him, give him the bad news and he shits himself and puts his hands up to the CIB. Sweet as a nut.'

'Have you got an answer for everything, Pat? A violent answer to everything?'

Her voice was flat and that was not wasted on him. 'Listen, Kate, we've got a lot going for us, and I don't want that geek of a husband . . .'

'Ex-husband, Pat.'

'All the better, ex-husband, to bugger it all up. Where there's a villain there'll always be an Old Bill. Our kind of partnership goes back to the start of skulduggery, my love. You know in your heat that you're not doing anything wrong. We are friends and lovers. I'm not asking you to tell me the secrets of the Serious Crime Squad. I'm not asking you to tap out on your little computer what they're trying to fit me up with next. We just enjoy each other's company.

'I love you, Kate, and I'm trying to help you that's all. I know that if you lost your job over me, we'd be finished for good. Because you'd always hold it against me.'

'We could finish it now.'

Patrick frowned. He was getting annoyed. He'd thought she felt a bit more for him than this.

411

'Well, that's entirely up to you, darlin'!'

Kate put her cigarette out and went to him. She sat on the arm of his chair and touched the lines of his face.

'I didn't really mean that, Pat, it was unfair.'

She could no more leave him now than she could walk past an injured child on the street. He was a part of her, a big part. But to keep him she had to let him do something that went against the grain.

'Let me think about it, please. Give me a couple of days?'

Patrick saw the confusion in her eyes and grasped her hand in his.

'I don't want to lose you, Katie. You've come to mean an awful lot to me.'

She kissed the top of his dark head.

'Same here.'

He pulled her on to his lap and kissed her hard. He wanted her to have something else to think about as well, just in case she forgot for a second what she would be giving up.

It was Friday 16 February 1990, and the blood testing had been going on for four days. The police were amazed at the response from the public. The men of Grantley seemed to be positively eager to have themselves eliminated from the inquiry. Thames News gave a report every day and even News at Ten had shown a film of the 'phenomenal' testing of a whole community.

There were already problems. The sheer magnitude of the task had caused a large backlog. The number of people taking the blood tests far exceeded the capacity of the people who carried out the testing of the blood. Still, even with this problem, Kate was happier than she had been for a long time. It was a chance to try and nail the man responsible and she was glad for that alone.

The fact that Leonora Davidson had been dead for two weeks now frightened her. She felt that with the closeness of the previous attacks the killer would be striking again soon.

The phone broke into her reverie and she answered it.

'DI Burrows here.'

'Kate? It's me, Dan.'

She had been expecting his call, and now that it had come she felt an overpowering rage. He had been visiting Lizzy when he knew Kate was gone from the house. Since his little escapade with the CIB he had been keeping a low profile where she was concerned.

'What can I do for you?'

Her voice was chillingly polite.

'I want to see you.'

'But I don't want to see you, Dan, not now, not ever. You went too far this time.'

The phone went quiet and Kate realised that she had let the cat out of the bag. She should not have let on she knew about what he had done. He would get in touch with the CIB and they'd know she was already on to them. It would damn her immediately.

'Dan? Are you still there?' The line was very quiet. Please God let him be there. Don't let him have gone. 'I think we should meet, talk this thing over.'

'I'll meet you tonight at the Bull in Bulphan, Kate. Eight o'clock.'

The line went dead and she felt herself exhale.

'You all right, Katie?' Caitlin smiled at her.

She nodded.

'I couldn't help overhearing your conversation – only your end, of course. If I was you now, from tomorrow I would carry out all other communication with him from a public pay phone. Know what I mean?'

Kate nodded again, and picking up her handbag from the floor she left the office.

So they were tapping her phones now. At work and also at home. It figured. She left the station and as she walked out wondered how many of her colleagues were in on this thing. Suddenly she was worried. Very worried indeed.

George had had a long bath and was sitting on the toilet, with the seat down, cutting his toenails when Elaine burst into the room.

413

'How long are you going to be? I'm off out in half an hour.'

'Not long, dear. Where are the girls taking you tonight?'

George smiled as he said 'girls', and pictured a crowd of big fat till girls drunk on Pernod and black, their raucous laughter escaping from heavily lipsticked mouths.

He stared straight into Elaine's face as she spoke and was grudgingly impressed with the way she lied so convincingly.

'Oh, I don't know yet, we don't decide till we get to the pub, bingo probably.'

She smiled back at him.

'I've run the bath for you anyway. Why don't you jump in it quickly? I won't be long now.'

Elaine hesitated for a few seconds and then slipping off her dressing gown dropped her eyes from his and put a foot gingerly into the water. She slowly climbed in and then relaxed gratefully into the hot steamy water. Her red hair was piled up on her head and George watched with morbid fascination as she closed her eyes and breathed regularly and deeply.

She looked dead.

She looked happy, dead.

Her breasts were rising and falling with each breath and the nipples had hardened at the sudden cold then heat. They were pointing up at the ceiling, big rosy tips that George suddenly longed to touch. The milky white skin that was once her best feature was jutting from the water in different places. Her pubic hair, that vivid red hair that had once driven him wild, was sparser now but still more luxuriant than most women's. He had seen a naked and relaxed Elaine many times since the New Year. He guessed that it was the man she was seeing who had given her a new lease of life.

George quite liked him, he thought. For making her happy. He could not make her happy.

'Are you staring at me again?'

The voice that could crack glass was back.

'I was just thinking how you would look on the beach in Spain, dear. You're looking ever so well, you know.'

Elaine squinted at him. Whenever George paid her a

compliment she was never sure if he was really laughing at her.

George sat back on the toilet seat and grinned at her.

'Not long now until your hols. I bet you're looking forward to them? I know I would be if I was you.'

'Yes, I'm looking forward to them, George. What will you do while I'm away?'

By the tone of the question, George knew it had not occurred to her before and he grinned again.

'I thought I might arrange a little surprise for your homecoming.'

Elaine sat up in astonishment, causing the water to overflow on to the carpet.

'What kind of surprise?' Her voice was suspicious.

'Now if I told you that it wouldn't be a surprise, would it?'

'Oh, George! Tell me!'

He laughed good-naturedly.

'No! Wait and see. I think you deserve a surprise, Elaine. A nice surprise.'

She felt a lump in her throat. Why was George being so good to her all of a sudden?

He stood up.

'Get yourself washed and I'll put the towel on the radiator for you so it will be nice and warm when you get out. Shall I make you a drink? Brandy and coke? I made some ice yesterday. Get you in the mood for your night out with the girls.'

Elaine stared at him.

George raised his eyebrows. 'Brandy and coke, OK?'

Elaine nodded and watched him practically skip out of the bathroom.

She picked up the soap and began to wash herself all over. She stood up and soaped between her legs. Her mind went to Hector then. If only she was married to Hector. If only she had never stood by George.

She smiled to herself ruefully. If regrets were pennies she would be a millionairess by now.

Down in the kitchen, George was taking the ice cubes from

their tray. He poured a generous measure of brandy into a tall tumbler and listened to the satisfying crackle as the ice cubes met the alcohol. Then he added a small dash of coke. He didn't want Elaine's amour to be disappointed, did he? Give her a few drinks and she'd be well away. George wondered idly who he could be.

He could follow her. He dismissed the idea, he wasn't really that interested. Whoever the man was, he got Elaine out of the house and that meant George could carry on his own business at his leisure. The thought of having something over Elaine appealed to him, but he might need her one day. Anyway, she deserved to enjoy herself. After all, he had his fun. Who was he to spoil things for her? And if it got serious and she left him, then he would help her pack her bag and kiss her goodbye.

He picked up the drinks and took them up to the bedroom. Elaine was drying herself when he came in. He gave her hers and raised his glass.

'Cheers. I thought I'd join you myself.'

'Cheers.' Elaine took a sip of her drink then grimaced and placed it on the dressing table. She pulled the towel around her tighter and tucked it in over her breasts.

'Did I tell you what happened today, George?' She sat on the stool by the dressing table.

'No.' He settled himself on the edge of the bed.

'Well, one of the fellows who deals with the deliveries went and took that test in the precinct . . .'

George's eyes gleamed. He was just going on to autopilot when her words penetrated his brain.

'Really! How thrilling! What happened?'

'Well, it seems it's a bit more complicated than people thought.'

'In what way?' He could feel a slight trembling in his hands and sipped his drink again. He almost loved her again. You could always depend on Elaine to find out what was going on.

'Well, they wanted to know his mother's full name, the address where he lived and phone number, plus his place of work and the phone number of that. The names of his children, then his post code! Oh, it was terrible, he said. He was so nervous he nearly forgot his mother's maiden name!' She picked up her drink and took a swig. It wasn't often she had George's undivided attention and she was quite enjoying regaling him with the story.

George, on the other hand, was fretting. She wasn't telling him quickly enough and knowing Elaine, she would draw out the story for maximum effect. He gritted his teeth and smiled at her.

'Is that all? I would have thought it would have been a bit more than that.'

'Oh, it was. They took his fingerprints and asked him if he had been questioned by them regarding the murders. They asked to see his passport but he only had his driving licence, and then they wanted to know what kind of car he drove and what was the registration? Then after all that he finally had the blood test. He said the woman who took the blood was really rough and his arm was swollen where the needle went in.'

Elaine chattered on but she'd lost George now. He was quietly processing exactly what she had said and trying to turn it to his own advantage. He stood up abruptly.

'I'd better let you get on, dear, you're off out soon and if you don't get a move on, you'll be late.'

Elaine glanced at the clock by the bed and gave a little squeal, causing George to close his eyes. Acting like a teenager did not sit well on Elaine, but she couldn't see that herself. Jumping up, she rushed to the wardrobe and took down a bright blue dress that was hanging on the outside. So busy was she taking off the plastic film, she did not even notice George slip from the room.

Twenty-five minutes later, when she'd left, George went down to his shed and brought out all his clippings. He had a whole scrapbook now and lovingly read every word, over and over again. In one local paper was a picture of Kate Burrows, the Detective Inspector who was working on his case. Beside her was her Chief Inspector, a Kenneth Caitlin. He studied the blurred black and white photos and grinned.

They couldn't catch a cold, George thought.

He smiled at the witticism and went back to the pictures of his victims. As always when he saw Geraldine O'Leary, he felt a twinge of sadness. Her poor children, to have a mother like that! He sipped the last of his brandy and shook his head. They really were much better off without her.

Later, after he had read his fill, he put on a nice video and, pouring himself another brandy, settled down to watch it. For the time being at least he was happy to be just an onlooker while others perpetrated the deeds on screen. But he knew that before long the urge would come over him, and he would have to go out once more.

The girl on the screen had become Leonora Davidson and the most violent of the men himself . . .

George felt the stirrings of excitement.

Once Tony had taken his test for him he would be as safe as houses. In his mind, he toyed with the notion of getting rid of Tony Jones permanently and decided not to make a decision just yet. He would see how it went.

But if he tried to blackmail him? Threatened to tell the police? George smiled grimly this time. He would cross that bridge when he came to it. At the moment he needed Jones, and until that need had been answered he had to keep on good terms.

Tony Jones was worried. Very worried. The more he saw on the news and in the papers about the blood testing, the more convinced he was that he would be caught out.

If he was caught and they put him on remand, Patrick Kelly would make sure he was dead within twenty-four hours. If he refused to help and George was caught, he would spill the beans and Tony would still be at the mercy of Patrick Kelly.

The news that Pat Kelly had sold off his massage parlours had rolled through London like a tidal wave. It was being said on the street that his daughter's death had made him chary of owning anything to do with sex. But at the same time, he had apparently begun to expand on his repo businesses.

Kelly was one of the hardest repomen in the country. It was rumoured he had even repossessed a jumbo jet for a British aircraft manufacturer who were owed hundreds of thousands of pounds by an African airline. Had repossessed it on the runway with all the passengers on board. Kelly had a reputation all right. He also knew all the right people, including the bird who was working on the murder inquiry. Barrow or whatever her name was. It was the talk of the town.

He looked out of the door of his shop again. George Markham was supposed to have been there an hour before. It was just after nine and he had closed the shop especially. Now there were men hanging around waiting for the doors to reopen and that bloody Markham was nowhere to be seen.

He had given Emmanuel the night off, with pay. He did not want anyone seeing or hearing his meet with Georgie. He was losing money hand over fist. It was Saturday night and all the nonces were out in force. Spending their cash on books, films and so-called marital aids. Tony Jones glanced at his watch again. It was nearly nine fifteen. Perhaps he wasn't coming? Had changed his mind? He felt relieved as he thought that.

A man banged on the window of the door and he went to it, staring through the reinforced metal glass. It was not George but a man called Merve the Perve. He was well known in Soho and a good spender. Tony shook his head and pointed to the handwritten sign: Closed from 8 to 10.

The old man gave him a two-fingered sign and Tony gritted his teeth. There went a good fifty quids' worth of business. He watched Merve walk away and sighed.

Then he saw George and quickly unbolted the door and let him in. The shop was in semi-darkness as they made their way silently to the back. George sat down without being invited, which was not lost on Tony Jones. The quiet meek little man was slowly metamorphosing into a dangerous individual. He was even scaring Tony.

'I have a list here of the questions being asked and the answers you will give. I understand they want a passport if possible, something with a picture on.'

He passed the paper to Tony.

The man glanced at it. George's neat handwriting filled both sides of the paper.

'I can get a passport, but it will cost you. I'll need a photo of you as well, and your own passport number.'

'I brought a yearly one I had done this morning, just in case.'

He took it from his inside pocket and gave it to Tony.

'How much more will this cost?'

'Say three grand for the lot.'

'All right, the money will be paid afterwards. When I'm sure it's all OK. Don't get it into your head to try anything. It's a funny thing, you know. Once you've killed you lose your fear of it. Killing is easy. It's become a kind of hobby for me now.'

George watched Tony for a while until his words had sunk in then said, 'I want you to take the test on Monday the nineteenth at about six o'clock in the evening. They are coming to my place of work at nine o'clock on Thursday the twenty-second. I want my piece of paper ready for them then, to say that I had it done before. I will meet you on the Duggan Road, just outside Grantley itself, in a pub called the Lion Rampant at eight thirty, I will bring half the money with me then.'

'Why on Monday at six o'clock?'

'Because that is when the police are winding up to leave the unit. If you get there for about half past five you should get in at about sixish. Being one of the last of the day I think they'll just want to get you in and out as quickly as possible. Also, if you have a passport you're home and dry. It's the ones without a positive ID who are being given a hard time.'

Tony Jones nodded.

'All right. But I can't get there on Monday. I'll need a few days to get the passport sorted out.'

George was annoyed.

420

'Well, when can you meet me then?'

'Wednesday. On Wednesday. We'll stick to the same plan of where to meet and that, but I need time to get this thing sorted. It's Wednesday or not at all.'

'All right, but just make sure you get it sorted by then.'

George stood up. 'When you've memorised the answers, get rid of the paper.'

He walked out of the tiny room without a by your leave and Tony Jones stared at the paper until he heard the shop door close. Pushing it into his pocket, he left the room and switched on the lights to reopen for business. As he worked, one thought kept recurring.

It was of the day that Tippy had walked in battered and cut. He should have realised then that the bloke was two sandwiches short of a picnic. If he could rattle an old tom like Tippy he was capable of anything.

How the hell had he got into all this?

George drove through London and out to Essex. He was listening to a talk show on Radio Essex as he hit the Dartford Tunnel. It was about the Grantley Ripper.

Women were phoning up, saying he should be castrated when he was caught, given a lethal injection, locked away in Rampton or Broadmoor.

George was enjoying listening to the silly suggestions. They would never catch him.

Kate had rung Patrick and told him about the meet with Dan at the Bull. She sat just inside the doorway, watching the people come and go, a feeling of dread on her. She had told Patrick that she would see Dan first, try and appeal to him. If that didn't work she would leave the pub and give Patrick a sign. He would be waiting with Willy, then he could have a word with Dan. One of his special words.

Kate hoped it would not come to that.

Dan came into the pub at ten past eight. He was wearing black trousers and a deep red sweater. He had taken his overcoat off as he walked in, and had it draped casually over his arm. Kate noticed more than one woman give him a second glance. Her big manly husband.

She felt like saying out loud, 'You couldn't afford him, girls. He wouldn't soil his hands on women from a backwater pub.'

It annoyed her that he could still make her feel inadequate.

He went to the bar without acknowledging her and came back with a Spritzer for himself and a vodka and tonic for her.

'Hello, Kate.' He sat beside her, his voice smug. He knew just how much he had over her.

Kate nodded to him. 'Dan.'

She watched his mouth on the rim of the glass. Once he had been everything to her. Now she was amazed to find that she felt nothing, not even contempt for him.

'Why did you do it, Dan?'

He thought for a while, searching her face for some kind of indication of what she was actually thinking.

'Because, Kate,' he pointed a finger at her, 'you pushed me too far this time.'

'*I* pushed *you* too far?' Her voice was incredulous.

He nodded, warming to his theme.

'That's right. I came to you for solace, if you like. I've always taken you for a good woman, but what do I find? I find the mother of my child with a bloody villain! My God, Kate, I just couldn't believe it. You had the gall to pass me over for a thug.'

He took another long drink of his Spritzer.

'It has nothing to do with you any more, Dan. My life's my own. I'm working on a big case . . .'

'Nothing to do with me? When my child is being neglected!'

Kate grabbed his hand and pushed it back on to the table with such force the glass he was holding spilt its contents over the red sweater.

'You listen to me, Danny Burrows. I put up with more than enough crap from you over the years, but this time, boy, it's over. It stops. If I lose my job, who's going to pay my mortgage? Not you, that's for certain. You couldn't pay your own way in a million years. That's why you fuck the Antheas of this world. You're a ponce, Dan, and I will not stand back and let you make a mockery of my life like you have of your own. I'm warning you . . .'

Kate was getting annoyed. She had known this was useless and now wondered why she had even tried to get him to see her side of it; he was incapable of real feeling. Intelligent feeling.

'You're warning me? That's a turn up for the book. You should be down on your bended knees, girl, because at this moment in time, I—' he poked himself in the chest '—can make or break you, Kate Burrows. Your career is in the palm of my hand.'

He held his hand in front of her face and clenched it into a fist.

Kate saw how much he was enjoying himself, and was saddened. Once, a long time ago, this man had been the most important thing in her life. She had slept with him, cooked for him and had his child; he had walked out on her and she had held a torch for him for so long. Now, she was seeing him as her mother had seen him and she felt that her life had been wasted because she would not let go of her futile dreams for too long.

She stood and picked up her cigarettes and bag.

'Where do you thing you're going?'

'This is getting us nowhere. You make all these accusations about me yet you can prove nothing. You know something, Dan? You bore me. You bore the arse off of me. I only wish I'd realised it ten years ago.'

She walked from the pub and Dan followed her. Outside in the gravel car park he caught up with her and, grabbing her arm, swung her round to face him. He slapped her. Not hard, but a stinging slap.

It was then he saw Willy and Patrick.

Kate saw his face change in the gloomy light of the car park and turned to see Patrick running across the gravel towards them.

'You fucking bitch, you set me up!'

As Dan turned to make his way to his car, Willy caught up with him and Kate watched as Dan was dragged towards Patrick's BMW. A young couple pulled into the car park and got out of their car. They were watching Dan and Willy, a shocked look on their faces. Kate went to them and got out her ID. 'Grantley police, we're apprehending a known drug dealer. Did you happen to see anyone on the road as you drove here?'

Both shook their heads, not wanting to get involved. Patrick walked sedately to the BMW with Kate, taking her arm and nodding at the couple. Willy had already forced Dan inside. Kate felt as if she was caught up in a nightmare. She went to the car and got in the front, Patrick got in the back with Dan, Willy wheelspun out of the car park and on to the Grantley Road. Kate twisted in her seat and looked at Dan. He was terrified.

Willy slowed the car and Patrick lit a cigarette. He passed it to Kate in the front seat and then lit one for himself. He puffed on it until the end glowed bright red.

Kate watched him and he winked at her.

Then he grabbed Dan's hair and held the cigarette a fraction of an inch away from his eyeball.

'I could blind you, Danny boy, I could blind you without even thinking about it.' Kate went to say something and Willy put his hand on her leg to warn her to keep silent.

Patrick carried on talking in his sing-song voice and Kate watched, fascinated now, as Danny sat stock still. Not moving a muscle.

'You see, you've annoyed me, and when I get annoyed I do terrible things. I could even cripple someone if they annoyed me enough. And you have annoyed me, Danny boy, believe me.'

'Wh-Wh-What do you want?' Dan's voice was high as a schoolgirl's.

'I think you know what I want, I think you know what your wife wants. And I think you know we're going to get it.

Because if needs be, I will hunt this country high and low for you, Danny, and I'll get you in the end. Like AIDS I am. You won't even know I'm there for years, but when I do show up the consequences will be devastating. Do you get my drift?'

Dan swallowed loudly. Kate heard it above the low drone of the car engine.

'Yes.'

'So you're going to be a good boy and tell the CIB that you gave them a load of old cod's, ain't you?'

'Yes.'

'Right. Willy, stop the car and let the man out.'

Patrick took the cigarette away from Danny's face and flicked the ash on the floor.

Willy stopped the car. Leaning over Dan, Patrick opened the door and pushed him out violently on to the road. He shut the door as they pulled away, leaving Dan lying in the road, so frightened he thought he was going to wet himself. He saw his overcoat being thrown out of the window and felt the sting of tears.

Kate had sat there and let it happen. He couldn't believe it.

But one thing was certain: he was going to do what Kelly said. As he had always admitted to himself, he was not the hero kind.

Kate stared out of the car, not sure if what she had witnessed had really happened.

'All right, Kate?' Patrick's voice was low.

She nodded.

He sighed. It was a shame they had had to do it in front of her.

'Look at it this way, Kate, if I hadn't've frightened him – and that's all I did, frighten him – you could kiss your job goodbye. He asked for that, girl. He damn' well asked for it.'

'Could you take me back to my car, please?'

'Turn the car round, Willy, Kate wants to get home.'

Patrick had a feeling of utter futility. He had been trying to help her, but maybe he had gone too far. Sometimes he forgot that she was from a different world. This night

425

would make or break them, he knew that, but either way she still had her job and that, he knew, meant a lot to her. He had given her that much at least.

Kate was still shaking when she got home. She went upstairs and locked herself in the bathroom, running herself a hot bath. She stepped into it and lay there, trying to work out her troubled thoughts.

Tonight she had seen another side to Patrick Kelly. It had not endeared him to her. She was finally seeing exactly what she was taking on, and it was frightening.

But for all that, in a funny kind of way, she had enjoyed seeing Dan get his come-uppance. All those years of being hurt by him, of knowing that he had used her. Seeing the contempt he had for her tonight had hurt her more than she had thought possible. He had enjoyed having something over her. She had not enjoyed what Patrick had done to him, but she had enjoyed seeing Dan's fear, seeing him grovel like that.

It was these feelings that frightened her more than anything.

George had had an accident. He had dropped his hot chocolate all over the living-room carpet and had spent the best part of an hour cleaning it. He had gone to the shed and got the Bex Bissel, starting to clean the carpet. Then the patch where the stain had been looked cleaner than the rest and he had ended up cleaning the whole carpet. Now, three hours later, he was finally finished and he was wondering if he still had time to watch his film when he heard the low throb of a taxi. He looked through the curtains as Elaine paid the man clumsily. She was as drunk as a lord.

The bloody bitch!

He watched her lurch from the taxi, clutching her bag, and trying to walk up the cement pathway to the front door. He could hear her fumbling for her keys and trying to place them in the lock. Everything seemed magnified a thousand times. The front door banged open and he heard her heavy footfalls approaching the lounge. He sat on an armchair waiting for her to come into the room, but she passed by it and made her way into the kitchen.

He heard the click of the fluorescent lights and her heels clattering on the linoleum, then he grimaced as he heard her retch into the spotlessly clean sink.

He stood up slowly and followed her. Standing in the doorway, he watched her back and shoulders heaving as she brought up port and brandy into the white sink.

He walked to her.

He saw the deep red stains in the sink like clotted blood and turned on the cold tap. He watched mesmerised as the stain became a light pink before swirling around and down the plug into the sewer.

Picking up a tea towel, he soaked it in cold water and placed it on Elaine's forehead. Then, holding the back of her neck tightly as she tried to push him away, he brought the sopping wet cloth down over her nose and mouth and pushed with all his might.

Elaine breathed in and felt the tiny droplets of water enter her nasal canal and burn as she breathed them inside. She tried to move her head and felt the vice-like grip of George's hand on the back of her neck.

She began to struggle as she realised through her drink-fuddled brain just what was going on.

George held the tea towel over her face, enjoying her panic, enjoying the pain and terror he was creating. This would teach her.

In her struggle Elaine knocked the mug rack by the sink flying on to the floor. The smashing mugs bounced and shattered, making a tremendous noise as the flying shards reached every corner of the kitchen.

George pushed her head down and under the rushing cold tap. The freezing water took the little breath she had left away. With one final surge of strength Elaine tried to bring her head up and felt the deadening pain as she came into contact with the stainless steel tap.

George heard the dull clang, and watched as red blood rapidly began to stain her orange hair. He felt her body relax as she lost consciousness, and held her for a few seconds. Then he slowly lowered her on to the floor, letting the tea towel drop from his hand into the sink.

Elaine lay on the floor amid the broken mugs. Her carefully applied makeup was streaked across her face. Mascara had come away from her lashes in lumps and now peppered the skin around her nose and cheeks. The deep red blood was running from the wound on her head and on to the pristine tiles into little red rivers that broke up and formed tiny map-like inlets.

George stared at her. Her orange hair was in wild disarray and her dress was soaked through. Her eyelids were flickering and when they opened he could see that she was unaware of what exactly had happened.

She closed her eyes again and groaned loudly. It was the groan that triggered him into action.

Going behind her, he lifted her bodily by linking his arms under her arms and across her enormous breasts, and dragged her through the chaos of broken mugs through to the lounge where he laid her on the carpet. Dragging one of the lace chair protectors off, he folded it up and placed it under her head to protect the carpet from the blood.

Then, rushing out to the kitchen, he got the first aid box from under the sink and tenderly dressed the cut. He was gratified to see it was only a flesh wound; the blood made it look more serious than it was.

He worked quietly and quickly. When he had finished, he placed a cushion under her head and slipped off her sopping dress. Then he covered her with a blanket, warm from the airing cupboard. Satisfied that he had done all he could, he went and started on the kitchen.

Sweeping up the broken mugs, the broom spread bloody water around the kitchen like an abstract painting. The different shades mesmerised George as he worked. When he finally washed the floor clean he was sorry to see it go: he liked the patterns it made and the colours it created and the smell of it – the richly scented smell of fresh blood.

He went back in to Elaine and held her pudgy hand. He

428

had nearly blown it, he knew that. If he'd killed Elaine, that would have been the end of him. She groaned again and opened her eyes. She had been unconscious for over an hour.

'Wha-What happened, George?' Her voice was still groggy with drink.

He smiled at her gently.

'I think you had too much to drink, my dear. You had an accident.'

Elaine stared at him with her compelling green eyes for a few seconds and George went cold. It was as if the whole night's events were written in them for all to see. Then she closed them tightly.

If she remembered what had taken place she didn't say so. George was even more worried. Supposing she did? What then?

'Shall I make you a nice hot drink?'

Elaine nodded painfully, her hand going up to her bandaged head.

He got up from the floor and went to the kitchen, his eyes boring into every corner to make sure he had picked up every bit of evidence.

While he was gone, Elaine lay passively on the floor.

Then, unannounced, a fat tear pushed its way from underneath her eyelid.

George had tried to kill her. She remembered it all. He must know about Hector.

When he came back with the steaming tea, she was crying loudly, her ample shoulders heaving once more.

Putting the tea on the table, he pulled her into his arms.

She knew.

'I'm sorry, Elaine, I am so very sorry for what I did. I thought you had a boyfriend or something. I realise that's ridiculous. Forgive me for a moment of madness and jealousy.'

Elaine sniffed loudly, gratified in a way that George could be jealous, but not at all sure she liked the 'ridiculous' bit.

He did not know for certain about Hector yet he had physically attacked her. He had hurt her.

She would have to be very careful in the future.

George watched her face and knew everything she was thinking. It was like watching a television screen. Thank God he hadn't killed her. For the Grantley Ripper to be caught like that!

But one thing he was sure of: he would have to play this one very carefully. Elaine was not going to forget this in a hurry.

She felt the change in George and shuddered. He was like before. When they had had the trouble. Only this time it was all her fault.

She closed her eyes. Poor George.

Chapter Twenty-three

It was Monday morning and George brought Elaine breakfast in bed. She felt and looked dreadful. Her head had swollen where it had hit the tap and the scab that had formed had dried on to the surrounding hair, making it impossible for her even to touch her head lightly. Once the effect of the drink had worn off she was left with a violent headache and George's solicitous manner was not helping.

He got on her nerves.

After his attack – and it was an attack, she told herself – she did not really want anything to do with him, She needed time alone to think it all through.

'I made you some eggs and bacon, Elaine, with a couple of lightly grilled tomatoes.' George's voice was once more meek and mild. 'I poached the eggs for you because of your diet.' He placed the tray across her knees and smiled at her shyly.

Elaine glanced at the food on the plate, anything rather than look into his face.

'I think you'll feel better after a couple of days off work, don't you?'

She picked up a fork and began to push the food around the plate, the livid blue of the willow pattern a focal point in her need to ignore George.

He hesitated for a few seconds, waiting for an answer. 'Well . . . I'll leave you to enjoy your breakfast then. I rang your manager and told him you had a bug. See you tonight. I'll cook you a lovely dinner.'

Please go, George, she thought.

He went and she felt a moment's lifting of her spirits as she heard the front door close.

Close, not slam, because George slamming a door would be like the Pope joining the Chippendales.

But he had attacked her.

She pushed the laden tray to the other side of the bed. George was capable of violence. He had attacked that poor girl on the train that time. The doctor had said that he was full of unhappiness and bitterness due to his childhood and his overbearing mother. That Elaine's condition and the impending birth had put a strain on him that had caused him to act out of character.

Why had she felt that it was all her fault?

Why had she stayed with him, stood by him?

Because she hadn't known what else to do, that's why. 'For richer for poorer, in sickness and in health.' Why hadn't it had anything about in prison or out of it in the ceremony?

Her head was aching. She closed her eyes and saw Hector. Good old Hector who had told her that he loved her. Hector who laughed all the time and wanted to have fun. Nothing more or less, just fun.

She smiled to herself slightly. And what fun they had had. She couldn't give Hector up! Hector was her life support. Her passport to a happier land.

She lay back against the pillows and surveyed her bedroom. It needed decorating. The whole house did. Years before George had been a handy DIY merchant. They had spent hours looking at paint charts and choosing colour schemes and papers. But that was before his trouble, as they referred to it – when it was ever referred to at all.

George had come out of prison a changed man. Never a gregarious person, he had nonetheless been a cheerful type once. But he had returned to her a sullen and unhappy individual, with a meekness that bordered on humility. Except she sometimes thought it was all a front. All he had been able to do was his gardening. It was as if the inside of the house was meaningless now, and that only the shell was to be maintained in any way.

She sometimes thought that was just like George himself. He had an outer shell that he wore day in and day out, but inside he was empty.

Empty and frightened.

When the murders had started in Grantley she had been inclined to think it was him, but she knew it couldn't be. George would never make a competent murderer. Everything he did just fell apart.

No, George was just a poor fool. But his outburst had proved to her that he did feel something. That he still looked on her as his wife.

The worst part of all the trouble that time had been the knowledge that he had been to a pornographic cinema. That, for some reason, had seemed worse to Elaine than the attack on the young girl.

A single fat tear careered from the corner of her right eye and snaked down her rounded cheek until she tasted the hot saltiness on her tongue.

Why had it all gone wrong? Where was the young girl who had waited so eagerly for her baby to arrive? When did she become a ridiculous middle-aged woman sneaking around to meet another man?

When, in God's name, would all this end?

Kate left her house at seven in the morning. It was foggy, the air laden with the smell of early spring. As she unlocked her car, she felt a man's presence and turned abruptly to face him. She thought it was Dan. Her mind had been so full of him all night, she had hardly slept. It was thinking about him and the lack of sleep that had driven her from home so early. She could not face Lizzy just yet.

She turned to look into the big moon face of Willy. She was startled, holding her hands to her chest instinctively.

'I'm sorry to scare you, I just wanted a word. I won't keep you long.'

He took Kate's arm and walked her along the road to Patrick's Rolls Royce. He opened the back and she sat inside. All her instincts told her not to be frightened, but she could not totally allay her fears. Willy started up the car and it rolled away noiselessly from the kerb. He put down the connecting window and began to speak.

'I know a little place where we can have a bit of breakfast if you like.'

Kate nodded to him, aware he was watching her in the mirror. 'A coffee would be nice, thanks, Willy.'

They drove in silence to a small transport cafe on the A13. He parked the Rolls where he could watch it from the window and took her inside. It was empty except for two women and one lone lorry driver, who gave Kate the once over as she sat down and Willy bought two coffees. Happier now she was within sight of people, she gradually relaxed. She lit a cigarette and sipped her coffee.

'I wanted to talk to you about last night, Kate. Can I call you Kate?'

She nodded. 'What about last night?'

'Well, after we dropped you off, Pat was really down. I think he knew he had made a mistake, letting you see what was going to happen, but you must understand him, Kate – Patrick had your best interests at heart. He was trying to save your job and your relationship with him. He has a bit of sway with the big boys, as you probably guessed. Once that pra— I mean, once your ex-husband gives them the news he was just trying to stir up hag, they'll close the case there and then, and it will never be referred to again.'

Kate sipped her coffee and lit another cigarette from the butt of the previous one.

Willy sighed. 'Pat wouldn't have hurt him, I know that for a fact. Sometimes you have to use a bit of friendly persuasion . . .'

'If that's friendly persuasion, I'd hate to see you do it to someone you didn't like!'

'But that's just it – we only scared him, that's all. It was Pat seeing him slap you in the car park, it made him mad. Madder than hell. He was just trying to help you, that's all.'

Kate sucked on her cigarette and the smoke billowed around her head like a cloud.

'You got to understand Pat. He comes from an area that was poor, and I mean poor. We had nothing. He's worked his arse off to get what he's got. He ain't bothered about people

434

like your old man. They're nothing to him, nothing at all. He did that last night for you.

'Pat hasn't put the frighteners on anyone before who wasn't directly involved in one of his businesses. In our game, someone gets out of order you threaten them with a bit of a slap. It's the law of the street and you live by it. I mean, it's not unknown for Old Bill to scare a suspect shitless until he's put his hand up for something he didn't commit. Look at them pub bombing blokes and that. The Old Bill beat the crap out of them. Well, with us, we just threaten.'

God forgive me for lying, he thought.

Still Kate was silent, and Willy was getting exasperated now.

'He only wanted you to keep your bloody job! He was worried about the way he'd compounded you . . .'

'Compromised, Willy. That's the word you're looking for.'

'Yeah, well, that and all then. But you know what I mean, girl, you're not a silly bird. You know the score. Your old man won't be any more or any less hurt by what happened to him. He was asking for it. I know it must have seemed a little scary to you, 'cos you're not used to it, but believe me, Pat wouldn't have bothered but for you. You and your job. He knows how much it means to you.'

'Can you take me home now, Willy? I have to get my car for work.'

He nodded and they drove back to Kate's in silence. The traffic was thick now and she felt the stares of the other motorists wondering who was in the large Rolls Royce. As she stepped out at the bottom of her street, she patted Willy's arm.

'You're a good friend to Patrick, you know.'

'I worship that man, Kate. I know the good in him. I think you do too, otherwise I don't think you'd have got involved with him in the first place. Don't take what he did last night too much to heart. He loves you, I know he does, and he just wanted to help you. He's a bit cack-handed in the way he goes about it, that's all.'

435

Coming from Willy this made her smile. A smile she had not thought she had in her at the moment. It was definitely food for thought.

Willy drove back to Patrick's with a heavy heart. He had tried. If Pat had known where he had gone, he would kill him stone dead. But he'd had to try.

Kate and Patrick were good together.

George sat at work listening to Peter Renshaw's voice go on and on about the 'night out'. It was finally decided they would hold it on the Wednesday night, just two days away. George forced himself to smile as Peter regaled him with anecdotes on the leaving dos he had attended in the past. From what George could gather there were about twenty-five people going to his, most of whom he had never spoken to in his life.

Mrs Denham came into the office.

'May I see you for a moment, Mr Markham, in my office.'

George followed her and watched Renshaw's eyebrows rise rudely. George was glad of a respite from Renshaw's almost frenetic bonhomie. The anecdotes and jokes bored him no end. Once inside the office, Mrs Denham offered George a seat and closed the door behind him.

He sat down and watched her bustle to her own seat, the beige silk suit she wore whispering against her tights as she sat down.

George smiled warily.

Josephine Denham smiled back. Just as warily. She cleared her throat nervously.

'It's about your redundancy – I have a note here of the amount you will be receiving.' She passed a slip of paper across the desk to George and he glanced at it.

'If you would like to leave earlier than stated, we would do everything we can to accommodate you. Jones is leaving at the end of the week . . .' Her voice trailed off as she looked at his shocked face.

'Twelve thousand pounds? I thought it would be more than this.'

George's mind was whirling now. Elaine would go mad. He had told her about twenty or twenty-five thousand, which had softened the blow as far as she was concerned. Twelve thousand pounds. That would do nothing, nothing.

Josephine Denham watched the confusion on George's face and felt a moment of sympathy. She had never liked him. Like most of the women in the firm, she had felt uncomfortable around him. Not that he had ever done anything, of course. It was just his way of looking at you. Of staring at you from beneath lowered eyelids. She felt a prickling sensation on the back of her neck now as she watched his expression turn from confusion to fury.

'I need more than this! Much more than this.'

'Look, Mr Markham, it's all worked out on your wages. You're . . .'

George interrupted her. 'I know all that. I work in accounts, remember? It's just that I thought it would be more! Much more. I need more than that, for Christ's sake. Can't you understand, you stupid bitch!'

Josephine Denham's eyes widened to their utmost and she stood up with what dignity she could muster.

'I understand that you're upset, Mr Markham, but talking to me like that won't help matters. I think it would be better if you went now and we talked it over another day. When you're feeling . . .'

George was breathing heavily. Twelve thousand pounds. The words were flying around his head, banging and thumping against his skull. Twelve thousand lousy pounds. It was like a chant.

He stayed in his seat. Josephine Denham was gone from his vision now. All he could see was the three thousand for the passport, and for Tony Jones to take his place in the testing.

The woman walked from the room and into the accounts offices. She pulled Peter Renshaw aside and after a hasty few words he followed her to her office.

It was empty. George had gone.

'I thought he was going to hit me!'

For once in his life Peter Renshaw looked at an attractive woman without seeing her breasts, eyes, hair, legs. He knew what was wrong with George. This place was his life. His refuge.

'Did it ever occur to you that maybe the man knows he's finished? That he'll never work again? That tens of young men and women are waiting to fill any job he might be eligible for? That he's got a wife and home?

'Of course it didn't, Mrs Denham, because you never think of anyone but yourself and this bloody firm. Well, when your turn comes – and it will, my love, make no mistake about that – I hope whoever axes you does it with a bit more tact.'

With that, he walked from the room and left Josephine Denham with her mouth agape.

On the table was the piece of paper she had handed to George. She picked it up and stared at it. Twelve thousand pounds. It wasn't much for fifteen years.

Elaine was fed up with lying in bed and had decided to get up. After making herself a cup of tea and reading the paper in the kitchen she decided she needed something to take her mind off things. She looked at the garden as she washed up her cup and a thought occurred to her. She could germinate the tomato seeds. Every year at this time George popped them into the airing cupboard ready to go into his greenhouse. Then all summer they would have big fat red juicy tomatoes.

She went upstairs and got dressed. Her aching head was feeling much better after a couple of aspirins. She pulled an old jumper carefully over her head and put on a pair of track suit bottoms. Elaine was a woman who needed to be doing something. That was why the house was so spotlessly clean. If she had five minutes to herself then her thoughts wandered to the way she lived and it made her depressed.

She made her way down to the garden shed. It smelt musty, like sheds should, and she looked around her. George had it quite cosy really. This was his little domain. His refuge. He spent a great deal of time here.

438

Suddenly, Elaine felt like an interloper. She shrugged. This was as much her shed as George's. He had the gardening sorted out like she did the house. His and hers.

Now, where were the seeds? She began by looking on the small shelves he had built. There were gladioli bulbs waiting to go into the ground. She would get him to put some by the front door this year, liven up the front of the house with a nice spray of colour. She was warming to her theme. Planning the garden would give her something else to think about. Once George was made redundant he would be spending a lot of time in the garden. He could replace the whole lot. Buy some nice rose bushes. She liked a nice rose and George was a good gardener. He was patient and thorough. There were never any weeds anywhere.

She began clearing the old desk of gardening debris, then opened it up to find his gardening magazines. She would flick through them and get some ideas. They could even have a bigger pond, with a nice rockery.

She pulled out the magazines and then went cold. She stared down at the books as if not quite sure of what she was seeing.

A girl was looking at her, a Chinese girl, nearly naked and with a chain around her neck.

She was smiling.

Elaine picked up the magazine and stared at it, feeling the bile rising in her stomach.

Underneath there was another one. This had 'Nazi Torturers' emblazoned across it. On the front were two women in SS uniforms dragging a scantily clad girl between them.

Elaine closed her eyes tightly and opened them again. It was no good, they were still there.

Slowly she removed all the magazines. Her heart was heavy now. Underneath the magazines were some scrap books and she took these out. Sitting in George's comfortable chair, she opened one. It was full of newspaper clippings about the Yorkshire Ripper, yellowing with age now and brittle-looking.

There were the photographs of his victims. Headlines screamed out at her: I WAS CHOSEN TO KILL. HER EYES DROVE ME CRAZY. RIPPER IN THE WITNESS BOX.

She closed the scrapbook and opened another one.

This time the cuttings were newer, all about the Grantley Ripper, and suddenly Elaine knew what had happened. It was crystal clear.

It was George who had murdered all these women.

He was sick.

He had attacked her!

Elaine hastily began to put the scrapbooks and magazines back where she had found them. She had to get the police. She was fumbling in her haste and only half aware of the shadow that passed the shed window. She did not even hear the shed door opening. She turned around and came face to face with George. So great was her terror that instead of screaming she groaned, holding on to the desk for support lest she faint away completely.

George was staring at her. And he was smiling. The little smile that just showed his teeth.

'Come and have a cup of tea, dear, you look as white as a sheet. You've had a shock, I think.'

Kate was in the canteen having her lunch when she was told there was a phone call for her. She went to the phone on the wall by the door and picked it up.

'Burrows here.'

'Kate? It's me, Dan.'

She felt a surge of apprehension as she heard the desolate tone of his voice. She pushed herself against the wall to try and muffle their conversation.

'Look, Dan. About what happened. I swear I had no idea . . .'

He cut her off. 'I know that. Let's face it, Kate, I asked for it. Well, you can tell that . . . your friend, that it's done. The CIB are off your back. I've been round to see Lizzy and told her that I'm going back to Anthea's.'

'And are you?'

'Yeah. I rang her this morning. We're going to have another try.'

It was a lie. Dan was going as far away from Grantley as possible. He didn't want any reminders of Patrick Kelly.

'I hope it works out for you, Dan, really I do.'

The line crackled, Dan had muttered something inaudible and Kate said his name down the phone line a couple of times before hanging up. She went back to her table and lit a cigarette. The canteen was filling up but the babble of voices and laughter went unnoticed by her.

She was still thinking about Patrick and what he had done. After Willy had dropped her off she had thought long and hard about Patrick and, much as she loved him, had admitted to herself he scared her.

The worst of it all was, scared of him, annoyed with him or anything else that she might feel, above all she wanted him. Desperately. It was this that scared her more than anything.

'Penny for them?'

Caitlin's voice was friendly.

'I wouldn't take money from an old man.'

He laughed in surprise. 'Is everything all right with the other business?'

She nodded and Caitlin grinned.

'Sure that Danny's an eejit. Imagine doing that. Still, the blood testing is going well, so that's something anyway.'

'It's certainly going better than anyone expected, that's for sure.'

'Did you hear about Spencer?'

Kate shook her head.

'Well, like all the male officers he got a letter, same as everyone else. He's doing his pieces! Thinks it's a deliberate slur on his character.'

Caitlin roared with laughter, bringing many eyes to rest on him and Kate.

'But it was what that Amanda said to him that's really caused the trouble.'

Kate was intrigued. She smiled at him. 'Go on then, tell me.'

Caitlin leant across the table and whispered: 'She said she had read a secret psychologist's report that stated the Grantley Ripper was a policeman in his late-twenties with a history of paranoia and violent and disruptive behaviour!'

Kate giggled. 'Well, if the cap fits!'

'My sentiments entirely!' Caitlin was roaring again. 'Sure she's a comical lass that one. So Kelly saw your old man then?'

He changed the subject so quickly he caught her offguard. 'Yes. It's all right.'

'That Patrick Kelly is a very astute man, you know. You just let him sort out everything. You're lucky to have such a good friend.'

She dropped her eyes.

'Come on, Kate, we've still got a good half an hour. Let me buy you a drink in the pub. My throat's as dry as a buzzard's crotch!'

Kate closed her eyes. 'You have a disgusting turn of phrase, you know.'

'Sure me wife, poor woman, used to say that. God rest her nagging soul.'

'You miss her, don't you?'

'I do, Katie, more every day. She had a tongue like an adder, but she was me wife. Come and have a drink, lass. This place gives me the heebie jeebies. All this youth makes me stomach turn.'

Kate stood up and followed him out of the canteen. She could do with a drink herself.

Elaine was sitting opposite George at the kitchen table. He had made her a cup of coffee and it stood in front of her, cold now, with a thick skin of milk floating on top. George had been silent, just smiling at her every now and then while he sipped his own coffee.

'Elaine.' His voice was so low she could barely hear him, but all the same she jumped in her seat.

'Don't be scared, Elaine. Would I hurt you? Now would I?'

She bit her lip.

'I didn't mean to murder anyone, believe me, my dear. It just happened.' He spread out his hands in front of him in a gesture of helplessness. 'I don't know what it is. I just see them – they're all whores, every last one of them.'

He was nodding to himself now and Elaine felt her nails bite into the flesh of her hands.

'Even that bitch O'Leary, with the children. They're much better off without her, believe me. You didn't see her like I did, Elaine. Sprawled out on the dirt. She had no tights on, you know, and the weather was freezing. She was a slut . . . a dirty stinking slut.'

Elaine put her hands over her ears to block out his voice. George stood up. Fear overtaking her, Elaine made a rush for the kitchen door. As she ran George grabbed at her hair. She shrieked as pain tore through her. Blood began to seep from her wounded head on to the vivid orange locks. George punched her to the ground, every movement calculated and controlled. He stood over her and shook his head.

'You've been a trial to me, Elaine, do you know that?'

Her lips were already swelling from his blows and she could taste the blood in her mouth.

'Why didn't you just divorce me? Why did you have to sit there all those years, a silent reminder of what I'd done?'

He gave her a vicious kick in the stomach and she gagged.

'Now I've got to kill you. You understand that, don't you? I couldn't possibly let you live now you know my little secret.'

He tutted a couple of times in exasperation. Elaine stared at her husband through watery eyes.

It dawned on her that George was as mad as a hatter and she was never going to see Hector, her friends, or anyone ever again. She was as good as dead already.

He stepped over her cumbersome body and walked out into the hall. Elaine could hear him whistling between his teeth, a habit that had grated on her nerves over the years. She saw, from her vantage point, that he was opening the coat cupboard in the hall and lifting up the floorboards. She

443

pulled herself painfully to her knees. Grabbing at the wall, she staggered upright. The floor was covered in blood, and as she swayed and tried to steady herself she felt droplets running down her chin and into the folds of her neck.

George pulled out his army knife and walked purposefully towards her. He was tutting again as if she was a recalcitrant child.

She heard him sigh and as she tried to run towards the back door felt the sharp slice as the knife went through the wool of her jumper and into her shoulder blade. She gathered up all her strength and tried to dodge around the kitchen table. The serrated edge of the knife was caught in the wool of her jumper and George watched in fascination as she staggered away, pumping out blood, the knife hanging half out of her back.

He shook his head. Elaine was always so difficult.

He watched her stagger for a few steps before she fell to her knees, her breaths coming in quick painful gasps.

He walked over to her and, pulling the knife gently from her jumper, raised it over his head. As he did so Elaine turned her head and looked into his face.

'George! Please . . . please, George . . . !'

She coughed and a trickle of blood seeped from the corner of her mouth. George planted the knife neatly into the middle of her shoulder blade, burying the blade up the hilt.

Elaine fell forward, and George watched her arms and legs twitch in the final throes of death. Finally he sighed.

Elaine was still, her cheek was pressed against the white tiles and her green eyes stared vacantly at the skirting board.

George knelt beside her body and tidied the orange hair, pushing it around her still face. Elaine had always been such a difficult woman but now she was at peace.

He made himself another cup of coffee and sat drinking it quietly, watching her body.

A little while later he began to whistle once more through his teeth. He had to make some plans now. He had to sort everything out.

At least this way he had saved her the knowledge of the

444

pittance that had been offered to him. She would never have let him live it down.

He glanced at the clock. It was three fifteen. He wouldn't be able to do anything just yet. He made himself a sandwich and took it into the lounge. He'd watch one of his films and relax. It had been a very trying day.

Tony Jones watched the man sitting opposite him. Larry Steinberg could get anyone anything. He was nicknamed 'Harrods' among the villains he dealt with because of this. If you wanted a Nepalese yak Larry would find one, and at a reasonable price. Tony watched the tiny man push his pince-nez up along the bridge of his nose, settling them just below the large lump in it.

'I had a bit of trouble with this one, Tone, but I managed it for you as quick as I could. Needs must when the devil drives, eh? What did you say you wanted it for?'

'I didn't.'

'Oh, well, you obviously have your own reasons. My friends in the passport office are getting very expensive these days. But for you, a good friend, I do it for the old price.'

Tony took a brown envelope from his inside pocket and placed it on the desk. Larry opened it and counted the money carefully. One thousand pounds exactly. Not a bad day's work. He opened a drawer and passed a small burgundy-coloured passport across the desk.

'I even got you one of the new EEC ones.'

Tony opened it and looked at his photograph staring out of the page.

'Thanks, Larry. I owe you one, I think.'

He stood up, putting the passport into his top pocket. Larry watched him leave the office and then walked to the window. From there he watched Tony cross the road and hail a black cab.

Larry was intrigued.

The details in the passport were of a George Markham, from Grantley in Essex. The man already had a one-year tourist passport, as well as a ten-year passport with eighteen

445

months on it. Larry knew that something not quite kosher was going down, but he was stumped as to what it was.

Something rang a warning bell in his head but he could not put his finger on it.

He went back to his desk and slipped the thousand pounds from the envelope into his wallet. At least he had been paid promptly. Nowadays that was something in itself.

Tony Jones walked into Sexplosion and poured himself a large scotch. He drank it down, the alcohol biting into his throat and stomach, burning his ulcer.

The enormity of what he knew about George Markham was weighing him down. He felt sick every time he thought about it.

All his life Tony had lived among villains, pimps and prostitutes. He had dealt with most of the so-called gang bosses in his time. In his business it was inevitable you would stumble across them at some time or another.

He had always prided himself on his ability to work side by side with the most violent men, keeping his business going and his head above water. He never made their Christmas card lists but they had afforded him a modicum of respect.

His shop was one of the oldest in the West End. His father had run it for years, before handing it over to his only son. Tony wanted to hand it over to his son one day. It was a lucrative business now that porn was more socially acceptable. He had dealt with prostitutes who would give Frank Bruno food for thought before fighting them and with pimps who would carve you up as soon as look at you. Yet none of these people had ever frightened him like George Markham, the little man with the funny smile.

He poured himself another stiff drink and Emmanuel waltzed into the back of the shop, his heavily mascaraed eyelids fluttering.

'I need a bit of help out here, Tone, if you don't mind. I've been run off my feet.'

Tony glared at the boy.

'Emmanuel, piss off and don't come in here again today

unless we get busted by the filth or Joan Collins comes in to buy a vibrator. All right?'

The boy pursed his cherry red lips and stormed out of the room. He could be so bitchy, could Tony Jones. He noticed a new customer in a neat brown suit and immediately cheered up. He liked the newies.

He smiled at the man. His nicest smile. He had all day. By the looks of it Tony was going to drink himself stupid. He'd been doing that a lot lately.

'Can I help you?'

The man in the brown suit smiled sheepishly.

Emmanuel smiled back widely. He was worth a fifty at least.

George had watched his film and was now feeling relaxed and cheerful. He turned off the video and sat smiling to himself. No more Elaine. No more having to be polite.

His face darkened. No more alibi.

Then he brightened. His mind was working overtime. If he planned everything just right, he could get away with it all.

If he went away for a while and then came back he could say that Elaine had left him. If he went to Edith's in Florida he could say it had happened out there. And now that he was redundant he could sell this house and be free. The more he thought, the more viable it all seemed.

He felt absolutely wonderful. He was so clever! He patted himself on the back. Cleverer than a bag of monkeys.

But what was he going to do with Elaine? He would have to hide her away somewhere. He thought of burying her in the garden but dismissed the idea immediately.

He would put her right under everyone's nose, and still they wouldn't find her. All he had to do was have a good old think . . .

The phone rang and he jumped in his seat. The harsh tones echoed around the silent house, upsetting George. He crept out into the hallway and picked up the offending instrument.

'Hello, George. Margaret here. How's Elaine?'

447

He felt his heart begin to race.

'Oh, she's fine, Margaret, feeling a bit better . . . I doubt she'll be in this week though.'

'Can I have a word?'

'She's sleeping at the moment. I'll tell her you called though, Margaret, she'll be sorry to have missed you.'

'Okey doke then, I'll ring her later in the week. 'Bye.'

George replaced the receiver.

The whole conversation had taken less than two minutes, but to him it had seemed like a fortnight.

He stormed out to the kitchen, his temper flaring. Elaine was still sprawled on the kitchen floor, her sightless eyes staring at the skirting board.

'That was your friend Margaret. Checking up on you as usual. Are you listening to me?'

George knelt down and pulled her head up by her flame-coloured hair. He looked ferociously into her face.

'You're nothing but trouble, Elaine. That's all you've ever been.'

Then, as if the reality of events suddenly hit him, he cradled her head in his arms and began to cry.

Evelyn heard the door knocker and went out to the hall to answer it. She could hear loud music coming from Lizzy's room and smiled to herself as she wiped her hands on her apron. The child was like a young girl should be now, and that thought cheered her.

She opened the front door. Patrick Kelly was standing there.

'Oh, hello. Kate isn't here, but come away in anyhow. I was just going to have a coffee.'

He walked into the hall, hearing the loud music coming down the stairs. Evelyn laughed.

'That's Lizzy. You're forgiven for thinking she might be a bit deaf!'

They went through to the kitchen and Patrick undid his coat and sat at the breakfast bar.

'I'm just making a nice lamb casserole for dinner.'

'It smells delicious.'

She poured out two coffees.

'I like to cook. It relaxes me.'

He took the coffee from her and sipped it.

Sitting opposite him, Evelyn lit herself a cigarette and blew out the smoke loudly.

'So what can I do for you, or is this a social call?'

Patrick smiled slightly. She was a game old bird.

'It's a bit of both actually. It's about your trip to Australia.'

'What about it?'

'Well, the truth is, I don't think that Kate can really afford it, can she?'

Evelyn took another drag on her cigarette. She knew that Kate couldn't afford it really, that she was trying to get a bank loan to pay for it. But she had told Lizzy she was going and there was no way that she would let her down, even if it meant selling the car and every bit of jewellery she possessed.

Patrick could gauge what Evelyn was thinking. He sighed. Taking an envelope from his pocket he placed it on the table.

'What's this?'

'That, Mrs O'Dowd, is two first-class tickets to Sydney, with a four-day stop over in Singapore. It's a long old flight to Oz, you know, and you'll be glad of the break, believe me. I want you to take these tickets and tell Kate that you had some money left over from . . . well, whatever you like. Let her think you paid for them.'

Evelyn fingered the thick brown envelope and looked into Patrick's eyes.

'Something's happened between the two of you, hasn't it?'

He nodded. It was pointless lying. He told her about Dan. Evelyn did not bat an eyelid all the time he spoke.

'That would go against the grain with Kate. It goes against the grain with me to be honest. But I'm a bit more of a realist than my daughter. I know that desperate times mean desperate measures. I'll give you a bit of advice where Kate is concerned, shall I? Always remember that her job is the most important thing in her life. She fought hard to get to where she is and I think that the fact she allowed herself to get involved with you, knowing your reputation, speaks volumes. She's had only one man in her life, Danny Burrows. Now she has you. Or maybe I should say had you? I don't know. Only Kate knows that.

'If you care about my daughter, and I think you do, then you should remember these facts. They'll stand you in good stead for the future. Kate's as honest as the day is long.'

Patrick at least had the grace to look away from her, and Evelyn admired him for that. She knew that he loved her daughter, could hear it in the way he spoke her name, see it in the way that he tried in his own way to make things right for her. Like the tickets to Australia. An expensive way to make amends, but Evelyn knew that was what he was trying to do. She opened the envelope.

The tickets were for 4 March 1990, from Heathrow. She looked at him and frowned.

He held out his hand and took the envelope from her. He placed it back in his pocket.

'I never said I wasn't going to accept them, did I?'

Her voice was softer now. She held out her hand and he gave her back the envelope. He left a few minutes later, lighter of heart.

Evelyn let him out and as she closed the door looked up the stairs. The thump-thump of Lizzy's music was still audible.

It was just as well the child had no idea he'd been here. Kate was astute enough to put two and two together. Evelyn only hoped she would believe her story about insurance money left over from her father's death.

She went into the kitchen and put the envelope into her apron pocket. It gave her a warm feeling knowing that it was there. She would see her other grandchildren and it would be thanks to Patrick Kelly.

No matter what anyone thought, she liked him. He was a product of the world they lived in and his lifestyle gave her not a smidgen of bad conscience.

As for what he had done to Dan . . . she shrugged. He'd been asking for that for years.

450

Her only regret was she hadn't been there to see it for herself.

Chapter Twenty-four

George looked at the clock. It was five-thirty-five and still dark. He rubbed at his eyes. They felt gritty and he could smell a funny smell on his hands. He leant out of bed and turned on the small bedside lamp. As the glaring brightness penetrated his eyes he grimaced.

His hands had rust-coloured stains on them. He held them up in front of him as if he had never seen them before and sat up in bed. He was fully dressed. He frowned.

Pulling back the covers, he slipped out of the sheets and stood uncertainly on the carpet.

His mouth felt dry and fluffy and he swallowed with difficulty. What he needed was a cup of coffee. He made his way downstairs humming to himself. He walked into the kitchen and turned on the fluorescent light. It flickered into life, illuminating Elaine's body. Ignoring her, he walked to the sink and filled the kettle. Stepping over her silent form, he made himself a strong, sweet coffee and took it to the kitchen table. Then he went into the lounge and brought back his Christmas cigars. He lit one and puffed on it for a few seconds to get it fully alight.

He sighed with happiness. Coffee and cigars. Cigars and coffee.

He grinned to himself. He was totally free now.

Finally he looked at Elaine.

Today she was going to disappear forever. He knew what he had to do. But first he needed a shower.

George had had his shower and was now in the process of putting Elaine into two large black bags. He covered her head and shoulders first. Her sightless eyes were getting on his nerves. Her head had stuck to the floor in a pool of blood that had congealed to a reddish-brown. It still had long strands of ginger-orange hair stuck in it. He would have to scrape it off the tiles. He finally had the bag over her head and tied it around her neck with string. Then he looked at her lower body. He had turned her over to make it easier for him and now her legs were wide open. He imagined her without her tracksuit bottoms and smiled to himself, feeling the familiar excitement. The blood everywhere was making him feel aroused.

He liked blood. He liked the sticky feel of it, like crimson semen. He pulled off her trainers and tracksuit bottoms, staring at her milky white legs as if fascinated. She had on a pair of white panties and her thick red pubic hair poked out of the sides with a jauntiness that pleased George immensely. Like this, Elaine was his perfect woman. Faceless, undemanding and completely available.

He poked a finger into her crotch, feeling the softness there. He ran his finger inside the silky material of her panties and round her pubic hair.

He licked his lips, feeling the sweat that was now beading them. He hooked his fingers into her panties and pulled them down her legs slowly, gently, revealing her most intimate parts.

He unzipped his trousers, locked in the almost sublime feelings of his fantasy world. He began to knead her thighs, feeling the cold strength of them. He tried to part her legs further to remove her panties, but they wouldn't budge! He pulled at them harder, trying to force them open.

George had not allowed for rigor mortis.

His breathing was laboured now, from his exertions and from his fantasies.

He frowned.

Elaine had always been the same: difficult. Even in death, she was still inaccessible.

He wiped a clammy hand over his face. Suddenly, the

chaos around him registered. He had better get cleaned up. He had plenty of time for fun.

Real fun, with better women than Elaine.

He began to bundle her into the other black bag, his movements more urgent now. Finally he sat back on his heels and stared at his handiwork. Elaine was trussed up like a chicken.

Standing up, he zipped his trousers back up, carefully tucking in his shirt first. He would have a nice cup of tea, then he would start the second phase of his operation.

Kelly was waiting outside the pub where Kate and Caitlin had gone for lunch. As she saw his black BMW she felt a lurch in her breast. Caitlin grinned at her and said: 'I think you've got company, Kate. I'll see you later.'

He waltzed into the pub and left her standing alone on the pavement. She could see Patrick's face through the windscreen and against her better judgement walked over to the car and got inside.

'Hello, Kate.' Patrick's voice was normal and she swallowed hard.

'Patrick.' She let him drive. The closeness of him made her feel breathless. She could smell his aftershave. Despite herself she was glad to see him. This fact, admitted to and accepted, annoyed her.

Patrick drove to his house and she got out of the car and followed him inside. They had barely spoken a word. In his dining room the table was laid for two and the smell of a delicious roast assailed her nostrils.

He held her seat for her and she sat down.

'I'm sorry, Kate. I know that what I did to Dan was wrong. But I swear I was just trying to help you, that's all. I wanted the CIB off your back and that was the only way. I had no intention of hurting him, just scaring him.'

Kate could hear the desperate tone in his voice. Could see the absolute honesty in his face. But she also could feel the pull that this man had on her. She looked around the beautiful room: at the plush carpet, the watercolours on the walls, at the expensive linen and cutlery, and knew that she had missed all this but most of all had missed the man. Missed him with all her being, no matter what he had done. He was like the breath of life to her and she needed him. Whatever the attraction was between them, it was powerful enough to make her admit that what he had done to Dan didn't really matter when he was with her, when he was close to her, when she could reach out and touch his face.

She looked at Patrick and he looked at her. It was more than an exchange of glances: it was like a tangible force, there between them. Each knew the other intimately, each felt the attraction that had brought her here today. Each wanted the rift between them breached so that they could get on with their lives.

Kate's eyes were like dark pools of liquid light. Patrick searched them for some sign that she had relented. That he was forgiven. As she picked up her wine glass and smiled at him, he felt as if someone had given him an injection of pure happiness.

'Cheers, Pat.' She sipped the heavy red liquid and as she did so knew that there was no going back. She had accepted his way of living one hundred per cent. Dan would be forgotten, everything would be forgotten, except for their urgent desire.

Patrick opened the serving dish that had been placed on the table by Willy just as they had driven up and filled Kate's plate with slices of beef.

As she took the plate from him their fingers touched and the jolt that went between them was like a physical pain.

'How's Willy?'

Patrick filled his own plate and grinned. 'He's fine.'

'Good. I rather like Willy.'

And she did. She knew that Patrick would go mad if he knew that Willy had been to see her, but it was the talk she had had with him that had helped her sort out her own mind.

'Can I see you tonight, Kate?'

456

She smiled, taking a mouthful of juicy beef and wiping her lips with a napkin.

'I don't see why not.'

Putting down his own knife and fork he walked around the table and took her in his arms. They did not kiss, but as he rubbed his face in the softness of her hair, she felt as if she had indeed finally come home.

He was dangerous to her, she knew that. But she was determined to have him.

An hour later she was back at work, lighter of heart than she had been for days and raring to go. She looked and felt great, something which was noticed by just about everyone in the incident room.

DS Spencer, still smarting from Amanda Dawkins' practical joke, whispered into Willis's ear: 'Screwing a villain seems to cheer her up no end.'

Willis gave him a dirty look. Spencer got on his nerves. In fact, Spencer got on everyone's nerves.

'Why don't you piss off, Spencer?'

Willis walked away from him. Collating all the blood tests was much harder than anyone had thought, but it had given them an added impetus. It was a new avenue. It was their big chance to catch the Grantley Ripper.

When a man was blood tested his fingerprints were taken also. If he had a record then the fingerprints were matched. It was another way of confirming their alibis. If a man had no criminal file then his passport or some other form of identification was necessary. A driving licence was adequate, but something with a picture on was much more solid. This is what was taking all the time. Not enough manpower to keep abreast of the mounting names. Still, it was better than nothing and much better than they'd had before.

Willis picked up yet another file. He was dealing with the known sex offenders. Due to a delay in the computer system, they had only just received all the names of sex offenders in the area who had been tried and convicted in other parts of the country. These were known as 'floaters', passing through on their way to another prison sentence. They were the flotsam and jetsam of the criminal world, hated by police and villains alike. The pile was in alphabetical order and Willis picked up the first file.

Name: Desmond Addamson.

Willis flicked through the file: rape, arson and flashing, along with robbery with violence. He had turned up in Grantley in the middle of January. Too late for the first murders. He picked up the phone. The man had better be checked out anyway. He would start with his probation officer. As he picked up the phone, he knocked the pile of files from his desk. He dropped the phone and tried to save them. Too late.

The files landed with a muted thud and papers were strewn everywhere. A small cheer went up from the others in the room and Willis smiled good-naturedly as he bent down to scoop up the papers. He would be there for ages putting all the papers back in their proper folders. He placed the last lot on the desk and there, staring up at him, was George Markham's face. Younger, with browner, thicker hair, but unmistakably George Markham.

Willis glanced at the photo without seeing it.

George had had a nice cup of tea and was now in the process of thinking how to get Elaine up into the loft. He had thought long and hard about where to put her and then it had come to him in a flash of inspiration. There was only one problem: Elaine was big. How was he to get her up there?

The answer was so cunning that he grinned with satisfaction. He was clever all right.

He stood up and looked at Elaine's body, wrapped in the incongruous plastic bags.

'I'm off out, dear, I won't be long.'

He went into the hall and put on his good overcoat. Then, carefully locking up, he drove to Grantley shopping centre, parked his car in the multi-storey car park and walked through the town centre to a small plant hire shop.

Stellman's Plant Hire had been in Grantley for twenty

years. It was the first time George had ever been in there and he stood uncertainly among the debris of lawnmowers and wallpaper strippers. A young man came up and smiled at him.

'What can I do you for?'

'I beg your pardon?' George's voice was timid once more.

'A joke, mate.' The boy stared at George and shrugged. 'What can I do for you, sir?' He tacked the 'sir' on the end at the last second.

'I . . . er . . . want to lift an engine out of a car. A friend of mine is going to put a new engine into my car, you see.' George's voice trailed off. He should have prepared what he was going to say.

The boy was all the business now.

'I see. You want the Haltrac.' Seeing George's confusion, he grinned. 'The small block and tackle. It will lift about a ton, but it's lightweight. Not like the old ones of years ago. You just set it up and Bob's your uncle. Manual lift, the lot. How long would you want it for?'

George smiled now. This was easier than he'd thought.

'Oh, a couple of days at most.'

'All right. I'd have it for the week, though. If it pisses down with rain then you won't be doing much. It's cheaper that way anyhow. It's eight quid a day, but only sixteen quid for the week. Plus VAT of course. Mustn't forget Maggie's curse, must we?'

George was overwhelmed. The boy could sell, that much was obvious. But at that moment George would have paid any amount for the tool in question, and in fact was shocked that it was so cheap.

'Whatever you think is best. Can I take it now?'

'Course you can.'

The boy began to make out the paperwork and George paid him in cash. He left, the Haltrac held firmly in his hands. He drove back home feeling quite lighthearted.

Once indoors he began the serious work of the day. First he opened the loft hatch and, after cleaning it thoroughly, placed it on his bed. No need to make everything dirty. He

459

hated mess of any kind. Then he brought the block and tackle up the stairs. He walked up the stainless steel, safety conscious steps that led to the square hole in the ceiling of the landing and began phase two of his operation.

Lifting himself into the loft, he looked around him critically. The roof sloped upwards and running parallel on each side were three sets of purlings, large pieces of wood that supported the roof joists. He went back down the ladder and returned with a length of half-inch-thick polyester rope in a lovely bright blue colour. He lashed this around the left-hand purling, tying it tightly, and did the same on the right-hand side, giving the rope a good hard tug to make sure it was secure. The purlings were eight feet from the floor and he balanced himself precariously on a large packing case to secure the rope.

He got off the packing case and jumped up, grabbing the centre of the rope to make sure it was secure. He held on to it for a few seconds, swaying, his feet off the ground. It was perfect.

He let got of the rope and dropped lightly on the balls of his feet. He felt quite gay. It was like when he was a child and they played on the bundle swings, hanging precariously above the ground, then that wonderful feeling of dropping on to terra firma. He smiled to himself and then repeated the whole process again, swinging for a few seconds more this time, swaying from side to side.

Then the significance of what he was doing penetrated his brain and he was businesslike once more. He went down the ladder and brought up the block and tackle. He placed the hook on the top of the tackle on to the rope, letting the tackle itself drop through the loft hole. He was ready.

He felt a thrill of anticipation course through his whole body. He went back to the kitchen. Holding Elaine's body through the plastic, underneath the arms, he began dragging her through the hall and up the stairs. Elaine's dead weight was more than he had bargained for and he had to leave her propped up on the middle of the stairs while he went for a cold drink. He was sweating like a pig. His euphoria was wearing off now and he was feeling positively disgruntled. Elaine always made everything so difficult. Every time he planned something, she messed it up.

He pursed his lips together into a hard line, the water forgotten in front of him as he brooded.

Half an hour later he was startled when the harsh trill of the telephone rang through the silent house. It was probably that nosy bitch again, Elaine's so-called friend. He pulled himself from his seat to answer the phone. The blood-spattered kitchen had not penetrated his consciousness yet.

'Hello.' His meek, humble voice was back.

'George?' His heart sank. It was Renshaw.

'You there, Georgie boy?'

'Yes. Hello, Peter.'

'Bad business that yesterday and I told that cow Denham what I thought about it as well. You're still on for tomorrow night though? Bugger the lot of them, we'll have a night to remember, what?'

'Tomorrow night?' George was puzzled.

'Your leaving do, of course.'

'Oh . . . Oh, yes. Yes, I'll be there.'

'Good. Meet you in the Fox Revived at eight thirty, OK?'

'Yes. That would be lovely.'

'I don't blame you for getting on your high horse, you know, George. That bitch needed taking down a peg or two. They all do in the end.'

'Quite.'

'See you tomorrow then?'

'Yes.'

The phone went dead and George replaced the receiver. Peter Renshaw was right. They did all need taking down a peg and he was the man to do it!

He walked up the stairs and stared at Elaine's grotesque form. She was another one. Ripping the top of the bag he watched, fascinated, as Elaine's orange hair tumbled into view. Then, taking the long hair in chunks, he wrapped it around his hands and dragged her bodily up the remaining stairs. The action forced her head from the bag and he laughed at her milky eyes. Glazed now and dry, they stared up at him passively.

With one final heave he had her on the landing. Then, pulling the tackle down, he hooked it into the rope that trussed her in the black bags. Satisfied, he went up the ladder and then, pulling the steps up behind him, picked up the slack rope that was attached to the pulley on top of the tackle and gradually pulled Elaine up into the loft.

It was easier than he'd expected. She lifted up as easy as pie and when she was dangling, her exposed head hanging sideways, staring at him as if in surprise, he tied the rope around one of the lower purlings and surveyed his handiwork. He felt almost gleeful again.

Elaine's body was swaying gently to and fro and he watched her in fascinated amusement. Her skin was a greeny-grey colour now and he thought she looked quite ill. He shrugged. The sooner he tucked her away the better.

But he had other things to do first. Placing the steps down once more, he climbed down and retrieved the loft hatch from the bed. Then he replaced it carefully, leaving Elaine dangling there in the dark loft. He took the steps and put them back in his shed then he walked purposefully into the kitchen. He looked around at the chaos and made little tutting noises before rolling up his sleeves and filling the sink with hot water.

He certainly had his work cut out for him today!

It took him all of three hours to clean the kitchen. The pristine white floor tiles would not come up to their usual standard. The blood left rust-coloured marks and finally he took out a bottle of Domestos and spread it liberally over the tiles. The thick liquid was then spread evenly, ammonia burning George's hands and eyes. Finally he was finished and the floor looked better. Much better. But the stains were still visible. He tutted again and shrugged. He had done his best.

He polished through the house and hoovered thoroughly. He changed the sheets on his bed, and the counterpane, then made himself an omelette. He glanced at the clock. It was seven fifteen.

Washing up his plate, he left it to drain. He went into the lounge, closed the curtains and put on the lamp. He turned on the television and put on channel 3, then page 251 on the Ceefax. He studied the holidays first, imagining himself in Thailand with some little Thai woman. He had read somewhere that you could pick up a bar girl for about two dollars a night. One day he would treat himself to that. It was a pity Elaine hadn't had a heart attack or something. He could have claimed the insurance money.

He flicked to the page of cheap flights. He saw what he wanted immediately: ORLANDO FLYDRIVE 21 NIGHTS 23 FEB.

Friday.

He would turn up at Edith's house, telling her how Elaine had left him for another man. In her delight at seeing him so unexpectedly, she would soon forget why he was actually there. He would have to box clever this end though, with Elaine's friends, but he would cross that bridge when he came to it. It's a shame her parents were dead. He could have said she was staying with them.

He picked up the phone by his side and dialled the number on the screen. People were there to take your calls until nine thirty. Within five minutes he was booked on a flight, had paid with his credit card and arranged to pick up his tickets and visa at Gatwick Airport.

He replaced the receiver and sat back in the chair. Tomorrow night he had his leaving do. He would go to that. That left tomorrow and Thursday to sort out the final details. He sighed with contentment.

Busy, busy, that was him. For the first time in his life he was at the centre of things and he loved it. He was in total control.

George phoned work at ten on Wednesday morning. He asked politely for Mrs Denham and waited nervously until her voice crackled over the line.

'Hello?'

'Mrs Denham, it's George Markham here.'

The line went quiet and he rushed on.

'I want to apologise about the other day. I'm afraid it all came as rather a shock . . .'

His voice was as sweet as honey.

'I understand. I think we had a communication breakdown somewhere.' George could hear the smile in her voice. 'If you would prefer not to come back to work, I can arrange it for you.' Her voice was hesitant again now.

'Is that really possible? Only my wife is dreadfully ill . . .'

'Of course, I'll arrange it immediately.'

George sensed that she was glad to be rid of him and his mouth set in a grim line.

'About the money . . .'

'Oh, that will be paid into your bank account in about three weeks' time. That's the earliest I can manage it, I'm afraid.'

'That's fine. Lovely. Thank you very much.'

'You're welcome. And good luck.'

'Thank you, 'bye.'

Josephine Denham replaced the telephone and felt a moment of exquisite pleasure. What she was doing for George Markham was not strictly allowed, but to get rid of that man she would do anything. He gave her the creeps. She wanted him paid off and out as soon as possible.

Tony Jones was nervous. He had been in Grantley since ten thirty in the morning, acclimatising himself to the place. What a dump! In Tony's estimation, the Smoke was the only place to be. All these green fields disturbed him. Full of cow shit more than likely.

He sat in the Wimpy Bar in the town centre and watched people coming and going for the blood testing. He licked his lips again, his hand going nervously to the passport in his jacket pocket. He had paid out a good slice of wedge for it, and had yet to recoup the money from George Markham. He felt an insane urge to walk into the police vehicle nearby and tell them he knew who the Grantley Ripper was. He knew it was the decent thing to do. But Tony Jones loved money more than anything.

He wanted the three thousand from George and then he would go and see Kelly and do some kind of deal. He knew Pat Kelly well enough to know that if he found out Tony had had the Ripper's name and had not furnished him with it immediately, then Tony Jones was as good as dead. Besides, there was the money Kelly was offering . . .

He'd get this blood testing out of the way first, then he would approach Kelly.

It was lunchtime and Tony noticed that the line of men going in for blood testing was getting longer. In their lunch hour? Tony shook his head in wonder. If he was one of them he would use it as an excuse to skive off for an afternoon or morning.

People amazed him, they really did. They never had their eye on the main chance.

He ordered another coffee and watched. It was going to be a long day.

George had bathed and felt rosy and pink. That's what his mother used to say. Rosy and pink after a nice hot bath. He dressed himself in a pair of pyjamas that had seen better days, and putting on his slippers set about getting the ladder so he could go once more up into the loft.

Elaine was still hanging there and George smiled at her. Poor thing! She must be frozen. Then, going to the corner of the loft, he rubbed his hands together and stood staring at the water tank.

Elaine's final resting place.

The houses in George's street had been built before the war and still boasted the old sixty-gallon water tanks. Most of the houses in the road had been modernised, but George and Elaine had never really bothered with theirs. The water tanks were so big, they'd been put in before the roof of the house went on. Consequently, when people modernised, they had to leave the old galvanised water tank in the loft, as there was no way to remove it. In George and Elaine's case, it still provided the water for the toilet and bath, and they had a small floor-mounted boiler in their kitchen to run the central heating. George lifted the lid off the tank and stared down into the water. A dead mouse floated on top. He picked it up by its tail and threw it into the corner, shuddering.

The tank was four feet by three feet and about three feet deep. George felt a moment of panic. Suppose she wouldn't fit?

Putting the hatch back, so he could move about more freely, George turned on the lights and began the job of getting Elaine's body down from the block and tackle. She dropped with a loud thud on to the dusty floor and he began the difficult task of dragging her to the tank.

The loft had been boarded out and around the sides were boxes of old photographs and clothes, old curtains, even an iron bedstead, unscrewed and leaning gently against the roof joists.

George dragged her body, his pyjamas already sweat-stained and covered in dust, over to the tank. Then, with a mighty heave, he pulled her up off the floor and pushed her head first inside. The water immediately overflowed from the tank and George cursed. The icy cold shock took his breath away. He lifted Elaine's legs and tried to push her into the tank. He tried to bend her in two but her fat belly would not allow this and still the water was spilling out everywhere. His slippers were soaked as were his pyjamas. The water was funnelling into the black sacks and making it even more difficult for him to grasp hold of her.

In the end, in sheer temper, he dragged her out of the tank and dumped her unceremoniously on to the soaked floor. His heart was crashing in his chest and he put his hand on it, feeling the thudding sensation of life with satisfaction.

Then he heard a low gurgling sound and his heart stopped dead. He flicked his head towards Elaine's body. Her face was on the floor, the skin squeezed up into grey wrinkles, and water was running out of the side of her mouth. All the gasses inside her and the trapped air were dislodged with the intake of water and she actually sounded as if she was groaning.

George felt a moment's sick apprehension before it dawned on him what was happening.

He prodded her with his slippered foot and she groaned again, accompanied this time by a loud breaking of wind.

He grinned, all the fear leaving him.

He had thought she was still alive!

He knew she would kill him for leaving her trussed up like a chicken overnight.

He began to laugh, a high cackling sound bordering on hysteria. She made the watery gurgle again and he had to sit on the edge of the water tank, tears streaming down his face. Oh, he hadn't had so much fun in ages.

He wiped his eyes with his hands and laughed himself hoarse. Then, finally, he calmed.

It was a quick change. From roaring good humour his face closed up and a cold calculating look appeared.

He knew what he had done wrong. He hadn't drained the water.

Picking up the ballcock in the water tank, he tied it with a piece of string so it was against the side of the tank. Then he opened the loft hatch and went down to the bathroom, opening the taps in the sink and bath. He did the same in the kitchen. He put the kettle on and had a coffee. His wet pyjamas were making him feel cold now and he slipped his overcoat over them to keep warm.

He drank hot coffee gratefully and then went back to work. The tank was empty now. He dragged Elaine up the side and pushed her into it head first. Then he went around the other side and, dragging her under her oxters, sat her upright in it, forcing her legs inside. Then he pushed her head down between her knees and shoved with all his might. She stayed as she was.

In the process of dragging her inside, the ballcock was dislodged from where he had tied it on the joist and he placed it now at the small of Elaine's back. It was far enough away from the water line there.

Finally George picked up the lid and popped it on the tank. He was happy again.

467

He tidied up the loft as best he could and then dropped himself down on to the landing. He had better get himself cleaned up. He was going out tonight.

He put the water back on and ran himself another bath. George's mind was on the night ahead.

Elaine was forgotten now as the water tank began to fill slowly, very slowly, because the ballcock was trapped in the small of her back.

Tony Jones sat in the small Portacabin, nervously practising the answers to the questions he knew they would ask.

He was so nervous that when they asked him his name he nearly said 'Tony Jones'. Now they were calling for George Markham and he was sitting there wondering why no one answered. He stood up uncertainly.

'Sorry, I was miles away.' He smiled at the two men.

'This way, sir.'

He followed them into the tiny office next door and sat down.

'My name's Doctor Halliday and I will be taking your blood. Would you mind removing your jacket, please?'

Tony smiled widely.

She wasn't a bad-looking sort. Bit on the thin side, but then, educated women always were. Or so he'd found, anyway.

He removed his jacket and rolled up the sleeve of his shirt, sorry now that he had not put on a cleaner one. He was conscious of the smell of stale sweat under his arms. He saw the doctor wrinkle her nose and felt himself blush. The older of the two policemen smiled at him and sat carelessly on the desk. Tony guessed he was enjoying his discomfort and frowned.

Bloody filth, they were all the same. He concentrated on the job in hand.

'Right, Mr Markham, where do you work?'

Tony took a deep breath and grimaced as the needle was plunged into his vein.

'I work at Kortone Separates.'

'Address?'

'Units 16 to 38, Grantley Industrial Estate.'

'Phone number?'

'04022 795670.'

Tony felt the doctor swab his arm and apply a small round plaster. He began to roll down his sleeve, glad to be putting his jacket on again. The other policeman came into the room. He smiled at the doctor, nodded at Tony and spoke to his colleague.

'He's the last one, we can shut up shop now.'

'Thank Christ. You going down the pub?'

'Yeah. Shall I get you a pint in?'

'All right, see you in about ten minutes.'

Tony was amazed as how easy it was.

The other man left and the policeman turned to Tony again. 'Got any identification please, sir?'

He produced the passport from his pocket andd the man glanced at it then took the passport number down.

'Would you sign this, sir, and then you can go.'

Tony signed the declaration and was outside the Porta-cabin within thirty seconds.

He couldn't believe it! No wonder they couldn't catch the Grantley Ripper. After what he had just witnessed, he would he amazed if they could catch the bus!

Shaking his head, he made his way to his car. He was meeting George at eight thirty. He looked at his watch. It was just after seven. Give him time to get a few drinks down him. He needed them.

George was ready. He checked himself over once more in the mirror and smiled.

Not bad. Not bad at all. He smoothed his scanty hair down with the palms of his hands and grinned. He was in the mood for an outing now. He was going on his holidays the day after tomorrow and the thought cheered him. Elaine was gone from his thoughts.

He imagined Edith's face when he knocked on her door.

He felt a little jiggle of excitement inside his chest. It was going to be a wonderful holiday.

He locked the house up carefully before leaving and drove out to the Lion Rampant. He arrived there just after seven thirty and walked into the deserted bar. Tony Jones was sitting tucked away in the corner. George walked to him and sat down opposite.

'You're early.'

'So I am. Would you like another drink?' Tony nodded, nonplussed at the gaiety in George's voice.

'I'll have a large scotch.'

George went up to the bar and got the drinks. When they were settled he smiled at Tony.

'Got the passport?'

'You got the money?' Tony's voice was hard and George pursed his lips.

'It's in the car.'

'Well, go and get it then.'

'Don't be silly, the barman's watching us like a hawk. People remember things, you know. He'll remember seeing us exchanging envelopes. No, we do the business outside.'

Tony screwed up his eyes and sipped his drink. It made sense.

'All right. I took the test. I tell you now it was difficult. They asked me lots of awkward questions . . .'

George was immediately alert.

'I hope you didn't muck it all up?'

Tony was aware of the underlying threat in his voice. 'They're due at my firm tomorrow. I don't want any worries, Tony.'

He realised his mistake. He was trying to impress on George that he had earned his money and all he had done was make him nervous. And George nervous made Tony nervous.

'Don't worry, I did a great job, I swear it. They never guessed a thing, honest.'

George visibly relaxed and so did Tony.

He kept forgetting that George was a murderer. A

470

dangerous man. If only he didn't look so nondescript. All the murderers he had ever read about or known – and he had known a few in his time – had looked a few sandwiches short of a picnic. But this bloke here, he looked like a flasher. A weekend pervie. He looked like a lot of things – but not a murderer.

He didn't look dangerous. But he was.

'Drink up and we'll get going. I have an appointment.'

Tony tossed back his scotch and they walked out into the cold air. He followed George to his car.

'Where's the money?'

George opened the door and motioned for him to get into the car. Tony sat in the passenger seat. The nervousness was back.

'Show me the passport, please.'

Tony slipped it from his pocket and George glanced at it in the dim glow of the car light.

'Where's the temporary one I gave you?'

Tony took that from his pocket. George put both passports into the glove compartment and then turned to face Tony.

'I'm not paying you a penny.'

'You what!'

'I said, I'm not paying you, Tony.' George grinned. 'Oh, come on, you never really thought I would, did you? I thought you were a man of the world.'

George chuckled. He was enjoying himself.

Tony's mind was reeling. He stared into George's eyes and realised he had been wrong earlier. George like this, with that horrible throaty chuckle and his feverish eyes, *did* look like a murderer. He looked diabolical.

Tony saw his mouth opening wider and the dark cavern that held his pink tongue seemed to draw him. He saw not only the money for the passport going down the Swanee, but also the blackmail money.

George held all the cards, because he knew Tony was frightened of him.

'Let's just say that we had a little misunderstanding regarding the money, shall we, Tony?'

471

He dropped his gaze and nodded.

George grinned to himself.

'Good man. Now if you don't mind, I have an important engagement.'

Tony slipped from the car and watched as George drove away. Then he went back into the pub and ordered himself another large scotch.

The barman looked at him curiously and Tony took his drink and went back to the corner table.

There was only one avenue left open to him: Patrick Kelly.

It wasn't just the money now, either. He wanted to see George get his come-uppance.

There was just one cloud on the horizon. How to give the name to Kelly without his own involvement being discovered. If Kelly found out that he had known the murderer of his daughter and had not told him . . . If he found out that he, Tony Jones, had taken the blood test for the man responsible . . . Tony felt faint with fright just thinking about it. How the hell had he got so embroiled?

A little voice in the back of his head said: 'Because you're greedy, Tony, that's why.'

He tossed back the drink and stayed sitting in the bar. There was a way to see Kelly and he would work it out, but it would take a bit of thinking about.

He was going to pay George Markham back a hundredfold and save his own skin at the same time.

George walked into the smoky heat of the Fox Revived and there was Peter Renshaw and a crowd of other men standing at the bar. Peter saw him and shouted: 'Here he is, the man of the moment!'

George smiled. All the others smiled back. He had a drink thrust into his hand and smiled again. He didn't mind the warehouseman being there now. In his euphoric state of mind they were his bosom pals. He was pleased with the turnout. If only Elaine could see him now. Why, there must be twenty-five men here. For his leaving do. For him.

Renshaw slapped his back and brought his red beery face close.

'We'll have a few more here and then we'll make tracks to a nightclub. I know just the place. Drink up, man. We're a good few ahead of you!'

One of the warehousemen, a large, bulky man called Pearson, winked at George and then shouted to the barmaid: 'Another round here, love.'

He belched loudly and George felt his familiar distaste, but tonight he fought it down.

He was going to enjoy himself if it killed him.

He drank his brandy straight down and felt another being pushed into his hand almost immediately. The pub was filling up and the noise was getting louder. People were coming and going. George's crowd had taken over the right-hand side of the bar. He was in the midst of the crowd. For the first time in his life he felt he belonged. The men from the warehouse made him feel welcome. They patted him on the back and wished him good luck. They made dirty remarks about Mrs Denham's breasts and George felt a part of it all. When they left an hour later, in two minibuses, he was elated.

Renshaw certainly knew how to enjoy himself, by God. George regretted now not going on all the other dos Renshaw had planned.

The minibuses stopped outside a club in the seedier part of Grantley. They piled out on to the dirty pavement, then Renshaw produced a pile of tickets and they all walked boisterously past the dark-suited men on the door. George had heard of the Flamingo Club, indeed he had once wanted to join it, but the fear of Elaine finding out had put him off. Now here he was, sitting at a table with his friends and waiting for the pretty girls in their scanty outfits to serve them drinks.

The lights dimmed and a spotlight came on, illuminating the tiny dance floor. All the men cheered as a woman walked out into the bright light. She was wearing a schoolgirl outfit and her hair was in two long plaits that somehow stood out from her head like a St Trinian's girl. She had large freckles painted over her nose and her breasts strained against the tunic.

George's eyes were shining with excitement.

The strains of 'Daddy's Gonna Buy Me a Bow-Wow' crackled out of the speakers.

The woman bent over, showing navy blue school knickers, pulling them away from her body. The men all shouted in satisfaction as the pink slit was revealed. George looked around him in wonderment. He was surprised to see another drink in front of him and drank from it greedily, smacking his lips together as he had seen the warehouseman do.

His eyes never left the stage now as the woman began undressing, the men cat calling and whistling. She walked over to their tables and, grinning, sat on one of the warehousemen's laps, her legs spread. She gently rubbed herself up and down his legs. Then, undoing her side buttons, she let her tunic top fall to the floor. Her large baggy breasts sprang free and she pushed them into the man's face. George was enthralled.

Getting up, she pulled the navy knickers up her belly, so the lips of her vagina poked out of the sides, then gradually she began to pull them down, her eyes roaming over the men as she did this as if it was a personal show for each of them.

Then the music stopped, the lights went off and she was gone, amid clapping, whistling and stamping of feet.

Next was a female impersonator. A few tables away was a crowd of young men on a stag night. They had been served chicken and chips in baskets and the man on the stage, his face garishly made up under a deep red wig, walked to one of the young men and said: 'Here, love, do you know the difference between a big cock and a chicken leg?'

The boy went red and shook his head, his friends roaring with laughter. The man put his arm around him and said, 'Want to come on a picnic?'

George laughed as hard as the rest of them. He was amazed to find that he now had three separate drinks in front of him. Peter caught his eye and winked and George felt sudden affection for him, his usual annoyance forgotten. Peter had arranged this and George would remember that to his dying day. He was where he should be. Among men who liked what he liked. Who saw women for what they really were.

The female impersonator was finished and another stripper came on. Peter Renshaw called to the impersonator and he walked over to their table in a parody of a woman's wiggle.

'Hello, Peter, how are you?'

'All right, Davey. We're on a leaving do. How much for the live show?'

The impersonator grinned.

'Same as usual, Peter. You do the whip round and I'll sort out the girls. Don't forget my drink on top, will you?'

Renshaw grinned. 'Good man.'

The impersonator laughed. 'Do you mind?'

'Come on, lads, get your dosh out, we've got ourselves a live show.'

He turned to George. 'Ever seen one before?'

He shook his head, amazed.

'You'll love it, Georgie boy. Great fun.'

He got up from the table and went to the others. Men were putting in money hand over fist. On his own table a pile of money now stood in the centre so George took out his wallet and put twenty pounds in the kitty. That was the average amount men were contributing.

Within minutes, Peter had arranged it all. George was impressed. The bouncers on the door had fifty each to lock up for the duration and the girls themselves had been paid. There was an air of expectancy in the club now.

George had removed his jacket. He licked a film of perspiration from his lips.

The spotlight was back on and two women were standing semi-naked, chatting together and smoking cigarettes while the floor was being set up. The young bridegroom-to-be and one of the warehousemen had been unanimously chosen to be the star performers and all the other men waited with bated breath for the real show to start.

475

The female impersonator came out with a microphone and announced that he would be the master of ceremonies. The young bridegroom and the warehouseman were stripped naked, the women put their cigarettes out and, plastering professional smiles on their faces, walked on to the stage area, smiling and waving at the audience.

George was mesmerised. The two women knelt down and took the men in their mouths. There were bets going on as to who would ejaculate first. The warehouseman was gripping the woman's hair and forcing his penis into her mouth. His cronies were shouting with excitement.

'Go on, my son!'

'Choke the fucking bitch!'

The warehouseman was making lewd faces and thrusting his hips around, loving the attention.

The young groom-to-be could not even get an erection. He was laughing and at the same time totally embarrassed. Finally, one of the other men at his table got up and, pulling off his trousers, lunged for the girl.

'Here you are, get hold of that.'

A loud cheer went up.

George watched, entranced, as the women were used by the men. Finally, the female impersonator called an end to everything and the men returned to their tables like conquering heroes.

The two women left the stage exhausted. Their elaborate hairdos were hanging in lank strands and their body make up was patchy and running with sweat.

All the men were ragging the warehouseman who was now dressing himself amidst shouting and swearing.

George sat among them. The show had excited him. His eyes were red-rimmed now and feverish. He had shouted himself hoarse along with all the other men.

In his wildest dreams he had never envisaged anything quite like this. For the first time in his life George was sharing his pastime with others. Others who were enjoying themselves with him.

He felt an absurd feeling of happiness that made him want

476

to cry. He felt the sting of tears and hastily blinked them away.

Peter Renshaw noticed and put his arm around his shoulder.

'Cheer up, Georgie boy. It's your leaving do.'

He faced Peter and said, 'This has been the best night of my life, Peter. Thank you. Thank you so very much.'

Peter Renshaw was gratified that George had had a good time. He had always felt a sadness in George, a strangeness that at times had bothered him. He smiled at him now. The drink was making them feel maudlin, he decided.

'Have another, Georgie boy, there's another stripper on in a minute.'

He nodded and picked up his drink.

Someone proposed a toast to George and, pink with happiness, he watched them all raise their glasses. Another round of drinks was delivered to the table and the men began some serious drinking.

A little while later the two women who had provided the show came to the table fully dressed for their money. The older of the two, a hard-faced blonde, held out her hand to Peter Renshaw.

'We want our money, mate, now.'

Her voice was weary.

'How about a please then, you old boot?'

This from the warehouseman who had taken part in the earlier proceedings.

The woman turned on him.

'Why don't you shut your mouth and give your arse a chance?'

All the men began laughing at this. The warehouseman picked up a pint of lager, gesturing to the other men at the table. They all did the same. Then, as if all of one mind, they threw the drinks over the two women, soaking them.

George's eyes were shining and he shouted, 'That'll teach you your manners, you piece of dirty scum!'

All the men laughed, mostly in amazement.

'That's right, Georgie, you tell 'em.'

'Smack her in the mouth.'

George heard the calls and preened himself.

The older woman wiped her face and held out her hand again. 'I want the money. Please.'

Peter, sorry for them now, handed it over. They walked back to their dressing room despondently. It was always the same after a live show. The men turned on you, because deep down they were ashamed of what they'd done. Once the excitement wore off, they blamed you for their own perversion. They'd go home now to their wives or their girlfriends, full of themselves. Tomorrow their night out would be the talk of their pub. But inside, deep down inside, they were ashamed of themselves. Ashamed of what they had done or witnessed.

The younger girl was in tears and the older woman put her arm around her.

'They're all wankers, darlin', don't let it get to you. We got ourselves a couple of ton, that's the main thing. My eldest boy wants a mountain bike, what you spending yours on?'

She tried to bring a bit of normality to the conversation. It was the only way to survive.

Chapter Twenty-five

Tony Jones had lain awake all night. His tossing and turning so disturbed his wife Jeanette that at three-thirty she got up and slipped into their daughter's old room, now the spare. Tony smiled despite himself. She liked her Sooty and Sweep did his Jeanette.

Finally, after many hours of restlessness, he had the glimmer of a plan. The main thing to bear in mind was that Patrick Kelly was not a man to cross. After the turn out with the rent boys, he knew without a shadow of a doubt that he would not make Kelly's Christmas card list. He shrugged mentally. He never had anyway. All the same Kelly would not forget his part in the rent boy business for a long time. If he went to the repoman with any old cock and bull story, Kelly would see to it that he did not live long enough to collect his reward. If Kelly even suspected that he knew the name of his daughter's murderer . . . Tony swallowed heavily.

But, and there was always a but, if he pretended that he had been going over his customer lists and happened to notice a George Markham from Grantley on it. Or better still on his mailing list. Yes, that sounded much better. As if he had never actually met the man.

He bounced the ideas around in his head for a while, finally convincing himself that if he played it just right, he would come out of it all with a good few quid and his neck intact. The latter being the most important.

He would put his plan into action first thing in the morning.

* * *

George woke up to a fine, crisp day and grinned to himself. The previous night's events bundled into his mind, crowding it with erotic images. George hugged himself in the warmth of his bed. All his life he had wanted to be part of the men's world, and always he had had to stand on the edge of it. Watching as an outsider. Last night it was as if a door had been opened and he had crept through it into the magic world of men together. He had been drunk on the mystery of it. At one point, he had experienced an ecstasy so acute he had felt tears sting his eyes.

He left the warmth of the bed and went into the bathroom. He had a long, leisurely bath as he dwelt on memories of the night before.

By nine he had finished packing, had ticked off everything on his carefully prepared list. He had everything from lightweight clothes to sunglasses. He had bought these a few years before. They were mirrored. He could watch and stare and no one knew what he was looking at. George kept them lovingly in a leather case.

He allowed himself the luxury of imagining himself on the golden beaches of Florida, watching all the girls and women. He'd watched the travel programmes, he knew what to expect. He felt a thrill of anticipation. He was flying out at seven thirty the following morning and had decided to stay overnight at the airport hotel. Start his holiday properly. He would have to check in to his flight at five thirty, so he would need a good night's rest, a good meal, and then he could get on the plane and relax.

He checked his passport, then the one Tony Jones had procured for him. He put them in his jacket pocket. Poor Tony Jones, he had been ripped off. But, he reflected, the pornographer had deserved it.

The house was beginning to feel claustrophobic. George bent his head to one side, a look of concentration on his face. He listened avidly. Nothing. He kept thinking he could hear Elaine calling.

He shrugged. Let her call, he just wouldn't listen. He took

his bags out to his car and then had an idea. He could go and visit his mother. He would like to see her before he saw Edith. Give her a nice surprise.

He grinned. If she knew he was going out to Edith's it would kill her. Maybe he would mention it. But then she would know where he was going. He frowned. He'd see how it went. Happy now that he had a plan in mind, he began to make himself ready in earnest. It was nice, he thought, to be busy. To be in demand. To be a . . . what did the youngsters call it nowadays? A free agent. He smiled to himself in satisfaction, that's just what he was.

Up in the top of the house Elaine's body shifted slightly with the pressure of the rapidly filling tank. The ballcock that had been trapped at the small of her back shifted position with her and the tank began to fill up faster.

Patrick Kelly had kissed Kate goodbye at six thirty and was on his way to see a man who had some news for him. Important news by all accounts. He clenched his fists in agitation. It had better be something concrete or he was going to explode.

The traffic into London was heavy, and Patrick's Rolls Royce was duly stared at and discussed. Every set of traffic lights had people trying to look inside, thinking it was someone famous. Patrick Kelly smiled to himself. He was famous to an extent, only not in the way these people thought. The Rolls drew up behind a funeral cortège and Patrick frowned. He felt, rather than saw, Willy shift gears and banged on the partition, sharply shouting: 'You bloody dare, Willy, and I'll murder you!'

Willy changed down again and sighed. They would be stuck here for ages now. Pat was like an old woman these days. Kelly shook his head in wonderment. He could just imagine the mourners' faces when a Rolls Royce wheelspun around them. Willy was an animal at times.

'Just take your time, we'll get there soon enough.'

'All right, Pat.' Kelly could hear the sullenness in Willy's voice and said, 'Show some respect. It's a funeral, for Christ's sake.'

Willy kept his own counsel, but deep inside hoped that Porsche would one day do a stretch limo so he could go to his own funeral in style, and with a bit of speed and panache. The first corpse to do a ton!

He didn't mention it to Pat though. He had a sneaky feeling he wouldn't laugh.

Kate sneaked into her house at seven, grateful that no one was up. As she showered she heard her mother get up and the distant clatter of breakfast being made. She went into her bedroom and messed up the bed, smiling as she did so. At her age she should not have to worry about spending the night with a man, but it was respect really. Respect for her mother and her daughter. She felt the glow that still surrounded her body. The night had been a long one. With Patrick sex was a labour of love, and she had missed him. Oh, how she had missed him. She relived in her mind the slow deliberate lovemaking. She knew she was undone and did not care.

Her mother had come up trumps over the Australia business. It was remarkable that she had kept that money secret for so long. Kate felt a great surge of affection for her, knowing that Evelyn was just trying to take the burden from her. Lizzy was like a dog with six lamp posts at the thought of going. It was as if after all the trouble they had been having, everything had finally come together. All Kate wanted now was the Grantley Ripper – and she would get him. And when she did, she would see him put away for ever. Then she could concentrate once more on her family and Patrick. She was looking forward to concentrating on him.

Lizzy knocked on her bedroom door and walked in. 'Oh, Mum, I just woke up and the first thing I thought was: This time next month, I'll be in Australia! I just can't believe it. A whole six weeks holiday in Oz! I can't wait.'

Kate smiled at her daughter in genuine happiness.

'Come here, poppet.' She put out her arms and Lizzy fitted herself into them.

482

'Were you with that man last night, Mum? That Patrick Kelly?'

Kate looked into her daughter's face, so much like her own, and sighed gently. She nodded.

'I think you should hang on to him, he's really sexy.'

Kate grinned. 'Oh, so you think that, do you?'

'Mmm, I do actually.' She kissed her mother's cheek and stood up, looking very young and innocent in her long white nightie that seemed to hide the womanly curves.

'I wouldn't mind going out with him myself!' She flounced from the room laughing. Kate laughed too, but uneasily. Knowing what she did about her daughter's sex life the remark hurt. Not because of Patrick, but as yet another reminder of the fact that her daughter was more experienced than she was sexually. Kate forced the thought from her mind. Lizzy was nearly a grown woman and she had had problems – ones that Kate blamed herself for.

She admitted to herself that she would be glad, in a way, to see her off at the airport. She needed space from Lizzy, as much as Lizzy needed space from her. The thought made her sad.

She comforted herself. She was looking forward to waking up with Patrick in the mornings. But, more than anything, she was looking forward to spending the nights with him.

Larry Steinberg ushered Patrick into his office and the two men shook hands. He had been here once before. Larry Steinberg dealt with the law, the unacceptable face of it. He was also a fixer, and had taken care of some things for Patrick that he had thought beyond the fixing stage. Patrick did not like him, but he had a grudging respect for him. And to Patrick, in business, respect was often preferable to liking.

He had called on Larry to defend a couple of his repomen a few years earlier. They had gone round a man's house to repossess his car and been met by a crowbar and a sawn-off shotgun. Not unusual in their game; people were often far from happy when repomen appeared. One of his men, however, had removed the crowbar from the punter's hand and then buried it in his skull, leaving the man scarred, semi-paralysed, and suffering from epilepsy.

Larry had arranged for the Attempted Murder charge to be quashed and for a pretty stiff out-of-court settlement that had guaranteed a satisfactory outcome for all concerned. The sawn-off shotgun had mysteriously disappeared from the armoury of the Metropolitan Police and had since been used on two different robberies, but that was not Patrick's business. One thing he knew for sure was that the man who had been hit with the crowbar was the man behind the robberies. He was a gas meter bandit gone big time, and with his pay off from Patrick's insurance and his medical records he was as safe as proverbial houses.

Larry blew his nose and sniffed loudly. His bulbous eyes were watering and he wiped them with his fingers. Patrick disguised his distaste as best he could.

'Right then, Larry, let's not beat about the bush – what you got for me?'

'It's to do with Tony Jones. He came to me a while ago for a passport.'

'What's that got to do with me?'

'The passport wasn't for him, it was for someone else, a bloke from Grantley.'

Patrick's ears pricked up.

'Go on.'

Larry Steinberg wiped his nose once more with a grubby handkerchief. He knew that if you drew your story out, people became impatient and listened better.

'He didn't pay me much, Mr Kelly.' His voice had taken on a whining tone.

Patrick closed his eyes.

'Look, Larry, you'll get the money on the fucker's head as soon as I have a face. Now tell me the geezer's fucking name! I ain't in the mood for games.'

Larry hurriedly obeyed.

'It was Markham. A George Markham'.

'Did Tony say why the bloke wanted a passport?'

484

Save the best till last, that was Larry's motto.

'That was the funny thing about it all – the passport had Tony Jones's photograph in it.' He watched Kelly's expression and gabbled on: 'Now be fair, Mr Kelly, I'm just a fixer. If you pay me enough I'll fix up anything, but I knew that there was something wrong with all this and that's why I'm telling you. At first I didn't think anything, you know yourself what it's like. Then I read about the blood testing in Grantley and it came to me like – well, like a vision from God . . .'

He shook his head for maximum effect. 'I've dealt with bank robbers who wanted to retire abroad, the scum of the criminal world. But my life, Mr Kelly, I would not cover for a sadistic murderer. I heard through the grapevine that you were looking for the man who took your young daughter's life and thought it was my duty to inform you of what I knew.'

Larry Steinberg himself actually believed this now, so good was his acting.

Patrick nodded.

'I hope I have been of some little help?'

'You'll get the money, Larry, if this is the man, I promise you that.'

He held out his hand and Larry shook it. Feeling the animal strength of Kelly, he shuddered inwardly.

Poor Tony Jones. Still, he reasoned, Kelly had shaken hands on it, and from him that was as good as a signed contract. Steinberg had to stop himself from rubbing his hands together with glee.

That would have been in bad taste, even for him.

Patrick left the office. Getting into his Rolls Royce, he shouted to Willy: 'Tony Jones's gaff, now!'

Willy started the car and Patrick filled him in on what had taken place as they drove. By the time they reached the sex shop, both were ready to commit murder.

Emmanuel had been on his own all morning and was exhausted. Tony hadn't even bothered to ring him to say when he would arrive. The only high spot had been two definite dates for later that night from two rather well-dressed city gents. Tony hated him procuring from the shop, even though it brought in business. He heard rather than saw Kelly and Willy come in. The door flew open, sending a display of *Masochist Monthly* magazines flying all over the floor.

'Where is he?' Patrick Kelly's voice was low and Emmanuel felt his fury.

'Who?' The boy's voice was high and squeaky.

'Tony fucking Jones, that's who. Who else would we come in here for? Princess Diana?'

'I don't know where he is. He didn't come into work today.'

Willy grabbed Emmanuel round the throat and shook him. 'Where's he live? I want his address now.'

A big man in working clothes walked into the shop and Patrick grabbed the front of his overalls and threw him out on to the pavement with such force he careered into some passers-by. By now the other shopkeepers had noticed what was going down and were watching the action from strategic points.

Emmanuel wrote down the address with shaking hands. His mascara was running into his eyes and making them sting.

Patrick took the proffered paper and nodded at Willy, who promptly set about tearing the shop apart. Emmanuel watched in terror.

Whatever Tony had done it must have been bad. He wondered briefly if he should start looking for another job.

When Willy had finished the two men left. Emmanuel looked at the debris around him and began to cry again. The other shop owners came in when the coast was clear and, under the guise of helping Emmanuel calm himself, tried to prise some gossip from him. He thought it was to do with the time Kelly came in looking for the rent boys and told them so. But it was obvious he didn't really know too much about anything.

The story hit the streets in Soho within the hour, it was the talking point of the day.

486

People nodded their heads sagely. Tony Jones had always courted trouble and now it had knocked on his door.

Tony himself heard the news ten minutes before Kelly and Willy arrived at his house. While they banged down his door, Tony and a very frightened Jeanette were on their way to their eldest daughter's in Brighton.

Nancy Markowitz, as she now liked to be called, sat drinking a cup of hot steaming tea. Her daughter-in-law Lilian was making the beds. Nancy scowled to herself. A cat's lick, that's what Lily gave the house. When she herself had been younger her house had shone out like a beacon, showing all the neighbours how a house should be cleaned. She passed a malevolent eye over the skirting boards in the front room. They could do with a good dusting. What she wouldn't have given then for a nice house like this!

She shook her head. Lily had always been lackadaisical, even her children had never looked right. Pasty-faced little buggers they'd been. Still were, in fact. Nancy sipped her tea. Like cat's piss, Lilian didn't even know how to make a decent cup of tea. More than likely poured water over tea bags. Real tea leaves would be too much of a chore for her . . .

She was taking her time making the beds. Nancy glanced at the clock. It was nearly twelve. She shook her head again. Imagine not making the beds till lunchtime. Lazy bitch.

She sat sipping her tea, building up in her mind every little thing she could against Lily; all the things she'd done or failed to do, real and imagined.

Nancy Markham had a knack of putting other people in the wrong. It had been a major asset all her life. It was her power over people and she used it, along with bullying and cajoling, to her own best advantage.

Lilian was actually lying on her own bed reading a magazine and having a cup of tea and a biscuit herself. Savouring the half hour away from her mother-in-law. It was the only time of the day she had wholly to herself, where her mother-in-law's voice wasn't intruding on her thoughts, her bell wasn't stopping her from working and her presence could not be felt like a malign force. Sometimes Lily thought that Nancy was a witch. Fanciful as that seemed it was the only logical reason why everyone should hate her so. Her own children included. How many times had Joseph promised, under cover of darkness and the duvet, that he was going to put her away in a home? And how many times had he come face to face with her and backed down? Too many times.

Though Lily admitted to herself that she would not relish the task herself. Nancy frightened her. She frightened her grandchildren. She frightened her son. Her son whom Lily had loved once with all her heart and now despised for his weakness, a weakness that she had played on herself since learning all the tricks from her mother-in-law. Even Elaine and drippy George had balked at Nancy coming to live with them.

Lilian tried to concentrate on her *Best* magazine. It didn't do to dwell on things in this house. It was oppressive enough. Still, the Rabbi was due tomorrow. Even though Nancy's following her Jewish faith annoyed Lily, it also gave her a free afternoon a week when she could go out of the house in peace, knowing that the young Rabbi would be too frightened to leave Nancy alone until she came back. She suppressed a grin. The poor boy's face when she finally arrived was a picture. Nancy, self-righteous and actually being friendly, was more scary than when she was her usual overbearing and evil self.

Lily forced her mind back to her magazine just as the doorbell rang. She pushed herself up on the bed. Who could that be? She jumped up and hastily brushed her clothes to get rid of any tell-tale biscuit crumbs. The bell rang again and she rushed from the room.

By now her mother-in-law's bell was also ringing. It was an old-fashioned school bell and Lily sometimes fancied that it tolled her life away. She hurried to the front door.

'Hello, Lily.' George stood on the step smiling at her.

'Oh . . . This is a surprise.'

He walked into the spacious hall.

488

'Where's Elaine?'

George visiting was a shock, but George without Elaine was an even bigger one.

'Oh, she's at work. I had a bit of time and I thought, I know, I'll go and visit poor Mother.'

Lily's face froze. Who on earth in their right mind would visit Nancy Markham, correction Markowitz, if they didn't have to?

Nancy's voice thundered from the front room.

'Lily, who is it? Who's knocking the bloody door down?'

She wished that the caller had been the young Rabbi; she'd have loved Nancy to drop her guard in front of him.

The bell began to ring furiously and George gestured with his head to the door on his right.

'I take it she's in there?'

He walked into the room.

'Hello, Mother.' His voice was meek once more. His mother always had that effect on him.

Nancy recovered her equilibrium fast.

'Oh, it's you, is it?'

George dutifully kissed her cheek. He could smell her lavender perfume and face powder.

'I thought I'd give you a little visit, see how you were faring.'

She snorted. 'I'm not ready for the knacker's yard yet, me boy, if that's what you're thinking.'

She rang the bell furiously again. George watched her large hand grasping the wooden handle and lifting it up over her shoulder then swinging it down towards the floor.

'Lily, bring in a pot of fresh tea.' They heard her scuffling across the hall from the kitchen. 'And make sure it's stronger than that gnat's piss you made earlier,' Nancy called.

She settled herself once more into her chair. So her son had decided to visit her, had he? A nasty smile played on her lips.

'Where's Ten Ton Tessie today?'

George smirked. She could be cruel, could his mother.

'Elaine's working, Mother.'

He sat himself down on the settee and glanced around the

room. It really was lovely; high-ceilinged, it still had the original ornamental cornice and ceiling roses.

'She wouldn't have come anyway.'

George dragged his eyes from the ceiling. 'Who?'

'Elaine, of course. Who'd you think?' Nancy patted her outrageous orange hair. 'So what brings you here anyway?'

'Mother, I only came to say hello.'

'Tripe. You've never visited me before. You're in some kind of trouble.'

'What kind of trouble could I be in?' George's voice was low.

Nancy shrugged. 'How should I know? Have you done something wrong, Georgie boy? You can always tell me, you know.' Her voice became confidential and wheedling.

George surveyed her and was surprised to find that his fear of her seemed to have diminished today. Normally her bullying voice would leave him a bundle of nerves, her malevolent expression would set his heart galloping in his chest, but today, all she did was make him want to laugh at her.

'Do you ever hear from Edith, Mother?'

He felt the temperature in the room drop to freezing point and continued, 'I hear from her sporadically. She's doing awfully well, you know.'

He watched his mother's mouth set in a grim line. He was enjoying himself.

'Why aren't you at work?' It was an accusation.

'I'm retiring.'

'Huh! Being made redundant more like. Elaine told Mouth Almighty and she told me.' She poked herself in the chest with a pudgy finger.

George felt his confidence waning.

'They didn't want you any more, that's the truth of it. How old are you now? Fifty-one . . . fifty-two. You're over the hill, my boy.'

George was getting upset. Why had he come here? He knew what would happen, what always happened. He clenched his fists. Nancy was warming to her theme.

'You've never had what it takes, Georgie. You never even had any friends . . .'

'I have got friends. Lots of friends, Mother. I was out with my friends last night. I do wish you wouldn't always try and upset me. You're such a bitter pill, Mother, no wonder no one ever visits you. How the hell Joseph and Lily put up with you I don't know.'

His sister-in-law was walking into the room with the tea tray when he said the last part and she nearly dropped the whole lot with fright.

'What did you say?' Nancy's voice was like granite.

But George was too far gone now.

'You heard me, Mother, you've got ears like an elephant's. Always flapping around, listening to everything.' He spied the white-faced Lilian with the tray and forced himself to smile.

'Here, let me help you with that, Lily.'

'Put it on the coffee table, please.' Her voice was breathless.

Nancy watched her son through narrowed eyes. She was shrewd enough to guess that if she carried on in her present vein he would leave, and she didn't want him to leave. He was the first of her children to visit willingly, out of the blue, without being summoned.

'Shall I pour?' George's voice was strong again.

The only sound in the room was the clinking of cups and spoons, and the heavy ticking of the long case clock.

Lily watched the two people in front of her. It was like some secret dance going on before her eyes. Her mother-in-law was subdued now, watching her son under lowered lids. Her yellowing skin had a grey tinge to it that had not been there earlier.

George, on the other hand, looked well. Great, in fact. She could not remember seeing him look better. He had an assurance about him that was at odds with his appearance. George even dressed humbly. It was an odd thing, and if Lily had not seen it for herself she would have sworn it was impossible. How could someone dress in a humble manner? Well, George did. Only today his white shirt, grey tie and navy blue hand-knitted tank top looked almost jaunty. She took her tea in silence.

There was a subtle shifting of position here and Lily was not sure whether or not she liked it. If George upset his mother, she, Lily, would be the recipient of Nancy's bad humour when he left.

'I'll take my tea out to the kitchen if you don't mind, I have things to finish out there . . .' She was gabbling. Awkwardly she left the room. Whatever the upshot she wanted no part of it – but she left the kitchen door wide open.

'Now then, Mother, this is nice, isn't it?' George's voice was determined.

Then Nancy smiled, a rare genuine smile. As it softened the hard lines of her face, George felt a lump in his throat. For a few seconds she looked young again. He saw the softness that she had sometimes displayed, that she had occasionally allowed through her veneer of hardness. It was the smile of the girl she had once been, a long, long time ago, before her marriage and her children and her other life.

Before the men.

George wished fervently he had known her then.

He had his illusions about his mother, he needed them. He could not accept that she had been an evil force since childhood. That she had been using men to her own advantage from the onset of adolescence. That Nancy Markham had spent her whole life using and abusing people, none more so than her own children.

'Over there in the sideboard are my photo albums. Bring them to me, Georgie.'

He collected the bulky albums and put them on his mother's lap.

'Sit down at my feet and we'll reminisce.'

George did as he was told, like the old days when her word was law.

Nancy began to flip the pages, her eyes soft with nostalgia.

'Here, look at this one, Georgie. Remember this?'

He knelt up and looked at the picture. It was of him, aged about five with his mother. She was wearing a two-piece swimsuit that had been racy in those days and peering into the camera with a sultry look. Her hair was perfect; her long shapely legs partly obscured by a little boy holding a large candyfloss. George saw his baggy shorts with sticklike legs emerging from them, his close-cropped hair and serious elfin face.

It was a day that had stuck in his memory because it had been a good day. A happy day. A rare day. The moment caught in his chest like a trapped bird, fluttering against his ribcage. He could smell the heat and the sand and the people. The donkeys, the candyfloss and the aroma of melting margarine in the jam sandwiches. Could almost taste the strawberry jam, gritty with sand from grubby fingers. Could almost touch once more the saltiness of the blue sea. It had been such a good day, from the train ride early in the morning to the sleepiness and exhaustion of lying in his crisp cold sheets ready to sleep the sleep of the dead. He could remember Nancy kissing him good night. Smiling down on him from her soft peachy face.

'Camber Sands that was, Georgie boy. Lovely days those were. I was a picture then. Could gather the looks and all, them days.'

'You still look wonderful, Mother.'

It was a kindly lie, what she wanted, expected to hear.

'Well, maybe not as good as I used to look but not bad for my age, eh?'

Her voice was softer too, almost jocular. When Nancy was talking about herself she was animated and happy.

She turned the page. This time the picture was of her alone. A head and shoulders shot. Lips just parted to show her perfect white teeth. Her deep copper-coloured hair framed her face and she had on bright orange lipstick. The picture had been hand coloured by the photographer and he had caught the exact shade of her hair and skin.

Nancy stroked the page with wrinkled fingers, caressing the photograph.

'I can remember this as if it was yesterday. The man who took the photograph said I should have been a model. Said I had a perfect bone structure.'

And he should know, thought George. He moved in with us for a while if I remember rightly. He squeezed his eyes tight shut. He could see that day so clearly. They had all had their photos taken and afterwards his mother had sent them home. He could picture Edith in his mind shepherding them on to the bus, then making them something to eat at home. Later on his mother had come back with the man, a large gregarious type with a tiny pencil moustache and a Prince of Wales checked suit. He had brought back their mother, rather drunk, and a parcel of fish and chips, which had endeared him to Joseph and George immediately as he had not forgotten them. He had also brought them a large bottle of Tizer, then made them all laugh with stories of his time in the army. Telling the two avid-eyed little boys about shooting the Boche.

Then, later that night, much later, George had woken with a tummy ache from the fish and chips and the Tizer. On his way to the toilet he had heard groans coming from his mother's room. Opening the door quietly he had investigated. He had seen his mother kneeling on the bed with the man. His hands were in her long thick hair, fanning it around her head, pulling on it. He was groaning.

'That's it, Nance. Take the lot, Nance.'

He could see his mother's naked body in the dim firelight, could see her head and mouth moving up and down on the man. Then the man had spied him. Pulling Nancy up by the air, he had dragged a sheet across himself to hide his nakedness. Too late George saw the fury on his mother's face.

'Get out, you nosy little bugger!'

Then she was scrambling from the bed, her face twisted in temper, her lipstick smudged around her chin. She was stalking towards him with her long-legged stride, her mouth like a big gaping cavern.

He had been three years old.

494

'Here, Georgie, look at this one.'

He was dragged back to the present.

'Look at my dress. I remember saving up for that dress for ages.'

George forced himself to look at the picture. He could feel the rapid beating of his heart subside.

'Who's the girl with you?'

'That, Georgie boy, is Ruth Ellis.'

He peered closely at the picture.

'I worked her club. It was called the Little Club, of all things. In Knightsbridge.'

Nancy looked at her son, a half smile on her face, enjoying the shock she was creating.

George peered at the photograph again.

'She ran a brothel.'

'Hardly a brothel, Georgie boy. More like a gentlemen's club.'

George looked into her face and saw the gleam in her eyes. She was using her past now, the past she would not have mentioned to a soul, to try and undermine him, intimidate him. From religious grandmother, the epitome of decency, she was reverting to the days of her whoring to bring him low. He knew her so well. How sanctimonious she could be. He remembered her berating Edith when she had fallen pregnant that time; remembered the false impression of genteel poverty she liked to give to the neighbours. Remembered how she had told all and sundry of Edith's fall from grace. Now her real life could be used to hurt one of her children, to wound, and she used it without a qualm. He felt an urge to strike her.

Nancy watched her son's face and guessed what he was thinking. The old malice was back in her now.

'Someone once said to me: "Nancy, you're sitting on a gold mine." How right they were. And do you know who said it? Your father's brother. I ran off with him. Your father hadn't died, Georgie. I dumped him.'

'You said he was dead! I believed . . .'

Nancy laughed again. 'He is dead now. He died about ten

years ago. The police traced me and told me. He died in a bedsit in South London. He'd been dead ten days before they found him. Cheeky buggers wanted me to pay for the funeral! I told them where they could get off and all. He was useless, Georgie, bloody useless. Couldn't even die properly. Alone to the last.'

He felt himself rise from the floor, aware that his legs had gone dead at some point from kneeling – and then he slapped her. He knew he had slapped her because he heard the crack as his open palm met her baggy flesh, felt the force of her head snapping back and heard her scream of outrage.

Lily, outside the door, was hopping from one foot to the other in agitation.

'You evil slut! You dirty filthy slut!' George had balls of spittle at the corner of his lips. 'My father was alive. He could have saved me from you. Could have saved all of us from your men friends and your evil ways. You let men touch me for money . . . Touch me and use me!'

His mind was like a burst sore, all his hatred spilling out. He was dangerously close to tears and swallowed them back.

'You fucking filthy whore! You stinking tart!'

All his life she had taken pleasure in hurting him, while she gave pleasure to others for a price. He felt bile rising in his throat, burning him. He pursed his lips together to stop it spewing out on to the woman sitting in front of him with the old mocking grin.

'None of my children ever had any gumption. You were all like him, weak and sickly. I hated you all.'

Her voice was filled with malice and something else.

It was fear.

She was scared of him, of what she had caused. Of what the outcome might be.

George dropped back into a seat. Suddenly he was exhausted. It had been a mistake to come here. He should have known that. She had stolen his childhood, his innocence and his father.

The last he could never forgive.

The number of times he had run away from her, only to be

brought back, when all the time he'd had a father he could have run to. A man to take care of him properly.

He looked at his mother as if for the first time. He finally hated her one hundred per cent. She disgusted him. She was a whore. They were all whores, every last one of them.

Suddenly he began to laugh, a high-pitched laugh bordering on hysteria, and it was that frightening sound that brought Lily bursting into the room.

The old bitch! All those years of her sanctimonious rambling, listening to Joseph pandering to her, coming second to the paragon of virtue who rang her bell like a demented school mistress and shouted, 'Get me this, get me that!' When in reality she had been a common prostitute!

'You lying old cow!' All Lily's hard-won refinement was gone now.

'You was on the bleeding bash!'

Nancy stared at her daughter-in-law, eyes like pieces of flint.

'You've driven us all up the bloody wall. Well, that's it now, my girl. It's a home for you. I don't care how much it costs. Wait till Joseph gets in! I'll give you Ruth Ellis! It's a pity they didn't bloody well hang *you*, you old bitch!'

George wiped his eyes with his handkerchief and with a final glance at his now terrified mother, walked from the room and out of the front door. Lily's shouting carried after him.

He started the car. On the back seat was his suitcase, packed and ready for his holidays.

Wait until he told Edith. George knew he would never see his mother again.

Patrick Kelly made his way to Brighton. It had not taken him long to find out the addresses of Tony Jones's family. If necessary he would take the elder daughter hostage until Jones came forward. It wouldn't take long for the whisper on the street to get back to him, Patrick knew that.

The Rolls Royce pulled up at an address in Steyning. Kelly nodded at Willy and they slipped from the car. Inside

497

the small bungalow Tony Jones was drinking scotch while his wife watched him. On his lap was his grand-daughter Melanie.

She loved her grandad and cuddled into his big flabby frame. It was Tony's daughter who answered the door and she stood by silently as they walked in.

Patrick nodded at the girl. She was not part of this, he knew that.

'Where is he, love?'

She pointed to a door at the end of the passageway. 'In there. Look, Mr Kelly, my daughter's in there . . .'

He ignored her and walked into the room.

'Hello, Tone, long time no see. I've come to take you for a little drive. Have a chat like.'

Tony Jones blanched. The little girl on his lap sensed his fear and hugged him tighter.

Kelly looked at the long blonde hair and enormous blue eyes. She could have been his Mandy as a child. He put out a hand and touched the soft downy head.

'Hello there, my darling. What's your name?'

The little girl looked up at the man and grinned, exposing tiny pearl-like teeth.

'Melanie Daniels and I'm three.'

'You're a big girl for your age, aren't you? Let Grandad get his coat, darlin', while me and you have a little chat.'

The child looked at her grandad and was glad when he nodded assent. She decided she liked the big man in the big coat. Willy watched fascinated as Patrick took the girl's tiny hand. He then accompanied Tony Jones while he got his coat. Tony opened his mouth to speak and Willy silenced him.

'You must have been barmy if you thought you could pull one over on Pat where that scumbag's concerned.'

Tony hung his head.

Melanie was sitting on Patrick's knee, regaling him with stories about her life.

'I've got a little cat called Sooty. Have you got a cat?'

Patrick shook his head.

'How about a little doggie? You got a little doggie?'

Patrick smiled at her with genuine good humour. She was an enchanting child.

'Can I make you a coffee, Mr Kelly?' Jeanette's voice was flat. She knew enough about Patrick Kelly to know her grand-daughter was safe. She had known Renée many years before. She knew that he would remember that.

'Why not? Patrick looked into her eyes. 'I'm sorry about this, Jeanette, but you know the score.'

She couldn't meet his gaze so got up and went to the kitchen. Willy and Tony came back into the room.

'And I go to play school.' Melanie was still chatting and Patrick was enjoying the conversation.

'Really? What do you do there?'

Melanie bit her top lip in consternation as she thought.

'We do singin' and paintin', sometimes. I can sing "The Wheels on the Bus", all the way through.' This last bit of information was given with a toss of her long blonde hair and Kelly laughed.

'You're a clever little girl, Melanie.'

'My grandad says I'm as pretty as a picture. And he sings me songs. Don't you, Grandad?'

Tony nodded his head, watching the scene in front of him.

Patrick looked at him as he spoke. 'And what songs does he sing you?'

'Can I sing one, Grandad? Please?'

Tony nodded again and she began to sing.

Patrick let Tony Jones sit stewing for another twenty minutes before he decided to leave. By this time Melanie had become so enamoured of him she screamed the place down because she wanted to go with them. Her cries followed them from the house.

She had insisted on a kiss from all three of them, and Willy had had to be scowled at severely by Patrick before he complied. Patrick, on the other hand, had stroked her hair and comforted her before leaving, enjoying the innocence and babyness of her; an innocence that had reminded him of another life, one where he had had a wife and a child.

In the car, he turned to Tony.

'A lovely child. You must be proud of her?'

Tony nodded, he couldn't answer.

'Wasn't she a lovely little thing, Willy?'

He half turned from his driving. 'Oh, yeah.'

Patrick continued conversationally.

'Imagine how you'd feel if someone took her, buggered her, and then left her for dead on a filthy floor. Half her skull battered away, hair stuck to the floor in a pool of blood. If you had to watch her die, slowly and painfully, in the hospital. Watch her fight for her life, after operations to cut her skull away bit by bit because her brain was so swollen inside her head. Makes you sick just thinking about it, don't it?'

Tony's nod was barely noticeable.

'Well, now maybe you'll understand why you're going to get the hiding of your fucking life, won't you? But first I want that cunt's address, phone number, post code. I want to know everything you know about him. All right?'

Tony nodded again.

At least Kelly hadn't said he was going to kill him. As far as Tony was concerned, that in itself was a result.

500

BOOK TWO

'"Hanging is too good for him,"
Said Mr Cruelty'
    – John Bunyan, 1628–88

'A rape! A rape!
Yes, you have ravish'd justice.
Forced her to do your pleasure'
    – John Webster, 1580–1625

'Life for life,
Eye for eye, tooth for tooth,
Hand for hand, foot for foot.
Burning for burning, wound for wound,
Stripe for stripe'
                – *Exodus*, 21, xxiii

Chapter Twenty-six

George booked himself into the Hilton Hotel at Gatwick. He was feeling upset. He knew he would not sleep.

He opened his suitcase. He had packed one of his favourite books and tonight he needed it. He needed the release from the real world. He opened the magazine at the centre pages. A girl was looking up at him. She had real auburn hair. George knew it was real because it was the same top and bottom.

He slipped off his clothes and hung them up neatly in the wardrobe, then relaxed on the bed in his underpants. This time tomorrow he would be in the USA. He allowed himself a grin. He'd be in Florida, starting a new life.

His tongue was just poking from the corner of his mouth now as he concentrated his energies, thinking up different situations and pastimes for the girl on the page.

George was beginning to feel better.

Patrick smiled at Tony Jones.

'So what you're saying is, Tony, you took the blood test for the bloke?'

He nodded, his eyes aimed at the floor.

'You actually went and took the blood test – the blood test that *I'm* paying for – so that piece of shite could walk free?'

'It wasn't like that, Mr Kelly. He had me by the bollocks . . .'

'I'll have you by them in a minute, mate.' Willy's voice was low and menacing.

Tony looked at Patrick in distress.

'I've been selling snuff movies. He bought them. Said he'd rope me into it . . .' His voice was desperate.

It was quiet for a while. Kelly and Willy both stared at the man in front of them with slitted eyes, as if trying to understand just what it was in front of them.

'Snuff movies? You sell snuff movies. You deal with scum who rent out little boys, you sell death, and you want me to be lenient with you? You want me to say, "Oh, don't worry, Tone, long as you make a good bit of bunce . . ."'

Patrick swung back his fist and began punching Tony Jones in the face and head. He could feel the bruising on his knuckles as they came into contact with the man's skull, felt the first trickle of blood as Jones' eyebrow split, and still he could not stop. Rage was inside his head, fuelled by the pictures of Mandy's broken face and body. The knowledge that she had been buggered, raped and humiliated by a sadist who had no more thought for her than he'd have had for a mad dog.

And it was all this man's fault! He pandered to him, was the means by which this George Markham fed his sick fantasies. Finally, spent, he walked to the corner of the lock-up garage. Outside he heard the scraping of the Rottweiler belonging to one of his repomen. It sniffed underneath the door, making tiny whining sounds. Every so often he heard Jimmy Danks quieten the beast. It occurred to Patrick that Tony could be dead soon.

He shrugged. He didn't really care at this moment. He blinked back tears; whether they were of rage or sadness he wasn't sure. All he could think about was his child. That took precedence over everything. There was nothing he could do to bring Mandy back. He accepted that, but he would find this George Markham and make him pay dearly for what he had done. Not just for Mandy but for all of them.

He heard a groan and turned to see Tony Jones regain consciousness. Patrick watched him pull himself up from the dirty floor and sit back on the brokendown chair. He opened the lock-up door and nodded at the man with the Rottweiler.

Then he took one last look at Tony Jones and, gesturing for Willy to follow, walked from the lock-up.

The dog was straining on its leash now, scenting the air. Its huge jaws were clamping down, making snapping noises. Kelly stood by his car in the deserted block and watched as the man took off the lead and let the dog run into the garage, closing the door behind it.

By the time Tony Jones realised what was happening, one hundred and twenty pounds of muscle had already launched itself at him.

Kelly and Willy drove away to sounds of his anguished screams. The dog's owner was rolling himself a cigarette. He waved to them cheerfully as they drove off.

George had dressed and left the hotel at eight thirty-seven. He could not relax tonight. Even the book had done little to make him feel better. His mother had upset him so much. He drove around for a while, his head whirling with the things she had said.

His father had not been dead. He remembered only a tall thin man with dark blond hair and a smell of tobacco about him. George remembered sitting with the man on a large easy chair. Then one day he had gone.

His earliest memory of his mother was of her picking him up and kissing him on the mouth, holding him to her tightly even though he had wanted to get away. Her arms had been like steel bands around him.

He shuddered.

A car hooted its horn and he broke out of his reverie to find that he was at a roundabout. He pulled away and took the first turning. He looked at the signpost and saw that he was on the A26 going towards Maidstone. That was how upset he was. He had been driving, unaware even where he was going.

Only his mother could upset him like that.

He pulled off at the slip road that led to Nettlestead. It was half past nine. George drove along slowly, trying to gather his thoughts.

Then he saw a woman about thirty yards in front of him.

She was standing by a large Range Rover, actually flagging him down!

George pulled up behind her and wound down his window. Cynthia Redcar rushed towards him, her large man's parka blowing open as she ran. She had been stranded there for thirty minutes.

'I say, I'm awfully sorry to trouble you, but my car's gone on the blink.'

George saw white teeth and abundant black hair. She had a long jawline and anyone looking at her would guess that she was a 'horsey' kind of person.

'Could you please take me to get some help? I must phone my husband, he'll be worried sick.' She smiled at him again.

'What seems to be the trouble?'

She pulled the parka around her slim frame and grimaced.

'I don't know a thing about cars, I'm afraid. It just cut out and died on me. Oh Christ, here we go again.' She ran back to the Range Rover at the sound of a child whimpering.

George got out of his car and ambled after her.

The woman was holding a boy of about eighteen months to her breast, stroking the dark head gently and crooning the way only mothers know how. She lifted her eyebrows at George. 'Poor little blighter's cold and hungry.' She picked up her bag from the back seat and set about locking the Range Rover. She stood in front of George ready and waiting, her eyebrows raised in query.

He really was an odd little man, she thought. Hardly said a word. She began to walk towards the Orion in a determined way. Opening the back doors, she placed the now quiet child across the back seat and slipped in beside him, talking softly and stroking his legs. George saw the child close his eyes and relax. He was entranced at the pretty picture it created.

The woman saw him looking and grinned. 'Another three like this at home, I'm afraid. I hope Dicky remembers to feed them! He can be so unreliable at times. I'll bet he fed the horses though, he'd never forget about them!' She laughed gaily. George stared at her and she felt the first prickle of unease.

'I say, I don't like to push, but if you could just drive me into the village?' Her eyebrows rose once more, this time in hope.

George was looking around him. The road was deserted. If she had been there for over half an hour then it was obviously rarely used. To the right-hand side were woods, to the left a cornfield. He could feel the familiar excitement mounting. He felt in the pocket of his coat and his hand grasped the handle of the knife. It felt cool to the touch. The road had lighting, but it was subdued, as if the planners knew that it would not be used very often.

'Do you live far?'

'No, about eight miles along the road. Trouble is the lighting packs up about a mile further on and I didn't fancy trekking along there in the dark.'

Her voice was so full of life. George imagined she would be a lot of fun to live with. Could see her playing games with her children, baking her own bread. She looked the type who worried about the ozone layer and tropical rain forests. Riding her horses.

He giggled.

'Are you all right? Only if I'm putting you to any trouble . . . ?' She sounded even more uncertain now and George saw her eyes scanning the road for any oncoming vehicles. His face set in a grim mask. The child began to snore gently and George grinned at her.

'Get out of the car.'

'I . . . I beg your pardon?'

He pulled her by the arm.

'I said, get out of the car.'

She went to pick up the child and George pulled the knife out. 'Leave him there.'

Cynthia Redcar stared at the man. The confusion in her dark eyes was apparent. George could practically smell her fear. She stumbled from the car.

'Take off your coat and cover him with it. He looks cold.'

Cynthia stood dumbstruck, staring at him.

507

George rolled his eyes. Why were women always so difficult?

He slapped her across the face, hard. 'Don't annoy me, I'm warning you. Just do as I say and everything will be fine.'

Cynthia took off her coat. The wind bit into her. She placed it gently over the child.

'Now shut the door and we'll go for a little walk.'

A minute later they were in the woods. In the dimness Cynthia felt his hand go to her breasts and instinctively she pushed it away.

'What's the little boy's name?' George's voice was low and menacing and Cynthia felt the threat like a physical blow.

'Please – please don't hurt James. I'll do anything, just don't touch my little boy.'

This was more like it.

'Take off your clothes.'

George watched her as she fumbled with the buttons on her jeans. As she pulled her jumper over her head. All the time her eyes were on him. He could see the shaking of her hands as she moved.

She had heavy baggy breasts. George guessed they were marked, could visualise the mauve veins in them from childbearing. Four children did she say she had? His mind was fuzzy again. It was the excitement from her fear. He loved the fear. He loved being in control. She was standing now in her bare feet, her hands across her breasts, trying to hide her nakedness.

'Lie down.'

'Please . . . whoever you are, don't do this.' Her voice was drenched with tears.

'Lie down.' He stepped towards her and she flinched as the blade of the knife neared her face.

She lay down on the damp cold ground, her hands between her legs. George surveyed her for a few seconds before he slipped off his overcoat and knelt in front of her, forcing her legs open with his knees.

'You're going to do some things for me, dear. And if, but only if, you do them very, very well, I'll let you go home.'

He unzipped his trousers.

Cynthia felt a wave of nausea wash over her.

George was happy again. Today had not been so bad after all.

Kate knocked at Patrick's door at nine thirty. He opened it to her himself.

'I got your message, Pat, is everything all right?'

'Yeah. I had a bit of business to attend to, that's all.'

They went into the drawing room and Patrick poured them both a drink. Kate slipped off her coat and placed it on a chair. She looked around the familiar room and felt a warm glow engulf her. She liked Patrick's house, liked it very much.

'Is it still cold out, Kate?'

'Yes, it's going to rain later by all accounts.'

She sat on the settee and sipped her drink. 'Are you sure you're all right, Pat?'

He jumped. He had been thinking about later, when he would finally get his hands on George Markham.

'Sure.' His voice was curt and he tried to calm himself.

'I had a bit of aggro with one of the repomen, that's all. It happens all the time.'

He should have left a message with her mother saying that he would see her tomorrow. He should not have arranged to see her tonight. They had been supposed to meet at eight and he had rung and told her mother to ask Kate to make it nine thirty instead. It was a mistake. If she knew what he was going to do tonight . . .

'What kind of trouble? Her voice was concerned. He looked at her and loved her so much he felt an urge to cry.

'Nothing to worry about, Kate. How's things with you?'

His voice was softer now. She watched him lighting a cigarette. His hands were trembling.

'All right. The blood testing is going great guns.'

'I'm sure it is.' His voice was hard.

He felt like telling her that it was all a waste of time, that the Grantley Ripper, George Markham, had paid a man to take the test for him. It was a bloody mockery, the lot of it.

'We're doing all we can, you know.' Kate's voice was soft and Patrick felt a moment's fleeting guilt. Then it was replaced by apprehension. If she only knew what he was going to do . . . It would be the end for them. What he had done to Danny Burrows would be nothing to how she would feel when Markham was found murdered. Patrick didn't care if he was caught, as long as the man paid the price.

Kate was worried. He looked as taut as a bowstring. It was as if he knew a devastating secret but couldn't tell anyone.

'Have you eaten, Pat?'

Patrick could not help smiling. She sounded just like his mother: whenever there was a crisis or an upset she wanted to feed everyone.

Food was a woman's way of healing.

If only it was that easy.

'Come here.' It was a command.

She put down her drink and went to him. She stood in front of him, her hands on her hips.

'I'm not sure I like your tone!'

She was laughing and Patrick felt a feeling in his gut, like a hand gripping his entrails.

He knew what she was trying to do. She thought he was having a bad day over Mandy and was trying to cheer him up.

She was good. Kate was a good woman.

He pulled her on to his lap and put his hand up her jumper, rubbing at the soft skin of her breasts.

'Oh, Kate . . .' It was a heartfelt cry, and she felt it like a physical blow.

'Patrick, tell me what's wrong. I want to try and help you. Are you in some kind of trouble?'

'No. Nothing like that, I swear to you.'

'Then why are you like this? Is it Mandy? It's as if you're on tenterhooks for some reason.' Her voice lowered. 'It is Mandy, isn't it?'

He could tell her the truth about that anyway.

'Yeah . . . it's about Mandy.'

'You're missing her? It's perfectly natural, you know. It often hits people suddenly. I've seen it before.'

Her earnest face stared into his and he felt his heartbeat speeding up.

He wanted to tell her that he missed her every second of the day; that it was there with him when he opened his eyes in the morning and when he closed them at night. Even his dreams were no escape from the feelings of futility. But now he had the perpetrator within his grasp and tonight he was going to commit murder. And he couldn't wait!

But he knew Kate would not understand his need. The need to destroy the man who had ravaged the only decent thing he'd had. It would cleanse him. He knew he could lie to himself, say he was ridding the world of a piece of shite. That's what Willy had termed it. But deep inside he knew that that was only a small part of it. Revenge was what he wanted. Revenge, and the feeling of blood on his hands.

Kate watched the emotions cross his face and her heart went out to him.

Then, suddenly, they were on the floor.

Her clothes were being pulled off her and he was inside her, thrusting away as if his life depended on it.

She had never known a loving so brutal and so beautiful. They came together in a shuddering climax and then lay there, holding one another tightly.

Patrick stared at her dark eyes and wished he did not have to do what he was going to do. Because if this exquisite creature ever found out, he would once more lose everything he had.

But even Kate's love wasn't enough. Revenge had a bitter taste already, but there was no going back.

George was humming softly to himself. Cynthia was quiet and pliable. He arranged her limbs once more to his satisfaction. She had muscular thighs. All the horse riding, he guessed. She had passed out with fright, and that had annoyed him. Because tonight he wanted, needed, a woman to beg.

His mother should beg really. Beg him to forgive her. But she wouldn't.

511

He felt the rage coming again, then he heard the noise. It was a child's crying.

James was awake.

Cynthia stirred beneath him. The crying of her child was penetrating somewhere in her unconscious. She opened her eyes and, remembering what had happened, looked at George, terrified.

The crying was getting louder. The little hiccoughing sobs were like knife blades in her heart.

How long had she been out? Had the man hurt James? She tried to push herself up.

George tutted to himself. He felt the woman's hands on his chest and the force as she tried to push him from her. An animal strength seemed to fill her body. Her child needed her. Her child was in danger.

They were all the same.

Cynthia brought up her knee. Panic over her child galvanised her into action. She caught George in the groin and he groaned, a white hot pain shooting into his testes. Lashing out with the knife, he swiped it cleanly across her throat, slicing the skin and veins as neatly as a surgeon.

Cynthia put her hands to her neck in shock. Bringing them away covered in blood. She opened her mouth but only a strangled gurgle escaped.

George watched her head snap back as she shuddered to her last sleep, the gaping wound spurting blood.

Then she was still, her eyes fastened on him.

George wiped the blade on the dirt beside him, then he stood up and rearranged his clothes. Picking up his overcoat, he slipped off the white cotton gloves and pushed them into the pocket. He walked to his car.

James was crying hard. He had woken up in a strange car with a strange smell and his mother was gone. He huddled into her coat, trying to breathe in his mother's perfume.

George opened the door and scooped him up. Then he walked back to Cynthia with him.

The child struggled, and George held him tighter.

'Be quiet!'

James gulped in a large draught of air and screamed. George dropped him on to the leaf-covered ground. The child was stamping his feet and screaming and he watched, fascinated at the strength in the little body. At the determination to get whatever it was he wanted.

He watched him stumbling around on fat little legs, trying to find something familiar. Fear and panic were making him clumsy. Then George tried to grasp his hand but the child would not let him.

He pulled his arms away, screaming louder and louder until finally George began to hit him.

On his way to the hotel George started humming again.

Patrick and Willy pulled into Bychester Terrace at two fifteen. As Patrick walked up the path, he felt a loosening in his bowels. He would be facing the murderer of his daughter in next to no time. He felt a heat inside him as he thought about it. The few hours with Kate had been tinged with despair. Now she was gone from his mind. All he could think about, all he could see, was the future without Mandy. His child.

He knew as he walked to the front door that the house was empty. It had that deserted air. He knocked anyway and waited.

The anger was back. The burning anger that started in his chest and wormed its way through his body, seeping into sinew and bone. Maddening him.

He wanted George Markham. He wanted to strangle the life from him slowly. He wanted to castrate him. He wanted to hurt him more than he had ever wanted anything in his life.

This man had used his daughter as if she was a piece of dirt, and Patrick Kelly would see that justice was meted out.

He walked around the back of the house, Willy following. As they passed the overflow pipe a trickle of water splashed on to them.

'Bollocks! That water's bloody freezing.' Willy's voice was a whisper.

Taking a glass cutter from his pocket he cut a hole in the back door. Within seconds they were inside the house.

It was empty all right.

Patrick cursed under his breath.

Turning on their torches, they began the search for a clue to where their man might be. By tomorrow night latest they would know every move he made. Patrick Kelly had already arranged for that in case tonight's visit drew a blank.

Elaine's handbag was in the hall cupboard and Willy rifled through it. Taking a shabby brown address book from it, he put the bag back where he'd found it. Patrick motioned that they were leaving.

He felt as high as a kite. The adrenalin was coursing through him. He had not got this close for the man to evade him now.

If it took him the rest of his life, he'd find him. Especially now he had his name.

Nancy lay in her bed contemplating the evening's events. She knew that Lily had never liked her, the feeling had always been mutual. But she had never fully realised the extent of her dislike until tonight.

For the first time in her life, Nancy Markham was frightened. She realised that at eighty-one her life was nearly over and if what had been threatened tonight came to pass, she would finish it in a home.

A home!

How dare that stinking slut threaten her with a home?

But she had.

And Joseph had agreed. Oh, not out loud, not in so many words. Her son was too much of a coward for that.

But he had agreed with his eyes. The eyes that were as grey and lifeless as his father's.

She clenched her fists in temper. When she thought of how she had fought to give them a decent life! And Nancy really believed that she had.

When she thought of the sacrifices she had made for them . . .

One of the things George had inherited from his mother was her capacity for fantasy.

Lily's voice was at full throttle in the room next-door.

'She goes this time, Joseph. She should have been put away years ago. You know that and I know that.'

Joseph stared up at the ceiling.

'She's as nutty as a bloody fruit cake. But she's cute.' Lily wagged her finger at him.

'Oh, she's cute all right. Well, I'm telling you now, Joseph Markham, I've had enough. I've had to put up with her all these years. It's all right for you, you're out all bloody day. Have you any idea what it's like, having to listen to that sodding bell, day in day out? Well, have you?'

He closed his eyes tightly.

'Even the children hate her. I never see them any more. She's driven them from the house.'

Suddenly, it was all too much for her and her voice quavered. She swallowed back her tears. Joseph turned to her and hesitantly took her in his arms. The display of affection was too much for her and the dam broke. Sobs were shaking her whole body and Joseph held her to him, seeing in his mind's eyes the girl she had been.

'Hush now. Hush now, Lily. Everything's going to be all right. I'll sort out somewhere for her tomorrow.'

She pulled away from him.

'Pr-Promise?'

'I promise.'

Now he had actually said it out loud, it was true. He'd see the doctor first thing in the morning. If he could, he'd get her put in council care. If he couldn't, then he'd pay for it. The time had come to let go. He had done all he could for her. Anything he owed her had been repaid in full. Over and over again.

It was funny, but after all that he had heard tonight, he had no fear of her any more.

It was as his wife had told her: she had finally fouled her nest.

He stroked Lily's hair and smiled to himself. It'd be nice to see the children more often.

In the Mile End Hospital two nurses stood over Tony Jones. He was heavily sedated. Jeanette had left the hospital ten minutes earlier.

'Poor man! He'll be scarred for life.'

'Those bloody dogs should be put down, all of them. To think it could be wandering around now. Imagine if it attacked a child!'

'Yeah. Didn't you think his wife was a bit funny?'

'In what way?'

'Well . . .' The other nurse lowered her voice confidentially.

'It's as if she knew he was going to be bad. She didn't seem surprised or shocked when she saw him.'

'Can't say I noticed really.'

'Oh, well, maybe it was just me.'

'Come and have a cuppa before we start the turns.'

Tony groaned in his drug-induced sleep and the two women watched him for a second. He settled down once more.

'Poor little thing. He'll know all about it when those stitches on his face begin to tighten.'

'Let's get that cuppa while we've still got the chance.'

Chapter Twenty-seven

George had just had his meal on the plane and was now watching a hilarious episode of 'Some Mothers Do Have 'Em'. Frank Spencer was a motorbike messenger for a firm called Demon King and was inadvertently delivering pornographic pictures instead of letters and parcels. Everyone on the plane was screaming with laughter and adjusting their headphones. George laughed more than any of them. He was really enjoying himself.

He had eaten all his meal, discovering he had a ravenous appetite when he had seen the Beef Stroganoff, Duchesse potatoes and peas. He had also had a small bottle of red wine.

He sat in a window seat looking down at the cottony clouds and felt a moment of euphoria. He was going to Florida, he was going to see Edith. His Edith. He was going to enjoy himself.

He thought about the night before and his happy expression faded for a second.

The memory of the child was troubling him.

Then he shrugged. All children got beaten at some point, by parents or by teachers. He knew this for a fact. Satisfied again that he had not done anything really wrong, he savoured once more the delights of the woman's body. He could feel his own excitement and forced those thoughts from his mind, concentrating on the clouds and the blueness of the sea that peeped through the whiteness every so often, reminding him that he was leaving England. England, Elaine, his mother . . . mustn't forget his mother . . . and all his troubles.

He would start again in Florida, he had decided. He would

sell the house. It was all his now. He experienced a small feeling of annoyance, just a flicker really, that Elaine had had to die like she did. Not because he felt any guilt, but because it had stopped him claiming the insurance money.

He had it all worked out. When he went back to sell the house he would say that Elaine had run off with someone. He gave his little grin. That would immediately win him sympathy. He would put the house up for sale and then return to Florida and Edith.

He would remove Elaine from her watery grave and bury her somewhere. He'd put her out with the garden rubbish in black bags and then dump her on the tip.

This made him want to laugh again. Elaine on the tip! Better than she deserved, maybe. He'd cross that bridge when he came to it. Either way, she was gone.

Beside him sat a little girl. She was sandwiched between George and her mother. Her mother was still laughing at Frank Spencer, showing pearly white teeth.

George decided he approved of her. She looked like a mother should. Flat-chested, clean and wholesome-looking. No make up or jewellery. The programme ended and Desmond Lynam came on the screen to talk about the next feature. George pulled off the headphones and relaxed. The little girl did the same. She smiled at him shyly. George smiled back, smelling the sweetness of the little body. He noticed she had a pack of cards and leant towards her.

'Would you like a game of snap?'

The child flicked back her long blonde hair disdainfully.

'I don't play snap. I play poker, pontoon or five card stud.' She saw the dismay on George's face and hurried on, 'I also play rummy and trumps.'

George smiled once more.

'How about a game of rummy, then?'

'All right.' She began to shuffle the cards expertly and he sighed.

Nothing and no one was ever what they seemed.

Five card stud indeed!

Kate looked down at the two bodies and felt sickness wash

over her. The woman was lying spreadeagled on the dirt floor, her neck a gaping wound. Blood had dried on her shoulders and breasts. Her mouth was in a perfect O. That was bad enough, but it was the child's body that affected her.

His little face was crushed completely, nose and cheeks collapsed in towards his brain. His tiny plump baby fingers were curled in his palms. He was lying huddled into his mother's body.

The pathologist shook his head.

'She's been dead longer than the child. My guess is he crawled to her for comfort then suffocated in his own blood.'

He pointed with his pen at the child's face. 'See here and here? Well, the blow caused the blood to flow down the back of his throat. His nose couldn't release it, no way. He practically drowned in his own blood. Poor little fucker.'

Kate wanted to cry. She wanted to cry desperately. But not here. She refused to though she guessed shrewdly that more than a few of the men around her were feeling the same.

Murdered people were bad enough, but murdered children? They were the worst.

When they had received the call that the Grantley Ripper had decided to expand his area, they had all felt a sense of shame. They hadn't stopped him and the man was on the move.

And the case had a new dimension. He killed little children now. Christ alone knew where he would strike next.

Kate heard the sound of sobbing and turned to the left. In a clump of yew trees stood DS Willis, head bent. Caitlin was patting him on the shoulder and lighting him a cigarette. It was the boy's first child corpse.

Kate felt a surge of affection for the young man. And for Caitlin. Much as he tried to be the hardfaced know-all, Kate was realising he was in fact quite a soft-hearted man. She looked at the two bodies and pictured the tiny child trying to find his mother's warmth. Crying, in acute pain, he had dragged himself to her. Believing, as all children believed, that she would protect him. Make him better. Only Mummy was already dead and the child's time was running out.

Dicky Redcar had alerted the police to his wife's disappearance at eleven-fifteen.

Two patrolmen had found the Range Rover at eleven forty-nine and assumed she had tried to walk and maybe gone to a friend's. There was no reason to suspect foul play. At one twenty-five they had begun a search; the bodies had been found just after two.

Kate had been alerted at five-thirty that the Grantley Ripper had decided to extend his operations. The DNA on the woman had been conclusive. It was the same man, and the only clue they had were his tyre tracks.

As Caitlin had remarked, unless they had a definite make on the car the tyre tracks were a piss in the ocean. How many dark-coloured saloons were there, for heaven's sake?

Kate saw Frederick Flowers arrive and heaved a sigh. The heavy mob was here. That meant the newspapers were already on to it.

Dicky Redcar was in shock. His three remaining children had been taken by relatives. His sister had wanted to stay with him, but he needed to be alone.

He sat in his study with a photograph of Cynthia and James on his lap. He could hear Major, one of his horses, whinnying outside the window.

The photograph showed Cynthia holding young James on a pony. He'd had a natural seat. All their children did. Rosie, nearly eleven, was already a name on the children's eventing circuit. Jeremy, aged nine, was following in her footsteps. Even Sarah was a natural at five. It was what they had lived for. The horses, the children and each other.

Since returning from the Falklands, he had given up his army career and they had settled down to their 'real life', as they referred to it. He had seen enough death and carnage out there. He'd never expected to see it at home.

There was a knock at the door and he closed his eyes.

He felt a shadow cross the window at his side and glanced up. Two men were standing there, smiling at him. Who the hell were they?

He rose from his seat and opened the window, putting the photograph on the sill.

'What do you want?'

'Hello.' The man was tall and slim with a ready smile. 'I wondered if we could have a word?'

The second man brought up a camera and the flash made Dicky Redcar reel.

Damned reporters!

'Go away! Leave me alone. I have nothing to say to you.'

'Come on now, sir, this is news. Five minutes and we'll be gone.'

Dicky stepped away from them as if they were the plague. He side stepped his chair and stumbled from the room. The two men watched him bolt and shrugged their shoulders at each other. The tall man put his hand inside the open window and picked up the photograph.

'Look what I've found.' He raised his eyebrows in delight. 'Not a bad-looking piece. Bit flat-chested, but you can't have everything. Shame about the kid. His face is a bit blurred. Come on, let's talk to the neighbours, see what we can gather. I hope he was a war hero, that always makes great copy.'

The two men slunk away.

Major whinnied again, wondering where his mistress was with his morning carrot.

Patrick was on a high. He had not slept from when he had left George Markham's, his energies set on finding out everything about him.

He was now sitting outside Kortone Separates, waiting for people to arrive for work. The address and phone number had been in Elaine's phone book.

A large man, slightly balding, drew up in the car park in a Granada and Patrick stepped from his Rolls-Royce. The early morning cold hit him, sending his breath into the sky life puffs of smoke.

'Excuse me. Can I have a word?'

Peter Renshaw turned to look at the man. His eyebrows rose at the sight of the Rolls Royce. What could he want?

'Yes? Can I help you?'

'Do you work there?' Patrick flicked his head in the direction of the factory opposite.

'Yes?' It was a question, coming out in a bewildered fashion.

'Do you happen to know a George Markham?' Patrick's voice was friendly, friendly and neutral.

The man's face relaxed.

'Old Georgie? Know him well.'

Patrick gave him a big smile.

He opened the door of the Rolls and got inside, motioning for Peter Renshaw to follow him.

Peter clambered in, without a trace of fear. He could smell the pure luxury of the car and relaxed into the leather upholstery with glee.

'Lovely motor.'

'Thanks. Can I get you a drink?' Patrick opened the small mini bar. It never failed to impress people, especially those in C-reg Granadas.

'Bit early for me, it's only eight twenty!'

'Fair enough.' Patrick poured himself a brandy and swirled it around the glass.

'I'm Patrick Kelly, I don't know if you've heard of me?' He watched the man's face drop. 'Don't worry, I've no grievance with you. It's George Markham I'm interested in. "Old Georgie" as you just referred to him, Mr . . .'

Peter Renshaw wished he'd taken the drink now. Patrick Kelly was serious trouble. What on earth could he want George for?

'Renshaw. Peter Renshaw. I don't really know George that well . . .'

He was babbling.

Patrick poured out another brandy and handed it to him. 'I think me and you need to have a little chat, Peter. I can call you Peter?'

Renshaw nodded. As far as he was concerned, Patrick Kelly could call him anything he liked!

The car purred to life.

'Where . . . Where are you taking me?'

'Just for a little drive. Now calm down. I think you're a

sensible man. I think I can trust you.' The threat was there as plain as daylight. 'I can, can't I?'

Peter drained the brandy at a gulp.

'Yes. You can trust me, Mr Kelly.'

'Call me Pat. All my friends do, and I want us to be friends, Peter. Now, starting from the beginning, I want you to tell me all you know about George Markham.'

'But what for?' It was out before he realised what he was saying.

'Because, Peter, I asked you. And as far as I'm concerned, that's reason enough. OK?'

He took a deep breath.

'I only know him as a colleague at work. He's a quiet little man. I suppose you could say I've always felt a bit sorry for him.'

Patrick's eyebrows rose.

A quiet little man? He wouldn't be quiet when he got his hands on him. He'd be screaming his head off.

He already had the make and reg of Markham's car. That had been the easy bit. The hard bit was finding out where the hell the little bastard was. But if he could locate the car, he could locate George Markham.

Until then, he would hound everyone he could. Use force if necessary.

All his men had the description and details of George Markham's car. He had been on to some friends in the Met and they were looking for it as well. Something had to give eventually.

Then he would have him in the palm of his hand.

Twenty minutes later, he dropped off Peter Renshaw outside Kortone Separates. It had been obvious he knew nothing of importance. Except that George was not coming back to work.

There was something going on here. Where was the wife? Was she with him? If so, they were looking for a couple.

In that case, Patrick would either have to get rid of her, or abduct George off the street.

Either way he'd get him.

Then the news of the murders came on the radio. Willy

turned it up and put it over the intercom. Patrick listened as the newscaster's voice droned on. He felt a coldness in his bowels. At the mention of the child he locked eyes with Willy in the mirror on the windscreen.

The filthy bastard!

It only added incentive.

Patrick felt Willy put his foot down and settled himself back in his seat. He stared at the passing scenery and then pulled the address book from his pocket.

'I think the brother's house next, Willy. We'll drag him out if necessary, and fuck the consequences. No more pussy footing around.'

Willy nodded. Those were his thoughts entirely.

Joseph had been ringing around all morning. Yellow Pages was choc-a-bloc with nursing homes. Like all good business-men he was finding out the rates before committing himself. Eighty-one his mother might be, but she could live for a good while yet. The council had informed him that she was not their responsibility and he had wondered briefly if they had ever met her. Once people had they generally kept well away.

She was shouting at Lily at the moment and the sound went through his skull. His wife had taken the school bell from her and now Nancy was demanding its return.

Lily had changed overnight. It was as if knowledge of his mother's past had wiped away all fear of her.

He picked up the phone and began to dial the number of the Twilight Home for the Elderly.

Then there was a banging at his door.

'I'll get it, dear.' Putting down the phone, he opened the front door and saw two men.

One was large with a bald head and a toothless grin. The other was tall, athletically built and very well dressed.

'Joseph Markham?'

'Yes. Can I help you?'

'Would it be possible for us to talk in the house, Mr Markham? It's about George.'

Without stopping to think, Joseph stepped out of the way so the two men could enter.

'Who's that at the bloody door?'

Nancy's voice was at fever pitch. She was convinced the men would be coming to take her away at any moment.

'My mother. She's . . . not very well.'

Willy frowned.

'She sounds all right.'

Patrick was having trouble controlling himself.

'Look, about George. We wondered if you knew where he might be? He's not at home. We really need to find him quite urgently.'

Joseph frowned.

'Not at home? He was here yesterday. He came to visit Mother.'

'Did he? Was he alone?'

'Oh, yes, Elaine was working. Look, what's all this about?'

Patrick walked towards the voice. He pushed the door open and walked inside.

Nancy saw him and immediately calmed herself.

Patrick watched her. It was as if a new skin grew over her in a matter of seconds. The wrinkles evened out and her face took on a sublime expression.

'How do you do? Won't you take a seat? Lily, make some tea.'

He smiled at the woman, a wide friendly smile. So this was the scumbag's mother.

Lily looked at the two men and her eyebrows rose in a question. Joseph, in the doorway, shrugged in bewilderment. But if they shut his mother up, they could stay all day as far as he was concerned.

'Make the tea, Lily.' His voice was low.

She went from the room.

Patrick and Willy sat down.

'We're friends of George's, Mrs Markham. We wondered if anyone knew where we could find him?'

Nancy Markham patted her outrageous hair and smirked. 'I think there must be some mistake.'

'Sorry?' Patrick smiled again.

The woman's face hardened.

'My son hasn't got any friends.'

Willy and Patrick exchanged glances.

No wonder the bloke was a nutter. The whole family seemed a few paving slabs short of a patio.

Out in the kitchen, Lily and Joseph made the tea.

'Who the hell are they?' hissed Lily.

'I don't know.'

'Well, don't you think you ought to find out then? After all, they are ensconced in our living room with your mother.'

Joseph allowed himself a small grin.

'I think she can look after herself, Lily, don't you?'

He put a few biscuits on a plate and added them to the tray. He would sit in and listen to the conversation. For some reason he didn't fancy confronting the two men. They looked as if they could take good care of themselves.

George got off the plane and smiled at the hostesses. He walked down the flight of stairs and lifted his face to the bright Florida sun. He was in America. Before he knew what was going on he had collected his luggage, changed some money and was on a courtesy bus to Lindo's car rental on Sandlake Road.

The driver of the bus was a large man in a leather baseball hat with 'Chicago Bulls' in blood red lettering across the front. His voice had a slow southern drawl and George was enjoying listening to it. It was so American.

'Orlando Airport is one of only three airstrips that is capable of landing the Space Shuttle in an emergency. As y'all know, Kennedy Space Centre is only twenty minutes' drive from here, so if ever the shuttle missed its target, we could land it here, safe and sound.' He paused for maximum effect then continued, 'If you look out of your window on the left you will see a B52 bomber. This was used in the Vietnam War and is now here purely for ornamental purposes.'

George stared enthralled at the bomber, as did most of the little boys on the bus.

'In England I understand you see dead cats and rabbits on your highways. Well, here in Florida, don't be surprised to find baby 'gators flattened in the middle of the road. The

526

'gators are night creatures by nature and are very rarely seen during the daylight hours. They provide a natural security for the Space Centre, as you can imagine.' He paused again and everyone laughed nervously.

'But if you go to Gatorland you can have your photo taken with them and see the 'gator wrestlin'. Refreshments are provided there and you can even eat 'gator burgers.'

George listened enraptured. Oh, why hadn't he come here before?

The journey from Orlando Airport to Lindo's took only ten minutes and he and the other passengers were soon standing on a large lot, with their cases at their feet, waiting for their designated cars. George gave his papers to a tall slim black man and gasped with surprise when he returned driving a Chevrolet Caprice. In America this was a small compact car; to George it was on a par with a Porsche or a Ferrari.

The black man in his Lindo's overalls showed him how to open the boot, or trunk as he called it, how to put the car on automatic cruising, how the lights worked and where the fuel tank was.

George listened raptly, smiling incessantly. The man stowed his case in the trunk and shook his head at George's obvious pleasure.

He thanked the man and promptly opened the door and sat in the passenger seat.

The black man grinned at him.

'Y'all better git used to drivin' on the left, boy. Lessen' you end up havin' an accident.'

George got out of the car sheepishly and walked around to the driver's side. He slipped a crisp five-dollar bill into the man's hand.

George was elated. He had his car hire agreement tucked away safely in his pocket, he had a map of Orlando from the car hire company and a wad of dollars in his pocket. He felt like a millionaire.

He studied the map to find Edith's address. It was on Apopka Vineland Road, Windermere, Orange County.

It was only a few miles from where he was!

He relaxed and started the car. As he drove carefully away, the little girl from the plane waved to him from her mother's Dodge. George gave her a little wave back. She had won three pounds fifty off him eventually.

He pulled out on to Sandlake Road and started the journey to his sister's, full of excitement.

The sights and sounds around him astounded his eyes and ears. Big billboards proclaimed the delights of 'Wet'n'Wild', 'Disney World', 'Universal Studios' and 'Gatorland', which he already knew about.

George drank it all in.

He drove past large shopping malls that put English shopping centres to shame. He saw tanned, healthy-looking people, milling around car parks, either getting in or out of cars. Someone on the plane had said that no one walked anywhere out here and George now understood why.

It was much too big.

He turned on his radio and caught the lunchtime news. He shook his head in wonder.

It was five o'clock in England now. The wonder of the aeroplane! In eight and a half hours he had travelled thousands of miles to another time zone.

He pulled into a large car park and studied his map. He was nearly there. Unlike in England, American roads had large signs going across them with the place names written in black lettering. It was almost impossible to get lost. No straining the eyes to find the road sign as you passed the corner of the road here. Oh, no. The name of the road was emblazoned across it!

He had only two more sets of traffic lights to go and then he was there.

He drove out of the car park and resumed his journey. Americans seeing the 'Dollar' sign on the car made allowances for him and waved good naturedly.

George beamed back at them, full of camaraderie. He liked Americans.

He drove into Apopka Vineland Road. It was clearly

residential, but not what he'd imagined. The houses were large and beautiful. Edith lived at number 22620. George could not imagine a house number so big. He drove along the quiet road slowly, taking in his surroundings.

Edith and Joss must have done very well indeed to be able to afford to live here. He thought of Joseph's large house back in England. It looked like a shack compared to the properties here. The numbers were in the 22600s now and George felt excitement pound within him.

Then he saw it.

He stopped the car and stared at Edith's house. It was large, like all the others, and set well back from the road. It had a long, sweeping drive that led up to a whitewood house that positively sprawled. It had to be at least eighty feet across. It had a deep cherry red roof from the centre of which rose a turret with windows round it, like an observatory. The windows all over the house had cherry red shutters and the double front door was cherry red as well. The gardens alongside the drive sloped down to the road and were a riot of shrubs and trees. George could see a lemon tree with a white seat beneath it. The lawns were cut to perfection and he could hear the faint sounds of the sprinklers as they watered the ground.

He wished his mother was sitting in the back, so she could see how well Edith had done for herself. But only for a second. If his mother had been here, the day would have been ruined.

She ruined everything.

He would send her a photograph of the house, though, to annoy her. He drove cautiously up the drive to the front door and stopped the car.

Then pandemonium broke out.

Two large Dobermans appeared around the side of the house as if by magic. George saw two sets of teeth coming towards him and immediately set about closing the electric windows, the dogs' ferocious barking sending chills of fear through him.

Then he heard a female voice. 'Dante . . . Inferno . . .

Here, boys.' The two dogs immediately stopped in their tracks and ran towards the sound, their small stumpy tails like lather brushes wagging as they made their way to the woman standing by the side of the house. It was Edith.

A changed Edith.

She was wearing a white dress with a thick black belt around her waist and black high-heeled shoes. She was slim and curvaceous. George was amazed. Edith had never had breasts. She looked better now than she had twenty years ago. He watched her put up her hand to shield her eyes as she tried to see who was in the car.

He opened the door and stepped out.

The bigger of the two dogs made as if to run at him and Edith called it back.

'Hello, Edith. Long time no see.'

He watched happily as her eyes opened wide and her mouth curved into a grin.

'George?' Her voice was husky with emotion.

He nodded and then she was running towards him and into his arms, the dogs following, sensing that he was a friend.

'Oh, George . . . George! It's so good to see you. Why didn't you ring me and let me know you were coming? Where's Elaine? How's everything back home?'

The words were tumbling out, tripping over each other as Edith led him into her house. Her heart was bursting with happiness. She had experienced so much with George, he was her closest relative. Her childhood confidant. The only part of life in England that she regretted leaving. Now he was here with her, her happiness knew no bounds.

George held her arm tightly as they walked into the beautiful house, a lump of emotion in his throat.

There was nothing like family.

Patrick and Willy were driving back to Grantley.

'I'm telling you, Pat, she was nuttier than a squirrel's posing pouch. And that bloke Joseph weren't much better.'

Patrick nodded absently. It had been a waste of time. They had known nothing.

But the man had to be somewhere. If he used his credit card then Patrick would be on to him. Oh, he knew all the faces that could help him. He wasn't a repoman for nothing. He could find just about anyone, given time.

But time was something he didn't have.

If Kate found out who the Ripper was, then the police would be looking for Markham as well. He could still get to him in prison, but it wouldn't have the personal touch. And Pat wanted to do this job himself.

Chapter Twenty-eight

Patrick answered the telephone. A female voice came down the line.

'Mr Kelly?'

He yawned. 'Speaking.'

'I'm Louella Parker from Colmby Credit. I have some information regarding a Mr George Markham.'

Patrick felt a surge of excitement.

'Go on.'

'Subject to the usual terms, of course.' The woman's voice was crisp. 'I do rather put myself out for these things.'

'All right, all right, don't make a meal of it. If you tell me what I want to know you'll get the dosh.'

The woman cleared her throat delicately and he was glad for a moment that she was on the other end of a phone line, otherwise he would have grabbed her throat and shaken the information out of her.

'George Markham booked a flight to Orlando by credit card on the twentieth of this month. He was due to leave on the twenty-third. The company he travelled with was Tropical Tours.'

Patrick was stunned.

The dirty bastard had outwitted him!

'Mr Kelly, are you still there?'

'What? Oh, yeah. Sorry.'

'I trust that's what you wanted to know?'

'Oh . . . yes. Yes. You'll get the money, Miss Parker, in the usual way.'

While the woman thanked him, he put the phone down gently and stared out of the library window.

He'd gone to the States?

Patrick began looking through the phone book for the number of Tropical Tours. Once he had established the flight number and whether or not George Markham had been aboard, he would plan his next move.

Frederick Flowers scanned the sea of faces in front of him. He always felt nervous when addressing the press. You never quite knew what you would be asked.

'Is this the work of the Grantley Ripper?' The scruffy, bearded man stared into Flowers's face.

'I really cannot divulge that sort of information, as well you know. At the moment we are liaising with the Kent Constabulary to ascertain whether it is the same person.'

'Why is Detective Inspector Kate Burrows here, then? Do you think that a female officer might handle the case differently? Better?'

Flowers made a conscious effort not to screw up his eyes in annoyance.

'Detective Inspector Burrows is a very capable police-woman, she is respected by her colleagues and myself. Her sex has nothing to do with it.'

The female reporter pressed on, undeterred. 'Nevertheless, it is unusual for a female DI to be on a case of this size.'

'My dear girl, I assume you are writing with a feminist slant? Well, can I go on record as saying that we are here to trap a cold-blooded callous murderer, not to discuss sexual politics.' He turned from the woman and looked around. 'Who's next?'

The reporters laughed.

'Have you any idea at all who the man is? Any leads?' a booming voice called from the back.

'Was the child molested at all?' called another.

Kate followed Caitlin out of the building and to their car. Caitlin lit one of his cigars.

'It's funny you know, Kate, but why would the man come here?'

534

'I thought that, Kenny. I wondered if maybe he was visiting over this way. Could he work here maybe? Has he family in the area? The murders in Grantley were obviously done by someone who knows the neighbourhood. Maybe he lives here now but was brought up in Grantley? Why kill the child so brutally?'

Caitlin shook his head.

'The blood testing is backlogged, did you hear?'

Kate nodded. 'I heard. We need more manpower on it.'

'It's the results that are taking all the time. Still, we'll keep at it. Time's the one thing we haven't got, but it's also all we've got, if you get my meaning.'

Kate smiled wanly.

'I keep thinking of that child. How can we not have anything to go on? Jesus Christ!'

'Look, girl, Peter Sutcliffe took years to find. Then there was Dennis Nilsen. He was even cooking the poor fuckers' heads and no one would have found him if he hadn't blocked up his drains with human flesh. Murderers like this only get caught quickly in books and on TV. Real life is a different thing altogether. This man is probably discussing the murders with his family, friends, workmates, acting like he's as shocked as them. But underneath it all he's laughing at them and us. Oh, yes, especially us. He'll read the papers and grin all over his face.

'But you mark my words, he'll do something wrong and when he does make a mistake, we'll be waiting for him. And do you know the first thing I'm going to do?'

'What?'

Caitlin leaned towards her and grinned.

'I'm going to smack him once for every corpse that I've seen with his handiwork on it and twice as hard and as long for the child. It's what will keep me going.'

Kate turned from him. Before she could answer the reporters began filtering out of police headquarters and she started the car. The last thing she wanted was to get caught by them.

Caitlin's words troubled her though. More than she cared to admit. She was aware that any suspect they had now could be in great danger. James Redcar had put a different light on this inquiry altogether. Everyone knew that even criminals had their own code of conduct when it came to a child murderer. As soon as the Grantley Ripper was identified, there'd be more than just the police out to get him. She just hoped they could get to him first.

As she drove back towards the Dartford Tunnel she saw a plane taking off from Gatwick and sighed.

How she wished she was on it.

Patrick went back through Elaine's address book and grinned. Willy grinned back.

'He's gone to his sister's. Well, we can soon put a stop to his gallop. Get me Shaun O'Grady on the blower, I've just had a great idea.'

While Willy dialled, Patrick poured out a fresh cup of coffee. He had the man now. He was convinced of it.

He thought fleetingly of Kate. If she ever found out what he was going to do, she would never forgive him.

His mouth hardened. This had nothing to do with Kate, this was family business.

He sipped the hot coffee and lit a cigarette. Willy handed the phone to him.

'Shaun? It's me, Patrick, how are you?'

Shaun O'Grady sat in his luxurious home in Miami and whooped with delight.

'Hiya, Pat. How's tricks?'

'I've got some trouble, Shaun, family trouble.'

Shaun O'Grady pushed the woman beside him away. He pulled himself up to a sitting position and gestured to her to light him a cigarette.

'What kind of family trouble?'

'It's Mandy. My Mandy. She's dead.'

'Dead?' O'Grady's gravelly voice was disbelieving. 'What happened? Was it an illness, what?'

He took the proffered cigarette and pulled on it deeply, his

536

eyes travelling around the large room without seeing anything. He had been dealing with Patrick Kelly for over fifteen years. Although the two men had met face to face only twice, they had built up a mutual respect and friendship over the long-distance telephone line.

Shaun O'Grady was an American version of Patrick Kelly. Except Shaun O'Grady had branched out into other areas that Kelly knew about only through word of mouth. One of which was a service providing professional hits.

As Kelly spoke, the woman watched O'Grady's face. Sighing heavily, she pulled on a negligee and left the room. She switched on the thirty-six-inch television in the bedroom and, sprawling on the bed, began watching 'I Love Lucy'.

She knew Shaun well and when his face had that look, it was best to keep out of his way.

'Pat, Pat, I'm heart sore for you.' O'Grady thought of his own three daughters ensconced in a large house in Palm Springs with his ex-wife. He might not spend much time with them, he was a busy man, but they were his children, his flesh and blood. He felt a moment's guilt as he recalled he hadn't seen any of them since the Christmas holidays.

'What can I do to help you? You name it.'

'Our man is at this moment in Florida. That's why I've called you, Shaun. I want him removed from the earth. I want him dead.'

'It's as good as done, Pat. Give me the details and I'll see to it at once.'

'I'll send the money within a few days . . .'

'There's no need for money.'

'Fair dos, Shaun, I'll pay. I'll ring through the details in a couple of hours.'

If it was one of his daughters . . . O'Grady closed his eyes. It did not bear thinking about. He began to jot down Edith's address and after a short exchange both men rang off.

O'Grady sat on his white leather Italian settee and stared at the Salvador Dali on his wall. He was fifty-eight, with a bald head, long baggy jowls and a large belly that nothing would get rid of. He had short stubby legs and arms.

He caught his reflection in the mirror and wiped his hand across the stubble on his jaw.

He thought of his ex-wife's house, with its comfortable battered furniture and his three young daughters. He heard Lucille Ball's voice coming from the bedroom and winced.

He had exchanged all that for a bimbo and a two million dollar bachelor pad.

The joke was that Noreen, his ex-wife, had never tried to stop his affairs, so why the hell had he dumped her?

He picked up the telephone again and dialled her number. The phone was answered by his youngest daughter, Rosaleen.

'Hello, Daddy!' He heard her put the phone on the table with a clunk and call to her mother.

'Mommy, Mommy, Daddy's on the phone!'

O'Grady tried to ignore the sound of surprise in the child's voice.

Noreen's gentle New England twang came on the line. Noreen had class, he admitted that to himself. He should never have divorced her.

'Hello, Shaun, this is a surprise.'

As he began to answer, the woman came out of the bedroom. She still had on the negligee and her impossibly long brown legs were visible through it. She pushed back thick black hair and lit a cigarette with natural grace.

O'Grady watched her, fascinated, then spoke into the phone. 'I'm coming up at the weekend to see the children. OK?'

'Fine. Let me know when you'll be picking them up and I'll make sure they're ready. They do miss you, you know.'

'I'll call back with the details, Noreen.'

'Fine.'

She put the phone down.

He immediately began dialling again, his eyes on the woman's buttocks, shimmering beneath the thin silk. He smiled at her and she half smiled back, retreating once more into the bedroom.

538

'Hello, Duane? Get yourself over here now, I have a job for you.'

He put down the phone and stubbed out his cigarette. He could hear Ricky Ricardo's laugh and guessed that the programme was coming to an end.

Tasha loved the old programmes: 'I Love Lucy', 'The Three Stooges'. He had bought her the Marx Brothers collection. She was twenty-five.

How old was Noreen now? Thirty-eight? Thirty-nine?

He would see more of the girls, he was determined on that. Christ, what Pat had told him made you think! Who said the screwballs were only in America.

George was the centre of attention and loving every second of it. Edith looked fantastic and he couldn't take his eyes off her. Her hair was perfectly coiffeured. He knew it must be dyed, but it was dyed a natural colour and it suited her. She did not look like a woman in her fifties. Joss, on the other hand, looked every bit of his sixty-five years. His face was deep brown and leathery. Both of them had American twangs which George found exciting and attractive.

Edith was talking nineteen to the dozen.

'I've been in touch with the children and they're both coming tomorrow. Joss Junior, as we call him, is flying from Denver – that's in Colorado. He works for a big drug company. And Natalie is driving up from Miami, she works for a cosmetics company there. She's a buyer, you know. Wait until you see them, George. They're beautiful.'

'I wish Elaine and I had been blessed with children, but after the boy died . . .' His voice trailed off and Edith looked at him with ready tears gathering in her eyes.

How could Elaine have left him? After all this time too. The woman was a heartless bitch and if she ever saw her again, which she admitted was unlikely, she would say so to her face. Poor George. He had no luck with women. First their tramp of a mother and now Elaine. She pursed her perfectly painted coral lips.

Joss's loud, booming voice broke into her thoughts. 'How about we take Georgie here into Orlando for a slap-up meal? We could go to the Mercado on International Drive.'

Edith smiled widely, displaying all her expensive dentistry. 'Oh, let's. George, they have thirty-two ounce steaks there.'

George was worried. 'I don't think I could eat all that, Edith.'

'You old silly, we share it! Come on, let's get ready.'

In the back of her mind, she hoped George had a decent suit with him. He looked so damned touristy.

Still, she reasoned, it was lovely to see him. She fought down the impulse to squeeze him to her again. She was so damned pleased to see him, she could take a big bite out of him. Instead she put her arm around him and kissed him lightly on the cheek.

'It sure is good to see you, George. So good.'

'And you, Edith, my dear. It's been far too long.'

She accompanied him to the spacious guest room. She was amazed that her brother, whom she had honestly thought she would never see again, was actually in her home. Her beautiful home that she hoped he told their mother all about when he went back. That would be one in the eye for the old bitch!

'How's Mother, George?' She sat on his bed, her face troubled now. Every time she thought of her mother, she thought of the child.

George sat beside her and took her hand. 'The same as always, Edith. Spiteful, nasty. She hasn't changed.'

'I bet.' Her voice was vehement. 'Does she know about Elaine? Leaving you, I mean?'

George shook his head vigorously. 'No. I was going to tell her, I visited her just before I flew out here, but we got into a bit of an argument.'

Edith's eyebrows arched.

'Don't you mean she argued with you?' The playfulness was back now.

George grinned. 'No. Actually, I told her what I thought of

her. I only wish I hadn't left it so long.' He rubbed a hand over his eyes. 'Edith, did you know that mother . . . was . . . well, a good-time girl?' He found it difficult to form the words. He found it even more difficult to understand Edith's laughter.

'What's so funny?' He was getting annoyed now.

'Oh, George, you always were the eternal innocent. I sometimes think that's why she picked on you so much. Don't you remember all the men she used to have around? Remember her fights with them and her drunken ramblings?'

'Of course I do, but I never thought she was . . . well, charging them.'

Edith sighed.

'You get changed, George, and we'll go out and have a big juicy steak and a really good time. Mother's thousands of miles away. She couldn't harm us now, even if she wanted to.'

George smiled his assent, but inside his head a little voice said: 'Can't she?' He would have been surprised to know that Edith was thinking exactly the same thing.

Alone in his room, he looked around at the blues and greens of the furnishings. On the hardwood floor, Indian rugs were placed at strategic points and the cover on the bed matched them perfectly. It really was a lovely room and a far cry from the house they had been brought up in.

He opened the wardrobe door and was surprised to find a bathroom in there. He filled the bath and poured in some bath salts he found on the window sill.

He was in America, in Florida with his Edith, Mother was not going to spoil it. He sank back in the water and let his mind wander on to other, more relaxing things.

Edith, more disturbed than she cared to admit, went to her own room and, opening her wardrobe, took down from the top shelf a little box. Placing it on her large oval bed, she opened it and took out the old black and white pictures.

There was George, in his short trousers and long grey school socks. There was Joseph and herself. She peered at each picture for a long while. In each and every photo, not one of the children was smiling.

Patrick was ecstatic. He had George Markham! He was disappointed that he could not put the man away himself, but he accepted that. He was grateful that he had done something. It was the frustration of knowing the man was somewhere safe, laughing up his sleeve, that had really got to him.

Now, though, he had him. Shaun O'Grady was going to see that he was no more. Just thinking about it gave Patrick a thrill.

If Kate knew what he had arranged today . . . He closed his eyes. Kate was good. Kate was everything that was right and decent and he loved her for those very qualities. Until they intruded on his concerns, that is.

He knew that if she had even an inkling that he knew the Grantley Ripper's name and whereabouts, she would create havoc. She wanted to bring the man to justice. Her justice.

Well, the man was getting Patrick's kind of justice and it had a much sweeter taste to it so far as he was concerned.

He clenched his fists. George Markham would soon be dead.

Dead, dead, dead!

He looked at Mandy's photograph on the mantelpiece and his face sobered. What he wouldn't give to have her back. Sometimes, late at night, when the house was quiet, he imagined he heard her voice.

He awoke, covered in sweat, hearing her crying. Calling out for him in distress. He would put his hands over his ears to blot out the noise.

It was then he imagined her terror.

The acute fear that must have enveloped her as the man began to pound her face with his fists. The thought of her lying there, on that dirty floor, while the bastard raped her . . .

He could still see her face, battered beyond recognition, as she lay in the hospital. He still heard the low buzz of the life support machine as it failed in its job. Saw her bruised body as it jerked with the electric shocks they'd used to try to resuscitate her heart.

Oh, George Markham had a big payout coming to him.

The telephone rang and he jumped.

'Hello?'

'Hello, Pat? It's me, Jerry. The fight's at the old hat factory near the Roman Road. I've faxed the directions through to you, OK? It's a nine-thirty start.'

Patrick closed his eyes, he had forgotten about the fight.

'Look, Jerry, I might not be able to make it. I've got a lot on here.'

'Okey doke. It's gonna be a good one though. If I see you, I see you then. Ta rah.'

He replaced the receiver and sighed. He had been looking forward to the fight. He liked illegal boxing matches. It was like the old-style bare knuckle fighting of years ago. No one knew where the matches were to be held until a couple of hours in advance. That way the Old Bill, by the time they did find out where the venue was, were too late to do anything about it. The crowd and the fighters were long gone.

Patrick poured himself another generous measure of whisky and glanced at his watch. He wished O'Grady would ring with the details so he could really relax. He took a large sip of his drink.

A little while later the phone rang again and Kelly picked it up. He was gratified to hear the distant whirring and clicking of a long-distance call.

'Hi, Pat. Can you hear me OK?'

'I can hear you, clear as a bell.'

'It's arranged. Your man will be out of the way in the next three days. It'll cost fifty thou – dollars that is. I have one of my best men working on it. He's already setting it all up.'

'I'll have the money with you in twenty-four hours. Thanks, Shaun, I won't forget what you've done for me.'

'Hey, what are friends for? I'll keep you posted, OK? You just try and get over your loss, Pat. I'll sort out everything this end.'

'Thanks, Shaun. 'Bye.'

'No problem. Talk to you soon.'

The line was dead.

He had George's address and now he knew when he was to die. Patrick smiled to himself. It wasn't too late to go to the boxing match after all. Might take his mind off everything for a while.

Willy pulled up outside the hat factory and Patrick helped Kate from the car. There were people everywhere. She was aware that their arrival had caused a stir and instinctively stayed close to Patrick. He pushed his way towards the entrance, greeting people here and there. Then they were inside. A haze of cigarette smoke hit them both full in the face and a little grizzled man ran towards them, a large grin splitting his face.

'Pat! Pat! You made it. Hello, my dear.'

'Jerry, this is Kate, a special friend of mine. Kate, Jerry. An old reprobate.'

Kate smiled and took the tiny hand in hers.

'How do you do?'

Jerry sized her up expertly. Not the usual tit and bum that Kelly saddled himself with, but not bad for her age.

'I do very well, my dear. Come, I've saved you some front row seats.'

Patrick held on to her arm as they moved through the crowd. Loud soul music was coming from speakers and everyone was shouting to be heard above it. The place was filled to capacity already and Kate was amazed at the sights and sounds around her. Touts were openly taking bets and when the large boxing ring came into view she was even more puzzled. Surely he hadn't brought her to an illegal boxing match?

Jerry ushered them to their seats. Kate looked at Patrick sternly.

'Is this what I think it is?'

He laughed. 'Yes. Quick, Kate, over there!'

He pointed. Sitting on the opposite side of the ring was Chief Constable Frederick Flowers and what looked to Kate like half the Serious Crime Squad. She waved weakly as Flowers whistled and called over to them, obviously the worse for drink. Patrick was laughing his head off and Kate turned on him.

'You brought me here deliberately, didn't you?' He saw the confusion in her eyes and was sorry he'd laughed.

'I didn't know they'd be here, Katie, I promise you. I was coming here on me own account and then I thought you'd enjoy it. I just wanted to be with you.' He smiled and put his hand to his heart like a schoolboy. 'Scout's honour.'

'Well . . . you said it would be an experience.'

'It will. Now then, how much shall we bet?'

Kate frowned. 'How about a fiver?'

'Listen, darlin', if I bet a fiver here my reputation would go down quicker than free Bushmill's at an Irish wake! I'm putting a ton on Rankin Rasta Dave, my love. He'll piss it.'

As he spoke, the '2001 Space Odyssey' theme came over the speakers and a large Rastafarian walked from the makeshift dressing rooms. Kate gasped with surprise. The man was huge, with enormous arms and legs. His hair was tied back in a pony tail of big fat dreadlocks like sausages. He had a handsome, proud face. The crowd was cheering or jeering depending on whether they had a bet on him.

Pat got up and said, 'You keep looking at him with love in your eyes while I go and put the bets on, all right?'

Kate grinned despite herself. She had never seen such a big man. He stood in the ring, jumping around, shadow boxing and flexing his oiled muscles. A woman nearby tapped Kate on the arm and shouted: 'He could put his boots under my bed any day of the week.'

Kate put her hand to her mouth with shock and then laughed outright. Then the music changed and she heard Dana singing 'All Kinds of Everything' and a mighty cheer went up.

Another large man climbed into the ring. He held enormous arms above his head in an arrogant stance. He had

545

a big, finely chiselled face surrounded by shaggy red hair. Little blue eyes like pieces of flint surveyed his opponent and, to the satisfaction of his supporters, obviously found him lacking. He held up a large gloved hand at the Rasta and spat on the floor aggressively.

Patrick slipped back into his seat. His voice startled her. 'That, Katie, is Big Bad Seamus. He's come over from Dublin especially to fight the Londoner, Rasta Dave. There's an awful lot of money riding here tonight.'

Kate looked at him, her eyes troubled.

'I can't believe I'm here. I've never seen anything like this in my life. They're going to batter each other's brains out, aren't they?'

Kelly grinned. 'I bloody hope so, girl. If they don't the crowd will tear them apart themselves.'

A small man in a dinner suit climbed into the ring and began announcing the rules of the fight which to Kate seemed to mean only one thing: anything was allowed bar sawn-off shot guns or knives. Then both men sat in their corners while a half-naked young girl walked around the ring to whistling and cat calling, holding up a piece of cardboard with 'Round 1' on it. A bell went and the two men came at each other like bulls in the proverbial china shop.

Kate watched, amazed, as they began to fight. The Rasta took the initiative from the first punch. He delivered pounding blows to the Irishman's head again and again. Kate watched in morbid fascination. The Irishman was up now. He lunged at the Rastafarian, head butting him sickeningly just below his eye. She watched the swelling rise and put her hand to her mouth. She closed her eyes tightly. This was barbaric. Two grown men pummelling the life out of one another. The atmosphere in the warehouse was charged and Kate glanced around her. She saw women standing up screaming at the two men; now that the fight was getting really violent it was as if they had been waiting for the real beating to begin. Kate's eyes were dragged towards Frederick Flowers, who had also leapt from his seat and was shouting advice into the ring.

'Nut the bastard back! Don't let the Irish ponce get away with that!'

The black man in the ring seemed to heed the advice and was once more hammering the life out of the Irishman.

Kate watched Flowers as if she had never seen him before. He had made press statements about illegal boxing matches, as he had on many subjects over the years. It was one of the things he was supposed to be stamping out. Out of uniform and with too much drink in him, he looked what he was, a cheap shyster. Gone was the aura of respectability, the wise demeanour he assumed all day as the Chief Constable. In its place was just another assumed persona. The 'I'm one of the lads really' character. There wasn't much to separate him and Patrick.

A dark-haired woman in her twenties brought Flowers a drink and he took it from her without acknowledging her presence. She sat in his vacated seat and pulled her skirt down ineffectively. She was definitely not Mrs Flowers. Kate had met Flowers's wife on two separate occasions. She was a very refined woman, given to wearing sombre plaids and sensible shoes.

Why had Patrick brought her here, anyway?

Somewhere in her mind, Kate heard a bell. She looked at the ring and saw the two men swaggering back to their respective corners.

'All right girl?' Patrick's voice was concerned.

Kate stared at him. Despite all the noise and confusion around them, he seemed to sense her feelings.

'Katie?' He raised his eyebrows a fraction and Kate looked away. Flowers now had his hand halfway up the bimbo's skirt. Patrick followed her gaze. Kate saw him grin and felt a tightening around her heart. He looked at her again.

'He's a right old slag is Freddie. That's not his bird as such, Kate. She charges about two ton a night. She's on the bash.'

His eyes went back to the ring. Another girl, black this time, was walking around the ring swinging her skinny hips, holding a piece of cardboard with 'Round 2' written on it.

The Irishman grabbed her as she passed and put her over his shoulder, pretending to bite her buttocks. The girl squealed with delight, loving all the extra attention.

Kate watched the Rasta put his whole head into a bucket of water and come up shaking his hair like a shaggy dog, sending droplets of water everywhere.

Patrick lit two cigarettes and passed one to Kate. She took it gratefully.

'Patrick . . .'

She was going to tell him she wanted to leave but the bell had gone again and it was too late. His whole attention was on the ring.

Kate watched, sickened, as the hammering and pounding started again, even harder this time. About two minutes into the round the atmosphere changed again, becoming charged with malice. The black man was different somehow. His punches were landing heavily on the Irishman's face. Kate saw the lumps form around his eyes and mouth. Then the crowd surged forward in their seats. The Irishman was down on one knee. The black fighter saw his chance and took it. Swinging back his enormous arm he began pounding it into the other man's face and head.

The crowd were ecstatic. Women as well as men were screaming out advice to the two fighters. Kate watched terrified as the black man dragged the Irishman up from the floor and, holding him up, began to pummel his face and body. The Irishman was out on his feet and still the merciless hammering went on. Finally, after what seemed an age, the Rasta threw the man on to the canvas, delivering a swift kick to the groin as his last shot.

The Irishman lay there as if crucified, his arms spread out on either side of him.

The crowd were going wild. In the back small fights had broken out among rival fans. In the ring the Rasta was walking round, arms held up in the air like a conquering hero. His dreadlocks had freed themselves and now flew this way and that around his face as he moved. A tall, good-looking white woman of about thirty climbed into the ring and threw herself into his arms, landing a smacking kiss on his swollen and bruised lips.

Patrick turned to face Kate. 'That's Veronica Campella, otherwise known as violent Veronica . . . She's his manager. Veronica's got one of the biggest stables in England and she knows her job all right. She got him a twenty grand purse for tonight. Not bad for two rounds, is it? She even takes her boys as far as China and the States for fights.' Kelly's voice was admiring.

Kate was silent as she saw the Irishman being helped from the ring. The Rasta went to him and they embraced like old friends. The Irishman was obviously a good loser.

'Can we go now, Pat, please?'

'There's another couple of fights on yet, Kate.' He looked at her closely. 'What's the matter?' His voice was genuinely puzzled.

'I just want to get out of here. It's horrible. All this,' she spread her arms out, 'makes me feel sick to my stomach.'

For a fleeting second she saw a flicker of annoyance cross Patrick's features. Then he seemed to remember who she was, because he smiled at her sadly.

'Not a very good idea this, was it?'

Kate picked up her bag from the floor and shook her head.

'Not really. I don't like legal boxing, Patrick. I can't stand any form of violence.'

'Then we'd better go, hadn't we?'

She knew that she had annoyed him for real this time. His voice was flat and he walked through the crowd ahead of her, nodding here and shaking hands as he went. As they left the heat and excitement of the hall and walked out into the cold air, Willy appeared as if by magic.

'How did you fare, Pat?'

'Not quite as well as I expected, Willy. You?'

Kate heard the tone of voice and gritted her teeth.

'Won meself a quick grand. I knew the soot could take him, Pat. I just knew it. That boy can fight!'

Patrick smiled at him. 'You stay and watch the rest of the action, Willy.'

549

'What about you two?'

Patrick sighed. 'I'm quite capable of driving me own car, Willy.'

Willy knew something was up. Kate looked like a wet weekend in Brighton and Patrick didn't look much better. He handed over the keys.

'Well . . . If you're sure . . .'

He didn't like Pat driving the Roller, she was his baby.

'Well, don't gun her, right? She ain't really used to you driving her. You have to know how to handle her . . .'

'Willy!' Patrick's voice was clipped.

'What?'

Patrick pushed his face close to the other man's and said, 'Good bye.'

With that he opened the passenger door for Kate and walked round to the driving seat. Kate got into the car in dead silence. Willy watched them closely all the time, shaking his head. Patrick started the engine and wheelspun the car out of the car park, sending stones showering everywhere. On the main road he settled down to sixty miles an hour and in the darkness Kate heard him laugh bitterly.

'What's the big joke?' Her voice was flat.

'That bloody Willy, sometimes I wonder why I've kept him on so long. He's more like me mother than me minder.'

'He's a good friend to you, that's why.' Kelly's criticism added to Kate's annoyance.

Patrick pulled the car into a layby and cut the engine.

'Listen here, I don't need this crap, Kate. From the moment you saw Freddie Flowers you've had the bleeding hump . . .'

Kate interrupted him.

'That's not true! You had the audacity to take me to an illegal boxing match, Patrick. Just because my Chief Constable was there and having the time of his life doesn't mean to say I had to. I thought it was barbaric, cruel and degrading, not just to the two men who fought, but to the people who paid money to see it.'

'What this boils down to, Kate, is this. We come from different worlds. I ain't apologising for taking you there, no matter what you say. I am what I am, Kate, you take me as you find me.'

'And the same goes for me, Pat, I'm not apologising either.'

They looked at each other in the dimness of the car, the atmosphere thick and pungent. Kate felt her heart hammering; she had to let him know what she was feeling. Suddenly, this wasn't about boxing any more, it was about them, the two of them as people. The differences between them.

Patrick lit them both another cigarette.

'What do you want from me, Kate?' It was a plea.

Kate paused.

'I want a bit of respect. I want to be cared for. But most of all, I want to feel that I am not compromising myself in any way by being with you. That . . . that . . . spectacle tonight made me feel physically ill. When they began to really pummel one another, it scared me.'

Kate heard the whirr of the electric window being lowered.

Patrick stared out on to the road. Cars whizzed by, their engines intruding now into their world. A cold breeze settled around them. Patrick sighed. It was the sigh of an old man.

'I'm sorry, Kate. You're right. What else can I say? I know we're different, but most of the time we're on the same wavelength. I've had to rethink a lot of life in the last few months. Like when I sold the massage parlours . . .' He paused to pull on his cigarette. 'I should never have taken you there tonight, I see that now. Even if you wasn't an Old – I mean a DI – you're not geared up for that type of thing. Renée wasn't, either. All I can say in my defence is . . .' He turned to face her. 'It's been a long time since I had a woman who didn't just go along with whatever I wanted to do.'

Kate searched his face in the darkness, she could make out his features, and her eyes caressed them one by one. He kissed her lightly on the lips and it was like an electric shock going through her body. 'I'm not sorry for being what I am, Kate, let's get that straight now. I'm apologising for not thinking about you and what you must be feeling. Does that make sense?'

Kate nodded.

'Well then, give us a proper kiss.'

He pulled Kate into his arms and kissed her hard on the mouth.

As they broke apart, Kate saw a head look in at the window.

'Is everything all right, sir?'

Neither of them had noticed the Panda car pull up behind them.

'Yes, thank you, officer, everything's fine. We're just going.'

Kate smiled at the officer and as Patrick pulled out of the layby she put her hand over his on the steering wheel.

'I don't want us to fight, Pat.'

'Let's just forget abut all this. Now, how about some food? What do you fancy? Italian, French, Spanish, chinky, what?'

Kate laughed. 'How about an Indian?'

'Trust you to say the one food I missed out! Tell you what, how about we skip the meal and just go home to bed?'

'No way.'

Patrick sighed. 'It was worth a try.'

Kate squeezed his hand gently. 'I never go to bed on an empty stomach.'

Suddenly she wanted him so badly she could taste it. She felt him put his foot down on the accelerator.

'Willy told you not to gun the car.'

He glanced at her and smiled.

'Willy didn't say anything about emergencies.'

Much later, as she lay beside him, the smell of him in her nostrils and the laziness that rough lovemaking brings enveloping her, she pondered her situation.

The warm loving individual beside her would murder the Grantley Ripper at the drop of a hat. He was capable of murder, she knew that. He had never made any secret of it.

Yet still she wanted him.

He stood for everything she disagreed with. The bed she was lying in was paid for through one or other of his borderline businesses, and he had taken her to an illegal boxing match. Yet one look at his handsome face and she could forgive him anything.

Anything? she asked herself again, and couldn't answer.

Not honestly anyway.

She snuggled down deeper into his arms. She felt his flaccid penis against her leg, moist and soft, and felt the thrill of him again. He woke momentarily and drew her towards him as if surprised to find her there. She kissed him on the mouth hungrily, trying desperately to empty her mind. He rubbed her breasts roughly and she responded by kissing him harder.

'Kate?'

'What?'

'You can deny this if you want, but I think that big Rasta turned you on.'

'Oh, you!'

He grabbed hold of her and kissed her again, slipping on top of her as if they were made to fit. She was glad of it.

Neither had mentioned the murders or the fight. It was as if they had an unspoken agreement to drop the subject. But even in the throes of orgasm, it was in the back of both their minds.

Eventually, it would all come up again. Their differences, their divided opinions on right and wrong, these would bring them into conflict.

And it would bring them grief.

Chapter Twenty-nine

Duane Portillo watched number 22620 Apopka Vineland Road. He sat opposite the house eating a sandwich and waiting for his quarry to show himself. He had been furnished with a description that fitted the man he had seen earlier perfectly. All he needed to establish now was that the guy was English. He bit into his sandwich, savouring the taste of moist chicken and crisp salad. He had been there over two hours and the two Dobermans had been watching him from the gates with beady eyes.

Duane approved of the dogs. If he had a house like that he would have had two similar dogs. He knew exactly what could happen to you if someone decided to rob you. He knew because he had been a robber himself for a while. Now he enjoyed the good life. He just let loose a few bits of lead and was paid a great deal of money. It was an arrangement that suited him. He would give this guy another thirty-six hours before he wasted him, Mr O'Grady's orders.

Duane guessed in his shrewd way that he was waiting for the money to arrive before committing himself. Mr O'Grady was one clever guy. Duane blessed the day he had met up with him.

Duane caressed the gun case on the passenger seat. It held his favourite weapon, a Ruger mini 14. It had an accurate range of four to five hundred yards and he used the .223 bullets that had been used in Vietnam. They could blow a man's brains out while sounding no louder than a whisper.

He finished his sandwich and started his car. He drove a few hundred yards down the road, turned the car around and watched the house from a different angle.

Sure enough, he saw what he was looking for.

He picked up his binoculars and watched the man through them. He didn't look like someone with fifty thousand dollars on his head. Duane shrugged mentally. Well, whatever the man looked like, it didn't matter. What did matter was that he had annoyed someone in England enough to merit his head being blown off. And Duane would do just that.

George had got up early and was enjoying the sunshine in the garden. He could not help looking at the swimming pool. Its water shone, blue and cool, and he wished he had the guts to jump in it. But George couldn't swim.

His niece and nephew were due later in the day and he was excited at the prospect of seeing them. Especially Natalie. He had seen photographs of her and she really was a good-looking girl.

Edith had informed him that she never rose before ten so he had the early morning to himself. Edith's housekeeper, a pretty Mexican woman, told him that he should go and explore and he thought he might just take her advice. He fetched his car keys and made his way from the house. The two Dobermans growled at him as he passed them and George hurriedly opened the gates and drove through. Then, shutting them carefully, he began to drive.

He was completely unaware of the large Buick trailing him. George drove towards Orlando itself, enjoying the clean sunshine of Florida. He had rolled up the sleeves of his shirt and now, with the sunroof open and a light breeze playing through his hair, he relaxed. After a while he found what he was looking for: the Orange Blossom Trail.

Last night at dinner, Edith and Joss had told him about the Orange Blossom Trail, saying its lovely name belied its function. It was downtown Orlando, where the tourists who flocked to Disney only went by accident. It was the Orlando version of Soho and George couldn't wait to get there.

He drove along enthralled. It was full of sleazy hotels

advertising blue movies and waterbeds. Women of every shape, colour and description stood around dressed in tiny bikinis, their bodies tanned to a leathery mahogany. Some of the women lounged against their own trailers, mobile homes that they used to entertain their customers, thereby saving on hotel bills. George drank it all in like a man dying of thirst. He smiled at different women and was pleased when they smiled back. He came across a place called the Doll's House which promised delights such as topless dancers and drinking partners.

George carried on driving, until he came to the heart of the Orange Blossom Trail. Gone now were the big hotels of International Drive and the shopping malls. Gone were the pleasant-faced people wishing you 'Have a nice day now'. Here were the shanties, with people slumped outside them in various states of drunkenness or drug-induced lethargy. Here, shoeless children watched vacant-eyed as an obviously strange car drove by. Here, dirty-looking men pushed themselves from walls and lurched towards George's car, causing him to put down his foot on the accelerator. Here was the last stop for the poor, the addicted and the criminal.

George looked around him now in dismay. Turning the car, he drove back to the Doll's House and parked. Within seconds, women and men were propositioning him. George stepped from the car, locking it, and began to stroll along. A young girl waved at him and began to walk leisurely towards him. George stopped to feast his eyes on her.

'Hi.'

'Hello, dear.'

'Why, yo' English. Are you from London?'

George smiled. 'Originally. I don't live there any more.'

The girl looked disappointed. She thought London was England. 'What you lookin' for? Maybe I kin' help you.'

George stood in the dirty, dusty street, in the hot sunshine, and felt a thrill of expectation.

'I'm looking for a little fun.'

The girl smiled, displaying crooked teeth. 'Well, you certainly came to the right place. My name's Loretta.'

'George.'

'Well, George, how about you and me go for a little walk? My trailer's just down the road a mite.'

George walked with her, listening to her chatter. She greeted people as she passed them. Her soft southern drawl was captivating, he decided. She was no more than eighteen. George climbed into the trailer behind her and she shut the door, turning to smile at him.

'Would you like a drink. I ain't got no icebox, but the beer's usually cold enough.'

He nodded at her and she bent over to open the cupboard under the tiny sink. George watched her bikini bottom ride up into the cleft of her buttocks. As she straightened up with the can of beer, a little smile on her face, she saw the man staring at her strangely.

Englishmen were so cold. Maybe it was the climate. She had heard that it rained all the time there.

'You OK?'

George smiled, his little smile that just showed his teeth. 'Perfectly.'

Duane sat watching in his Buick. He lit himself a cigarette and settled down to wait for the Englishman to do his business.

Jack Fenton was a retired Army corporal who had lived in Bychester Terrace for ten years. He was not a man to mix very much with his neighbours, but he knew their comings and goings. His wife Daisy said he was nosy, but as far as Jack was concerned he was just observant.

Like the other night when he'd heard a car pull up late in the night, a Rolls-Royce no less, and two men going into the Markhams' next door. That had thrown him, he admitted. The Markhams kept themselves to themselves, and in Jack's book that was how it should be. But all the same he would have liked to know who the men were. It was a lovely car. In the end he had put it down to rich relations.

Now their overflow pipe was another matter. He had

558

noticed when he had gone down to get his newspaper and his Woodbines that their overflow was causing a bit of distress. There was a large puddle around the side of the house. He had knocked but got no answer. So after a strong cup of tea he had informed his wife that he was just going next door for a recce. He still used army slang to the annoyance of Daisy, who hated the armed forces with all her heart.

Pulling on his wellingtons Jack went next door. It was a fine crisp morning and he took a few deep lungfuls of air, feeling the burn as it went down his throat. Then he began to cough dangerously so took out his Woodbines, puffing on one until it controlled the tickle. He surveyed the offending overflow pipe, the Woodbine clamped firmly between his teeth.

A blockage somewhere, he would lay money on it. He opened the back gate and walked into the garden, ducking to avoid the falling water. If George and Elaine weren't careful they'd end up with damp in their walls.

Then he saw the Markhams' back door.

He walked purposefully towards it and shook his head. There was a perfect round hole cut in the glass by the door handle.

He himself still had the original wire-reinforced glass in his door. The Markhams had a hardwood back door with four glass panels in the top.

Jack wasn't surprised when the door opened. He walked into the kitchen, his nose quivering like a bloodhound's.

The place was spotless.

He walked into the lounge and found the same. Nothing had been touched.

There was something strange afoot here or his name wasn't Jack Fenton. Picking up the telephone he dialled the police. Then he sat at the kitchen table and waited patiently for them to arrive.

A Panda car finally came over an hour later. Jack opened the door and showed them the evidence in silence. The two young PCs dutifully looked around and declared him right. There had been some kind of break in.

'Do you know where the occupants of the house are?'

Jack looked at them as if they were imbeciles. They didn't total his age between them.

'They're at work, of course.'

'Where do they work? Do you know?'

'Course I know. I'm their neighbour, aren't I?'

The elder of the two PCs took a deep breath.

'Well, if you'd be so kind as to tell us?'

'Her, that's the wife, Elaine, she works at the supermarket in town. What's it called? Lowprice or whatever. As for George, he works on the Industrial Estate at Kortone Separates.'

'Thank you. Did you notice anything suspicious at all, before you saw the window?'

'Well, I don't know if this means anything, but I saw a Rolls Royce here the other night. Two men got out of it and knocked here.'

'Are you sure it was a Rolls Royce?'

'Course I'm sure. I just said so, didn't I?' His strident voice was beginning to get on the PCs' nerves.

'You want to get a plumber in, boys, that overflow's going to do some damage, I tell you. Well, I'm off home. I only live next door if you need me.'

He left the house, shaking his head sadly. He had expected detectives at least.

PC Dendy radioed the break-in to the information room. The duty officer sent a constable to Lowprice to speak to Mrs Markham and was told she had been off sick for a week. The constable had then gone to Kortone Separates and been told Mr Markham had recently retired.

Puzzled, he radioed both messages in, and the desk sergeant, being a suspicious man, had a talk with plain clothes. There was more going on here than met the eye. Rolls Royces turning up in the middle of the night? Holes cut in windows and the video still in the front room? Neither occupant of the house to be found? One sick and one retired? It didn't add up.

Caitlin was told about the mysterious case in his coffee

break and would have laughed if it hadn't been for one thing: the Rolls Royce. A deep red Rolls Royce, Kelly's car.

He got the address from the desk sergeant and drove around to Bychester Road himself. The PCs were surprised to see him.

'Has anyone been back yet?'

'No, sir. It doesn't look as if anything's been taken.'

'I want you to search this place thoroughly. The house and the shed and the garage. Thoroughly, mind.'

'What are we looking for, sir?'

Caitlin smiled. 'That's just it, lads. I don't really know.'

He was outside in his car smoking one of his cigars when a PC came outside and tapped on the window.

'I think you'd better have a look at this, sir, I don't know if it means anything.'

Caitlin followed him through the house and up the garden to the shed. There were all George's magazines and scrapbooks.

Caitlin nodded to himself. His hunch has been right. There was only one thing wrong: it seemed Patrick Kelly had found the Grantley Ripper first.

He went out to his car and radioed in.

Kate was there within ten minutes with her squad. They began systematically to tear the house apart. No one was really sure what they were looking for until DS Willis and DS Spencer went up into the loft.

'Cor! What's that bloody awful smell?'

Spencer turned on the light as he spoke and Willis pulled the lid off the water tank.

Spencer watched as he staggered backwards, his hands over his mouth, until he dropped out of sight through the loft entrance.

The other detective sergeant went to the tank and put his handkerchief over his nose.

Elaine was lying on her side, her head at an impossible angle. Her eyes were milky white and bulbous. Her waterlogged skin was purple-grey and swollen.

He fainted just as Kate and Caitlin climbed into the loft.

Kate called through the hatch: 'Someone get up here and remove Spencer, please, and call the pathologist.'

Kate and Caitlin took one glance at Elaine and then looked at each other. This was the Grantley Ripper's home all right, complete with dead wife.

The only question was, where was George Markham?

In Caitlin's mind there was another question. Where the hell was Kelly?

He made a mental note to have the Rolls Royce part omitted from the next-door neighbour's statement. Until he knew more, anyway.

He stared at Kate, a look of sadness on his face. She instinctively put her hand on his arm, assuming that he was sad for the poor woman in front of them.

It never occurred to her that the sympathy could have been for her.

The mood in the incident room was one of pure elation. They had the Grantley Ripper.

Kate allowed Caitlin to give her a glass of whisky. Everyone was patting themselves on the back, laughing and joking.

She picked up her phone as it rang. It was Frederick Flowers, and Kate held her arms up for hush as she put the phone on to the intercom.

'Well done, one and all. I knew you'd catch him. I'm releasing the news to the press in a couple of hours. You can all be very proud of yourselves.'

As he rang off, an almighty cheer erupted from everyone. Caitlin kissed Kate on the cheek and she hugged him. It was over. All they had to do was find him, and now they had his name, that was a formality.

Then Amanda Dawkins tapped Kate on the shoulder. The girl's serious expression made her frown.

'What's up?'

'I think you'd better put a stop to the party, ma'am. George Markham was blood tested. It was a negative.'

'What!'

Kate's shout cut through the noise around her and gradually it died down. She took the piece of paper from Amanda and read the results wearily.

George Markham had tested negatively.

They had been celebrating too soon.

She passed the paper to Caitlin, who stared at it for a long time.

'Shit . . .' The word was drawn out from between his lips.

'I can't believe it. I just can't believe it.' Kate's voice was low. She clenched her fist. 'I thought we had him there!'

The policemen and women began to whisper amongst themselves as the news penetrated them. The atmosphere in the room went flat in a matter of seconds.

Kate took a swig of her scotch, she needed it now. 'So if he's not the Grantley Ripper, he's murdered his wife and gone on the trot. It's a different case entirely?'

'That's about the strength of it, yeah.' Caitlin's voice was low. 'Those videos and books, though. Jasus, I would have laid money on him being our man.'

Then another thought occurred to him.

Patrick Kelly also thought he was the man.

Kate watched him as he rushed from the room. If she had not been so disturbed by the news of George's negative test, she might have wondered what was wrong with him.

She was more annoyed that he had left it to her to break the news to Flowers.

How could they have assumed so much before confirming it? She finished the scotch in one gulp and picked up the phone. She did not relish this job one bit.

Patrick Kelly had spoken to Caitlin and assured him that he knew nothing about a George Markham. The next-door neighbour was probably half asleep and had made a mistake. He listened to Caitlin tell him about the negative blood test and made the appropriate noises of dismay at their mistake. Then he put the phone down and smiled to himself. George Markham's little plan had paid off.

He knew, and Tony Jones knew, that George's blood test

563

would have been positive. Now Tony Jones was in hospital and George Markham was about to meet his maker. All in all this hadn't been a bad day.

Kate arrived at his house by cab two hours later.

'Hello, Patrick. I've had a terrible day. Pay the silly cabman before I arrest him!'

'Are you drunk?' Kelly's voice was shocked.

'A bit. And if I have my way, I'll be drunker.'

He took her arm and helped her across the hall and up the stairs.

'Where are we going?' Her voice had taken on an aggressive tone.

'I'm going to put you in the shower, my girl. Now get up them stairs.'

Willy walked out into the hall and Kelly snapped at him, 'She's pissed. Pay the cab, then get her some coffee.'

Willy nodded and watched Patrick half carry and half drag a drunken Kate up the stairs.

In the bedroom, he let her flop on to the bed and began to pull her clothes off. She was compliant now. The aggression had turned to a weary resignation.

'We thought we had him, Pat, but we didn't. We didn't . . . All we had was another murderer. He'd murdered his wife . . .'

'All right, all right, calm down.'

He hoisted her naked off the bed and walked her into the en-suite bathroom. Turning on the cold tap, he held her under the shower. The freezing water made her gasp for breath and she tried to leap out of the shower tray. Patrick held her in there with difficulty, the white silk shirt he was wearing getting soaked.

'Let the water run over you, Kate, it'll make you feel better.'

'You bloody bastard! Let me out of this shower now! It's fr-fr-freezing.'

Kelly watched the goose bumps appearing all over her skin as if by magic and stifled a grin. Her nipples were enormous!

He was still holding her under the flowing water when,

about five minutes later, he heard Willy bring the coffee into the bedroom. Turning off the shower, Patrick wrapped her in a large bath towel.

'Come on then, into the bedroom.'

'Flowers told me off good and proper today. Not Kenneth Caitlin, though. Oh, no. Only me.'

He poured out a strong coffee, but when he took it over to the bed she was already asleep.

Her long hair was plastered across her body. Droplets of water made her skin look pearly. The bath towel barely covered her. Never had she looked so vulnerable or so desirable. For a fleeting second, looking down at her, he was sorry for what he had done. He knew, without a shadow of a doubt, that George Markham was her man. But he could never tell her.

There was something he could do, though, and that was put Frederick Flowers in his place. The thought consoled him for a while.

Kate finally opened her eyes three hours later. She looked around her, trying to get her bearings. Then she saw Patrick.

'Hello, love, feeling better?'

She pulled herself up on the bed.

'I feel rough actually.'

'I'll ring down for some fresh coffee.'

While he called the kitchen Kate pulled the damp towel around her more tightly, catching sight of herself in the mirror opposite the bed. She frowned. She looked terrible. Patrick sat beside her on the bed.

'I'm sorry about that Markham bloke.'

'Oh, don't remind me about it, please.'

He kissed her bare shoulder.

'If only we'd checked the blood tests before we put the finger on him, Pat. I feel such a bloody fool, but I would have sworn on a stack of bibles he was our man. The snuff movies, the books. It all fitted in. He'd even been in prison for attempted rape and battery. We found that out too late as well.'

'Well, he murdered his wife.'

565

Kate cut him off. 'But did he? For all we know someone else murdered her and Markham, dumping his body elsewhere. Until we find him or his body we don't know anything.'

Willy knocked on the door and brought in the coffee. 'Phone call from the States, Pat.'

He leapt off the bed and out of the room. 'Shall I pour, ma'am?'

'Yes please, Willy. I don't feel very steady at the moment.'

'I paid your cab for you. You was very drunk, you know.'

'I know.'

She took the cup from him.

'You look like you've been done and left!'

Kate couldn't help smiling. 'I feel like it, Willy.'

He pointed a short fat finger at her. 'Then let that be a lesson to you. Never have liked to see a woman in drink, it's horrible.'

'I'll bear that in mind in future.'

Willy left the room and Kate sipped at her coffee. God knows how the others must be feeling, they had been even drunker than her. Once the initial shock had worn off they had all started in on some serious drinking. The last she remembered was Caitlin slipping off his chair. One and all they'd been blotto.

But, by Christ, why not? After the news they'd had, they damned well needed something.

She closed her eyes as frustration assailed her again. All day the picture of James Redcar's tiny body had haunted her.

Patrick came back into the room, sat down beside her and slipped the towel from her breasts, caressing them.

'I think me and you could do with cheering up a bit. I know a little game you might like to play. Take your mind off your troubles for a bit.'

'What's that?'

'It's called lorries and garages. I don't know if you've ever played it before?'

Kate looked at him with one eyebrow raised.

'I can't say I have, no.'

'Well, do you see this?' He put her hand on his erect member. 'This is my lorry, right. And I have to find somewhere to park it. Get my drift?'

Kate roared with laughter.

'Oh, Patrick, I need you tonight. I need you so much.'

He looked down into her brown eyes. The lashes were glistening with tears and he felt an overwhelming sadness. Kate was hurting, and he could stop the hurt with a few words. The solving of this case was everything to her, and he could tell her everything she wanted to know.

Instead he began to kiss her, losing himself in her sweet-smelling body as he felt her respond to him. Felt her tongue slip between his lips. Her nails travel down his back and under his body to cup his testicles.

Then she was shuddering beneath him. He watched her face as she thrust her hips into him and he loved her then. Loved her to death.

Soon it would be all over, and Kate would never be any the wiser.

At least, that was his prayer.

Amanda Dawkins had stayed relatively sober. She sat on in the incident room collating everything she had about George Markham. She stared at the picture of him from his file. He had attacked a young girl on a train eighteen years earlier. It had been a vicious assault, and he had been sent to Broadmoor. He had been in and out in three years. His wife had given birth to a stillborn son, and that had helped with his release.

Amanda shook her head as she read his statement: 'The girl was asking for it, she was smiling at me. Egging me on.'

How many times did a policeman hear that?

She looked at his picture again. At the nondescript man staring out at her. He had lifeless grey eyes and a weak, almost non-existent chin. He did not look like a sexual pervert at all. He looked like someone's uncle.

She poured another scotch into the paper cup by her side. They'd really thought they had him.

Her eyes travelled to the pictures on the wall. Cynthia Redcar and her young son were now added to them. The picture of the little boy's battered face seemed to be imprinted on her mind. Who the hell could hurt a child like that?

She dragged her eyes back to the file in front of her. There had been ructions earlier over this. Caitlin and Kate had wanted to know why George Markham had not been brought to their attention. Amanda had been sorry for Willis then. He had knocked over a whole stack of files and got them all mixed up together. He had then shoved them into a filing cabinet and promptly forgotten them. It was only when they had tapped into the central computer that they had found out they had already been sent a copy of Markham's file, along with many others. Caitlin's swearing could be heard all over the building.

Amanda sipped her scotch and looked at the statement again. George Markham's handwriting was spidery, barely legible. Then she sat forward in her seat with a jolt. As she scrambled through the paperwork in front of her, her heart began to pound.

Then she found what she was looking for: George Markham's blood testing statement. He had signed it in a large childish script.

She held the two signatures together, her hands shaking. Then she downed the scotch in one gulp and picked up the telephone. Kate's mother answered. Leaving her home number, Amanda told Evelyn that Kate was to ring her as soon as she got in.

Kate was home at one-thirty, the day's events a blur, except for Patrick's lovemaking. She walked into the house and straight up the stairs to her bedroom. The note on the table by the phone went unnoticed.

She heard the alarm go off at six and pulled herself from bed. Her mouth felt dry, as if it was full of cotton wool. She pulled on her dressing gown and padded into the bathroom. She needed a good hot shower and at least one pot of coffee to get herself set up for the day ahead. After yesterday's fiasco, she knew that today was not going to be a good one.

In the shower she soaped her body absentmindedly. Patrick had made her feel good. He had held her and told her he loved her, and she had needed that so much. He had been so understanding with her that she felt almost as if he knew what she was going through, as if he had an affinity with her, a special knowledge.

She was so lucky to have him.

She wrapped herself in a large bath towel and, pushing on her slippers, walked down the stairs to make her coffee. It was six fifteen.

As she walked past the telephone she saw the piece of paper that her mother had left for her and picked it up and read in the hallway light.

She dialled the number.

'Hello, Amanda?'

'Oh, Kate, I've been worried out of my mind! Look, I think George Markham *is* our man . . .'

'What!' Kate's voice rose.

'I went back through his files. The signatures on his statements are different. He must have had someone take the test for him.'

As the enormity of what Amanda was saying penetrated, Kate felt a surge of excitement.

'Who else have you told?'

'No one.'

'Oh, Amanda, you're brilliant! I'll see you in about twenty minutes, OK?'

'OK.'

'And, Amanda . . . thanks a million.'

'Any time. Oh, and one last thing. I put a call out for his car again. I told them to concentrate on the Kent area. That's obviously the last place he was.'

'Great, Amanda. You'll make DI yet, my girl.'

The two women laughed and said goodbye. Kate put down the phone and did a little jig. She had known he was the man. She had known it in her heart. He was wily. He must have a very good friend if he would take a blood test for him. Especially a blood test on a murder case. A man who could arrange a bluff like that was obviously not lacking in imagination.

She threw on her clothes, pulled on her coat and picked up her bag, her coffee left by the phone to go cold. Forgotten now.

She would find George Markham wherever he was. Find him and put him away.

The earlier depression had disappeared. Kate felt wonderful.

Chapter Thirty

Ratchette and Caitlin were both looking at her expectantly.

'I have proof that George Markham is our man.'

She watched their eyes widen.

'Last night, Amanda Dawkins checked through George Markham's file. It seems the signatures on his statements for the blood testing and his previous arrest differ. I can only assume he had someone else take the blood test for him. He's definitely our man.'

Caitlin's face lit up.

'I knew he was the bugger we were after. I just knew it in me guts.'

'Well, we have Amanda Dawkins to thank for this. She saw what was under everyone else's nose. I think she deserves to take full credit.'

Ratchette smiled gently.

'Another good woman coming up in the ranks, eh, Kate? This is excellent news. I'll get on to Flowers immediately.'

'Make sure he knows it was Dawkins. I think she did an exceptional job.'

'I will. So where will you go from here?'

'Amanda Dawkins put another call out on Markham's car. This time she asked them to concentrate on the Kent area. That was obviously his last port of call. I can only guess his wife was on to him, he murdered her, and now he's trying to disappear. At some point someone would have wanted to know where she was. She'd been dead a few days so he has a head start on us. My guess is he picked on Cynthia Redcar while in Kent. God knows where he'll strike next.'

'Well, you follow up any avenues you have to. And tell

Dawkins well done. I'll see her myself later. Now I think you'd better tell all the officers on the case. A bit of morale boosting wouldn't go amiss today.'

Caitlin left the office with Kate and put his arm around her shoulders. 'Sure you women like to stick together. If it had been me and Ratchette you'd have accused us of pushing you out.'

Kate grinned at him.

'Kenny?'

'What?'

'Up yours. That's how you would have answered me if I'd accused you of pushing me out!'

Caitlin laughed out loud. 'You're learning, Katie, and that young Amanda did good. It'll be one in the eye for Spencer anyway.'

They walked into the incident room and Caitlin called for silence.

'I have an announcement for you all that I think will take the sour expression off your faces.'

Everyone stood staring at him.

'Thanks to a certain young lady,' he pointed to Amanda Dawkins, who went red with embarrassment, 'we have reason to believe that George Markham *is* our man.'

There was a murmur of surprise.

'It seems he got someone to take the blood test for him. The signatures on his statements don't match. We must concentrate on finding out who that was, and on looking for George Markham. One can only lead to the other.'

The telephone rang and Amanda Dawkins picked it up, glad of something to do. Everyone was grinning at her.

'Today we will concentrate on people who knew the Markhams: workmates, friends, relatives. Anyone at all. Let's get going!'

The excitement was back in the air. Cigarettes were being lit with a flourish, the disappointment of the night before evaporated. Kate watched the change in her team and felt the adrenalin in her own veins.

They would find George Markham. She was convinced of it.

Patrick ate a hearty breakfast and went into work. He had managed to shrug off his feelings of despondency over Kate. Had convinced himself that what she didn't know couldn't hurt her. Once George Markham was out of the way, he would be able to relax once more. His debt to his daughter would be paid in full. He could live again.

He smiled at the men in his office and they smiled back, wondering who had put the smile on his face in the first place.

'Gentlemen,' he announced, 'I am officially calling off the hunt for the murderer of my daughter. The man who gave me the information will be paid in full in a few days.'

He saw the men's faces drop.

'Now then, down to business. Larry, I want you to go down to Colchester today and repossess a Jag. The owner is a Paki and he ain't paid more than one instalment on it. The credit company think he may have ringed it. I want you to find out.

'There's also a large warehouse in Surrey that needs to be cleared out, mainly colour tellies and video equipment. The whole lot is to be moved from there and impounded. I'm saying this only once, so listen good. Only a telly or a video apiece can go astray. If I hear that any of the stuff's being sold on the side there'll be trouble. Right, Jimmy?'

He hung his head. Pat sussed all right. Everyone laughed.

'Now we've got a lot of furniture snatchbacks today, you know the score. Council flats with leather settee suites and solid oak dining tables, mainly catalogue collection, so look after the gear right. There's a list outside for each of you, with a route map. Take the big removal vans. It's the after Christmas rush at the moment so there's plenty of work. Don't hassle the occupants of the places unless you have to. I heard through the grapevine that Dinny Morris's lot slapped a young bird the other week, I don't like that kind of behaviour. You'd throw a paddy if someone came to take your furniture away, try and remember that. Have a bit of sympathy for them.'

The men looked at Jimmy again.

'I don't know why you're all looking at me! I'd never slap a bird.'

'Not unless you was living with her anyway.'

Ronalld Baker's voice was hard and the men looked uneasy. Jimmy lived with Ronald's youngest sister.

'All right, keep your family feuds outside this office and this company. Lastly, I want you to tell your teams that when they are debt collecting I want all the money paid in pronto. I keep hearing how the men are keeping the Saturday collections at home until the Monday morning. That's got to stop from now on. I know every scam in the book, and a couple of the collectors have pissed money up the wall by Monday then sworn black was blue they never collected it. Any more stories like that and they're out, along with their team leader which will be one of you.'

He lit himself a cigarette slowly to let his words sink in. 'Other than that, I don't think I've got anything else to say.'

The men stood up and began making their way to the door.

'Can you stay behind for a minute, Ronnie?'

He resumed his seat and waited for the room to empty.

'I've got a special job for you.'

'What kind of job?' Ronnie's voice was neutral.

'A very lucrative job. Are you game?'

Ronnie nodded his head. His thin-lipped mouth had a tight roll-up stuck in the corner. It moved up and down as he spoke. Kelly could never remember seeing it lit.

'In Spain there's a certain old lag who owes a considerable amount of money to a friend of mine. He wants the debt collected this week.'

Ronnie nodded again. 'How much is my bunce?'

'Your take will be ten per cent as is usual in these cases. The amount to be collected is eighty grand.'

Ronnie nodded again.

'Who's the lag?'

Patrick took a deep breath. 'William Carlton.'

Ronnie's taciturn expression never wavered. 'Tell the bloke I want twenty per cent and he supplies the shooter. I'll bring the money back by boat.'

'That can all be arranged. You're to go tomorrow morning.'

'Fair enough.'

Ronnie stood up. 'One more thing, Pat. Jimmy will be out of work for a good few months soon. I thought I'd let you know so you could replace him.'

Patrick nodded. 'What's the rub?'

'He gave me sister a kicking Saturday, thinks no one knows about it, but she phoned me mum. I can't swallow no more, Pat. She's only twenty-two and five months pregnant. The slag won't even marry her.'

'What about your sister, can't she leave him?'

'She won't. Thinks the sun shines out of his arse. She's only a kid, Pat. Don't know what's good for her yet.'

Patrick stood up and shook the man's hand.

'Thanks for letting me know. I'm sorry to hear about Clare, she's a good kid.'

'Thanks, Pat. I'm glad you found the scumbag who done your Mandy. Fucking real, ain't it? The shite that's knocking about these days. No one's safe.'

Patrick saw him to the door and sat back at his desk. Well, the piece of scum who'd killed his Mandy had had his card marked for sure. His days were numbered.

Patrick began to whistle through his teeth as he studied his books.

Hector Henderson was worried. Very worried. He had not heard from Elaine for over a week. He had gone round to Margaret Forrester's house and been informed that Elaine was off work ill. Some kind of 'flu'. Except she'd had all day to ring him while George was out at work, and nothing. Nothing at all.

He chewed on his thumbnail, his big fat face shining with a film of sweat. Suppose she didn't want to see him any more? He chewed harder at the thought, causing his ill-fitting teeth to make tiny popping noises as they rattled against his gums. Since the New Year he had become fond of Elaine. More than fond in fact. He would even go so far as to say he loved her.

Yes, it was no use denying it, he thought the bally world of her.

She was a good handful was old Elaine, a good laugh, and a very accommodating woman. Bet she could cook too. Stood to reason, the size of her. If only she wasn't married to that George chap.

He sighed. Elaine might leave him, though. The only thing was, how was he going to convince her to throw the man out? He looked around his little bedsit. They couldn't live here. Perhaps if Elaine sold her house they could buy a nice flat. He nodded to himself. That would be the best bet. After all, he didn't want to see her husband with nothing. The last time he had seen her she had been like a ripe plum, ready for the picking, and he had picked her all right. He smiled to himself. Surpassed himself in fact. She did like the old one-eyed snake did Elaine! That was another of her attractions.

He settled himself back in the large armchair. He was worrying over nothing. Elaine had told him in no uncertain terms that she loved him. She was probably lying in bed at this very moment, half dead with 'flu' and a raging temperature. He pictured this in his mind. That was why she hadn't been in touch, bless her heart. He scolded himself for his earlier, unworthy thoughts. His Elaine was a diamond, a 24-carat diamond. She would see him all right. She would get him out of this dump.

She had to. He was depending on it.

He was startled by a knock on the door. He sat quietly for a few minutes. If it was that old bitch for her rent money she usually gave a warning shout. Nothing. He felt his panic subside. Perhaps it was Elaine?

He leapt from his chair as the knocking began again, his eyes taking in the chaos of the room. He could have kicked himself, he should have tidied up a bit. He glanced in the piece of broken mirror on his mantelpiece. Hurriedly tidying his hair, he opened the door with a flourish, a big smile on his large round face.

'Mr Henderson?'

Hector nodded cagily, racking his brains to think if he was in any kind of debt.

'I'm Detective Inspector Burrows and this is my colleague, Chief Inspector Caitlin. We would like to have a few words with you.'

Hector stared at the tiny cards in their hands.

'What about?'

'Elaine Markham. We understand from Margaret Forrester that you were close friends.'

Hector stood aside to let them in. Caitlin's nose wrinkled at the sour smell.

'I'm afraid we have some bad news for you, Mr Henderson. Elaine Markham has been murdered.'

Kate watched the shock and disbelief on the man's face and felt sorry for him.

'No . . . No, it can't be true. Not Elaine.'

His voice was a distraught whisper. All his dreams were dissolving in front of his eyes. A proper home, a wife, a companion for his old age. Hector knew as sure as eggs were eggs that Elaine Markham was his last chance.

'Murdered, you say?'

Caitlin nodded.

'Well, it wasn't me. I haven't seen her for over a week.'

Hector was now out to save his skin. Maybe they thought he had done it?

'We have a good idea who murdered her, Mr Henderson, you're not a suspect. We just want you to tell us all you know about Elaine Markham and anything she might have told you about her husband.'

Hector Henderson nodded slowly. He looked around the grubby room and sighed. It had all been too good to be true. His dancing clothes hung from the picture rails around the room, mocking him, and he felt an urge to cry.

Elaine had been a good egg. She would have seen him all right.

Inside the trailer it was hot. Loretta lay on the bed, watching

577

the Englishman. As he brought his arm up to run his hand through his hair she flinched.

'Don't worry, my dear, I wouldn't hurt you.'

He smiled at her, displaying his tiny teeth.

Loretta took a large swallow. She put a hand between her legs to try and ease the burning.

'Let me drink my beer, and then we'll get back down to business.'

Loretta closed her eyes. She ached all over.

The Englishman was cold, as she had first thought. Cold and callous. Never before had she had to endure the things he wanted from her, and she had done them all, she'd had to do them. This man was frightening in his intensity. He took his sex seriously. He had lain on top of her and pounded into her, as if he knew exactly what would hurt most.

Luckily for Loretta, she lay passively, letting him do just what he wanted; some inbred cunning told her that this was not a man to fight with. Even when he dug his fingers hard and spitefully into her genitals, she had just whimpered, biting down the scream that was trying to emerge.

She did not want to upset this guy.

George looked into the young fresh face. A trickle of blood ran down from her swollen lip.

She really was quite a pretty little thing.

'Turn over on your stomach, dear.'

Loretta did as he asked and as she felt him straddle her she bit down once more on her bottom lip. Big fat tears squeezed out from beneath her closed lids. As she felt the sharp pain of George's penis entering her anal passage she began to beg him to stop, her words becoming incoherent as the pain engulfed her again.

George looked down at the long tanned body and smiled.

Outside in the Florida sunshine, Duane yawned and settled himself more comfortably in his seat.

This guy certainly liked his money's worth.

Kate came back into the station at two thirty. She had just got herself a coffee when Amanda came to her desk.

'His car's been found. In Gatwick Airport car park. Caitlin's on his way down now, he'll wait for you outside.'

Kate picked up her bag and rushed from the room. They made their way to Gatwick in record time, barely exchanging a word.

Both were filled with the same thought: He'd left the country. Either that or someone had left his car here for him. They already knew they were dealing with a clever man.

The flights were being checked, as were the ferries. He did not know yet that his wife's body had been found. George Markham was still in the clear so far as he knew. The press hadn't got so much as a whiff of this one.

In the car park George's car was opened. In the back was Cynthia Redcar's parka. It had a little plastic toy in the pocket. Looking at it, Kate felt a wave of sadness.

Later, the car had just arrived at the forensics workshop and Kate and Caitlin were watching it being dusted for prints, before being stripped, when the call came through.

George Markham had gone to Orlando on a charter flight three days previously.

Cynthia Redcar had been his last little fling before boarding. He was due back on 16 March. He was on a fly drive holiday. That meant he could be anywhere.

But they were interviewing his brother soon. Maybe he could shed some light on the trip. There had been no address books in the Markham house. Joseph Markham's address had been found on an old letter.

First though, they were going to Kortone Separates.

George arrived back at Edith's happy and relaxed, and full of good-natured bonhomie as he embraced his nephew, Joss Junior.

'Natalie is just coming down now, George. She's so excited.'

George heard her footsteps on the stairs and turned in their direction, a large smile on his face. When she walked into the room his face froze.

579

In the flesh, Natalie was the living image of his mother. She looked nothing like the photograph he'd seen the day before. Her hair was the same deep red, her eyes the same greeny-blue. George felt his heartbeat quicken. He half expected her to say something cutting as Nancy would have. Instead she ran towards him and embraced him, enveloping him a cloud of Giorgio perfume. George automatically put his arms around her slim waist. He could smell the slightly musky smell of her sweat. Not unpleasant, he decided, but womanly.

'Oh, Uncle George, I've heard so much about you. I feel as if I know you already!'

Her voice was pure American, as was Joss's, and the reminder of Nancy evaporated. George caught Edith's eye and realised she knew what he was thinking.

Joss Senior came into the room with a jug of martinis. 'Who wants a drink?' he boomed.

Everyone moved outside to the sunshine and George listened to all the family chit chat. Joss Junior, unlike his namesake, was very subdued. In fact he reminded George of himself when younger. George smiled at him now and then and the boy coloured slightly and nodded back.

Edith thought her heart would burst.

She had all the important people in her life around her, something she was sure she would never experience again.

'Where did you go today, George?'

He blanched. 'Oh, I just drove around, you know. Had a little look about.'

Natalie squealed, 'I know, let's take him to MGM tomorrow. Oh, Uncle George, you'll just love the studios.'

George beamed. He liked Florida right enough. It really brought him out of himself. An hour later he was half listening to Joss, Joss Junior and Edith chatting while he watched Natalie swimming in the pool.

She was Nancy Markham all over again, from the big fat breasts to the jutting hip bones. George watched her closely and nodded to himself. She had her grandmother's lust for sex too. That was evident in every move she made. A flicker of repugnance crossed his features. He watched her pull herself from the pool and dry herself, rubbing hard at her skin with the towel, causing her breasts to shimmy in their tiny top.

They were all the same. Every last one of them. Abruptly he got up and went to his room.

Edith, Joss and their children all gave one another puzzled looks.

'I think the flight probably caught up with him,' said Edith. It sounded lame even to her own ears.

George locked himself into his bathroom. He sat on the toilet seat, his mind filled with thoughts of his niece's body and presence. Erotic visions played in front of his eyes. He felt the familiar urge rising in him. He would show them. He would show them all. They were all bloody whores!

His mother, Edith, Elaine . . . he pictured all the women he had murdered, and then somewhere, tacked right on the end, was his niece Natalie. In his mind's eyes he saw her beneath him, begging for him to stop hurting her, and he smiled.

Downstairs Natalie sat with her family, feeling safe and secure. Happy to be with them and part of their lives.

George heard her tinkling laughter; it wafted up to him on the heavy Florida air, and somewhere in his mind he decided she was laughing at him.

Well, he would teach her a lesson she would not forget.

Edith watched her children with pride. She had spent a lifetime protecting them. She did not even guess that the biggest threat her daughter had ever faced was sitting upstairs in her own home.

Peter Renshaw was nervous. Kate could sense the sweat coming from his pores.

'I understand you were quite friendly with Mr Markham?'

'I knew him as a workmate, that was all.'

Kate frowned. He was hiding something.

'Look, Mr Renshaw, I understand you arranged his leaving party for him. I got the impression that you were one of the few people who was actually close to George Markham.'

'Look, why is everyone interested in George all of a sudden? What's he supposed to have done?'

Renshaw's voice was high and uneasy.

'What do you mean by everyone? Who else has been looking for him?'

'No one. No one at all. Why would anyone want him?'

Kate watched him chew his fingernail.

'Listen here, Mr Renshaw.' She stressed the 'Mr'. 'You can either chat to me here or I can haul your fat arse into the station. It's up to you. But I warn you now – I don't like people holding out on me. Now who else was looking for George Markham?'

'If I tell you, do you promise me you'll keep it to yourself?' His bulbous eyes were pleading.

Kate nodded.

'It was a local hard man . . . Patrick Kelly. He pulled me up a few days ago.' He looked at Kate and stood up. 'Here, are you all right?'

'Patrick Kelly?' she whispered.

Renshaw nodded. Then watched as she stormed from the room. He shook his head. He hoped to Christ she kept her promise.

Kate drove back to Grantley at record speed. Patrick had already seen Renshaw. He already knew who they were looking for. George Markham was in America and Patrick had taken a call from the States . . . She felt icy fingers at the back of her neck. Hadn't he told her he would pay his daughter's murderer out? Hadn't he told her that?

He had known where George Markham was all along. He had made love to her knowing that. Knowing he had murder planned. .

Patrick must have thought she was the most stupid bimbo he had ever come across in his life. He'd been laughing at her. If he knew where Markham was then Markham was a dead man – unless she did something about it.

She drove as fast as she could to Grantley Police Station and went in search of Caitlin. By this time she was in a fury so passionate it was making her shake.

Patrick Kelly had a lesson to learn: never to mug off Kate Burrows again!

Caitlin was in the incident room, thick grey cigar smoke curling around his weather-beaten face. He took one glance at Kate's expression and hurriedly bundled her from the room, much to the chagrin of the other officers present, who could smell a rat before it was stinking.

Spencer glanced at Amanda Dawkins. 'She looked fit to do murder. I wonder what's going on?'

Amanda shrugged. 'How the hell should I know?'

Caitlin had taken Kate to an empty interview room. Now she stood facing him. It was all as clear as day. Even Caitlin had known what was going on. She could have cried with temper.

'You know, don't you?'

He was nonchalant. 'Know what, Katie?'

'Don't you bloody "Katie" me, Kenneth Caitlin. You know what I'm going to say, don't you? By Christ, I must be some kind of dunce. I should change my name to Detective Inspector Thicko.'

Caitlin sat down at the table and puffed on his cigar. 'Sit down, woman, and tell me what's on your mind.'

Kate placed both hands on the table and looked into Caitlin's face.

'Last night I was at Kelly's when he had a call from the States. This morning I find out that that's where George Markham has gone. Now I don't know about you, but that tells me that George Markham is a dead man.'

'It could be a coincidence.'

'Coincidence my arse! When I think of all the work that's gone into this case. The blood testing, the man hours . . . And all the time we were working for Patrick fucking Kelly!'

Caitlin's eyes widened to their utmost. Two swear words in one sentence from Kate Burrows told him just how annoyed

583

she was. 'Well, he won't get away with it, matey. I'm going to see Flowers. I want some answers, and I want them now!'

She slammed out of the interview room and Caitlin followed her as fast as he could. He finally caught up with her in the car park where he banged on the window of her car and motioned for her to unlock the passenger side.

'Bugger off!'

Caitlin watched the small car drive away, and sighed. Then he went to his own car and began following her. She'd need all the help she could get when she saw Frederick Flowers.

The episode in the car park had been witnessed by the occupants of the incident room.

Spencer shook his head.

'That's why women should never have been allowed in the police force. They're too emotional. Look at the way she was carrying on.'

The others allowed their eyes to peruse the ceiling.

Frederick Flowers was sitting in his office nursing a hangover when his secretary's chirpy tones informed him that Detective Inspector Kate Burrows was demanding to see him. He winced. That bloody woman got on his nerves. Before he could put her off, Kate herself stood in front of him, sending his office door crashing against the wall. The noise whiplashed in his aching head. The door opened again and Flowers relaxed slightly at the sight of Caitlin.

Kate was firing on all cylinders.

'You listen to me now! George Markham, whatever he's done, is in mortal danger and we must do something about it. Patrick Kelly has sworn he's going to kill him and I know he will. He is aware of George Markham's whereabouts, and we have a duty to protect that man so he can stand trial.'

Her chest was heaving and Flowers took a crafty peek at it before answering. Like this, with two red temper marks on her cheeks and her face glowing, he could see what Kelly saw in her. Her dark silky hair had been hastily pinned up in a French pleat and shone in the weak February sun.

'You have no proof of this, Burrows, it's all conjecture on

584

your part. From information I have received, Markham is on a fly drive holiday to his sister's. The finding of his wife's body will not be in the newspapers and Markham will fly back to England none the wiser that we have tumbled him. As he steps off the plane on to British soil he will be arrested.'

'But that's just it! He'll be coming back to England in a bloody coffin.' Kate clenched her fists. 'I have every reason to believe that Patrick Kelly has put a price on his head.'

Caitlin closed his eyes. Oh, Katie, he thought, you stupid woman.

'Look, Burrows, I think you're overwrought. I think you should go home and have a good think about all you've just said. They're very serious allegations and unless you have concrete evidence I would advise you to keep your thoughts to yourself. Patrick Kelly is not above suing us for defamation of character. I might add that after listening to your hysterical ramblings, I wouldn't blame him.'

Kate opened her mouth to speak. Flowers held up his hand for silence, but she ignored him.

'You're all in on it, aren't you?' Her voice was low and bitter. 'Oh, I know that no one could actually put your faces in the frame, no more than they'll be able to put Kelly's. But you all know the score, don't you? You're all quite willing to let him collect his debt, aren't you?'

Her voice was disgusted and Caitlin at least had the grace to look away.

'I must have been living in some kind of fools' paradise. I honestly believed in my work. You must all think I'm a cretin.' She poked a finger at Flowers and he flinched as it came within an inch of his face. 'Well, I'll settle you lot if it's the last thing I do.'

Flowers found his voice.

'Are you threatening me? Because if you are, you listen to me and listen good, Burrows. I know that you, a Detective Inspector, have been seen with Patrick Kelly on more than one occasion. Now I'd say that constitutes a slur on your integrity, don't you?'

She was dumbstruck.

'You've known him a lot longer than I have, Flowers,' she said at last.

Flowers grinned.

'Sure I know Kelly, he's a well-known figure, but think about this very carefully, Burrows. I'm not sleeping with him, am I? My husband has not made a statement to the CIB to that effect.'

Kate felt an anger born of futility engulf her. 'You dirty stinking bastard!'

'As from now, Burrows, you're off this case and suspended from duties. Caitlin, take her away, for goodness' sake.'

He flapped his hand in a gesture of dismissal and Kate found her eyes filled with tears of frustration.

'Shall I tell you something, Flowers? For the first time in my life I realise just what you are. You're quite willing to let a man be murdered in cold blood, aren't you? It means nothing to you, does it? You're even willing to sacrifice my career so your friend Kelly can get even with Markham.'

Caitlin pulled her by the arm. He had stood silently all through the exchange, but now he realised he had to get her home and talk some sense into her. He owed her that at least.

'Come on, Katie, before you say some more things you'll regret.'

'Regret?' She laughed out loud. 'The only regret I have is getting mixed up with you lot.'

Caitlin's voice was firmer now.

'Shut your bloody mouth up and give me your keys. I'll drive.

In the car, neither of them spoke until Caitlin turned off the dual carriageway and down a country lane, stopping at a small public house.

'Come on, Kate, we're going to have something to eat and drink, and a talk.'

She followed him, her shoulders slumped inside her jacket. She knew she was beaten. Nothing in all her experience had prepared her for something like this.

Sitting in the comfortable bar, Caitlin ordered two roast dinners and a bottle of Chianti. Then he added two large scotches.

Absentmindedly Kate said, 'We'll be over the limit.'

'Let me worry about that.'

Finally, with her drink untouched in front of her, Caitlin began to talk to her.

'Look, I know how you're feeling, believe me. I've experienced the same thing myself. What you seem to have forgotten is that George Markham was a murderer of the worst kind. He took seven lives, Katie, and God himself only knows how many more he would have taken. He raped and murdered innocent girls and women. He was a sadist.'

She interrupted him.

'You just said he *was* a murderer. You used the past tense, Kenny. Is he already dead then?'

'Oh, that was just a slip of the tongue, Kate. What I'm trying to say is that, noble as your sentiments are, they're wasted on him.'

'Flowers has sewn me up nice and tightly, hasn't he? You all have. You, Flowers, and let's not forget Kelly, shall we?'

'Kelly's daughter was brutally murdered, Kate. Even if he does have Markham taken out, think of the alternative. All the money it would cost to keep him locked up for the rest of his life, because that's what would happen.

'You disappoint me, Kate. I always thought you were a sensible woman. You're putting your career on the line for a piece of filth. If he was put in prison in the morning all he could look forward to is years of abuse from prisoners and staff alike. Years ago he attacked a young girl on a train and beat the frigging crap out of her. His wife gave birth to a dead child over it. We're not dealing with a blagger here now, Kate, we're dealing with a sadistic rapist.'

'That's just it, though. I know what we're dealing with, and no matter how you, Flowers, Kelly or bloody King Street Charlie dress it up, it's still condoning murder!'

Caitlin shook his shaggy head. His hair was sticking up in all directions where he had run his hands through it. 'Kelly was the one who paid for the blood testing, Kate. It was him who got it okayed. He tried hard to help find the killer.'

'I know he paid for the blood testing.' Her voice was bitter.

587

'How good of him. Just so he could find out who did it for his own ends!'

'You still don't know for certain if he has put a price on the man's head. Like Flowers said, it's all conjecture on your part.'

She sneered, 'Oh, grow up, Kenny, for Christ's sake. You know as well as I do that Markham's a dead man. But just to be on the safe side, I'm going to see the Golden Boy myself.'

Kate stood up. Snatching her keys off the table, she stormed from the pub. Caitlin did not attempt to follow her this time. Instead he poured her drink into his glass and cancelled one of the dinners.

He had done his bit. Now it was up to her.

Kelly was like a cat on hot bricks. He had arranged the payment of the fifty thousand dollars, a minuscule amount for what he wanted done. Now all he wanted was confirmation of the hit. Every time the telephone rang he rushed to answer it, a feeling of excitement in his breast.

He couldn't relax until that piece of scum was dead. His eyes went automatically to Mandy's photograph. The familiar lump came to his throat.

He saw her as she had been when she was eleven. Her hair a mass of blonde around a tiny heart-shaped face.

'Mummy won't b coming home any more, Princess.' The feel of her little skinny sobbing body had helped to allay his own grief. He had had to pick himself up and brush himself down for Mandy's sake. He had comforted her through the inevitable nightmares and depressions. He had tried his hardest to be a good father to her. To be there for her always. To protect her.

And for what? For that ponce to batter her brains out on a filthy floor while he raped her. It would have been better if she had been in the car with his wife. At least that way she would have died without all the shame and fear. It would all have been over in seconds.

Willy knocked softly on the door and stepped into the room. 'Any news yet, Pat?'

He shook his head.

'Never mind, no news is good news. Can I get you a coffee or anything?'

Kelly looked at Willy's big moon face and felt a surge of affection.

'I love you, Willy, you know that?' The words were quietly spoken and the minder knew their significance. Together they had been through the worst life has to offer.

Willy smiled. 'I never had you down as a shirtlifter, Pat.'

Kelly laughed painfully.

'Oh, Willy, only you could get away with that.'

'Have a nice cup of coffee, Pat, it'll settle your nerves.'

'All right. Shove a drop of brandy in it, would you?'

Willy opened the door. Looking back over his shoulder, he said in his best man to man voice. 'I recipcreat your sentiments entirely.'

'It's reciprocate, Willy.'

'Oh, who gives a toss, Pat? You know what I mean.'

Kelly smiled to himself. Kate had been right: Willy was the best friend he had. Sometimes he thought he was the only friend he had. The only genuine one anyway.

As if his thoughts had conjured her up, Kate's car screeched to a halt outside.

One look at her dark expression told him everything and he braced himself for the onslaught he knew was to come. A brief of his had once told him: 'Deny, deny, and deny again.' Well, he'd need to use that tack now.

Kate pushed past Willy and into the entrance hall of Patrick's house.

'Where is he?'

Willy was so shocked he just pointed to the library door. She stormed in there to see Patrick sitting behind his desk, casually smoking a cigarette.

'Hello, Kate.' He stood up, smiling at her widely.

'Don't you bloody "hello" me! I've just had the Third World War with Frederick Flowers over you. I've sussed you out, Patrick Kelly.'

'I don't know what you're talking about.'

'Oh, don't you? Well, let me enlighten you then. When I was here yesterday you had a call from the States. And George Markham, the man we want for our inquiries into the Grantley Ripper murders, is in the States. Florida to be exact.'

He butted in, 'What's this got to do with me?'

Kate pushed her face towards his.

'You swore to me that you would get him for what he did to Mandy.'

'Can you blame me? Well, can you? How would you feel if it had happened to Lizzy?

'All that aside, Kate, I have many business dealings in America and Europe. Don't you come round here reading the riot act to me over a fucking phone call!'

'You're just like Dan, do you know that? Attack as the best form of defence. Well, the minute I hear that George Markham has been hurt, I'm going to the newspapers, Pat. I mean it. I'll scream it from the bloody roof tops.'

He shook his head sadly.

'I don't know what you're talking about, Kate.' His soft voice belied his eyes, which were like granite.

'You're disgusting, do you know that? What did I ever see in you? Maybe it was pity because of your daughter, I don't know. But one thing I do know – the thought of you touching me now makes me sick to my stomach.'

She spoke through clenched teeth and the vehemence of her voice cut Patrick to the bone.

'I think you'd better go, Kate. Before we both say things we'll regret.'

'Oh, don't worry, I'm going. The sight of you makes me want to spew. But remember what I said, Pat. As soon as I hear Markham's dead, I open my mouth. You can tell Flowers that and all, when you speak to him. I'll go as high as the DPP or the Chief Justice. I'll even go to the blasted Queen.'

The phone on his desk rang shrilly and he looked at it for a second before answering. O'Grady's American twang wafted over the distance.

'One moment, please.' Putting his hand over the mouth-piece he looked into Kate's eyes.

'I think you had better go, before I throw you out.'

Giving him one last look she walked from the room. Patrick waited until she had slammed the door before he spoke to the man on the other end of the phone.

'Sorry about the delay. What's the score?'

He watched through the window as Kate got into her car and drove away. He felt as if a crucial part of himself had gone with her.

'It's all set up for tomorrow morning. As soon as the deed is done I'll be in touch.'

'Can't it be done today?'

'No can do, Pat. Stop worrying. The man will be well out of the ball game tomorrow. A professional job like this takes planning. That's what you pay for.'

'Tomorrow it is then.'

He replaced the receiver and Willy walked in with the tray of coffee.

'It's tomorrow, Willy.'

He nodded and poured, adding a liberal amount of brandy. Then, sighing, he said, 'I take it you're not seeing Kate any more then?'

Kate drove home and let herself into her house. It was quiet. Too quiet. She went into the kitchen and made herself a cup of tea. She sat at the table drinking it, still with her coat on. She could not take in the events of the last few hours. Everything had gone wrong. Terribly wrong.

Her job was on the line, she was finished with Patrick, everything she believed in was being trampled underfoot. She put her arms on the kitchen table and cried.

Last night she had slept with a murderer. A man who could pay money for the ending of another man's life. The logical part of her brain told her that Patrick was settling the score for his daughter's death in the only way he knew how. To him there was only black and white. You destroy something of mine, I destroy something of yours.

But inside herself, Kate knew this thinking went against the grain of her profession, her beliefs. Patrick Kelly still lived by the old adage: 'An eye for an eye'. And that was wrong. It had to be wrong. Otherwise all she had instilled in her own child, all she had lived and worked for, counted for nothing.

Yet still a tiny nagging doubt burned into her. Supposing he was right?

If her child was murdered could she honestly say she could forgive? Would she be happy knowing the perpetrator of the deed was alive, locked up maybe but alive, while her child was dead? She remembered reading somewhere that the mother of one of Myra Hindley's victims had even found out when Hindley's mother had died and had turned up at the funeral to berate her.

As a mother herself, she could understand that feeling of hatred.

But murder?

She licked away the salt tears from her mouth.

Flowers was quite willing to use her association with Patrick Kelly for his own ends. He had dropped her from the case, and despite all her shouting about the DPP and the Lord Chief Justice she knew that she was finished. If she went to the papers it would cause a stink for a few days, but that would be all. Because Patrick Kelly would look like a hero to everyone. A vigilante who had taken the law into his own hands. Were there many men who would not sympathise with him?

He would be like a modern day Robin Hood while she would come out of it as the bitter mistress who had been dumped and was trying to get her own back.

Between them, Kelly, Flowers and Caitlin had her right where they wanted her. But the worst of it was that, for all Patrick had done and was going to do, she still wanted him.

Chapter Thirty-one

Edith was worried – about what she was not really sure. Since George's weird reaction to Natalie, she had felt a shiver of apprehension go through her every time they were together. It was nonsense, of course. George was her closest living relative. Her child was like his child.

She shrugged. He had just been overcome, that was all. The flight, the excitement, they had taken their toll.

Today, at lunch, he seemed a bit more relaxed. Edith watched him as he stared across the table at her daughter. It seemed to her, though, that he stared at Natalie for too long. She had to force herself to look away from George and concentrate on Joss when he was talking.

George, like herself, had obviously noticed Natalie's startling resemblance to their mother. Over the years it had distressed her too, so she could guess how he was feeling. But inside Natalie was the antithesis of their mother. She was kind, considerate, caring; she had a lot of friends, real friends, that bore evidence to this. She was a beautiful person inside and out. And if the talks they had had were to be believed, she was still a virgin.

No, Natalie had none of her grandmother's licentiousness. A deeply religious girl, she lived a good, clean, wholesome life. They would never have to worry about Natalie.

Unaware of the stir she was creating, Natalie was listening to her father telling one of his long boring golf stories. She was a good daughter who laughed in all the right places and Joss loved her for this alone. His son on the other hand looked bored, as did George and Edith. He brought the story to a premature ending and concentrated on his steak.

George still watched Natalie closely, unaware that Edith was watching him.

Every movement the girl made was his mother's, even the way she brushed her hair from her face. Her shoulders in the lightweight dress were his mother's. They looked too fragile to hold up the enormous breasts.

George cut into his steak so hard he scraped his knife across the plate, causing more than one set of teeth to be set on edge.

'How long are you staying, Uncle George?' Joss Junior was not really interested but felt the question was expected from him.

'For a couple of weeks. If I like it I might sell up and move out here. I have nothing at home any more.'

Edith's heart immediately went out to him. Poor George. No wonder he was acting so strangely. Elaine leaving him must have been a bitter blow.

'Well, you're welcome to stay here as long as you want, until you find a place of your own.'

George smiled at her gratefully and Joss Senior chewed harder on his steak.

Edith's brother troubled him. He was too damn' meek and mild. His eyes went to his son and he swallowed hard. He had often wondered who the boy took after; now he knew. Try as he might he could not really love his only son. There was something disturbing about him. He felt the same about George Markham. But he was Edith's brother, her closest family, and he would accommodate him.

There was something funny about Edith's family. About the set up. The mother had been as mad as a hatter, the other children like scared mice. The eldest, Joseph, had seemed to him more like his mother's lover than her son. From the bits and pieces that Edith had let drop over the years he knew they'd all had a terrible upbringing. He remembered when he had gone to tell Nancy Markham he was marrying Edith. Her malice as she'd told him about her daughter's illegitimate child had shocked him.

594

She was sick in the head, Nancy Markham. No wonder the children all turned out weird. Except for Edith. She had been the sweetest girl he had ever known, and even though over the years he had systematically cheated on her with everyone and anyone, he still loved her. He still thought of her as that same sweet girl he married. But Edith had a distaste for sex, touching, even kissing. Oh, she had tried to hide it, but he knew. You always know when your attentions are welcome and when they're not. But she was a damn' fine wife and mother and that was the main thing.

Natalie watched her uncle eating and smiled at him. She had heard stories about her Uncle George all her life. He was her mother's closest living relative. She knew her grandmother was alive. They heard from her only occasionally, and after a communication her mother was always jumpy for a few weeks.

Her greeny-blue eyes surveyed the room around her. She loved this house. She loved being inside it with her family. One day, when she met the right man, she would own a house just like it and she'd fill it with children and laughter. She smiled to herself at the thought.

Until then she had her job and her dogs. It was Natalie who had named the Dobermans. She had read Dante's *Inferno* and it had made a great impression on her. Dobermans to her were devil dogs. But she loved them, as she loved all animals.

George watched his niece. When she had smiled at him then he had been convinced that it was his mother sitting opposite him. George felt the strangeness that came over him at times. As if he was hand in hand with reality one minute and left out, floating in limbo, the next. The room had taken on smoky edges. Nothing looked solid any more. His mind was filled with thoughts, crowded with them as if they didn't have enough room to manoeuvre. Flickering pictures entered this brimming morass. He saw Geraldine O'Leary with her long beautiful hair lying beneath him. He saw Mandy Kelly and he saw Elaine. They all drifted in and out of his mind, and after every vision this girl was before him. He

595

felt an urge to take his steak knife and push it through her throat. Let the blood bubble from the wound, strangling his mother's voice.

He could hear her now: 'Who's Mummy's little soldier, Georgie?'

He could smell the sheets on the bed, scented with Lux flakes. He could hear the dreadful ack-ack of the anti-aircraft fire. The bombs were going to land on their house but Mother made them stay in bed while she drank tea and smoked. He could feel the ache in his bowels and the red rawness of his rectum where the tubing had been forced past his sphincter. Sweat was pouring from his brow. He could feel it running on to the pillows with his frightened tears. Why didn't she come? Why didn't she comfort him? He was Mummy's little soldier, wasn't he?

'George . . . George. Joss is talking to you, dear.'

He was dragged back to the present and looked around the table, bewildered.

'Are you feeling all right, George?' Edith's voice was concerned.

Joss Junior glanced at his watch. 'I really have to go soon, Mother, if I'm to catch my plane.'

Edith was immediately concerned. George took the opportunity to try and pull himself together.

'Natalie's company gave her the week to see her uncle. I wish yours had done the same.'

Joss Junior smiled. 'Well, Ma, I'm doing an important job. They can't afford to let me have too much time off.'

Edith was gratified to hear this.

'Your father and I will run you to the airport. Finish your meal.'

Natalie stretched in her chair, pushing her long tapering fingers through her hair in a completely feminine gesture. Edith and Joss Senior watched her with pride. George watched her with hatred. Joss Junior took no notice of her whatsoever.

'Do you want to drive to the airport with us, George?'

'No. I think I'll just relax, Edith. I feel so tired.'

'Do you want me to stay here with Uncle George?' Natalie's voice was concerned.

'No. You leave your uncle, let him have a rest, Natalie. Come with us and see your brother off at the airport.'

For some reason, Edith did not want George and her daughter left alone.

George smiled at them as he waved them off a little later. Then, climbing into his car, he made his way to the Orange Blossom Trail.

Duane Portillo watched the little family climbing into the large Lincoln Continental. A few minutes later he followed George Markham out towards the Orange Blossom Trail.

Linette Du Bouverie was what was known on the trail as an 'ornery' whore. She was petite and a natural redhead. But she sure was 'ornery'. She was known as the loudest, most foul-mouthed and argumentative woman on the Trail. Her vicious mouth was hated by other whores, pimps and police, in that order. She was a heroin addict and needed her daily fixes desperately. Linette would take a man on for a measly five dollars if necessary.

Today she was banging on the door of the little one-roomed apartment of Elvis Carmody.

Elvis was a pusher of uncertain creed. He had black wiry hair and the reddish skin colour of a Mexican. His mother, a hooker, used to joke that he was her Heinz 57. She never knew who fathered him. Elvis had built himself a business of sorts. He supplied heroin, crack, dope, uppers, downers . . . anything, in fact, that he could lay his hands on. He opened the apartment door to Linette and whistled at her through his teeth.

'You look terrible, baby!'

She walked into the room on her high heels. She was having trouble focusing properly in the dim light. Somewhere in the room she heard the rustle of bedclothes and, peering through the dimness, made out the shape and face of a little Puerto Rican hooker named Marigold. She swore under her breath. If Elvis had just had some ass he was not going to come across to her and give her a little bit on account.

'What can I do for you, Linette?' Already Elvis wanted rid of her.

'I need a fix. I'll pay you in about an hour, man, there's nothing going down in the street just yet. Once it's dark the place will be buzzing.'

Elvis lit a Marlboro and blew out the smoke noisily. 'No way, baby, you still owe me twenty bucks from yesterday.'

Linette felt her famous temper rising. Going to the bed, she grabbed Marigold's hair.

'You'd give her some, though, wouldn't you, you motherfucking creep? I'll pay you the goddam' money, but first I need me a little bit on account.'

Elvis walked to her and untangled her fingers from the girl's hair. Marigold had not batted an eyelid.

Taking Linette by the scruff of her neck, he ran her to the doorway and threw her on to the dirty floor outside.

'Why don't you quit annoying people, Linette? If you didn't have such a bad attitude, people might be more inclined to help you.'

He shut the door on her. Dragging herself up, she threw herself at the wood, kicking and pummelling the door. There were tears of frustration in her dark green eyes.

'I'll cut your motherfucking throat, you stinking creep!'

There was no answer from the room. Feeling sorry for herself, Linette walked from the building into the bright sunlight outside.

George saw a tiny, slim girl of about twenty-five lounging against a wall. Her red hair was catching the rays of the sun and she was dressed in a green suede hot pants suit. Her ample breasts practically spilled out of the material and he smiled at her. His secret smile that just showed his teeth.

Linette, knowing a punter when she saw one, smiled back. Her sweetest smile.

George opened the window of his car. Linette ambled over to him.

'Hello there.'

George smiled again, wider this time. 'Hello, dear.'

'How would you like some company?'

'Get in.'

Linette walked round and got inside the car. 'Drive to the Lazy Q. We can get a room there, movies, anything you want.'

George was already on his way. Linette lit a cigarette and smiled to herself as they neared the motel. He knew where he was going so he wasn't that green. She wondered how much she should hit him for. She could already feel the sweating that told her she needed a fix. And soon.

The man who gave them the key was now watching an episode of 'Married with Children'. George wondered briefly if he ever left the TV set. Up in the room, Linette picked up the phone and ordered a bottle of bourbon. It would ease her nerves till she could score some smack.

While she waited for it to come she slipped off her clothes. George watched her, fascinated. It was as if she did not even realise he was there. She had not attempted to make conversation. He sat on the bed and took out some small change. Putting two fifty cents into the meter on the television, he turned the knob and a porno film flickered into life on the screen. Linette answered the door to the boy with the bourbon, naked except for her shoes. Linette never removed her shoes. Ever.

She looked at George. 'I need ten dollars.'

He calmly peeled the money off a large roll and gave it to her. The young black boy watched her in total fascination as she swayed towards him, naked except for her high heels.

'Here you are, boy. Take a good look. And when you get paid, child, you come and see Linette.'

'Yes, ma'am.' This was said with every bit of manliness the fourteen year old could muster.

Linette shut the door and laughed. She cracked the top and drank the whisky from the bottle.

'That's a lot of money you got there, honey.'

George took off his clothes and folded them neatly on a chair.

'How much do you want?'

She liked his meekness. 'I charge sixty dollars, the best lay you're ever gonna get.'

George handed three twenty-dollar bills to her.

He watched the film for a moment. It was of a woman, a dog and a large black man.

Linette sat beside him on the bed. Pushing her breasts against his arm she stroked his flaccid penis. She wanted this over with as quickly as possible.

'Come on, baby, Linette ain't got all night.'

George could smell her sweat. Her hair was lying across his arm and he could see her rosy nipples. Her hand on his penis had deep red-painted nails. She looked just like his mother. She even smelt like his mother. He pushed her hand away from him impatiently.

'Don't touch me like that.'

George's voice was hard. Linette fell backwards with the force of his push.

'Who the hell you think you're pushing, you little shit!' Her natural antagonism was surfacing.

George faced her. She was standing now, the whiskey bottle still in her hand. Her legs were long and shapely in the green high heels. She took another long pull of the Jim Beam. George stood up and faced her.

She was just like his mother. Just like Natalie. They were all whores, every last one of them. Give themselves to anyone who had a couple of pounds. All women were the same. They were whores. Well, he knew what to do with whores, didn't he? Hadn't he shown them in Grantley? Grabbing her hair, he punched her in the face, putting all his weight behind the blow. He watched, a smile on his face, as Linette staggered backwards and fell against the wall. The blow had hit her in the mouth and she leant against the wall, her breasts heaving. She poked a little pink tongue out of her mouth and tasted the blood that was seeping from her lip. She watched warily as he walked towards her. He was naked and his stomach wobbled as he walked.

As he lifted his fist again Linette kicked out. George felt a stinging sensation and when he looked down he had a cut across his stomach.

Linette Du Bouverie kept a blade in the toe of each shoe, a trick she'd learned in prison.

That's why Linette never took her shoes off. George watched the blood begin to run and looked at the woman in astonishment. He lurched at her, putting up his hands to seize her hair, and grabbed empty space.

Linette kicked out at him again. This time she caught his back. A long searing pain engulfed him. She had ripped the skin right across the kidney. It was a deep cut of half an inch. As he dropped to his knees Linette took another long pull of whiskey, then smashed the bottle against the chest of drawers by the bed. His back was bleeding profusely now.

Using all the strength that he could muster, George slammed his fist into her solar plexus. Linette doubled up as she tried to breathe. George pulled himself up to his feet; his hands were covered in blood.

On the screen, the black man, the woman and the dog careered around, impervious to what was going on.

'You friggin' creep, nobody hits me, nobody. Not you, not anyone.' Her mouth was a twisted gash. This time the blade caught him across his thighs, the blood spurted out in crimson droplets, the skin opening slowly, as if shy about revealing the flesh beneath. George dropped to his knees once more, for the first time realising he was up against a will much stronger than his own. This woman was of the same calibre as his mother. Pulling his head back by his hair, Linette grinned at him as she brought the jagged edge of the Jim Beam bottle across his throat.

George dropped to the floor, his face turned towards the television. His last sight was of the woman grunting as the black man pushed his impossibly large member inside her, the little dog yapping as it ran around their bodies.

Linette sat on the bed, dropping the bottle on to the carpet. She placed a bloody hand on to her breast to stem the beating of her heart. Looking down at George, she drew her lips back from her teeth in disgust.

Linette had been physically and mentally abused all her short life. Her father had been the main offender, her brothers had followed his example. Her mother had turned a blind eye. When Linette had left home at fifteen, she had been thrust into a world where only her looks and her sex had been her saving graces. She had taken her first fix and turned her first trick within thirty-six hours of hitting the streets. Selling her body was all she could do. Allowing men a free licence with it was all she had ever known. But once she'd left home, Linette had always balked at being beaten. It was the thing she hated most. Sexually, she'd do anything for money. Anything. But a man or woman beating up on her was an admission of failure. If she could keep herself protected then she still had a certain amount of self respect. It was important to her. Her violent reputation had stood her in good stead over the last few years. A violent whore was not wanted by a pimp, a violent whore would not get robbed by another whore. The law of the streets was strength, and even though she was tiny, she was strong and she could look after herself. The man on the floor was nothing to Linette, he was a trick, a John, a means to an end. Without looking at him again she got up from the bed and went to the shower. She washed the blood from her body, then calmly got dressed, brushed her hair and repaired her makeup, feeling the slight swelling already around her eye. She took all George's cash and traveller's cheques. She left the credit cards; she'd quickly become a suspect if she tried to use them. Taking one last look at herself in the mirror, she left the room, shutting the door quietly behind her. Ten minutes later she was at Elvis's, George's eight hundred dollars assuring her of a very warm welcome. As she pushed the needle into her arm, she felt the first waves of euphoria rushing to her brain; she breathed in deeply and let the good feelings flow.

George Markham was already gone from her mind.

Duane Portillo watched Linette walk from the hotel. He sat up in his seat and waited for George to emerge. But George did not come out.

George still lay on the floor of the motel room, still staring, vacant eyed, at the blue movie. The blood had long ceased pumping. The girl on the film seemed to be staring back at him, her face a mask of pretended pleasure.

But George couldn't see her. It was a shame really. He would have loved it.

Edith was getting worried. They had got back from the airport and George was nowhere to be seen. Every time she heard a car she rushed to the window to see if it was him.

'Oh, for Christ's sake, Edith, he's a grown man,' Joss told her. 'He's probably gone out for a beer and got talking to someone.'

She did not bother to answer. She tutted. Imagine thinking George would get talking to someone. Sometimes she didn't think that Joss realised just what was going on around him. George talking to strangers indeed!

Natalie kissed them good night and went up to bed. Edith watched her walk up the stairs and felt the pride she always felt in her children.

She had done well for them. She had always looked after them and protected them.

The police answered the call at eleven thirty. The hotel manager had dragged his eyes away from the television set at eleven-twenty to go and rout out room number 14. They had been in there for over five hours. He now had another couple who wanted the room. He asked them to wait and went up and knocked on the door.

It was deathly quiet.

He unlocked the room with his master key. He was not too shocked at what he found. He told the couple to come back another time, and hid George's credit cards before he phoned the police.

Edith was informed at twelve ten precisely.

Duane Portillo watched the proceedings before he left the

scene. He went straight to Shaun O'Grady with his story. Shaun scratched his head in bewilderment.

'You mean the guy you was gonna kill has been killed! By a goddam whore, for Chrissakes!'

Duane nodded. He couldn't quite believe it himself.

Shaun O'Grady saw the funny side.

'Well, who the hell would credit that?'

Duane Portillo laughed too. It sure had been a weird day.

Kate was helping Lizzy sort out what clothes she was taking. Since she had been dropped from the Grantley Ripper case, she had tried to assume an air of nonchalance but it had gradually been slipping away from her.

'Mum?'

'What, love?'

Lizzy turned her mother to face her.

'What's wrong really? Have you had a tiff with Patrick?'

Kate felt an urge to cry and laugh at the same time. A tiff? Lizzy sat on her bed and looked at her mother.

'Please tell me what's wrong with you, Mum. I can't stand seeing you so unhappy.'

Kate looked into the dark eyes so like her own and felt a rush of love for her daughter.

As she tried to speak her voice broke and Lizzy pulled her into her arms. Kate sobbed her heart out on her daughter's shoulder.

Somewhere a little voice was saying that this was wrong. That it was she who should be comforting her daughter. But it felt so good to have someone to hold her, and kiss her hair, and tell her everything was going to be all right. Even though she knew in her heart that nothing would ever be all right again. That all she had wanted and held dear was destroyed. That she had been used by a man she loved so desperately that she would still have him now, if he came to her.

Lizzy stroked her mother's hair and sighed gently. It felt good to be able to help her for once; to feel that she was in control of the situation. That her mother could let down her defences and admit that she was not Wonder Woman, that she had problems too.

It made her seem more human somehow.

Lizzy knew with the awareness of womankind that she could help her mother by holding her and loving her. For the first time ever, they were equals. They had healed a breach that spanned fifteen years. In spite of all her heartache, it felt good to Kate. It felt very good.

Later on, in her lounge with her mother and Lizzy, Kate heard the shock statement on News at Ten. She was drinking a bacardi and coke, having just got out of the bath. Lizzy had run it for her, filling it with the fragrance of lavender to make her feel calmer.

She had needed all her calm when Sandy Gall started speaking.

'A British tourist was murdered today in Florida by a prostitute. George Markham was savagely slashed to death and his throat cut. From the reports we have had in so far, Mr Markham, who was fifty-one years old, had been wanted by the British police in connection with the murders of six women and a child. He is believed to have been the Grantley Rapist. The police here have confirmed that they wanted to interview him on his return from Florida.

'In the Lebanon today . . .'

'Jesus suffering Christ!' Evelyn's voice was shocked and low.

Kate stared at Sandy Gall's face for a moment. Then, jumping from her seat, she went to the hall and phoned Caitlin's home number. It was answered on the second ring.

'I take it you've heard the news, Katie?'

'It's true then?'

'Oh, it's true all right. It seems he got his come-uppance. He was murdered by a known prostitute called Linette something or other. She told police that he attacked her and it was self-defence.'

Kate nodded into the phone, forgetting Caitlin couldn't see her.

'Are you still there, Kate?'

605

'Yes. Oh, Kenny, I feel such a fool.'

She heard the smile in his voice as he answered. 'I told you not to jump in at the deep end, but you wouldn't listen, would you?'

'No.'

'Look, Katie, have another few days off. I'll speak to Flowers for you. You're a good policewoman and I know he doesn't want to lose you. Now this Ripper thing is over, I think we can all relax.'

Kate said goodbye and hung up.

She felt such a blasted fool. She had accused Patrick Kelly of trying to murder the man. She had gone to his house and shouted her mouth off. She could hear everything she'd said and her face burned with humiliation.

He must feel disgusted with her. And who in their right mind could blame him?

She put her head against the coolness of the wall and sighed. Everything had gone wrong and it had been her fault. She was suspended from work, but more importantly to her she had botched up the only chance of real happiness she'd had.

As Patrick would say, she was a 24-carat fool.

Her mind was filled with thoughts of the nights she had spent with him. The excitement. The closeness. The shared love.

He had told her he loved her, and how had she repaid him?

Patrick took the call at seven fifteen.

Willy watched him exclaim: 'You're joking!'

O'Grady's voice crackled over the line.

'No, Pat, it was a classic, I tell you. I waited until I could get the full facts before phoning you. The man picked up a prostitute on the Orange Blossom Trail. That's Florida's answer to Soho, you know. Well, it seems things got a bit out of hand and he attacked her. That's always a whore's defence, of course: The man attacked me, so I pulled a knife, a gun, whatever.

'By all accounts she said she never reported it to the police because she knew that they wouldn't believe her. When it came on CNN today that the man was wanted in England as a serial killer, this place went wild. The woman's a frigging national heroine, for Chrissakes.'

'Jesus, I can't believe what you're telling me. Markham murdered my daughter. I would have followed him to the ends of the earth. But to have that happen to him . . . I mean, it's just unbelievable.'

O'Grady's voice was quiet.

'Believe it, buddy. He's dead. Now you just go on living your life. I'll see that the money's returned to you tomorrow. I've got to give my guy something though. He still trailed him, you know.'

'Anything you say, Shaun.'

Kelly replaced the receiver and stared at it for a few seconds as if not sure he had really had the call.

He stared at Willy. 'You're not going to believe this.'

'Try me.'

Edith looked down at George's body and felt the sting of tears.

'Is this your brother, ma'am?' The policeman's voice was low and reassuring.

She nodded.

She looked at the man as he gestured to the mortuary assistant to cover George's face again. Suddenly she felt very old and frightened.

'Ma'am, I have some more distressing news for you.'

'What? What could be worse than this?'

'We have been notified by the British police that your brother had murdered seven people, including his own wife and a young child. It seems the British cops were waiting for him to return to Britain to arrest him.'

Edith realised she had known this inside all along. She still read the English papers, knew all about this Grantley Ripper. Deep down in her heart she had known it was her brother. She looked into the policeman's sympathetic face.

'Joss, please take me home.'

He pulled himself wearily from his seat and took his wife's arm. In their car Edith spoke.

'I know what George did was wrong and I'll regret his coming here for the rest of my life. But, Joss, only I know why he was like he was. And knowing what I know, all I can do is pity him.'

Her husband said nothing.

If the whore who had done it would come forward, Joss would shake her by the hand.

Joseph Markham and his wife watched the news in stunned silence. Both looked over to Nancy and saw that her face was grey and drawn.

Lily was the first of the three to come to herself. 'How will we ever live this down?' she shrieked. 'Your brother, the Grantley Ripper!'

'Oh, be quiet, Lily. George was always a stupid fool. All my children were useless,' snapped Nancy. 'Look at him.' She flicked her head at Joseph. 'He sits there like a big lummock. His brother is a murdering rapist and he just sits there. At least George had some life in him.'

'We'll have to sell the house, I can't live here now. The neighbours will be laughing up their sleeves. Every time we leave the house people will be pointing at us, talking about us.'

'I knew there was something wrong with George, I told the policeman that the other day. My sons are spineless nobodies. All my children are. Not one of them inherited a thing from me. They're all like their father. He was just the same.'

Joseph Markham listened to his wife's high-pitched voice and his mother's deep-throated tirade and finally, after thirty years, he spoke up.

'SHUT UP, THE PAIR OF YOU!'

Nancy and Lily both stared at him in shock.

'You,' he pointed to his mother, 'are going in to that home, first thing in the morning. I can't wait another week to get shot of you.'

She opened her mouth to speak and Joseph raised his hand menacingly.

'I told you to shut up, woman.'

His wife's mouth dropped open.

'The house is being sold, Lily, and you will get half the money. I am buying myself a flat and neither of you two will have the address. I've spent all my life listening; first to you, Mother, then to Lily, and finally to the blasted pair of you. I must be the only man in Christendom nagged in stereo.

'Well, the buck stops here. George murdered all those people, including Elaine, and neither of you two even care. You're worried about the neighbours. Fuck the neighbours! I couldn't care less about them. My brother is dead, six women and a child have been murdered by him. So why don't you two just shut your bloody stupid mouths up and think about other people for once?'

He began to walk from the room.

'Where are you going?' Lily's voice was frightened.

'Where the hell do you think? I'm going to phone poor Edith. She must be in a terrible state. Then I'm going to get my coat and go to a hotel. I'll be back tomorrow to arrange for her to be put away – as far away as possible, I might add – and to sort this lot.' He gestured around him with his hands.

Ten minutes later, they heard his car splutter to life and drive away.

'This is all your fault!' Lily turned on her mother-in-law.

'Why don't you piss off?' Nancy's voice was bored-sounding.

Lily pursed her lips. There had been too much swearing tonight for her liking. Just as she and Joseph were getting on a good footing, this had to happen!

As he drove along Joseph tried to piece together the night's events in his mind.

George had finally gone over the top. Why hadn't anyone noticed? He had been left too much to his own devices, Joseph supposed. They rarely visited except for Christmas. He was George's elder brother and should have looked out for him more.

609

Well, his mother had gone too far this time. He must have been mad to put up with her all these years. His threat to Lily was shallow, he wouldn't leave her, but he had a sneaky feeling that letting her think he would might augur better for their future.

Edith was in a terrible state, she was barely coherent. And deep down inside Edith knew, as he did, that it was their mother's fault. He remembered shamefully how they had held George down while he was a child. How she had gradually strangled every natural instinct in them.

Joseph pulled the car over and sat for a few minutes. His hands were shaking on the steering wheel.

Into his mind came a picture of George when he was a small boy, in his National Health glasses and long grey socks. They had been playing hide and seek while their mother was out working and George was laughing his head off. Real, robust, childish laughter. Joseph remembered it clearly because it had happened so rarely.

The Markowitz children had had nothing to laugh about most of the time.

Joseph wept.

He wept for the George he had known. The little boy he should have protected more. The little boy who used to cry every night, who was frightened of his mother and yet loved her so much. No matter what she did to him.

Patrick Kelly slept heavily that night, a long blissful sleep, the first since his daughter had been murdered.

His last thought as he drifted off was of Kate. He wished she was beside him, but after what she had said, he knew the gulf between them was too wide.

Kate Burrows was a luxury he couldn't afford. Tomorrow he would get out his little black book. Go back to the women who understood him. Who wanted nothing more from him than a good time.

He didn't need Kate Burrows. She was a forty-year-old woman while he could have any gorgeous girl he wanted. And have them he would. He would become a playboy again.

He smiled to himself at the thought. That would please Willy. He had always enjoyed observing his boss's affairs.

Kate Burrows could get stuffed.

Happy he had sorted his life out, Patrick slept.

Kate lay awake, her mind in a turmoil, her body aching to be touched. To be comforted by Patrick Kelly's lovemaking.

Chapter Thirty-two

4 March 1990

Kate was in the airport lounge watching Lizzy and her mother checking in for their flight. She stood by as their baggage was tagged and taken from them. A feeling of desolation assailed her. She would be alone for six weeks.

All she had was her work, and she was not happy with that, she admitted to herself. She wished she was getting on the plane with them. That she was going somewhere where she could forget the last few months.

Lizzy and Evelyn approached her. Kate watched the tall slim girl, who caught more than a few male eyes, and the stooped little woman beside her.

When had her mother developed a stoop? When had she become old?

She walked with them towards passport control, chatting about nothing. She was dreading saying goodbye, but knew that they had to go. Her mother would see her other child and the grandchildren whom she had only seen in photos and spoken to rarely, when funds allowed. She still had all their letters and had chronicled their ages from lovingly preserved school photos.

Dear Grandma . . . Now she would see them for herself. Kate was glad for her really. It was only selfishness that wanted her to stay at home.

They were at passport control now. Kate pulled her mother into her arms and kissed her hard.

'Have a good time, Mum. Look after my baby for me.'

Evelyn looked into Kate's face and said seriously, 'Haven't I always? You look after yourself.'

Lizzy was crying and Kate smiled at her, a single tear escaping from the corner of her own eye.

'Goodbye, baby.'

Lizzy threw herself into her mother's arms and hugged her.

'Oh, Mum, I wish you were coming with us. Will you be all right on your own?'

Kate kissed her again.

'You just go and have a good time. Enjoy it. Before you know it, you'll be back home.'

Evelyn stroked Kate's face. 'You ring that Patrick Kelly, you hear?'

'Oh, Mum! Get yourselves through and send me a card from Singapore.'

'It was him who paid for this, you know. I didn't have any money at all. If I had done, I'd have spent it years ago. You know that. Did you know we're going first class? He did this to try and help you when Lizzy was bad.'

Kate stared at her mother for a few seconds then Evelyn took Lizzy's arm and they walked through to the departure lounge.

Kate's head was whirling. Patrick had paid for the holiday. It was the final humiliation. She had accused him of everything heinous under the sun and he had spent a fortune on airplane tickets and hotels for her mother and child.

Oh, the generosity of him. The concern for her. And she had taken what he had offered and thrown it back in his face.

She watched them till they were out of sight, then drove home to her empty house. As she put her key in the lock she felt it was mocking her.

At five fifty-five she poured herself the first drink. At seven she was in a drunken sleep.

Oprah Winfrey stared into the camera and smiled. Her studio audience was finishing its applause and the opening credits had been rolled.

'Thank you.' She looked around at her audience. 'Five

614

weeks ago in Windermere, Florida, a man attacked a prostitute. The woman, Ms Linette Du Bouverie, fought the man off, killing him. She left the scene of the crime because she was frightened of the consequences. She was later identified by a young man who worked at the hotel who had delivered a bottle of Jim Beam to the room. It turned out that Ms Du Bouverie had in fact killed a vicious serial killer from England. Tonight we hear from women who have killed the men who attacked them. Let us start by giving a big hand to Linette Du Bouverie.'

The audience went wild.

Linette walked out on to the stage and smiled. She was pretty and petite and looked like everybody's next-door neighbour.

Elvis watched her smile at the camera and laughed out loud. That Linette was some bad dude.

Kate came home from work and made herself a coffee. In the month that Lizzy and her mother had been away, her routine had not changed at all. The empty house seemed to mock her and she put the radio on as she did every night to fill up the hollowness with sound. What she would not give to have Lizzy's music blaring out now!

The phone rang and she picked it up. It was Amanda Dawkins.

'Hello, love.'

'I wondered if it was all right if me and Phil popped round tonight, Kate? We've got a great video and a bottle of wine.'

She smiled into the phone.

Amanda did this every so often, came around with her boyfriend as if she knew that Kate was lonely and needed a bit of company.

'That would be lovely, Amanda, as long as you're sure you haven't got anything better to do?'

'We'll see you about half past eight.'

'What's the video?'

'*Beaches* with Bette Midler.'

615

'I bet Phil didn't pick that one!'

'You guessed exactly right! If he'd have chosen it, we would have watched *Nightmare on Elm Street* or *Hallowe'en*!'

'See you later then.'

She had a sandwich and went upstairs for a bath.

Patrick Kelly glanced at the girl beside him. Leona had the biggest blue eyes he had ever seen in his life, and the biggest breasts. She faced him and smiled, displaying white teeth. 'Would you like another glass of wine?'

'Please.'

She had a little lisp that had sounded enchanting when he first met her. Now it was beginning to get on his nerves.

Leona was one of a series of women he had been dating since his break up with Kate. Patrick was hoping against hope that one of the bevy of lovelies would take his mind off her once and for all. He had hoped Leona would be the one to pull him out of himself.

He poured her a glass of white wine. It was cheap Liebfraumilch. There was no way he was going to give her expensive wine. She drank it down in two gulps. He watched her do it, leaving a thick red line on the rim of the glass.

'How old are you, Leona?'

'Twenty-one, why?'

'I just wondered, that's all.'

Kelly sipped his own wine and racked his brains for something to talk about.

Leona watched his troubled face. This was their third date and he hadn't tried it on once. This was a novelty to Leona and she wasn't sure if she was glad or not. He was a damn' sight better looking than most of the men she dated.

She made a golden rule of going to places where the clientèle were men who were rich, getting on, and not too fussy. She was astute enough to know that with her looks and body she could have her pick of them.

She drove a brand new Golf Gti, had her own flat, bought

and paid for, and relied heavily on men like Patrick Kelly to supplement her lifestyle. Leaving school with no qualifications, and nothing going for her except a pretty face and a double D bra size, she had quickly assessed her position and cashed in on her only assets.

So far, along with the flat and the car, they had taken her around the world.

She could like this Kelly, though. He was a good-looking man with an air about him that she liked. She was quite looking forward to getting into bed with him. He seemed very generous as well, which to Leona was the most important thing.

She watched him struggling to find something to talk about. 'Tell me all about yourself, Patrick.'

She relaxed into her chair. Someone had told her once that the secret of keeping a man happy was to get him started on his favourite subject: himself. This had been proved correct over and over again; it kept them occupied for hours. Leaving Leona to think about *her* favourite subject: herself.

Patrick still struggled while he told her bits and pieces. He didn't want to share any part of his personal business with her. He didn't really want her there at all.

He couldn't be bothered to make the effort to chat. He took the bull by the horns.

'Want to come to bed?'

Leona shrugged.

'OK.'

She followed him up the stairs, pricing everything she saw on the way.

He was rich all right.

Phil studied Kate and Amanda as they watched the film. He smiled to himself. Women loved nothing more in a film than a good death. It amazed him. He had sat through *Terms of Endearment* and *Who Will Love My Children?*. Both films Amanda had loved while he had hated them. Deathbed scenes weren't his favourite subject. He would much rather be watching *Predator*, there was plenty of death in that, but it was not slow and lingering enough for Amanda. Or Kate for that matter. Women liked a good bout of cancer or some-one coughing up a lung. That appealed to them.

He cracked open another lager and poured out more wine for the two women. Kate and Amanda had a box of Kleenex on the settee between them and every so often a little hiccough could be heard.

Kate gazed at the screen and sniffed. She loved a good weepy, and it was nice to cry in company. Bette Midler was on the beach with her best friend's daughter, trying to make friends with her before her mother died.

She sipped her wine and wiped her eyes again. She felt so lonely. So very, very lonely.

She got up from the settee and went out to the kitchen. She had made some sandwiches earlier and now took the cling film off them and brought them into the lounge.

Phil, his bright copper-coloured hair shining in the light from the television screen, grinned at her as he took the plate and started to eat.

Kate hoped they wouldn't stay too late tonight. She liked to go to bed and read for a while until she dropped off. Amanda had really come up trumps for her since the Grantley Ripper inquiry, and Kate appreciated that. But sometimes you can be lonely even when you're in a crowd, and that was just how Kate was feeling. For the first time ever she had more than enough time to devote to herself and every second of it was a form of torture.

She knew what was wrong with her, and knew who could cure it. But she could not bring herself to dial his number or go to his house.

Patrick was lying on his bed naked, smoking a cigarette. Leona was still undressing. He noticed she was hanging her clothes in his wardrobe and grinned ruefully to himself. She obviously thought she was set for a good few months. He watched her as she turned to face him with her incredible breasts, a half smile on her face, waiting for the effect they always had on men.

Especially older men.

Patrick took one look at her and his heart sank down to his boots.

What was he trying to prove?

Like the others he had had in recent weeks, Leona did nothing for him whatsoever. He saw her mouth twitch with disappointment and felt a moment's sympathy for her.

She walked timidly towards him. 'Don't you like me?' Her voice was small.

'Of course I like you, you're beautiful.'

She pouted prettily and rubbed his flaccid penis. 'Leona wants to play!'

Patrick sighed. What he wouldn't give for a pack of cards or a draughts board!

She pulled his foreskin back, slowly and expertly, and Patrick felt the first stirrings inside him. He closed his eyes. When he felt the wet heat of her mouth enveloping him he groaned.

Leona sucked away as if her life depended on it. For the first time ever she had to take the initiative, and she didn't like it at all. One look at her boobs generally had them champing at the bit. She felt him stiffening in her mouth and fought down the urge to heave.

Leona hated oral sex. She usually saved it for when the man was getting tired of her. It normally gave her the edge then.

Her dark blonde hair fell over her face and she cupped his testicles as gently as possible. Then, satisfied he was hard enough, she climbed on top.

She was as dry as a bone, but nevertheless forced him inside her. As she moved up and down, her breasts brushing against his chest, Patrick opened his eyes.

Instead of long, silky dark hair there was thick blonde hair. Instead of Kate's small pointed breasts with their cherry red nipples there was an enormous pair, hanging over his face. Instead of dark brown eyes looking into his there was a pair of startled-looking blue ones.

Patrick Kelly lost his erection in record time.

619

Leona felt him deflate inside her and leapt off him in temper. How dare he? After all she had done!

She sat on the side of the bed, her arms crossed over her breasts and a frown on her pretty face.

'I'm sorry, love, I'm tired that's all.'

Leona glared at him. One thing Leona was sure of: her body was the best thing this creep had ever seen in his life. He must be a homosexual or something. She shuddered, wishing now she'd made him use a Durex.

She looked at him through slitted eyes.

'Are you a poofta, Mr Kelly?'

Patrick stared at the girl as the words penetrated. Then, to the amazement of both of them, he began to laugh. He laughed so loudly that Willy, who was in the library downstairs enjoying a brandy while he read the racing paper, looked up at the ceiling, pleased that Patrick was having such a good time.

He laughed so much that big fat tears rolled down his face.

As far as Leona was concerned, enough was enough. She dressed herself as quickly as possible. Standing over the bed, her dignity back now, along with her clothes, she poked a perfectly manicured fingernail into his chest.

'I've heard about men like you. You should come out into the open. It's not a crime any more. They call it coming out of the wardrobe. I'll bill you for my time in the morning.'

With that she went down the stairs to call a cab.

Patrick lay against the pillows. He could still smell her perfume.

He began to laugh again at her words. Then, abruptly, he stopped laughing.

In reality, she could have been his Mandy. Mandy had had a lot more savvy, he knew that, but she was the same age. What would he have thought if he had found out his daughter was sleeping with a man over twenty years her senior? And not for love either, but for a few quid and a good time.

He closed his eyes and rubbed his fingers against them, trying to blot out the image of those breasts. He felt the loneliness as it welled up inside. He should have Kate beside him. But after what had happened between them? He knew that she had thought the worst of him and admitted to himself that he was glad now that Markham had died through another's means. He was glad that he was not the cause of the man's death.

He had hoped against hope that Kate would have rung him up when she heard the news and said she was sorry. Then they could have got back on their old footing. But nothing. Not a word. And being the kind of man he was, he had had too much pride to get in touch with her.

What she had said to him had hurt because it was true. She had sussed him out all right. It was only after he knew Markham was dead, when the euphoria had worn off, that he'd realised that revenge is not as sweet as you first imagine. It had come out in all the papers about the man's terrible childhood. His sister in America had spilled the beans. Wanting to set the record straight, she said.

Kelly had read the stories and felt a funny kind of sorrow for the man. He was sick in the head. But he had already known that, hadn't he? When he was planning to kill him.

He shifted uneasily in the bed. Kate had been right. The man had needed help. He wished that she was here beside him. He had wanted Kate beside him from the minute he had seen her. He admitted that to himself now.

What was it his old mum used to say?

'God pays back debts without money.'

Well, both he and George Markham had more than paid the price.

Kate and Amanda looked at each other as the film ended and both started to laugh through their tears. Phil stood up and put on the overhead light.

'You women amaze me. Imagine watching something that makes you sad!'

'Oh, Phil! That was a lovely film.'

He walked out to the hall and was just at the bottom of the stairs, going up to the bathroom, when the phone rang. Without thinking, he picked it up.

'Hello?'

The line was quiet and he spoke again.

'Hello, who is this?' He heard the noise as the connection was broken.

Kate came out to the hall.

'Who's that?'

Phil shrugged. 'Wrong number.' He carried on walking up the stairs to the bathroom and Kate went back to make some coffee.

Patrick Kelly lay in bed with the phone in one hand and his fingers on the receiver rest.

He was fuming. It hadn't taken her long to get someone else!

He glanced at the clock. It was just after eleven fifteen. Probably interrupted their lovemaking. The snidey bitch! To think he had thrown out a perfectly good woman because of her. Because he was silly enough to fancy himself in love with her.

Well, that was the finish as far as he was concerned. That would teach him to think that he could ever replace Renée.

Face it, boy, he told himself, you're on your Jack Jones and the sooner you realise that, the better.

Downstairs, Willy helped himself to another brandy. The girl had gone and Patrick had tried to use the phone. Willy had heard the bell as he'd picked it up, and then again as he'd put it down.

He shook his head sagely.

Patrick Kelly's trouble was he didn't know when he was well off. And he had been well off with that Burrows piece. Willy had liked her himself. She wasn't that well stacked but she'd had class.

He sipped some more of his boss's brandy and went back to reading his paper.

Kate was at work on a series of burglaries that had been happening over a two-year period. They all had the same

MO. It was a lone man and he broke in while the woman was sleeping, sexually assaulting his victim before he trashed the bedroom, taking money and jewellery. It was the assaults that bothered her. He used the burglary as a blind. He was working up to a full-scale rape, she would lay money on that.

The phone rang.

'Burrows.'

'Hello, Kate.'

She took the phone from her ear and stared into the mouthpiece before answering.

'Is that you, Willy?'

'Yes.'

The line went quiet.

'Well, what can I do for you?'

'I wondered if I could see you, like?'

'What about?'

'Well, I don't like to talk about it over the phone. Can we meet, please?'

Kate licked dry lips.

'Where do you want us to meet?'

'How about the Cartella restaurant? Tonight at eight thirty?'

'Is this something to do with Patrick?'

Willy swallowed deeply and she heard the sound over the phone.

'Oh, no. He'd kill me if he thought I'd rung you up.'

Kate felt her heart sink down to her boots. So he didn't even want her name mentioned. Well, she couldn't blame him.

'See you at eight thirty then.' Before Kate could answer, the phone went dead.

Meet Willy for a meal? She pushed the thought from her mind and went back to the papers in front of her. She'd decide later what she was going to do.

Patrick walked into the drawing room and grinned. 'Where you going, all poshed up?'

Willy had on a dinner jacket and smelt like a poke of devils.

623

'I've got a date, actually.'

'A what! You ain't been out on a date for years.'

'Well, there's always a first time, ain't there? I got meself a right classy bird for the evening.'

Patrick laughed out loud.

'Good bleeding luck to you and all. How much is she rushing you?'

Willy looked annoyed.

'If you don't mind, Pat, just 'cos you spend most of your time with bimbos don't mean we all have to. This is a very respectable woman. Got a good job and everything. In fact, if you saw her you'd fancy her.'

Patrick looked at him and smiled. Willy usually went out with women who made a Japanese Tosa look good. But he kept his own counsel.

'Well, you use the Rolls, Willy, that'll impress her.'

'Thanks, Pat. What time's your table booked for?'

'A quarter to eight. Don't worry about driving me, I'm quite capable of taking one of the motors.'

'Okey doke then, Pat.'

Willy watched Patrick leave the house and then sat down for a minute. He hoped Kate turned up.

Kate decided she would meet Willy. If nothing else at least she could find out how Patrick was. The thought of being seen with him in public worried her, though. He looked like a bad accident, did old Willy, lovely as he was inside.

She had bought herself a new trouser suit. It was deep red and showed off her dark hair perfectly. She slipped it on with a white camisole top underneath, then stepped back from the mirror and admired herself.

Not bad.

She pulled up in the car park of Cartella at eight twenty and there, waiting for her in Patrick's Rolls Royce, was Willy. As she locked her car he walked over to her.

'You look lovely, Kate.'

She grinned at him, the overpowering smell of his aftershave making her cough. He looked almost presentable in his dinner jacket and she felt an enormous surge of affection for him. As they walked into the restaurant she took his arm. He patted her hand and smiled at her.

Patrick smiled at the girl opposite him. She really was very lovely. Since he had phoned Kate's house that night and a man answered, he had gone all out to have a good time.

He had met Michelle three days before. She was stunning, and he had watched every pair of male eyes assess her as they walked to their table. She was five foot ten, slim, and like her predecessors had enormous breasts. In the white sheath dress she was wearing, though ostensibly covered up, her breasts were actually in full view of everyone because of the way the dress moulded her tanned and healthy body. She had long blonde hair and violet eyes.

For the first time in months Patrick felt he might actually get to like a girl. Michelle was a career woman. She was personal secretary to the managing director of an export firm and Patrick had met her by accident in the man's office. Unlike her predecessors, she had a brain in her head and her talk stimulated him.

She chose her own food and Patrick was gratified at her appetite. He hated women who picked at their dinner, worried that every mouthful would be an extra pound in weight. Especially when the meal cost a small fortune.

But Michelle was the kind of woman who lived life to the full.

'I've never been here before. Do you use this restaurant a lot? The maître d' seemed to know you.'

Patrick had the grace to blush.

The maître d' also knew how many women he had brought here. At one time they had run a book in the kitchen on how long a particular girl would last. Michelle deserved better than that. It was the reason he had never brought Kate here.

'It's local, you know. I don't always fancy driving into the Smoke.'

She chatted on and Patrick watched her, fascinated. She really was a lovely girl.

As Willy and Kate walked into the restaurant, arm in arm, the maître d' walked towards them with a happy smile on his face. It was Friday night, the place was packed, and he could hear the cash tills ringing. Pierre, real name Albert Diggins, had a part ownership of the Cartella, and now it was really paying its way, he was a happy man. He walked towards Kate and Willy, wondering briefly what such an attractive woman was doing with such an ugly man.

'Name, monsieur?'

'It's Gabney. Mr William Gabney. I reserved a table for two.'

'Ah, the special table. I remember the booking, I took it myself.'

He smiled widely enough to encompass them both and any strangers in the vicinity. Gabney's was the champagne table that was costing the man a hundred pounds already.

'Please, follow me.'

He swept out his arm. Kate, stifling a smile, followed with Willy. She was still holding his arm when Patrick Kelly looked up from his steak and saw them. He nearly choked.

Kate looked into his face and saw her own shock mirrored there. She watched the blonde goddess sitting opposite him get up out of her seat and playfully pat him on the back while he coughed. The action caused the girl's breasts to shimmy in such a way they caught the eye not only of Willy and every other male diner in the place but also of Pierre, who walked into a chair, doing himself a painful injury.

Kate didn't know how she kept her head. Clutching her arm tighter, Willy followed a practically cross-legged Pierre to their table.

It was only about six feet from Patrick's and the champagne was already there on ice.

Pierre made a big deal out of opening it, hoping to entice some of the other diners into ordering the same thing. It was Cristal and Kate sipped the bubbling liquid nervously. She was sitting opposite Patrick and they glanced at one another surreptitiously.

Michelle knew something was up and looked behind her.

'Do you know that woman or something?'

Patrick coloured. 'I know her slightly.'

Michelle laughed. 'I think you know her a bit better than slightly, don't you?'

He nodded.

Willy sipped his champagne and watched Kate's face. He was sorry now he'd brought her here. Kate looked at him and shook her head.

'I'm sorry, Willy, I have to go.'

She stood up and walked out of the restaurant. In the foyer she went straight into the ladies' room. She leant against the sink, her face burning with humiliation. She looked at herself in the mirror.

She looked good, she knew that, but no one could compete with the girl Patrick was sitting opposite. Poor Willy. She had walked out on him in front of everyone.

Why on earth had she decided to come?

She splashed some cold water on to her face to try and calm herself down. She put on a film of red lipstick and walked from the ladies' room.

Patrick was waiting for her.

She looked straight into his eyes.

'Hello, Kate.'

'Patrick.'

She felt as if a hot mist was gradually filling her head. His closeness was making her feel physically ill. She had to use all her willpower not to reach out and touch his hair, the lines of his face.

She looked down at the floor, unable to face him.

'How are you?'

'Fine. And you?' Kate marvelled at how normal her voice sounded.

'All the better for seeing you.'

Her eyes dragged themselves to his face of their own volition.

'I've missed you, Kate.'

Patrick was doing what he'd sworn he would never do. If

627

she walked away now, he would feel humbled and humiliated for the rest of his life.

Kate looked into his face.

'Really?'

'Really. I love you, Kate.'

'What about Titsalina in there then?' She gestured with her head towards the dining hall. 'Do you love her as well?'

Patrick felt a moment's euphoria.

She was jealous.

Kate saw his smile and regretted the words immediately.

'No, actually, Kate, I don't. It's you I want. I can't eat, I can't sleep, I can't even bonk since we split up, if you must know.'

Kate laughed. Patrick could be so comical. Here he was begging her to have him once more, and it had been her fault they had split up in the first place!

'So what are we going to do?'

'We're going to walk out of this restaurant and go home. Home to my house, Kate.'

'But what about Willy and that . . . girl.'

'I'll sort Willy out. As for Michelle, she told me to come out here. A clever girl that, she'll go far.'

Kate looked into the blue depths of Patrick's eyes and admitted the truth to herself. She needed this man. When he was there she felt alive, really alive, and she wanted that feeling for the rest of her life.

'I've missed you, Patrick.'

As they stood there Willy came out to them.

'I'll drop Michelle off home in the Roller.'

'Thanks, Willy.' Patrick and the big man shook hands, each grasping the other's wrists.

Willy went red. 'I knew that if you two just saw each other you'd be all right.'

Kate smiled at him and he went back into the restaurant.

'Right then, shall we go home?'

Kate took the proffered arm.

'Yes, let's go home, Pat.'

In the car park they stopped by Kelly's BMW. He took her in his arms and kissed her.

Willy watched them through the window of the restaurant. They fitted together perfectly, like two pieces of a jigsaw. He held up his glass in a silent toast: To Pat and Kate.

Martina Cole

GOODNIGHT LADY

SHE KNOWS EVERYONE'S SECRETS . . .

The infamous Briony Cavanagh: quite a beauty in her day,
and powerful, too. In the sixties, she ran a string of the most
notorious brothels in the East End. Patronised by peers and
politicians – even royalty, some said. Only Briony knew
what went on behind those thick velvet curtains, those
discreet closed doors, and Briony never opened her mouth –
unless she stood to benefit.

Only Briony knew the hard and painful road she'd travelled
to get there. From an impoverished childhood that ended
abruptly with shocking betrayal, she had schemed and
manipulated, determined to be mistress of her own fate.

But her flourishing business brought her into contact with
the darker side of life at the violent heart of London's
gangland. Along with her material success came risk and
danger. And the Goodnight Lady had her own secret place, a
place in her heart that was always shadowed with loss . . .

'Move over Jackie [Collins]!' *Daily Mirror*

'Sheer escapism . . . gripping . . . will definitely keep you
guessing to the end' *Company*

'Graphic realism combined with dramatic flair make this a
winner' Netta Martin, *Annabel*

FICTION / GENERAL 0 7472 4429 4

CATHERINE ALLIOTT
THE OLD-GIRL NETWORK

A SPARKLING FRESH TALENT FOR ALL JILLY COOPER FANS

Why didn't anyone warn her that the path to true love would be filled with potholes?

Dreamy, scatty and impossibly romantic, Polly McLaren is a secretary in an advertising agency, but the day a stranger on a train catches her eye, her life changes for ever. This American Romeo, who's recognised her old school scarf, begs Polly to help him find his missing Juliet. Over an intoxicating dinner at the Savoy, Polly agrees to play Cupid – St Gertrude's girls must, after all, stick together – and her investigations begin. The last thing she needs now is trouble from the men in her life . . .

. . . like Harry Lloyd Roberts – Polly's madly attractive but infuriatingly elusive boyfriend. It's he who goads her into turning detective – on the grounds that it might give her something to do for a change. Not to mention distract her from his own lustful pursuits . . .

. . . and Nick Penhalligan – Polly's rude, arrogant and ridiculously demanding boss, who's not best pleased that her mind is everywhere but on her job. But even he gets entangled when the old-girl network turns into a spider's web of complications, deceit and finally, love.

FICTION / GENERAL 0 7472 4390 5

A selection of bestsellers from Headline

LAND OF YOUR POSSESSION	Wendy Robertson	£5.99	☐
TRADERS	Andrew MacAllen	£5.99	☐
SEASONS OF HER LIFE	Fern Michaels	£5.99	☐
CHILD OF SHADOWS	Elizabeth Walker	£5.99	☐
A RAGE TO LIVE	Roberta Latow	£5.99	☐
GOING TOO FAR	Catherine Alliott	£5.99	☐
HANNAH OF HOPE STREET	Dee Williams	£4.99	☐
THE WILLOW GIRLS	Pamela Evans	£5.99	☐
MORE THAN RICHES	Josephine Cox	£5.99	☐
FOR MY DAUGHTERS	Barbara Delinsky	£4.99	☐
BLISS	Claudia Crawford	£5.99	☐
PLEASANT VICES	Laura Daniels	£5.99	☐
QUEENIE	Harry Cole	£5.99	☐

All Headline books are available at your local bookshop or newsagent, or can be ordered direct from the publisher. Just tick the titles you want and fill in the form below. Prices and availability subject to change without notice.

Headline Book Publishing, Cash Sales Department, Bookpoint, 39 Milton Park, Abingdon, OXON, OX14 4TD, UK. If you have a credit card you may order by telephone – 01235 400400.

Please enclose a cheque or postal order made payable to Bookpoint Ltd to the value of the cover price and allow the following for postage and packing:

UK & BFPO: £1.00 for the first book, 50p for the second book and 30p for each additional book ordered up to a maximum charge of £3.00.

OVERSEAS & EIRE: £2.00 for the first book, £1.00 for the second book and 50p for each additional book.

Name ....

Address ....

....

....

If you would prefer to pay by credit card, please complete:
Please debit my Visa/Access/Diner's Card/American Express (delete as applicable) card no:

Signature .... Expiry Date..............